W. E. B. GRIFFIN

Three Complete Novels

W.E.B. GRIFFIN

THREE COMPLETE NOVELS

THE CORPS:

BATTLEGROUND
LINE OF FIRE
CLOSE COMBAT

G.P. PUTNAM'S SONS   NEW YORK

G. P. PUTNAM'S SONS
Publishers Since 1838
200 Madison Avenue
New York, NY 10016

Library of Congress Cataloging-in-Publication Data

Griffin, W.E.B.
[Corps. Bks. 4–6]
The corps : three complete novels / W.E.B. Griffin.
p. cm.
Contents: Battleground—Line of fire—Close combat.
ISBN 0-399-14013-1
1. United States. Marine Corps—History—Fiction. 2. United
States—History, Military—20th century—Fiction. 3. World War,
1939–1945—Fiction. 4. War stories, American. I. Title.
[PS3557.R489137C68 1995]   94-33371 CIP
813'.54—dc20

Printed in the United States of America
1 2 3 4 5 6 7 8 9 10

THE CORPS *is respectfully dedicated to the memory of*
Second Lieutenant Drew James Barrett III, USMC
Company K, 3rd Battalion, 26th Marines
Born Denver, Colorado, 3 January 1945
Died Quang Nam Province,
Republic of Vietnam, 27 February 1969
and
Major Alfred Lee Butler III, USMC
Headquarters 22nd Marine Amphibious Unit
Born Washington, D.C., 4 September 1950
Died Beirut, Lebanon, 8 February 1984

"Semper Fi!"

And to the memory of Donald L. Schomp
A Marine fighter pilot who became a legendary
U.S. Army Master Aviator
RIP 9 April 1989

CONTENTS

BATTLEGROUND

I

(ONE)
Midway Atoll
0455 Hours 4 June 1942

William Charles "Bill" Dunn, USMCR, of Point Clear, Alabama, was twenty-one years old, five feet six inches tall, and weighed 142 pounds; he'd been a First Lieutenant, USMCR, twelve days, and a Naval Aviator not quite six months; and in all that time—in all his twenty-one years, even—he'd never had a night as hard as the last one. By the time he threw off the sheet that morning and swung his feet onto the floor, he did it with the sinking conviction that he was a coward. That conviction didn't come as a surprise to him. The thought, if not the conviction, had been there when he crawled into bed, and more times than he wanted to count he'd woken up during the night with it.

Just about every time he did that, he'd had to rush to the head to move his bowels. As far as he was concerned, that made him—literally—"scared shitless." It did not strike him as amusing. Now that his bowels were empty, he had an urge— suppressed only with enormous effort—to throw up. And every couple of minutes he felt a cold and clammy sweat on his back and on the seat of his skivvy shorts.

The reason his body was acting so wild was that today he was going, as the Naval Service so quaintly put it, "In Harm's Way." The Japanese were about to attack the islands where Dunn was stationed, with the objective of capturing them; the United States Navy was determined not to lose them. Both sides had sent formidable naval forces toward the area. And both forces were closing in on one another. Bill Dunn's role in this vast exchange was to fly a single seater fighter off this tiny little airfield to see if he could shoot at least some of the Japanese airplanes down.

All for the sake of a circular atoll surrounding a pair of tiny dots of land (total area, two square miles) lying just east of the International Date Line, 1,300 miles Northwest of Pearl Harbor. The dots themselves were named Eastern Island (1.25 miles long) and Sand Island (1.75 miles); and the whole thing, including the atoll, was called Midway.

Midway had been an American possession since just after the Civil War. But, with the exception of a cable station, it had been essentially abandoned and forgotten until 1936. That year, Pan American Airways instituted scheduled service between Hawaii and the Philippine Islands using Midway as a midpoint stop. Once that facility was in place, the strategic importance of Midway began to grow apparent, until in 1939, the Navy Hepburn Board (named after its senior member), charged with evaluating Navy facilities in the Pacific in case of war, determined that those tiny dots of land were "second only in importance to Pearl Harbor" itself.

In 1940, the Navy started construction of extensive facilities to service both aircraft and submarines on Midway. A Navy dock was completed on 1 September 1940, and on 29 September, about a third of the 3rd USMC Defense Battalion arrived with one battery of two five-inch naval cannons and some machine guns to defend the atoll.

The decision was made to build an airstrip (only facilities for seaplanes were originally planned) and Army Engineers began to dredge the channel between the islands and undertook other construction work.

The Japanese, meanwhile, attacked Midway at 2135 hours 7 December. The destroyers *Sazanami* and *Ushio* under Captain Koname Konishi shelled the tiny islands for twenty-three minutes, causing minimal damage. The three- and five-inch naval cannon of the 6th Defense Battalion (which had replaced the 3rd) returned the fire and claimed damage to both vessels.

This first Japanese attack was hardly more than a nuisance, but other attacks, including an amphibious assault, were expected. And so by the end of May, Midway had received meaningful reinforcement: The Marine Corps had furnished five anti-aircraft batteries, ranging in size from twenty-mm to three-inch; two companies of the 2nd Marine Raider Battalion; and even a platoon (five) of light tanks.

During the same time, the small airstrip on Eastern Island had become home to an odd mixture of aircraft: In addition to the original fourteen Navy Consolidated PBY Catalinas, there were two Royal Dutch Navy Catalinas, which had attached themselves for service after they were unable to return to their base; the U.S. Army Air Corps had flown in from Oahu four twin-engine Martin B-26 Marauder medium bombers and seventeen four-engine heavy bombers, Boeing B-17 ''Flying Fortresses''; while the Navy had sent six torpedo-carrying Grumman TBF Avengers.

Most of the aircraft, however (sixty-four), were Marine: nineteen Douglas SBD-2 Dauntless dive bombers; seventeen (virtually obsolete) Vought SB2U-3 Vindicator dive bombers; twenty-one (obsolete) Brewster Buffaloes; and seven of the new Grumman F4F-3 Wildcat fighters.

In the days before this particular morning, Navy Intelligence, whose information in this instance Bill Dunn trusted, had provided a good deal of information about the enemy, all of it alarming:

Their Midway Strike Force, under Admiral Chuichi Nagumo, was built around four aircraft carriers: The Akagi (at 36,500 tons, Japan's largest carrier); *Kaga* (36,000 tons); and *Hiryu* and *Soryu* (both much smaller at 16,000 tons). The force also included two battleships, three cruisers, destroyers and other screening vessels, and transports for 1,500 men of the Special Naval Landing Force and 1,000 soldiers of the Ichiki Detachment.

There were going to be large numbers of Japanese aircraft: ''Probably in excess of one hundred,'' the skinny, bespectacled, school-teacherish Navy full Lieutenant Intelligence Officer had announced at the most recent briefing, sounding as bored as a guide in the Atlanta Zoo telling visitors about the wonders they could find in the reptilarium.

If the Japanese followed their usual practice, based upon the normal complement of aircraft aboard their carriers, three types of aircraft would be in the striking force, and in roughly equal numbers.

There would be an element of Nakajima B5N1 Torpedo Bombers, single engine, low wing monoplanes, which some Navy Intelligence bureaucrat had decided should be known as Kates. Since torpedoes cannot sink an island, even little, bitty ones like Sand and Eastern Islands, Intelligence had cleverly deduced that the Kates would probably be operating in their bomber and not their torpedo role. That meant the Kates would have large bombs, probably enormous bombs, slung beneath their fuselages, and they would carry three men aboard, instead of the usual two. When it was used to deliver torpedoes, the pilot aimed the single torpedo Kates could handle; when it was used as a bomber, there was a bombardier. The pilot could also fire the two 7.7mm machine guns in his wings. And there was always a gunner, who fired a single 7.7mm machine gun from the back seat.

They could also, according to the Atlanta Zoo guide, expect an element of Vals.

The Val was officially the Aichi D3A1 Navy Type 99 Carrier Bomber Model 11. Bill Dunn vaguely remembered hearing someplace that Type 99 (or was it Model 11?) made reference to the year in the Japanese calendar, which was different from the calendar used in the West.

He did remember that the Val had a nonretractable landing gear . . . the wheels had pants. These made Vals look something like the Gee-Bee Racer Jimmy Doolittle used to fly in air races. Jimmy Doolittle was one of Bill Dunn's childhood heroes.

Bill hadn't thought of Jimmy Doolittle in years, until word had come six weeks ago that Doolittle had flown B25s off an aircraft carrier, bombed Tokyo, and wound up a Brigadier General with the Medal of Honor. He didn't understand how the hell Doolittle had managed to get B25s off an aircraft carrier; it was hard enough getting a Wildcat off.

The news of the Tokyo raid brought back to him his adolescent hero worship of Doolittle racing his Gee-Bee around pylons. The Gee-Bee was much like the Wildcat, a little airplane with a big engine, and thus very fast. And correspondingly hard—dangerous—to fly.

By the time Bill Dunn was fifteen, he knew he would never emulate his father and his two brothers who'd been football heroes at the University of Alabama: He weighed 105 pounds and was dubbed "The Runt." Things were in fact looking bad for him in the manhood department in general until the U.S. Navy—specifically, the Naval Air Station, Pensacola—came to his rescue. The Navy showed him a way to do manly things, even if he wasn't going to be well over six feet and two hundred pounds when he reached full growth.

The Navy hoped to build auxiliary and emergency landing strips on land the Dunns owned just across the border from Florida in Alabama. Though the Navy had no funds to lease, much less buy, the necessary land, the Admiral at Pensacola thought there was a good chance that he could appeal to the Dunn family's patriotism.

The Admiral had read his history and suspected—correctly—that Lieutenant Cassius Alfred Dunn, gunnery officer of the Confederate Ship *Alabama,* probably had a familial connection with the Dunns of Mobile and Point Clear, shipping agents and land owners. The *Alabama,* under Admiral Raphael Semmes, was the greatest Naval Raider of all time.

"You must come see us at Pensacola," the Admiral said to C. Alfred Dunn IV, Bill's father. "And bring your boy. I think he'd like it."

When the Dunns came to Pensacola, the Admiral laid on them a little demonstration of the capabilities of the Grumman F3F-1, the last Navy biplane fighter to be produced. Bill Dunn's awe of the F3F-1 was exceeded only by his shocked realization that the pilot who climbed out of the cockpit and walked over to be introduced to the Dunn family was no taller and not much heavier than he was.

I bet they called him "Runt" too, when he was fifteen.

That summer, and the next, Bill spent long hours with his feet dangling off the family pier, watching the sun set over the smooth waters of Mobile Bay. A lot of the time he was there he was thinking about flying. He would have cheerfully swapped all his worldly possessions, present and future, for a chance to climb in the cockpit of a fast and powerful little airplane and shove the throttle as far forward as it would go.

The dream endured . . . though he changed part of it. By the time he entered the University, he'd decided that if there was anything in the world better than being a Naval Aviator, it was becoming a *Marine* Naval Aviator.

Now that he was a Marine Naval Aviator and rated in the Grumman F4F, which was a little larger than the Gee-Bee, but just about as fast, he understood that flying hot aircraft as fast as they would go, as close to the ground as you could get them, was a pretty dumb thing to do. He realized now why there had been such a hell of a hue and cry to stop the National Air Races because those guys had kept flying into each other, the pylons, or the ground.

The Val, like the Kate, had two forward firing 7.7mm machine guns in the wings and a single 7.7mm in the aft cockpit. It could carry about nine hundred pounds, total, of bombs, a big one under the fuselage and two smaller ones under the wings.

Neither the Val nor the Kate was any match for the *Wildcat,* which was faster, and far more heavily armed (six .50 caliber Browning machine guns) and armored. One on one, that is.

Was one Wildcat equal to two Vals? Or three?

That was an uncomfortable question.

And that wasn't the whole problem.

"We may certainly expect the Vals and Kates to be accompanied by a roughly equal number of Zeroes," the Navy Zoo Guide had said matter-of-factly.

The Zero (technically the Mitsubishi A6M2 Model 21) was an interesting airplane . . . interesting, that is, if you could sit back and compare it dispassionately with the Wildcat. It was a low wing monoplane fighter, with a fourteen-cylinder radial engine that gave it a top speed of about 315 mph at 16,000 feet. The Wildcat had a top speed a couple of miles an hour faster at 18,000.

But if you could not consider it dispassionately—for example, if you were about to go fight twenty-five to thirty-five of them—the Zero seemed immensely formidable. From everything Bill Dunn had heard, the Zero was a better airplane than the Wildcat. That the Navy pretended otherwise did not change the facts. The Navy also pretended that the Brewster F2A Buffalo was only "marginally inferior" to the Wildcat, and that was bullshit, pure and simple.

It was common knowledge, anyhow, that the Zero was far more maneuverable than the Wildcat, except at sea level, where the more powerful Wildcat engine gave it an edge. And in addition to the two 7.7mm machine guns it had in the wings, it had two 20mm machine cannon. The projectile from a 20mm machine cannon had greater range than a .50 caliber bullet. Thus a Zero pilot could shoot at a Wildcat before the Wildcat pilot could shoot at him; and because it was larger, a 20mm did more damage.

If it was true that no matter how bad a situation is, it could always be worse, Bill thought, *then whenever we sally forth into harm's way, I could be flying a goddamned Buffalo. There are three times as many (twenty-one) Buffaloes on Midway as there are Wildcats.*

The Navy didn't want the Buffaloes, of course, knowing that they are no fucking good. So naturally, they are good enough for the Marines. But at least I will be flying a Wildcat.

Which raises the interesting question, how come?

Did Major Parks put me into a Wildcat because he felt I can fly one better than the other guys? Or because he thought, being the nice guy he is, that I stand a slightly better chance of living through this morning flying a Wildcat than I would flying a Buffalo?

And that raises the question of relative pilot skill, which is a real chiller. Christ only knows how much time Major Parks and Captain Armistead and the other old timers have—several thousand hours anyway—but Mrs. Dunn's Little Boy Billy has 312.5 hours, which ain't very much, especially considering how little of that is in the Wildcat, and that somehow Navy Intelligence has learned enough about the Japs to estimate their average carrier pilot has 800 hours, including some in combat. I have zero hours in combat.

After he rolled out of bed, Dunn dressed quickly by pulling on what the Marine Corps called a "Suit, Flight, Tropical," and which he somewhat irreverently thought of as his rompers. Next came ankle high boots, which he thought of as his clodhoppers, because the rough side of the leather was on the outside. Some of the guys flew with low-quarter shoes, but he preferred the clodhoppers. He slipped a leather flight jacket over the flight suit, and then put on a shoulder holster with a Colt Model 1911A1 pistol in it.

Some of the guys carried .38 Special caliber revolvers, which were somewhat smaller weapons, arguing that they didn't get in the way as much as the Colt. Bill carried the Colt because that's what they had issued him, and because he thought the chances of his ever having to take it from the holster to shoot anybody with it ranked right up there with his chances of being named Pope.

Last came a canvas helmet with flaps folded up so his ears were free. It always reminded him of the helmet he'd worn to grammar school, goggles in place, imagining that he was Jimmy Doolittle flying the Gee-Bee to racing glory around the pylons.

He looked at the photograph of his parents standing outside St. Luke's on some long ago Sunday morning. It shared a folding leather frame with a photograph of Miss Sue-Anne Pendergast, who had been the 1941 Queen of the Mobile Mardi Gras. Sue-Anne was a nice looking girl . . . for that matter, a nice girl, period. But she was not, as Bill suggested to his peers, his beloved, almost his fiancée.

He had known Sue-Anne all of his life. They'd climbed trees and gone swimming and thrown mudballs at each other since about the time the two of them could talk. Now she was doing her bit for the Boys In Service by writing him faithfully once a week. While she signed her letters, "Love," it wasn't the sort of love Bill had so far in his life been denied.

Another of the reasons it was a dirty rotten fucking shame he was probably going to get killed today was that he was, with one exception, a virgin. Just before he'd dropped out of college to join the Marines, he and half a dozen fraternity brothers had gone down from Tuscaloosa to the Tutweiler Hotel in Birmingham, where they had pooled their money and hired a whore from the bellhop. He was so drunk he didn't remember much about it, except that it was not what he expected it to be, and not very pleasant either.

It seemed to Bill common justice that a man should be able to get decently laid before he got himself killed. But that hadn't happened.

The Officer's Mess was an open-sided tent with benches and tables, the food was served cafeteria style. Breakfast was the standard fare: Spam and powdered eggs served any way you wanted them, which meant that you could either have little squares of fried Spam with powdered eggs on the side, or you could have the Spam cut up and mixed into powdered eggs. Plus toast, with your choice of apple or cherry flavored jelly. And coffee, with your choice of canned cow or no canned cow.

He had taken a mug of black coffee and a piece of cold toast and walked out to the flight line. He was afraid that he would throw up and didn't want to vomit in the cockpit.

The plane chief was there, looking over the armorer's shoulders as he checked the Brownings and the links and placement of the belted .50s. They exchanged salutes. The plane chief, a stocky Italian from Florida whose name was Anthony Florentino, was about as old as Bill was, and took his work and the Marine Corps seriously. He was a corporal.

"Good morning, Sir," he said.

"Good morning. Everything shipshape?"

"Yes, Sir. Just checking the guns, Sir."

Funny, it looked to me like you were playing chess.

"You got the word, Sir, that we're to start engines at 0540?"

"No, I didn't."

Jesus, I have to take another dump!

"The Skipper wants the engines warmed up for when the word comes, Sir."

He looked at his watch. It was 0533. In seven minutes he would have to climb in that cockpit and hope that he didn't have nausea or diarrhea.

He walked around the plane and did the preflight, trying to act as nonchalant as possible. When he finished he had four minutes to wait. He leaned against the Wildcat, just behind the cowl flaps.

"I didn't see you in the mess, I wondered where you were," Major Parks said, startling him. He hadn't seen The Skipper coming up.

"Good morning, Sir."

"Everything all right? You feeling OK?"

"Yes, Sir, fine."

"You got the word about warming the engines?"

"Yes, Sir. I was about to get in."

"A PBY radioed at five-twenty-five that it had spotted the Japanese fleet," Parks said. "I expect word anytime now that the Navy radar has picked up aircraft. I want to get off the ground as soon as we get a heading. Hit them as far away from here as possible."

"Yes, Sir."

"You're a good pilot, Bill. That's why I put you in a Wildcat. You don't get excited. That's a good thing for a fighter pilot. Excited pilots forget what they've been taught."

"Yes, Sir."

Translated, that means you have had second thoughts about putting me in a Wildcat, because I am very likely to get excited and forget what I've been taught, and would probably change your mind if there was time and put me in one of the goddamned Buffaloes. That being the case, you have decided to inspire the troops with confident words.

Shit!

Major Parks touched his arm.

"Good luck," he said. "Good hunting."

"Thank you, Sir."

Major Parks was both a professional warrior and a realist. He knew that until the shooting actually started there was no way to predict how Lieutenant Dunn, or any of his pilots, would behave in combat. Even so, he had a belief that he could devise guidelines that would give him some indication—a hint if not a prediction—about which pilots could handle best the stress and terrors of combat. With that goal in mind, he had collected as much data as he could about the behavior of British fighter pilots during the Battle of Britain, the battle Churchill had described both accurately and eloquently: "Never in the history of human conflict have so many owed so much to so few."

Parks wondered what the few were really like.

Not without difficulty, he had learned that by and large they were no older than his young officers, and they'd been trained no better. They had also gone up against pilots with more experience than they had, yet they'd done very well.

He'd found two notable differences between the British pilots and his own, perhaps the most important being that the English were defending their homes, literally fighting above their mothers and their girlfriends, where his kids would be fighting halfway around the world from theirs. They would be protecting their mothers and their girlfriends, too, but abstractly, over a wide and empty ocean.

Secondly, the Brits had flown Spitfires against Messerschmidts. Both were splendid aircraft; it was a matter of opinion which was the better. One could charitably call the Wildcat the equal of the Zero, and perhaps when they had enough experience against the Zero to make a bona fide analysis, it would turn out to be so. But that could not be said about the Buffalo, which was hopelessly outclassed by the Zero, and probably by even the Kate.

With no data worth a damn to really go on, Parks realized he would have to go with his gut feeling. He thought that commanders had probably been forced to go on their gut feeling from the beginning of time, but that offered little reassurance. His gut feeling (which he desperately hoped was not wishful thinking) was that his kids—and perhaps Bill Dunn in particular—would acquit themselves well.

He had given Bill Dunn one of his precious few Wildcats because of that gut feeling. And perhaps, he thought, because sometimes when he saw Dunn on the flight line, a spunky little crew-cutted, clean-cut kid who looked more like a cheerleader than a Marine Officer, he reminded him of those young English kids standing beside their Spitfires in an East Anglian field.

(TWO)

Lieutenant Bill Dunn watched The Skipper walk down the flight line to the next aircraft, which happened to be a Buffalo, and pause for a word with its pilot.

I can't remember that guy's name! I'm about to go get killed with him, and I can't even remember his name. I wonder if he knows mine?

He climbed up on the wing root.

Corporal Florentino had already opened the canopy. As Bill lowered himself into the seat, Florentino climbed onto the wing root and watched, prepared to help, as Bill fastened his shoulder and lap belts, and then as Bill set the clock, the altimeter, and the rate of climb indicator to zero. He waited until Bill had checked the stick and rudder pedals for full movement, and then jumped off the wing root.

Bill checked the emergency canopy release and the fuel gauge, then glanced out the canopy.

"Ignition switch off, throttle open, mixture at idle cut off," he called. "Pull it through."

Florentino grasped a propellor blade and pulled on it, then the next blade, and the next, until the engine had been turned through five revolutions. Otherwise, oil that had accumulated by gravity in the lower cylinders would still be there when the engine fired. Since oil does not compress, lower link rods would have been bent or broken.

Bill put the Fuel Selector Valve handle to MAIN TANK and turned the crank opening the engine cowl flaps. He checked the propeller circuit breaker switch and then set it on AUTOMATIC. Outside, Corporal Florentino had charged the starter mechanism with a Type C cartridge, a kind of super-sized blank shotgun shell. When it fired, its energy would turn the engine over until it started.

Bill set the supercharger on LOW, pushed the Carburetor Air handle in so that air would be delivered directly to the engine, and set the throttle for 1000 rpm.

He looked to make sure that no one was near the propellor and that a ground crewman had a fire extinguisher ready to go.

"Clear!" he called.

Florentino made a wind-it-up motion.

Bill turned the battery switch to ON, turned on the Emergency Fuel Pump, and watched as the fuel pressure gauge rose to fifteen pounds. Then he held the primer switch on for three seconds, turned the ignition switch to BOTH, and fired the starter cartridge.

The propellor began to turn, and then there was the sound, rough, of the engine catching. The Wildcat shuddered, and the engine gave off a small cloud of blue smoke. He moved the mixture control to AUTO RICH and flicked the primer switch a couple of times until the engine smoothed out.

He idled the engine at 1000 rpm, and then teased the throttle further open until it indicated 1200 rpm. There was nothing to do now but wait for the oil pressure and inlet temperature needles to "move into the green." This made reference to little green arcs painted on gauges and dials to show where the indicator needle should point, if things were as they were supposed to be. There were also little red arcs that indicated a dangerous temperature, or pressure, or the like.

The oil pressure gauge almost immediately indicated 70 psi (Pounds Per Square Inch) and then the oil inlet temperature gauge needle came to life. It slowly began to move across the dial to the green arc, stopping at an indication of 86° Fahrenheit.

Then he checked the magnetos, which provided the ignition spark to the engine, by switching from their normal BOTH position first to LEFT and then to RIGHT. The tachometer showed a drop of less than 100 rpm, which meant he had no problem there.

The goddamn airplane is not going to suffer some fatal internal malady and keep me on the ground. That would have been nice. Not exactly heroic, but nice.

He let it run another minute and then shut it down. It was warmed up and ready to go. He sat in the cockpit for another minute, listening to the creak of metal as it cooled, and then a Jeep came down the flight line with Captain John Carey at the wheel. He signaled down the flight line. Dunn had expected this. The word had come, and there would be last minute instructions and probably a pep talk.

"We've been over this before," Major Parks conceded. "You all know where you're supposed to be when we get in the air. What we have now is where the enemy is: bearing 310, about 90 miles. Radar reports too many of them to count."

Now he's going to say, "Go out there and give them hell, men! Win one for the Gipper! Semper Fi! To the Halls of Montezuma!"

Major Parks said, "I'll see you all later at the debriefing."

Bill was a little surprised to find himself trotting, almost running, back to the Wildcat. As he climbed in, he saw for the first time that something had been stenciled below the canopy: 1ST LT W C DUNN USMCR CPL A M FLORENTINO, USMC.

That wasn't there yesterday. He must have painted it on there last night. And I didn't see it before because I had other things on my mind, like getting killed.

"Great-looking sign, Florentino," Bill said when the plane captain appeared at the side of the cockpit.

"Thank you, Sir."

He fastened his seat and shoulder harness again and went through the start-up procedure. The engine caught immediately and quickly smoothed down. He checked the Manifold Pressure Regulator and the Propeller Operation; then he de-sludged the supercharger. After that he followed the Buffalo which had been parked beside him toward the runway.

When he was lined up with the runway, he went through the final take-off checklist, which takes longer to describe than to do: He checked to see that the indicator in the wing root showed the wings were properly spread and locked. He locked the tail wheel; made sure the sliding portion of the canopy was locked open; set the aileron and elevator tabs in NEUTRAL and the rudder tab a couple of marks to the right. He checked to see that the fuel selector switch was on the main tank and that the cowl flaps were open. He made sure the propellor governor control was pushed all the way in; that the supercharger was set to LOW, the mixture control set to AUTO RICH, and the Emergency Fuel Pump to ON. He pushed the Carburetor Air Control all the way in and finally pushed the throttle to FULL.

The engine roared, the plane began to strain against the brakes, and the needle on the Manifold Pressure Gauge rose to indicate about fifty-two inches. He released the brakes and the Wildcat started to move down the runway, as if it was chasing the Buffalo in front of it.

He dropped his eyes momentarily to check the oil and fuel pressure, the oil and cylinder head temperatures, and the indicated airspeed. The needles were all in the green. He thought he saw the airspeed indicator needle flicker to life, which usually happened about 40 knots, but he wasn't sure. It didn't really matter. He would sense in the seat of his pants when the Wildcat wanted to fly.

The rumble of the landing gear suddenly stopped. The Wildcat, having reached an airspeed of about 70 knots, had decided to fly. Without thinking about it, Bill swapped hands on the control stick, using his left hand on the stick to counter the Wildcat's tendency to veer to the right on take-off and freeing his right hand to crank up the landing gear. It took twenty-seven revolutions of the crank, hard turns, to get it up.

When he had finished and put his right hand back on the stick, he looked around for Major Parks, spotted his Wildcat, and maneuvered to get into his assigned position behind him. He was not at all surprised when he was in position and had adjusted the throttle, the mixture, and the trim, to see that he was climbing at 1,000 feet per minute, indicating 125 knots, and with his cylinder head temperature right at 215° Centigrade. That's what the book said was the most efficient climbing attitude, and Major Parks flew by the book.

As they passed through 12,000 feet, he put the black rubber mask over his face, readjusted his headset to accommodate it, and turned on the oxygen. It felt cool in his mouth and throat, and somehow alien. At 14,000 Parks leveled his flight out.

Several minutes after that, Parks wiggled his wings, seeming to point with his right wing tip. Bill followed the line down, and there they were, two thousand feet below them.

He was surprised at the color scheme. The Kates' fuselages, wings, and rear appendages were painted a lemon yellow. And the red ball of Japan was not readily visible on either fuselage or wings. From the windscreen forward, the Kates were painted black. And so was the bomb hanging under the fuselage.

Jesus Christ, there's a lot of them!

I'll be goddamned, the Zeroes are *below them! What the hell is that all about? Didn't they think we'd try to intercept?*

Following Parks's lead, he put the Wildcat into a dive, correcting without thinking about it for the Wildcat's tendency to drop the right wing and turn the nose to the right.

As he approached his first target, Bill could clearly see the aft-facing gunner bringing his machine gun to bear on him.

That bastard is shooting at me!

That triggered two other—alarming—thoughts:

Christ, I didn't test my guns!

I forgot to pull my fucking goggles down!

The Wildcat shook with the recoil of the .50 caliber Browning machine guns in the wings. And two other thoughts came:

Jesus, my tracer stream is way out in front of him!

I'll be goddamned! He blew up! How the hell did that happen?

And then he was through the layer of Kates and approaching the layer of Vals beneath them.

I fucked that up! I didn't get a shot at any of them, and here come the fucking Zeroes!

Our Father, who art in heaven—

I don't think I can turn this sonofabitch enough to lead him—

I'm skidding all over the fucking sky! You're a real hot pilot, Mr. Dunn. In a pig's ass you are!

Oh, shit, there goes one of our guys. His right fucking wing just came off!

For yea, tho' I walk through the valley of the shadow of death—

That's right, you miserable cocksucker, just stay right there another five seconds, four, three—

Gotcha!

Holy shit, there's somebody on my tail! A fucking Zero, what else?

I can't get away from him.

Our Father, who art in heaven, hallowed—

Chop the fucking throttle, stupid! Put it in a skid, let him overshoot you!

Oh, my God, the windshield's gone. I can't see a fucking thing. I'm going to die. Where the fuck are those goggles? Where the hell is that Zero? Why does my leg feel wet? Did I piss my pants?

Not unless you're pissing blood, you didn't.

I thought it was supposed to hurt when you got wounded.

Oh, shit, it hurts! I wonder if it's broken?

(THREE)

"How do you feel, Dunn?" the tour guide from the Atlanta Zoo asked, pulling up a folding metal chair to the side of Dunn's bed. "Well enough to talk to me?"

What if I said "no"?

"Yes, Sir."

"The more you can tell me about what happened out there, the better," the tour guide said. "You want to take it from the beginning?"

"We were at fourteen thousand, about thirty miles out, when Major Parks spotted them. He showed us where they were and went into a dive, and I went after him."

"And?"

"And that's all I remember."

"Come on."

"I remember being surprised that the Zeroes were on the bottom of the formation, not the top."

"OK. That was unusual. They apparently intended to use the Zeroes to strafe the field here. I guess they didn't think we had anything to send up against them. When you went in the dive, then what happened?"

"I shot at a Kate."

"You got it. It was confirmed."

"The Kates were on top. Then there was a layer of Vals. I went right through them without firing a shot. And then I was in the Zeroes."

"And?"

"I don't know. I don't remember much."

"You are credited with shooting down one of them. You don't remember that?"

"Who says I shot down a Zero?"

"I don't immediately recall."

"The Skipper?"

"Major Parks didn't make it back, I'm sorry to say."

"Shit."

"I was hoping that perhaps you might have seen him go in."

"I saw somebody go down. His right wing, most of his right wing, came off. I don't know who it was."

"When was that?"

"I don't know. Toward the beginning."

"That was the only time you saw one of ours go down?"

"Yes."

"You're sure?"

"I told you, that was it. How many of ours went down?"

"A good many, I'm sorry to have to tell you."

"How many is a good many?"

"We lost fifteen. Two Wildcats—not counting yours, although yours has been surveyed and is a total loss—and thirteen Buffaloes."

"We only had nineteen Buffaloes with us."

"In addition to yourself, Captain Carey, Captain Carl, and Lieutenant Canfield came back. Of Major Parks's flight, I mean."

"You mean the rest are dead?"

"Do you remember when you were hit?"

"You mean everybody but the four of us is dead?"

"I'm afraid so."

"Oh, my God!"

"Do you remember being hit?"

"No. I remember the windshield going."

"In other words you don't know who shot you down, whether it was a Zero or some other type aircraft?"

"It had to be a Zero. I was in the Zeroes."

"But you don't know for sure?"

"I don't even know how I got back here."

"You came back and made a wheels-up landing."

"I found my way back here by myself?"

"How else?" the Naval Intelligence debriefing officer asked, a tinge of sarcasm in his voice.

"The last thing I remember is when I lost my windshield. And got hit."

"You don't remember heading back here?"

"The last thing I remember is trying to pull my goggles down after the windshield went."

"You were apparently flying with the canopy open—"

Christ, I forgot to close the canopy, too?

"Was I?"

"The shell, most likely a 20mm, apparently entered the cockpit from the side—"

"Just one round?"

"There were others. In the engine nacelle. Another just forward of the seat. But the one—the one which entered the cockpit—apparently exploded going through the windshield, from the inside out?"

"Yeah," Bill said, understanding.

"What they took out of your face and leg, legs, was debris from the windshield and control panel. Perspex and aluminum fragments."

"Then it was a Zero."

"Presumably." The Intelligence officer looked directly at him. "You have no memory of breaking off the engagement and heading back here?"

"No."

"Could you determine, do you have any memory of determining, from your instruments, or from a loss of control, that your aircraft was no longer airworthy?"

"No," Bill said, and then, thinking aloud, "That's an odd question."

"You were seen leaving the area."

"So?"

"The officer who saw you leave could not tell whether you had lost your windshield. You were too far apart."

"Who was that?"

"I don't think we'd better get into that."

"But he thought I was running, right?"

"Were you?"

"I don't know."

"That's not a very good answer, you realize?"

"Sorry about that."

"You don't seem overly disturbed at what could be an accusation of cowardice in the face of the enemy."

"Fuck you, Lieutenant."

"You can't talk to me that way!"

"If I'm to be charged with cowardice in the face of the enemy, what's the difference what I say to you?"

After a long pause, the Naval Intelligence Officer said, "I didn't say anything about you being charged with anything."

"No witnesses, right? Everybody's dead?"

"If you're through with my patient, Lieutenant," another voice said, from behind Dunn, "I'd like to put him aboard the PBY."

"You're being flown to Pearl Harbor," the Intelligence Officer said to Dunn.

"I'd prefer to stay with the squadron," Bill said.

"You won't be flying for a while. Three weeks anyway," the voice behind him said.

"And there's no squadron to stay with," the Naval Intelligence Officer said.

"Moving is going to be painful," the voice behind him, now much closer, said. "I can give you some morphine, if you like."

"How painful?"

"You're pretty well stitched up, particularly on the legs. Any movement will be painful."

"Then you'd better give me the shot," Bill Dunn said.

II

When the knock came at his door, Captain Fleming Pickering, USNR, was relaxing with his jacket off and his tie pulled down, tilting back in a chair, his feet on the windowsill of his seventh-floor suite, and balancing a cup of coffee on his stomach. Even that way he looked tall and distinguished; and it would have taken a moment of indecision before you concluded he was a man in his early forties. At first glance he appeared younger than that.

Rooms—much less suites—in the Menzies Hotel, now the Headquarters of General Douglas MacArthur, Supreme Commander, South West Pacific Ocean Areas, were not ordinarily assigned to lowly Navy Captains. But Captain Pickering was not an ordinary officer, or for that matter, an ordinary man.

Six months before, he had been Chairman of the Board, Pacific & Far East Shipping Corporation. He had been known as Captain Pickering then, too, preferring the title to the more grandiose Commodore which many ship owners adopt, whether or not they have ever gone to sea. Fleming Pickering had received his Master, Any Ocean, Any Tonnage, license from the U.S. Coast Guard when he was twenty-six. He was entitled to be called Captain.

The Corporation he chaired was in many ways as singular as he was. P&FE did not for instance issue an annual stockholders' report detailing the financial condition of its assets (which included fifty-two ships and a good deal of real estate in the United States and abroad). The majority stockholders did not consider such a report necessary. Captain Pickering and his wife owned seventy-five percent of the outstanding shares, and controlled voting rights to the other twenty-five percent, which had been placed in trust for their only child.

Captain Fleming Pickering, USNR, was, in other words, an important and influential man in his own right. But what made him unique, in the military pecking order, were the orders he carried in his pocket:

THE SECRETARY OF THE NAVY
WASHINGTON, D.C.

30 JANUARY 1942

CAPTAIN FLEMING W. PICKERING, USNR, OFFICE OF THE SECRETARY OF THE NAVY, WILL PROCEED BY MILITARY AND/OR CIVILIAN RAIL, ROAD, SEA, AND AIR TRANSPORTATION (PRIORITY AAAAA-1) TO SUCH POINTS AS HE DEEMS NECESSARY IN CARRYING OUT THE MISSION ASSIGNED TO HIM BY THE UNDERSIGNED.

UNITED STATES NAVAL COMMANDS ARE DIRECTED TO PROVIDE HIM WITH SUCH SUPPORT AS HE MAY REQUEST. OTHER UNITED STATES AGENCIES ARE REQUESTED TO CONSIDER CAPTAIN PICKERING THE PERSONAL REPRESENTATIVE OF THE UNDERSIGNED AND TO PROVIDE TO HIM APPROPRIATE SERVICES AND AMENITIES.

CAPTAIN PICKERING HAS UNRESTRICTED TOP SECRET SECURITY CLEARANCE. ANY QUESTIONS REGARDING HIS MISSION WILL BE DIRECTED TO THE UNDERSIGNED.

FRANK KNOX
SECRETARY

Very soon after the attack on Pearl Harbor, Navy Secretary Frank Knox came to realize that the information about Naval operations in the Pacific he was getting—and would get—from regular Navy officers was understandably slanted to reflect well on the U.S. Navy. These reports tended to gloss over any facts or opinions that might suggest that the Navy was less than perfect. What he needed, he concluded, was someone to report to him directly, and someone who not only was not a member of the Navy establishment, but who would know what he was looking at.

Knox met Pickering through their mutual friend, Senator Richmond Fowler (Republican–California). He decided immediately that Pickering was the man he was looking for. It was less Pickering's nautical experience that appealed to him than Pickering's strongly stated conviction that after Pearl Harbor, Knox should have resigned and the admirals at Pearl Harbor should have been shot. It was *in vino* truth: The day Secretary Knox met him, Pickering was treating a sorely bruised male ego with large doses of Old Grouse Scotch whiskey. The P&FE Chairman, a much decorated Marine corporal in France during the First War, had just been told the Marine Corps could not use his services in World War II.

Two weeks later, Knox offered Pickering a commission as his personal representative, with captain's stripes to go with it. To Knox's surprise, Pickering immediately accepted. Shortly thereafter he left for the Pacific.

"Come!" Captain Pickering called; and carefully, so as not to spill the coffee, he looked over his shoulder.

A youthful-looking Navy officer somewhat hesitantly stuck his head in the door.

"Captain Pickering?"

"Yes," Pickering said. "Come on in."

His visitor's sleeves, Pickering saw with surprise, carried the stripes of a full commander. He didn't look old enough to be a commander, Pickering thought. Even more surprising was the manner in which the commander carried his large, apparently full briefcase. It was attached to his wrist by a chain and a handcuff.

"You *are* Captain Pickering?" the young-looking commander asked.

"Guilty," Pickering said. "Who are you?"

"Sir, may I trouble you for some identification?"

"Jesus," Pickering said, and carefully removing himself from the tilted back chair, went to his uniform jacket and took out a wallet. The breast of the jacket carried ribbons for both valor and for wounds received in action in what had now become the First World War. He offered the young commander his Navy Department identification card, and then, because he already had his hands on it, his local identity card.

That one, with red diagonal stripes across the photograph and data blocks, told the Military Police he had been authorized unlimited access to all areas of MacArthur's headquarters. The red stripes seemed to awe people, Fleming had noticed. It should satisfy this young man.

"Thank you, Sir, I just had to be sure."

"I understand," Pickering said. "Now who are you?"

The commander did not reply. Instead, he reached into an interior pocket of his uniform jacket and came out with an envelope. As he did so, Pickering saw the butt of a revolver and the straps of a shoulder holster.

"This is for you, Sir," the commander said.

"What is it?"

"Captain, I suggest that when you've read that, you burn it as soon as you can," the commander said.

Pickering tore the envelope open. Inside was another envelope. He opened that and took out a thin sheath of onion skin carbon copies of a typewritten document. There was no heading, and neither was there what he expected to find, in these circumstances, the words TOP SECRET stamped in red ink on the top and bottom of each page.

"What the hell is this?" Pickering asked. "It doesn't even look like it's classified." When there was no immediate reply, he added, a little coldly, "And for the last time, Commander, who are you?"

"I think you'll understand when you read it, Sir," the commander said. "Sir, I'm a friend of a friend."

Pickering ran out of patience. Both his eyes and his voice were cold when he replied, "In case you haven't heard, Commander, I'm a friendless sonofabitch around here."

While Pickering had established a good, even warm, relationship with MacArthur, the officers on MacArthur's staff were barely able to conceal their hostility toward a man who was not part of their clique; was not subject to their orders; and who could be accurately described as Frank Knox's spy.

The commander baffled him with a warm smile. "That's not exactly the scuttlebutt I heard, Sir," he said, adding, "Our mutual friend is Captain David Haughton. If you don't mind, Sir, I won't give you my name. Then you can truthfully say you never heard of me."

"OK, sure," Pickering said, far less icily. Captain David Haughton was Administrative Assistant to Secretary of the Navy Frank Knox. If Haughton was involved, there was certain to be a satisfactory explanation for all this.

"I'll say 'Good morning,' Sir," the commander said. "I hope to meet you—for the first time—while I'm in Melbourne."

Now Pickering chuckled.

"We can walk through the looking glass together, right?" he said.

"Sir?" the commander asked, confused.

"*Alice in Wonderland?* Lewis Carroll?"

" 'Curiouser and curiouser,' Sir." the commander replied, now understanding.

"I would say 'Good-bye,' " Pickering said, "but you're not here, right?"

The commander smiled again and walked out of Pickering's suite. Pickering unfolded the sheets of onion skin and started to read them. The salutation was brief, and it was meaningful only to him. He was obviously FP. EF was Ellen Feller, who had been assigned as his secretary when he had been in Washington. But Ellen Feller was more than that, actually; for she'd been his administrative assistant, with the same relation to him as David Haughton had to Secretary of the Navy Knox. Ellen was now in Pearl Harbor, serving as his conduit to Knox, when she wasn't working as a Japanese language linguist in the ultrasecret Navy cryptographic office. The Commander, Pickering now guessed, was some sort of officer courier between Pearl Harbor and MacArthur; that would explain the pistol and the briefcase.

FOR FP FROM EF

This is a back channel summary prepared for PH by an officer here and sent to you on PH's authority.

A Midway-based PBY spotted the transport element of the Japanese assault force 700 miles West of Midway at 0900 3 June. B-17's were immediately dispatched from Midway. They later reported hits which still later proved to be wishful thinking. At 0145 4 June, another PBY hit a Japanese oiler with a single bomb as the Japanese moved closer.

At 0555 4 June, Navy landbased radar on Midway picked up reflections from a large aerial force about ninety miles away. Four Army Air Corps B-26 Marauders and six Navy TBF Avengers were launched from Midway against the carrier(s) which had presumably launched the Japanese aircraft.

Marine fighters and dive bombers on Midway were airborne within ten minutes of the alert. Major Floyd Parks led seven Buffaloes and five Wildcats directly toward the Japanese aircraft. Captain Kirk Armistead led the remaining Wildcat and a dozen Buffaloes to a position ten miles away, where it was believed another flight of Japanese would be found.

Thirty miles off Midway, Parks found a 108-plane Japanese force, divided into three waves of thirty-six planes each, and attacked. Several minutes later, Armistead joined up. They shot down sixteen horizontal bombers of the first Japanese echelon, and eighteen of the second echelon of dive bombers.

Fifteen of the twenty-five Marine fighter pilots were shot down, including Major Parks. Only three of the pilots with Parks survived the attack. Thirteen Buffaloes and two of the four Wildcats went down. For all practical purposes, Marine Fighter Squadron VMF-221 has been wiped out.

The Japanese force, although weakened, continued onto Midway and dropped its bombs. They destroyed the powerhouse on Eastern Island and the PBY hangars and some fuel tanks on Sand Island. Thirteen Americans were killed and eighteen wounded.

Meanwhile, the Marine dive bombers sent to attack the Japanese aircraft carrier approached their target. Major Lofton R. Henderson led the first, faster, echelon of SBD Dauntless Dive Bombers, and Captain Elmer C. Glidden led the slower Vought SB2U-3 Vindicators.

Apparently because neither he nor any of his pilots were really proficient in the Dauntless, Henderson ordered that greater accuracy would be obtained by glide (as opposed to dive) bombing. At 0800, from 8,500 feet, he began a wide "let down" circle. At 8,000 feet, Japanese fighters from the carriers attacked his force.

Henderson's plane was the first to take fire and begin to burn.

Captain Glidden's echelon, arriving shortly afterward, began to dive bomb at five-second intervals. Of the sixteen planes in both echelons, eight were lost. Damage to the enemy was minimal.

Fifteen B-17s from Midway arrived at 0810, somewhat naively trying to hit now wildly maneuvering warships from 20,000 feet.

We believe that on learning that he had lost about a third of his attacking force, Admiral Nagumo ordered a second attack. This required that he put his aircraft carriers into their most vulnerable condition, as they were refueled and rearmed. He apparently decided the prize, the neutralization and capture of Midway, was worth the risk.

At 0940 the first torpedo bombers from American aircraft carriers arrived above the Japanese carriers, whose decks were crowded with aircraft being rearmed and refueled.

Fifteen Devastator torpedo bombers from Hornet attacked first. They were all shot down. Fourteen Devastators from Enterprise attacked next. Ten of these were shot down. Next came a dozen Devastators from Yorktown. Eight of them were shot down.

It was a slaughter, and little damage was done to the Japanese fleet.

Thirty-seven Dauntless dive bombers from Enterprise under Lieutenant Commander Clarence McCluskey remained available. McCluskey led half in an attack on the carrier <u>Kaga</u>, and ordered Lieutenant Earl Gallagher to attack the carrier <u>Akagi</u> with the remainder. They sank both Japanese carriers.

Next, seventeen Dauntlesses from Yorktown dive bombed the carrier <u>Soryu</u>, causing severe damage, and she was later sunk by the submarine <u>Nautilus</u>. Finally, the fourth, and last, Japanese aircraft carrier, <u>Hiryu</u>, was successfully attacked and sunk.

I regret to inform you that Kate torpedo planes broke through the defenses of <u>Yorktown</u> and sank her, with great loss of life.

The entire Japanese fleet has withdrawn beyond range of our land- and sea-based aircraft. We believe that Admiral Nagumo has transferred his flag to the cruiser <u>Nagara</u>.

KLW

Pickering strongly suspected that the two ''we believe'' statements, that Nagumo had ordered a second attack on Midway and that he had transferred his flag to the cruiser *Nagara,* meant that ''we''—almost certainly a Naval Intelligence officer in Hawaii—had obtained the information from interception and decryption of Japanese radio messages.

Navy cryptographers had broken several important Japanese codes. Keeping that knowledge from the Japanese was of great importance. Reference would not be made to it even in documents which would be hand carried by officer couriers.

He considered briefly, and then forced from his mind, the painful images of the terrible loss of American life, and wondered what he should do with the information he had been given.

It took him just a moment to decide to give it to General MacArthur. Commander Nameless certainly was carrying with him, among other things, the official Navy after-action report. But that was certain to be wordy, and written in the knowledge that in addition to being at war with the Japanese, the Navy felt itself to be at war with the Army.

What he had in his hand was what General MacArthur wanted—and certainly was entitled to have—a concise, unvarnished description of the first major Japanese naval defeat of the war.

He picked up the telephone.

''Yes, Sir?'' a male American voice answered. The hotel's Australian switchboard operators had recently been replaced by U.S. Army Signal Corps soldiers.

''Six One Six,'' he said. That was MacArthur's private number. It wasn't much of a secret, but there were few who dared to call it directly and run the risk of annoying The General.

''Six One Six, Sergeant Thorne speaking, Sir.''

''This is Captain Pickering, Sergeant. I'd hoped to speak to The General.''

''Sir, the General is in his quarters, and will go from there to the Briefing Room. Shall I switch you, Sir?''

''No, thank you,'' Pickering said. ''I'll try to see him at the briefing.''

He quickly pulled up his tie, shrugged into his uniform jacket, tucked the onion skin sheets of paper in the side pocket, and left his suite.

(TWO)

The Briefing Room, once one of the Menzies Hotel's smaller ''Function'' Rooms, was on the mezzanine floor. Pickering momentarily debated going down the stairs, which would almost certainly be quicker, but decided against it. Around Supreme Headquarters, SWPOA, it would not be considered good form for a Navy Captain to race down five flights of stairs three steps at a time, when an oak paneled elevator was available.

His hope was to meet MacArthur as The General strode off the elevator reserved for his use and marched toward the briefing room. With a little luck, he would be able to ask for a couple of minutes.

Luck went against him; MacArthur was nowhere in sight. So he had no choice but to get in line with the others waiting to pass the muster of the MPs guarding the door to the Briefing Room. Once inside, he took a seat at the rear, beside the door. The man in the seat beside him was a Cavalry Colonel who nodded coldly at him.

Pickering wondered what the Cavalry Colonel's function was. The only U.S. Cavalry in the Orient had been the 26th Cavalry in the Philippines. They had been dismounted and their horses butchered and issued as rations fairly early on in the war.

The door beside him was flung quickly open, hitting Pickering on the shoulder. An officer stepped inside; he was wearing a tropical worsted uniform and the golden fourragère and four-starred lapel insignia of an aide-de-camp to a full general.

"Gentlemen," Lieutenant Colonel Sidney L. Huff announced with a shade more than necessary pomp, "The Supreme Commander."

The thirty-odd men in the room quickly rose to their feet and came to attention.

The Supreme Commander, General Douglas MacArthur, strode into the room and marched down the aisle between rows of folding metal chairs. He was wearing an Army Air Corps leather flight jacket with a zipper front, the four silver stars of his rank pinned to its epaulets; a somewhat battered brimmed cap with faded gold ornamentation around the headband that he had designed for himself when he had been Marshal of the Philippine Army; and wash-faded khakis. Another four stars were pinned to each collar of the shirt. He was tieless, and he had a long, thin, black cigar in his hand.

The corncob pipe he was famous for was most often seen when the Supreme Commander was in public. This gathering was the antithesis of public. Every man in the room—from the three sergeants functioning as orderly, stenographer, and handler-of-the-maps, through the assorted majors, wing commanders, and colonels, to the dozen general and flag officers of five different nations—not only held a TOP SECRET security clearance, but appeared on a list, updated daily, of those authorized to be present at what the schedule called "THE SUPREME COMMANDER'S MORNING BRIEFING."

An Australian Military Police Captain had checked each man against the list before permitting him to enter the room.

The front row was furnished with two blue leather armchairs. There was a table at each end of the row and between the chairs. The center table held a silver thermos of water, two glasses, a telephone, and an ash tray. The table at the left held a coffee cup and saucer; a cigarette box; an ash tray; a lighter; and another telephone. The table at the right held a coffee cup and saucer; a larger (big enough for a corncob pipe) ash tray; a small cigar box; a sterling silver lighter; a glass holding four freshly sharpened pencils; and a small notepad in a leather folder on which was stamped "Douglas MacArthur" and four silver stars.

When he reached his chair, General MacArthur looked around the room at his senior officers, all standing to attention. He found the face he was looking for, toward the rear.

"Captain Pickering," he said. "May I see you, Sir?" He smiled at everyone else. "Good morning, gentlemen," he added. "Take your seats, please."

He sat down.

Captain Pickering came down the aisle to MacArthur.

"Have a seat, Fleming," MacArthur said cordially, gesturing at the other blue leather armchair. The second chair was ordinarily reserved for Mrs. MacArthur. Although she had no official function and no security clearance, she went anywhere in HQSWPOA The General felt like taking her. When she was not present, The General awarded the privilege of sitting beside him to whichever of his officers was at the moment highest in his favor.

To the barely concealed disappointment and displeasure of his generals and admirals, that officer had very often been Captain Fleming Pickering. There were a number of reasons for their annoyance, starting with Pickering's relatively low rank. For another, the initials following his name were USNR; he wasn't even a professional Navy Man. And neither was he actually a member of the staff. Technically, he was assigned to the Office of the Secretary of the Navy, half a world away in Washington, D.C.

"Thank you, Sir," Pickering said and sat down.

MacArthur gestured to the orderly, a swarthy-skinned, barrel-chested Filipino Master Sergeant, who immediately approached the table beside MacArthur and filled the cup with steaming coffee.

MacArthur gestured with his finger that the service should be repeated for Captain Fleming. Then he turned to his side and picked up the small cigar box, opened it, and extended it to Pickering, who took one of the cigars, nodded his thanks, and bit off the end.

So far as MacArthur was concerned, it was simple courtesy. He had mentioned idly, in conversation, that among many other obvious regrets he had about leaving the Philippines, he was going to miss his long-filler, hand-rolled El Matador cigars. The next day, a half dozen boxes of El Matador had been delivered to his office, courtesy of Captain Pickering, who had found them through his contacts in Melbourne. When a friend (and he had come to think of Pickering as a friend) gives you boxes of cigars, and you are smoking one, how could a gentleman not offer him one?

So far as ninety percent of the people in the Briefing Room were concerned, it was one more manifestation of the incredible way that man Pickering (often that Goddamned Sonofabitch Pickering) had wormed his way into The General's intimate favor.

The General waited until his Filipino orderly held a flame to Captain Pickering's El Matador, then nodded at the portly U.S. Army officer in tropical worsted blouse and trousers standing almost at attention beside a lectern.

"Willoughby," he said. "Please proceed."

Colonel Charles A. Willoughby stepped behind his lectern. Willoughby had been MacArthur's Intelligence Officer (G-2) in the Philippines, had escaped with him from Corregidor, the island fortress at the mouth of Manila Bay, and was now the SWPOA G-2.

"General MacArthur," he began, "gentlemen. This morning's briefing is intended to bring you up to date on the Battle of Midway."

He nodded at the sergeant standing by the map board, who removed a sheet of oil cloth covering a map of the Pacific Ocean from the Aleutian Island chain off Alaska to Australia. When the sergeant was finished, Willoughby walked to the map.

"The intelligence we have developed," Colonel Willoughby said, "indicates that Admiral Yamamoto, commanding the entire Japanese fleet, is aboard the battleship *Yamoto* somewhere in this general area."

He pointed roughly between Midway and the Aleutian Islands.

You phony sonofabitch, Captain Fleming Pickering thought, in disgust. *"Intelligence we have developed"* my ass. *You didn't develop a goddamn bit of that. It came from the Navy. After the fact, of course, much later than they should have told us,* but *they came up with it.*

"The Japanese fleet was divided into two strike forces," Willoughby went on. "One intended to strike at the Aleutian Islands, and the other to attack and occupy Midway. As The General predicted when we first developed this information, the Aleutian operation was in the nature of a feint, a diversion, and their real ambition, as The General predicted, was to attack and occupy Midway, rather than, as some senior Navy officers believed, to launch another attack at the Hawaiian islands.

"The Midway Strike Force, under Admiral Nagumo, was made up of two battleships, four aircraft carriers, with a screening force of three cruisers, a half dozen destroyers and other ships, and of course the troop transports and other ancillary vessels."

The Supreme Commander leaned his head toward Captain Pickering and, covering his mouth with his hand, waited until Pickering had leaned toward him, and then said,

"Mrs. MacArthur would be pleased if you would come for a little supper and bridge."

"I would be honored, Sir."

"And could you have that Korean Signal Officer come too? After supper, of course?"

"I'm sure I can, Sir."

The "Korean" Signal Officer was Lieutenant "Pluto" Hon, a New York-born, MIT-educated mathematician, assigned to the staff as a cryptographic officer and Japanese-language linguist. A mere lieutenant was far too low in the military social hierarchy to be asked to dine with The Supreme Commander and his lady, but his bridge playing skill got him into The Supreme Commander's suite for bridge after dinner.

"Good," MacArthur said. "I'll give *you* to Jeanne this time, and he and I will whip you badly."

"Sir, will you take a look at this, please?" Pickering asked.

"Something you want, Pickering?" MacArthur asked, suspiciously.

"Something that just came to hand, Sir," Pickering said, and handed the onion skins to him.

MacArthur took the sheets from him. Pickering saw the distress in Colonel Willoughby's eyes that showed he no longer had The Supreme Commander's attention.

MacArthur read the summary carefully, grunting once or twice, and shaking his head.

"You believe this is accurate?" he asked.

"Yes, Sir. I think that's the best information presently available."

"You're an amazing fellow, Fleming," MacArthur said. "I'd love to know where you got this."

MacArthur handed the onion skins back to Pickering and stood up. Pickering saw in that—with relief—that MacArthur did not expect an answer.

Colonel Willoughby interrupted himself in mid-sentence as everybody in the room stood up and came to attention.

"Willoughby, something has come up. Captain Pickering and I have to leave. That was a first-class briefing. Make me a one-page summary, would you please, at your first opportunity?"

"Yes, Sir," Colonel Willoughby said.

"Keep your seats, gentlemen," MacArthur ordered, and then marched back up the aisle with Pickering and then Lieutenant Colonel Huff trailing after him.

"What was that you gave The General?" Huff asked.

"I'm sorry, Sid," Pickering said. "I can't tell you."

"I'm The General's aide," Huff argued.

"I'm sorry, Sid," Pickering repeated.

He saw the anger in Huff's eyes.

He really hates me, Pickering thought. *Hell, if I was in his shoes, I'd hate me, too. But he really doesn't have the Need to Know what those onion skins say, and I don't want him asking questions, of me or anyone else, about how I got them.*

The elevator was waiting. They rode up in it to MacArthur's office.

"Sid," MacArthur ordered, as he swept through the outer office, "will you get us some coffee, please? And have Sergeant Thorne bring his book? And then see that we are not disturbed?"

"Yes, Sir," Huff said.

Pickering saw that Sergeant Thorne already had his stenographer's notebook and a half dozen sharpened pencils in his hand. He still had time to make it to the inner door and open it for MacArthur.

Once in his office, MacArthur waved Pickering into a leather sofa. He walked to his desk, laid his gold encrusted cap on it, and then sat on the forward edge of the desk, supporting himself with his hands, looking upward, obviously deep in thought.

A staff sergeant appeared with a silver coffee set, put it on the coffee table in front of the sofa, and left.

When the door closed, MacArthur looked at Pickering.

"Pickering," he said solemnly, "my heart is so filled with thoughts of the nobility of the profession of arms that words may fail me."

Pickering, not having any idea how he was expected to respond to an announcement like that, fell back on the safe and sure: "Yes, Sir," he said.

"The first message," MacArthur went on, now looking at Sergeant Thorne, "is to Admiral Nimitz."

"Yes, Sir," Thorne said.

"My dear Admiral," MacArthur began. "Word has just come to me of your glorious victory and of the incredible courage and devotion of your men which made it possible."

He stopped abruptly. He looked at Pickering. "Pour some of that coffee for us, will you please, Fleming? Thorne, will you have some coffee?"

"Not just now, thank you, Sir," Sergeant Thorne said.

MacArthur pushed himself off the desk and walked to the window.

"Read that back, please," he said.

Sergeant Thorne did so.

"Strike 'admiral,' make it 'Chester,'" MacArthur ordered. "Strike 'made it possible.'"

"Yes, Sir," Sergeant Thorne said.

MacArthur walked to the coffee table, picked up the cup Pickering had just poured, and stood erect.

"Read it, please."

"My dear Chester, Word has just come to me of your glorious victory and of the incredible courage and devotion of your men."

"Move 'has just come to me' to the end of the sentence," MacArthur ordered, "and read that."

"Word of your glorious victory and of the incredible courage and devotion of your men has just come to me."

MacArthur considered that a moment.

"Better, wouldn't you say, Fleming? Not yet quite right, but a decent start."

"I think that's fine, General," Pickering said.

"I would be grateful for any suggestions you might care to offer," MacArthur said. "This sort of thing is really very important."

Gracious and considerate, Pickering thought. *But important?*

And then he realized why it was important.

And not only as a footnote in the History of World War II, he thought, *when someone got around to writing that. That cable is an olive branch being offered to the Navy. Nimitz is supposed to be a salty sonofabitch, but he's human, and getting a cable from MacArthur addressed, 'My dear Chester' and using phrases like 'glorious victory' and 'the incredible courage and devotion of your men' is going to have to get to him.*

Is MacArthur aware of that? Is that the reason for this? Or is it just what he said, that his heart was 'filled with thoughts of the nobility of the profession of arms' and nothing more?

It's probably both, Pickering decided. *And I'm going to give him the benefit of the doubt and think it is mostly emotion. But he is not unaware of the ancient tactic of putting your enemy off guard, either.*

"General, I wouldn't presume to attempt to better that," Pickering said.

MacArthur didn't hear him.

"The Battle of Midway will live in the memory of man—strike 'memory of man,' make it 'hearts of our countrymen, alongside Valley Forge,'" he dictated. "Got that, Thorne?"

"Yes, Sir."

"I am having trouble," MacArthur said, "recalling significant U.S. Naval victories. If only he'd said something, I could compare that to 'Don't give up the ship,' or 'Damn the torpedoes, full speed ahead.'"

For God's sake, Pickering. Don't chuckle. Don't even smile. He's deadly serious.

"If I may say so, Sir, Valley Forge seems appropriate. A small band of valiant men, with inadequate arms, showing great courage against overwhelming odds."

MacArthur considered that for a moment.

"Yes," he said. "I see what you mean. Valley Forge will do. Thorne, add 'forever' after 'live'—'will live forever.'"

"Yes, Sir," Sergeant Thorne said.

"Read the whole thing back," MacArthur ordered.

Master Sergeant Thorne stood almost at attention before General MacArthur's desk as The Supreme Commander read the fifth—and Thorne hoped last—neatly typed version of his Personal for Admiral Nimitz.

MacArthur handed it back to him.

"Give that to Captain Pickering, please."

Pickering read it, although he knew it by heart.

"I think that's fine, Sir," he said. "The language is magnificent."

"From the heart, Pickering. From the heart."

Sergeant Thorne put his hand out for the Message Form.

"I can take it downstairs, Sir," Pickering said. "I have to see Lieutenant Hon anyway."

Downstairs was the Cryptographic Office and Classified Document Vault in the hotel basement.

"Very well," MacArthur said.

"Sir, I have the Personal for General Marshall ready, too," Sergeant Thorne said.

"Well, give that to the Captain, too," MacArthur said. "Two birds with one stone, right?"

Thorne left the office and returned with two envelopes. One was sealed. He took the Personal for Admiral Nimitz Message Form from Pickering and sealed it in the other.

"If that's all you have for me, Sir?" Pickering said.

"I appreciate your assistance, Fleming. See you at six?"

"And I'll tell Lieutenant Hon to stand by from seven, Sir?"

He involuntarily glanced at his watch. It was quarter to two. He had been in MacArthur's office for nearly three hours. That seemed incredible. There had been interruptions, of course, but they hadn't taken much time at all. There had been two calls from Mrs. MacArthur and a dozen officers seeking decisions. MacArthur had wasted little time making them. Most of that time had been spent composing MacArthur's Personal for Admiral Nimitz.

"Seven," MacArthur confirmed.

(THREE)

First Lieutenant Hon Song Do, Signal Corps, U.S. Army Reserve (his very unlikely nickname was "Pluto"), and Captain Fleming Pickering, USNR, had an unusual relationship for an Army first lieutenant and a Navy captain. This had its roots in Hon's duties at SWPAO. There was virtually nothing classified SECRET or above in Supreme Headquarters SWPAO with which Lieutenant Hon was not familiar.

Lieutenant Pluto Hon was carried on the books as a cryptographic-classified documents officer. He was one of half a dozen so designated; and he performed those duties carefully and diligently. Only a very few people knew his primary function, however; for Pluto Hon had a MAGIC clearance. He was thus privy to the same information made available in Melbourne solely to MacArthur himself; his Intelligence Officer, Colonel Charles Willoughby; and Captain Fleming Pickering, Personal Representative of the Secretary of the Navy.

Hon, a mathematician at the Massachusetts Institute of Technology before the war, was directly commissioned into the Army's Signal Corps, where mathematicians were critically needed for cryptographic operations. It had then been learned that not only was he fluent in written and spoken Japanese, he was steeped in the subtleties of Japanese culture.

When word of Hon's knowledge of Japanese culture reached the cryptographic-intelligence community, he was quickly transferred from Fort Monmouth, New Jersey, to Pearl Harbor, where the Navy code-breaking operation was located, and then to MacArthur's headquarters.

In one of the most closely held secrets of the war, Navy cryptographers at Pearl Harbor had succeeded in breaking many—though by no means all—of the Japanese military and diplomatic codes. The operation involved with decrypting the Japanese messages was called MAGIC; it was a major American triumph.

Still, once the intercepted messages were decrypted, most of them did not make complete sense; for the intercepted messages were all deeply impregnated with Japanese culture and traditions. Thus analysts were needed who were not only familiar with the language but who could almost feel and react to the messages the way a Japanese would.

Lieutenant Hon was also one of the very few people who had unquestioned access to the Classified Documents Vault. When a TOP SECRET document was signed out, and later returned, it was his duty to make sure it had been returned in its entirety. It would be impossible to do that without counting pages and looking at the maps.

Additionally, he had other duties involving Captain Fleming Pickering, USNR, personally. Since Pickering had been charged by Secretary of the Navy Frank Knox to provide his assessment of what was going on, and since very often his assessments were not flattering to any number of highly placed people, these assessments had to be kept secret not only from the enemy but from everybody in Supreme Headquarters SWPOA as well.

Hon personally encrypted all communications between Pickering and Secretary Knox, and was thus privy to information known only to Pickering.

And on top of that, they had become friends. Pickering not only genuinely liked the outsize Korean, he felt a little sorry for him: The nature of Hon's duties shut him off from other junior officers; and off duty, he was in Australia. Australians did not like Asiatics—there were rigid immigration and even tourist regulations against them. It made no difference to them that Pluto Hon was a native-born American and an officer in the United States Army.

Lieutenant "Pluto" Hon stood up when Pickering walked into his tiny office. He was eating a Hershey bar.

"Good afternoon, Sir."

Hon had a thick Massachusetts accent. Pickering, a Harvard man himself, knew the dialect well. Hon was also a large and tall man, which Pickering thought of as another inconsistency. Orientals were supposed to be slight.

"How goes it, Pluto?" Pickering said. "I don't suppose you've got another Hershey bar?"

Hon took a small box of them from a desk drawer and handed it to Pickering.

"Aren't they feeding the brass these days?" Hon asked.

"I was sitting at the foot of the throne," Pickering said, as he unwrapped the Hershey bar. "The emperor was not hungry, so we didn't eat."

Pluto chuckled. "I also have peanuts," he said.

"Thank you, this will hold me. I'm eating at the palace, too. Where you will play bridge starting at about seven."

"I don't mind," Hon said. "He's one hell of a bridge player."

"Tonight it's the Empress and me against you and the throne," Pickering said.

"What have you got for me to brighten my otherwise dull day?"

"Two personals," Pickering said. "Oh, and before I forget it . . ."

He took the onion skins from his pocket and handed them to Hon.

"Burn those for me, will you?"

Hon took them and matter-of-factly started to read them.

"This must be the straight poop," he said. "KLW is a Lieutenant Commander named Ken Waldman. In Magic."

"How can you be sure?" Pickering asked, and then, without waiting for a reply, asked, "You know him?"

"Who else would have this much hard data this quick? Yeah, I know him. He was at MIT, too."

He held one sheet of the onion skin over a metal waste basket and touched the flame of his Zippo to it. It caught fire so quickly that Pickering suspected it had been chemically treated to do that.

Hon lit another sheet.

"You get this from that commander who flew in this morning?"

"Yeah. A commander."

"Mine had a briefcase chained to his wrist and a gun," Hon said. "He stopped in here and asked where he could find you before he gave me his stuff."

"Must be the same guy."

"What's the personals?"

"One to Nimitz. Powerful words of congratulation," Pickering said, and handed the envelope to Hon.

Hon tore it open and started to read it.

"What's the other one?"

"Personal to Marshall."

"What's it say?"

"I don't know, it's sealed," Pickering said, and handed it to him.

Hon read it, raised his eyebrows, and handed it to Pickering. "Based on my vast professional military experience, I don't think he's going to get away with that."

Pickering was reluctant to take the document, but curiosity overwhelmed his reticence. His curiosity was rationalized by his orders stating that it would be presumed he had the Need to Know anything that interested him. And as Hon turned to his cryptographic machine to encode the Personal to Nimitz, he read the Personal to Marshall.

FROM SUPREME HQ SWPOA

TO WAR DEPARTMENT WASH DC

FOLLOWING EYES ONLY GENERAL GEORGE C. MARSHALL CHIEF OF STAFF

PERSONAL FOR GENERAL MARSHALL

MY DEAR GEORGE X I HAVE TODAY DISPATCHED VIA OFFICER COURIER INITIAL PLANS FOR AN OPERATION I WOULD LIKE TO COMMENCE AS SOON AS I CAN OBTAIN AUTHORITY FROM THE JOINT CHIEFS OF STAFF X IT IS MY INTENTION TO STRIKE IN THE NEW BRITAIN DASH NEW IRELAND AREA USING THE US 32ND AND 41ST INFANTRY DIVISIONS AND THE AUSTRALIAN 7TH DIVISION ALL PRESENTLY IN AUSTRALIA X ONCE DRIVEN FROM NEW BRITAIN DASH NEW IRELAND THE JAPANESE WOULD BE FORCED BACK TO TRUK X TO ACCOMPLISH THE INITIAL ASSAULT AND FOR A PERIOD NOT TO EXCEED THIRTY DAYS THEREAFTER MY PLAN WOULD REQUIRE THE USE OF PAREN A PAREN ONE INFANTRY DIVISION TRAINED AND EQUIPPED FOR AMPHIBIOUS OPERATIONS X PAREN B PAREN AIR COVER FROM CARRIER BASED AIRCRAFT X PAREN C PAREN A SUITABLE NAVAL FORCE TO BOMBARD THE HOSTILE SHORE AND GUARD SHIPPING LANES X ONCE THE BEACHHEAD IS ESTABLISHED I CAN QUICKLY BEGIN AERIAL OPERATIONS FROM EXISTING FIELDS AND WILL NOT HAVE FURTHER NEED OF NAVAL ASSISTANCE X I MOST EARNESTLY SOLICIT NOT ONLY YOUR SUPPORT BUT ONCE YOU HAVE READ THE DETAILED PLANS YOUR WISE COUNSEL AS TO THEIR EFFICACY X TIME IS OF THE ESSENCE X WITH MY MOST SINCERE EXPRESSION OF REGARD I REMAIN AS ALWAYS FAITHFULLY DOUGLAS X END PERSONAL TO GENERAL MARSHALL

"The Navy's not going to loan him the First Marines and a couple of aircraft carriers," Hon said when he was sure Pickering had had time to read the Personal to Marshall. "Are they?"

His fingers were still flying over the cryptographic machine's typewriter keys as he talked. Hon always baffled Pickering when he did that. How could one part of his brain type while another part engaged in conversation?

"Not willingly," Pickering replied.

"And he doesn't know that?"

"I think he knows it," Pickering said. "I am always astonished when I find something he doesn't know."

And, he thought, *after that cable The Emperor just sent him, when Admiral Nimitz bitterly objects to this plan, he will not be as abrupt as he would otherwise have been.*

"It doesn't even make much sense, does it?"

"Yeah. I think it does. But I agree with you that the Navy will have a fit when they get this. I think they'd rather scuttle an aircraft carrier than loan it to MacArthur."

"What is that shit all about?" Pluto asked. "Can't the brass understand they're on the same side? That the goddamn Japs are whose throats they're supposed to cut?"

"Yours—and mine—Pluto, is not to reason why," Pickering said. "Can I change my mind about those peanuts?"

III

"Bingo!" Technical Sergeant Harry Rutterman, USMC, said softly, nodding his head with satisfaction.

Rutterman, a wiry man in his early thirties, raised his eyes from his desk and looked down the narrow, crowded room to an office at the end. The door was cracked open. That meant Captain Ed Sessions was in there; if he was gone, the door would have been closed and locked with iron bars and padlocks.

Rutterman lifted himself out of his chair and took the uppermost of a stack of yellow teletype sheets from his desk. He was wearing green trousers and a khaki shirt. His field scarf was pulled down, which was unusual for a regular Marine non-com; the manner in which he was armed would also be considered unusual elsewhere in the Corps. The pistol was a standard issue Colt Model 1911A1, but instead of the flapped leather holster and web belt, its standard accoutrements, Rutterman had his pistol in a skeleton holster clipped to the rear of the waistband of his trousers; the pistol was inside his trousers with only the butt in sight.

He went to Captain Sessions's door, rapped it with his knuckles, and announced, "Rutterman, Sir."

"Come," Sessions answered, and Rutterman pushed the door open.

Captain Edward M. Sessions, USMC, was a tall, lithely muscular young officer, not exactly handsome, but attractive to women all the same. Like Rutterman, he had removed his blouse and pulled his tie down; and like Rutterman, he was armed in a manner not common in the Corps. He was wearing a leather shoulder holster, which held a short-barrelled Smith & Wesson .357 Magnum Revolver.

He had expected to spend his career as a Marine officer who followed the usual progression: from infantry platoon leader, to assistant staff officer of some sort at battalion level, and then to executive officer and company commander. He had in fact commanded a platoon, but while serving as an assistant S-2 of Third Battalion, Second Marines, he had attracted the attention of the Marine Intelligence Community by the literary quality of the routine reports and evaluations he was required to write.

These were written in a style that was the antithesis of the fancy prose that the word "literary" usually calls to mind. His words were short and simple; he came right to the point; and there was little chance of mistaking what he meant.

Instead of returning to a line company following his eighteen-month assignment as an assistant S-2, he was relieved from the assignment after only a year. First, he was sent to the University of Southern California at Los Angeles for six months intensive training in Japanese, and then he was assigned to Marine Corps Headquarters in Washington. He was put to work synopsizing Intelligence reports and translating Japanese documents that had come into American hands.

He had done that for six months when a far more experienced officer, a captain, fell ill three days before he was to board the Navy Transport Chaumont. The Captain was being sent to China (where the Fourth Marines were stationed in Shanghai) to have a close look at the Japanese Army. Having no one else to send, they ordered Lieutenant Sessions to go in his place.

He performed far better than anyone expected. In his basic mission, he handled efficiently and accurately the more or less routine business of seeing how the Japanese Army was organized and equipped. And in a far more important and dramatic way, he knew what to do when the Japanese harassed a Marine convoy by dispatching Chinese "bandits" to rob it on a remote highway.

There was a nasty firefight, during which Sessions proved that he had the one characteristic the Marine Corps seeks in its officers above all others, the ability to function well and calmly under fire.

His promotion to captain came a full year before those who had been promoted to first lieutenant with him; by then it was clear that his career would henceforth be in the Intelligence field. At least twice a day, he dwelled on the thought that he would much rather be a line company commander in one of the regiments. But he was a Marine officer, and good Marine officers do—without complaint and to the best of their ability—what they are ordered to do.

"This is interesting, Harry," Captain Sessions said to Sergeant Rutterman. "The powers that be have determined that former members of the Abraham Lincoln Brigade are to be considered potentially subversive, are not to be granted security clearances, and are to be 'assigned appropriately.'"

"Interesting," Rutterman agreed. "Where'd that come from?"

"This came from G-2," Sessions said, "but it says, 'on the recommendation of the Attorney General.' That means it came from J. Edgar Hoover; I doubt if the Attorney General ever heard of the Abraham Lincoln Brigade."

Rutterman snorted.

"Have we got any, do you think?" Sessions asked.

"You mean us? Or the Corps generally?"

"In the Corps. I don't think we have any, Harry."

"There was 3000, 3500 of them. I'm sure that there's some in the Corps. But I'll bet most of them have already been tagged as Reds. What's that got to do with us?"

"Nothing that I can see; it's a Counterintelligence matter. Unless you were in Spain fighting fascism and haven't told me. I think we were just on the distribution list."

Rutterman nodded.

"What have you got, Harry?"

"I think I have a Japanese linguist for Major Banning," Rutterman said, handing Sessions the sheet of teletype paper.

Major Edward J. Banning, one of the most knowledgeable-about-the-Japanese officers in the Marine Corps, had been the S-2 of the 4th Marines in Shanghai. He had gone with the Regiment to the Philippines when it had been transferred there just before the war had broken out.

He had been blinded by concussion during a Japanese artillery barrage on Leyte, and evacuated with other blinded men by submarine from Corregidor. His sight had returned as the submarine approached Pearl Harbor. After a month's recuperative leave he had returned to duty, and almost immediately he'd been ordered back to the Pacific as commanding officer of the purposely obfuscatorily titled "Special Detachment 14."

The mission of Special Detachment 14 was to support an organization known as "The Coastwatcher Establishment" of the Royal Australian Navy. When the Japanese had begun their march toward Australia down the islands, the Australians had left behind on the captured islands a motley collection of ex-colonial officials, plantation managers, and the like. They had been equipped with radios and were reporting on Japanese shipping, troop movements, and other matters of critical intelligence importance.

One of Captain Fleming Pickering's first reports from Australia to Secretary of the Navy Knox had informed him both of the existence of the Coastwatcher Organization and of the barely concealed hostility between it and the U.S. Navy. He recommended, strongly, that Knox establish a special unit—not subordinate to "Pearl Harbor brass hats"—to work with the Coastwatchers.

Properly handled, Pickering wrote, the Coastwatcher Establishment would be of enormous value. Knox responded by charging Marine Corps Intelligence with the responsibility of working with the Coastwatchers. The orders to the again purposefully obfuscatorily named Marine Office of Management Analysis had been to set up an outfit, with whatever priorities and funds were required, to do what Captain Fleming Pickering thought should be done. Special Detachment 14 had been the result.

There was a more or less standing requisition from Major Ed Banning for two kinds of specialists: radio technicians and Japanese-language linguists. What Banning wanted, the Marine Office of Management Analysis tried very hard to send him.

"Think?" Captain Sessions asked. "Does he speak Japanese or not? And assuming he wasn't in the Abraham Lincoln Brigade?"

"He's an officer candidate," Rutterman said. "They started sending a bunch of them through Boot Camp at Parris Island."

"So? What's the problem?"

"For one thing, he's five months, maybe a little more, away from being available for assignment. After he finishes Parris Island, he has to go through Officer Basic School at Quantico. And by that time, we'd have to fight for him anyhow; they'd want to send him to a Division. And Banning needs him now."

"So we take him and send him to Banning now," Sessions said. "As an enlisted man." He heard what he had said, and added: "That sounds a little ruthless, doesn't it? But Banning really needs linguists. 'For the good of the Corps,' all right?"

"Those guys who enlisted as officer candidates have a deal, Captain," Rutterman said. "They either get the bar, or they get discharged."

"And then what?" Sessions asked.

"They report him to his draft board, and he goes in the Army."

"What about a direct commission?"

"Two weeks ago, that would have been the answer; but now the word is every second john goes through Basic School at Quantico. No exceptions. We'd only pick up a couple of weeks, *if* we could get a slot for him at Quantico. Of course, if we did that, got him a direct commission, he would belong to us, and we could probably keep him."

"Damn!" Sessions said. "And there are some other questions. Is he for real? Can he get a security clearance?"

"He's got a security clearance. Permanent SECRET. The FBI ran a complete background investigation on him when he first applied for the officer candidate program. Before they called him for active duty."

"So it would be reasonable to presume that his story that he lived in Japan for—how many years?"

"Ten, in all."

". . . checked out. And if that's the case, maybe he really does read and write Japanese."

"Yes, Sir."

"I think I better go see the Colonel," Sessions said. "And you better come with me."

The Colonel was Lieutenant Colonel F.L. Rickabee, USMC, who was carried on the Table of Organization and Equipment of Headquarters, United States Marine Corps, as a Management Analyst in the office of the Assistant Chief of Staff for Logistics. This had absolutely nothing whatever to do with his actual duties.

Colonel Rickabee, a tall, slight man who was in civilian clothing and didn't, truth to tell, look much like a Marine on a recruiting poster, heard out Captain Sessions and Technical Sergeant Rutterman.

"Ed, there's a courier plane to Parris Island at ten o'clock. Get on it. Go see this young man. First see if he really is fluent in Japanese. If he is, offer him instant sergeant's stripes and five-day delay en route home leave if he waives his current rights as an officer candidate. Tell him we'll arrange a commission for him later. If he gets on his high horse, Rutterman here will personally take him to 'Diego or 'Frisco and load him on the first plane for Australia as a private. Questions?"

"Sir, where are you going to get the authority to promote him to sergeant?" Sessions asked.

"The same place I got the authority to put him on the next plane to Major Banning. Banning desperately needs linguists. This linguist Rutterman found just may keep some Marines alive if I can get him to Banning. If I have to explain that to General Holcomb personally, I will. Questions?"

Captain Sessions was aware that two mornings a week, Lieutenant Colonel Rickabee went to Eighth and "I" Streets, S.E., in Washington. There, with the sliding doors to the Commandant's Dining Room closed, he took breakfast alone with the Commandant of the United States Marine Corps, newly promoted Lieutenant General Thomas Holcomb. If the Commandant was out of town for longer than a couple of days, Rickabee either went wherever he was, or had a private meeting with whoever was running the Marine Corps in Holcomb's absence.

"No, Sir," Sessions said, and then had a second thought. He glanced at his watch. "Sir, it's five past nine. I'm not sure I can make that ten hundred courier."

Colonel Rickabee looked thoughtful for a moment, and then dialed a telephone number from memory.

"Charley, Fred Rickabee. I'm sending an officer, Captain Ed Sessions, to Parris Island on your ten o'clock courier plane. See that it doesn't leave until he gets on it, will you?"

There was a pause, and then Rickabee said, "I don't care who gets thrown off, Sessions goes. And when he comes back, he'll be bringing a private with him. Questions?"

There was another pause.

"I've always been an unreasonable prick, Charley, you know that," Rickabee chuckled. He put the phone in its cradle and looked at Captain Sessions. "Questions?"

"No, Sir."

"Good job, Rutterman," Rickabee said, "finding this guy."

Then he dropped his eyes to the papers, most of them stamped TOP SECRET, on his desk, and shut Captain Sessions and Technical Sergeant Rutterman off from his attention.

(TWO)
Headquarters, 2nd Training Battalion
United States Marine Corps Recruit Depot
Parris Island, South Carolina
1555 Hours 15 June 1942

"Colonel Westman for you, Sir," Major H.B. Humphrey's clerk, a small, stocky, young Corporal in tailored khakis, announced, putting his head in the door.

"Thank you," Humphrey said, reaching for the telephone on the desk of his office. The desk, like the building, was new. The building was so new it smelled of freshly cut pine. The interior walls of the hastily thrown up structure had not been finished; between the exposed studs the tar paper under the outer sheeting was visible.

Photographs of the chain of command—President Roosevelt, Secretary of the Navy Frank Knox, the Commandant of the Marine Corps, and the Commanding General of Parris Island—hung from bare studs. These photos were as much *de rigueur* for a battalion commander's office as the National Colors, the Marine Corps flag, and the battalion colors.

In addition to the desk and its chair, the office was furnished with a small safe, a filing cabinet, and two folding metal chairs.

"Major Humphrey, Sir," he said to the telephone.

He wondered what the hell Colonel Westman wanted. Westman was the Parris Island G-2 Intelligence Officer. There was very little that a training battalion had to do with Intelligence. For that matter, Humphrey had wondered idly more than once what the Parris Island G-2 did at all. The function of a G-2 in the Marines was to provide the Corps with whatever information he could lay his hands on about the enemy. There was no enemy anywhere close to Parris Island.

"One of your boots has attracted the attention of some people who sit pretty close to the divine throne, Humphrey," Colonel Westman announced without any preliminaries. "A man named Moore. John Marston Moore. An officer candidate. You know him?"

Humphrey thought it over a moment.

"No, Sir."

"I have had two telephone calls," Westman said. "The first was official. From Washington. A captain named Sessions was on his way down here to 'deal with' Private Moore. I was told it would behoove me to grease this captain's ways, and if necessary, to run interference for him."

"Sir, I don't think I understand . . ."

"The second call was back channel. From . . . an old friend of mine. An aviator. He said he thought I should know that this Captain Sessions who's coming on the courier plane works for Lieutenant Colonel Rickabee. That name mean anything to you?"

Humphrey thought about that for a moment.

"Sir, there was a Major Rickabee in the class ahead of me at the Command and General Staff College. That was '39. Thin officer. Not very . . . outgoing. I've met him, but I can't say I know him."

"That's him. A very interesting man. I served with him years ago in Santo Domingo. I hear he now has very interesting duties. You take my meaning?"

"No, Sir, I'm afraid I don't."

"He sits at the foot of the divine throne. OK?"

"I take your meaning, Sir."

"I think it would behoove you to give Captain Sessions whatever he asks for, Humphrey. If he asks for anything you don't feel you can give him, call me."

"Aye, aye, Sir. You don't know what he wants with Private Moore?"

"I was not told," Colonel Westman said. "When I asked, I was told that if Captain Sessions wanted me to know, he would tell me."

"Jesus Christ!"

"I had precisely the same reaction, Humphrey," Colonel Westman said. "I would like an after action report, if I don't hear from you in the interim."

"Aye, aye, Sir. When does Captain—Sessions, you said, Sir?—get here?"

"Sessions," Westman confirmed. "The courier plane is due here in thirty minutes."

"Thank you for the advance warning, Sir."

"Good afternoon, Major," Colonel Westman said, and hung up.

Major Humphrey called for his clerk, learned to his scarcely concealed annoyance that the battalion sergeant major had business on Main Post . . . which meant that he was already hoisting his first brew of the afternoon at the Staff NCO Club . . . and was not available.

"Find out what platoon a man named Moore, John Marston Moore, is in," Major Humphrey ordered. "Then send word I want him available; and that I want to see his Drill Instructor here, right now. And then go to personnel and get his record jacket."

"If I leave, Sir, there will be no one to answer the telephone."

"I know how to answer a telephone," Major Humphrey said, more sharply than he intended. "Get moving."

"Aye, aye, Sir."

Staff Sergeant J.K. Costerburg, Private John Marston Moore's Drill Instructor, was not very helpful: Moore had not given him any trouble, but on the other hand he hadn't been an outstanding trainee, either. There had been genuine concern that he was going to have trouble on the rifle range for a while, but he'd finally shaped up. He kept to himself.

"Sir, he's just not . . . *out of the ordinary,*" Staff Sergeant Costerburg said, almost visibly pleased that he'd found the right words.

Private Moore's record jacket, which included a synopsis of the FBI Complete Background Investigation, was more illuminating: Moore was the second of three children born to the Reverend Doctor and Mrs. John Wesley Moore. He had been born in Osaka, Japan, twenty-two years before. There was a notation that under a provision of the Immigration & Naturalization Act of 1912, as amended, Moore was considered to be a native-born American, as his father's service abroad as a missionary representative of the Methodist Episcopal Church was considered to be service abroad in the interest of the United States.

He had lived in the United States, in Washington and Philadelphia, from 1922 until 1929 (Humphrey checked the dates and did the mental arithmetic and came up with from the time he was two until he was eight), and then had returned to Japan with his family, staying there until 1940, during which time he had matriculated at the University of Tokyo. On his return to the United States, he had entered the University of Pennsylvania as a junior and graduated in June of 1941 with a Bachelor of Arts degree in Oriental Languages.

He applied for the Marine Officer Candidate Program in January 1942 and was accepted. He was sworn into the Marine Corps Reserve in February, and ordered to active duty 1 April.

Humphrey was aware that people who spoke Japanese were in great demand, and that a young officer who spoke Japanese would almost certainly be given duties to take advantage of his skill, but that did not explain the attention being paid to him by a lieutenant colonel who "sat at the foot of the divine throne."

He now knew a little something about Private John Marston Moore, but he had no idea what that little something meant. And there was no time to really think it through; for he was still examining the contents of his record jacket when Colonel Westman called again.

"The plane was early," Westman announced by way of greeting. "He's on his way in my staff car with one of my lieutenants."

"Thank you, Sir," Humphrey said. For a reply he got the clatter and click of a telephone being replaced in its cradle.

Captain Sessions appeared ten minutes after that. He was a stranger to Humphrey, but he had a manner that suggested that he had been a Marine before the war.

That didn't annoy Humphrey; but there was something about his attitude that did. He was polite, but superior. It was an attitude that Humphrey had sensed in other officers who worked in Headquarters, U.S. Marine Corps, and who seemed to be very much aware of their own importance.

"Sir, my name is Sessions," Sessions had begun. "I understand that someone telephoned to alert you that I was coming."

"They didn't tell me why," Humphrey said.

"I want to look at the service records of Private John Marston Moore, and then I'd like to talk to him, Sir."

"Have you got some kind of orders, Captain? Or at least some identification?"

"Yes, Sir," Sessions said. He handed Humphrey a small leather folder. It contained a gold badge, and an identity card sealed in plastic with Sessions's photograph and name—but not, Humphrey noticed with curiosity, his rank. And it was not a Marine Corps identity card. It bore the seal of the Navy Department, and the legend CHIEF OF NAVAL INTELLIGENCE. It identified Sessions as Special Agent, not as a Marine Captain.

"That ought to do it," Humphrey said, and then blurted, "I've never seen anything like that before."

"There's not very many of them," Sessions said, matter-of-factly.

"I've got Moore's record jacket here," Humphrey said.

"May I see it, please?" Sessions replied. "And then could you send for him, please, Major?"

"I've got him standing by," Humphrey said. "Is this boy in any kind of trouble, Captain?"

"Not so far as I'm concerned," Sessions replied, and then smiled. "I was about to put that same question to you, Major."

(THREE)
United States Marine Corps Recruit Depot
Parris Island, South Carolina
1615 Hours 15 June 1942

Private John Marston Moore, United States Marine Corps Reserve, had practiced the maneuver, but he had never before rendered the rifle salute to a real officer: He marched through the door identified by a stenciled sign as that of MAJOR H.B. HUMPHREY, USMC, BATTALION COMMANDER, with his piece at right shoulder arms, determined to do so to the best of his ability.

He stopped eighteen inches from the Major's desk, with his heels together and his feet turned out equally and forming an angle of 45 degrees. He then moved his left hand smartly to the small of the stock, forearm horizontal, palm of the hand down, the first joint of his left forefinger touching the cocking piece of his Springfield Model 1903A4 rifle.

"Sir," he barked, looking at Major Humphrey, a thin, leather-skinned man of about thirty-five who wore his hair so short his scalp was visible, "Private Moore, J.M., reporting to the battalion commander as ordered."

Ordinarily, Private Moore had learned, persons in the Naval Service of the United States do not salute indoors, except when Under Arms. He was obviously, with the Springfield, Under Arms, but he had also learned in his six weeks of service in the Marine Corps that things were most often not as one expected them to be. He had asked the staff sergeant in the outer office what he was supposed to do with the rifle. The reply—"Get your ass in there and report to the Major"—had not been very helpful.

Major Humphrey touched his eyelid with his right hand, fingers together and straight, palm down.

The salute had been returned.

Private Moore cut his left hand smartly back to his right side, fingers extended and together, so that his thumb touched the seam of his utility trousers. He then looked six inches above Major Humphrey, in the prescribed position of attention.

"Order arms," Major Humphrey ordered, and then followed this command immediately with, "stand at ease."

Private Moore moved the Springfield so that it cut diagonally across his body, the center of the rifle just below his chin, held at the point of balance by the left hand. He moved his right hand from the butt on the rifle to a point one-third down from the muzzle, and then moved the rifle beside his right leg, checking the movement with his left hand. When the butt touched the floor, he moved his left hand so that its thumb touched the seam of his utility trousers. Then he leaned the Springfield forward, put twelve inches between the heels of his boots, and set his left hand in the small of his back. He was now At Ease.

"He's all yours, Captain," Major Humphrey said.

"Good afternoon, Moore. How are you today?" the Captain asked.

His tone was conversational, even friendly, which was almost astonishing, but what was genuinely astonishing was that the Captain had asked the question in Japanese.

"Very well, thank you, Sir," Private Moore said.

"Could you reply, please, in Japanese?" the Captain asked.

Moore did so.

"Do you read and write Japanese with equal fluency?"

"Yes, Sir."

"Major," the Captain said, switching to English, "I wonder if there's some place I could talk to Private Moore privately?"

"You can use my office, of course," Major Humphrey said.

"Very kind of you, Sir. Thank you, Sir," the Captain said, and then waited for Major Humphrey to get up and leave.

It was not lost on Private Moore that no matter what their ranks, the captain was giving orders, however politely, to the major, and that the major didn't much like it.

Sessions waited until Major Humphrey had left the office, closing the door behind, and then turned to Moore. He opened his mouth, as if to speak, then chuckled.

In English, he said, "I was about to ask you how you find boot camp, but I suppose when you open your eyes in the morning, there it is, right?"

Now he laughed, almost a giggle.

John Marston Moore had no idea how to react. There was no emotion on his face at all. Sessions saw this.

"My name is Sessions," he said. "I'm from Headquarters, USMC."

"Yes, Sir?"

"You're posing something of a problem to the Marine Corps," Sessions began seriously, but then his eyes lit up in amusement. "Usually, with a private, and especially here, that works the other way around, but in this case, you're causing the problem."

"Sir?"

"I'm going to have to take your word that you read and write Japanese," Sessions said. "I suppose I should have brought some document in Japanese for you to read from, but I left Washington in rather a hurry and didn't think about that. And the way I write Japanese . . . that wouldn't be a fair test."

Moore had just decided that Marine Captain or not, this man was an amiable idiot, when Sessions met his eyes. The eyes were both intelligent and coldly penetrating; not the eyes of a fool.

"You do read and write Japanese with fluency, right?" Sessions asked.

"Yes, Sir."

"OK. You ever read any Kafka, Moore?"

"Sir?"

"Franz Kafka? Everyman's problems with a mindless bureaucracy? They kept telling him he was guilty, but they wouldn't tell him of what?"

"Yes, Sir, I know who you mean."

"This is going to be something like that, I'm afraid," Sessions said. "There is a Marine Corps unit somewhere which has a priority requirement for a man with your Japanese language skills. I can't tell you what that unit is, where it is—except somewhere in the Pacific—or what it does, because that's all classified."

"Sir—" Moore began hesitantly, and then plunged ahead. "Sir, I was told that I've been granted a SECRET security clearance."

"Yeah, I know. But then there's TOP SECRET, and above TOP SECRET are some other security classifications. In this case, your SECRET clearance wouldn't get you in the door."

"Yes, Sir."

"I don't suppose," Sessions said, "that based on what little I'm able to tell you, you would be disposed to volunteer for service with this unit, would you?"

I am being asked to do something. This is the first I have been asked, as opposed to being told, to do anything since I got off the Atlantic Coastline train in Yemassee, South Carolina.

An image of that scene popped into his mind, complete to sound and smell; it was the start of his first night of active duty in the Marine Corps.

They had gotten off the chrome-and-plastic, air-cushioned, air-conditioned ACL cars and transferred to ancient, filthy wooden passenger cars resurrected from some railroad junk yard for the spur line trip to Port Royal. From Port Royal, they had been moved to Parris Island, like cattle being carried to the slaughter house, in an open trailer truck.

In Port Royal, he heard for the first time the suggestion that he might as well give his soul to Jesus, because his ass now belonged to the Marine Corps. Those words had subsequently been repeated many times.

From the moment he boarded the spur line train in Yemassee, his every action had been ordered, usually at the top of some uniformed sadist's lungs, his language punctuated with obscenities.

He had once been ordered by a corporal to run around the barracks with a galvanized bucket over his head, his piece at port arms, shouting, "I am an ignorant asshole who can't tell the difference between his piece and his prick." He'd done it, too.

He had only been permitted to stop when he ran full bore into a concrete pillar and nearly knocked himself out. He could not recall, now, the offense.

And now I am being asked *to do something. I am not prepared to make a decision.*

"Sir, I don't know what you're asking me to do."

"Let me throw one more thing into the equation," Captain Sessions said. "It would also mean, for the time being, that you would give up your commission. One can be arranged at a later date, but you would not get one now."

"Sir—"

"The bone I am authorized to throw to you is sergeant's stripes, effective immediately, and a five-day delay en route leave, not counting travel time."

"Sir, I don't mean any disrespect, but could you tell me why I should do something like this? I'm almost through here. When I finish at Quantico, I'll be an officer."

He had clung to that, the belief that when he had endured all that Parris Island, specifically all that his Drill Instructor and his assistants, could throw at him, he would be granted a commission. An officer, even a lowly second lieutenant, was not required to obey the orders of enlisted men.

Captain Sessions didn't reply. He shrugged and opened his mouth as if to speak, but then closed it again.

"Couldn't this assignment wait until I get my commission, Sir?" Moore asked.

"No," Sessions said simply, "it couldn't. You're needed now."

"Captain, what if I tell you 'no'?"

Sessions shrugged his shoulders again, almost helplessly. He did not respond to the question, but after a moment, he said: "I suppose that in your shoes, I would react exactly the way you are. And I would probably snicker, at least privately, if someone like me announced the reason you should do what you're being asked to do is that you're a Marine, and when the Corps asks Marines to do something, they do it."

"I've only been in the goddamned Marine Corps six fucking weeks!" Moore heard himself blurt and was horrified.

The consequences of making a statement like that, especially to an officer, boggled the imagination.

Sessions, to Moore's genuine surprise, did not flare back at him. He looked at him and chuckled.

"Six weeks is long enough, don't you think? Don't you think that six weeks has changed you forever?"

"Oh, Christ," Moore said, and heard himself chuckle. "Yes, Sir, I think I have been permanently changed."

"For what it's worth," Sessions went on, "I've learned that you get back from the Corps whatever you put into it. Sometimes a little more."

He believes that. This man is not a fool, not one of the cretinous savages they make into drill sergeants. He's well educated—Christ, talking about Franz Kafka and Everyman at Parris Island! And he speaks Japanese, and not at all badly. And whatever this is they want me to do, it's important. He really did come down here to see me from Washington.

And what happens if I say 'no'? Since it is important, then obviously they will be annoyed that I have refused. So far as they're concerned, I'm a Marine and Marines do whatever they are asked, or told to do. I will have, so to speak, in their judgment, let the side down. And equally obviously, the consequences of that would be very unpleasant. Am I a Marine? Why do I have the insane urge to go along with this?

Possibly because he is the first man in authority to talk to me as if I were a

*human being, perhaps even an intellectual equal, since I got on that fucking train
from Yemassee to Port Royal.*

*Fuck it! Why not? What the fuck have I got to lose? The fuckers are right, my
fucking ass really* does *belong to the fucking Marine Corps!*

Why, John Marston Moore! Listen *to your* language!

"Yes, Sir," Moore said. "Whatever it is you want me to do, Sir, is fine with
me."

He had no idea what sort of response his patriotic, "Aye, Aye, Sir! Semper Fi,
Sir! We Are All Marines In This Together, Sir!" decision would produce in Captain
Sessions, but the one he got was not at all what he expected:

"OK," Sessions said, matter-of-factly, even coldly. "That's it. But don't feel
noble. What you just did made you a sergeant and got you five days at home. If
you had decided the other way, you would have been on a plane tomorrow as a
private."

"Yes, Sir," Moore said, more as a reflex action than a reply.

"This is very serious business, and we can't take any chances with it whatever.
Between now and tomorrow, I will come up with some sort of credible story for
you to tell your parents when you go home. But from this moment on, you're
operating under a whole new set of restrictions. For example, you will not tell
anyone that you were pulled out of boot camp and made a sergeant, or that you
even met me. If anyone asks you any questions, your response will be, simply, 'I'm
sorry, I can't talk about that.' Clear?"

"Yes, Sir."

"Just so that I'm sure you understand me, that includes everybody here, including
Major Humphrey. Clear?"

"Yes, Sir."

Sessions got up, walked to the door, and opened it.

"Major Humphrey? May I see you a moment, please, Sir?"

Humphrey came into his office, uneasy, Moore saw, about taking his own chair
behind his desk.

"Something I can do for you, Captain?" he asked.

"Yes, Sir. There are several things I'd be grateful if you would do for me. From
this point on, you will consider this conversation classified Top Secret."

"OK," Humphrey said. Moore had the feeling that Humphrey had only with
effort kept himself from saying 'Yes, Sir.' There was now a tone of command, *I
Will Be Obeyed,* in Sessions's voice that had not been there before.

"Sergeant Moore will not be returning to his platoon," Sessions said. "I will
take his service records jacket with me . . ."

"*Sergeant* Moore?" Major Humphrey interrupted.

Captain Sessions ignored him. "In the next day or two, there will be a TWX from
Enlisted Personnel routinely transferring him. You are to discuss the circumstances of
Sergeant Moore's departure with no one."

"I understand, Captain," Humphrey said. "Colonel Westman, the G-2, has asked
me for an after action report."

"I'll go see Colonel Westman when I leave here. You are not to tell him anything.
I'll make sure he understands that I'm responsible for that decision."

"Whatever you say, Captain."

"I don't want the people in his platoon, boots or Drill Instructors, discussing the
unusual circumstances of Sergeant Moore's departure," Sessions said. "Do you see
any problem there?"

"No, that can be handled, I think. I'll have to tell my sergeant major something.
You understand, he will be curious."

"OK. Tell him that there's been an administrative fuck-up—that shouldn't surprise him—and that we're quietly trying to make it right. I would rather you talk to him than me. And also, by the time Sergeant Moore and I get on the courier plane in the morning, I want him to be wearing the insignia of his rank. Which means that someone is going to have to go to his platoon and get his gear and run the shirts and blouses past a seamstress."

"I think the Gunny can handle that without trouble, Captain," Humphrey said.

"Another practical matter. Where is Sergeant Moore going to spend the night?"

"There's a guest house. I don't suppose too many eyebrows would be raised if he was in one of those rooms. He could be waiting for his wife, or mother, whatever."

"Particularly if he went to his room and stayed there until I fetched him in the morning, right?"

Humphrey nodded.

"How is he going to eat?"

"There's a snack bar," Humphrey said.

"Could I stay there, too?"

"It's an enlisted guest house," Humphrey said.

"OK. I'll get a room in the transient BOQ. Moore, you will be taken to the guest house. Your gear will be delivered to you there. You will take supper and breakfast in the guest house. You will not leave your room for any other purpose. I will fetch you at about eight-thirty tomorrow morning. You are to make no telephone calls, or communicate with anyone but myself. I will get you a number where I can be reached. Clear?"

"Aye, aye, Sir."

"Questions?" Sessions asked.

Christ, he thought, *I sound just like Colonel Rickabee.*

There were no questions.

(FOUR)
Enlisted Guest House
United States Marine Corps Recruit Depot
Parris Island, South Carolina
0730 Hours 16 June 1942

Sergeant John Marston Moore was unable to resist the temptation to examine himself carefully in the cheap and somewhat distorting full-length mirror mounted on the door of the closet in his room at the guest house.

He had last examined himself in a small and even more distorting mirror in the head of his barracks twenty-six hours before, after shaving. What had then looked back at him was a hollow-eyed, sunken-cheeked individual in baggy utilities. He had looked very much like every other boot in his platoon, except that he was taller than most of them, and the weight loss and musculature hardening of the physical conditioning had made him look skinnier.

What looked back at him now was a sergeant of the United States Marine Corps, wearing a stiffly starched khaki shirt and a sharply creased green uniform. He moved slightly, so that his left shoulder pointed at the mirror and looked at the reflection of his new chevrons.

Then he met his eyes in the mirror and shook his head. He looked closer. He still had what he thought of as a "boot head"—a head an electric clipper had shorn of all hair, down to the skin, in ninety seconds. His head was by no means recovered from that outrage.

With the boot head I still look like a boot.

He went to the double bed where he had passed the night, picked up his fore-and-aft cap, put that on, and examined himself in the mirror again. That was better. The cap concealed the top of his head from view.

He had woken in the bed at four o'clock, conditioned by six weeks of waking at that hour to the shrill blast of a whistle and the ritual admonition to drop his cock and pick up his socks.

For a moment, he hadn't known where he was, for the room was pitch dark. There had always been some kind of light in the squad bay, if only what came into the long, narrow, and crowded room from the head. And then he had remembered what happened, out of the blue, the previous afternoon.

They would have wondered, the guys in the platoon, what the fuck had happened to Moore, J. He was known as Moore, J. because there were two Moores in his platoon. The other one, from Connecticut, was Moore, A. Moore, J. had never learned what Moore, A.'s "A" had stood for.

"What the fuck happened to Moore, J.?"

"Who the fuck knows. They sent for him. Company, I think."

"What the fuck did he do?"

"Who the fuck knows?"

Eventually, someone's curiosity would overwhelm his good sense and he would ask, waiting until he thought one of the DI's assistants was in an unusually kind mood.

"Sir, permission to speak, Sir?"

"Speak, Asshole."

"Sir, whatever happened to Moore, J., Sir?"

"If the Marine Corps wanted you to know, Asshole, I would have told you. What are you doing, Asshole, writing a book?"

"Yes, Sir. Sorry, Sir. Thank you, Sir."

He had not been able to get back to sleep. After a while, he had gotten out of the double bed and stood at the window in his underwear and looked out at the deserted streets.

Then the sounds of mating had come through the thin walls from the next room. He remembered hearing them the night before, waking him about half past nine.

Someone, he had thought, *was making up for lost time.*

It had been funny for a moment . . . and then somehow erotic, as his mind's eye filled with what was going on next door. And then finally it was terribly sad, although he didn't quite understand why that should be the case. The Marine Corps, he had noticed from signs at the Reception Desk, seemed determined that no Marine should share one of its Parris Island Enlisted Guest House rooms with a lady to whom he was not legally joined in marriage.

He hadn't thought much about sex since he'd been at Parris Island. For one thing, there hadn't been time to think about sex or anything else. For another, he had always been exhausted; he had woken up exhausted. And he thought it was possible . . . he had learned that at Parris Island anything was possible . . . that they did indeed lace the chow with saltpeter as the folklore had it.

There was a knock at the door. He looked at it in astonishment. Since he had been at Parris Island, closed doors, what few of them there were, had been flung open whenever they were noticed.

The door opened. It was the Sergeant Major.

"Good morning," the Sergeant Major said. "You're up."

"Yes, Sir."

The Sergeant Major smiled. He was a bald, barrel-chested man, whose blouse wore the hash marks, one for each four years of service, of two decades in the Marine Corps.

"Sergeant, sergeants do not say 'Sir' to other sergeants," he said. "Only boots do that."

Moore took off his fore-and-aft cap and rubbed his boot head.

"It'll grow back," the Sergeant Major, understanding the gesture, chuckled. "Keep your cap on when you can. Let's catch some breakfast."

Moore had been given a room on the upper floor of the two-story, newly constructed, frame building. As he followed the Sergeant Major down the stairs to the first floor, they ran into Captain Sessions coming up.

"Good morning, Sir," the Sergeant Major said. "I thought I would make sure that Sergeant Moore got his breakfast."

"My mission, too," Sessions said. "The corporal in the BOQ said it would be all right for me to eat in the snack bar."

"Yes, Sir. It's run by the Base Exchange. Neutral territory."

"Good morning, Moore. You packed?"

"Yes, Sir."

"Then let's eat."

"Would I be in the way, Sir?" the Sergeant Major asked.

"Not at all," Sessions said.

"I've got a staff car, too, Sir. I thought I could take you and Sergeant Moore to the airfield. And then you could turn Colonel Westman's car loose."

"Fine," Sessions said.

"I always feel sorry for colonels who have to walk, Sir," the Sergeant Major said, solemnly.

"I'm sure you do, Sergeant Major," Sessions said, and then laughed. "Take Moore to the snack bar, and I'll go tell the colonel's driver he can go."

The breakfast fare was simple, but the eggs and the hash-brown potatoes were served on plates, and they sat at chairs at four-place tables covered with white oil cloth, and the china coffee mug had a handle; and that combined to make it, Moore thought, the most elegant meal he'd had since he left Philadelphia.

And there was something else. A newspaper. *The Charleston Gazette.* He hadn't seen a newspaper since coming to Parris Island, either.

There was a photograph on the front page of a tall, skinny American officer, a lieutenant general, Moore could now tell. He was seated at a table on what looked like a porch, wearing a tieless, mussed khaki shirt. There were three other American officers sitting with him. On the other side of the table were Japanese officers.

JAPS RELEASE PHOTO OF WAINWRIGHT SURRENDER, the headline over the picture said. Under it, the caption read: "War Department officials confirmed that Lieutenant General Jonathan M. Wainwright, U.S. Commander in the Philippines, sits (center, left) in this photograph, which the Japanese claim depicts General Wainwright's surrender to Japanese General Mashaharu Homma (center, right) May 5. The photo was obtained via neutral Sweden."

"That's a bitch, isn't it?" the Sergeant Major said, tightly.

"I think that must be the toughest thing an officer ever has to do," Sessions said. "God, what a humiliation!"

"It was on the radio last night that General Sharp surrendered Mindanao," the Sergeant Major said. "That's it. The Japs now own the Philippines."

"I know some of the people who are now prisoners," Sessions said, sounding as if he was thinking aloud, "if they're still alive."

"Yes, Sir, I know," the Sergeant Major said.

"How do you know that?" Sessions asked.

Moore sensed that Sessions had been made uneasy by the apparently innocent statement and wondered why.

"I'm an old China Marine, too, Captain. In my last hitch I was the S-3 Operations Sergeant for the 4th."

"Were you?" Sessions asked, and now the suspicion in his voice was evident.

"Yes, Sir. The 4th was a good outfit. Good people. I had sort of a special buddy. Guy named Killer McCoy."

"You're moving into a mine field, Sergeant Major," Sessions said, softly. "Sometimes, playing auld lang syne is not the thing to do."

"Oh, I don't mean to . . . I wasn't trying to pump you for poop, Sir. Really. It was just that Killer and I had the same ideas about who was a good Marine officer and who wasn't."

"Which means?"

The Sergeant Major hesitated momentarily, and then met Sessions's eyes.

"I got three, four staff NCOs who could have taken care of Sergeant Moore for you, Sir. I sort of wanted to do it myself. You know, any friend of The Killer's . . ."

Sessions looked at the Sergeant Major for a long moment before he replied.

"That's very kind of you, Sergeant Major. I'm touched. Thank you."

"No thanks necessary, Sir," the Sergeant Major said. "There's not many of us old China Marines left now. I figure we should try to take care of each other, right?"

"You didn't get this from me, Sergeant Major," Sessions said. "But the Killer made it out. He's with the 2nd Raider Battalion."

"I hadn't heard that. Thank you, Captain."

"What's the word on the courier plane?" Sessions said, obviously changing the subject.

"We better get out to the airport by say nine-fifteen, Sir."

Sergeant John Marston Moore had no idea what the conversation between the Sergeant Major and Captain Sessions was all about, but he understood that Captain Sessions had done something—probably in China, there was all that talk about Old China Marines—that had earned him the respect of the old Marine non-com. And he had the feeling that earning the Sergeant Major's approval didn't come easily.

He wondered about "The Killer." If he was the "special buddy" of the sergeant major and held in high regard by Captain Sessions, "The Killer" was obviously one hell of a Marine. Hash marks from his wrist to his shoulder, a breast covered with twenty, thirty years' worth of campaign ribbons, barrel chested and leather skinned, with a gravel voice to match.

There was something really admirable about these professional warriors, Moore thought. They were latter day Centurions. Or maybe gladiators? Whatever they were, they weren't like ordinary men. For them, war was a way of life.

Captain Sessions looked at his watch.

"Well," he said. "Let's get the show on the road. It never hurts to be early."

"You're all packed, right?" the Sergeant Major asked Moore.

"All packed," Moore replied, stopping himself just in time from replying, "Yes, Sir."

"Go get your stuff then," the Sergeant Major said. "I'm parked right out in front."

"One late thought," Captain Sessions said. "There's always one late thought, too late to do anything about. Have you been paid? Have you got enough money to carry you, Moore? Enough for the train ticket between Washington and Philadelphia?"

"The train ticket between Washington and Philadelphia"? I'm actually leaving Parris Island and going home. Why is that so incredible?

"I haven't been paid, Sir," Moore said. "But I have money."

"You're sure?"

"Yes, Sir."

"Go get your gear, Moore," Captain Sessions said.

IV

As the Sergeant Major drove them to the small airfield that served the Parris Island Recruit Depot, Sergeant John Marston Moore, USMCR, wondered what his father was going to say about his turning down an officer's commission and then going off to God only knows where in the Pacific. His father—to put it mildly—had not been pleased when he joined the Marine Corps in the first place; and he'd probably go into a righteous rage that he was not going to be an officer, at least not for the foreseeable future. To make matters worse, John couldn't even tell his father the reason why he'd made his choice.

All the same, there was no sense worrying about his father. . . . He'd learned not to worry about things he had no control over. And besides, no matter how used his father was to getting his own way, he could not bend the U.S. Marine Corps to his will.

Moore had flown only twice before in his life, both times during the family's last trip home from Japan: They'd left the ocean liner in San Francisco, and then they'd flown on from there via Chicago to New York. The flight from San Francisco to Chicago had been on Transcontinental & Western Airlines, and from Chicago to New York on Eastern. The airplanes had been essentially identical, large, twenty-odd-passenger Douglas DC-3s. Eastern had called theirs "Luxury Liners of the Great Silver Fleet."

John Marston Moore knew he would never forget that trip. He still had a flood of memories from it. He even remembered the name stenciled on the Eastern airplane's nose; it was *The City of Baltimore*. He also recalled watching his father take his mother's hand, bow his head, and mouth a prayer as the TWA airplane started down the runway in San Francisco.

He hadn't forgotten, either, the justification his father put forth for the extra expense of flying: "The Lord is a hard taskmaster," he would intone in his most virtuous voice, "who wants all that I can give Him. 'Missions' needs me in Philadelphia as soon as I can reach there. I've already spent a great deal of time at sea on the voyage from Yokohama, and that has kept me out of touch with 'Missions' for weeks. If I take the train, I'll be traveling another five days, while it will only take thirty-six hours by airplane. Obviously, taking the plane is the clear will of the Lord."

By then, John Marston Moore had long since decided that the Reverend Doctor John Wesley Moore was a pious hypocrite. A number of arguments supported this judgment. His father, for example, had delayed their departure from Japan for nearly three weeks, so they could return to the United States in first class aboard the *Pacific Princess,* the flagship of the Pacific & Far East Shipping Corporation fleet. The alternative would have been to travel on one of the Transpacific freighters which made their comfortable but spartan passenger accommodations available to missionaries and their families at reduced rates.

"Your Uncle Bill would insist," the Reverend Doctor Moore told John Marston Moore and his sisters. "He would know how much I need the rest."

Uncle Bill—William Dawson Marston IV—was president of the family business, Dawson & Marston Paper Merchants. Dawson & Marston had been in business in Philadelphia since 1781, on Cherry Street, near the Schuylkill River. If John Marston Moore had been a betting man, he would have laid five to one that the first time Uncle Bill heard about the first-class cabins on the *Pacific Princess* was when the bill arrived for payment at Dawson & Marston.

John knew no one in the world who could muster the audacity to ask his father the obvious question: "You could have flown alone at one third the cost, and then the family could have followed by train . . . why didn't you do that?" If someone by chance had dared to ask him such a thing, his father would have replied—with a perfectly straight face, believing every word that poured from his lips—that it was clearly his Christian duty to be with his family and protect them from the well-known hazards of a transcontinental journey.

The Reverend Doctor Moore's concept of his clear Christian duty to his family had also been behind their twelve-room house in Denenchofu; the chauffeured Packard; the semiannual vacations in first-rate hotels in Australia and New Zealand; the monthly crates of canned goods that arrived from Boston; and everything else that made their life saving infidel souls for the Lord in far off Japan far more comfortable than any of their co-religionists in America would have imagined.

It was not as if he was living high on the hog on funds intended to educate and convert Asiatic heathens . . . he did not misappropriate funds; he'd never dream of defrauding "Missions." He was in fact on the whole a very good man. Still, though the salary and living allowance he was paid by "Missions" was not at all generous, the Reverend Doctor Moore didn't complain about his stipend, neither did he make any attempt to live on it. John long ago concluded that most of what "Missions" paid his father went to feed the servants.

Though it was only peripherally connected with most other functions of the Methodist Episcopal Church, "Missions" was more formally known as "The William Barton Harris Methodist Episcopal Special Missions to the Unchurched Foundation." It was founded in 1866 by a grant from Captain James D. Harris of Philadelphia.

Harris Shipping predated the American Revolution and was prosperous before the Civil War. But the war had swelled its coffers beyond anyone's imagination. On Captain Harris's death, the foundation received his entire estate, his wife having died the year before he did; and they'd lost their only son, William Barton Harris, in the Civil War.

The stated purpose of Missions was "to bring the Gospel of Jesus Christ and the Hope of Eternal Life to those who would not normally receive the blessing, such as Merchant Seamen, heathen Asiatics, the natives of the Caribbean Islands, and the former slaves now residing in those same islands."

While it was to be guided by the principles of Methodism, and it was "to be hoped that principal officers will be Methodist Episcopal Clergy and that the Foundation will be supported by the ever increasing generosity of Methodists," it was not to "become part of, or subject to the direction of, any local or national Methodist Episcopal organization." A key phrase of the bequest went on to state, "if at any time it becomes evident that the Foundation cannot continue its Christian mission, as specified herein, its assets will be liquidated and conveyed to the Philadelphia Free Public Library."

The rumor, Uncle Bill had once told John Marston Moore, was that "The Captain" had not seen eye to eye with his Bishop and was not about to give him control of his money. But whatever the truth, "Missions" had evolved into an organization with three major arms: The Seaman's Mission provided services to merchant seamen from Boston to Charleston—primarily cheap, clean YMCA-like accommodations and other related socio-religious services; the Caribbean Mission operated schools and social services in the Caribbean; and the Asiatic Mission performed a similar function in the Orient.

Each arm was headed by a Methodist clergyman, while another served as Superintendent; and two of the seven trustees were also Methodist clerics. The other five trustees were a Presbyterian Minister; an Episcopal priest; and three laymen. From the beginning, one of these had either been a Marston or someone married to a Marston. Uncle Bill had succeeded his father as a Missions Trustee.

Philadelphia Methodist and social circles showed very little surprise when the son-in-law of William D. Marston III, a longtime Missions trustee, was married and ordained during the same week that he joined Missions; neither was there much surprise when years later the now Reverend Doctor John Wesley Moore, brother-in-law of Missions trustee William D. Marston IV, was named to head the Asiatic Mission.

But Philadelphia Methodist and social circles would have been surprised, John Marston Moore knew, if it ever became generally known how well the Reverend Doctor John Wesley Moore lived while serving the Lord. His father, of course, was ready with an explanation for it—if that ever became necessary: Though *he* was perfectly willing to live a life of austerity, indeed poverty, while in the Service of the Lord, not only had his beloved wife and adored children *not* been so moved to serve the Lord, but the Lord, in his infinite wisdom, had moved his brother-in-law, that fine Christian gentleman, to extraordinary generosity toward his sister and nieces and nephews.

John Marston Moore wondered now and again just how much of Dawson & Marston Paper Merchants, founded A.D. 1781, his parents actually owned. And for that matter, he had questions about the amounts involved in the trust funds that had been set up for him and his sisters by grandparents on both sides of the family. But the few times he'd asked, he was told that he need not just now concern himself with that sort of thing. "The Lord has done very well, so far, wouldn't you agree, John, providing for your needs?"

If John Marston Moore didn't know his father as well as he did, he would never have believed it possible for anyone to be such a good man—perhaps even close to a saintly man—and still be a pious hypocrite. But the younger Moore had pages of illustrations in his own personal book of memories demonstrating the truth of that hypothesis.

One evening, for instance, while his father was literally warming in his hand a snifter of Rémy Martin cognac at the Union League Club, John Marston Moore had been forbidden to live in a fraternity house at the University of Pennsylvania, because it was common knowledge that the fraternity houses were awash with intoxicants. As the only son of a Man of God of Some Position, he had to be quite careful of appearances.

The airplane parked in front of the wood frame, single-story Operations Building at the airfield was much smaller than the Douglas DC-3s of TWA and Eastern. Captain Sessions identified it for him as a Beech Aircraft D-18. The legend MARINES was painted on the fuselage.

There were more than a dozen would-be passengers already in the wooden operations building hoping to get one of the eight seats on the airplane. Since three of these men were officers senior to Captain Sessions, Moore wondered if that meant they would have to travel to Washington as he had come to Parris Island, by train.

But he quickly found out that the seats on the Beech were assigned not by rank but by priority. It did not surprise him, however, that Captain Sessions had a priority: The first two names called out to board the plane were Sessions and Moore.

As they filed out to the plane, one of the pilots handed each of them a brown bag containing a baloney sandwich and an apple. The pilots were both Marine sergeants; Moore found that very interesting. He thought that only officers were permitted to fly.

If there were sergeants who did things like fly airplanes, perhaps there were other things a sergeant—Sergeant John Marston Moore, for example—could do besides screaming obscenities at boots or conducting close order drill. That made him feel a good deal better about having given up—at least for the time being—his promised officer's commission.

Once they found seats, Moore saw that compared to the plushness of the planes he was used to, the D-18 was rather crudely finished inside. But that didn't bother him. The very idea of flying from South Carolina to Washington on a military airplane was exciting. He tried to muster what savoir faire he could to conceal this from Captain Sessions.

But just after the pilots walked down the narrow aisle to the cockpit and sat down to start the engines, curiosity overwhelmed him, and he turned to Captain Sessions.

"Sir, I thought all pilots were officers."

"Just most of them," Sessions replied. "In the Army," he went on, "they all are. But both the Navy and the Marine Corps have enlisted pilots; oddly enough, they're called 'Flying Sergeants.' Don't worry, Moore, I personally would rather be flown around by a Flying Sergeant than by some kid fresh out of Pensacola."

After the airplane took off, it flew right over the Recruit Depot. Moore could see the small arms ranges, and even platoons of boots marching around on the parade ground. The thought ran through his mind that it was conceivable that he was looking down at his old platoon.

The flight to the Anacostia Naval Air Station just outside Washington was much too short for Moore's liking. The day was clear, and there was something very nice indeed about being able to look down at the lush spring country. It didn't bother him at all that the sandwiches were dry, the apple mushy, and the coffee in the thermos jug lukewarm.

Technical Sergeant Harry Rutterman was waiting for them when the airplane landed. As they got out of the airplane, he came up to them and saluted Captain Sessions, who smiled as he returned it.

"Nice flight, Sir?"

"Why do I suspect that your meeting me has nothing to do with your all-around admiration for me as an officer and human being?" Sessions replied.

"The Captain, Sir, has for some reason a suspicious nature where I am concerned."

"Come on, Rutterman," Sessions said with a smile. "What's going on?"

"The Colonel wants you right now," Rutterman said. "He even sent his car. I'll take care of Sergeant Moore from here."

"Brief me on that," Sessions said, and then, "Excuse me. Moore, this is Sergeant Harry Rutterman."

Rutterman gave Moore a broad smile, and then—unintentionally, Moore decided—he crushed his hand in an iron handshake.

"Welcome to Never-Never Land, Sergeant," he said.

"OK, Rutterman," Sessions said. "Enough!"

"Yes, Sir," Rutterman said. "As of this morning, Private Moore was transferred to Baker Company, Headquarters Battalion, here. Then, recognizing the enormous contribution to the Corps he is about to make, they promoted him to Sergeant. Then they transferred him to Marine Barracks, Navy Yard, Philadelphia. I checked the travel times. He has forty-eight hours to get here from Parris Island, and twenty-four to get to Philadelphia after he leaves here. When his orders get to Philadelphia, he'll have seven days to get to San Diego. I got him an airplane ticket from New York to Los Angeles, which will put him there in about thirty-six hours. He has to take the train from Los Angeles to 'Diego. So I didn't put him on leave. I mean, why? What's important is that he gets on the plane in 'Diego on the twenty-first, right? This way, he won't get charged any leave time."

"I don't think I want to hear about this," Sessions said.

"It's all according to regulations, Captain," Sergeant Rutterman said, sounding slightly indignant.

"The trouble is, Sergeant, that you read things in regulations that no one else can see," Sessions said. "But he has a seat on the courier from San Diego on the twenty-first, right? That's all locked in?"

"As well as it can be, Sir. You know what happens, sometimes. An unexpected senior officer shows up wanting a seat . . ."

"What's his priority?" Sessions interrupted.

"Six As," Sergeant Rutterman had replied. "The Colonel had to make a couple of phone calls himself, but he got it."

Sergeant John Marston Moore wondered what in the world they were talking about.

"What else can we do?"

"Odd that you should ask, Sir—"

"If you're about to suggest that out of an overwhelming sense of duty, you would be willing to take the Sergeant out there yourself, to make sure he doesn't get bumped out of his seat by 'an unexpected senior officer . . .'"

"That thought . . ."

"No, Goddamn it," Sessions said, but was unable to contain a smile. "We must have somebody already out there who can get him through Outshipment despite your 'unexpected senior officer.'"

"I'll think of someone, Sir," Rutterman said.

"Don't be downcast, Rutterman," Sessions said. "It was a good try. One of your better ones."

"Thank you, Sir," Rutterman said.

Sessions turned to Moore.

"I don't suppose you understood much of that, did you, Moore?"

"No, Sir. I'm afraid . . ."

"Sergeant Rutterman will make it all clear, beyond any possibility of misinterpretation . . . Right, Rutterman?"

"Aye, aye, Sir."

". . . before he puts you on the train," Sessions concluded.

"Yes, Sir," Moore said.

Sessions met his eyes.

"Most of this will make sense when you get where you're going and learn what's required of you," Sessions said. "Until you get there, you're just going to have to take my word that it's very important, and that the security of the operation is really of life-and-death importance . . ."

"Yes, Sir," Moore said.

"Damn," Sessions said. "Security clearance! What about that? A lousy SECRET won't do him any good."

"The Colonel had me get the full FBI report on Moore . . ."

"They gave it to you?" Sessions asked, surprised.

"They owed us one," Rutterman said. "And he reviewed it and granted him a TOP SECRET. What more he may have to have, he'll have to get over there."

Sessions looked thoughtful for a moment, and then put out his hand.

"Good luck, Sergeant Moore. God go with you."

Moore was made somewhat uneasy by the reference to God. It was not, he sensed with surprise, simply a manner of speech, a cliche. Sessions was actually invoking the good graces of the Deity.

"Thank you, Sir," he said.

Rutterman had a light blue 1941 Ford Fordor, with Maryland license plates. But a shortwave radio antenna bolted to the trunk and stenciled signs on the dashboard (MAXIMUM PERMITTED SPEED 35 MPH; TIRE PRESSURE 32 PSI; AND USE ONLY 87 OCTANE FUEL) made it rather clear that while the car had come out of a military motor pool, for some reason it was not supposed to look like a military vehicle.

When they got to Union Station, Rutterman parked in a No Parking area and then took a cardboard sign reading NAVY DEPARTMENT—ON DUTY—OFFICIAL BUSINESS from under the seat and put it on the dashboard.

"If you don't think you'd lose control and wind up in New York or Boston, why don't you buy a Club Car ticket and have a couple of drinks on the way?" Rutterman suggested. "Otherwise, you're liable to have to stand up all the way to Philly."

"You reading my mind?" Moore asked.

"And I do card tricks," Rutterman said with a smile.

Moore bought his ticket and then, bag in hand, headed for the gate.

"You don't have to do any more for me, Sergeant," Moore said. "I can get on the train by myself."

"I want to be able to say I watched the train pull out with you on board," Rutterman replied.

A hand grabbed Moore's arm, startling him.

It was a sailor, wearing white web belt, holster and puttees, and with a Shore Patrol "SP" armband. Moore saw a second SP standing by the gate to Track Six.

"Let me see your orders, Mac," the Navy Shore Patrolman said.

Moore took from the lower pocket of his blouse a quarter-inch thick of mimeograph paper Rutterman had given him on the way to the station and handed it over.

"And your dog tags, Mac," the SP said.

"Slow day?" Sergeant Rutterman asked. "Or do you just like to lean on Marines?"

"What's *your* problem, Mac?" the SP asked, visibly surprised at what he obviously perceived to be a challenge to his authority.

"My problem, Sailor, is that I don't like you calling Marine sergeants 'Mac.'"

"Then why don't you show me your orders, *Sergeant?*" the SP said, as the other SP, slapping his billy club on the palm of his hand, came up to get in on the action.

Rutterman reached in the breast pocket of his blouse and came out with a small leather folder. He held it open for the SP to read.

Moore saw that whatever Rutterman had shown the SP, it produced an immediate change of attitude.

"Sergeant," the SP said, apologetically, almost humbly, "we're just trying to do our job."

"Yeah, sure, you are," Rutterman said, dryly. "Can we go now?"

"Yeah, sure. Go ahead."

Rutterman jerked his head for Moore to pass through the gate.

"Goddamned SPs," he muttered.

"What was that you showed him?" Moore asked.

"You forget you saw that," Rutterman said. "That's not what you're supposed to do with that."

"What was it?" Moore asked.

"What was what, Sergeant?" Rutterman asked. "Didn't Sessions tell you the way to get your ass in a crack around here is to ask questions you shouldn't?"

His voice was stern, but there was a smile in his eyes.

"Right," Moore said.

Rutterman boarded the train with him, saw that he was settled in an armchair in the club car, and then offered him his hand.

"I'll give you a call tomorrow or the next day," he said. "To tell you how the paperwork is moving."

"I'll have to give you my number," Moore said.

"I've got your number," Rutterman smiled, then shook his head. "Don't forget to get off this thing in Philadelphia."

"I'll try," Moore said. "Thank you, Sergeant."

"What for?" Rutterman replied, and then walked out of the club car.

(TWO)
Headquarters, First Marine Division
Wellington, New Zealand
0815 Hours 16 June 1942

On Sunday 14 June, when the first elements of the First Marine Division (Division Headquarters and the 5th Marines) landed at Wellington, New Zealand, from the United States, they found on hand to greet them not only the Advance Detachment, which had flown in earlier, but an officer courier from the United States, who had flown in more recently.

The officer courier went aboard the USS *Millard G. Fillmore* (formerly the *Pacific Princess* of the Pacific & Far East lines) as soon as she was tied to the wharf. He was immediately shown to the cabin of Major General Alexander A. Vandergrift, the Division Commander.

In the courier's chained-to-his wrist briefcase, in addition to the highly classified documents he had carried from the States on a AAAAAA priority, there was a business-size envelope addressed to the First Division's Deputy Commander, Brigadier General Lewis T. Harris, and marked "Personal."

Since it took a few minutes to locate the Division's Classified Documents Officer, who had to sign for the contents of the courier's briefcase, General Harris, who was in General Vandergrift's cabin at the time, got his "personal" letter before the other, more official documents were distributed.

The letter was unofficial—a "back channel communication" written by a longtime crony, a brigadier general who was assigned to Headquarters, USMC. Harris tore it open, read it, and then handed it wordlessly to General Vandergrift.

Washington, 11 June

Brig Gen Lewis T. Harris
Hq, First Marine Division
By Hand

Dear Lucky:

Major Jake Dillon, two officers, and six enlisted Marines are on their way to New Zealand to "coordinate Marine public relations." The Assistant Commandant is very impressed with Dillon, who used to be a Hollywood press agent. He feels he will be valuable in dealing with the more important members of the press, and making sure the Navy doesn't sit on Marine accomplishments.

He will be on TDY to Admiral Ghormley's Commander, South Pacific, Headquarters, rather than to the First Division, which takes him neatly out from under your command while he is there.

If I have to spell this out: This is the Assistant Commandant's idea, and you will have to live with it.

Regards,
Tony

The Division Commander read the letter, looked at Harris, snorted, and commented, "*I* don't have to live with this press agent, Lucky, *you* do. Keep this character and his people away from me."

The First Division was already prepared to deal with the public as well as the enemy. One of the Special Staff sections of the First Marine Division was "Public Information." It was staffed with a major, a captain, a lieutenant, three sergeants, three corporals, and two privates first class. It was natural, therefore, that the question, "just what the hell is this about?" should arise in General Harris's mind.

"Aye, aye, Sir," he said.

Major Dillon, accompanied by two lieutenants, four sergeants, and two privates first class, arrived by air (priority AAA) in Wellington on Tuesday, 16 June 1942.

He presented his orders to the G-1, who as Personnel Officer for the Division, was charged with housing and feeding people on temporary duty. The G-1 informed Major Dillon where he could draw tentage for the enlisted men, and in which tents he and his officers could find bunks. He told Major Dillon to get his people settled and to check back with him in the morning.

The G-1 then sought audience with the Assistant Division Commander, who he suspected (correctly) would be curious to see Major Dillon's orders, which included a very interesting and unusual paragraph: *3. Marine commanders are directed to give Major Dillon access to classified information through* TOP SECRET.

The G-1, who had earned the reputation of not bothering the Assistant Division Commander with petty bullshit, was granted an almost immediate audience with General Harris. After he read Major Dillon's orders, Harris inquired, "Where did you say you put this messenger from God? Get him in here right now."

This proved not to be possible. For Major Dillon and his officers were not at the Transient Officer's Quarters. Nor were they engaged in helping the enlisted men erect their tents. Indeed, according to the Quartermaster, nobody asking to draw tentage had been to see him. When the G-1 somewhat nervously reported these circumstances to General Harris, the General replied, "You find that sonofabitch, Dick, and get him over here."

The G-1 and members of his staff conducted a search of the area, but without success.

At 0915 the next morning, however, General Harris's sergeant reported that a Major named Dillon was in the outer office, asking if the General could spare him a minute.

"Ask the major to come in, please, Sergeant," Harris replied.

Major Dillon marched into Harris's office, stopped eighteen inches from his desk, came to rigid attention, and barked, "Major Dillon, Sir. Thank you for seeing me."

General Harris's first thought vis-à-vis Major Jacob Dillon was: *The fit of that uniform is impeccable. He didn't get that off a rack at an officer's sales store. Give the devil his due. At least the sonofabitch looks like a Marine.*

General Harris let Major Dillon stand there for almost a minute—which seemed like much longer—examining him.

"Stand at ease, Major," Harris said, and Dillon snappily changed to a position that was more like Parade Rest than At Ease, with his hands folded in the small of his back.

"Colonel Naye finally found you, did he?" Harris asked softly.

"Sir, I wasn't aware the colonel was looking for me."

"Where the hell have you been, Dillon? Where did you lay your head to rest, for example?"

"At the Connaught, Sir," Dillon said.

"At the where?"

"The Duke of Connaught Hotel, Sir."

"A hotel?" Harris asked, incredulously.

"Yes, Sir."

"Just to satisfy my sometimes uncontrollable curiosity, Major, how did you get from here to town? And back out here?"

"A friend picked us up, Sir. And arranged for the rooms in the Connaught. And has arranged a couple of cars for us."

"'Rooms'? 'Us'? You took your officers with you?"

"Yes, Sir. And the men. I thought they needed a good night's sleep. It's a hell of a long airplane ride from Hawaii, Sir."

It had previously occurred to General Harris that if Major Dillon and his two commissioned and six enlisted press agents, and their 1240 pounds of accompanying baggage and equipment had not traveled to Wellington, New Zealand, by priority air it would have been possible to move nine real Marines and 1240 pounds of badly needed equipment by air to Wellington.

With some effort, General Harris restrained himself from offering this observation aloud.

"I wouldn't know," he said. "We came by ship. Who's going to pay for the hotel, just out of curiosity?"

"That's going to require a sort of lengthy answer, Sir."

"My time is your time, Major. Curiosity overwhelms me."

"For the time being, Sir, those of us who are still on salary are splitting the expenses for everybody."

"Still on salary?"

"Most of us are from the movies, Sir," Dillon said.

What the hell does that mean? Tony's letter, come to think of it, said this guy was a Hollywood press agent.

"But one of the photographers and two of the writers came from Pathe—the newsreel photographer—and the wires. AP specifically. Their salaries stopped when they came in the Corps. The rest of us are still getting paid, so we decided to split the tab for Sergeant Pincney and the lieutenants."

"Let me be sure I have this right," Harris said. "Your two officers are having their hotel bills paid by your enlisted men?"

"General, it sounds a lot worse than it is," Dillon said.

"Fortunately, it's none of my business, since you're not in the 1st Marines," Harris said. This had just occurred to him; it was a little comforting. "But what is my business is your mission here. Can you explain that to me?"

"Well, Sir. When we—the 1st Marines—make their first landing, the men I have with me, broken down into two teams, will go ashore with the first wave. Each team will have a still and a motion picture photographer and a writer. The film they shoot, and the copy the writer writes, will be made available to the press on a pool basis ... and flown to the States, to see what mileage they can get out of it in Washington."

"You're aware, of course, that we have our own PIO people?"

"Yes, Sir. I tried to make that point to General Frischer. I didn't get very far.

And to tell you the truth, Sir, I didn't mind getting shot down. I wanted to come over here."

"You did? Why?"

"I'm a Marine, General," Dillon said.

"I was about to ask about that. I heard you were a Hollywood press agent."

"Yes, Sir. Before that I was a Marine. A China Marine. Then I got in the movie business, and then I came back in the Corps."

"To be a press ag—a public information officer?"

"That was the Deputy Commandant's idea, Sir. I thought, still think, that I could be of more use with stripes on my sleeve."

I like the sound of that. Maybe this character isn't a complete asshole after all.

"Well, Major, I'm sure the Deputy Commandant is right. Now, what can I do for you?"

"Not a thing, Sir. I'm going to try to stay out of your hair as much as possible."

It was an ill-chosen figure of speech. General Harris suffered from advanced male pattern baldness and was somewhat sensitive on the subject. Major Dillon promptly made it worse:

"The only thing on my schedule right now is to see your Division PIO," he said. "To assure him that I'm going to stay out of his hair, too. And then I want to see Jack NMI Stecker. *Major* Stecker."

"I'm acquainted with Major Stecker," Harris said. "What do you want from him?"

General Harris was more than "acquainted" with Major Jack NMI Stecker. Given the chasm between officer and enlisted ranks, they were—as much as possible— lifelong friends. For nearly a quarter of a century, Harris had believed that one of the few mistakes Jack Stecker made in his Marine career was turning down the appointment he was offered to Annapolis in 1918.

At nineteen, Stecker won the Medal of Honor . . . for really incredible valor in France. With the Medal came the Annapolis appointment. But Stecker turned it down to marry his childhood sweetheart, which meant that he would spend his Marine Corps career as an enlisted man.

It was folklore in the Marine Corps that many senior non-coms were just as qualified to command companies and battalions as any officer. Harris believed that one of the few men of whom this was really true was Jack NMI Stecker. And Harris put his belief in action; he went to Marine Corps Commandant Slocomb to make this announcement—a dangerous deviation from the sacred path of chain of command. Even so, his move resulted in the gold leaf now on Jack NMI Stecker's collar points, and his assignment as a battalion commander in the 5th Marines.

"Jack and I were pretty close when he was Sergeant Major of the 4th Marines in Shanghai . . ."

If you and Jack NMI Stecker were really close, that means you really aren't an asshole, Major, after all. I'll call Jack and ask him about this guy.

". . . and I hope to talk him into letting me send some of my people down to his battalion to see if he can make Marines out of them."

Good thinking. If anyone can turn feather merchants into Marines, Jack Stecker can.

"The PFCs, you mean?"

"No, Sir. Everybody *but* the PFCs. They at least went through boot camp at San Diego. I mean the sergeants and the lieutenants. Some of them have only been in the Corps a month."

"And they haven't been—the officers—to Basic School? Or the others to boot camp?"

"No, Sir. General Frischer said that since they wouldn't be commanding troops, it wouldn't matter."

"They were commissioned, or enlisted, directly from civilian life, to do this? And they were sent here without any training whatever?"

"Yes, Sir, that's about the size of it."

I don't think I will bother General Vandergrift with the details of this operation. He has enough to worry about as it is; he doesn't need this proof positive that the rest of the Corps has gone insane. He told me to keep this press agent and his people away from him, and I will.

"Thank you for coming in to see me, Major," General Harris said. "Unless you have something else?"

"Just one thing, General. I know that I must look like a feather merchant to you, but to do my job, I have to know what's going on."

"I will see that you are invited to attend all G-3 staff meetings, Major. And anything else I think would interest you."

"Sir, with respect," Dillon said, even more uneasily, "the general doesn't really know what would interest me or wouldn't."

You arrogant sonofabitch!

"What are you suggesting, Major? That you be given carte blanche to just nose around here wherever you please?"

"I'll try to stay out of people's hair as much as possible, General."

There was a perceptible pause as Harris thought that over. Finally, remembering that Dillon's orders had as much as authorized him to put his goddamned feather merchant's nose into any goddamned place where he goddamned pleased, and that Tony had written that this whole goddamned cockamamie operation was the Deputy Commandant's own personal nutty goddamned idea, he said, calmly and politely, "Very well, Major. I'll have a memo prepared authorizing you to attend any staff conferences that you desire to attend."

(THREE)
Buka, Solomon Islands
16 June 1942

Buka is an island approximately thirty miles long and no more than five or six miles wide. The northernmost island in the Solomons chain, it lies just north of the much larger Bougainville; and it is 146 nautical miles southeast of Rabaul, on New Britain.

In June of 1942 the Japanese had at Rabaul a large, well-equipped airbase, servicing fighters, bombers, seaplanes, and other larger aircraft. There was, as well, a Japanese fighter base on Buka, and another on Bougainville.

When the Japanese invaded Buka in the opening days of the war, an Australian, Jacob Reeves, who had lived on the island, volunteered to remain behind as a member of the Coastwatcher Service. He was commissioned into the Royal Australian Navy Volunteer Reserve and given a radio, a generator, and some World War I small arms. Thus equipped, he was expected to report on Japanese ship and air movement, from Rabaul down toward the Australian continent. Prior to his commissioning, Reeves had no military experience; and he knew nothing about the shortwave radio except how to turn it on and off.

Inevitably—in early June—what he called the "sodding wireless" failed. Following the orders he had been given for such an occurrence, he—actually he and the girls—stamped flat the grass in a high meadow, forming enormous letters thirty feet tall, R A.

He'd been told that if he went off the air, the Coastwatcher Service would fly over his hideout as soon as possible to look for indication that he was still alive and needed help. There were ten codes in all (Lieutenant Commander Eric Feldt, Royal Australian Navy, commanding the Coastwatcher Service, did not believe his men could remember more than that): R A stood of course for radio; P E would indicate his supply of petrol for the generator which powered the wireless was exhausted; and so on.

As he waited for the Coastwatcher Service to act on his stamped-in-the-grass message, Reeves wondered what the response would be.

His reports on Japanese activity, he knew, had been of great value both tactically and for planning purposes. Now that they were interrupted, getting his wireless station up and running again would be a matter of some priority.

He was well aware that they did not have many options. The only way he could see to get him up and running again was to send him another radio. There were a number of problems with that; most notably: The only way to get him one would be to drop it by parachute. But if the airplane was seen by the Japanese, they would certainly launch fighters to shoot it down.

And even if the plane made it to the meadow, the odds that the dropped radio would survive the shock of landing were slim. If, indeed, he could find it at all.

All the same, he was not surprised on 6 June to hear the sound of the twin engines of a Royal Australian Air Force Lockheed Hudson transport. Five minutes later, he saw the Hudson make a low level pass over the meadow. As it passed, four objects dropped from the aircraft. A moment later these were suspended beneath white nylon parachute canopies.

He was surprised when he made out human forms beneath two of the parachutes. He had mixed emotions about that. On one hand, it probably meant they were sending him people who knew something about how the sodding wireless and its sodding generator worked. And that, of course, would be helpful.

But on the other hand, it would mean he would have to care for two men who had probably never in their lives been out of Sydney or Melbourne, much less been in a jungle. *How can I feed them?* he asked himself. *More important, how can I conceal them from the sodding Nips?*

And then when he made his way to the first one, what he found was a sodding American Marine—a *boy!*—wearing, in the American way, the upside down stripes of a sergeant. The other one turned out to be an American Marine officer, a lieutenant. That one managed to go into the trees, breaking his arm in the process. These two were the first Americans Sub Lieutenant Reeves had ever met. It didn't take him long to conclude that they were an odd, childish lot.

When he reached the boy sergeant, Reeves told him there were Nips snooping around the area, and that they would, unfortunately, have to count as lost the one who landed in the trees.

"We're Marines," the boy told him. "We don't leave our people behind."

It never came to a test of wills; for one of the girls found Lieutenant Howard. As far as Reeves was concerned, that was fortunate. For he not only subsequently grew rather fond of the boy, Steve Koffler, but at the time Reeves was reasonably sure that Koffler would have insisted on looking for his lieutenant even to the point of turning his submachine gun on Reeves.

Not long after that, they found they had to get rid of a Nip patrol who'd heard the Lockheed and probably seen the parachutes; and Koffler did what had to be done then with skill and courage. But the boy threw up when it was over . . . after he looked down at the corpse of a Japanese he'd wounded, and then, because it was necessary, killed.

Later, when Lieutenant Howard explained the reasons for their coming to Buka, the explanation made enough sense to Reeves that he put aside his earlier fears and objections about them.

According to Howard, Reeves's observation point was considered vital. With the three of them there, the odds that it could be kept operational were made greater.

Meanwhile, some weeks before, a small detachment of U.S. Marines was attached to the Coastwatcher Organization. When word that Reeves's wireless was out reached Commander Feldt, Feldt decided to send two men from the Marine detachment to Buka, together with the latest model American shortwave wireless. Koffler was chosen to go because he was not only a radio operator, he was a highly skilled technician as well (he'd been an Amateur Radio Operator before the War), while Howard had once taught courses in recognition of Japanese aircraft and naval vessels. Because of that, and because Koffler couldn't tell the difference between a battleship and an intercoastal freighter, Howard was asked to join him.

The village looked like a picture out of *National Geographic* magazine: A clear stream, about five feet wide and two feet deep, meandered through the center of a scattering of grass-walled huts. The village was populated with about twenty brown-skinned, flat-nosed people, most of whom had teeth died blue and then filed to a point. Cooking fires were burning here and there; chickens were running loose; and bare-breasted women were beating yamlike roots with rocks against other rocks. Most of the men and some of the women were armed with British Lee-Enfield rifles; and many carried web ammunition bandoliers.

Sergeant Stephen M. Koffler, USMC, of East Orange, New Jersey, and Detachment A of Marine Corps Special Detachment 14, had been eating bacon and pork chops and ham and sausage for most of the eighteen years and six months of his life; but if it were in his power he would never do so again.

He had never given pork much thought before. It had always been there in the refrigerated meat display of Cohen's EZ-Shop Supermarket on the corner of Fourth Avenue and North 18th Street, ready to be wrapped and taken to the cash register. All you had to do was pay Mrs. Cohen, who worked the register, and then take the bacon home and put it in a frying pan.

He had spent most of the morning watching the conversion of a living, breathing, squealing, hairy, ugly pig into edible meat products; and he hadn't liked what he had seen at all.

The pig had been brought into the village shortly after dawn by a visibly proud and triumphant Petty Officer First Class Bartholomew Charles Dunlop, Royal Australian Navy Volunteer Reserve. Petty Officer Dunlop, who was known as "Charley," was a native of the island of Buka. When he brought in the pig, he was wearing his usual uniform. That consisted of a brassard around his upper right arm, onto which was sewn the insignia of his rank, and a loin cloth. The loin cloth was something like a slit canvas skirt; and the brassard was placed just below two copper rings. His teeth were black and filed into points. And there were decorative scars on his forehead, his cheeks, and bare chest.

Petty Officer Dunlop was carrying a 9mm Sten submachine gun, two Lee-Enfield .303 Caliber rifles, and a two-foot-long machete. The rifles belonged to the other two members of the detail, who were actually carrying the pig. They were uniformed like Dunlop, except that they had no insignia brassards. Canvas webbing ammunition belts, however, were slung across their chests.

They carried the pig, squealing in protest, on a pole run between his tied-together legs.

"Roast pork tonight!" Petty Officer Dunlop announced triumphantly. "And would you look at the size of the bugger!"

Petty Officer Dunlop had been educated at the Anglican Mission School on Buka, and spoke with the accent of a Yorkshireman.

Steve Koffler had not seen many pigs, except in photographs, but the one Charley seemed so proud of didn't seem as large as the ones Steve was used to. It was about the size of a large dog.

"It's beautiful, Charley," Steve said.

"Where's the officers?"

Steve shrugged and nodded vaguely toward the jungle.

How the hell am I supposed to answer that? Out there in the bush someplace?

"I didn't go with them," Steve said, explaining: "I've got to make the 1115 net call. They weren't sure they'd be back in time."

"Well, we'll have a jolly little surprise for them when they do come home, won't we?"

The women of the village, beaming, quickly appeared and watched as the pig was lowered to the ground and the pole between its legs was removed. A length of rope appeared, and this was tied to the pig's rear feet. The pig was then hauled off the ground under a large limb.

A woman produced a large, china bowl and carefully placed it under the pig's head. It looked to Steve like one of those things people put under their beds before there was inside plumbing.

Then with one swift swipe of his machete, Charley cut the pig's throat. The squealing stopped, and arterial blood began to gush from the pig's throat as the pig jerked in its death spasms.

It was only with a massive effort that Steve managed not to throw up. He had to tell himself again and again that he could not humiliate himself, the Marine Corps, and the white race by tossing his cookies.

The butchering process was performed by the women (hunting was a male responsibility; everything else was women's business). It was worse than even the throat-cutting. Intestines (steaming, despite the heat) spilled from the carcass. The hide was peeled off. The carcass was cut into pieces. And at one point Steve realized with something close to horror that one particularly obscene-looking hunk of sickly white stuff was what he knew as bacon.

Next fires were built; then large steel pots full of water were either suspended over them or set right onto the coals. In one of them, eventually, they dropped the pig's head. Once the water started boiling, the head turned over and over.

By the time the officers returned, just before 1100, the butchering was just about finished. The bacon and hams (they were too scrawny to be *real* hams, Steve thought, but that's what they were) had been suspended over a smokey fire; and the rest of the meat was either being slowly broiled over coals or boiled and rendered. Nothing, Steve saw, was going to be wasted.

Both Reeves and Howard looked exhausted when they arrived. Without a word, Howard dropped his web belt and his Thompson by the creek; and fully clothed, except for his boondockers, he lowered himself into it, carefully holding his splinted arm out of the water. Reeves ordered tea for himself and slumped onto the ground, resting his back against a tree.

They had nothing to report about their patrol—a case of no news being good news: They'd detected no signs of the Japanese looking for them.

Steve took his wristwatch from his pocket, and then from the condom where he stored it. There were two watches in the village, his and Lieutenant Howard's. Since there was no chance of getting replacements, and since there were two times each day that were critical—1115 and 2045—it was crucial that the watches be protected.

The dial read 1059. If he was lucky, the watch was accurate within five minutes. He went in search of Petty Officer Second Class Ian Bruce. He found him in the grass commo shack, already in place on the generator, his skirt spread wide (it wasn't hard to tell that he was a man), ready to start pumping the bicycle-like pedals of the device that provided power for the Hallicrafters shortwave transceiver.

The watch hands now indicated 1102. Steve made a wind-it-up motion with his hand. Ian started pumping the pedals. In a moment, the needles on the Hallicrafter came to life. It was now 1103.

Fuck it, close enough.

Steve put his fingers on the telegraph key.

FRD1.FRD6.FRD1.FRD6.FRD1.FRD6.

Royal Australian Navy Coastwatcher Radio, this is Detachment A, Special Marine Detachment 14.

Today, for a change, there was an immediate response:

FRD6.FRD1.GA.

Detachment A, this is Coastwatcher Radio, Townesville, Australia, responding to your call. Go ahead.

FRD1.FRD6.NTATT.

Coastwatcher Radio, this is Detachment A. No traffic for you at this time.

FRD6.FRD1.NTATT.FRD1 CLR.

Detachment A, this is Coastwatcher Radio. No traffic for you at this time. Coastwatcher Radio Clear.

"Fuck!" Sergeant Koffler said, and signaled for Ian Bruce to stop pedaling. He had hoped—he always hoped—that there would be some kind of message. And he was always disappointed when there was not.

He got to his feet and walked out of the hut. Lieutenant Reeves was nowhere in sight, and Lieutenant Howard was asleep on the bank of the stream. There was no point in waking him up; there had been no traffic.

He walked to one of the charcoal fires. The pig's ribs were getting done. They *looked* like spareribs now, Steve thought, not like parts of a dead animal.

And they smelled good. His mouth actually salivated.

He wondered how much salt from their short—and dwindling—supply Lieutenant Reeves would permit them to use to season the spareribs.

V

(ONE)
The Club Car "Curtis Sandrock"
The Pennsylvania Railroad "Congressional Limited"
16 June 1942

Sergeant John Marston Moore, USMCR, had been in his chair less than half an hour when he had occasion to dwell on the question of saltpeter.

It had been commonly accepted by his peers at Parris Island that the Corps liberally dosed the boots' chow with the stuff. The action was deemed necessary by the Corps, the reasoning went, in order to suppress the sexual drives of the boots, who were by definition perfectly healthy young men who would have absolutely no chance during the period of their training to satisfy their sexual hungers.

Save of course by committing what his father called the sin of onanism, and what was known commonly in the Corps as Beating Your Meat, or Pounding Your Pud—a behavior that was high on the long list of acts one must not be caught doing by one's Drill Instructor . . . considerations of finding someplace to do it aside.

John Moore now realized that all he knew about saltpeter was what he had heard at Parris Island. That is to say, he had no certain knowledge whether such a substance really existed; or if it did exist, whether it did indeed suppress sexual desires, once ingested; or whether the Corps really fed it to their boots.

It was possible, of course.

There was the question of homosexuality, for instance. He had heard that because of the absence of women, a lot of the men in prisons turned queer. . . . There was a large number of other things Parris Island and prison had in common, too. The Corps could certainly not afford to have its boots turn to each other for sexual gratification. Several times the pertinent passages from The Articles for the Governance of the Naval Service, known as "Rocks and Shoals," had been read out loud to them. These described the penalties for taking the penis of another male into one's mouth and/or anus. In the eyes of the Corps, this was a crime ranking close to desertion in the face of the enemy and striking a superior officer or non-commissioned officer.

And if one was to judge from the training time allocated to inspiring talks from Navy Chaplains and incredibly graphic motion pictures taken in Venereal Disease wards, the Corps had a deep interest in even the heterosexual activities of its men. After they were freed from Parris Island, the Corps did not want them to rush to the nearest brothel and/or to consort with what it called "Easy Women." Easy women were defined as those who would infect Marines with syphilis, gonorrhea, and other social diseases, thereby rendering them unfit for combat service.

The conclusions Sergeant Moore reached as he accepted a second rye and ginger ale from the club car steward was that (a) it was likely that the Corps had been feeding him saltpeter at Parris Island; (b) that it had worked, because he could not now recall any feelings of sexual deprivation while he was there; and (c) that once one was taken off saltpeter, one's normal sexual drives and hungers returned within a day.

With a vengeance, he thought, as he tried to fold his leg over the first erection he'd had in weeks. It seemed to have a mind of its own, determined to make his trousers look like an eight-man squad tent, canvas tautly stretched from a stout center pole.

The source of his sexual arousal, he was quite sure, was not what the Corps would think of as an Easy Woman. In the training films, Easy Women had without exception earned the cheering approval of the boots with their tight sweaters, short skirts, heavily applied lipstick, and lewdly inviting mascaraed eyes. Most of them had cigarettes hanging from their mouths, and one hand attached to a bottle of beer.

This woman demonstrated none of these characteristics. She wore very little makeup. She held her cigarette in what Sergeant Moore thought was a charming and exquisitely feminine manner. She wore a blouse buttoned to her neck, a suit, and a hat with a half-veil. She was old—at least thirty, John judged, maybe even thirty-five—but he charitably judged that her hair, neatly done up in sort of a knot at the back of her head, was prematurely gray.

And the final proof that she was a lady and not an Easy Woman came during the one time she raised her eyes from *The Saturday Evening Post* to look at him. It was clear from her facial expression that he was of absolutely no interest to her at all.

But despite all this, he found her exciting and desirable. This struck him with particular urgency after she stood to take off her suit jacket: The light then was such that her torso was silhouetted by the sun; the absolutely magnificent shape of her breasts had, for ten seconds or so, been his to marvel at.

And when she sat down and crossed her legs, there was a flash of thigh and slip, of lace and soft white flesh; and instantly, in his mind's eye, she was as naked as the lady in the club soda ad, sitting on a rock by a mountain lake.

At that instant the sexual depressant effects of saltpeter were flushed from his system as if they were never there, and Old Faithful popped to a position of attention that met every standard of the Guide Book for Marines for stiffness and immobility.

Had the opportunity presented itself, Sergeant John Marston Moore, USMCR, would cheerfully have gone with her then . . . even if the price was the loss of all his money, contraction of syphilis, gonorrhea, all other social diseases, and any chances he had after the war to meet Miss Right and have a family of his own.

He tried, very hard, not to let her know he was watching her. This involved adjusting his head so that he could see her reflection in a mirror on the club car wall. Despite his care, she did catch him looking at her once; in a flash, he desperately spun around in his chair.

A little later, he managed to catch another reflection of her in the glass of his window, but that was nowhere near as satisfactory as the mirror reflection.

Between Baltimore and Philadelphia, she spoke to him. Her voice was as deep, soft, throaty, and sensual as he knew it would be.

"Excuse me," she said, waving *The Saturday Evening Post* at him. "I'm through with this. Would you like it?"

"No!" he said abruptly, with all the fervor the Good Marine had shown in the training film when the Easy Woman offered him a cigarette laced with some kind of narcotic. "It'll make you feel real good," she'd told him breathily.

"Sorry," the woman said, taken aback.

You're a fucking asshole, Moore, J. Out of your cotton-picking fucking mind!

"I don't read much," he heard himself say.

The absolutely beautiful woman smiled at him uneasily.

"Excuse me," Sergeant John Marston Moore, USMCR, said. Then he got up and walked to the vestibule of the car, where he banged his forehead on the window, and where he stayed until the train pulled into the 30th Street Station in Philadelphia.

The woman got off the train there. Fortunately, Moore decided, she didn't see him hiding in the vestibule corner. He exhaled audibly with relief. And then, for one last look at the beautiful older woman as she marched down the platform and out of his life forever, he stuck his head out the door.

She was standing right there, as the porter transferred her luggage into the custody of a Red Cap.

He pulled his head back as quickly as he could.

When it began to move again, and the train caught up with her on the platform, she looked for and found Sergeant John Marston Moore. She smiled and waved.

And smiled again and shook her head when, very shyly, the nice-looking young Marine waved back.

"North Philadelphia," the conductor called, "North Philadelphia, next."

(TWO)
U.S. Marine Barracks
U.S. Navy Yard
Philadelphia, Pennsylvania
18 June 1942

While the staff sergeant who dealt with Sergeant John Marston Moore, USMCR, could not honestly be characterized as charming, in comparison to the sergeants who had dealt with Moore at Parris, he seemed to be.

"You're Moore, huh?" he greeted him. "Get yourself a cup of coffee and I'll be with you in a minute."

He gestured toward a coffee machine and turned his attention to a stack of papers on his crowded desk. The machine was next to a window overlooking the Navy Yard. As he drank the coffee, Moore watched with interest an enormous crane lift a five-inch cannon and its mount from a railroad flatcar onto the bow of a freighter.

He found the operation so absorbing that he was somewhat startled when the staff sergeant came up to him and spoke softly into his ear.

"You could have fooled me, Moore," he said. "Even with that haircut, you don't look like somebody who was a private three days ago."

Moore was surprised to see that the staff sergeant was smiling at him.

"Thank you," Moore said.

"I checked your papers out pretty carefully," the staff sergeant said. "Everything's shipshape. Shots. Overseas qualification. Next of kin. All that crap. Once you get paid, and after The Warning, all you have to do is get on the airplane at Newark airport on Friday morning."

" 'The Warning'?" Moore asked.

"Yeah, The Warning," the staff sergeant said. "Come on."

He gestured with his hand for Moore to follow him. He stopped by the open, frosted glass door to a small office and tapped on the glass with his knuckles.

A captain looked up, then motioned them inside.

"Sergeant Moore, Sir, for The Warning."

"Sure," the captain said, and looked at Moore. "Sergeant, you have been alerted for overseas movement. It is my duty to make sure that you understand that any failure on your part to make that movement, by failing to report when and where your orders specify, is a more serious offense than simple absence without leave, can be construed as intention to desert or desertion, and that the penalties provided are greater. Do you understand where and when you are to report, and what I have just said to you?"

"Yes, Sir," Sergeant Moore replied.

"Where's he going?" the captain asked, curiously.

The staff sergeant handed the captain a sheaf of papers.

"Interesting," the captain said.

"Ain't it?" the staff sergeant agreed. "Look at the six-A priority."

"I'd love to know what you do for the Corps, Sergeant Moore," the captain said. "But I know better than to ask."

That's good, Moore thought wryly, *because I have no idea what I'm supposed to do for the Corps.*

The captain then surprised him further by standing up and offering Moore his hand.

"Good luck, Moore," he said.

Moore sensed that the good wishes were not merely sincere, but a deviation from a normal issuing of The Warning, which he now understood was some sort of standard routine.

"Thank you, Sir."

The staff sergeant handed the captain a stack of paper, and the captain wrote his signature on a sheet of it.

That's a record that I got The Warning, Moore decided.

The staff sergeant nudged Moore, and Moore followed him out of the office. They went to the Navy Finance Office where Moore was given a partial pay of one hundred dollars.

The staff sergeant then commandeered an empty desk and went through all the papers, dividing them into two stacks. Moore watched as one stack including, among other things, his service record, went into a stiff manila envelope. The sergeant sealed it twice: He first licked the gummed flap and then he put over that a strip of gummed paper.

He surprised Moore by then forging an officer's name on the gummed tape: "Sealed at MBPHILA 18June42 James D. Yesterburg, Capt USMC"

Yesterburg, Moore decided, was the captain who had given him The Warning and then wished him good luck.

"Normally, you don't get to carry your own records," the staff sergeant said, handing him the envelope. "But if you do, they have to be sealed. There's nothing in there you haven't seen, but I wouldn't open it, if I was you. Or unless you can get your hands on another piece of gummed tape."

Moore chuckled.

"These are your orders," the staff sergeant said as he stuffed a quarter-inch-thick stack of mimeograph paper into another, ordinary, manila envelope. "And your tickets, railroad from here to Newark; bus from Newark station to the airport; the airplane tickets, Eastern to Saint Louis, Transcontinental & Western to Los Angeles; and a bus ticket in LA from the airport to the train station; and finally your ticket on the train—they call it "The Lark"—from LA to 'Diego. In 'Diego, there'll be an RTO office—that means Rail Transport Office—and they'll arrange for you to get where you should be. OK?"

"Got it," Moore said.

"There's also Meal Vouchers," the staff sergeant said. "I'll tell you about them. You are supposed to be able to exchange them for a meal in restaurants. The thing is, most restaurants, except bad ones, don't want to be run over with servicemen eating cheap meals that they don't get paid for for a month, so they either don't honor these things, or they give you a cheese sandwich and a cup of coffee and call it dinner. So if I was you, I would save enough from that flying hundred they just gave you to eat whatever and wherever you want. Then in 'Diego, or Pearl Harbor, or when you get where you're going, you turn in the meal tickets and say you couldn't find anyplace that would honor them. They'll pay you. It's a buck thirty-five a day. Still with me?''

''Yeah, thanks for the tip.''

''OK. Now finally, and this is important. You've got a six-A priority. The only way you can be legally beat out of your seat on the airplane is by somebody who also has a six-A priority *and* outranks you. Since they pass out very few six-As, that's not going to be a problem. If some colonel happens to do that to you, you get his name and telephone Outshipment in 'Diego, the number's on your orders, and tell them what happened, including the name of the officer who bumped you. In that case, no problem.''

''I understand,'' Moore said.

''But what's *liable* to happen,'' the staff sergeant went on, ''is that *you're* going to bump some captain or some major—or maybe even some colonel or important civilian —who doesn't have a six-A, and he's not going to like that worth a shit, and will try to pull rank on you. If you let that happen, your ass is in a crack. You understand?''

''What am I supposed to say to him?''

''You tell *him* to call Outshipment in 'Diego, and get *their* permission to bump you. Otherwise, 'with respect, Sir, I can't miss my plane.' Got it?''

''Yes, I think so.''

''Somebody pretty high up in the Corps wants to get you where you're going in a hurry, Sergeant, otherwise you wouldn't have a six-A. And they are going to get very pissed off if you hand the six-A to somebody who didn't rate it on their own.''

''OK,'' Moore said.

''Well, that's it,'' the staff sergeant said. ''Good luck, Moore.''

''Thank you,'' Moore said, shaking his hand.

''Oh, shit. I just remembered: You're entitled to a couple of bus and subway tokens. We'll have to go back by the office, but what the hell, why pay for a bus if you can get the Corps to pay, right?''

''I've got a car.''

''Oh, shit! I knew there would be something!''

''Something wrong?''

''You want the Corps to store it for you, you'll be here all goddamned day.''

''It's my father's car.''

At breakfast, Moore had been surprised at his father's reaction to his mother's suggestion—''Dear, couldn't John use the Buick to drive down there?'' He would never have bothered to ask for it himself, for the negative response would have been certain.

''I suppose,'' the Reverend Doctor Moore had said, after a moment's hesitation, ''that would be the thing to do.''

There was not even the ritual speech about driving slowly and carefully, which always preceded his—rare—sessions behind the wheel of his father's car. It was a 1940 Buick Limited, which had a new kind of transmission that eliminated the clutch pedal and little switches on the steering wheel that flashed the stop and parking lights in the direction you intended to turn. His father was ordinarily reluctant to entrust such a precision machine into the hands of his rash and reckless—as he considered it—son.

And yet, to his astonishment, his father hadn't even put up a ritual show of resistance.

As he put his mind to that, it occurred to Moore that this was not the first time his father had behaved oddly since he had come home from Parris Island. For instance, there had hardly been any questions about why he was going overseas now as a sergeant, rather than to Quantico for officer training.

His father was probably concerned that he was going to be killed in the Orient, Moore decided, and was going out of his way to be kind and obliging. But he sensed there was something else, too; he had no idea what.

"Jesus, you had me worried for a minute," the sergeant said, and then offered his hand again, and repeated, "Good luck, Moore."

Moore had not been able to get his father's car onto the base. It was parked just outside.

And he had to show his orders to the Marine Guard at the gate as he left. He remembered at the last moment that his orders now were the ones the staff sergeant had just given him, not the ones Tech Sergeant Rutterman had given him only a couple of days before.

He took them from the smaller manila envelope and handed them to the guard, who scanned them quickly.

"OK, Sergeant," he said. "If you have to go, that's the way."

Moore smiled at him, but didn't know what he meant. As he walked to the car, he read the orders for the first time.

Marine Barracks
U.S. Naval Station
Philadelphia, Penna

16 June 1942

Letter Orders:
To Sergeant John M. Moore, 673456, USMCR

1. You are detached this date from Headquarters Company, Marine Barracks, Phila. Pa., and assigned 14th Special Detachment, USMC, FPO 24543, San Francisco, Cal.

2. You will proceed by government and/or civilian rail, air and sea transportation via USMC Barracks San Diego, Cal., and Pearl Harbor, T.H. Air Transportation is directed where possible, with Priority AAAAAA authorized by TWX Hq USMC dated 15 June 1942, Subject: "Movement of Moore, Sgt John M." to final destination.

3. USMC Barracks San Diego, Cal., and Pearl Harbor, T.H., and all other Naval facilities are directed to report via most expeditious means to Hq USMC ATTN: GHV3:12 the date and time of your arrival and departure while en route. Once travel commences, any delay in movement which will exceed 12 (twelve) hours will be reported to Hq USMC ATTN: GHV3:13 by URGENT radio message.

By Direction:
Jasper J. Malone
Lieut. Colonel, USMC

He realized that he knew nothing more now than he had been told by Captain Sessions at Parris Island. He didn't know what Special Detachment 14 was; where it was; or what he would be doing there when he got there. The only thing he knew for sure was that the Corps was going to a hell of a lot of trouble to get him there as quickly as possible.

It was disturbing.

Disturbing, shit! It's frightening.

He looked at his watch. It was quarter to four. All of his business at the Marine Barracks had taken far less time than he had expected, and planned for. It would take him ten minutes to drive down Broad Street to the Union League, where he was to meet Uncle Bill for dinner. That meant he would arrive two hours and five minutes early.

And two hours and five minutes was not enough time to find a movie and watch through the whole thing. It was enough time to take the car home and ride back downtown on the train. That would make the car available to his father when he returned from the Missions office.

Alternatively, he could make profitable use of the time . . . the Reverend Moore believed that profitable use of one's time was a virtue and thus the waste of one's time was a non-virtue, and consequently sinful . . . by making a farewell visit to the Franklin Institute or the Philadelphia Museum of Fine Art.

Or he could go to the Trocadero Burlesque Theater, which was within walking distance of the Union League Club. There, while munching caramel-covered popcorn, he could watch an Easy Woman take her clothing off . . . perhaps as many as four Easy Women in the nearly two hours he had. That was about as close as he was going to get to a naked woman in the foreseeable future.

It was also possible—unlikely, but possible—that he might encounter a real Easy Woman in the Tenderloin, as the area was known . . . a woman in a short skirt and tight sweater who would leer at him and entice him to a cheap hotel as her contribution to the war effort.

He parked the Buick behind the First Philadelphia Trust Company and walked down 12th Street to the Trocadero. He encountered no real Easy Women on the street, and the Easy Women on the stage seemed not only a little long in the tooth but bored as well. One of them actually blew a chewing gum bubble as she moved around on the stage.

And the Easy Women did not appear one after the other. Their performances were separated by comedians and intermissions, during which the audience was offered special deals on wristwatches, fountain pen and pencil sets, and illustrated books portraying life in Wicked Paris—offered today only, by special arrangement to Trocadero Theater patrons.

An hour after he went into the Trocadero, he got up and walked out. He walked back to Market Street and then up toward Broad Street. Just as he came to John Wanamaker's Department Store he saw the incredibly beautiful older woman from the train.

She walked purposefully out of Wanamaker's and turned toward Broad Street. She glanced at him but he felt sure she made no connection with the train.

Why should she? My God, she's beautiful!

I'm not following her. She's going in the same direction I am.

He almost caught up with her as she waited for the traffic light on Broad Street, but he slowed his pace so that he was still behind her when the light changed. He was sure she hadn't noticed him.

She turned left, and he followed her, for that was his direction too. He was going to meet Uncle Bill at the Union League Club for dinner.

I wonder what the hell that's all about?

She walked past the Union League, moving in long graceful strides, her smooth flowing musculature exquisitely evident under her straight skirt. Quickly consulting his watch, Sergeant John Marston Moore decided there was no reason he could not walk for a couple of minutes down South Broad before returning to the Union League to meet his Uncle Bill.

She came to the Bellevue-Stratford Hotel. The doorman spun the revolving door for her, and twenty seconds later for Sergeant John Marston Moore.

She crossed the lobby and went into the cocktail lounge. Sergeant John Marston Moore visited the Gentlemen's Room, relieved his bladder, and then washed his hands. He examined his reflection in the mirror over the marble wash basin.

Just what the fuck do you think you're doing?

He went into the cocktail lounge and took a seat at the bar.

"What can we get the Marine Corps?"

"Rye and ginger," he said, sweeping the room in the mirror behind the bar.

She was at a small table away from the lobby, near a door that led directly to the street. A waiter was delivering something in a stemmed glass. She took a cigarette from her purse, lit it with a silver lighter, and exhaled through her nose.

Like Bette Davis. Except that compared to her, Bette Davis looks like one of those cows in the Trocadero.

"Seventy-five cents, Sir."

He laid a five-dollar bill on the bar. When the waiter brought the change, he pushed the quarter away and put the singles in his pocket. When he found the beautiful older woman in the mirror again, she was looking at him, via the mirror.

And she was smiling.

In amusement, he thought, *not in encouragement, or enticement.*

He found his pack of Chesterfields and lit one with his Marine insignia decorated Zippo, pretending to be in deep thought. He was unable to keep his eyes away from the mirror. Sometimes he got a profile of her face. Twice his eyes were drawn to her legs; they were crossed beneath the table, ladylike, but they still offered a forbidden glance under her skirt.

You are not only about to make a flaming ass of yourself, but you are going to embarrass that nice woman.

He drained his rye and ginger ale.

I will leave by the side door, so that she can't help but see me leave and will understand that I am leaving, and not making eyes at her, or anything like that.

He determinedly kept from looking at her as he walked to the side door. As he reached the door, a half dozen people started to come into the bar from the street. He had to stop and wait for them. He glanced at her. She was no more than five feet away.

She was looking up at him. She smiled.

"The Club Car, right?" she asked. "You don't read very much, right?"

"I just came in for a drink," he blurted.

"I thought it was something like that," she said.

Christ, she knows I followed her in here!

"I have to meet someone for dinner," Moore said. "Just killing a little time."

"So do I, unfortunately," she said, more than a little bitterly. "Have to meet someone for dinner, I mean."

She ground her cigarette out in the ash tray and then looked up at him. Their eyes locked for a moment, and John felt a constriction in his stomach.

She broke eye contact, fished in her purse, and came up with another cigarette.

She just put one out. What is she so nervous about?

He held his Zippo out to her. She steadied his hand with the balls of her fingers. It was an absolutely innocent gesture, yet it gave him immediate indication that he was about to have an erection.

She raised her eyes to his again.

"Well, nice to see you again," she said.

There was nothing to do now but leave.

"I'll remember it a long time," he heard himself say.

She laughed softly, deeply.

"Oddly enough," she said. "I think I will, too."

As if with a mind of its own, his hand went out.

She caught it, as a man would, and shook it. But of course she wasn't a man, and the warm softness of her hand made his heart jump.

"Good-bye," she said as she took her hand away. "And good luck."

He didn't trust his voice to speak. He nodded at her, and then went through the door onto the street.

I'm in love.

No, you're not, asshole. All it is is that you're not getting saltpeter in your chow anymore.

For Christ's sake, she's thirty, you never saw her before the train, and you'll never see her again.

You are an asshole, Sergeant Moore. There is absolutely no doubt of that.

He walked up to Broad Street and turned north, back to the Union League Club.

What did she mean "unfortunately" she had to have dinner with someone? Was she suggesting that she would rather have dinner with me?

Back to Conclusion One, Sergeant Asshole, you're an asshole.

"May I help you, Sir?" the porter asked, barring his access to the Union League.

"I'm meeting Mr. Marston," John said. "William Marston."

"Mr. Marston is in the bar, Sir," the porter said, pointing.

William Dawson Marston IV, forty-six, a tall and angular man in a nicely tailored glen plaid suit, was sitting in a leather upholstered captain's chair by a small table, his long legs stretched straight in front of him and crossed near his ankles.

He smiled and waved when he saw his nephew, then made a half gesture to get up.

"Sit you down, Johnny my boy, and have a drink."

"Hello, Uncle Bill."

"Christ, you even look like a Marine," Marston said.

"Thank you."

"What will you have to drink?"

"Rye and ginger."

"Ginger ale will give you a hangover," Marston said. "I'm surprised you haven't learned that yet. Or are you that impossible contradiction, a teetotal Marine?"

"What would you suggest?" John asked.

A waiter had appeared.

"Bring us two of these, will you please, Charley?" Marston said.

"What is it?" John asked.

"Scotch and water. Very good scotch, and thus with very little water. They call it 'Famous Grouse.'"

That will not be Uncle Bill's second drink. More likely his fifth or sixth.

"I have been here some time," Marston said, as if he had read Moore's mind. "Absorbing some liquid courage. That would annoy your father, but if you report on our conversation, you may feel free to tell him that yes indeed, Uncle Bill was at the bottle."

"Why should I report on our conversation?"

"When you learn the topic, you will understand," Marston said.

He looked around impatiently for the waiter, then turned back to John.

"When are you leaving, John?"

"Thursday."

"Where are you going? Did they tell you?"

"Not specifically. Somewhere in the Pacific, obviously. From here to San Diego, and then to Hawaii."

The waiter appeared. Marston picked up his glass immediately and took a swallow.

"Not surprisingly, when I spoke with him, your father was rather vague about your status," he said. "How is it you're not an officer?"

"I can't talk about that," John said.

"You in some sort of trouble?"

"No. I've been led to believe the commission will come along later."

John sipped his scotch. He would have preferred rye and ginger ale.

But he's probably right about the ginger ale giving me a hangover.

"Getting right to the point," Marston said. "There are those, including your father, who would hold that this is absolutely none of my business, but I have chosen to make it my business: Has your father discussed your trust fund, funds, with you?"

"No," John replied, and then asked, "Is there any reason he should have?"

"That sonofabitch," Marston said, bitterly.

"Excuse me?"

"I shouldn't have said that," Marston said. "I beg your pardon. I really hope you can forget I said that."

"What about my trust fund?"

"Funds, plural. Three of them. Together, two comma trust funds."

"Two comma?"

"Think about it."

What the hell does "two comma" mean? Then he understood. *When figures in excess of $999,999.00 are used, for example, $1,500,000.00, there are two commas.*

"What about my trust funds?"

"There are three," William Dawson Marston said. "The first is payable on your achieving your majority—how long have you been twenty-one, Johnny?"

"I'm twenty-two," John said.

"Then you should have had the first one turned over to you. You say that hasn't happened?"

"No. I don't know what you're talking about."

"The second is payable on your marriage, or your twenty-fifth birthday, whichever comes first. And the third on your thirtieth birthday, or the birth of your first issue, whichever comes first. Your father hasn't mentioned any of this to you? Even in his marvelously opaque way?"

"No."

"Then I'm very glad that I decided to butt in," Marston said.

"I don't understand you," John said.

"I need another drink," Marston said. "You ready?"

John looked at his glass. It was three quarters full.

"No, thank you," he said, and then changed his mind. "Yes, please, I think I will."

Marston held his glass over his head and snapped his fingers loudly until he had the waiter's attention.

Father often says that Uncle Bill is crude on occasion.

John took a deep swallow of his drink.

"I love my sister," Marston said seriously, and then unnecessarily adding the explanation, "your mother. I really do. But she has a room temperature IQ, and when your father and/or the Bible are concerned, she is totally incompetent to make decisions on her own."

I wonder why I have not leapt loyally, and angrily, to Mother's defense?

"If she has ever raised with your father the question I just raised—and I will give her the benefit of the doubt on that subject—your father doubtless explained that you're only a child, and not nearly as well equipped to handle your financial affairs as he is. And she was surely reassured by those words."

"Why are you bringing this up?" John asked.

"You may have noticed over the years that I am not among your father's legion of admirers," Marston said.

"No, Sir, I never thought anything like that."

"To put a point on it, I can't stand the sonofabitch," Marston said, and then quickly added, "Hell, there I go again. Sorry."

"I think I better get out of here," John thought out loud.

"Keep your seat!" Marston said, so loudly that heads turned. "I have started this, and I *will* finish it."

"I don't like the way you're talking about my parents."

"I'm talking about your money. Two comma money."

"I don't understand," Moore said.

"That's the root of the problem," Marston said. "I presume that you have considered the possibility—God forbid, as they say—that you won't come back from the war alive?"

"Yes, of course."

"And I presume that the Marine Corps encouraged you to prepare a will?"

"Yes."

"And I will bet you a doughnut to a bottle of scotch that you left all your worldly possessions to your parents, yes?"

"Something wrong with that?" John asked, a little nastily.

"Nothing at all, so long as you know what you're doing," Marston said. "But at the time you signed your will, you thought that your worldly possessions consisted of your civilian clothing and your ten thousand dollars' worth of government life insurance, no?"

"Yes," John agreed.

"You now know that your estate will be somewhat larger than you thought it would amount to. I want to make sure that you understand you can dispose of your estate in any manner you see fit. You can for example leave all or part of it to your sisters. Or to your rowing club. Or the Salvation Army. Even—God forbid—to Missions."

"Jesus Christ!" John said.

"Him, too, I suppose. But you would have to route that through some churchly body, I think."

John looked at his uncle. Their eyes met. They smiled.

"I'm sure I don't have to say this, but I will. I don't want any part of it," Marston went on. "I want you to come home from this goddamned war and spend it yourself. Preferably on fast women and good whiskey. At least for a while. I . . ."

He reached over and snatched up John's Zippo. He ran his fingers over the Marine Corps insignia.

"This is all I want in way of remembrance, Johnny. May I have it?" Marston's voice broke, and John's eyes teared. "I'll give it back when you come home."

"Of course," he said, and his voice broke.

There was a full minute's silence as they composed themselves. John broke it: "What should I do? About the trust funds?"

"Change your will as soon as you can," Marston said. "If you're curious about the numbers . . . hell, in any case, go to the Trust Department of the First Philadelphia and ask for Carlton Schuyler . . ."

He interrupted himself to take a card and write the name on it.

"Schuyler's a good sort, and he's probably already a little nervous that your father's 'handling' your affairs for you. If I know it's not legal, he damned well does too. Anyway, Schuyler will have the numbers and can answer all your questions."

Moore nodded, and then asked: "When I have all this information, what should I do with it?"

"You're asking my advice?" Marston asked. "You sure you want to do that?"

"Yes."

"OK. Have Schuyler set up another trust for you, using the assets of the trust fund that should have been turned over to you. Let the bank manage your assets while you're away. I've asked about this. It's a common practice for people in the service. Put all of it, save, say, a thousand dollars, in the trust."

"I don't quite understand," Moore confessed. "What would the difference be? I mean, it's already in a trust . . ."

"Your father has access to it the way it is now. This way he couldn't touch it."

It was a long moment before Moore replied, "I see."

His uncle nodded.

"And why everything but a thousand dollars?" Moore asked.

"Good whiskey and wild women, Johnny, are expensive. Have a good time before you go over there."

"Christ!"

"I didn't exactly have Him in mind," Marston said. "I was thinking more of the long-legged blondes you might bump into. Pity you're not going through San Francisco. The long-legged blondes around the bar at the Andrew Foster Hotel are stunning."

Like that woman, that stunning woman, in the bar at the Bellevue-Stratford?

"OK," John said. "I'll do it first thing in the morning."

"Then I accomplished what I set out to do," Marston said.

"Thank you," John said.

"You mean that, Johnny? Or was I putting my nose in where it had no business?"

"I mean it," John said. "But what I don't understand is why? I mean, why did my father do what he did? Why is he always doing something like that?"

"In this case, it's pretty obvious. Neither his mother or your grandfather left him or your mother very much in their wills. They left everything in trust to the grandchildren. I won't say—though I have a damned good idea—why they chose to do that, but they did."

"Tell me what you think."

"They didn't particularly like *him,* obviously, and they knew that leaving the money to your mother would be the same thing as leaving it to him. Ten minutes after she got it, he would have talked her out of it."

"Oh."

"In his mind, he was right about not bothering you with the details of your inheritance. He was *protecting* you. He's been that way as long as I've known him. He really never questions the morality of anything he does. He thinks I like to buy his goddamned first class cabins on the *Pacific Princess,* and pay his tailor bills, for example. But I shouldn't have called him a sonofabitch, even if he is a sonofabitch, and I'm sorry."

John chuckled.

Marston smiled at him.

"Finish your drink, and we'll have dinner. I'm not sure I'll be able to find the dining room as it is."

William Dawson Marston IV found the dining room without trouble, and he got through the cherrystone clams and half his steak; but then, without warning, he lowered his chin to his chest, dropped his wineglass, and went to sleep.

John was alarmed, but quickly learned that the Union League was prepared for such eventualities. The maître d'hôtel and an enormous chef quickly appeared, hoisted Marston to his feet, and carried him out of the dining room.

"We'll just put Mr. Marston up overnight, until he feels better," the waiter said softly in John's ear.

John was back across Broad Street and almost to the First Philadelphia Trust Company parking lot before he realized that the last thing he wanted to do now was get in the car and go home, where he would probably have to face his father.

If I go back to the bar in the Bellevue-Stratford, maybe she'll be there.

There you go again, Sergeant Asshole! For one thing, she won't be there, and for another, what do you think you would do if she was?

He went back to the bar in the Bellevue-Stratford and she was not there.

Well, asshole, what did you expect?

He took the same seat at the bar he had before.

"Scotch," John said. "Famous Grouse, if you have it. With a little water."

He laid money on the bar, but when the bartender delivered the drink, he said, "It's on the gentleman at the end of the bar."

John, uncomfortable, looked down the bar. A middle-aged, silver-haired stout Irishman waved friendlily at him.

Well, he doesn't look like a pervert.

He waved his thanks.

"I wondered if you would come back in here," the beautiful older woman said, behind him.

"Jesus!"

"How was your dinner?"

"The food wasn't bad," John said.

"But the rest was awful?" she asked. "Mine, too."

"Can I get you a drink?"

"Yes, please," she said. "But I insist on paying."

"I can pay," he said. "I want to."

"I think I have a little more money than a Marine Sergeant," she said.

"Don't be too sure," he said. "You weren't at my dinner."

"It was a money dinner? Have you noticed that talking about money at dinner ruins the taste of the food?"

He laughed.

"Yes," he said. "Is that the voice of experience?"

"Yes," she said. "Unfortunately. Over a Bookbinder's lobster, my soon-to-be ex-husband and I fought politely over the division of property."

"I'm sorry," John said.

"Yes, Miss?" the bartender asked.

"What are you drinking?" she asked John.

"Famous Grouse," he said.

"Fine," she said to the bartender. She turned to John. "Why is it that now that I see you again I don't think you're a lonely marine, far from home and loved ones?"

"I'm from here," he said. "That may have something to do with it. And I just had dinner with my uncle."

She chuckled. "You are also far more articulate than you were on the train," she said. "What was with you on the train?"

"I thought you had caught me staring at you," he said.

"I had," she said. "Why were you?"

"Because you're the most beautiful woman I've ever seen."

"I can't believe that," she said.

"Why did you come back in here?" John asked.

"Ooooh," she said, and then looked at him. "Right to the bone, right? OK. I thought maybe you would be in here."

"I am."

"Did you come in here to pick up a girl?"

"I came in because I didn't want to go home and face my father," John said evenly.

"You did something wrong?"

"He did."

"That's the money you were talking about?"

He nodded.

"And because I had the crazy idea you might be here."

"I am," she said.

"I think maybe I'm dreaming and will wake up any second," John said.

"It's like a dream for me too," she said. "A bad dream. I had the odd notion that when I met my husband, that we could . . . patch things up. But what he wanted was the Spode . . . his beloved saw the Spode and wanted it . . . You know what I mean by Spode?"

"China."

". . . and the monogrammed silver. I mean, after all, it would have no meaning for me anymore, would it? I'll certainly remarry in time, won't I?"

"I'm sorry," John said.

"And then here I am, in a bar, more than a little drunk, with a Marine. A boy Marine. Bad dream."

"I'm not a boy," John said, hurt.

"Yes, you are," she said, laughing.

"Well, fuck you!"

There you go, asshole. You fucked it up. Why the fucking hell did you say that?

"Sorry," he said, in anguish.

She opened her purse and he thought she was looking for a cigarette and remembered that Uncle Bill had taken his Zippo so he couldn't light it for her.

But her hand came out of the purse with a five-dollar bill. She dropped it on the bar and stood up.

Now she's going to walk out of here, and I will never see her again.

She looked into his face.

"Come on," she said. "Let's get out of here."

She walked to the side door; and in a moment he followed her. She waited for him to open the door for her, and walked out. Then she put her hand on his arm.

"As long as we both understand this is insane . . ." she said.

"Where are we going?"

"Rittenhouse Square," she said. "We—*I*—have an apartment there."

There was a hand on Sergeant John Marston Moore's shoulder and a voice calling gently, "Hey!"

He opened his eyes. He was lying belly down on a bed, his arm and head hanging over the edge. He could see a dark red carpet and a naked foot, obviously a female foot. This observation was immediately confirmed when he saw that the leg attached to the foot disappeared under a pale blue robe.

He remembered where he was, and what had happened, and rolled over onto his back.

She was standing there, holding a cup of coffee out to him.

I don't even know her name!

"Hi!" she said.

"Hi," he replied, looking into her eyes. "What's that?"

"Coffee," she said.

"Coffee?"

"You said you had your father's car. I don't want you driving drunk."

"You're throwing me out?"

"I'm sending you home."

"Why?"

"Didn't we both get what we were looking for?"

"We gave each other what the other needed would be a nicer way to put it."

"All right," she said. "Yes, we did. I hope I did. I know you did. But now it's time to come back to the real world."

"And for me to go home."

"Right."

"I don't want to go home. I want to stay here with you, forever."

"That's obviously out of the question."

He sat up. She tried to hand him the cup and saucer. He avoided it.

She touched the top of his head.

"You are really very sweet," she said.

He tilted his head back to look up at her. She smiled.

He reached up for the cord of her robe.

"Don't do that."

He ignored her.

The robe fell open when he pulled the cord free.

He put his arms around her and his face against her belly.

He heard her take in her breath, and her hand dropped to the small of his neck.

"Oh God!" she said.

Her navel was next to his mouth and he kissed it.

"I'm going to spill the coffee."

"Put the coffee on the floor and take the robe off."

"And if I do, then will you go?"

"No."

She dropped to her knees and put the cup and saucer on the floor, shrugged out of the robe, and then turned her face to him and kissed him.

"Oh, Baby, what am I going to do with you?"

"I don't know about that," he said. "But I know what I'm going to do to you."

He put his hands on her shoulders and moved her onto the bed and looked down at her.

"God, you're so beautiful!" he said.

"So are you," she said.

And then he surprised her very much by pushing himself off the bed. She raised her head to look at him. He walked to the other side of the bed and sat down and reached for her telephone.

"Father," he said into it. "Uncle Bill and I have had a long talk and a lot to drink, and I think it would be best if I stayed over with him at the Union League, rather than driving."

There was a pause, and then Sergeant John Marston Moore, USMCR, said: "You're going to have to understand, Father, that I'm no longer a child. I can drink whatever and whenever I wish."

There was another pause.

"There's something else, Father. My orders have been changed. I have to leave tomorrow afternoon. When Mother's awake, please tell her that I'll be out there sometime before noon to pack. I have to see Mr. Schuyler at First Philadelphia, first."

One final pause.

"I think you know why I have to see Mr. Schuyler, Father," John said.

A moment later, he took the receiver from his ear and looked at it.

It was clear to Barbara Ward (Mrs. Howard P.) Hawthorne, Jr., that John's father had hung up on him. There was pain in his eyes when he turned from putting the receiver in its cradle and looked at her.

"Oh, Baby," she said. "Whatever that was, I'm sorry."

"Do you think you could manage to call me 'Darling,' or 'Sweetheart,' or something besides 'Baby'? . . . I'll even settle happily for 'John.' "

She held her arms open.

"Come to me, my darling," she said.

He didn't move.

"I thought you wanted me to leave."

She put her arms down and pulled the sheet up and held it over her breast.

She found his eyes and looked into them and said, "I want what's best for you."

"You're what's best for me."

"You really have to leave tomorrow? Which is really, now, today?"

"No. Thursday."

"Then why . . . ?"

"I want to be with you until I go."

She took her eyes from his and lowered her head and fought the tears. Then she raised her eyes to his again and opened her arms again and said, "Come to me, John, my darling, my sweetheart."

And this time he went to her.

VI

(ONE)
Headquarters
Marine Air Group Twenty-One (MAG-21)
Ewa, Oahu Island, Territory of Hawaii
1325 Hours 19 June 1942

Lieutenant Colonel Clyde G. Dawkins, USMC, Commanding MAG-21, was a tall, thin, sharp-featured man who wore his light brown hair so closely cropped that the tanned and sun-freckled flesh of his scalp was visible.

He was wearing a stiffly starched khaki shirt with a field scarf tied in a tiny knot. A gold collar clasp held the collar points together and the knot in the field scarf erect. He had heard somewhere that the collar clasp was now frowned upon; but that brought the same reaction from him as the suggestion from Pearl Harbor that since *Navy* Naval Aviators were now discouraged from wearing their fur-collared leather flight jackets when not actually engaged in flying activities, it behooved him to similarly discourage *Marine* Naval Aviators from wearing their flight jackets when not actually on the flight line: He said nothing; thought, *Fuck You;* and wore both a collar clasp and his leather flight jacket almost all the time, fully aware that if he did so, the Marine Naval Aviators of MAG-21 would presume it was not only permissible but encouraged.

He was not at all a rebel by nature. He did not relish defying higher authority, even when he knew he could get away with it. But he was a practical man, and the wearing of flight jackets by aviators seemed far more practical and convenient than forcing his officers to waste time taking off and putting on their uniform tunics half a dozen times a day. And the gold collar clasp, in his judgment, struck him as a splendid means to keep an officer's collar points where they belonged, even if some people in The Corps thought of it as "civilian-type jewelry." An officer with one of his collar points in a horizontal attitude looked far more slovenly than one with his collar points fixed in the proper attitude with a barely visible piece of "civilian jewelry."

The officer standing somewhat uncomfortably before Lieutenant Colonel Dawkins's desk had performed well in the Battle of Midway. His name was Captain Thomas J. Wood. He was young and newly promoted; he was wearing a fur-collared flight jacket and a collar clasp; and he was standing with his hands clasped together behind him in the small of his back.

But there was something about him—an impetuosity, an indecisiveness—that Dawkins did not like. Dawkins believed that a good officer made decisions slowly, and then stuck by them.

"It's time to fish or cut bait, Tom," Dawkins said, not unkindly.

"Uh . . . Sir, I decline to press charges."

"So be it," Dawkins said.

"Sir, I saw what I saw, but I can't . . ."

"That will be all, Captain," Dawkins said. There was now a hint of ice in his voice. "You are dismissed."

The captain came to attention.

"Yes, Sir," he said. He did an about-face and started to march out of the room.

"Ask Major Lorenz to come in, please," Dawkins called to him.

"Aye, aye, Sir."

Major Karl J. Lorenz, who was the Executive Officer of MAG-21, walked into the office. Lorenz looked, Dawkins often thought, like a recruiting poster for the Waffen-SS—in other words like an Aryan of impeccable Nordic-Teutonic heritage, blond-haired, blue-eyed, fair-skinned, and lithely muscular.

"You wanted me, Skipper?" he asked.

"Close the door, please," Dawkins said.

Lorenz did so.

"After some thought," Dawkins said, "he declined to press charges."

"Huh," Lorenz said thoughtfully. "Probably a good thing, Sir. It would have been hard to make those charges stick."

"*Not* a good thing, Karl," Dawkins said.

"You think we should have tried him?" Lorenz asked, surprised.

"I think before young Captain Wood started running off at the mouth, he should have made up his mind whether or not he was prepared to carry an accusation of cowardice through."

"Oh," Lorenz replied. "Yes, Sir, I see what you mean."

"He doesn't really know any more than I do—and I wasn't there—if Dunn ran away from that fight or not. Cowardice in the face of the enemy . . . that's the worst accusation that can be made."

"I presume you told Wood that?"

"No. I didn't want to influence his decision, one way or the other."

"Can I ask what you *think?*"

"I already told you, I don't think Wood really knows. Or, if you were asking, do I think Dunn ran?"

"Yes, Sir."

"I think we're going to have to give him the benefit of the doubt. He says he doesn't remember when, or under what conditions, he broke off the engagement. I don't think he does. He lost his windscreen and he was wounded. The question is, when did that happen? Before or after he started back to Midway? He didn't run before the fight. He got a Kate. There's no question about that. And then he got a Zero. Again, confirmed beyond any question. And then the next time he's seen, he's on his way back to Midway. Close enough to be recognized beyond any doubt, but too far away for anyone to be able to state with certainty that he had, or had not, already lost his windshield."

"I realize, Sir, I haven't been asked, but in those circumstances I would be prone to give him the benefit of the doubt."

"Ascribing Wood's charges to post-combat hysteria?"

"Something like that, Sir."

"Unfortunately, although he elected not to pursue them, Wood's charges are going to be remembered by a lot of people for a long time—made worse in the retelling, of course."

"What are you going to do with Dunn, Sir?" Lorenz said, after a moment.

"You and I are about to visit Lieutenant Dunn in the hospital; there I will express my pleasure that he will be discharged tomorrow, present him with his Purple Heart Medal, and inform him that he is now assigned to VMF-229. I think he will understand why it would be awkward for him to return to VMF-211. I hope he doesn't ask me for an explanation."

"Two-twenty-nine, Sir?" Lorenz asked, surprised.

Dawkins nodded. "Two-twenty-nine."

"Sir, we haven't activated VMF-229 yet."

"It is activated," Dawkins said and paused to look at his watch, "as of 1300 hours today. Its personnel consists of one officer, absent in hospital, and one officer, en route, not yet joined. See that the order is typed up."

"Who did you decide to give it to, Sir?"

"A good Marine officer, Major," Dawkins said, "is always willing to carefully consider the recommendations of his superiors."

"Sir?"

Dawkins chuckled, opened a desk drawer, and handed Lorenz a sheet of yellow teletype paper.

ROUTINE

CONFIDENTIAL

HQ USMC WASH DC 1445 14JUNE42

COMMANDING OFFICER

MAG-21 EWA TH

CAPTAIN CHARLES M. GALLOWAY, USMCR, HAVING REPORTED UPON ACTIVE DUTY, HAS BEEN ORDERED TO PROCEED BY AIR TO EWA FOR DUTY AS COMMANDING OFFICER VMF-229. WHILE THIS ASSIGNMENT HAS THE CONCURRENCE OF THE COMMANDANT AND THE UNDERSIGNED YOU ARE OF COURSE AT LIBERTY TO ASSIGN THIS OFFICER TO ANY DUTIES YOU WISH.

D.G. MCINERNEY BRIG GEN USMC

"I will be goddamned," Lorenz said.

"I thought you might find that surprising," Dawkins said.

"The last time I saw Charley, I thought they were going to crucify him," Lorenz said. "And I mean, literally. What the hell does that 'concurrence of the Commandant' mean?"

"I think it means that Doc McInerney went right to the Commandant. They had Charley flying a VIP R4D around out of Quantico." The R4D was the Navy designation of the twin-engine Douglas transport aircraft called DC-3 by the manufacturer and C-47 by the Army Air Corps. "What I think is that McInerney went to the Commandant and told him how desperate we are for people with more than two hundred hours in a cockpit. As furious as the Navy was with him, nobody but the Commandant would dare to commission him."

"The last I heard, they wouldn't let him fly—hell, even taxi—anything. He was still a sergeant, and they had him working as a mechanic on the flight line at Quantico. But this sort of restores my faith in the Marine Corps," Lorenz said.

"'*Restores*' your faith, Major?" Dawkins asked wryly. "That suggests it was lost."

"Well, let's say, the way the brass let the Navy crap all over Charley, that it *wavered* a little."

"Oh ye of little faith!" Dawkins mocked, gently.

"When's he due in?"

Dawkins shrugged helplessly. "The TWX didn't say," he said. "And knowing Charley as well as I do, that means one of two things: He will either rush over here as fast as humanly possible, or else he will still be trying to find a slow ship the day the war's over."

Lorenz laughed.

Dawkins stood up.

"Let's go pin the Purple Heart on Lieutenant Dunn," he said.

(TWO)
U.S. Naval Hospital
Pearl Harbor, Oahu Island, Territory of Hawaii
1505 Hours 19 June 1942

When Lieutenant Colonel Dawkins pushed open the door to his room, First Lieutenant William C. Dunn was lying on his back on the bed; his bathrobe was open and his legs were spread; and he was not wearing pajama pants. Dunn was obviously not expecting visitors.

What Dawkins could see, among other things, were several bandages in the vicinity of Dunn's crotch. One of these was large, but most were not much more than Band-Aids. He could also see a half-dozen unbandaged wounds, their sutures visible, on his inner upper thighs. The whole area had been shaved and then painted with some kind of orange antiseptic.

He was almost a soprano, Dawkins thought. *Whatever had come through the canopy of Dunn's Wildcat had come within inches of blowing away the family jewels. From the number of fragments, it was probably a 20mm, which exploded on contact.*

Soon after the door opened, Dunn covered his midsection with the flap of his hospital issue bathrobe; and then when he saw the silver leaf on Dawkins's collar, he started to swing his legs to get out of bed.

"Stay where you are, Son," Dawkins said quickly, but too late. Dunn was already on his feet, standing at attention.

"Well, then, stand at ease," Dawkins said. "Does all that hurt very much?"

"Only when I get a hard-on, Sir," Dunn blurted, and quickly added, "Sorry, Sir. I shouldn't have said that."

"If I had been dinged in that area, and it still worked," Dawkins said, "I think I would be delighted."

"Yes, Sir," Dunn said.

"Do you know who I am, Son?"

"Yes, Sir. You gave us a little talk when we reported aboard."

"And this is my exec, Major Lorenz," Dawkins said.

Lorenz gave his hand to Dunn.

"How are you, Lieutenant?"

"Very well, thank you, Sir."

"Why don't you let me pin this thing on you," Dawkins said. "And then you get back in bed."

He took the Purple Heart Medal from a hinged metal box, pinned it to the lapel of Dunn's bathrobe, and then shook his hand.

"Thank you, Sir."

"That's the oldest medal, did you know that?" Dawkins said. "Goes back to the Revolution. Washington issued an order that anyone who had been wounded could wear a purple ribbon—and in those days that meant a real ribbon—on his uniform."

"I didn't know that, Sir," Dunn admitted.

"You have literally shed blood for your country," Dawkins said. "You can wear that with pride."

Dunn didn't reply.

"Why don't you get back in bed?"

"I'm all right, Sir. And they have been encouraging me to move around."

"They tell me you're being discharged tomorrow," Dawkins said.

"I was about to tell you that, Sir, and ask you what's next."

"You've been assigned to VMF-229," Dawkins said.

"Pending court-martial, Sir?"

"No charges have been, or will be, pressed against you, Dunn," Dawkins said.

"But they don't want me back in the squadron, right, Sir?"

"*I* ordered your transfer to VMF-229," Dawkins said. "The commanding officer of VMF-211 had nothing to do with that decision."

"Yes, Sir," Dunn said, on the edge of insolence, making it clear he did not believe that answer.

Dawkins felt anger swell up in him, but suppressed it.

"VMF-229 is a new squadron. It was activated today. Right now, you are half of its total strength. The commanding officer is en route from the States. I assigned you there because I wanted someone with your experience . . ."

"My Midway experience, Sir?" Dunn asked, just over the edge into sarcasm.

"When I want a question, Son," Dawkins said icily, "I will ask for one."

"Yes, Sir."

"You will be the only pilot in the squadron who has even seen a Japanese airplane, much less shot two of them down," Dawkins said. "I want the newcomers to look at you and see you're very much like they are. To take some of the pressure off, if you follow my meaning. Additionally, perhaps you will be able to teach them something, based on your experience."

"Yes, Sir."

"I'm personally acquainted with your new commanding officer, Captain Charley Galloway," Dawkins went on. "I will tell him what I know about you, and the gossip. And I will tell him that I personally feel you did everything you were supposed to do at Midway, and then, suffering wounds, managed to get your shot-up aircraft back to the field."

Dunn for the first time met Dawkins's eyes.

"Now, you may ask any questions you may have," Dawkins said.

"Thank you, Sir," Dunn said after a moment. "No questions, Sir."

"Unsolicited advice is seldom welcome, Dunn, but nevertheless: Do what you can to ignore the gossip. Eventually, it will die down. You now have that clean slate everyone's always talking about, new squadron, new skipper. If I were Captain Galloway, I'd be damned glad to be getting someone like you."

"Colonel, I really don't remember a goddamned thing about how I got back to the field," Dunn said.

I believe him.

"The important thing is that you got back," Dawkins said.

"Sir, where is VMF-229?"

"Right now, it's on a sheet of paper in Major Lorenz's OUT basket," Dawkins said. "When you get out of here, check into the BOQ. When Captain Galloway gets here, or something else happens, we'll send for you. Take some time off. I was about to say, go swimming, but that's probably not such a hot idea, is it?"

"No, Sir," Dunn said.

For the first time, Dawkins noticed, *Dunn is smiling. I think it just sank in that he's not going to be court-martialed, and maybe even that someone doesn't think he's a coward.*

"Check in with the adjutant, or the sergeant major, once a day," Dawkins said.

"Aye, aye, Sir."

Dawkins put out his hand.

"Congratulations, Lieutenant, on your decoration," he said. "And good luck in your new assignment."

"Thank you, Sir."

Major Lorenz offered his hand.

"If you need anything, Dunn, come see me, or give me a call. And congratulations, too, and good luck."

"Thank you, Sir," Dunn repeated.

(THREE)
U.S. Naval Hospital
Pearl Harbor, Hawaii, Territory of Hawaii
1535 Hours 19 June 1942

Lieutenant Colonel Dawkins and Major Lorenz left the room, closing the door after them. Dunn lowered his head to look at his Purple Heart Medal—he had seen the ribbon before, but not the actual medal—then unpinned it and held it in his hand and looked at it again. It was in the shape of a heart and bore a profile of George Washington.

He picked up the box it had come in and saw that it contained both the ribbon and a metal pin in the shape of the ribbon, obviously intended to be worn in the lapel of a civilian jacket.

"You're a real fucking hero, Bill Dunn," he said wryly, aloud. "You have been awarded the 'Next Time, Stupid, Remember to Duck Medal.'"

He chuckled at his own wit. Then he put the medal in the box, snapped the lid closed, walked to the white bedside table, and put it in the drawer. As he was closing the drawer, the door opened again.

Lieutenant (Junior Grade) Mary Agnes O'Malley, Nurse Corps, USN, entered the room, carrying a stainless steel tray covered with a wash-faded, medical green cloth.

"Hi," she said and smiled at him.

Lieutenant Dunn was strongly attracted to Lieutenant (j.g.) O'Malley, partly because she was a trim, pert-breasted redhead, and partly because he had heard that she fucked like a mink. He'd heard it so often at the bar in the Ewa Officer's Club that it had to be something more than wishful thinking.

"Hi," he replied.

He thought she looked especially desirable today. When she put the cloth covered tray down on his bedside table, she leaned far enough over to afford him a glimpse of her well-filled brassiere, and the soft white flesh straining at it.

Despite her reputation, Lieutenant (j.g.) O'Malley had so far shown zero interest in Dunn. In his view there were two reasons for this. First, since someone as good looking as Lieutenant (j.g.) O'Malley could pick and choose among a large group of bachelor officers, she would naturally prefer a captain or a major to a lowly lieutenant. Second, but perhaps most important, he knew that his reputation had preceded him: She had certainly heard the gossip that he had run away from the fight at Midway. To a young woman like Lieutenant (j.g.) O'Malley—for that matter, to any young woman—a lowly lieutenant with a yellow streak was something to be scorned, not taken to bed.

"What did the brass want?" she asked.

"The war is going badly," he said. "They came for my advice on how to turn it around."

"I'm serious," she said, gesturing for him to get on the bed. "What did they want?"

"They gave me my 'You Forgot to Duck Medal.'"

"What?"

"Colonel Dawkins gave me the Purple Heart," Dunn said. "And my new assignment. Why should I get in bed?"

"Because I'm going to remove your sutures," she said. "Or some of them, anyway. Where's your medal?"

"In the table drawer."

"Can I see it?"

"You've never seen one before?"

"I want to see yours."

You show me yours and I'll show you mine.

He went to the bedside table and took the box out and handed it to her.

She opened it and looked at it and handed it back.

"Very nice. You should be proud of yourself."

"All that means is that I got hit," he said.

"You realize how lucky you were that it wasn't worse, I hope?"

Does she mean that the 20mm didn't hit me in the head? Or that it didn't get me in the balls?

"Yeah, sure I do," he said.

"Get in the bed and open your robe," she said.

"I'm not wearing my pajama bottoms."

She tossed him the faded green medical cloth.

"Cover yourself," she said. "Not that I would see something I haven't seen before."

He got on the bed, arranged the cloth over his crotch, and opened the robe.

She pulled on rubber gloves, an act that he found quite erotic, dipped a gauze patch in alcohol, and then proceeded to mop his inner thighs.

He yelped when, without warning, she pulled the larger bandage free with a jerk.

"Still a little suppuration," she observed, professionally. "But it's healing nicely. You were *really* lucky."

Without question, that remark makes reference to the fact that I didn't get zapped in the balls.

As she scrubbed at the vestiges of the tape that had held the bandage in place, he got another glimpse down the front of her crisp white uniform at the swelling of her bosom. He could smell the perfume she'd put down there, too. With dreadful inevitability he almost instantly achieved a state of erection.

Lieutenant O'Malley seemed not to notice.

"Where are they sending you?" she asked, as she jerked the smaller bandage free.

"VMF-229," he said.

"Where's that? Or is that classified?"

"Colonel Dawkins said that right now it's in the exec's desk drawer," Dunn said. "It was activated today. Right now it's me and a captain named Galloway, who's en route from the States."

"Galloway?" she asked. "Does he have a first name?"

Dunn thought a moment. "Charley, I think he said. Mean anything to you?"

"I don't know," she said. "I used to date a Tech Sergeant Charley Galloway. He was a pilot. I wonder how many Charley Galloways there are in the Marine Corps?"

Socialization between commissioned officers and enlisted personnel was not only a social no-no in the Naval Service but against regulations, and thus a court-martial offense. The announcement startled him.

"You used to date a sergeant?" he blurted.

"My, aren't you the prig? Haven't you ever done anything you shouldn't?" she asked as she dabbed at the gummy residue of the second bandage. "I think we'll just leave the bandage off of that."

"I didn't mean to sound like a prig," he said. "I guess I was just a little surprised to . . . hear you volunteer that."

"Well, I didn't think you would tell anybody," she said. "You mean you never heard of Sergeant Charley Galloway?"

And then, all of a sudden, he realized that he had. He hadn't made the connection before because of the rank.

"I reported aboard VMF-211 after he left," Dunn said. "That Galloway?"

She chuckled.

"That Galloway," she confirmed.

"The scuttlebutt I heard was that he and another sergeant put together a Wildcat from wrecks of what was left on December seventh, wrecks that had been written off the books, and that he flew it off without authority to join the Wake Island relief force at sea."

"The *Saratoga,*" she said. "Task Force XIV. They started out to reinforce Wake Island, but they were called back."

"I heard that he was really in trouble for doing that," Dunn said. "That they sent him back to the States for a court-martial. What was that all about?"

"He embarrassed the Navy brass," she explained. "First of all BUAIR." (The U.S. Navy Bureau of Aeronautics, which is charged with aviation engineering for the Marine Corps.) "They examined the airplanes after the Japanese attack and said they were total losses. But Charley and Sergeant Oblensky . . ."

"Who?"

"Big Steve Oblensky. He was VMF-211's Maintenance Sergeant."

"I know him," Dunn said. "As far as I know, he still is."

"So after the brass said all of VMF-211's planes at Ewa were beyond repair, Big Steve and Charley got one flying; and then Charley flew it out to *Sara,* which was then a couple of hundred miles at sea. The whole relief force was supposed to be a secret, especially of course, where *Sara* was. So the brass's faces were red, and since the brass never make a mistake, they decided to stick the old purple shaft in Charley."

"Why did he do it?"

"Hell," Lieutenant (j.g.) O'Malley said, "the rest of VMF-211 was on Wake and had already lost most of their planes. Charley figured they needed whatever airplanes they could get. The only aircraft on *Sara* were Buffaloes. They could have used Charley's Wildcat, if the brass here hadn't called the relief force back."

Dunn grunted.

It had occurred to him that despite the smell of her perfume, her well-filled brassiere, and the other delightful aspects of her gentle gender, Lieutenant (j.g.) O'Malley was talking to him like—more importantly, thinking like—a fellow officer of the Naval Establishment, even down to an easy familiarity with the vernacular. It was somewhat disconcerting.

"We don't know if we're talking about the same man," he said.

"Probably, we're not," Mary Agnes O'Malley replied, matter-of-factly, "considering how pissed off the brass was at Charley. It's probably some other guy with the same name."

He sensed that she was disappointed.

She put the alcohol swab on the tray and picked up a pair of surgical scissors. Next she bent low over his midsection; and he sensed, rather than saw—her head was in the way, and he was unable to withdraw his eyes from her brassiere—that she was cutting the sutures.

The procedure took her a full ninety seconds. Sensing that she was concentrating, he did not attempt to make conversation.

She straightened, finally, and he was suddenly sure from the look in her eyes that she knew he had been looking down her dress.

She laid the scissors down and picked up surgical forceps and a pad of gauze.

"Now we pull the thread out," she said, and bent over him again. "It shouldn't hurt, so don't squirm."

"Okay."

The green surgical cloth was somehow displaced. He grabbed for it in the same moment she did. She got to it first and put it back in place. In doing so, her hand brushed against it.

"Christ, I'm sorry!" Dunn said.

"Don't be silly," she said professionally.

"I thought, I heard . . ." Bill blurted, "that when something like that happens, a nurse knows where to hit it to make it go down."

She chuckled, deep in her throat.

"I wouldn't want to hurt it," she said, matter-of-factly. "I think it's darling."

He felt a nipping sensation, and then a moment later, another one, and then a third. He realized that she was pulling the black sutures from his flesh.

She stood erect and wiped two short lengths of thread from her fingers with a cloth, and then a third from the forceps. She looked down at him.

"We're supposed to be very professional—I think the word is 'dispassionate'— when something like that happens," she said. "But the truth is, sometimes that doesn't happen. Especially when the patient is sort of cute."

Her fingers slid up his leg, found his erection, and traced it gently.

"You're going to be discharged tomorrow, which means that if you ask for one, they'll give you an off-the-ward pass until 2230."

She took her hand away, wiped the forceps with the gauze again, and bent over him. He felt another series of nips in the soft flesh of his groin, and then she stood up again.

"Cat got your tongue?" she asked.

"I don't suppose you could have dinner with me tonight?"

"I think that could be arranged," she said.

"Put your hand on it again."

"We'd both be in trouble if somebody saw us," she said, and then ran her fingers over him again.

"What time?"

"I go off at 1630," she said. "How about 1730 at the bar?"

"Fine."

"My roommate has the duty tonight," she said.

"She does?"

"If we have gentlemen callers, we're supposed to leave the door open," she said. "But I always wonder, when the door is closed, how anybody could tell if we have anybody in there or not."

"I can't see how they could tell," he said.

"Well, maybe you might want to get a bottle of scotch and pick me up at my quarters. We could have a drink, and then go to dinner. Or would you rather eat first?"

"What kind of scotch?"

"I'm not fussy," she said.

"You better stop that, or I'm going to . . ."

She immediately took her hand away.

"We wouldn't want to waste it, would we?" she asked. "Now be a good boy and let me finish this. Before old Shit-for-brains wonders why it's taking me so long and sticks her nose in here."

(FOUR)
Apartment "C"
106 Rittenhouse Square
Philadelphia, Pennsylvania
22 June 1942

Barbara Ward (Mrs. Howard P.) Hawthorne, Jr., slid the frosted glass door open and stepped out of her shower. She took a towel from the rack and started to dry her hair. Then she stopped and wiped the condensation from the mirror over the wash basin.

She resumed drying her hair as she examined herself in the mirror.

It's not at all bad looking, she thought, *they're not pendulous, and the tummy is still firm, but ye old body is thirty-six years old. Nearly thirty-seven, not thirty-two, as you told John.*

When he is thirty-seven—she did the arithmetic—*you will be fifty-one. Fifty-one! My God, you're insane, Barbara!*

She finished drying herself, put the towel in the hamper, and went into the bedroom. There she took a spray bottle of eau de cologne and sprayed it on herself, and then she took a bottle of perfume, which she dabbed behind her ears and in the valley between her breasts. She pulled on her robe, walked back to the bathroom, and began to brush her hair, looking into the reflection of her eyes in the mirror.

Why did you put perfume on? There will be no one to smell it. Specifically, John has probably nuzzled you between the breasts for the last time. He is at this very moment ten thousand feet in the air over Western Pennsylvania, or Ohio, or some-place, on his way to the war. Even if he survives that, the chances of his coming back to you are very slim.

What he got was what he wanted, a willing playmate in bed for four days. But when he comes back, what he is going to want is a quote nice unquote girl his own age, not some middle-aged woman who he picked up—or vice versa—in a bar.

He says he loves you . . .

And he probably really thinks he does, because he would not say something like that unless he meant it. But what he is really doing is mistaking lust, and a little tenderness, for love.

He's not much used to love, that's for sure. From everything he told me, his father is really a despicable human being. He got no love from him. Or anything like tenderness, either, for that matter. Nor from his mother, either, I don't think. I got the idea that, in the Moore house, hugging and kissing were unseemly.

And while I am not all that experienced in the bed department myself, it was perfectly obvious that he can count his previous partners on the fingers of one hand. He had an enthusiasm factor of ten and an experience factor of one. Maybe minus one.

I am absolutely convinced that no one ever did to him some of the things . . .

So why did you do them?

He probably can hardly wait to get back to the boys.

"So how was your leave?"

"Great. I met this older woman. Not bad looking. But talk about hot pants! Talk about blow jobs! I'm telling you, she couldn't get enough, wouldn't let me alone. Once she did it while I was sleeping."

I did do it to him while he was sleeping, and I loved it. Which goes to show, therefore, that beneath your respectable facade, you are an oversexed bitch.

Or, more kindly, just your normal, run-of-the-mill, unsatisfied housewife, whose husband has been off gamboling with a sweet young thing for the past five months. Or maybe longer. Only he and the sweet young thing know for sure.

After she finished brushing her hair and rubbing moisturizer into her face, she took a paper towel and wiped the mirror clean of vestigial condensation, and then went into the bedroom. She lay on the bedspread and turned on the radio; then she turned it off and went into the living room and took the bottle of scotch—from where John had left it—from the mantelpiece and carried it into the kitchen and poured two inches of it into a glass.

She took a sip, and then a second, larger sip, and then she exhaled audibly.

God, I wish he was here!

The door bell went off. It was one of the old-fashioned, mechanical kind, that you "rang" by turning a knob.

She looked at the clock on the wall. It was quarter to nine.

Who the hell can that be?

Did that damned fool somehow not go? Did the airplane turn back for some reason and land at Newark again? If that happened, he would just have time to come back here now.

She went to the door, just reaching it as the bell rang again.

She opened the door to the length of the chain and peered through the crack and saw the last person in the world she expected to see, Howard P. Hawthorne, Jr.

"It's me, Barbara," Howard said, quite unnecessarily.

"So I see," she said, instantly hearing the inanity in her voice.

"May I come in, or . . . have you guests?"

She closed the door, removed the chain, and opened it fully.

"Come in, Howard."

"Thank you," he said.

"I'm having a drink," she said. "Would you like one? What do you want?"

"Scotch would be fine, thank you."

"You're welcome to a scotch, but that's not what I meant to ask."

"Oh. Yes, I see. I wanted to talk to you."

"Well, come in the kitchen while I make your drink. We can talk there."

"Thank you," Howard said, and then asked, "I'm not interrupting anything, am I? Interfering with your plans?"

"My plans are to go to bed," she said. "I've had a busy day."

She poured whiskey in a glass and handed it to him. With the familiarity of a husband, he turned to the refrigerator, found ice, and then squatted looking for the little bottles of Canada Dry soda habitually stored on the lower shelf.

His bald spot is getting bigger.

He opened the soda bottle, mixed his drink, and stirred it with his index finger. Then he raised his eyes to hers.

"I know," he said. "I was here earlier."

"Cutesy-poo think of something else of mine she wanted from the house?"

"I was worried about you," he said.

"I'm touched, but there is no cause for concern. I was visiting friends in Jersey."

"I know about him, Barbara," Howard said evenly.

Oh my God!

"I beg your pardon?"

"I said I know about you and the—young soldier."

Not very much. John is a Marine, not a soldier.

"And I said, 'I beg your pardon?' "

"Honey . . ."

"Don't you call me 'Honey,' you sonofabitch!"

"Sorry."

He took a swallow of his drink.

"Barbara, you're well known in Philadelphia," he said. "You must have known that someone would see you, recognize you . . ."

Great, now I will be known as the Whore of Babylon as well as Poor Barbara, whose husband dumped her for young Cutesy-poo.

"I have no idea what you're talking about. Who saw me? What soldier?"

"The young one," he said. "The one you had dinner with two nights ago in the restaurant in the Warwick."

"God," she heard herself say, "people have such filthy minds!"

"I don't understand that," Howard said.

"I'm guilty, Howard. I did have dinner in the Warwick two nights ago. But he's not a soldier. He's a Marine."

"What's the difference?"

"In this case, the difference is I'm nearly old enough to be his mother."

"You're not that old," he said. "You're thirty-eight."

Thirty-six, Goddamn you!

"I had dinner with Bill Marston's nephew, Johnny Moore. He's a sergeant in the Marines and about to go overseas, since you seem so hungry for the sordid details. And if I had had him when I was eighteen, I would be old enough to be his mother. He's eighteen. Or maybe nineteen."

"How did that come about?"

"I don't even know why I'm discussing this with you," Barbara said. "You have given up any right to question anything I do. I would love to know who carried this obscene gossip to you, though."

"Friends," he said.

"Some friends!"

"The same friends who have been telling me all along that I was making an ass of myself with Louise," Howard said.

She met his eyes.

"Tell me about this . . . young man, Barbara."

"I'll be damned! What if I said, 'tell me about Louise, Howard'?"

"Then I would say it's all over," he said.

"Since when?"

"Since about nine o'clock this morning," Howard said. "I told her I was going to see you, and she said if I came over here, it was all over between us. And . . . here I am."

"You've been trying to find me all day?"

He nodded.

After a moment, Barbara asked, "What did you think you were going to do here?"

"I realize that I've hurt you, Barbara . . ."

"Huh!" she snorted.

"I didn't want you to hurt yourself."

She exhaled audibly.

"With . . . my young man, you mean?"

He nodded.

"Bill Marston found out that Johnny's father was—I don't know how to put this—fooling around with Johnny's trust fund."

"His father? Who's his father?"

"The Reverend John Wesley Moore," Barbara said. "He's with that Methodist Missions thing. What do they call it? The Harris Methodist Missions to the Un-churched, something like that."

"The missionaries, right? In the Orient someplace?"

"Right."

"What about it?"

"Bill Marston found out that Johnny's father had not turned over a trust fund from his grandparents to the boy. So, since the boy is on his way overseas, he decided he had to tell him. And did."

"The father, the *minister,* was stealing the kid's money?" Howard asked.

He's interested. More important, he believes me.

"I don't know if 'stealing' is the right word, but he didn't turn it over to him when he should have."

"I'll be damned!" Howard said, outraged.

He's really angry. Why am I surprised? Before Cutesy-poo came along, he never did anything dishonorable.

"So the boy was upset, obviously," Barbara said. "He's really very sweet. He's on a home leave before going overseas, and he couldn't even go home."

"That's absolutely despicable!"

"So I felt sorry for him. And had dinner with him. And took him to the movies."

"Where was the boy staying?"

"Bill got him a room in the Union League."

"And that's where you heard about this?"

"Yes. I met Bill on Broad Street. He was with the boy. And he insisted I have a drink with them . . ."

"In his cups again, I suppose?"

"Don't be too hard on Bill, Howard. It was a terribly hard thing for him to have to do."

"I've always liked Bill Marston. He just can't handle the sauce, that's all."

He's not at all suspicious. He wants to believe what I'm telling him. He's a fool. Obviously. Otherwise Cutesy-poo couldn't have got her claws into him the way she did.

"Where's the boy now?"

"On his way to the Pacific. That's what I was really doing in New Jersey today, Howard. Putting him on the plane. Bill couldn't get off . . ."

"That was very kind of you, Barbara."

"He had nobody, Howard. I have never felt more sorry for anyone in my life."

"I should have known it was something like this. I'm sorry, Barbara."

"It's all right."

He smiled at her.

"I'm sorry things . . . didn't work out between you and Louise."

"And I would expect you to say something like that," he said. "It could have been worse. I could have actually married her."

"And it's really all over?"

"It's really all over."

"So what are you going to do?"

He looked at his watch and drained his glass.

"I don't really know. Except that right now, I'm going to leave here and see if I can catch the 9:28 to Swarthmore," he said.

"You'll never make the 9:28," Barbara said.

"There's another train at 10:45."

"You left some things here. Shirts and underwear. Why don't you stay here?"

"Barbara—"

"What?"

"That's very decent of you."

"Don't be silly."

"But where would I sleep? There's only one bed in this place."

"I know you don't think I'm very smart, Howard, but I really can count," Barbara said.

(FIVE)
The Andrew Foster Hotel
San Francisco, California
22 June 1942

The tall, long-legged blonde shifted on the seat of the station wagon so that she was facing the driver. Her fingers gently touched the beard just showing on his upper jaw, and then moved to trace his ear. When he jumped involuntarily, she laughed softly.

"I learned that from my husband," Mrs. Caroline Ward McNamara, of Jenkintown, Pennsylvania, said to Captain Charles M. Galloway, USMCR, whose home of record was c/o Headquarters, USMC, Washington, D.C.

Mrs. McNamara was wearing a pleated plaid skirt, a sweater, a string of pearls, and little makeup, all of which tended to make her look younger than her thirty-three years. Captain Galloway, who was wearing a fur-collared horsehair leather jacket, known to the Supply Department of the U.S. Navy as "Jacket, Fliers, Intermediate Type G1," over a tieless khaki shirt, was twenty-five. He was a tanned, well-built, pleasant-looking young man who wore his light brown hair just long enough to part.

The jacket was not new. It was comfortably worn in; the knit cuff on the left sleeve was starting to fray; and here and there were small dark spots where oil or AVGAS had dripped on it. Sewn to the breast of the jacket was a leather badge bearing the gold-stamped impression of Naval Aviator's Wings and the words CAPT C M GALLOWAY, USMCR. The leather patch was new, almost brand-new. The patch had replaced one that had identical wings but had designated the wearer as T/SGT C M GALLOWAY, USMC.

Captain Galloway had been an officer and a gentleman for just over a month. Before that, since shortly after his twenty-first birthday, in fact, he had been an Enlisted Naval Aviation Pilot (all Marine fliers are Naval Aviators), commonly called a "Flying Sergeant." He had been a Marine since he was seventeen.

"You learned that from your husband?" Charley Galloway asked, turning to Caroline McNamara. "How to play with his ear, or how to bullshit your way into a hotel?" The hotel they had in mind was the Andrew Foster, one of San Francisco's finest, and therefore also probably already stuffed to the brim with people who had thought to make reservations.

Her fingers stopped tracing his ear.

"Well, fuck you," Caroline said, very deliberately.

"Oh, Christ," he said, sounding genuinely contrite. "Sorry."

In Caroline's mind, Charley's language was too loaded with vulgarisms. A dirty mouth was certainly understandable, she knew, considering his background. But for his own good, now that he was an officer, he should clean it up. Since he did not like to hear her use bad language (except in bed, which was something else), she had settled on doing that as the means to shame him into polishing his own manners.

Every time he said something like "bullshit," she came back with "fuck." He really hated that; and so words like bullshit and asshole were coming out far less often now than they did not quite four months before, when they first met.

At that time Caroline had been divorced for not quite five months. It was far from a glorious marriage, of course; but it ended more or less satisfactorily, as far as she was concerned. . . . In other words, she came out of it, as she put it, "with all four feet and the tail," meaning that she got the house in Jenkintown, the cars, and almost all of the bastard's money. Her prosperous stockbroker husband had an understandable reluctance to reveal in court that the person he'd been having an affair with also wore pants and shaved.

During the divorce process, she had scrupulously followed her lawyer's advice to do nothing "indiscreet," correctly interpreting that to mean she should keep her legs crossed. When she met Charley Galloway, then Technical Sergeant Galloway, she had been chaste for more than eighteen months.

He had flown into Willow Grove Naval Air Station, outside Philadelphia, in a Marine version of the Douglas DC-3 transport, acting as both pilot-in-command and instructor pilot to two young Marine aviator lieutenants, one of whom, Lieutenant Jim Ward, was her nephew.

Jim had called from the airport, and Caroline had driven out to Willow Grove to fetch him and the others home. The moment she saw Charley Galloway, she knew he might be just the man to break her long period of celibacy. After all, she would probably never see him again.

Until she met him, she had come to believe—after all manner of sobering, painful experience—that the real love of her life was a delightful, wholly improbable fantasy. But what happened between them, the very first time, told her that that very delightful and improbable fantasy had landed six hours before at Jenkintown.

It wasn't long after that before she started worshiping him.

Jimmy Ward worshiped him, too, which had been at first rather difficult to understand. Enlisted men are supposed to worship officers, not the other way around. But when she asked him about it, Jimmy explained that Charley probably would have been an officer—he had all the qualifications—if it hadn't been for what he'd done a few days after Pearl Harbor.

He and another sergeant had put together a fighter plane from parts of others destroyed by the Japanese. Charley had then flown it out to the aircraft carrier *Saratoga,* then en route to reinforce Wake Island. Half of Charley's squadron was on Wake Island. Charley was riding, so to speak, to the sound of the guns.

The reinforcement convoy was ordered back to Pearl Harbor. And so an act that was to Jimmy's mind heroic—dedication worthy of portrayal on the silver screen by Alan Ladd and Ronald Reagan—became quite the opposite. An *enlisted man* had made flyable an airplane *commissioned officers,* in their wisdom, had concluded was beyond repair. He had then had the unbridled gall, against regulations and policy, to decide all by himself to take the airplane off to war.

The only reason that they hadn't court-martialed him, Jimmy Ward told her, was that the witnesses were either dead or scattered all over the Pacific and could not be assembled.

So what they had done was take him off flight status and return him to the States for duty as an aircraft mechanic. It was only a critical shortage of pilots that had found him—the very morning of the day Caroline met him—back in a cockpit. The Marines were demonstrating parachute troops to the press and couldn't run the risk of having a less than fully qualified pilot fly the plane.

After their first night together, Caroline couldn't have cared if Charley was a PFC. Or what anyone thought about her taking up with an enlisted man eight years younger than she was.

On the twelfth of June, ten days before Caroline and Charley were driving into San Francisco, she went to Quantico to be with him. But he wasn't there.

And then two days later he showed up as Captain Galloway, USMCR, having been pardoned and commissioned by the Commandant of the Marine Corps himself. There was a price, however. He had five days leave, plus travel time, to report to

San Francisco, there to board a plane for Hawaii, and there to assume command of a newly activated Marine fighter squadron.

Caroline decided she didn't give much of a damn what anyone—God included—thought about her traveling across the country with a man to whom she was not joined in holy matrimony. She was going with him.

And given a little more time, she thought, she would have been able to clean up his vocabulary so that even the Protestant Episcopal Bishop of Philadelphia could have found no fault with it.

Unfortunately, there was hardly any time left at all. And then there was the matter of finding a room to make time in.

" 'Conspire' is the word you were looking for," Caroline said. "We are going to 'conspire' our way into the Andrew Foster Hotel."

"You think it would really work?" Charley asked.

"They make mistakes," Caroline said. "Everybody does. All we have to do is make them think they made one with us, and we get a room."

"Sounds like bull—aloney to me," Charley said.

"Better," she chuckled, "better."

"This hotel is important to you, isn't it?" Charley asked. "What did you do, stay there with your husband?"

"No," Caroline lied, easily. "With my parents."

My conscience, she thought, *is clear. I don't want him in there thinking of me being there with Jack. All I want him to remember about the Andrew Foster Hotel is the luxury, and the food, and the two of us together in one of those lovely beds. Or together in one of those marvelous marble-walled showers with all the shower heads. I don't think Charley has ever seen anything like that. I want him to remember us there.*

"And you think that would work?"

"Yes, I do," Caroline said, trying to put more conviction into her voice than she felt.

"OK, Baby," Charley said. "If that's what you want, we'll give it a shot."

"Good," she said.

"We'll have to pull over somewhere and get a tunic and a tie out of my bag," Charley said. "I can't walk in a fancy hotel wearing a flight jacket. I wish I could shave. I feel as cruddy as the car."

The light oak bodywork of the 1941 Mercury station wagon was covered with five days and several thousand miles of road grime. They had driven practically nonstop from Quantico, Virginia. There had been a light rain during the night, and the half-moon sweep of the wipers showed by contrast just how dirty the rest of the vehicle was.

"Well, when we get to our room, Mommy will wash your ears," Caroline said. "Or anything else you think needs it."

"I told you to knock off that 'Mommy' shit," Charley said, coldly. "I don't think it's funny."

Caroline did not respond with a dirty word of her own. She was wrong, and she knew it.

Why did I say that? I know it angers him. There's probably something Freudian in that Mommy shit. Obviously. We both know I'm thirty-three and he's twenty-five. There is probably a hint somewhere in there of perversion, too. Charley can't understand why I stayed married to Jack for so long after I learned that he was homosexual. First she was married to a fairy, he thinks, and now she's shacked up with a Marine eight years younger than she is and doesn't give a damn who knows it. Obviously, there is something strange about that dame. Strange is not all that far from perverse.

Charley pulled off the highway and stopped.

"I won't say that again, Baby," Caroline said.

And now he will take affront at 'Baby'! Why did I say that? What the hell is the matter with me?

"Forget it," Charley said, and smiled at her. "My bag will be the one on the bottom, right?"

"Probably," she smiled. "Would you like me to drive? I know where the Andrew Foster is."

"Go ahead," he said.

He got in the back and she slid behind the wheel.

There were four men behind the marble reception desk of the Andrew Foster Hotel, flagship of the forty-two-hotel Foster chain, atop San Francisco's Nob Hill. Three wore formal morning clothes, wing collars and tailed coats. The fourth man, older than the others, wore a double-breasted gray coat and striped trousers and had a rose-bud pinned to his lapel.

"Madam, I'm terribly sorry," one of the men in formal clothing said to Caroline McNamara. "I just don't seem to be able to find any record of your reservation."

"Well, as long as you can put us up, I suppose no harm is done," Caroline said.

"That, Madam, I'm afraid, is going to pose a problem," the desk clerk said. "The house, I'm afraid, is absolutely full. I'll call around and see if we can't find something for you . . ."

"Excuse me," the older man said to the desk clerk. "There has been a cancellation." He handed the clerk a key. "Why don't you put this officer and his lady in 901?"

"Yes, of course," the desk clerk said and snapped his fingers for a bellman.

"Thank you," Caroline said.

"I'm sorry about the mix-up with your reservation," the older man said. He nodded at her, and then at Charley, and disappeared through a door in the paneled wall behind the counter.

Nine oh one turned out to be a corner suite consisting of a sitting room, a bedroom, and a butler's pantry.

As soon as Caroline tipped the bellman and he was gone, Charley said, "Jesus, what do you suppose this is going to cost us?"

"What you are supposed to say, Darling, is 'I was wrong and you were right, and I'm sorry I doubted you.'"

"Consider it said," Charley said. "And what do you think it's going to cost?"

"Do you really care?" Caroline asked. "And anyway, I've got a bunch of traveler's checks."

"No. What the hell," Charley said. "Why not?"

"Why not, indeed?"

"I'm going to take a shower," Charley said, and headed for the bathroom. In a moment, he was back. "Hey, look at this, they even give you a bathrobe!"

He held a thick, terry cloth robe in his hands, embroidered with the logotype, "ANDREW FOSTER HOTEL San Francisco."

"Between the hotel and me, Darling, you'll have everything your heart desires," Caroline said.

As soon as I hear the shower running, I'm going to get in there with him. Surprise, surprise!

She looked around the room, hoping that there would be something to drink—preferably something romantic or erotic, like cognac. She was disappointed, but not surprised, to find a liquor cabinet full of glasses, but no booze. She considered calling room service, but decided that getting in the shower with him was the highest priority. She could call room service later.

She found the bottle of scotch they'd bought in Nevada and set it on the bar. Then she changed her mind and took it and two glasses to the bedside table. And then, after taking Charley's clothes from where he had tossed them on the bed and throwing them onto the floor, she took off her clothes, added them to the pile, and went into the bathroom.

When she opened the glass door, she found him shaving. He told her he'd learned how to do that in boot camp at Parris Island when he had first joined the Corps. She found it delightfully masculine.

She wrapped her arms around him from the back.

"I'll wash yours if you wash mine," she said.

"Mine's already clean," he said.

"Bastard!"

He turned and put his arms around her.

"Christ," he said. "This is like a dream."

"If it is, I don't want to ever wake up."

"We have fifty-six hours," Charley said, "before I have to report to Mare Island."

"Say, 'Caroline, you were right about driving straight through so that we would have some time in San Francisco.'"

"You were right, Baby," he said.

"Fifty-six hours?" Caroline said. *"However* are we going to pass all that time?"

"Well, for openers, I'm clean enough," he said, and turned the shower off. "How about a quick game of Hide the Salami?"

"And then what?" she said, dropping her hand to his midsection.

"And then another game of Hide the Salami," Charley said. "The second time we'll start keeping score."

"You're on," she said.

There came the sound of chimes.

"What the hell is that?" Charley asked.

"I think it's the doorbell."

"One of the characters in the fancy costumes is out there, and he's about to tell us they've made a mistake and we'll have to get our asses out of here."

"We're going to have to see what it is," Caroline said.

"Yeah," Charley said.

He turned her loose and stepped out of the shower, put one of the terry cloth robes on, and went out of the bathroom.

Caroline got out of the shower, quickly toweled herself, and pulled on a robe. She wiped the steam from the mirror and looked at herself.

I can't go out there looking like this!

But, of course, she had to. Charley was ill-equipped to deal with people who managed a world-class hotel like the Andrew Foster.

She went out of the bathroom.

There were three people in the sitting room. Two bellmen, one of whom was stocking the liquor cabinet with liquor, and the other in the act of taking the cellophane from a large basket of fruit. Caroline also saw a bottle of champagne in a cooler.

"I'm so sorry to disturb you, Madam," the third man announced; he was the older man who had announced the reservation cancellation downstairs. "But when I checked, I found that the bar wasn't stocked, and I thought I'd better remedy that."

"Thank you," Caroline said.

"And I wanted to make sure you understood that because of our mix-up about your reservation, your bill will be for the room you reserved; I mean to say there will be no increase in price."

"Oh, hell," Charley said. "I can't let you do that."

"It's the pleasure of the Andrew Foster," the old man said.

"No," Charley said. "That would be stealing. I mean, we didn't really have a reservation. I don't mind talking you out of a room, but I couldn't cheat you out of any money that way."

I can't believe, Caroline thought, *that he just said that!*

"Your husband, Madam, is obviously an officer and a gentleman," the old man said.

Charley is really a gentleman, Caroline thought. *And touchingly, innocently honest. And not, of course, my husband.*

"My husband is on his way to the Pacific," Caroline said. "I wanted to spend our last night, our last two nights, in this hotel. I didn't much care what I had to do to arrange that."

"The Andrew Foster is honored, Madam. And so you shall. As guests of the inn."

"We want to pay our way," Charley said.

"I would be very pleased if you would be guests of the inn," the old man said.

"Why would you want to do that?" Caroline asked.

"How could you fix it with the hotel?" Charley asked.

"I noticed your wings, Captain. I gather you're an aviator?"

"Yes, Sir, I am."

"Are you familiar with the F4F Wildcat?"

"Yes, Sir, I am."

"Charley's on his way to take command of an F4F squadron," Caroline blurted. *My God, don't you sound like a proud wife!*

"My grandson, my only grandchild, is training to be an F4F pilot," the old man said. "I don't suppose you've ever run into a second lieutenant named Malcolm Pickering, have you? They call him 'Pick.'"

"He's a Marine?" Charley asked.

"Yes. He's at Pensacola right now."

"No, Sir, I don't know him," Charley said. "Sorry."

"Nice boy. His father was a Marine in the first war, so of course, he had to go into the Marines, too."

"Yes, Sir," Charley said. "That's understandable."

"I don't know anything about the sort of training they give young men like that, or about the F4F," the old man said. "I don't want to know anything I shouldn't know, classified information, I think they call it, but I really would like to know whatever you could tell me."

"Yes, Sir. I'll be happy to tell you anything you'd like to know."

"Perhaps at dinner," the old man said. "If you did that, I'd consider it a fair swap for you being guests of the inn so long as you're here."

"You don't have to do that," Charley said. "And, how the hell could you square that with the hotel?"

"I can do pretty much what I want to around here, Captain Galloway," the old man said, with a chuckle. "My name is Andrew Foster."

"I'll be goddamned!" Charley said.

"I live upstairs," Andrew Foster said. "Just tell the elevator man the penthouse. My daughter, Pick's mother, lives here in San Francisco. I'd like her to join us, if that would be all right with you."

"Certainly," Caroline said.

"Eight o'clock?" Andrew Foster asked.

"Fine," Caroline said, softly.

"My daughter, of course, knows as little about what Pick is doing as I do, and my son-in-law hasn't been much help."

"I'm sorry?" Caroline asked.

"My son-in-law, who is old enough to know better, and had more than enough to keep him busy here, couldn't wait to rush to the colors."

"He went back in the Corps?" Charley asked.

"The Marine Corps wouldn't have him back," Andrew Foster said. "So he went in the Navy. The last we heard, he's in Australia."

VII

"The Lark," as the train from Los Angeles to San Diego was called, was probably one hell of a money maker, Sergeant John Marston Moore thought; it probably should have been called "The Pigeon Roost."

There was not an empty seat on it; and the aisles and even the vestibules between the cars were jammed with people standing or, if they could, sitting on their luggage. At least half of the passengers were in uniform; and there was something about most of the civilian women that told Moore they had some kind of a service connection. They were either wives or girlfriends of servicemen.

He had recently become convinced that air travel was not only the wave of the future, but the only way to travel. Having a good-looking, solicitous stewardess serving your meals and asking if you would like another cup of coffee was far superior to this rolling tenement, where if you were lucky you could sometimes buy a soggy paper cup of coffee and a dry sandwich from a man who made his way with great difficulty down the crowded aisle.

When nature called, he waited half an hour for his turn in the small, foul-smelling cubicle at the end of the car; and then when he made his way back to his seat, he found a sailor in it, reluctant to give it up.

The ride wasn't smooth enough, nor his seat comfortable enough, for him to sleep during the trip; but he cushioned his head with his fore-and-aft cap against the window and dozed, floating in memories of the time he and Barbara spent together. Aware that it was ludicrous to dream of his return from the war before he had actually gone overseas, he nevertheless did just that.

By then, certainly, the temporarily delayed commission would have come through. He would be Lieutenant Moore, possibly even Captain Moore. In any case, an officer. That would certainly tend to diminish the unfortunate differences in their ages. One simply could not treat a Marine lieutenant, or a Marine captain, like a boy. He even considered growing a mustache—once the commission came along, of course.

But most of the images he dwelt on concerned the scene that would take place once he and Barbara went behind a closed and locked door somewhere, either in the apartment on Rittenhouse Square, or preferably, in some very nice hotel suite.

The astonishing truth was that physical intimacy—he did not like to think of it simply and crudely as "sex," because all that he and Barbara had done together was much more beautiful than that—between people who were in love with each other was everything—and more—than people said it was.

Such images were pleasant. But the ride was long, and the seat uncomfortable, and he was glad to hear the conductor announce their imminent arrival in San Diego. Somewhat smugly, he did not join in the frenzied activity to reclaim seabags and luggage and get off The Lark. When all these people left the train, the station was going to be as crowded as the train had been. If he just sat and looked out the window and waited, by the time he got to the station, much of the crowd would be dispersed.

Finally, he jerked his seabag from the overhead rack, carried it out of the car with his arms wrapped around it, hoisted it to his shoulder in the vestibule, and went down the stairs to the platform.

A hundred feet down the platform toward the station, he was surprised to see a Marine with corporal's stripes painted on his utility jacket sleeves holding up what looked like the side of a cardboard box. Written on that in grease pencil was, Sgt. J. M. Moore.

He walked up to him.

"My name is Moore."

"I was beginning to think you missed the fucking train," the corporal said. "Come on, the Gunny's outside in the truck."

He tossed the sign under the train and started down the platform. Outside the main door was a Chevrolet pickup truck, painted in Marine green. A short, muscular Gunnery Sergeant, a cigar butt in his mouth, was sitting on the fender.

"You Moore?" he asked as he pushed himself off the fender.

"Right."

"I was beginning to think you either couldn't read or missed the fucking train," the Gunny said. "My name is Zimmerman. The Lieutenant, Lieutenant McCoy, sent me to meet you. Throw your gear in the back and get in."

"Right," Moore said. "Where are we going?"

"Would you believe the San Diego Yacht Club?"

Moore smiled uneasily. Obviously, he was not supposed to ask where he was going, otherwise he would not have been given a sarcastic reply.

"Sorry," he said.

Gunnery Sergeant Zimmerman grunted and got behind the wheel, Moore got in the other side, and the corporal got in beside him, next to the window.

As they drove away from the station, Zimmerman said, "I checked out how those fuckers at Outshipment work, the way they handle people like you with priorities like yours."

"Oh?"

"What they do when you report in is send you over to the transient barracks, and then get you put on some kind of detail. Then, when they're making up the manifest for the flight, they see who else is on it with rank and no priority, or not so high a priority. If there ain't anybody, then they call you back from the transient barracks and you get on the plane. But if there is some commander or some colonel who's going to give them trouble about being bumped by a sergeant, they 'can't find you' on your detail, you miss the flight, the commander or the colonel gets on it, they don't get no trouble, and everybody's happy."

"I see."

"So I told the Lieutenant, and he said 'fuck 'em, stash him until thirty minutes before the plane leaves and then take him right to operations. Then they can't lose him, he'll be there.'"

"I understand," Moore said, although he wasn't absolutely sure he did.

"So I asks the Lieutenant where he wants you stashed, and he says take you over to the boat, he'll call Miss Ernie and tell her you're coming."

"The boat?"

"I told you, we're going to the Yacht Club," Gunny Zimmerman said, impatiently.

"How'd you know when I was arriving?"

"You ask a lot of fucking questions about things that are none of your fucking business, don't you?" the Gunny replied.

"Sorry," Moore said.

The corporal beside him snorted in amusement.

"Miss Ernie"? "The Yacht Club"? Am I being a snob because I suspect that the yacht club he's referring to is not what usually pops into my mind when I hear the words "yacht club"? Odds are that this yacht club is going to turn out to be a Marine bar somewhere, with a picture of a naked lady and the standard Marine Corps emblems hanging above the bar, and whose proprietress, Miss Ernie, will bear a strong resemblance to Miss Sadie Thompson?

And then another question popped into his mind: *Lieutenant McCoy? He did say "Lieutenant McCoy," didn't he? He damn sure did! Killer McCoy? Am I really going to get to meet the legendary Killer McCoy?*

Discretion, however, overwhelmed his curiosity. Having just been told by the Gunny that he asked too many fucking questions about things that were none of his fucking business, he decided that it would be best to just ride along in silence.

Fifteen minutes later, he was more than a little surprised when the Gunny turned the pickup truck off the highway and through two large brick pillars. On each of these was a bronze sign reading, SAN DIEGO YACHT CLUB—PRIVATE—MEMBERS ONLY.

Three minutes after that, they stopped at the end of a pier.

"You carry his seabag onto the boat for him," Gunny Zimmerman ordered the corporal, "and you come with me."

They walked down the pier until they came to the stern of a large yacht, on whose tailboard was lettered in gold leaf, "LAST TIME, San Diego."

The corporal went up a ladder carrying Moore's bag and went aboard. Gunny Zimmerman touched Moore's arm in a signal to stop.

What the hell is going on? This thing is at least fifty feet long. Without question, by any definition, a yacht.

A startlingly beautiful young woman wearing white shorts and a red T-shirt emblazoned with the insignia of the U.S. Marine Corps appeared at the stern rail. She had jet black hair cut in a page boy, and the baggy T-shirt seemed to do more to call attention to a very attractive figure than to conceal it.

"Hi!" she called down.

"The Lieutenant call, Miss Ernie?" Gunny Zimmerman asked.

"Yes, he did. And I told you the next time you called me 'Miss Ernie' I was going to throw you in the harbor," she said. She looked at Moore. "Hi! Come aboard. I've been expecting you."

"Go aboard. I'll be back for you in the morning," Gunny Zimmerman ordered.

"You want a beer, Zimmerman?" the girl asked.

"Got to get back, Miss Ernie," Zimmerman said. "The Lieutenant said he might be a little late."

"There, you did it again!" she said.

"Jesus Christ, Miss Ernie," he said uncomfortably, "you're the Lieutenant's *lady.*"

"Just don't stand close to the edge of the dock, Zimmerman," she said. "You're warned."

Zimmerman hid his face from the young woman. "You watch yourself with that lady, Moore," he said, with more than a hint of menace.

And then he marched back up the pier to the truck.

As Moore walked to the ladder, the corporal came down it.

"Nice!" he said, as he walked past Moore.

The black-haired girl was waiting on the deck with her hand held out.

"I'm Ernie Sage," she said. "As Zimmerman so discreetly put it, I'm Ken McCoy's 'lady.' Welcome aboard."

"How do you do?" Moore said, taking the offered hand. "I'm Sergeant Moore."

"Have you got a first name?"

"John."

"Would you like a beer, John? Or something stronger?"

"I'd love a beer. Thank you."

As he followed her down the deck to the cabin, Moore observed that she was just as good looking from that perspective.

She opened a refrigerator door and took out a bottle of beer.

"Mexican," she said. "Ken says it's much better than the kind they make in 'Diego. Would you like a glass?"

"The bottle's fine, thank you," he said.

"Where are you from?"

"Philadelphia," he said.

"Oh, I'm from Jersey. Bernardsville. I've spent some time in Philly. I used to go with a guy—nothing serious—who was at U.P."

"I went to the University of Pennsylvania," he said.

"And then you joined the Corps?"

He nodded.

"Ken's from Norristown," she said. "But he's only been back once since he joined the Corps."

"Oh," Moore said, aware that he was tongue-tied.

"I told Whatsisname, Zimmerman's driver, the one he won't let drive, to put your bag in a cabin—second door to the right when you go below—so if you'd like, when you finish your beer, you could have a shower."

"I need one," Moore said. "I've been traveling for forty-eight hours."

"And you've been on The Lark," she said with a smile. "Anyone who's been on The Lark needs a long, hot shower."

She smiled at him, and he smiled back. He had no idea who this young woman was, but he liked her.

Sergeant John Marston Moore, USMCR, came back in the cabin just as Second Lieutenant Kenneth R. McCoy, USMCR, entered it from the deck.

Lieutenant McCoy, who was in dress green uniform, looked not unlike other second lieutenants Moore had seen. That is, he was young—*about my age,* Moore thought—and trim, and immaculately shaven and dressed. But there was one significant difference. Above the silver marksmanship medals which all second lieutenants seemed to have—although McCoy seemed to have more of these, all EXPERT—he had five colored ribbons, representing medals. Moore had seen very few second lieutenants with any ribbons at all.

Moore didn't know what all of them represented, but he did recognize two. One was the Pacific Theater of Operations Campaign Medal. McCoy's had a tiny bronze star, signifying that he had participated in a campaign. And on top was the ribbon representing the Purple Heart. This second lieutenant had already been to the war in the Pacific and had been wounded.

Miss Ernestine Page kissed Lieutenant McCoy. It was a *wifely* demonstration of affection, Moore judged, although it had been made clear that whatever her relationship was with Lieutenant McCoy, she was not his legal spouse.

"I'm Ken McCoy, Moore," he said. "I'm a friend of Captain Sessions. Ernie been taking good care of you?" He put out his hand. His grip was firm, and there was something about his eyes that made Moore decide that this was a good man.

"Yes, Sir, she has."

"Let me get a beer, Baby, and get out of this uniform," McCoy said. "Give Moore another one."

"Aye, aye, Sir. Right away, Sir."

McCoy patted her possessively on the buttocks.

"Be nice," he said.

"I'm always nice," Ernie Page said.

"How about eighty percent of the time?" McCoy said, and, carrying a bottle of beer, went below. By the time Moore had finished his second beer, McCoy reappeared, wearing shorts and a T-shirt. He looked even younger than he had before.

He caught Moore's eye.

"Why don't I loan you a pair of shorts and a T-shirt?" he asked.

"I don't want to trouble you, Sir."

"You'll trouble me in your greens," McCoy said. "Come on."

He took two fresh bottles of beer from the refrigerator and led Moore below again. He sat on the double bed in the cabin as Moore changed out of his greens.

"Zimmerman tell you about Outshipment? The way those feather merchants handle difficult passengers like you?"

"Yes, Sir."

"And that we figured out how to—fuck them—get you on your way to Australia?"

"Yes, Sir," Moore replied, and then took a chance. "Is that where I'm going, Sir, to Australia?"

"Sessions didn't tell you? What the hell is the big secret? He told me you were going to Australia when he called and asked me to make sure you got on the plane."

"No, Sir, he didn't tell me."

"OK. Well, keep your mouth shut, about where you're going, and who told you."

"Yes, sir."

"You're going to Australia. You know the outfit?"

"My orders say 'Special Detachment 14.' I don't know what that means, Sir."

"Well, I guess that's the reason for the secrecy. So I won't go into that. But your new CO is one of the good guys. His name is Major Ed Banning. I used to work for him in Shanghai. So did Captain Sessions. For that matter, so did Zimmerman. What he's doing is very important, and the reason you're travelling on a Six-A priority is that he needs someone, yesterday, who speaks Japanese."

Moore nodded.

And then he put everything together.

"Lieutenant, are you the one they call 'Killer McCoy'?"

The friendly smile that had been in McCoy's eyes vanished. Moore did not like what he saw in them now.

"Where did you hear that?" McCoy asked, and his voice was as cold and menacing as his eyes.

Moore knew that it had been the wrong question to ask, and tried to frame a reply that would be placating. When he did not immediately reply, McCoy, now visibly angry, asked, "Did that fucking Zimmerman run off at the fucking mouth again?"

Moore didn't reply instantly.

"I asked you a question," McCoy snapped.

"No, Sir. I heard that at Quantico. There was a Master Gunnery Sergeant there . . ."

"Name?" McCoy snapped.

"I don't remember his name, Sir," Moore said, and then remembered. "He said he was the S-3 Sergeant of the 4th Marines . . ."

"Nickleman," McCoy interrupted. "He always had a bad case of runaway mouth."

". . . and he was talking about the 4th Marines, and Shanghai, with Captain Sessions."

McCoy stared at him for a long moment. Gradually, the cold fury in his eyes died, and blood returned to his lips.

"I'm sorry, Sir, if . . ." Moore began.

McCoy waved his hand to shut him off.

"To answer your question, Sergeant," McCoy said. "There are some people who call me 'Killer,' including people who should know better, like Mike Nickleman and Captain Sessions. I don't like it a goddamn bit. But you didn't know, so don't worry about it."

Moore's mouth ran away with him. "Why do they call you that, Sir?"

The ice came instantly back into McCoy's eyes, and his lips drew tight and bloodless again. He looked at Moore for a long moment, and then shrugged.

"OK. Let me set that straight. I had to kill some people in China. I didn't want to. I had to. It just happened that way. Some Italians, the Italian equivalent of Marines. Three of them. And about a month later, when Sessions and Zimmerman and I were fucking around in the boondocks, trying to find out what the Japs were up to, we had to kill some Chinese. They were supposed to be bandits, but what they were was working for the Kempae Tai—Japanese secret police. There was about twenty of them got killed. The word got back to Shanghai and some wiseass— I still don't know who—in the 4th heard about it. He didn't know what we were really doing up there, just that we got in a fight with Chinese bandits, so what he did was have a sign painted, 'Welcome Back, Killer' and hung it in the club. The name stuck. It makes me sound like a fucking lunatic, like I go around getting my rocks off knifing and shooting people."

"I'm sorry, Sir, that . . ."

McCoy held up his hand to cut him off again, and then, switching to Japanese, which startled Moore, said, "I'd be damned surprised, Moore, if you haven't figured out you're now in the Intelligence business, that we both are. Rule One in the Intelligence business, and I'm surprised Captain Sessions didn't tell you this, is to disappear into the wallpaper. The one thing you can't afford, in other words, is to have people point you out and say, 'there he is, Killer McCoy, who killed all those people.' Understand?"

"Yes, Sir," Moore replied in Japanese. "I understand."

McCoy looked at him appraisingly for a moment before he went on. "Well, we know that you speak Japanese, don't we? And damned well. Where'd you learn that?"

The subject of Killer McCoy, Moore understood, was closed.

The truth of the story is that he is called "Killer" because, very simply, he has killed people. Three Italians, probably by himself, and "about twenty" Chinese with Captain Sessions and Gunny Zimmerman. It would be hard to believe if I hadn't seen his eyes. I would hate to have Killer McCoy angry with me. Or, hell, just be in his way.

"I'm fairly fluent, Sir. I lived in Japan for a while," Moore replied in Japanese.

"There's damned few people in the Corps who speak Japanese," McCoy said, "for that matter, anything but English. On the other hand, about one Jap—or at least, one Japanese officer—in three or four speaks English. You'd be surprised how important that is."

"Yes, Sir."

"Well, what happens now is that in the morning, Zimmerman will go to Outshipment at the Seaplane base. When he finds out they're making up the manifest for the Pearl Harbor flight, he'll send his driver out here to pick you up. So you'll have to be dressed and ready after, say, seven o'clock in the morning. Standing by. You show up with your orders and they'll have to put you on the plane."

"Yes, Sir."

"Any questions?"

"No, Sir."

"Not even about the boat? Or Ernie?" McCoy asked, wryly.

"They're both . . . very nice . . . Sir."

"Yes, they are," McCoy chuckled.

As if on cue, Ernestine Sage appeared at the door.

"Dorothy and Marty just came home," she said. "He brought abalone. Unless you two would rather stay here and tell some more dirty stories in Japanese."

McCoy switched to English. "Ernie thinks that whenever people speak Japanese around here they're talking dirty," he said. "Not true, of course. I'm perfectly willing to say in English that she has a marvelous ass and spectacular boobs."

"You bastard!" she said, but Moore saw that it was said with affection.

Dorothy and Marty turned out to be a First Lieutenant and his wife, who was heavy with child. The lieutenant's tunic had no campaign medals above his marksmanship badges. And although first lieutenants outrank second lieutenants, it was immediately apparent not only that McCoy gave the orders on board the *Last Time,* but that the lieutenant was just about as impressed with Lieutenant McCoy as Sergeant Moore was.

"I didn't mean to disturb you . . ." the lieutenant said.

"No problem," McCoy said. "Ground rules: This is Sergeant Moore. John. You didn't see him here. You don't ask him where he came from, or where he's going. But feel free to talk about the Raiders. He's cleared for at least TOP SECRET. Moore, this is Marty Burnes and his wife, Dorothy."

Lieutenant Burnes crossed the cabin to Moore and gave him his hand.

"How are you, Moore?"

"How do you do, Sir?"

"Hello," Mrs. Burnes said.

"Hello."

"Is he going to have to call you two 'Sir' all night?" Ernie Sage asked.

"Whatever he's comfortable with," McCoy said.

"I think we can dispense with the customs of the service, tonight," Lieutenant Burnes said to Moore.

"Yes, Sir."

"Hell, he's as bad as Zimmerman," Ernie laughed. "You better not start calling me 'Miss Ernie,' John."

"No, Ma'am," Moore said, but he said it as a joke, and they all laughed.

"I filled the car with gas, Ken," Marty Burnes said.

"You didn't have to do that," McCoy replied.

"Well, hell, we used it."

"Otherwise I would probably have had Little Martin, or Little Mary," Dorothy said, patting her swollen belly, "on the bus on the way to the Maternity Clinic."

"What did the doctor say?" Ernie Sage asked.

"Three weeks," Dorothy said.

"Your mother called," Ernie said. "I told her where you were. You better go call her. She's concerned."

Dorothy heaved herself with effort to her feet and went to a telephone at the far end of the cabin.

"Ken and Ernie took us in," Burnes said to John Moore. "We couldn't find a place to stay, and Dorothy wanted to have the baby here. If it wasn't for Ken and Ernie, Dorothy would have had to go back to Kansas City."

"Ernie took you in," McCoy corrected him. "This is her boat."

"Go to hell!" Ernie said, and then looked at Moore. "The boat belongs to a friend of a friend of my mother's. And since we're being such a stickler about the

facts, my mother pretends that I am not living in sin with Ken. But, romantic fool
that I am, I pretend that this is our first home, Ken's and mine, our barnacle-covered
little boat by the side of the bay."

Moore smiled at her.

"Tell him about the Raiders," McCoy said.

Burnes looked at him in surprise.

"He's going to meet a friend of mine where he's going," McCoy explained.
"He'll be curious."

"Then why don't *you* tell him about the Raiders?" Ernie challenged.

"Because I am only a second lieutenant. Everybody knows that second lieutenants
can't find their ass with both hands. Isn't that so, Sergeant Moore?"

"Yes, Sir. We were taught that at Parris Island," Moore said.

"I'm almost glad you're not staying here longer," Ernie Sage said. "I think you
and Ken would be dangerous if you had time to get your act together."

"Give the sergeant a beer, Dear," McCoy said, sweetly, "while Lieutenant Burnes
tells him all about the Raiders."

"Aye, aye, Sir," Ernie Sage said. "Right away, Sir."

(TWO)
U.S. Navy Base
San Diego, California
0815 Hours 25 June 1942

Sergeant John Marston Moore, USMCR, was the fifth person to board the seaplane,
a U.S. Navy Martin PBM-1. Boarding was supposed to be in order of priority, in
which case Moore would have been first. But among those ordered to proceed via
air to Pearl Harbor, Territory of Hawaii, by government air transport were a Vice
Admiral of the U.S. Navy and a Brigadier General, USMC, whose priorities guaran-
teed them a seat.

Rank hath its privileges and the admiral and the general and their aides-de-camp
were boarded first. Moore stepped inside the fuselage of what had been designed
as a Patrol Bomber. A sailor in undress blues, with the insignia of an Aviation Motor
Machinist's Mate First Class sewn to his sleeve, showed him where to stow his bag
and where to strap himself in for the take-off. He found himself seated next to the
admiral.

"Good morning, Son," the admiral said.

"Good morning, Sir," Moore replied.

"First flight?"

"No, Sir."

"Then you can reassure me," the admiral said. "I am not wholly convinced that
something this big is really meant to fly."

I will be damned. He really went out of his way to be nice to me.

The sailor, a red-haired man in his late twenties who was obviously the crew
chief, waited until all the passengers had come aboard and then passed out yellow,
inflatable life preservers, first giving simple instructions about using them, and then
checking the passengers to see that they had each put them on correctly.

Then he climbed a ladder in the front of the fuselage. A moment later, the
airplane shuddered as first one and then the second of its engines started. The plane
immediately began to move, but with a curious motion that made Moore wonder
for a moment if he was going to get seasick.

Next, one at a time, the engines roared and then slowed to idle. Then they both revved together, and the seaplane began to pick up speed. The noise of the engines was deafening, and the noise was compounded by a series of metallic crashes as the hull encountered swells. Then suddenly there was only the sound of the engines, and the crashing of the hull against the water was gone.

Through the window on the far side of the cabin, Moore saw that the float—there was one on each side—which had kept the wing from dipping into the water was retractable. As he watched, it moved upward and outward until it formed the tip of the wing.

He turned in his seat and looked through the window behind him. They were already out over the Pacific. Some ships were visible, and the wakes of small boats; and then, suddenly, there was nothing outside the window but an impenetrable gray haze.

"I am solemnly assured by my Naval Aviator friends," the admiral said, "that the young men who drive these things are extensively trained in navigation."

They looked at each other and smiled.

Moore put his head back against the metal wall of the fuselage.

He had really had a good time the night before, he thought. And not only because Ernie Sage and Lieutenant McCoy had gone really out of their way to make him comfortable. More than that, they had made it sort of a party for him.

And what he'd heard about the Marine Raiders had been fascinating. With obvious pride in what he was doing, Lieutenant Burnes had explained that they were sort of American Commandos whose mission it was to make surprise landings—raids, hence the name—on Japanese-held islands. The idea was not to capture the islands, but to blow up enemy installations and supplies, and then leave. That, Burnes said, would force the Japanese to station troops wherever they had supply depots or airfields so they could protect them from the Raiders, troops that otherwise could have been used to invade New Guinea or even Australia.

As he went on, Burnes had mentioned on more than one occasion the 2nd Raider Battalion Commander, Major Evans Carlson, and Carlson's executive officer, Captain James Roosevelt, who was the son of the President. Every time the names of these two came up, his voice dropped to nearly reverential tones.

It was also pretty clear that Burnes was very impressed with the legendary Killer McCoy, who had taken out three Italian Marines with a knife, and then killed the Chinese bandits, and who had been wounded in the Philippines. So, Moore admitted, was he.

Moore could also see that Lieutenant McCoy wasn't quite so boyishly enthusiastic about the Raiders as Burnes was. McCoy never said so directly, and his face was in no way easy to read; but Moore sensed that as far as McCoy was concerned, the Raiders might as well be a gang of ten-year-old boys playing war games. At the same time, it was more than pretty clear to Moore that Burnes had no idea McCoy was involved with Intelligence. He wondered what McCoy was doing that had an Intelligence connection, but obviously he couldn't ask.

In fact there was no sense wondering what kind of Intelligence work McCoy was doing, or what he himself would be doing once he got to Australia. The only thing he knew about Intelligence was what he had learned watching spy movies, and McCoy was certainly not going to tell him what Intelligence was like in the real world.

But it had really made him feel good to see how Lieutenant McCoy and Ernie and Lieutenant Burnes and his wife had behaved to each other.

It would, he thought before he dozed off, be that way with Barbara when he came back. He would be an officer then, and maybe they could all get together and have a welcome home party.

(THREE)
Headquarters
Marine Air Group Twenty-One (MAG-21)
Ewa, Oahu Island, Territory of Hawaii
1105 Hours 27 June 1942

"The Colonel will see you now, Sir," the staff sergeant said.

Captain Charles M. Galloway, USMCR, hoisted himself out of a battered, upholstered armchair whose cushions had long ago lost their resiliency, nodded at the sergeant, walked to the commanding officer's door, and rapped on the jamb with his knuckles.

"Come," Lieutenant Colonel Clyde G. Dawkins ordered.

Galloway marched into the office, came to attention eighteen inches from Dawkins's desk, and announced, "Captain Galloway reporting as ordered, Sir."

"Good morning, Captain, welcome aboard."

"Thank you, Sir."

"You get settled all right, Charley?"

"I told the kid in the truck to take me to the NCO billet," Galloway said.

"Did you really?" Dawkins chuckled. "Well, I guess being an officer—a squadron commander—will take some getting used to. But I'm sure you can handle it, Charley. Stand at ease, for Christ's sake. Sit down, as a matter of fact."

He pointed to an armchair, and Charley sat down. Its cushions were as exhausted as the cushions on the chair in the outer office.

"Thank you, Sir. That was after he told me he'd never heard of VMF-229."

Dawkins laughed.

"That's because most of VMF-229 resides in Karl Lorenz's desk drawer," he said. "You remember Lorenz, of course?"

"Yes, Sir. Sure."

"Right now VMF-229 consists of you, another officer, and eleven F4Fs on a wharf at Pearl Harbor, covered with all the protective crap they put on them when they ship them as deck cargo."

Galloway's eyebrows rose.

"What about men?"

"Lorenz levied the other squadrons for personnel for you. They came up—after a lot of breast beating—with a list of sixteen enlisted men. Some of them are alleged to be mechanics, and there is an alleged clerk, an alleged truck driver, *and* an alleged armorer. None of them is more than a buck sergeant. You have authority, of course, to draw whatever equipment and personnel is authorized for a fighter squadron."

"How much of what is authorized is going to be available when I go try to draw it?"

"Not much, Charley," Dawkins said. "Supply is a little better than it was, but not much."

"What about pilots?"

"Right now there's two of you. They dribble in all the time. Sometimes one at a time on a courier plane, sometimes two dozen when a carrier or cruiser from 'Diego or 'Frisco puts into Pearl, sometimes lately, three or four at a time on tin cans and merchantmen. As you get your planes operational, I'll see that you have pilots. They won't have much time, I'm afraid, they'll be right out of Pensacola."

"Ouch," Galloway said. "I've got some pilots, pretty good pilots, coming. General McInerney authorized me to steal five from Quantico and Pensacola."

"Only five?"

"I sent him nine names. I didn't have to ask for volunteers. When the word got out I was getting a squadron, people came looking for me. Everybody wants to get over here, even if it means being in a squadron commanded by a flying sergeant."

"Hold it right there, Captain," Dawkins said sharply. He had just been thinking that Captain Charles M. Galloway looked like everything one expected a Marine captain to look like. He was erect and trim, neatly barbered, in a well-fitting uniform. There was an aura of competence and command about him.

"Sir?"

"That's the last time I ever want to hear you refer to yourself as a 'flying sergeant,'" Dawkins said. "I don't even want you *thinking* of yourself as a 'flying sergeant.' When you pinned those bars on, you stopped being a flying sergeant. Is that clear enough for you, Captain?"

"Aye, aye, Sir."

Dawkins held Galloway's eyes with his own for a long moment.

"Scuttlebutt going around is that someone interesting personally gave you those bars, Charley. Anything to that story?"

"Yes, Sir. They had me flying a VIP R4D out of Quantico. I'd just come back from a round robin, Pensacola, New River, Philadelphia, and back to Quantico. When I parked the airplane, the Operations Officer told me to report to the VIP quarters. I walked in expecting some congressman or movie star needing a ride, and what I got was the Commandant."

"No crap?"

"Him and General McInerney. Five minutes later, I was a captain."

"Just like that?"

"He gave me a little speech, Sir, that I won't forget for a while."

"Oh?"

"He said that, acting on General McInerney's recommendation, and against his own better judgment, he was going to give me captain's bars, and that I goddamn well better forget thinking I was Errol Flynn or Ronald Reagan and start acting like a Marine captain."

"Sounds like sound advice," Dawkins chuckled. "Christ, you really had the Navy mad at you. For a while, there was guilt by association."

"Sir?"

"There was talk—serious talk—about court-martialing Lenny Martin for being conveniently absent when you flew that F4F out of here to rendezvous with Task Force XIV. 'Dereliction of Duty' was the way they put it."

Captain Leonard Martin had been the senior officer of VMF-211 present (and thus in command) when Galloway reported that he and the maintenance sergeant, Technical Sergeant Stefan "Big Steve" Oblensky, had repaired one of the shot-up F4Fs and that he intended to fly it out to the *Saratoga*.

Captain Martin had reminded Tech Sergeant Galloway that BUAIR engineers had officially classified the F4F as totally destroyed and that therefore, it was obviously unsafe to fly. He had also pointed out that even if there had been an officially flyable aircraft available, orders would have to be issued before it could be flown anywhere. And obviously, since the location of *Sara* was a closely guarded secret, Tech Sergeant Galloway had a practically nonexistent chance of finding it.

Quite unnecessarily, he had informed Tech Sergeant Galloway that his intended flight was against regulations and thus forbidden. And then, as he shook Tech Sergeant Galloway's hand, he had mentioned idly, in passing, that he had business at Pearl Harbor and would not be at the airfield at the time Galloway said he wanted to take off.

"Sir, is Captain Martin—still in trouble?"

"Not anymore, Charley. He was shot down at Midway."

"Shit!" Galloway said bitterly, adding, "I hadn't heard that."

"He was flying a goddamned Buffalo. We lost all of them but one."

"He was a good guy," Galloway said, softly.

"Most of them were," Dawkins said.

Galloway looked at him with a question in his eyes, and then put it in a word: " 'Most'?"

"I didn't mean that the way it sounded," Dawkins said. "But I was thinking—speaking ill of the dead—that it is possible to be both a dead hero and a prick. But you've touched on something else that needs to be discussed."

"I'm afraid you've lost me, Sir."

"The other officer presently assigned to VMF-229, Captain, is First Lieutenant, USMCR, William C. Dunn. He was also at Midway with VMF-211. Flying an F4F. He has—confirmed—both a Kate and a Zero."

"Dunn?" Galloway asked, thoughtfully. "I don't think I remember . . ."

"Nice-looking young kid. He came aboard after you were returned to the States in such glory," Dawkins said dryly. "He took what we think was a 20mm round, an explosive shell, in his windscreen. It almost turned him into a soprano. He managed to get the airplane back to Midway, totalling it on landing. It was full of holes, in addition to the 20mm, I mean."

"Sounds like a good man," Charley said.

"Very possibly he is," Dawkins said carefully. "But there is some question, I'm afraid serious question, about whether he took the round that filled his crotch with shrapnel and fragments while he was engaging the enemy, or after he'd already decided to fly back to Midway."

"You're saying he ran?"

"Listen carefully. What I said was 'serious question.' The officer—there was more than one, but the officer who made the most serious accusations—decided, on reflection, not to bring charges against him."

"Who was that?"

"I don't think giving you his name would be appropriate," Dawkins said.

"What has . . . you said 'Dunn'? . . . got to say for himself?"

"Dunn says that he has no memory of flying back to Midway at all."

"What do you think?"

"I believe that Dunn doesn't remember flying back to Midway."

"How come I get this guy?"

"I'm giving him the benefit of the doubt," Dawkins said.

Galloway started to say something and changed his mind. Dawkins saw it.

"Say it, Charley."

"Nothing, Sir."

"Say it, Charley," Dawkins repeated.

"Actually, I was thinking two things, Sir. The first was that when a good Marine gets an order, even one he doesn't think he can handle, he says 'Aye, aye, Sir' and does his best."

"You mean you don't think you can handle a squadron?"

"I can handle a squadron. But there are squadrons and squadrons, and it looks like mine is staffed with sixteen enlisted Marines who are almost certainly the ones their squadron commanders figured they could do without; plus pickled aircraft that I have to unpickle with somebody else's rejects; plus, of course, an officer one jump ahead of a court-martial."

"Is that all one thought? You said you had two?"

"I was thinking, Colonel, that you wouldn't screw me unless you had no choice. But if the brass *is* making you set me up to fuck up so I can be relieved, why don't we just jump to that? Give the squadron to somebody else, and just let me fly. I didn't ask for the bars; all I ever wanted to do is fly fighters. I mean, I'll take a bust back to sergeant . . ."

"That's quite enough, Captain," Dawkins said furiously. "Shut down your mouth. How *dare* you suggest, you sonofabitch, that I would be party to something like that?"

"Sorry, Sir," Galloway said after a long moment, during which he realized that Dawkins was waiting for a response.

"You're going to have to learn, Galloway, to engage your brain before opening your mouth," Dawkins said more calmly. "Just for your information, I was given the option of *not* giving you VMF-229. I'm giving it to you because you're the best man I have available to take the job."

"Yes, Sir."

"I wish I had an operational squadron I could just turn over to you, fully equipped with flyable aircraft, qualified mechanics, and whatever else is called for. I don't. All I have to give you is what I told you, airplanes sitting on a wharf and a handful of half-trained kids to get them up and running. I'll do my damnedest to get you anything else you think you need, but the shelves are pretty goddamned bare."

They looked at each other without speaking for a long moment.

"Can I have Oblensky, Sir?"

"What?"

"Tech Sergeant Oblensky, Sir," Galloway said. "I know he's here. I asked."

Dawkins looked unhappy. He made three starts, stopping each time before a word left his mouth, before asking, "Do you think it is a good idea, Captain, theoretically or practically, for a non-commissioned officer to be assigned to a squadron commanded by an officer with whom he served as a non-com? Who was his best pal when they were sergeants together?"

"From what you've told me about the men you're going to give me, Sir," Galloway said, "I'll either have to have Big Steve, or somebody like him, or get those airplanes flyable myself."

"Captain Galloway, if I hear that you have been seen with a wrench in your hand, you will spend the rest of this war with a wrench in your hand. Clear?"

"Does that mean I get Oblensky, Sir?"

"I finally have something in common with the Commandant, Galloway. Acting against my better judgment, I'm going to give you something I don't think you should have."

"Thank you, Sir."

"That will be all, Captain Galloway. Thank you."

VIII

PFC Alfred B. Hastings, who was seventeen and had been in the Corps not quite five months, had just about finished drying with a chamois a glistening yellow 1933 Ford convertible coupe, when he noticed that his labor had attracted the attention of an officer.

The Ford was parked in the shade of Hangar Three. When Hastings was finished, his orders were to return the car to the other side of the hangar, to a parking space lettered MAINTENANCE NCO.

For a long moment, PFC Hastings pretended he did not see the officer, who was a captain and an aviator. He did that for two reasons. First, he had slipped out of the sleeves of his coveralls and tied them around his waist, which left him in his sleeveless undershirt and thus out of uniform. Second, despite the dedicated efforts of his drill instructors at the San Diego Recruit Depot to instill in him a detailed knowledge of the Customs of the Service as they applied to military courtesy, he was not sure what was now required of him.

The basic rule was that officers got saluted by enlisted men. But it wasn't quite that simple. You were not supposed to salute indoors unless you were under arms. That meant actually carrying your rifle, or a symbol of it like a cartridge belt. And you were not supposed to salute when you were on a labor detail. The NCO in charge of the labor detail was supposed to do that, first calling "attention" and then saluting the officer on behalf of the entire labor detail.

I suppose, PFC Hastings finally decided, *that since I am the only one on this labor detail, I am in charge, and supposed to salute. And that sonofabitch obviously isn't going to go away. He's looking at the car like he never saw a '33 Ford before.*

And I don't think anybody ever got in real trouble in the Corps for saluting when they really didn't have to.

He gave the chrome V-8 insignia on the front of the hood a final wipe, stepped back a foot; and then, as if he had first noticed the officer just then, he popped to attention and saluted.

"Good afternoon, Sir!" PFC Hastings barked. At the same moment, he realized that coming to attention had rearranged his hips so that the bottom of his coveralls was sliding down off them.

"Good afternoon," Captain Charley Galloway said, crisply returning the salute and doing his best not to laugh. "Stand at ease and grab your pants."

"Aye, aye, Sir. Thank you, Sir."

PFC Hastings quickly untied the sleeves of his coveralls, shoved his arms through them, and buttoned the garment as regulations required. When he looked up, he saw that the Captain was carefully inspecting the Ford's interior. He took a chance.

"Nice car, isn't it, Sir?"

"Yes, it is," Galloway said, smiling at PFC Hastings. "And Sergeant Oblensky lets you take care of it for him, does he?"

"Yes, Sir," PFC Hastings said, a touch of pride in his voice. "I try to keep it shipshape for him, Sir."

"And you seem to have done so very well," Galloway said.

"Thank you, Sir."

"Do you happen to know where Sergeant Oblensky is?"

"Yes, Sir. He's inside, in the hangar, I mean."

"Would you please find Sergeant Oblensky and tell him I'd like a word with him, please?"

"Aye, aye, Sir," Hastings said, and started to walk away, then stopped. He had forgotten to salute; and he also hadn't done what Sergeant Oblensky had told him to do with the car when he had finished washing it.

"Sir, I'm supposed to put the car back in Sergeant Oblensky's parking space."

"It'll be all right here," Galloway said. "Just go get him, please."

"Aye, aye, Sir," Hastings said, and this time remembered to salute.

Galloway, fighting the urge to smile, returned it; and then when the kid had disappeared, at a fast trot, around the corner of the hangar, he leaned over the mounted-in-the-front-fender spare tire and raised the left half of the hood.

The engine compartment of the nine-year-old Ford was as spotless as the exterior. The first time Charley had seen the Ford's engine it was a disaster; where it wasn't streaked with rust it had been coated with grease. Now it looked as good as it must have looked on the showroom floor. Better. And mechanically it was better too. The engine had not just been completely rebuilt, it had been greatly modified. The heads had been milled to increase compression. The carburetor had been upgraded. There had even been thought about "blowing" the engine, getting an aircraft engine supercharger from salvage, rebuilding it, and adapting it to the flathead Ford V-8. That probably would have happened had the war not come along.

Captain Galloway lowered the hood, fastened it in place, and stood erect. Technical Sergeant Stefan Oblensky appeared at the corner of the hangar.

He was known as "Big Steve" because he *was* big. He stood well over six feet, had a barrel chest, and large bones. He was almost entirely bald, and what little hair remained around his ears and the back of his neck was so closely shorn as to be nearly invisible.

He was forty-six, literally old enough to be Charley's father. Seeing him, Charley realized with surprise that he had forgotten both how old and how big Big Steve was. And how formidable appearing in his stiffly starched, skin-tight khakis, his fore-and-aft cap perched on his shining, massive head.

There was no suggestion on his face that he had ever seen Captain Charles Galloway before in his life. He raised his hand in a crisp salute.

"Good afternoon, Sir. The captain wished to see me?"

Charley returned the salute.

"Good afternoon, Sergeant," he said. "Yes, I did."

"How may I help the captain, Sir?"

"I think we might as well start by putting this back in my name," Galloway said, waving at the Ford. "Does it run as good as it looks?"

"I don't think the captain will have any complaints, Sir."

"Well, then get in, Sergeant, and we'll go see the Provost Marshal."

"Sir, with the captain's permission, I'll have to inform the maintenance officer that I will be out of the hangar."

"That won't be necessary, Sergeant. I've explained to your squadron commander that we have some business to take care of."

"Yes, Sir."

That's bullshit.

What I did, with absolutely no success, was try to placate his squadron commander after he had been told five minutes before that he had just lost his Maintenance NCO to VMF-229, and that the decision was not open for discussion or reversal. When I walked out of his door, the man was still steamingly pissed off—not only at his Wing Commander but, if possible, even more at Captain Charles M. Galloway, CO, VMF-229. I wonder why I didn't tell Big Steve that he now works for me?

Obviously, because I don't want him to think that Santa Claus has come to town, and that he now has a squadron commander in his pocket.

Galloway got behind the wheel of the Ford. Oblensky, after first removing it from a well-filled key ring, handed the ignition key to him.

The engine started immediately. Galloway slipped it in gear and made a U-turn away from the hangar.

"I heard you were back," Oblensky said.

It starts. "You," not "the captain." No "Sir."

"I got in yesterday," Galloway said. "I got a ride on an Army Air Corps B-17."

"Do they give them guns and ammo now?" Oblensky asked.

Again, no "Sir," Galloway thought. *What the hell is he talking about?*

And then he remembered. During the attack on Pearl Harbor, a flight of B-17s had arrived in Hawaii. Since they had left the United States in peacetime—and to decrease the parasitic drag the weapons would cause if in place—their .50 caliber Browning machine guns had been stowed inside, and they had carried no ammunition for them. They had arrived in the middle of a battle absolutely unable to defend themselves.

"These had ammo," Galloway answered, remembering. "The side positions were faired over, and their guns were on the deck. The turrets were operational."

"I heard they were giving you a squadron."

Of course you did. If you could find out from the Navy the course of the Saratoga *at sea, it was no problem at all for you to find out from the sergeant in Colonel Dawkins's office that I was going to get VMF-229.*

"VMF-229," Galloway said.

It was not far from the hangar to the Provost Marshal's office. Oblensky did not attempt further conversation.

There was a lanky buck sergeant on duty. He stood up behind his desk when Galloway walked into the small frame building.

"Good morning, Sir," the sergeant said. "Can I help you?"

"I want to register a car," Galloway said. "You got the papers, Sergeant Oblensky?"

"Yes, Sir," Oblensky said, taking the vehicle registrations, military and civilian, from his wallet and handing them over.

"Sir," the Provost Marshal Sergeant said, "if the captain is buying the car from the sergeant, you'll need a notarized bill of sale."

"I'm not buying it," Galloway said. "I already own it. I gave Sergeant Oblensky a power-of-attorney to use it when I went to the States."

"It's on file," Oblensky said. "Look under 'Oblensky.'"

"Let me check," the sergeant said, and he went to a vertical file cabinet. In a moment, he found what he was looking for. He returned with a manila folder, reading from it as he walked.

"You're Tech Sergeant Galloway, Sir?"

"No. I'm Captain Galloway. But I was a Tech Sergeant when I signed that power-of-attorney."

"Yes, Sir. That's what I meant, Sir. I'll get the forms, Sir."

He went into a small storeroom.

"I think he knows who you are," Oblensky said, softly.

"Who am I?"

"I mean, I think he knows what happened, who you are," Oblensky said.

The sergeant came out of the storeroom with several printed forms and a small metal plate. He sat down at the typewriter and fed the forms into it. He asked for Galloway's serial number and unit.

"There's a new regulation, Sir," the sergeant said. "You'll need your CO's permission to have a car on the base."

"Colonel Dawkins, you mean?"

"No, Sir, your squadron commander will do."

"I command VMF-229," Galloway said.

"Yes, Sir," the sergeant said, visibly surprised.

Big Steve was right. That guy did make the connection. It will be interesting conversation at the Staff NCO Club tonight—for that matter at the Officer's Club, too—and all over the base by tomorrow:

"Remember that story about the Flying Sergeant of VMF-211 who fixed up the F4F the Japs got on December 7? Fixed it up and flew it out to the Saratoga *at sea and really pissed the Navy off? The guy they sent back to the states for court-martial? Well, he's back, and guess what, he's a* captain, *no shit, and a squadron commander!"*

The sergeant came from his typewriter and handed Galloway forms to sign and then the small metal plate.

"You screw this on top of the Hawaiian plate, Sir," he said. "That'll be fifty cents, please."

Galloway handed him two quarters.

"Thank you," he said.

"Excuse me, Sir," the sergeant said. "You used to be a flying sergeant with VMF-211, right?"

"Right."

"I thought I remembered the name," the sergeant said.

Would you like my autograph? How to Succeed in the Corps: Really *fuck up!*

He became aware that Oblensky was tugging at the small metal plate, and released it to him. When they went outside, Oblensky opened the rumble seat, took a screwdriver from a small tool roll, and replaced the tag (for enlisted men) above the license plate with the new officer's tag Galloway had just been given.

"Thank you, Steve," Galloway said. "And also for keeping the car so shipshape."

"Don't be silly," Oblensky said. "I was using it, wasn't I? I owe you."

I'm not very good at this psychological bullshit, "How the wise commissioned officer should deal with the enlisted swine." Fuck it!

"Steve, I had you transferred to VMF-229," Galloway said. "Is that going to cause any problems?"

"You're starting with problems," Oblensky said. "What you have is fourteen pickled F4Fs on a wharf at Pearl, Christ only knows what shape they're in; a dozen—maybe fifteen, sixteen—kids who are not sure what a wrench is used for; and a young pilot scuttlebutt says runs from fights."

"I mean with you and me," Galloway said.

Oblensky's eyes narrowed. Galloway knew him well enough to know that meant he was angry. Very angry.

"I don't think I deserved that, *Captain* Galloway," he said, coldly, after a moment. "I would have thought you know me well enough to know that I have been in the Corps long enough to know where the line is between those of us who wear stripes and those of you who wear bars."

"Christ, Steve!"

"If the captain can remember not to call the sergeant by his Christian name where other people can hear him, the sergeant will remember not to remember that he knew the captain when he was a wiseass little fucker who made tech sergeant before he was old enough to be a pimple on a buck sergeant's ass."

"I'll keep that in mind, Sergeant Oblensky."

"The captain would be wise to do just that," Oblensky said.

They met each other's eyes for a moment, and then, Oblensky first, they smiled at each other.

"Thank you, Steve," Galloway said.

"When does my transfer come through?"

"I don't know about the paperwork, but you're in VMF-229 as of now."

"In that case, why don't we ride over and see what shape our airplanes are in? Unless there's something I don't know about, that would seem to be our first order of business."

They got in the Ford. En route to the wharfs at the Pearl Harbor Naval Station, Oblensky asked, "Remember when we painted this thing? And that Lieutenant Commander wanted to know where we got the paint, and you showed him the can from Sears, Roebuck?"

Galloway chuckled. The paint can from Sears had been labeled, HIGH GLOSS YELLOW ENAMEL. $5.95. After they'd bought it, Oblensky had dumped the contents into a five gallon can of Navy yellow paint intended to paint lines on hangar and flight line floors. He had then refilled it—"borrowed" it from Navy stocks—with a very high quality aviation paint that was reported to be worth sixty dollars a gallon on the civilian market.

The Ford's new paint job had been spectacular, as the Lieutenant Commander had noticed. He had run right down to Sears to get a gallon of their $5.95 "High Gloss Yellow Enamel" to paint his own car. His Studebaker, somehow, hadn't come out looking nearly as nice as Galloway's Ford, and he had been disappointed and mystified.

His own reaction at the time, Charley remembered, was that was the sort of stupid behavior you expected from a fucking officer. He was aware now that he had switched sides, that he was now a fucking officer, and considered fair game by old-time non-coms like Big Steve.

"I got some more bad news for you," Oblensky said. "Your Lieutenant Dunn's been fucking your girlfriend."

"You mean Ensign O'Malley?"

"Yeah. You mean you forgot her?"

"She was never my girlfriend, Steve."

"Well," Oblensky chuckled. "You were pretty fucking chummy, as I remember."

In the early morning of December 7, 1941, Technical Sergeant Galloway had been in bed with Ensign O'Malley in a cabin in the hills Technical Sergeant Oblensky had borrowed for the weekend from an old and now retired Marine Corps buddy. When Oblensky had burst into the room to tell Galloway that the Japanese were attacking the Naval base at Pearl Harbor, Ensign O'Malley had been performing on Technical Sergeant Galloway's body a sexual act that he had not even heard of previously, not even in the French movies he had sometimes seen on stag night in the Staff NCO Club.

"What about Flo?" Galloway asked, to change the subject. "You still see her?"

Flo was Lieutenant Florence Kocharski, Navy Nurse Corps, a lady a few years younger and not much smaller than Oblensky. They had met when Oblensky had gone to the Naval Hospital for his annual physical. It had taken them about twenty minutes to decide that it was time to break a rule both had followed for more than twenty years: Officers do not become involved with enlisted personnel.

"I knew you'd get around to asking that, sooner or later," Oblensky replied.

It was not the reply Galloway expected.

"Is there some reason I shouldn't have asked? You were pretty fucking chummy, too, as I remember."

"Off the record, Captain?"

"Off the record."

"We got married," Oblensky said. "The day after you flew out to the *Saratoga*."

"Married?" Galloway asked, in disbelief.

"We were going to get married when one of us retired anyway," Oblensky said. "We both got our twenty-years in, and then some. So when this goddamned war came along, and they weren't going to let us retire, we figured, fuck 'em. We got married. Flo knew a priest who can keep his mouth shut, and we didn't put ranks or whatever on the marriage license."

"You mean you got married without permission?"

"They don't let officers marry enlisted men, or vice versa, you know that."

"Well, you know I like Flo," Galloway said, honestly. "So the first thing I've got to say is 'congratulations.' "

"Why don't you just stop there, then?"

"Christ, what are you going to do if they find out?"

"Hope they don't, for openers," Oblensky said. "I don't think they'd court-martial us."

"Goddamn, Steve, I don't know."

"After Flo and Hot Pants O'Malley dropped us back at the base on seven December," Oblensky said carefully, "Flo went down to Battleship Row. She was on board *West Virginia* taking care of some sailors when there was a secondary explosion . . . one of the five-inch magazines blew up. She caught some fragments and got burned a little, but she was still able to work, so she stuck around for a while. Some Commander saw her and put her in for a medal and the Purple Heart. We figured the Navy and/or the Corps would look pretty fucking silly court-martialing a wounded hero for marrying a Marine. Or vice versa, a Marine for marrying a wounded hero."

"They're going to be pissed," Galloway said.

"Well, they were pissed at you, too, and now look at you," Oblensky said.

"I didn't think to ask," Galloway said. "Were you in trouble because of what I did?"

"They were pretty excited for a while right afterward," Oblensky said. "But you were the one who flew the airplane, not me. I don't expect to get promoted any time soon, though."

"What are you going to do about the paperwork?" Galloway asked. "Who's the dependent, for example? You, or Flo?"

"We've been a little wary about getting into that," Oblensky said. "The only thing we did was change our life insurance. She gets mine, and I get hers, if anything happens. I changed my home of record to her brother's, in Chicago. And we didn't say we were married. You can leave your insurance to a friend."

"Let me look into this, Steve."

"Don't rock the fucking boat, Charley," Oblensky said.

"I won't, trust me."

"I guess I have to, don't I?" Oblensky said. "You don't seem very pissed off that Hot Pants is fucking Lieutenant Dunn."

Just in time, Galloway stopped himself from saying, "I met somebody special in the States."

I can't tell him about Caroline. If I told him that I actually met a woman from a background like that, that she drove across the country with me, that we stayed at the Andrew Foster Hotel as the guests of Andrew Foster, he would think it was one-hundred-percent bullshit, probably concocted because he had just told me Hot Pants O'Malley is now screwing this guy Dunn. If he believed there really was a woman named Caroline who drove out to the West Coast with me, he would be sure she was some tramp I met in a bar. He would not believe the suite in the Andrew Foster at all. Not that he thinks I'm an imaginative liar, but because all of that belongs to a world that he can't even imagine.

Instead, Galloway said, *"You* seem pissed off about it."

"Pussy's in short supply in Hawaii, as you damned well know. A girl like that, she can do great things for morale. But it seems to me that if she wants to pass it around, she could find somebody who's not afraid to fight to pass it out to."

Oh, shit! I can't let him get away with that!

After a moment, Oblensky sensed the tension.

"I say something wrong?" he asked.

"Yeah, Steve, you did," Galloway said. "Did you really think I would just sit here, as your commanding officer, and let you accuse one of your officers—one of my officers—of cowardice?"

"Everybody knows he ran away from Midway," Oblensky said.

"No, goddamnit, everybody doesn't know that. Colonel Dawkins doesn't know, I don't know, and you goddamned sure don't know. You keep your mouth shut about Lieutenant Dunn. Not only in front of me, but everywhere."

Oblensky looked at him in surprise, but said nothing.

"There is an expected reply from a non-com when an officer gives him an order," Galloway said, coldly.

Oblensky wet his lips. There was a just perceptible pause before he said, "Aye, aye, Sir."

That was pretty chickenshit of you, Charley Galloway, pulling rank on him that way, Galloway thought. And then he thought: *Fuck him. He was wrong. And that's why they give officers rank, to use it.* And then he had a final, more than a little satisfying, even a little smug, thought: *I didn't handle that badly at all. Maybe I just can hack it as an officer, a squadron commander.*

(TWO)
Officer's Club
Pearl Harbor Naval Base
Oahu, Territory of Hawaii
1630 Hours 27 June 1942

Uniform Regulations of the United States Naval Base, Pearl Harbor, specified the white uniform for wear after 1700 hours in social situations, e.g., while dining in the Main Officer's Club. But because there were exigencies of the service which brought officers to Pearl Harbor without their whites—such as for example the fact that there was a war on—there was a caveat: The words "whenever possible" had been added.

It was a loophole through which most Marine and many Naval aviators leapt en masse. White uniforms were expensive to begin with, they soiled easily and often permanently, and as a general rule of thumb they could be worn only once before requiring a trip to the laundry/dry cleaners.

When Captain Charles M. Galloway came into the Main Officer's Club, he saw at the bar another Marine officer dressed as he was. They were both wearing a tropical worsted uniform, shirt, trousers, and the khaki necktie that the Corps called a "field scarf"—for reasons Galloway never understood. "TWs" were not only more comfortable than whites, they did not require very extra careful movement of cup or fork to the mouth, and could often be worn three times before a visit to the dry cleaners.

That has to be Lieutenant William C. Dunn, Galloway thought. *He's a first john aviator, "a good looking kid," as Colonel Dawkins called him, and he is rubbing knees with Mary Agnes O'Malley.*

As he walked to the bar, Charley noticed that Dunn was wearing his wings, but no ribbons. He was entitled to wear the Purple Heart after the Japs almost turned him into a soprano.

As soon as Lieutenant (j.g.) Mary Agnes O'Malley, Nurse Corps, USN, recognized Charley, she discreetly withdrew the knee she'd draped over Lieutenant Dunn's and smiled at Galloway. There was, Charley thought, more than a little hint of naughty invitation in her eyes.

"Well, look at what the tide threw up on the beach!" she cried, and got off the bar stool.

Just looking at her, you'd never guess what she likes to do—have done to her—in the sack. I wonder if she's doing that to Dunn? Or got him to do it to her?

"Hello, Mary Agnes," Galloway said. She stood on her tiptoes and gave him her cheek to kiss, managing in the maneuver to rub her breasts against his abdomen.

"Charley, this is Lieutenant Bill Dunn," Mary Agnes said, touching Dunn's shoulder with her hand. "Bill, this is Captain Charley Galloway."

"Hello, Dunn," Charley said, offering his hand.

"Good evening, Sir."

Christ, you can cut that Rebel accent with a knife! He sounds like he thinks there's no "e" in "evening" and that "Sir" is spelled "Suh."

"I sort of hoped you would be here," Galloway said. "So I would have my chance to hold my very first officer's call."

It was an attempt at humor, and it failed.

"Yes, Sir," Dunn said, adding, with absolutely no suggestion of invitation in his voice, "Would you join us for a drink, Sir?"

"Oh, of course, he will," Mary Agnes said. "Charley and I are old friends, aren't we, Charley?"

"Absolutely," Charley said. He caught the bartender's eye. "Another round here, please. I'll have whatever the lieutenant's drinking."

"I'll just get in the middle," Mary Agnes said. "Move over a stool, Bill."

Dunn shifted to the adjacent stool; Mary Agnes sat on the one he vacated; and Galloway slid onto the one where she had been sitting. It was still warm from her body, which served to trigger a remarkably clear image of what that bottom looked—and felt—like when not covered with the crisp white of a Navy Nurse's dress uniform.

Galloway looked past Mary Agnes at Dunn.

"I left a message for you at the BOQ," he said. "Did you get it?"

"Yes, Sir. Hangar Three at 0730. I'll be there, Sir."

"I talked Colonel Dawkins out of Technical Sergeant Oblensky," Galloway said. "You know him, I guess? Big Steve?"

"Yes, Sir."

"I told him to find us someplace for a squadron office . . ." Galloway said.

"Yes, Sir," Dunn said, when Galloway paused momentarily to take a breath.

". . . and I'd be surprised if he didn't have us one by 0730 tomorrow," Galloway finished.

"Yes, Sir."

He doesn't like me. I wonder why? I don't think Hot Pants is likely to have told him much about us, if anything. Maybe because he heard I used to be a flying sergeant? And he's not thrilled by having an ex-sergeant for a CO?

"When I was a flying sergeant in VMF-211," Galloway said, "I got to know Oblensky pretty well. He's what they call 'The Old Breed'; he's been in the Corps since Christ was a corporal. Damned good man."

"So I've heard, Sir," Dunn said.

The bartender delivered the drinks.

"Here's to old friends," Mary Agnes said, raising her glass. "The best kind."

"How about here's to VMF-229?" Galloway said. "And particularly to its pilots, both of whom are here with you?"

"All right," Mary Agnes said agreeably; and then realizing what Charley meant, she added, "Is that right? All the pilots there are is you two?"

"That's right," Galloway said and then added to Dunn, "But there was a radio this afternoon . . ." He stopped, took a sheet of yellow paper from his hip pocket, handed it to Dunn, and continued, ". . . with these names on it. They'll be in the next couple of days."

Dunn took the sheet of teletype paper, read it, and handed it back.

"Know any of those people?" Galloway asked.

"I knew a Dave Schneider, went through Advanced with him at Pensacola, but they sent him on to multiengine. Not an F4F pilot."

"It's probably the same guy," Galloway said. "He was learning to fly R4Ds when I met him."

Galloway had met Lieutenant David Schneider on a very important day in his life. Not only was it the first time he had been permitted to fly since he had landed the Wildcat on *Sara*'s deck, but it was the day he met Mrs. Caroline Ward McNamara.

Headquarters, USMC had laid an important mission on Quantico. They were to furnish an R4D to drop parachutists at the Marine Corps Parachute School at Lakehurst, New Jersey. It was important because Major Jake Dillon, a legendary Hollywood press agent who had come back into the Corps when the war started—he had once been a staff sergeant with the 4th Marines in Shanghai—had arranged for *Time-Life* to do a major story on what were being called "ParaMarines."

Colonel Robert T. "Bobby" Hershberger, of the 1st Marine Air Wing, decided that he could not entrust flying the plane to the only two pilots he had who were checked out in the R4D. Lieutenants David Schneider and James L. Ward simply didn't have the necessary experience. On the flight line, however, wrench in hand, removed in disgrace from flight status, was a Tech Sergeant named Charley Galloway who not only had several hundred hours in R4Ds but had graduated from the U.S. Army Air Corps School for dropping people and equipment by parachute from R4Ds.

After a somewhat heated telephone conversation with Brigadier General D. G. McInerney, during which both officers said things they immediately regretted, it was decided that the situation required Galloway's restoration to flight duty for the Lakehurst mission. It was either that or run the risk of allowing a new R4D with MARINES lettered on the fuselage and a load of parachutists aboard to crash in flames before *Time*'s, *Life*'s, and *The March of Time*'s still and motion picture cameras.

Lieutenants Schneider and Ward were called into Colonel Hershberger's office and told that they would fly the mission with Technical Sergeant Galloway, who would be Pilot-in-Command.

Lieutenant Schneider, who was an Annapolis graduate and a career officer, was very unhappy to find himself under the orders of a Flying Sergeant. And he did nothing to conceal his unhappiness. On the other hand, Lieutenant Ward, who was a reservist, was not knocked out of joint because he had to learn from someone who knew more than he did, whatever his rank. And far more importantly, Ward had a just-divorced aunt named Caroline Ward McNamara, to whom he introduced Technical Sergeant Galloway in Philadelphia.

"Schneider's an absolute asshole," Dunn said. "Annapolis. The reason he hates this war is because they have to let civilians into the Corps to fight it. Civilian savages pissing on the Corps's sacred potted palms, so to speak . . ."

Then Dunn saw the look on Galloway's face and stopped.

"My mouth ran away with me, Sir, I'm sorry."

The test of a truly intelligent man, Galloway remembered hearing somewhere, *is the degree to which he agrees with you.*

"The thing about Lieutenant Schneider, Lieutenant Dunn," Galloway said sternly, "is that he not only is a skilled, knowledgeable pilot, but, in my judgment, he is one of those rare people who are natural fliers. With those characteristics in mind, I asked Lieutenant Schneider to join VMF-229, even though he *is* personally an *absolute* asshole. Fortunately for you—and for me too—you outrank him."

Dunn's eyes widened, and then for the first time he smiled.

"Yes, Sir, that thought has occurred to me."

We're going to get along, Galloway thought, *this Rebel kid is all right.*

Mary Agnes swung around on the stool so that she faced Galloway and her knee pressed against his leg.

"Why don't we carry our drinks into the dining room and find a table?" she asked. "They've got a band in there, and I'd like to dance."

"On the table?" Galloway asked.

Her knees pressed harder against his leg, and her hand came down to rest on it.

"No," she said, giving his leg a little squeeze. "With you, silly."

(THREE)
**The Elms
Dandenong, Victoria, Australia
1730 Hours 28 June 1942**

When the telephone rang, Captain Fleming Pickering, USNR, was in the library of The Elms, sitting in a high-backed red leather armchair, jacketless, his shoes off, his tie pulled down, and his feet on a footstool. He was just about ready to take his first sip of his first drink of the day.

He eyed the instrument with distaste; it was sitting out of reach on a narrow table across the room. It had been a busy day, and it was his considered judgment that anything anyone on the phone wanted could wait until tomorrow morning.

The telephone kept ringing. There was a staff of four at The Elms: a housekeeper, a maid, a cook, and a combination yardman, chauffeur, and husband to the housekeeper. They were all personal employees of Captain Pickering. The house was leased from a Melbourne banker Captain Pickering knew from before the war.

The Vice-chairman of the Board of the Pacific & Far Eastern Shipping Corporation (that is to say, Mrs. Fleming Foster Pickering) had arranged for the salary and expense allowance of Chairman of the Board Fleming Pickering to continue while he was on "military leave" from his duties. After having been assigned quarters (a small, two-room hotel suite to be shared with a portly Army Colonel who snored) Captain Pickering had decided that since he damned well could afford something more comfortable, there was no reason not to leave the colonel to snore alone.

Besides, he rationalized, he needed a place where he could discreetly meet people in connection with his duties. The brass hats of MacArthur's Palace Guard could give lessons in plain and fancy gossiping to any women's group he was familiar with. The gossip was at the least annoying, but it could also spread information that deserved to be sat upon, and at worst it could cost people their lives.

"Christ," Pickering asked rhetorically, vis-à-vis his domestic staff, "where the hell are they all?"

He hauled himself out of the chair and walked across the two-story library in his stocking feet and picked up the telephone.

"Captain Pickering."

"Major Banning, please."

It was an American voice.

"I'm sorry, Major Banning isn't here at the moment. I expect him within the hour. Can I take a message?"

"Am I correct, Captain, that you're an American officer?"

"Yes, I am."

"This is Commander Lentz, Captain, of Melbourne NATS."

It took Pickering a moment to decode the acronym: Naval Air Transport Service. Next it occurred to him—after a moment spent digesting the superior tone of the commander's voice—that the NATS officer had jumped to the wrong conclusion: *Lentz thinks I'm a Marine captain, and thus inferior in rank, rather than what I really am, an exalted four striper.*

"How may I help you, Commander?"

"We've got an enlisted man down here, Captain, one of your sergeants . . ."

Bingo, I was right. He thinks I'm a Marine. Actually, I wish to God I was.

". . . he just came in from Hawaii on the courier plane. He's headed for some outfit called Special Detachment 14. Ordinarily, I would have sent him over to the transient detachment, but he's traveling on a Six-A priority, so I tried to find this Special Detachment 14 . . ."

"He's there now, Commander? Is that what you're saying?"

"You people really ought to make an effort to keep us up to date on your phone numbers," Commander Lentz said. "I spent an hour on the telephone before I managed to get through to some sergeant, who said Major Banning could be reached at this number."

"Tell the sergeant I'll be there in about thirty minutes to pick him up," Pickering said.

"You're going to come get him yourself?"

"Certainly," Pickering said. "I think it behooves those of us who are Naval officers to concern ourselves with the welfare of the enlisted men of our sister service, don't you, Commander?"

Commander Lentz was not stupid.

"Yes, Sir," he said. "Of course I do, Sir. Sir, it won't be necessary for the Captain to come himself. I'll arrange transportation if the Captain will give me an address."

"I'll be there in thirty minutes, Commander. I know where you are," Pickering said and hung up. His annoyance at having to drive into town was easily overwhelmed by his pleasure at having pricked the Commander's balloon of self-importance.

He was sitting on the footstool in front of the red leather chair tying his shoes when Mrs. Hortense Cavendish, the housekeeper, came in. She was a plump, gray-haired, motherly woman in her late fifties.

"I'd hoped to be back before you got here," she said.

"No problem."

"I bought a couple of nice, fresh barons of lamb," she said. "I know you like to feed Major Banning well when he comes. And Charley and I were in the country buying them, which is why we weren't here."

"I've got to go into town," Pickering said. "There was another young Marine for Major Banning on the courier plane. I'm going to fetch him."

"Couldn't Charley fetch him?"

"I'll get him," Pickering said. "What this boy needs after flying from the States is a hot meal, not a wild ride through Melbourne on the wrong side of the road with a crazy Australian at the wheel."

She laughed.

"There's plenty of food," she said. "I'll just slice the barons before I serve them."

"I'm not going to bring him here," Pickering said, as he stood up. "The one thing that kid does not need is dinner with a Navy brass hat. I'll get him a hotel and let Banning take care of him in the morning."

He drained his glass of scotch and walked out of the library.

First Lieutenant Hon Song Do, Signal Corps, U.S. Army Reserve, arrived at The Elms ten minutes after Pickering left, and Major Edward J. Banning, USMC, arrived five minutes after that. Both men were there at Captain Fleming Pickering's invitation.

Major Banning had called Captain Pickering on the telephone that morning to tell him he had "something interesting" and was about to fly to Melbourne to show it to him. Pickering asked him then to go directly to The Elms, not only because he liked Banning and wanted to have him to dinner, but also because he liked to keep Banning away from MacArthur's headquarters as much as possible. If the gossips didn't see him, they didn't ask questions. Pickering had also asked Pluto for dinner, not only because he—and Banning—enjoyed Hon's company, but also because he believed that Hon should know about anything "interesting" Banning had found.

After Mrs. Cavendish told them that Captain Fleming would be a little late, she set out a half gallon bottle of scotch, a soda siphon, and a silver champagne cooler full of ice for them in the library.

Major Banning had been driven to The Elms from the airfield in a Ford station wagon bearing the insignia of the Royal Australian Navy. He had just flown in from Townesville, Queensland, where he commanded Special Detachment 14, USMC. The very existence of Special Detachment 14 was classified CONFIDENTIAL. Its presence in Australia was classified SECRET. Its mission, "to support the Coast-watcher Establishment, Royal Australian Navy and to perform such other intelligence gathering activities as may be directed by Headquarters, USMC," was classified TOP SECRET.

Lieutenant Commander Eric A. Feldt, Royal Australian Navy, who commanded the Coastwatcher Establishment, had surprised a large number of Australians and Americans by taking an immediate liking to Major Banning. He had previously run off every other American officer sent to work with the Coastwatchers. In the process he often used language so colorful that some thought it inappropriate for a senior naval officer.

But Captain Pickering heard from Rear Admiral Keith Soames-Haley, RAN, a pre-war friend of long standing, that Feldt had described Major Banning as "the first sodding American officer I've met who could find his sodding ass with both hands."

Admiral Soames-Haley and Captain Pickering both agreed that the rapport between Feldt and Banning was probably based on the mysterious chemistry that sometimes developed between seemingly dissimilar men—each surprisingly recognizing in the other a deep-down, kindred soul, the two of them bobbing along alone and unappreciated in a sea of fools.

Soames-Haley and Pickering also agreed that the friendship between the two men almost certainly had much to do with the long years that Banning had spent in the Orient before the war. Banning understood the Japanese as well as Feldt did—which is to say as well as any Westerner could. Both officers spoke fluent Japanese. And finally, Feldt probably felt a connection with Banning because of Banning's personal stake in the war: Banning had been forced to leave his Russian-born wife behind in Shanghai when war came.

Whatever the reasons, both Saomes-Haley and Pickering were truly delighted that the problems of Australian-US Cooperation vis-à-vis the Coastwatchers was solved. Soames-Haley was all too aware of how valuable that cooperation would be to both allies. For his part, he was not just eager, he was hungry to get his hands on some of the logistical largess available from Americans with the right connections. The Coastwatcher Organization needed desperately the latest communications equipment, as well as access to aircraft and submarines. And for his part, Pickering was fully aware of the value of the intelligence that would now flow from the Coastwatchers. Now that Banning was close to Feldt, and not regarded by him as one more arrogant, sodding American over here to tell us how to run the sodding war, the intelligence Feldt could provide would arrive far more quickly than through standard channels.

Major Banning had been met at the airport by a RAN Lieutenant, and transported to The Elms in a RAN Ford station wagon, because Commander Feldt had spread the word that Banning was "not too sodding stupid for an American." This was, for Feldt, praise of the highest order. Commander Feldt was highly regarded by his peers in the RAN, and any friend of his . . . Lieutenant Pluto Hon had driven to The Elms in a 1941 Studebaker President, which had the letters USMC on its hood and the Marine Corps insignia stencilled on its doors.

One of the sixteen enlisted men assigned to Special Detachment 14 was Staff Sergeant Allan Richardson, who was a scrounger of some reputation. Richardson had learned that shortly after the war broke out, a transport under charter to the U.S. Navy and loaded with equipment intended for the Chinese had been diverted to Melbourne. The cargo, which included a large number of Studebaker trucks and twenty President sedans, had been off-loaded and turned over to the only U.S. Navy group then in the area, a small Hydrographic Detachment. Richardson reasoned—correctly—that since Special Detachment 14 needed vehicles and had none, and since it was, furthermore, under the control of Captain Pickering, all it would take to get the needed vehicles would be a call from Captain Pickering to the Commanding Officer of the Hydrographic Detachment, a Lieutenant (j.g.). As a general rule of thumb, Lieutenants (j.g.) tend to comply with requests of Naval Captains.

Captain Pickering made the call. Special Detachment 14 got all the trucks and sedans it needed, plus one additional President. Two days after he made the telephone call on behalf of Staff Sergeant Richardson, Richardson gave Pickering the extra President, now bearing USMC insignia.

Pickering's rank entitled him to a staff car. Nevertheless, in order to avoid worrying about a driver, he had borrowed a Jaguar drophead coupe from a pre-war business associate for his personal transportation. Consequently, he promptly turned the Studebaker over to Lieutenant Pluto Hon. Pickering was immensely fond of Lieutenant Hon; he also felt himself to be in Hon's debt, for many courtesies rendered.

It did not surprise Pickering at all that Commander Lentz was waiting at NATS Melbourne, a small frame building plus a warehouse on Port Philip Bay. What surprised Commander Lentz was Captain Pickering's automobile; he was expecting either a Navy or an Army staff car, with a driver; and so a frown crossed his face when the Jaguar drophead coupe with Victorian license plates pulled into his OFFICIAL VISITORS parking space.

But Commander Lentz noticed the gold braid and the four gold stripes on Pickering's sleeves when he stepped out of the car, and he was suddenly all smiles.

"Captain Pickering? Commander Lentz, Sir."

"How are you, Commander?" Pickering replied, returning Lentz's salute with a far more crisp salute than was his custom.

Sergeant John Marston Moore, USMCR, stood at attention beside his seabag.

"Welcome to Australia, Sergeant," Pickering said.

"Yes, Sir. Thank you, Sir."

"Put your gear in the back," Pickering said, and then turned to Commander Lentz. "Do I have to sign for him or anything?"

"No, Sir. Nothing like that. I hate for you to have to have driven all the way down here, Sir. I would have been happy to arrange . . ."

"No problem," Pickering interrupted him. "Thank you for your diligence in finding somebody to take care of the sergeant, Commander."

"My pleasure, Captain."

Pickering got behind the wheel, and after John Moore got in beside him, he drove off.

"My name is Pickering, Sergeant."

"Yes, Sir."

"That's a long flight. I suppose you're tired, Sergeant? Sergeant what, by the way?"

"Moore, Sir."

"Are you tired?"

"I'm all right, Sir," Moore said, although that wasn't the truth. He had had trouble staying awake waiting for Captain Pickering.

"You don't have to be afraid of me, Sergeant," Pickering said. "I'm one of the *good* Naval officers."

"Sir?"

"Major Banning, your new CO, identifies good Naval officers as those who have previously been Marines. I was a Marine Corporal in what is now known as World War I."

Moore looked at him directly, for the first time, and saw that Pickering was smiling. He smiled back.

"And I have a boy about your age in the Corps," Pickering said. "What are you, twenty-one, twenty-two?"

"Twenty-two, Sir."

"How long have you been in the Corps?"

"About four months, Sir."

"You made buck sergeant in a hurry," Pickering said. But it was more of a question than a statement.

"When they took me out of boot camp to send me here, they made me a sergeant, Sir. I was originally supposed to go to Quantico and get a commission."

"Oh, really? You went to college, then?"

"Yes, Sir. Pennsylvania."

"Well, I'm sorry about the commission. But the Corps needed your skill here and now. What is that?"

"Sir?"

"Why did they take you out of boot camp and rush you over here?"

"Captain, I was told not to talk about anything connected with my transfer here."

"I understand, but, for all practical purposes, I'm Major Banning's commanding officer."

"Captain, with respect, I don't know that."

Pickering chuckled. "No, you don't. Good for you, Sergeant."

"Are we going to Special Detachment 14 now, Sir?"

"They're in Townesville, in Queensland, sort of on the upper right-hand corner of the Australian continent. What we're going to do is get you a hotel room. Have you got any money?"

"Yes, Sir."

"You're sure? Don't be embarrassed."

"I've got money, thank you, Sir."

"OK. So we'll get you a hotel. You can have a bath, and get something to eat, and in the morning, we'll get you together with Major Banning."

"Yes, Sir."

"I suppose I'd better have a set of your orders, and your service records, if you have them."

"Yes, Sir, they're in my bag."

IX

(ONE)
The Elms
Dandenong, Victoria, Australia
1845 Hours 28 June 1942

Major Ed Banning and Lieutenant Pluto Hon were on the wide veranda of The Elms when Pickering drove up. It was a pleasant place to watch darkness fall.

They both stood up as soon as the Jaguar drophead stopped. Banning set his drink on the wide top of the railing, and Hon stooped and set his on the floor.

"Good evening, Sir," they said, almost in unison.

Charley Cavendish, in a striped butler's apron, came from inside the house.

"I'd have been happy to go to town for you, Sir," Charley said.

"I know. Thank you, Charley. It was no trouble. I hope you have been taking care of these gentlemen? Lemonade, tea, that sort of thing?"

"Of course, Sir."

"Major Banning," Pickering said dryly, "the Marine Corps, in its infinite wisdom, has seen fit to increase your troop strength with a Sergeant John M. Moore. I just put him in a hotel. Here's his paperwork."

"How did you wind up with Sergeant Whatsisname, Captain?" Major Banning asked, as he took the service record envelope from Pickering.

"Moore is his name," Pickering said. "I wound up with him, Major, because you have failed in your obligation to keep Melbourne NATS up to date on your telephone numbers. I know this because a Lieutenant Commander named Lentz called up here and chewed me out about it."

"What?" Banning asked incredulously.

"At the time, he thought I was a Marine and one of your subordinate officers," Pickering said.

"And you didn't tell him?"

"Not at first," Pickering said, "but I think I ruined his supper when I dropped 'we Naval officers' into the conversation later on."

"Captain, I could have gone down there and picked him up," Pluto Hon said. "You should have called me."

"Then I wouldn't have had a chance to rub all my gold braid in the Commander's face," Pickering said. "Besides, it was no trouble."

"Well, I'm sorry that this guy bothered you, Captain," Banning said.

"He didn't really bother me. And I was interested to learn how much trouble he had finding Special Detachment 14. That's the way it's supposed to be."

Banning had meanwhile torn open the envelope and was scanning through Moore's service record with a practiced eye.

"Well, he's not a radio technician," he said, and then a moment later, "nor even an operator. And they didn't send him to parachute school. According to this, he just got out of boot camp. How come he's a sergeant?"

"He said they took him out of the officer candidate program to send him here. And made him a sergeant instead," Pickering said.

He held the service record envelope upside down and shook it. A business size envelope fell out. On it was written, "Major Ed Banning, USMC Special Detachment 14, Personal."

"And what have we here?" Banning said and tore it open.

Washington, 16 June 1942
Major Ed Banning

Dear Ed:

You have no idea how much trouble it was to find the young man probably now standing in front of you. He knows nothing about radios, I'm afraid, or about parachuting, or for that matter, about the Marine Corps, since I plucked him out of Parris Island before he finished boot camp.

But he speaks fluent Japanese, and I thought you could find some use for him. The FBI had quite a dossier on him (and his family) who were Methodist missionaries in Japan before the war, and he comes to you with a permanent TOP SECRET clearance.

If you can't use him, I'm sure the First Division, which should be in New Zealand by now, could. But you have the priority, so here he is. I'm working on radio people, parachute qualified, for you, but they're in nearly as short supply.

I wish I was there, instead of here. I don't suppose you could arrange something for me, could you?

Best Regards. Semper Fi!

Edward Sessions, Captain, USMC

Banning handed the letter to Pickering, who read it and handed it to Pluto Hon.

"I guess we'd better send him to the 1st Division," Banning said. "Before I came here, I thought that I would need a Japanese linguist, linguists, which is why Ed Sessions went to all this trouble to get this guy for me. But it hasn't turned out that way. A couple of Feldt's people and I can handle what translations we get into. It would be nice to have another linguist, particularly an American, but the First Marine Division really needs him more than I do. What I really need is radio operators, technicians."

"If you don't want him, Major, can I have him?" Pluto Hon asked.

"What do you want him for?" Pickering asked.

"Analysis," Hon said.

"You're talking about MAGIC?" Pickering asked.

Hon nodded. "Analysis needs someone who understands the Japanese mind, their culture."

"Christ, we can't get him cleared for that," Pickering replied.

"He doesn't have to know what it is, where it came from," Hon argued. "All he has to do is compare the intercepts with the translations we get from Pearl, and tell me if that's the translation he would have made."

"I'll have to think about that," Pickering said. "For one thing, we don't know if he speaks Japanese well enough to be of any use to you."

"Let me talk to him a couple of minutes, and I'd know," Hon said.

Pickering looked at Hon a moment, and realized that Hon really wanted Sergeant Moore.

"Well, that's easy enough to arrange. I put him in the Prince of Wales Hotel. We'll call him up and let you talk to him. But first things first. I need a drink. Unless what you've got that's 'interesting,' Ed, won't wait?"

"It'll wait long enough for a drink, Sir. I left it in the library."

"Well, let's go into the library and have a look," Pickering said. "It'll give us an excuse to get close to the liquor, anyway."

They picked up their empty glasses and followed him into the house.

"I'm going to take my coat off," Pickering said, as he did so. "Why don't you two relax, too?"

Then he went to the liquor and made drinks.

When he turned from the table, he saw that Pluto Hon was standing by the telephone.

"I found the number, Sir. Would you like me to dial it for you?"

Pickering nodded, and signaled for Hon to dial the telephone. Then he walked to him and took it from him.

"Sergeant Moore, please. I think he's in 408," he said, and then a moment later: "This is Captain Pickering, Sergeant. They taking care of you all right?" And then: "There's someone here who wants to talk to you." He handed the phone to Hon.

In Japanese, Pluto Hon said, "Welcome to Australia, Sergeant. I suppose that you're pretty beat after that long flight. How long did it take you to get from the States?"

Banning walked quickly to the telephone and put his head close to Pluto's so that he could hear Moore.

"Yes, Sir, I'm pretty . . ."

"In Japanese," Hon interrupted him, in Japanese. "If you will, please, Sergeant."

"Yes, Sir," Moore said, in Japanese. "I'm pretty tired, it was a long flight. And in Hawaii, I got off one plane and thirty minutes later got on another one."

"Where did you live in Japan?" Pluto Hon asked.

"In Denenchofu, Sir. Tokyo."

"And how long were you in Japan?"

"On and off, all my life, Sir."

"You went to school there? I mean Japanese schools?"

"Yes, Sir."

"The University?"

"Yes, Sir. And elementary and middle schools, too. Sir, who am I talking to?"

"My name is Hon, Sergeant. Your commanding officer is here and wants to talk to you."

He handed the phone to Banning, who didn't expect it.

"Sergeant, I'm sorry there was no one at NATS to meet you," Banning began, in English, and then switched to Japanese. "I'll be down to fetch you in the morning. Get yourself some dinner and a good night's sleep."

"Yes, Sir."

"Welcome to Australia, Sergeant," Banning said. "Good night." He hung the phone up, and turned to Pluto. "I didn't want to talk to him."

"I wanted you to be able to tell the Captain how well that kid speaks Japanese," Hon said, unabashed.

"Does he? Speak it well, I mean?" Pickering asked.

"He didn't learn that pronunciation in Japanese 202 at Princeton," Hon said. "He's been in Japan on and off all his life. He went to school there. Japanese schools, I mean. Including the University. I'd really like to have him, Captain."

"He went to Pennsylvania, too, he told me," Pickering said, "so he probably didn't graduate from University in Tokyo. So what? But I'm more than a little uneasy about giving him access to the MAGIC intercepts, even if he doesn't know what they are."

"I could have a fatherly little chat with him, Captain," Banning said. "And tell him that if it ever comes to my attention that he has discussed in any way what Hon gives him to do, or what he's learned, or thinks he's learned, with anyone but

Pluto, you, or myself, I will see that he spends the next twenty years in solitary confinement at the Portsmouth Naval Prison.''

''On the way to the hotel, he wouldn't even discuss Special Detachment 14 with me,'' Pickering said. ''I don't think he would have a loose mouth. OK, Pluto. You can have him. But you have that talk with him, Ed, anyway. And don't say Portsmouth. Tell him we'll have him shot.''

Banning looked quickly at Pickering and saw that he was serious.

''Aye, aye, Sir,'' Banning said.

Then Pickering changed the subject. ''Let's see what you have, Ed, that's so interesting.''

''Aye, aye, Sir,'' Banning repeated.

He pulled a leather briefcase from under the couch and took a large manila envelope from it.

''Would you like me to keep my eyes to myself, Captain?'' Pluto Hon asked.

''Oh, no, Pluto,'' Pickering said. ''You only thought I asked you here just for dinner.''

Banning chuckled, and spread a dozen ten-inch-square aerial photos out on a library table.

Three of the photos showed a dense cloud of smoke from a grass fire rising from a field, and then, in photographs apparently taken a day or two later, the same field. There were tracks from a truck or some other vehicle crisscrossing the now blackened grassy area.

''What am I looking at?'' Pickering asked.

''That's a field on an island called Guadalcanal,'' Banning said. ''It's one of the larger islands in the Solomons chain. . . . Here, I have a map, too.''

He took a map from his briefcase, spread it on the table, and pointed out the position of Guadalcanal in relation to New Britain and New Ireland islands, and to the islands nearer to it, New Georgia, Santa Isabel, Malaita, Tulagi, and San Cristobal.

''That field is near Lunga Point, on the north shore of Guadalcanal,'' Banning said, ''between the Matanikau and Tenaru Rivers.''

''I heard the Air Corps had taken some aerials of that area,'' Pickering said. ''Is that what these are?''

''No, Sir. These came from the Australians. Feldt passed them to me.''

''And does Feldt also think the Japanese are about to build a fighter strip there?''

''Feldt thinks—he's familiar with Guadalcanal—that *when* the Japanese build a field there, it will be able to handle any aircraft in the Jap inventory.''

''Jesus,'' Pickering said softly. ''If they get a fighter field going there, they can cover that whole area. And we don't have anything to stop them, and won't until we get that field on Espíritu Santo built . . . and God only knows how long that will take. Can I have these?''

''Yes, Sir, of course. We have Coastwatchers on Guadalcanal, but not in that area. We've radioed them to see what they can find out. But it will take them a couple of days to move over there.''

'' 'We'?'' Pickering quoted.

''I should have said, 'Commander Feldt,' '' Banning said.

''Hell, no. 'We' is fine. 'Them' and 'us' is just what I didn't want to hear. I was asking, are any of the Coastwatchers American?''

''No, Sir. The only Marines we have actually in place are Lieutenant Howard and Sergeant Koffler, and they're on Buka, to the Northwest.''

''I thought you told me you were going to try to . . . what's the word? 'insert'? . . . some more of our people.''

''So far, no luck,'' Banning said. ''Which translated means that Feldt has shot down every proposal I've made.''

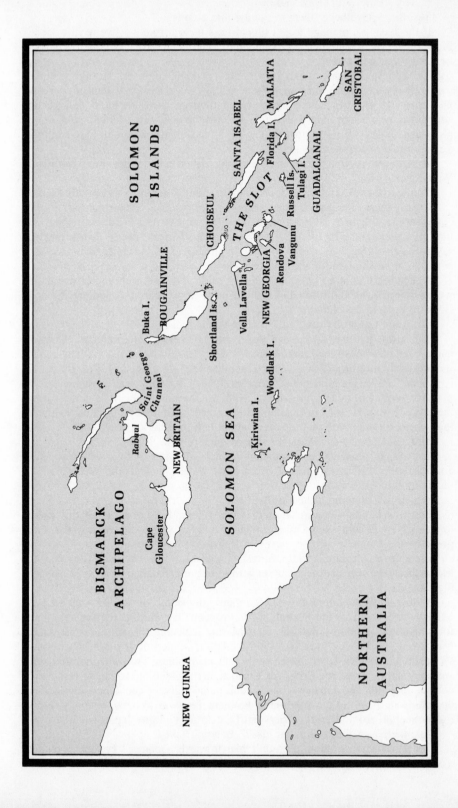

"It's his show," Pickering said.

"Yes, Sir. I have been operating under that premise."

"If the Japanese manage to get this airfield up and running, we're in trouble," Pickering repeated, and then asked Banning, "Did Feldt have anything to say about how long that will take?"

"I asked him the same question. 'I'm not a sodding engineer,' he said. 'But they can probably start to land fighters there in maybe six weeks. It depends on what they are using, whether real engineers, with bulldozers and other heavy construction equipment, or whether they will just try to level the field with ordinary soldiers and picks and shovels. If they move in engineers and their equipment, they can build a real airfield in two months or so.'"

"Off the top of your head, Ed, how long will it take to get these pictures to Washington?"

"You're going to send those to Washington, Sir?" Banning asked, surprised.

"I really meant the pictures our Army Air Corps took," Pickering said.

"If they sent them by officer courier, maybe four, five days," Banning said. "Are they that important? To get them to Washington, I mean, rather than a message saying we think the Japs are about to build an airfield on Guadalcanal? A message could be in Washington in a matter of hours."

"A picture, to coin a phrase," Pickering said, "is worth a thousand words. If I were Admiral King and wanted to sell President Roosevelt on something, I'd think I'd want to have the pictures."

"Sir, I don't quite follow you," Banning admitted.

"The Army and the Navy are at war again," Pickering said, bitterly. "Does the name Ghormley mean anything to you?"

"Admiral Ghormley?"

"Yeah," Pickering said. "On nineteen June, Ghormley was appointed Commander, South Pacific, under Admiral Nimitz. Ghormley's all right. I went down there to see him. He was in London on December seventh, and isn't infected with that sense of humiliation that the other admirals from King on down seem to feel."

"Sir?" Banning said, asking for an explanation.

"The others seem to feel that their primary mission in this war is to make amends for Pearl Harbor," Pickering said, bitterly, "ahead of all other considerations, including the best way to fight a war."

"Which is?" Banning asked softly.

"Early this month, when was it Pluto? MacArthur radioed Marshall for permission to attack New Britain–New Guinea. Which would, if successful, remove the threat posed by the Japanese airbase, *bases*, at Rabaul on New Britain."

"Eight June, Captain," Pluto furnished the date. "It was an EYES ONLY for Marshall, and he sent an officer courier with some pretty detailed plans to Washington the same day."

"MacArthur wanted to use two U.S. Infantry divisions," Pickering went on, "the 32nd and the 41st, plus the Australian 7th. Problem One was that they're not trained for amphibious landings. But the First Marine Division, by definition, is. And it was already on its way over here. So MacArthur wanted the 1st Marines to make the landing, and then be replaced by the others. Problem Two was that the beach was way out of range for Army Air Corps fighters. Once the force was ashore, of course, and took the Japanese bases, land-based fighters could be flown in and operate from them. So the solution to Problem Two was to have the Navy furnish fighter support from aircraft carriers until the Army took the Japanese airbases."

"And the Navy didn't like that idea?" Banning asked.

"The Pearl Harbor admirals didn't like it worth a damn," Pickering replied.

"Admiral Ghormley, on the other hand, thought MacArthur's plan made more sense than anything else he'd heard . . ."

"Excuse me, Sir," Banning interrupted. "What had he heard? What does the Navy want to do?"

"I'm telling you all this more to get it straight in my mind than for any other reason," Pickering said, a little sharply. "Let me do it my way, please, Banning."

"Sorry, Sir," Banning said, genuinely contrite.

"Ghormley, as I was saying, not only thought MacArthur's plan made more sense than the Navy's, but fired off radios saying so. More important than Ghormley, so did General Marshall. And you know that Marshall and MacArthur agree on damned little. The day MacArthur's courier officer—he was really more than a courier; he was one of the assistant G-3s, a really bright lieutenant colonel, who knew what was in his briefcase. Anyway, the day he got to see the Chief of Staff in Washington, Marshall presented MacArthur's plan to Admiral King. Since New Britain was in MacArthur's territory, logically the operation should be under his command. But he threw in a bone for King: King would appoint an Admiral to actually run the operation, under MacArthur."

"And?" Banning asked.

"On June twenty-fifth, King gave the Navy's plan to Marshall. Instead of MacArthur—or an Admiral under MacArthur's orders—attacking New Britain, King wanted a force under Admiral Nimitz—in other words, not under MacArthur—to make an attack in the Solomons and the Santa Cruz islands, as a first step toward taking New Britain. King wanted MacArthur to stage a diversionary attack against Timor, near the Australian Coast."

"And, of course, the Army doesn't like the Navy's idea?" Banning asked rhetorically.

"No," Pickering replied. "And with good reason. They think that the thing to do is hit New Britain first—specifically, the big Jap base at Rabaul. Our land-based bombers could support the attack, and probably take the airbases out long enough so they wouldn't pose much of a problem for us while we're getting ashore. Then, once we had captured the airbases and got them up and running, Army fighter planes could relieve the Navy's carrier-based fighters. And then once we had Rabaul, we could keep the Japs from supplying or reinforcing their other bases within bomber range. They'd be rendered impotent.

"There's no argument over the importance of Rabaul, just when and how to take it. The Navy wants to start with Tulagi and move to Rabaul gradually. The Army agrees that it would be easier to take Tulagi first than it would be to take Rabaul, but argues that as we move northward to Rabaul afterward, all our operations would be under attack from Rabaul-based bombers. And, further, as soon as the Japanese see what our obvious plans are, they would have time to reinforce Rabaul with both ground and air forces."

"So what's going to happen?" Banning asked.

"Theoretically, the matter is still under consideration by the Joint Chiefs of Staff," Pickering said drily.

" 'Theoretically'?" Banning asked.

"King apparently thinks he will prevail when the decision is made by the President. He's ordered Nimitz to prepare to attack in the Solomons, with or without MacArthur's support. Nimitz relayed that order to Ghormley. So the First Marines are either about to start making up the Operations Orders for the invasion of Guadalcanal, or they already have them now."

"How do you know that?"

"Don't ask, Major," Pluto Hon said softly. "You really don't want to know."

"What do you think's going to happen, Captain?" Banning asked.

"Franklin Roosevelt hates MacArthur, and he loves King and the U.S. Navy. He is probably going to rationalize his decision to go with King by deciding that Marshall's agreement with MacArthur on this is based on Marshall hating the Navy even more than he hates MacArthur. Logic will have little to do with it."

"Jesus!" Banning said softly.

"And of course," Pickering added, "Admiral King is certainly going to walk into the Oval Office and dramatically throw the aerial photographs the Air Corps took of this field on Guadalcanal onto the presidential desk. It will be an effective cap to his argument."

"Isn't it?" Banning asked.

"If we had Rabaul, the Japs could not supply an airfield on Guadalcanal," Pickering said. "And it seems to me that if a B-17 could take pictures of the field on Guadalcanal, B-17s could bomb it, too."

Banning looked as if he was going to say something, but had then decided against it. He held his glass up.

"May I have another of these, Sir?"

"Sure, Ed," Pickering said. "You don't have to ask. Help yourself." Then he added: "But in any event, the more information we have about the field on Guadalcanal, and the sooner we get it, the better."

Banning, halfway across the room to the liquor, stopped and turned.

"At this moment, as I am about to help myself to another belt of your splendid booze, and about to sit down to a baron of lamb—Mrs. Cavendish told me about the lamb—at least four Coastwatchers are slopping through some of the nastiest mountain jungle in the world to get us that information, Captain."

Pickering grunted. And then he said, "Christ, I'd like to sit all four of them—plus Lieutenant Howard and Sergeant Koffler—down to dinner with King, MacArthur, and the other prima donnas."

Banning chuckled. "Chunk of fire-blackened wild pig, cold rice, and washed down with a nice canteen cup of Eau de chlorine, '42."

Pickering laughed. "Yeah," he said.

(TWO)
Headquarters, 1st Marine Division
Wellington, New Zealand
0815 Hours 29 June 1942

"Gentlemen," Major General A. A. Vandergrift's aide-de-camp announced, "the commanding general."

The thirty-odd officers in the room, almost all of them field grade, the half dozen senior non-commissioned officers, and the one PFC (there to operate a slide projector), came to attention.

Major General Vandergrift strode into the room.

"Take your seats, gentlemen," he said conversationally, as he stepped behind a rather crude lectern. A bedsheet had been thumbtacked to the wall behind him.

"This won't take long," Vandergrift began when the noise of folding chairs scraping on the floor had died down. "We have a lot to do, and precious little time to do it in, and we can't afford the luxury of wasting any time at all. I have just returned . . ."

He stopped and looked directly at Major Jake Dillon, who was seated in the last row of folding chairs.

"Major, I certainly don't mean to embarrass you, but what are you doing in here?"

"Sir," Brigadier General "Lucky Lew" Harris said, as he got to his feet, "I asked Major Dillon to attend."

Vandergrift's eyebrows rose in surprise.

"Then I suppose we can presume Major Dillon is cleared for TOP SECRET," Vandergrift said, "which is how this meeting is classified, and that he has a Need to Know."

"Yes, Sir," General Harris said.

He suspected, correctly, that the only reason General Vandergrift had not asked Major Dillon, more or less politely, to get his ass out of the room was that Vandergrift paid more than lip service to the military adage that an officer should not be reprimanded or, especially, humiliated, in front of his juniors. Vandergrift was not going to ask his Deputy, before the General and Special Staff officers of the Division, "just what the *hell* did you do that for?"

He probably won't even ask me later, privately. He knows that I know he's displeased. He ordered me to keep Dillon away from him. I wonder if I should tell him about Dillon's orders, which require us to let him stick his goddamned nose in wherever he pleases?

"As I was saying," Vandergrift resumed, "I have just returned from meeting with Admiral Ghormley, COMSOPAC, at his headquarters in Auckland. Admiral McCain, who is COMAIRSOPAC, was also there." (Commander, Air, South Pacific.)

The room was now absolutely quiet.

"Admiral Ghormley has ordered me to prepare the division, less the 7th Marines, which, as most of you know, is on Samoa, for combat in the Solomon Islands on 1 August. For those of you who don't already know, the 1st Marines and our artillery—the 11th Marines—are presently at sea and due to arrive here by the tenth of July. We will be augmented by the 2nd Marines, which will ship out of 'Diego on one July; by the 1st Raider Battalion, now en route; and by 3rd Defense Battalion, which is in Hawaii. When they will ship out of Hawaii isn't known; shipping is in critically short supply. We will probably also have the 1st Parachute Battalion. Because there are no transport aircraft for them, they will function as regular infantry."

There were muted sounds of surprise, audible exhaling and shaking heads. The people in the room were professionals. They knew the division's state of preparedness and its logistical problems. All that added up to the almost unarguable fact that the Division was simply not ready to enter combat in less than two months.

"Son," General Vandergrift addressed the junior Marine present, "would you put map one up on the screen, please?"

The overhead lights went out, and a white beam of light erupted from the slide projector against the bedsheet on the wall, and then a black-and-white map appeared.

"This, obviously, is Guadalcanal," General Vandergrift said, standing in front of the map and pointing to the island that always reminded Lucky Lew Harris of a tapeworm. He had been infested with tapeworms several times during his Marine service in Latin America. They had left an indelible, unpleasant memory with him.

"While our intelligence, putting it kindly, ranges from lousy to nonexistent," General Vandergrift went on, "we have reason to believe the Japanese are building an airfield here, on the Northern side of the island, near Lunga point."

He paused, and then said, "The comment vis-à-vis our intelligence was not intended as a criticism of Colonel Goettge. I meant to say that there is very little intelligence available to anybody over here, including Admiral Ghormley and General MacArthur."

"Not that MacArthur would give it to the Marines if he had it," someone muttered.

Vandergrift's face tightened.

"I will not ask who made that remark," he said, icily furious. "But I will observe that anyone who makes a similar remark in the future does so at his own, considerable peril."

It had recently become rumored throughout the Marine Corps—and Lucky Lew Harris had taken the trouble to check it out and verify it—that MacArthur had not recommended the 4th Marines, who had fought on Bataan and Corregidor, for the Presidential Unit Citation. The citations had been passed out to almost every other unit in the area. MacArthur was reported to have explained his action, or lack of it, by saying, "The Marines have enough decorations as it is."

The crack, Harris thought, *is understandable. And probably true.*

When Harris met General Vandergrift at the airport after his return from meeting Admiral Ghormley, Vandergrift told him that MacArthur was opposed to the Solomon Islands operation for two reasons, tactical and personal; he didn't think it was the way to fight the war, and he wasn't to be in command of it.

Under those circumstances, MacArthur would be reluctant to give the Marines the time of day. And the General knows that. But he certainly had to say what he said. If that had been me, I would have called Motor Mouth to attention and really eaten his ass out.

"Now, across this body of water, about twenty-three miles from the airfield we believe they are building near Lunga point," Vandergrift went on, pointing again, "we find these tiny islands off Florida Island, Tulagi and Gavutu. We *know* the Japanese have built a seaplane base on Tulagi, and they have some other installations in the area. The seaplanes could raise hell with our landing craft, so we have to take Tulagi and Gavutu first, by which I mean several hours before we land on Guadalcanal itself, in the Lunga point area.

"A few more points about my general thinking. I think we should divide the division into two regimental combat teams—there would be about 4500 men in each—for the main landing on Guadalcanal. We will use the Raiders and the Paratroops, probably reinforced by one of the battalions of the 5th Marines, for the Tulagi-Gavutu landings, and the RCTs for the landing on Guadalcanal itself.

"What I'm going to do now is turn this over to General Harris and the G-3, and for the next hour—and no more than that—I want you to discuss the major problems as you see them. And then I want you to get to work. As I said before, we have a lot to do, and damned little time to do it in."

He turned from the lectern. Someone called, "Atten-hut!" and everyone came to attention. Vandergrift marched out of the room. General Harris walked to the lectern.

"Take your seats," he ordered. "Try turning the lights on to see if we can still see the map."

(THREE)
**The Prince of Wales Hotel
Melbourne, Victoria, Australia
0930 Hours 29 June 1942**

Major Edward Banning had called Sergeant John Marston Moore, USMCR, at half past six, and somewhat brusquely ordered him to have a quick breakfast, settle his hotel bill, and be waiting for him in the lobby with his gear when he came to pick him up.

"Aye, aye, Sir."

Banning had hung up without a further word.

By 0715 Sergeant Moore had complied with his orders, by dressing hurriedly, gulping down a breakfast identified on the menu as "scrambled eggs with bangers," and paying for his hotel room with a twenty-dollar bill. The cashier looked with great suspicion at that, but he reluctantly accepted it.

When Major Banning did not show up by 0800, Moore checked with the desk to make sure there had been no calls or messages for him. He did so again at 0830, again at 0900, and was about to check again when he saw the Marine officer walking quickly across the sidewalk to the revolving glass door of the hotel. There was little doubt in his mind that it was his new commanding officer, so he stood up, almost in the formal position of Attention.

Each man examined the other carefully. Moore would have been flattered to know that Banning was pleased with what he saw, a tall, good-looking, physically fit kid with intelligent eyes, who really didn't look as if he was fresh from boot camp at Parris Island.

And Moore saw a tall, stocky, tanned man who met his expectation of what a Marine field grade officer should look like. But as a recent graduate of Parris Island, where the only major he had ever seen was on the reviewing stand at a parade, this was not a comforting appreciation. He was more than a little in awe, something approaching fear, of Major Banning.

"Sergeant Moore?" Banning asked.

"Yes, Sir."

Banning offered his hand. There was a momentary test of grip-strength, which Banning, surprising neither of them, won. Banning was further pleased that when he looked intently into Moore's eyes, the kid didn't blink.

"You've had breakfast? Got your bill paid?"

"Yes, Sir."

"Grab your gear, then. I'm parked illegally."

He marched out of the hotel lobby. Moore grabbed his gear and scurried after him.

Banning led him to a Studebaker parked in a No HALTING zone. Marine insignia were on the hood and doors. Banning held open the back door and gestured for Moore to put his gear in the back seat. When he had done so, Banning slammed the door, pointed to the front seat, and said, "Get in."

"Yes, Sir."

Banning got behind the wheel, punched the ignition button, and then looked at Moore.

"Sorry to be late, Sergeant. Captain Pickering had an appointment with General MacArthur at 8:30 and his car wouldn't start. So I had to drive him over there before I came for you."

"Yes, Sir."

Banning had expected to see more of a reaction to the words "General MacArthur" than he got.

Either he's stupid, which I doubt. Or he didn't hear me, which is unlikely. Or he is simply unable to comprehend what I said. It's like being told that someone you know has just had lunch with Saint Peter, if not God himself.

Moore did indeed hear what Banning said. He had also noticed that Banning was wearing the Purple Heart ribbon, making him the second man he'd met (Lieutenant "Killer" McCoy was the first) who had actually seen combat in this war. He supposed that Banning had been wounded in the Philippines, which, aside from Wake Island, was the only place the Marines had seen ground combat so far. But if that was so, he wondered, how had Banning escaped when the Philippines fell?

It was at once possible and incredible to consider that the man driving him around in a Studebaker had actually escaped from Corregidor.

He had not made a response because he could think of none to make.

Banning drove to a hill outside Melbourne overlooking Port Philip Bay and pulled the Studebaker off the road.

"There goes your plane," Major Banning said, pointing. Moore followed the finger and saw a Navy Martin PBM-3R Mariner moving across the blue waters of the bay.

I've ridden on a plane like that, he thought, and then, *Major Banning said, "your plane," so that must be the very plane, headed back for Hawaii.*

The Mariner rose into the air, and then with a tremendous splash fell back into the water. It repeated this twice more before it rose finally into the air. Then it banked, and passed right over them.

Banning offered Moore a cigarette, and then held his Ronson out to light it for him.

"I don't think anyone has to tell you that you're now on the perimeter of the intelligence business, Moore, do they? I mean, you're a bright young man, you *did* think there was *something* a little odd about the way they took you out of Parris Island and sent you here? *Flew* you here, ahead of some pretty senior officers?"

"Yes, Sir."

"And would it be a reasonable statement that you don't know diddly-shit about the Intelligence business? Or for that matter, about the Marine Corps?"

"Yes, Sir."

"You have seen the spy movies, of course, where the sneaky little Jap with the buckteeth and the thick glasses has the plans for the latest aircraft carrier in his briefcase? And is foiled at the last moment by Commander Don Winslow of the U.S. Coast Guard?"

Moore chuckled. "Yes, Sir."

"Commander Winslow of the Coast Guard" was a popular children's radio program.

"Well, for openers, you couldn't get the plans for an aircraft carrier in a boxcar, much less a briefcase. And then, in the real world, I have come to know a number of Japanese Intelligence types who are as large as I am, have perfect teeth and eyesight, and are probably a lot smarter than I am. And I know from personal experience that our Intelligence, and Counterintelligence, fucks up by the numbers far more often than it works at all."

Moore looked at him, expecting Banning to be smiling. He was not.

"For example," Banning said, "all that effort by all those people to get you over here as soon as humanly possible was a waste of time, money, and airspace. I can't use you." He waited for a moment until that announcement had time to sink in, and then added, "Comment?"

Oh, shit! What happens to me now?

"I don't know what to say, Sir."

"But finding you and sending you here the way they did was sound, a good idea, and well carried out."

"Sir?" Moore asked, wholly confused.

"What I'm doing, what Special Detachment 14 is doing, in other words, is very important. Importance is normally judged by how many American lives can be saved, or how many of the enemy can be killed, by what you're doing. Are you still with me?"

"You're saying, Sir, in effect, 'damn the expense'?"

"Just about. When something important is at stake, you can't worry about what it costs, or anything else. So here you are, and I can't use you."

"Sir, what happens to me now?"

"I wondered when you were going to get around to asking that," Banning said. "One of two things: We send you down to the First Division, the initial elements of which just arrived in New Zealand. Your Japanese language skills can be put to good use there."

"Yes, Sir."

"Or, we keep you here," Banning said.

"Sir, I thought you said you don't need me."

"You might be of value working for Captain Pickering, or more precisely, for an officer who works for Captain Pickering."

"May I ask doing what, Sir?"

"It has to do with intelligence, and it has to do with your knowledge of Japanese, and the Japanese culture."

"Sir, I don't understand."

"I said before, if you remember, that importance is usually judged by how many American lives can be saved, or how many of the enemy can be killed. Do you remember that?"

"Yes, Sir."

"What you would be involved in could literally affect the outcome of the war," Banning said evenly.

"I still don't understand, Sir."

"No, you don't. And I will not entertain any questions about what that is."

"Sir, I don't really . . ."

"That's the whole idea, Moore. You're not supposed to know what's going on. You would be expected to do what you were told, and not only not ask questions, but not try to guess. It's that important."

"Wow!"

"No romance. Nobody in a trench coat, but—and I tell you this because it would be self-evident—real world intelligence at the highest level. There would be a high degree of risk to you."

"May I ask how, Sir?"

"If I, or anyone else, ever learned that you had run off at the mouth about any aspect of this operation, you'll be shot. There would be no court-martial, nothing like that. The burden of proof of innocence would be on you. You would be shot out of hand, and your family would get a telegram from the Secretary of the Navy expressing his deep regret that you had been lost at sea. Something like that."

Moore, his eyes wide, looked at Banning for confirmation that he had correctly heard what Banning had just said.

"Yes," Banning said, reading Moore's mind. "I'm serious. Deadly serious, pun intended."

"Sir, when they took me out of Parris Island, they—Captain Sessions—led me to believe that I could ultimately get a commission."

"Maybe you could in the 1st Division," Banning said. "But no way in the billet I'm talking about."

Moore exhaled audibly.

"You want some time to think this over?" Banning said.

If I was this kid, I would think, "Fuck you, Major. Send me to the 1st Marine Division and give me that gold bar I was promised."

"No, Sir," Moore said. "If you think I could do what you want me to do, I'll try. I think I can keep my mouth shut."

"So does Captain Pickering," Banning said. "Don't disappoint him. He told me that you remind him of his son, who's a Marine officer. He wouldn't like to have you shot. But he would, and I'd probably have to do it."

"I understand, Sir."

"The mission of Special Detachment 14 is classified TOP SECRET," Banning said. "What we do is support the Australian Navy's Coastwatcher Operation. What they do is have people on Japanese-occupied islands. What *they* do is furnish intelligence information, generally about Japanese air and sea activity, but also about Japanese troop installations, and that sort of thing."

"Am I going to be working with the Coastwatchers, Sir?"

"No. I don't need you. I need radio operators and radio technicians. Who are parachutists. You're none of those things. But having you assigned to Special Detachment 14 will be what is known as a good cover assignment. People who think you're already assigned to a highly classified activity won't be prone to ask questions, or even wonder, about what you're really doing."

"I think I understand, Sir."

"We're in Townesville, Queensland, up North. You will stay here, ostensibly to function as our rear area. Meet courier planes, receive and transship equipment, that sort of thing."

"Yes, Sir."

"There is a headquarters company at Supreme Headquarters, but if we put you in there, questions will obviously be asked as to what exactly you would be doing. So, for the time being, you will live at The Elms."

"Yes, Sir."

"You're not going to ask what 'The Elms' is?"

Moore looked at Banning and smiled, "Sir, you just told me not to ask questions."

Banning chuckled.

"OK, Sergeant, one point for you. 'The Elms' is an estate Captain Pickering has leased, not far from here. He has more money than God, and he was not prepared to share the Spartan quarters provided for Navy captains with an Army colonel who snores. It's equipped with a housekeeper and some other servants, and it's enormous. You'll have no problems making yourself invisible there."

"My God!" Moore said.

"And living there will get you out of the clutches of the headquarters company commander, who would, I'm sure, love to have a Marine sergeant for his guard details. MacArthur is about to move his headquarters to Brisbane—that move is classified SECRET, by the way—so other arrangements will have to made for you when that happens."

"Yes, Sir."

"The officer you will be working for is Lieutenant Hon. He's in the Army Signal Corps and is a cryptographic-classified documents officer at Supreme Headquarters, South West Pacific. He also has other duties he performs for Captain Pickering. You spoke with him on the telephone last night."

"He speaks perfect Japanese," Moore thought aloud.

Banning chuckled again. "He said the same thing about you, which is why you're not on your way to the First Marine Division."

Banning turned the ignition key and started the engine, and then turned and looked at Moore.

"One question, Moore."

"Yes, Sir?"

"Do you believe me when I say we'll have you shot if you breach security? Or do you think this is some sort of bullshit line I'm handing you?"

Moore met Banning's eyes.

"I believe you, Sir."

"Good," Banning said.

He put the gearshift in reverse and turned the Studebaker around.

(FOUR)
Headquarters, 1st Marine Division
Wellington, New Zealand
1605 Hours 29 June 1942

"General," Harris's sergeant said, putting his head in Harris's office door, "Major Dillon is here and wants to know if you can see him for a minute."

I want to see that sonofabitch about as much as I want to break both my legs.

"Ask him to come in, please, Sergeant," Harris said.

Major Dillon, to Harris's surprise, was wearing utilities. Both the utilities and his boots were muddy.

It actually looks like the sonofabitch has been out in the boondocks.

"Hello, Dillon," Harris asked. "What can I do for you?"

"Good morning, Sir," Dillon said, assuming the position of Parade Rest.

"Pull up a chair," Harris said. "But don't get too comfortable. I've got people coming to see me right about now."

Jake Dillon was no fool. He had not been a fool when he was a staff sergeant in Shanghai, and he'd learned a good deal more about people during his time in Hollywood. He was fully aware that General Harris didn't like him personally and regarded his official function as that of a parasite on the body of the First Marine Division specifically and the Corps generally.

"May I get right to the point, Sir?" Dillon asked.

"You'd better," Harris said, tempering it with a faint smile.

"Sir, I've got a pretty good friend in MacArthur's headquarters."

"Why doesn't that surprise me, Major Dillon?" Harris said and immediately regretted it. He saw in Dillon's eyes the hurt the sarcasm had caused.

"Sir, I think he could be helpful with regard to intelligence," Dillon went on.

"He's an intelligence officer?" Harris asked, wondering if Dillon really didn't know that intelligence officers pass out information outside their own headquarters only when specifically ordered to do so, and then did so reluctantly.

"No, Sir. He's . . . Frank Knox sent him over to keep an eye on MacArthur for him."

"You *are* referring to *Secretary of the Navy* Frank Knox and *General* MacArthur?" Harris asked. Dillon nodded, completely oblivious to the oblique reprimand. "And how do you know this?"

"It was all over Washington, General," Dillon said confidently.

This sonofabitch probably was privy to all the high level gossip in Washington. I wouldn't really be surprised if he calls the Secretary of the Navy by his first name.

"Who are we talking about, Dillon?"

"Fleming Pickering, General. He's a Navy Captain. He owns Pacific & Far East Shipping."

"And how do you know Captain Pickering?" Harris asked.

"I used to shoot skeet with him in California," Dillon said. "He's a big skeet shooter. I met him through Bob Stack."

I am about to lose my temper. How dare this sonofabitch waste my time like this?

"The actor, you mean?" Harris asked, evenly.

"Yes, Sir. We had a team for a couple of years, me, Stack, Clark Gable, Howard Hawks—the director—and Pickering."

"Major," Harris said, his voice low and icy, "are you actually suggesting to me that because a Navy captain shot skeet with you and some other Hollywood types before the war, he would make intelligence available to you that we could not get through official channels?''

''No, Sir. Not because of the skeet. He was a Marine. He was a corporal in War One. He and Doc McInerney and Jack Stecker were buddies at Belleau Wood. He's got the Silver Star and the Croix de Guerre. He was wounded a couple of times, too.''

''By 'Doc McInerney,' Major, I gather you are referring to *General* McInerney?''

''Yes, Sir,'' Dillon said. ''And Captain Pickering's boy is in the Corps. The last I heard he was a second lieutenant learning to fly Wildcats at Pensacola.''

I'll be goddamned. This guy Pickering might be damned useful.

''Sergeant!'' Harris raised his voice. His sergeant quickly appeared at his door. ''Send for Major Stecker, 2nd Battalion, 5th. Get him in here right away. And then pass the word to Colonel Goettge that I may want to see him within the next half hour.''

''Aye, aye, Sir.''

X

(ONE)
The Elms
Dandenong, Victoria, Australia
1430 Hours 1 July 1942

When Mrs. Cavendish put her head in the library and told him that there was a telephone call for him, Sergeant John Marston Moore, USMCR, was sitting at a typewriter set up on a heavy library table. He was writing to his beloved, and he was having difficulty. It was a love letter, of course, and he was highly motivated to write it, but neither his passionate intentions, nor the typewriter, nor the privacy of being alone in the house (except for the servants) seemed to help.

There didn't seem to be a hell of a lot one could say on the subject, beyond the obvious, especially for someone who had absolutely no flair for the well-turned romantic phrase. He couldn't even call to mind much of the established literature on the subject, from which he would have eagerly and shamelessly plagiarized.

He got as far as "How do I love thee, let me count the ways—" and then his mind went blank. A phrase—"Thus have I had thee" from a poem he thought was called "Cynara" by Ernest Dowson—kept coming into his mind. But he wasn't sure that was the title, that Ernest Dowson had actually written it; and not only couldn't he remember what came after "Thus have I had thee," but those words seemed to paint an erotic picture, in the biblical sense ... as in "Thus have I had thee, standing up against the refrigerator in the apartment on Rittenhouse Square." And the last thing in the world he wanted to do was let Barbara think that all he was interested in was the physical side of their relationship.

That was fine, marvelous, splendid, of course, but his love for her was more than that. He loved her because ... He knew the one thing he could not write to her about was what he was doing now in Australia. Even if he could, he still didn't have all that squared away in his mind. So much had happened to him so quickly, so much that was so extraordinary, and so much he could only guess at, that his confusion was certainly understandable.

Major Banning had driven him from the hill overlooking Port Philip Bay to The Elms. And Lieutenant Hon had been waiting for them there, sitting on the wide veranda of the mansion drinking a beer.

It was the most cordial greeting Moore had ever received from an officer.

"I'm very glad to meet you, Sergeant," he said in Japanese, extending his hand before Moore could even begin to salute. "I owe you a big one."

He looked over Moore's shoulder at Major Banning and explained his last remark: "The Captain called early this morning and said, 'Pluto, I've been thinking. Wouldn't it be more convenient if you moved into The Elms with the Sergeant? Would you mind?'"

Banning laughed.

"I told him that no sacrifice for the war effort, like moving into The Elms, was too much to ask of me."

"That was very noble of you, Pluto," Banning said, in Japanese.

"And I owe it all to you, Sergeant. So welcome, welcome!"

"Thank you, Sir."

Soon after that, a motherly gray-haired woman came onto the veranda, and was introduced as Mrs. Cavendish, the housekeeper.

"Let me show you where you'll be staying, Sergeant, and then we'll serve lunch," she said.

Moore expected that he would be given a servant's room, probably on the third floor of the mansion. But he was taken instead to a large and airy room on the second floor complete with an enormous tiled bath.

"Get yourself settled," she said. "If you have any soiled clothing, or something that needs pressing, just leave it on the bed."

A luncheon of roast pork, green beans, applesauce, coffee, and apple pie was served in the dining room. The tableware was silver, the plates were fine china, the napkins and tablecloth linen, and the glassware that elegantly cradled Moore's beer was Czechoslovakian crystal.

After lunch, they drove into Melbourne to the Menzies Hotel. Lieutenant Hon told Moore to drive: "That's the best way to learn the route. If somebody else is driving, your mind goes to sleep."

At the Menzies, Hon told him to park in an area marked, RESERVED FOR GENERAL STAFF OFFICIAL VEHICLES.

"Our boss, Moore, ranks right under the Emperor in the pecking order around here. And this is his car."

"Yes, Sir."

At the elevator bank, where Banning left them, Moore saw that one elevator bore a sign, RESERVED FOR GENERAL MACARTHUR. He hoped that he would get a chance to see him.

That would be something to write and tell Barbara about. Oh, shit! I can't do that, either.

They rode the elevator to the basement, and then walked past an OFF LIMITS sign down a low, brick-lined corridor to a steel door guarded by two soldiers armed with Thompson submachine guns.

"This the new man, Lieutenant?" one of the soldiers asked.

"Sergeant Moore, Sergeant Skelly," Lieutenant Hon replied.

"Welcome to the dungeon, Moore," Sergeant Skelly said. "The way this works is that you have to show your dog tags to the guard on duty and then sign the register. He'll check your signature against the one on file, and let you in. If you take anything TOP SECRET out of here, it has to be logged out, and you have to be armed, and you have to carry it in a handcuff briefcase."

"A what?"

Hon leaned behind Sergeant Skelly's desk and picked up a leather briefcase from a stack of them. Attached to the handle was a foot-long length of stainless steel cable welded to half of a pair of handcuffs.

"There's a couple of .45s in our safe," Hon explained.

"You also have to log out CONFIDENTIAL and SECRET," Sergeant Skelly went on, "but you don't need the pistol or the briefcase."

"OK," Moore said.

Hon bent over the register and signed his name, then showed Moore where he was to sign. Sergeant Skelly pushed a 3 × 5 inch card across the small desk to Moore.

"Sign it," he said. "This is the one we keep on file."

Moore signed it.

Sergeant Skelly then went to the steel door and unlocked it with a large key.

"Come by the NCO Club, Moore, and I'll buy you a beer."

"Thank you," Moore said.

When the door had closed behind them, Lieutenant Hon said, "I don't think that would be a very good idea, Moore."

"Yes, Sir."

"I won't tell you to be a teetotal, although that might be a good idea. And I know it would be a good idea if you let Skelly think you are."

"Yes, Sir."

Hon led him to another steel-doored room, the key to which he had on a cord around his neck. Inside was a small room furnished with a small table and two filing cabinets with combination locks.

"Captain Pickering has the only other key to this room and is the only other person to know the combinations," Hon said. "You won't take anything out of here that I don't give you. Understood?"

"Yes, Sir."

"Turn your back, please, while I open this," Hon said, matter-of-factly.

Moore complied.

"OK, you can turn around," Hon said after a moment. "Sit down."

Moore sat down at the small table.

Hon handed him two sheets of paper, both stamped top and bottom, TOP SECRET. They were in Japanese calligraphs.

"We're going to run a little experiment," Hon said. "First, you are going to translate these. Then I am going to give you somebody else's translations. I want to see if they're different, and if they are, whether you think your translation is more accurate than the other guy's. Clear?"

"Yes, Sir. I think so."

"How long do you think it will take you?"

Moore glanced at the calligraphs.

"Ten, fifteen minutes, Sir."

"Can you type?"

"Yes, Sir."

"Well, I'll go see about scrounging a typewriter. For the time being, do these in pencil."

"Yes, Sir."

Hon took a lined pad and a Planter's peanuts can full of pencils from the top of one of the filing cabinets and put them on the table. Then, without a word, he walked out of the room. The door closed and Moore heard the key turning in the lock. He was locked in.

He picked up a pencil and started to read the calligraphs. He became aware of a strange feeling of foreboding and decided it was because he didn't like being locked behind a steel door with no way that he could see to get out.

He read both documents quickly, to get a sense of them, and then again more carefully.

They were obviously Japanese Army radio messages. The first was from the 14th Army in the Philippines to Imperial Japanese Army Headquarters in Tokyo. It was signed HOMMA. The second message was a reply to the first. It was signed, IN THE NAME OF HIS IMPERIAL MAJESTY.

He began to write his translation. It was hardly, he thought, a matter of world-shaking importance. It dealt with captured American weapons, ammunition, and food supplies. Not surprisingly, there was a comment to the effect that most weapons of all descriptions had been destroyed before the American surrender. Another stated that there was a large stock of captured ammunition, mostly for large caliber artillery, but that it was in bad shape, and that the possibility had to be considered that it had been . . . he had to search for the right, decorous words in English, for what popped into his mind was "fucked up"—*tampered with? rendered useless? sabotaged?*—by the Americans.

There was another comment that captured American food supplies were scarce, in bad shape, and inadequate for the feeding of prisoners.

The reply from Imperial Japanese Army Headquarters was brief, and far more formal. It directed General Homma to . . . again he had to search for the right words—to *inspect and rehabilitate? evaluate and repair? inspect and salvage?*—the captured artillery ammunition as well as he could using—*facilities? assets? capabilities?*—available to him. It reminded General Homma that shipping, of course, had to be allocated on the priorities of war. And finally, somewhat insultingly, Moore thought, it reminded Homma of the—*duty? obligations? price to be paid? sacrifices expected?*—of soldiers under the Code of Bushido.

Finally, he was finished. He looked at what he had written and heard his mother's voice in his ear, "Johnny, I can't understand how you can do that calligraphy so beautifully, but hen scratch when you write something in English."

He hoped that Lieutenant Hon would have no trouble reading his handwriting and was considering copying what he had written more neatly, when he heard the key in the lock of the steel door. It creaked open—*dungeon-like,* Moore thought—and Hon came back into the room. Moore started to get up.

"Keep your seat, nobody can see us in here," Hon said, and then asked, "Finished?"

Moore handed him the sheets of lined paper.

Hon read them carefully, then opened one of the filing cabinets again and handed Moore two more sheets of paper with TOP SECRET stamped on them.

They were someone else's translations of the two messages. Moore read them, wondering how different they would be from the translation he had made. There were minor differences of interpretation, but nothing significant. Moore felt a sense of satisfaction; he had obviously done as well as whoever had made the other translation.

"OK. Now tell me what the messages mean," Hon said.

"Sir?"

"Tell me what they mean," Hon repeated.

Moore told him and could tell by the look on Lieutenant Hon's face that he was disappointed.

"Look beneath the surface, beneath the obvious," Hon said.

"Sir, I don't quite understand."

"Forget you're a sergeant, forget that you're an American. Think like a Japanese. Think like General Homma."

How the hell am I supposed to do that?

When there was no response after a moment, Hon said, "OK. Try this. What, if anything, did you notice that was unusual, in any way, in either message?"

Jesus Christ, what is this, Twenty Questions?

He went over the messages in his mind, then picked up the original messages in Japanese and read them again.

"Sir, I thought it was unusual . . . I mean, Homma is a general. Why the reminder about the Code of Bushido?"

"Good!" Hon said, and made a "keep going" gesture with his hands.

Off the top of his head, Moore said, "If I was General Homma, I'd be a little pissed—*insulted* that they had given me the lecture."

"Good! Good!" Hon said. "Why?"

"Because it was discourteous. Not maybe the way we would look at it, but to a Japanese . . ."

"OK. Accepting it as a given that the IJAGS . . ."

Hon pronounced this "Eye-Jag-Ess," saw confusion cloud Moore's eyes, and translated:

"—the Imperial Japanese Army General Staff—did insult General Homma by discourteously reminding him about Bushido. He is a General officer who has to be presumed to know all about Bushido." Hon now switched to Japanese: "Why would they do this? In what context? Reply in Japanese."

Beats the shit out of me, Moore thought and dropped his eyes again to the calligraphs.

"The context is in . . ." he said.

"In Japanese," Hon interrupted him.

". . . reference to a shortage of shipping," Moore finished, in Japanese.

"Is it?"

"Homma's message to—What did you say, 'Eye-Jag-Ess'?—said that the food he captured from us was inadequate to feed the prisoners," Moore said. He had in his sudden excitement switched back to English. Hon did not correct him.

"And?"

"IJAGS's reply was that there was a shortage of shipping, and then reminded Homma of the Code of Bushido."

"Right. And how, if you know, does the Code of Bushido regard warriors who surrender?"

"It's shameful," Moore said. "Disgraceful. A failure of duty. More than that, there's a religious connotation. Since the Emperor is God, it's a great sin."

"Meaning what, in this context?"

Moore thought that over, and horrified, blurted, "Jesus, meaning, 'fuck the prisoners, they're beneath contempt, let them starve'?"

"That's how I read it," Hon said. "You did notice that there was just a hint of sensitivity to Western concepts of how prisoners should be treated—the Geneva Convention, so to speak—the reference to the shortage of shipping, which IJAGS uses to rationalize not shipping food?"

"My God!"

"Why are you surprised?" Hon asked. "You grew up there."

Moore's mind was now racing.

"I still can't accept this," he said. "Jesus Christ, can't we complain to the International Red Cross or somebody? Maybe they'd arrange to let us send food."

"We cannot complain to anybody," Hon said.

"Why not?"

"We cannot complain to anybody," Hon repeated. "And stop that line of inquiry."

"We have their goddamn messages," Moore plunged on. "Why the hell not?"

Hon held up both hands, palms out, to shut Moore up.

"In about ten seconds, that will occur to you. And in ten seconds, Major Banning's warning to you will move from the realm of the hypothetical to cold, cruel reality."

Moore looked at him, confusion all over his face. And then, in five seconds, not ten, he understood.

"We've broken their code, haven't we? That was a coded message, and we intercepted it and decoded it, right?"

"Since I didn't hear the question, Sergeant Moore—if I had, I would have to inform Major Banning—I obviously can't answer it."

"Jesus!" Moore exhaled.

"Apropos of nothing whatever, the correct phraseology is 'encrypted' and 'decrypted,'" Hon said. "The root word is 'crypt,' variously defined as 'burial'; 'catacomb'; 'sepulcher'; 'tomb'; and 'vault.'"

"And they don't know we can do that, do they?" Moore asked, more rhetorically than anything else.

"I hope you're about to get your mouth under control, Sergeant Moore," Hon said, "because I feel my memory is returning."

Moore exhaled audibly.

"Jesus Christ!" he said.

"Yeah," Hon said. "OK, Sergeant, we will now proceed to Lesson Two in Pluto Hon's Berlitz in the Basement School of Languages. Just one more thing, apropos again of nothing whatever. There is a security classification called TOP SECRET-MAGIC. There are four people in this headquarters with access to TOP SECRET-MAGIC material: General MacArthur, his G-2, Colonel Charles A. Willoughby, Captain Fleming Pickering, and me. You will not, repeat, not have access to TOP SECRET-MAGIC. I mention it only because if anyone other than the people I just mentioned ever even mentions MAGIC to you, you will instantly tell me or Captain Pickering. Clear?"

What I just read is MAGIC. *There's no question about that.*

"Yes, Sir."

Hon met his eyes for a moment, and then nodded.

"Lesson Two deals with administrative procedures," Hon said. "If you look under the table, you will find a wastebasket. In the wastebasket is a paper bag. The bag is stamped TOP SECRET-BURN in large letters. It is intended for TOP SECRET material that is to be burned. TOP SECRET material includes this lined pad you have been writing on. Not just the pages you wrote on, but the whole pad, because your pencil made impressions on pages underneath the top one. Clear?"

"Yes, Sir."

"I'm about to give you a key to the dungeon and the combination to one of the file drawers. You will memorize the combination. When you come to work here—which will be at any hour something comes in—if I'm not here, you will find that material in your drawer. You will make your translation—one copy only—and when you leave, you will put that in your drawer with the original material and make sure it is locked. Then you will take your notes, if you made any, or if you have written on a pad, anything at all, put them in the burn bag, and, accompanied by one of the guards, take it to an incinerator and burn it. You'll find a supply of burn bags in your drawer. Clear?"

"Yes, Sir."

"You will not, repeat not, burn anything that I give you."

"Yes, Sir."

"You will not take anything from this room, except burn bag material in a burn bag, unless specifically directed to do so by either Captain Pickering or myself."

"Yes, Sir."

"The people around here have been told that you are a cryptographic clerk-typist. If anyone, *anyone,* ever asks you what you're really doing in here, you will tell me instantly. If I'm not available, find Captain Pickering and tell him."

"Yes, Sir."

"To my considerable surprise, when I went to scrounge a typewriter, I managed to get two. I carried one down here. When you are doing MAGIC . . . Shit!" Hon stopped abruptly, and then continued, "When you use the typewriter to do translations for me, you will use a ribbon reserved for that purpose and kept in your file drawer. When that wears out, you will dispose of it via the burn bag. But you will not leave the ribbon in the typewriter when you leave the room . . . even to take a leak. Clear?"

"Yes, Sir."

Lieutenant Hon handed him a large key.

"Wear this on your dog tag chain," he said. "And for Christ's sake, don't lose it."

"No, Sir."

"OK. Go get the typewriter outside, and the box of ribbons, and bring them in here. Then we'll show you the incinerator, and the procedure to burn things. And finally, we'll get the other typewriter, before the supply officer changes his mind, and lock it in the car."

The phone was ringing.

Moore left his—mostly failed—love letter and walked across the library to the telephone.

"Sergeant Moore, Sir."

"Major Banning, Sergeant. I understand you have the car out there?"

"Yes, Sir."

"Is there any reason you could not drive to the airport and pick up some people, and then run past the Menzies and pick me up?"

"No, Sir."

"There'll be two Marine officers waiting for you. A Colonel Goettge and a Major Dillon. Can you leave right now?"

"As soon as I hang up, Sir."

"I'll be waiting in front," Banning said and hung up.

Moore went back to the typewriter, pulled his letter to his beloved from it, read it with very little satisfaction, and started to tear it up. Then he changed his mind.

He laid the letter on the table, took a pen, and wrote, "Duty calls. I have to run. I love you more than life itself."

He addressed an envelope, wrote "free" where a stamp would normally be placed, stuffed the letter in it, and put it in his pocket. There was an Army Post Office Box at the airfield. He would mail the letter to Barbara first and then go pick up the officers.

As he drove the Studebaker to the airport, he thought that "I love you more than life itself" was a pretty well-turned phrase and was sort of pleased that Major Banning's call had rescued him from more time at the typewriter.

(TWO)
Supreme Headquarters, Southwest Pacific
Hotel Menzies
Melbourne, Victoria, Australia
1600 Hours 1 July 1942

When Lieutenant Pluto Hon heard the key turning in the steel door, he quickly covered what he was working on with its Top Secret cover sheet and stood up. There were only three people with a key to the room, and he had told Sergeant John Marston Moore to stay at The Elms until he sent for him. Ergo, whoever was unlocking the door had to be Captain Fleming Pickering, USNR.

"How are you, Pluto?" Pickering greeted him with a smile. "What can I do for you?"

"Sir, I just asked your clerk to let me know when you had a free minute. You didn't have to come down here."

"So she said," Pickering said. "What's up?"

"Well, first, did Major Banning get to you?"

"About tonight?"

"Yes, Sir."

"Yes, he did. And you're invited, too, of course. Is that what you wanted to ask?"

"No, Sir," Hon said, and then with obvious reluctance he plunged ahead: "Sir, I'm sorry I let my mouth run away from me and asked you for Sergeant Moore."

"Oh? How come?"

"Sir, and it's obviously my fault, it's already gotten out of hand."

"How?" Pickering asked evenly. Hon felt the normal warmth leave Pickering's eyes.

"Sir, he's already guessed that what I gave him to analyze was an intercept."

"Guessed?"

"I suppose 'deduced' would be a better word."

"How was his analysis?" Pickering asked.

Hon hesitated.

"Well?" Pickering asked, impatiently.

"Sir, what popped into my mind sounds flippant. And I realize this is not the place to sound flippant."

"What popped into your mind?"

" 'The true test of a man's intelligence is how much he agrees with you,' " Pluto quoted. "I gave him the MAGIC intercept from Homma to IJAGS, and the reply about prisoner rations in the Philippines."

"Refresh my mind?"

"The one Pearl Harbor thought was a reprimand to Homma, and wondered what about."

"And the one you thought meant, 'prisoners have no right to eat'?"

"Yes, Sir."

"And he agreed with you?"

"Yes, Sir. I had to prompt him a little. But just a little. I didn't give him any . . ."

"I'm sure you didn't," Pickering said. "And he went from that to figure out where it came from?"

"Yes, Sir. I probably handled that badly. I'm very sorry, Sir. I decided I had better tell you."

"Yeah, sure," Pickering said. He reached inside his uniform jacket and came out with a cigar case. He took a long time removing a narrow, black cigar; he then carefully trimmed it with a pocket knife and lit it with a wooden match.

Finally, he exhaled through pursed lips, examined the coal at the end, and said, "We both—me especially—should have seen that coming. Now that I really think about it, it was inevitable. OK. So where does that leave us? Worst possible scenario: What's the greatest damage?"

Pickering paused, not long enough for Pluto to respond, and then answered his own question. "We have added one more man to the loop. I mean the cryptographers at Pearl and here. They know about the existence of MAGIC. So now Moore does too. The only difference between him and them is that he is now analyzing instead of decrypting. They don't have to know that. We won't tell Pearl Harbor . . . we won't volunteer the information, in other words. If we did they would shit a brick. If they find out, I'll take the heat. I'll tell them I ordered you to bring him in on this. I'll say I did so because it occurred to me that if you were unavailable, broke your leg or something, I would need an analyst. That's true, come to think of it."

"Yes, Sir," Pluto said uneasily.

"In for a penny, Pluto, in for a pound," Pickering said. "I'll tell Banning what *I've* done, and tell him to bring Moore in on anything he thinks Moore should know. As far as Moore is concerned, just let things go as they are. As far as you're concerned," he paused and smiled, "since we now have proof positive that he's highly intelligent, just put him to work. To coin a phrase, two minds are better than one."

"Yes, Sir," Hon said.

(THREE)
The Elms
Dandenong, Victoria, Australia
1805 Hours 1 July 1942

Sergeant John Marston Moore helped Mr. Cavendish carry Colonel Goettge's and Major Dillon's luggage to their rooms, and then went to his. Obviously, a sergeant was out of place with visiting brass hats, even under the strange circumstances he was now in.

When I get hungry, he decided, *I'll go down the back stairs and see what there is to eat in the refrigerator.*

He had just taken his shoes off and settled himself on the bed when there was a knock at the door.

They probably want me to drive somebody somewhere—maybe go get Captain Pickering or Lieutenant Hon—or maybe serve drinks.

It was Major Banning.

"Yes, Sir?"

"Come with me," Banning said. "I want to show you something. Save your questions until I tell you."

"Aye, aye, Sir. Give me a moment to get my shoes on."

He followed Banning down the back stairs to the kitchen, and then to a small room off the kitchen he had not known existed.

It was not much larger than a closet, and it held a small table with a lamp on it and a simple cushioned chair. Banning put his finger over his lips, ordering silence, and then pointed to foot-square ducts in the walls. Moore realized first that the other end of one of the ducts opened into the library, and then he remembered seeing it when he had been browsing among the books. It had been hardly visible among the books. He remembered that there was another duct in the dining room.

Banning touched his ear and pointed toward the duct opening on the library. Moore realized that he could hear, faintly, but clearly, Major Dillon talking to Colonel Goettge about Captain Pickering's estate in San Francisco. Obviously, anything said in the library and dining room could be heard in the small room.

Banning signaled that they should leave the room, and when they had done so, he closed the door after them. He went to a coffee pot, helped himself, and then leaned against a work table under a large rack of pots and pans.

"I think that's where the butler sat," Banning said. "So he could hear when the lord of the manor needed more ice or when it was time to serve dessert."

"Interesting," Moore said.

"When you sit in there and listen, you're probably going to hear all sorts of interesting things."

The notion of eavesdropping on people, especially on Captain Pickering, made Moore uncomfortable.

"Sir?"

"I want you—as a matter of fact, Captain Pickering wants you—to sit in there and listen."

"Aye, aye, Sir."

"Put your trench coat away," Banning said, laughing. "This is not high level espionage. You made quite an impression on Pluto—Lieutenant Hon. He told Captain Pickering he thought you have a good analytical mind and that with your knowledge of how the Japanese think and behave, you were probably going to be damned useful. Obviously, the more you know, the more useful you will be. There will be things discussed in there tonight that you should know, and which would not be discussed if you were in there, even serving drinks, which was my original idea. Understand? Or would you rather pass canapés?"

"No, Sir," Moore said with a chuckle.

"There are certain things you should keep in mind," Banning said. "Priorities, primarily. And something you should always have in the back of your mind when you're involved with intelligence: Who knows what, and who isn't supposed to know what. You work for Captain Pickering. Or you work for P1—Lieutenant Hon, which is saying the same thing. Captain Pickering's interests are therefore your highest priority. Captain Pickering is here as the Secretary of the Navy's personal representative. That means he is authorized access to any information the Navy has. He has also become quite close to General MacArthur, who has given him access to everything in Supreme Headquarters. If you think that through, you'll understand that there's damned little he does not know.

"I don't know—it's none of my business—what information he's been getting from the Secretary of the Navy, or how much of that, if any, he is authorized to pass on to General MacArthur. Or—frankly—since he has apparently decided MacArthur is right and Admiral King is wrong, how much he has passed on to MacArthur without being specifically authorized to do so.

"Colonel Willoughby, who is MacArthur's intelligence officer, will be here in a little while. He is not authorized to know what Pickering may or may not have told MacArthur, but what MacArthur has decided to tell him anyway will be interesting.

"And finally, Colonel Goettge: He is obviously not privy to what either Pickering knows or what MacArthur knows. He has no Need to Know, for one thing, and for another, in a sense, at least as far as MacArthur and Willoughby are concerned, he's the enemy. The First Marine Division is under COMSOPAC . . ."

"Excuse me?"

"COMSOPAC. Commander, Southern Pacific—Admiral Ghormley. And Admiral Ghormley is under Admiral Nimitz. Admiral Nimitz is the senior Naval officer in the Pacific and is thus MacArthur's opposite number. There are two wars out here: between us and the Japanese, and between the Army and the Navy to see who fights the war, and where it is fought, and how."

Banning could see in Moore's face that the kid was both a little stunned by what he'd just been told and was suppressing only with an effort the urge to ask questions.

"And there is one more thing," Banning said, somewhat reluctantly. He was a good officer, and good officers do not criticize second lieutenants, much less lieutenant colonels, before enlisted men. But this was the inevitable exception that proved the rule. It had to be done.

"There are intelligence officers and intelligence officers," Banning went on. "Colonel Goettge is very good at what he does—Division Intelligence Officer. What that means is that he advises the Division Commander of his assessment of enemy capabilities and intentions, based on what information he has been given, and what he's been able to develop himself, say from prisoner interrogation, that sort of thing.

"But he has not been trained in, and has no experience with, the kind of—I guess the word is 'strategic'—intelligence that we're dealing with here . . ."

He stopped when he saw confusion clouding Moore's eyes. He realized that he'd been beating around the bush; this was not the place to be doing that.

"To put a point on it, Moore," he said. "In my opinion, Colonel Goettge is not as good an intelligence officer as he thinks he is . . . nor as knowledgeable, nor for that matter as bright. Keep that in mind."

"Yes, Sir," Moore said. Astonishment was all over his face. He never imagined he'd hear an officer say such a thing about another officer.

"Question?" Banning asked. "Questions?"

"Several hundred," Moore said.

"But one in particular?"

"Why am I being told all this?" Moore asked, and then remembered to append, "Sir?"

" 'In for a penny, in for a pound,' " Banning quoted Pickering. "You're now part of the team, Sergeant. In Captain Pickering's judgment, since you have been made aware of the price of a loose mouth, it makes more sense to bring you in on anything and everything that will help you do your job—which you now know is analysis of intercepted enemy messages—than it would be to make a decision every time something came up whether or not you should be told about it."

"I see," Moore said thoughtfully.

"Just one more thing: You are never, under any circumstances, to tell anyone that you have been given access to MAGIC."

"Aye, aye, Sir."

(FOUR)

Even after all that Major Banning had explained to him in the kitchen earlier, Moore sat for a long time in the butler's cubicle listening to the conversation in the library before he even began to understand what was going on. But finally, it began slowly to make sense:

In about a month the 1st Marine Division would invade several islands in the Solomons. Colonel Goettge, who was the Intelligence Officer of the 1st Marines, had very little intelligence information, maps or anything else, that the Division would need in order to launch the invasion. So he was understandably desperate for whatever information he could get. He'd come to Melbourne after Major Dillon told him that he and Captain Pickering were old friends, and that Pickering could be prevailed upon to use his influence at MacArthur's SHSWPA (Supreme Headquarters, South West Pacific Area).

That wasn't all Moore learned that evening. There were fireworks too.

"Hell, it's all over Washington, Flem, that you and Dugout Doug are asshole buddies," Major Dillon said at one point.

And Captain Pickering jumped all over Major Dillon almost before the words were out of Dillon's mouth.

If Captain Pickering's furious defense of MacArthur's brains and personal courage and his outrage that Major Dillon would dare call him "Dugout Doug" was not so intense, actually frightening, the ass-chewing he gave Dillon would have been funny. Moore was almost pleased to learn that the dignified Naval officer who was now his boss had a completely unsuspected flair for obscenely colorful phraseology. It would have been the envy of any Parris Island Drill Sergeant. Among other things— and there were *many* other things—he told Major Dillon that he wouldn't make a pimple on a real Marine's ass.

But the ass-chewing he gave to Major Dillon was frightening . . . so frightening that at one point Colonel Goettge even tried to apologize and leave.

Probably, Moore decided, because he didn't want to risk exacerbating the already hostile relations between SHSWPA and the Navy, which of course included the Marines.

"No, Colonel, you stay," Captain Pickering told him. "I certainly don't hold you responsible for Diarrhea Mouth here. Let's have another drink to calm down, and then try to figure out how to help the 1st Division."

Five more people came in the library before they all went in for dinner: Colonel Willoughby, who spoke—Moore noted—with a faint German accent and who was introduced as the SHSWPA G-2; then two women, a U.S. Navy Nurse and some kind of Australian Navy enlisted woman; and finally two Australian Navy Officers.

One of them was introduced as "Commander Feldt."

"Commander Feldt, Colonel," Pickering explained to Goettge, "commands the Royal Australian Navy Coastwatcher Establishment."

Moore tried to get a look at Commander Feldt through the duct, but was unable to see him. He decided that the other Australian officer worked for Feldt, or with him anyhow.

The women baffled him for a long time; but from what was said, he eventually understood that they were the girlfriends of two Marines who were off on some island with the Coastwatchers. And that answer raised another fascinating question: What were these women doing at a dinner where all sorts of classified information was being discussed?

The answer to that, when he finally thought of it, was quite simple. Captain Pickering decided who could be told what. In this case, obviously, he had decided that these two women—who were in uniform themselves and whose men were off on a secret mission—could be trusted to keep their mouths shut about that mission, and for that matter, about anything else.

Proof of that came a little later, just before they went into dinner and the women went to "powder their noses."

"Nice girls," Colonel Willoughby said approvingly.

"*Women,* Colonel," Commander Feldt corrected him, somewhat nastily. "Daphne has already lost one man, her husband, to this sodding war."

"He was a Coastwatcher?"

"No," Feldt answered. "He was a sergeant in the sodding Royal Signals. Our sodding politicians sent most of our men to sodding Africa, which is where he caught it."

He paused, apparently having seen something on Willoughby's face. "Did that remark offend you, Colonel?"

By now Moore was convinced that Feldt was more than a little drunk.

"No, of course not," Willoughby replied, somewhat unconvincingly.

"I was thinking of a conversation I had yesterday with Banning," Feldt went on, "as I watched her walk out of here just now."

"Oh?" Willoughby asked uneasily.

"He asked me what I thought the chances were of getting them back alive—Banning's men on Buka, Lieutenant Howard and Sergeant Koffler, who has been comforting the widow Farnsworth in her grief. I told him the truth: From slim to sodding none."

"Is it that low?" Willoughby asked.

"Commander Feldt underestimates the Marine Corps," Major Banning said, trying to temper Feldt's bitterness.

"Sod you, Banning," Feldt said cheerfully. "What I was thinking, Colonel, was that it is a bit much to ask of a pretty young *woman* like Yeoman Farnsworth to lose two men to this sodding war."

"I think they'll come back," Pickering said. "They are both very resourceful young men."

"I think we had better change the subject," Banning said. "They're liable to walk in here any moment."

"They wouldn't hear a sodding thing they haven't sodding well thought of at least once a sodding day themselves," Feldt said. "What the hell are they doing here anyway? Whose brilliant sodding idea was that?"

"Mine, actually," Pickering said.

Feldt snorted. "Until just now, Pickering, when you said that, I was beginning to believe I had finally met one American who really had enough brains to pour piss out of a sodding boot."

"Banning suggested that the company of a pretty woman just possibly might put you in a mellow frame of mind," Pickering said.

"Shit!" Feldt said. "Why? Banning, you bastard, what do you want from me?"

The women came back in the room. There was an awkward silence, and then Feldt said, "Major Banning was about to tell me what he wants from me."

"A dozen Coastwatchers to be attached to the 1st Marine Division," Banning said.

"That's a marvelous idea," Colonel Goettge said enthusiastically. Moore sensed that it was the first time he had heard of the idea.

"What for?" Feldt asked.

"Captain Pickering and I think they could be very helpful to Colonel Goettge," Banning said. "Dealing with the natives, among other things. Colonel Goettge doesn't speak Pidgin too well."

"I'll bet he sodding well doesn't," Feldt snorted. "From what I've seen, he's living proof of the old saw that 'intelligence officer is a contradiction of terms.'"

"That's quite enough, Feldt," Pickering snapped. "You're in my home, and you owe the colonel an apology."

There was a long, silent moment.

"No offense, Goettge," Feldt said finally. "A little down-under humor."

"No offense taken, Commander," Goettge said.

Neither of them sounded at all sincere.

"Interesting thought, Major," the other Australian officer said, in an obvious attempt to spread oil on the troubled waters.

"Don't encourage Banning, for Christ's sake," Feldt said. "There's no telling what the bastard'll ask for next." He fell silent for a moment, and then said, "OK. I don't know about a dozen. But I can come up with six or eight people."

"Why don't we go in to dinner?" Captain Pickering suggested.

"Are you trying to separate me from the booze, by any chance, Captain?"

"Absolutely not," Pickering replied. "You give us eight Coastwatchers to attach to the 1st Marine Division, and I'll give you all the sodding booze you can sodding well handle."

There was a moment's silence, and then Feldt laughed.

"You're a devious bastard, Pickering," he said. "I like you."

(FIVE)
The Elms
Dandenong, Victoria, Australia
0805 Hours 2 July 1942

When Major Jake Dillon, more than a little hung over, went down to breakfast, he was surprised to find Fleming Pickering's driver, or orderly, or whatever the hell he was, sitting at the dining room table finishing up what looked like steak and eggs.

Until he had been accused (with justification) of helping himself to the booze, Corporal Jake Dillon of the 4th Marines had once served as an orderly to a captain named Jerold in Shanghai. Corporal Dillon had not eaten steak and eggs at the captain's table. What he ate was leftovers, and he had done that standing up in the kitchen.

Sergeant John Marston Moore started to get to his feet when he saw Dillon.

"Good morning, Sir."

"Keep your seat, Sergeant," Dillon said. "Finish your breakfast."

"I'm just about finished," the kid said. And then he seemed to be stretching his leg under the table. After a moment, Jake understood there was a button on the floor, to summon the help. Proof came a moment later when the door to the kitchen opened and Mrs. Cavendish came out.

"Good morning, Sir," she said. "I hope you slept well."

"Like a drum," Dillon said.

"And what may I get you for breakfast?"

"What the sergeant was eating looks fine, thank you."

"Tea or coffee?"

"Coffee, please."

"Don't drink that," Mrs. Cavendish said to Moore, as he raised his cup toward his lips. "I'll bring you a fresh cup, hot."

She took the cup and saucer from him and went into the kitchen.

"Pretty soft berth, huh?" Dillon said to Moore.

"Sir?"

"I was an orderly once, a long time ago. My officer made me eat in the kitchen." He saw in Moore's face that he had interpreted the remark as a reprimand, and added: "Hey, I don't give a damn where you eat. I told you, I used to be an enlisted man. Hell, I was a sergeant a lot longer than I've been an officer. I was just saying that it looks as if you fell into a pretty soft berth."

"Yes, Sir."

"How long have you been working for Pickering?"

"Not long, Sir."

"Well, don't fuck up, Kid, and get yourself sent down to the 1st Division. They're living in tents, and they are not eating steak and eggs for breakfast."

"Yes, Sir."

Dillon heard the sound of footsteps, turned his head, and saw that Colonel Goettge and Major Banning were coming into the dining room. Moore saw them, too, and started to get up again.

"Good morning," Dillon said. "I told Captain Pickering's orderly to sit down and have a cup of coffee. I hope that's all right, Colonel."

Moore looked at Banning and saw a small smile around his lips and eyes.

"Sure," Colonel Goettge said. "Why not? Good morning, Sergeant. Take your seat."

"Yes, Sir."

Colonel Goettge, Moore thought, *has good reason to be in a good mood. He came here expecting damned little, and he was going to get far more than he could have hoped for.*

Before the evening was over, in addition to the Australians of the Coastwatcher Establishment who were going to be attached to the 1st Marine Division, Colonel Goettge had been offered:

—Intelligence briefings on the Solomon Islands by both the SHSWPA Intelligence Section and the Royal Australian Navy;

—the latest aerial photographs available, Australian and American;

—the latest maps, and in quantities sufficient to equip the Division. The number of maps required had really surprised Moore;

—permission to send a liaison officer to SHSWPA to ensure that any new intelligence developed would quickly get to the division.

Captain Pickering had been even more obliging about that. When Colonel Goettge admitted that he didn't have an officer of high enough rank to send to Melbourne, Pickering had volunteered to send a radio message to the Secretary of the Navy asking that an officer of suitable rank and experience be flown immediately from the United States.

Captain Pickering walked into the dining room.

"Good morning, gentlemen," he said, as everyone stood up. He walked to the head of the table and sat down. He looked at Moore.

"You look a little beat this morning, Sergeant," he said. "The scuttlebutt is that you were out until the wee hours carousing. Anything to that?"

"No, Sir."

"But you would characterize how you spent last night as interesting?"

"Fascinating, Sir."

Major Dillon snorted. Colonel Goettge smiled tolerantly.

"Well, I hope you can see well enough to drive these gentlemen around town today. They have several errands to run. They'll tell you what they are."

"Aye, aye, Sir."

"But check in every hour or so with Lieutenant Hon, Moore," Pickering said. "I think he may have something he wants you to do."

"Aye, aye, Sir."

"We keep Sergeant Moore pretty busy around here," Pickering said, a smile around his eyes, "with one thing or another."

"Well, whatever you have him doing," Major Dillon said, "it's still a soft berth compared to living in a tent in the mud at Wellington. I just told him, 'don't fuck up, Kid, you've got it made.'"

"You really think so, Jake?" Pickering asked, innocently.

XI

Yeoman Daphne Farnsworth, Royal Australian Navy Women's Volunteer Reserve, walked up to Sergeant John Marston Moore, USMCR. Sergeant Moore was then leaning on the front fender of the Studebaker Commander outside a frame building on a wharf on Port Philip Bay.

Moore recognized her immediately. Last night she was sitting in the dining room directly across from the duct in the butler's cubicle. She had lost her husband in action in Africa, he remembered, and was now a Marine's girlfriend . . . or, in Commander Feldt's words, he was "comforting her in her grief." He also remembered all too clearly what else Commander Feldt said with such bitter cynicism about the Marine, a Sergeant named Koffler now on some Japanese island: His chances of returning alive ranged from "slim to sodding zero."

"Comforting her in her grief" could have meant something sordid. But looking at her the night before, Moore decided she was a nice girl, and that whatever was going on between her and Sergeant Koffler was not cheap.

Looking at her now—just as he realized she had never seen him—the same thing occurred to him again. She was a nice girl, with warm, intelligent eyes. *And damned good-looking.*

"I should be very surprised," she greeted him with a smile, "if you are not Sergeant Moore."

She has a very nice voice.

"Guilty."

"Come with me, Lieutenant Donnelly wants to see you."

"Yes, Ma'am," he said.

She looked at him strangely, and then smiled.

Moore followed her into the building. Lieutenant Donnelly, a tall, sharp-featured, skinny officer with a very pale complexion, and black, unruly hair, had an office on the second floor. Moore recognized Donnelly as the other Australian Navy officer who had been at dinner.

I remember you from last night, but how the hell do you know who I am? And what's this all about, anyway?

"I'm Sergeant Moore, Sir."

"That'll be all, Love," Donnelly said to Yeoman Farnsworth. "Close the door, please."

When the door had closed behind her, Lieutenant Donnelly said, without smiling, "Put your eyes back in their sockets, Sergeant. She already has a Yank Marine sergeant."

Moore looked at him in shock.

"Listen carefully," Lieutenant Donnelly said. "The airfield at Lunga Point is being built by the 11th and 23rd Pioneers, IJN. Estimated strength 450. They are equipped with bulldozers, rock crushers, trucks, and other engineer equipment."

Moore was completely baffled. It showed on his face as he looked at Lieutenant Donnelly.

"What did I just say?" Lieutenant Donnelly asked.

"Something about Pioneers," Moore said lamely, embarrassed.

"Christ!" Donnelly snorted in disgust. He handed Moore a sheet of paper. On it, Moore read what Donnelly had just said. "Try committing that to memory."

Moore read the sheet of paper again. And then again, and again, very uncomfortable under Donnelly's impatient glare. Finally, he said, "I think I have it, Sir."

"Try it," Donnelly said.

Moore repeated what he had memorized.

"Once more, to set it in your head," Donnelly ordered.

Moore repeated it again.

"OK. Repeat that to Major Banning," Donnelly ordered. "Tell him that Commander Feldt said, 'it's as good as gold.'"

"'It's as good as gold,'" Moore dutifully parroted. "Sir, I don't know when I'm going to see Major Banning."

"You are going to see him right away," Donnelly said. "You get in your car and you go over to the Hotel Menzies, and you repeat to him what you just memorized. And then you forget it, OK? Understand?"

He's talking to me like I'm a backward child. Probably because I am acting like one.

"Sir, I'm driving some American officers around."

"Well, Sergeant, they're just going to have to bloody well wait for you. I'll have Daphne—Daphne being the Yeoman you were ogling—to look out for them and tell them what's happened."

"Aye, aye, Sir," Moore said.

When he got to the Hotel Menzies, Moore realized that he had no idea where to find Major Banning.

Lieutenant Hon will know, he decided. He rode the elevator to the basement and made his way to the steel-doored room.

"I thought you were playing chauffeur?" Hon greeted him.

"I was outside the Australian Navy building when Lieutenant Donnelly sent for me. He gave me a message for Major Banning. Made me memorize it. And then told me to deliver it. I don't know where he is, Sir."

"What's the message?" Hon asked. He saw the look of concern on Moore's face. "Hey, I'm cleared for everything."

"The airfield at Lunga Point is being built by the 11th and 23rd Pioneers, IJN," Moore recited. "Estimated strength 450. They are equipped with bulldozers, rock crushers, trucks, and other engineer equipment."

"Christ!" Hon said, "that's bad news."

"Commander Feldt said 'that's as good as gold,'" Moore added.

Hon looked at Moore thoughtfully. "You don't have the faintest idea what that means, do you?"

"No, Sir."

Hon went to an open file drawer, took from it and unfolded a map of Guadalcanal, and pointed to Lunga Point.

"That's Lunga Point," he said. "We already heard—had aerial photos—that the Japanese had burned the grass off a flat area, a plain, here. Feldt sent Coastwatchers he had on Guadalcanal across the island from here," he pointed, "through the jungle to see what was going on. And now we *know*—Feldt said his information was 'as good as gold'—that the Japanese are making a real effort to build a major airfield there. Pioneers are what we call Engineers. They've got 450 Engineers in there with rock crushers and bulldozers."

"I realize I must sound stupid, but is that really so important?"

"If they can base aircraft there—even fighters, but especially bombers—we're in real trouble. Always keep that airfield in the back of your mind when you're reading the MAGICs. Let me know if anything—*anything*—arouses your curiosity."

"Yes, Sir. Sir, what do I do about getting this to Major Banning?"

"He and Captain Pickering are on their way down here," Hon replied, and then handed Moore a sheet of onion skin. "I just got my hands on this."

OPERATIONAL IMMEDIATE

TOP SECRET
WASH DC 0015G 2JUL42
FROM: THE JOINT CHIEFS OF STAFF
TO: EYES ONLY
ADMIRAL NIMITZ COMPOA PEARLHARBOR
INFORMATION: EYES ONLY
GENERAL MACARTHUR SHSWPA MELBOURNE
VICEADMIRAL GHORMLEY COMSOPAC AUCKLAND
1. NO FURTHER DISCUSSION OF OPERATION PESTILENCE OR ALTERNATIVES THERETO IS DESIRED.
2. DIRECTION OF THE PRESIDENT, EXECUTE OPERATION PESTILENCE AT THE EARLIEST OPPORTUNITY BUT NO LATER THAN 10 AUGUST 1942.
FOR THE CHAIRMAN, THE JOINT CHIEFS OF STAFF:
HANNEMAN, MAJGEN, USA, SECRETARY, JCS

"What's 'Operation Pestilence'?" Moore asked, as he handed the onion skin back.

"The invasion of the Solomon Islands," Hon replied. "Or three of them, anyway. Tulagi, Gavutu, and Guadalcanal. Where the Japs are building this airfield. MacArthur and Ghormley think it's a lousy idea."

The steel door creaked open.

"You should have bolted that," Hon said.

Captain Fleming Pickering and Major Ed Banning came into the tiny room.

"What was that, Pluto?" Pickering asked.

"Nothing, Sir," Hon said. "This just came in, sir. I thought you would want to see it right away."

Pickering took the onion skin. His eyebrows rose as he read it. He handed it to Banning.

"Does General MacArthur have that yet?"

"He and Mrs. MacArthur are having lunch with the Prime Minister. One of the crypto officers is on his way over there with it."

Pickering grunted. "What brings you here, Moore?"

"He has a message for me," Banning answered for him. "Let's have it, Sergeant."

"The airfield at Lunga Point is being built by the 11th and 23rd Pioneers, IJN. Estimated strength 450. They are equipped with bulldozers, rock crushers, trucks, and other engineer equipment," Moore recited, and added, "Commander Feldt says 'that's as good as gold.'"

Pickering snorted. "Repeat that, please," he said.

Moore did so.

"What can they accomplish in a month, five weeks?" Pickering asked.

"They can probably have it ready for fighters," Banning replied. "I don't know about bombers."

"They already have float mounted Zeroes on Tulagi," Pickering said thoughtfully.

Then he looked at Moore. "You'd better get back to driving Colonel Goettge around," he said. "I don't have to tell you, do I, that Colonel Goettge is not to know about this? Or what you just relayed from Commander Feldt?"

"No, Sir," Moore said. He started to walk out of the room.

"Moore!" Banning called, and Moore turned. Banning held out a thin stack of envelopes to him. "Mail call. It came in on this morning's courier."

"Thank you, Sir."

In the elevator en route to the lobby, Moore thumbed through the half dozen envelopes. There were two letters from his mother; one each from his two sisters; one from Uncle Bill; and one with the return address, Apartment "C", 106 Rittenhouse Square, Philadelphia, Pennsylvania.

His heart jumped. He resisted the temptation to tear Barbara's letter open right there.

I'll save it until I'm alone.

He raised it to his nose and thought he could smell, ever so faintly, Barbara's perfume and then he put the letters in the inside pocket of his uniform jacket.

He walked out of the Menzies Hotel, got in the Studebaker, and drove back to where he was supposed to be waiting for Colonel Goettge and Major Dillon.

They were outside, waiting for him, and Colonel Goettge was visibly annoyed that he had been kept waiting.

"Sergeant," Goettge said, somewhat snappishly, "I thought that you were aware I have a luncheon appointment with Colonel Willoughby."

"Sorry, Sir," Moore said. "I had to do something for Major Banning."

"So we have been informed," Goettge said, as he got in the car. Moore closed the door after him and drove back to the Menzies Hotel.

"Don't disappear again without letting me know," Colonel Goettge said, as Moore held the rear door open for him.

"No, Sir," Moore said.

Moore watched the two of them disappear into the lobby and then took the stack of envelopes from his pocket. He was hungry and knew that he should try to eat, but that could wait.

He carefully opened the letter from Barbara, sniffing it again for a smell of her perfume, and then unfolded it. It was brief and to the point:

Philadelphia, June 23, 1942

Dear John,

There is no easy way to break this to you, so here goes: My husband and I have reconciled.

I'm sure, when you think about it, that you will realize this is the best thing for all concerned. And I'm sure you will understand why I have to ask you not to write to me.

You will be in my prayers, and I will never forget you.

Barbara.

He felt a chill. He read the letter again, then very deliberately took his Zippo from his pocket and set the letter on fire, holding it by one corner until it became too hot, and then dropping it on the floorboard, wondering, but not caring, if it was going to set the carpet on fire.

Then he banged his head on the steering wheel until the tears came.

(TWO)
Aotea Quay
Wellington, New Zealand
5 July 1942

It was cold, windy, and raining hard on the Quay, and Major Jake Dillon's allegedly rainproof raincoat was soaked through.

What he faced, he thought more than a little bitterly, was one hell of a challenge for a flack. Even a flack like him . . . The *Hollywood Reporter* had once run a story about the gang that showed up every Saturday at Darryl Zanuck's polo field. The cut line under a picture of Jake Dillon and Clark Gable on their ponies read, "The King of the Movies and the King of the Flacks Playing the Sport of Kings."

For once, Jake Dillon thought at the time, the *Reporter* had stuck pretty close to the facts. He hoped there was still some truth in the line about him . . . The King of Flacks would need every bit of his royal Hollywood experience if he was going to make a success of what he had in mind to do:

He was going to put together a little movie about the Marine invasion of Bukavu, Tulagi, and Guadalcanal. He'd made the decision solely on his own authority; nothing about it was put on paper; and he didn't tell anyone about it except his cameramen.

His film would come in addition to the footage the combat cameramen shot when the invasion was actually in progress. As soon as possible, that would be sent undeveloped to Washington, where somebody else would soup it, screen it, and do whatever they decided to do with it, passing it out to the newsreel companies and whatever.

What Jake Dillon had in mind was to have his people shoot newsreel feature stuff—as opposed to hard news. The emphasis would be on the ordinary enlisted Marine. They'd follow the 1st Division as the Division prepared to go to the Solomons, and then of course, they'd be with them when they got there.

He had a number of scenes in mind. Training shots, primarily. Life in tent city here in New Zealand. Life in the transports en route to the rehearsal in the Fiji Islands, and then as they sailed for the Solomons, and then after they landed. Human interest stuff.

In point of actual fact, it would be the first movie that he had ever produced. But he had been around the industry for a long time and knew what had to be done and how to do it. The idea was not intimidating; God only knew how many successful movies had been produced by ignoramuses who couldn't find their own asses with both hands without the assistance of a script, a continuity girl, and two or three assistant directors to put chalk marks on it for them.

He learned early on in Hollywood that a good crew makes all the difference when you are shooting a movie. If you have a crew who know what they are doing, all you have to do is tell them what you want, and they do it. And even if it was a damned small one, he had a good crew here with him.

They understood what he wanted to do; and, just as important, they thought it was a pretty good idea.

That meant, for example, that he could tell them that he wanted to show equipment being off-loaded from transports, and they would go shoot it for him. He didn't have to stand around with a script and a megaphone in his hand, yelling at somebody to get a tight shot of the sweating guy driving the truck. His people made movies for a living; they knew what was needed, and how to get it.

As Dillon walked down the Quay, he thought, *If I was making a movie called*

"The Greatest Fuck-Up Of All Time," I could finish principal photography this morning right here on this goddamned dock.

Jake Dillon had seen some monumental screw-ups in his time, but this took the goddamned cake: The ships carrying the supplies of the 1st Marine Division had not been "combat-loaded" when they sailed from the United States. That meant they all had to be reloaded here, since they could not approach the hostile Solomon Island beaches the way they were originally loaded.

The term "combat-loaded" refers to a deceptively simple concept: Logisticians and staff officers spend long hours determining what equipment will be needed during the course of an invasion, and in what order.

As a general rule of thumb, the ships carrying the invasion force would have in their holds supplies for thirty days' operations. Adequate stocks of ammunition, obviously, had to be put on the beach before the chaplain's portable organ, or the Division's mimeograph machines. But the barges and small boats ferrying supplies from the ships to the beach would be a narrow pipeline. Thus it would not be prudent to fill that pipeline with ammunition and nothing else. For other supplies were no less vital: The men had to eat, for example; so there had to be rations in the pipeline. And all the complex machinery on the beach needed its sustenance too—what the services call POL (Petrol, Oil, and Lubricants). And so on.

When the obvious priorities had been determined, then the loading order was fine tuned. This wasn't simply a case of saying off-load so much ammunition, then so many rations, then so many barrels of POL, and repeating the process until all the important supplies are ashore, after which you could off-load the nonessentials, like typewriters.

For example, while a radio operator receiving messages intended for the Division Commander could take them down by hand, he would be far more efficient in terms of speed and legibility using a typewriter. So, while a typewriter might not seem to be as necessary in the early stages of an invasion as, say, a case of hand grenades, at least one typewriter would head for the beach early on, probably with the first ammunition and rations supplied.

When all the priorities had been established and fine tuned, the ships of the invasion force were ready to be "combat-loaded." This followed the logic of "Last On, First Off": Once The Division was on the Solomon Islands beaches, the supplies needed first would be loaded on last.

Doing this was proving far more difficult than it sounded—the combat-loading planning for an amphibious invasion has been described as a chess game that cannot be won.

One major problem the 1st Marine planners faced—though it was by no means their *only* major problem—was that since the ships were not originally combat-loaded back in the States, the supplies had to be removed from the holds of the ships and sorted out before they could be reloaded.

This problem was compounded by the Wellington Longshoreman's Union, which had very strong views about how ships should be unloaded and loaded; and by whom; and on what days during what daylight hours. They had come to an understanding with management regarding the role of longshoremen in the scheme of things only after long hours on the picket line and extensive negotiations over many years. They had no intention of giving up these hard earned prerequisites for anything as insignificant as a war with the Japanese Empire.

The Americans solved the labor problem by using a cut-the-Gordian-knot approach: American Marines were unloading the ships around the clock, seven days a week. At the same time, they let it be known that armed Marines were posted at various spots around the Quay, with orders to shoot at anyone or anything interfering with unloading and loading of the ships.

Jake hoped the threat would suffice. While it wouldn't have bothered him at all if half the longshoremen in Wellington got shot between the eyes, the flack in him was concerned with how "MARINES MASSACRE THIRTY NEW ZEALAND LONGSHOREMEN IN LABOR DISPUTE" headlines would play in the papers in the States.

Technically, it was not his problem, since he was not the PIO for the 1st Marine Division. But he was over here to "coordinate public information activities," and he suspected that if there was lousy publicity, he would get the blame.

While the supplies were being off-loaded for sorting, another major problem had come up: There was no way to shelter the off-loaded supplies from the dismal New Zealand July winter weather (the seasons were reversed down under). It was raining almost constantly.

For openers, the supplies for the First Marine Division—not only rations but just about everything else, too—were civilian stuff. The quart-size cans of tomatoes, for example, had been bought from the Ajax Canned Tomato Company, or somesuch. These cans had been labelled and packed with the idea in mind that they would wind up on the shelves of the "Super-Dooper Super-Market" in Olathe, Kansas. They had paper labels with pictures of pretty tomatoes attached to the metal with a couple of drops of cheap glue. There were six cans to a corrugated paper carton. The carton was held together with glue; and a can label was glued to the ends.

As soon as the cases were off-loaded from the cargo holds of the ships onto Aotea Quay and stacked neatly so they could be sorted, the rain started falling on them. Soon the cheap glue which held the corrugated paper cartons together dissolved. That caused the cartons to come apart. Not long after that, instead of neatly stacked cartons of tomato cans, there were piles of tomato cans mingled with a sludge of waterlogged corrugated paper that had once been cartons.

And then the rain saturated the paper labels and dissolved the cheap glue that held them on the cans . . .

The people in charge of the operation had put a good deal of thought and effort into finding a solution to the problem. But the best they had come up with so far was to cover some of the stacks of cartons with tarpaulins; and when the supply of tarpaulins ran out, with canvas tentage; and when the tentage ran out, with individual shelter-halves. (Each Marine was issued a small piece of tentage. When buttoned to an identical piece, it formed a small, two-man tent. Hence, "individual shelter-half.")

As he walked down the Quay, Jake Dillon saw this wasn't going to work: There were gaps around the bases of the tarpaulin-covered stacks. The wind blew the rain through the gaps, and then the natural capillary action of the paper in the corrugated paper cartons soaked it up like a blotter. Moisture reached the glue, and the glue dissolved. The cartons collapsed, and then the stacks of cartons.

Major Jake Dillon found Major Jack NMI Stecker standing behind the serving line in a mess fly tent—essentially a wall-less tent erected over field stoves. A line of Marines was passing through the fly tent, their mess kits in their hands. As soon as they left the fly tent, rain fell on their pork chops and mashed potatoes and green beans.

It was the first time in Dillon's memory that he had ever seen Jack Stecker looking like something the cat had dragged in. He looked as bedraggled as any of his men. In China with the 4th Marines, Master Gunnery Sergeant Jack Stecker used to come off a thirty-mile hike through the mud of the Chinese countryside looking as if he was prepared to stand a formal honor guard.

He walked up and stood beside him.

"Lovely weather we're having, isn't it?" Dillon said.

"There's coffee, if you want some," Stecker replied, and then walked a few feet away; he returned with a canteen cup and gave it to Dillon.

Dillon walked to the coffee pot at the end of the serving line and waited until the KP ladling out coffee sensed someone standing behind him, looked, and then offered his ladle.

The coffee was near boiling; Dillon could feel the heat even in the handle of the cup. If he tried to take a sip, he would give his lip a painful burn. This was not the first time he had stood in a rain-soaked uniform drinking burning-hot coffee from a canteen cup.

But the last time, he thought, *was a long goddamned time ago.*

"What brings a feather merchant like you out with the real Marines?" Stecker asked.

"I'm making a movie, what else?"

Stecker looked at him.

"Really? Of this?"

"What I need, Jack, is film that will inspire the red-blooded youth of America to rush to the recruiting station," Dillon said. "You think this might do it?"

Stecker laughed.

"Seriously, what are your people doing?"

Dillon told him about the movie he had in mind.

"I suppose it's necessary," Stecker said.

"I'd rather be one of your staff sergeants, Jack," Dillon said. "I was a pretty good staff sergeant. But that's not the way things turned out."

"You were probably the worst staff sergeant in the 4th Marines," Stecker said, smiling, "to set the record straight. I let you keep your stripes only so I could take your pay away at poker."

"Well, fuck you!"

They smiled at each other, then Stecker said bitterly: "I'd like to make the bastards who sent us this mess, packed this way, see your movie."

"They will. What my guys are shooting—or a copy of it, a rough cut—will leave here for Washington on tomorrow's courier plane."

"No kidding?"

"Personal from Vandergrift to the Commandant," Dillon said.

"Somehow I don't think that was the General's own idea."

"No. But Lucky Lew Harris thought it was fine when I suggested it."

Stecker chuckled. "I guess that explains it."

"Explains what?"

"I saw General Harris for a moment this morning," Stecker said. "I asked him how things went when you took Goettge to Australia. He said, 'very well. I'm beginning to think that maybe your pal Dillon might be useful after all. He's really not as dumb as he looks.'"

"Christ, I better go buy a bigger hat," Dillon said. "How much did he tell you about what's going on?"

"You mean about the airfield the Japs are building?"

Dillon nodded.

"That we better go try to stop them, whether we're ready or not."

"And we're not ready, right?"

Stecker waved his hand up and down the Quay.

"What do you think?"

"Well, there'll at least be the rehearsal in the Fiji Islands."

"And because we're not even prepared for a rehearsal, that will be fucked up. And we'll go nevertheless."

"What's going to happen, Jack?"

"You know what the Coast Guard motto is?"

"'*Semper Paratus'?*" Dillon asked, confused.

"No. Not that one, anyhow. What the Coast Guard says when a ship is in trouble. They have to go out. Nothing's said about having to come back."

"You think it's that bad?"

"Even after Wake Island and what happened to the 4th Marines in the Philippines, half the people in the Division think the Japs are all five foot two, wear thick glasses, and will turn tail and run once they see a real Marine. Not only the kids. A lot of the officers, who should know better, think this is going to be Nicaragua all over again."

"Jesus, you really mean that?"

"Yeah, but for Christ's sake, don't tell anybody I said so."

"Of course not," Dillon said.

"Are you going to go?"

"Sure, of course."

"You're not going to inspire . . . what did you say, 'red-blooded American youth'? . . . to rush to the recruiting station with movies of dead Marines floating around in the surf."

Dillon didn't reply for a moment. Then he said, "Straight answer, Jack: I'm not going to show them movies of dead Marines. I'm going to find me a couple, maybe three, four, good-looking Marines who get themselves lightly wounded, like in the movies, a shoulder wound . . ."

"A shoulder wound is one of the worst kinds, nearly as bad as the belly, you know that."

"I know that, you know that, civilians don't know that," Dillon replied. ". . . and maybe have a medal to go with it" he went on, taking the thought forward. "Then I'm going to bring them to the States and send them on a tour with movie stars. People will be inspired to buy War Bonds. Red-blooded American youth will rush to Marine recruiting stations."

Stecker turned to look at Dillon, who saw the contempt in his eyes.

"Most heroes I've known are as ugly as sin and would lose no time grabbing one of your movie stars on the ass," Stecker said. "What are you going to do about that?"

"Present company included, I suppose," Dillon said. It was a reference to Stecker's World War I Medal of Honor. "I'd love to have you on a War Bond tour. Do you suppose you could arrange to get yourself shot in the shoulder, Jack? *After* you do something heroic?"

"Fuck you, Jake."

"Like I said, Jack, I'd much rather be going to Guadalcanal as one of your staff sergeants. It didn't turn out that way, so I try to do what the Corps wants me to do as well as I can."

Stecker met his eyes.

"Yeah," he said. "I know."

He handed Dillon his empty canteen cup.

"I am now going out in the rain again," he said. "Somebody once told me that a good Marine officer doesn't try to stay dry when his men are getting wet."

"Nobody has to tell you what a good Marine officer should or should not do," Dillon said.

"What the hell is that?"

"It was intended as a compliment."

"Don't let it go to your head, Major, but I almost wish you were one of my staff sergeants," Stecker said, and then he touched Dillon's arm and walked out from under the fly tent and into the rain.

(THREE)
Headquarters, VMF-229
Marine Corps Air Station
Ewa, Territory of Hawaii
7 July 1942

If Captain Charles M. Galloway, commanding officer of VMF-229, had been called upon to describe his present physical condition, he would have said that his ass was dragging. He was bone tired and dirty. He had been flying most of the morning. He was wearing a sweat- and oil-stained cotton flying suit. His khaki flight helmet and goggles were jammed into the left knee pocket of the flying suit, and his fore-and-aft cap stuck out of the right knee pocket. He carried his leather flying jacket over his shoulder; his index finger was hooked in the leather loop inside the collar.

He needed a long shower and some clean clothes, he knew, and he would dearly like to have a beer. But beer was out of the question: He would probably put another two hours in the air this afternoon, and you don't drink—not even a lousy beer—and fly.

The door to the Quonset hut which housed both the squadron office and the supply room of VMF-229 was padlocked when Charley Galloway walked up to it. He glanced at his watch and saw that it was just after 1200.

PFC Alfred B. Hastings, Galloway decided angrily, had elected to have his luncheon, and fuck the phone, let it ring. He immediately regretted his anger. Hastings, who had transferred into VMF-229 with Tech Sergeant Big Steve Oblensky, had been promoted from being Oblensky's runner to Squadron Clerk. His only qualification for the job was that he could type, but he had proved to be a quick learner of the fine points of Marine Corps bureaucracy and had been doing a good job. Galloway knew how late at night the kid worked, and obviously he had to eat sometime.

Galloway dipped his hand into the open flap of his flight suit and came out with his dog tag chain. It held his dog tags and four keys—one to his BOQ room; one to the Ford; one to the padlock on the squadron office door; and one to the padlock on the safe in the squadron office. He opened the lock and went inside.

The handset of the telephone was out of the cradle. Not by accident. PFC Hastings had been told by Technical Sergeant Oblensky that it was better to have the brass *annoyed* that you were on the phone when they called than *pissed* because there was no answer when it rang—clear proof that the rule that Squadron Offices would be manned around the clock was being violated.

Captain Galloway walked to the squadron safe, knelt by it, unlocked the padlock, opened the door, and reached inside and took a bottle of Coke from an ice-filled galvanized iron bucket, which at the moment was all the safe held. He knocked the cap off by resting the lip on the edge of the safe and hitting it with the heel of his hand.

He walked to his desk, sat down in the battered, but surprisingly comfortable, office chair Oblensky had scrounged somewhere and then had reupholstered, leaned back in it, swung his feet on the desk, and took a pull at the neck of the Coke. After a moment, he burped with satisfaction.

On his desk, neatly laid out, was a half-inch-thick stack of papers. From experience, he knew that just about every sheet there would require his signature—on the original and the standard four onion skins. Whatever it was, it would have to wait.

His hands were dirty, oily; it would offend the high priests of the bureaucracy if an official document with oily fingerprints on it appeared in their IN baskets for movement to the OUT basket and forwarding to higher headquarters.

He looked at the handset of the telephone and after a moment leaned forward and hung it up. By the time he had rested his back against his chair and raised the Coke bottle to his lips, it rang.

He leaned forward and picked it up.

"VMF-229, Captain Galloway, Sir."

"You guys must live on the phone," his caller said. "I been calling for an hour."

"Well, it'll keep your index finger in shape," Galloway said. "Who's this?"

"Lieutenant Rhodes, at NATS Pearl. I got a couple of warm bodies for you."

"I don't suppose there's any way you could get them a ride over here?"

"No. Not today, anyway. That's why I called."

"What kind of warm bodies?"

"Two intrepid birdmen, fresh from the States. They went into Hickam Field, and the Air Corps sent them here."

"Instead of here. That figures."

"You going to come get them? Or should I put them in the transient BOQ?"

"I'll send somebody for them. Thanks very much."

"Anytime."

Galloway put the phone back in its cradle and talked out loud to himself: "I will not send somebody for them, because I don't have anybody to drive a vehicle to send for them . . . even if I had a vehicle, which I don't." He thought that over, and added, "Shit!"

He drained the Coke and dropped the bottle with a loud clang into the object he now knew—as a commanding officer charged with responsibility for government property—was not a wastebasket but a "Receptacle, Trash, Office, w/o Liner Federal Stock Number Six Billion Thirteen." Then he swung his feet back onto the floor, burped again, and stood up. He looked at the telephone, took the handset out of the cradle, and laid it on the desk.

He went to PFC Hastings's desk and left him a note. "1205 I went to pick up some replacements at NATS. CMG."

Then he went out of the Quonset hut, closed the padlock, and walked to his Ford. Regulations required that officers leaving installations be in the properly appointed uniform of the day. An exception was made only for officers who were actually engaged in preparing for flight duty, or who were returning from such duty; these men were permitted to wear uniforms appropriate for such duty. Captain Charles M. Galloway decided that he met the criteria for exception. He had been flying, and he was preparing to fly again.

He took his fore-and-aft cap from the knee pocket of his flight suit, put it on, and then slipped his arms into the leather flight jacket and zipped that up. Then he got behind the wheel of the Ford and drove off.

The Marine MP on duty outside the Navy Air Transport Service terminal eyed Galloway suspiciously as he pulled up in the yellow Ford.

"I've got two warm bodies inside," Galloway said when the MP walked up to the car. "Can I leave this here a minute?"

"No, Sir," the MP said. "That would be against regulations. But on the other hand, if I checked around inside, which would take me about two minutes, I wouldn't see it, would I?"

"Thanks," Charley said, and got out of the car.

He smiled when he saw the two warm bodies, the intrepid birdmen fresh from the States, sitting on wooden benches inside the terminal. He knew both of them.

And when they saw him, they both stood up. First Lieutenant James G. Ward, USMCR, smiled and waved. First Lieutenant David F. Schneider, USMC, just about came to attention.

If he outranked Jim Ward, Galloway thought, *he would bark "attention" and announce that he was "Lieutenant Schneider reporting for duty as ordered with a party of one."*

"Welcome to sunny Hawaii," Galloway said, extending his hand. "How was the flight?"

"Long," Jim Ward said.

"Very nice, thank you, Sir," Lieutenant Schneider said.

Oh, that's the way he's decided to play this. He probably sat with his thumb up his ass for a long time, trying to figure the best way to behave when reporting to a squadron commanded by an ex-sergeant.

"I've got a car outside. You can flip a coin to see who gets to sit in the rumble seat. Need any help with your gear?"

"I can manage, thanks," Ward said.

"No, Sir. Thank you, Sir," Schneider said.

He led them outside.

"Great car!" Jim Ward said. "I always wanted one of these. Yours?"

"Yeah. I bought it when I was with VMF-211, tore it apart, and rebuilt it."

Captain Galloway suspected that Lieutenant Schneider was not nearly as enthusiastic about a nine-year-old yellow Ford roadster as Lieutenant Ward was. And he saw that Schneider was almost visibly relieved when Ward settled himself in the rumble seat with their luggage. Riding in the rumble seat of a nine-year-old yellow Ford roadster was not the sort of thing that Lieutenant Schneider felt was appropriate for a Marine officer, especially one who had entered the service from Annapolis.

Galloway got behind the wheel.

"Following the sacred military custom of 'do as I say, not what I do,'" he said, "be advised that wearing flight suits off the flight line is a no-no. A couple of the guys have got themselves written up by the MPs and Shore Patrol."

"What happens then?" Ward asked.

"I reply by endorsement that the offenders have been hung, then drawn and quartered. It's a pain in the ass. We have only one kid for a clerk, and he's not all that good with a typewriter. So don't get caught."

"Got you," Jim Ward said. He leaned forward from the rumble seat and thrust an envelope, a thick one, firmly sealed with scotch tape, at Galloway.

"What's this?"

"A little note from Aunt Caroline," Jim Ward said.

"You hang on to it," Galloway said. "I'm greasy and so is the flight suit. I was about to take a shower when they called and said you were here."

"We could have waited," Schneider said.

"I figured to hell with it," Galloway said. "I'm going to fly again this afternoon anyway."

"We have planes?" Ward asked eagerly.

"Wildcats," Galloway said. *"New* Wildcats. And if you talk nicely to Sergeant Oblensky, he will have your name painted on it, and you can send a picture home to Mommy."

"Who is Sergeant Oblensky?" Ward asked.

"The maintenance sergeant. Best one in the Air Group. At the moment, he's also the first sergeant, the mess sergeant, the supply sergeant, and the motor sergeant."

"How is that, Sir?" Schneider asked.

"Because we don't have anybody else to be the first sergeant, the mess sergeant, the supply sergeant, or the motor sergeant. I'm working on it, so far with a monumental lack of success."

"I see," Schneider said.

"Where we're going now is to Ewa, where I will show you MAG-113 Headquarters,"—Marine Air Group 113; a MAG is the next superior headquarters to a squadron, the aviation equivalent, so to speak, of an infantry battalion—"then the BOQ, and then our squadron office. Then we'll go to the flight line, where I'll get out. You will then drive back to MAG-113. The Skipper—Lieutenant Colonel Clyde D. Dawkins—always wants a personal look at the new meat. When he's finished with you, go to the BOQ and get yourself set up there. And then go to the squadron office, where PFC Hastings will do all the necessary paperwork on you. I'll meet you there, and we can go to the club for our one daily beer and supper. OK?"

"Sounds fine to me," Ward said.

"The penalty for dinging your skipper's little yellow car is death by slow castration," Galloway said. "A word to the wise, so to speak." They chuckled.

"I suppose your flight physicals are up to date?"

"Yes, Sir," they chorused.

"OK. Make sure Hastings gets a copy. And your orders, too, of course. Then in the morning, we'll go flying. Local area checkout if nothing else. There are two IPs. Me and a Lieutenant name of Bill Dunn. He got a Betty and a Zero at Midway. Good pilot. Pay attention to what he says. I do."

"He's almost halfway to being an ace," Ward thought aloud.

"Before you fly away on dreams of glory," Galloway said, "he also took a 20mm round in his window at Midway that damned near made him a soprano, and he totalled the airplane when he set it down. Most of the pilots of VMF-211 who took off for Midway didn't come back. Bear that in mind, too."

There was a moment's silence and then Schneider said, "Sir, we're hardly presentable. To report to the Group Commander, I mean."

"Lieutenant," Galloway said, "we are blessed with a Group Commander who is wise enough to know how mussed people get flying here from the States. He wants a look at your balls, not the crease in your trousers."

Jim Ward laughed.

"Yes, Sir," Schneider said.

If first impressions are important, Galloway thought as he drove the Ford convertible down the taxi road behind the flight line, *Big Steve just blew it so far as Schneider is concerned.*

Technical Sergeant Oblensky was sitting on the ground in the shade of a Wildcat, his back against the left wheel, with a bottle of Coke resting on his belly. He was wearing service shoes and what had originally been khaki trousers, now somewhat raggedly cut off just above the knees. And nothing else. The belly on which the Coke bottle sat sagged over the trouser waistline. His massive chest was streaked with grease and what probably was hydraulic oil, and he needed a shave. His head and neck were sweat streaked.

As Galloway stopped the car and he and the others got out, Oblensky pushed himself to his feet and sauntered over. He glanced at the two young officers with Galloway and dismissed them as unimportant; then he looked at Galloway.

"Those fucking guns need a good armorer," he announced. "Peterson came back this morning with three of his guns jammed after three, four rounds."

There were four .50 caliber air-cooled Browning machine guns on F4F-4 aircraft.

"What's the problem? More important, what do we do about it?"

"If I knew what the problem was, I'd fix it," Oblensky said. "What I did was call a pal—used to be a China Marine, now he's a Gunny with the 2nd Raider Battalion, guy named Zimmerman. He said if I could get them over there, he'd have a look at them.''

"OK," Galloway said.

"But I'd have to give him a little present."

"What's he want?"

"An auxiliary generator," Oblensky said. "They're living in tents. He's got a refrigerator someplace, but he needs juice to run it."

"Jesus, Steve, we only have two."

"I think I know where I can get another one."

"Where?"

"You don't want to know, Captain."

"And if you get caught?"

"Then I guess you'd still have some fucked up Brownings, Captain."

"Then be careful," Galloway said.

Big Steve nodded.

Galloway glanced at Ward and Schneider. He saw fascination in Ward's eyes and disbelief in Schneider's, as both came to comprehend what had just been discussed.

"Gentlemen," Galloway said, "I'd like you to meet Technical Sergeant Oblensky, the squadron maintenance sergeant. Sergeant, this is Lieutenant Ward and Lieutenant Schneider; they've just reported aboard."

Big Steve extended his hammy, greasy hand to Ward and Schneider in turn. Ward shook the hand with visible pleasure; Schneider managed a smile only with an almost visible effort.

"Welcome aboard, Sirs," Big Steve said. "The Skipper's told me about you. We didn't expect you so soon."

"I told them you'd paint their names on their airplanes, so we could take a picture," Galloway said.

"Consider it done. Tomorrow, for sure," Big Steve said. He smiled, turned, and pointed at the Wildcat behind him. "This one's ready for a test hop, and if they can replace one more jug in that fucked-up engine in Six-Oh-Three, that'll be ready this afternoon, too." (A "jug" is the engine's cylinder and piston assembly.)

"Is that what you want me to do, Steve, test-fly this one?"

"Lieutenant Dunn took Lieutenant Peterson out again. He said if you got hung up, he'd test-fly this one when he got back."

"What I'd like, Steve, is for six-oh-three to be ready for a test hop when I bring this one back," Galloway said.

"You want to trust Neely to replace the jug himself? I mean, I got to see about that other auxiliary generator."

"We have to push him out of the nest sometime, Steve."

"OK. I'll tell him to have it ready when you get back," Oblensky said. "Things are probably going to be a little tight. You want to change your plans for tonight, Captain?"

Shit! I forgot all about that!

Mrs. Stefan Oblensky, aka Lieutenant Commander Florence Kocharski, United States Navy Nurse Corps, had requested the pleasure of the company of Captain Charles M. Galloway, USMCR, at dinner at the family residence where she and Technical Sergeant Oblensky cohabited with the blessings of God but in contravention of the Rules & Customs of the United States Naval Service.

Charley looked at Big Steve's face.

I can't turn him down again. They've asked me four times, and I've had to turn him down three.

"Hell, no," he said. "I'll be there."

XII

Lieutenant David F. Schneider reached out and touched Lieutenant Jim Ward's arm as Ward tried to operate the door latch of Galloway's 1933 Ford convertible. Ward turned and looked at him.

"Don't you really think it would be a good idea if we took a shave and got into a fresh uniform before we go in here?"

"You heard what the man said. The man said the colonel is smart enough to know you lose the crease in your trousers when you spend twelve hours in an airplane. And the man, if I have to point this out, is now our commanding officer."

"But he hasn't changed much," Schneider said, "has he?"

"Meaning what?"

"You did understand that he gave that bare-chested gorilla of a sergeant of his permission to steal an auxiliary power unit generator someplace, from somebody who certainly needs it?"

Ward didn't reply.

"So that he can swap it to some other sergeant in the 2nd Raiders," Schneider went on, "for doing something to the machine guns that he's not competent, or too stupid, to do himself? The last I heard they call that 'misappropriation of government property.'"

"I don't know what you're talking about," Jim Ward said.

"You were standing right there!" Schneider said indignantly, and then understood. "Oh," he said in disgust. "I see."

"I don't think you really do, Dave," Ward said. "Let me tell you something about yourself, Dave. Most of the time you're a pretty good guy; but hiding inside you—I guess all the time—is a real prick struggling to get out. I don't like you much when that happens."

Schneider looked at Ward for a time, and then he said slowly, "Your attitude wouldn't have anything to do with the relationship between Galloway and your Aunt Caroline, would it?"

"Probably that has something to do with it," Ward said. "But what I think it is, what I hope it is, is loyalty to my commanding officer."

Schneider snorted.

"You weren't sent here," Ward said. "You volunteered, so you could get out of flying R4Ds and into fighters. Galloway fixed it. If it wasn't for him, you'd still be at Quantico. You knew what Charley—Captain Galloway—was like when he let you volunteer. All you had to say was no."

"I can't believe that you are actually condoning what you saw him do with your own eyes."

Ward turned away and managed to get the door open. Then he walked quickly around the front of the car and intercepted Schneider as he was getting out.

"I never thought I would enjoy something like this," he said, "but I was wrong. You will recall, Lieutenant, that I am senior to you. By the authority therefore vested in me by the goddamned Naval Service, Lieutenant, I order you (a) to get back in the car; (b) to shut your fucking mouth; (c) and to sit there and don't move until I send for you. And be advised, Lieutenant, that if it comes down to it, I will swear on a stack of Bibles that when Sergeant Oblensky spoke with us, he was dressed like a fucking recruiting poster and said not one fucking word about a goddamned generator. You got that, Lieutenant?"

"Jim," Schneider said. "Obviously, I . . ."

"Your orders, Lieutenant, are to sit there with your fucking mouth shut," Ward said, spun on his heel, and walked to the door.

(TWO)
Threshold, Runway 17
Ewa Marine Corps Air Station
Oahu, Territory of Hawaii
1450 Hours 7 July 1942

Captain Charles M. Galloway, USMCR, had a dark secret, a true secret, shared with no one else. He wasn't sure if it was a character flaw, or whether it was something that happened to other people, too. But he knew that he didn't want it known, and that he could never ask anyone else if they were similarly affected. Or maybe similarly afflicted.

The cold truth was that in situations like this one—in the cockpit, with all the needles in the green, in the last few instants before he would shove the throttle forward and then touch his mike button and announce to the tower, with studied savoir faire, "Five Niner Niner rolling"—he was afraid.

He could tell himself that it was irrational, that he was a better pilot than most people he knew, that the aircraft he was about to fly was perfectly safe, that he had so many hours total time; and he could even remind himself that a study by the University of California had proved beyond reasonable doubt that a cretin (defined as the next step above morons) could be taught to fly; but it didn't work. At that moment—and all those other times—he had a very clear image of the airplane going out of control, smashing into the ground, rolling over, exploding. And it scared him. Sometimes his knees actually trembled. And more than once he had taken his hand from the stick so he could try to hold his shaking knees still.

Today, as he sat there waiting, he reminded himself of the command decision he had made vis-à-vis himself and Lieutenant Bill Dunn: who would fly what and why. Dunn was a good pilot, and he had done something Galloway had not done. He had met the enemy in aerial combat and shot down two airplanes. Galloway believed that there was no way to vicariously experience what it was like to have someone shooting at you.

That did not change, however, his belief that good pilots were a product of two qualities: natural ability and experience. He really believed that he was a better natural pilot than Dunn, and there was no question that he had much more experience.

The mission of VMF-229 at the moment was to become operational, which is to say its eighteen F4F-4 Wildcats and their pilots had to be made ready to go where the squadron was ordered to go, and to do what the squadron was ordered to do.

All his pilots were of course rated as Naval Aviators. Someone in authority had decreed that they were qualified to fly. But with Galloway's certain and Bill Dunn's possible exception, the pilots VMF-229 had so far were for all practical purposes novices. They were highly intelligent young men in superb physical condition who had passed through a prescribed course of training. But none of them had been flying for more than a year; and none of them, so far as Galloway had been able to determine, had ever been in trouble in the air.

And they were all impressed with Lieutenant Bill Dunn—understandably . . . if, in Galloway's judgment, rather naively. Dunn had *been in combat,* and he'd been *hit* and *wounded,* and he'd returned alive and *with two kills.*

All the same, just as soon as Big Steve Oblensky was able to make flyable two of the Wildcats they had trucked to Ewa from the docks at Pearl Harbor, Galloway flew against Dunn in half a dozen mock dogfights. He had no trouble outmaneuvering him the first time out, or the second, or the third; and he was starting to wonder if he should, so to speak, throw a dogfight, because consistently whipping Dunn was likely to humiliate him.

Then he thought that through and realized that humiliating Dunn was precisely the thing he *should* do. As the privates in a rifle squad should think, *believe,* that their sergeant was the best fucking rifle shot in the company, so should the lieutenant pilots of a fighter squadron *believe* that The Skipper was the best fucking airplane driver in Marine Aviation.

That policy seemed to have worked out well, even better than Galloway foresaw. For one thing, Dunn wasn't impressed with his own heroic accomplishment at Midway. So he was not humiliated when he was bested by a pilot who'd been flying when he was trying out for the junior varsity football team in high school.

For another, as the other pilots drifted into the squadron, Dunn let each of them know that The Skipper was really one hell of a pilot. Coming as it did from a pilot who had been wounded and scored two kills at Midway, Dunn's opinion was taken as Gospel.

And Galloway didn't let either himself or Dunn sit and rest on their accomplishments. He believed the simple old Marine Corps adage that the best way to learn something was to teach it. So he had Dunn up all the time teaching techniques of aerial combat and gunnery to the kids, honing his own skills in the process, and picking up time, which meant experience.

As for Galloway, whenever possible he did the test flying himself—simply because he was the best qualified pilot to do it. Most test flights were simply routine. If everything worked, they could be flown by one of the University of California's cretins. It was only when something went wrong that experience became important. An experienced pilot often sensed when something was about to go wrong, and so he could act to reduce the risk to the airplane before things went seriously bad. Even when some major system failed unexpectedly, an experienced pilot could often recover, and put the airplane back on the ground in one piece, while a pilot without his experience was likely not only to get himself killed, but to send the airplane to the junkyard, as well.

No aircraft assigned to VMF-229 had been lost—or even seriously damaged— during test flights. In Galloway's view this was a pretty good record . . . especially when you considered that three times the test pilot—C. M. Galloway—had lost power on take-off: When the fan of a Wildcat stopped spinning, the Wildcat didn't want to fly anymore; as soon as the power quit, the nose got heavy, and it started to stall. (Although the manual usually read like a sales brochure for Grumman, it nevertheless warned—in small print—that the aircraft became ''excessively nose heavy in a power loss situation.'') And then, even if you could keep it from stalling by getting it into a glide, the Wildcat sank like a rock.

Despite all that, Galloway somehow managed to bring each of those three aircraft down without cracking up the aircraft or the test pilot.

And so as Galloway sat there in the cockpit of the Wildcat he was testing that afternoon, cleared by the tower as Number One for take-off, and with all the needles in the green, it started to hit him that his anxious feelings, viewed objectively, just might be pretty goddamned ridiculous.

Captain Galloway pressed his mike button.

"Ewa," he said confidently, "Five Niner Niner. I'm experiencing a little roughness and low oil pressure. I want to check it out a moment."

"Roger, Five Niner Niner. Do you wish to leave the threshold at this time?"

"Five Niner Niner, negative. I think I'll be all right in a minute."

It would be a mistake I would regret all my life, correction, for all eternity, *however the fuck long that is, if I took this bird off and crashed in flames with a letter from my girlfriend I hadn't read in my pocket.*

He put his finger in his mouth, caught the index finger of the pigskin glove on his right hand between his teeth, and pulled the glove off. Then he repeated the process with the glove on his left hand. He took the envelope from his pocket and sniffed it.

I am probably fooling myself, but I think I can smell her perfume.

The envelope contained what Charley thought of as "ladies' stationery," a squarish, folded, rather stiff piece of paper. The outside bore a monogram. Scotch-taped to the inside was a small piece of jewelry, a round gold disc on a chain.

Jenkintown, June 30 '42

My Darling,

 This is an Episcopal serviceman's cross. I know you're not an Episcopalian; and now that I'm divorced (and for other reasons), I am a fallen Episcopalian woman. But I wish you would wear it anyway, to know that I am praying for you constantly.

 It has occurred to me that the only time you will ever notice it is when it gets in your way when you're taking a shower. But perhaps that will remind you of the showers you have shared with someone who loves you and lives for the moment when she can feel your arms around her again.

    All my love, now and forever,
    Caroline

Charley Galloway reached up and shoved his goggles up on his forehead. For some reason, his eyes were watering. He pried the medallion loose from the Scotch tape and looked at it. He tried to open the clasp on the gold chain, but couldn't manage it. There was no way he could get that fragile gold chain over his head. So he leaned forward and looped it around the adjustment knob of the altimeter on the control panel, then tugged on it to make sure vibration wouldn't shake it off.

He wiped his eyes with his knuckles, put his goggles back in place, worked his hands back into his gloves, and put them on the throttle and the stick. He inched the throttle forward and turned onto the runway. Then he moved the throttle to full take-off power, and pushed his mike button.

"Ewa," he said, with practiced savoir faire, "Five Niner Niner rolling."

Four hundred yards down the runway, he spoke to the engine.

"Don't you dare crap out on me now, you sonofabitch!"

A moment after that, F4F-4 tail number 40599 of VMF-229 lifted off into the air.

(THREE)
Headquarters, MAG-21
Ewa USMC Air Station
Oahu, Territory of Hawaii
1445 Hours 7 July 1942

Lieutenant Colonel Clyde D. Dawkins, USMC, commanding, MAG-21, was by no means unhappy with First Lieutenant James G. Ward, USMCR. He would have been happier, of course, if Ward had another five hundred hours of flight time, all of it in F4F-4s; but compared to the other replacement pilots they were getting fresh from Pensacola, Ward was a grizzled veteran.

He liked his attitude, too, which was not surprising, since Charley Galloway had recruited him. Galloway would not recruit a fool or a troublemaker.

"Captain Galloway until recently was a flying sergeant. Is that going to pose any problems for you?"

"Yes, Sir," Ward replied. "I mean I knew he was a flying sergeant. He was a sergeant when he taught me to fly the R4D, Sir." The question had obviously surprised him. "I don't know what you mean about problems, Sir."

"Well, Mr. Ward, there are some officers, generally very stupid officers, who resent Mustangs. I'm pleased to see that you're not one of them."

"No, Sir. I consider myself very fortunate to have a squadron commander who knows what he's doing."

Dawkins restrained a smile at the honest naïveté of the remark.

"Mr. Ward," he said sternly, "you are not suggesting, I trust, that there are squadron commanders who do not know what they are doing?"

Ward flushed.

"Sir," he began lamely.

"I know what you mean, Mr. Ward," Dawkins laughed. "That works both ways. I'm glad to have Charley Galloway as one of my squadron commanders. I share your opinion that he knows what he's doing. I will refrain from comment on my other squadron commanders."

"Yes, Sir," Ward said. His relief was evident on his face.

"I thought there were two of you?" Dawkins said.

"Yes, Sir. Lieutenant Schneider is outside."

Dawkins stood up and offered his hand. "Welcome aboard, Mr. Ward. We're glad to have you. I'm available to my officers for any reason, around the clock."

"Thank you, Sir."

"Would you send Mister—what did you say, 'Schneider'?—in, please?"

"Yes, Sir."

Lieutenant Colonel Dawkins was initially very favorably impressed with First Lieutenant David F. Schneider, USMC. He was a well-set-up young man; he looked remarkably crisp for someone who had just flown from the States to Hawaii. And he wore an Annapolis ring. Colonel Dawkins had been commissioned from Annapolis.

There were very few officers in the pre-war Navy who were not Annapolis graduates.

There was a theory . . . it was soon to be tested in the crucible of war . . . that the real value of Annapolis graduates to the country did not derive from their experience manning the ships of the peacetime Navy, but from the fact that they would now serve as the firm skeleton for the flesh and musculature of the enormous Navy that would be required to win the war.

Some of this would come from the presumed professionalism and Naval expertise that could be expected of a man who had spent his life, from the age of seventeen or eighteen, in Naval uniform. The rest would come because the Annapolis graduates —from ensigns, to first lieutenants, USMC, to admirals—would serve as role models for an officer corps that would be seventy or eighty percent civilian Marines and sailors. Dawkins privately thought that this was the more important of the two.

Even if they had difficulty admitting this in person to a graduate of Hudson High, virtually all Annapolis graduates both admired and tried hard to adhere to the code West Point put in words, *Duty, Honor, Country.*

And so Dawkins felt at first that Galloway was fortunate to have someone like Schneider in his squadron. He even imagined, somewhat wryly, that Schneider might be able to temper Charley Galloway's policy that he had greater right to any government property that was not chained to the ground or under armed guard than whoever it was issued to.

He was so impressed with Schneider that he almost passed over the question he had asked Lieutenant Ward, and in fact every other officer newly assigned to VMF-229. But in the end, he did ask him:

"Captain Galloway until recently was a flying sergeant. Is that going to pose any problems for you?"

"No, Sir. Not for me, Sir."

Why don't I like that response? What did he say? "Not for me"?

"Not for you? Is that what you said, Mr. Schneider? Are you suggesting that it might be a problem for Captain Galloway?"

"Sir," Schneider said, with a disarming smile, "I'm a regular. I know that before Captain Galloway was commissioned, a good deal of thought went into it. I certainly don't mean to suggest that Captain Galloway is not a first rate squadron commander."

"But?"

"Sir, what I'm saying, badly I'm afraid, is that I really wish I hadn't served with Captain Galloway when he was an enlisted man."

What bothers me about that? Dawkins wondered, and then he understood: *You didn't serve with Charley Galloway, Lieutenant, with him on your wing, or vice versa. He was your IP. By definition, IPs are superior to their students. I'm getting the idea, you presumptuous puppy, that you think an officer of suitable grade should have been assigned to instruct an officer and a gentleman and an Annapolis graduate such as yourself.*

"Because you will always think of him as a sergeant, you mean?"

"No, Sir. Because I think he may remember that I was one of his officers. And that might be a little awkward for him."

So you're a fucking liar, too, Mr. Schneider? I'll be goddamned! And an arrogant sonofabitch, too, if you really thought you were going to take me in with that bullshit.

"I think I take your point," Dawkins said. "Well, let me give it a little thought. Perhaps we could quietly arrange a transfer for you to one of the other squadrons."

"I wouldn't want any special treatment, Sir."

"I understand," Dawkins said. "We're talking about the good of the service, aren't we?"

"I think so, Sir."

What I don't understand is how this asshole fooled Charley Galloway. Maybe there's something here I'm missing. But if Galloway hasn't figured this self-serving prick out, I will transfer him for the good of the service. Charley has enough on his mind without worrying about this back-stabbing prick. He'll spend the rest of this fucking war test-flying Piper Cubs in Kansas.

"Well, that seems to be about it, Mr. Schneider," Dawkins said. "Unless there's something on your mind?"

"I hate . . ."

"Let's hear it?"

"My Uncle Dan is over at Pearl, Sir. On the CINCPAC staff. I wonder if there's any chance that I could get over to see him for a couple of hours before I begin my duties here?"

"Your Uncle Dan? I know a *Karl* Schneider . . ."

"This is my mother's brother, Sir. Daniel Wagam. Admiral Wagam."

You didn't lose any time letting me know that, did you?

Dawkins looked over Schneider's head at the clock on the wall. It was twenty after three. Certainly, Galloway wasn't going to put Schneider in a cockpit today. For one thing, it was too late. For another, Schneider was just off a long plane ride from the States. What Galloway probably had in mind was taking this prick and the nice kid over to the club so they could meet the other squadron officers. That could wait.

"Why don't you call and see if Admiral Wagam has time for you?" Dawkins said. "If he does, we'll get you a ride over there. I'm sure the admiral could arrange to get you back here by 0500 tomorrow, don't you think?"

"Yes, Sir. I'm sure he'd be able to do that."

Dawkins pointed to his telephone.

"Help yourself, Mr. Schneider."

(FOUR)
Headquarters, VMF-229
Ewa USMC Air Station
Oahu, Territory of Hawaii
1640 Hours 7 July 1942

When Captain Charles M. Galloway walked into his headquarters, two people were waiting for him, Lieutenant Jim Ward and PFC Alfred B. Hastings. Both rose to their feet.

Galloway was starting to wonder where Schneider was when he noticed that PFC Hastings was holding something in his hand. It was a piece of cardboard, a laundry shirt stiffener, on which he had drawn a rather nicely done skull and crossbones, the international symbol of danger; an oak leaf, the insignia of majors and lieutenant colonels; and an arrow pointing to Galloway's office.

"Stand at ease," Galloway said sternly. He smiled at Ward, winked at PFC Hastings, and walked into his office.

"Good afternoon, Sir," he said.

Lieutenant Colonel Clyde W. Dawkins was sitting in Charley's chair with his feet on Charley's desk. "You look like shit, Charley," he replied. "How many hours were you up today?"

"Six, I guess. Maybe a little more."

"Well, cut it down," Dawkins said. "I don't want to find myself writing 'pilot fatigue' as the probable cause of your fatal accident."

"Aye, aye, Sir."

"Close the door," Dawkins said.

Charley did so.

Dawkins was not through with him.

"What the hell is the matter with you?" he demanded. "You didn't start flying last week. You know better."

"Big Steve had a bunch of airplanes that needed test flying. I flew them," Galloway answered.

"How many have you got operational?"

"Eighteen, Sir. All of them," Galloway said, not without a hint of pride in his voice. "I have more operational aircraft than I do pilots."

"Christ, that was quick," Dawkins said.

"Big Steve's as good as they come."

"Yeah, but he's got a commanding officer who takes dumb chances test-flying them when he should know better."

"Yes, Sir," Galloway said.

"OK. Tomorrow you don't fly. Tonight, go get drunk. Consider that an order."

"Aye, aye, Sir. Actually, Sir, that thought had gone through my mind."

"I'm serious about this, goddamn you. I want *you* commanding VMF-229, not some kid six months out of Pensacola."

"Yes, Sir."

"But that's not the reason I am here, instead of inside a cold martini," Dawkins said. "I have interviewed your two new officers, Captain. The one outside seems to be a nice enough kid. Maybe too nice. Tell me about the other one."

Galloway hesitated.

"Out of school, Charley. Consider me your friendly parish priest. Bare your soul."

"The miserable sonofabitch knows how to fly," Galloway said.

"Really?" Dawkins asked doubtfully.

"He's really good," Charley said. "I need pilots like that. And I can handle the sonofabitch part."

"Did you know his uncle is an admiral? Admiral Wagam at CINCPAC?"

"No, but it doesn't surprise me. He's trade-school," Charley said, and then heard what he had said. "Sorry, Sir."

"Some of us trade-school graduates are sterling fellows," Dawkins said. "But— and I wouldn't want this to get around—a very small percentage are genuine pricks. I think your man Schneider is one of them."

"I can handle him, Sir," Charley said.

"Well, that's what I came to find out. If he starts giving you trouble, let me know."

"Aye, aye, Sir."

"He's over at Pearl with his uncle the admiral," Dawkins said. "I'm not sure if that's because they have a close-knit family or because he wanted me to know that his uncle is an admiral. But I told him he could go, and to be back at 0500. Will that cause any problems for you?"

"No, Sir."

Dawkins looked into Galloway's eyes for a moment, and then snorted. He swung his feet off the desk.

"You know what will cause a real problem for you, Captain?"

"Sir?"

"If I don't see you at the club tonight, really spiffy in your whites, having trouble with slurred speech and the other effects of alcohol."

"Well, Sir, that will cause a problem," Charley said. "While I'm sure my speech will probably get a little slurred as the night progresses, I hadn't planned to go to the club. I would really much rather not go to the club."

"I don't want to hear about it, Captain. Neither do I want to hear that, clear-eyed and bushy-tailed, you went anywhere near an airplane tomorrow."

"Aye, Aye, Sir."

"You've done a good job here, Charley," Dawkins said. "Christ, I didn't think you'd have eighteen operational aircraft for another two weeks."

"That's Big Steve, Sir, not me."

"Bullshit. But it raises a question. How much flying are you giving your people?"

"Sir?"

"How many hours a day are they flying?"

"No more than four, Sir."

"Do as I say, not as I do, right? Cut down your flying hours, Charley. I mean that."

"Aye, aye, Sir."

"I've enjoyed our little chat, Captain," Dawkins said. "We must have another, real soon."

He walked to the door, opened it, and walked through. Lieutenant Ward and PFC Hastings came to attention. He walked past them, then stopped and turned, and went back to Hastings.

"Captain Galloway's been telling me of your good work, Son," he said. "Keep it up!"

"Yes, Sir," Hastings said. He glowed with pride.

What the fuck was that all about? Charley wondered. *I didn't say a word to him about Hastings. Was that just apply-anywhere bullshit? Or was it Lesson Three in how to be a good commander?*

He saw Jim Ward looking into the office.

What the hell do I do with him tonight?

He waved him into the office.

"Dave went to Pearl Harbor," Jim Ward said. "He got permission from the colonel."

"So I hear. Did you get settled in the BOQ?"

Ward nodded. Somewhat uneasily, he said, "Did you know his uncle is an admiral?"

"No. Not until just now."

"This is going to sound ridiculous," Jim Ward said. "But I promised Aunt Caroline I would ask. Six hours after I got here. Are you wearing your necklace?"

Charley pulled the zipper of his flying suit down and pointed to the medallion.

"Oh," Ward said, smiling. "I thought it might be something like that. Are you Episcopal?"

"No. But do you think God really gives a damn?"

Jim Ward looked startled for a moment, then replied, "Hell, no."

Galloway made up his mind what he was going to do with Jim Ward.

"You can meet the rest of the guys tomorrow," he said. "Tonight we're going to go have dinner with some friends of mine."

"Won't I be in the way?"

"No. I don't think so," Charley said. "Come on, let's get out of here."

PFC Hastings rose once again from behind his typewriter as they walked into the outer office.

"Two things, Hastings," Charley said.

"Yes, Sir?"

"I don't want to hear that you've been here after 1730."

"Sir, I've got a lot to do."

"It'll wait."

"Aye, aye, Sir. And the second thing?"

"Cut a promotion order for the colonel's signature," Galloway said. "Make yourself a corporal."

"Aye, aye, Sir."

(FIVE)
Near Waialua, Oahu
Territory of Hawaii
1800 Hours 7 July 1942

Greeting her dinner guests, Lieutenant Commander Florence Kocharski, Nurse Corps, USN, was attired in sandals and a shapeless, loose-fitting cotton dress printed with brightly colored flowers, called a *Muumuu*. Over her ear she had a gardenia stuck through her silver hair.

"Hi, Charley," she said and let him kiss her cheek.

He handed her a brown paper sack which obviously contained bottles.

"Flo, this is Jim Ward," Charley Galloway said. "He's a friend of mine. I didn't think you would mind if I brought him along."

"No, of course not," Flo said, not very convincingly. "There's enough food to feed an army. How are you, Lieutenant?"

"I said 'friend,' Flo," Charley said. "His aunt is my girl. He introduced us."

Technical Sergeant Stefan Oblensky, USMC, attired in sandals, short pants, and a gaily flowered loose fitting cotton shirt, appeared behind her.

"Jesus, Charley!" he said, his tone torn between hurt and anger.

"I'm going to say this again," Galloway said. "Jim is a friend. More than a friend. Damned near family. My girl is his aunt."

"Yeah, sure," Big Steve said, far from mollified.

"And I told him what's going on here," Charley said. "He knows how to keep his mouth shut."

"What the hell," Flo said. "What's done is done. Come on and we'll open the jug." She put her arm around Jim Ward. "I know more about your aunt than I really want to know," she said. "He doesn't talk about her much, but once he gets started, you can't shut him up."

Jim smiled at her shyly.

"He told me about you, too," he said.

"He did? What?"

"About you being on the *West Virginia* on Pearl Harbor Day and getting the Silver Star."

"Like I say, sometimes you can't shut him up," Flo said.

With her arm still around his shoulders—she was just as tall as he was, and outweighed him by twenty pounds—Flo marched Jim Ward across the small living room of the frame cottage and into the kitchen.

She took the two bottles of scotch from the bag, opened one, and set out glasses. Then she reached under the sink and opened an insulated gray steel container, labeled MEDICAL CORPS USN, and took ice from it.

"No refrigerator," she said, as she dropped ice cubes in the glasses, "and the head is that small wooden building out there. But what the hell, what do they say, 'Be It Ever So Humble'?"

"It's very nice," Jim said.

"It belongs to a guy, retired Marine, who lets us use it," she said.

"Charley told me you were up here on Pearl Harbor Day," Jim said.

"He told you that, too, did he? He say who he was with?"

Jim shook his head "no."

Flo laughed. "Then I won't."

"Then you won't what?" Charley said, coming into the kitchen.

"I won't tell him who you was with on Sunday, December seven."

Galloway chuckled. "I was hoping you would," he said. "I was hoping you would have a motherly word to him about the dangers of getting involved with certain members of the Navy Nurse Corps."

"Don't play Mr. Innocent with me, Charley. The way I remember that, nobody had to drag you up here."

"This was all, Jim, pre-Caroline, when I was a footloose and carefree flying sergeant, like skinhead here."

"I told you, Charley," Flo said, "I don't like you to call Stefan that."

"Well, 'Curly' sure doesn't fit," Galloway said, unabashed.

"Who are you talking about?" Jim asked.

"One of Flo's angels of mercy," Charley said.

"Angel, my ass," Flo said. "I'm always wondering if she won't say something to somebody about Stefan and me, out of pure bitchiness."

"Does she know about you?" Charley asked.

"Not that we're married," Flo said. "But I have to let them know where I am. I'm assistant chief nurse. She knows damned well that I'm not coming up here alone to count the pineapples; she knows I'm still 'dating' Stefan. She's always making some sweet little crack, you know, 'give my regards to Sergeant Oblensky,' like that."

"I don't think she'll say anything," Charley said. "You know too much about her."

"I know more about her than you think I do," Flo said, "but now that she's running around with that lieutenant of yours, no telling what she's liable to do."

By then, she had finished making the drinks. She handed them out.

"Well, welcome to our happy home," she said.

"Thank you," Jim said.

"I'm getting really sick of the whole goddamned thing," Big Steve said, "hiding out like we're doing something wrong. I'm pretty close to telling them. 'We're married. Fuck you, what are you going to do about it?' "

"Watch your mouth, Honeybun!" Flo snapped.

"They wouldn't court-martial us," Big Steve went on. "That's bullshit."

"Maybe not. You can never tell," Charley said. "But they'd sure as hell transfer one of you. Probably you. You'd spend the war changing Yellow Peril engines at Quantico or Pensacola. You could kiss these weekends up here good-bye."

"What the hell's the difference? Here or Pee-Cola? The fuckers won't let me fly anymore anyway."

"You're too goddamned old to fly, you old fart," Charley said, laughing. "The Corps's not flying Spads anymore."

"I don't know what the hell is with you two," Flo said, angrily. "Watch your mouths, there's a lady present!"

"Sorry," Big Steve said, contritely.

"Just watch it!" she said. Then, "Charley's right, Honeybun. Be grateful for what we have. Don't do something dumb."

"Just because he's an officer now don't make him smart," Big Steve said.

"The hell it doesn't!" Charley protested, jokingly. "We officers have to know how to read and write and how to tie our own shoes. Don't we, Flo?"

"You tell him, Charley," Flo said, laughing.

"If you're so fu—smart, Captain, Sir," Big Steve said, "tell me about Guadacanal."

"About what?"

"Guadacanal," Big Steve said, triumphantly.

"Never heard of it," Charley confessed.

"Well, for your general information, Captain, Sir, it's an island. The Japs are building a fighter base on it, and the First Marine Division is going to take it away from them.''

This scuttlebutt has the ring of truth to it, Charley decided.

''Where is this island?'' Charley asked.

Big Steve shrugged his massive shoulders.

''It's in the Solomon Islands, Charley,'' Flo said, softly. ''Down by Australia. And it's *Guadalcanal,* with an 'L.' I heard the same thing. They've been levying us for doctors and corpsmen. I heard they're going to invade this place right after the first of the month.''

''You heard that too, huh, Honey?'' Big Steve asked.

Charley looked at Jim Ward.

''Jim, do I have to tell you not to repeat this scuttlebutt?''

''No, Sir. Of course not.''

''I don't even know where the Solomon Islands are,'' Charley said, as much to himself as to the others.

''Wait a minute,'' Big Steve said. ''I brung some maps. I was going to ask Flo.''

He left the kitchen. They heard him a moment later walking across the living room, and then they heard the screen door screeching.

''Straight poop, would you say, Flo?'' Charley asked softly.

She nodded. ''I don't know where he heard it, but I'd bet on my information.''

The screen door slammed again, and then Big Steve called for them to come into the living room. They went in, to find him fastening the corners of a large map to the floor with ashtrays and a bottle.

They all got on their knees and examined the map.

''There it is,'' Flo said, pointing. ''And those itsy-bitsy little islands near it. Tulagi and Gavutu. I heard that, too.''

''God,'' Charley said thoughtfully. ''It's a long way from nowhere, isn't it?''

There was no reply, except a grunt from Big Steve. And then Charley asked for a sheet of paper and a pencil. When Flo produced both, he laid the paper on the map and copied the scale from it.

Then he began moving the paper around on the map.

''What the *hell* are you doing?'' Big Steve asked, taking the words from Jim's mouth.

''Ssssh, Honeybun,'' Flo said.

Finally, Charley sat back on his heels.

''Well, if this is the place the First Marine Division is going, they're going without VMF-229,'' he said.

''How can you tell that?'' Jim asked, curiously, not as a challenge.

''Because it's out of fighter range from any land airbase we control,'' Charley said. ''Which means they're going to have to use carrier-based aviation. And VMF-229 is not carrier qualified. I think only Dunn and me ever were.''

Big Steve grunted again.

''And, if your date is anywhere near close, Flo, there's no way we could qualify in time.''

''Why not?'' Big Steve asked. ''All you'd need is, what? Two, three days to shoot some landings.''

''We'd need a carrier to shoot them on,'' Charley said. ''There's no carrier here right now. And even if there was, there's no way we could be qualified, and put aboard, and still steam that far in time to make the invasion.''

''Huh!'' Big Steve said, disappointed.

''But I tell you what *could* happen,'' Charley said thoughtfully. ''They are going to need fighters on that island when they take it.''

''Why, if we take it?'' Jim asked.

"Because all of those islands are within fighter range of each other. They will be within range of land-based Japanese aircraft. And they're not about to leave aircraft carriers in the area; they'd be too vulnerable to the Japs."

"OK," Big Steve said. "So what? What are you driving at?"

"They could load us on one of those escort carriers, and then catapult us off that onto this island when they have captured the airfield."

"I thought you said nobody but you and Dunn was carrier qualified," Flo asked.

"Nobody else is, but that wouldn't matter. If they were to catapult us off one of the escort carriers, we wouldn't go back to it. The hard part of carrier operation is landing—the approach and the arrested landing. Getting catapulted off a carrier is something else. It's scary, especially the first time. You go from zero to ninety knots in a second. But then you're flying."

Big Steve snorted.

Galloway looked at him and shrugged.

"I was just thinking out loud."

"I was just thinking," Big Steve said, "that you may not be so dumb after all—for an officer, that is."

"You have just been complimented," Flo chuckled. "Enjoy it, Charley."

"I'll drink to that," Charley said, and then looked at Jim Ward. "But you will not. You are flying tomorrow. You will be practicing the technique of taking off short. And you will be as baffled as any of your peers when they start wondering out loud what that crap is supposed to be all about—as opposed to mock dogfights, which are a lot more fun."

"Aye, aye, Sir."

"Let's eat," Flo said. "We've having a Hawaiian Luau. Except it's a pork loin. I can't stand the sight of one of those poor baby pigs with apples in their mouths."

(SIX)
Officer's Club
U.S. Navy Base, Pearl Harbor
Oahu, Territory of Hawaii
2130 Hours 7 July 1942

Although he was of course delighted to see his sister's son, Rear Admiral Daniel J. Wagam was also a little annoyed at the way the kid popped up unannounced out of nowhere, expecting to be entertained.

The Admiral had been working his ass off since the Eyes Only EXECUTE OPERATIONAL PESTILENCE radio had come in five days before, and it seemed obvious that the work days were going to grow longer rather than shorter as things finally started to mesh.

The truth of the matter was that the Pacific Fleet and attached Marine Forces were not prepared—in any way—to stage an amphibious assault on an island in the Hawaiian chain, much less on three islands a quarter of the world away in the Solomons.

There was not enough of anything that would be needed. About the only thing that was not in short supply was senior officers. A whole flock of commanders and captains and even a dozen or so flag officers had been called back from retirement. They had come back into uniform willingly, even eagerly, and their expertise was most welcome. But at times, Admiral Wagam had reluctantly concluded, they were like a bunch of goddamned old maids.

By his own actual calculation, Admiral Wagam was spending two-thirds of his time establishing shipping priorities and scheduling convoys and the other third settling disputes over Naval protocol between the retreads, who were exquisitely sensitive to the prerogatives of rank and time in grade.

Most often, the disputes had to do with the assignment of creature comforts—who had a permanently assigned staff car with driver, and who didn't, that sort of thing. But the worst fights were over quarters—where the most desirable rooms in the Bachelor Officer's Quarters were assigned, or in cottages, in the case of captains and flag officers. These assignments were ordinarily made on the basis of rank, and within rank, on the basis of time in grade. Now and again, however, some of the retreads came to believe that the assignment they had been given was beneath their dignity and inappropriate to their rank and seniority.

As Admiral Wagam knew only too well, "seniority" was not as simple a concept as it might at first appear to be. For instance, seniority could not be established solely by date of promotion; for this would have made virtually all of the retreads senior to virtually all of the officers in a particular grade who had not retired. Some of the retreads had retired as early as 1935.

Thus it had been necessary to make up a seniority list for the retreads. Clerks had dug into the records to see how much time in grade Captain So-and-so had at the time of his retirement. This would be added to the time he now had on active duty since being recalled. This produced a seniority list based on time in grade, not date of promotion.

It had not been possible, however, to merge this list with a similar list prepared for nonretired officers, and announce that Captain A, who had never retired, and who had five years, nine months, and *eleven* days of service as a captain, therefore outranked Captain B, a retread, who had five years, nine months, and *one* day of service as a four striper. When this happened, Captain B would very often make it known that the list be damned, when he retired, Captain A was a lowly lieutenant commander, a none-too-bright one, as he recalled; and he had no intention of taking orders from the young pup now.

And it wasn't a question of simply reminding Captain B that he was back in the Navy and expected to take orders, although Dapper Dan Wagam had done just that several times. Even when there was no question of seniority, a good many of the retreads seemed to have an uncontrollable urge to question the orders they had been given. Even when he himself was giving the orders, he'd come to expect from these guys a moment of smug hesitation, then something like, "Well, in my experience, we did . . . or did not . . ." Or, "In the *Old* Navy, they . . ." When they believed that they were being forced by an unappreciative Navy to take orders from some young pup still wet behind the ears, their obedience ceased being cheerful and willing. "After all," they were quick to point out, "we were *asked* to return to duty."

It often lent an entirely new meaning, Wagam had concluded, to the word "grudging."

And since he was on the bridge of a desk, rather than at sea, Admiral Wagam had, he believed, more than his fair share of the retreads. Indeed, very few of *them* were actually being sent to sea, although virtually all of them had volunteered—often two or three times a week—to take a command.

When his sister's son, First Lieutenant David F. Schneider, USMC, showed up, Admiral Wagam was trying to recover from yet another bad day. For one thing, he was frustrated that he'd failed to solve logistical problems there was no satisfactory solution for—there was simply not enough available tonnage for OPERATION PESTILENCE; and consequently, the First Marine Division was going to assault a hostile shore inadequately supplied. And for another, he'd been forced to handle no less than three retreads who truly believed that their professional reputations were being demeaned by the duties he had assigned them.

But Admiral Wagam was as gracious to David Schneider as he could be under the circumstances. He realized his problems were certainly not David's fault; but more to the point, his sister was hell on wheels when she felt one of her children had been slighted. . . . So he personally showed David around the office, to give the boy some understanding of what he was up to.

He did not, of course, mention OPERATION PESTILENCE, which was classified TOP SECRET.

And then he took him to dinner in the Flag Officer's Mess and introduced him around. It would have been nice if David could have written his mother that he had been introduced to Admiral Nimitz, but Nimitz apparently had elected to eat in his quarters.

Nimitz was probably eating alone, or as alone as the CINCPAC ever got to be, Admiral Wagam thought, *as opposed to having a working dinner. If it had been a working dinner, he probably would have been invited.*

And then he sent him on his way:

"David, I'd like to send you back to Ewa in my car, but I'm going to need it."

"I understand."

"There's a bus that runs between here and Ewa. Among other places, it stops at the Main Club."

"I can manage, Uncle Dan."

"I would suppose there will be a number of officers from MAG-11 at the club. Ask around. The odds are you can find a ride back with one of them."

"Thank you."

"Give your mother my love when you write."

"Yes, Sir, I'll do that."

XIII

(ONE)

First Lieutenant William C. Dunn, Executive Officer, VMF-229, was sitting at the bar with Lieutenant (j.g.) Mary Agnes O'Malley, Nurse Corps, USN, having an after-dinner cognac. Dunn had learned that an after-dinner cognac—for that matter, any kind of alcohol at any time—seemed to trigger in Mary Agnes lewd and carnal desires. As they sipped their cognacs, her arm was resting on his upper leg, and her hand was gently stroking his inner thigh. She was fully aware what this did to him. And he knew that once there was proof positive, so to speak, that she had flipped his HORNY ON switch, and the mechanism had been activated, she would look into his eyes with pleasure and understanding, and purse her lips in promise of what was to come. And probably even give it a friendly little pat on the head. *Good doggie.*

Dunn had recently been giving a good deal of thought to his relationship with Mary Agnes O'Malley.

For starters, he was the envy of most of his peers, even the noble minded who chose to believe she wasn't really giving him any. The ratio of young bachelor officers in the Naval Establishment around Pearl Harbor to good-looking, socially acceptable females—or for that matter, to any kind of females—was probably two-hundred-fifty to one. Phrased another way, the odds against a first lieutenant hooking up with a good-looking, firm-breasted, blonde-headed nurse who fucked like a mink were probably on the order of a thousand to one.

What did every red-blooded Marine Aviator want? A nymphomaniac whose father owned a liquor store. Mary Agnes's father didn't own a liquor store, but there didn't seem to be any question that if she wasn't really a nympho, she was pretty damned close.

But Bill Dunn kept remembering from college some great philosophical truth—he forgot who said it—to the effect that the only thing worse than not realizing one's dreams was to realize them: Here he was with a good-looking woman who couldn't wait to get him in bed every night. There she would eagerly perform sexual acts he had seen before only in stag movies. And he was unhappy with the situation.

Even the sex, once the novelty wore off, was becoming a chore. He was regarding it lately as his duty, his more and more reluctant holding up of his end of the bargain.

The sad truth was that Mary Agnes O'Malley was dumber than dog shit. It was a realization he'd come to somewhat belatedly, probably because intellectual attainment was not high on his original list of priorities. But it didn't take him long to begin to think that it was entirely within the realm of possibility that an original idea and a cold drink of water *would* actually kill her.

Mary Agnes O'Malley read *Photoplay* and *Screen Life* magazines for intellectual stimulation; she was a veritable fountain of information regarding the private life of movie stars. She had read somewhere, for instance, that actor Tyrone Power had entered the Corps and was in flight training. Her dream was that Power would be assigned to Hawaii and Dunn would introduce them. She spoke of this often.

If that happened, Lieutenant Power—or Captain Power, whatever he was—would probably set the minimum time record for the Marine Aviator getting his ashes hauled after arrival in the Territory of Hawaii.

But in the meantime, Mary Agnes made it plain that Lieutenant Bill Dunn was all that her heart—and other anatomical parts—desired. This was not because she found him a charming companion, or even an outstanding lover, but because he looked, as she often told him, just like an actor named Alan Ladd.

Dunn knew that if he really wanted to break it off with Mary Agnes, he could do it relatively easily. He could just call her and say that he had the duty and could not make it over to Pearl. She was dumb, but she was capable of understanding that. He was convinced that if he did this five nights in a row, say, no matter how determined she was not "to cheat" on him, she would have a snifter or two of Hennessey VSOP, her blood would start to boil, and some other soul would find himself sneaking up the back stairs to Room Eleven, Female Officer's Quarters Fourteen.

But in his own eyes he had no character. Or phrased less delicately, he was letting his dick do his thinking for him. He made "Sorry, I have the duty" telephone calls at least four times—for two nights in a row, twice. But that was as far as logic could go, vis-à-vis overwhelming the sinful lusts of the flesh.

No matter how high his original resolve and how firm his original intentions, by the third day, he was unable to refute the whispers in his ear, *Billy-Boy, they are not pulling your chain with that "Live Today For Tomorrow We Die" shit. The piece of ass you are so casually rejecting may well be the last piece you are ever offered. Tomorrow morning, you may crash in flames. Or they may tell you to get your ass aboard a carrier; and away you will sail to your hero's death. With that in mind, does it really make any sense to spend your last night alive or ashore in your room with a portable radio for company, when you can play Hide the Salami and other games in Mary Agnes's perfumed bed?*

Dunn noticed First Lieutenant David Schneider within sixty seconds or so of the moment Schneider walked into the bar of the Main Club. Schneider caught Dunn's attention because he was wearing a white uniform. Officers wearing white uniforms outnumbered officers wearing greens about ten to one, but Schneider's white uniform was the only one—Marine or Navy—with gold Naval Aviator's wings pinned to it.

I wonder who that horse's ass is? was Bill Dunn's first thought. If you were an aviator, you could get away with not wearing whites.

His second thought immediately followed the first: *He probably just got here. He's probably, as a matter of fact, one of the two we got today.*

When Dunn had signed out in the squadron office for the Main Club at Pearl Harbor, PFC Hastings told him VMF-229 had two new officer pilots.

"If you don't stop that, I'm going to bust my zipper," First Lieutenant Dunn said quietly to Lieutenant (j.g.) O'Malley, removing her hand from his crotch.

"Promises, promises," she replied and pursed her lips at him.

"Excuse me," he said, getting up.

"Where are you going?"

"I think the guy in whites down at the end of the bar is one of ours," he said. "I'll be right back."

Mary Agnes looked toward the end of the bar and saw First Lieutenant David Schneider.

"Oh, he's cute!" she exclaimed, "He looks just like John Garfield."

Dunn reached Schneider in time to see the bartender fill the lieutenant's glass with ginger ale. He was a little surprised, because there was no darker liquid already in the glass.

"Good evening," Dunn said.

Schneider nodded an acknowledgment, but did not speak.

"Is your name John Garfield, by any chance?"

"No, it is not."

"Just get in? To VMF-229 by any chance?"

Dunn saw that the question made the lieutenant uncomfortable.

Obviously, he can't answer that question. Japanese ears are everywhere. Loose lips sink ships. And I probably look like a Jap spy in disguise.

"My name is Dunn. I'm Exec of VMF-229."

"Oh," Schneider said, straightening. "Yes, Sir. My name is Schneider, Sir. I reported aboard today, Sir."

Dunn gave him his hand.

"How do you do, Sir?"

"I heard there were two of you?"

"Yes, Sir. Lieutenant Jim Ward was on the same set of orders."

"He here with you?"

"No, Sir. I believe he stayed aboard Ewa."

"Oh, now I know who you are. The Skipper stole you from Quantico, right?"

"We were stationed at Quantico, yes, Sir."

"Now, don't misunderstand this. This is a simple suggestion. I'm about to return to Ewa. I have a car. If you need a ride?"

"Yes, Sir, thank you very much. Actually, I came in here hoping to get a ride."

"Well, then, come on down the bar while I finish my drink."

"Won't I be in the way, Sir? Two's company, and so on?"

"Not at all," Bill Dunn said. "The lady and I are just friends."

This is despicable of you, Billy Dunn. But on the other hand, what a clever sonofabitch you are sometimes.

"Lieutenant O'Malley, may I present Lieutenant Schneider, who joined the squadron today?"

"Pleased to meet you, I'm sure," Mary Agnes said. "Did anyone ever tell you you look just like John Garfield?"

Dave Schneider flushed. "No, I can't say that anyone has."

"Don't you think he does, Bill?"

"Spitting image," Bill Dunn said. He was pleased to see that Lieutenant Schneider did not seem to be able to keep his eyes away from Mary Agnes's tunic, where her bosom placed quite a strain against the material; it sort of made her gold buttons stand to attention.

He beckoned to the bartender.

"We'll have a round," he said.

"Sir," Dave Schneider said uncomfortably, "I was led to believe we'd be flying tomorrow."

"One cognac won't hurt you," Bill Dunn said. "And we can't welcome you aboard with ginger ale."

"Yes, Sir," Dave Schneider said.

"And another part of the welcome aboard ritual is a dance with Lieutenant O'Malley," Dunn said. "Mary Agnes is something like the squadron mascot, isn't that so, Mary Agnes?"

"Oh, it is not," she said. "You make me sound like a cocker spaniel. But I do like to dance."

How about a bitch in heat?

(TWO)
Headquarters, RAN Coastwatcher Establishment
Townesville, Queensland
1945 Hours 15 July 1942

Both Major Ed Banning, commanding officer of U.S. Marine Corps Special Detachment 14, and Lieutenant Commander Eric Feldt, Officer Commanding, Royal Australian Navy Coast Watcher Establishment, were waiting at the small Townesville air strip when the Royal Australian Air Force Lockheed Hudson came in low over the sea and touched down.

As the twin engine bomber-transport taxied to a parking place, Banning put the Studebaker President in gear and bounced over the grass to it.

By the time the rear door opened, and Captain Fleming Pickering, USNR, was emerging from it, Banning and Feldt were standing on either side of the spot where his feet would alight. After Feldt saluted elaborately, in the British palm-out manner, the hand quivering, he barked, "Sir!"

Banning extended a towel-wrapped bottle in an ice-filled cooler. The cooler had begun life as a tomato can.

"It's beer," he said. "But you can't fault our good intentions."

"I expected at least a band," Pickering said, taking the bottle from the can and removing the towel. "What am I supposed to do, bite the cap off?"

"Sir!" Feldt barked again, and bowing deeply handed him a bottle opener.

Pickering opened the beer bottle, took a pull from the neck, and offered the bottle to Feldt.

"Very good of you, Sir," Feldt said, taking a pull at the beer and handing it to Banning. "And may I say how honored we all feel that you could find time in your busy schedule to honor us with a visit."

Pickering appeared to be thoughtfully considering the remark. Finally, smiling, he said, "Yes, I think you may."

Feldt laughed with delight.

The pilot, a silver-haired Wing Commander, the co-pilot, a Squadron Commander, and the crew chief, a sergeant, came out of the airplane. Banning introduced them, and then said, "I think, Wing Commander, that you may unload the emergency rations for these starving savages."

"Very good, Sir," the Wing Commander said.

The sergeant went back in the Hudson and started handing boxes out. There was a case of scotch, a case of bourbon, six cases of beer, and a wooden case marked Moet & Chandon.

"Do you sodding Americans do everything backward? Christmas is in *December*," Feldt said.

"A small contribution to the *enlisted* mess," Pickering said. "Knowing as I do that a fine Christian officer such as yourself would never allow alcohol to touch his lips."

"I can get it down without it coming near my lips," Feldt said. "Anyone who comes between me and the bubbly does so at his peril."

"What's up, Boss?" Major Ed Banning asked.

"Never treat with the natives until you've plied them with alcohol," Pickering said. "And always hope that no one has warned them to beware of Americans bearing gifts."

"Why don't I like the sound of that?" Feldt asked.

"Because you're prescient," Pickering said. "You intuit that I am here to tell you how to do your job."

Feldt continued to smile, but the warmth was gone from his eyes.

"Will it wait until after dinner? Or should I more or less politely tell you to climb back on the sodding airplane and bugger off now?"

"That would depend on dinner," Pickering said. "What are we having?"

"Probably very little," Banning said. "I told them to go ahead and eat if we weren't back by 1830."

"We ran against a forty-knot headwind all the bloody way," the Wing Commander said. "We had to set down and refuel."

"Then I suppose we'll have to drink our dinner," Pickering said. "How are we going to get all that in the car?"

"We'll take the booze, naturally, and leave you and Banning here," Feldt said. "There's such a thing as going too sodding far with this international cooperation crap."

"Why don't you and the Wing Commander and Captain Pickering take half of the booze, and then send the car back to pick up the rest of us and the rest of the booze?" Ed Banning suggested.

"Why don't we leave the Wing Commander, too?" Feldt said. "That way there would be no witnesses when I remind the Captain that the understanding was that he would keep his sodding nose the hell out of my business?"

"That," Pickering said, after a moment, "as you suggested, can wait until after dinner."

"It's a pity, really," Feldt said. "I was on the edge of almost liking you, Pickering. A man, even a sodding American, can't be all bad if he brings me Moet & Chandon."

"Into each life," Pickering intoned sonorously, "some rain must fall."

"Get in the car, you sodding bastard," Feldt said. "You drive. The sodding steering wheel is on the wrong side."

Lieutenant Commander Eric Feldt rose somewhat unsteadily to his feet.

"If you will excuse us, gentlemen," he said, "the time has come for me to tell Captain Pickering to bugger off before I am too pissed to do so."

"Ed," Pickering said, as he stood up from the dinner table, "you and Wing Commander Foster, too."

Feldt looked, not at all friendly, at Wing Commander Foster.

"You, too, Wing Commander?" he asked. "I wondered what the hell a Wing Commander was doing chauffeuring Pickering around."

Wing Commander Foster was aware of Lieutenant Commander Feldt's reputation even before Air Vice-Marshal Devon-Jaynes and Captain Fleming Pickering warned him that Feldt was difficult. As they all ate dinner, while Feldt bitterly criticized everyone involved in the war except the Japanese, Foster had managed to keep his mouth shut—though with an effort.

But now, momentarily, he lost control.

"One does what one is ordered to, Commander," he said icily. "In this instance, I am here at the direction of Air Vice-Marshal Devon-Jaynes."

"Air Vice-Marshal Devon-Jaynes?" Feldt replied. "Well, sod him, too."

He turned and marched out of the room. Pickering shook his head and made a gesture with his hand to Wing Commander Foster, signifying both an apology for Feldt and an order to say nothing more.

"Sorry, Sir," Foster said.

"Commander Feldt," Pickering said, touching Foster's arm, "is both a remarkable man, and a man whose contributions to this goddamn war cannot be overstated."

"Yes, Sir," Foster said, and then followed Pickering into Feldt's office. Banning brought up the rear.

Feldt was standing behind his desk, pouring scotch into a glass.

"I presume," he said nastily, "that since the Wing Commander is here at the direction of Air-Vice Marshal Whatsisname that he has the sodding Need to Know whatever it is we're going to talk about?"

"Wing Commander Foster has a TOP SECRET OPERATION PESTILENCE clearance," Pickering said evenly. He took a business-sized envelope from his inner jacket pocket and handed it to Feldt. "That's an authorization from Admiral Boyer to give Wing Commander Foster access to Coastwatcher classified information through TOP SECRET."

Feldt looked at the envelope, and then tossed it unopened on his desk.

"I'll take your word for it," he said. "OK. Let's get to it."

"Why don't we uncover the map?" Pickering said.

"Why don't we?" Feldt said. He turned around and faced the wall behind his desk. A four-by-six-foot sheet of plywood, hinged at the top, lay against the wall. With some difficulty, Feldt raised it, then attached a length of chain which held it horizontally, exposing the map beneath.

The map displayed the Solomon Islands area from New Britain and New Ireland in the North, through Santa Isabel and Guadalcanal in the Southeast, and the upper tip of Australia to the Southwest. It was covered with a sheet of celluloid, on which had been marked in grease pencil the location of the thirty or more Coastwatchers, together with their radio call signs.

"Why don't you have a look at that, Wing Commander?" Pickering said.

Foster went to the map and studied it carefully in silence for more than a minute.

"This is the first time I've seen this . . ." he said.

"We don't publish it in the sodding *Times,* for Christ's sake," Feldt said.

". . . and I had no idea how many stations you have," Foster concluded, ignoring him.

"Not as many as we would like. Or had," Feldt said. "Note the red Xs."

There were a dozen or more locations which had red grease pencil Xs drawn through them.

"No longer operational, I gather?" Foster said.

"No longer operational, for one reason or another," Feldt said. "Betrayed by natives. Or felled by one sodding tropical disease or another. Or equipment failure. Or the sodding Japs just got lucky and found them."

"We are going to land on Guadalcanal, Tulagi, and Gavutu on August first," Pickering said. He stopped and then went on. "Actually, I don't think there is any way they can make that schedule. There's going to be a rehearsal in the Fiji Islands first. And then they'll probably land on Guadalcanal on seven August or eight August."

"If then," Ed Banning said, a little bitterly. "I heard what a mess things are in in New Zealand."

"It'll have to be by then," Pickering replied. "If the Japanese get that airfield near Lunga Point on Guadalcanal operational—even for Zeroes, not to mention bombers—I hate to think what they could do to an invasion fleet."

"The point of all this?" Feldt asked.

"At the moment, the bulk of Japanese aerial assets are in—or around—Rabaul. When they attack the invasion fleet, or the islands themselves after we land, they will use planes based at Rabaul. The more warning we have, obviously, the better. I am concerned with Buka."

"Buka is up and running," Feldt said.

Foster searched on the map and found Buka, a small island at the tip of Bougainville.

"Here?" he said, but it was more of a statement than a question.

"Buka is the only Coastwatcher station, Wing Commander," Feldt said, "manned by U.S. Marine Corps personnel. Do you suppose that has anything to do with Captain Pickering's concern?"

Banning looked at Pickering and actually saw the blood drain from his face.

"There is a point, Eric," Pickering said icily, "when you cross the line from colorful curmudgeon to offensive horse's ass. At that point I will not tolerate any more of your drunken, caustic bullshit. You have passed that point. Do you take my meaning?"

"Not really," Feldt said, unrepentant. "Explain it to me."

"Let me put it this way: How would you like to spend the rest of this war counting life preservers in Melbourne?"

"Don't you threaten me!"

"If I don't have an apology in thirty seconds, I'm going to pick up that telephone and call Admiral Boyer and tell him that I have reluctantly come to agree with him about the necessity of relieving you."

"Sod you, Pickering."

"We're not going to need the thirty seconds, I see," Pickering said. He walked to the desk and reached for the telephone.

He had it halfway to his ear when Feldt stayed his hand.

"It's the booze, for Christ's sake."

"Then leave the goddamned booze alone!"

"I have this terrible tendency to lubricate myself when I find myself writing letters that go, 'Dear Mrs. Keller, I very much regret having to inform you that information has come to me indicating that your husband has been captured and executed by the Japanese . . .'"

Pickering put the telephone back in its cradle, but did not take his hand off it, nor take his eyes off Feldt.

Feldt avoided Pickering's eyes and looked at Wing Commander Foster.

"When they catch one of our lads, Wing Commander, what the Nips do—after interrogation, of course—is put him down ceremonially. First, they make him dig his own grave; and then they behead him, after making sure their chap with the sword is of equal or superior grade. After that, they pray over the grave. Did you know that?"

"No," Foster said quietly, "I did not."

Feldt looked at Pickering.

"Letting the side down, in my cups, I look for someone, a friend, against whom I can vent my 'caustic bullshit.' Ed Banning usually gets it. I don't know how or why he puts up with it. And I certainly can understand why you won't, Pickering. But for the record, I am fully aware that Buka would not be up and running if it weren't for your two lads. They have balls at least as big as any of my lads, and the one thing I was not suggesting was that they don't."

Pickering looked into his eyes for a moment, then took his hand from the telephone and straightened up.

"Let's talk about Buka," he said.

"I gather you accept my apology?"

"Oh, was that an apology?" Pickering asked lightly.

"As close as I know how to come to one."

"In that case, yes," Pickering said.

"Let's talk about Buka," Feldt said.

"We can't afford to lose it," Pickering said. "Worst possible case, we can't afford to lose it in the last few days before and the first few days following the invasion of Guadalcanal. Every plane the Japanese launch from Rabaul to attack the invasion force will pass over Buka. If we know the type of aircraft, how many, and when they're coming, we can have our fighters in the air to repel them. If we don't have that intelligence from Buka, a lot of people are going to be killed, and ships we can't afford to lose will be sunk."

"So?"

"I want to reinforce it," Pickering said. "I've discussed this with Admiral Boyer and he agrees. Wing Commander Foster has been directed to provide aircraft to drop another team, or teams, in."

"Sod Admiral Boyer," Feldt said. "No."

"You have reasons?" Pickering asked. Banning saw his face pale again.

"If there is anybody in Australia or New Zealand who knows his way around Buka, I haven't been able to find him," Feldt said. "And Christ knows, it's not for want of trying."

"What's your point?"

"There is only one spot on Buka where we could parachute a team in with any chance of them surviving the landing. We already used it to put your lads in there. The Nips know we used it. They are now watching it. So we can't use that again. The sodding island is covered with dense jungle, except where the Nips are. You jump a team in there, what you're going to have is three skeletons in trees. And even if by some miracle that didn't happen, and they got to the ground in one piece, they still wouldn't know the island, would they? They'd never be able to get from where they were dropped to where they could do any good. Either the jungle would get them, or the natives—you understand that the natives are still reliably reported to be cannibals?—or the sodding Nips, of course."

Pickering nodded, and then said softly, "It might become necessary to send in one team after another until one made it."

"You are a cold-blooded bastard, aren't you, Pickering?" Feldt asked softly.

"A lot of lives are at stake," Pickering replied. "We simply can't afford to lose that early intelligence."

"Are you looking for advice? Or did you come here to tell me when we are going to start dropping parachutists?"

"Advice."

"OK. Form your teams. Banning's already done that, anyway. Lay on an airplane, have it ready around the clock. For that matter, if you have the clout, lay on a submarine, or maybe a PT boat, in case we decide the best thing is to put them ashore and not parachute them in. If Buka goes down, then we start sending people. Not before. This isn't the Imperial sodding Japanese Navy; our lads don't want to die for their emperor, and I will be damned if I'll ask them to."

Pickering pursed his lips for just a moment.

"OK," he said. "We'll do it your way. And pray that Buka doesn't go down."

Feldt nodded.

"Since you've been so sodding agreeable, I'm going to offer you some of my bubbly. You understand I wouldn't do that for just anybody, Pickering."

(THREE)
Company Grade Bachelor's Officer's Quarters #2
Supreme Headquarters, South West Pacific Area
(Formerly, Commerce Hotel)
Brisbane, Australia
0430 Hours 22 July 1942

As often happened when the telephone rang in the middle of the night, and he made a grab for it, Lieutenant Pluto Hon, BS, MS, PhD (*summa cum laude,* Mathematics), Massachusetts Institute of Technology, knocked the unstable fucking museum piece off the bedside table and had to retrieve it from under the bed before he could answer it. The unstable fucking museum piece held its cone-shaped mouthpiece atop a ten-inch Corinthian column, and the ear piece hung from a lifeboat davit on the side.

"Lieutenant Hon, Sir."

"What the hell was that noise?" Captain Fleming Pickering asked.

"I knocked the phone over, Sir."

"Pluto, I'm really sorry to wake you at this ungodly hour, but something has come up, and I really want to have a word with you before I go."

"No problem, Sir. Where?"

"Here. On the way to the airport. Is that going to be a problem?"

"No, Sir. I'll catch a ride out there as soon as I can."

"No. I called Moore and told him to pick you up on his way out here. He should be at the hotel in ten, fifteen minutes."

"I'll be waiting for him, Sir."

"Thank you, Pluto. I am really sorry to have to do this to you. But I think it's important."

"No problem, Sir."

I have just spoken to the only officer in the grade of Army captain or above at the Emperor's Court who would dream of apologizing for waking a lowly lieutenant up. I am really going to miss Captain Pickering.

Pickering was leaving Brisbane to join the Guadalcanal invasion fleet in time for the rehearsal in the Fiji Islands. Hon suspected he would not be back for a long time, if ever.

Pickering hadn't come right out and said so, but there was little doubt in Hon's mind that when the rehearsal was over, Pickering was going with the invasion fleet to Guadalcanal instead of resuming his duties as the Secretary of the Navy's personal representative to the Emperor. Hon thought it was entirely likely that Pickering wouldn't stop there—watching the landing from the bridge of the command ship USS *McCawley*—but would actually go ashore with the Marines.

Pickering's contempt for the brass hats—at least for their petty bickering—at SHSWPA and CINCPAC had been made clear in the reports he had written (and Hon had read in the process of transmission) to Secretary of the Navy Frank Knox. And Pickering had also taught Hon that there was still life in the old saw, "Once A Marine, Always A Marine." Pickering thought of himself as a Marine. He felt a tie of brotherhood with the men who were actually invading Guadalcanal and Tulagi. The notion of returning to the cocktail party circuit in Australia while they were going in harm's way was repugnant to him.

In Hon's opinion, it would not be at all hard for Pickering to convince himself that he could best discharge his duty by going ashore with the Marines. If he was actually on the scene, he'd be in a better position to keep Frank Knox informed than if he were back in Australia—or at least so he would rationalize. Hon half expected that Pickering would actually suggest this plan to Knox in one of his reports. When he didn't, Hon suspected it was because he knew Knox would immediately forbid him to go anywhere near Guadalcanal.

If he decided to go ashore with the invasion force, there was nobody in the Pacific with the authority to stop him. His orders made it absolutely clear that he was subordinate only to Frank Knox.

Lieutenant Pluto Hon got out of the narrow iron bed, with its lumpy mattress, and took a very quick shave over the tiny sink in his room. The toilet and bath, in separate rooms, were down the corridor. About the only good thing Hon could think to say about the Commerce Hotel was that it was only a block and a half from the new Supreme Headquarters, South West Pacific Area. After the move from Melbourne, that was established in an eight-story building from which an insurance company had been evicted for the duration.

Before the war, the Commerce Hotel had apparently catered to traveling salesmen on very limited expense accounts. It was, of course, good enough for company grade officers assigned to the Emperor's Court.

He dressed quickly, ran down the stairs rather than wait for the small, creaking elevator (which often did not answer the button, anyway), and was standing outside on the sidewalk when Sergeant John Marston Moore pulled up in the Studebaker President sedan Banning's sergeant had scrounged for them.

Hon got in the front seat beside him.

Moore had really been screwed by the move from Melbourne, he thought. In Melbourne, he'd lived in a large room at The Elms. In Brisbane, the only property Pickering could find was a small house, called Water Lily Cottage, out by the racetrack. There was not only no room for Moore there, but when Pickering had ordered Hon to find someplace decent for Moore to live in and give him the bill, Hon had been unable to find any kind of a room at all.

So Moore lived outside of town with the other headquarters enlisted men in an old Australian barracks. When he didn't have the Studebaker, he had to ride back and forth to work on Army buses, when they were running. Worse, in the barracks, a headquarters company commander and a first sergeant, who could not be told what Moore was doing, saw in him just one more sergeant who could be put to work doing what sergeants are supposed to do, like supervising linoleum waxing and serving as sergeant of the guard.

Captain Pickering spoke several times with the headquarters commandant about his needing Moore around the clock, which meant he would not be available for company duties. The last time he made such a call, he told the headquarters commandant he would register his next complaint with General Sutherland. And that worked. But with Pickering gone, it would happen again. Lieutenant Hon could not register complaints with MacArthur's Chief of Staff, "Dick, I'm having a little trouble with your headquarters commandant."

"I think we're going to miss Captain Pickering, Lieutenant," Moore said as they pulled away.

"Don't read my mind, please. Lowly sergeants should not be privy to the thoughts of officers and gentlemen."

"I went by the shop," Moore said, chuckling. "To see if there was anything for the boss. Nothing."

"Nothing?"

"Two more of Feldt's Coastwatchers are—'no longer operational.'"

"Buka?"

"Buka's all right. Should I tell the boss?"

"Not unless he asks. What can he do anyway?"

There were lights on all over Water Lily Cottage when Moore turned off Manchester Avenue into the driveway. Pickering's borrowed Jaguar drophead coupe was parked in the driveway ahead of them.

Pickering came out onto the porch in his shirt-sleeves as Hon got out of the car.

"Come on in, the both of you," he said. "There's time for coffee, and I want you to meet someone."

There was a woman in Water Lily Cottage. She had apparently spent the night, for she was wearing a bathrobe. It covered her from her neck to her ankles. She was, Hon quickly judged, in her thirties. Her dark hair was parted in the middle, brushed tightly against her scalp, and drawn up in a bun at the back. She wore no makeup.

Jesus, what's the boss been up to? I can't believe he's been screwing this dame.

"Gentlemen," Pickering said, "I'd like you to meet Mrs. Ellen Feller. She got in last night from Pearl Harbor."

I would never have thought she was an American, Hon thought, and then revised his opinion of her sexual desirability. Even the padded bathrobe could not conceal an attractive breastworks, which was apparently unrestrained by a brassiere.

I still don't think he's been screwing her. But on the other hand, I was twenty before I was willing to admit that my parents hadn't had me via immaculate conception.

Ellen Feller's smile, which accompanied the hand she gave Hon, was somewhat the wrong side of being friendly and inviting.

"Ellen and I go back pretty far," Pickering said. "She was my secretary in Washington."

"We're old friends," Ellen Feller added, quietly demure. Then she turned to Moore. "I believe I know your father," she said. "The Reverend John Wesley Moore, isn't it? Of Missions?"

"Yes, Ma'am," Moore said, visibly surprised.

"Of what?" Pickering asked.

"Missions, Sir," Moore furnished. "The William Barton Harris Methodist Episcopal Special Missions to the Unchurched Foundation."

"My husband and I were in China before the war," Mrs. Feller said, "with the Christian and Missionary Alliance. I met your father, and your mother, too, I believe, in Hong Kong."

"Ellen will be working with you," Pickering said, obviously impatient with missionary auld lang syne. "She's a damned good linguist, and a damned good analyst, and more to the point, she's MAGIC cleared."

I'll be damned.

But then another thought struck him, *It makes a lot of sense though.*

The high-ups in the intermingled and confusing multiservice command structure of communications intelligence had to send someone else with a MAGIC clearance to MacArthur's headquarters. They didn't know that Pickering had brought Sergeant John Marston Moore in on the most important secret of the war in the Pacific, which meant they believed only two underlings, Hon himself and Major Ed Banning, even knew what MAGIC was.

That made a total of four people in the Emperor's Court who were cleared to read intercepted messages between the Japanese Imperial General Staff and Japanese Naval Headquarters and units at sea: The American Emperor himself, of course; MacArthur's G-2, newly promoted Brigadier General Charles M. Willoughby (who to Hon's private amusement spoke with an unmistakable German accent); and Banning and Hon.

Even taking very seriously the cliché that the more people in on a secret, the greater the chance the secret will soon be out, it just didn't make sense not to send at least one other person to Brisbane. For the most basic of reasons: If a Brisbane bus ran over Lieutenant Hon while Banning was up at Townesville, as he was most of the time, and a hot MAGIC came in, it would not reach MacArthur or Willoughby until Banning could fly down from Townesville to decrypt it for them.

As a practical matter, of course, Sergeant Moore would have filled in. Hon had given him a crash course in operation of the cryptographic equipment, and he knew what to do with MAGIC messages. But *they* didn't know that.

And so they sent someone else in; and not the kind of person Hon might have expected—a Navy Lieutenant Commander or an Army Signal Corps Lieutenant Colonel, the rank a sop to the rank consciousness of MacArthur's headquarters, where daily Hon was made to realize that a lowly lieutenant was of no consequence whatsoever. Instead, they sent a civilian, and even more incredibly, a female civilian.

"There was a chance for Ellen and me to talk last night," Pickering continued. "So it was fortunate that she came in when she did. I'm sure everybody would have been confused had she come in this afternoon." He stopped for a time to gather his thoughts. "Her coming," he went on after a moment, "might cause us a few minor problems. But let's deal with who's in charge first. Pluto, that's you. You're doing a fine job, and there's no one better qualified. Unfortunately, you're a lowly first lieutenant. I've been—punching pillows is what it feels like—trying to get you promoted to at least captain. For reasons that escape me, that has so far proven impossible. I left word with Ed Banning that he is to continue trying."

"That's very good of you, Sir, but . . ."

"Oh, bullshit . . . sorry, Ellen. *Nonsense,* Pluto. You're well deserving of promotion, and we all know it. But anyway, you are outranked not only by Ed Banning, obviously, but by Ellen as well."

"Sir?"

"What is it they said you are, Ellen?"

"An assimilated Oh Four, Captain."

"You know what that means, Pluto?" Pickering asked.

"Yes, Sir. Mrs. Feller is entitled to the privileges of a major, Sir. Or a Navy lieutenant commander."

"OK. That may come in handy for billeting, or whatever. And I don't give a damn who anyone at the Palace thinks is running things. But between you and Ellen, so far as MAGIC is concerned, you're in charge, Pluto. I have also left word with Ed Banning making that clear."

"Yes, Sir."

"You remain, Sergeant Moore," Pickering said, "low man on the totem pole, outranked by everybody."

"Yes, Sir. I understand."

"But since I suspect that moron at Headquarters Company will have you on a guard roster the moment he hears I've left, I want you to clear your things out of that barracks and move in here. I had to take a six-month lease on this place, and there's no sense letting it go to waste."

"Yes, Sir."

"Mrs. Feller will also be living here. I have assured her that you are a well-bred gentleman who will not be bringing any wild Australian lasses home for drinking parties late at night."

"No, Sir."

"There's only two bedrooms, Pluto," Pickering said. "I'm afraid you're stuck with the Commerce Hotel. The important thing, I think, is to keep Moore out of the hands of Headquarters Company—without calling attention to him."

"Absolutely, Sir," Hon said.

"Take Mrs. Feller to the bank later today or tomorrow and see that she is authorized to draw on our account," Pickering said. "And on that subject, Banning has been spending a lot of money. I have asked for more, and it should be coming quickly. If, however, one of the officer couriers does not bring you a check within the next week, radio Haughton. The one thing I do not want to do is run out of money for Banning and Feldt."

"Yes, Sir."

"Can you think of anything, Pluto? Or you, John?"

"No, Sir," Moore replied immediately.

"No, Sir," Hon said, a moment later.

"Ellen?"

"Credentials for me, Captain."

"Oh, yeah. There's a Major Tourtillott who handles that sort of thing. Ellen needs what you and Banning and Moore have. Anywhere in the building, at any time. If Tourtillott gives you any trouble, see Colonel Scott, who works for Sutherland. If he gives you trouble, radio Haughton."

"Yes, Sir," Hon said.

"The liaison officer, Captain," Ellen Feller said.

"Oh, yeah. Thank you. That's important. I suggested to Frank Knox that he send a liaison officer between here and CINCPAC. Ellen tells me that Colonel Rickabee found one. He should be coming in soon. He is not, repeat, not, to be made a member of your happy circle. He's not cleared for MAGIC, or for what Banning is doing. I mention that solely because Rickabee's name may come up. Or because I'm afraid the poor bastard may be another orphan around here and may seek company in his misery."

"I understand, Sir," Hon said. He looked at his watch. "Captain, what time is your plane?"

Pickering looked at his watch.

"Christ," he said. "And I didn't give you the coffee I promised."

"No problem, Sir."

"Moore can drive me to the airport, Pluto. You don't have to go."

"I'd like to see you off, Sir, if that would be all right."

"Why thank you, Pluto," Pickering said. He looked at Ellen. "Sorry to have to leave you in the lurch like this."

"Take care of yourself, Fleming," Ellen Feller said.

Why does the way she said that make me suddenly think that they have been making the beast with two backs? . . . Even after the modest declaration she just gave about how my-husband-and-I-were-missionaries-in-China and Fleming-and-I-are-just-old-friends?

Because you're a dirty-minded young man, Pluto Hon, who hasn't had his own ashes hauled in so long you probably wouldn't know what to do with an erection.

"Where's your bags, Sir?" Hon asked.

"I'll get them," Moore said.

"I'll carry my own damned bags, thank you," Captain Pickering said.

(FOUR)
Headquarters, VMF-229
Ewa USMC Air Station
Oahu, Territory of Hawaii
1555 Hours 25 July 1942

Corporal Alfred B. Hastings, USMC, followed Captain Charles M. Galloway, USMCR, into his office.

"Whatever it is, Corporal Hastings, fuck it," Captain Galloway said. "Your beloved commanding officer has had it for today."

Galloway's cotton flight suit was sweat soaked. His hair was matted on his skull, and his hands and face were covered with a film of oil. He looked exhausted. He settled himself like an old man in the chair behind his desk.

"It's the colonel, Sir," Hastings said. "He said for you to phone him the minute you got in."

"Did he say what he wanted?"

"No, Sir, but he's called three times."

Galloway pointed to the telephone on his desk. Hastings took the handset from the cradle, listened for a dial tone, handed the handset to Galloway, and then dialed a number.

"This is Captain Galloway, Sergeant. I understand the colonel wants to speak at me."

Hastings left the room. He returned a moment later with a bottle of Coke, which he set on Galloway's desk. Galloway covered the microphone with his hand.

"Bless you, my son," he intoned solemnly.

"Yes, Sir," Hastings said, smiling.

"Galloway, Sir," Charley said to the telephone. "I just got in."

"And how many hours is that today, Captain Galloway?" Lieutenant Colonel Clyde W. Dawkins asked, innocently.

"I haven't checked my log book, Sir."

"But you can tell time and count, right? Up to say five hours and forty-five minutes?"

What the hell has he done? Gone and checked the goddamned board?

"Was it that much, Sir?"

"You know goddamned well it was," Dawkins said. "On the other hand, if you're dumb enough not to believe me when I say I don't want you flying more than four hours, maybe you *are* too dumb to count."

"Yes, Sir."

"But that is not the reason, at least the main reason, I wanted this little chat with you, Captain Galloway."

"Sir?"

"Knowing as I do your penchant for obeying only those orders you find it convenient to obey, I suppose it's hoping too much to expect you to have a white uniform for formal occasions?"

"Sir, I have a set of whites."

"Just in passing, I believe the regulation says you are required to have *two* sets. Is the one set you have suitably starched and pressed for wear at a formal occasion, for example, taking cocktails and dinner with an admiral?"

Charley took a quick mental inventory of his closet in the BOQ. His whites, never worn, were there, still in the bag they'd come in. If they weren't pressed, he had an iron.

"Yes, Sir," he said.

"Good. The admiral will be pleased. He is sending his car for us at 1830. Try not to spill tomato juice on your whites between now and then. With you owning only one set, that would pose a problem."

"What admiral is that, Sir?"

"Take a guess."

Since Charley was reasonably convinced that for reasons he could not imagine, Dawkins was pulling his chain about dinner with some admiral, he could not resist the temptation:

"Admiral Nimitz?"

"No. Close, but no. Guess again."

Christ, he's serious!

"I have no idea," he confessed.

"I'll give you a hint: How many officers do you have with uncles who are admirals?"

"Oh, Christ! What's he want?"

"I don't know. What I do know is that his aide was over here around noon—in his whites by the way, with the golden rope and everything—bearing an invitation for you and me to take cocktails and dinner with the admiral at his quarters. The admiral is sending his car for us, and the uniform is whites."

"Jesus!" Charley said.

"Have you been saying unkind things to Lieutenant Schneider, Charley?"

"No. I was just flying with him, as a matter of fact. He's doing very well, and I just told him so. He's going to be all right, Colonel."

"Well, he is not, repeat not, to be informed of where you and I are going tonight. The way the aide put it was, 'the admiral thinks that it would be best if Lieutenant Schneider didn't hear of this.' "

"I wonder what the hell is going on?"

"Considering how you ignore me when I tell you I don't want you flying more than four hours a day, *I* wonder if you will be able to keep our dinner plans a secret from Lieutenant Schneider."

That won't be a problem. Schneider at this very moment is probably already showered, shaved, shined, and doused with cologne, and breathing through flared nostrils as he arranges tonight's rendezvous with Mary Agnes O'Malley; he won't surface until tomorrow morning, looking wan, exhausted, and visibly satiated.

"That won't be a problem, Sir."

"You told me that keeping your flying under four hours a day wasn't going to be a problem, either, as I recall," Colonel Dawkins said. "My quarters, not a second after six-thirty. We don't want to keep the admiral waiting, do we, Charley?"

Colonel Dawkins hung up while Charley was on the "No" of "No, Sir."

At 1825 Admiral Daniel J. Wagam's aide-de-camp arrived at Lieutenant Colonel Dawkins's BOQ in the Admiral's Navy gray Plymouth staff car. Captain Charles M. Galloway arrived a moment later in his nine-year-old yellow Ford roadster. By the time Charley found a place to park the Ford, Colonel Dawkins had emerged from the building and was standing by the Plymouth.

The admiral's aide, a Lieutenant (j.g.), got in the front seat beside the driver, affording Captain Galloway, in deference to his rank, the privilege of riding in the back. Charley had often wondered why in military protocol the back seat represented privilege and prestige. If he were the brass hat, he would have chosen to ride in front, where there was often more room and you could see better.

After considerable idle thought, he'd finally figured out an answer that made sense: It went way back, to horse-drawn carriages. The front seat then had been less comfortable, and often out in the rain.

The services were very reluctant to change tradition. Charley knew that chances of his ever having to take a swipe at somebody with a sword were pretty goddamned remote. But a sword, in the pattern prescribed for Marine officers, was like his white uniform, yet one more thing he had had to buy when he took the commission.

The crown of his white brimmed hat cover had embroidered loops sewn to it. These were not the gold embroidered loops ("scrambled eggs") worn by senior officers on their caps. So anyone could tell at a glance whether or not he was looking at some lowly company grade officer. The loops went back to the days when Marines were posted as sharpshooters in the rigging of sailing ships. The officers then had fixed knotted rope to their headgear so the sharpshooters would not shoot them by mistake. Charley somewhat irreverently wondered if that now sacred tradition had come into existence after too many officer pricks had been popped "by mistake" by their men in the rigging.

"You should not have shot Lieutenant Smith in the head, Private Jones. You could see that he was an officer. He had rope on his hat."

How come, Charley wondered, *only the officers wore rope loops? Why not all Marines? Or in those days, was it considered OK to shoot enlisted Marines by mistake?*

Admiral Wagam's aide turned around on the front seat.

"Colonel, by any chance do you know Commander C.J. Greyson?"

"Yes, I do," Colonel Dawkins replied. "He was a classmate."

"Yes, Sir. I knew that. I didn't know if you knew Charley."

"Knew him well. We were both cheerleaders."

You were what? Cheerleaders? *Jesus! Siss Boom Bah! Go Navy!*

"Charley's my brother, Sir."

"Oh, really?"

"He's on the staff of COMDESFORATL now, Sir. I had a letter last week." (Commander, Destroyer Force, Atlantic.)

"Well, when you write him, please give him my best regards," Dawkins said.

Back in Central High School, those of us who played varsity ball thought the male cheerleaders were mostly pansies. But I guess things are different at the United States Naval Academy, huh?

"Yes, Sir, I'll be happy to."

"You went to the Academy?"

"Yes, Sir. '40."

Lieutenant (j.g.) Greyson smiled at Charley.

"I understand you were directly commissioned, Sir."

"Well, the Commandant had to make a choice," Charley said. "It was either commission me, or send me to Portsmouth."

Lieutenant (j.g.) Greyson looked uncomfortable and turned to the front again.

"Watch it, Charley," Dawkins said, softly and sternly; but he was unable to suppress a smile.

In 1937–39, when he was still a Captain, Rear Admiral (upper half) Daniel J. Wagam and his family occupied the quarters he shared now with Rear Admiral (lower half) Matthew H. Oliver.

(Rear Admirals, upper half, are equivalent to Army and Marine Corps Major Generals. Rear Admirals, lower half, are equivalent to Army and Marine Corps Brigadier Generals. Army and Marine Corps Major Generals wear two silver stars as the insignia of their rank, while Army and Marine Corps Brigadier Generals wear just one star. All Rear Admirals, however, wear the same two stars that Major Generals wear. This practice is said to annoy many Army and Marine Corps Brigadier Generals, particularly when they learn that they actually outrank the Rear Admiral, lower half, whom they have just saluted crisply.)

Though the Pearl Harbor officer corps had tripled or quadrupled in size since 1939, there were now very few dependents. That meant that many former family quarters were now occupied by "unaccompanied" officers. It had worked out remarkably well.

Placing "unaccompanied officers" in family quarters afforded senior officers with quarters appropriate to their rank. This was valuable not only because these provided greater creature comforts—such as privacy and luxury—than can be found in Bachelor Officer quarters, but because these also gave them a place where they could hold private meetings over drinks, or drinks and dinner.

Admiral Wagam's quarters were a four-bedroom house. He occupied the master bedroom, Admiral Oliver the guest room, and their aides-de-camp occupied what he still thought of as Danny's and Joan's rooms. The admiral's children were now waiting out the war with their mother, near Norfolk, Virginia.

Three Filipino messboys took care of the housekeeping and cooking. (Two of them were assigned as a prerogative of rank to Admiral Wagam and one to Admiral Oliver.) The loyalty and discretion of Filipino messboys was legendary. Admiral Oliver was not senior enough to have a permanently assigned staff car and driver. Admiral Wagam's driver lived over the garage.

Admirals Wagam and Oliver got along splendidly. When one or the other of them wished to hold a meeting in the house, he simply asked the other if it would be possible for him to eat in the Flag Mess that night. Neither, both being gentlemen, ever asked who was being entertained. It might be CINCPAC himself, for example; or it could be an old family friend—female—with whom the admiral had a platonic relationship but did not wish to wine and dine at the mess because of the way people talked. No matter who it was, each admiral could count on the discretion of the other.

A white-jacketed, smiling Filipino messboy had the front door of Admiral Wagam's quarters open even before Lieutenant Greyson could put his finger on the highly polished brass door bell.

Greyson waved Dawkins and Galloway through the door.

"I'll tell the Admiral you're here, gentlemen," he said, and went to the closed door to the study and knocked.

In a moment, Admiral Wagam emerged, carrying a leather briefcase.

"Lock that up, will you please, Dick?" he said, as he handed the briefcase to his aide-de-camp.

"Aye, aye, Sir."

"Gentlemen," Admiral Wagam said, smiling at Dawkins and Charley. "Welcome. I'm glad you were able to come tonight."

"Very good of you to have us, Sir," Dawkins said.

"Dick's been telling me, Colonel, that you and his brother are classmates."

"Yes, Sir. '32."

"I'm '22," the admiral said, and turned to Galloway.

"And the famous—or is it infamous—Captain Galloway. I've been looking forward to meeting you, Captain. I was present, Captain, for the famous 'Q.E.D.' remark."

"Sir?" Galloway asked, wholly confused.

"I was in Admiral Shaughn's office when word came that you were flying that F4F out to the *Saratoga*. Captain Anderson of BUAIR [Bureau of Aeronautics] was there, sputtering with rage. He said, 'Admiral, this simply can't be. My people have certified all of VMF-211's aircraft as totally destroyed.' And Admiral Shaughn replied, *'Quod erat demonstrandum, Captain, Quod erat demonstrandum.'* What made it even more hilarious was that Anderson didn't have any Latin, and it had to be translated for him."

"Yes, Sir," Charley said, still wholly confused.

"He didn't know that *'Quod erat demonstrandum'* meant 'the facts speak for themselves'?" Dawkins asked. "Really?"

You made that translation for me, Charley realized. *Thank you, Skipper.*

"He hadn't the foggiest idea what it meant," Admiral Wagam said, chuckling. "And he gave an entirely new meaning to the word 'ambivalent.' Like everybody else . . . Anderson is really a nice fellow, personally . . . he was hoping that Galloway would make it onto *Sara.* But on the other hand, if he *did,* in an airplane Anderson's BUAIR experts had certified was damaged beyond any possibility of repair, he was going to look like a fool."

Admiral Wagam laughed out loud. "Which Galloway did, of course, making him look like a fool. No wonder BUAIR was so angry with you, Galloway. Well, it turned out all right in the end, didn't it? All's well that ends well, as they say."

"Yes, Sir," Charley said.

"Let's go in the living room and have a drink," Admiral Wagam said. "I've been looking for an excuse since three o'clock."

A small, pudgy Filipino messboy in a starched white jacket was waiting for them behind a small, well-stocked bar. Through an open door, Charley saw a dining room table set with crystal and silver. A silver bowl filled with gardenias was in the center of the table.

"We've got just about anything you might want," the Admiral said, "but Carlos makes a splendid martini, and I've always felt that a martini is just the thing to whet the appetite before roast beef."

"A martini seems a splendid notion, Admiral," Dawkins said.

"Yes, Sir," Charley said.

"Four of your best, Carlos, please," the admiral ordered. "And I suggest you have a reinforcement readily available."

I could learn to like living like this, Charley thought. But this was instantly followed by two somewhat disturbing second thoughts: *Jesus, Caroline's house in Jenkintown is bigger than this. And so is Jim Ward's parents' house. And compared to the apartment on the top floor—the* penthouse—*of the Andrew Foster Hotel, this place—this* Admiral's Quarters—*is a dump.*

Carlos filled four martini glasses from a silver shaker, and the Admiral passed them around.

The Admiral raised his glass, and looking right at Charley, said, "To youth, gentlemen. To the foolish things young men do with the best of intentions."

"Admiral," Colonel Dawkins said, "with respect, I would prefer to drink to the wise elders who keep foolish, well-intentioned young men out of trouble."

"Colonel, I normally dislike having my toasts altered, especially by a Marine, but by God, I'll drink to *that,"* Admiral Wagam said, taking a sip and beaming at Dawkins.

Charley and Lieutenant (j.g.) Greyson dutifully sipped at their martinis.

"So you have the feeling, do you, Colonel . . ." Admiral Wagam said, interrupting himself to turn to the messboy: "Splendid, Carlos. Splendid."

"Thank you, Admiral," Carlos beamed.

". . . that senior officers rarely get the appreciation they should," Admiral Wagam went on, "for—how should I put this?—*tempering the enthusiasm* of the young men for whom they are responsible?"

"Yes, Sir," Dawkins beamed. "I was just this afternoon having a conversation with Captain Galloway about his excessive enthusiasm for flying."

"At the expense of his duties as commanding officer, you mean?"

"No, Sir. I can't fault Captain Galloway's command. What I was trying to do was point out that all work and no play makes good squadron commanders lousy squadron commanders."

The Admiral grunted. "There was a study, a couple of years back, Medical Corps did it on the quiet. They found out that a newly appointed destroyer captain on his first voyage as skipper averaged five point three hours sleep at night. A man, especially an officer in command, can't function without a decent night's sleep. There's such a thing as too much devotion to duty, Galloway. You listen to Colonel Dawkins."

"Yes, Sir."

"That sleep requirement apparently doesn't apply to aides, Admiral?" Lieutenant (j.g.) Greyson asked.

"Aides have very little to do," the Admiral replied. "They can get their necessary sleep while standing around with their mouths shut." He put his arm around Greyson's shoulders. "I learned that from a distinguished sailor, Mr. Greyson. Your father. I was his aide when he told me that."

A second messboy appeared in the door to the dining room.

"Excuse me," he said. "Admiral, dinner is served."

"Hold it just a moment, Enrique," Admiral Wagam said. "I need another one of Carlos's martinis."

Charley glanced at Dawkins. Dawkins, just barely perceptibly, shrugged his shoulders, signifying that he had no idea what the hell this was all about, either.

The admiral passed out four fresh martinis.

"Let me offer another toast," he said. "Prefacing it with the observation that, obviously, it is not for dissemination outside this room. To the officers and men of VMF-229, who will sail from Pearl Harbor aboard the escort carrier *Long Island* two August. May God give you a smooth voyage and good hunting."

"Hear, hear," Colonel Dawkins and Lieutenant (j.g.) Greyson said, almost in unison.

"Thank you," Charley said.

"Although I am afraid he sometimes qualifies as one of the foolish, overly enthusiastic young men we were talking about a moment ago, my nephew tells me that VMF-229 is the best fighter squadron in Marine Aviation. Do you think I should believe him, Captain?"

"Sometimes even foolish young men have it right, Admiral," Charley said.

"Is that another example of that famous Marine modesty, Captain?" Admiral Wagam asked, as he put his hand on Charley's arm and led him into the dining room.

"A simple statement of facts, Sir," Charley said.

The admiral took his seat at the head of the table and pointed to the chair where Charley was to sit. Dawkins went to the far end of the table. Greyson sat across from Charley.

"I'm a little surprised you haven't asked where you're going," Admiral Wagam said.

"Sir, I thought that would be classified," Charley said.

"It is, of course," Wagam said. "And I suppose that disqualifies you as a foolish young man. Only a foolish young man would ask, right?"

"Yes, Sir."

"But let me put you on the spot, Galloway. Where do you think you'll be going? What's the scuttlebutt?"

Wagam saw Galloway's discomfiture.

"I will neither confirm nor deny, Galloway. But sometimes it is of value to know what people think, what they are guessing."

Galloway looked at Dawkins for help. Dawkins shrugged again, barely perceptibly. Galloway interpreted this to mean, "Tell him what you think."

"Sir, I think that once the 1st Marine Division has secured the airfield on Guadalcanal, we'll be flown off the *Long Island* onto the island."

Admiral Wagam audibly sucked in his breath.

"And when does the scuttlebutt have it that the 1st Marines are going to invade, what did you say, Guadalcanal?"

"Yes, Sir. Guadalcanal. Shortly after the first of the month, Sir."

"Goddamn it, I'd love to know where you got that!" Admiral Wagam exclaimed, and then immediately regained control of himself. He held out his hand in a stop gesture. "If you were about to answer me, belay it. We will now change the subject."

"Yes, Sir," Charley said, and put a fork to the shrimp cocktail the messboy had set in front of him.

There was no question in his mind now that Big Steve's scuttlebutt, and his own studied guesses, were right on the mark. VMF-229 was going to Guadalcanal to operate off a captured Japanese airfield. Presuming, of course, that the 1st Marine Division could capture it.

"You're a bachelor, I understand, Galloway," the admiral said.

"Yes, Sir."

"In wartime, there are a number of advantages to being a bachelor," the admiral said.

"And in peacetime, there are a number of advantages to being a bachelor," Dawkins said.

The admiral gave him a frosty look.

"Spoken like a longtime married man, Colonel," he said. "I share that opinion, to a degree. But what I had in mind was that a bachelor can devote his full attention to his duties, where a married man is always concerned with the welfare of his family. Wouldn't you agree?"

"Yes, Sir. I take your point."

"But what you said just made me think of something else," the admiral said. "My wife would probably kill me if she heard me say this, but I would say—how can I phrase this delicately?—Would you agree, Colonel, that the pain of separation from one's wife is less for people like you and me, who have been married for a long time, than it would be for someone who has recently married and then is almost immediately separated from his bride?"

"Yes, Sir. I agree. And I think you phrased that very delicately, Admiral."

"Yes," the admiral agreed.

The messboys appeared, removed the silver shrimp cocktail bowls, and served the roast beef, roasted potatoes, and broccoli with hollandaise. A bottle of wine was introduced, opened, sipped by the admiral, and then poured.

The admiral raised his glass.

"To marriage, gentlemen. A noble institution. But one into which, I don't think, speaking of foolish young men with the best of intentions, Lieutenant David Schneider should enter at this point in his life and career."

Jesus Christ, what's this?

"I wasn't aware he was contemplating marriage." Colonel Dawkins said.

"He is," the admiral said, sawing at his roast beef. "He is now experiencing the ecstasy of what he really believes is true love. True love at first sight, to put a point on it."

"I'll be damned," Dawkins said.

Not Mary Agnes, for Christ's sake!

"The young lady in question is a Navy Nurse," the admiral said. "Lieutenant (junior grade) Mary Alice O'Malley."

Holy Christ!

"Mary *Agnes*, Sir," Lieutenant Greyson corrected him.

"Mary *Agnes*, then," the admiral said, a trifle petulantly. "David came to me last night and told me that he intended to apply for permission to marry. He tells me that he has stolen the affections of this young woman away from your executive officer, Captain Galloway; and for that reason, and others, he fears that his application will be delayed by you. He therefore sought my good offices to overcome your objections." He looked at Galloway. "Was he correct? Would you have, by fair means or foul, put obstacles in his path?"

"Yes, Sir, I would have."

"Good. Then we are all on the same wavelength," the admiral said. "What we have to do now is come up with a plan that will both keep him from making a fool of himself and keep both of us out of the line of fire. Just between us, gentlemen, I don't intend to spend the rest of my life explaining to my sister why I stood idly by and watched her precious Davey-boy marry a peroxide blonde floozie who is seven years older than he is, and who has been satisfying the sexual desires of every other junior officer in Pearl Harbor." The admiral paused and looked at Captain Charles M. Galloway, USMCR. "Including some squadron commanders who should have known better, even when they were in enlisted status."

XIV

(ONE)
Marine Corps Liaison Office
Princeton University
Princeton, New Jersey
27 July 1942

When his sergeant major loudly bellowed, "telephone for you, Major, Sir," Major George F. Dailey, USMC, a curly haired, slightly plump man six months shy of his thirtieth birthday, was sitting at his desk in shirt-sleeves in surrender to the heat.

Sergeant Major Martin was more than a little deaf. He was an Old Breed Marine recalled from the Fleet Reserve. He originally retired, after twenty-five years of service, the year before Dailey was commissioned.

"Thank you, Sergeant Major," Dailey said, and picked up the telephone.

"Major Dailey speaking."

"Major George Frederick Dailey?"

"Yes."

"What was your mother's maiden name?"

"I beg your pardon?"

"I asked what was your mother's maiden name?"

"Who is this, please?"

"My name is Rickabee. I'm a lieutenant colonel on the headquarters staff."

He means, Daily realized, genuinely surprised, *Headquarters, United States Marine Corps staff.* The Director, Central North East Region, Officer Procurement—Dailey—had never before heard directly from Headquarters, USMC.

"Cavendish, Sir," Dailey said.

"OK," his caller said. "I want you to catch a train as soon as you can, Major, and come down here. We're in Temporary Building T-2032 on the Mall. Take a cab from the station. Write that down. T-2032. My name is Rickabee." Rickabee obligingly spelled his name.

"Sir, would . . . day after tomorrow be all right?"

"I'm talking about this afternoon."

"Sir, that would be difficult. I have a . . ."

"Get your ass on a train and get down here this afternoon, Major," Colonel Rickabee said, and then hung up.

Dailey held the telephone in his hand for a moment before replacing it in the cradle. Then, for another minute, he looked out his window at the Princeton campus. Then he called for Sergeant Major Martin. He had to call three times before the old Marine appeared at his door.

"They want me to come to Washington," he said. "You'll have to reschedule whatever's on the schedule for this afternoon."

Major Dailey was himself a Princetonian, and he supposed that had more than a little bit to do with his first assignment in wartime. He understood the importance of officer procurement, of course, and why it made a good deal of sense to have a professional, such as himself, deciding which eager young man had the stuff required of a Marine officer and which did not. All the same, he would have much preferred to be in the Pacific as a fighter pilot, but that was out of the question.

At one time Major Dailey was a fighter pilot. He had gone from Princeton to Quantico, after which he'd done two years duty with troops. And then, just after he had been promoted to first lieutenant, he was sent to flight school at Pensacola. He flew for not quite four years, and loved every moment of it. But then he was called in after his annual flight physical and told that he had a heart murmur, and he had better give serious thought to what he wanted to do in the Corps now that he was no longer physically fit to fly.

He seriously considered resigning—he had no interest in the infantry or artillery, which seemed his other options. If he no longer could fly, what good to the Corps could he be? But a full bull colonel he had a lot of respect for told him the Corps needed unusually bright, well-educated officers in procurement, logistics, or intelligence even more than it needed yet one more aviator. So he decided to put off resigning for a couple of years to see what happened.

The Corps sent him back to college for six months for a crash course in the German language, and then sent him to the U.S. Embassy in Berlin as an Assistant Naval Attache. His promotion to captain came along when it was due, and he was not blind to the fact that a six-room apartment on Onkle Tomallee in Berlin-Zehlendorf was considerably more comfortable than a BOQ in Quantico.

He came home in 1940 and did an eighteen-month tour in Headquarters, USMC, essentially studying German tactics for review by G-3. And in November, 1941, he was promoted to Major (in the reserve; he was still only a Captain on the numerical list of regular Marine Corps Officers). When war came, he expected to be assigned some sort of duties which would take advantage of his European experience, but that didn't happen.

They sent him to Princeton to serve as President of the Officer Selection Board for the area, and to modify (that is to say, condense) the Platoon Leader's Training Program at the university. He was led to believe that the decisions he made about what could be cut from the pre-war program would set the pattern for other programs across the country.

He didn't like the prospect of sitting out the war in Princeton, but he was able to resign himself to it, particularly in the belief that his assignment probably would not last long. The projected growth of the Corps boggled the mind . . . they were now talking of hundreds of thousands of Marines—*divisions* of Marines. And certainly, they would need an officer of his rank and experience doing something besides selecting potential officers.

He expected to be reassigned, in other words. But the suddenness of the event, and the assignment itself, were startling.

At 1615 that afternoon, Lieutenant Colonel Rickabee ushered Major Dailey into the office of Brigadier General Horace W.T. Forrest, USMC, Assistant Chief of Staff for Intelligence. To Dailey's surprise, Rickabee was not only not in uniform, he had a large revolver ''concealed'' in the small of his back under his seersucker jacket.

Dailey noticed on General Forrest's desk both his Officer's Service Record and another file, marked SECRET, and DAILEY, GEORGE F.

He could not remember afterward what questions General Forrest put to him, and thus not his answers, but he remembered clearly how the interview ended:

''He'll do,'' General Forrest announced. ''You brief him. I'm too busy, and I don't want him contaminated by those bastards in G-1.''

''Aye, aye, Sir,'' Colonel Rickabee said, smiling, and then signaled for Dailey to leave. When he came out of General Forrest's office, Dailey saw that he was carrying both the files that the General had apparently been reading.

In the unmarked (but obviously government owned) car they drove back from Eighth and "I" Streets to Rickabee's office on the Mall, Rickabee gave him the first inkling of the billet that General Forrest had now officially given him.

"You know the good news–bad news routine?" Rickabee asked.

"Yes, Sir."

"The good news is that you are, effective today, a lieutenant colonel and on leave. The bad news is that when you come off your leave you will be in San Diego, about to board an airplane for Pearl Harbor. Your ultimate destination is Brisbane, Australia, where you will be the Marine liaison officer between CINCPAC—Admiral Nimitz—and The Supreme Commander, Southwest Pacific Area—General MacArthur."

"Why is that bad news, Sir?"

"Haven't you ever heard that primitive cultures always shoot the bearers of bad news?" Rickabee said.

Despite what General Forrest said about contamination, Lieutenant Colonel Dailey was briefed by a team of officers of the Office of the Assistant Chief of Staff for Personnel. The lieutenant colonel in charge told him (and Dailey believed him, and could not help but be flattered by the statement) that G-1 had been looking all along for a suitable assignment for him ... God knew the Corps needed experienced officers; but, until the day before, there had been "a G-2 Hold" on his records; and as long as that was there, he could not be reassigned without G-2 concurrence; and that had not been given.

"We didn't even propose you for this billet, frankly," the lieutenant colonel said. "We thought it would be a waste of time with the G-2 Hold. So, wouldn't you know, G-2 proposed you to us. We're delighted, of course. And I suppose I will have to take back all the unpleasant things I've been saying about G-2."

The G-1 lieutenant colonel went on to describe the bad feeling between General MacArthur's and Admiral Nimitz's headquarters. This was recently brought to a head when SHSWPA (Supreme Headquarters, South West Pacific Area) formally charged that CINCPAC had been denying MacArthur information he was entitled to have; or at least was delaying it until it was too late to act upon.

"That brought the Secretary of the Navy in on this, Dailey," the lieutenant colonel said. "He sent word down that he didn't want MacArthur to have grounds to even suspect that anything was being kept from him; he ordered that an officer be assigned to Brisbane to do nothing but pass information between CINCPAC and SHSWPA; and he specified a Marine. We thought of you right away, of course, with your diplomatic experience ... but with that G-2 Hold?" he shrugged. "Anyway, here you are."

Lieutenant Colonel Dailey took a seven-day leave, spending it with his mother in Greenwich, Connecticut. And then returned to Washington, where Colonel Rickabee informed him that he would travel at least as far as Pearl Harbor with a briefcase chained to his wrist.

"Two birds with one stone," Rickabee explained. "And it will free the seat the officer courier would normally occupy."

At Anacostia Naval Air Station, Dailey asked Rickabee about the G-2 Hold. He did that just before he got on the plane to San Diego, reasoning that it was too late for Rickabee to do anything about it, even if he did make him mad.

"I presume the G-2 Hold situation has been resolved, Colonel," he said. "May I ask what it was, specifically?"

"I see that our friends in personnel have diarrhea of the mouth again," Rickabee said.

"What I'm asking, Colonel, is whether there is some sort of cloud over me."

"No. I assure you there is not."

"Then may I ask why there was a hold?"

"Am I to suspect, *Colonel*," Rickabee replied, "that your conscience is bothering you vis-à-vis your relationship with Fraulein Ute Schellberger?"

"I wondered if that was a matter of official record," Dailey confessed. For an instant it all seemed perfectly clear. That's why he was sent to Princeton. If there was anything worse for a young officer on attache duty than getting drunk and pissing in the Embassy's potted palms, it was getting involved with a German blonde.

"Well, it bothered the FBI some, frankly," Rickabee said. "But then I told them that so far as the Corps was concerned, we would have been worried if a red-blooded young bachelor Marine officer far from home had *not* been fucking the natives, and that we were convinced you had not become a National Socialist."

"Christ!" Dailey had said.

Rickabee smiled at him.

"I can't tell you how relieved I am to hear that," Dailey said.

"You didn't hear anything from me, Colonel," Rickabee said. "Understood?"

"Understood."

"And now you are wondering, naturally, how come you were given this assignment? And are too polite, or too discreet, to ask?"

"Yes, Sir."

"There are several things going on over there in which we have an interest. Since you have no need to know what they are . . ."

"I understand, Sir."

"We may need replacements for the incumbents. An ideal replacement would be an officer of appropriate grade, who had already gone through the FBI's screening and been declared ninety-nine and forty-four one-hundredths percent pure on the morals scale—like Ivory soap. And who was not only over there, but in a position to know more of what's going on than, say, a battalion commander. Or for that matter, a division G-2. A liaison officer, for example."

"I think I understand, Sir," Dailey replied, very seriously.

"Think of yourself as a spare tire, Colonel. I devoutly hope we never have to take you out of the trunk."

"Yes, Sir."

(TWO)
Cape Esperance
Guadalcanal, Solomon Islands
7 August 1942

At 0200, the Amphibious Force of OPERATION PESTILENCE, Transport Groups X and Y, reached Savo Island, which lies between Guadalcanal and Florida islands. The skies were clear, and there was enough light from a quarter moon to make out both the land masses and the other ships.

The fifteen transports of Transport Group X carried aboard the major elements of the 1st Marine Division and were headed for the beaches of Guadalcanal. These turned and entered Sealark Channel, which runs between Savo and Guadalcanal.

Meanwhile, Transport Group Y sailed along the other side of Savo Island, that is, between Savo and Florida Island, and headed toward their destinations, Florida, Tulagi and Gavutu islands. Transport Group Y consisted of four transports carrying the 2nd Battalion, 5th Marines, and other troops, and four destroyer transports carrying the 1st Raider Battalion. These were World War I destroyers that had been converted for use by Marine Raiders by removing two of their four engines and converting the space to troop berthing.

The Guadalcanal Invasion Force was headed for what the Operations Plan called "Beach Red." This was a spot about 6,000 yards East of Lunga Point, more or less directly across Sealark Channel from where the Tulagi-Gavutu landings were to take place. The distance across Sealark Channel was approximately twenty-five miles.

Three U.S. Navy cruisers and four destroyers began to shell the Guadalcanal landing area at 0614. It had already been bombed daily for a week by U.S. Army Air Corps B-17s. At 0616, one cruiser and two destroyers opened fire on Tulagi and Gavutu.

By 0651 the transports of both groups dropped anchor 9,000 yards off their respective landing beaches. Landing boats were put over the side into the calm water, and Marines began to climb down rope nets into them.

Minesweepers working the water between the ships and their landing beaches encountered no mines, but a small Japanese schooner carrying gasoline wandered into Sealark Channel. It was set afire and quickly sunk by Naval gunfire and machine gun fire from Navy fighter aircraft and dive bombers. These were operating from carriers maneuvering seventy-five miles away from the invasion beaches.

The Navy sent forty-three carrier aircraft to attack the Guadalcanal invasion beach, and forty-one to attack Tulagi and Gavutu. Eighteen Japanese seaplanes at Tulagi were destroyed.

At 0740, B Company, 1st Battalion, 2nd Marines, went ashore near the small village of Haleta, on Florida Island. They encountered no resistance.

At 0800, the First Wave of the Tulagi Force, Landing Craft carrying Baker and Dog Companies of the 1st Raider Battalion, touched ashore on Blue Beach. A Marine was killed almost immediately by a single rifle shot, but there was no other resistance on the beach. The enemy had elected to defend Tulagi from caves and earthen bunkers in the hills inland and to the South.

The Landing Craft returned to the transports, loaded the Second Wave (Able and Charley Companies, 1st Raiders), and put them ashore. Then a steady stream of Landing Craft put 2nd Battalion, 5th Marines on shore.

Once on Tulagi, the 2nd Battalion, 5th Marines crossed the narrow island to their left (Northwest), to clear out the enemy, while the Raiders turned to their right (Southeast) and headed toward the Southern tip of Tulagi. About thirty-five hundred yards separated the Southern tip of Tulagi from the tiny island of Gavutu (515 by 255 yards) and the even smaller (290 by 310) island of Tanambogo, which was connected to Gavutu by a concrete causeway.

The Raiders encountered no serious opposition until after noon. And 2nd Battalion, 5th Marines, encountered no serious opposition moving in the opposite direction until about the same time.

Off Guadalcanal, at 0840, the destroyers of the Guadalcanal Fire Support Group took up positions to mark the line of departure for the Landing Craft, 5000 yards North of Beach Red. Simultaneously, small liaison aircraft (Piper Cubs) appeared over Beach Red, and marked its 3200-yard width with smoke grenades.

At exactly 0900, all the cruisers and destroyers of the Guadalcanal Fire Support Group began to bombard Beach Red and the area extending 200 yards inshore.

The Landing Craft carrying the first wave of the Beach Red invasion force (the 5th Marines, less their 2nd Battalion, which was at that moment in the process of landing on Tulagi) left the departure line on schedule. When the Landing Craft were 1300 yards off Beach Red, the covering bombardment was lifted.

At 0910, on a 1600-yard front, the 5th Marines began to land on the beach, the 1st Battalion on the right (West) and the 3rd Battalion on the left (East). Regimental

Headquarters came ashore at 0938, and minutes later it was joined by the Heavy Weapons elements of the regiment.

Again, there was virtually no resistance on the beach.

As the Landing Craft returned to the transports to bring the 1st Marines ashore, the 5th Marines moved inland, setting up a defense perimeter 600 yards off Beach Red, along the Tenaru River on the West, the Tenavatu River on the East, and a branch of the Tenaru on the South.

Once it had become apparent that they would not be in danger from Japanese artillery on or near the beach, the transports began to move closer to shore, dropping anchor again 7000 yards away.

At about this point, serious problems began with the off-loading process, in many ways duplicating the disastrous trial run in the Fiji Islands.

The small and relatively easy to manhandle 75mm pack howitzers (originally designed to be carried by mules) of the 11th Marines (the artillery regiment) had come ashore with the assault elements of the 5th Marines.

The 105mm howitzers now came ashore. But their emplacement was hindered because there were not enough drop-ramp Landing Craft to handle their "prime-movers," the trucks which tow the cannon. The "prime mover" for the 105mm howitzer was supposed to be a 2½-ton, 6×6 truck. The 11th Marines had been issued instead a truck commonly referred to as a "one-ton." Instead of the six (actually ten) powered wheels of the "deuce and a half," it had only four powered wheels to drive it through mud, sand, or slippery terrain.

It was this much smaller, inadequate, one-ton "prime mover" for which there were insufficient drop-bow Landing Craft to move immediately onto Beach Red.

So when the 105mm howitzers arrived on the beach, the only vehicles capable of towing them inland to firing positions were the few, overworked, Amphibious Tractors. These had a tank-like track and could negotiate sand and mud.

They were pressed into service to move the 105mm howitzers. In doing that, however, their metal tracks chewed up the primitive roads and whatever field telephone wires they crossed, effectively cutting communication between the advanced positions, the beach, and the several headquarters.

Within an hour or so of landing on the beach, moreover, the Marines were physically exhausted. For one thing, because of the long time they had spent aboard the troop transports, they had lost much of the physical toughness they'd acquired in training.

For another, as they moved through sand and jungle and up hills carrying heavy loads of rifles, machine guns, mortars and the ammunition for them, Guadalcanal's temperature and high humidity quickly sapped the strength they had left.

And there was not enough water. Although Medical Officers had strongly insisted that each man be provided with two canteens (two quarts) of drinking water, there were not enough canteens in the Pacific to issue a second canteen to each man.

The Navy was asked to provide beach labor details of sailors to assist in unloading the supplies coming ashore from the Landing Craft, and then to move the supplies off the beach to make room for more supplies. The Navy refused to do this.

Marines exhausted by the very act of going ashore were thus pressed into service unloading supplies from Landing Craft.

But first there were no trucks to move the supplies off the beach, and then when the "one-ton" trucks finally began to come ashore, these proved incapable of negotiating the sand and roads chewed up by Amphibious Tractors.

The result was a mess. Landing Craft loaded with supplies were stacked up off the beach. They were unable even to reach the beach, much less rapidly discharge their cargoes.

Meanwhile, starting at 1145, Navy SBD dive-bombers attacked Gavutu across the channel. Ten minutes later, the Navy started a five minute barrage of the island, creating huge clouds of smoke and dust.

By 1500, both Tulagi and Gavutu were "secured."

On Guadalcanal itself, the main invasion force spent the rest of the afternoon and the night trying—with little success—to clear up the mess on the beach itself, and to set up a perimeter defense around the beach and the six hundred yards the Marines had moved inshore.

There was no question that the Japanese would try to throw the Marines back into the sea. The only question was when.

(THREE)
Buka, Solomon Islands
0745 Hours 8 August 1942

"I rather think that's more than one, wouldn't you agree?" Sub-Lieutenant Jacob Reeves, Royal Australian Navy Volunteer Reserve, said, turning to Miss Patience Witherspoon and nodding vaguely toward the far-off sound of aircraft engines to the North.

Reeves was a bit old—forty-one—to be a Sub-Lieutenant, the lowest commissioned rank in the Royal Australian Navy; and his uniform fell far below the standards usually expected of an officer on duty. He was wearing a battered and torn, brimmed uniform cap; an equally soiled khaki uniform tunic with cut off sleeves; and khaki shorts and shoes whose uppers were spotted with green mold. His hair tumbled down his neck; and he was wearing a beard. A 9mm Sten submachine gun and a large pair of Ernst Leitz Wetzlar binoculars hung from his neck on web straps.

He and Miss Witherspoon were standing beneath an enormous tree, down from which hung a knotted rope.

"Oh, yes, Sir," Miss Witherspoon replied. "That's certainly more than one. A great many, I wouldn't be surprised."

"Well, then, I suppose I'd better go have a look, and you had better wake up the sodding Yanks, don't you think?"

"Yes, of course," Miss Witherspoon said. "I'll fetch them."

Lieutenant Reeves reached for the knotted rope. And then hanging on to it, he agilely climbed the trunk of the enormous tree, disappearing in a moment into the foliage.

Miss Witherspoon, who was eighteen, ran quickly and gracefully to Sergeant Stephen M. Koffler's hut down a narrow dirt path cut through lush vegetation. She ducked through the low entrance and knelt by his bed.

She giggled. Sergeant Koffler was also eighteen, and Miss Witherspoon was more than a little attracted to him. He was on his back, asleep. He was wearing only his U.S. Marine Corps issue skivvie shorts. The anatomical symbol of his gender, gloriously erect, poked through the flap in his skivvie shorts.

Miss Witherspoon, tittering, put one hand to her mouth, and with the other gave Sergeant Koffler's erection a friendly little pat. Sergeant Koffler gave a pleasant little grunt. Miss Witherspoon patted him again, just a little harder, but enough to waken him. He reached down and caught her wrist.

"God*damn* it, Patience!" Sergeant Koffler said, sounding more exasperated than angry.

"Lieutenant Reeves sent me to fetch you," Miss Witherspoon said, pronouncing the rank title in the British manner—Lef-ten-ant. "There's a large number of aircraft."

"Be right there," Koffler said. "Make sure Lieutenant Howard is up."

"Right you are," Miss Patience Witherspoon said cheerfully. Smiling, she backed out of the hut.

Steve sat on the edge of his bed. Miss Patience Witherspoon herself had constructed it of narrow tree trunks driven into the ground; a sort of "spring" of woven strips of bark supported a thin mattress. The mattress was covered with a surprisingly clean white sheet. The mattress and the sheet had also been made by Miss Witherspoon, who also washed them regularly.

Sergeant Koffler pulled on a pair of shorts that had once been a pair of "Trousers, Utility, Summer Service"; and then a pair of socks. He jammed his feet into his just-about-rotted through ankle high shoes, once a pair of "Shoes, Service, Dress." When he graduated from Parris Island these had worn a shine he could actually see his reflection in. Last he picked up his weapon where it lay under his bed.

The truly astonishing thing about Miss Patience Witherspoon, Sergeant Koffler thought for perhaps the hundredth time, was not her teeth, which were stained blue-black and filed into points; or even her breasts, which she made no effort to conceal, and which were elaborately decorated with scar tissue; or even that she lusted absolutely shamelessly after him. The truly astonishing thing about her was the way she talked.

Miss Witherspoon sounded almost exactly like Miss Daphne Farnsworth, who was the only other female subject of his Most Britannic Majesty Steve Koffler had come to know intimately. Miss (actually Yeoman, Royal Australian Navy Volunteer Reserve) Farnsworth had neat, pure white, intact teeth, and her breasts, which she modestly concealed virtually all of the time, were not only unscarred, but in Steve's opinion, they were an absolute work of art.

Without really being aware that he was doing it, Steve removed the magazine from his Thompson .45 ACP caliber submachine gun, worked the action, and then replaced the magazine. If necessary, it would fire.

The moment he ducked through the entrance to his hut, he heard the sound of aircraft engines. The hut was constructed of narrow tree trunks, covered with a thatch of enormous leaves. The sound had not penetrated the thick leaves of the hut.

He started to trot toward the Tree House, slinging the Thompson over his shoulder on its web strap as he ran. A hundred yards up the path, he encountered First Lieutenant Joseph L. Howard, USMCR, commanding the Marine Garrison on Buka Island.

Sergeant Koffler saluted crisply, and his salute was as impeccably returned.

"Good morning, Sergeant," Lieutenant Howard said. "You are to be commended on your shipshape appearance."

"Thank you, Sir. I try to set an example for the men."

Lieutenant Howard was dressed and shaved and coiffured exactly as Sergeant Koffler was. That is to say, he was wearing rotting shoes; cut-off utility pants; and no shirt. A Thompson was slung over his shoulder. The last time either of them had a haircut or a shave was two months before in Australia, on June 6, the night before they jumped into Buka. And there were in fact no other men to set an example for. What was carried on the books as "Detachment A of USMC Special Detachment 14" consisted of Lieutenant Howard and Sergeant Koffler.

But at least once a day, they went through a little routine like this one. It was ostensibly a joke, but there was more to it than that. It reminded them that they were in fact Marines, part of a fellowship greater than two individuals living in the jungle on an island neither of them had heard of three months before; dodging the Japs; and with chances of getting home alive ranging from slim to none.

Two days before, after supper, Lieutenant Howard had told both Reeves and

Koffler that in the very early hours of 7 August, OPERATION PESTILENCE, the invasion of the Solomon Islands of Tulagi, Gavutu, and Guadalcanal by the 1st Marine Division, would begin.

The great majority of Japanese bombers intending to strike at the invasion force would come from their major base at Rabaul or from its satellite installations; the flight path of these bombers would take them over Buka. Thus the importance of the Coastwatcher station on Buka could hardly be overstated. If the Americans in the invasion fleet knew when the Japanese could be expected, they could launch their aircraft in time to intercept them. This early warning would be of even greater importance once the Americans got the Japanese-started airfield on Guadalcanal completed and operational.

"How come you never said anything about this before?" Sergeant Koffler had inquired.

"In case either of you were captured by the Japs," Howard had explained, "you couldn't have told them because you didn't know."

"You knew," Koffler pursued. "What if you got caught?"

"I couldn't let myself get caught, Steve," Howard said, softly.

"What were you going to do, shoot yourself?"

"Let it go, Steve," Howard had said.

The sound of aircraft engines was now quite definite, Howard thought, but it was still sort of fuzzy, suggesting that there were a large number of aircraft some distance off, rather than one or two aircraft somewhat closer.

When they reached the tree, Howard gestured for Koffler to go ahead of him, and Koffler scurried quickly up the knotted rope and out of sight. Since the arm he'd broken when they first landed was now pretty well healed, Howard was able to follow him.

A platform had been built in the tree a hundred feet off the ground. It was large enough for three or four people to stand or sit comfortably. Reeves was sitting with his back against the trunk, when Steve Koffler stepped from a limb onto the platform.

He handed Koffler his binoculars and pointed north. Steve followed the directions and thought he could pick out, far off and not very high in the air, specks that almost certainly were aircraft. He leaned his shoulder against the trunk to steady himself, and with some difficulty found the specks through the binoculars. They were still too far away to see clearly, but he could now see that they were flying in formation, a series of Vs.

Lieutenant Howard touched his arm; he wanted the binoculars. Steve handed them to him.

Howard hooked the eyepieces under the bones above his eyes, took a breath, let half of it out, and held the rest, much the same technique that a skilled rifle marksman uses to steady his sight picture before firing.

"There's a bunch," he said. "What do you think they are, Steve?"

"Too far away to tell," Steve replied.

"If they were Bettys, for example, how could you tell?" Howard asked innocently.

"Shit," Koffler chuckled, realizing that he was being tested. Since they had been on Buka, they had been training each other—not just because there wasn't much else to do. Koffler had rigged up a simple buzzer and taught Howard Morse code, and Howard had not only sketched various Japanese aircraft, but had called forth their characteristics from memory and passed them on to both Koffler and Reeves.

"Well?" Howard went on.

Koffler pushed himself away from the tree and came to attention—except for a broad, unmilitary smile.

"Sir," he barked. "The Japanese Mitsubishi G4M1 Type 1 aircraft, commonly

called the Betty, is a twin-engine, land-based bomber aircraft with a normal complement of seven. It has an empty weight of 9.5 tons and is capable of carrying 2200
pounds of bombs, or two 1700-pound torpedoes, over a nominal range of 2250
miles at a cruising speed of 195 miles per hour. Its maximum speed is 250 miles
per hour at 14,000 feet. It is armed with a 20mm cannon in the tail, and four 7.7mm
machine guns, one in the nose, one on top, and two in beam positions." He paused
just perceptibly, and barked "Sir!" again.

Lieutenant Reeves applauded.

"Very good, Sergeant," he chuckled. "You win the prize."

"I'm afraid to ask what the prize is," Steve said, leaning against the tree again.

"How about Patience?" Howard asked innocently. "I've noticed the way she
looks at you."

"Shit!" Steve said. "You know what she did to me just now?"

"Tell me," Howard said.

"No. Shit!"

"You might as well let her," Howard said. "You're going to have to sooner or
later. And besides, you're a Marine sergeant now. It's time you lost your cherry."

Reeves laughed. Steve Koffler glowered at Howard.

Pretending not to notice, Howard put the binoculars back to his eyes. He studied
the sky intently for thirty seconds, and then handed the binoculars to Reeves.

"I make it Betty," he said. "Large Force. I count forty-five."

"That's a bit, isn't it?" Reeves said, and put the binoculars to his eyes. Thirty
seconds later, he took them away. "Vs," he said. "Five to a V. Nine Vs. Forty-five
Bettys. Looks like they're climbing slowly."

He handed the binoculars to Koffler, who waved them away.

"You better see who you can raise, Steve," Howard said.

"Aye, aye, Sir," Steve said, and left the platform for the limbs of the tree, and
then started climbing down.

"Why don't you go along with him?" Reeves said. "I'll stay and see if anything
else shows up. Send Patience up."

"All right," Howard said.

"We can't have her distracting our operator, can we?" Reeves chuckled. "And
if there's anything I don't recognize, I'll send her after you."

Howard climbed out of the tree and walked quickly to the village. He saw two
men tying the long wire antenna for the Hallicrafters radio in place in two trees on
opposite sides of the cleared area. The antenna lead wire rose from the center of
one hut.

The antenna was erected only when they intended to use the radio. Otherwise,
like the other parts of the radio, it was neatly stored and packed, ready to be carried
into the jungle if the Japanese should send a patrol into the area.

When he entered the hut, Howard saw that Koffler had the radio just about set
up. A muscular native, named Ian Bruce, was already in place at the generator,
which looked something like the pedals of a bicycle, waiting for orders to start
grinding. Koffler was carefully checking his connections for corrosion. He glanced
up at Howard when he sensed his presence, but said nothing.

Howard walked to the set itself and glanced down at the message pad. There was
nothing Koffler had written on it that needed correction. All the message consisted
of was the time, the type and number of aircraft, and their relative course. In
Australia, or if the connection to Australia could not be completed, in Pearl Harbor,
there were experts who would understand this information and relay it.

Koffler screwed a final connection in place, went outside to quickly check on the
antenna, and then squatted on the floor by a packing case which held the transceiver,
the key, and two sets of headphones. He picked up one set of headphones (which

Howard now thought of as "cans," which is what Koffler called them) and handed them to Howard. He put the second set on and made a winding motion with his finger. Ian Bruce smiled and began to pedal the generator; there was a faint, not unpleasant whine.

In a moment, the dials on the Hallicrafter lit up and their needles came to life.

Koffler put his fingers on the key.

The dots and dashes went out, repeated three times, spelling, simply, FRD6. FRD6. FRD6.

The code name for the Coastwatchers Organization was Ferdinand. It was a fey title, chosen, Howard suspected, by Lieutenant Commander Eric Feldt himself. Ferdinand was the bull who would rather sniff flowers than fight. The Coastwatchers were not supposed to fight either.

There was no response to the first call. Koffler's finger went back to the key.

FRD6. FRD6. FRD6.

This time there was a reply. Howard had learned enough code to be able to read the simple groups.

FRD6.KCY.FRD6.KCY.FRD6.KCY.

KCY, the United States Pacific Fleet Radio Station at Pearl Harbor, Territory of Hawaii, was responding to Ferdinand Six.

That radio room leapt into Joe Howard's mind. Before the war, as a staff sergeant, he had been stationed at Pearl Harbor; and he had been sergeant of the guard at CINCPAC, Commander in Chief, Pacific. He saw the immaculate officers and the even more immaculate swabbies at their elaborate shiny equipment in a shiny, air-conditioned room with polished linoleum floors. Air-conditioned!

Now Koffler's hand came to life. Howard could not read what was going out over the air. Koffler was proud of his hand. He could transmit fifty words a minute. He was doing so now. Even repeated three times, the message didn't take long.

Then there was a reply, slow enough for Howard to understand it.

FRD6, KCY. AKN. SB.

Ferdinand Six, this is CINCPAC Radio. Receipt of your last transmission is acknowledged. Standing By.

Koffler's fingers flew over the keys for a second or two.

FRD6 CLR.

Detachment A of Special Marine Corps Detachment 14 has no further traffic for the Commander in Chief Pacific Fleet and thus clears this communications link.

Koffler put his fingers in his mouth and whistled shrilly. When he had Ian Bruce's attention, he signed to him to stop cranking the generator. Then he looked at Howard.

"No traffic for us, I guess," he said.

Howard shrugged.

"I mean, I guess if there was bad news at home or something, they'd let us know, right?"

"Yeah, sure they would, Steve," Howard said.

(FOUR)
Radio Room
USS *McCawley*
1033 Hours 8 August 1942

"Sir," the Radio Operator 2nd Class sitting at the console called out, "I've got a Top Secret Operational Immediate from CINCPAC." Operational Immediate is the highest priority message, taking precedence over all others.

A tall Lieutenant Junior Grade went to his position and stood over him as the radio operator typed out the rest of the message. The moment the radio operator tore it from the typewriter, he snatched it from his fingers and took it to the cryptographic compartment.

Five minutes later, a Marine corporal in stiffly starched khakis stepped onto the bridge of the *McCawley*. He was armed with a .45 pistol, its holster suspended from a white web belt with glistening brass accoutrements.

He walked to Rear Admiral Richmond K. Turner, Commander, Amphibious Forces, South Pacific.

"Sir, a message, Sir," he said.

"Thank you," Admiral Turner said, and took it and read it.

OPERATIONAL IMMEDIATE

TOP SECRET

FROM CINCPAC

TO COMAMPHIBFORSOPAC

INTELSOURCE 1 INDICATES YOU MAY EXPECT ATTACK BY FORTY FIVE BETTY AIRCRAFT AT APPROXIMATELY 1200 YOUR TIME. END

Admiral Turner handed the sheet of paper to his aide-de-camp.

"See that the word is passed to the fleet," he said. "Tell the carriers I want to know when they launch their fighters. Tell them I think this is reliable, and I want to go with it."

"Aye, aye, Sir."

(FIVE)
USS *McCawley*
Off Beach Red
Guadalcanal, Solomon Islands
8 August 1942

At 1600 Admiral Fletcher received word from General Vandergrift that the 1st Battalion, First Marines had captured the Japanese airfield on Guadalcanal, relatively intact. The field was renamed Henderson Field in honor of Major Lofton R. Henderson, USMC, who had died at Midway. In Vandergrift's opinion, the airfield could be repaired enough to accept fighter aircraft within forty-eight hours.

At 1807, Admiral Fletcher radioed Admiral Ghormley stating that in repelling the Japanese aerial attack at noon, he had lost twenty-one of his ninety-nine aircraft. He stated further that the necessary maneuvering of the ships of the invasion fleet during the invasions had reduced his fuel supply to a level he considered inadequate. He further stated that there was a strong probability that a second Japanese attack by air or sea would be made against his fleet. Unless permission to withdraw the invasion fleet was immediately granted, this attack would result in unacceptable losses to his Task Force.

At 2325 hours, General Vandergrift, having been ordered to report to Admiral Fletcher, came aboard the *McCawley*. There Admiral Fletcher informed General Vandergrift that he had received permission from Admiral Ghormley to withdraw from the Guadalcanal area. At 1500 9 August (the next day), he went on to say, ten transports, escorted by a cruiser and ten destroyers, would depart from the beachhead. The balance of the invasion fleet would sail at 1830.

General Vandergrift is known to have protested that the off-loading of the 1st

Marine Division and its supporting troops—including the heavy (155mm) artillery, along with considerable quantities of ammunition and supplies, including rations—had not been completed. Admiral Fletcher's reply to the protest has not been recorded.

General Vandergrift returned to the invasion beach on Guadalcanal shortly after midnight.

(SIX)
Headquarters, First Marine Division
Beach Red
Guadalcanal, Solomon Islands
1830 Hours 9 August 1942

Division Sergeants Major have far more important things to do than escort individual replacements to their assigned place of duty. But in the Marine Corps, as elsewhere, there is an exception to every rule, and this was an exceptional circumstance.

For one thing, Major General A.A. Vandergrift had personally told his sergeant major to "take this gentleman down to Colonel Goettge and tell him I sent him."

The gentleman in question was more than a little out of the ordinary, too. He was in his forties, silver-haired, tall, erect, and with a certain aura of authority about him that the sergeant major's long military service had taught him came to men only after a lifetime of giving orders in the absolute expectation that they would be obeyed.

The gentleman was wearing Marine utilities, loosely fitting cotton twill jacket, and trousers already sweat stained. The outline of a Colt .45 automatic pistol and two spare magazines for it pressed against one of the baggy pockets of the utilities. The outlines of two "Grenades, Hand, Fragmentation" bulged the other trousers pocket. A Springfield Model 1903A3 .30-06 caliber rifle hung with practiced ease from his shoulder on a leather strap. And the outline of a half dozen five-round stripper clips of rifle cartridges pressed against the material of the right breast pocket of his utility jacket.

There was a small silver eagle pinned to each of the utility jacket's collar points. Fleming Pickering looked for all the world like a Marine Colonel engaged in ground combat against the enemy. Considering his age and rank and his casual familiarity with the Springfield, other Marines would probably guess that he was a regimental commander, rather than a staff officer.

But the Sergeant Major had learned that he was not a Marine. The silver eagles on his collar points were intended to identify him as a Navy Captain. And the Sergeant Major had also heard that Captain Fleming Pickering was the only man in the United States Naval Service on Guadalcanal, sailor or Marine, who had not been ordered there. He was on Guadalcanal because he wanted to be. According to the General's orderly, who overheard a great deal, and who was a reliable source of information for the Sergeant Major, no one—not General Vandergrift, not even Admiral Chester W. Nimitz, the overall Pacific Ocean Areas (POA) Commander-in-Chief back in Pearl Harbor—could order him off, or for that matter, order him to do anything.

The Sergeant Major was just about convinced that he liked this Navy VIP. This was unusual for him. His normal reaction to Naval officers generally, and to Naval VIPs specifically, was to avoid the sonsofbitches as much as possible.

One reason he sort of liked this one was because he was here on the beach, in Utilities, carrying a Springfield over his shoulder, and a couple of grenades in his pocket. The rest of the fucking Navy was already over the horizon and headed for

Noumea . . . after leaving Marines on the beach, less their heavy artillery and most of their rations and ammunition.

But the primary reason that the Sergeant Major decided that this Navy captain was the exception to the general rule that Navy captains are bad fucking news was that this captain enjoyed the friendship and respect of one of the sergeant major's few heroes, Major Jack NMI (for "No Middle Initial") Stecker.

Major Stecker, who had commanded the 2nd Battalion, 5th Marines, in the invasion of Tulagi the day before, came into the Division Command Post on Guadalcanal a few minutes after Captain Pickering showed up on the island.

There is, of course, by both regulation and custom, a certain formality required in conversation between Sergeants Major and Majors, but the Sergeant Major and Jack NMI Stecker had been Sergeants Major together longer than Jack Stecker had been an officer. When the Sergeant Major inquired of Major Stecker vis-à-vis Captain Fleming W. Pickering, he was perhaps less formal than Marine regulations and custom required.

"Jack," the Sergeant Major inquired, "just who the fuck is that swabbie trying to pass himself off as a Marine?"

Stecker's voice and eyes were icy: "He's someone an asshole like you, *Sergeant,* better not let me hear calling a swabbie."

"Sorry, Sir," the Sergeant Major replied, coming to attention. Stecker's temper was a legend. It was always spectacular when aroused, and it usually lasted a long time.

This time it began to pass almost immediately.

"Captain Pickering, Steve," Major Stecker went on, "won the Croix de Guerre at Belleau Wood. Everybody in his squad was dead, and he had an 8mm round through each leg when we got to him, and twenty-four German Grenadiers needing burying."

"He was a Marine?" the Sergeant Major asked, so surprised that there was a perceptible pause before he remembered to append, "Sir?"

Stecker nodded. "You ever hear what they say, Steve, 'Once a Marine, always a Marine'?" he asked, now conversationally.

"Yes, Sir."

"Captain Pickering is one of the good guys, Steve. Don't forget that."

"I won't, Sir."

"If you had taken a commission when they offered you one, you stupid sonofabitich, you wouldn't have to call me 'Sir.'"

"Calling *you* 'Sir' doesn't bother me, Major."

"Do what you can for Captain Pickering, Steve," Stecker said. "Like I said, he's one of the good guys."

The G-2 (Intelligence) General Staff Section of Headquarters, 1st Marine Division was set up in its own tent fifty yards from the Division Command Post, which had been established in a frame building that had survived both the pre-landing bombardment and the invasion itself.

A labor detail, bare chested, sweat soaked, looking exhausted, had just about completed a sandbag wall around the tent. In Captain Pickering's opinion, the wall would provide some protection from small arms fire, and from shrapnel from incoming mortar or artillery rounds landing nearby, but that was about all. A direct hit from an artillery shell would be devastating. What was needed, he thought, based on his World War I experience, was a hole in the ground, timbered over, and with a four- or five-foot-thick layer of sandbags on top.

Colonel Frank B. Goettge, the G-2, was standing before a large, celluloid-covered map mounted on a sheet of plywood. He was watching one of his sergeants mark on it with a grease pencil, when the Sergeant Major and Captain Pickering came in.

"The General, Sir," the Sergeant Major said when Goettge looked at him, "asked me to bring this gentleman to you. Captain Pickering, this is Colonel . . ."

"I have the pleasure of Captain Pickering's acquaintance," Goettge said, walking to Pickering, smiling, and offering his hand. "Good to see you, Sir. And a little surprised."

"I'm a little surprised myself," Pickering said, shifting his shoulder to indicate the Springfield. "I would have given odds I'd never carry one of these things again."

"I don't mean to sound facetious, Sir," Goettge said, "but what did you do, miss the boat?"

"Something like that," Pickering said. "I just couldn't bring myself to sail off into the sunset with the goddamned Navy."

"Is there anything I can do for you, Sir?" Goettge asked, in some confusion.

"Tell me how I can make myself useful to you," Fleming Pickering said, "and stop calling me 'Sir.'"

"I don't understand . . ."

"I asked General Vandergrift where he thought I could be helpful, and he sent me to you," Pickering said.

"For 'duty,' so to speak?"

"Anywhere where I can earn my rations—I understand, by the way, there are goddamn few of those. I'm a little long in the tooth to go on patrol, but if that's all you've got for me . . ."

Colonel Goettge looked at Pickering intently. He had not had time to digest the presence of Captain Fleming Pickering, much less the reason for his presence, whatever that may be. He knew Pickering was wrapped in the mantle of the Secretary of the Navy and that he personally owned the Pacific & Far East Shipping Corporation. And yet, here he was in Goettge's bunker with a rifle slung over his shoulder.

I'll be damned, he's dead serious about going out into the boondocks of this goddamned island with that rifle, as if he was still an eighteen-year-old Marine corporal.

"Even if I couldn't think of half a dozen ways where you can really be of help around here, Captain," Goettge said, "I think we're both a little too long in the teeth to go running around in the boondocks."

Pickering nodded.

"Thank you, Sergeant Major," Goettge went on. "Please tell the General 'thank you' for Captain Pickering."

"Aye, aye, Sir," the sergeant major said, and then he added: "If I can help in any way, Captain, you just tell me what and how."

XV

As the 1940 Packard limousine passed out of the gates of the White House onto Pennsylvania Avenue, The Honorable Frank Knox, Secretary of the Navy, pulled a handkerchief from the cuff of his rumpled seersucker suit jacket, removed his Panama hat, and mopped at his forehead. Since the handkerchief was already damp with sweat, he did little but rearrange beads of sweat.

As he did now and again in such weather, Knox let his mind dwell on Thomas Jefferson and George Washington. *They must have really been marvelous practical politicians,* he thought, *right up there with Franklin Delano Roosevelt in their ability to talk people into doing foolish things against their better judgment.*

There was no other reason he could think of why the fledgling nation established its capital in a steaming swamp on the Potomac River. Certainly, Adams and Stockton and the other founding fathers must have known that the logical place for the capital was Philadelphia. Or New York. Or Boston. Or Richmond, for that matter. Anywhere but where they agreed to put it.

It was a thought that kept popping into Secretary Knox's mind over the last week, during which the temperature in Washington had rarely dipped below ninety-five degrees Fahrenheit and ninety-five percent humidity.

"Mr. Secretary?"

Knox turned to look at Captain David Haughton, USN, his administrative assistant, a tall, slender officer in a mussed, sweat-soaked khaki uniform. Haughton extended a fresh handkerchief to him.

"Thank you," Knox said. As he mopped at his forehead again, he saw that Haughton had half a dozen handkerchiefs in the open briefcase he held on his lap, in addition to the probably five pounds of paper, all stamped TOP SECRET, and the snub-nosed .38 Colt revolver. In the summer, he carried the revolver in the briefcase, because the shoulder holster was too visible under khaki and white uniforms.

Knox spoke aloud what came into his mind: "What the hell would I do without you, David?"

"Probably a lot better, Mr. Secretary," Haughton said. "May I respectfully suggest that you get someone who could really take care of you, and perhaps arrange to send me to sea?"

"You can suggest it all you want, but you're stuck with me."

"Yes, Sir."

"Where now?" Knox asked.

"Across the street, Sir," Haughton said, and pointed toward the elegant brick facade of the Foster Lafayette Hotel. "Senator Fowler."

"I'd forgotten," Knox confessed.

"He didn't offer to come to your office, Mr. Secretary," Haughton said. "He usually does."

"No problem. We're here," Knox said, and then added, chuckling, "He has a nicer office than I do, anyway."

Senator Richmond K. Fowler, Republican of California, maintained a suite in the Foster Lafayette. Not an ordinary suite—though God knew suites in the Lafayette were as large and elegant as they came—but an apartment made up of a pair of suites. It was furnished with antiques that were the personal property of old Andrew Foster himself.

Fowler was quite wealthy, and unlike some of his peers in the Senate, he made no effort at all to conceal it. In many ways he was like Knox: He considered public service a privilege; living in Washington, D.C., even as well as he did, was the terrible price he had to pay for that privilege.

Fowler was also, in Knox's opinion, one of the better senators. He was enormously influential, but rarely used his influence like a club, or a baton of power. For example, he did not make telephone calls to the Secretary of the Navy—or to other senior executive department officials—just to hear the sound of own voice, to remind himself of his own importance, or as a fishing expedition. He called only when he had something to say, or wanted specific information he could not get elsewhere. Consequently, his calls were put through to Knox—and to others—when other senators would be told the Secretary had just left for a meeting.

Even more rarely, he requested a personal audience with Knox. He understood his time was precious, and that he could usually accomplish in ninety seconds on the telephone business that would take thirty minutes or an hour from the Secretary's available time if they met face to face.

So when he did ask to see Knox personally, the Secretary of the Navy was usually willing to give him the time he needed, if at all possible. There was some business that should not be discussed on the telephone. Fowler had proven over the years that he knew what that was.

The limousine pulled up before the marquee of the hotel, and a doorman, sweating in his uniform coat, opened the door.

"Welcome to the Lafayette, Mr. Secretary," he said.

"Thank you," Knox said and offered his hand. "How are you? Hot enough for you?"

"I didn't think I'd be this hot until after Saint Peter pointed toward the basement," the doorman said. He waited until Captain Haughton was out, and then spoke to the chauffeur: "Pull it up there where it says DIPLOMATIC CORPS ONLY."

A bellman spun the revolving glass door for Knox as he approached, and then smiled at him as he came through. Knox walked across the quiet, heavily carpeted lobby to the bank of elevators.

"Eight," Captain Haughton ordered.

By the time the elevator reached the eighth floor, there had been a telephone call from the doorman. A large, very black man wearing a gray cotton jacket and a wide smile was standing by the open door of Senator Fowler's suite when the elevator door opened.

"Hello, Mr. Secretary Knox, Sir. Nice to see you again, Sir. And you too, Captain Haughton. The Senator's waiting for you."

"Hello, Franklin," Knox said. "How do you manage to look so cool on a day like this?"

"I just don't go outside in the heat, Sir," Fowler's butler chuckled.

Senator Richmond K. Fowler was in the sitting room. He was not alone. A tall, shapely, aristocratic woman was with him. She had silver hair, simply but elegantly coiffured, and she was wearing a cotton suit, with a high-necked white linen blouse under it. For jewelry, she wore a simple wedding band, a single strand of pearls, and a small, cheap pin on the lapel of her jacket. It held two blue stars on a white background and signified that two members of her immediate family were serving their country in uniform. Secretary Knox had not previously had the honor of the lady's acquaintance, but he knew who she was.

Her father owned the Foster Lafayette Hotel (and forty others), and her husband owned the Pacific & Far Eastern Shipping Corporation. She was, *pro tempore,* in her husband's absence, Chairman of the Board of P&FE. Her name was Patricia Foster (Mrs. Fleming) Pickering.

She stood up as Knox and Haughton entered the room, and the Secretary liked what he saw. Nice-*looking woman,* he thought. This was immediately followed by, *Her presence here is not coincidental. I wonder what she wants?*

"Hello, Frank," Senator Fowler said, walking up to him and offering his hand. "Thank you for finding time for me." He looked at Captain Haughton, nodded, and said, "Haughton."

"Senator," Haughton replied.

"I was right across the street," Knox said. "And anytime, Richmond."

"I don't believe you know each other, do you?"

"I know who the lady is," Knox said. "How do you do, Mrs. Pickering? I'm pleased that I'm being given the chance to meet you."

"How do you do, Mr. Knox?" Patricia Pickering said, giving him her hand.

She's striking now, Knox thought. *She must have been a real beauty when she was twenty.*

She turned to Haughton. "My husband has often spoken of you, Captain Haughton. How do you do?"

"Very well, thank you," Haughton said.

"Would you do any better if we got you something cold to drink?"

"Oh, yes, Ma'am," he said.

"Franklin?" Patricia Pickering said, and the butler appeared.

"I hope that offer includes me," Knox said.

"Oh, yes. We intend to ply you with liquor and anything else that might please you," she said.

"Do you really?" Knox said, taken a little aback.

"I've been drinking—what is this, Franklin?"

"An Orange Special, Miss Patricia."

"Orange juice, club soda, and a hooker of rum," she said. "I can't handle gin, for some reason."

"That sounds wonderful," Knox said.

"Make a pitcherful, please," she ordered.

"Patricia is in town for a meeting of the War Shipping Board," Senator Fowler said.

"That's not quite true," she said. "What I did, Mr. Knox, was take one of the three airline ticket priorities they gave P&FE to send people to the WSB meeting, so that I could come here and see Senator Fowler."

"But you are a member of the War Shipping Board," Fowler protested.

"Yes, I am. In the same way that I am chairman of P&FE," she said. "But I don't like sailing under false colors."

"I don't think I know quite what you mean, Mrs. Pickering," Knox said. There was something about this woman, beyond her grace and her beauty, that he instinctively liked.

"I am not foolish enough to think that I can run P&FE, Mr. Knox," she said evenly. "And only fools think I do. Despite the title. My position, I've come to think, is analogous to that of the King. I understand that every day they bring him a red box containing important state documents. They make sure he knows what's going on. But they don't let him run the British Empire."

"Well, then, may I say that you make a lovely queen?" Knox said.

She smiled at him, a genuine smile. "Richmond is supposed to be the politician," she said. "Saying, as a reflex action, what he thinks people want to hear."

"She was a sweet child when I first met her, Frank," Fowler said. "And then she married Flem Pickering, who has poisoned her against public servants."

"That's not true," she said. "Flem Pickering proposed because my father had already told me about public servants."

"I'm afraid to ask what he told you," Knox said.

"He started by saying that one should regard them as used car salesmen in one-tone shoes," she said. "And then, I'm afraid, he became somewhat cynical."

Knox laughed.

"But here you are, seeing Senator Fowler," he said.

"My father and my husband feel he's the exception to the rule," she said. "And he tells me you are, too."

Franklin, the butler, appeared with a pitcher and glasses on a tray. It occurred to Knox that since there hadn't been time to make it, obviously Franklin had prepared it beforehand, probably on orders from Patricia Pickering.

Knox took one of the glasses and raised it. "Your health, Ma'am."

"Thank you," she said. "Would that include my peace of mind?"

"Certainly," Knox said, smiling.

"You can do something about that," she said. "You can tell me where he is and what he's doing."

"He's in the Pacific, as you know," Knox said. "As my personal representative."

"A week ago, I had a message from him saying that he was going to sea for a while and would be out of touch," Patricia Pickering said. "And now the radio tells me that we have invaded Guadalcanal in the Solomons. And I have learned that my husband is no longer in Australia. I want to know where he is and what he's doing. And Richmond tells me that you're the only man who knows."

"Are you sure he's no longer in Australia?" Knox replied. "I'm curious. How could you know that?"

"The *Pacific Endeavor* is now in Melbourne. I radioed a message there to be relayed to my husband; and her master replied that his whereabouts are unknown to our agent there. And that MacArthur's headquarters denied any knowledge of him."

Use of Maritime Radio for transmission of personal messages had been forbidden since the United States had entered the war, but Knox was not surprised to hear what she just told him. The master of the *Pacific Endeavor* was not going to ignore a message from her owner, or refuse to do whatever the message ordered him to do, whether or not the U.S. Navy liked it.

Patricia Pickering read his mind. "Please don't tell me I wasn't supposed to do that."

"I have the feeling, Mrs. Pickering," Knox said, "that anything I say wouldn't make very much difference to you."

"I would take your word if you tell me there were good reasons why my husband disappeared from the face of the earth," she said. "Is that what it is?"

"David," Knox said, turning to Captain Haughton, "would you show Mrs. Pickering our last message from Captain Pickering?"

Haughton opened his briefcase, took out a two-inch-thick sheaf of papers, looked through it, and pulled a file from it. The file cover sheet was marked with diagonal red stripes across its face and Top Secret was stamped at the top and bottom. He handed it to Patricia Pickering.

Aboard USS McCawley
Off Guadalcanal
1430 Hours 9 August 1942

Dear Frank:

This is written rather in haste, and will be brief because I know of the volume of radio traffic that's being sent, most of it unnecessarily.

As far as I am concerned the Battle of Guadalcanal began on 31 July when the first Army Air Corps B-17 raid was conducted. They have bombed steadily for a week. I mention this because I suspect the Navy might forget the bombing in their reports. They were MacA's B-17s and he supplied them willingly. That might be forgotten, too.

The same day, 31 July, the Amphibious Force left Koro in the Fijis, after the rehearsal. On 2 August, the long awaited and desperately needed Marine Observation Squadron (VMO-251, sixteen F4F3-Photo recon versions of the Wildcat) landed on the new airbase at Espiritu Santo. Without the required wing tanks. They are essentially useless until they get wing tanks. A head should roll over that one.

The day before yesterday, Friday, Aug 7, the invasion began. The Amphibious Force was off Savo Island, on schedule at 0200.

The 1st Marine Raider Bn under Lt Col Red Mike Merritt landed on Tulagi and have done well.

The 1st Parachute Bn (fighting as infantrymen) landed on Gavutu, a tiny island two miles away. So far they have been decimated, and will almost certainly suffer worse losses than this before it's over for them.

The 1st and 3rd Bns, 5th Marines, landed on the Northern Coast of Guadalcanal, west of Lunga Point, to not very much initial resistance. They were attacked by Japanese twenty-five to thirty twin-engine bombers from Rabaul, at half past eleven.

I can't really tell you what happened the first afternoon and through the first night, except to say the Marines were on the beach and more were landing.

Just before eleven in the morning yesterday (8 Aug), we were alerted (by the Coastwatchers on Buka, where Banning sent the radio) to a 45-bomber force launched from Kavieng, New Ireland (across the channel from Rabaul). They arrived just before noon and caused some damage. Our carriers of course sent fighters aloft to attack them, and some of our fighters were shot down.

At six o'clock last night Admiral Fletcher radioed Ghormley that he had lost 21 of 99 planes, was low on fuel, and wants to leave.

I am so angry I don't dare write what I would like to write. Let me say that in my humble opinion the Admiral's estimates of his losses are over generous, and his estimates of his fuel supply rather miserly.

Ghormley, not knowing of this departure from the facts, gave him the necessary permission. General Vandergrift came aboard the McCawley a little before midnight last night and was informed by Admiral Fletcher that the Navy is turning chicken and pulling out.

This is before, I want you to understand, in case this becomes a bit obfuscated in the official Navy reports—before we took such a whipping this morning at Savo Island. As I understand it we lost two US Cruisers (Vincennes and Quincy) within an hour, and the Australian cruiser Canberra was set on fire. The Astoria was sunk about two hours ago, just after noon.

In thirty minutes, most of the invasion fleet is pulling out. Ten transports, four destroyers, and a cruiser are going to run first, and what's left will be gone by 1830.

The ships are taking with them rations, food, ammunition, and Marines desperately needed on the beach at Guadalcanal. There is no telling what the Marines will use to fight with; and there's not even a promise from Fletcher about a date when he will feel safe to resupply the Marines. If the decision to return is left up to Admiral Fletcher, I suppose that we can expect resupply by sometime in 1945 or 1950.

I say "we" because I find it impossible to sail off into the sunset on a Navy ship, leaving Marines stranded on the beach.

I remember what I said to you about the Admirals when we first met. I was right, Frank.

Best Personal Regards,

Fleming Pickering,
Captain, USNR

Patricia Pickering looked at Frank Knox.

"I didn't know that we lost three cruisers. My God!"

She may not consider herself qualified to run Pacific & Far East Shipping, Knox thought, *but she knows what a cruiser is, and what the loss of those three cruisers means to the Pacific Fleet.*

"That was very bad news," Knox said.

"And they had to leave, to avoid the risk of losing even more ships?"

"Your husband doesn't think so," Knox said. "I don't want to sit here in Washington and judge the decisions made on the scene of battle by an experienced admiral whose personal courage is beyond question."

"And my husband? Do I correctly infer that he went ashore on Guadalcanal and is there now?"

"I'm afraid so."

"God *damn* him!" Patricia Pickering said furiously. "The old fool!"

"Apparently, there *is* someone more annoyed with Captain Pickering than I am," Knox said. "I didn't send him over there to shoulder a rifle."

She smiled at him.

"They're mad, you know. Anyone who is, or who ever was, a Marine is mad. And I am blessed—or cursed—with two of them."

"Blessed, I would say," Knox said. "Wouldn't you, really?"

She smiled at him again. "What happens now?"

"That message came in just as Haughton and I were leaving for the White House. As soon as we get back to the office, Captain Haughton is going to radio orders for Captain Pickering to be withdrawn from Guadalcanal as soon as possible. How long would you say it's been, Mrs. Pickering, since someone read the riot act to your husband?"

"Much too long, Mr. Knox," Patricia Pickering said.

"My heart won't be in it, frankly," he said. "But under the circumstances—I used to be a sergeant myself, you know—I don't think I've forgotten how to chew somebody out."

Mrs. Fleming Pickering surprised the Secretary of the Navy. She moved her head quickly to his and kissed him on the cheek.

(TWO)
Near Lunga Point
Guadalcanal, Solomon Islands
1440 Hours 12 August 1942

Captain Fleming Pickering, USNR, stood on the bed of a Japanese Navy Ford truck and watched as Marines worked to put the finishing touches on the airfield the Japanese had begun. He was wearing sweat-streaked utilities; on his head was a soft utility cap (instead of the steel helmet he was supposed to wear). A Springfield 1903 .30-06 rifle was cradled like a hunting rifle in his arms.

This airfield, in his judgment, was the reason for OPERATION PESTILENCE. Even before it was ready to handle aircraft it was named "Henderson Field" by General Vandergrift in order to honor Major Lofton Henderson, USMC, who had been killed after some spectacularly heroic airmanship at Midway. Whoever controlled this airfield was going to be able to control the Solomons, and thus New Guinea and Australia, and very likely the outcome of the war.

There was no doubt in Pickering's mind that the Japanese Imperial General Staff was at least as aware of the importance of this airfield as Frank Knox's personal snoop. And thus there was no question in his mind that they were going to make a valiant effort to take it back. Soon they would try to throw the First Marine Division back into the sea. He was surprised that there had not already been a violent counterattack, if not by the Japanese actually on Guadalcanal, then by Japanese naval and air forces.

So far, OPERATION PESTILENCE had gone much better than Pickering had expected, particularly after the Navy had sailed off to protect its precious aircraft carriers, taking with them a long list of material and equipment that was desperately needed on the island.

The area held by the Marines was now about 3,600 yards wide and 2,000 yards deep. Not all of the perimeter was occupied, however; that is, not every part of the perimeter was protected by trenches and foxholes. The entire beach line was so defended; but at the ends of the beach, the foxholes and machine gun emplacements extended only 500 yards or so away from the water. The cannon of the 11th Marines, in fortified positions, were in place on the forward line; and there were fortified positions scattered among the artillery emplacements.

Facing inland, the Marines held positions from 700 yards to the right of the mouth of the Kukum River to the right bank of Alligator Creek (also called "The Tenaru River") on the left. "Henderson Field" was within this area, roughly in the middle, and about 1200 yards from the beach. Division Headquarters had been set up about equidistant between Lunga Point on the beach and Henderson Field.

The invasion of Guadalcanal had taken the Japanese by surprise. Their major troop units there had been the 11th and 12th Naval Rikusentai companies, about 450 men in all. The nearest American equivalent of these units would be Naval Construction Battalions. But the Rikusentai were neither trained nor equipped the way the American Sea-Bee's were—to fight as infantry as well as to build. Thus when the invasion began, the Japanese Rikusentai units on Guadalcanal had scattered to the boondocks—specifically to somewhere near Kukum.

Fortunately for the Marines, whose own engineer equipment had never been off-loaded from the invasion fleet, they left behind all of their engineer equipment, as well as large quantities of food and other equipment, and even cannon. That wasn't the end of the bounty, though: A Japanese communications radio, far superior to anything the Marines had, had been captured intact and converted to American use.

And Marines of Lieutenant Jim Barrett's machine-gun platoon, M Company, 5th Marines, had captured two Japanese 3-inch Naval cannon, found ammunition for them, and pointed their ad hoc coast artillery battery seaward from the beach. They would be used against the Japanese warships everyone knew would soon appear offshore.

The large stocks of food the Rikusentai left behind would probably keep the 1st Marine Division from starving, Pickering thought. The departing fleet had carried away with it most of the rations it was supposed to have put ashore for the Marines.

Though the Rikusentai had rendered unusable the truck Pickering was standing on—the tires had been slashed and sand poured into the gas tank and engine oil filter—they didn't have time to sabotage most of the other trucks they left behind. So these were either intact or repairable. And so were several small bulldozers and other engineer equipment. Without the Japanese equipment, completing the airfield would have been impossible.

The Japanese plan for constructing the field involved starting from both ends and working toward a natural depression in the middle. Since the Japanese had not yet filled in the depression by the time the invasion came, when the Marines started work, that was their first order of business. One of the officers told Pickering that the job required moving 100,000 cubic yards of dirt. After that, the Marines extended the runway to 2600 feet, which was the minimum length required for operation by American airplanes.

But all that was now just about completed—*with more help from the Japanese than the U.S. Navy,* Pickering thought bitterly. The proof seemed to be that a Navy Catalina amphibious long range reconnaissance airplane was overhead, acting as if it wanted to come in for a landing.

Pickering jumped off the bed of the derelict Japanese truck, and walked to the Henderson Field control tower—obligingly built by the Rikusentai. They neglected to destroy it before heading for the boondocks.

Antennae had already been erected and strung. And when Pickering entered the building, a ground-to-air voice radio was in operation, manned by a Marine aviator who had obviously come ashore with the invasion force.

He looked at Pickering curiously, even with annoyance; but Lieutenants do not casually ask officers wearing silver eagles on their caps what the hell they want. So he returned his attention to the Catalina overhead, holding his microphone to his mouth.

"Navy two oh seven, I repeat the airfield is not, repeat not, ready to accept aircraft at this time."

"It looks fine to me," a metallic voice replied. "I repeat, I am exceedingly reluctant to land this aircraft on the water."

"Oh, shit!" the Marine Lieutenant said, and then pressed the TRANSMIT button on his microphone. "Navy two oh seven, the winds are negligible, the altimeter is two niner niner niner. Be advised that the runway may be soft, may be obstructed, and has vehicular and personnel traffic all over it. That said, you are cleared as number one to land, to the north, at your own risk. I say again, at your own risk."

"Henderson," the metallic voice replied cheerfully, "Navy two oh seven, turning on final."

Pickering went to the window of the control tower and noticed that some glass panes were missing. This was not due to any kind of bombing or shelling of the field, however. There was a jar of putty on the floor. The Rikusentai had not completed installing the glass when the Americans arrived.

Once its gear unfolded from the boat-shaped fuselage, the Catalina banked, lined up with the runway, lowered its flaps, and dropped toward the ground. It touched down, bounced back into the air, and then touched down again and stayed down.

When it completed its landing roll, stopped, and began to turn, there was shouting and applause; and any vehicles with horns blew them.

Henderson Field was now in operation, and the men who made it so were delighted with themselves, with Naval Aviation, and with the world in general.

In fact, everyone in sight seemed pleased—with the exception of the Marine Aviator who had been on the radio. He started down from the tower as the Catalina taxied toward it. Pickering followed him.

The pilot parked the Catalina and shut the engines down. A moment later, he emerged from a door in the fuselage, wearing a large grin.

He was a Lieutenant, one grade senior in rank to the Marine Aviator First Lieutenant who greeted him, "What's wrong with it? I want to get you out of here as soon as I can. Before the Japs start throwing artillery at us."

"Nothing's wrong with it, Lieutenant," the Naval Aviator said.

"You said you couldn't land it on water."

"I said, I was *'exceedingly reluctant'* to land it on water," the Navy pilot said. "My name is Sampson, Lieutenant William Sampson, USN, in case you might want to write that down in some kind of log. I believe this is the first aircraft to land here."

"You sonofabitch!" the Marine Aviator said.

If it was Lieutenant Sampson's notion to remind the Marine Lieutenant that it was a violation of Naval protocol to suggest to a senior Naval officer that his parents were unmarried, he abandoned it when he saw Pickering . . . when he saw specifically the silver eagle on Pickering's cap.

He saluted. "Good afternoon, Colonel."

Pickering returned the salute. He did not correct Lieutenant Sampson's mistake.

"Welcome to Guadalcanal," Pickering said. "Do you have business here? Or was your primary motive turning yourself into a footnote when the official history is written?"

"I'm Admiral McCain's aide, Sir. I have a bag of mail for General Vandergrift."

"I've got a Jeep," Pickering said. "I'll take you to him."

"That's very good of you, Sir."

A Jeep bounced up to them, and an officer in Marine utilities, wearing a Red Cross brassard on his arm, got out from behind the wheel.

"Have you got any space on that airplane to take critically wounded men out of here?"

"I can take two, Sir," Sampson replied. "That's all."

"When are you leaving?"

"Just as soon as I can deliver something to General Vandergrift."

"I can have them aboard in ten minutes," the doctor said.

"My crew will help you, Sir," Sampson said, and then looked at Pickering, who gestured toward the derelict Japanese Ford truck and his Jeep.

(THREE)
G-2 Section
Headquarters, 1st Marine Division
Near Lunga Point, Guadalcanal
1710 Hours 12 August 1942

Captain Fleming Pickering, USNR, did not hear Major General Alexander A. Vandergrift enter the map room of the G-2 section.

The title "map room" was somewhat grandiose: A piece of canvas (originally one of the sides of an eight-man squad tent) had been hung from a length of communications wire, dividing the G-2 Section "building" in two. The G-2 building was another eight-man squad tent, around which had been built a wall of sandbags. When there was time, it was planned to find some timbers somewhere and build a roof structure strong enough to support several layers of sandbags. At the moment, the roof was the tent canvas. Because of the sandbag walls, an artillery or mortar shell landing outside the tent would probably not do very much damage. But the canvas tenting would offer no protection if an artillery or mortar shell hit the roof.

Pickering was on his knees, working on the Situation Map. Specifically, he was writing symbols on the celluloid sheet that covered the Situation Map. This in turn was mounted to a sheet of plywood leaning against the sandbag walls. When there was time, it was planned to find some wood and make some sort of frame, so that the Situation Map would not have to sit on the ground.

In his hand, Pickering held a black grease pencil. He was marking friendly positions and units on the map. In his mouth, like a cigar, was a red grease pencil, which he used to mark enemy positions. A handkerchief, used to erase marks on the map, stuck out of the hip pocket of his utility trousers. He was not wearing his utility jacket. The Map Room of the G-2 Section was like a steam bath, and Captain Pickering had elected to work in his undershirt.

General Vandergrift walked to a spot just behind Pickering so that he could examine the map over Pickering's shoulders. Vandergrift's face, just starting to jowl, showed signs of fatigue. He stood there for more than a minute before his presence broke through Pickering's concentration. And then, startled, Pickering looked over his shoulder. A split second later, he realized who was standing behind him.

He rose quickly to his feet and came to attention.

"I beg your pardon, Sir."

Vandergrift made an "it doesn't matter" wave of his hand.

"Is that about it?" he asked, with another gesture at the map.

"Yes, Sir."

"Where's Colonel Goettge?" Vandergrift asked. "For that matter, where's the sergeant who normally keeps the Situation Map up to date?"

"Colonel Goettge is out with a patrol, Sir. I suppose I'm in charge."

"Say again?"

"Colonel Goettge is out with a patrol, Sir. He and the sergeant and some others."

Vandergrift's eyes tightened.

"I thought that's what you said," he said. "Tell me about it."

If I knew him better, I could answer that question without beating around the bush: "I think Goettge's gone off the deep end, General."

But that's not the way it is. He doesn't know me. All he knows is that I am a rich man, highly connected politically, who was sent over here to serve as Frank Knox's eyes and ears, and didn't even do that somewhat ethically questionable task well. A wiser man than I am would not take advantage of his position—no one had the authority to tell me to stay on the McCawley—to make a gesture of contempt for Navy Brass by staying with the Marines here.

What standing I have in his eyes, if any, is because Jack NMI Stecker told him that I was a pretty good Marine Corporal a generation ago.

I would not tolerate criticism of one of my officers from an ordinary seaman; why should General Vandergrift tolerate my unpleasant, and very likely uninformed opinion of one of his colonels?

Christ! I wish I knew this man better!

Although he had had only brief contact with General Vandergrift, Fleming Pickering had already formed strong opinions about him. The first was that he was competent, experienced, and level-headed. The second was that if the opportunity came, they could become friends.

Vandergrift reminded Pickering of a number of powerful commanders he had known and respected. The first of these was his own father, whose first command, at twenty-one, had been of a four-master Brigantine. And there was the master of the Pacific *Emerald,* on which Fleming Pickering, also at twenty-one, had made his first voyage with his brand-new third mate's ticket; this man had taught Pickering just about all there was to know about the responsibility that went with authority. Pickering had himself earned his any-tonnage, any-ocean Coast Guard Master Mariner's ticket at twenty-six. Since then, he'd come to know well maybe a half dozen other masters in command of Pacific & Far East Shipping Corporation vessels whom he held in serious respect. (Most of the others he employed were better than competent, but not up to the level of the six.)

And Vandergrift reminded Pickering of Pickering himself. Pickering had long believed that there were only very few men who were born to accept responsibility and discharge it well. Such men had a strange ability to recognize similar characteristics in others; they formed a kind of fraternity without membership cards and titles. Thus he had the strong conviction that he and General Vandergrift were brothers.

"Sir," Pickering said, "two days ago, a Japanese warrant officer, a *Navy* warrant officer, was captured by 1st Battalion, 5th Marines. During his interrogation, he said there were a large number of Rikusentai . . ."

"What?"

"Rikusentai, Sir. They're Naval Base troops. Sort of soldiers. Not Marines, Sir. They take care of housekeeping, construction. That sort of thing. They're in the Navy, but not sailors."

Vandergrift nodded.

"The warrant officer said there were a number of Rikusentai, and at least as many civilian laborers, wandering around in the bush near Matinikau. Here, Sir," Pickering said, pointing to the map. "In this general area. And he felt they could be induced to surrender. He said they were starving."

"He was unusually cooperative for a Japanese Naval officer, wasn't he?" Vandergrift said.

"He was originally pretty surly, as I understand it, Sir. But he was in bad shape. What used to be known as shell-shocked."

"You saw him, Pickering?"

"Yes, Sir. The 5th sent him up here."

"And?"

"What the warrant officer said was corroborated, Sir, by another prisoner. A Navy rating. Not captured at the same place. And not one of the warrant officer's men. He said there were both Rikusentai and civilian laborers in the area here," he pointed at the map with the red grease pencil, "at the mouth of the Matanikau River, in the vicinity of Point Cruz."

"And Colonel Goettge apparently believed both of them?"

"Yes, Sir. I assume that he did."

"Tell me about the patrol," Vandergrift said.

"Colonel Goettge had previously ordered a patrol under First Sergeant Custer. As originally set up, Custer was to take about twenty-five men into the Point Cruz-Mouth of the Matanikau River area. But then Colonel Goettge decided to lead the patrol himself."

"Did he offer any explanation for his decision?" Vandergrift asked, evenly.

"He apparently felt that the mission was too important to be entrusted to First Sergeant Custer, Sir."

What he did was act like an ass. He had no business going on patrol himself.

"Twenty-five men, you say? All from the 1st of the 5th?"

"No, Sir. He took several men from here, clerks and scouts. And Lieutenant Cory, our linguist. And Dr. Pratt, the 5th's surgeon."

"In other words, Captain Pickering, instead of a patrol of scouts and riflemen under a First Sergeant, we now have a patrol substantially made up of technicians of one kind or another, under the personal command of the Division Intelligence Officer?"

Pickering didn't reply.

Vandergrift met his eyes.

"And he left you in charge?" Vandergrift asked.

"Not in so many words, Sir."

"You just decided to fill the void left by Colonel Goettge when he went on this patrol of his?"

"I'm trying to make myself useful, Sir."

"Yes, of course you are. Actually, I came here to see you."

"Sir?"

Vandergrift reached in the cavernous pocket of his utility jacket and handed Pickering a crumpled sheet of paper.

URGENT

CONFIDENTIAL

NAVY DEPARTMENT WASHDC 10AUG42

TO: COMMANDING GENERAL
      FIRST MARINE DIVISION

INFORMATION; CINCPAC

1. BY DIRECTION OF THE SECRETARY OF THE NAVY CAPTAIN FLEMING PICKERING USNR IS RELIEVED OF TEMPORARY ATTACHMENT 1ST MARINE DIVISION AND WILL PROCEED BY FIRST AVAILABLE AIR TRANSPORTATION TO WASHINGTON DC REPORTING UPON ARRIVAL THEREAT TO THE SECRETARY.

2. THE OFFICE OF THE SECRETARY OF THE NAVY WILL BE ADVISED BY RADIO OF RECEIPT OF THESE ORDERS BY CINCPAC, COMMGEN FIRST MARINE DIVISION AND CAPTAIN PICKERING. OFC SECNAV WILL BE SIMILARLY ADVISED OF DATE AND TIME OF CAPTAIN PICKERING'S DEPARTURE FROM 1ST MARDIV AND ARRIVAL AND DEPARTURE FROM INTERMEDIATE STOPS EN ROUTE TO WASHINGTON.

DAVID HAUGHTON, CAPT, USN, ADMINISTRATIVE ASST TO SECNAV

"It may be some time before you go home, Pickering," General Vandergrift said. "I have no idea when the field will be able to take anything but fighters. That Catalina coming in here was an aberration."

"Yes, Sir."

"In the meantime, I am sure that you will continue to make yourself useful," Vandergrift said. "When Colonel Goettge and his ... what did you call them, Pickering?"

"Rikusentai, Sir."

"... Rikusentai. When he returns, would you tell him I would like to see him, please?"

"Aye, aye, Sir."

Their eyes met briefly, but long enough for Pickering to understand that Vandergrift shared his opinion that Division Intelligence Officers should not shoulder rifles and go off into the boondocks like second lieutenants. And there was confirmation, too, of Pickering's conviction that if there was only the opportunity, he and Vandergrift could become friends.

(FOUR)
G-2 Section
Headquarters, 1st Marine Division
Guadalcanal
2250 Hours 13 August 1942

Major Jake Dillon, USMCR, a Leica 35mm camera suspended around his neck, a Thompson .45 caliber submachine gun cradled in his arm, pushed aside the canvas black-out flap and stepped into the G-2 section.

"Where can I find Captain Pickering?" he demanded of the Marine buck sergeant sitting by the three field telephones on a folding wooden desk.

A very tall, very thin Marine with sergeant's stripes painted on the sleeve of his utility jacket followed Dillon into the room. He was unarmed, and looked haggard and shaken, shading his eyes against the sudden brightness of the hissing Coleman lanterns.

The Marine sergeant started to rise to his feet. Dillon waved him back in his chair.

"The Captain's in there, Sir," he said, pointing to the map room. "I think he's asleep."

Dillon motioned for the sergeant who had come with him to follow him. Then he pushed the canvas flap aside.

Captain Fleming Pickering, USNR, was not only asleep, he was snoring. He was fully dressed, except for his boondockers, which were on the floor beside him. Next to the boondockers was a .45 Colt automatic pistol, the hammer cocked. His Springfield rifle hung from its sling on a length of steel pipe near his head.

His bed was two shelter halves laid on communications wire laced between more steel piping. A Coleman lantern hissed in the corner of the room.

Jake Dillon looked quickly around the room, walked quickly to the "bed," and placed his foot on Pickering's pistol.

"Flem!" he called. He immediately had proof that stepping on the pistol had been the prudent thing to do. It was the first thing Pickering reached for.

"It's me. Jake Dillon."

"What the hell do you want?" Pickering asked, a long way from graciously. He stretched a moment, and then sat up, swinging his feet to the floor and reaching for his boondockers. "What time is it?"

"Nearly eleven," Dillon replied, then checked his watch and corrected himself. "Ten-fifty."

Pickering looked at the sergeant.

"This is Sergeant Sellers, Flem," Dillon said. "He's one of mine."

Pickering nodded at the sergeant curtly.

"He was with Goettge," Dillon added.

Pickering's face lit up with interest.

"You were with Colonel Goettge, Sergeant? Where is he?"

"He's dead, Sir. Just about everybody is dead," the sergeant said.

"Christ!" Pickering said softly. "Everybody?"

The sergeant nodded dazedly.

"Just about everybody," he said.

"I thought you had better hear this, Flem, right away," Dillon said.

Pickering looked at Sergeant Sellers and saw in his face—especially in his eyes—the absent look that comes into men's eyes when they have seen something horrifying.

This guy is right on the edge of shock!

Pickering reached under his commo wire and shelter halves bed and came out with a musette bag. He opened the straps and took from it a bottle of Old Grouse scotch, thickly padded with bath towels. He took the top off and extended it wordlessly to Sergeant Sellers.

Sellers looked at it for a moment before somewhat dreamily reaching for it and putting it to his lips. He took a healthy pull and then coughed and then handed the bottle back to Pickering.

"You need some of this, Jake?" Pickering asked.

Resisting the temptation to reach for the bottle, Dillon shook his head no. Liquor, like everything else, was in short supply on the island.

"Sure?"

Dillon reached for the bottle and took a sip.

Pickering took the bottle from him, and began to wrap it in the towels again.

"You were with Colonel Goettge's patrol, Sergeant?" he asked, gently.

"Yes, Sir."

"How did that happen, Jake?"

"I heard about the patrol and told Goettge I'd like to send one of my people along. He said, 'sure.'"

Pickering had a sudden, furious thought: *Was that simple stupidity, or did Goettge want to make sure his Errol Flynn-John Wayne heroics were properly photographed for posterity?*

He immediately regretted the snap decision: *There you go again, Pickering, from all your vast experience as a corporal twenty-odd years ago, judging a man who spent that much time learning his profession. Who the* hell *do you think you are?*

"Can you tell me about the patrol, Sergeant? You say you're just back?"

"Yes, Sir," Sergeant Sellers replied, and then fell silent.

"Start from the beginning, why don't you? You went with Colonel Goettge on the ramp boat from Kukum?"

That much Pickering already knew. When the Navy sailed away from Guadalcanal, they did so in such haste that a number of the landing boats normally carried aboard the transports were left behind. Before the Naval bombardment, there had been a small village called Kukum. The village was almost totally destroyed, but it remained a good spot for keeping the boats the Navy left behind. So Vandergrift formed there an ad hoc unit, "The Lunga Boat Pool," made up of the boats and their mixed Navy and Coast Guard crews.

"That was about eighteen hundred?" Pickering pried gently. He knew what time Goettge left.

Fucking around with one thing and another, including taking his own combat correspondent with him, Goettge's ramp boat left at least two hours too late to do any good once he got where they were headed.

"That's about all we know, Sergeant," Pickering said, gently. "Could you fill me in from there?"

"Well, it was dark when we got there, Sir."

"You mean at the Matanikau River?"

Pickering knew that too. Following First Sergeant Custer's original plan at least that far, Goettge had told him he planned to go ashore about two hundred yards west of the mouth of the Matanikau.

"Yes, Sir. That's probably why we ran aground. It was dark and we couldn't see."

"Where did you run aground?"

"About fifty yards offshore, Colonel," Sergeant Sellers said. Pickering did not correct him. "The . . . watchacallem? The guy who runs the boat?"

"The coxswain," Pickering furnished.

"The coxswain said it was a sandbar."

"What happened then?"

"Some of the guys went over the sides and tried to rock it free, but when that didn't work, we all went into the water and waded ashore."

"What happened to the ramp boat?"

"A couple of guys stayed behind and kept rocking it. I guess they finally got it loose. We could hear it after a while; we couldn't see it, it was too dark. We could hear it going away."

"So there you were on the beach?"

"So they talked it over."

" 'They'?"

"Colonel Goettge and the officers," Sellers said. "I was there with them."

"And?"

"They decided it was too late, too dark, too, to do anything. Except find some place to spend the night. And then go on patrol in the morning. So Colonel Goettge and Sergeant Custer started walking toward the coconut trees . . ."

"What coconut trees?"

"There was a grove of coconut trees. It was dark on the ground, Colonel, but we could see the tops of the trees . . . You know what I mean?"

"Yes, I think so. Then what happened?"

"That's when the Japs started shooting," Sellers said, very quietly, barely audibly.

"Was anyone hit?"

"Colonel Goettge. He got it first. Then Sergeant Custer," Sellers said. "They went down right away. Christ! Then the Doc ran out to help them . . ."

"That would be Captain Pratt, the surgeon?"

"I think that was his name," Sellers said. "And then Sergeant Caltrider shot the Jap."

"What Jap was that?"

"The one we brought with us. The Jap warrant officer."

"Sergeant Caltrider shot him?"

"Blew the cocksucker's head off," Sellers said. "The bastard led us into a trap. That's what it was, a trap. He deserved it, the cocksucker."

"Was Colonel Goettge badly wounded?"

"Killed. Had half of his face shot away. Sergeant Custer, too. He was hit four, five times. Killed him right away."

"And Doctor Pratt?"

"Him, too."

"And what were the rest of you doing?"

"One of the guys ran back in the water and fired his rifle, to get the ramp boat to come back. The rest of us just laid there. Jesus, there was no place to get out of the line of fire. It was like they were waiting for us, knew where we would be, and when we got where they wanted us, they opened up with everything they had."

"Did the boat come back?"

"No, Sir. Either he didn't know we wanted him to, or he could see what was going on and figured we were all dead."

"Then what?"

"We just laid there. Christ, we couldn't even see where they were to shoot back at them. I mean, we knew where they were, but we couldn't see them."

"But they knew where you were?"

"The only reason I'm alive is because of the way the beach sloped. There was just enough sand to hide behind."

"Where was Captain Ringer? Did you see him?"

Ringer was the S-2 of the 5th Marines. In Pickering's judgment, if any staff Intelligence officer should have gone out on this patrol—and he didn't think any should have—it should have been under the command of an infantry platoon leader. It should have been Ringer. And now he thought, unkindly, that since Goettge had insisted on going himself, Ringer should have stayed behind.

"Yes, Sir. He sort of took over after the colonel was killed. Him and Lieutenant Cory."

"What were they doing at this time?"

"Well, the first thing he did was send a corporal down the beach for help. And then, I guess it was about an hour later, Sergeant Arndt volunteered to swim back for help. I went with him."

"You swam back?"

"Yes, Sir. We ran into a Jap—I think he was as lost as we were—and Arndt killed him. And then we found a boat and paddled most of the way back."

"Most of the way?"

"Sergeant Arndt thought we would probably get shot by our own guys, so we paddled out to one of the landing boats we knew was anchored off shore, and then we got them to start it up and take us in."

"Where is Sergeant Arndt now?"

"They took him to the 5th Marines Command Post, Sir."

"I was there, Flem," Jake Dillon said. "I thought you had better hear this, so I brought him here."

"Yeah," Pickering said.

He looked at Sergeant Sellers.

"Is that about it, Sergeant? Is there anything else?"

Sellers met his eyes but didn't speak for a moment.

"Sir, as we were swimming away," he said finally, hollow voiced, "we could make out . . . the Japs came out of the boondocks, Sir, from the coconut trees and the other side of them. They . . . They went after the people on the beach, Sir. Not only with rifles and pistols. I mean, they were using swords. We could see the swords, reflections from them, I mean. And we could hear our guys screaming."

From a remote portion of his brain, dimmed by more than two decades, and intentionally hidden on top of that, Pickering's memory brought forth the sound of the screams men made when their bodies were violated by sharpened steel. Some of the Marines at Belleau Wood, Corporal Fleming Pickering among them, had armed themselves with intrenching shovels. They sharpened the sides with sharpening stones. These had been more effective than the issue bayonets and trench knives.

"Sergeant," Pickering said after a moment, "I'm going to leave you here for a while. Lie down on my bed. Help yourself to some of the whiskey, if you want. But I think that some other officers will want to talk to you, so go easy with the whiskey."

That's so much bullshit. Debriefing should be performed by Intelligence Officers. All of ours are now dead.

"Jake, you stay with him. I'm going to see General Vandergrift."

"Aye, aye, Sir."

XVI

"I'd like to see the General, please," Captain Fleming Pickering said to the sergeant in the Division Command Post.

"He's in there, Sir," the sergeant said, pointing, "with Colonel Hunt. I'll see if he can see you."

Colonel Guy Hunt was the regimental commander of the 5th Marines.

If he's here, Pickering reasoned, he knows what has happened.

"Keep your seat, Sergeant," Pickering said, and walked into Vandergrift's office.

Both Hunt and Vandergrift looked with annoyance at Pickering when he walked in. Officers, even Navy Captains, do not enter the "office" of the commanding general of the 1st Marine Division without permission.

Vandergrift met Pickering's eyes.

"For reasons I suspect you already know, Captain," Vandergrift said after a moment, "please consider yourself the acting G-2 of this division."

Oh, shit! I am no more qualified to be the Division G-2 than I am to flap my wings and fly.

"Aye, aye, Sir."

"I know you know Colonel Hunt, Pickering. Do you know Marine Gunner Rust?" (Marine Gunners were almost always veteran Master Gunnery Sergeants promoted to warrant officer rank.)

"No, Sir."

"Rust, this is Captain Pickering. He and Jack NMI Stecker were at Belleau Wood together."

"I know the captain by reputation," Rust said and gave Pickering his hand.

"How much do you know about what's happened to Goettge's patrol, Pickering?" Vandergrift asked.

"I just finished talking to Sergeant Sellers, Sir. He swam back with Sergeant Arndt."

"Sellers?" Master Gunner Rust asked.

"He's one of Major Dillon's combat correspondents," Pickering explained.

"Christ, another feather merchant who went along!" Rust exploded.

"A technician, maybe," Pickering heard himself say, angrily. "Or a specialist. But feather merchants, in my book, are those who head in the other direction from the sound of the guns."

Rust glowered at Pickering for a moment, and then shrugged.

"I beg the captain's pardon," Rust said.

"Not mine," Pickering said. "I know I'm a feather merchant. But that Four-Months-in-the-Corps Hollywood photographer has no apologies to make for his behavior on this patrol."

Pickering glanced at Vandergrift and found the general's serious eyes on his.

"Speaking of this patrol, Pickering," Vandergrift said, "we were just discussing the possibility of sending a patrol out to look for survivors. What's your feeling about that?''

"Sir, I don't feel qualified to . . .''

"I make the decisions about who is and who is not qualified to offer an opinion, Captain. I asked for yours.''

"Based on what Sergeant Sellers told me, I don't think there will be many survivors, if any," Pickering said. "And I would presume the Japanese will be waiting for us to do something. At night, Sir, in my opinion, it would be suicidal. I think we could, should, send a strong patrol over there at first light."

"I agree," Vandergrift said. "I appreciate the offer, Rust, but that makes it three to one against your idea."

"Yes, Sir," Rust said.

"You can head it up yourself, Rust, if you like," Vandergrift said. He turned to Colonel Hunt. "All right with you, Guy?''

"Yes, Sir. A *strong* patrol, Rust. They'll be expecting you.''

"Aye, aye, Sir.''

"Guy, why don't you and Rust go set it up?" Vandergrift said. "Let me know before you take off. I want a word with Captain Pickering.''

Hunt and Rust left the room. Then Colonel Hunt returned. He offered his hand to Pickering.

"Good luck, Captain," he said. "Thank God we have somebody like you to step into the breach.''

"Thank you, Sir," Pickering said.

Hunt left again. Pickering looked at Vandergrift.

"That was gracious and flattering," Pickering said. "But I am not qualified to step into Goettge's shoes.''

"You weren't listening carefully, Captain," Vandergrift said. "The operative words were '*somebody* like you to step into the breach.' I don't have anyone else. You don't expect to lose your division G-2 like this. Nor the 5th Marines' G-2, who would have been my choice for a temporary replacement.''

"I'll do my best, Sir. But you need a professional.''

"I'll send a radio asking for one, of course," Vandergrift said. "But until he arrives, or until I have to order you off the island, you're it.''

"I'll need some help, Sir.''

"Jack Stecker? Am I reading your mind?''

"Yes, Sir.''

Major Jack NMI Stecker had commanded 2nd Battalion, 5th Marines, when they invaded Tulagi. During the battle, Stecker had personally taken out a sniper-in-a-bunker who had been holding up the 2nd Battalion's advance by standing in the open and shooting him, offhand, in the head from a distance of 200 yards. The story had not surprised Pickering when he heard it.

"General Harris won't like losing Stecker, but he'll have to live with it. Tulagi is secure, and Stecker will be of more value to the division working with you here. I'll send a boat to Tulagi at first light to fetch him. He's not going to be happy about it, either, but that's the way it's going to have to be.''

"What he really won't like is working for me," Pickering chuckled. "In France, in 1918, he was my sergeant when I was a corporal.''

Vandergrift looked at Pickering, and then smiled. "I think they call that the fortunes of war, Captain," he said, in mock solemnity, and then went on, changing the subject, "There's something I feel I should tell you: How well do you—perhaps that should be, 'did you'—know Lieutenant Cory?''

"You're speaking of the 5th Marines Japanese language officer?" Vandergrift nodded. "Not well, Sir.''

"He is another of your Four-Months-in-the-Corps Marines, Pickering. He came in April. Direct commission. He was previously employed by the Navy. In Washington. Something to do with communications intelligence. Something hush-hush. I received a special message about him. I was directed to take whatever action was necessary to keep him from falling into Japanese hands."

"Jesus!" Pickering said, not aware he had spoken.

My God, he might have known about MAGIC! *What idiot assigned him to an infantry regiment here?*

"From your reaction, I gather you might know what that's all about," Vandergrift said. " 'Whatever action' was not defined. Did it mean that I should make an effort to see that he did not go on patrols like this one? Or was more unpleasant action on my part suggested?"

"Sir, there are some classified matters which would justify any action to keep people privy to them out of enemy hands."

"Are you in that category, Captain?"

"Yes, Sir."

"Then it won't be necessary for me to tell you not to put yourself in a position where you might fall into enemy hands, will it?"

"No, Sir."

"Unless there's something else going on that I don't know about, I think the thing for you and me to do is try to get some sleep. There's nothing else that can be done about Goettge and his people tonight."

"Yes, Sir," Pickering said. "Sir, is our communications in to Pearl Harbor?"

"As far as I know."

"I have a message to send," Pickering said. "I have authority, Sir . . ."

"I know all about your authority, Pickering: You don't have to ask my permission to radio the Secretary of the Navy, and I don't have the authority to ask what you're saying to him."

He thinks, Pickering thought, *that I am going to radio Washington that Cory may have been captured by the Japanese. I hadn't even thought about that. But I'll do that, too.*

"With your permission, Sir?" Pickering said.

Vandergrift smiled, nodded, and waved his hand in a gesture of dismissal.

"For what it's worth, I share Colonel Hunt's sentiments about you, Pickering," Vandergrift said.

(TWO)

The duty officer in the communications section of Headquarters 1st Marine Division was a second lieutenant. He was dozing, but woke up when Pickering entered the small, sandbag-walled room.

"May I help you, Colonel?" he asked, getting to his feet.

"I'm Captain Pickering. I need to send a radio, classified TOP SECRET. Are you a crypto officer?"

"Yes, Sir, I am, but . . . Captain, what's your authority?"

Pickering took his orders, wrapped in waterproof paper, from his pocket and showed them to the young officer.

"If that won't do it for you, Lieutenant, call General Vandergrift."

"This will do, Sir. Where's the message?"

"I haven't written it yet," Pickering said. "Sergeant, you want to get up and let me at that typewriter?"

The sergeant, who had been monitoring his radio, waiting for traffic, looked at the lieutenant for guidance. The lieutenant nodded. The sergeant got up, and Pickering sat down at the typewriter. There was a blank sheet of paper in it.

Pickering looked at the lieutenant.

"The priority immediately below 'Operational Immediate' is 'Urgent,' right?"

"Yes, Sir."

Pickering tapped the balls of his fingers together impatiently as he mentally composed the message, and then he began to type. He typed with skill. He had taken up typing to pass time as a junior officer at sea. It wasn't too much later than that when he learned that doing the typing himself was much faster than dictating to a secretary.

URGENT

FROM: HQ FIRST MARINE DIVISION

TO: CINCPAC

0045 13AUG42

FOLLOWING CLASSIFIED TOP SECRET FROM CAPTAIN FLEMING PICKERING USNR FOR EYES ONLY SECNAVY WASHINGTON DC

1. LOSS IN COMBAT OF COLONEL FRANK GOETTGE 1ST MARDIV G2, CAPTAIN WILLIAM RINGER 5TH MARINES S2 AND 1STLT RALPH CORY 5TH MARINES LANGUAGE OFFICER REQUIRES IMMEDIATE ACTION TO AIRSHIP QUALIFIED REPLACEMENT PERSONNEL.

2. DESPITE URGENT NECESSITY TO FURNISH 1ST MARDIV WITH QUALIFIED PERSONNEL I URGE IN STRONGEST POSSIBLE TERMS THAT EXISTING POLICIES PROHIBITING ASSIGNMENT OF PERSONNEL WHO HAVE HAD ACCESS TO HIGHLY CLASSIFIED INFORMATION TO DUTIES WHERE THEY MAY FALL INTO ENEMY HANDS BE STRICTLY OBSERVED.

3. PENDING ARRIVAL OF QUALIFIED REPLACEMENT, THE UNDERSIGNED HAS TEMPORARILY ASSUMED DUTIES OF 1ST MARDIV G2.

SIGNED FLEMING PICKERING CAPTAIN USNR

END TOP SECRET EYES ONLY SECNAV FROM PICKERING CAPT USN G2 1ST MARDIV

He tore the paper from the typewriter and read it.

If that second paragraph doesn't tell Haughton that some damned fool assigned Cory, who almost certainly knew about MAGIC, *to an infantry battalion, he's not as smart as I think he is.*

He handed the sheet of paper to the lieutenant.

"Encrypt it and get it out as soon as you can," he said.

"Yes, Sir," the lieutenant said. He read the message.

"My God, they're all dead? What the hell happened?"

"It's a long, sad story, Lieutenant," Pickering said and walked out of the commo bunker.

(THREE)
Supreme Headquarters Southwest Pacific Area
Brisbane, Australia
13 August 1942

On the plane from Pearl Harbor, Lieutenant Colonel George F. Dailey, USMC, seriously considered doing something about the pristine newness of his silver oak leaves. The problem was that he didn't know what would do the job . . . He didn't think that rubbing them—on a carpet, say—would effectively dim their gloss. And working on them with, say, a nail file, would probably produce a silver lieutenant colonel's leaf that looked like somebody had worked it over with a nail file.

Before he fell asleep, he thought that when he got to his new billet in Australia, *before* he actually reported in, he would find some sand and rub it into his insignia with his Blitz cloth. The idea was amusing. After eight years in the Corps, he'd worn out probably twenty Blitz cloths in practically daily use putting a high shine on his insignia. He would now use one to dull it.

Lieutenant Colonel Dailey's concern was based less on personal vanity than on his belief that he could function better in new duties if it was not immediately apparent that he had been promoted so recently. After all, he reasoned, he had been a lieutenant colonel only thirteen days. And he wanted to do well in his new billet.

When he actually reached Brisbane, so many things happened so quickly that he forgot about taking the shine off his new silver oak leaves.

For one thing, there was a general's aide-de-camp, a lieutenant, waiting for him at the airport, with a 1940 Packard Clipper staff car, a driver, and an orderly.

"Colonel," the lieutenant said, "on behalf of Supreme Headquarters, SWPA, and General Willoughby specifically, welcome to Australia. The General asked me to express his regret that he couldn't meet you here himself, but he's tied up with the Supreme Commander at the moment."

The Supreme Commander, of course, was General Douglas MacArthur. General MacArthur was a full, four-star general. Dailey had never seen a four-star general. There were no four-star generals in the Marine Corps. The Commandant of the Corps was only a three-star lieutenant general. And until recently, his title had been Major General Commandant, and he had had but two stars.

"It's very good of you to meet me," Dailey said.

"I'll have the sergeant get your luggage, Sir," the aide said, "and then we'll try to get you settled. General Willoughby hopes we can do that by sixteen hundred, so there will be a chance for him to have a quick word with you before you see the Supreme Commander—he'll take you to see him—which we have penciled in for sixteen forty-five."

My God, I'm going to meet MacArthur!

"If I'm to see the General," Dailey said, "either general, I really am going to have to have a uniform pressed."

"No problem, Sir," the aide said. "There's a valet service in Lennon's. I'll have a word with the manager and explain the situation."

"Lennon's?"

"Lennon's Hotel, Sir. Sometimes irreverently known as 'The Lemon.' It's the senior staff officer's quarters, Sir."

"Splendid," Dailey said. He was human. He was not yet really accustomed to being addressed as "colonel," and liked the sound of it; and the phrase "senior staff officer" had a nice ring to it, too, especially since it had been made clear that he was regarded as such by at least one general officer of General Douglas MacArthur's general staff.

Lennon's Hotel turned out to be very nice. It was a rambling, turn-of-the-century structure with high ceilings and a good deal of polished brass and gleaming wood. As General Willoughby's aide led him across the lobby, Dailey saw a bar, and then smiled when he saw the brass sign above its door: GENTLEMEN'S SALOON.

It was well patronized in the middle of the afternoon, Dailey saw, by men wearing a wide variety of uniforms. He did not see a Marine uniform, however, and wondered how many—if any—other Marines were assigned here. The subject had not been mentioned in the briefings he had been given in Washington and at CINCPAC in Pearl Harbor.

At 1555 hours, General Willoughby's Packard Clipper deposited Lieutenant Colonel Dailey at the main entrance to Supreme Headquarters, South West Pacific. It was a modern office building. Dailey wondered what it had originally been, but a new sign, reading SUPREME HEADQUARTERS, SOUTH WEST PACIFIC AREA, had been placed on the building wall over the spot where he was sure the building's name had been chiseled into the marble.

General Willoughby's aide read his mind: "It used to be an insurance company, Colonel. The Aussie military does things right. When they need a building, they just tell the occupants to get out."

"I see," Dailey said.

He saw one more thing of interest before an Army Military Policeman in a white cap cover pushed open the door for them. He saw a Studebaker President pull into a parking spot marked RESERVED FOR SENIOR OFFICERS. A Marine Corps emblem was on its door, and the letters USMC were painted on the hood. A Marine sergeant, carrying a briefcase, got out and headed for the entrance. Obviously, there was at least one other Marine officer assigned here, one senior enough to have his own staff car and driver.

"I see that I am not alone," he said to the aide. "There's a Marine."

"He's one of the cave-dwellers, Colonel."

"I beg pardon?"

"Classified documents and cryptography are two floors underground. They call the people who work down there in the dark 'cave-dwellers.'"

"I see."

"I think I heard someone say that that sergeant is a Japanese-language linguist."

"I see," Dailey said. He was about to ask how come a sergeant had a staff car when the obvious answer came to him. It belonged to a Marine officer of appropriate rank. He wished they'd gotten into that in the briefings. He would have liked to know if he was junior to or senior to the other Marine officer. Or officers.

The elevator took them to the eighth floor.

Brigadier General Charles Willoughby greeted Dailey cordially, offered him coffee, quite unnecessarily apologized for not having met him personally at the airport, and asked if he found his quarters satisfactory.

And he asked an odd question:

"Does the phrase MAGIC mean anything to you, Colonel?"

"No, Sir. I can't say that it does."

"It's of no importance," Willoughby said.

Dailey was no fool. He knew that General Willoughby had not asked him about MAGIC, whatever the hell that was, because it was "of no importance," but very probably because it *was* important, and he expected Dailey to know what it was.

I wonder what the hell MAGIC *is, and why haven't I been told about it?*

At 1643, they were in General Douglas MacArthur's outer office. General Willoughby introduced Dailey to Lieutenant Colonel Sidney Huff, MacArthur's aide-de-camp. Dailey was reminded again what august company he was now keeping. A *lieutenant colonel* for an aide-de-camp!

At 1645 exactly, Colonel Huff formally announced, "The Supreme Commander will see you now, gentlemen."

General Douglas MacArthur looked exactly like the picture of him that had been on the cover of *Life* magazine. When he rose from behind his huge, mahogany desk, he was wearing a khaki shirt open at the neck and pleated khaki trousers. The famous, battered, heavily gold embroidered cap was sitting in MacArthur's IN basket. Dailey looked for but did not see MacArthur's famous corncob pipe.

"General, may I present Lieutenant Colonel Dailey? Colonel, the Supreme Commander."

Dailey remembered that it was the Army's odd custom to salute indoors, and did so. MacArthur returned it with a vague gesture toward his forehead and then offered that hand to Dailey.

"We are very pleased to have you here, Colonel," he said.

"I am honored to be here, Sir."

"To clear the air between us, Colonel . . ." MacArthur said, interrupting himself to say, "Please, be seated. There's coffee of course, but it's nearly seventeen hundred—what is it you sailors say? Time to sink the main brace?—and at that hour I always like a little pick-me-up."

"Thank you, Sir."

"There is no naval officer for whom I have higher professional or personal regard than Admiral Chester Nimitz," MacArthur said, coming very quickly to the reason why Dailey was there. "I regard him as a brother."

"Yes, Sir."

"There has been some unfortunate talk of friction between us. That's absolute rot. We *have* had some frank interchanges of thought, where we both approached problems from our different perspectives. Which is as it should be. We have resolved our differences without an iota of rancor. Isn't that so, Willoughby?"

"Absolutely, General."

"I don't know how that sort of thing gets started," MacArthur said. "All I know is that it does, and that it's circulated so quickly that the Signal Corps should find out how and adapt the technique for themselves."

Dailey understood in a moment that the General had been witty, and he was expected to at least chuckle and smile. He did so.

"General Willoughby's got you settled all right, I presume. Decent quarters, a car, that sort of thing? Is there anything I can do to make Admiral Nimitz's representative here feel more welcome than General Willoughby has?"

"My quarters are fine, Sir. General Willoughby has been most gracious."

"No car, General," Willoughby said. "I didn't think about that."

"Sid, get on the phone and tell the headquarters commandant to arrange for a car for Colonel Bailey . . ."

"It's 'Dailey,' General," General Willoughby said.

"Dailey then," MacArthur said, his tone making it clear that he did not like to be either interrupted or corrected. "Effective immediately."

"Yes, Sir," Huff said, and started to leave the room.

"Sid," MacArthur called after him, "Tell Sergeant Gomez that I have just decreed that it is seventeen hundred. He has his orders to be executed at that hour."

A moment later, a stocky Filipino Master Sergeant rolled in a tray loaded with liquor bottles, glasses, and a silver bowl full of ice.

Five minutes or so later, one of the four telephones on MacArthur's desk rang. Huff grabbed it on the second ring.

"Office of the Supreme Commander, Colonel Huff."

He listened, then covered the mouthpiece with his hand.

"General, it's Lieutenant Hon. He has two MAGICs."

There's that word MAGIC *again. And it's obviously important, or they wouldn't be telling General MacArthur about it.* Them. *He said* MAGICs. *Plural. What the hell does it mean?*

"Ask him to bring them up," MacArthur ordered. "Tell him General Willoughby is here."

Huff nodded.

"Come up, Hon. General Willoughby is here."

MacArthur looked at Dailey.

"Take your time, Bailey. Finish your drink. But when Pluto—Lieutenant Hon. Unusual fellow. He has a PhD in Mathematics from MIT; splendid bridge player— gets here, I'll have to ask you to excuse me."

"Yes, of course, Sir."

"Do you play bridge, by chance, Bailey?"

"Yes, Sir. I do."

"Well, Mrs. MacArthur and I like to think we play well. We'll have to try that some evening."

"I would be honored, Sir."

"Make a note, Sid, to ask Colonel Bailey, when he's had time to settle in, for bridge."

"Yes, Sir."

A minute later, there was a knock at the door. A very large Asiatic of some sort wearing the insignia of an Army Signal Corps First Lieutenant walked in the room. He held two TOP SECRET cover sheets in his hand.

"Nothing startling, I hope, Pluto?" General MacArthur said.

"I would say 'interesting' rather than 'startling,' Sir."

"Well, let's see them," MacArthur said. "Sid, you make sure Bailey here gets a car."

"Yes, Sir."

"Glad to have you here, Bailey," MacArthur said.

"Thank you, Sir," Dailey said. Huff ushered him out of the room.

(FOUR)

Sergeant John Marston Moore, USMCR, noticed Lieutenant Colonel George F. Dailey outside the building and wondered idly who he was. But then he put him out of his mind. The only thing really unusual about him was that he had aviator's wings on his blouse. There were Marine officers commonly in and out of SWPA, for one reason or another, but this was the first aviator that Moore could remember seeing.

He got into the elevator and rode it down to the basement. He showed his identity badge to the MP buck sergeant on guard in the passageway outside the elevator. Although they knew each other, he examined it carefully. And then Moore signed himself into the commo center.

"They were looking all over for you last night and this morning," the MP sergeant said. "You were supposed to be charge-of-quarters."

"I was moved out of the barracks," Moore said.

"I guess nobody told them. They were pissed."

"Fuck 'em," Moore said.

"They were pissed, you better watch out," the MP sergeant said. "The whole fucking war will be lost because you weren't there to answer their fucking phone."

Moore chuckled, nodded at him, and went down the corridor. There was a steel door at the entrance to the cryptographic section. It was guarded by another MP, this one a corporal. He had another IN/OUT log.

Moore went through that security check, and then unlocked the steel door where he, Pluto Hon, and, at least in theory, Mrs. Ellen Feller plied their trade.

When he turned and locked himself inside, Pluto said, "I gather the Deaconess didn't come with you? Prayer meeting, no doubt?"

"She's playing tennis," Moore said. "She said that if it was anything interesting, I should bring it out to the house."

For what Moore thought were obvious reasons, Mrs. Feller did not like to spend any more time than she had to in their cubicle.

"Tennis? That's new."

"There's half a dozen courts at the racetrack. She asked around, and they let her join."

"War is hell, isn't it, Moore?"

"She has nice legs," Moore said, and immediately wondered why he had volunteered that. It was sure to result in a crack from Pluto. It came immediately.

"It's not nice to notice married women's legs, Moore," Pluto said, mockingly stern. "And how did you get to see them? Is something that I don't know about going on at Water Lily Cottage between you and the Deaconess?"

"She bought tennis clothes. You know. And she asked me if I thought they were too daring."

"And were they?"

"Come on. No, of course not. They were hardly shorter than a regular dress."

"But short enough for you to notice her legs, right?"

"I knew I made a mistake the minute I said that," Moore said. "What came in?"

I hope that gets him off the subject.

Hon pushed a TOP SECRET cover sheet off a thin sheaf of papers fresh from the crypto machine. He handed these to Moore.

"The Nips may finally be getting off the dime," he said.

Moore read the intercepts.

The most significant one was on top. It was from the Imperial General Staff in Tokyo, addressed to Vice Admiral Nishizo Tsukahara, commander of the 11th Air Fleet; and to Lieutenant General Harukichi Hyakutake, who commanded the 17th Army, whose headquarters were in Rabaul.

It relieved the Navy of responsibility for dealing with the Americans on Guadalcanal, Tulagi, and Gavutu, and gave it to the 17th Army.

"What does Pearl Harbor make of this? I mean, wasn't it expected?" Moore asked. "The Navy doesn't have any troops they could use on Guadalcanal. If anyone is going to be able to throw us off, it will have to be the Jap Army."

"Pearl Harbor expected it," Hon said. "Read the other ones."

The next intercepted message, also from the Imperial General Staff, was to a convoy of ships at sea. It directed the convoy commander to divert to Truk and off-load the Ichiki Butai.

"That's the 28th Infantry, 7th Division, right?" Moore asked. "The ones that were on Guam?"

"Right. First class troops. Colonel Kiyano Ichiki. Two thousand of them."

The Japanese Army, Moore had learned, had the interesting habit of officially referring to outstanding units by the name of the commanding officer.

The next intercepts, two of them, were an offer from the Japanese Navy to General Hyakutake of a battalion of Rikusentai "for use in connection with your new responsibility"; and his acceptance.

The last two intercepts placed an infantry brigade in the Palau Islands under Hyakutake's command and assigned the Ichiki Butai to him as soon as they reached "their next destination," which of course a previous intercept had identified as Truk.

"OK," Moore said. "What are we looking for?"

"You tell me. You're the one always noticing things you shouldn't, like missionary ladies' legs."

"Ah, come on, Lieutenant!"

"I'll give you a hint," Hon said. "Numbers. Ratios. That's two hints."

"I don't know what you mean."

"What do we have on Guadalcanal?"

"I don't know," Moore replied, then thought about it and came up with an answer: "Less than a division, since they didn't all get to land. Is that what you're driving at?"

"Plus the Raider Battalion, plus the Parachute Battalion, less the troops that didn't make it onto the beach. A Division, about. Ten, twelve thousand troops."

"OK."

"I personally thought the estimate of Japanese on Guadalcanal at the time of the invasion was high, but let's say it really was six thousand. For the sake of argument, let's say there are four thousand effectives—I don't think there are . . ."

"OK," Moore said, grasping Hon's line of thought.

"OK, what?"

"How many Japs in a brigade?"

"For the sake of argument, three thousand. It's like one of our regimental combat teams. Basically an infantry regiment that they've augmented with artillery, and maybe some tanks, and some service troops."

"Three thousand in the brigade in the Palau Islands, plus two thousand in the Ichiki Butai on Truk, plus what? Five, six hundred in the Rikusentai battalion? Five thousand five hundred people. Plus the four thousand you say may be left on Guadalcanal. Ninety-five hundred, ten thousand."

"At the most optimistic," Hon said, "they would have as many people there as we do. Much more likely, a couple of thousand less."

"And you can't push an Army back in the sea unless you outnumber them—what? Two to one?"

"Question," Hon said. "Are we missing intercepts that authorize more troops than these? Probable answer, probably not. We know about the two divisions they intend to stage through Rabaul to use in New Guinea. So again, probably not."

"Question," Moore picked up, "Do they not know how many men we have on Guadalcanal? Probable answer, they know damned well."

"So?"

"Question, do they really think they are so much better soldiers than we are that they can kick us off Guadalcanal with the troops they have and the ones they're sending? Answer: I don't know. They are not stupid, but when they get their pride going, all bets are off."

"How about this? Question, are they only sending five thousand troops because they don't have shipping to transport any more than that? Probable answer, I haven't the faintest idea. Maybe there are enough ships and they intend to use them to move those two divisions from Rabaul to New Guinea with them, leaving Guadalcanal until later."

"So what we're looking for is shipping information?" Moore asked.

"One other thing. I have seen nothing in any of these intercepts that suggests the Japs are worried about our getting that airfield up and running. Does that mean they don't think we can do it? Or they don't understand what it will mean?"

"How much more is there to go through?"

"I've got another thirty intercepts."

"I'll get on them," Moore said.

"The reason I was hoping you would bring the Deaconess with you was so that she could help. Why should we do all the work? She's making all the money."

"Lieutenant," Moore said, in mock shock and outrage, "that's very ungentlemanly of you."

"*I* haven't been admiring her legs. *I* don't have to be gentlemanly."

"I'll take the intercepts out to the cottage."

"I thought you said she was playing tennis?"

"You don't play tennis all afternoon."

"OK," Hon said. "Now listen to me, John. I'm not pulling your leg. I don't trust that woman. She looks to me like she has taken postgraduate courses in how to take credit for what other people have done, while simultaneously keeping her own ass out of the line of fire."

"You better go deeper into that," Moore said.

"So far, she has not put her ass on the line with any analysis we've taken to the Emperor. Think about it. So far we have been right. She's getting credit for that, because they think she's in charge. But if we had been wrong, I think she would have said, 'Lieutenant Hon never discussed that with me.' "

"You really think she's that much of a bitch?"

"Yeah."

"Well, there's something damned cold about her, I'll admit that."

"I want to make sure she reads every goddamned thing that comes through here. I don't want her to be able to say she never saw something."

"What are you going to do about the Emperor?"

"I'm going to call Sid Huff and tell him I have some MAGIC. What you read. Before we offer an analysis, I want the Deaconess's two cents."

"I'm on my way," Moore said.

"Take a pistol and use the chain on the briefcase. Do it by the book, Sergeant."

"OK."

"Do I have to tell you that making a pass at the Deaconess would earn you a prize for Stupid Action of the Century?"

"Jesus Christ, that never entered my mind."

"Bullshit. That leg crack didn't just pop into your head."

"Believe what you want. But rest assured, the lady's virtue is in no danger from me."

"OK. One final thing. Did you know that you're on the AWOL report this morning?"

"I heard they were looking for me."

"Well, you are. I think I fixed it. But you better not go anywhere near the headquarters company barracks until I know for sure."

"Don't worry about that either," Moore said.

He picked the briefcase off the floor, opened it, and set it on the table. Hon put the intercepts into it—it looked more like fifty or sixty than thirty, Moore thought. And then Moore closed the briefcase and snapped the handcuff around his wrist. Hon took a .45 Colt automatic from a file cabinet. Moore hoisted the skirt of his tunic and put the pistol in the small of his back under his trouser waistband.

"You're going to shoot yourself in the ass one day doing that," Hon said.

Then he picked up the telephone and dialed a number.

"Colonel Huff? Sir, this is Lieutenant Hon. I have several MAGIC messages that I believe should be brought to the Supreme Commander's attention."

Moore unlocked the steel door and let himself out. When he reached the security post by the elevator, an Army technical sergeant from headquarters company was waiting for him.

"Sergeant Moore, you went AWOL last night."

"There's been a mistake, Sergeant," Moore said. "I don't live in the barracks anymore. I'm not supposed to be on your duty rosters."

"You tell that to the first sergeant, Sergeant. He told me to find your ass and bring you home."

"I'm sorry," Moore said. "I can't do that." He held up the briefcase.

"I don't give a shit about any fucking briefcase," the sergeant said. "You come with me."

"I'll have to tell my officer where I'm going," Moore said and went back to the office. Hon was locking the steel door when he got there.

"There's a tech sergeant out there who wants to haul me off to headquarters company," he said.

"Oh, shit!" Hon said. "Come on."

The tech sergeant was waiting at the outer security point with his arms folded.

"All right, Sergeant, what's this all about?"

"Sir, I'm here to return Sergeant Moore to Headquarters Company. We're carrying him as AWOL."

"That's in error. Sergeant Moore is not attached to Headquarters Company."

"Sir, I got my orders."

"And I have mine, Sergeant. Mine are to dispatch Sergeant Moore, with a briefcase full of classified documents, to—to who is none of your business. But to someone who ranks much higher around here than the first sergeant of Headquarters Company. For that matter, than the Headquarters Company commander. You will not interfere with that. If necessary, I will have this MP place you under arrest. Do you understand me, Sergeant?"

"Yes, Sir."

"All right, Moore, get going," Hon said.

"Yes, Sir."

"Sergeant, you will return to Headquarters Company. You will tell your first sergeant that (a) Sergeant Moore is no longer his responsibility and (b) if he ever does something like this again around here, I will be forced to bring the matter to the attention of Captain Pickering—that's Navy Captain Pickering—and I think he would speak to General Sutherland about it. You understand that?"

"Yes, Sir."

"You may go, Sergeant."

"Yes, Sir."

That may work, Hon thought. *If it doesn't,* fuck *it, I'll go to Sutherland.*

As Moore was unlocking the door of the Studebaker, the Marine Aviator lieutenant colonel he had seen before walked up to him.

"Good afternoon, Sergeant," he said.

Moore straightened and saluted.

"Good afternoon, Sir."

"I'm delighted to see a familiar uniform around here," Dailey said. "I'm Colonel Dailey. I've just been assigned here as the CINCPAC liaison officer."

"Yes, Sir," Moore said. He remembered the radio Captain Pickering had sent SECNAV asking that a liaison officer be assigned.

"What have they got you doing around here, Sergeant?"

"I work for Major Banning, Sir."

"Major Banning is assigned to this headquarters?"

"No, Sir. I mean, he works with SWPA, Sir. But he's not assigned here."

"Oh?"

"He commands Special Detachment 14, Sir."

"I see," Dailey said. "Do you happen to know, Sergeant, who is the ranking Marine officer here?"

"I suppose that would be Major Banning, Sir."

Well, that's nice to know, too, Dailey thought. *Since this man Banning is only a major, that makes me the senior Marine officer present.*

"When you see Major Banning, Sergeant, would you please tell him we bumped into each other, and that I'd like to meet him?"

"Yes, Sir, I'll do that."

"Thank you, Sergeant."

Dailey smiled at Moore and went back to the front door to wait for the car and driver that had been assigned to the CINCPAC liaison officer by General Douglas MacArthur's personal order.

He wondered what Special Detachment 14 was and what it did around here.

(FIVE)
Water Lily Cottage
Manchester Avenue
Brisbane, Australia
1730 Hours 13 August 1942

Ellen Feller was annoyed when she returned from the Doomben Tennis Club to see that the Studebaker was not there. She parked the Jaguar drophead coupe Fleming Pickering had left for her to use and went into the house.

She wondered why it should annoy her that the car—and thus, Sergeant John Marston Moore—was not there. She concluded that it was because it left her with the choice of either driving to the Lennon Hotel for dinner, which she did not like to do alone, or making herself something to eat, alone, here. Neither option was appealing.

She was desperately thirsty. The water at the tennis courts tasted as if it had been stored for a decade in a rusty barrel; and of course the Turf Club was closed for the duration, so there was no place to get even a soft drink.

She found a bottle of water in the refrigerator. And beer. She shrugged and reached for a beer bottle and opened it. And since there was no one around to see her, she drank from the neck. It was good beer, more bitter than American beer, and reminded her somewhat of the beer she'd grown to like in China.

On the sly, of course, she thought. *The wife of the Reverend Glen T. Feller of the Christian & Missionary Alliance could not afford to have the recent heathen see her sucking on a bottle of beer.*

I wonder what that bastard is up to these days?

The Reverend Feller had elected to go about The Lord's Work during the war years by bringing the Gospel to the Indians in Arizona.

Which is probably where he has the jade he smuggled out of China when we left. I know it's nowhere around Baltimore or Washington. If it was, I would have found it.

He's probably waking up right about now in bed with some well-muscled, smooth-skinned young Indian lad in whom he was taking a special interest.

Well, what's wrong with that? There is a lot to be said for being in bed with well-muscled, smooth-skinned lads. Like Sergeant John Marston Moore, for example.

Oh, God, is that why I was so annoyed when I found out he wasn't here? Am I in that dangerous condition again? That's absurd. I know better. Only a stupid ladybird dirties her own nest, to coin a phrase.

She finished the bottle of beer and was surprised at how quickly she did it.

It was the lousy undrinkable water at Doomben. I'm dehydrated. I'm not even very sweaty.

She tested this theory by raising her arm and sniffing her armpit. There was an unpleasant odor, but not what she expected after an hour and a half on the court with an Australian woman who was built like a boxcar but who moved around the court with really amazing speed and grace.

Ellen opened the refrigerator door again and started to reach for another bottle of beer, and then changed her mind.

It will make me flatulent and probably keep me up all night.
There was a quart can of Dole's pineapple juice in the refrigerator.
Moore's, she thought. *Lieutenant Hon got it for him somewhere.*
Well, fuck him, I'm thirsty.
There you go again, Dear. Thinking dangerous thoughts.
She took the can of pineapple juice from the refrigerator, punched a hole in the top with a beer can opener, and then poured it in a glass and added ice cubes.

After that she walked into the living room, to the array of bottles on a table, and went through them. She could find neither gin nor vodka, but there was a bottle of rum. She carried that back into the kitchen.

I wonder what that will do to pineapple juice? For that matter, what does straight rum taste like?
She took a pull from the neck of the rum bottle.
God! That's awful! It burns like cheap whiskey!
She poured rum into the pineapple juice, stirred it with her finger, and then licked her finger.
Not bad!
She took a tiny sip from the glass, then a much larger one. She was pleased with the taste.

She put the glass on the table and went into the refrigerator again, looking for something she could make for dinner after she had her shower. She saw the remnants of a leg of lamb.

Nothing in the world tastes worse than cold lamb!
In the pantry, she found a dozen cans of chicken and dumplings, furnished, she supposed, by Lieutenant Hon.

I wonder what he does about his sinful lusts of the flesh? God knows, no respectable Australian girl would dare to be seen with an Oriental, even one wearing an American officer's uniform.

I wouldn't mind trying a few relatively hairless muscular young male bodies again; but that would be even more stupid than doing something with John Marston Moore.
She took one of the cans of chicken and dumplings from the pantry, carried it into the kitchen, and set it on the sink. Then she picked up her drink and finished it.

She could feel the warmth spread through her body.
You have another one of those, Dear, you'll have trouble finding the bathroom. And God knows how you'll manage to get in and out of the tub.
She put more ice, pineapple juice, and rum into the glass, stirred it with her finger, licked her finger, took one little sip, added another little drop of rum, stirred, licked, and tasted again. Satisfied, she carried it with her out of the kitchen and into the master bedroom, where she would have it when she finished her bath.

She undressed, and put the soiled tennis dress and her underclothes in the hamper. When she turned, she saw her reflection in the mirror over the chest of drawers. She remembered what Fleming Pickering said the night he saw the same thing, the night she arrived in Australia: "I wondered what they would really look like."

She smiled to herself. Making love to Fleming Pickering had been a wise move. He regarded their sex together as far more important than she ever dreamed he would. It was the first time he had been unfaithful to his wife, he told her, and she believed him. But Ellen was truly surprised to hear it. Someone as good looking and as rich and prominent as Fleming Pickering should have had women jumping into his bed the moment word got out that Mrs. Pickering wasn't in it.

Anyway, doing it had accomplished her intentions. It put Fleming Pickering permanently in her corner. It was sort of a living, breathing insurance policy. And she needed that. There was still a chance—more and more remote as time passed, to be sure—that the smuggled jade would become a matter of official attention. If it did, she would need a bit of insurance.

Back in China before the war, Ken McCoy told her that the Marines knew all about the jade. McCoy was a member of the 4th Marine's escort detachment then. They were guarding the missionaries from the mission to Shanghai when they had to get out.

But she didn't know exactly what he meant: The junior officers of the guard detachment? Or just the other enlisted men? Or Captain Ed Banning, who had been the 4th Marines Intelligence Officer? She hadn't thought to ask until it was too late.

For a while, Ellen Feller thought the whole matter of the jade was water under the bridge. So far as getting in trouble for smuggling it out of China was concerned, at least. Getting her fair share of the money from her husband would have to wait until the war was over.

But then she'd taken a job as a Japanese language translator with Naval Intelligence in Washington, and both McCoy and Banning had turned up again. McCoy by then had been commissioned, and Banning had been promoted to major.

She hadn't thought that McCoy would be a problem. She could buy his silence in Washington the same way she had bought it in China . . . *Here come those smooth, muscular young male body thoughts again, Dear . . .*

But Banning was one of those moral, highly principled men who would have loved to blow the whistle on her. His sense of right and wrong would have been offended if he ever found out that his Marines had risked their lives to protect jade that missionaries were illegally removing from China to line their own pockets.

But nothing was ever said about that. Ken McCoy kept his mouth shut, apparently. And just as apparently, Major Ed Banning did not know about the jade. Otherwise he *would* have blown the whistle.

Now, Ellen thought, as she walked into the bath and turned on the water, *the whole affair is almost certainly buried forever. Even if something happens—and as stupid as the Reverend Glen T. Feller can sometimes be, that is a real possibility— and the smuggled jade comes to light, it probably won't touch me. I am now a respected, responsible senior civilian employee of Naval Intelligence, and if I say I don't know a thing about any jade, I will be believed. Especially if Captain Fleming Pickering comes to my aid, as he would probably do in any case. But he certainly will do that now that he's been in my bed.*

As she adjusted the temperature of the water, she decided to shower rather than have a bath. So she pulled the thingamabob on the faucet. At that moment her lovemaking with Fleming Pickering flashed again into her mind. And it brought with it another one of those dangerous thoughts about smooth young muscular male bodies generally and Sergeant John Marston Moore specifically.

In bed, Fleming Pickering was everything that she hoped he would be, and more. He held his age well. Even his body had been firmer and more youthful than she expected.

It wasn't that he left me unsatisfied, but that he whetted my appetite; opened the floodgates, so to speak.

But I am not a fool. I am not going to risk what I have so carefully built up for so long by behaving like a bitch in heat. While it would be very nice to actually have John Marston Moore's smooth and muscular young body in my bed, I am going to have to do that in fantasy.

She turned the shower head so that it produced a strong, narrow stream of water, rather than a spray; and then she directed the stream where she thought it should go.

Sometimes, under the right circumstances, the fantasy is better than the actuality.

She sat down in the tub, slid against the sloping back side, and spread her legs. The stream of water struck the tub eight inches from the right spot.

"Damn!"

She stood up and moved toward the shower head again.

The screen door slammed, and a moment later, the front door. Sergeant John Marston Moore did that every time he came home. Thus every time he came home, the whole damned house shook.

She inhaled deeply. After that, she changed the shower flow back into a spray, and shifted the head again, so that it flowed onto her hair, instead of halfway down the tub. Then she picked up the soap and went ahead with her shower.

Fate, she thought. *Kismet. I really didn't want to do it that way, anyway.*

XVII

Three or four hairs popped up from the aureola of Sergeant John Marston Moore's nipples. Ellen Feller thought they were adorable. She toyed with them with her fingernail, watching them spring back into little coils when she turned them loose.

"Baby," she said, "if we're going to do this again, you're going to have to use something."

"I beg your pardon?"

"I don't want to find myself in the family way," Ellen said.

I should have thought of that before. God, was it the rum? Or how excited his shyness made me? For a while there, I was beginning to think that he was either a fairy or a virgin.

"Oh," he said. "I see what you mean. Are we going to do it again?"

"You don't sound very enthusiastic. You did a minute or two ago."

"I mean, is it smart? What if we got caught?"

"Who's going to catch us? Or *didn't* you like it?"

"It was great," Moore said.

And fuck you, Mrs. Howard P. Hawthorne. You are not the only fish in the sea. And your teats aren't as nice, either.

"It was great for me, too," she said. "I can't believe it happened."

"Me, either."

"You must think me terrible, giving in to you the way . . ."

"No. Not at all."

"I didn't have any idea you . . . were thinking of me in that way."

"It was the tennis dress," he said. "When you showed me your tennis dress."

"What about my tennis dress?"

"I thought your legs were great," he said.

I'll be damned. He's blushing again. How sweet!

"You really think so?" she asked, and threw the sheet off them.

"They're beautiful," he pronounced.

"Yours aren't so bad, either," she said, and ran her hand over his hip and then down his leg.

"There's a pro station at the barracks," he said. "But, Christ, I hate to go out there."

"What?"

"There's a pro station. When they give out the you-know-whats, at the barracks. But I hate to go out there."

"Maybe you could buy some at a drugstore. What do they call them here, 'chemists'?"

"Yeah."

"Is there any chance that Hon is going to show up here?" she asked.

"I don't think so. He's going to play bridge with General MacArthur."

Thank God for small blessings!

"But he's going to want to know what we thought of the intercepts in the morning," Moore added.

"We'll have time," she said. "We have plenty of time. For everything. But what are we going to do about that?"

"About what?"

"You know very well what I mean," she said.

She moved her hand to his stirring erection and felt it stiffen to her touch.

"I don't know," he said, and blushing again, which pleased her very much, he added: "I could get dressed and go look for a chemist's."

"We don't know if chemists even sell them," she said.

"That's right."

"There is one thing I could do," she said. "But I'm afraid you'd think I was terrible."

"I would never think that."

"Oh, you're just saying that. You probably already think I'm really terrible."

"No."

"Close your eyes, then," she ordered.

He closed his eyes.

A moment later, she said, "Open them."

He opened them.

"Did you like that?"

"Oh, yes."

"You want to watch me do it?"

"Yes."

After a moment she stopped.

"Some women like to do that," she said. "I love it."

"I love it when you do it."

"And some men like to do it to women."

"Do they?"

"Do you want to do it to me?"

"Do you want me to?"

"Oh, yes, Baby."

"Then, OK."

"Close your eyes again."

He felt her shifting around on the bed.

What the hell, guys are always talking about it. It probably won't kill me.

(TWO)
The Office of the Secretary of the Navy
Washington, D.C.
1605 Hours 15 August 1942

Captain David Haughton, USN, signed the receipt for the TOP SECRET Eyes Only SecNav radio, smiled at the messenger, said "Thank you," and waited until the messenger had left before lifting the cover sheet and reading the document.

"Jesus Christ," he muttered, frowning and shaking his head.

Then he stood up, went to the door to the Secretary's office, opened it, and stood there until the Secretary of the Navy sensed his presence and raised his eyes to him.

"Something important, David?"

"Guadalcanal has been heard from, Mr. Secretary."

"Do you mean Pickering's received the 'come home, all is more or less forgiven' radio? Or something else?"

Haughton handed him the Eyes Only.

Knox's face tightened as he read it. He looked up at Haughton.

"What is this, David, do you think? A blatant defiance of the radio? Who the hell does he think he is? 'The undersigned has temporarily assumed duties of First Marine Division G-2.' By what authority?"

"Sir, I don't know. But I would be inclined to give Captain Pickering the benefit of the doubt. The second paragraph caught my eye."

Knox read the Eyes Only again.

"Good Christ, do think he's trying to tell us that Goettge or one of the other officers had a MAGIC clearance?"

"Mr. Secretary, he didn't say 'Killed in Action,' he said 'lost in combat.' That suggests the possibility that they may have been captured. If you go with that line of reasoning, paragraph two makes some sense."

"How quickly can you find out if any of these people had access to MAGIC?"

"They're not on the list I'm familiar with. Maybe Naval Intelligence has added some others—cryptographers—that sort of thing. And I think, Sir, that we may have to consider the possibility that Captain Pickering brought Colonel Goettge, officially or otherwise, in on it."

It was a moment before Knox replied.

"That's one of your 'worst possible scenarios,' David, right?"

"Yes, Sir."

"Well, I thank you for it. I appreciate why you had to bring that up. I am unable to believe that he would do that. He knows what's at stake."

"Yes, Sir."

"Find out from Naval Intelligence . . . you had better check with the Army, too, while you're at it. And in person. Stay off the phone. See if any of these names ring a bell."

"Yes, Sir."

"Let me know the minute you find out, one way or the other."

"Yes, Sir."

"I just thought of another worst possible case scenario, David," Knox said. "Pickering gets himself captured."

"I think we have to consider that possibility, Sir."

"Send an urgent radio to Admiral Nimitz. Tell him to get Pickering off Guadalcanal now. I don't care if he has to send a PT boat for him. I want him off of Guadalcanal as soon as possible."

"Yes, Sir."

"Sir," Captain David Haughton, USN, reported to the Secretary of the Navy not quite two hours later, "I think I've come up with something."

"Let's have it. I'm due at the White House in fifteen minutes."

"Neither Colonel Goettge nor Captain Ringer was cleared for MAGIC. And it is my opinion, and that of the Chief of Naval Intelligence, Sir, that it is unlikely that either of them ever heard more than the name."

"Unless, of course, Pickering talked too much to Goettge."

"I think we can discount that, too, Sir. Colonel Goettge visited Captain Pickering in Australia. While he was there, he apparently picked up on the word. MAGIC, I mean. He sent a back channel communication to General Forrest—the Marine Corps G-2—"

"I know who he is," Knox said impatiently.

"Yes, Sir. He said that he had heard the word MAGIC and wanted to know what it was. He and General Forrest are old friends, Sir."

"I know how it works. Get on with it."

"Forrest is MAGIC cleared. He replied to Goettge that he had never heard of AGIC, and then reported the message to the Chief of Naval Intelligence."

"What you're suggesting is that if Pickering had told Goettge, there would have been no back channel message to General Forrest?"

"Yes, Sir."

Knox considered that a moment.

"OK," he said finally. "But what the hell was Pickering driving at? If, indeed, he was suggesting anything at all?"

"Lieutenant Cory, Sir, was a civilian employee of Naval Communications Intelligence, here in Washington."

"So I *am* going to have to tell the President that MAGIC has been compromised?"

"I don't think so, Sir. What's happened, Sir, I think, is that if anything Naval Intelligence erred on the side of caution to preserve the integrity of MAGIC."

"I don't understand a thing you just said."

"Lieutenant Cory did *not* have a MAGIC clearance."

"Thank God!"

"But the crypto people, the intelligence people, the intelligence *community*, I guess is what I'm trying to say, being the way they are, it occurred to somebody that he might have heard the name at least, and possibly had guessed what it was all about."

"So?"

"So a special radio was sent to General Vandergrift directing him to make sure that Lieutenant Cory did not fall into enemy hands."

"How was he supposed to do that?" Knox asked.

"I didn't get into that, Sir."

"Well, he didn't, did he? Cory may well indeed be a prisoner of the Japanese?"

"I think we have to consider that possibility, Sir."

Knox snorted.

"You're suggesting that Vandergrift told Pickering about the message vis-à-vis Cory? And *that's* what Pickering was driving at?"

"Yes, Sir, that's what I think."

"This is not enough to take to the President," Knox decided aloud. "But I want Nimitz radioed tonight, Dave, telling him to get Pickering off Guadalcanal."

"I took care of that, Sir," Haughton said, and handed him an onion skin.

URGENT
WASHINGTON DC 1710 15AUG42
SECRET
FROM: NAVY DEPARTMENT
TO: CINCPAC PEARL HARBOR TH
FOR THE PERSONAL, IMMEDIATE ATTENTION OF ADMIRAL NIMITZ
INASMUCH AS THE PRESENCE OF CAPTAIN FLEMING PICKERING USNR, PRESENTLY ATTACHED TO HEADQUARTERS 1ST MARINE DIVISION, IS URGENTLY REQUIRED IN WASHINGTON, THE SECRETARY OF THE NAVY DIRECTS THAT EXTRAORDINARY EFFORT CONSISTENT WITH CAPTAIN PICKERING PERSONAL SAFETY BE MADE TO WITHDRAW THIS OFFICER FROM GUADALCANAL BY AIR OR SEA, AND THAT HE BE ADVISED OF PROGRESS MADE IN COMPLIANCE WITH THIS ORDER.
DAVID HAUGHTON, CAPT USN, ADMIN ASST TO SECNAV

(THREE)
Temporary Building T-2032
The Mall
Washington, D.C.
1750 Hours 15 August 1942

Lieutenant Colonel F.L. Rickabee, USMC, was in his shirt-sleeves, his tie was pulled down, and he was visibly feeling the heat and humidity, when Brigadier General Horace W. T. Forrest, Assistant Chief of Staff, Intelligence, Headquarters, USMC, walked into his office.

"Good evening, Sir," he said, standing up. "I hope the General will pardon my appearance, Sir."

"Don't be silly, Rickabee," Forrest said. "Christ, I hate Washington in the summer."

"I don't put any modifiers on the basic sentiment, Sir," Rickabee said dryly.

Forrest looked at him and chuckled.

"There's ice tea, Sir, and lemonade, and I wouldn't be at all surprised if someone defied my strict orders and hid a bottle of spirits or two in one of these filing cabinets."

"I'd like a beer, if that's possible."

"Aye, aye, Sir," Rickabee said. "Excuse me."

He went through a wooden door and came back in a moment with two bottles of beer and a glass.

"Keep the glass, thank you," General Forrest said. He raised the beer bottle.

"Frank Goettge," he said and took a pull.

"Frank Goettge," Rickabee parroted and took a sip. "Was there any special reason for that, Sir?"

"Frank's dead. Or at least missing and presumed dead."

"Jesus Christ! What happened, Sir?"

"I don't know. I know only that. I got it from the Commandant thirty minutes ago. He got it from the Secretary of the Navy. There have been no after-action reports, casualty reports, anything else. I can only presume that Frank Knox got it directly from that commissioned civilian he sent over there . . . what's his name?"

"Pickering, Sir."

". . . as his personal snoop. Pickering is on Guadalcanal. Did you know that?"

"No, Sir. I did not."

"The Secretary of the Navy has directed the Commandant to replace Colonel Goettge immediately with a suitably qualified officer. Don't waste our time suggesting yourself. You're cleared for MAGIC. You can't go."

"Yes, Sir."

"What about Major Ed Banning? He was S-2 of the Fourth Marines. He could handle it, and he's in Australia."

"Banning's cleared for MAGIC, too, Sir."

"I didn't know that."

"Captain Pickering had him added to the list."

"Damn that man!"

"I don't think the Secretary would want us to send Banning in any event, Sir. He sent him over there."

"That's right, isn't it? I'd forgotten."

"Sir, isn't there someone in the First Division who could take over?"

"I asked the same question. Do you know Captain Ringer, Bill Ringer?"

"Yes. That's right. He's there, too, isn't he? S-2 of the 5th."

"He's dead, or missing, too. And a Lieutenant named Cory. You know Cory?"

"He was a civilian here. Navy communications. He was commissioned only a couple of months ago."

"Knox's aide—Haughton. He's not his aide. What do they call him?"

"Administrative Assistant, Sir."

"Haughton was all exercised that Cory might have had access to MAGIC."

"Did he?"

"No. What I would really like to know is what the hell went on over there to take out the Division Two, the 5th Marines Two, and a Japanese linguist all at once. The last after-action report I saw didn't show a hell of a lot going on over there."

"And the Commandant didn't know?"

"You mean did he know and wouldn't say? I don't think he knew a thing more than he told me. We were talking about Major Banning."

"Banning is out, Sir."

"Yes, of course," Forrest said. "I must be getting senile. Suggestions, Rickabee?"

"We have a man in Brisbane. His name is Dailey. Lieutenant Colonel. Ex-aviator. He was in Berlin before the war as an assistant Naval attache."

"What's he doing in Brisbane?"

"He's liaison officer between MacArthur and Nimitz."

"How do you know about him?" Forrest asked, and when Rickabee hesitated, snapped, "Come on. I've got to get back to the Commandant tonight with a name."

"Sir, I sort of stashed him over there."

"Stashed?"

"As a replacement, Sir, a supernumerary, in place. In case anything happened to Ed Banning. Or some other people. He has gone through the FBI background check."

"MAGIC?"

"No, Sir. I would be surprised if he ever heard the term. But, if it came to that, I would feel easy about clearing him for access to MAGIC."

"Could he handle being a division two?"

"I think so, Sir. He wouldn't be a Frank Goettge . . ."

"You just lost your supernumerary, Rickabee. Now, what about a regimental two to replace Captain Ringer?"

"Sir, I have no idea what to do about that."

"Don't try to tell me you don't have any linguists you can spare."

"I *don't* have any linguists I can spare, General," Rickabee said. "Wait a minute . . ."

"Well?"

"I found a kid at Parris Island. He was supposed to go to Quantico for a commission. But Banning wanted a linguist, so we put sergeant's stripes on him and sent him to Australia."

"He's a linguist?"

"Yes, Sir. Fluent Japanese. Reads and writes."

"How critically does Banning need a linguist?"

"I'm sure he would say he needs one desperately, Sir."

"I'm asking you."

"I think if Banning doesn't have this kid, General, and needs a linguist, he will either do it himself or he'll find someone in Australia. Secretary Knox sent Pickering's secretary over there, now that I think about it. She's a Japanese-language linguist. She's cleared for MAGIC, too."

"I presume the sergeant has had no access to MAGIC?"

"I'm sure he hasn't, Sir."

"I want his name and serial number, and the supernumerary's name and serial number. You have them, I presume?"

"Yes, Sir. Sir, the order to appoint a liaison officer between CINCPAC and MacArthur came from the Secretary. He might not like having him reassigned."

"Let him make that decision. I'll make a note of what this officer is doing on the buck slip I give to the Commandant. Is there someone around here who can type it up for me? It would save me a trip to Eighth and 'I.' "

"Yes, Sir. That'll be no problem."

(FOUR)
Headquarters, First Marine Division
Guadalcanal, Solomon Islands
17 August 1942

Both Major General Alexander Archer Vandergrift, the division commander, and Captain Fleming Pickering, USNR (acting) Division G-2, went down to the beach when the destroyers appeared on the horizon.

Vandergrift was wearing sweat-streaked, soiled khakis and a steel helmet; and he was armed with a .45 Colt automatic pistol suspended from a web pistol belt. Pickering was wearing utilities, a utility cap, and carried a Springfield rifle in the crook of his arm.

There were four destroyers.

"They're older than most of the boys, Fleming, do you realize that?" Vandergrift said to Pickering.

"I thought they looked familiar," Pickering said. "I remember seeing them."

"In France?"

"No. They had some tied up in Washington state. And somewhere on the East Coast. Virginia. I remember thinking that it was a stupid idea, they'd never get them ready for sea again after tying them up for twenty years. I'm glad to see I was wrong."

Vandergrift snorted.

The destroyers came in in a line. The first in line slowed; water was churning at its stern as the engines were put in reverse.

One, and then another, and finally a line of landing craft from the Lunga Boat Pool headed away from the beach toward the destroyers.

Pickering handed a pair of binoculars to General Vandergrift.

The General examined them before he put them to his eyes.

"Leitz 8×50s," he said. "Why do I suspect these aren't issue?"

"My father gave those to me when I got my first officer's license. They don't wear out. I thought they might come in useful."

Vandergrift took the binoculars from his eyes and handed them back to Pickering.

"If the Japanese know about those destroyers, they're in trouble," he said.

Pickering looked through them at the landing craft. Each carried a half dozen Marines, most of them wearing only their undershirts. They were a work party, men taken from their units to function as stevedores.

During the planning process for this operation, the Marines had asked for sailors to manhandle supplies; but the Navy had refused. That question, he thought, would have to be resolved before the next Marine amphibious landing.

As they handed the binoculars back and forth, Pickering and Vandergrift watched sailors on the deck of the nearest destroyer unlashing 55-gallon barrels and then manhandling them to the rail. Life boat davits had been jury-rigged to lower the barrels into the landing craft.

Five minutes later, the first landing barge started for the beach.

"There's an officer standing next to the coxswain," Vandergrift said, handing the binoculars back to Pickering.

"And for the rest of his career, he can command attention in the officer's club by beginning a sentence, 'When I was on the beach at Guadalcanal . . .' " Pickering said.

"Fleming, have you ever heard that old saw about people who live in glass houses?" Vandergrift said.

Pickering looked at him in surprise and saw Vandergrift smiling at him.

"Touché, General," Pickering said.

We have become friends, Pickering thought. *It didn't take long.*

When the landing barge touched on the beach and dropped its ramp, a dozen Marines who had been waiting on shore went up the ramp and began rolling the 55-gallon barrels onto the beach.

The officer who had been standing next to the coxswain came ashore. When he arrived, he spoke to another officer, who looked around and then pointed to Vandergrift and Pickering.

The officer made his way up the beach to them. He was wearing a steel helmet, and he carried a pistol on a web belt. He even wore canvas puttees. His khaki uniform was starched. There was a crease in his trousers.

"Natty, wouldn't you say?" Vandergrift said softly.

The officer saluted. Vandergrift and Pickering returned it.

"Sir, I'm Lieutenant Goldberg. I'm executive officer of the *Gregory.*"

"We're very glad to see you, Mr. Goldberg," Vandergrift said. "Welcome to Guadalcanal. I really regret the division band is otherwise occupied. You really deserve a serenade."

"Thank you, Sir."

"What have you got for us, Mr. Goldberg?"

"Each of us is carrying 100 drums of AvGas, Sir, and eight drums of Aviation lubricants. We also have some aircraft bombs, one hundred pounders, and linked .50 caliber ammo. And there's some tools."

"Chamois? I especially asked for chamois."

"Yes, Sir, there are several cartons of chamois."

"Thank God, for that. The AvGas wouldn't have done us any good without a means to filter it."

"There's chamois, Sir," Goldberg said. "And we're carrying some tools. The *Little* and the *Calhoun* have some ground crewmen aboard, too."

"At the risk of repeating myself, Mr. Goldberg, you are very welcome indeed."

"And I have this for you, General," Goldberg said and handed Vandergrift an unsealed envelope.

Vandergrift took a sheet of paper from the envelope, glanced at it, and handed it to Pickering.

"I got my copy of this last night," he said. "I don't think you've seen it."

Pickering took it. It was a radio message, all typed in capital letters.

URGENT
SECRET
FROM: CINCPAC
TO: COMMANDER DESTROYER FORCE TWENTY
INFORMATION: COMMANDING GENERAL FIRST MARINE DIVISION
1. BY DIRECTION OF THE SECRETARY OF THE NAVY YOU WILL TRANSPORT FROM YOUR

DESTINATION TO SUCH PLACE AS WILL BE LATER DIRECTED CAPTAIN FLEMING PICKER-
ING, USNR, PRESENTLY ATTACHED HQ FIRST MARDIV.

2. YOU WILL ADVISE CINCPAC, ATTENTION: IMMEDIATE AND PERSONAL ATTENTION OF
CINCPAC, WHEN YOU HAVE SAILED FROM YOUR DESTINATION WITH CAPTAIN PICKERING
ABOARD.

BY DIRECTION: D.J. WAGAM, REARADM USN

Pickering looked at Vandergrift, who smiled.

"Lieutenant Goldberg, may I present Captain Pickering?" Vandergrift said.

"How do you do, Sir?" Goldberg said. His surprise was evident. He had not
expected to see a Navy Captain in Marine Corps utilities, carrying a Springfield
rifle like a hunter.

"I think I've just been sandbagged, as a matter of fact," Pickering said.

"That boat is about ready to go back out to the *Gregory,* Captain Pickering.
Don't you think you had better get on it? I'm sure her captain wants to get underway
as soon as possible."

Pickering didn't reply.

"Major Stecker was good enough to pack your gear, Captain," Vandergrift said,
and pointed to the landing barge.

Pickering saw Jack NMI Stecker handing a bag to one of the Marines on the
barge. It was the bag he brought with him from the command ship USS *McCawley*
when he'd come ashore.

"I know I've been sandbagged," Pickering said. "I gather there is no room for
discussion?"

"Thank you for your services, Captain Pickering," Vandergrift said. "They have
been appreciated by all hands."

Vandergrift handed Pickering the Ernest Leitz binoculars.

"General, I would be honored if you would hang on to those," Pickering said.

Vandergrift looked at the binoculars and then met Pickering's eyes.

"That's very kind of you, Fleming, thank you," he said. He put out his hand to
Pickering.

Pickering had to grab the Springfield rifle with his left hand in order to take
Vandergrift's hand with his right.

Then he held the rifle up.

"I won't need this anymore, will I?"

"Why don't you take it with you?" Vandergrift said. "If nothing else, you could
hang it on your wall. Then for the rest of your life, you could command attention by pointing to it and beginning a sentence, 'when I was on the beach at Guadalcanal . . .'"

"Touché, again, General."

"Bon voyage, Fleming," Vandergrift said. "I look forward to seeing you again."

He touched Pickering's arm and then walked away.

(FIVE)
Water Lily Cottage
Manchester Avenue
Brisbane, Australia
0815 Hours 17 August 1942

Mrs. Ellen Feller had just about finished dressing when she heard the crunch of tires on the driveway. A few seconds later, the double slamming of the front doors told her that Sergeant John Marston Moore had returned to the cottage.

The slamming doors annoyed her. She was already annoyed. Lieutenant Pluto Hon had been summoned to Townesville by Major Ed Banning—for reasons Banning had not elected to tell her. And that meant she was going to have to spend all day in the dark, damp cell two floors underground at SHSWPA. And probably do the same thing all day tomorrow, too. Someone had to be available to deliver MAGIC intercepts to Generals MacArthur and Willoughby, and since Banning and Hon were in Townesville, and Moore was officially not supposed to know even what MAGIC meant, that left her.

When she looked at her watch and saw that it was only a quarter after eight, she was even more annoyed. She had told him to pick Hon up at the Commerce Hotel and deliver him to the airport; then to stop at the Cryptographic Facility, pick up what had come in, and run it through the machine; and then, 'about nine, Baby, come pick me up.'"

She decided she knew what was in his mind, the horny little devil, and while that was flattering, now was not the time. She had just spent an hour washing and doing her hair, and if *that* happened, as appealing as it was, she would have to go through the whole process again, starting with the shower.

The door to her bedroom was flung open.

"You ever think of knocking?"

"Sorry," he said, visibly unrepentant. "Take a look at these."

There was something important in the overnights, she thought. *He doesn't have that delightfully shyly naughty look in his eyes.*

She took the two sheets of onion skin from him, and read them.

URGENT
SECRET
HQ USMC WASHDC 2205 15AUG42
VIA: SUPREME HEADQUARTERS
      SOUTHWEST PACIFIC AREA
TO: COMMANDING OFFICER
      USMC SPECIAL DETACHMENT 14
1. ON RECEIPT OF THIS MESSAGE SGT JOHN M. MOORE IS DETACHED FROM USMC SPECDET 14, ATTACHED HQ FIRST MARDIV, AND WILL PROCEED THERETO IMMEDIATELY.
2. YOU ARE AUTHORIZED TO INFORM SHSWPA THAT AN URGENT REQUIREMENT FOR JAPANESE-LANGUAGE LINGUISTS EXISTS WITHIN FIRST MARDIV AND REQUEST OF THEM HIGHEST POSSIBLE AIR TRANSPORTATION PRIORITY FOR SERGEANT MOORE.
BY DIRECTION: H.W.T.FORREST, BRIGGEN USMC
          ACOFSG-2
URGENT
CONFIDENTIAL
HQ USMC WASHDC 2207 15AUG42
TO: LT COL GEORGE F. DAILEY

CINCPAC LIAISON OFFICER

SUPREME HEADQUARTERS SOUTHWEST PACIFIC AREA

INFORMATION: CINCPAC ATTN: CHIEF OF STAFF

COMMANDING GENERAL 1ST MARINE DIVISION

1. ON RECEIPT OF THIS MESSAGE YOU ARE DETACHED FROM PRESENT DUTIES AND WILL PROCEED IMMEDIATELY TO HEADQUARTERS FIRST MARDIV FOR DUTY AS ASSISTANT CHIEF OF STAFF, G-2. THIS MESSAGE CONSTITUTES AUTHORITY FOR AAAA AIR TRAVEL PRIORITY.

2. YOU ARE AUTHORIZED TO INFORM SHSWPA THAT THE EXIGENCIES OF THE SERVICE MAKE THIS TRANSFER NECESSARY AND THAT A LIAISON OFFICER TO REPLACE YOU WILL BE ASSIGNED AT THE EARLIEST POSSIBLE TIME.

3. IF POSSIBLE, AND TO THE DEGREE THAT IT WILL NOT REPEAT NOT INTERFERE WITH YOUR MOVEMENT TO FIRST MARDIV, YOU ARE DIRECTED TO FACILITATE THE MOVEMENT TO FIRST MAR DIV OF SERGEANT J.M.MOORE, PRESENTLY ASSIGNED USMC SPECIAL DETACHMENT 14.

BY DIRECTION OF BRIG GEN FORREST:

F L RICKABEE, LTCOL, USMC

"I called Townesville," Moore said. "They either don't know where Banning is, or he doesn't want it known."

"I wonder why Rickabee signed the one to Dailey?" Ellen said, thoughtfully, "and General Forrest the one about you? And the one about you is classified Secret, and the one to Dailey only Confidential?"

"What the hell difference does it make?" Moore asked, but he took the onion skins from her hand. "Probably because everything about the detachment is classified Secret but the name," he said.

"Obviously, you don't want to go," Ellen said. "Is that why you tried to call Banning?"

"I *can't* go, for Christ's sake," Moore said. "I'm privy to Magic."

"Not officially," she thought out loud.

"That's not the point," he said. "I *know* about Magic."

"The point is, they—Rickabee and Forrest—don't know that. That's why they're sending you to Guadalcanal."

She thought: *And if it comes out that Fleming Pickering compromised Magic by letting you in on it, he's in trouble. I don't want to see that happen.*

Banning is supposed to be clever. Let him see if he can find a solution to this.

"I think the thing for you to do is make yourself scarce until we can get in contact with Major Banning," Ellen said.

"Too late. That was the first thing I thought of. But Dailey's caught me."

"How?"

"His orders didn't have to go through crypto. So as soon as they came in, the message center gave them to him ... Christ, *that's* why they classified them Confidential, so they wouldn't have to go through crypto ..."

Ellen thought about that quickly, and said, "Yes. Probably."

"I had just run the radio to Banning through the crypto machine and was trying to get him on the telephone, when an MP came to the cell and said I had a visitor at Outer Security."

"Dailey?"

"Yeah. Pumped full of his own importance. You could practically hear the Marine Corps Drum and Bugle Corps playing the Marine Hymn in the background."

She smiled, and their eyes met.

I'm going to miss him.

"What did he say?" she asked.

" 'Sergeant Moore,' " Moore quoted sonorously, " '*I* have been ordered to Guadalcanal by *Headquarters, USMC. You* are to accompany me. We leave *immediately.*' "

She smiled at him again.

"I didn't tell him I had just decrypted my own orders; I told him I worked for Banning, and he would have to talk to him."

"And?"

" 'Sergeant, I am the ranking Marine officer present. I will see that Major Banning is informed of what has transpired,' or bullshit to that effect."

"My God!"

"I tried refusing," Moore said. "Politely. I told him that Major Banning had told me to take orders from nobody else."

"And?"

Moore pointed toward the window. Ellen went and pushed the curtain aside. There was a 1941 Ford staff car in the drive. It had MILITARY POLICE painted on the doors. An MP wearing a white helmet liner was sitting on it. Another rested his rear end on the front fender.

"They're going to take me to the airport," Moore said. "Dailey apparently rushed to tell Willoughby, or maybe Sutherland, of his orders ... for all I know, The Emperor himself may have gotten into the act by now. Anyway, a B-25 is going to fly us to Espíritu Santo. The field at Guadalcanal won't take a B-25 yet. So from Espíritu Santo, we'll go by Catalina."

"He didn't put you under arrest?" Ellen asked.

"No. Except by inference. The MPs are to 'help me gather' my gear and get me to the airport."

"I don't see what else you can do," Ellen said.

"I've got to go, there's no question about that. And what you have to do is one of two things: Call Willoughby now, tell him you have just heard about this, and that I'm into MAGIC."

"I don't think that's smart," Ellen said. "I think a decision like that should be made by Major Banning."

"That's 'B,' " Moore said. "Get on the phone and keep trying to get through to Banning."

"I will," she said. "That's the way to handle this."

The horn on the MP car blew.

"Shit," he said.

He walked out of her bedroom and across the living room to his bedroom and began stuffing his belongings into his seabag.

Ellen stood in his doorway and watched.

"Is there anything I can do to help?"

"I can handle it," he said.

Inasmuch as she was unaware how many times Private John Marston Moore had, under the skilled eye of a Parris Island Drill Instructor, packed and unpacked, packed and unpacked a seabag until he had it right, Ellen was genuinely surprised to see how quickly and efficiently he packed his gear.

He finally picked up the seabag and bounced it three or four times on the floor. This caused the contents to compact. He reached inside, removed a precisely folded pair of pants, reached under the skirt of his blouse, and came out with a Colt .45 and four extra magazines. He put these in the bag, replaced the pants on top, and closed the bag.

"I decided I needed that pistol more than one of the classified documents messengers," he said. "So I signed it out before I left the basement. If they come looking for it, send them to Guadalcanal."

My God, he really is going to the war! He is too beautiful to be killed!

She stepped into the room and closed the door after her.

She walked up to him and put her hand on his cheek, then raised her head and kissed him lightly on the mouth.

"Do you think they'll wait another five minutes, Baby?" she asked, dropping her hand down his body, pushing aside the skirt of his blouse, and finding the buttons of his fly. "Or will they break the door down?"

When he was gone, she decided calmly that it was probably a good thing. Their relationship could easily have gotten out of hand.

If only Fleming Pickering hadn't been such a damned fool and brought him into MAGIC!

The thing to do about that, she decided, *is nothing. The chances that John Moore will fall alive into Japanese hands are negligible to begin with. And even if he does, he is only a sergeant. Sergeants are not expected to be privy to important secrets.*

She would have to make that point to Banning. Hon would argue against it, but Hon was a lieutenant and Banning a major. The important thing to do was to protect Fleming Pickering. Banning, for his own reasons, would understand that, and he almost certainly would be able to convince Pluto Hon as well.

That *was* going to be possible, she decided. Fleming Pickering would be protected . . . and it followed that he would be available to protect her, if need be.

She had—years ago, she couldn't remember where—heard someone described as "being able to walk around raindrops." She was a little uneasy about thinking that she was one of these people, but the facts seemed to bear it out. Just when things started to get out of hand, something happened that put them in order again.

XVIII

(ONE)
Aboard USS *Gregory* (APD-44)
Coral Sea
0735 Hours 18 August 1942

Captain Fleming Pickering stood in the port leading from the Chart Room to the bridge until the captain turned, saw him, and motioned him to come in.

"Permission to come onto the bridge, Sir?" Pickering asked. He was wearing borrowed khakis that were just a bit too tight for him.

"Captain, aboard this tin can, you have the privilege of the bridge at any time."

"That's very kind of you, Captain," Pickering said, coming onto the bridge. "But—in the olden days—when I was a master and carrying supercargo, I always wanted the bastard to ask."

The USS *Gregory*'s Captain, a Lieutenant Commander, laughed.

"I appreciate the sentiment, Sir, but I repeat: You have the privilege of this bridge whenever you wish. Can I offer you some coffee?"

"No, thank you. I just had a potful for breakfast."

"And you slept well, Sir?"

"Like a log. Despite the fact that I felt like an interloper in your cabin."

"My pleasure, Sir. I rarely use it at sea, anyway."

"You're very gracious."

"We seldom have a chance to show our party manners to a VIP, Sir."

Christ, is that what I am?

"Beautiful day," Pickering said.

"We're making good time, too, Sir. Did you check the chart?"

"We're making, if I haven't forgotten how to read a chart, better than twenty knots?"

"We are making 'best speed consistent with available fuel,' Sir," the captain said, then took a sheet from his shirt pocket and handed it to Pickering.

> URGENT
> SECRET
> FROM: CINCPAC
> TO: COMMANDER DESTROYER FORCE TWENTY
> 1. GREGORY IS DETACHED FROM DESFORCE TWENTY. GREGORY IS TO STEAM FOR BAKER XRAY MIKE AT BEST SPEED CONSISTENT WITH AVAILABLE FUEL.
> 2. DESFORCE TWENTY WILL PROCEED TO BAKER XRAY MIKE IN COMPLIANCE WITH PRESENT ORDERS.
> 3. PASS TO CAPTAIN PICKERING ARRANGEMENTS FOR HIS FURTHER MOVEMENT BY AIR HAVE BEEN MADE.
> BY DIRECTION: D.J. WAGAM, REARADM USN

Pickering went to the heavy plate glass windows of the bridge and looked out. There was no other vessel in sight on the smooth, blue swells of the sea.

"Where, or what, is Baker XRay Mike?"

"Espíritu Santo, Sir. They've got a pretty decent airfield up and running there."

"Is this what the Navy calls 'flank speed'?" Pickering asked.

"She'll go a bit faster than this, Captain. But the ride gets a little rough, and the fuel consumption goes way up. I dislike not having enough fuel in the bunkers."

"That was a question, not a criticism. I've never been on one of these before."

"You know what they are?"

"High speed transport," Pickering said. "Right?"

"That's something of a misnomer, Sir. They removed half the boilers and converted that space to troop berthing. It's high speed relative to a troop transport, not compared to anything else. She's considerably slower than she was before they removed half her boilers."

"Well, whoever's idea it was, it seems to be a good one. They couldn't start landing aircraft on Henderson until they got some fuel in there, and they couldn't risk sending a transport."

"The original idea, as I understand it, Sir, was that the APDs would be used to transport the Marine Raiders. We even trained with them for a while. You familiar with the Raiders, Sir?"

"Yes," Pickering said. "A little."

Franklin Roosevelt copying—or trying to best—the British again. They almost wound up being called The Marine Commandos.

"What happened to the idea of using these ships to transport Raiders?" Pickering asked.

"Well of course, in a sense, we did. We are. We put the Raiders ashore on Tulagi. But that was a conventional amphibious assault. What I meant, Sir, was that I think the idea for the conversion of these ships was to transport the Raiders on raids."

"That isn't going to happen?"

"There is some scuttlebutt, Sir, that the Second Raider Battalion was to be landed yesterday on Makin Island from submarines. I emphasize, Sir, that it's scuttlebutt, and probably shouldn't be repeated."

Meaning, of course, that you know goddamn well the Second Raider Battalion was landed yesterday on Makin by submarine, but are afraid that when your VIP supercargo has a few drinks with the brass, he will report that you told him.

"I know an officer with the Second Raiders," Pickering thought aloud, and then corrected himself. "I have a friend who is an officer with the Second Raiders."

I know Colonel Evans Carlson and Captain Roosevelt, whose father is our Commander-in-Chief, and a dozen other Raider officers. But I'm not sure—I frankly doubt—if they would appreciate me going around announcing that I'm a friend of theirs. Killer McCoy, on the other hand . . .

"And actually, he's more my son's friend—they went through officer candidate school at Quantico together—than mine. Very interesting young man. He was an enlisted man with the Fourth Marines in China before the war. They call him 'Killer' McCoy."

"Your son is a Marine, Sir?"

"Yes, he is."

"With the First Division?"

"No. Thank God. He's just finished flying school. Actually, the last I heard, he'd just finished F4F training. I expect he's on his way over here, or will be shortly."

"The F4F is supposed to be quite an airplane," the captain said.

Thank you, Captain, for your—failed but noble—attempt to reassure the father of a brand-new Marine Corps fighter pilot that all is right with the world.

"Bridge, Lookout," the loudspeaker above Pickering's head blared suddenly. "Aircraft, to port. On the deck."

The captain ran to the port to the open portion of the bridge, rested his hands on the steel surrounding it, and looked out.

Aware that his function as supercargo was to stay the hell out of people's way, Pickering successfully resisted the temptation to look for himself. He backed up until his back touched the aft bulkhead of the bridge.

The captain turned around. "Sound General Quarters," he ordered. "All ahead full. All weapons to fire when ready." He looked at Pickering, and over the clamor of the General Quarters bell, said, "It's an Emily. Obviously on a torpedo run."

Then he turned to look at the aircraft again.

The Emily, Pickering knew, was the Kawanishi H8K2, a four-engine flying boat which had obviously borrowed much of its design from Igor Sikorski's Pan American Airways flying boats. It was fast—he recalled that it cruised at 290 mph—had a range of 4000 miles, and could carry either two of the large, excellent, 1780-pound Japanese torpedoes, or just over two tons of bombs.

It's spotted the Gregory, Pickering realized, *and has decided an American destroyer all alone on the wide sea is just what she is looking for.*

With the element of surprise on the side of the bomber, a destroyer made an excellent torpedo target. On the other hand, hitting an aircraft with the 40mm Bofors and .50 Caliber Brownings on a destroyer was very difficult, even if they could be brought to bear in time. An aircraft slowed to a speed that allowed it to safely and accurately launch a torpedo was a little more vulnerable, but not much.

Thirty seconds later—it seemed like much, much longer—there was a sudden, violent eruption of noise and sound on the bridge. Explosions followed, and smoke, and shattering glass. And before Pickering regained his senses, there was another explosion and then a water spout thirty feet off the port rail; and a moment later a hundred feet off the starboard rail, another.

The captain was wrong, Pickering decided, even as he looked down at his body and saw with surprise that his upper chest and right arm were bloody, *the sonofabitch was not on a torpedo run. Her pilot opted for a bomb run. Maybe he didn't have any torpedoes. So he came in far faster than he would have if he were dropping a torpedo.*

He looked for the captain and found him almost immediately. He was on his back on the deck, his eyes and mouth open in astonishment, his shirt a bloody mess. He was very obviously dead.

There had been six, seven, eight people on the bridge a moment before. Now Pickering saw only two others on their feet. The talker, his earphones and microphone harness in place, leaned against the aft bulkhead not far from Pickering, a look of shock and horror on his face. A sailor, whose function Pickering did not know, stood with his back to the forward bulkhead, his face blackened, his arms wrapped tightly around his chest.

The helmsman was crumpled on the deck by the wheel, and the others were scattered all over the rest of the bridge. One sailor was crawling toward the chartroom port.

A bomb didn't do this, Pickering thought. These were small, explosive shells. He remembered then that the Emily carried five 20mm cannon and four 7.7mm machine guns. The Emily had strafed the *Gregory* before, during, and after the bombing run.

He tried to push himself off the bulkhead, and heard himself moan with pain. He looked again at his arm, and saw that it was hanging uselessly.

I am about to go into shock.

There was confirmation of that. He felt light-headed and was chilled.

He finally managed to stand erect and went to the talker, who looked at him but did not see him.

"Get the executive officer to the bridge," he ordered. When there was no response, when the talker's eyes looked at him but did not see him, Pickering slapped him hard across the face. The talker looked at him like a kicked puppy, but life came back in his eyes.

"Get the executive officer to the bridge," Pickering repeated. The talker nodded, and Pickering saw his hand rise to the microphone switch.

As Pickering went to the other sailor, he slipped and nearly fell in a puddle of blood.

"Take the wheel," Pickering ordered.

"I'm the ship's writer, Sir."

"Take the goddamned wheel!"

"Aye, aye, Sir."

Pickering went to the window of the bridge. Only shards remained of the thick glass. Dead ahead, he could see the Emily, still close to the sea, making a tight turn. He was about to make another bomb run.

An officer, a nice-looking kid in a helmet, appeared on the bridge.

"Mother of Christ!" he said, looking around in horror.

"Get the executive officer up here!" Pickering shouted at him.

"Sir, I . . . Mr. Goldberg's dead, Sir. I came up here to report."

"Can you conn this vessel?"

"No, Sir. I'm the communications officer."

"Get someone up here who can," Pickering ordered. "Get people up here. I need someone on the telegraph, someone on the wheel."

"Aye, aye, Sir," the communications officer said, then turned and left the bridge. Pickering saw that he stopped just outside and became nauseous.

He returned his attention to the Emily, which was now in level flight, low on the water, making another bombing run to port.

"Prepare to come hard to port," Pickering said.

"Damage report, Captain," the talker said.

"What?"

"Damage control officer reports no damage, Sir."

"Tell him to get up here!" Pickering said, then: "Hard to port."

"Hard to port it is, Sir."

The *Gregory* began to turn, heeling over. It was now pointing directly at the Emily.

Pickering saw four dark objects drop from the airplane, and watched in fascination as they arced toward the ship.

And then he saw something else: Red tracers from a Bofors 40mm cannon splashing into the sea, and then picking up, moving toward the Emily. When she was just about overhead, the line of tracers moved into the Emily's fuselage, and then to her right wing. The wing buckled as the airplane flashed over.

Pickering ran to the exposed portion of the bridge, his feet slipping in the pool of blood now spreading from under her captain's body. He looked aft. The Emily had already crashed. As he watched, what was left of it slipped below the water, and the dense cloud of blue-black smoke that had been rising from her wreckage was cut off. For a moment, there were patches of burning fuel on the water, but they started to flicker out.

He returned to the bridge. A lieutenant whom he remembered seeing in the wardroom at dinner the night before came onto the bridge.

"I'm the damage control officer, Sir."

"Can you conn this vessel?"

"Yes, Sir."

"Sir, you have the conn," Pickering said, and then put his hand out to steady himself. He really felt faint.

"I have the conn, Sir," the lieutenant said, ritually, and then Pickering heard him say, "Help the Captain, Doc. Stop that bleeding."

(TWO)
Aboard USS *Gregory* (APD-44)
Coral Sea
1425 Hours 18 August 1942

Pickering was in the Captain's cabin, in the Captain's bunk, his back resting on pillows against the bulkhead. He was naked above the waist. His arm, in a cast, was taped to his chest. He appeared to be dozing.

The lieutenant walked to the bunk and looked down at him.

"How do you feel, Sir?"

Pickering looked at him for a moment without recognition, and then, with an effort, forced himself awake.

"Oh, it's you," he said cheerfully. "Mr. 'No Damage to Report, Sir.'"

"Sir," the Lieutenant said, obviously hurt. "I didn't know what had happened on the bridge, Sir. Except that Mr. Goldberg had been killed on the ladder."

"I shouldn't have said that," Pickering said. "I'm sorry. I had a tube of morphine; I must still be feeling it."

"Are you still in pain, Sir?"

"Every time I breathe. That's a hell of a place to be stitched up." He changed the subject: "What shape are we in?"

"We're about five hours out, Sir, from Espíritu Santo. There's some things that have to be decided."

"Are you the senior officer?"

"No, Sir. You are."

"I'm supercargo."

"Sir, I checked the manual. Command passes—in a situation like this—to the senior officer of the line. Captain, that's you, Captain."

"What is it?"

"The bodies, Sir. I have them prepared, Sir."

"Where are they?"

"The captain and three others are in sick bay, Sir. The others are in the Chief's quarters."

"If you're suggesting a burial at sea . . ."

"That's your decision, Captain."

"If we're only five hours out, I think we should take them to Espíritu Santo," Pickering said. "I have no intention of conducting a burial at sea."

"Aye, aye, Sir," the Lieutenant said. "And we seem to have forgotten the report, Sir."

"I don't know what you're talking about."

"Mr. Norwood, the communications officer, has prepared it, Sir," the Lieutenant said, and handed it to him.

OPERATIONAL IMMEDIATE
SECRET
FROM USS GREGORY
TO: CINCPAC
1. GREGORY ATTACKED 0750 HOURS 18AUG42 POSITION WHISKEY ABLE OBOE SLASH

NAN NAN CHARLEY BY ONE REPEAT ONE EMILY. MODERATE TO SEVERE DAMAGE TO BRIDGE. EMILY SHOT DOWN.

2. CASUALTIES: CAPTAIN, EXECUTIVE OFFICER, TWO ENLISTED KIA. THREE OFFICERS AND SEVEN ENLISTED WIA.

3. GREGORY PROCEEDING BAKER XRAY MIKE.

PICKERING, CAPTAIN, USN, COMMANDING

"It's 'USNR,' not 'USN,'" Pickering said. "I'm not a regular."

"Yes, Sir. I'll have that changed."

"What about the wounded?"

"One of them is in pretty bad shape, I'm afraid. We're hoping he makes it. There's medical facilities at Espíritu. The others will be all right, Captain."

"*Captain,*" Pickering said thoughtfully, sadly, and paused, and then went on: "The captain died quickly. I don't think he knew what hit him."

"Mr. Goldberg, too, Sir. He was . . . whatever got him, got him in the head."

"Jesus Christ!" Pickering said.

"Captain, can I get you something to eat? A tray, maybe. A sandwich? You really should have something."

"What I really would like is a drink," Pickering replied.

"I wish I could help you, Sir."

"Is there any medicinal bourbon aboard?"

"Yes, Sir."

"How much?"

"There's four cartons, Sir. I think they pack them forty-eight of those little bottles to a carton."

"Enough for one per man?"

"Yes, Sir. More than enough, Captain."

"Issue one bottle per man. If there is any left over, bring me a couple."

"Aye, aye, Sir."

(THREE)
Water Lily Cottage
Manchester Avenue
Brisbane, Australia
1925 Hours 18 August 1942

There was the sound of tires crunching on the driveway. Major Ed Banning went to the window, pushed the curtain aside, and saw the Studebaker President stopping in the drive.

"Pluto," Banning said, turning to Mrs. Ellen Feller. She was sitting on the couch, holding a tea cup and saucer in her hand.

"I presumed he would come here to discuss this situation with you," Ellen Feller said. "Didn't you?"

Banning didn't reply. He went to the door and opened it as Hon bounded onto the porch.

"I gather you've heard about Moore?" Banning greeted him.

"Yeah," Pluto said. "Take a look at this."

He handed Banning a sheet of onion skin, walked into the room, and nodded at Ellen Feller.

"Major Banning and I have been talking about what to do about Sergeant Moore," she said.

"And?"

"We've decided the best thing is to do nothing," Ellen said.

"What is this thing?" Banning asked, confused.

"The Signal Corps monitors the Navy frequencies when they can," Hon explained, "and they copy what they think might be interesting. Operational Immediates, for example. The crypto officer handed me that the moment I walked in. *Before* he told me that he had to fill in for the missing Sergeant Moore."

"But what the hell *is* this?"

"Read the signature," Pluto Hon said.

Banning did so.

"I'll be damned," he said.

"May I see that?" Ellen Feller asked, rising to her feet and walking to Banning. Banning handed her the Operational Immediate message radioed from the USS *Gregory* to CINCPAC after the Emily attack.

"Well, we knew that Mr. Knox told CINCPAC to take him off Guadalcanal," Ellen Feller said. "He was apparently on this ship, and I suppose that as the senior officer aboard, he would naturally take command if the captain was killed."

Banning ignored her.

"I don't suppose you know off-hand what Baker XRay Mike is. Or where?"

"Espíritu Santo," Hon said. "With great reluctance, the Navy Liaison Officer told me."

"Well, thank God, Captain Pickering is all right," Ellen said.

Banning looked at her but said nothing.

"Lieutenant Hon," Ellen said. "As I was saying, Major Banning and I have been discussing Sergeant Moore."

"What do you mean by that?" Hon asked.

"We can't let it get out that Moore knew . . . more than a sergeant should have been permitted to know . . . can we? I mean, the greater priority is to protect Captain Pickering, isn't it?"

He looked at her for a moment before replying. Then he asked, "Are you suggesting that we should not do whatever the hell has to be done to get Moore the hell off Guadalcanal?"

He looked at Banning, who met his eyes, but said nothing. Hon looked back at Ellen Feller.

"The only way," she said, "we can, as you put it, get Moore the hell off Guadalcanal is to make it known that he has had access to MAGIC. That will get Captain Pickering—for that matter, all of us—in a great deal of trouble."

"Your discussion, I'm afraid, Mrs. Feller," Pluto Hon said, coldly, "is academic."

"What does that mean?" Banning asked.

Hon handed him a sheet of paper.

URGENT

TOP SECRET

SERVICE MESSAGE

FROM: OFFICER IN CHARGE SPECIAL COMMUNICATIONS FACILITY JKS-3 SHSWPA BRIS-BANE

TO: OFFICER IN CHARGE SPECIAL COMMUNICATIONS FACILITY JKS-1 CINCPAC PEARL HARBOR

1. FOLLOWING TOP SECRET EYES ONLY TO BE RELAYED URGENT TO CAPTAIN FLEMING PICKERING USNR SOMEWHERE ENROUTE VIA BAKER XRAY MIKE TO OFFICE SECNAV WASHINGTON: BEGIN MSG ONLY ENLISTED MEMBER JKS-3 EN ROUTE VIA AIR GUADAL-CANAL ON ORDERS ACOFS G2 HQ USMC SIGNATURE PLUTO END MSG.

2. IMPORTANCE OF DELIVERY AS SOON AS POSSIBLE CANNOT BE OVEREMPHASIZED.
HON 1STLT SIGC USA

Ellen Feller stepped behind Banning and read the message over his shoulder.

"You had no authority to do that!" she flared.

"This has gone out, Pluto?" Banning asked.

"Yes, Sir."

"If you did so in the presumption that I would agree with it, you were absolutely right, Lieutenant," Banning said.

"It's insane," Ellen said. "The people in Hawaii aren't stupid. They are going to know exactly what this means."

"I hope so," Pluto said. "MAGIC is too important to risk being compromised."

"I can't imagine what Captain Pickering is going to think when he gets that," she said.

"He's probably going to wonder why we let it happen," Banning said.

"What could we do? How could we stop it?" she snapped.

"Since Pluto and I were gone, obviously, we couldn't."

"You're not suggesting that I could have stopped him from going?"

Banning didn't answer.

"You tell me, Banning," she flared, "how I could have stopped him from going."

"You could have hid him under your bed, if nothing else, until Colonel Dailey was gone."

She snorted contemptuously.

"Or in it," Banning added, nastily.

"How dare you talk to me like that?"

"For your general information, Mrs. Feller," Banning said evenly, turning to meet her eyes, "at my request, the Army Counterintelligence Corps has been providing security for this house since Captain Pickering rented it. He's a splendid fellow, but he's a little lax about classified document security. They kept it up after Captain Pickering left and turned the house over to you and Sergeant Moore. The CIC people go through the house every time it's left empty, to make sure there's nothing classified lying about. They're very thorough in their surveillance. They even write down which bedrooms are used by whom, and they've been furnishing me a daily report."

(FOUR)
Henderson Field
Guadalcanal, Solomon Islands
1045 Hours 19 August 1942

A bag of official mail and six insulated metal boxes marked with red crosses and the legend, HUMAN BLOOD RUSH, were aboard the PBY-5 Catalina from Espíritu Santo. There were also three passengers.

One of the passengers was wearing a steel helmet and a Red Cross brassard on the sleeve of his obviously brand-new USMC utilities.

The Navy Medical Corps, Lieutenant Colonel George F. Dailey thought approvingly, was just about as efficient in sending replacements for lost-in-action physicians as Marine Corps intelligence had been in getting him and Sergeant Moore to the scene of battle.

Sergeant Moore did not favorably impress Lieutenant Colonel Dailey. When he was told that he was going to be given the opportunity to serve the Corps and the nation doing something far more important than shuffling classified documents, Moore's behavior in Brisbane was really distressing, not at all that expected of a Marine sergeant. He didn't want to go. And while Dailey was not prepared to go so far as to suggest cowardice, he was convinced that if he hadn't sent the Army Military Policemen to "help him collect his gear" there was more than a slight chance that Moore would not have shown up at the airport. At least until after the plane to Espíritu Santo had left.

As the Catalina landed, Dailey saw that there were no other airplanes on the field, and wondered why. If the Catalina could land, why not fighters?

The pilot taxied up to the control tower and shut down the engines. A crewman opened the door and made a gesture for the passengers to get out.

"Welcome to Guadalcanal," he said. "Cactus Airlines hopes you have enjoyed your flight."

There were two Jeeps sitting by the control tower. A medical officer wearing a Red Cross brassard sat on the hood of one of them. Surprising Dailey, he had a .30 caliber carbine slung over his shoulder. A major leaned against the other Jeep. A 35-mm camera was hanging around his neck, and a Thompson .45 caliber submachine gun was cradled in his arm.

The major smiled and pushed himself erect.

"Well, I'll be damned, look who's here! I warned you not to screw up, Sergeant." Moore saluted.

"Hello, Major Dillon," he said.

"Major," Dailey said. "My name is Dailey."

Dillon did not salute. He offered his hand, and announced, "Jake Dillon, Colonel."

The medical officer, and a Corpsman who appeared from inside the control tower building, went to the Catalina. The refrigerated blood containers were handed out and put into the medical Jeep. The doctor who had been on the plane from Espíritu Santo climbed out.

He shook hands with the doctor who had been waiting with the Jeep, then he stepped up to the front seat. The corpsman climbed over the rear and sat down precariously on one of the blood containers. The Jeep drove off.

The pilot came out the door.

"Just the man I'm looking for," Dillon said, and took an insulated Human Blood container from the back of his Jeep. A failed attempt to cross off HUMAN BLOOD with what appeared to be grease pencil had been made.

When he looked closer, Dailey saw that the grease pencil had also been used to write, EXPOSED PHOTOGRAPHIC FILM. For Public Relations Section, Hq USMC, Washington DC on several sides of the container.

"Hello, Major," the pilot said.

"You don't have any film for me, by any chance, do you?"

"There's four boxes for you at Espíritu, but I didn't have the weight left."

"Christ, I'm running low."

"I had the medic and those two to carry. They had the priority. Next time, I hope."

"If you can't bring all of it, bring at least one. Or open one. Bring what you can. I'm really running low. And film doesn't weigh that much."

"I'll do what I can, Jake."

"Thank you," Dillon said, and walked back to Dailey and Moore.

"I think I know where Sergeant Moore is going," Dillon said. "Is there any place I can carry you, Colonel?"

"I'm reporting for duty as Division G-2," Dailey said.

"I thought that might be it," Dillon said. "Hop in, I'll give you a ride."

"Thank you," Dailey said. "What's your function around here, Major?"

"I'm your friendly neighborhood Hollywood press agent," Dillon said, as he got behind the wheel.

"I'm afraid I don't understand?"

"I've got a crew of combat correspondents recording this operation for posterity," Dillon said.

"How is it you know Sergeant Moore?"

"I was in Melbourne—with Frank Goettge, the man you're replacing—a while back. At Fleming Pickering's place. Moore worked for him." He turned to look at Moore in the back seat. "You knew he was gone from here, didn't you?"

"I knew he was going, Sir," Moore said. "I didn't know he was gone."

"Well, don't worry, they'll find a lot for you to do here. You heard what happened to Colonel Goettge and the others?"

"No, Sir."

Dillon told them.

When they reached the G-2 Section, Dillon got out of the Jeep.

"Major Jack NMI Stecker is acting G-2," he said. "I'll introduce you. He'll be damned glad to see you."

"Why do you say that?"

"Because they took him away from his battalion to put him in G-2 when Goettge got himself killed, and he's very unhappy about that."

Dillon entered the G-2 section. It was dark inside, and it took a moment for his eyes to adjust. Before they did, before he could make out more than shadowy bodies, he called out: "Christmas present, Jack. Your replacement."

There was silence for a moment, and then a dry voice said, "At least he didn't go 'Ho, Ho, Ho.' I suppose we should be grateful for that."

Major Dillon's eyes had by then become acclimated to the lower light. He could now make out a familiar face.

"I beg your pardon, General. I didn't know you were in here."

"I wonder if that would have made any difference?" General Vandergrift asked, and then advanced on Dailey.

"I'm General Vandergrift, Colonel," he said, offering his hand. "I hope that wasn't more of Major Dillon's Hollywood hyperbole, and you are indeed the intelligence officer we've been promised."

"Sir," Dailey said, coming to attention, "Lieutenant Colonel Dailey, Sir. Reporting for duty as G-2."

"I'm very pleased to meet you, Colonel," Vandergrift said. "Welcome aboard. This is Major Stecker, who has been filling in."

Stecker offered his hand. Vandergrift spotted Moore, and offered him his hand.

"You came in with Colonel Dailey, Sergeant?"

"Yes, Sir."

"He was Flem Pickering's—I don't know what, *orderly,* I guess—in Australia," Dillon volunteered.

"Is that what you've been doing, Son?" Vandergrift asked. "Orderly?"

"No, Sir. I'm a Japanese-language linguist, Sir."

"In that case, I'm sure Major Stecker is even more glad to see you than he is to see Colonel Dailey," Vandergrift said. He looked at Major Jake Dillon and shook his head.

"Think about it, Jake," he said. "Did you really think they would airship an orderly in here?"

Stecker walked over to Moore and examined him closely.

"Give me a straight answer, Sergeant. How well do you speak—more important, how well do you read—Japanese?"

"Fluently, Sir."

"Sergeant!" Stecker said, raising his voice.

A head appeared from behind the canvas that separated the outer "office" from "the map room."

"Sir?"

"Take the sergeant here up to the First Marines. He's a Japanese-language linguist."

"Belay that, Sergeant," General Vandergrift said. "I'm sure you have more important things to do, and Major Dillon has just kindly offered to take the sergeant, haven't you, Major?"

"Yes, Sir," Dillon said. "I'd be happy to."

"Sergeant," Jack Stecker said, "there's several boxes of stuff at the First, taken from the bodies of Japanese. We haven't had anybody who can read it. I want anything that looks official, anything that can help us identify enemy units, anything that would be useful to know about those units. Do you understand what I'm talking about?"

"Yes, Sir. I think I do."

"If you come across something, give it to Captain Feincamp. He's the S-2. I'll get on the horn and tell him you're coming."

"Aye, aye, Sir."

"Anything that *looks* to you like it might be interesting. Don't bother with actually translating it. Just make a note of what it is. I'll decide whether or not you should make a translation."

"Aye, aye, Sir."

"Have you got a weapon?"

If I tell him about the .45, he's probably going to take it away from me.

Sergeant John Marston Moore, surprised with how easily it came, lied.

"No, Sir."

"Sergeant!" Stecker raised his voice again, and again the head appeared at the canvas flap.

"Sir?"

"Give the sergeant that extra Thompson."

"Aye, aye, Sir."

"You *can* use a Thompson?" Stecker asked Moore.

"Yes, Sir."

"I think that probably I'll have you—Colonel Dailey will have you—work here. But right now, we need to go through the stuff the First has collected."

"Yes, Sir."

The sergeant appeared and handed Moore a Thompson submachine gun and two extra magazines.

"Thank you."

"Drive slow, Jake," Stecker said. "Sergeant Moore is a very valuable man. We can't afford to lose him."

"Right," Dillon said. "OK, Sergeant. Let's go."

An alarm went off in the back of General Vandergrift's head. Something was wrong, but he couldn't put a handle on it.

Stecker's words, he finally realized. *"We can't afford to lose him."*

It was that, and the reference to Flem Pickering. And what Flem had said about Lieutenant Cory, whose place this young sergeant was taking.

The morning he left, Pickering had told him about MAGIC, and about his concern that Cory might have known about it. If Cory had that knowledge, he should never have been sent to Guadalcanal.

The sergeant, obviously, does not know about MAGIC. For one thing, that sort of secret is not made known to junior enlisted men. For another, he worked for Fleming Pickering. Therefore, if he knew, Pickering would have made sure he would not be sent to Guadalcanal.

But this lieutenant colonel: He was an intelligence officer, he's senior enough to have had responsibilities which would have given him the Need to Know. And they rushed him here to replace Goettge. Since so few people actually knew about MAGIC, *it was possible that whoever had rushed him over here hadn't even considered that possibility.*

And this fellow—General Vandergrift had made a snap, and perhaps unfair, judgment that Lieutenant Colonel Dailey was not too smart; otherwise he would not have been assigned as a liaison officer to SHSWPA—*if he was privy to* MAGIC, *it might well have been decided to send him to Guadalcanal anyway.*

"Colonel," General Vandergrift asked. "Does the phrase MAGIC mean anything to you?"

"No, Sir," Lieutenant Colonel Dailey replied. "I've heard the word, Sir, but . . ."

"It's not important," General Vandergrift said.

(FIVE)
S-2 Section, First Marines
Guadalcanal, Solomon Islands
2005 Hours 19 August 1942

Sergeant John Marston Moore, USMCR, sat on the dirt floor of the S-2 bunker in the brilliant light of a hissing Coleman gasoline lamp. His legs were crossed under him, and his undershirt was sweat soaked. He had long before removed his utility jacket. The Thompson submachine gun Major Stecker had given him now rested on it.

He was about two-thirds of the way, he judged, through the foot-and-a-half-tall pile of personal effects removed from Japanese bodies; and he had been at it steadily since shortly after eleven, less time out for "dinner"—a messkit full of rice, courtesy of the Japanese; a spoonful of meat and gravy, courtesy Quartermaster Corps, U.S. Army; and two small cans of really delicious smoked oysters, again courtesy of the Japanese.

He had found virtually nothing that Major Stecker could possibly use. He had learned that the Marines already knew the identity of the Rikusentai engineers— the 11th and 23rd Pioneers—who had been building the airfield.

He had been able to augment this by finding, in written-but-not-mailed letters home, references to the names of the commanding officers. He had written them down. He couldn't see how the names of three or four junior Japanese officers would be of much use, except perhaps as a psychological tool for prisoner interrogation.

That seemed to be a moot point. For one thing, Moore had learned there were damn few prisoners. The story of the Japanese warrant officer who led Colonel Goettge and the others into the trap had quickly spread through the division. The Marines had decided that discretion—*don't take a chance, shoot the fucker!*— overwhelmed the odd and abstract notion that prisoners had an intelligence value.

Tell that to Colonel Goettge!

For another, there seemed to be very few people around capable of interrogating prisoners at all, unless they happened to speak English, much less of outwitting them with psychological tricks.

He had spent long hours reading letters from home. It had been emotionally unnerving. He had lived in Japan. Tokyo was really as much home to him as

Philadelphia. When he found an envelope bearing a Denenchofu return address, he knew it was entirely possible that he and the writer, somebody's mother, had met and bowed to each other at the door of a shop.

Much of the stuff was stained with a dark and sticky substance, now beginning to give off a sickly sweet smell, that he could not pretend was mud or oil or plum preserves.

Moore heard someone coming into the sandbagged tent. He turned and looked over his shoulder. It was Captain Feincamp, the First Marine's S-2, and he had with him a lieutenant and a technical sergeant, a balding, lean man in his late thirties.

"How you coming, Sergeant?" Feincamp asked.

"I haven't found anything interesting so far, Sir," Moore replied.

"He's a linguist," Captain Feincamp explained to the lieutenant. "They just flew him in. There's a replacement for Colonel Goettge, too."

And then he explained to Moore the reason why the lieutenant and the technical sergeant were there.

"They just came off patrol, Sergeant," he said. "They ran into some Japs and had themselves a little firefight. I think maybe you'd better listen in on this."

"Yes, Sir," Moore said, grateful for the chance to stop rummaging through personal effects.

He spun around on the dirt floor.

The lieutenant and then the technical sergeant handed him several wallets and some more personal mail.

"We're the first ones back, I suppose," the lieutenant said. "Maybe you can make something out of this shit."

Moore took it, glanced through it, and quickly decided it was more of the same sort of thing he'd been looking at for hours.

Feincamp produced a map. The lieutenant looked at it for a moment, and then pointed.

"Right about here on the beach, Captain," he said. "Captain Brush called a lunch break. I told him that I'd been there before, and twenty, thirty minutes inland was an orange farm . . ."

"A what?"

"Orange trees."

"Orange *grove*," Feincamp provided.

"Yes, Sir. Well, the captain said we could walk another half hour if it meant fresh fruit, so we started inland. Ten, fifteen minutes later, right about here . . ." he pointed, "all hell broke loose. We lost Corporal DeLayne right away. He took a round in the head."

"The big blond kid?"

"Yes, Sir."

"Damn."

"So Captain Brush told me to take a squad around here, on the right flank, and the rest started for where the fire was coming from. Straight ahead. When we started that, they started withdrawing, and we started after them."

Moore saw that the technical sergeant was admiring a Japanese helmet he had taken as a souvenir.

"So then it was sort of like the wild west for maybe twenty minutes. But we whipped their ass!"

"Casualties?"

"A pisspot full of them. We counted thirty-one Japs, and I'm sure we missed some."

"I was speaking of Marines," Feincamp said coldly.

"Three KIA, Sir. Three wounded."

"Sergeant," Moore suddenly interrupted, "let me see that helmet, please?"

The technical sergeant looked at him doubtfully.

"Huh?"

"May I please see the helmet?" Moore asked.

"You want a helmet, Sergeant, you just take a walk up the beach."

"Give him the helmet, Sergeant," Captain Feincamp ordered softly.

The technical sergeant reluctantly handed it over.

"What is it, Sergeant?" Feincamp asked, after a moment.

"This isn't a Rikusentai helmet, Captain," Moore said.

"It isn't a what?" the lieutenant asked.

Moore ignored the question.

"Were the Japanese all wearing helmets like this?" he asked.

"They was—the ones that *was* wearing helmets—were wearing helmets like that," the technical sergeant said.

"With this insignia?" Moore pursued, pointing to a small, red enamel star on the front of the helmet.

"I don't know," the lieutenant said. "What was that you said before?"

"The Rikusentai, the construction troops who were building the airfield, are in the Japanese Navy. The Navy insignia is an anchor and a chrysanthemum. This is an Army helmet."

"Meaning what?"

"Meaning, possibly," Moore thought aloud and immediately regretted it, "that the Ichiki Butai is already ashore."

"What the fuck is whatever you said?" the technical sergeant asked.

"The Ichiki Butai is an infantry regiment—the 28th—of the 7th Division. First class troops under Colonel Kiyano Ichiki. The Japanese are going to send them here from Truk. If I'm right, and they're already here, that *would* be important."

"How the hell do you know that?" Captain Feincamp asked. "What units the Japs intend to send?"

"I know, Sir. I can't tell you how I know."

"The captain," the technical sergeant said furiously, "asked you a question. You answer it!"

Captain Feincamp raised his hand to shut off the technical sergeant.

"How do we know the Japs didn't issue Army helmets to—what was it you called them?" Captain Feincamp asked.

"The Rikusentai, Sir," Moore furnished. "It's possible, of course. But that Major in G-2 . . ."

"Major Stecker?"

"Yes, Sir, I think so. He told me to look for anything out of the ordinary."

"Captain," the lieutenant said thoughtfully. "I have something . . . I mean, out of the ordinary. The Japs we killed seemed to be heavy on officers. Maybe half of them were."

"You just forgot to mention that, right?" Feincamp said, sarcastically.

"Sorry, Sir. I didn't think it was important."

"What I think you had better do, Lieutenant," Feincamp said, "is get down to Division G-2, and tell Major Stecker what happened . . . No, tell the new G-2; I forgot about him. I'm going to send your sergeant and Sergeant Moore back down the beach to see what else Moore can come up with."

"Aye, aye, Sir."

"I don't think I have to tell you, Moore, do I, what to look for?"

"No, Sir."

(SIX)

Aside from perhaps four hours familiarization at Parris Island, the only experience Sergeant John Marston Moore, USMCR, had with the U.S. Submachine Gun, Caliber .45 (Thompson) was vicarious. He had watched half a dozen movie heroes—most notably Alan Ladd—and as many movie gangsters—most notably Edward G. Robinson—use the weapon against their enemies with great skill, élan, and ease.

They were now forty minutes down the beach toward the site of the encounter between Able Company, First Marines, and the Japanese; and he really had had no idea until that moment how heavy the sonofabitch was.

He had opted to leave his utility jacket in the S-2 Section of the First Marines, which he now recognized to be an error of the first magnitude. The canvas strap of the Thompson had worn one shoulder and then the other raw. And as they made their way down the sandy beach, the two spare 20-round Thompson magazines he carried, plus the .45 pistol and its two spare magazines, had both banged against him, in the process wearing raw and badly bruising the skin and muscles of his legs and buttocks.

He had also quickly learned that the good life he had been living in Melbourne and Brisbane had not only softened the calluses he had won at Parris Island—the balls of his feet and the backs of his ankles had quickly blistered, and the blisters had broken—but it had softened him generally.

To the technical sergeant's great and wholly unconcealed annoyance and contempt, he had absolutely had to stop every five minutes or so to regain his breath. His heart pounded so heavily he wondered if it would burst through his rib cage.

Twenty minutes down the beach, they began to encounter other members of Captain Brush's patrol. Five minutes after that, they encountered Captain Brush himself, bringing up the rear.

When the technical sergeant responded to, "Sergeant Ropke, where the *hell* do you think you're going?" by informing him of their mission, Captain Brush assigned a Corporal and a PFC to go with them.

Fifteen minutes after that, they reached the site of the action. It was marked by Japanese bodies scattered over the beach in various obscene postures of death. Even more obscene, in Moore's judgment, were the three-quarters-buried bodies of the three Marines who had been killed.

They had been buried with one boondocker shod foot sticking out of the ground so that their bodies could be more easily found later.

In the clothing of the third body Moore examined, that of a Japanese Army Captain, he found positive proof that the Ichiki Butai had indeed been landed on Guadalcanal. He also found in the calf of the Captain's boot a map which looked to him like a Japanese assessment of the Marine defense positions on the beachhead.

He gave this to the technical sergeant, and oriented the map for him.

"Jesus Christ!" the technical sergeant said, after carefully examining the map. "They did a good fucking job with this!"

Moore spent another twenty minutes searching for the bodies of Japanese officers, and then searching the bodies for materials he thought would be important. Finally he had a Japanese knapsack full of documents, maps, and wallets.

They started back. Five minutes down the beach, after the first time he stopped to catch his breath, the technical sergeant relieved him of the Thompson.

"Let me carry the Thompson," he said, not unkindly. "That shit you picked up is slowing us all down."

I should be embarrassed, ashamed, humiliated. I am not. I am simply grateful that I don't have to carry that sonofabitch anymore!

Ninety seconds after that, there was a faint suggestion of something—some *things*—flying through the air in high arcs. And a moment after that, there were two almost simultaneous flashes of light, and then a moment later, a third.

And then something like a swung baseball bat hit Sergeant John Marston Moore twice, once in the calf of his left leg and once high, almost at the hip joint of his right leg.

This was followed immediately by a loud roar, and the sensation of flying through the air. He landed on his back, and the wind was knocked out of him.

After a moment, while he was still trying to figure out what was happening, he became aware of people running out from the woods onto the beach. Two of them had rifles, and the third a pistol.

He rose on his elbow for a closer look.

He saw that the Corporal and the PFC who had been sent with them were down on the beach, crumpled up, and that the technical sergeant was trying, without much success, to get to his feet.

Moore rolled over onto his stomach and took the .45 Colt automatic from where it had been bruising his buttocks raw and sore and worked the action and held it in two hands and shot at the three men running onto the beach. He shot until two of them fell, and until the slide locked in the rear position indicating that the last of the seven rounds in the magazine had been expended.

He searched desperately for a spare magazine.

There was a short, staccato burst of .45 fire, accompanied by orange flashes of light, and then another. The technical sergeant had gotten the Thompson into action.

By the time Moore found a fresh magazine, ejected the empty magazine, inserted the fresh magazine, let the slide slam forward, and then looked for a target, there was none.

What he saw was the technical sergeant, bleeding profusely from cuts or wounds on the neck and face, crawling over to him.

"You all right?" the technical sergeant said.

"I think I broke both legs."

"It'll be all right. They probably heard the fire, they'll send somebody back for us."

"Bullshit," Sergeant John Marston Moore said.

"Yeah, probably," the technical sergeant said. "But maybe when it gets light in the morning, they will."

One of the two Marines who had been sent with them—Moore couldn't tell which—moaned and then began to whimper.

They will find my body on this fucking beach in the morning, Sergeant John Marston Moore thought, *unless the tide comes in and washes it out to sea for the sharks to eat.*

Two minutes after that, there was the unmistakable sound of a Jeep in four-wheel drive making its way through soft sand.

When the Corpsmen loaded Sergeant John Marston Moore onto the litter, he screamed with pain.

They loaded the technical sergeant in the other litter. And then, because they didn't know what else to do with them, they laid the bodies of the PFC and the Corporal on the Jeep hood. The PFC's body started whimpering again.

"Jesus," Moore heard one of the Corpsmen say, "I thought he was dead."

(SEVEN)

"The Doc tells me you took grenade fragments in your legs," Major Jack NMI Stecker said to Sergeant John Marston Moore. "That's better than getting shot."

"What?" Moore asked incredulously. His legs were now one great sea of dull aching pain, with crashing wavelets of intense, flashing, toothache-like agony.

"There's often less tissue damage; and they can repair a jagged wound easier than a smooth one. The worst is a slice."

"I hurt," Moore said. "Why won't they give me something for the pain?"

"I told them not to, until I could get here and talk to you," Stecker confessed. "I want to hear more about Ichiki Butai."

"You *sonofabitch!*" Moore flared. The moment the words were out of his mouth, he realized with horror what he had said. Marine Sergeants do not call Marine Second Lieutenants, much less Marine Majors, sonsofbitches. Moore realized that he was horror stricken, but not repentant. Under the circumstances, if Jesus Christ himself was responsible for the withholding of painkillers, he would have questioned the parentage of the Son of God.

Major Jack NMI Stecker did not seem to take offense.

"Yeah," he said. "Are they or aren't they?"

"They were all Ichiki Butai," Moore said. "I think it was a headquarters team or something. I saw two lieutenant colonels, three majors, five or six captains. A bunch of senior NCOs."

"OK, Sergeant. I've got what linguists I could scrounge up working on those documents."

"How did you know about Ichiki Butai?" Moore asked.

"I've seen the Order of Battle," Stecker said. "What interests me is how you knew what you told Captain Feincamp."

"I want something for this fucking pain!"

"Son," a vaguely familiar voice asked. "Does the word MAGIC mean anything to you?"

"I *hurt!* God*damn* it, doesn't anybody care?"

"I'm General Vandergrift, Son. You can tell me. Do you know what MAGIC means?"

"Yes, Sir, General, I know what MAGIC is."

"All right, Doctor. Do what you can for this boy," General Vandergrift said.

Moore felt a surprisingly cool rubber mask being clamped over his mouth. Then there was a rush of cool air. It felt good. He took a deep breath.

"Well done, Lad," he heard General Vandergrift say. "Well do . . ."

XIX

Captain Charles M. Galloway slid open the canopy of his Wildcat, then lowered the left wing just a little, just enough to give him a good look at Henderson Field.

A Douglas SBD-3 Dauntless was just about to touch down. Another Dauntless— the last of a dozen—was just turning on final.

Galloway turned to his right, saw Jim Ward looking at him, and gestured to him to go on down. Ward nodded and peeled off. The other three Wildcats in the first five-plane V followed Ward.

As the first planes of VMF-229 landed, Galloway flew two wide three-sixties, mostly over the water (there was no reported anti-aircraft fire, but why take a chance?). And then Bill Dunn, leading the second five-plane V, pulled up alongside him. Galloway signaled for him to land. Dunn nodded, and gave the signal to his wing man. He peeled off and made his approach, followed by the others. Dunn remained on Galloway's wing tip.

Soon it was the two of them alone above the field.

Two mother hens, Galloway thought, *making sure the little chickies get home safe.*

Except this isn't home and it isn't safe.

Charley reached his left hand down beside his seat, found the charging handle for the outboard .50 Caliber Browning in the left wing, and turned it ninety degrees, putting the weapon on SAFE. Then he found the inboard handle, and rotated that. He put his left hand on the stick, put his right hand down beside his seat, and repeated the action, putting the guns in the right wing on SAFE.

Then he looked over at Dunn, held up his index finger, and then pointed it at himself.

Me First.

He could see Dunn smiling.

Charley peeled off and put the Wildcat into a dive.

There are two ways to lower the landing gear of a Grumman F4F. The means specified in *AN 01-190FB-1 Pilot's Handbook of Flight Operating Instructions for Navy Model FM-2 Airplanes (As Amended)* specifies that the pilot will turn the landing gear handcrank located on the right side of the cockpit approximately twenty-eight times until the crank handle hits a stop indicating the landing gear has been fully extended.

The second way was not listed in any pilot's manual. The technique was not only not recommended, it was forbidden. It was the technique Charley Galloway used— and, he was sure, most of the pilots of VMF-229. Charley had explained it to them back at Ewa, so they would know what they were forbidden to do . . .

He released the landing gear handcrank brake just before he came out of the dive. Following Newton's Law that a body in motion tends to remain in motion, when he pulled out of the dive to make his final approach, the forces of gravity pulled the landing gear out of the retracted position.

You had to be very careful that the rapidly spinning handle didn't get your arm, which would probably break it, but on the other hand, you didn't have to turn the damned crank twenty-eight times with your right hand while flying the airplane with your left.

Charley touched down; and twenty seconds later, Bill Dunn touched down behind him. Before he finished the landing roll, the humid heat began to get to him. He felt his back break out in sweat.

He was not very impressed with the airfield. It looked to him like a half inch of rain would turn it into a sea of mud. And he understood that a half inch of rain a day was not at all uncommon on Guadalcanal.

The entire runway was lined with spectators. Not solidly, but every couple of yards there seemed to be a Marine. They were smiling, and a few of them even waved.

Charley waved back, and even forced a smile.

The Marines looked like hell. They looked exhausted and underfed and filthy. And they regarded the arrival of the first combat aircraft as something more important than it really was.

It was actually a desperate attempt to stop a major Japanese effort to throw the Marines off Guadalcanal and reclaim the airbase.

That effort was about to get underway. Charley Galloway had private personal doubts that nineteen F4Fs and a dozen SBD-3s were going to be able to do much to stop it. Not to mention anything else they scraped off the bottom of the barrel.

Just before they'd left the *Long Island,* he heard that the Army Air Corps was sending a squadron of Bell P-400s to Guadalcanal. The reaction of the group was that the goddamned Army Air Corps was butting in on the Marine Corps' business.

Galloway's reaction was that the Marines, and maybe especially MAG-21 in particular, could use all the help they could get; but they weren't going to get very much from a squadron of P-400s. He knew the story of the P-400.

Technical Sergeant Charley Galloway first heard about the aircraft in 1939. Curious about it, he managed to have a little engine trouble over Buffalo, New York, which gave him a chance to sit down at the Bell plant and have a look at the plane that began life as the Bell P-39 Aircobra.

He had not been impressed. It was a weird bird, sitting on what looked to Charley like a very fragile tricycle landing gear. It had a liquid cooled Allison engine, mounted amidships, *behind* the pilot. The prop was driven by a shaft. The shaft was hollow, and carried a 37mm cannon barrel. There was no turbocharger, giving it, consequently, low to lousy performance at high altitudes.

All of which, in the final analysis, meant that nobody wanted the damned things.

The English wouldn't have anything to do with them. So the Aircobras that were supposed to go to them were sent to the Russians. Though Charley couldn't say for sure, it was entirely possible that the Russians, as desperate as they were for anything that would fly, didn't want them either. And so somebody had turned them over to the Army Air Corps.

Their reputation was so bad they'd even changed the name from P-39 to P-400. The only thing that surprised Charley was that the Marines hadn't wound up with them. The Marines normally got what the Army and the Navy didn't want.

It was not the sort of thing you talked to your men about, to bolster their morale, so Charley kept his mouth shut.

A familiar bald head and naked barrel chest appeared on the side of the runway, directing Charley to taxi to a sandbag revetment.

Tech Sergeant Big Steve Oblensky climbed up on the wing root before Charley stopped the engine.

"Well, I see you all got here," he said.

"There was some doubt in your mind?"

"Only about you," Big Steve said.

"What shape are we in?"

"Great. We have to pump fuel—the fuel there is—by hand through chamois. That runway's going to be a fucking muddy . . ."

" 'The fuel there is'?" Charley quoted, interrupting him.

Big Steve waited until Charley hauled himself out of the cockpit before replying.

"Those converted tin cans that brung us here," he said, "carried 400 barrels of Avgas. That's not much. Some of it they already used to refuel the Catalinas that have been coming in."

"You're telling me we have less than 22,000 gallons of gas?"

"Maybe a little more. They're bringing in a little all the time, but when we start using it . . ." Oblensky gestured at the aircraft that had just flown in. "And I just heard that the Army is sending in a half dozen P-400s tomorrow."

"Jesus Christ," Charley said.

There was the sound of aircraft engines, a different pitch than a Dauntless or Wildcat made. Charley looked up at the sky and saw a Catalina making its approach.

We make fun of them, he thought. *Aerial bus drivers. But it has to take more balls to fly that slow and ungainly sonofabitch in and out of here than it does to fly a Wildcat.*

"And there's no fucking chow," Oblensky said, almost triumphantly. "We're eating captured Japanese shit."

"Well then, I guess we better hurry up and win the war," Charley said. "I wouldn't want you writing Flo that we officers are starving your fat ass."

(TWO)
U.S. Navy Hospital
San Diego, California
0905 Hours 24 August 1942

The nurse bending over the chest of Captain Fleming Pickering, USNR, was a full lieutenant who had been in the Navy for six years. She was competent, aware of this, and had a well-deserved reputation among her peers as being both hard nosed and unable to suffer fools.

She looked over her shoulder when she sensed movement behind her, and barked, "You'll have to leave. Who let you in here, anyhow? Visiting hours start at oh nine thirty."

Pickering laughed, and it hurt.

"Lieutenant," he said, "may I present the Secretary of the Navy?"

"Bullshit," the lieutenant said and chuckled, then looked, and said, "Oh, my God!"

"Please carry on," Frank Knox said. "How are you, Fleming?"

"I'm all right," Pickering said, and then, "Jesus Christ, take it easy, will you?"

"You want an infection? I'll stop."

"I thought they had some new kind of miracle drug—Sulfa?—you could just sprinkle on it," Pickering said, looking down at his chest.

"It's bullshit," she said. "What I'm doing works."

"It should, it hurts like hell."

"Be a big boy, Captain, I'm just about finished."

"So, I suspect, am I. Finished, I mean," Pickering said, looking at Knox.

"No," Frank Knox said. "I checked with the hospital commander. Despite your *grievous and extremely painful wounds,* you'll live. You should be out of the hospital in two weeks."

"That's not what I meant," Pickering said.

"I know what you meant," Knox said.

"I'm not finished?"

"I bring the personal greetings of the President of the United States," Knox said. "That sound like you're finished?"

"It sounds suspicious."

"Take a look at this," Knox said, and walked to the bed and handed Pickering a sheet of paper.

URGENT

CINCPAC 0915 22AUG1942

SECRET

PERSONAL FOR SEC NAVY

INFORMATION: CHIEF OF NAVAL OPERATIONS

1. CAPTAIN FLEMING PICKERING, USNR, DEPARTED PEARL HARBOR VIA MARINER AIRCRAFT FOR SANDIEGO NAVAL HOSPITAL 0815 22AUG1942. THE PROGNOSIS FOR HIS RECOVERY FROM WOUNDS TO THE CHEST AND FRACTURED ARM IS QUOTE GOOD TO EXCELLENT END QUOTE.

2. IN VIEW OF CAPTAIN PICKERINGS UNIQUE ASSIGNMENT THERE IS SOME QUESTION OF THE AUTHORITY OF THE UNDERSIGNED TO DECORATE THIS OFFICER, AND THE MATTER IS THEREFORE REFERRED FOR DETERMINATION.

3. IF CAPTAIN PICKERING WERE SUBORDINATE TO CINCPAC, THE UNDERSIGNED WOULD AWARD HIM THE SILVER STAR MEDAL WITH THE FOLLOWING CITATION: CITATION: CAPTAIN FLEMING PICKERING, USNR, WHILE ABOARD THE USS GREGORY IN THE CORAL SEA ON 18 AUGUST 1942 WAS ON THE BRIDGE WHEN THE GREGORY WAS ATTACKED BY ENEMY BOMBER AIRCRAFT. WHEN THE CAPTAIN AND THE EXECUTIVE OFFICER OF THE GREGORY WERE KILLED IN THE ENEMY ATTACK, AND DESPITE HIS GRIEVOUS AND EXTREMELY PAINFUL WOUNDS, INCLUDING A COMPOUND FRACTURE OF HIS ARM CAPTAIN PICKERING ASSUMED COMMAND OF THE VESSEL. REFUSING MEDICAL ATTENTION UNTIL HE COLLAPSED FROM LOSS OF BLOOD, CAPTAIN PICKERING MANEUVERED THE SHIP DURING THE CONTINUING ATTACK WITH CONSUMMATE MASTERY, WHICH NOT ONLY SAVED THE SHIP FROM FURTHER ENEMY DAMAGE BUT RESULTED IN THE DESTRUCTION OF THE ENEMY AIRCRAFT, A FOUR-ENGINED JAPANESE HEAVY BOMBER. HIS CALM COURAGE, ABOVE AND BEYOND THE CALL OF DUTY IN THE FACE OF ADVERSITY INSPIRED HIS CREW AND REFLECTED GREAT CREDIT UPON THE OFFICER CORPS OF THE UNITED STATES NAVAL SERVICE. ENTERED THE FEDERAL SERVICE FROM CALIFORNIA NIMITZ, ADMIRAL, USN, CINCPAC

Pickering handed the message back to Knox.

"Before you start handing out any medals, you better look at this," Pickering said. It was handed to me a few minutes ago, just before Florence Nightingale came in here."

"Will you hold still, please?" the nurse snapped.

Pickering handed Knox the radio message Lieutenant Pluto Hon had sent to MAGIC headquarters in Pearl Harbor.

Knox glanced at it and handed it back.

"I've seen it," Knox said. "How do you think they knew where to deliver it?"

"You don't know what it means," Pickering said.

"I've got a damned good idea," Knox said. "I also have this."

He handed Pickering another radio message.

URGENT

SECRET

HQ FIRST MARDIV 0845 20AUGUST 1942

SECNAV WASHINGTON DC

PLEASE PASS URGENTLY TO CAPTAIN FLEMING PICKERING USNR SERGEANT J M MOORE USMCR HAS BEEN AIRLIFTED ON MY AUTHORITY TO USNAVAL HOSPITAL PEARL HARBOR FOR TREATMENT OF WOUNDS SUFFERED IN COMBAT 19 AUGUST 1942. THE RABBIT DID NOT GET OUT OF THE HAT. BEST PERSONAL REGARDS SIGNED VANDERGRIFT MAJGEN USMC

BY DIRECTION: HARRIS BRIGGEN USMC

"I wonder what he means about the rabbit in the hat," Knox said. "That sounds like Magic."

"It never entered my mind that boy would be sent to Guadalcanal," Pickering said. "How the *hell* did that happen?"

"No one knew any reason he should not have been sent. Not even me."

"I thought it was necessary that Hon have some help."

"So did I. That's why I sent your secretary over there."

"I didn't know she was coming," Pickering said.

"I told myself that," Knox said.

"I think you should know that I would do the same thing again, under the same circumstances."

"Except that next time, you might bring me in on it?"

"Yes. I am sorry about that. If it had been compromised, it would have been my fault."

"Who else knows?"

"Just Vandergrift."

"OK," Knox said.

The nurse finished cleaning the wounds on Pickering's chest.

"I'm going to send a nurse in to give you a sponge bath," she said. "And this time, you will not run her off."

"Yes, Ma'am," Pickering said.

"You're on the way to recovery. Don't screw it up by getting yourself infected," the nurse said.

"No, Ma'am," Pickering said, and then to Knox: "I don't suppose you know how badly Moore was hurt?"

"He's well enough to be flown home; I ordered that."

"That kid should be an officer," Pickering said.

"Why don't you make up a list of things you think the Secretary of the Navy should do?" Knox said, and then called after the nurse, "Lieutenant, there's a Captain Haughton and a lady out there. Would you send them in, please?"

"Yes, Sir."

Captain David Haughton held the door open for Patricia Pickering to enter her husband's hospital room.

She looked at him. Tears welled in her eyes.

"You goddamned old fool, you!" she said, and walked to the bed and kissed him.

"Haughton," the Secretary of the Navy ordered. "Give him the medal. I think we can dispense with the reading of the citation."

(THREE)
Buka, Solomon Islands
1105 Hours 24 August 1942

"Here you go, Steve," First Lieutenant Joseph L. Howard, USMCR, said to Sergeant Stephen M. Koffler, USMC, handing him a limp, humidity-soaked piece of paper. He had had to be very careful as he encrypted the message so that his pencil would not tear through the paper.

Koffler smiled at him and laid the paper on the crude table. Koffler, Howard thought, looked like hell. There were signs of malnutrition and fatigue. There was a good chance that Koffler had malaria. There was no question that he had a tape worm, and probably a half dozen other intestinal parasites.

Koffler thought much the same thing about Joe Howard, who was down to probably one hundred thirty pounds, and whose eyes were deeply sunken and unnaturally bright.

But, like Howard, he kept his thoughts to himself. Talking about it wasn't going to fix anything.

"Hey!" Koffler called. Ian Bruce was sitting on the generator. He smiled, exposing his black, filed to a point teeth, and began to pump slowly but forcefully.

There was a whine; and after a moment, the dials on Koffler's radio began to glow a dull yellow. The yellow turned almost white, and the needles came off their pegs.

Koffler put earphones on his head and arranged his own pad of paper on the table. He had attempted to dry out his paper on a heated rock. The result was that the paper had shrunk and twisted.

Koffler reached for the key.

The dots and dashes went out, repeated three times, spelling out simply, FRD6. FRD6. FRD6.

Detachment A of Special Marine Corps Detachment 14 is attempting to establish contact with any station on this communications network.

This time, for a change, there was an immediate reply.

FRD6.FRD1.FRD6.FRD1.FRD6.FRD1.

Hello, Detachment A, this is Headquarters Royal Australian Navy Coastwatcher Establishment, Townesville, Australia, responding to your call.

As Koffler reached for the RECEIVE/XMIT switch, there was another reply.

FRD6.KCY.FRD6.KCY.FRD6.KCY.

Hello, Detachment A, this is the United States Pacific Fleet Radio Station at Pearl Harbor, Territory of Hawaii responding to your call.

"What's that?" Joe Howard asked.

"We got both Townesville and Pearl Harbor," Koffler said. Meanwhile his fingers were on the key.

FRD1.FRD1.SB CODE. KCY.KCY.PLS COPY.

Townesville, stand by to copy encrypted message. CINCPAC Radio, please copy my transmission to FRD1.

FRD6.FRD1. GA.

Townesville to Detachment A: Go ahead.

KCY.FRD6.WILL COPY YRS FRD1.GA.

CINCPAC to Detachment A. As requested we will copy your transmission to FRD1. Go ahead.

Koffler put the sheet of damp paper Howard had given him under his left hand, then pointed his index finger at the first block of five characters.

As his right hand worked the telegrapher's key, his index finger swept across the coded message. It is more difficult to transmit code than plain English, for the simple reason that code doesn't make any sense.

It took him not quite sixty seconds before he sent, in the clear, END.

FRD6.FRD1.VRF.

Detachment A, this is Townesville. I am about to send to you the material you just transmitted to me for purposes of verification.

FRD1.FRD6.GA

Townesville, this is Detachment A. Go ahead.

Koffler picked up a stubby pencil carefully.

We're running out of pencils, too. If something doesn't happen, if they don't send us some supplies, I'll be taking traffic from the Townesville and the Commander-in-Chief, Pacific by writing it with a sharp stick in the dirt floor.

After the message was received, Koffler handed it to Howard, who checked it against his original. Then Koffler began to write down the verification from Pearl Harbor.

The message informed both the Royal Australian Navy Coastwatcher Establishment and the Commander-in-Chief, Pacific, that Detachment A had observed, beginning at 1025 hours, a fleet of approximately ninety-six Japanese aircraft, consisting of approximately thirty Aichi D3A1 "Val" aircraft; ten Mitsubishi G4M1 Type 1 "Betty" Aircraft; fifteen Nakajima B5N1 "Kate" aircraft and approximately forty-one Mitsubishi A6M2 Model 21 "Zero" aircraft, flying at altitudes ranging from 5,000 to 15,000 feet, on a course which would probably lead them to Guadalcanal.

Howard wanted to make sure the message had been correctly transmitted. It took a little time.

FRD6.KCY ?????????

Detachment A. This is CINCPAC Radio. What's going on? We haven't heard from you in ninety seconds.

KCY.FRD6. FU FU.

CINCPAC Radio. This is Detachment A. Fuck You Twice.

"OK, Steve," Howard said. "Tell them we verify."

FRD6.FRD1.KCY. OK VRF. SB.

Detachment A to Townesville and Pearl Harbor. Verification is acknowledged. Detachment A is standing by.

FRD1.FDR6. SB TO COPY CODE.

FDR6. GA.

A minute later, Sergeant Stephen Koffler asked rhetorically, as he scribbled furiously, "what the hell are they sending us, the goddamned Bible?"

The message took three minutes to take down.

FDR1.FDR6. CLR.

Townesville to Detachment A. We have no further traffic for you at this time and are clearing this channel.

FDR6.FDR1. CLR.

Detachment A to Townesville. OK, Townesville, Good-bye.

KCY.FD6. FOLLOWING FOR COMMANDING OFFICER. PASS TO ALL HANDS. WELL DONE. NIMITZ. ADMIRAL.KCY CLR.

FRD6.KCY. GRBL. RPT.

Detachment A to CINCPAC Radio. Your last transmission was received garbled. Please repeat it.

KCY.FD6. FOLLOWING FOR COMMANDING OFFICER. PASS TO ALL HANDS. WELL DONE. NIMITZ. ADMIRAL.KCY CLR.

"I'll be goddamned," Sergeant Koffler said, and sent: FRD.6.KCY.CLR.

"Ian!" he called to the now completely sweat-soaked man pumping the generator. When he had his attention, he made a cutting motion across his throat.

"About fucking time!" Ian Bruce replied.

Steve handed the sheet of paper to Joe Howard.

"You think that's for real?" he asked.

"I can't imagine CINCPAC Radio fucking around," Howard said, seriously. "I'll be damned."

"What was the long code?" Steve asked.

Howard handed it to him.

Deeply regret am unable to relieve or reinforce at this time. Cannot overstate importance of what you are doing. Hang in there. Semper Fi. Banning.

"That's all there was?" Koffler asked.

"That's not enough?" Howard asked.

"You know what I meant," Koffler said. "I thought he was sending the goddamned Bible."

"That was all, Steve."

"Are we going to get out of here?"

"Until we got that 'Well Done' from the Commander-in-Chief Pacific, I thought so," Howard said. But when he saw the look on Koffler's face, he quickly added, "Just kidding, for Christ's sake."

"I was thinking of Daphne this morning," Koffler said. "I can't remember what she looks like. Ain't that a bitch?"

"When you see her, you'll know who she is," Howard said seriously. "Let's go get something to eat."

(FOUR)
Headquarters MAG-21
Henderson Field
Guadalcanal, Solomon Islands
1215 Hours 24 August 1942

First Lieutenant Henry P. Steadman, USMC, reminded Lieutenant Colonel Clyde W. Dawkins, USMC, Commanding, Marine Air Group 21, of First Lieutenant David F. Schneider, USMC. Like Lieutenant Schneider, Steadman was a graduate of the United States Naval Academy and a brand-new replacement from the States; and the similarity did not please him.

When he saw Steadman with apparently nothing to do sitting on a folding chair just outside the sandbagged frame building which was serving as his headquarters, Lieutenant Colonel Dawkins ordered, "Steadman, pass the word to the pilots there'll be a briefing in ten minutes, will you?"

Lieutenant Steadman rose to his feet, looked baffled, and inquired, "The enlisted men, too, Sir?"

Dawkins's temper escaped.

"No, *of course* not," he said, with withering sarcasm. "I certainly have *no* intention of letting any of *my* flying *sergeants* in on *officer type* secrets like who and where we are going to fight."

Steadman's face colored.

"Sorry, Sir."

"You stupid little sonofabitch," Dawkins went on, his anger not a whit diminished, "if you don't know it yet, I'll spell it out for you: There's not a flying sergeant around here who can't fly rings around you. I would cheerfully trade two of your kind for one flying sergeant. You better write that on your goddamned forehead, I don't want you to forget it."

"Yes, Sir. I mean, No, Sir. I won't forget that, Sir."

"Go!" Dawkins ordered, extending a pointed finger at arm's length.

Lieutenant Steadman took off at a trot.

I really shouldn't have blown my cork that way, Dawkins thought, but then reconsidered: *That arrogant little asshole needed that. It just may keep him alive through the next couple of days.*

Ten minutes later, the pilots of MAG-21 were gathered in the tent that served as the briefing room. Three of the four sides had been rolled up, leaving only one narrow end wall behind the area that in a theater would have been the stage. Here, a bed removed from an otherwise destroyed Japanese Ford truck had been set up as a very rudimentary platform. It faced rows of simple plank benches. On the platform was a tripod made of two-by-fours. The tripod held several maps, now covered by a sheet of oilcloth.

Dawkins stepped into view from behind the canvas wall and made the slight jump onto the "stage."

"Ten-HUT!"

That was Galloway, Dawkins thought. For one thing, the command sounded like it came from a Marine, not from a recent graduate of the University of Michigan Naval ROTC program. And for another, a million years before the war, back when he was Technical Sergeant Galloway of VMF-211, Galloway had always taken pride in being the first to spot the commanding officer and issue the command that brought everybody to their feet and to attention.

Out of the corner of his eye, he spotted Galloway at the rear of the tent, standing beside Lieutenant Bill Dunn and Captain Dale Brannon, U.S. Army Air Corps.

Brannon commanded the somewhat grandiosely named 67th Pursuit Squadron, which had arrived at Henderson 21 August. Brannon's group, more or less informally, was put under MAG-21's command. It had only five airplanes, Bell P-400s. In Dawkins's opinion the P-400 was only marginally superior to the F2A-3 Buffalo, which was arguably the worst plane either side sent into combat in the Pacific.

Dawkins felt sorry for Brannon and his pilots; they would be going into combat almost literally with one hand tied behind them. Not only was the P-400 inferior to the Zero, but Dawkins had just learned that the oxygen system installed on the P-400s when they were supposed to go to the English could not be serviced by the equipment on Guadalcanal. That would limit them in altitude to maybe 12–13,000 feet. The book said that oxygen should be used over 10,000. The only hope Brannon and his pilots would have was in their superior armament (superior to the F4F, anyway): In addition to six .50 caliber Browning machine guns, the P-400s had a 20mm cannon, which fired through the propellor hub.

A hit with an explosive 20mm projectile was far more lethal than, say, ten hits with a .50 caliber solid nose or tracer bullet.

Dawkins was not surprised, somehow, when he noticed that Brannon and Galloway had taken up with each other.

All the pilots, Marine and Army, were dressed in gray tropical areas Naval aviator flying suits and boondockers. Dawkins would not have been surprised, either, to learn that the Army pilots' flight suits had come to them via Charley Galloway's VMF-229. Just before they left Ewa, a highly excited Navy supply officer at Pearl Harbor appeared, trying to locate a barrel-chested, bald-headed Marine Technical Sergeant who had been drawing supplies—including leather jackets and flight suits—with requisitions that turned out to be fraudulent. Dawkins told him he couldn't call to mind, offhand, if he had a barrel-chested, bald-headed Technical Sergeant or not. But if one turned up, he promised to let the Navy supply officer know right away.

Although there were some .38 Special caliber revolvers around, Galloway and Dunn and most of the others had Model 1911A1 Colt autoloaders in shoulder holsters.

Captain Brannon and his officers were all wearing battered leather-brimmed caps, from which the crown forms had been removed, ostensibly so that earphones could be worn over them. Dawkins recognized them for what they really were. They were pilots' hats, so that no one could mistake their wearers for some pedestrian soldier. Dawkins thought it was a classy idea—though he would not have shared this opinion with Brannon.

Galloway had a utility cap at least four sizes too small for him perched on top of his head. He had pinned to it his gold Naval aviator's wings and his railroad tracks. Dunn and most of the others wore khaki fore-and-aft caps, carrying the Marine insignia and the insignia of their rank.

I wonder what's going to happen to Dunn today? He's going out as Charley's exec, not as just one more airplane driver.

"Take your seats," Dawkins ordered. "Good afternoon, gentlemen."

There was a chorus of "Good afternoon, Sir," from the pilots, as they settled onto the plank benches.

"I am sorry to have to tell you that Captain Frankel is not available. Word has reached me that he was out carousing all night, and will not be sober until much later this afternoon. Consequently, I will handle this part of the briefing," Dawkins announced, straight-faced.

There was another chorus, this time of chuckles. There was, of course, no place to carouse; and even if there were, Captain Tony Frankel, MAG-21's S-2, was an absolute teetotal, and everybody knew it. And most of the pilots knew that Frankel had caught some kind of bug and had a spectacular case of the running shits. The scuttlebutt was that the Doc said he didn't know what it was, although he didn't think it was dysentery. Whatever it was, the Doc had grounded him.

Dawkins grabbed the oilcloth covering the maps and threw it over the back of the tripod.

A map showing the area from New Britain in the North to San Cristobal island, southwest of Guadalcanal, was now visible.

"For those of you who may have been wondering where the U.S. Navy is . . ." Dawkins began, and waited for the laughter to subside, "I have it on pretty reliable authority that as of midnight last night, Task Force 61 was in this area, about 150 miles east of here."

He used a pointer to show where he meant; it was made of a shortened pool cue, to which was fixed a .30'06 cartridge case and bullet.

"Task Force 61 consists of three smaller forces, each grouped around a carrier. *Saratoga* is out there, and *Enterprise*. *Wasp* and her support ships left the area yesterday so she could refuel; no estimate on when she will return.

"And we had, as of 2400 last night, *precisely* located the Japanese Navy as being *right* here," Dawkins said and waved the pointer over the map from New Britain to San Cristobal. His pilots correctly interpreted the move to mean that as of 2400 no one had any idea where the Japanese were.

More chuckles.

"At 0910 this morning," Dawkins went on, and his changed tone of voice indicated that the witty opening remarks were now concluded, and this was business, "a Catalina found the aircraft carrier *Ryujo* and its support vessels right about here.

Just to the right—ten, fifteen miles—there's a transport force. Intelligence thinks it is safe to assume that the transports carry troops to be landed on Guadalcanal.''

The tent was now dead quiet.

''At 1030 this morning, F4Fs operating off *Sara* shot down an Emily here. The *Saratoga* was then twenty miles away, which means the Emily got pretty close before they found it.

''About an hour ago, another Catalina found the *Ryujo* again, still on a course that would bring her to Guadalcanal. Nobody's said anything, but you don't have to be Admiral Nimitz to guess that *Enterprise* has mounted a rather extensive search operation, so as not to lose *Ryujo*. It's just as clear that *Sara* is preparing a strike. Or vice versa, with *Sara* looking and *Enterprise* preparing to launch an attack.

''We also have word that at about half past ten the Japs sent a hell of a lot of airplanes, about a hundred of them, down this way from Rabaul. The word comes from what CINCPAC chooses to call an Intell Source One. That means they think the poop is the straight stuff. *I* think it probably comes from the people the Australians left behind when the Japs occupied the islands between here and New Britain/New Ireland.''

Dawkins paused until the murmur died down, and then went on: ''About forty Zeroes escorting thirty Vals, ten Bettys, and fifteen Kates. Now, the odds are that their scouts are going to find *Sara* or *Enterprise,* or both, in which case I think we can presume that a good many of them will divert to make their attack. But some of them, maybe even most of them, will continue on to hit us. It's also just possible that they may *not* find either of our carriers. In that case, they will *all* come here, probably with all the aircraft *Ryujo* can launch coming with them.

''The best guess we can make of their ETA here is a few minutes after two. It's now,'' he paused to look at his watch, ''1225. At 1300 we're going to start launching the SBDs as our scouts, in thirty-five minutes in other words. At 1330, we will start launching the fighters. First, VMF-211. And at 1345, VMF-229.

''If things go as scheduled—and they rarely do—at 1400 the SBDs should be at altitude here,'' he pointed again, ''in a position to spot either the planes from *Ryujo* or the planes from Rabaul, or both. VMF-211's F4Fs should be about here, just about at the assigned altitude. And Captain Galloway and his people should be about here, *almost* at assigned altitude.

''We've been over this in some detail, so I'll just touch the highpoints: When the SBDs *positively* locate the stream of attacking aircraft, or when it is *positively* located by aircraft from *Lexington* and/or *Sara,* they will start to look for the *Ryujo,* fuel permitting. Fuel permitting is the key phrase. I don't want to lose any aircraft because they ran out of go-juice. When the SBDs *start* to run low on fuel, they *will* return here to refuel. I don't want any stupid heroics out there. I think I can guarantee there will be ample opportunity for the SBDs to take on an aircraft carrier, or carriers. It doesn't have to be this afternoon. Unless, of course, our estimates are way off, and you find them sooner than we think you will and can attack and still have enough fuel to get home safely.

''The mission of the fighters is right out of the book. They will locate, engage, and destroy the enemy. And they will do that in the knowledge that if they run out of fuel doing so, a scorned woman's fury can't hold a candle to that of your friendly commanding officer.''

There was a murmur of chuckles.

''And something you haven't heard before: Stay off the radio unless you have something to say.''

More chuckles.

''No damned idle chatter,'' Dawkins went on firmly. ''When this thing starts, all

I want to hear on the radio is business. I want a word with the squadron commanders and the execs. The rest of you may go.''

"Ten-HUT!" somebody bellowed. Dawkins was surprised. He was looking at Charley Galloway, and Galloway didn't even have his mouth open when the command came.

Colonel Dawkins jumped off the truck bed, walked behind the tent wall to wait for his squadron commanders and their executive officers.

(FIVE)
Headquarters MAG-21
Henderson Field
Guadalcanal, Solomon Islands
1715 Hours 24 August 1942

Lieutenant Colonel Clyde W. Dawkins had decided early on that squadron commanders, and certainly air group commanders, really had no business being present when individual pilots were being debriefed by intelligence officers. With The Skipper standing there, pilots would be far less prone to tell the truth, the whole truth, and nothing but the truth, than if they were talking alone, and more or less in confidence, to the debriefing officer.

He decided that the debriefing of First Lieutenant William C. Dunn, USMCR, however, was going to be the exception to this rule. He sent word that when Dunn was to be debriefed, he wanted to be there.

The debriefings were conducted on the bed taken from the Japanese Ford truck. The debriefing officer had set up a folding wooden table in front of the map tripod Dawkins had used in the pre-flight briefing. He sat behind the table. As the pilots came in, one by one, to be debriefed, he waved them into another folding chair in front of his "desk."

Knowing the setup, Dawkins came into the tent carrying his own chair, a comfortable, cushioned, bentwood affair left behind by some departed Japanese officer.

He came around the tent wall as Dunn entered the tent from the other, open, end.

Dunn looked beat. He was hatless. His flight suit had large damp patches around the armpits and on the chest. When he came closer, Dawkins saw that his face was dirty; and, although Dunn had obviously made a half-assed attempt to wash, the outline of his goggles was clearly evident on his face.

Dawkins, smiling, made a gesture to Dunn to come onto the platform. And then he sat down, backwards, on his Japanese chair, resting his arms on the back.

Dunn eyed the debriefing officer suspiciously.

"Sir, where's Captain Frankel?" he asked.

When he was tired, Dawkins had noticed, Dunn's Southern accent became more pronounced. That had come out, "Suh, Whea-uh is Cap'n Frank-kel?"

"He's got the GIs, Bill," Dawkins said. "You know that."

"Don't I know you, Lieutenant?" Dunn asked, but it was more of a challenge than a question.

"Yes," the debriefing officer said. "I debriefed you after Midway."

"I thought I recognized you. I didn't like you then, and I don't like you now. Colonel, do I have to talk to this sonofabitch?"

Ah thought ah recog-nazed you. Ah didn't lak you then an ah don' lak you now. Cunnel, do ah have to talk to this som'bitch?

"With Frankel down with the GIs, I borrowed him to do the debriefing. It has to be done. You don't have to like him, Bill," Dawkins said calmly, "but you do have to answer his questions. Sit down!"

Dunn looked at him with contempt in his eyes, as if he had been betrayed.

"Sit down, Bill," Dawkins ordered again, calmly.

Dunn met Dawkins's eyes for a moment, and then shrugged and sat down.

"Before we begin, Lieutenant Dunn," the debriefing officer said, "I'd like to say this: If there ever were any questions raised at Midway about your personal behavior, your courage, to put a point on it, your behavior today has put them to rest for all time."

"Jesus!" Dawkins snorted.

"My report will indicate," the debriefing officer plunged ahead, a little confused by Dawkins's snort, "that you shot down four aircraft today, two Zeroes, and one each Betty and Val; that all kills were verified by at least two witnesses. That places you, Lieutenant, one aircraft over the five required to make you an ace. I would be very surprised if you were not given a decoration for greater valor in action, and it probably means a promotion."

"Fuck you," Bill Dunn said very clearly. "Stick your medal and your promotion up your ass."

"That's enough, Bill," Dawkins said. There was steel in his voice. Their eyes locked for a long moment.

"Yes, Sir," Dunn said, finally.

"Get on with it, Lieutenant," Dawkins ordered the debriefing officer.

"Well, as they say," the debriefing officer said, "let's take it from the top. In your own words, from take-off until landing. When I have a question, I'll interrupt? OK?"

"Every other pilot who made it back has been in here. How many times do you have to hear the same story?"

"Bill, goddamnit, do what he says," Dawkins ordered.

"You took off at approximately 1420, is that correct?" the debriefing officer began.

"Yeah."

"Was that the originally scheduled take-off time?"

"No," Dunn said, "we were supposed to take off earlier, at 1345, but the Colonel changed his mind, and held us on the ground. The SBDs hadn't found the Japs, and he wanted to conserve fuel. We took off when the goddamned radar finally found the Japs."

"Was the take-off according to plan? And if not, why not?"

"No. When the scramble order came, everybody tried to get into the air as quickly as possible. The Japs were just about over the field; there was no time to screw around waiting for the slow ones."

"And was the form-up in the air according to plan? And if not, why, in your opinion?"

"No. And I just told you. The Japs were over Henderson. It would have made absolutely no sense to try to form up as the schedule called for. And some airplanes are faster than others. Mine was faster than most."

"So, in your own words, tell me what happened to you after you took off."

"I guess I was eighth, ninth, tenth, something like that, to get off the ground . . ."

"Do you remember who was first?" the debriefing officer interrupted.

"Captain Galloway and his wing man, Lieutenant Ward. When the Black Flag went up, they were sitting in their aircraft with their engines already warmed up. They were moving within seconds."

"By the Black Flag, I presume you mean the Black Flag raised above the control tower signifying 'Condition I, Airbase under attack.'"

"Is there another black flag?"

"And once you were in the air, what did you do?"

"I started the climb," Dunn said. "Alone. I had been in the climb two, three minutes when I saw Lieutenant Schneider forming on my wing."

"That would be Lieutenant David F. Schneider?"

"Yes."

"Go on."

"Well, we finally got to 10,000 feet. By that time the bombers, the Bettys, had dropped their bombs, and were headed home."

"And how high would you estimate the Bettys were?"

"They were at nine thousand feet, I guess, and they were in a shallow dive, apparently to gain speed."

"There were no other enemy aircraft in sight?"

"There were Zeroes to the right," Dunn said. "They had seen us and were trying to keep us away from the Bettys. Captain Galloway and Ward headed for the Zeroes. I headed for the Bettys."

"Why?"

"Because it was pretty clear to me that was what Captain Galloway wanted me to do. He would take care of the fighters while I attacked the Bettys."

"Where was Lieutenant Schneider?"

"Shit. While *we* attacked the Bettys. He was on my wing. I told you that."

"And you did, in fact, attack the Bettys successfully. I have been told that you attacked from above . . ."

"Yeah."

"And that your stream of fire caused an explosion in the engine nacelle . . ."

"The one Schneider got, he took the vertical stabilizer off. Then it blew up."

"We were talking about yours."

"I got the engine. Schneider got the vertical stabilizer on his and then probably the main tank."

"Right. I have that. And then what happened?"

"Then the Zeroes showed up. Some of them apparently stayed to deal with Captain Galloway and Ward, but most of them tried to protect the bombers, and came to where we were."

"And then what happened?"

"I don't know. We got into it."

"Witnesses to the engagement have stated that during that engagement, you shot down two Zeroes. And you don't know what happened?"

"We were all over the sky. The only thing I know for sure is that Schneider got one, beautiful deflection shot, and he blew up."

"I thought you said Schneider was on your wing."

"I also said we were all over the sky. I don't know where Schneider was most of the time, except when I saw him take the Zero with the deflection shot."

"But you do remember shooting at at least two Zeroes?"

"I shot at a lot more than two. I'm sure I hit some of them, but I couldn't swear to anything but that I hit one good and he started to throw smoke and went into a spin."

"You did not see him crash?"

"No."

"Did you see Captain Galloway crash?"

"No. I saw Captain Galloway on fire and in a spin, but I did not see him crash."

"Was that before or after you shot the Zero you just mentioned, the one you said began to display smoke and entered a spin?"

"Before."

"Did you see Lieutenant Ward during this period?"

"I don't know. I saw a plane that could have been either him or Captain Galloway. I can't say for sure. They both came to help us when the Zeroes came after us."

"But you are sure that it was Captain Galloway you saw, in flames, and in a spin?"

"Yes."

"How can you be sure?"

"I'm sure, goddamn you. Take my word for it."

"Tell me about the Val," the debriefing officer said.

"He was a cripple," Dunn said. "I saw him down on the deck as I was coming home."

"Let's get into that. Why did you disengage?"

"My engine had been running on Emergency Military Power too long. I was losing oil pressure. My cylinder head temperature needle was on the peg. And I had lost fuel. A fuel line fitting had ruptured. I didn't know that. All I knew was the LOW FUEL light came on. Two of my guns had either jammed or were out of ammunition. So I started home."

"But you saw the Val and attacked it?"

"Why not?"

"Was attacking the Val wise, Bill?" Dawkins asked. It was the first time he had spoken.

"I was a little pissed at the time," Dunn said.

"Because of Captain Galloway?" Dawkins asked.

"He was one hell of a Marine, Colonel," Dunn said, and Dawkins saw tears forming in his eyes.

"Getting back to Captain Galloway," the debriefing officer said. "At the time Captain Galloway was reported hit, it has been reported that he had engaged a Zero and seriously damaged it. Did you see any of that?"

"Yeah," Dunn said. Dawkins saw that he was having trouble getting the lump out of his throat. Finally he cleared his throat. His voice was still unnatural.

"I am sure beyond any reasonable doubt that the Zero Captain Galloway was engaging the last time anybody saw him was in flames, missing his left horizontal stabilizer, out of control, and a sure kill."

"Very well, we'll put that down as 'confirmed.'"

"Thank you ever so much," Dunn said sarcastically.

"That makes it three and a half for Captain Galloway and two and a half for Lieutenant Ward, right?" Dawkins asked.

"Yes, Sir," the intelligence officer replied.

"What was the total, Sir?" Dunn asked. "Not, now that I think about it, that I give a flying fuck."

"Eleven this morning," Dawkins said. "And seven this afternoon. That makes eighteen. I think that's probably the most aircraft ever destroyed in a twenty-four hour period by any squadron—Marine, Navy, or Air Corps."

"We get a gold star to take home to Mommy?"

Dawkins ignored him.

"We lost five. Captain Galloway, of course."

"Of course."

"Close your mouth, Dunn," Dawkins snapped, and then went on. "Galloway, missing and presumed dead. Jiggs. We know he's dead. Hawthorne, ditto. Ward, pretty well banged up on landing. And Schneider, wounds of the legs and a broken ankle. Six aircraft lost or seriously damaged. That's not a bad score, Lieutenant."

"It didn't come cheap," Dunn said, "did it?"

"I don't want to wave the flag in your face, Dunn, but don't you think Charley went out the way he would have wanted to?"

"Charley didn't want to go out at all," Dunn said. He stood up. "I'm going to the hospital to see Jim Ward and Schneider," he said.

"I spoke to Ward," Dawkins said. "He asked me if it would be all right with you if he wrote his aunt and told her what happened to Charley. Charley apparently had her listed as 'friend, no next of kin.' I told him I thought you would be grateful."

"Yeah, sure," Dunn said.

"The other letters, you're going to have to write yourself, Bill. In my experience, it's best to do it right away. It doesn't get any easier by putting it off."

It took a moment for Dunn to take Dawkins's meaning. It is the function of the squadron commander to write letters of condolence to the next of kin of officers who have been killed. In accordance with regulations, Lieutenant William C. Dunn had acceded to the command of VMF-229 when the previous commander had been declared missing and presumed killed in action.

"As soon as I see the guys in the hospital, Sir," Dunn said. "I'll get on it."

"We're not through here, Lieutenant," the intelligence officer said.

"Yes, you are," Dawkins said. "Go ahead, Bill."

(SIX)
160 Degrees 05 Minutes 01 Seconds East Longitude
09 Degrees 50 Minutes 14 Seconds South Latitude
1820 Hours 24 August 1942

Captain Charles M. Galloway, USMCR, had a pretty good idea that he was going to die before the sun, now setting, rose again. It could come violently, and soon . . . in minutes. Or more slowly . . . he might last the night.

He could think of two possible violent deaths. The most probable, and the most frightening, was from a shark attack.

At the moment he was floating somewhere in the Southwest Pacific. God knows where. It was a circumstance that flung the thought of sharks right out there in the forefront of his mind.

He remembered hearing somewhere a peculiar theory about shark attacks. Peculiar or not, at the moment he took some small comfort from it. This theory held that when a shark bites something—or in this case, someone—it considers to be dinner, the force of the bite is so violent that the person bitten doesn't feel any pain.

The shark bite was somewhat analogous to a gunshot wound. When you're shot, the pain comes later, after the shock has passed. When a shark bites, according to the theory, there'd be no pain at all: a shark would tear away so much flesh—the powerful jaws of a shark could tear away half a leg, or so he had been told—that you passed out from loss of blood before the shock went away and the pain came.

The other sudden, violent death he could think of would be self-induced. He still had his .45 automatic. It had been underwater since he had gone into the drink, of course, but he thought it would still fire. After all, he reasoned, ammunition was designed to resist the effects of water. The cartridge case was tightly crimped against the bullet, and the primer was coated with shellac.

Although they were badly puckered and a dead-fish white, his fingers still functioned. He was reasonably sure he could get the .45 out of its holster, work the action, put the barrel against his temple or into his mouth, and then pull the trigger and see what came next.

It wasn't an idea that attracted him very much, even under the circumstances. In fact, the idea was repugnant. It literally made him shiver. When he was a young marine, for reasons that were never made clear, an old staff sergeant blew his brains all over the wash basins in a head at Quantico. The memory was bright in Charley's mind; he didn't want to go out that way, even if logic told him there wasn't much difference between a shattered head and having half your abdomen ripped off by a shark.

Given the imminent certainty of his death, he thought, it would have been better if he had been killed in the air. That almost happened. Now that he had time to go over it in his mind, he was more than a little surprised that it didn't:

He saw a Zero, a thousand or so feet below him, on Bill Dunn's tail. Bill was firing at a Val and didn't see him. Charley put his Wildcat in a dive and went after the Zero, to get him off Bill's tail.

He got him, almost certainly a sure kill. But as he started to climb out again, another sonofabitch came out of nowhere. Before he knew that anyone was anywhere near him, it was all over.

Parts of the engine nacelle suddenly flew off; a moment later, the engine stopped. Probably 20mms, hitting and shattering jugs, and freezing the engine.

Because he was in a climb when the power stopped, he decelerated rapidly. Moments later, the expected shudder announced a stall. And a moment after that, yellow flames came from the engine.

The nose went down, and the Wildcat began an erratic spin to the right. He reacted automatically. First, he shut off the fuel selector valve. There were probably shattered lines, but it probably wouldn't hurt. Then he pushed the stick full forward— the priority was to pick up airspeed and restore lift—and applied full left rudder.

He didn't remember how many turns he made—five, anyway, probably six—but getting out of the spin took a long time. By then he had a chance to look at the instrument panel. Most of the gauges were inoperative, and there were bulges and tears in the control panel itself, telling him that either explosive rounds had gone off behind it, or that the 20mms that killed the engine had sent shrapnel and/or engine parts into the back of the panel.

He had no doubt that it was time to get out of the Wildcat.

He held the stick between his knees, so that he could pull both of the canopy jettison rings simultaneously. If you didn't do that, the canopy might well jam on the remaining pin, trapping you in the cockpit; or else it might drag off into the airstream and hang there like an air brake, making control difficult or impossible.

The canopy blew off without trouble. All he had to do after that was unfasten his seat and shoulder harness, and climb out.

That turned out to be harder than he thought it would. He'd been a pilot for a long time, but he was still surprised at the force of the slip stream when he lifted his head and shoulders above the windscreen.

He went over the left side, bounced on the wing, then fell free. He watched the tail assembly flash over his head, alarmingly close, and then he pulled the D-Ring.

A moment after that, there was a dull flapping, thudding noise, and then a hell of a jolt as the canopy filled with air and suddenly slowed his descent.

For a while there was still some horizontal movement. When he bailed out, he was probably making right about a hundred knots. So when it opened, the parachute had to stop the forward motion before it started to lower him to the water.

He swung like a pendulum for maybe twenty seconds under the parachute, and then he looked down and saw the water. For a moment, it looked very far away, but the next it rushed up at him with alarming speed. Then he went in.

He remembered, at the last possible instant, to close his mouth. He even tried to get his hand up to hold his nose, but there wasn't time.

All of a sudden, he was in the water. It was like hitting hard sand. It wasn't at all cushiony, like water is supposed to be.

He remembered to get out of the parachute harness as quickly as he could. He worked the quick-disconnect mechanism and made sure he was free of the straps before swimming to the surface.

If you got tangled in the parachute harness, the shroud lines, or the parachute canopy itself, you could drown.

When he was on the surface, and sure that he was away from the parachute, which was floating on the surface of the water, he fired the CO_2 cartridge and inflated his life vest.

The sea moved in large, gentle swells. Nothing at all was in sight, not even aircraft in the distance. Using his hands, he turned himself around. He could see no land on the horizon. He was therefore at least seven or eight miles from any land—and probably a hell of a lot farther than that. In any event, he was too far away to try to swim anywhere, even if he knew where he should go; and he didn't.

He never felt so alone in his life.

He told himself they would probably look for him, either airplanes from his squadron, or Catalinas, or maybe even with Navy ships. But then he told himself that was wishful thinking.

If anyone watched him go down, they would have seen he was in bad trouble, and they'd probably figure he died in the crash.

He was in the water about an hour when the wind picked up and started making whitecaps. That seemed to put the cork in the bottle. He was a tiny little speck floating around in the great big ocean. It was difficult, but possible, for someone to spot the brilliant yellow life preserver against a calm blue sea; there was no chance anyone—from four, five thousand feet—could make out a couple of square feet of yellow among the whitecaps.

When darkness fell, Charley told himself that with a little bit of luck, he would be asleep when the shark—sharks—struck. That would be a better way to go than putting the .45 in his mouth, or of being sunburned to death when the sun came up again in the morning. He was already desperately thirsty, and that could only get worse, not better.

He went to sleep thinking of Caroline. They were in the marble-walled shower of the Andrew Foster Hotel in San Francisco, with the water running down from the multiple shower heads over them.

(SEVEN)
USN Patrol Torpedo Boat 110
160 Degrees 05 Minutes 02 Seconds East Longitude
09 Degrees 50 Minutes 14 Seconds South Latitude
0505 Hours 25 August 1942

At 0400, Ensign Keith M. Strawbridge, USNR (Princeton, '40), relieved PT 110's skipper, Lieutenant (j.g.) Simmons F. Hawley III, USNR (Yale '40); but Hawley elected to remain on the bridge.

Ensign Strawbridge wasn't sure whether Lieutenant Hawley was staying because there was no sense trying to go below and get some sleep; or because he didn't really trust him to assume command of the boat; or whether—despite the heat, it was a pleasant night, reminding both of them of sailing off Bermuda—he just decided to stay for the pure pleasure of it.

After all, he was the captain. PT 110 was, in the law, a man of war of the United

States Navy; and Sim Hawley was therefore invested with the same prerogatives of command as the captain of the Aircraft Carrier USS *Saratoga.*

If he wanted to stay on the fucking bridge of his man of war and play his fucking harmonica, there was no one to say him nay.

Having just asked his executive officer if he thought bathing the harmonica in fresh water would be a good idea, to combat the rust from the salt spray, Captain Hawley was startled and somewhat annoyed by a report from Motor Machinist's Mate 3rd Class James H. Granzichek (Des Plaines, Ill. Senior High '41).

"Hey, Mr. Hawley," he called. "Check out whatever the fuck that is on the left. The yellow thing."

Hawley did not like being addressed as "Hey, Mr. Hawley." He preferred to be referred to as "Captain," but thought it would be rather bad form to suggest it, much less order it. He also could not see where it was necessary for the men to use "fuck" every time the proper word did not immediately come to mind. And there was a proper Naval term for "on the left." Granzichek should have said, "to starboard." Or was it, "to port"?

But he looked for the yellow thing. First with his naked eyes, and then, when that didn't work, through his binoculars. The boat was shaking so much he couldn't hold the binoculars still.

"All engines stop," he ordered.

MMM3 Granzichek hauled back on the throttles that controlled the twin Packard engines of PT 110. She slowed, and then began to move side to side in the swells. This action tended to make Ensign Strawbridge feel a bit queasy, but it permitted Captain Hawley to see through his binoculars.

"Good God," he exclaimed. "It's a man in a life jacket."

"No shit?" MMM3 Granzichek asked, reaching for the binoculars. A moment later, he reported, "I think he's dead. He's not moving or waving or anything."

"May I have a look now, please?" Ensign Strawbridge asked, a trifle petulantly. Granzichek handed him the binoculars.

"How would you say, Granzichek," Captain Hawley asked, "would be the best way to take him on board?"

Granzichek, Captain Hawley reasoned, had been aboard PT 110 for three and a half months. He himself had assumed command only last Monday. Experience tells.

"Pull up alongside him, catch him with a boat hook, and then get a line on him," Granzichek said.

"Very well, then let's have a go at it," Captain Hawley ordered.

URGENT
CONFIDENTIAL
FROM PTSQUADRON-30
TO COMMANDING OFFICER
VMF-229
VIA CINCPAC
1. PT 110 OF THIS SQUADRON RECOVERED AT SEA AT 0530 THIS MORNING CAPTAIN CHARLES M. GALLOWAY, USMCR.
2. CAPTAIN GALLOWAY IS SUFFERING FROM EXPOSURE AND DEHYDRATION BUT IS OTHERWISE IN GOOD HEALTH. HE HAS BEEN TRANSFERRED TO HOSPITAL SHIP USS CONSOLATION, WHO WILL ADVISE YOU OF ARRANGEMENTS TO RETURN HIM TO DUTY.
BY DIRECTION:
J.B. SUMERS, LTCOM USNR

LINE OF FIRE

I

In the early months of 1942, a Major of the U.S. Army Ordnance Corps in Australia was forced to reconsider his long-held belief that he'd passed the point where the Army could surprise him.

The Pacific & Far East Shipping Corporation's freighter *John J. Rogers Jr.* docked at Melbourne after a long and perilous voyage from Bremerton, Washington. In addition to desperately needed war matériel, it off-loaded 800 identical, sturdy wooden crates. Each of these was roughly three feet by three feet by four feet, weighed 320 pounds, and was strapped with steel, waterproofed, and otherwise prepared for a long sea voyage.

These crates were loaded aboard trucks and taken to the U.S. Army Melbourne Area Ordnance Depot, a requisitioned warehouse area on the outskirts of the city. Because they were in waterproof packaging and inside storage space was at a premium (and because the Ordnance Corps Major could not believe the shipping manifest), the crates were placed on pallets—each holding four of the crates—and stored outside under canvas tarpaulins.

It was two weeks before the Ordnance Corps Major could find time to locate the shipment, remove the tarpaulin, cut the metal strapping, pry open the crates, then tear off the heavy tar-paper wrapping.

He found (as the manifest said, and indeed as was neatly stenciled onto the crates in inch-high letters) that each of the crates did indeed contain US SABERS, CAVALRY MODEL OF 1912, w/SCABBARDS, 25 EACH.

The sabers and their scabbards were packed five to a layer, and each crate held five layers. It took him a moment to do the arithmetic:

If he had 800 crates, and there were twenty-five cavalry sabers, with scabbards, in each crate, that meant he had 20,000 cavalry sabers, with scabbards. They all looked new; they had probably never been issued. The Ordnance Major was aware that the last horse-cavalry unit in the U.S. Army, the 26th, had been dismounted in the Philippines; their mounts were converted to rations for the starving troops on Bataan; and the cavalrymen went off to fight their last battle as infantrymen.

On the face of it, cavalry sabers were as useless in modern warfare as teats on a boar hog. A lesser man than the Ordnance Corps Major would have simply pulled the tarpaulin back in place and tried to forget both the US SABERS, CAVALRY MODEL OF 1912, w/SCABBARDS and the goddamned moron who used up that valuable-as-gold shipping space sending them all the way to Australia.

But the Ordnance Major was not such a man.

He gave a good deal of thought to how he could make them useful, yet the best he could come up with was to convert them to some kind of fighting knives, perhaps like the trench knives of World War I. On investigation, however, this proved to be impractical. The blades were too heavy and the hilts too awkward.

He'd just about concluded that the sturdy crates the goddamned sabers were packed in had more potential use to the war effort than the sabers, when he had another idea. This one seemed to make sense.

And so a contract was issued to an Australian firm (before the war it had made automobile and truck bumpers) to convert the sabers into Substitute Standard machetes—at a cost of U.S. $2.75 each. The blades were cut down to sixteen inches and portions of the hilts were ground off. The scabbards, meanwhile, were run through a stamping press. In one operation the press cut the scabbard to size and sealed its end.

And so when First Lieutenant Joseph L. Howard, USMCR, Commanding Officer of Detachment A, USMC Special Detachment 14, decided he needed a dozen machetes for a military operation, he was given MACHETES, SUBSTITUTE STANDARD, w/SHEATHS which had begun their military careers as US SABERS, CAVALRY MODEL OF 1912, w/SCABBARDS.

Actually, he got more than a dozen. Lieutenant Howard had had previous experience with the U.S. Army Ordnance Corps (as a sergeant), and he'd learned then that he was lucky to get half—or a quarter—of what he'd requested.

This request proved an exception to that rule. He requisitioned one hundred machetes, and he got one hundred MACHETES, SUBSTITUTE STANDARD, w/ SHEATHS.

The mission Lieutenant Howard drew the machetes for involved a parachute drop of both personnel and equipment. Since there were no specially designed cargo containers, or parachutes, available for the equipment (most importantly, shortwave radios), ordinary personnel parachutes had to be adapted.

Cushioning the radios against the shock of landing was rather simply accomplished by wrapping them securely in mattresses.

But that wasn't the only problem. The standard personnel parachute was designed for a standard soldier carrying normal equipment—that is to say, it could handle a "drop weight" of 200 to 225 pounds. The mattress-wrapped shortwave radios weighed approximately 110 pounds.

Since lightly loaded parachutes fall more slowly than heavier ones, and thus drift more, Howard's radios would not fall to earth anywhere near his personnel.

This was a matter of critical concern, because Lieutenant Howard intended to drop upon a small landing area in the mountains of Buka Island.

Approximately thirty miles long and no more than five miles wide, Buka is the northernmost island in the Solomons chain. That places it just north of the much larger Bougainville and 146 nautical miles from the Japanese base at Rabaul on New Britain.

On Buka, there was a Japanese fighter base and a garrison of Japanese troops variously estimated from several hundred to several thousand.

There was additionally a detachment of the Royal Australian Navy's Coastwatcher Establishment. This consisted of one officer, Sub-Lieutenant Jakob Reeves, RAN Volunteer Reserve, and approximately fifty Other Ranks, all of whom had been recruited from the native population.

Sub-Lieutenant Reeves remained behind when the Japanese occupied Buka; he was provided with a shortwave radio and a small quantity of arms and ammunition; and he was ordered to report on the movement of Japanese ships and aircraft from Rabaul, Bougainville, and of course from Buka.

From the beginning, these reports had been of enormous value for both tactical and planning purposes. But by June 1942, when Lieutenant Howard was preparing his drop, their importance had become even more critical: The United States planned to land on the island of Guadalcanal and to capture and make operational an airfield the Japanese were already building there. The invasion of Guadalcanal was not only the first Allied counterattack in the Pacific War, some considered it to be the campaign that could decide the outcome of the entire war in the Pacific.

Since there were no Allied air bases within fighter range of Guadalcanal, initial aviation support for the invasion of Guadalcanal would fly from aircraft carriers. But launching and recovering aircraft from carriers was a difficult, time-consuming operation, and aviation-fuel supplies were finite. These difficulties could be minimized, however, if the Navy could be informed when Japanese aircraft took off from Rabaul or other nearby bases and headed for the invasion area. That was the function of the Coastwatcher Station on Buka.

Unfortunately, Sub-Lieutenant Reeves' shortwave radio went off the air during the preparations for the invasion. The Coastwatcher Establishment saw two likely explanations for Reeves' absence: One, the radio itself had broken down (this was the most hopeful scenario). Or two (and much worse), the Japanese had captured Sub-Lieutenant Reeves.

An overflight of his location, conducted at great risk, returned with aerial photographs of a grassy field. The grass had been stamped down to form the letters RA, for radio. Sub-Lieutenant Reeves needed another radio. Good news, considering the alternative.

USMC Special Detachment 14, whose mission in Australia was to support the Coastwatcher Establishment, had a number of brand-new, state-of-the-art Hallicrafters communications radios; and it would be a fairly easy thing to air-drop one to Sub-Lieutenant Reeves. The problem was that Reeves' knowledge of radios was minimal. He almost certainly would not know how to set one up and get it operational. Thus, the planners decided to send someone to Buka who could handle such things.

Additionally, the planners felt it would be useful to have a second aircraft spotter on Buka. Not only could Sub-Lieutenant Reeves use the help, but there was the further question of what to do should he become *hors de combat* from either enemy action or tropical illness—more a certainty than a probability.

It was decided, consequently, to parachute a radio operator-technician into Buka with the radios. Sergeant Steven M. Koffler, USMC, was a parachutist as well as a radio operator-technician. Unfortunately, he couldn't tell the difference between a bomber and a scout plane, and there was no time to teach him. Neither did Sergeant Koffler have the tropical jungle survival skills he was sure to need.

On the other hand, though Lieutenant Howard was not a parachutist, he not only had the necessary survival skills, he had as a sergeant taught classes in identification of Japanese aircraft and warships. And so Howard volunteered to jump in with Sergeant Koffler and the replacement radios.

When faced with the question of ballast for the cargo parachutes (to bring their drop weight up to the norms for personnel parachutes), Lieutenant Howard suggested small arms and ammunition. For these were heavy, fairly indestructible, and valuable to Ferdinand Six—the radio call sign for Sub-Lieutenant Reeves' detachment.

But Lieutenant Commander Eric Feldt, Royal Australian Navy Volunteer Reserve, disagreed. Feldt, who was commanding officer of the Coastwatcher Establishment, pointed out that the mission of the Coastwatchers was not to fight the Japanese but to hide from them. Ferdinand was the bull who preferred to sniff flowers rather than fight, he reminded Lieutenant Howard and Major Edward F. Banning, USMC, the commanding officer of USMC Special Detachment 14.

A small quantity of small arms and ammunition should be dropped to replenish losses, he maintained. But what Howard and Koffler certainly needed were machetes. Machetes were not only useful for hacking through the jungle, they made effective— and *silent*—weapons.

Major Banning deferred to Commander Feldt's expertise. And the mattress-wrapped radios were ballasted primarily with MACHETES, SUBSTITUTE STANDARD. Their scabbards were left behind.

The airdrop on Buka went off more or less successfully. And Sub-Lieutenant Reeves was on the whole pleased to have what Feldt and Banning sent him. He was, as expected, delighted with his new radios. On the other hand, he entertained early doubts about the wisdom of dropping a pair of sodding Yanks in his sodding lap. He was not on Buka to nursemaid sodding children. One of them didn't even know enough about parachutes to keep from breaking his arm on landing.

The Other Ranks of Ferdinand Six, however, had no complaints about the drop, and they were especially overjoyed with the MACHETES, SUBSTITUTE STANDARD. Their own machetes were in short supply and worn out, while the new ones were high-quality steel of a more modern and doubtless better design. There were even enough of them to equip the women and the older boys with one. The men, as a general rule of thumb, went about with two.

(TWO)
Ferdinand Six
Buka, Solomon Islands
28 August 1942

The commanding officer of the U.S. Marine Garrison on Buka Island and the senior representative of His Britannic Majesty's government there—that is to say, Lieutenant Joe Howard and Sub-Lieutenant Jakob Reeves—elected to locate their command conference at a site where the subjects to be discussed and the decisions made relative thereto would not become immediately known to their respective commands.

They selected for this purpose the tree house, a platform built a hundred feet off the ground in an ancient enormous tree. Large enough for three or four people to stand or sit comfortably, the tree house was their primary observation post. Since it was normally manned from daybreak to dark, as soon as Sub-Lieutenant Reeves finished climbing up the knotted rope, he ordered the man on duty, Petty Officer Ian Bruce, Royal Australian Navy Native Volunteer Reserve, to go catch a nap.

Petty Officer Bruce was armed with a Lee-Enfield Mark I .303 rifle and two MACHETES, SUBSTITUTE STANDARD, and he was wearing a loincloth and what might be described as a canvas kilt. He was a dark-skinned man with a mass of curly hair; his teeth were stained dark and filed into points; and his chest and face were decorated with scar patterns.

"Yes, Sir!" PO Bruce replied crisply, in Edinburgh-accented English. He and many of his fellows had been educated in a mission school operated by Protestant nuns from Scotland.

He went nimbly down the rope, and then Lieutenant Joe Howard climbed up.

Howard, who wore a three-month-old beard, was dressed in Marine Corps utilities. The trousers had been cut off just over the knees, and the sleeves torn out at the shoulders. He was armed with a Thompson .45 ACP caliber machine gun and what had once been a U.S. Army Cavalry saber.

He found Reeves sitting with his back against the trunk of the tree. He was wearing a battered and torn brimmed uniform cap, an equally soiled khaki uniform tunic, the sleeves of which had been cut off, and khaki shorts and shoes, the uppers of which were spotted with green mold. His hair hung down his neck, and he was wearing a beard even longer than Howard's. A 9mm Sten submachine gun and a large pair of Ernst Leitz Wetzlar binoculars hung from his neck on web straps.

"I passed the distillery on the way here," Reeves said. "It's bubbling merrily."

"Sugar we have, salt we don't," Howard said.

"Yes," Reeves agreed. "And what do you infer from that?"

"That we can either die drunk or go get some salt. And maybe some other things."

Reeves chuckled. Despite his initial doubts, he had come to admire Joe Howard since he dropped from the sky three months before. In fact, he'd grown fond of him.

"The last time the cannibals attacked a Japanese patrol," Reeves said evenly, "they had three hundred people up here for a week."

"But they didn't find us."

"They came pretty sodding close."

"We need salt," Howard repeated. "And we really could use a couple of hundred pounds of rice. Maybe even some canned smoked oysters, some canned crab. Koffler said he would really like to have a Japanese radio. I'm not even mentioning quinine or alcohol or other medicine."

"If I were the Japanese commander, and I heard that an outpost of mine had been overrun by cannibals who made off with smoked oysters, medicine, and a radio, I think I'd bloody well question if they were really cannibals."

"I think they know, Jake. By now, they must."

"And if they suspected that the cannibals were led by an Australian, or for that matter by an American Marine—and I think probably by now they've heard us talking to Pearl, which would suggest an American presence—then one thought that would occur to me would be to arrange an ambush for the cannibals the next time they came out of the sodding jungle."

"We need salt," Howard said.

"You keep saying that, mate."

"That's not debatable."

Reeves shrugged, granting the point.

"Which means we have to get some from the Japs. We would get the same reaction from stealing a fifty-pound bag of salt as we would carrying off whatever we find."

"The last time we were lucky."

"Where does it say you can't be lucky twice in a row?"

"In the sodding tables of probability, you jackass!" Reeves said, chuckling.

"I'll take Ian Bruce," Howard said. "And a dozen men. I can make it back in six days."

"No," Reeves said, smiling, but firmly.

"Jake, that sort of thing is my specialty."

"I know Buka. You don't," Reeves said. "For one thing."

"We can't afford to lose you, Jake. If you weren't around, the natives would take off, and Christ knows, I wouldn't blame them."

"Precisely my point," Reeves said. "Except that they wouldn't just take off. There would be a debate whether they should convert you to long pig or sell you to the Japanese."

"You don't mean that," Howard said.

"About the long pig? Or selling you to the Japanese?" Reeves asked. "Yes, I do, mate. Both. My use of the word 'cannibal' was not to be cute. You don't think the good nuns put those scars on Ian's face, do you?"

Their eyes met for a moment and then Reeves went on:

"We'll leave Ian Bruce here with Steve Koffler, one or two other men, and most of the women. That'll keep the station up, and there'll be enough people to carry things off if the Nips should luck upon them while we're gone."

Howard thought that over for a minute and then looked at Reeves again.

"Ian and Koffler have become friends. We'll leave Patience behind too. The two of them might just get Koffler off safe in case the Nips do come. Do you disagree?"

Though Miss Patience Witherspoon was also educated by the nuns in the mission school, she immediately forgot all they taught her about the Christian virtue of chastity the moment she laid eyes upon Sergeant Steven M. Koffler, USMC. Not only were Patience and Koffler both eighteen years old, she found him startlingly attractive.

Her unabashed interest in Sergeant Koffler had not been reciprocated, possibly because Patience's teeth were stained dark and filed to a point, and her not-at-all-unattractive bosom and stomach, which she did not conceal, were decorated with scar tissue.

Lieutenant Howard did not know, and did not want to know, whether time had changed Koffler's views about Patience. And if his views had changed, whether she crawled into his bed at night.

But, he realized, Reeves was right again. If the requisitioning mission went bad, or if the Japanese should luck upon this place while they were gone, Ian and Patience were Koffler's best chance of survival. Perhaps his only chance.

"No, you're right, of course," Howard said.

"And of course, with you along with us, we will have the benefit of your warrior skills."

"Bullshit."

"I wouldn't want this to go to your head, old boy, but the chaps are beginning to admire you. Very possibly it's your beard. Theirs don't grow as long as ours. But in any event, if we both go, and if something unpleasant should happen to me, I think—I said *think*—that the chaps would probably come back here with you."

Howard met his eyes.

"I was thinking we should leave at first light tomorrow."

"No. I think we should leave now. That way we can move the rest of the day and through the night, and then sleep all day tomorrow."

Reeves stood up.

"I'll have a word with Ian," he said. "And you can have a word with Koffler."

(THREE)
Henderson Field
Guadalcanal, Solomon Islands
28 August 1942

The twin-engine, twenty-one-passenger Douglas aircraft known commercially as the DC-3 and affectionately as the Gooneybird was given various other designations by the military services that used it: To the U.S. Army, for instance, it was the C-47; to British Empire forces it was the Dakota; and the U.S. Navy—and so The Marines—called it the R4D.

An hour out of Espíritu Santo for Guadalcanal the crew chief of the MAG-25 (*M*arine *A*ir *G*roups consisted of two or usually more Marine aircraft squadrons) R4D came out of the cockpit and made his way past the row of high-priority cargo lashed down the center of the fuselage. At the rear of the cabin, a good-looking, brown-haired, slim, and deeply tanned young man in his middle twenties had made himself a bed on a stack of mailbags.

The other two passengers, a Marine Lieutenant Colonel and an Army Air Corps Captain, both of whom carried with them the equipment, clothing, and weapons specified by regulation for officers assigned to Guadalcanal, were more than a little curious about the young man dozing on the mailbags.

For one thing, he had boarded the aircraft at the very last moment; the pilot had actually shut down one of the engines so the door could be reopened. For another, his only luggage was a bag made out of a pillowcase, the open end tied in a knot. He was wearing khaki trousers and a shirt, the collar points of which were adorned with the silver railroad tracks of a captain, and Marine utility boots, called "boon-dockers." All items of uniform were brand new. In fact, the young Captain had even failed to remove the little inspection and other stickers with which military clothing comes from stock.

The crew chief, a staff sergeant, started to reach for the Captain's shoulders to wake him, but stopped when the Captain opened his eyes.

"Sir," the crew chief said, "Major Finch wants you to come forward."

"OK," the young Captain said, stretching and then getting to his feet.

He followed the crew chief back up the cabin to the cockpit door. The crew chief opened the door, held it for the Captain, and then motioned him to go first.

The Captain went as far forward as he could go, then squatted down, placing his face level with the Major's in the pilot's seat.

"You wanted to see me, Sir?"

"Oh, I got curious. I sort of expected you would come here on your own to say thank you."

"I am surprised the Major has forgotten what he learned in Gooneybird transition: 'Unauthorized visitors to the cockpit are to be discouraged.'"

The Major laughed.

"Speaking of unauthorized, Charley, how much trouble can I expect to get in for giving you this ride?"

"None, Sir. I'm still assigned to the squadron. I'm just going home."

"Why does that sound too simple?" the Major asked. He looked at the copilot, a young first lieutenant. "Mr. Geller, say hello to Captain Charley Galloway, of fame and legend."

"How do you do, Sir?" Lieutenant Geller said, smiling and offering his hand.

"You may have noticed, Mr. Geller, what a superb R4D pilot I am . . ."

"Yes, Sir, Major Finch, Sir, I have noticed that, Sir," Lieutenant Geller said.

"The reason is that my IP was Charley here."

"At Fort Benning," Galloway said, smiling, remembering.

"We drove the Air Corps nuts," Finch said. "Here I was, a brand-new *major,* and *Sergeant* Galloway was teaching me—and ten other Marine officers—how to fly one of these. The Army doesn't have any flying sergeants."

Lieutenant Geller dutifully laughed.

"I think maybe I should have busted my check ride," Finch said. "Then maybe I would be flying fighters instead of this."

"But tonight you will be back on Espíritu Santo," Galloway said, "drinking whiskey with nurses and going to bed in a cot with real sheets."

"I understand creature comforts are a little short at Henderson," Finch said.

"You haven't been there?" Galloway asked, surprised.

"This is my first trip."

"Creature comforts *are* a little short at Henderson," Galloway said. "Let me give you a little protocol: *Nice* transient copilots, Mr. Geller, pump their own fuel out of the barrels into the tanks."

"No ground crews?" Finch asked.

"And no fuel trucks. What gas there is comes in on High Speed Transports . . ."

"What's a High Speed Transport?" Geller asked.

"A World War One destroyer with half its boilers removed and converted to troop space," Galloway explained. "High Speed only in the sense that they're faster than troop transports.

"Anyway, gas comes in fifty-five-gallon barrels lashed to the decks. The Navy either loads them into landing barges, or, if time is short, throws them over the side—they float, you know—and then the Marines take over—getting it to shore, off the barges and to the field. The heat and humidity are really nasty. You don't have to move many fifty-five-gallon barrels of AvGas very far before your ass is dragging. So please, Mr. Geller, don't stand around with your finger up your ass watching somebody else fuel this thing up."

"No, Sir," Geller said.

"How come there's no Navy shore parties to handle supplies?" Finch asked.

"You've been in The Corps more than three weeks, Jack," Galloway said. "You should know that the Navy doesn't give The Corps one goddamn thing it doesn't have to."

"That sounds a little bitter, Charley," Finch said. There was just a hint of disapproval in his voice.

"*Sailors* I get along with pretty well," Galloway said. "It's the *Navy* I have problems with."

Finch chuckled, then asked, "Are you going to tell me why you needed this off-the-manifest ride to Henderson?"

"Because some Navy two-striper on Espíritu decided that I should get back to Guadalcanal on one of those High Speed Transports."

"What's wrong with that?"

"I get seasick," Galloway said.

"Bullshit."

"My executive officer is a brand-new first lieutenant with maybe 350 hours' total time. And he's one of my more experienced pilots."

"Now that we're telling the truth, are you all right to fly? Or did you just walk out of the hospital?"

"I'm all right. I didn't get hurt when I went in. I got sunburned and dehydrated, that's all."

"Is that straight, Charley?"

"Yeah, I'm all right."

"What happened, Charley?"

"I really don't know. I never saw the guy who got me. A Zero, I'm sure. But I didn't see him. The engine nacelle started to come off, and then the engine froze. And caught fire. So I remembered what *my* IP had taught me about how to get out of an F4F and got out."

"How long were you in the water?"

"Overnight. A PT boat picked me up at first light the next morning."

"Jesus!"

"God takes care of fools and drunks," Galloway said. "I qualify on both counts."

Geller, Finch noticed, *is looking at Galloway as if he was Lazarus just risen from the dead.*

"Tell me about Henderson," Major Finch asked, sensing that Galloway would welcome a change of subject.

"It's not Pensacola," Galloway replied. "The Japs started it, and had it pretty well along when we took it away from them—which is obviously why we went in half-assed the way we did. If they'd gotten it up and running, Jesus Christ! Using captured construction equipment, our guys made it more or less usable."

"Why captured construction equipment?" Geller asked.

"Because the construction equipment the First Marines took with them never got to the beach. It, and their heavy artillery, and even a bunch of Marines, sailed off into the sunset the day after they landed because the Navy didn't want to risk their precious ships. Right now, at least half of the ration is captured Jap stuff."

"My God!" Finch said.

"Actually, some of it's not bad," Galloway went on. "I mean it's not just rice. There's orange and tangerine slices, crab and lobster and shrimp, stuff like that."

"What's the field like?" Finch pursued.

"Twenty-six hundred feet," Galloway answered. "They're working to lengthen it. It gets muddy when it rains, and it rains every day. We have a lot of accidents on the ground because of the mud."

"Dirt? Not pierced-steel planking?"

"Dirt. And there's talk—maybe they even started on it—of making another strip for fighters, a couple of hundred yards away."

Galloway suddenly stood up. His legs were getting cramped.

"Would you like to sit in here, Sir?" Geller asked politely.

"No. No, thank you," Galloway said, and then smiled. "Tell me, Mr. Geller, have you ever seen a P-400?"

"What the hell is a P-400?" Finch asked.

"No, Sir," Geller said.

"It used to be the P-39," Galloway said. "The story is they renamed it the P-400 because everybody knew the P-39 was no goddamned good. They were supposed to be sent to Russia—"

"That's the low-wing Bell with the engine behind the pilot, and with a 20mm cannon firing through the propeller nose?" Geller interrupted.

"Right. The cannon was supposed to be used against German tanks. But then somebody told them a 20mm bounced off German tanks, so the Russians said, 'No, thank you.' So then the British were supposed to get them. They flew just enough of them—one, probably—to learn they were no good. So they said, 'No, thank you,' too. So they sent them to Guadalcanal."

"To the Marines?" Geller asked.

"No. There's an Army Air Corps squadron. They have a high-pressure oxygen system, said to be very effective to twenty-five thousand feet, which would be very helpful; the Japanese often come down from Rabaul at high altitude. Except we don't have the gear to charge the oxygen system, so they can't fly above twelve, fourteen thousand feet. And aside from that, it's not a very good airplane in the first place."

"Then why the hell are you so anxious to get back to this paradise?" Finch asked, without thinking, and was immediately sorry.

The Marine Corps finally did something right and made Galloway a captain and gave him a squadron, Finch thought. *He wants to get back because good Marine captains—and Galloway is probably a better captain than he was a tech sergeant—want to be with their squadrons.*

Not surprising Finch at all, Galloway ignored the question.

"We have pretty good Intelligence," Galloway went on. "The Australians left people behind when the Japs started taking all these islands."

"I don't follow you, Charley," Finch said.

"They left behind missionaries, government employees, plantation owners, people like that. They commissioned them into the Australian Navy and gave them shortwave radios. Just as soon as the Japs take off, we know about it. And we get en route reports, too. Which gives us enough time to get the Wildcats into the air and at altitude before they get there. The P-400s and the dive bombers—we had thirty Douglas SBD-3s; there were eighteen left the last time I was there—take off and get the hell out of the Japs' way."

"You mean the P-400s are useless?"

"No. Not at all. They're useful as hell supporting the First Marine Division. But they can't get up high enough to attack the Japanese bombers, and they're no match for the Japs' Zeroes. So they get out of the way when the Japs have planes in the area. I really feel sorry for those Air Corps guys. The P-400 is the Air Corps version of the Buffalo."

Finch knew all about the Buffalo. It was a shitty airplane. VMF-211 flew them in the Battle of Midway (VMF is the designation for Marine Fighter squadrons). For all practical purposes the squadron had been wiped out. The only survivors were the pilots lucky enough to have been assigned Wildcats.

Galloway lost a lot of buddies with VMF-211 at Midway, he thought. *We all did. In the old days, you knew just about every other Marine Aviator.*

"You want to drive this awhile, Charley?" Finch asked as he started to unfasten his seat and shoulder harness. "I need to take a leak and stretch my legs."

He got out of his seat and Galloway slid into it. Finch paused to take down a Thermos bottle of coffee from its rack and pour an inch of it into a cup. He drank that. Then he poured more into the cup and leaned over to hand it to Galloway.

Galloway's hand was on the throttle quadrant. Apparently the synchronization of the engines was not to his satisfaction.

Ordinarily, Finch thought, *my ego would be hurt and I would be pissed. But in this case, in the interest of all-around honesty, I will concede that Captain—formerly Tech Sergeant—Charley Galloway has forgotten more about flying the R4D than I know.*

"Coffee, Charley?" he asked, touching Galloway's shoulder.

Finch brought the R4D in low over the ocean, making a straight-in approach toward Henderson Field, which was more or less at right angles to the beach. He called for wheels down as he crossed the beach, and maintained his shallow angle of descent until he reached the runway itself.

There was no chirp as the wheels touched down, just a sudden rumbling to tell him that he was on the ground.

He chopped the throttles, put the tail on the ground, and applied the brakes, stopping before he reached the control tower, which was to the right of the runway. To his left he saw parts of three hangars, but couldn't tell if they were damaged or simply under construction.

He saw other signs of damage around. There was an aircraft graveyard to the left. People were cannibalizing parts from wrecks, including the P-400s Galloway talked about.

A FOLLOW ME jeep appeared on the runway, and he followed it toward the control tower. A Marine in the jeep jumped out and showed him where he was to park the airplane.

He spotted a familiar face, or more accurately a familiar hairless head, thick neck, and massive chest belonging to Technical Sergeant Big Steve Oblensky. He was glad to see him. Tech Sergeant Oblensky had been very kind to a very young Lieutenant Finch when he reported to his first squadron. Oblensky's uniform consisted of utility trousers, boondockers, and a Thompson submachine gun slung from his bare shoulder.

Oblensky, who had more than enough time in The Corps to retire, had been a Flying Sergeant when Major Finch was in junior high school. Long ago he'd busted his flight physical, but had stayed in The Corps as a maintenance sergeant. He had been Maintenance Sergeant of VMF-211, Finch recalled, until Charley Galloway stole him when he formed his VMF-229.

He was not surprised to see Oblensky. Half the crates lashed down the center of the fuselage were emergency shipments of aircraft parts, and Big Steve was not the sort of man to order emergency shipments only to see them diverted by some other maintenance sergeant. Or for that matter, by the MAW Commanding General.

"Shut it down, Geller," Finch ordered and got out of his seat.

When he reached the rear door of the aircraft, he saw a sight he never expected to see. Technical Sergeant Oblensky ran up to his squadron commander, Captain Charles M. Galloway. But instead of saluting him, he wrapped his arms around him, lifted him off the ground, and complained, "You little bastard, we all thought you was dead!"

"Put me down, for Christ's sake, you hairless ape!"

Major Finch recalled that Galloway and Oblensky had been in VMF-211 for a long time before the war. Galloway had then been a technical sergeant.

Oblensky set Galloway back on his feet. But emotion overwhelmed him again. He swung his massive fist at Galloway's arm in a friendly touch, or so he intended. It almost knocked Galloway off his feet.

"Goddamn—it's good to see you!"

"Christ, watch it, will you?" Galloway complained.

But he was smiling, Finch noticed.

"Hello, Oblensky, how are you?" Finch called as he climbed down the stairs to the ground.

Oblensky looked, and when recognition dawned on his face, he came to attention and threw a very crisp salute.

"Major Finch, Sir. It's good to see you, Sir."

Finch returned the salute.

Oblensky is obviously glad to see me. But not as glad as he is to see Galloway. Whatever the reason, whether because they were sergeants together, or because Charley is just back, literally, from the mouth of death, I'm just a little jealous.

"There's some stuff on board for VMF-229, Oblensky," Finch said as the two shook hands.

"I better get it," Oblensky said, then turning to Galloway, he remembered the appropriate military courtesy before he went on. "Captain, Ward and Schneider are flying out on this thing. I mean, if you wanted to say hello or so long, or something, Sir."

He pointed to a fly tent erected behind the control tower, between the tower and the tree line. Galloway saw a half dozen jeeps near there, each rigged for stretchers. Several of these had red crosses painted on their hoods.

"How bad are they hurt?" Galloway asked.

"Mr. Schneider's got a busted ankle and took some hits in the legs. Mr. Ward busted his ribs and took some little shit, shrapnel, glass, whatever, in the face. He's not so bad off. I don't know why they're evacuating him."

"And the others?" Galloway asked softly.

"Mr. Jiggs and Mr. Hawthorne didn't make it, Sir," Oblensky said. "Everybody else is all right."

Galloway turned to Finch.

"Thank you for the ride, Sir," he said.

"Anytime, Charley," Finch said, putting out his hand. "Be careful. Get to be one of those old, *cautious* birdmen we hear about."

Galloway freed his hand and saluted, then walked off toward the fly tent.

He found First Lieutenant James G. Ward, USMCR, sitting on a cot, holding his shirt on his lap. He was bare-chested except for the adhesive tape wrapped around his upper torso; his head was wrapped in bandages; the parts of his face that were visible looked like someone had beaten him with a baseball bat; and his neck and shoulders were decorated with a dozen small bandages.

What did that idiot say? "He's not so bad off"? What's bad off, then?

"Hello, Jim," Galloway said. "I'd ask how you are, except that I'm afraid you'd tell me."

Ward, startled, jumped to his feet.

"My God, am I glad to see you!"

"Yeah, me too," Galloway said.

He was fond of Jim Ward for many reasons . . . and not just because Jim Ward was responsible for his initial meeting with Mrs. Carolyn Ward McNamara, who was Jim's aunt. Carolyn's last letter to Galloway was signed, *"all of my love, my darling, always, to the end of time."* And Galloway felt pretty much the same about her.

"These idiots want to evacuate me!" Ward said indignantly, gesturing toward a group of medical personnel at the far end of the fly tent.

"Really? I wonder why?"

"All I've got is some busted ribs."

"Have you looked in a mirror lately?"

"I took some shards from the windscreen," Ward protested. "And I guess I banged my face against the canopy rails or something. But the bandages and the swelling will be gone in a week." He saw the look on Galloway's face and added indignantly, "Go ask them if you don't believe me."

"Where's Schneider? More importantly, how is Schneider?"

First Lieutenant David F. Schneider, USMC, a graduate of the Naval Academy and the nephew of an admiral, had only one redeeming feature, in Galloway's judgment. The arrogant, self-important little shit had a natural ability to fly airplanes.

"He's in pretty bad shape," Jim Ward said. "He broke his ankle. I mean bad. And he took a bullet and some shrapnel in his leg. They've been keeping him pretty well doped up."

He pointed to a cot at the far end of the fly tent near where the medical personnel were gathered.

"You stay here," Galloway ordered. "I'll ask why you're being evacuated."

"I can fly *now,* for Christ's sake."

"Yeah, sure you can," Galloway said.

He walked to the foot of Schneider's cot. Schneider's face looked wan, and his eyes, though open, seemed to be not quite focused on the canvas overhead. A cast covered his foot and his left leg nearly up to his knee; and his upper right leg was covered with a bandage from his knee to his crotch. Like Ward, he was peppered with small bandages.

"Hey, Dave, you awake?" Galloway called softly.

Schneider's eyes finally focused on Galloway and recognition came. He smiled and started to push himself up on the cot.

"We heard you were alive, Sir. I'm delighted."

"What happened to you?"

"I took some hits in the leg, Sir. And as I was landing, I found that I was unable to operate the right rudder pedal. I went off the runway and hit a truck, Sir."

"How's the truck?" Galloway asked jokingly.

"I understand it was one of the trucks the Japanese rendered inoperable, Sir," Schneider said, seriously. "I regret that I totaled the aircraft, Sir."

"Well, by the time you get back, we'll have a new one for you."

"Yes, Sir."

"Anything I can do you, Dave?"

"No, Sir. But thank you very much."

"I just came from Espíritu Santo, Dave. What they'll probably do is keep you there no more than a day and then fly you to the new Army General Hospital in Melbourne."

"Not to a Navy hospital, Sir?" Schneider asked, disappointed.

Galloway knew the reason for Schneider's disappointment: Ensign Mary Agnes O'Malley, NNC, might not be serving at the hospital where he was assigned. Mary Agnes O'Malley was a sexual engine who ran most of the time over the red line, and in recent times she liked having Schneider's hands on her throttle.

Jesus, as doped up as he is, he's still thinking about Mary Agnes, hoping she'll be there to nurse him in a way not ordinarily provided. Sorry, Dave, even if you go to a Navy hospital, and Mary Agnes was there with her libido in supercharge, it'll be some time before you'll be bouncing around on the sheets again.

"Hey, Dave," Galloway said. "Hospitals are hospitals."

"Yes, Sir."

A small-boned little man in utilities walked up to the cot, swabbed at Schneider's arm with a cotton ball, and then gave him an injection. At first Galloway thought he was a Navy corpsman, but then he saw a gold oak leaf on the little man's collar. He was a lieutenant commander.

He was not wearing a Red Cross brassard, Galloway noticed, and there was a web belt with a Colt .45 automatic pistol in its holster dangling from it.

He looked at Galloway coldly and walked away. When Galloway looked down at Schneider again, his eyes were closed. Galloway walked after the doctor.

"Got a minute, Doctor?"

The little man turned and again looked coldly at Galloway.

"Certainly I have a minute. Obviously there is very little for me to do around here. What's on your mind?"

"Lieutenant Ward, over there," Galloway said, jerking his thumb toward Ward, "doesn't think he really has to be evacuated."

"What are you, his priest or something?"

"I told him I would ask, Commander," Galloway replied.

"OK. He has broken ribs. He can't fly with broken ribs, OK? His nose is broken, OK? And there is a good chance he has some bone damage in that area. We won't know until we can get a good EN&T guy to take a good look at him, OK? In addition to that, he has a number of small penetrating wounds, each of which, in this fucking filthy humid environment, is likely to get infected, OK? So I made a decision, Chaplain: Either I let this guy hang around here, and not only get sicker, OK? And take up bed space I'm going to need soon, OK? And eat rations, which we don't have enough of as it is, OK? Or I could evacuate him, OK? I decided to evacuate him. OK?"

"OK," Galloway said. "Sorry to bother you."

"I don't know how long you've been around here, Chaplain," the doctor said. "But you better understand that these pilots are all crazy. For example, I just got word that a lunatic in the hospital on Espíritu Santo went AWOL to come back here. The son of a bitch was suffering from exposure and dehydration after he got shot down and floated around in the goddamned ocean for eighteen hours."

"You don't say?"

"Anything else on your mind, Chaplain?"

"No, thank you very much, Doctor."

The doctor turned and walked away. Galloway went back to Jim Ward.

"What did he say, Skipper?"

"He said get on the airplane, Mr. Ward. He said unless you do, your wang will turn black and fall off."

"Come on, I can fly."

"Have a good time in Australia, Jim," Galloway said.

"Oh, shit!" Jim Ward said, resigned to his fate.

* * *

When Lieutenant Colonel Clyde W. Dawkins, USMC, wearing a sweat-soaked tropical areas flight suit and a .45 automatic in a shoulder holster, raised his eyes from his desk, he saw Captain Charles M. Galloway, USMCR, standing at the entrance to his tent. Though Dawkins looked hot and hassled, his voice was conversational, even cordial, when he spoke:

"Please come in and have a seat, Captain Galloway, I'll be with you in just a moment."

"Thank you, Sir," Galloway said.

Galloway was worried. He had served under Dawkins for a long time, and he knew Dawkins: When he was really pissed, before he really lowered the boom, he assumed the manner of a friendly uncle.

A full two minutes later, Dawkins looked at him.

"I must confess a certain degree of surprise, Captain Galloway. From the description of your physical condition and mental attitude furnished by the medics on Espíritu Santo, I expected a pathetic physical wreck, eyes blazing with a maniacal conviction that the entire war will be lost unless he is there to fight it himself."

"Sir, I'm all right. All I was doing was sitting around reading three-month-old copies of the *Saturday Evening Post.*"

"In case this has not yet come to your attention, Captain, the Naval Service, in its wisdom, has certain designated specialists, called doctors, who determine if people are fit, or not fit, to return to duty. What makes you think your judgment is superior to theirs?"

Galloway opened his mouth to reply, but Dawkins went on before he could. "How the hell did you get back here, anyway?"

"I caught a ride, Sir."

"And did you really think you could get away with just getting on a plane and coming back here?"

Galloway made no reply.

"They want you court-martialed for breaking into some supply room. What the hell is that all about? What did you steal, anyway?"

Galloway waved his hand, indicating his uniform.

"They wouldn't give me my uniform back, Sir."

Dawkins glowered at him for a full thirty seconds, and then said, "If I wasn't so glad to see you, you sonofabitch, I'd *personally* kick your ass all over this airfield, and *then* send you back there in irons."

"I thought I should be here, Sir," Galloway said.

"Are you really all right, Charley?"

"I looked like a corpse when they fished me out of the water, and I never want to get that thirsty again, but yes Sir, I'm all right."

"What do you mean, you looked like a corpse?"

"My skin was all puckered up."

"You realize how lucky you were?"

"Yes, Sir."

"Jiggs and Hawthorne weren't lucky," Dawkins said.

"Yes, Sir. Oblensky told me."

"And you know about Ward and Schneider?"

"Yes, Sir. I just saw them. Ward's unhappy about being evacuated."

"Well, following the sterling example of his squadron commander, he'll probably go AWOL and come right back."

"I didn't have the chance to ask Big Steve about aircraft," Galloway said, hoping to change the subject.

"You have eight left. Christ only knows when we'll get more. I think the Air Corps is down to about six of their P-400s. Have you seen Dunn?"

"No, Sir. I came right here."

"He is now officially an ace. I put him in for a DSC," a Distinguished Service Cross. "They bumped it down to a DFC," a Distinguished Flying Cross.

"You should have known they would," Galloway said.

Dawkins nodded. "That's why I put him in for the DSC. If I'd have put him in for a DFC, they would have bumped it down to a Good Conduct Medal."

Galloway chuckled.

"You're credited with three and a half," Dawkins said.

"Anything unusual I should know?"

Dawkins shook his head.

"Same drill. We generally get thirty minutes' notice from the Coastwatcher people, via either Pearl Harbor or Townsville. That gives us enough time to get off the ground and to altitude. By then the radar can usually give us a vector. We shoot them down or they shoot us down. That will go on until one side or the other runs out of airplanes. Right now, unless we get some help from the Navy, that looks like us."

"There was a bunch of F4F pilots on Espíritu. Right out of Pensacola."

"That's academic. We don't have airplanes for them to fly."

Their eyes met for a moment, and then Galloway said, "I suppose I better go see Dunn and let him know I'm back."

As the next senior officer present for duty, First Lieutenant William Charles Dunn, USMCR, assumed command of VMF-229 after Galloway was shot down and presumed dead. Bill Dunn was twenty-one years old; he stood five feet six, weighed no more than 135 pounds, and looked to Dawkins like a college cheerleader. He became an ace the day he took over VMF-229.

Dawkins nodded, and then stood up and offered his hand.

"I'm glad you came through, Charley. God knows how, but I'll deal with the people you've pissed off."

"Thank you, Sir."

Galloway had gone no farther than two hundred yards from Dawkins' tent when a siren began to wail. He looked at the control tower. A black flag—signifying *air base under attack*—was being hoisted on the flagpole.

He started to trot toward the area where the aircraft of VMF-229 were parked in sandbagged revetments. Then, realizing that he really had no reason to rush to his airplane, he slowed to a walk: The F4F with CAPT C. GALLOWAY USMCR painted below the canopy track was now at the bottom of the sea.

Soon he heard the peculiar sound of Wildcat engines starting, and then the different sound of R4D engines being run up to takeoff power. He looked down the runway in time to see the R4D he'd flown in to Guadalcanal begin its takeoff roll. A moment later it flashed over his head.

No more than sixty seconds later, the first F4F with MARINES painted on its fuselage bounced down the runway and staggered into the air, followed almost immediately by half a dozen others.

From his position, he could not see into their cockpits and identify their pilots.

He kept walking toward the squadron area.

The next time the Japanese come, I will bump one of my eager young lieutenants out of his seat. Will I be doing that because I really think that a squadron commander's place is in the air with his men? Or was that doctor on Espíritu right, that anyone who does such things when he hasn't been ordered to is by definition out of his mind?

II

(ONE)
U.S. Marine Corps Recruit Depot
Parris Island, South Carolina
31 August 1942

Prior to his enlistment in The Marine Corps, George F. Hart, USMCR, was employed by the Saint Louis, Missouri, Police Department. Specifically, the twenty-four-year-old fifth son and eighth child of Captain (of the Saint Louis police) and Mrs. Karl J. Hart was the youngest (ever) detective on that organization's Vice Squad. Law enforcement was something of a family tradition.

After immigrating to the United States from Silesia, George's paternal grandfather, Anton Hartzberger, joined the force a month after he became an American citizen. He retired as a sergeant.

Two of Anton's sons, George's father and his Uncle Fred (legally Friedrich), went on the cops, as did two of George's brothers and a pair of cousins. Uncle Fred was a harness bull sergeant and happy to be where he was ... though he thought it would be nice if he made lieutenant later, because of the pension. George's father, Karl, was promoted to Captain shortly after he was placed in charge of the Homicide Bureau; and he had ambitions for higher rank. But he believed his ambitions were damaged all along by the perception that he was one more stupid Kraut—of which, it must be admitted, the Saint Louis police had a more than adequate supply.

When Georg Friedrich Hartzberger was in the eighth grade, Sergeant Karl Hartzberger took his wife and his children to a judge's chambers. They emerged the Hart family, with all their given names Anglicized.

After he graduated from high school, George found employment as a truck driver's helper for a well-known Saint Louis brewery—despite misgivings that he wasn't big or strong enough to handle it.

Legally, he should have been over twenty-one before taking employment in the alcohol industry. But that provision of law was enforced by the police department, none of whose members saw reason to inquire just how old Captain Hart's kid was.

And so for close to three years, he manhandled beer kegs and cases of bottled beer from loading dock to truck, and from truck to saloon or store basements, or to wherever those in the business of slaking the thirst of their fellow citizens chose to keep their supplies of brew.

George Hart was sworn in as a police officer when he was twenty-one. By then the regimen of beer-keg tossing had given him a remarkable musculature. While he wasn't built like a circus strongman—as many of his coworkers were—he was extraordinarily strong. For example, he could (and often did, when sampling his employer's wares) cause an *unopened* beer can to explode by crushing it in his hand.

He had also been inside just about every hotel, motel, restaurant, tavern, bar and grill, saloon, and whorehouse in both Saint Louis and East Saint Louis, its neighbor across the river in Illinois.

The usual period of rookie training—riding around with an experienced officer so as to become familiar with the city and with police procedures—was very short for Officer Hart. He already knew the city, and there wasn't much about the police department that he hadn't already learned before he joined the cops.

Afterward, he was assigned as a plainclothes officer to the Vice Squad. The mission of the Vice Squad was the suppression of gambling, prostitution, narcotics, and crimes against nature. As a practical matter, as long as the girls in the houses behaved themselves (which meant they didn't roll their clientele or sell them narcotics), the whorehouses were left pretty much alone. Nor did the police get very excited about a bunch of guys sitting around playing poker or shooting craps.

For the most part that left the drug dealers, the fairies, and the pimps—especially black pimps who preyed on young women, especially really young, fourteen-, fifteen-year-old white country girls who came to Saint Louis seeking fame and fortune. And also, for obvious reasons, the Squad came down hard on badger operations: A guy takes a girl to a hotel room expecting to get a five-dollar piece of ass; instead he finds some guy waving a badge at him, saying he's a cop, and wanting twenty bucks not to run him in and cause him severe public humiliation. And then there were the fucking unwashed hillbillies who came to Saint Louis to find a job, found that a job meant work, and decided it was easier to rent out their fourteen-year-old daughters to make their moonshine money. These guys really offended Officer George Hart's sense of decency.

Hart had been working plainclothes Vice about six months when he was awarded his first citation. He was in a bar down by the river, just nosing around, when two guys stuck it up. One of them had a .38 Smith & Wesson Military and Police, the other one had a .22 Colt Woodsman. Hart wasn't going to do anything about it except remember what they looked like, but a uniform walked in off the street and tried to be a hero. When the robbers shot him, there was nothing Hart could do but shoot the robbers. He killed one; the other would be paralyzed for the rest of his life.

Four months after that, he was in another bar, just nosing around, when a guy came looking for his wife. He found her where he thought she would be, with some other guy, and shot her. He then saw Hart taking out his pistol and was making up his mind whether to shoot the boyfriend or Hart, when Hart shot him.

He already had a citation, so they bent a few civil service rules and made him a detective and kept him in Vice.

He was a detective three weeks when he tried to arrest an unimpressive-looking guy he caught in the act of selling a bag of marijuana leaves. Confident of both his professional skill and his unusual strength, he attempted to make the felony arrest without calling for assistance from other police officers.

Not only did the marijuana vendor successfully resist arrest, he sent Detective Hart to Sacred Heart Hospital with a broken nose, several broken ribs, and three broken fingers on his right hand. When he was subsequently apprehended, it was learned that he had been taught the fine points of street fighting in Tijuana, Mexico, where he was ultimately deported.

After Hart's broken appendages and ribs were healed, Sergeant Raphael Ramirez gave Detective Hart off-duty instruction in the manly art of self-defense as practiced in the Mexican-American neighborhoods of El Paso, Texas, where Sergeant Ramirez lived before moving to Saint Louis and joining the cops.

Detective Hart proved to be an apt pupil. He was never again injured in the line of duty.

Then the goddamn war came along.

Near the courthouse there was a bar, Mooney's, where most of the patrons were either cops or otherwise connected with the law enforcement community. Civilians (unless they were young, female, and attractive) quickly sensed they were not welcome. The other exception was members of the Armed Forces, possibly because they are by definition not civilians.

The Army, Navy, and Marine Corps recruiting offices were in the courthouse, and the enlisted personnel of these offices felt quite at home in Mooney's. Over a period of time, Detective Hart struck up an acquaintance with Staff Sergeant Howard H. Wertz, USMC, one of the Marine recruiters.

They were of an age, shared a Teutonic background, and even looked very much alike. When they were together, Detective Hart talked to Sergeant Wertz about the cops, and Sergeant Wertz talked to Detective Hart about The Marine Corps.

Now and again the question of Detective Hart's possible military service came up. Though it had been decided early on that police work was an essential service and its practitioners exempt from the draft, in Sergeant Wertz's judgment the draft deferment for police officers would not last long. Soon they too would be summoned by their friends and neighbors to military service.

After a while Sergeant Wertz suggested to Detective Hart that he might not have to worry anyhow, since he might not pass the physical examination. Whether Hart was fit for service or not, Sergeant Wertz suggested, would be a good thing to know. A few days after that, he told Detective Hart he had a buddy at the Armed Forces Induction Center who would run Detective Hart through the examination process "off the books," as a special favor.

The results of the physical were a mixed blessing. Detective Hart was in really splendid physical condition, which was nice to know. At the same time they were a little unnerving, for if Sergeant Wertz was correct and the police deferment was eliminated, Hart would go into the Armed Forces.

Perhaps it might be a good idea, Sergeant Wertz suggested, to start looking around to see what Detective Hart could get from the services in exchange for his immediate enlistment, rather than waiting for his Draft Board to send him the *Your Friends and Neighbors Have Selected You* postcard.

Two days after that, Sergeant Wertz told his friend Detective Hart the good news: The Marine Corps just happened to be looking for a few good men with police backgrounds who would be utilized in law enforcement areas. The only problem was that "The Program" (as Sergeant Wertz called it) was nearly full and about to close. So Hart would have to make up his mind quickly.

When Detective Hart consulted him, his father was enthusiastic: "If you have to go, George, and it looks like you'll have to, that's the way to do it. Otherwise they'll hand you a rifle and turn you into cannon fodder."

Private Hart was in The Marine Corps three days when he learned from a personnel clerk at Parris Island that the Marines not only did not have a law enforcement recruitment program, they'd never had one. In other words, he was like anyone else who had enlisted in The Corps: He'd be assigned where The Corps decided he would be of the greatest value. In his case it was The Marine Corps' intention to hand him a rifle, teach him how to use it, and assign him to a rifle company as a rifleman—a/k/a cannon fodder.

One of the reasons Private Hart looked forward to graduation from Parris Island was that afterward he would be given a short leave. During that time he planned to return to Saint Louis, locate Staff Sergeant Wertz, and break both of the sonofa-bitch's arms.

But Staff Sergeant Wertz was not the only Marine noncom who, in his view, deserved such treatment.

Private George F. Hart, USMCR, was in the fifth week of his recruit training when he decided to render as-painful-as-possible bodily harm to Corporal Clayton C. Warren, USMC. He did not actually intend to *kill* Corporal Warren, who was one of the assistant drill instructors of his platoon, but the thought of breaking Corporal Warren's arm was, well, satisfying.

Though every man in the platoon had the same wish, Private Hart believed he was the only one with the necessary expertise to (a) do it and (b) get away with it. He wished to do so for two reasons. One was personal, and the other was For the Good of the Service (at least as he saw it).

And today was the day.

The first time Private Hart saw Corporal Clayton C. Warren at Parris Island, he thought the guy was one of the hillbilly pimps he had made in Saint Louis. Warren bore an astonishing physical resemblance—tall, bony, sharp-featured, no chin, and a large, fluid Adam's apple—to a shitkicker from Arkansas or someplace like that who had prostituted his fifteen-year-old *wife* rather than get a goddamn job.

And when Corporal Warren first opened his mouth, thus proving he was indeed a hillbilly shitkicker, the likeness was even more astonishing. Hart had to remind himself that *his* shitkicking hillbilly was doing three-to-five; it couldn't possibly be the same man.

Hart understood the necessity and value of the rigorous recruit training program of The Marine Corps. In his judgment, it had three aims: First was to bring the recruits up to a standard of physical strength and endurance which would permit them to fight the enemy; many of them had never lifted anything much heavier than a schoolbook. Second, it was intended to give them the necessary military skills, from the obvious (how to accurately fire and care for a rifle) to the less obvious (how to live in the field on nothing but what you carried on your back). Many of Hart's fellow recruits had never held a firearm until they came to Parris Island; and they'd never slept anywhere but on a soft bed.

Third, and most important, was to teach a bunch of civilians discipline: that is, to do whatever they were told to do, to the best of their ability, whenever they were told to do it. This was surely the most difficult training task the drill instructors and their assistants faced, and Hart was well aware that not many students were going to like the curriculum.

All of this having been said, it was Hart's judgment that The Marine Corps had made a mistake (despite the Parris Island Holy Writ that this kind of mistake was not possible). They had placed at least part of the responsibility of turning civilians into Marines into the hands of a semiliterate, sadistic, hillbilly shitkicker who got his rocks off by humiliating and physically abusing anyone he suspected of having more brains than he did. That meant all but one or two of the men in the platoon.

Corporal Clayton C. Warren, USMC, was not only a really vicious prick, but a dangerous one. On three occasions, for instance, Hart saw him actually trip men running up an inclined log on the obstacle course. One of the men broke his arm; it was only luck that the other two suffered only minor sprains and abrasions.

And he took delight in making trainees run around the drill field with their rifles held over their heads until they collapsed from exhaustion. A few times this was punishment for some sort of offense, but often it was because Corporal Clayton C. Warren, USMC, just liked to see people run until they dropped.

There was a long list of similar outrages, all falling under the category of acts against the general Good of the Service.

Hart's personal troubles with Corporal Clayton C. Warren, USMC, were based on Warren's notion that Hart was a fucking college boy. This category of *Homo sapiens* seemed to trigger Warren's most intense feelings of inferiority, and thus his most vicious impulses.

There were a dozen fucking college boys in the platoon—real and perceived: Corporal Clayton C. Warren's definition of a fucking college boy was anyone older than eighteen who could read without moving his lips. And yet—even taking into consideration that Warren was likely making him paranoid—Hart was convinced that Warren had him identified as the most offensive of all the fucking college boys.

Warren's actual offenses against Hart himself began with blows to the face (three times, with his fist); to the solar plexus (three times); to the kidneys (twice). He'd kicked Hart in the shins (three times); in the head, while doing push-ups (twice); and once in the side during a rest break.

He also described Hart's relationship with his mother in words that Hart found insufferable—even considering the source, and his experience as a vice cop.

According to the mimeographed Training Schedule thumbtacked to the barracks wall, the second period of post-lunch instruction today was Hand-to-Hand Combat. There was a similar period yesterday. Hand-to-Hand Combat was one of Corporal Warren's favorites. He could hurt people with the blessing of The United States Marine Corps.

Yesterday he dislocated the shoulders of three recruits, skillfully stopping just short of pulling their joints apart. Still, he'd strained them enough to leave enough pain to last for days.

He also ground into the dirt the faces of each student he honored with Hands-on Instruction—with sufficient force to embed pebbles and twigs in their skin.

Corporal Warren's method of instruction went something like this: The trainees would be seated in a semicircle on the ground; Corporal Warren would select one of them—"You, motherfucker!" He'd then instruct the trainee in the Approved Marine Corps Technique of killing the enemy with a knife.

The trainee would be handed a sheathed trench knife. Similarly armed, Corporal Warren would attack the trainee. In a second or so the trainee would find himself on his back, with Corporal Warren's sheathed knife pressing painfully against his Adam's apple.

"You're dead, cocksucker!"

Next Corporal Warren would tell the trainee to attack him, to demonstrate the proper method of defense against a knife attack.

"Now really try to kill me, shitface!"

The trainee—who was not only in awe of Corporal Warren but traumatized by the situation—would make a clumsy attempt to stab Warren with his sheathed knife. He would immediately find himself on his back, with Warren's knee grinding one side of his face into the ground, or else on his stomach, with Warren twisting his arm to the point of shoulder dislocation.

"You're dead, you stupid motherfucker!"

Private Hart noticed with satisfaction that today's instruction period was going very much like yesterday's. He also noticed that the drill instructor, who sometimes watched Corporal Warren in action, seemed to be occupied with the other half of the platoon.

"You, college boy!" Corporal Warren said, indicating Private Hart.

Private Hart rose to his feet. Corporal Warren threw him a sheathed trench knife.

"Try to kill me, college boy!"

Private Hart successfully resisted the terrible urge to obey the order, and moments afterward found himself on his back with Corporal Warren's sheathed knife pressing painfully against his Adam's apple.

"Fucking fairy motherfucker, you're dead!"

He spat in Private Hart's face and then contemptuously got off him.

Private Hart had dropped his knife.

"Pick it up, college boy, and really try to kill me!"

Hart picked up the knife. He crouched and spread his arms, then advanced on Corporal Warren.

Warren smiled.

Private Hart threw the trench knife from his right hand to his left. When Corporal

323 ≡ L I N E O F F I R E

Warren's eyes followed, for a split second, the passage of the knife, Private Hart kicked Corporal Warren in the groin.

As Warren's eyes, now registering shock, returned to him, Hart took one step toward him, grabbed his right arm, twisted it, flipped Warren over his extended right leg, and followed him to the ground as he fell. He placed his knee between Warren's wrist and elbow and tensed his muscles to break the arm.

He felt a hard blow in the back, between the shoulder blades, and felt himself flying through the air.

What the hell?

His face slid a foot through the dirt and pebbles. The breath was knocked out of him.

He heard the crunch of boots on the dirt and a pair of highly shined service shoes and the cuff of sharply creased khaki pants appeared in his view.

"On your feet!"

He recognized the voice of the drill sergeant before he saw his face.

Shit, he saw what happened. He kicked me.

Private Hart, breathing hard, came to attention.

"Look at me," the drill instructor said evenly.

He was a leathery-faced, leanly built staff sergeant in his early thirties. His eyes were gray and cold.

"Try *me,* tough guy," the drill instructor said, and Hart felt a jabbing at his stomach. He looked down and saw that he was being offered a trench knife, butt first. The sheath had been removed.

He looked into the drill instructor's face again.

He looks, Hart thought, *more contemptuous than angry.*

"Go on, tough guy, take it," the drill instructor said, and jabbed Hart in the stomach again with the butt of the trench knife.

Hart shook his head and blurted what came into his mind: "I don't have anything against you."

The drill instructor's eyes examined him with renewed interest.

"Meaning you think you could hurt me?"

Again, Hart blurted what came into his mind:

"I don't know. But I've got no reason to cut you."

There was a moment's silence.

" 'Ten'hut!" the drill instructor barked. "Fow-wud, Harch! Double-time, Harch!"

Hart's compliance was Pavlovian. He started double-timing across the parade ground. After a moment, he became aware that the drill instructor was double-timing a step or two behind him, just within his peripheral vision.

He came to the end of the parade ground, then crossed a narrow macadam road and moved between two barracks buildings.

"Column left, Harch!" the drill instructor ordered when they reached the far end of the long frame building. "Detail, halt!"

Hart stopped and stood at attention. The drill instructor stepped in front of him.

What the fuck do I do now? Let him beat me up?

"Who taught you to fight?" the drill instructor demanded, and then, without waiting for a reply, "What did you do before you came in The Corps?"

"I was a cop."

"A cop?"

"A detective," Hart said.

"Where?"

"Saint Louis."

"Were you really going to break his arm?"

"He's a vicious, sadistic sonofabitch," Hart heard himself say. "Yeah, I was going to break his arm. Nobody calls me a motherfucker."

"He's on his way out of here," the drill instructor said. "Before the war, there's no way an asshole like Warren would have made corporal, much less been assigned here. But he *is* here, and you just made him—made a DI—look like an asshole in front of the platoon. Maybe I should have let you break his arm—we could have said it was an accident."

Jesus Christ, he's talking to me like a human being.

"I'll fix it with the Captain somehow," the drill sergeant said, obviously thinking out loud. "If I can get you transferred to another platoon, can you keep your mouth shut about what happened?"

He looked intently at Hart, as if finally making up his mind.

Hart nodded.

"Thank you," he said.

"Stick your thanks up your ass. I'm not doing this because I like you. I'm doing it because it's the best thing for The Corps."

(TWO)
Royal Australian Navy Coastwatcher Establishment
Townsville, Queensland
30 August 1942

The letters USMC were stenciled on both sides of the hood of the gray 1941 Studebaker President, and a stenciled Marine Corps globe and anchor insignia were on each rear door.

The driver was a Marine, a tall, muscular man in his early thirties. He wore a green fore-and-aft cap adorned with the Marine insignia and the golden oak leaf of a major. Otherwise, he was substantially out of uniform. Instead of the forest green tunic prescribed for officers during the winter months in Australia, he wore a baggy, off-white, rough woolen thigh-length jacket that was equipped with a hood and was fastened with wooden pegs inserted through rope loops. The letters RAN, for Royal Australian Navy, were stenciled on the chest.

The passenger, a lean, sharp-featured man of about the same age, wore an identical duffel coat and a Royal Australian Navy officer's brimmed cap, the gold (actually brass) braid of which was both frayed and green with tarnish. There was no visible means to determine his rank.

Lieutenant Commander Eric Feldt, RAN, Commanding Officer of the Royal Australian Navy Coastwatcher Establishment, turned to Major Edward J. Banning, USMC, Commanding Officer of USMC Special Detachment 14, gestured out the window, and inquired, "Is that for you?"

Banning, who had heard the engines, leaned forward to look out the window, and saw what he expected to see. A United States Army Air Corps C-47 had begun its approach to the landing field.

"I don't expect anyone," Banning said.

"But we couldn't expect the Asshole to let us know he was coming, could we?"

Under practically any other circumstances, Major Ed Banning's sense of military propriety would have been deeply offended to hear a brother officer call another officer an anal orifice. And he would have been especially offended when the insult came from a foreigner, and the officer and gentleman so crudely characterized was a full colonel of the U.S. Marine Corps.

But at the moment, Major Banning was not at all offended. For one thing, he had a profound professional admiration and a good deal of personal affection for Commander Feldt. And for another, so far as Banning was concerned, Feldt's vulgar characterization fit to a T Colonel Lewis R. Mitchell, USMC, Special Liaison Officer between the Commander in Chief Pacific Ocean Areas (CINCPAC—Admiral Chester W. Nimitz) and the Supreme Commander, Southwest Pacific (SWPOA—General Douglas MacArthur).

Banning knew far more about Colonel Lewis R. Mitchell than Mitchell would have dreamed possible, including the fact that Mitchell had been given his present assignment in the belief that he could do less damage to the war effort there than he had been causing as one of a half dozen colonels assigned to the Personnel Division at Headquarters, USMC.

"You really think it's Mitchell?"

"Who else would it be? That's a sodding Dakota, not a puddle-jumper. If it were your Nip, he'd be in a puddle-jumper."

The "your Nip" reference was to First Lieutenant Hon Song Do, Signal Corps, U.S. Army.

"I'm telling you for the last fucking time, Eric!" Banning flared furiously. "Don't you *ever* refer to Pluto as a Nip, mine or anyone else's!"

"Sorry," Feldt said, sounding genuinely contrite. It did not satisfy Banning.

"For one thing, he's a serving officer. For another, he's a friend of mine. And finally, for Christ's sake, he's *Korean,* not Japanese."

Pluto Hon had made a good many trips by puddle-jumper from MacArthur's headquarters to Townsville to deliver to Banning classified messages that could not be entrusted to ordinary couriers. It was a long way to fly in a Piper Cub. Pluto Hon was a good man, a good officer, and he was *not* a fucking Nip.

"I'm really sorry, old boy," Feldt said. "That just slipped out."

"That's your fucking trouble!"

Feldt did not respond.

Banning decided he had gone far enough. In fact, he was chagrined that he had lost his temper.

"Well, what do you say?" he asked. "Should we go down to the field and see if that *is* the Asshole?"

"Sod him," Feldt said. "Let him walk."

"We'd just have to send one of the men back for him," Banning replied as he braked and prepared to turn around. "And if one of my guys were out of uniform, say wearing one of these RAN sleeved blankets, the Asshole would have apoplexy."

Feldt and Banning had been en route from the Coastwatcher Establishment antennae farm to their headquarters when Feldt had spotted the airplane. The airfield was in between; it took them only a few minutes to reach it.

By then the C-47 had landed and taxied to the transient ramp. The door opened as Banning stopped the Studebaker at the hurricane fence between the parking lot and the field itself.

As Banning walked to the policeman guarding the gate, Colonel Lewis R. Mitchell climbed down the short ladder, tugged at his trench coat to make sure it was in order, and marched toward the terminal.

He looks like an illustration: "Field Grade Officer, Dress Uniform, Winter," Banning thought.

He intercepted him and saluted crisply.

"Good afternoon, Sir."

Colonel Mitchell returned the salute but said nothing.

What he's doing is mentally composing something memorable to say to me about the duffel coat.

Colonel Mitchell's lips worked as if he was distinctly uncomfortable.

"Major Banning," he said finally, "a communication has arrived which I have been instructed to place before you."

What the hell is he talking about?

"Yes, Sir?"

Mitchell reached into the inside pocket of his blouse, removed an envelope, handed it to Banning, and then adjusted his uniform again.

The envelope was unsealed. It contained a single sheet of paper. From its feel, even before he saw the red TOP SECRET classification stamped on it, Banning knew that it had come from the Cryptographic Room. The paper was treated somehow to aid combustion. When a match was touched to it, it almost exploded.

URGENT

HEADQUARTERS USMC WASH DC 29 AUG 1942 1105

TO: HEADQUARTERS SOUTHWEST PACIFIC AREA
ATTN: (EYES ONLY) COLONEL L.R. MITCHELL USMC

1. Reference your radio 25Aug42 subject, "Request for clarification of role SWPOA-CINCPAC liaison officer vis a vis USMC Special Detachment 14 and RAN Coastwatcher Establishment," which has been referred to HQ USMC for reply.

2. You are advised that you have no repeat no role vis a vis USMC Special Detachment 14 or RAN Coastwatcher Establishment. You are further advised that Commanding Officer USMC SPECDET 14 is under sole and direct repeat sole and direct command of the undersigned and therefore not subject to orders of any USMC officer in CINCPAC or SWPOA, regardless of position or rank.

3. In order to insure that there is absolutely no misunderstanding, you are directed to personally make the contents of this message known to Major Edward Banning, USMC; LTCOM Eric A. Feldt, RAN; and 1st Lt S.D. Hon, SigC, USA.

4. Lt Hon is directed to inform the undersigned of date and time he has seen this message. Major Banning is directed to inform the undersigned of the date and time he has seen this message, and to inform the undersigned when its contents were made known to LTCOM Feldt. A consolidated reply, classified Top Secret, will be dispatched by urgent radio.

5. You are further advised that your raising of this question has called into doubt your ability to perform the duties of your present assignment.

FOR THE COMMANDANT

HORACE W.T. FORREST
MAJOR GEN, USMC
ASSISTANT CHIEF OF STAFF, G2, USMC

Banning raised his eyes to Colonel Mitchell's.

"Yes, Sir," he said.

"I apparently overstepped my authority and responsibility as I understood it . . ." Mitchell said.

Jesus Christ, I actually feel sorry for him.

". . . and if an apology is in order, Major, please consider one extended."

"No, Sir. No apology is required, Sir. They should have briefed you."

"Is that Commander Feldt in the car?"

"Yes, Sir."

"If you will give me that message back, I will show it to Commander Feldt and then see about getting back to Melbourne."

"Colonel," Banning said, "unless you have some pressing business in Melbourne, why don't you spend the night with us, and let us show you what we're doing here?"

"In light of that message, that strikes me as—"

"Sir, it was a question of Need to Know. With respect, Sir, you have not been cleared for what we're doing here."

"I have a TOP SECRET clearance," Mitchell said. "I'm the liaison officer between the two senior headquarters in the Pacific, and I'm the senior Marine officer present at SWPOA."

Banning, aware that he was about to lose his temper, spoke very carefully.

"Colonel, you have two choices. You can get back on that airplane or you can spend the night with us, let us show you why this is all so important."

"You had something to do with that message I just got, didn't you, Major? It was not just a reply to my radio, was it?"

"Sir, when you told me what you wanted me to do, and I told you what you asked was impossible, and when I learned you had sent that radio, I sent a back-channel message—"

"Who told you about my radio? That Oriental cryptographer?"

"That Oriental cryptographer"? Fuck you, Asshole!

Banning came to attention.

"Sir, I will bring this message to Commander Feldt's attention and arrange to have the confirmation of its receipt radioed to General Forrest. Good afternoon, Sir."

He saluted, and without waiting for it to be returned, executed a perfect about-face movement and then marched toward the Studebaker.

"Now see here, Banning!" Colonel Mitchell called after him.

Banning reached the Studebaker, got behind the wheel, and drove off.

"The Asshole, I gather, is not coming to tea?" Commander Feldt asked.

"Sod him," Major Banning said.

The story that ended with the arrival of Colonel Mitchell in Townesville had its start some months earlier with what Banning now recognized to be a hell of a smart idea on the part of Secretary of the Navy Frank Knox. At the beginning of the war, Knox realized that he was going to read very few honest reports on the functioning of Navy in the Pacific so long as those reports were written by Navy captains and admirals.

Knox concluded that if he was going to get anything like what he actually needed, he'd have to find someone who was not a member of the Navy establishment, yet who understood the Pacific and the Navy's responsibilities there. He found him, in spades, in the person of Captain Fleming W. Pickering. In addition to having been an any-tonnage, any-ocean master mariner (hence Captain) since he was twenty-six, Pickering was Chairman of the Board of Pacific & Far East Shipping Corporation.

Pickering, in other words, had all the necessary credentials that Knox required.

It is a sign of Frank Knox's considerable integrity that he actually chose Fleming

Pickering for the job; for their initial encounter was not pleasant, Fleming Pickering being a notably outspoken man with very strong views indeed. They met in connection with Pickering's refusal to sell his forty-two-vessel cargo fleet to the Navy (he did sell the Navy his twelve-vessel passenger-liner fleet). During their meeting (it took place not long after the attack on Pearl Harbor), Pickering told Knox that he should have resigned after that fiasco, and they should have shot the admirals in charge.

Peace between the two was arranged by their mutual friend, Senator Richmond F. Fowler (R., Cal.), and Pickering was commissioned into the Navy as a Captain on Knox's personal staff. He left almost immediately for the Pacific, where he filed regular reports on what the Navy and Marine Corps were actually doing—as opposed to what they wanted Frank Knox to know about.

Unfettered by the restraints he would have endured had he been under the command of CINCPAC, and with a wide network of friends and acquaintances in Australia and elsewhere in the Far East, Pickering put his nose in wherever he wanted to.

Very soon after he learned of the Royal Australian Navy Coastwatcher Establishment, he realized its great intelligence value. And it didn't take Pickering long after that to realize that he and Lieutenant Commander Eric Feldt were both just about equally contemptuous of the brass hats the Navy sent to work with the Coastwatchers.

As a result, a lengthy radio message from Pickering to Navy Secretary Knox resulted in the formation of Marine Corps Special Detachment 14, Major Edward S. Banning, commanding, under the Marine Corps Office of Management Analysis (its name was purposely obfuscatory). Banning's mission was not only to get along with Commander Feldt at any cost, but to provide him with whatever personnel, matériel, and money Feldt felt he could use.

Shortly after he took command of Special Detachment 14, Banning was made aware of one of the great secrets of the war, a secret that Pickering was also privy to.

Navy cryptographers at Pearl Harbor had broken many (but *not* all) of the codes of the Imperial Japanese General Staff. Decoded intercepts of these messages were furnished to a very few senior officers (in SWPOA, for instance, only General MacArthur and his intelligence officer, Brigadier General Charles A. Willoughby, got them). The operation had its own security classification: TOP SECRET—MAGIC. And the only cryptographic officer at SWPOA (South West Pacific Ocean Area) cleared to decrypt MAGIC messages was a Ph.D. in mathematics from MIT, First Lieutenant Hon Song Do, Signal Corps, U.S. Army. Banning joined "Pluto" Hon on the MAGIC list, as a stand-in for Pickering.

Meanwhile, Fleming Pickering and Douglas MacArthur grew friendly—bearing in mind that to call any relationship with the General "friendly" might be stretching the truth. It was MacArthur's view (and Pickering agreed with him) that the Navy was telling him (like Frank Knox) only what it wanted him to know, and only when it wanted to tell him. As a result, a radio message brought the appointment of Marine Lieutenant Colonel George F. Dailey as liaison officer between CINCPAC and SWPOA, with orders to keep MacArthur as fully briefed as possible.

Dailey had a second function . . . though he wasn't aware of it. A former Naval attaché, he had the security and intelligence background that would enable him, if necessary, to replace Banning as both Commanding Officer of USMC Special Detachment 14 and as Pickering's stand-in on the MAGIC list. Since he had no Need to Know, he was told little about the Coastwatcher Establishment and nothing whatever of MAGIC—not even of its existence.

That issue became moot when the intelligence officer of the First Marine Division was killed in the opening days of the Guadalcanal operation. Officers at Headquarters

USMC Personnel, unaware of Dailey's standby role as Banning's replacement, saw only a qualified replacement for the dead First Marine G-2. And so they ordered Dailey to Guadalcanal. And—either taking care of one of their own or (in Banning's judgment) getting rid of the sonofabitch—they ordered Colonel Lewis R. Mitchell to Australia to replace Lieutenant Colonel Dailey.

By the time Mitchell arrived, Captain Pickering had gone to Guadalcanal (where he figured he would be more useful than he was in Melbourne). With Pickering's departure Banning lost his own one-man-removed access to Navy Secretary Knox. And he also had to deal with Mitchell. Colonel Mitchell might not have been a problem—except that he turned out to be what Banning considered the most dangerous of men, a stupid officer with ambition.

Soon after his arrival, Mitchell somehow learned of a priority air shipment of radio equipment Banning had ordered for Feldt from the United States. In short order he demanded to know:

(a) what the equipment was to be used for;

(b) why it was necessary to have it shipped with the highest air priority;

(c) why he had not, as Senior Marine Officer present, been consulted;

(d) what was this half-assed Coastwatcher operation all about anyway; and,

(e) since the United States was paying all the bills, why a U.S. officer was not in charge.

Banning, as politely as possible, told him he did not have the Need to Know.

That resulted in a radio message from Mitchell to CINCPAC "requesting clarification of his role vis-à-vis USMC Special Detachment 14 and the Australian Coastwatcher organization."

When Pluto Hon showed this to Banning and asked what he should do about it, Banning told him to delay transmission for twenty-four hours while he considered his choices.

Banning saw two options: He could go directly to General MacArthur. Or he could send a back-channel message to the Office of Management Analysis.

On the one hand, going to MacArthur could raise more problems than it solved: MacArthur believed in the chain of command. Since colonels are *de facto* smarter than majors, majors do not question what colonels do.

On the other hand, back-channel messages are not filed and therefore do not have to be phrased in military-acceptable terminology:

> URGENT
> FROM CO USMC SPECDET 14
> VIA CINCPAC MAGIC
> TO MARINE OFFICE MANAGEMENT ANALYSIS
> EYES ONLY COLONEL RICKABEE
>
> MITCHELL REALLY DANGEROUS X HE WILL SEND MESSAGE CINCPAC TOMORROW RE-
> QUESTING CLARIFICATION OF HIS ROLE VISAVIS EVERYTHING HERE X CAN YOU GET
> HIM OFF MY BACK X REGARDS X BANNING END

(THREE)
The Foster Lafayette Hotel
Washington, D.C.
1415 Hours 31 August 1942

Senator Richmond F. Fowler (R., Cal.), was a silver-haired, erect sixty-two-year-old. Despite his attire—he wore a sleeveless undershirt and baggy seersucker trousers held up by suspenders—he still managed to look dignified when he opened the door of his apartment himself in response to an imperious knock.

Fowler occupied a six-room suite on the eighth floor of the Foster Lafayette. It was a corner suite, and so half its windows gave him an unimpeded view of the White House on the other side of Pennsylvania Avenue. Though the suite's annual rental was not quite covered by his Senatorial salary, this was not a problem. The Senator had inherited from his father *The San Francisco Courier-Herald,* nine smaller newspapers, and six radio stations. And it was more or less accurately gossiped that his wife and her brother owned two square blocks of downtown San Francisco and several million acres of timberland in Washington and Oregon.

A tall, distinguished-looking man in his early forties was standing in the corridor. He was wearing a khaki uniform, shirt, trousers, and overseas cap. The U.S. Navy insignia and a silver eagle were pinned to the cap, and silver eagles were on his collar. The right armpit area of the shirt was dark with sweat. The left sleeve had been cut from the shirt at the shoulder to accommodate a heavy plaster cast which covered the arm from the shoulder to the wrist.

The two men looked at each other for a long time before Senator Fowler finally spoke.

"I am so glad to see you, you crazy sonofabitch, that I can't even be angry."

"May I come in, then?" the other man asked with gentle sarcasm.

"Are you all right, Fleming?" Fowler asked, concern coloring his voice.

"When I get out of these fucking clothes, and you get me something cold—and heavily alcoholic—I will be."

"You want to get in bed? Should I call a doctor?"

"I want a very large glass of orange juice, with ice, and a large hooker of gin," Captain Fleming Pickering, USNR, said, as he walked into the sitting room of the suite. "I have been thinking about that for hours."

"Can you have alcohol?"

"Hey, I have a broken arm. That's all."

"A *compound fracture* of the arm," Senator Fowler said. "Plus, I have been told, a number of other unnatural openings in the body."

With his good hand Pickering started to shove an overstuffed chair across the room.

"What are you doing? Let me do that!" Fowler said and walked quickly to him.

"Right in front of the air-conditioning duct, if you please," Pickering said.

"You'll catch cold," Fowler said.

Pickering ignored him. He took off his cap, tossed it onto a couch, then unbuttoned and removed his shirt and dropped it onto the floor. In a moment his khaki trousers followed.

Fowler looked at him with mingled resignation and alarm.

Pickering suddenly marched into one of the bedrooms and came back a moment later with a sheet he had obviously torn from the bed.

He started to drape it over the upholstered chair.

Fowler, seeing what he wanted to do, snatched it from him and arranged it more neatly.

Pickering collapsed into the chair.

"Anything else I can get you, Flem? Are you in pain?"

"How about a footstool and a pillow?" Pickering asked. "And of course the iced orange juice with gin."

Fowler delivered the footstool and the pillow, which Pickering placed on the arm of the chair, and then he lowered his encased arm onto it.

"You look like hell. You're as gray . . . as a battleship."

"I was feeling fine until they opened the door of the airplane and that goddamned humidity swept in like a tidal wave," he said. "I honest to God think the humidity is worse in Washington than it is in Borneo. Or Hanoi."

"You really want a drink?"

"It will make the gray go away, trust me."

Fowler shook his head and then walked into the kitchen, returning with a bowl of ice and a silver pitcher of orange juice. He went to a bar against the wall, put ice and orange juice in a large glass, and picked up a quart bottle of Gilbey's gin.

"I don't feel comfortable giving you this gin."

"Please don't make me walk over there and do it myself."

Fowler shrugged and splashed gin into the glass. He stirred it with a glass stick and then walked to Pickering and handed it to him.

"I knew that sooner or later you would turn me into a criminal," Fowler said.

"Meaning what?" Pickering asked, and then took several deep swallows of the drink.

"Harboring and assisting a deserter is a felony."

"Don't be absurd. All I did was leave the hospital. My orders permit me to go when and where I please."

"I don't think that includes this. The hospital didn't plan to release you for at least another two weeks."

"Yeah, they told me."

"Does Patricia know about it?"

"We stopped for fuel at Saint Louis. I called her from there."

"And what did she say?"

"She was unkind," Pickering said.

"Are you going to tell me what this is all about?"

"Well, I was getting bored in the hospital."

"That's not it, Flem."

"I want out of the Navy. I told Frank that when I saw him in California. When nothing happened, I tried to call him. But I can't get the sonofabitch on the telephone."

Frank Knox was Secretary of the Navy.

"Did he tell you he'd let you do that?"

"He said we would talk about it when I got out of the hospital. I am now out of the hospital."

"I don't think it's going to happen. You were commissioned for the duration plus six months. What makes you think the Navy will let you out?"

"The Navy does what Frank tells it to. That's why they call him 'Mr. Secretary.' "

"What do you plan to do, enlist in The Marines?"

"Come on, Richmond."

"Well, what?"

"Go back to running the company. That way I could make a bona fide contribution to the war."

"Why do I think I'm not getting the truth?"

Pickering started to get out of the chair.

"What are you doing?"

"I need another of these," Pickering said, holding up his glass.

Fowler was surprised, and concerned, to see that he had emptied it.

"I don't think so," Fowler said.

"Richmond, for Christ's sake. I'm a big boy."

"Oh, God. Stay where you are. I'll get it for you."

. Making the second drink just about exhausted the orange juice. Fowler was about to call down for a fresh pitcher when Pickering said, "I want to see Pick before he goes over there."

That, Fowler decided, *sounds like the truth.*

He carried the glass to Pickering and handed it to him.

"Well?"

"Thank you."

"That's not what I mean. You wouldn't let Knox send Pick out to the hospital. For God's sake, he doesn't even know you're home. Or that you've been wounded."

"It would upset him."

"That's what sons are for, to be upset when their fathers are wounded."

"The odds are strongly against Pick coming through this war."

"Every father feels that way, Flem. The truth is that most people survive a war. I don't know what the percentage is, but I would bet that his odds are nine to one, maybe ninety-nine to one, to make it."

"Most fathers haven't been where I have been, and seen what I have seen. And most sons are not Marine fighter pilots. Jesus, do you think I *like* facing this?"

"I just think you're overstating the situation," Fowler said, a little lamely.

"Just before the *Gregory* was hit, her captain told me what a fine airplane the F4F is. It's probably the last thing he ever said; he was dead a minute later. He was trying to do what you're trying to do, make the Daddy feel a little better. It didn't work then and it's not working now. But I appreciate the thought."

"Goddamn it, Flem, I'm calling it like I see it."

"So am I, goddamn it, and I'm calling it how I see it, not how I would like it to be."

"Well, I think you're wrong."

Pickering shrugged and took another swallow of the orange juice and gin.

"Have I still got some uniforms here?"

"No, I gave them to the Salvation Army. Of course you do."

"How about having the house tailor sent up here? I need to have the sleeves cut out of some shirts."

"Sure."

"I mean now, Richmond."

"You're leaving? You just got here."

"I want to go see Frank. To do that, I'll need something more presentable than what I walked in here wearing."

"Seeing Frank can wait until tomorrow. For that matter, I'll call him and ask him to come here."

"Call downstairs for the tailor. Do it my way."

"Yes, Sir, Captain," Fowler said. He walked to a table and started to pick up the telephone. Instead he picked up a copy of *The Washington Star* and carried it back to Pickering.

"Here's the paper," he said, unfolding it for him and laying it in his lap.

There were two major headlines:

BATTLE RAGES ON GUADALCANAL
WILLKIE HEADS OVERSEAS

A photo of a Consolidated B-24 four-engine bomber converted to a long-range transport was over the caption,

Republican Party head Wendell Willkie will travel in this Army Air Corps transport on his around-the-world trip as personal representative of President Franklin D. Roosevelt. He will visit England, North Africa, China and the Soviet Union.

"There are not enough bombers to send to the Pacific," Pickering said bitterly. "But there are enough to give one to a goddamn politician to go all over and get in the goddamned way."

Fowler ignored him.

"Are you hungry, Fleming? Have you eaten?"

"No, and no. But I suppose I'd better have something. How about having them send up steak and eggs?"

Fowler nodded and picked up the telephone. He called the concierge and asked him to send up the tailor, and then called room service and ordered steak and eggs for Pickering. After a moment's indecision he added, "And send two pitchers of orange juice, too, please."

He walked back to Pickering, thinking he could turn the pages of the *Star* for him. Pickering had fallen asleep. His head sagged forward onto his chest. His face was still gray.

"Christ, Flem," Fowler said softly. He walked into the bedroom and came back with a light blanket, which he draped over him, and then he went to the air conditioner and directed its flow away from Pickering.

Then he walked to his own bedroom, in a far corner of the apartment, and closed the door. He took a small address book from the bedside table, found the number he was looking for, and picked up the telephone.

"Office of the Secretary of the Navy, Chief Daniels speaking."

"This is Senator Fowler. May I speak to Mr. Knox, please?"

"One moment, please, Senator. I'll see if he's available."

"Richmond?"

"He's here, Frank."

"Let me speak with him."

"He's asleep. More accurately, he passed out in an armchair in my sitting room."

"How is he?"

"He looks like hell."

"Shall I send a doctor over there?"

"I don't think that's quite necessary. And there's one in the hotel if it should be."

"Do you have any idea what this is all about? What's he up to?"

"Two things. Apparently, you told him you would discuss his getting out of the Navy when he got out of the hospital. He says he is now out of the hospital."

"I'd hoped he would forget that."

"He says he wants to go back to running Pacific & Far East Shipping so that he can make a bona fide contribution to the war effort."

"I wonder what he thinks he's been doing so far?" Secretary Knox asked, and then went on, without waiting for a reply. "There are a number of reasons that's not possible. I suppose I should have told him that when I saw him. But he was a sick man . . . ."

"He's still a sick man. I told him, for what it's worth, that I didn't think you'd let him out."

"It's now out of my hands, if you take my meaning."

Fowler took his meaning. There was only one man in Washington who could override Frank Knox's decisions as Secretary of the Navy. He was Franklin Delano Roosevelt.

"You told him?"

"He's being Machiavellian again. He has his own plans for Pickering."

Fowler waited for Knox to elaborate. He did not.

"He is also very anxious to see his son," Fowler said. "His idea is to see you, get out of the Navy, and then go to Florida."

"I offered to have the boy flown to San Diego!"

"I think he wants to see him alone. He's managed to convince himself that the boy will not come through the war."

"He's not the only father who feels that way. You heard what our mutual friend's son has been up to?"

That was an unmistakable reference to James Roosevelt, a Marine Corps Captain. Captain Roosevelt had recently participated in the raid on Makin Island.

The Marine Corps had somewhat reluctantly formed the 1st and 2nd Raider Battalions. They were the President's answer to the British Commandos. The 1st was one of the units participating in the Guadalcanal operation. At about the same time, the son of the President of the United States was paddling ashore from a submarine with elements of the 2nd Raiders to attack Japanese forces on Makin Island.

"I also heard the Germans have taken Stalin's son prisoner. Do you think our mutual friend—make that 'acquaintance'—has considered the ramifications of that?"

"I have brought it to his attention," Knox said, then went on: "Technically, I suppose you know, Fleming Pickering is AWOL."

"I don't think you could make the charge stick. And he has a lot of friends in high places."

"And doesn't he know it?" Knox said, and then went on, again without waiting for a response: "I'm on my way to the White House. I'll get back to you, Richmond. Keep him there. I don't care how, keep him there."

"I'll do what I can," Fowler said, and hung up.

III

(ONE)
Headquarters, 2nd Raider Battalion
Camp Catlin, Territory of Hawaii
31 August 1942

When Gunnery Sergeant Ernest W. Zimmerman, USMC, Company A, 2nd Raider Battalion, was summoned to battalion headquarters, he suspected it had something to do with Sergeant Thomas Michael McCoy, USMCR.

Zimmerman was stocky, round-faced and muscular. And he'd been in The Corps almost exactly seven years, having enlisted as soon as possible after his seventeenth birthday. He'd celebrated his twenty-fourth birthday a week before aboard the submarine USS *Nautilus* on the way home to Pearl Harbor from the raid on Makin Island. At the time he was nursing a minor, though painful, mortar shrapnel wound in his left buttock.

Sergeant McCoy—four inches taller and forty-two pounds heavier than Gunny Zimmerman—had celebrated his twenty-first birthday the previous January in San Diego, California. He was then in transit, en route to the Portsmouth U.S. Naval Prison in the status of a general prisoner. There was little question at his court-martial at Pearl Harbor that he had in fact committed the offense of ''assault upon the person of a commissioned officer in the execution of his office by striking him with his fists upon the face and other parts of the body.''

He had also been fairly charged with doing more or less the same thing to a petty officer of the U.S. Navy in the execution of his office of Shore Patrolman, both offenses having taken place while PFC McCoy was absent without leave from his assignment to the 1st Defense Battalion, Marine Barracks, Pearl Harbor.

The Marine Corps frowns on such activity. Thus PFC McCoy was sentenced to be dishonorably discharged from the Naval Service and to be confined at hard labor for a period of five to ten years.

However, very likely because it was conducted during the immediate post–Pearl Harbor–bombing period when things were quite hectic, the court-martial failed to offer the accused certain procedural aspects of the fair trial required by Rules for the Governance of the Naval Service.

These errors of omission came to light while the Record of Trial was being reviewed by the legal advisers to the Commander in Chief, Pacific Fleet. It was therefore ordered that the findings and the sentences in the case be set aside.

Another trial was impossible, not only because of the possibility of double jeopardy, but also because the witnesses were by then scattered all over the Pacific.

PFC McCoy was released from the San Diego brig and assigned to the 2nd Raider Battalion, then forming at Camp Elliott just outside San Diego.

There PFC McCoy met Gunnery Sergeant Zimmerman. He almost immediately posed a number of disciplinary problems for Gunny Zimmerman. For instance, while he had apparently learned his lesson about striking those superior to him in the military hierarchy, on two occasions he severely beat up fellow PFCs with whom he had differences of opinion.

But what *really* annoyed Gunny Zimmerman about PFC McCoy's behavior was that it was seriously embarrassing to a Marine officer. Normally, this would not have bothered Gunny Zimmerman—indeed, under other circumstances, he might have found it amusing—but this particular officer was Second Lieutenant Kenneth R. McCoy, USMCR, PFC McCoy's three-year-older brother. Lieutenant McCoy and Gunny Zimmerman had been friends before the war, when Zimmerman had been a buck sergeant and McCoy a corporal with the 4th Marines in Shanghai.

There were very few people in The Corps who enjoyed Ernie Zimmerman's absolute trust and admiration, and Lieutenant "Killer" McCoy was at the head of that short list.

Since all other means of instilling in PFC McCoy both proper discipline and the correct attitude had apparently failed, Zimmerman decided that it behooved him to rectify the situation himself.

He accomplished this by going to the Camp Elliott slop chute, where he politely asked PFC McCoy if he could have a word with him. He led PFC McCoy to a remote area where they would not be seen. He then removed his jacket (and, symbolically, the chevrons of his rank) and suggested to PFC McCoy that if he thought he was so tough, why not have a go at him?

When PFC McCoy was released from the dispensary four days later—having suffered numerous cuts, bruises, abrasions and the loss of three teeth: after a bad slip in the shower—he'd undergone a near miraculous change of attitude.

The change was not temporary. Within three weeks, with a clear conscience, Gunny Zimmerman recommended PFC McCoy for squad leader. The job carried with it promotion to corporal.

And Corporal McCoy performed admirably on the Makin raid. Because of his size and strength, Zimmerman had given McCoy one of the Boys antitank rifles. The Boys, which looked like an oversize bolt-action rifle, fired a larger (.55 caliber) and even more powerful round than the Browning Heavy .50 caliber machine gun.

Although he could not prove it—there were other Boys rifles around—Zimmerman was convinced that McCoy was responsible for shooting up a Japanese four-engine Kawanishi seaplane so badly that it crashed while trying to take off from the Butaritari lagoon.

Nothing heroic. Just good Marine marksmanship, accomplished when the target was shooting back.

And when they were in the rubber boats trying to get off the beach back to the submarine—a disaster—McCoy really came through, really acted like a Marine. His had been one of the few boats to make it through the surf, almost certainly because of his enormous strength. Then, when they reached the sub, which was all that was expected of him, McCoy volunteered to go back to the beach for another load—despite his exhaustion.

Again nothing heroic, but good enough to prove that McCoy had the stuff Marine sergeants should be made of. After they were back at Camp Catlin, Colonel Carlson asked him if anyone should get a promotion as a reward for behavior during the raid. The first name Zimmerman gave him was Corporal McCoy's.

Word reached Gunny Zimmerman an hour before his summons to battalion headquarters that Sergeant McCoy had apparently strayed from the path of righteousness. He'd had a telephone call from another old China Marine, now working with the Shore Patrol Detachment in Honolulu. The Shore Patrol sergeant informed him that Sergeant McCoy apparently took offense at a remark made to him by a sergeant of the Army Air Corps. He expressed his displeasure by breaking the sergeant's nose. He then rejected the invitation of the Shore Patrol to accompany them peaceably.

Zimmerman's old China Marine pal told him, not without a certain admiration, that it took six Shore Patrolmen to subdue and transport Sergeant McCoy to the confinement facility. He was now sleeping it off there.

There seemed little doubt that before the day was over Sergeant McCoy would once again be Private McCoy. Unless, of course, Colonel Carlson wanted to make an example of him and bring him before a court-martial.

In Zimmerman's opinion, busting McCoy would be sufficient punishment. He would be humiliated and taught a lesson. And then in a couple of months they could start thinking about promoting him again.

The facts were that he had been a good corporal and would almost certainly have been a good sergeant.

Good sergeants are hard to find, Zimmerman thought. *Sending him to the brig for thirty days will teach him nothing he doesn't already know, and it might make his attitude worse.*

With a little bit of luck, maybe the sergeant major, or maybe even one of the officers, will ask me what I think should be done to McCoy. Or maybe even I can take a chance and just tell the sergeant major what I think.

Zimmerman went into battalion headquarters, walked up to the sergeant major's desk, and stood waiting while the sergeant major went very carefully over a paper that had been typed up for the Colonel's signature. He finally finished and looked up at Zimmerman.

He smiled.

"How are you, Ernie?" he asked. "How's the ass these days?"

"I sit on the edge of chairs."

"Your Purple Heart came through," the sergeant major said. "You are now a certified wounded hero."

Is that what this is about? Maybe he hasn't heard about McCoy yet.

"Did you send for Zimmerman?" a voice called from the office. On its door a sign hung, EVANS CARLSON, LTCOL, USMC, COMMANDING.

"He just this second came in, Sir," the sergeant major called back.

Colonel Carlson appeared at his office door. He was lean and tanned, and he was wearing sun- and wash-faded utilities.

"Morning, Gunny," he greeted him. "How's the . . . damaged area?"

Zimmerman popped to attention.

"Morning, Sir," he said. "No problem, Sir."

"Get yourself a cup of coffee, if you'd like, and come on in. Something's come up."

"Aye, aye, Sir," Zimmerman said.

Though he didn't really want it, he took a cup of coffee. The reason was that he considered the offer—the suggestion—an order, coming as it did from the Colonel. At the same time, the *friendliness* of the Colonel's gesture made him a little uncomfortable.

Colonel Carlson often made him uncomfortable. Zimmerman was on the edge of being an Old Breed Marine. He hadn't been to Nicaragua or any of the other banana republic wars, but he *had* been in The Corps seven years, most of that time in China, and in all that time he had never met another lieutenant colonel—for that matter, a major or a captain—who treated enlisted men the way Colonel Carlson did.

It was sort of hard to describe why. It wasn't as if Carlson treated the enlisted men as equals, but neither did he treat them the way they were treated elsewhere in The Corps, the way Zimmerman had been treated for seven years.

Colonel Carlson talked to enlisted Marines—not just the senior staff noncoms, but the privates and the corporals, too—like they were *people,* not *enlisted men.* Like he was *really* interested in what they had to say.

The motto of the Raiders was "Gung Ho!" Most people in the Raiders, even the ones who had been in China and had picked up a little Chinese, thought that meant

"Everybody Pull Together." Zimmerman knew better. He spoke pretty good Chinese, three kinds of it. What *Gung Ho* really meant was more like "Strive for Harmony."

When they were training for the Makin Raid back at Camp Elliott, outside 'Diego, Zimmerman talked about that with McCoy—*Lieutenant* McCoy, the Killer, not Sergeant Shit for Brains McCoy, now behind bars in Honolulu.

The Killer spoke even better Chinese than Zimmerman did, plus Japanese and German and Polish and Russian. So he knew what *Gung Ho* really meant, but he told Zimmerman to keep it to himself.

"What I think is really going on, Ernie," the Killer told him, "is that the Colonel is terrifically impressed with the way the Chinese do things. The Chinese communists, I mean."

"You're not telling me he's a communist?"

It would not have surprised Zimmerman at all if the brass had sent Killer McCoy to the 2nd Raider Battalion to see if he thought Colonel Carlson was a communist.

"No. I don't think so. But there are people in The Corps who do."

"Then how come they gave him the Raider Battalion if they think he's a communist?"

"There are also a lot of people who don't think he's a communist, like Captain Roosevelt's father, for example."

Captain Roosevelt was Executive Officer of the 2nd Raider Battalion. His father was Commander in Chief of the Armed Forces of the United States of America. As a Captain, Colonel Carlson had commanded the detachment of Marines assigned to protect the President at White Sulphur Springs, where the President often went to swim with other people crippled by infantile paralysis.

"We're sort of special Marines, Ernie, *Raiders,*" the Killer said. "The Colonel thinks that the kind of discipline the Chinese communists have would work better for us than the regular kind."

"We're *Marines,* not fucking Chinese communists," Zimmerman protested. "Does he really want to do away with ranks and have just leaders and fighters and technicians, and no saluting, and no officers' mess, and the other bullshit that I been hearing?"

"I think he's been talked out of that," McCoy said. "But I know he wants to make sure the enlisted men use their initiative. There's nothing wrong with that, is there?"

"What does that mean, 'use their initiative'?"

"You tell some PFC to fill sandbags and make a wall of them, he does it because you're a sergeant and he's a PFC and PFCs do what sergeants tell them to do. The Colonel figures he'll get a better wall if the sergeant tells the PFC they need a sandbag wall because that will keep people from getting their balls blown off . . . and then the sergeant helps the PFC make it. Understand?"

"Sounds like bullshit to me."

"That's what I thought when I first heard about it," the Killer said. "But now I suppose I've been converted. Anyway, Ernie, it doesn't make any difference what you think."

"It don't?"

"You're a Marine, a gunny. Marine gunnies do what they're told, right?"

"Fuck you, Ken," Zimmerman said, chuckling.

"That's 'fuck you, Lieutenant, Sir,' Sergeant," the Killer replied.

The funny thing, Zimmerman realized, was that over the months he too had become converted to the Colonel's way of doing things. It seemed to work. Everybody in the Raiders did "pull together" or "strive for harmony," depending on how well you spoke Chinese and translated *"Gung Ho!"*

That was very much on his mind on Makin, when things were going badly and he wouldn't have given a wooden nickel for their chances of getting off the fucking beach alive.

He came across Captain Roosevelt then, and the first thing he thought was that only in the United States of America would the son of the head man have his ass in the line of fire. Then he changed that to "only in The Marine Corps" and finally to "only in the Raiders."

Zimmerman realized that he was now a genuine fucking true believer Gung Ho Marine Raider . . . he was also a guy who had spent five and a half of his seven years in The Corps in the Fourth Marines in Shanghai, where officers were officers, and enlisted men were enlisted men.

He was not at all comfortable when he stood in Colonel Carlson's office door and the Colonel waved him into a chair without even giving him a chance to report to the commanding officer in the prescribed manner.

"I didn't know you'd done any time with Marine Aviation, Zimmerman," the Colonel said.

"I never did," Zimmerman said, so surprised that he added "Sir" only after a perceptible pause.

"Curious," Colonel Carlson said and handed him a teletype message.

PRIORITY
CONFIDENTIAL
HQ FLEET MARINE FORCE PACIFIC
1405 30 AUG 1942

To: COMMANDING OFFICER
        2ND USMC RAIDER BATTALION

Info: COMMANDING OFFICER
        21ST MARINE AIR GROUP

1. ON RECEIPT THIS MESSAGE FOLLOWING NAMED ENLISTED MEN ARE DETACHED COMPANY "A" 2ND RAIDER BN AND ASSIGNED HQ 21ST MARINE AIR GROUP.

ZIMMERMAN, ERNEST W 286754 GYSGT
MCCOY, THOMAS M 355331 SGT

2. CO 2ND RAIDER BN WILL ARRANGE TRANSPORT BY MOST EXPE-DITIOUS MEANS, INCLUDING AIR, FROM PRESENT STATION TO RE-CEIVING UNIT. PRIORITY AAA IS AUTHORIZED.

BY DIRECTION: C.W.STANWYCK LTCOL USMC

"The Twenty-first MAG is on Guadalcanal," Colonel Carlson said.

"Yes, Sir, I know."

"Then this doesn't surprise you, Gunny? You knew about it?"

"No, Sir. I mean, no, Sir, I didn't know anything about this."

"I'm curious, Gunny," Carlson said, conversationally. "If this question in any way is awkward for you to answer, then don't answer it. But would you be surprised to learn that Lieutenant McCoy had a hand in this somewhere?"

The question obviously surprised Zimmerman. He met Carlson's eyes.

"Sir, nothing the Kill—Lieutenant McCoy does surprises me anymore. But I don't think he's behind this. I think I know where it come from."

"You did know, didn't you, Gunny, what Lieutenant McCoy was doing, *really* doing, when he was assigned here?"

Zimmerman's face flushed.

"I had a pretty good idea, Sir," he said uncomfortably.

"Lieutenant McCoy is a fine officer," Carlson said, "defined first as one who carries out whatever orders he is given to the best of his ability, and second as a gentleman who is made uncomfortable by deception. You know what I'm talking about, Gunny?"

"Yes, Sir. I think so, Sir."

"I saw Lieutenant McCoy in the hospital just before they flew him home. He told me then what he'd really been doing with the Raiders. I then told him I had been aware of his situation almost from the day he joined the Raiders."

Zimmerman looked even more uncomfortable.

"I told him I bore him no hard feelings. Quite the contrary. That I admired him for carrying out a difficult order to the best of his ability. If certain senior officers of The Corps felt it necessary to send in an officer to determine whether or not the commanding officer of the 2nd Raider Battalion was a communist, then it was clearly the duty of that officer to comply with his orders."

"The Killer never thought for a minute you was a communist, Sir," Zimmerman blurted.

Carlson smiled.

"So I understand," he said. "And I hope you have come to the same conclusion, Gunny."

"Jesus, Colonel!"

"I also told Lieutenant McCoy that whatever his primary mission was, he had carried out his duties with the Raiders in a more than exemplary manner, and that I considered it a privilege to have had him under my command."

"Yes, Sir."

"The same applies to you, Gunny. I wanted to tell you that before you ship out."

"Colonel," Zimmerman said, the floodgates open now, "the Killer told me he arranged for me to be assigned to the Raiders in case he needed me for something he was doing. He didn't tell me what he was doing, and the only thing I ever did was take some telephone messages for him. I didn't even know what the fuck they meant."

"Hence my curiosity about your transfer," Colonel Carlson said. "You said, didn't you, a moment ago, that you thought you knew what was behind the transfer?"

"Yes, Sir. I mean, I don't know for sure, but what I think is . . . when they were forming VMF-229 at Ewa, they was having trouble with their aircraft-version Browning .50s. A tech sergeant named Oblensky, an old China Marine, was. He come to me and McCoy—*Sergeant* McCoy—and me went over there and took care of it for him."

"And you think Sergeant—Oblensky, you said?"

"Yes, Sir. Big Steve Oblensky."

"—was behind this transfer?"

"Yes, Sir. He goes way back. He's too old now, but he used to be a Flying Sergeant. He was in Nicaragua, places like that, flying with General McInerney. He knows a lot of people in The Corps, Sir."

Brigadier General D. G. McInerney was not the most senior Marine Aviator, but he was arguably the most influential.

"And you think that based on Sergeant Oblensky's recommendation, General McInerney, or someone at that level, convinced Fleet Marine Force Pacific that MAG-21 needs you and Sergeant McCoy more than the 2nd Raider Battalion does?"

"Yes, Sir. That's the way I see it."

"I think you're probably right, Gunny," Colonel Carlson said, standing up and offering his hand to Zimmerman. "We'll miss the two of you around here, but I'm sure you'll do a good job for MAG-21."

Zimmerman got quickly to his feet and took Carlson's hand.

"I don't suppose I got anything to say about this transfer, do I, Sir?"

"Yes, of course you do. You've been given an order, and when a good gunny gets an order, he says, 'Aye, aye, Sir.'"

"Aye, aye, Sir."

"Good luck, Gunny. And pass that on to Sergeant McCoy, please."

"Aye, aye, Sir."

Zimmerman did an about-face and marched to the office door. As he passed through it, he suddenly remembered that Sergeant McCoy was at the moment behind bars in Honolulu charged with drunkenness, resisting arrest, and Christ only knows what else.

(TWO)
Armed Forces Military Police Detention Facility
Honolulu, Oahu, Territory of Hawaii
31 August 1942

Sergeant Thomas M. McCoy, USMCR, had not been provided with a pillow or any other bedclothes for his bunk, a sheet of steel welded firmly to the wall of his cell.

He had remedied the situation by making a pillow of his shoes; he'd wrapped them in his trousers. And his uniform jacket was now more or less a blanket.

He was very hung over, and in addition he suffered from a number of bruises and contusions. The combined force of Navy and Marine Corps Shore Patrolmen, augmented by two Army Military Policemen, had been more than a little annoyed with Sergeant McCoy at the time of his arrest.

They had used, with a certain enthusiasm, somewhat more than the absolute minimum force required to restrain an arrestee. Sergeant McCoy's back, hips, buttocks, thighs, and calves would carry for at least two weeks long thin black bruises from nightsticks, and both eyes would suggest they had encountered something hard, such as a fist or elbow.

When the door of his cell, a barred section on wheels, opened with an unpleasant clanking noise, Sergeant McCoy had been awake long enough to reconstruct as much as he could of the previous evening's events and to consider how they were most likely going to affect his immediate future in The Marine Corps.

Even the most optimistic assessment was not pleasant: He would certainly get busted. Depending on how much damage he'd done to the Shore Patrol—the bloody gashes on the fingers of his right hand suggested he'd punched at least one of the bastards in the teeth—there was a good chance he would find himself standing in front of a court-martial, and would probably catch at least thirty days in the brig, maybe more.

On the premise that the damage was already done and that nothing else could happen to him, he ignored whoever it was who had stepped into his cell. When whoever it was pushed on his shoulder to wake him, he ignored that, too.

"Wake up, McCoy," the familiar voice of Gunnery Sergeant Zimmerman said as his shoulder was shaken a little harder.

He doesn't sound all that pissed, McCoy decided. And then there was another glimmer of hope: *Zimmerman ain't all that bad compared to most gunnies. Maybe I can talk myself out of this.*

He straightened his legs. That hurt.

Those bastards really did a job on me with their fucking nightsticks.

He pushed himself into a sitting position and looked at Zimmerman, a slight smile on his face.

He saw that Zimmerman had a seabag with him and that Zimmerman was in greens, not utilities.

That's probably my bag. He looked and saw his name stenciled on the side.

"You look like shit," Zimmerman said.

"You ought to see the other guy, Gunny."

"Anything broke?"

"Nah," McCoy said.

"I got your gear," Zimmerman said, kicking the seabag. "Shave and get into clean greens. I'll be back in five minutes. It stinks in here."

"How the hell am I supposed to shave? There's no water or nothing in here."

"Big, tough guy like you don't need any water or shaving cream."

Zimmerman turned around and struck one of the vertical cell bars with the heel of his balled fist. It clanked open. The moment Zimmerman was outside the cell, it clanked shut again.

Exactly five minutes later he was back. McCoy had changed into a clean set of greens.

"Where we going, Gunny?"

"I told you to shave."

"And I told you there's no water, no mirror, no nothing, in here. How the fuck . . . ?"

Zimmerman hit him twice, first in the abdomen with his fist, and then when he doubled over, in the back of his neck with the heel of his hand.

McCoy fell on the floor of the cell, banging his shoulder painfully on the steel bunk and nearly losing consciousness. He was conscious enough, though, to hear what Zimmerman said, almost conversationally:

"I thought I already taught you that when I tell you to do something it ain't a suggestion."

McCoy heard the sound of Zimmerman's fist striking the cell bar again, then he saw the cell door sliding open, and then closing again.

After a moment McCoy was able to get into a sitting position, resting his back against the cell wall. He took a couple of deep breaths, each of which hurt, then he pulled his seabag to him, unfastened the snap from the loop, and dug inside for his razor.

(THREE)
United States Naval Air Station
Lakehurst, New Jersey
1705 Hours 31 August 1942

Second Lieutenant Malcolm S. Pickering, USMCR, glanced over at his traveling companion, Second Lieutenant Richard J. Stecker, USMC, saw that he was asleep, and jabbed him in the ribs with his elbow.

Pickering, a tall, rangy twenty-two-year-old with an easygoing look, was considered extraordinarily handsome by a number of females even before he had put on the dashing uniform of a Marine officer. Stecker, also twenty-two, was stocky, muscular, and looked—on the whole—more dependable. They were sitting in adjacent seats toward the rear of a U.S. Navy R4D aircraft. To judge from the triangular logotype woven into the upholstery of its seats, the R4D had originally been the property of Delta Air Lines.

"Hey! Wake up! I have good news for you!"

"What the hell?" Stecker replied. He had not been napping. He had been sound asleep.

" 'You too can learn to fly,' " Pickering read solemnly. " 'For your country, for your future.' "

"What the hell are you reading?" Stecker demanded.

" 'Whether you're sixteen or sixty,' " Pickering continued, " 'if you are in normal health and possess normal judgment, you can learn to fly with as little as eight hours of dual instruction.' "

Stecker snatched the *Life* magazine from Pickering's hand.

"Jesus, you woke me up for that?" he said in exasperation, throwing the magazine back in his lap.

"We have begun our descent," Pickering said. "If you had read and heeded this splendid public service advertisement by the Piper people, you would know that."

"Where the hell are we?" Stecker said, looking out the window.

"I devoutly hope we are over New Jersey," Pickering said. He picked up the magazine, found his place, and continued reading aloud: " 'In the future a huge aviation industry will offer great opportunities to pilots of all ages. Visit your Piper Cub Dealer. He will be glad to give you a flight demonstration and tell you how you can become a pilot now.' "

"Will you shut the hell up?"

"It says right here, 'flying saves you time, gas, and tires.' How about that?"

"You're making that up."

"I am not, see for yourself," Pickering said righteously, holding up the magazine. Stecker did not look. He was staring out the window.

"I see water down there," he announced.

"And clever fellow that you are, I'll bet you've figured out that it's the Atlantic Ocean."

"You're in a disgustingly cheerful mood," Stecker said.

"I have visions of finally getting off this sonofabitch, and that has cheered me beyond measure. My ass has been asleep for the last forty-five minutes."

"And your brain all day," Stecker said triumphantly, and then added, "There it is."

Pickering leaned across him and looked out the window. The enormous dirigible hangar at Lakehurst Naval Air Station rose surrealistically from the sandy pine barren, dwarfing the eight or ten Navy blimps near it, and making the aircraft—including other R4Ds—parked on the concrete ramp seem toylike.

The Naval Aviators here are at war, Stecker thought. *Every day they fly Navy blimps and long-range patrol bombers over the Atlantic in a futile search, most of the time, for German submarines that are doing their best to interrupt shipping between the United States and England.*

"How'd you like to fly one of those?" Stecker asked. "A blimp?"

"Not at all, thank you. I have had my fucking fill of the miracle of flight for one day."

It was about 1300 miles in straight lines from Pensacola, Florida, to Lakehurst, N.J.

Using 200 knots as a reasonable figure for the hourly speed of the Gooneybird, that translated to six and a half hours. It had taken considerably longer than that. There had been intermediate stops at the Jacksonville, Florida, Naval Air Station; at Hurtt Field, on Parris Island, S.C.; at The Marine Corps Air Station, Cherry Point, N.C.; the Norfolk NAS, Va.; and Anacostia NAS, Md.

They had taken off from Pensacola at first light, just after four A.M. It was now nearly four P.M., or actually five, since they had changed time zones.

"I mean, really," Stecker said.

"Not me. I'm a *fighter* pilot," Pickering said grandly.

"Oh shit," Stecker groaned.

The Gooneybird flew down the length of the dirigible hangar, then turned onto his final approach. There was the groan of hydraulics as the Gooneybird pilot lowered the flaps and landing gear.

"You know, it actually rains inside there," Stecker said.

"So you have told me. Which does not necessarily make it so."

"It really does, jackass."

"Another gem from R. Stecker's fund of useless knowledge," Pickering said, mimicking the dulcet voice of a radio announcer, "brought to you by the friendly folks at Piper aircraft, where you too can learn to fly."

With a chirp, the Gooneybird's wheels made contact with the ground.

"The Lord be praised, we have cheated death again," Pickering said.

"Jesus Christ, Pick, shut up, will you?" Stecker said, but he was unable to keep a smile off his lips.

They taxied to the transient ramp at one end of the dirigible hangar. A two-story concrete block there was dwarfed by the building behind it.

The plane stopped. The door to the cockpit opened, and a sailor, the crew chief, went down the aisle and opened the door. He was wearing work denims and a blue, round sailor's cap. A blast of hot air rushed into the cabin.

He unstrapped a small aluminum ladder from the cabin wall and dropped it in place.

Pickering unfastened his seat belt, stood up, and moved into the aisle. When the other passengers started following the crew chief off the airplane, he started down the aisle.

"Put your cover on," Stecker said. "You remember what happened the last time."

"Indeed I do," Pickering said. It wasn't really the last time, but the time before the last time. He had exited the aircraft with his tie pulled down, his collar unbuttoned, and his uniform cap (in Marine parlance, his "cover") jammed in his hip pocket.

He had almost immediately encountered a Marine captain, wearing the wings of a parachutist—Lakehurst also housed The Marine Corps' parachutists' school— who had politely asked if he could have a word with him, led him behind the Operations Building, and then delivered a brief inspirational lecture on the obligation of Marine officers, even fucking flyboys, to look like Marine officers, not like something a respectable cat would be ashamed to drag home.

Dick Stecker, who'd listened at the corner of the building, judged it to be a really first-class chewing-out. He'd also known it was a waste of the Captain's time and effort. It would inspire Pickering to go and sin no more for maybe a day. He had been right.

If I hadn't said something, he would have walked off the airplane again with his cover in his pocket and his tie pulled down.

When Stecker got off the plane, he found Pickering looking up like a tourist at the curved roof of the dirigible hangar. From that angle it seemed to soar into infinity.

He jabbed him in the ribs.

"I'll go check on ground transportation. You get the bags."

Pickering nodded.

"Big sonofabitch, ain't it?"

Stecker nodded.

"It really does rain in there?"

"Yes, it does," Stecker said, and then walked toward the Operations Building.

There were a corporal and a staff sergeant behind the counter with the sign TRANSIENT SERVICE hanging above it.

Wordlessly, Stecker handed him their orders.

"Lieutenant," the corporal said, "you just missed the seventeen-hundred bus. The next one's at nineteen-thirty."

"That won't cut it," Stecker said. "Sorry."

"Excuse me, Sir," the corporal said politely, turned his back, and gestured with his thumb to the sergeant that the Second Lieutenant was posing a problem.

The sergeant walked to the counter.

"Can I help you, Lieutenant?"

"I'm on my way to the Grumman plant at Bethpage, L.I. I need transportation."

"Yes, Sir. The way you do that is catch the bus to Penn Station in New York City. And a train from there. You just missed the seventeen-hundred bus, and the next one is at nineteen-thirty."

"If I wait for the nineteen-thirty bus I won't get out there until midnight."

"Sir, you just missed the bus."

"We're scheduled for an oh-six-hundred takeoff, Sergeant. I am not about to get into an airplane and fly to Florida on five hours' sleep. If you can't get us a ride, please get the officer of the day on the telephone," Stecker said.

The sergeant looked carefully at the Lieutenant's orders and then at the Lieutenant and decided that what he should do was arrange for a station wagon. This was not the kind of second lieutenant, in other words, who could be told to sit down and wait for the next bus.

"I'll call the motor pool, Sir. It'll take a couple of minutes."

"Thank you, Sergeant."

"Yes, Sir."

Dick Stecker was less awed with the sergeant—for that matter, with The Marine Corps—than most second lieutenants were. For one thing he was a regular; the service was his way of life, not an unwelcome interruption before he could get on with being a lawyer, a movie star, or a golf professional.

More important, he was a second-generation Marine. He had grown up on Marine installations around the country and in China. While he and Pick Pickering both believed that there were indeed three ways to do things—the right way, the wrong way, and The Marine Corps Way—Pickering viewed The Marine Corps Way as just one more fucking infringement on his personal liberty, and Dick Stecker regarded The Marine Corps Way as an opportunity.

Their current situation was a case in point. The Marine Corps seemed for the moment to have misplaced them—as opposed to having actually *lost* them. So far as they knew, immediately on certification as qualified in a particular aircraft, every other Marine Corps Second Lieutenant Naval Aviator had been transferred to an operational squadron for duty.

Most F4F Grumman Wildcat pilots were assigned to the Pacific, either to a specific squadron or to one of the Marine Air Groups. The Marine Corps had lost a lot of pilots in the battles of the Coral Sea and Midway and in connection with the invasion of Guadalcanal.

It followed that Lieutenants Stecker and Pickering, duly certified as qualified to fly Wildcats, should have been on their way to the Pacific some time ago. Or failing that, they should have been assigned to one of the fighter squadrons forming in the United States for later service in that theater.

But that hadn't happened. They were "temporarily" assigned to the Naval Air Station, Pensacola, Florida (where they'd learned how to fly less than a year before), picking up brand-new Wildcats at the Grumman factory and ferrying them all over the country.

This bothered "Pick" Pickering no end. He wanted to be where the fighting was, not cooling his ass in the United States. He also wallowed in fear that they would be permanently assigned to Pensacola as instructor pilots, spending the war in the backseat of a Yellow Peril teaching people how to fly, while the rest of their peers were off covering themselves with glory in the Pacific.

Dick Stecker had a pretty good idea about why they were doing what they were doing. And while Pickering had listened politely to Stecker's explanation, he didn't accept a word of it. Possibly, in Stecker's view, because it was too simple:

Dick Stecker received his commission from the United States Military Academy at West Point. Since very few Marine officers took their commissions from the Army trade school, this screwed up The Marine Corps' Pilot Procurement Program scheduling insofar as Lieutenant Stecker was concerned.

Pickering received his commission from the officer candidate school at Quantico. The idea of becoming a Marine Aviator never entered his mind until he was given a chance to volunteer for pilot training as an alternative to what The Corps had in mind for him: mess officer.

Before coming into The Corps, Pickering had worked in hotels; he knew how to run bars and kitchens. The Corps needed people with experience in those areas, and The Corps was notoriously nonsensitive to the career desires of newly commissioned second lieutenants, even those whose announced intention was to start fighting the Japs as soon as possible.

But Pickering had a friend in high places. Long before he himself had been commissioned and learned how to fly, Brigadier General D. G. McInerney had been a sergeant at Belleau Wood in 1917. One of his corporals then had been Pick Pickering's father, currently a reserve Navy officer on duty somewhere in the Pacific. The elder Pickering and McInerney had maintained their friendship over the years.

While acknowledging that The Corps did need mess officers, General McInerney decided it needed pilots more, and would just have to make a mess officer out of some other lieutenant who did not possess young Pickering's splendid physical attributes, high intelligence, and tested genetic heritage.

Lieutenants Stecker and Pickering both arrived at Pensacola for training at the same time. Lieutenant Stecker did not think this was pure coincidence. Dick Stecker's father, Jack (NMI) Stecker, now an officer with the First Marine Division on Guadalcanal, had also been at Belleau Wood with General McInerney.

After Pickering and Stecker arrived at Pensacola, their basic flight training was not conducted in accord with the rigidly structured and scheduled system that other young pilots were subjected to. For one thing they were not assigned to a large class. And while they completed the exact syllabus of training everyone else was given, they did not do it as part of any particular training squadron. They took some ground school courses with one training squadron, other ground school courses with other training squadrons. And when it came time for them to actually climb into an airplane, *their* instructor pilots were not just instructor pilots but *senior* instructor pilots. Even though the normal duties of senior instructor pilots were supervision of other instructor pilots and giving check rides, they could and did fit two orphans into their available time, for The Good of The Corps. It was a secret only to Lieutenants Stecker and Pickering that General McInerney inquired every week or so into their progress.

When they completed the course, they did not march in dress whites in a graduation parade to the stirring strains of "Anchors Aweigh" and the Marine Hymn played by a Navy band. Their wings of gold were pinned on one Tuesday afternoon in the office of a Navy captain who seemed baffled by what was going on.

After that they were recommended for fighter training ... probably, in Dick Stecker's judgment, because none of their IPs felt comfortable announcing that one of *his* students didn't have that extra something special required of fighter pilots— especially with General McInerney in the audience.

And when they went down the Florida peninsula for Wildcat training, they again received the prescribed training, but they got it from pilots who were not only qualified IPs, but were also functioning in operational squadrons. So they were taught *the way it really is,* rather than the way the Navy brass thought it should be.

In fact, because of the quality of their instruction, they were just a shade better pilots than other young aviators of equivalent experience. Pickering considered that he was fully qualified to battle the Dirty Jap right now; Stecker was perfectly happy with the opportunity to get more hours in the Wildcat.

Stecker walked back out to the transient parking ramp. Pickering was nowhere in sight. After a moment, though, Stecker saw him standing near the open door to the dirigible hangar, talking to a Naval officer.

He just doesn't want to believe it really does rain inside there. Well, screw you, pal, you are about to learn that it does.

(FOUR)
Buka, Solomon Islands
31 August 1942

Sergeant Steven M. Koffler was awakened in his quarters by Miss Patience Witherspoon. She squatted by his bed and squeezed his shoulder. Miss Witherspoon herself had constructed the bed, of woven grass ropes suspended between poles.

He opened his eyes and looked at her.

The fucking trouble with her, he thought, for perhaps the one-hundredth time, *is her fucking eyes. They're clear and gray. It's as if a real girl is looking out at me from behind that scarred face.*

"There are engine noises, Steven," she said in her soft, precise voice.

"Right," he said.

He swung his feet out of bed and jammed them into his boondockers. They were green with mold, and he had no socks. The three pairs he'd had when they jumped in had lasted just over a month.

He picked up his Thompson submachine gun and checked automatically. As usual the chamber was clear, with a cartridge in the magazine ready to be chambered. He slung the strap over his shoulder before he noticed Patience holding something out to him.

It was his other utility jacket, in no better shape than the one he'd been sleeping in, but Patience had obviously washed it for him.

"I'll save it for later," he said. "Thank you."

"Don't be silly," Patience said, modestly averting her eyes.

He took Mr. Reeves' German binoculars from the stub of a limb on one of the poles that held the hut together and hung them around his neck.

Then he walked to the tree house—there was no real reason for haste. Using the knotted rope, he walked up the tree side to the observation platform.

"What have we got, Ian?" he asked.

"Rather a lot, I would say," Ian replied. "They should be in sight any moment now."

Steve could hear the muted rumble of engines and decided Ian was right. There were many of them.

And a moment later, as he scanned the skies, he saw the first of them. He handed the binoculars to Ian Bruce.

"Never let these out of your hands, Koffler," Mr. Reeves had told him just before

he and Howard went off into the boondocks. *"Ian is a rather good chap, but a curious one. Give him half a chance and he'll try to take them apart to see what magic they contain to make things bigger."*

When Ian handed them back a moment later, Steve noticed that the last tiny scrap of leather had finally fallen off the side of the binoculars. A thumbnail-sized area that had been glue still held on. But tomorrow that too would disappear and the binoculars would be green all over.

"Twenty to thirty, I would say," Ian said. "And I thought I could make out another formation a bit higher."

Steve put the binoculars to his eyes again. The spots in the sky were now large enough to be counted. Six 5-plane V's. Thirty. Almost certainly Bettys.

The Betty (designated the Mitsubishi G4M1 Type 1 aircraft by the Japanese) was the most common Japanese bomber. Koffler knew a good deal about the Betty: He could recite from memory, for example, that it was a twin-engine, land-based bomber aircraft with a normal complement of seven. It had an empty weight of 9.5 tons and was capable of carrying 2200 pounds of bombs, or two 1700-pound torpedoes, over a nominal range of 2250 miles, at a cruising speed of 195 miles per hour. Its maximum speed was 250 miles per hour at 14,000 feet. It was armed with four 7.7mm machine guns, one in the nose, one on top, and two in beam positions, plus a 20mm cannon in the tail.

He knew this much about the Betty because there was very little to do on Buka. You could not, for example, run down to the corner drugstore for an ice-cream soda, or—more in keeping with his exalted status as a Marine sergeant—down to the slop chute for a thirty-five-cent two-quart pitcher of beer.

So, to pass the time, you exchanged information with your companions.

Thus Steve learned from Mr. Reeves that when Australians went rooting, they weren't jumping up and down cheering their football team. "Rooting" was Australian for fucking. He also learned that the American equivalent to the Australian term "sodding" was somewhere between "fucking" and "up your ass."

Mr. Reeves also explained to Lieutenant Howard and Sergeant Koffler the Australian system of government and its relationship to the British Crown. Steve never knew that Australia was started as a prison colony. He had too much respect for Mr. Reeves to ask him if his ancestors were guards or prisoners.

Lieutenant Howard, in turn, explained the American system of government to Mr. Reeves, who actually seemed interested.

Lieutenant Howard also shared his detailed knowledge of Japanese aircraft with Mr. Reeves and Sergeant Koffler. And Sergeant Koffler tried to explain the theory of radio wave transmission, but with virtually no success.

He gave the binoculars back to Ian, who kept them to his eyes until he was able to announce, with certainty, "Bettys. I make them thirty-five."

"I counted thirty," Steve said, putting the glasses to his eyes again. Ian was right. There were thirty-five.

And the aircraft flying above them were Zeroes.

The Zero was the standard Japanese fighter aircraft, also manufactured by Mitsubishi, and officially designated the A6M. It was powered by a Nakijima 14-cylinder 925-horsepower engine, and was armed with two 20mm Oerlikon machine cannon and two machine guns, firing the British .303 rifle cartridge.

According to Lieutenant Howard it was a better airplane than anything the Americans or the English had. It was more maneuverable, and the 20mm cannons were not only more powerful but had greater range than the .50 caliber Browning machine guns on Navy and Marine aircraft.

"I count forty Zeroes," Steve said. "I'll get started. If anything else shows up, let me know."

"Right!" Ian said crisply.

Steve went down the knotted rope and walked to where the radio was kept, broken down. That way they could run with it if that became necessary.

He spotted Edward James and whistled at him. When he had his attention, he made a cranking motion with his hands.

Edward James popped to attention and saluted crisply.

"Sir!" he barked.

When he popped to attention, one of the two MACHETES, SUBSTITUTE STANDARD, he had hanging from his belt swung violently.

"Another inch and you'd have cut your balls off," Steve said. It took Edward James a moment to make the translation into what he thought of as proper English.

"Quite, Sir," he said.

He then disappeared into the bush. When he returned a moment later he was carefully carrying a device that looked something like a bicycle. It was in fact the generator that powered Steve's radios. They originally jumped in with two. But one of these was now worn out beyond repair—both physically (the bearings were shot) and electrically (the coils were shorted). How long the other would last, nobody knew. Steve would not have been surprised if it failed to work now.

By the time Edward James returned with the generator, Steve had the radio connected to the antennae. Edward James proudly connected the generator leads to the radio and then went to string the antennae between trees.

Steve took out the code book—also on its last legs and just barely legible—and wrote out his message. He then encoded it.

By the time he was finished, Edward James was back. Steve made the cranking motion again.

"Right, Sir!" Edward James said. He got aboard the generator and started slowly and powerfully pushing its pedals. In a moment the dials on the radio lit up. Steve put earphones on his head, adjusted the position of the telegraph key, and threw the switch on the Hallicrafters to TRANSMIT. Then he put his hand on the key.

The dots and dashes went out, repeated three times, spelling simply:

FRD6. FRD6. FRD6.
Detachment A of Special Marine Corps Detachment 14 is attempting to establish contact with any station on this communications network.

This time, for a change, there was an immediate reply.

FRD6.KCY.FRD6.KCY.FRD6.KCY.
Hello, Detachment A, This is the United States Pacific Fleet Radio Station at Pearl Harbor, Territory of Hawaii, responding to your call.
KCY.FRD6.SB CODE.
CINCPAC Radio Pearl Harbor, stand by to copy encrypted message.

When he was at Pearl Harbor, Lieutenant Howard once told him, he'd pulled guard duty a couple of times—he was sergeant of the guard—and got a look at CINCPAC Radio. It was in an air-conditioned building, so the equipment wouldn't get too hot. It made it nice for the operators too.

FRD6.KCY. GA.
CINCPAC Radio to Detachment A: Go ahead.

The information that thirty-five Bettys, escorted by forty Zeroes, out of Rabaul and on a course that would take them to Guadalcanal, had just passed overhead at approximately 15,000 feet was encoded on a sheet of damp paper. Sergeant Koffler put the sheet under his left hand and pointed his index finger at the first block of five characters.

As his right hand worked the telegrapher's key, his index finger swept across the coded message. It is more difficult to transmit code than plain English, for the simple reason that code doesn't make any sense.

It took him just over a minute, not quite long enough for the Japanese to locate the transmitter by triangulation, before he sent, in the clear, END.

FRD6.KCY.AKN.CLR.
Detachment A, this is Pearl Harbor. Your transmission is acknowledged. Pearl Harbor Clear.

Steve made a cutting motion across his throat, and Edward James stopped pumping the generator pedals.

Steve watched as Edward James proudly disconnected the generator leads from the Hallicrafters and then smiled at him.

As Edward James left the hut, Miss Patience Witherspoon came in. She carried a plate on which was a piece of cold roast pork (though it took quite a stretch of his imagination to identify it as such) and a baked vegetable, something like a stringy sweet potato, also cold. It tasted like stringy soap.

"Perhaps," Patience said gently, once she saw the look on his face, "they will be able to get something you will like from the Japanese."

And perhaps they've already had their heads cut off by the fucking Japs . . . after telling them where to find us, when the Japs sliced their balls off.

Ah, shit, she means well. I don't want to hurt her feelings.

"This is fine, Patience," he said. "And I'm starved."

She lowered her head modestly and crossed her hands over her breasts. The motion served to bring her breasts to Koffler's attention.

If they weren't all scarred up, they wouldn't look so bad; nothing wrong with their shape, or the nipples.

And then he had a thought that really frightened him: *With the officers gone, no one would ever know if I fucked her.*

IV

Fleming Pickering made a grunting noise and opened his eyes. *It could very well be a groan of pain,* Senator Richmond Fowler thought.

"I seem to have dropped off," Pickering said, pushing himself up in the armchair. "How long was I out?"

"Passed out is more like it," Fowler said. "A couple of hours. How do you feel?"

"Will you stop hovering over me like Florence Nightingale? I'm fine."

"I probably shouldn't tell you this, but you look a hell of a lot better than when you walked in here."

"I feel fine," Pickering said. He sniffed under his armpit. "I smell like a cadaver but I feel fine."

"I was wondering about that," Fowler said. "How do you manage bathing?"

"I take a shower with my arm raised as far as I can, and very carefully. Would you like to watch?"

"I'll pass, thank you just the same. I can live with the smell for a while. And besides, you might want something sent up to eat."

"Was the tailor here?"

"Yes. He did three shirts for you."

"Then I think I'd rather eat downstairs in the grill," Pickering said. He pushed himself out of the chair and walked into the bedroom.

In a moment, Fowler heard the sound of running water. Not without difficulty, he resisted the temptation to go in and help. Fleming Pickering was a big boy.

Five minutes later there was indication that not all was well.

"Oh, shit!" Pickering's voice came from the bedroom, filled with disgust.

Fowler went quickly in. Pickering, stark naked, dripping, stood in the door of the bath, examining water-soaked bandages scattered over his chest and upper stomach. Fowler saw streams of watery blood running down his body.

"I don't suppose you have any adhesive tape?" Pickering asked.

Fowler picked up the telephone.

"This is Senator Fowler. Find Dr. Selleres and send him up here immediately."

"That wasn't necessary," Pickering said.

"Trust me. I'm a U.S. Senator," Fowler said.

Pickering looked at him and chuckled. " 'The check's in the mail,' right? 'Your husband will never find out'?"

"Speaking of wives, I just spoke with yours."

"How'd she know I was here?"

"Where else would you be? Aside from St. Elizabeth's?"

St. Elizabeth's was Washington's best-known mental hospital.

"And?" Pickering replied, not amused.

"And she says, when you get a chance, call."

"I will," Pickering said.

He put his hand to his chest and jerked off one of the bandages. Fowler saw that the wound beneath was still sutured.

"You were almost killed, weren't you?"

"That's like being pregnant, you either are or you aren't. No. I wasn't. I don't think I was ever in any danger of dying."

"I saw the Silver Star citation. You passed out from loss of blood."

"I think that was shock from the arm," Pickering said matter-of-factly. "And I didn't pass out. I just got a little light-headed. Where did you see my citation?"

"Knox sent me a copy. He thought I would be interested."

"Christ, *Knox.* I forgot all about him."

"You will see him tomorrow."

"How do you know that?"

"He called me. How did he know you were here? Same answer. Where else would you go?"

"Is he annoyed?"

"I don't think 'annoyed' is a strong enough word."

"When do I see him?"

"Half past five."

"In the afternoon, obviously. Am I being forced to cool my heels all day, until half past five, as a subtle expression of displeasure?"

"At half past five we are having drinks and a small intimate supper with the President."

"Are you kidding?"

"No. I am not. Knox will be there. And Admiral Leahy. No one else, I'm told."

"What's that all about?"

"I have no idea. When the President's secretary calls me and asks if I am free for drinks and supper, I say, 'Thank you very much.' I don't ask what he has in mind."

"I had hoped to be well on my way to Florida by half past five tomorrow."

"You'll have plenty of time to see Pick. One more day won't matter."

"He is liable to be on orders any day. Considering the shortage of pilots over there, they may not give him much of a pre-embarkation leave, possibly only three or four days. I *don't* have plenty of time."

A knock at the door kept Fowler from having to reply. He went to answer it, and Pickering went into the bathroom and wrapped a towel around his middle.

Or tried to. It was a difficult maneuver with one arm in a cast.

"Hello, Fleming," Dr. Selleres, the house physician, said. He spoke with a slight Spanish accent.

"How are you, Emilio? You brought your bag, I hope? I seem to be leaking all over the Senator's floor."

Dr. Selleres walked to him, took a quick look, and shook his head.

"I'm surprised you were discharged from the hospital," the doctor said. "These wounds are still suppurating."

"They can suppurate as well here as they could in a hospital," Pickering argued reasonably.

"Did you get the cast wet, too?" Selleres said, feeling it. "I don't suppose you've heard of this marvelous new medical technique we have called the sponge bath?"

"I needed a real bath," Pickering said.

"Or so you thought," Selleres said. "Lie down on the bed and I'll do what I can to clean up the mess you've made of yourself."

Once he had Pickering down, the doctor checked his heart and blood pressure and peered intently into his eyes. Fowler was surprised that Pickering didn't protest.

353 ≡ L I N E O F F I R E

Selleres then swabbed the wounds with an antiseptic solution and applied fresh bandages.

"If you don't kill yourself falling down in a shower or doing something else equally stupid, you can have those sutures looked at in four or five days," Dr. Selleres said.

"I love your bedside manner," Pickering said, smiling at him.

"If I wasn't in love with your wife, you could change your own bandages," Selleres said. "Shall I give her any kind of message when I talk to her?"

"You're going to talk to her?"

"Patricia called and made me promise to check on you in the morning. The Senator had told her you were passed out and wouldn't stir before then. Now I can call her tonight and tell her, unfortunately, that you're going to live."

"Do what you can to calm her down, will you, please?"

"Don't I always?" Selleres said. He put out his hand. "Welcome home, Flem. It's good to see you. And I heard about the Silver Star. Congratulations."

"Thank you," Pickering said. Fowler saw that he was embarrassed.

When he had gone, Pickering got off the bed, tried to fasten the towel around his waist, failed, swore, and walked naked out of the bedroom to the bar in the sitting room.

"Not that it seems to bother you," Fowler said, "but would you like some help getting dressed?"

"I can handle everything but a towel," Pickering said. "Towels having neither rubber bands nor buttons."

He made himself a drink and carried it back into the bedroom. Fowler, after making himself a drink, went to the doorway, leaned on the jamb, and watched Pickering dress. He did not offer to help, although it was obvious that Pickering was having a hell of a hard time pulling his cast through the sleeve of a T-shirt and then forcing it over his head.

"Would you please put braces on my trousers?" Pickering asked as he pulled on boxer shorts.

Fowler went to the dresser and picked up a pair of suspenders.

"If you manage that without too much difficulty, I'll let you put the garters on my socks," Pickering said.

"How do you cut your food?" Fowler asked.

"The same way I tie my tie," Pickering said. "I have some kind soul do it for me."

"We don't have to go out to eat, you know. There's room service."

"Tell me about what Leahy's doing," Pickering said, ignoring the offer.

"What do you want to know?"

"I'm just curious. His role seems to fascinate all the admirals."

"You ever meet him?"

Pickering nodded.

"A couple of times. When he was Governor of Puerto Rico. Interesting man."

"A good man," Fowler said. "The first time I met him was when he was Chief of Naval Operations. If it wasn't for him, the way he fought for construction funds, made Congress understand, we would have a very small Navy right now to fight this war."

"So what's he doing now?" Pickering asked, sitting on the bed and pulling black socks over his feet.

Fowler dropped to his knees and strapped garters on Pickering's calves.

"His title is Chief of Staff to the Commander in Chief of the Armed Forces of the United States . . ." Fowler said.

"Which the Navy brass in the Pacific thinks means that he's the senior uniformed officer of the Armed Forces, Army and Navy. Is that the situation?"

". . . which sounds very impressive," Fowler went on, ignoring the question. "There was an initial perception that he was to rank above both King and Marshall." Admiral Ernest King was the Chief of Naval Operations; General George C. Marshall was the Chief of Staff of the Army. "He had seniority over both officers, having retired from being Chief of Naval Operations in 1939."

"But?" Pickering interrupted again.

"But Roosevelt quickly torpedoed that," Fowler went on, "—note the Naval symbolism—by saying that Leahy is going to be his legman. His legman *only*."

"I am just a simple sailor," Pickering said. "Unversed in the Machiavellian subtleties of politics. I don't know what the hell you're talking about."

"It means that the master of that art, Machiavellianism, our beloved President, has done it again."

"Done what again?"

"Kept his subordinates off balance. He's very good at that. Marshall and King don't know what to think: Just what authority does Leahy have? Is he speaking as Admiral Leahy, who has a lot of rank but no legal authority? Or is Leahy speaking with the authority of the President?"

"So what exactly does he do?"

"Whatever the President tells him to do."

"Now that I have this explanation, I realize that not only doesn't it have anything to do with me, but that I really don't give a damn about White House or Army/ Navy politics."

"You're in the Navy, you should be interested."

"I keep telling you that I'm getting out of the Navy," Pickering said.

"And I keep telling you," Fowler said, getting off his knees, "that I don't think Frank Knox is going to let you go. Can you get your pants on by yourself or will you need help with that, too?"

"If you've put the braces on my pants, I can handle putting them on."

(TWO)
Pennsylvania Station
New York City, New York
31 August 1942

"Thanks for the ride, Boats," Lieutenant Stecker said to the bosun's mate who had driven them to Manhattan from Lakehurst.

"Yes, Sir," the bosun said. "You go right through that door and you'll see where you turn in your travel vouchers for a ticket—the sign says 'Rail Transportation Office.'"

"Thanks again," Stecker said and closed the station wagon door.

He picked up his small bag and stood there smiling and waving until the station wagon had driven away.

Lieutenant Pickering stepped off the curb, put his fingers to his lips, and whistled. The noise was startling. In a moment a taxi pulled to the curb.

Pickering bowed Stecker into the cab.

"Foster Park Hotel, please," Pickering said to the driver, and then turned to Stecker. "I don't understand why we didn't have the station wagon drop us at the hotel."

"Because that was not some seaman second class," Stecker explained, "who would not give a damn if you told him to drop you in the middle of the Holland Tunnel. That was a boatswain's mate second class. Boatswain's mates second class do not normally chauffeur people around."

"So?" Pickering asked.

"So he probably was driving us because nobody else could be found to drive us. He did not mind doing so, because he thought we really had to catch the train to Long Island. Still with me?"

"To repeat, so?"

"So now he is returning to Lakehurst thinking he has made a small contribution to the war effort by giving up an evening drinking beer and taking two Marine officers to catch a train. On the other hand, if he dropped us at the hotel, bosun's mates being the clever fellows they are, he would have deduced that we were not bound for Long Island. He would have reported this fact to the chief who runs the motor pool. *'Those two fucking jarhead flyboy second johns didn't go anywhere near fucking Penn Station.'* And the next time we asked for wheels at Lakehurst, we would be told, politely, of course, to go fuck ourselves."

Stecker looked at Pickering to judge his reaction to what he thought of as his Lesson 1103 in The Practical Aspects of Military Service. It was immediately apparent that Pickering hadn't heard at least half of what he had said. Pickering was looking out the window.

Then he leaned forward and slid open the panel between the backseat and the front.

"Where are we going?"

"Foster Park Hotel, Sir."

"By way of Greenwich Village? Jesus, do we look that stupid?"

"This is a shortcut I know, Sir."

"Stop at the next cop you see," Pickering said.

The taxi made the next right turn and then turned right again, now headed uptown toward Central Park.

"A guy's got to make a living," the cabdriver said.

"You picked the wrong sucker," Pickering said. "I used to live here."

"You sure don't sound like no New Yorker."

"Oh, shit," Pickering said, laughing, and then slid the window closed and moved back onto his seat. "Did you hear that? That was a New York apology. Our driver is a mite pissed because I don't sound like a New Yorker; I made him waste his time trying to cheat us because I don't sound like a New Yorker."

"Did you hear what I said about why we're in this cab in the first place?"

"What does it matter?"

Stecker shook his head in resignation and leaned back against the cushion.

Like the other forty-one hotels in the Foster chain, the Foster Park Hotel provided its guests quiet elegance and every reasonable amenity. Andrew Foster learned early on in his career that a large number of people were willing to pay handsomely for hotel accommodations so long as the hotel was centrally located and offered first-class cuisine, well-appointed rooms and suites, and round-the-clock staffing. In every Foster hotel, for example, a room service waiter was on duty on every floor around the clock; a concierge was on duty in the lobby day and night; and complimentary limousine service was provided to and from railroad stations and airports.

Foster Hotels were not, in other words, the sort of places sought out by second lieutenants looking for a cheap place to rest their weary heads for a night.

A bellman, wearing a short red jacket, black trousers, and a pillbox cap tilted at the prescribed angle, rushed to open the door of the taxi when it pulled to the curb before the Foster Park Hotel marquee. As soon as he saw the two second lieutenants emerging from the car, his face showed that he was obviously aware that the Foster Park Hotel was doubtless beyond their limited means.

"May I help you, gentlemen?" he asked politely.

"We can manage, thank you," Pickering said.

"Are you checking in with us, Sir?" the bellman asked in a tone suggesting that this was highly unlikely. Even sharing a small double, a night at the Foster Park would cost these guys half their month's pay.

"I devoutly hope so," Pickering said.

At that point the doorman entered the conversation. He wore a black frock coat, striped trousers, and a gray silk hat, and was far too dignified either to open doors or to wrestle with luggage.

"Good evening, Mr. Pickering. How nice to see you, Sir."

"Hello, Charley, how are you?" Pickering said.

The doorman snatched Stecker's small bag from his hand and passed it to the bellman.

"Put the gentlemen's luggage in 24-A," the doorman ordered as he relieved Pickering of his small bag and gave it to the bellman.

Twenty-four-A and 24-B were a pair of terraced four-room suites that overlooked Central Park. The only more prestigious accommodation in the Foster Park was 25, the Theodore Roosevelt Suite, whose nine rooms occupied the entire front of the 25th floor.

The doorman walked quickly to open the door for the two lieutenants.

"Is there anything I can do for you, Mr. Pickering?" he asked as Pickering walked past him.

"Don't get between me and the men's room," Pickering said. "The last time I met nature's call was somewhere over Maryland."

The doorman chuckled.

"I believe you know where to find it, Sir."

"How could I forget?" Pickering said.

The resident manager of the Foster Park Hotel, in a gray tailcoat and striped trousers, was standing a discreet distance from the entrance to the gentlemen's facility when Lieutenants Pickering and Stecker came out.

"Good evening, Mr. Pickering," he said. "A pleasure to have you in the house, Sir."

"And it's always a pleasure to be here."

"There are no messages, Sir, I checked. And I had a small bar set up in 24-A. If there is anything else?"

"Very kind of you. I can't think of a thing. Thank you."

"Have a pleasant evening, Sir."

"We're going to try," Lieutenant Stecker said.

"Starting, I think," Pickering said, "with a snort in the bar."

There were perhaps two dozen people in the dimly lit bar, mostly couples and quartets sitting at tables, but with several pairs of single men at tables and two other single men sitting at the bar.

There were also two strikingly attractive young women sitting together at a table in the corner.

The bartender addressed Pickering by name, adding, "Famous Grouse, an equal amount of water, and a little ice, right?"

"You have the memory of an elephant," Pickering said. "Give my cousin one of the same."

"I'm not related to him," Stecker said, almost a reflex action, and then: "Did you see what's sitting in the corner?"

"Yes, indeed. I think he works for the Morgan Bank."

"I meant the blonde and her friend," Stecker said, even as he realized that Pickering had again successfully pulled his chain.

"Oh," Pickering said. "Her."

The bartender delivered the drinks. Pickering sipped his and then got off the stool.

"You keep the target under surveillance while I check on the car," he said. "Try not to slobber and drool."

He walked out of the bar carrying his drink, then through the lobby to the revolving door to the street. When he caught the doorman's eye, he motioned him over.

"What's up?" the doorman asked, his tone considerably less formal than it had been.

"The two ladies in the bar," Pickering said. "Are they what I think they are?"

The doorman now looked distinctly uncomfortable.

"Jesus, Pick."

"Answer yes or no."

"Yes and no. They are. But they aren't working the bar, Pick. I know better than that."

"Tell me, Charley."

"I don't know if they're free-lancing, working the bars at the Plaza or the St. Regis, or whether they're a couple of Polly Adler's girls. Or somebody else's. They come in every couple of nights, have a couple of drinks, and leave. They never so much as make eyes at any of our guests."

"They know you know?"

"Sure."

"I want to go to bed," Pickering said, and then when he saw the look in Charley's eyes, added, *"Alone.* And early. My buddy, on the other hand, is randy. Since we have to get up at four goddamn A.M., I'm in no mood to prowl the nightclubs. Getting the picture?"

"Sure. Which one?"

"He likes the blonde."

"Who wouldn't? That'd be expensive, Pick."

Pickering reached into his trousers pocket and came up with a wad of bills. He counted out three twenty-dollar bills and handed them to Charley.

"Not that much, Pick. All he's going to do is rent it for a little while."

"I don't want him to know that, right? If there's any left over, leave it in an envelope at reception."

"I understand."

"Get rid of the other one."

"You must be tired."

"I'm in love."

"No shit?"

"No shit."

"Hey, I'm happy for you, Pick."

"I appreciate this, Charley."

"Don't be silly. Anytime. Anything, Pick."

Pickering smiled at him, touched his arm, and walked back toward the bar.

Charley signaled with his finger to the bellman standing on the other side of the lobby to join him.

"There's a blonde in the bar," he said. "Tell her there's a telephone call for her. Bring her here. If I'm not back, tell her to wait."

"OK. What's going on?"

"None of your goddamn business," Charley said. He went to the concierge's desk.

"Mr. Pickering's guest will probably ask a young lady to join him for a nightcap in 24-A."

"I understand," the concierge said. "I'll take care of it."

Charley the doorman and the concierge had been employees of the Foster Hotel Corporation long enough to know that Andrew Foster had one child, a daughter. His daughter had one child, a son. The son's name was Malcolm S. Pickering. Charley the doorman met Pick Pickering when Pick was sixteen and was spending the summer at the Foster Park learning the hotel business: first as a busboy; later, when he proved his stuff, as a baggage handler; and finally, before the summer was over, as a bellman.

(THREE)
Bethpage Station
Long Island Railroad
0530 Hours 1 September 1942

Second Lieutenant Malcolm S. Pickering, USMCR, reached into the passenger compartment of the Derham-bodied Packard Straight Eight 280 limousine and pushed at the shoulder of Second Lieutenant Richard J. Stecker, USMC. When this failed to raise Stecker from his slumber, he pinched Stecker's nostrils closed, which did.

"Jesus Christ!" Stecker said, sitting up abruptly and knocking Pick's hand away.

"And good morning to you, Casanova," Pick said. "Nap time is over."

Stecker snorted.

"You have a hickey on your neck," Pick said.

"Fuck you."

"That was simply an observation, not an expression of moral indignation. I'm *glad* you had a good time . . . you *did* have a good time?"

"None of your fucking business."

"You sounded like you were having a good time. It sounded like a first-class Roman orgy in there."

"Do I detect a slight hint of jealousy?" Stecker asked as he climbed out of the limousine. "You had your chance. She told you she had a girlfriend she could call."

"*I* paid attention to the Technicolor clap movies I was shown. *I* don't go around picking up fast women in saloons, thus endangering *my* prospects for a happy home full of healthy, happy children borne for me by the decent, wholesome girl of my choice after the war."

"Oh, shit!" Stecker said. "And just for the record, she's a legal secretary."

"I gather you intend to see her again?" Pick asked.

"Jesus Christ," Stecker said angrily, suddenly remembering. "I didn't get her phone number!"

"She's probably in the book," Pick said.

"Yeah," Stecker said. "Christ, I hope so."

"Will there be anything else, Mr. Pickering?" the chauffeur of the Foster Park limousine said.

"No, I don't think so. Thank you very much. I'm sorry you had to bring us out here at this ungodly hour."

"No problem, Mr. Pickering, glad to be of service."

"When you see Charley," Pickering said, "tell him I said thank you very much."

"I'll do that, Mr. Pickering. And you take care of yourself."

"Thank you," Pickering said as he shook the chauffeur's hand.

Pickering and Stecker picked up their bags, walked twenty yards to the head of the taxi line, and climbed in the first one.

"Grumman," Pickering told the driver. "Use the airfield entrance."

At least, Stecker thought, *he remembers that much. We did not roll up to the airfield gate in the limousine.*

In Stecker's opinion, the key to success as a second lieutenant was invisibility. Second lieutenants should be neither seen nor heard. With Pickering, that was difficult. Pick was a living example of Scott Fitzgerald's line about the rich being different from you and me.

During their basic flight training at Pensacola, second lieutenants were furnished quarters, two men to a tiny two-room apartment in a newly constructed, bare-frame wooden bachelor officer's quarters building. Such facilities proving unsatisfactory to Second Lieutenant Pickering, he rented a penthouse suite in the San Carlos Hotel in downtown Pensacola and commuted to flight school in his 1941 Cadillac convertible.

The two of them made a deal: Stecker paid for their liquor (acquired tax-free at the Officer's Sales Store). In exchange he got to live in the suite's second bedroom. He did not want to be a mooch, but he couldn't refute Pickering's argument that he was going to have to pay for the suite whether the second bedroom was used or not. So why not?

Not without a little surprise, Stecker quickly learned that Pickering was not a mental lightweight or even someone taking a free ride from his wealthy parents. For instance, the Cadillac had not been a gift. It was purchased from Pick's earnings during his last college summer vacation. He had worked as head bellman in a Foster hotel. Stecker was astonished to learn not only how much head bellmen earned, but how important a head bellman is to a successful hotel operation.

Pick had also worked in hotel kitchens enough to have made him a professional-level chef. Stecker never ceased to be amazed that Pickering could tell the precise doneness of a grilled steak—rare, medium, or medium-rare—by touching it with the tip of his thumb.

For a while grilling steaks for Pensacola maidens on the terrace of their hotel suite was a very profitable enterprise, carnally speaking. But then Pick fell in love.

Not with one of the maidens, but with a widow (a *young* widow, his age) who wanted nothing to do with him. Part of Pick's infatuation with her, Stecker suspected, was that she spurned his attentions. A most unusual occurrence where Pick was concerned; from what Stecker had seen, females ran toward Pickering with invitation in their eyes, not away from him.

The widow, Martha Sayre Culhane, was the daughter of the Number-Two Admiral aboard Pensacola NAS, Rear Admiral R. B. Sayre. Her husband, a Marine First Lieutenant, a Naval Aviator, had been killed on Wake Island.

Pick was of course a formidable suitor, but he got no further with Martha Culhane than some dinner dates and movies. And she flatly refused to marry him.

Stecker was absolutely convinced that she had not let Pickering into her pants.

But he was faithful to her, witness last night, when a smashingly beautiful woman with an uncontrollable lust for Marine Aviators had a friend who felt very much the same way. Pick hadn't even wanted to meet her.

That was either incredibly stupid or admirable.

Because Stecker had grown very fond of Pickering, he gave his buddy the benefit of the doubt. It was admirable. Sir Pick, riding off to the Crusades, vowing to stay chastely faithful to Maid Martha while she remained pure and untouched in Castle Pensacola.

Stecker looked out the window and saw they were riding beside the hurricane fence that surrounded the Grumman plant. Up ahead he could see the floodlighted area around the gate. Since the cab was not permitted inside the fence, they got out of it by the gate.

Stecker saw a white-hat inside the guard shack. That was unusual. Although there was a small Navy detachment assigned to the factory, the security force was civilian. The officers and white-hats were here to get aircraft through the production lines and out to the fleet and air bases, not to guard the plant.

Pickering paid the cabdriver, and Stecker walked to the gate, taking a copy of their orders from his pocket as he did so.

"Excuse me, Sir," the white-hat said, saluting as he came out of the guard shack. "Is your name Pickering?"

"He's Pickering," Stecker replied with a gesture in the general area of the taxi. He was suddenly afraid that something unpleasant was about to happen. The insignia on the white-hat's sleeve identified him as an aviation motor machinist's mate first class. Sailors holding the Navy's second-highest enlisted grade are not ordinarily found in guard shacks at quarter to six in the morning.

"You're Lieutenant Stecker, then, Sir?"

"Right."

"Wait right there please, Lieutenant," the white-hat said, and went back in the guard shack. Stecker saw him pick up a telephone and dial a number.

The white-hat came back out of the guard shack as Pickering walked up. The white-hat saluted him. Stecker found nothing wrong with the return salute Pickering rendered.

He returns *salutes just fine. What gets him in trouble are those vague gestures supposed to be salutes that he* gives *those senior to him in the military hierarchy.*

"Gentlemen," the AMMM1st said, "the senior naval representative aboard would like a word with you. If you'll come with me I have transport."

The transport turned out to be a Chevrolet pickup truck painted Navy gray. When they had all crowded into the cab, Stecker said, "I wonder why I have this feeling that we're in trouble?"

"May I speak freely, Sir?"

"Please do."

"Where the fuck have you two been? They've been looking for you since yesterday afternoon."

"Who is 'they'?"

"First it was Lieutenant Commander Harris. Then, when you didn't show up last night, Commander Schneebelly. He's the senior naval representative, and he's been shitting a brick."

"Do you have any idea what it's all about?"

"I know there was a message from the Navy Department. I don't know what was in it. Where the hell have you been? Night on the town? I hope she was worth it."

"This officer was carousing and consorting with loose women," Pickering said piously. *"I* myself went to bed early, and of course, *alone.* I should have known that if I associated with *him,* he would sooner or later get me in trouble."

"Why don't I believe that, Lieutenant?" the petty officer asked.

"That he would get me in trouble?"

"That you went to bed early and alone. You could have come out here and done that."

"I have to keep an eye on him. He tends to run amok."

"This may not be as funny as you seem to think it is," Stecker said. "Did you do anything at Pee-cola I don't know about?"

"Can't think of a thing," Pick said truthfully.

The pickup pulled up before the Operations Building, a Quonset hut.

"Here we are," the petty officer said. "Good luck. Commander Schneebelly sometimes gets a little excited."

They stepped out of the truck and walked into the Quonset hut.

A chief petty officer was leaning on a counter. He stood erect when he saw them.

"Good morning, Chief," Stecker said.

"Mr. . . . ?"

"Stecker, and this is Mr. Pickering."

"Commander Schneebelly will see you now, gentlemen," the chief said, pointing to a closed door.

Motioning Pickering to follow him, Stecker walked to the door and knocked.

"Come!"

"Stand at attention when we get in there and keep your mouth shut," Stecker said softly, and then opened the door and marched in.

He came to attention before Commander Schneebelly's desk.

"Sir, Lieutenants Stecker and Pickering reporting as ordered, Sir."

Commander Schneebelly was short and plump; he wore both a pencil-line mustache and aviator's wings.

He pursed his lips.

"Stand at ease, gentlemen," he said softly, and then far less softly, "Where the hell have you two been?"

"Sir, our orders state 'not later than zero six-thirty' this morning," Stecker said. "Sir, with respect, it's zero five fifty-five."

"That's not what I asked, Mister!" Commander Schneebelly snapped. "And I can tell time, thank you. Don't tell me what your orders say. I asked you, *where have you been?*"

"Permission to speak, Sir?" Pickering said, and Stecker winced.

"Speak!"

"Sir, this is all my fault. We spent the night at my grandfather's house. Lieutenant Stecker wanted to come right out here, but I talked him out of it."

Commander Schneebelly considered that for a moment.

"Goddamn it, Mister, don't you have the brains you were born with? Doesn't your grandfather have a telephone? Is there some reason you couldn't have called out here and said that you would report in this morning?"

"No excuse, Sir," Pickering said.

"Goddamn it, son, you're an officer in the Naval Service. You've got to learn to think."

"Yes, Sir."

Commander Schneebelly glowered at both of them for another thirty seconds. But it seemed longer. He then handed Pickering a sheet of teletype paper.

URGENT
NAVY DEPT WASH DC 1530 31AUG42

TO: FLAG OFFICER COMMANDING
      NAS PENSACOLA FLA
      SENIOR NAVAL REPRESENTATIVE
      GRUMMAN AIRCRAFT CORPORATION
      BETHPAGE LI NY

1. THIS MESSAGE CONFIRMS VARIOUS TELEPHONE CONVERSA-
TIONS OF THIS DATE BETWEEN CAPT D.W. GOBLE, AND COMM F.L.
TAYLOR, NAS PENSACOLA; COMM J.W. SCHNEEBELLY AND LTCOM
B.T. HARRIS, OFFICE OF NAVAL REPRESENTATIVE, GRUMMAN AIR-

CRAFT CORP BETHPAGE LI NY AND CAPT J.T. HAUGHTON, OFFICE OF SECNAV.

2. THE SECRETARY OF THE NAVY DESIRES THE PRESENCE OF 2ND LT M.S. PICKERING, USMCR AND 2ND LT RICHARD J. STECKER, USMC IN WASHINGTON, D.C. NOT LATER THAN 1600 1 SEPTEMBER 1942.

3. SENIOR NAVREP GRUMMAN WILL AT THE EARLIEST POSSIBLE TIME DIRECT SUBJECT OFFICERS TO SCHEDULE AN INTERMEDIATE STOP AT ANACOSTIA NAS ARRIVING THERE AT NOT LATER THAN 1600 HOURS DURING FERRY FLIGHT BETHPAGE DASH PENSACOLA AND BE PREPARED TO SPEND NOT MORE THAN TWENTY-FOUR HOURS IN WASHINGTON.

4. SENIOR NAVREP GRUMMAN WILL BY THE MOST EXPEDITIOUS MEANS, PREFERABLY TELEPHONE, INFORM OFFICE SECNAV OF (A) TRANSMITTAL TO SUBJECT OFFICERS OF ORDERS IN 2. AND 3. ABOVE; (B) OF DEPARTURE OF SUBJECT OFFICERS FROM BETHPAGE AND ESTIMATED TIME OF ARRIVAL AT ANACOSTIA.

BY DIRECTION:

HAUGHTON, CAPT, USN, ADMINISTRATIVE OFFICER TO SECNAV

Pick read it and then looked at Commander Schneebelly.

"May I show this to Mr. Stecker, Sir?"

Schneebelly made an impatient gesture signifying that he might.

What the hell is this? Stecker wondered.

"What the hell is this all about?" Commander Schneebelly asked. "Do you know?"

"No, Sir," Stecker said.

"No, Sir," Pickering parroted.

"I have been just a little curious," Schneebelly said, "and so, I am sure, have people at Pensacola. What possible interest could the Secretary of the Navy have in two second lieutenants?"

Neither Stecker nor Pickering replied.

"All right. Now let me tell you what's going to happen. I have personally drawn up a flight plan for you. It is approximately 230 air miles between here and Anacostia, passing over Lakehurst NAS. At a cruising speed of 280 knots, that indicates an approximate flight time of forty-eight minutes. We will figure on one hour, just to be safe. We will also schedule your arrival time at Anacostia for 1500 hours, rather than 1600. That means you will take off from here precisely at 1400 hours. Between now and 1400, you will ensure that your uniforms are shipshape, and get yourselves haircuts. You will not leave the plant grounds, and you will keep me, and/or the chief, advised of your location at all times. Clear? Any questions?"

"Sir, what about test-flying the airplanes?" Stecker asked.

"The airplanes will have been test-flown before you sign for them. I'll do it myself, as a matter of fact."

"Sir, with respect, I'd prefer to do that myself."

"No one particularly cares what you would prefer to do, Mister."

"Sir, with respect, that's called for by regulations."

"You really are a wise guy, aren't you, Mister?"

"I don't mean to be, Sir."

"Very well, Mister, you will conduct the pre-ferry test flight."

"Thank you, Sir."

"Chief!" Commander Schneebelly called, raising his voice.

The door opened and the chief stuck his head in.

"Chief, these officers are going to conduct pre-ferry test flights of their aircraft and then they are going to get haircuts and have their uniforms pressed. Would you please go with them and see that they have every possible assistance?"

"Aye, aye, Sir."

"Don't let them out of your sight, Chief."

(FOUR)
The Foster Lafayette Hotel
Washington, D.C.
1710 Hours 1 September 1942

There was a knock. And Senator Richmond F. Fowler went to the door of his suite to answer it.

Two young men were standing in the hotel corridor. One wore a suit that bulged under the left armpit. The other was a Lieutenant Commander of the United States Navy in high-collared whites. From his shoulder was suspended the golden cords of an aide to the President of the United States.

The collars of both were wilted by sweat, and there were sweat-soaked patches under the jacket armpits.

"Good evening, Senator," the Secret Service agent said. "I'm Special Agent McNulty of the Presidential detail."

Fowler nodded at him but did not speak.

"We have a White House car, Senator, whenever you and Captain Pickering are ready," Secret Service Agent McNulty said.

"Please thank the President," Senator Fowler said, "and tell him that both the Captain and I are quite able to walk across the street and would prefer to do so."

"There has been a change of plans, Senator," the Naval aide said. "I'm Commander Jellington, Sir, the President's Naval aide."

Fowler looked at him and waited for him to go on. When he did not, Fowler said, "Is the change of plans really a matter of national security, Commander? Or are you going to tell me what the change is?"

"Dinner will be aboard the *Potomac,* Senator," McNulty answered for him.

"Hence, the *Naval* aide, right?" Fowler said. "Come in."

"Thank you, Sir," they said almost in unison.

"Actually, Sir," Commander Jellington said, "the President sent me to be of whatever assistance I could to Captain Pickering."

"Rendering assistance to Captain Pickering is right up there with trying to pet an alligator—a *constipated* alligator," Fowler added. "You stand a good chance of having the friendly hand bitten off at the shoulder."

He led the two down a corridor to the sitting room, which was on the corner of the building.

"There has been a change of plans, Fleming," Fowler announced to what looked like an empty room. "We are going to dine on the *Potomac.*"

"What does *that* mean?" Pickering's voice came from a high-backed leather chair placed directly in front of the room's air-conditioning duct.

"The *Potomac* is the Presidential yacht, Sir," Commander Jellington said.

Pickering rose from the chair. He was dressed in a T-shirt and boxer shorts. He was shoeless, but wearing calf-high black stockings held in place by garters. Bandages across his chest could be seen through the thin cotton of the T-shirt.

Neither the Naval aide nor the Secret Service agent seemed to notice anything out of the ordinary.

"Good afternoon, Captain Pickering," the Naval aide said. "Sir, I'm Commander Jellington. The President thought I might in some way be helpful to you."

"Whenever you and the Senator are ready, Sir," Agent McNulty said, "we have a White House car."

"The last I heard," Pickering said, glowering at Senator Fowler, "this was going to be cocktails and a simple supper across the street." He gestured with his right arm toward the White House; in his hand he held a bottle of Canadian ale. "And starting at half past six. It's only five something."

"The President has apparently changed his mind," Fowler said. "We are going to dine aboard the *Potomac*. And may I suggest that it behooves you, Captain, as a Naval officer, to manifest a cheerful and willing obedience to the desires of your commander in chief?"

"That sonofabitch," Captain Pickering said. "I should have known he'd pull something like this."

The eyes of Special Agent McNulty widened. He was not used to hearing the President referred to in such terms, much less by someone about to be honored with the great privilege of an intimate dinner with the President aboard the Presidential yacht.

"I think we should all remember that Captain Pickering is a wounded hero," Senator Fowler said, a touch of amusement in his voice, "just recently released from the hospital. And we all know that wounded heroes are a little crazy and have to be humored, don't we?"

"Fuck you, Senator," Captain Pickering said.

McNulty was more than a little uncomfortable. It was one of those situations not neatly covered by regulations and policy.

On one hand he took very seriously (his wife said "religiously") his duty to protect the President of the United States from all threats, real or potential: Here was a man who'd obviously been drinking, who angrily referred to the President as "that sonofabitch," who was just out of the hospital, and was quite possibly at least a little off the tracks, mentally speaking. A rational man did not say "Fuck you!" to a man like Senator Richmond Fowler.

On the other hand Senator Fowler seemed more amused than disturbed by Pickering's behavior, and it could be presumed that the Senator was at least nearly as concerned with the safety of the President as the Secret Service.

McNulty realized that he had two options: He could get on the phone and tell the supervisory agent on duty that he had a potential loony here who'd been at the bottle and should not be allowed anywhere near the President. The trouble was that the loony was not only the President's personal invitee, but a very close personal friend of Senator Fowler. Indeed, he was living in the Senator's hotel suite; and the Senator had *not* gone bananas when this Pickering guy told him to fuck himself.

Option two was to say nothing but keep a close eye on him.

"Commander," Senator Fowler said, "Captain Pickering has a nice fresh uniform in that bedroom. Perhaps you'd be good enough to help him into it?"

"You stay where you are, Commander!" Captain Pickering ordered. He marched across the room, entered the bedroom, and closed the door.

A moment later it opened again.

"Commander," Captain Pickering said, almost humbly, "if you wouldn't mind, I could use some help."

"Yes, Sir," the Naval aide said.

Special Agent McNulty decided that for the time being, option two seemed best.

"I'll give you a hand, Jellington," he said and followed him into Captain Pickering's bedroom.

(FIVE)
The Washington Navy Yard
1750 Hours 1 September 1942

Two limousines drove onto the wharf, where they were immediately stopped by neatly dressed men in business suits. The first limousine held a Naval aide to the President of the United States and a member of the Secret Service Presidential Security detail. There was a wave of recognition; then the limousine, a Cadillac, was given a wave of permission to drive farther down the wharf.

Instead, the Secret Service agent got out of the Presidential 1941 Cadillac.

He indicated the second limousine, a 1942 Packard 280.

"Senator Fowler and Captain Pickering are in that one," McNulty said to his Secret Service colleagues. "I'll identify them for you."

One of his colleagues asked the obvious question: "Why aren't they riding in the White House car?"

"Because the Senator's Packard is *air conditioned,* and the White House car *isn't,*" McNulty said.

He opened the front-seat passenger door in time to hear Senator Fowler say, "Now for God's sake, Fleming, when we go on board, watch your mouth. You've been at the sauce all afternoon."

"Just pull up behind the other car," McNulty said to Fowler's chauffeur.

There was a twenty-foot-high wall of corrugated paper boxes on the wharf, leaving just enough room for a car to pass between it and the small white ship tied up at the wharf.

Or a truck, Fleming Pickering decided, once he was out of the Packard. *That stuff is intended for a ship's galleys. This place really is a working Navy yard, not just a place for the President to park his yacht.*

He looked down the hull of the *Potomac.* Perfect paint. Not a speck of rust. A lifeboat, forward, had been swung out on davits. The tide was such that the main deck was within a couple of inches of the wharf; a simple gangplank was in place.

I wonder how they get Roosevelt on here when the Potomac *is much lower or higher than the wharf?*

The answer came immediately: *Hell, a couple of Secret Service guys make a basket of their hands and carry him on. How else? Christ, maybe Fowler's right and I am half in the bag.*

"Right this way, please, gentlemen," Commander Jellington said, and led them to the gangplank.

Two sailors in undress white uniforms stood at either side of the gangplank at parade rest.

Join the Navy and see the Potomac, Pickering thought cynically and then was immediately ashamed of the cynicism.

The sailors came to attention as he started onto the gangplank.

"Good evening," Pickering said and smiled at them.

A full Lieutenant and two more sailors stood on the deck at the end of the gangplank.

At the last moment Pickering remembered his Naval courtesy, and that the *Potomac* was legally a ship of the line.

"Permission to come aboard, Sir," he asked.

"Granted."

Pickering saluted the National Colors and then the officer of the deck.

"The President asks that you join him on the fantail, Sir," the officer of the deck said, and gestured toward the stern of the ship.

Canvas had been hung from the overhead to the rail along the dock side of the *Potomac,* obviously to shield the vessel from the eyes of the curious. But when he reached the fantail, he saw the river side was open. Or at least only covered by mosquito netting.

The President was sitting in an upholstered wicker chair, facing away from the wharf.

What the hell is the protocol? Do I just walk in and say hello?

There was another Naval officer on the fantail, wearing a somewhat wilted white uniform, with four stars on each shoulder board, the insignia of a full admiral.

Admiral William D. Leahy, Chief of Staff to the President, was sitting on a wicker couch and holding a glass of what looked like iced coffee.

He looks, Pickering thought, *a good deal older than the last time I saw him.*

He then remembered hearing somewhere that while Leahy had been Ambassador to Vichy France, his wife had suddenly taken ill and died. It was said that Leahy had taken it badly.

That probably explains why he looks so old, Pickering thought. Then he wondered, *What the hell am I supposed to do? Salute him?* Jesus *Christ, what am I doing in the Navy?*

Franklin Delano Roosevelt solved Pickering's dilemma. He looked over his shoulder, saw him, and smiled.

"Fleming, my dear fellow!" he said. "How good to see you! Come in and sit down by me."

"Good evening, Mr. President," Pickering said. Something was tugging at his hat. He had without thinking about it tucked it under the cast on his left arm. He looked and saw a white-jacketed Navy steward smiling at him.

"Let me have that, please, Sir."

Pickering raised his arm, and the uniform cap disappeared. He then walked across the deck to Roosevelt.

Roosevelt offered his hand. The grip was surprisingly strong.

"Good evening, Mr. President," Pickering repeated.

Jesus, he does get to me. I already said that.

"I believe you know Bill Leahy, don't you, Fleming?"

"I have had that privilege," Pickering said. "Good evening, Admiral."

"Pickering," Leahy said.

"Sit down and tell me your pleasure," Roosevelt said. "Does your medical condition permit alcohol?"

"It demands it, Sir," Pickering said.

The steward who had snatched his cap was back at his side.

"What may I get you, Sir?"

"Scotch, please. Water. Not much ice."

"And there is my favorite Republican," Roosevelt said, beaming at Senator Fowler. "Richmond, it's good to see you."

"Mr. President," Fowler said formally, making a nod that could have been a bow.

While Pickering was lowering himself into the wicker chair beside Roosevelt, he felt the *Potomac* shudder as the propellers were engaged.

Christ, they were waiting for us to get under way!

"How are you, Admiral?" Fowler asked.

"Very well, thank you, Senator."

"Richmond," the President said, "could I ask you to excuse us a moment? There's a little business I'd like to get out of the way, before we . . ."

"Of course, Mr. President," Fowler said.

One of the stewards held open for Fowler a sliding glass door to an aft cabin and then stepped inside after him. A second steward put a glass in Pickering's hand and then followed the first into the aft cabin.

"I'd like you to do something for me, Fleming," Roosevelt said, laying a hand on Pickering's arm.

"I'm at your command, Sir."

"But there are a few matters I'd like to get straight, if you will," Roosevelt said, "about your previous contributions to the war effort."

"Of course, Mr. President."

"I understand that you met with Bill Donovan right after the war started, isn't that so?"

"Yes, Sir, it is."

William S. Donovan, a New York lawyer, had been asked by Roosevelt to establish an organization to coordinate all United States intelligence activities (except counter-intelligence, which was handled in the U.S. and Latin America by J. Edgar Hoover's FBI). The organization evolved first into the Office of Strategic Services (OSS) and ultimately into the Central Intelligence Agency (CIA).

"I understand that your talk with Donovan didn't go well."

"That's correct, Sir."

Where the hell did he hear that? Did Donovan tell him? Or Richmond Fowler?

Roosevelt laughed.

"Forgive me. But you and Bill are the immovable object and the irresistible force. I'm really not at all surprised. I would love to have been a fly on the wall."

"Actually, Sir, it was quite civil. He asked me to become sort of a clerk to a banker whom I knew, and I respectfully declined the honor."

Pickering sensed Leahy's eyes on him, glanced at him, and was surprised to see what could have been a smile on his lips and in his eyes.

"And then, as I understand it," Roosevelt went on, "when you went to The Marines and offered your services, they respectfully declined the honor?"

"They led me to believe, Mr. President," Pickering replied, smiling back at Roosevelt, who was quietly beaming at his play on words, "that as desperate as they were for manpower, there was really no place in The Corps for a forty-six-year-old corporal."

"And then you went to Frank Knox, and he arranged for you to be commissioned into the Navy?"

That wasn't the way it happened. Frank Knox came to me and asked me to accept the commission.

"Yes, Sir," Pickering said.

"Admiral Leahy and I have just about concluded that was a mistake," Roosevelt said.

"So have I, Mr. President. I—"

"I don't think the President means to suggest that you're not qualified to be a Naval captain, Captain," Leahy broke in quickly. "I certainly don't. Your conduct aboard the *Gregory* put to rest any doubts about your competence. And I was one of those who never had any doubts."

"I didn't mean that the way it sounded, Fleming," Roosevelt said.

"I respectfully disagree, Admiral," Pickering said. "I should not be a Naval officer, period."

"Now with *that,*" Roosevelt said, "I agree."

"As soon as I can discuss the matter with Secretary Knox, Mr. President, I intend to ask him to let me out of the Service."

"I know," Roosevelt said. "He told me. I'm afraid that's quite impossible, Fleming. Out of the question."

"I don't quite understand," Pickering said.

"You're familiar, of course, with the Office of Management Analysis in Headquarters, U.S. Marine Corps?"

Pickering thought a moment, came up with nothing, and replied, "No, Sir. I am not."

"Does the name Rickabee mean anything to you, Pickering?" Leahy asked.

"Yes," Pickering replied immediately. "Yes, indeed. Outstanding man."

"He heads the Office of Management Analysis," Roosevelt said a trifle smugly.

"Yes, Sir," Pickering said, feeling quite stupid. He had never actually met Lieutenant Colonel F. L. Rickabee, USMC, but he had seen how efficiently the man could operate. He had, in fact, vowed to find Rickabee in Washington, to shake his hand, and say thank you.

Among the long list of Navy brass actions in the Pacific that were outrageously stupid in Fleming Pickering's view was their handling of the Royal Australian Navy Coastwatcher Establishment.

When the Japanese began their march down the Solomon Islands chain toward New Guinea, Australia, and New Zealand, the Australians hastily recruited plantation managers, schoolteachers, government technicians, shipping officials, and even a couple of missionaries who had lived on the islands. They hastily commissioned these people as junior officers in the Royal Australian Navy Volunteer Reserve and left them behind on the islands, equipped with shortwave radios and small arms.

They were in a position to provide—at great risk to their lives—extremely valuable intelligence regarding Japanese Army and Navy movements, strength, location, and probable intentions. But the Navy arrogantly judged that information coming from natives who were not professional Navy types couldn't possibly be genuinely valuable.

Later, when the value of the Coastwatcher-provided intelligence could no longer be denied, the Navy brass decided that it was now far too important to be left to the administration of the lowly Royal Australian Navy Reserve Lieutenant Commander who was in charge. The U.S. Navy would take over and do it right, in other words.

Pickering heard of the situation from an old friend, Fitzhugh Boyer, who had been Pacific & Far East Shipping's agent in Melbourne and was now a Rear Admiral in the Royal Australian Navy. Fitz Boyer introduced him to Lieutenant Commander Eric Feldt, who was running the Coastwatcher Establishment, and who cheerfully confessed to being a little less than charming to the detachment of U.S. Navy officers who had shown up in Townsville to take over his operation.

Fitz Boyer told Pickering that it was unfortunately true that Feldt did indeed tell the captain who led the detachment that unless he left Townsville that very day, he was going to tear his head off and stick it up his anal cavity.

That same day Pickering fired off an URGENT radio to Frank Knox, recommending that a highly qualified intelligence officer be sent to Australia as soon as possible, with orders to place himself at Feldt's disposal, and with the means to provide Feldt with whatever assistance, especially financial, Feldt needed.

Nine days later, Major Edward J. Banning, USMC, former Intelligence Officer of the Fourth Marines in Shanghai, got off a plane in Melbourne carrying a cashier's check drawn on the Treasury of the United States for a quarter of a million dollars. He was accompanied by a sergeant. Within days the balance of Marine Corps Special Detachment 14, along with crates of the very best shortwave radios and other equipment, began to arrive by priority air shipment.

Banning and Feldt were two of a kind; they hit it off immediately. Not only that, Banning and his detachment proved to be precisely what Pickering had hoped for but thought he had little chance of getting.

Soon after a pair of U.S. Marines was parachuted onto Buka Island to augment the Coastwatcher operation there, Pickering confessed to Banning that he was astonished at the high quality of the people Frank Knox had sent him; and he was equally surprised that they'd arrived so quickly. And Banning replied that the man responsible was Rickabee.

"Mr. Knox is a wise man," Banning said. "He gave this job to Colonel Rickabee, together with the authority, and then let him do it."

That was the first time Pickering heard of Rickabee. But before he was ordered home, he'd had many other dealings with the man; and each contact confirmed his first impression: Rickabee was a man who got things done.

"Colonel Rickabee and you have many things in common, Fleming," Roosevelt said, smiling. "For instance, some people—not *me,* of course, but *some* people— think you both have abrasive personalities."

Roosevelt waited for a reply, got none, and then went on.

"Another way to phrase that is that neither of you can suffer fools. As I'm sure you've learned, fools find that attitude distressing. That doesn't bother you, I know, but it does affect Rickabee."

"I don't think I follow you, Mr. President."

"When Admiral Leahy let the word out that the promotion of Lieutenant Colonel Rickabee to brigadier general was being considered, it was not greeted with enthusiasm. Quite the reverse."

"I think he would make a splendid general officer," Pickering said.

"So do I," Leahy said. "I've known him for a long time. Even before I was Chief of Naval Operations, he did special jobs for me. And he has done special jobs for me since."

"We have reached a certain meeting of the minds vis-à-vis Colonel Rickabee," Roosevelt said. "General Holcomb, the Marine Commandant, has recommended his promotion to colonel. Though I was prepared to send his name to the Senate for confirmation as a brigadier general without the approval of The Marine Corps, Admiral Leahy tells me that would have been counterproductive . . . and not only because it would have caused a lot of talk, which is exactly what Rickabee and the Office of Management Analysis does not want or need."

Jesus Christ, what bullshit! Pickering fumed. *A damned good man can't get promoted because of the prima donnas!*

"Colonel Rickabee's promotion doesn't solve the problem," Admiral Leahy said. "Which is, in rank-inflated Washington, that a general officer is needed to head up the Office of Management Analysis."

"Yes," Pickering thought out loud, "I can understand that."

"Good," Roosevelt said. "That's where you come in, Fleming."

"Sir," Pickering said, surprised, "I wouldn't have any idea whom to recommend for that. Nor would I presume to make such a recommendation."

"That's been done for you," Roosevelt said. "What Leahy and I have concluded is that the man in charge of the Office of Management Analysis should be someone who not only has experience at the upper levels of the Navy Department, say working closely with the Secretary of the Navy . . ."

Christ, he's not talking about me, is he?

". . . but who has also had firsthand experience with the war in the Pacific, and most importantly . . ."

Jesus H. Christ, he is!

". . . is a Marine with extensive combat experience, say someone who won the Distinguished Service Cross in the First World War, and who in this war has been awarded the Silver Star, the Purple Heart, and the Legion of Merit."

What's he talking about, the Legion of Merit?

"Are you beginning to get the picture, Fleming?" Roosevelt asked.

"Mr. President . . ."

Roosevelt reached to the table beside him, opened an oblong box, and took a medal on its ribbon from it.

"Captain Pickering," he said, motioning for Pickering to lean over to him. He pinned the medal to Pickering's uniform. "It is my great privilege, on the recommendation of the Commanding General, First Marine Division, to invest you with the Legion of Merit for your distinguished service as Acting G-2, First Marine Division, during combat operations on Guadalcanal."

"I don't deserve a medal for that," Pickering protested. "I was just filling in—the G-2 was killed—until they could get someone qualified in there."

"I think we can safely leave that judgment to General Vandergrift," Roosevelt said. "He made that recommendation, of course, without being aware that Admiral Leahy and I had something in mind for you."

"Mr. President, you can't really be thinking of—"

"Your name was sent to the Senate this afternoon, Fleming, for their advice and consent to your commission as Brigadier General, USMC Reserve. Now I realize that Richmond Fowler and I agree about very little, but I rather suspect that when I ask him to support your nomination, he'll come along . . . in a bipartisan gesture."

"I will be hated in The Marine Corps," Pickering said.

"Possibly," Admiral Leahy said. "But you're already hated in the Navy, so nothing is lost there. And no Marine is likely to criticize a fellow Marine with a record like yours. General Vandergrift does not hand out decorations like the Legion of Merit lightly."

The President raised his voice slightly.

"Commander Jellington!"

The glass door to the cabin slid open.

"Yes, Mr. President?"

"Commander, would you ask the other gentlemen to join us, please?"

"Yes, Mr. President."

Even though both Brigadier General D. G. McInerney, USMC, and Commander Jellington, USN, had given him an intense briefing on protocol in the presence of the President of the United States, the first of the President's other guests promptly forgot all he'd heard when he walked onto the fantail of the *Potomac* and saw Fleming Pickering with his arm in a cast.

"Jesus *Christ,* Dad!" he demanded. "What *happened* to you?"

V

(ONE)
Ferdinand Six
Buka, Solomon Islands
4 September 1942

As Sergeant Steven M. Koffler, USMC, knelt before the key of his Hallicrafters and waited for the dials to come to life, he was suffering from a severe case of the I-Feel-Sorry-for-Me syndrome.

In his judgment, with the exception of the inevitable failure of the Hallicrafters (which could happen at any time), everything that could go wrong had gone wrong.

When the officers left seven days ago to see what they could steal from the Japanese, they planned to be back in five or six days. They were now overdue. That probably meant they were not going to come back.

And that meant that the Japanese would probably be here sooner rather than later.

Although he was a uniformed member of an armed force engaged in combat against enemy armed forces and thus entitled under the Geneva Convention to treatment as a prisoner of war, Koffler was well aware that the Japanese had different views of such obligations than Americans.

Back in Townsville, to make sure that Sergeant Koffler and Lieutenant Howard really knew what they were letting themselves in for, Commander Feldt had explained the differences in some detail:

If the Japanese captured them, presuming they did not kill them outright, Koffler and Howard should hope for a Japanese officer who believed they were indeed U.S. Marines and thus entitled to treatment as fellow warriors.

That meant he'd have them executed according to the Code of Bushido: First they would dig their own graves. Then a member of the Japanese Armed Forces of equal or superior rank would behead them with a Japanese sword. Following the execution, prayers would be said over their graves, and entries would be made in official Japanese records of the date and place of their execution and burial. Presuming the records were not destroyed, that would be handy, after the war, for the disinterment of their remains and their return to the United States.

It was equally possible, Commander Feldt went on matter-of-factly, that they'd be regarded as spies and not soldiers. In that case, they'd be interrogated—read tortured—then executed in a less ritualistic manner. With a little luck they'd get a pistol bullet in the ear. More likely they'd serve as targets for bayonet practice. Of course, no record would be kept of their execution or place of burial. Thus they'd be listed officially as missing in action and presumed dead.

Later, Lieutenant Howard pointed out why Commander Feldt had gone so thoroughly into the unpleasant details: He wanted to make sure they knew how important it was for them not to get captured.

"So far as Feldt is concerned," Lieutenant Howard said, "we should have absolutely no contact with the Japs. None. But if we are captured, we should not give them any information. When the Cavalry was fighting the Apaches after the Civil War, they always saved one cartridge for themselves. The Apaches were worse than the Japs. They liked to roast their prisoners over slow fires. You understand?"

"Yes, Sir."

The dials came to life. Koffler threw the switch to TRANSMIT and worked the key. The dots and dashes went out, repeated three times, spelling out, simply, FRD6. FRD6. FRD6.

Detachment A of Special Marine Corps Detachment 14 is attempting to establish contact with any station on this communications network.

There was no reply. He put his hand on the key again.

FRD6. FRD6. FRD6. FRD6. FRD6. FRD6.

There was a reply:

KCY.???.KCY.???.KCY.???
This is the United States Pacific Fleet Radio Station at Pearl Harbor, Territory of Hawaii. Is there someone trying to contact me?
KCY.FRD6.KCY.FRD6.KCY.FRD6.
FRD6.KCY. FRD6.KCY URSIG 2X1.GA.
Detachment A of Special Marine Corps Detachment 14, this is the United States Pacific Fleet Radio. Your signal is weak and barely readable. Go ahead.

Fucking radio. Fucking atmospherics. Fucking sunspots. Fuck fuck fuck.

KCY.FRD6.SB CODE.
CINCPAC Radio Pearl Harbor, stand by to copy encrypted message.
FRD6.KCY. RPT URSIG 2X1. GA.
Detachment A of Special Marine Corps Detachment 14, this is the United States Pacific Fleet Radio. Repeat, your signal is weak and barely readable. Go ahead.

After six tries, Detachment A of Special Marine Corps Detachment 14 was able to relay to the United States Pacific Fleet headquarters in Pearl Harbor that an enemy bomber force of twenty Betty bombers, escorted by an estimated thirty Zero fighters, had passed overhead at an approximate altitude of 13,000 feet on a course that would take them to Guadalcanal.

FRD6.KCY. AKN. CLR.
Detachment A, this is Pearl Harbor. Your transmission is acknowledged. Pearl Harbor Clear.
KCY. FRD6. FU2 AND GOOD AFTERNOON. FRD6.CLR.

FU was not in the list of authorized abbreviations, but it was not difficult for the United States Pacific Fleet operator in Pearl Harbor to make the translation; every radio operator knew what it meant. He had just been told to attempt a physiologically impossible act of self-impregnation. Since regulations did not permit the transmission of personal messages and/or greetings, the Pearl Harbor operator concluded that wherever FRD6 was, and whoever he was, he had really stuck his neck out by getting drunk on duty.

(TWO)
Foster Lafayette Hotel
Washington, D.C.
1525 Hours 4 September 1942

Because Fleming Pickering ate lunch late that afternoon, when there was a knock at Senator Fowler's door, he thought it was the floor waiter come to remove the remnants of the tray of hors d'oeuvres they had sent him from the Grill Room.

But it wasn't the floor waiter, it was the concierge. He was helping a mousy-looking little man carry two large stacks of cardboard boxes. Each box bore the corporate insignia of Brooks Brothers.

He knew what they were.

"Put them in that bedroom, please," he said, pointing.

When he signed the receipt the mousy-looking man handed him, he said, "Please tell Mr. Abraham that I'm grateful for the quick service. And for sending you down here personally."

"Our pleasure, Captain Pickering," the mousy little man said. "You told Mr. Abraham, 'as soon as possible.' And I had a nice lunch on the train."

Once they were gone, Pickering looked at the boxes now neatly stacked on the bed and the chest of drawers, shook his head, exhaled audibly, and went back into the sitting room.

Yesterday afternoon, after Pick and Jack Stecker's boy left, Dr. Selleres got him to the office of an orthopedic surgeon. Selleres' pretext was to make a more comfortable cast for Pickering's arm. But his actual motive was to have the arm X-rayed—which was done. Then it was placed in a much less substantial cast than the Navy had given him at San Diego.

Though Pickering had been reluctant to go, he was now pleased that he did. For one thing, Selleres got on the phone afterward and assured Patricia that her husband's arm was well on the way to recovery ... and not about to fall off or develop gangrene. But more important, he could now put his arm through a shirtsleeve.

Pickering, who was wearing a light seersucker robe, boxer shorts, and a pair of the Foster Lafayette's throwaway cotton shower slippers, went back to the leisurely postprandial rest that the man from Brooks Brothers had interrupted. He poured himself another cup of black coffee—the last the silver pitcher held—sat down on the couch, put his feet up on the coffee table, and picked up *The New York Times*.

There came another knock at the door.

That has *to be the floor waiter.*

"Come in."

He heard the door open and sensed movement in the room, but no one appeared to roll the room service cart away.

"Get me another pot of coffee, would you, please? I won't need any sugar or cream."

"General Pickering, I'm Captain Sessions, Sir, from Management Analysis."

Pickering looked over his shoulder. A tall, well-set-up young man was standing in the open door. His black hair was styled in a crew cut, and he was wearing a well-fitting, if sweat-dampened, green elastique summer uniform. He carried a heavily stuffed leather briefcase and a newspaper.

"I thought you were the floor waiter," Pickering said. "Come in, please." Then he blurted what he was thinking: "That's the first time anyone has called me that. 'General.'"

"Then I'm honored, General."

"I'm about to order some coffee. Can I get you anything?"

"Would iced tea be possible?"

"How about a cold beer, Captain? That's what I really want."

"A general officer's desire is a captain's command, Sir."

Pickering chuckled.

Nice kid. He's not much older than Pick.

Pickering picked up the telephone. "This is Captain—strike that—*General* Pickering. Would you send the floor waiter to clear things away, please? And have him put a half dozen bottles of Feigenspan ale in a wine cooler with some ice." He stopped. "That all right? Feigenspan?"

"Just fine, Sir."

"Thank you," Pickering said to the telephone and hung it up. "What can I do for you, Captain?"

"Colonel Rickabee's compliments, Sir. He asked me to express his regrets for not coming here himself. He's playing golf with the Deputy Commandant."

Playing golf? Jesus Christ!

"War is hell, isn't it, Captain?"

"General, with respect, Colonel Rickabee regularly meets with the Commandant; or if the Commandant is not available, with the Deputy Commandant. The back nine holes at the Army & Navy Country Club is a fine place to hold a confidential conversation."

"My mouth ran away with me," Pickering said. "Sorry."

"I can understand why it sounded a bit odd, General."

"We're back to, 'what can I do for you, Captain?'"

"There's a good deal of paperwork to be signed, General—"

"I'll bet," Pickering interrupted.

Sessions smiled, and then went on, "—but first things first. Has the General seen *The Washington Star*?"

Pickering shook his head and reached for the newspaper Sessions extended to him.

"It's on the lower right-hand corner of the second section, General."

Pickering found what Sessions thought he should see:

SHIPPING MAGNATE ENTERS MARINE CORPS

Washington Sept 3—The White House this afternoon announced that it had been advised by the Senate of its consent to the appointment of Fleming Pickering as Brigadier General, USMC Reserve.

Presidential Press Secretary Stephen Early said that Pickering, an old and close friend of the President, will head the Marine Corps Office of Management Analysis, which has responsibility for increasing efficiency of Marine Corps' supply acquisition and distribution.

Pickering, who before the war was Chairman of the Board of Pacific & Far East Shipping Corporation, has been serving as a temporary Captain, U.S. Navy Reserve, and only recently returned from the Pacific, where he was a Special Representative of Navy Secretary Frank Knox on logistics matters.

"Both the President and Secretary Knox felt that Pickering would be more effective as a Marine officer," Press Secretary Early reported. "He brings to his new duties not only his extensive shipping experience, but those of his previous service as a Marine."

He said that Pickering was three times wounded and earned the Distinguished Service Cross and the Croix de Guerre as a Marine in France in World War I.

"And like the President," Early added, "he has a son in The Marine Corps." Captain James Roosevelt participated in the recent Marine Corps raid on Makin Island. Second Lieutenant Malcolm S. Pickering recently completed training as a Marine Corps fighter pilot and is believed en route to the Pacific.

Pickering will assume his new duties, according to Early, "just as soon as he can get into uniform."

"Not that I am one to believe much that I read in any newspaper," Pickering said, "but this really strays from the truth, the whole truth, and nothing but, doesn't it?"

"Actually, we were very pleased with it, General."

"We? Who's we?"

"Colonel Rickabee and me, Sir. He saw it first and told me to get a copy before I came over here."

"Just for openers, I am not an old and close friend of Mr. Roosevelt."

"And the Office of Management Analysis does not, as you know, Sir, have anything to do with logistics," Sessions said, smiling. "But it is almost always to our advantage if people have the wrong idea. And, General, with respect, there are people in this town who would kill to have *The Star* report that they are old and close friends of Mr. Roosevelt."

Pickering considered that and chuckled.

"I'm sure you're right, Captain," he said. "You're an interesting young man. What's your background? How'd you get involved . . . in your line of work?"

Before he could reply, there was another knock at the door.

"May I, Sir?" Sessions asked.

He went to the door and opened it. The floor waiter and a busboy came in, wheeled the floor service tray out, and left behind a tray of pilsener glasses and two silver champagne buckets, each holding three bottles of ale buried in ice.

"Help yourself," Pickering said, "there's an opener on the bar."

"This is very nice," Sessions said, indicating the champagne buckets.

"They are very nice to me here, probably because my wife's father owns the place."

"Yes, Sir, I know," Sessions said, opening a bottle of ale and handing it to Pickering. He glanced at Pickering as he spoke and saw coldness in his eyes.

"General, we have to know all there is to know about our people. That applies to everybody."

"I'm sure," Pickering said. "You were telling me how you got into this?"

"I served in China, Sir. With then Captain Ed Banning."

"You know Ed Banning?"

"I'm privileged to be his friend, Sir."

"That speaks highly of you, Captain."

"Sir, this may be a little out of line, but I think I should return the compliment. Ed Banning thinks the world of you."

"Two questions at a tangent, Captain?"

"Yes, Sir?"

"What about our two people on Buka? You know about them?"

"Yes, Sir. They're still there. Banning is trying to figure out a way to relieve them."

Pickering nodded. "I said two questions. I meant three. Number two: When you were in China, did you happen to meet a young man, a corporal, named McCoy?"

Sessions smiled. "Sir, I am happy to report that I am the man, over his bitter objections, who sent the Killer to Officer Candidate School."

"He went to OCS with my son. But I guess you know that."

"Yes, Sir."

"Do you happen to know where McCoy is? The reason I ask—"

"Sir, the Killer's one of us—"

"I suppose I should have guessed that," Pickering said.

"He's on convalescent leave, Sir."

"He was wounded?" Pickering asked, concern in his voice.

"On the Makin raid. But not seriously. The Colonel thought he was entitled to the full thirty days of convalescent leave. He ordered him to take it."

"Question three: Sergeant John Marston Moore?"

"Philadelphia Naval Hospital, Sir. He took some pretty bad shrapnel wounds on Guadalcanal."

"Is he going to be all right?"

"He'll be on limited duty for a while, Sir. But he will be all right."

"What else do you know about Moore?" Pickering asked innocently. But Sessions knew the question behind the question. He decided to answer it fully.

"He's privy to MAGIC, Sir. You authorized that clearance."

"And didn't tell anybody. Which is why he was sent to Guadalcanal, why he's in the hospital."

"Yes, Sir. I'm familiar with the details."

"You're apparently on the MAGIC list?"

"Yes, Sir. Colonel Rickabee and I both, Sir."

"Not McCoy?"

"No, Sir. Lieutenant McCoy does not have the Need to Know, Sir."

"I appreciate your candor in answering these questions, Captain."

"General, you're the boss."

"Two parts to that statement," Pickering said, "both of which I'm having difficulty accepting."

"Well, then, Sir, why don't we make it official?"

"I beg your pardon?"

"One of the things the General has to do to become a general, General, is sign his resignation from the Navy and his acceptance of his commission as a Marine general. Plus no more than four or five hundred other forms, all of which I just happen to have with me, all neatly typed up."

Smiling, he held up the briefcase.

"I even have two spare fountain pens," Sessions went on, "and these." He took from the briefcase two pieces of metal, each the size of a license plate. They were painted red and had a silver star fastened to their centers.

"What's that?" Pickering asked, even as he belatedly recognized the plates for what they were.

"That is what brigadier generals mount on their automobiles, fore and aft. I also drew your General's Flag, and the National Colors from Eighth and Eye before I came over here. But I left those in the car." Headquarters, United States Marine Corps, is at Eighth and I streets, in the District of Columbia.

"What am I supposed to do with a General's Flag?"

"It will be placed in your office, General, which at this very moment is being equipped with the appropriate furniture."

"And who got thrown out of his office so I could have one?"

"A Colonel LaRue, Sir," Sessions replied immediately. "The Colonel is the Marine representative to the Inter-Service Morale and Recreation Council. He was, Sir, very much aware that he was the senior officer in our little building. I don't think Colonel Rickabee was heartbroken when he had to tell him that we required his office space for our General, General."

"Oh, Christ," Pickering said, shaking his head.

"We'll still be pretty much sitting in each other's laps, Sir, but at least there will be nobody in the building but us from now on."

"Well, that's something, I suppose."

"Sir, Colonel Rickabee suggested that we drive down to Quantico this afternoon if you feel up to it."

"Oh? Why?"

"Uniforms, Sir. Colonel Rickabee said to tell you that the concessionaire there, a fellow named A. M. Bolognese, not only has very good prices, but is an old friend of his. He could probably turn out some uniforms for you in a couple of days."

Pickering gestured toward the bedroom.

"They just arrived. I called Brooks Brothers and they sent a man down on the train with them."

Sessions laughed. "Major Banning said that was the way you were, Sir. By the time he thought of something, you'd done it."

"I wish I'd known about this man with the good prices. I hate to think of the bill I'm going to get from Brooks Brothers."

"What exactly did you order, Sir?"

"I told them to send me whatever I would need."

"General, while you're signing all this stuff, why don't I take a look at it?"

"Somebody who knows what he's doing should," Pickering said. "Thank you."

"You'll find a little red pencil check mark every place you're to sign your name, General," Sessions said, going to a desk and unloading the briefcase. "Everything is in at least four copies, all of which have to be signed."

"What if I had broken my right arm?"

"Then you would make a mark, Sir, and I would sign everything, swearing that was your mark."

Pickering laughed.

"OK, Captain," he said and walked to the table and sat down.

Sessions uncapped a fountain pen and handed it to him. "If you run out of ink, Sir, there's a spare pen."

"You think two is going to be enough?"

"With a little luck, Sir."

By the time he'd taken the documents from one stack, signed his name in the places marked, and put them on a second stack, Pickering had concluded that Sessions was not exaggerating about how many there were. His fingers were stiff from holding the pen.

He got up and walked into the bedroom. The cardboard boxes had been opened, emptied, and piled by the door. An incredible amount of clothing was now spread out on the bed. And still more clothing was hanging from doorknobs and the drawer pulls of the two chests of drawers.

Sessions, who was bent over the bed, pinning insignia to an elastique tunic, looked over his shoulder at Pickering.

"They took you at your word, Sir. There's everything here but mess dress."

"Is mess dress expensive?"

"Yes, Sir. Very expensive."

"Then it was a simple oversight which Brooks Brothers will remedy as soon as humanly possible."

"The only thing we don't know is whether or not it will fit you, Sir."

"It should. I've been buying clothing there since I was in college."

Sessions handed him a shirt.

"There's only one way to know for sure, General."

Three minutes later, Flem Pickering was examining Brigadier General Fleming Pickering, USMCR, in the full-length mirror on the bathroom door.

I feel like one of the dummies in the Brooks Brothers windows. I may be wearing this thing, but I am not, and there is no way I could be, a Marine general.

That Navy captain business was bad enough, but at least I have the right to wear those four gold stripes. I am an any-ocean, any-tonnage master mariner, entitled to wear the four stripes of a captain.

This is different.

"That fits perfectly," Sessions said. "Let's see about the cover."

He handed him a uniform cap. The entwined golden oak leaves decorating its brim—universally called "scrambled eggs"—identified the wearer as a general officer.

Pickering put it on and examined himself again.

The hat makes me look even more like a Brooks Brothers dummy.

"Looks fine, Sir," Sessions said.

"Looks *fraudulent,* Captain," Pickering said.

There was another knock at the door.

"Shall I get that, General?"

"Please," Pickering said. "Thank you."

He turned from the mirror and started gathering up the other uniforms on hangers and putting them into closets. Then he went back to the mirror and looked at himself again.

"Good afternoon, General," a strange voice said. "I'm Colonel Rickabee."

Pickering turned. A tall, thin, sharp-featured man was standing in the door to the bedroom. He was wearing a baggy, sweat-soaked seersucker suit and a battered straw snap-brim hat. In one hand he carried a well-stuffed briefcase identical to Sessions', and in the other he held a long, thin package wrapped in brown waterproof paper.

"I'm very happy to meet you, Colonel," Pickering said. "But I'm afraid I have to begin this conversation with the announcement that I feel like a fraud standing before you in a Marine general's uniform."

Rickabee met his eyes for a moment and then walked into the room. He put the briefcase on the floor and the long, thin package on the bed. He took a penknife from his pocket and slit the package open.

He pushed the paper away from a Springfield Model 1903 .30-06 caliber rifle, picked it up, and handed it to Pickering.

"The General inadvertently left this behind when he checked out of the hospital, Sir. I took the liberty of having it sent here, Sir."

Pickering took the rifle, and then (in Pavlovian fashion) worked the action to make sure it was unloaded. After that he raised his eyes to Rickabee.

"Thank you, Colonel," he said. "It means a good deal to me."

"I thought it would, General," Rickabee said. "That's almost certainly the only Springfield in the United States which has seen service on Guadalcanal."

Pickering met his eyes again and after a moment said, "General Vandergrift told me to take it with me. When they ordered me off the island."

"Yes, Sir. So I understand. May I say something, General?"

Pickering nodded.

"If General Vandergrift and Major Jack Stecker both think of you as a pretty good Marine, Sir, I don't think you should question their judgment."

It was a long time before Pickering spoke. Finally he said, "Funny, Colonel, I have been led to believe—by the President, by the way—that you have an abrasive personality. That wasn't abrasive, that was more than gracious."

Rickabee met his eyes for a moment and then changed the subject.

"I see the General has dealt with the uniform problem."

"Before I knew about the man at Quantico with the good prices."

"Well, at least you're in the correct uniform for me to welcome you back into The Corps."

"Thank you," Pickering said. "I was just wondering what to do with my Navy uniforms. Send them home, I guess. Or find somebody who can use them."

"Thank you, Sir," Rickabee said. "We accept."

"You know someone who can use them?"

"Down the line, I'm sure, they can be put to good use," Rickabee said.

"I see," Pickering said, shaking his head. "OK. They're yours."

"Sessions has told the General, I hope, that we're setting up an office for him?" Pickering nodded.

"There has been a slight delay. The former occupant squealed like a stuck pig and complained to everybody he could think of," Rickabee said with obvious delight. "He lost his last appeal and has been ordered to clear out by noon tomorrow. If the General has some reason to come into the office tomorrow, we will of course make room for him, but I would respectfully suggest that he wait one more day."

"Are you going to keep talking to me in the third person?"

"Not if the General does not wish me to."

"The General does not," Pickering said with a smile.

"Aye, aye, Sir."

"I thought that tomorrow I would go into Philadelphia to see Sergeant Moore. Is there any reason I can't do that?"

"You can go just about anywhere you want to, General," Rickabee said. He picked the briefcase up from the floor, unlocked it, opened it, and handed Pickering an envelope. "Your orders came in this morning, Sir."

Pickering opened the envelope.

THE WHITE HOUSE
Washington, D.C.

3 September 1942

Brigadier General Fleming W. Pickering, USMCR, Headquarters, USMC, will proceed by military and/or civilian rail, road, sea and air transportation (Priority AAAAA-1) to such points as he deems necessary in carrying out the mission assigned to him by the undersigned.

United States Armed Forces commands are directed to provide him with such support as he may request. General Pickering is to be considered the personal representative of the undersigned.

General Pickering has unrestricted TOP SECRET security clearance. Any questions regarding his mission will be directed to the undersigned.

W. D. Leahy, Admiral, USN
Chief of Staff to the President

When Pickering finished reading the orders, Rickabee said, "They're much like your old orders, except that Leahy has signed these."

"It sounds as if we work for Leahy."

"Sometimes we do," Rickabee said matter-of-factly. "In any event, this should answer your question about whether or not you can go to Philadelphia."

"It's a personal thing. That boy worked for me. If I had done what I was supposed to do, he would never have been on Guadalcanal."

Pickering saw in Rickabee's eyes a sign that he hadn't liked that statement.

"OK," he said. "Let's have it."

"Nothing, Sir."

"Rickabee, if we're going to work together, I'm going to have to know what you're thinking."

Rickabee paused long enough for Pickering to understand that he was debating answering the challenge.

"Would you mind changing the last part of what you said to read, 'He would never have been on Guadalcanal, where he might have been captured and compromised MAGIC'?" Rickabee asked finally.

Pickering's face tightened. He was not used to having his mistakes pointed out to him. He felt Rickabee's eyes on him; they were wary and intent.

"Yes, I would," Pickering said, "but only because it reminds me of how incredibly stupid I can sometimes be. Still, consider it changed, Rickabee."

"I felt obliged to bring that up, Sir," Rickabee said. "And there is one other thing . . ."

"Let's have it."

"Ed Banning tells me you have a somewhat cavalier attitude toward classified documents."

"He never said anything to me about that!" Pickering protested.

"He and Lieutenant Hon kept a close eye on you, Sir. And just to be doubly sure, he had your quarters kept under surveillance."

Jesus, he's not making this up.

"I didn't know that."

"He didn't want you to," Rickabee said. "But we're not going to be able to do that here."

"I'll be more careful."

"General, you are authorized an aide-de-camp and an orderly. With your permission I would like to charge them with the additional responsibility of making sure that nothing important gets misplaced."

"I feel like a backward child," Pickering said.

"I don't see Japanese lurking in the bushes," Rickabee said. "Or, for that matter, Germans. J. Edgar Hoover is doing a good job with counterintelligence. But other agencies don't particularly like our little shop. They could do us a lot of damage, Sir, if they could show that our security isn't ironclad."

"Other agencies like who, for example?"

"All of them. Any of them. Maybe in particular the FBI, and Donovan's people, whatever they're calling themselves this week, and of course, ONI."—the Office of Naval Intelligence.

"In other words you're telling me the same thing is going on here that's going on in the Pacific? There are two wars? One against the Japanese and the other against ourselves?"

"Yes, Sir, I'm afraid it is."

Good Christ, I'm stupid. Why should I think things would be any different here? And he's right, of course. Bill Donovan would love nothing better than to run to Franklin Roosevelt with proof that I was endangering security, and/or behaving like a blithering idiot.

"If you feel it's necessary, Colonel, you can lock me in a sealed room at night."

"That won't be necessary, Sir. But I would like to be careful, by having your aide—"

"I don't suppose Lieutenant McCoy would be available for that, would he?"

"What I was thinking, Sir, was Sergeant Moore. We can commission him—he was in line for a commission before we sent him to Australia—and he's cleared for MAGIC."

"Yes, of course," Pickering said. "That's a good idea."

"And I'll work on the orderly/driver/clerk, whatever we finally call him. We've been recruiting people with the right backgrounds. There's three or four going through Parris Island right now, as a matter of fact."

"I leave myself in your hands, Rickabee," Pickering said. "My orders to you are to tell me what I can do to make myself both useful and harmless."

Rickabee looked into his eyes for a moment and then smiled.

"As far as useful, Sir—was that Feigenspan ale I saw in the cooler in the other room?"

(THREE)
The 21 Club
21 West 52nd Street
New York City, New York
5 September 1942

Ernest J. Sage stepped out of a taxi and rather absently handed the driver a five-dollar bill.

"Keep it," he said.

Ernest Sage was forty-eight years old, superbly tailored, slightly built, and very intense. His hair was slicked back with Vitahair because he liked it that way, and not because it was the number-three product in gross sales of American Personal Pharmaceuticals, Inc., of which he was Chairman of the Board and President.

"Good afternoon, Mr. Sage," the 21 Club's doorman said. After somewhat belatedly recognizing Sage, he rushed to the cab.

"Howareya?" Ernest Sage said, managing a two-second smile as he walked quickly across the sidewalk and down the shallow flight of stairs behind the wrought-iron grillwork.

Ernest Sage was late for an appointment. He disliked being late for any appointment.

The man inside the door was quicker to recognize him than the outside man had been. He had the door open and was smiling by the time Sage reached it.

"Good afternoon, Mr. Sage," he said, with what looked like a warm, welcoming smile.

"Howareya?" Ernest Sage replied. "I'm late. Has anyone been asking for me?"

"No, Sir, Mr. Sage."

"I'll be in the bar."

"Yes, Sir, Mr. Sage. I'll take care of it."

He made his way to the bar. At its far end was the man Ernest Sage was meeting. He was sitting on a barstool with his back against the wall . . . on a *very special and particular* barstool. This one was reserved by almost sacred custom for humorist Robert Benchley, or in his absence for another of a small group of 21 Club regulars—newspaper columnists, actors, producers, or a select few businessmen who'd earned the favor of the Kriendler family, the owners of 21.

The individual sitting there now was not famous or even well known. But he had obviously earned the approval of the Kriendler family. As evidence of that, a smiling Al Kriendler was in the process of handing him a drink.

Sage remembered hearing that Bob Kriendler was about to go in The Marine Corps. Perhaps he was already in . . . *Does that explain why Al's personally handing him a drink? Or is he just showing his respect to a nice-looking kid in a Marine uniform?*

The young man was wearing the summer uniform prescribed for first lieutenants of The United States Marine Corps—khaki shirt, trousers, and necktie with USMC tie clasp.

"Hello, Ken," Ernest Sage said, touching his back. "Sorry to be late. The goddamned traffic is unbelievable."

"Hello, Mr. Sage," First Lieutenant Kenneth R. McCoy, USMCR, said. "No problem. I just got here."

"Oh, you know each other?" Al Kriendler said.

"For reasons that baffle me," Ernest said, "Ernie thinks the sun rises in the morning because Ken wants it to."

"Well, I would say Ernie has very good taste," Al Kriendler said.

The bartender, who was familiar with Ernest Sage's drinking habits, slid him a Manhattan with an extra shake of Angostura bitters.

Ernie Sage—properly Ernestine Sage—was Ernest Sage's only child, and Ernest Sage loved her very much. At the same time he was aware of the facts of growth and maturity. And so he had pondered the inevitability of her one day transferring her affections to a young man.

Though he'd dwelt at length on every possible Worst Case, he'd never dreamed that the reality would be as bad as it turned out. It was not that he didn't like Ken McCoy. Ken McCoy was beyond question a really fine young man.

Ernest Sage would have been happier, of course, if there had been some family in McCoy's background—some money, frankly—and if he had a little better education than Norristown, Pennsylvania's, high school offered. But such things weren't insurmountable, in his view. In fact, under other circumstances, he could have resigned himself to Ken McCoy. Ernie could have done a hell of a lot worse.

But the circumstances were that the war was not even a year old, that he saw no end to it, that Ken McCoy was already wearing three Purple Hearts and a Bronze Star for valor in combat, and that his nickname in the Marines was "Killer."

Purple Hearts and Bronze Stars and nicknames weren't in themselves hugely significant. But in Ernest Sage's mind, they added up to a significant conclusion: The chances of Ken coming through the war alive and intact ranged from slim to none.

In Worst Possible Case Number Sixty-six, for instance, Ken came home missing a leg, or blind. And Ernie was condemned to a life of caring for a cripple.

If that makes me a heartless prick, so what? I'm worried about the life my daughter will have. What's wrong with that?

The funny thing was that Ken McCoy not only understood Sage's concerns but agreed with them. And yet Sage almost had a harder time dealing with that than if Ken had run off with her to a justice of the peace the day after he met her.

"I'm not going to marry her, Mr. Sage," Ken had told him. "Not while the war is on. I don't want to leave her a widow."

It was another reason he genuinely liked Ken McCoy.

The real problem, in fact, wasn't McCoy, it was Ernie. She had reduced the situation to basics. She was a woman in love. What women in love do is stick to their man and have babies. She didn't even much give a damn whether she was married to Ken or not—she wanted his baby.

"Look, Daddy," she had told him over lunch in the Executive Dining Room of the American Personal Pharmaceuticals Building. "If Ken does get killed, I would at least have our baby. . . . And it's not as if the baby and I would wind up on charity."

Ernest Sage had clear and definite ideas about moral values and a good moral upbringing. He had, for example, taught Sunday School classes for six goddamned years in order to set a proper example for his daughter. So it wasn't at all easy for him to go to her lover to discuss her intention to become pregnant by him. But Ernest Sage did that. He had to.

And again Ken McCoy surprised him . . . and made him uneasy—not because Ken was going to do his daughter wrong (he wasn't), but because he kept acting just exactly the way Ernest Sage himself would have acted if he had been in the boy's shoes.

"Yeah, I know she wants a kid," Ken said. "But no way. That'd be a rotten thing to do to her."

That was why Ernest Sage couldn't help liking and admiring Ken McCoy. Ken was very much like himself—a decent man with enough intelligence to see things the way they were, not through rose-colored glasses.

Goddamn this war, anyway!

"Miss Sage is here, Mr. Sage," one of the headwaiters said softly in his ear. "Your regular table be all right, Sir?"

Women were not welcome at the bar. Since they weren't actually *prohibited,* however, Ernie felt free to sit there, to hell with what people think. But whenever he could, her father tried to make her sit at a table.

"Yeah, fine," Sage said, looking toward the entrance for his daughter. She was tall and healthy looking, slender but not thin; her black hair was cut in a pageboy. She wore a simple skirt and blouse, with a strand of pearls that had belonged to her maternal grandmother.

He waved. She returned it, but there was a look of annoyance on her face when she saw the headwaiter rushing to show her to a table.

He noticed, too, that male eyes throughout the room followed her.

She stood by the table until they joined her.

"Hi, baby," Ken McCoy said.

"Is that the best you can do?" Ernie Sage asked.

"What?"

She grabbed his neatly tied necktie, pulled him to her, and kissed him on the mouth.

"Jesus Christ," he said, actually blushing when he finally got free.

"Hi, Daddy," Ernie said, smiling at him and sitting down.

When she smiled at him, he could not be angry with her.

"What may I get you, Miss Sage?" a waiter asked.

"What's good enough for The Marine Corps is good enough for me."

"Bring us all one," Ernest Sage said.

"Thank you for asking how my day was," Ernie said. "My day was fine. I was told my copy for Toothhold was 'really sexy.' I wonder what that man does behind his bedroom door if he thinks adhesive for false teeth is sexy?"

"My God, kitten!" Ernest Sage said.

Ken McCoy laughed. "Don't knock it until you try it."

"OK, darling, I'll bring some home. There's a case of it on my filing cabinet."

Ernie McCoy was a senior copywriter at the J. Walter Thompson advertising agency. Ernest Sage took a great deal of pride in knowing that she had the job on her own merits and not because American Personal Pharmaceuticals billed an annual $12.1 million at JWT.

"I learned something interesting today," Ernest Sage said, "which I saved until we could all be together."

"What's that?" Ernie asked.

"There was a story in the *Times* that Fleming Pickering has gone into The Marines. As a general."

"I thought he was a captain in the Navy," Ernie said, looking at McCoy for an explanation.

"I know," McCoy said. "He called me today."

I'll be goddamned, Ernest Sage thought. *He didn't call me. I haven't heard from the sonofabitch since the war started, and we have been friends since before our kids were born. And if he called Ken McCoy, that means he called him at Ernie's apartment, which means he knows they're living together. Well, why the hell should that surprise me? Flem arranged for that boat they were shacked up in at the San Diego Yacht Club. Goddamn him for that, too.*

It had been a longtime, pleasant, and not entirely unreasonable fantasy on the part of Mr. and Mrs. Ernest Sage and Captain and Mrs. Fleming Pickering (the ladies had been roommates at college) that one day Ernestine Sage and Malcolm S. Pickering would find themselves impaled on Cupid's arrow, marry, and make them all happy grandparents.

Instead, Pick Pickering joined the Marines, made a buddy out of Ken McCoy when they were in Officer Candidate School, and took him to New York on a short leave. Pick moved into one of the suites in the Foster Park and passed word around New York that he was in town and having a nonstop party over the weekend. Ernie Sage went to the party and bumped into Ken McCoy. End of longtime, pleasant, and not entirely unreasonable fantasy. Start of unending nightmare. As soon as Ernie saw Ken, she knew he was the man in her life. With that as a given, there was absolutely no reason not to go to bed with him four hours after they met.

"I *waited,* Daddy," Ernie said. "Until I was sure. I'm *sure.*"

If it wasn't for my goddamned father, Ernest Sage often thought, *I could at least threaten to cut her off without a dime.*

When Ernie was four, Grandfather Sage set up a trust fund for the adorable little tyke, funding it with 5 percent of his shares (giving her 2.5 percent of the total) of American Personal Pharmaceuticals, Inc. Control of this trust was to be passed to her on her graduation from college, her marriage, or on attaining her twenty-fifth year, whichever occurred first. Ernie had graduated Summa Cum Laude from college at twenty.

"Oh?" Ernest Sage asked.

"What did he want?"

"Well . . . I'm sorry about this. It's orders. I can't go to Bernardsville with you this weekend."

"Why not?"

"I've got to go to Philadelphia and then to Parris Island."

"You're on leave, hospital *recuperative* leave," Ernie said angrily. "You're supposed to have thirty days!"

"Come on, baby, I was only dinged," McCoy said.

Yeah, Ernest Sage thought, *and if whatever it was that dinged you in the forehead had dinged you an inch deeper, you'd be dead. They don't hand out Purple Hearts for dings.*

"What are you going to do in Philadelphia?" Ernie asked.

She doesn't argue with him. She'll argue with her mother and me till the cows come home. He tells her something and that's it.

"A guy's in the hospital there I have to see," McCoy began, then interrupted himself. "You know him, baby, as a matter of fact. Remember that kid who we put up on the boat? Moore? On his way to Australia?"

"Yes," Ernie said, remembering. "What's he doing in Philadelphia? *In the hospital in Philadelphia?*"

"He got hurt on Guadalcanal," McCoy said.

"Oh, God!" Ernie said. "Was he badly hurt?"

"Bad enough to get sent home."

"I thought he was going to *Australia!*" Ernie said, making it an accusation.

"Until this morning I thought he was in Australia," McCoy said.

"Why are they sending you to see him?"

"They're going to commission him," McCoy said. "Pickering was going there to swear him in, but it turns out he has an infection and they won't let him travel."

"An infection?" Ernest Sage asked.

McCoy nodded. "He says it's not serious, but—"

"Patricia told your mother," Sage said to Ernie, "that Flem just walked out of the hospital in California. Before he was discharged, I mean. He's a damned fool."

"Daddy!"

"Well, he is," Sage insisted, and then thought of something else. "What do you have to do with him, Ken?"

"He's now my boss," Ken said.

"I still don't understand why you have to go to Philadelphia," Ernie said.

"I told you. Moore's getting commissioned. I'm going to swear him in, take care of the paperwork."

"I want to go," Ernie said.

McCoy considered that a moment.

"If he's in the hospital, I want to see him," Ernie went on.

"From Philadelphia, I'm going to Parris Island," McCoy said.

"For how long?"

"Couple of days. I'm driving."

"Any reason I can't go?"

"Yes, there is."

"Well, I can at least go to Philadelphia."

"All I'm going to do is swear him in, handle the paperwork, and then head for Parris Island."

"Today's Friday. Tomorrow's Saturday. We could have all day in Philadelphia, and then you could drive to Parris Island on Sunday," Ernie said reasonably.

He shrugged, giving in.

"Your mother will be disappointed," Ernest Sage said. "And where would you stay in Philadelphia?"

"I don't know. The Warwick, the Bellvue-Stratford . . ."

"You're not married, you can't stay in a hotel together," Ernest Sage blurted.

"Talk to Ken about us not being married," Ernie said. *"I'm* not the one being difficult on that subject."

"Jesus, baby! We've been over that already!"

"What we're going to do, Daddy, is spend the night in Bernardsville and drive to Philadelphia in the morning. Why don't you call Mother and ask her to meet us somewhere for dinner? The Brook, maybe, or Baltusrol?"

There is absolutely nothing I can do but smile and agree, Ernest Sage decided. *If I raise any further objections, she won't go to Bernardsville at all.*

"Baltusrol," he said. "They do a very nice English grill on Friday nights."

He raised his hand, caught the headwaiter's attention, and put his balled fist to his ear, miming his need for a telephone.

As he waited for the telephone, he had a pleasant thought: *What did he say? That Fleming Pickering is now his boss? Jesus, maybe they'll give him a desk job.* But an unpleasant thought immediately replaced it: *Bullshit! Flem Pickering was supposed to be working for the Secretary of the Navy, which any reasonable person would think meant shuffling paper in Washington, and the next thing we hear is that he got all shot up and earned the Silver Star, taking command of some goddamn* destroyer *when the captain was killed.*

He looked at his daughter. She was feeding Ken McCoy a bacon-wrapped oyster. If he'd been an angel, her look couldn't have been more transfixed.

All I want for you, kitten, is your happiness.

"Elaine," he said a minute later to the telephone, "we're in Jack and Charley's, and what Ernie wants us to do is have supper at Baltusrol."

"Yes, I know you've made plans for the weekend, but something has come up."

"Elaine, for Christ's sake, just get in the goddamn car and go to Baltusrol. We'll see you there in an hour."

"You want an oyster, Daddy?"

"Yes, thank you, kitten."

VI

Both Gunnery Sergeant Ernest W. Zimmerman and Sergeant Thomas McCoy were considerably relieved when the R4D made contact again with the earth's surface. It was Gunny Zimmerman's third and Sergeant McCoy's second flight in a heavier-than-air vehicle. Though these previous experiences had a happy outcome (they survived them), that success did not relieve their current anxieties. In fact, if they'd had a say in the matter, both would have traveled by ship from Hawaii to wherever The Corps was sending them.

They were not given a choice. Their orders directed them to proceed by the most expeditious means, including air; and a AAA priority had been authorized.

They flew from Pearl Harbor to Espíritu Santo aboard a Martin PBM-3R Mariner, the unarmed transport version of the amphibious, twin-engine patrol bomber. Flight in the Mariner was bad enough, both of them privately considered during the long flight from Pearl, but if something went wrong with an amphibian like that—should the engines stop, for example—at least it could land on the water and float around until somebody came to help them.

The flight from Espíritu Santo in the R4D was something else. It was a land plane. If they went down in the ocean it would sink, very likely before they could inflate the rubber rafts crated near the rear door.

During the flight they were warm, though not uncomfortably so. But by the time the R4D completed its landing roll and taxied to the parking ramp, they were covered with sweat, and wet patches were under their arms and down the backs of their utility jackets.

The crew chief came down the fuselage past the crates of supplies lashed to the floor and the bags of mail scattered around, and pushed open the door.

By the time Zimmerman and McCoy stood up, a truck was backed up to the door. That meant they had to climb onto the bed of the truck before they could get to the ground. The Marine labor detail on the truck bed unloading the cargo were mostly bare-chested, wearing only utility trousers and boondockers. They were tanned and sweaty.

The sergeant in charge of the detail told Zimmerman where he could find the office of MAG-21. They put their seabags onto their shoulders and started to walk across the field.

The office turned out to be two connected eight-man squad tents, with their sides rolled up. The tents were surrounded by a wall of sandbags.

A corporal sat on a folding chair at a folding desk, pecking away with two fingers on a Royal portable typewriter. When Zimmerman walked into the tent, he saw another kid, bare-chested, asleep on a cot.

"Can I help you, Gunny?" the corporal asked.

"Reporting in," Zimmerman said, and handed over their orders. The corporal read the orders and then looked at Zimmerman.

"Sergeant Oblensky around?" Zimmerman asked.

The corporal ignored him.

"Lieutenant?" the corporal called.

The blond-headed kid on the cot raised himself on his elbows, shook his head, and then looked around the tent, finally focusing his eyes on Zimmerman.

"Do something for you, Gunny?" he asked.

Jesus, he's an officer. He don't look old enough to have hair on his balls.

"Zimmerman, Sir. Gunnery Sergeant Ernest W. Reporting in with one man."

"My name is Dunn," the kid said. "I'm the OD. Welcome aboard. Now, where the hell did you come from?" He looked at the corporal. "Those the orders?"

"Yes, Sir," the corporal said and handed them to him.

He read them and then looked up. "MacNeil," he asked, "where's the skipper?"

"On the flight line, Sir. Him and the exec, both."

"See if you can find him," Dunn ordered. "Or the exec. One or the other."

"Aye, aye, Sir."

"I don't understand your orders," Dunn said to Zimmerman. "A transfer from the 2nd Raider Battalion to an air group seems odd, even in The Marine Corps."

"Yes, Sir," Zimmerman agreed.

Lieutenant Colonel Clyde W. Dawkins, a tall, thin, sharp-featured man in his thirties, appeared a few minutes later, trailed by Captain Charles M. Galloway. Both were wearing sweat-darkened cotton flying suits. Dawkins also wore a fore-and-aft cap and a Smith & Wesson .38 Special revolver in a shoulder holster, while Galloway had on a utility cap that looked three sizes too small for him, and a .45 Colt automatic hung from a web pistol belt.

Zimmerman and McCoy popped to attention. Dawkins looked at them and smiled.

"Stand at ease, Gunny," he said, and then asked Dunn, "Where's MacNeil?"

"I sent him to look for you, Sir. These two just reported in." He handed Dawkins the orders.

Dawkins read them and made very much the same observation Dunn had: "I don't understand this. A transfer from the 2nd Raider Battalion to the 21st MAG?"

He handed the orders to Galloway and looked quizzically at Zimmerman.

"It wasn't my idea, Colonel," Sergeant McCoy volunteered. "I didn't ask to come to no fucking air group!"

"Shut your mouth!" Zimmerman said as Galloway opened his mouth to offer a similar suggestion.

Colonel Dawkins coughed.

"We've met, haven't we, Gunny?" Galloway said to Zimmerman.

"Yes, Sir. I went down to fix your Brownings when you was at Ewa."

"I thought that was you," Galloway said. "Oblensky at work, Colonel."

"Oh?"

"The gunny was good enough, in exchange for a portable generator, to make our Brownings work. I remember Oblensky saying at the time, 'We need him more than the Raiders do.'"

"Oh," Dawkins said. "And was Sergeant Oblensky right, would you say, Captain Galloway?"

"I think Sergeant Oblensky has managed to convince somebody that we need him, both of them, more than the Raiders, Sir."

"Persuasive fellow, Sergeant Oblensky," Dawkins said. "I wondered what happened to that generator. One moment it was there, and the next, it had vanished into thin air."

"On the other hand, Colonel, the gunny here, and his right-hand man, I guess, did make those machine guns work."

"That's a Jesuitical argument, Captain, that the end justifies the means," Dawkins said, trying without much success to keep a smile off his face. He turned to Sergeant McCoy. "Did I hear you say, Sergeant, that if things were left up to you, you would not be here in the fucking air group?"

"No, Sir. I mean, I didn't ask for this, Sir."

"Well, we certainly don't want anyone in our fucking air group who doesn't want to be in our fucking air group, do we, Captain Galloway?"

"No, Sir."

"Since Sergeant Oblensky, Captain Galloway, is your man, I will leave the resolution of this situation in your very capable hands."

"Aye, aye, Sir," Galloway said.

"Might I suggest, however, that since the sergeant doesn't want to be in our fucking air group, he might be happier in the 1st Raider Battalion. Only the other day, Colonel Edson happened to mention in passing that he had certain personnel problems."

"That thought ran through my mind, Sir," Captain Galloway said.

"How about that, Sergeant?" Colonel Dawkins asked solicitously. "How you would like to go to the Raider Battalion here on Guadalcanal? The Fucking First, as they are fondly known."

"I'd like that fine, Sir," Sergeant McCoy said happily. "I'm a fucking Raider."

Colonel Dawkins was suddenly struck with another coughing fit. Motioning for Lieutenant Dunn to follow him, he quickly left the tent; and a moment later they were followed by Captain Galloway, similarly afflicted.

Colonel Dawkins was first to regain control.

" 'I didn't ask to come to no fucking air group,' " he accurately mimicked Sergeant McCoy's indignant tone, " 'I'm a fucking Raider.' "

That triggered additional laughter. Then there was just time for the three officers to hear, inside the tent, Sergeant Zimmerman's angry voice . . . "When I tell you to shut your fucking mouth, asshole, you shut your fucking mouth." . . . when another sound, the growling of a siren, filled the air.

All three of them were still smiling, however, when they ran to the revetments and strapped themselves into their Wildcats.

(TWO)
**Royal Australian Navy Coastwatcher Establishment
Townsville, Queensland
6 September 1942**

Staff Sergeant Allan Richardson, USMC, senior staff noncommissioned officer of USMC Special Detachment 14, did not at first recognize the single deplaning passenger of the U.S. Navy R4D as a field-grade officer of the USMC.

Although Sergeant Richardson was himself grossly out of the prescribed uniform—he was wearing khaki trousers, an open-necked woolen shirt, a Royal Australian Navy duffel coat, and a battered USMC campaign hat—he had been conditioned by nine years in the prewar Corps to expect Marine officers, especially field-grade Marine officers, to look like officers.

The character who stepped off the airplane was wearing soiled and torn utilities, boondockers, no cover, and he was carrying what looked to Richardson's experienced eye like a U.S. Navy Medical Corps insulated container for fresh human blood. A web belt hung cowboy-style around his waist, and two ammunition pouches and a .45 in a leather holster were suspended from it.

Richardson stared at the insulated containers until he was positive—red crosses in white squares were still visible under a thin coat of green paint—that the containers had almost certainly been stolen. By then the character was almost at Richardson's Studebaker President automobile. When Richardson looked at him, he saw for the first time that not only was USMC stenciled on the breast of the filthy utilities, but that a major's golden oakleaf was pinned to each collar point.

At that point Richardson did what all his time in the prewar Corps had conditioned him to do: He quickly rose from behind the wheel, came to attention, and saluted crisply.

"Good afternoon, Sir!"

"Thank Christ, a Marine," Major Jake Dillon, USMCR, said with a vague gesture in the direction of his forehead that could only kindly be called a return of Sergeant Richardson's salute.

Dillon, a muscular, trim, tanned man in his middle thirties, opened the rear door of the Studebaker, carefully placed the ex–fresh human blood container on the seat, and closed the door.

"How may I help the Major, Sir?" Richardson asked.

"I'm here to see Major Banning," Dillon said as he walked around to the passenger side of the car and got in.

"Who, Sir?"

Richardson had heard Dillon clearly. Indeed, Major Ed Banning himself was the one who sent him to the airport when they heard the R4D overhead. But as a general operating principle, the personnel of USMC Special Detachment 14 denied any knowledge of the detachment or its personnel.

"It's all right, Sergeant. My name is Dillon. I'm a friend of Major Banning's."

When he detected a certain hesitancy on Sergeant Richardson's part, Dillon added: "For Christ's sake, do I look like a Japanese spy?"

"No, Sir," Richardson said, chuckling. "And you don't look like a candy-ass from MacArthur's headquarters, either. The Major really hates it when they show up here."

Dillon smiled.

"I'll bet," he said. "I'll also bet that you would be able to put your hands on a cold beer to save the life of an old China Marine, wouldn't you?"

"I don't have any with me in the car, Major, but I'll drive like hell to where you can get one."

"Bless you, my son," Dillon said, making the sign of the cross.

"That wasn't the regular courier plane, was it?" Richardson asked a minute or so later as he headed for the Coastwatcher Establishment. But it was really a statement rather than a question.

"No, that was a medical evacuation plane from Guadalcanal, headed for Melbourne. I asked them to drop me off."

"No cold beer on Guadalcanal?"

"No cold beer, and not much of anything else, either," Dillon said. "The goddamn Navy sailed off with most of our rations still on the transports. We've been living on what we took away from the Japs."

"Yeah, we heard about that," Richardson said.

When Major Edward F. Banning, USMC, Commanding Officer of USMC Special Detachment 14, glanced into the unit's combined mess hall and club, he saw Major Dillon sprawled in a chair at the table reserved for the unit's half-dozen officers. He was working on his second bottle of beer.

Sergeant Richardson, smiling, holding a bottle of beer, was leaning against the wall.

When Banning walked into the room, Richardson pushed himself off the wall and looked a little uncomfortable.

"I'm afraid to ask what you've got in the blood container, Jake," Banning said.

"There was film in it," Dillon replied. "Richardson put it in your refrigerator for me."

"What kind of film?"

"Still and 16mm. Eyemo."

"That's not what I meant."

"Of heroic Marines battling the evil forces of the Empire of Japan. With a cast of thousands. Produced and directed by yours truly. Being rushed to your neighborhood newsreel theater."

"You may find it hard to believe, looking at him, Sergeant Richardson," Banning said, "but this scruffy, unwashed, unshaven officer was once famous for being the best-turned-out Marine sergeant in the Fourth Marines."

"Don't give me a hard time, Banning," Dillon said.

"We was just talking about the Fourth, Sir," Richardson said. "We know people, but we wasn't there at the same time."

"How are you, Jake?" Banning asked, walking to him and shaking hands. "You look like hell."

"I was hungry, dirty, and thirsty. Now I'm just hungry and dirty, thanks to Sergeant Richardson."

"Well, I'll feed you, but I won't give you a bath."

"You got something I can wear until I get to Melbourne? My stuff is there."

"Sure. Utilities? Or something fancier?"

"Utilities would be fine," Dillon said.

"See what you can do, Richardson, will you?" Banning ordered. "Major Dillon will be staying in my quarters."

"Aye, aye, Sir," Richardson said. "You want to give me that .45, Major, I'll get it cleaned for you."

Dillon hesitated, then stood up and unfastened his pistol belt.

"Bless you again, my son," he said.

"Anytime, Major," Sergeant Richardson said with a smile and then left.

Dillon looked at Banning.

"I think I better go have that bath now, while I'm still on my feet."

"You sick, Jake, or just tired?"

"I hope to Christ I'm just tired. What you can catch on that fucking island starts with crabs and lice and gets worse. They've got bugs nobody ever heard of, not to mention malaria."

"If you want a *bath,*" Banning said, as he led Dillon, still clutching his beer bottle, from the mess hall, "I'll ask Feldt. All I have is a shower."

"Shower's fine. How *is* Commander Charming?"

"He might even be glad to see you, as a matter of fact," Banning said. "You didn't show up here in a dress uniform, taking notes, and telling him how to run things."

"Speak of the devil," Dillon said as he saw Commander Feldt coming down the corridor. He raised his voice slightly. "Well, there's the pride of the Royal Australian Navy."

"Hello, Dillon," Feldt said, offering his hand. There was even the suggestion of a smile on his face. "How are you?"

It was not the reception Dillon expected. He wouldn't have been surprised if Feldt completely ignored him, and even less surprised if Feldt was grossly insulting and colorfully profane.

"Can't complain," Dillon said.

"You *look* like something the sodding cat dragged in."

Commander Feldt then disappeared.

Three minutes later, in Banning's room, he surprised Dillon again. The shower curtain parted and a hand holding a bottle of scotch appeared.

"Have a taste of this, Dillon," Feldt said. "It might not kill the sodding worms, but it'll give them a sodding headache."

"Bless you, my son," Dillon said.

"Sod you, Dillon," Feldt said, but there was unmistakable friendliness and warmth in his voice.

When Dillon came out of the shower, Feldt was sprawled on Banning's bed, holding the bottle of scotch on his stomach. Banning was sitting on his desk.

"So how are things on Guadalcanal?" Feldt asked.

I am probably, Dillon realized, *the first man he—or Banning, for that matter—has talked to who has been on the island.*

"What I really can't figure is why the Japs haven't gotten their act together and thrown us off," Dillon said.

Feldt grunted.

"Are those stories true about the Navy sailing away with the heavy artillery, et cetera, or are you sodding Marines just crying in your sodding beer again?"

"They're true," Dillon said. He walked naked to the bed, took the bottle from Feldt, and drank a swallow from the neck. "If it wasn't for the food the Japs left behind, the First Marine Division would be starving. And if it wasn't for the engineer equipment the Japs left behind, Henderson Field simply wouldn't exist. The fucking Navy sailed off with almost all of our engineer equipment still aboard the transports."

Feldt looked at him a moment and then swung his feet off the bed.

"Cover your sodding ugly nakedness, Dillon," he said. "I asked one of the lads to fix you a steak."

"Thank you," Dillon said.

"Just for the record, you have the ugliest, not to mention the smallest—I will not dignify it by calling it a 'penis'—pisser I have ever seen on a full-grown man."

"Sod you, Eric," Dillon said.

"But for some inexplicable reason, I am glad to see you. What are you doing here, anyway?"

"Flacking," Dillon said as he pulled an undershirt over his head.

"What in the sweet name of Jesus is 'flacking'?"

"I am a flack," Dillon replied. "What flacks do is 'flack,' hence 'flacking.'"

"What is this demented sodding compatriot of yours rambling about, Banning?"

"I'm a press agent, Eric," Dillon said. "My contribution to the war effort will be to (a) encourage red-blooded American youth to rush to the Marine recruiter and (b) shame their families, friends, and neighbors into buying war bonds. That's what flacks do."

"I don't think he's trying to pull my sodding leg, Banning, but I haven't the faintest sodding idea what he's talking about."

"Neither do I," Banning said.

"I'm on my way home with six wounded heroes, two of whom I have yet to cast," Dillon explained as he pulled utility trousers on. "Said wounded heroes will be put on display all over America, with a suitable background of flags and stirring patriotic airs."

"You don't sound very enthusiastic about it, Jake," Banning said.

"I almost got out of it," Dillon said. "I almost had Vandergrift in a corner."

Major General Alexander Archer Vandergrift, USMC, was Commanding General, First Marine Division.

"You almost had *Vandergrift* in a corner?" Banning asked incredulously.

"I went and asked him if I could have a company," Dillon replied and then stopped. *The alcohol is getting to me,* he thought. *I'm running off at the mouth.*

"And?" Banning pursued.

"He said, 'Thanks very much, but captains command companies and you're a major.' And I said, 'I would be happy to take a bust to captain, or for that matter back to the ranks.'"

"And?"

"He said he would think about it, and I really think he did. But then we got a fucking radio from Headquarters, USMC. The Assistant Commandant is personally interested in this fucking wounded-hero war bond tour, it seems, and he wanted to know what was holding it up. And that blew me out of the fucking water."

"It's important, Jake," Banning said, more because he felt sorry for Dillon than because he believed in the importance of war bond tours.

"Bullshit," Dillon said. "They have civilians in uniform who could do as well as I can. I'm a Marine. Or I like to think I am."

"Yours not to reason why, old sod," Feldt said, "yours but to ride into the sodding valley of the pracks."

"Flacks," Dillon corrected him automatically.

"Flacks, pracks, flicks, pricks, whatever," Feldt said cheerfully. "You about ready to eat?"

"I'm a prick of a flack, who used to be a flack for the flicks," Dillon heard himself say.

Jesus, I'm drunk!

"Actually, old sod, I would say you're a prickless prack," Feldt said. And then he laughed. It was the first time Dillon could remember hearing him laugh.

The steak was not a New York Strip, charred on the outside and pink in the middle. It was thin, fried to death, and (to put a good face on it) chewy. But it covered the plate.

And it was the first fresh meat Jake had in his mouth for six weeks. He ate all of it with relish.

"Jesus, that was good!"

"Another, old sod?" Feldt asked.

"No, thanks."

"You haven't told us what you're doing here, Jake," Banning said.

"Well, I'm on my way home. I thought maybe you'd want me to call your wife—"

Dillon stopped abruptly.

Too late, Dillon remembered that Mrs. Edward F. Banning did not get out of Shanghai before the Japanese came. She was a White Russian refugee whom Banning had married just before the Fourth Marines were transferred from Shanghai to the Philippines.

You're an asshole, Dillon, and don't blame it on the booze.

"—Shit! Ed, I'm sorry!" he went on, regret in his voice. "That just slipped out."

"Forget it," Banning said evenly.

"Or get you something in the States," Dillon went on somewhat lamely.

"Send us Pickering back," Feldt said. "If you want to do something useful."

"Amen," Banning said, as if anxious to get off the subject of Mrs. Edward F. Banning. "The minute he left, the assholes in MacArthur's headquarters held a party, and then they started working on us."

"That figures," Dillon said. "I'll make a point to see him, talk to him."

"I don't think it will do any good," Banning said.

"I don't know. It sodding well can't do any sodding harm," Feldt said. "That *would* be a service, old sod."

"Consider it done," Dillon said. "He still works for Frank Knox. Hot radios from the Secretary of the Navy often work miracles. Is there anything in particular?"

"Ask him to get that sodding asshole Willoughby off our back," Feldt said.

Newly promoted Brigadier General Charles A. Willoughby, USA, was MacArthur's intelligence officer. He was one of the "Bataan Gang," i.e., the men who escaped by PT Boat with MacArthur from the Philippines.

"Since he is the theater intelligence officer," Banning said, "Willoughby feels that all intelligence activities should come under him. In his shoes I would probably feel the same way. But it really isn't Willoughby who's the problem so much as the people he has working for him."

"Willoughby," Feldt insisted, "is a sodding asshole, and so are the people working for him."

"They want us to route our intelligence through SWPOA," Banning said. (MacArthur's official title was Supreme Commander, *S*outh *W*est *P*acific *O*cean *A*reas.)

"So Willoughby can look important," Feldt said.

"Do you?"

"Yes and no," Banning said. "When possible, the Coastwatchers communicate with CINCPAC Radio directly. We monitor everything, of course. So if our people can't get through to them, we relay to CINCPAC. If that happens, we send a copy to SWPOA." (CINCPAC: Commander in Chief, Pacific, the Navy's headquarters at Pearl Harbor.)

"Willoughby wants our people to communicate with SWPOA, and he'll pass it on to CINCPAC," Feldt said. "We have been ignoring the asshole, of course."

"So far successfully," Banning said. "But, oh how we miss Captain Pickering. He could get Willoughby off our back."

"Speaking of 'our people,'" Dillon said, remembering the two boys on Buka. *It was one thing,* he thought, *to have your ass in the line of fire in a line company on Guadalcanal—having your ass in the line of fire was what being a Marine was really all about—and something entirely different to be one of two Marines on an enemy-held island with no chance of being relieved.*

"Good lads," Feldt said. "Every time I want to say something unpleasant about you sodding Marines, I remind myself there is an exception to the rule."

"So far they're all right, Jake," Banning said. "All right being defined as the Japs haven't caught them yet. Buka, right now, is probably the most important station."

"How are they?" Dillon asked. When neither Feldt nor Banning immediately replied, he went on: "I'm headed for the Fourth General Hospital. Barbara's there. She'll ask me about Joe."

"Lie to her," Feldt said. "That would be kindest."

Lieutenant (J.G.) Barbara T. Cotter, NNCR, was engaged to First Lieutenant Joseph L. Howard, USMCR, who was now on Buka with Sergeant Steven M. Koffler.

"Why are you going to the Fourth General?" Banning asked.

"I have four wounded heroes; I need two more. I'm going to hold an audition at the hospital to fill the cast. Don't change the subject. Tell me about Joe and Koffler. I don't want to lie to Barbara."

"They are on the edge of starvation," Feldt said. "They are almost certainly infested with a wide variety of intestinal parasites. The odds are ten to one they have malaria, and probably two or three other tropical diseases. They have no medicine. For that matter they don't even have salt. They are already two weeks past the last date they could possibly be expected to escape detection by the Japanese."

"Jesus!" Dillon said.

"Tell Barbara that if you like," Feldt said in a level voice.

"What about getting them out?"

"Out of the sodding question, old sod," Feldt said.

"Well, what the hell are you going to do when they are caught?" Dillon asked angrily. "You just said—Banning just said—that Buka is, right now, the most important station."

"When Buka goes down, Jake," Banning said, "we will start parachuting in replacement teams. The moment we're sure it's down, we start dropping people. Giving Willoughby his due, he has promised us a B-17 within two hours when we ask for one."

"A B-17? Why a B-17?"

"Because when we jumped Joe and Koffler in there—Christ, two Jap fighter bases are on Buka—we used an unarmed transport. It was shot down. Fortunately, after Joe and Koffler jumped."

"And nothing can be done?"

"I don't know. We haven't given it much thought," Feldt said, thickly sarcastic. "But perhaps someone of your vast expertise in these areas has a solution we haven't been able to come up with ourselves."

"Eric, I'm sorry you took that the wrong way," Dillon said.

Feldt didn't reply; but a moment later he stood up and leaned over to refresh Dillon's glass of scotch.

"What makes you think you can get a replacement team on the ground?" Dillon asked after a long silence.

"The operative word is 'teams,' plural," Banning replied. "We have six, ready to go. We will jump them in one at a time until one becomes operational. And then we'll have other teams standing by to go in when the operating team goes down."

"Jesus Christ!" Dillon said.

"If we're not able to inform CINCPAC and Guadalcanal when the Japanese bombers take off from Rabaul and the bases near it, our fighters on Henderson Field and on carriers will not be in the air in time to deflect them. That would see a lot of dead Marines," Banning said. "Viewed professionally, the mathematics make sense. It is better to suffer a couple of dozen losses to save a couple of hundred, a couple of thousand, lives. The only trouble is that I—Eric and I—know the kids whose lives we're going to expend for the common good. That makes it a little difficult, personally."

Dillon raised his eyes to Banning's.

"So tell Barbara the truth, Jake. Tell her that we continue to hear from Joe at least once a day, and that so far as we know he's all right."

"Speaking of the truth, old sod," Feldt said, "Banning told me a wild tale. He claims you've dipped that miniature wick of yours into most of the famous honey pots in Hollywood."

The subject of Buka was closed, and Jake knew that he could not reopen it.

"I cannot tell a lie, Commander Feldt," Dillon said. "The story's true."

(THREE)
United States Naval Hospital
Philadelphia, Pennsylvania
0930 Hours 6 September 1942

"May I help you, Lieutenant?" Lieutenant (J.G.) Joanne McConnell, NNC, asked.

"We're looking for Sergeant Moore, John M.," McCoy said. "They told us he was on this ward."

"He is, but—this isn't my idea—the rule is no visitors on the ward before noon."

"This is official business," McCoy said.

"Nice try," Lieutenant McConnell said. "But I don't think Commander Jensen would buy it. Maybe you, but not the lady. Commander Jensen runs a tight ship."

"Who's he?"

"She. She's supervisory nurse in this building."

McCoy took a wallet-sized leather folder from his pocket, opened it, and held it out for Lieutenant McConnell to see.

It held a badge that incorporated the seal of the Department of the Navy, an identification card with McCoy's picture on it, and the statement that the bearer was a Special Agent of the Office of Naval Intelligence.

"If the Commander shows up, you can tell her I showed you that and asked you where I can find Sergeant Moore, and that you told me."

"I never saw one of those before," Lieutenant McConnell said. "I hope he's not in some kind of trouble?"

"No. As a matter of fact, I'm about to make him an officer and a gentleman."

"He's a really nice kid," the nurse said.

"What shape is he in?"

"He still has to walk with a cane, but he's going to be all right."

"Why isn't he on recuperative leave?"

"He is. He was gone for a couple of days, but then he came back. He has family in Philadelphia, but—I didn't ask why he came back."

"Where is he?"

"Six-sixteen, second door from the end of the corridor on the left."

"Is he in there alone?"

"The scuttlebutt is that there was a telephone call from some captain in the office of the Secretary of the Navy ordering him a private room. It is one of the reasons he is not one of Commander Jensen's favorite people."

"Real chickenshit bitch, huh?" McCoy said.

"Ken!" Ernie Sage said.

"You said that, Lieutenant," Lieutenant McConnell said, smiling, "I didn't."

Sergeant John Marston Moore, USMCR, wearing a T-shirt and hospital pajama pants, was in bed when McCoy pushed open the door and walked in.

The top of the bed was raised to a nearly vertical position. And spread out before him on the food tray was the balsa-wood framework of a model airplane wing, to which Moore was attaching tissue paper covering.

He looked up with curiosity, then annoyance, and finally surprised recognition as the Marine officer and the girl walked into the room.

"Jesus!" he said.

"And the Virgin Mary," McCoy said. "I thought I told you to remember to duck, asshole."

"Ken!" Ernie said, and then, "Hello, John, how are you?"

"Surprised," Moore said. He looked at McCoy and went on, "I read in the papers about the Makin Island raid. I thought you would have been in on that."

"He was," Ernie said. "And almost got himself killed."

"No, I didn't," McCoy said.

Ernie walked to the bed and handed Moore a package. He removed the covering. It was a box of Fanny Farmer Chocolates; its cover didn't fit very well.

"Well, thanks," Moore said a little uncomfortably.

"I told you he wouldn't want candy," McCoy said.

"Don't be silly. I love chocolate," Moore lied, and quickly opened the box to prove it.

A pint flask of scotch lay on top of the chocolates. His face lit up.

"I hate people who are always right," Ernie said.

"He's a Marine. Marines always know what's important."

"God!" Ernie replied.

"Speaking of Marines," Moore said. *"General* Pickering. What's that all about?"

"He told me he called you," McCoy said.

"He called, but all he did was ask how I was, and if he could do anything for me. He didn't even tell me he was a general. I saw that in the newspaper. And he didn't tell me you were coming, either."

"Well, he's now a brigadier general; he's our boss; and just as soon as we finish the paperwork, he will have an aide-de-camp named Lieutenant Moore."

Moore didn't seem especially surprised.

"I wondered what they were going to do with me," he said.

"Now you know," McCoy said. "As soon as you get out of here, you go to Washington."

"I can leave here today," Moore said.

"You're entitled to thirty days' recuperative leave," McCoy said. "You want to tell me about that?"

"What do you mean, tell you about it?"

"Why aren't you out chasing skirts, getting drunk?"

"I can't chase too well using a cane. And when I get drunk, I fall down a lot."

"I mean, what the hell are you doing here making model airplanes?" McCoy pursued.

"Ken, that's none of your business!" Ernie snapped.

Moore looked at McCoy for a full thirty seconds, and then shrugged his shoulders.

"Going home was a disaster," he said. "For reasons I'd rather not get into. Before I went over there, I was . . . involved with a woman. Unfortunately she was a married woman. More unfortunately, she went back to her husband. So that leaves what? There's a couple of bars outside the gate here where you can go and have a couple of drinks without being treated like a freak—"

"What do you mean, a freak?" Ernie asked.

"Wounded guys are still a novelty," Moore said. "I am uncomfortable in the role of wounded hero . . . because I know goddamn well I'm no hero."

"You got the Bronze Star," McCoy said evenly.

"Not for doing anything heroic," Moore said, and then closed off further discussion of the subject by going on, "so I drink in local bars at night and make model airplanes during the day. Or is that against Marine Regulations?"

"I have to make him wear his ribbons, too," Ernie said. "I'll tell you what you're going to do today, John. You're going to put on your uniform and spend the day with us. I don't care if either one of you like it or not, I want to be the girl who has two wounded heroes on her arm."

McCoy saw Moore's eyes light up at the suggestion.

"You're going to be here all day?" Moore asked.

"Ken has to go to Parris Island tomorrow," Ernie said.

"I don't suppose I could go with you, could I?" Moore asked.

The door burst open.

Commander Elizabeth H. Jensen, NNC, a short, plump woman in her thirties, marched into the room. She folded her arms across her amply filled stiff white uniform bosom, glowered at McCoy, and announced, "I would like to know exactly what you think you are doing in here!"

"We are about to have a drink to begin the day, Commander," McCoy said, taking his credentials from his pocket and holding them up before Commander Jensen's eyes, "but aside from that, what else we're doing in here is none of your business. If I need you, however, I'll send for you."

(FOUR)
United States Army 4th General Hospital
Melbourne, Australia
7 September 1942

Now shorn, shaved, and dressed in a splendidly tailored officer's green elastique uniform, Major Jake Dillon sat with his hand wrapped around a glass of scotch at a small table in the Officer's Club. Two young and quite attractive members of the Navy Nurse Corps sat on either side of him.

He had flown in this morning from Townsville on a Royal Australian Air Force airplane that Commander Feldt arranged.

One of the nurses was Lieutenant (J.G.) Joanne Miller, NNCR, a tall, slim nurse-anesthesiologist who wore her fine blond hair in a bun. The other was Lieutenant (J.G.) Barbara T. Cotter, NNCR, a psychiatric nurse. She was also a blonde, but her hair was shorter. She was also not quite as tall as Lieutenant Miller, and a bit heavier—but by no means unpleasantly so. The two were part of a very small group of Navy nurses-with-special-training temporarily assigned to the Army Hospital. They were roommates and had become friends.

The U.S. Army 4th General Hospital was one of the very few facilities in Australia that had never been a major logistical problem. The Royal Melbourne Hospital was originally completed in late 1940. It was an enormous, fully equipped medical establishment that had simply been turned over to the United States Army for the duration of the war. The only thing it lacked was officer's billeting and an officer's club; but it was no problem to convert facilities originally intended for use by the medical school to those purposes. That was where Dillon and the two nurses were now sitting.

"There's a pretty one, Jake," Lieutenant Miller said, nodding toward a tall, good-looking Marine first lieutenant coming into the room, walking with a cane. He wore parachutist's wings pinned on his tunic.

"You stay away from that guy, honey," Dillon said, recognizing the officer.

"Why do you say that, Jake?" Lieutenant (J.G.) Barbara T. Cotter, NNCR, asked, surprised.

After a moment Jake Dillon said, "I don't know. There's something about that guy I don't like."

"You know him?"

Dillon nodded. "I met him once in the States. I just remembered where."

"I thought your criterion was 'handsome hero,'" Joanne Miller said.

" 'Handsome, *wounded* hero,' " Jake corrected her and then looked at Barbara Cotter. "Handsome, honey, not pretty."

"Sorry. It's just that I've never been out with a man when *he* was looking for handsome men," Barbara said, and both women laughed.

"Thanks a lot, girls," Jake said. "Buy your own booze."

"I guess the one at the end of the bar won't qualify, huh, Jake?" Barbara asked. Jake looked in the direction of her nod.

An officer, an aviator, was standing at the bar looking down at his drink. He had a large bandage over his nose; the adhesive tape holding it extended to his jawline and temples. Under the bandage, his face was a large bruise from the lip line to above his eyes.

"Jesus, what happened to him?" Dillon asked.

"It's not as bad as it looks," Joanne said. "He slammed his face into a control panel. There were some fractures in the nasal passage area; they went in and straightened things out."

"I know him," Jake said, surprise in his voice. "Excuse me."

He got up and went to the young officer at the bar.

"I'm Jake Dillon, Lieutenant. Don't we know each other?"

The young officer looked at him.

"No, Sir. I don't think so."

"Lakehurst," Dillon insisted. "Charley Galloway? A light colonel—what the hell was his name?—jumped out of your airplane and his chute didn't open?"

Recognition came.

"Yes, Sir," Lieutenant Jim Ward said. "You were the press agent—excuse me, public relations officer, right?"

"I don't think press agent is a dirty word," Dillon said. "I thought it was you." They shook hands.

"If you're alone," Dillon said, "I'm not. Want to join us?" He nodded toward the table where the girls were sitting.

"That's the best offer I've had in a long time," Ward said.

"The smaller one is taken," Dillon said.

"I admire your taste."

"Not by me, but taken," Dillon said.

As they walked to the table, Dillon saw the parachutist officer glance at them, and then saw recognition in his eyes. He did not respond.

"Ladies, I would love to introduce this wounded, handsome hero to you, but I just realized I've forgotten his name," Dillon said.

"Jim Ward," Ward said.

"He's a pal of a pal of mine," Dillon went on. "Captain Charley Galloway."

The women rather formally shook hands with Ward.

"We've met before too," Joanne said. "I passed the gas when they fixed your face. Are you supposed to be drinking?"

"Well, I hadn't planned on driving anywhere," Ward said.

"Speaking of Charley?" Dillon said.

"He's on the 'Canal," Ward said. "Commanding VMF-229."

"Christ, I wish I'd known that," Dillon said. "I just came out of Henderson." Ward looked at Dillon with an interest he had not shown before.

"What were you doing on Guadalcanal?" he asked.

"I suppose most people would say I was getting in the way," Dillon replied, and went on: "How's Charley doing?"

"He was shot down. He floated around all night and then a PT boat picked him up. Aside from that, he's fine."

"What happened to you?" Dillon asked.

"I made a bad landing," Ward said. "And bumped my nose on the control panel."

"He lost—temporarily, by the grace of God—the use of his right eye when his windshield was shot away," Joanne said matter-of-factly. "Plexiglas fragments. When he landed, his gear collapsed, and the airplane's nose hit the ground with such force that the seat was ripped loose. The main reason they sent him here was that they couldn't believe he walked away from that crash with nothing more than broken ribs and a broken nose."

"Jesus," Dillon said.

"I really hope your deep research into my background also came up with the fact that I'm single, available, and that dogs and old ladies like me," Jim Ward said.

"So how are you?" Dillon asked.

"Until about five minutes ago I was feeling sorry for myself," Jim Ward said.

"Why?" Joanne asked.

"Just before I came in here tonight, I was told that I couldn't go back to the squadron until my ribs healed, and that for the next three to four weeks I will be an assistant morale and welfare officer of the detachment of patients. Among other things I am to make sure the bingo games are honest."

"Be grateful, for Christ's sake," Dillon said.

Lieutenant Jim Ward looked directly at Lieutenant Joanne Miller.

"Oh, I am now," he said.

She looks uncomfortable, Dillon thought, *but not displeased.*

"Excuse me, Major," the officer wearing parachutist's wings and walking with a cane said, "but aren't you Major Dillon?"

"That's right."

"Correct me if I'm wrong, Sir, but haven't we met?"

"Yeah. At Lakehurst," Dillon said. "We were just talking about that."

"Why don't you pull up a chair, Lieutenant? And sit down?" Joanne Miller said.

Why the hell did I do that? she thought. *Because I wanted him to take the strain off his leg? Or because ol' I-bumped-my-nose-on-the-control-panel here is making a pass at me? Or because I don't like my reaction to the pass? I will not get emotionally involved with him or any of the others. I don't want to go through what Barbara's going through.*

"With the Major's permission?" the parachutist officer asked.

"Yeah. Go ahead. Sit down," Jake said. "The ladies are Lieutenants Miller and Cotter. You remember Jim Ward?"

"No, I can't say that I do," the parachutist said, glancing at Ward and dismissing him. "I'm Dick Macklin," he said to the women. "I'm very pleased to meet you."

Dillon did not like the way Macklin was smiling at Barbara Cotter.

He remembered now why it was he didn't like Lieutenant Macklin. Not specific details, just that when they had been at Lakehurst, Macklin had been chickenshit. He was perfectly willing to throw an enlisted man to the wolves so he would look good—a PFC or a corporal, Jake now remembered, although he couldn't come up with a face or a name.

All good Marine officers have contempt for such officers. But in Jake Dillon's case, the contempt was magnified by his own experience with chickenshit officers. He had far more time in The Corps as a sergeant than he did as a field-grade officer and gentleman.

If you make a pass at Barbara, I'll break your other fucking leg. Why did I tell this sonofabitch it was all right to sit down? As a matter of fact, if you make a pass at either one, I'll break your other fucking leg.

"May I ask, Sir," Macklin said, "if you're a fellow patient?"

"Just passing through," Dillon said.

"On your way to Guadalcanal?"

"No," Dillon said.

"We had press people with us," Macklin said. He raised his stiff leg. "That's where I caught this. I went in with the first wave of parachutists when we hit the beach at Gavutu."

"Then we went in at about the same time," Dillon said, wearing a patently insincere smile. "I went in to Tulagi with Jack Stecker's 2nd Battalion of the Fifth."

"Really?" Barbara Cotter asked. It was the first time Jake had said anything about what he had done at Guadalcanal. Without thinking about it, she'd decided that as a press agent, Jake had gone in after the beach had been secured.

"Jack Stecker and I were sergeants in the Fourth," Dillon said. "He let me tag along."

That's not surprising, Barbara thought.

Jake was like Joe Howard. Both were Marine Mustangs (officers commissioned from the ranks); she knew the type. They felt somehow cheated if they weren't where the fighting was. This was admirable, unless of course you were in love with one of them, in which case they were damned fools.

Barbara hadn't believed a word Dillon told her about Joe Howard being all right. What she didn't already know, or guess, about the Coastwatchers and Joe's chances of survival, she had learned from Yeoman Daphne Farnsworth, Royal Australian Navy Women's Volunteer Reserve. Daphne not only worked with the Coastwatchers, she had become involved with Sergeant Steve Koffler before the two Marines parachuted onto Buka.

"What happened to you, Ward?" Macklin asked, obviously not wanting to swap war stories with Dillon.

"I thought the guy said 'stand up,' " Jim Ward said. "What he said was 'shut up.' "

"He got hurt flying out of Henderson with VMF-229. With Charley Galloway," Dillon said. "You remember Charley, don't you, Macklin?"

"No, Sir," Macklin said, searching his memory.

Jim Ward not only remembered Lieutenant Macklin from Lakehurst; he'd picked up on Dillon's contempt; and was just as annoyed as Dillon with Macklin's raised-leg, look-at-me-the-hero attitude.

"Sure, you do," Ward said. "He was our instructor pilot on the Gooneybird. *Tech Sergeant* Galloway?"

"Oh, yes, of course."

"Captain Galloway, now," Jim Ward added. "My squadron commander."

"Really?" Macklin asked.

From the look on Macklin's face, Ward saw that he had struck home. Nothing else he could have said would so annoy a Regular Marine officer with a commission from Annapolis than to be told that a technical sergeant he had tried to push around now outranked him as an officer and a gentleman.

Meanwhile, Lieutenant Richard B. Macklin might not have been a prince among men, or even a very decent human being, but he was no fool. He saw that his high hopes to get to know one of the nurses, perhaps even carnally, were not going to come to fruition.

Although Dillon had claimed that the blonde with the big boobs was taken, she kept looking at Dillon with something like affection. And the other one kept stealing looks at the aviator.

He had been done in, he realized, by the natural tendency of female officers to be attracted to field-grade officers and/or aviators. He didn't understand this—as far as he was concerned, it took far more courage to jump out of an airplane than it did to fly one—but that was unfortunately the way things were.

"How long are you going to look like that?" Dillon asked Ward.

"I beg your pardon?"

Joanne Miller understood the question.

"He ought to look more or less human in a week or ten days; at least the black-and-blue will have gone away," she said. "The ribs will take six weeks or so to heal."

"I can fly now," Ward said. "I didn't want to come here and they shouldn't have sent me."

That's not bullshit intended to impress the girls and me, Jake decided. *This kid is a Marine.*

"Where are you from, Ward?"

"Philadelphia. Or just outside. Jenkintown."

"Right. Where Charley's girlfriend is from, right?"

"She's my aunt," Jim Ward said.

"What about you, Macklin? Where are you from?"

"California, Sir. Near San Diego."

"Where'd you go to school?"

"The Naval Academy, Sir."

Jake Dillon Productions, Jake thought, *has just completed final casting of his epic motion picture, or at least newsreel feature epic,* Wounded Marine Heroes of 1942.

But I won't tell either of them just yet. Ward will be genuinely pissed when he hears what I'm going to do to him. And I suspect that Macklin will be so pleased I'm taking him out of harm's way that he'll piss his pants.

He remembered a story going around the aid stations on Gavutu and Tulagi about the 2nd Parachute Battalion officer who'd taken a minor flesh wound to his calf and had to be pried, screaming and hysterical, from a piling on the seaplane wharf where he had been hit.

There was absolutely no question in Jake's mind that that officer was now sitting at his table.

VII

Sergeant Steven M. Koffler, USMC, woke suddenly and sat up, frightened. His guts were knotted and he had a clammy sweat.

It was from a nightmare, he concluded after a moment, although he couldn't remember any of it.

The feeling of foreboding did not go away. Something was wrong. There was enough light in the hut for him to see that Patience was gone. That was not unusual. Since she had moved in with him, she habitually rose before he did and was out of the hut before he woke.

But then, slowly, it came to him, what was wrong. He heard no noise. There was always noise, the squealing of pigs, the crying of children, the crackling of a fire, even hymn singing.

That image sent his mind wandering: *They don't sing hymns here, like in church. It has nothing to do with God. It's just that "Rock of Ages" and "Faith of Our Fathers" and "God Save the King" and "Onward Christian Soldiers" and the other ones are the only music these people have ever heard.* He corrected himself: *Plus the Marine Hymn, which of course me and Lieutenant Howard taught them.*

Why can't I hear anything?

He felt another wave of fear and reached for the Thompson. He checked the action and then stuck his feet in his boondockers and stood up.

He went to the door of the hut and looked out. No one was in sight.

Where the fuck is everybody?

With his finger on the Thompson's trigger, he left the hut, took one quick look to confirm that no one was visible, then ran into the jungle behind the hut. He moved ten feet inside it, enough for concealment, and then he moved laterally until he found a position where he could observe the other huts.

There was no one there. The fires had gone out.

Even the fucking pigs are gone!

The sonsofbitches ran off on me!

Well, what the hell do you expect? he asked himself. *If I wasn't here, they're just a bunch of fucking cannibals; the Japs don't give a shit about cannibals unless they're causing trouble. The worst thing the Japs would do would be to put them to work.*

With me here, they're the fucking enemy. The Japs would kill them, slowly, to show they're pissed off. And they'll do it so it hurts, to teach the other cannibals it's not smart to help the White Man. Like cutting off their arms and legs, not just their heads, and leaving the parts laying around.

A chill replaced the clammy sweat.

What the fuck am I going to do now?

He was suddenly, without warning, sick to his stomach. When that passed, he had an equally irresistible urge to move his bowels.

He moved another fifteen yards through the jungle and watched the camp for another five minutes. Finally he walked out of the jungle and started looking in the huts.

The radio was still there.

Why not? What the hell would they do with the radio?

And he found some baked sweet potatoes, or whatever the hell they were, and some of the smoked pig.

A farewell present? Merry Christmas, Sergeant Koffler? How the fuck long are those sweet potatoes and five, ten pounds of smoked pig going to last me?

Oh, shit!

There came the sound of aircraft engines, a dull roar far off.

Fuck 'em! What the fuck do I care if the whole Japanese Air Corps is headed for Guadalcanal?

He walked to the tree house. They'd left him the knotted rope, he found to his surprise. He used it to walk up the trunk.

"Good morning, Steven," Patience Witherspoon said. She was sitting on the floor of the platform, wearing an expression that said she expected to be kicked.

Ian Bruce was leaning against the trunk.

"You heard the engines, Sergeant Koffler?"

"Fuck the engines, where the hell is everybody?"

"The men went to seek Lieutenant Reeves," Ian said. "The women have gone away from here."

"Gone where?"

"You would not know where they have gone," Ian said with irrefutable logic. *"Away."*

"Why?"

"If it has not gone well with Lieutenant Reeves, the Japanese will come looking for us. If they find this place, with the radio, they may believe there were no other white men. You will come with us to where the women are making a camp. We may be able to hide you."

"You think something fucked up, went wrong, don't you?"

"I think something has fucked up. Otherwise Lieutenant Reeves would have returned when he said he would return."

"Why wasn't I told?"

"Because I knew you would forbid it," Ian Bruce said. "Lieutenant Reeves left you in charge; he told me I was to take your orders as if they had come from him."

"What are you doing up here, then?" Steve asked.

"Watching for the Japanese aircraft," Ian said. "We will need the binoculars."

"They're in my hut," Steve replied automatically.

"I will get them," Patience said, and quickly got to her feet and started down the knotted rope.

"If we're going to hide in the goddamned jungle," Steve asked, "why are we bothering with this shit, anyway?"

"Because," Ian Bruce said, again with irrefutable logic, "we do not know that Lieutenant Reeves is dead. We only believe he is. Until we know for sure, or until the Japanese come, we will do what he wishes us to do."

"Semper Fi, right?"

"I do not understand."

"Yeah, you do," Steve said.

"Is that English?"

"It's Marine," Steve said. "It means . . . you do what you're expected to do, I guess. Or try, anyway."

"I see," Ian Bruce said solemnly.

(TWO)
USMC Replacement Depot
Parris Island, South Carolina
2250 Hours 7 September 1942

Because he was on a routine check of the guard posts, the officer of the day happened to be at the main gate when the 1939 LaSalle convertible pulled up to the guard and stopped. It had been a long and dull evening and showed little prospect of getting more interesting.

"Hold it a minute," the OD said to his jeep driver.

"Aye, aye, Sir," the driver said and stopped the jeep.

The OD got out and walked toward the LaSalle. The driver was apparently showing his orders to the guard, for the beam of the guard's flashlight illuminated the interior. The OD saw that the car held two lieutenants, neither of whom was wearing his cover.

But what the hell, it's almost eleven o'clock.

"Welcome to sand flea heaven," the OD said. "Reporting in?"

"Just visiting," McCoy replied.

He was a first lieutenant, the OD saw, not any older than he himself was. But he was wearing a double row of ribbons, including the Bronze Star and what looked like the Purple Heart with two clusters on it. The other one was a second lieutenant, and he too was wearing ribbons signifying that he had been wounded and decorated for valor.

Am I being a suspicious prick, or just doing my job? the OD wondered as he reached to take the orders from the guard.

The orders were obviously genuine. They were issued by Headquarters, USMC, and ordered First Lieutenant K. R. McCoy to proceed by military or civilian road, rail, or air transportation, or at his election, by privately owned vehicle, to Philadelphia, Penna., Parris Island, S.C., and such other destinations as he deemed necessary in the carrying out of his mission for the USMC Office of Management Analysis.

What the hell is the Office of Management Analysis?

"Well, as I said," the OD said, smiling, "welcome to sand flea heaven."

"I know all about the sand fleas," McCoy said, smiling. "But how do I find the BOQ?"

"How do you know about the sand fleas and not the BOQ?" the OD asked, and immediately felt like a fool as the answer came to him: This guy was a Mustang. He had gone through Parris Island as an enlisted man before getting a commission. He knew about sand fleas. But Marine boots do not know where bachelor officers rest their weary heads.

"Follow the signs to the Officer's Club," the OD said. "Drive past it. Look to your right. Two-story frame building on your right."

"Thank you," McCoy said.

The guard saluted. McCoy returned it. McCoy drove past the barrier.

"Interesting," the OD said to the guard. "Did you see the ribbons on those officers?"

"Yes, Sir. And one of them had a cane, too."

"I wonder what the hell the Office of Management Analysis is?" the OD asked, not expecting an answer.

"I'll tell you something else interesting, Sir," the guard said. "The sergeant major is looking for them. At least for Lieutenant McCoy. He passed the word through the sergeant of the guard we was to call him, no matter when he came aboard.''

"Him? Not the OD? Or the General's aide?''

"Him, Sir.''

"Well, in that case, Corporal, I would suggest you get on the horn to the sergeant major. Hell hath no fury, as you might have heard.''

"Aye, aye, Sir.''

"Does this place fill you with fond memories?'' McCoy asked as they drove through the Main Post, an area of brick buildings looking not unlike the campus of a small college.

"I would rather go back to Guadalcanal than go through here again,'' Moore said.

"How's your legs?''

"I won't mind lying down.''

"Well, you wanted to come.''

"And I'm grateful that you brought me. I was going stir crazy in the hospital.''

"I think what you need, pal, is a piece of ass. I also think you're out of luck here.''

"Says he, the Croesus of Carnal Wealth,'' Moore replied.

"What?''

"Says he, who doesn't have that problem.''

"What Ernie and I have is something special,'' McCoy said coldly.

"Hell, I realized that the first time I saw you two looking at each other in San Diego,'' Moore said. "My reaction then, and now, is profound admiration, coupled with enormous jealousy.''

"Your lady really did a job on you, huh?''

"When I got her letter, in Melbourne, I was fantasizing about getting to be an officer and marching into the Bellvue-Stratford in my officer's uniform with her on my arm. . . . 'Dear John,' the letter said.''

"Hell, your name *is* John,'' McCoy said. "And you have your officer's uniform, three sets of khakis, anyway. . . .''

"And thank you for that, too. I wouldn't have known where to go to buy them.''

"Horstmann Uniform has been selling uniforms to The Corps since Christ was a corporal,'' McCoy said. "And as I was saying, your Dear John letter lady is not the only female in the world.''

"So I keep telling myself,'' Moore said.

"Well, there's the club, and it looks like it's still open. Would you like a drink?''

"I'll pass, thank you,'' Moore said. "But go ahead if you want to.''

"I've got a couple of pints in my bag,'' McCoy said. "I didn't really want to go in there anyway.'' A moment later he said, "That must be it.''

Moore looked up and saw a two-story frame building. McCoy drove around behind it and parked the car. Since he'd packed Moore's two spare khaki uniforms in his own bag, there was only one to carry.

A corporal was on duty in the lobby of the Bachelor Officer's Quarters.

McCoy told him they were transients and needed rooms; and the corporal gave them a register to sign, then handed each of them a key.

"End of the corridor to the right, Sir. Number twelve.''

"Thank you,'' McCoy said and walked up the stairs.

Halfway down the corridor he swore bitterly: "Shit! Sonofa*bitch!*''

Moore saw the source of his anger. A neatly lettered sign was thumbtacked to one of the doors. It read, RESERVED FOR KILLER MCCOY.

He walked quickly to the sign and ripped it down. He started to put his key to the lock in the door, but it opened before he could reach it.

"Well, if it isn't Lieutenant McCoy," a man wearing the three stripes up, three lozenges down insignia of a sergeant major said, standing at rigid attention. "May the sergeant major say, Sir, the Lieutenant looks just fine?"

"That fucking sign isn't funny, goddamn you!" McCoy flared. "What the hell is the matter with you, anyway?"

The sergeant major was not as taken aback as Moore expected him to be. He seemed more hurt and disappointed than alarmed by McCoy's intense and genuine anger.

"Aw, come on, Ken," he said.

McCoy glowered at him for a moment and finally said, "I don't know why the hell I'm surprised. You never did have the brains to pour piss out of a boot. How the hell are you, you old bastard?"

"No complaints, Ken," the sergeant major said with obvious affection in his voice, taking McCoy's hand.

And then he saw Moore, and a moment after that, there was recognition in his eyes.

"I believe I know this gentleman, too, don't I?"

"I don't think so," McCoy said. "Moore, this is Sergeant Major Teddy Osgood. We were in the Fourth Marines together."

"Yeah, sure," Moore said. "I remember you now, Sergeant Major. When I left here—"

"Oh?" McCoy asked, curious.

"Captain Sessions came down here and pulled me out of boot camp," Moore explained. "The sergeant major . . . how do I say it?"

"Handled the administrative details," the sergeant major furnished.

"I remember you telling Captain Sessions that you had known the Killer— Ooops!—*Lieutenant* McCoy in China."

"If you think that was funny, you asshole, it wasn't," McCoy said.

But he was not, Moore saw, furious anymore.

"I see neither one of you paid attention when you went through here. Is that *three* Purple Hearts, Ken?"

"Two of them are bullshit," McCoy said. "Moore took some mortar shrapnel on Guadalcanal. He needs to lie down."

"This is a field-grade officer's suite, all kinds of places to lay down," Osgood said. "Would you like a drink, Lieutenant?"

"Yes, thank you, I would," Moore said.

"Get in bed, I'll make the drinks," McCoy said.

"That Captain said you was with the 2nd Raider Battalion," Osgood said to McCoy.

"I was."

"You were on the Makin Island raid?"

McCoy nodded.

"And now?"

"I'm doing more or less what Captain Sessions does," McCoy said.

"Yeah, I figured that. When the TWX came in saying you was coming, the G-2 shit a brick. What the hell do you people do, anyway?"

McCoy didn't immediately reply. He dug in his bag, fished out a pint of scotch, poured some in a glass, and handed it to Moore, who by then had crawled onto one of the beds.

"The name is the Office of Management Analysis," he said finally. "We're sort of in the supply business."

"Yeah, sure you are. That's why every time we get some boot who speaks Japanese, who has civilian experience as a radio operator, or who's lived over there, we notify you, right? So they can pass out rations, right?"

"Right," McCoy said.

"Well, I got a dozen, thirteen people, lined up for you to talk to tomorrow, three who speak Japanese . . . what do you call them?"

"Linguists," McCoy said.

". . . half a dozen amateur radio operators, and a couple of guys who are going to cryptography school."

"Great," McCoy said. "Everything laid on for me, us, to talk to them?"

"You tell me when and where and I'll have them there."

"You got someplace?"

"Yeah. I'll take care of it," Osgood said. "I'll send a car for you in the morning. You have to make your manners with the G-2, I guess?"

"I suppose we'll have to," McCoy said.

"There's another guy, Ken. He don't speak Jap, and he's no radio operator, but he's interesting."

"Why interesting?"

"Well, for one thing, he used to be a cop. Actually a vice squad detective. Saint Louis."

"A vice squad detective?" Moore asked, laughing.

"Maybe *he* could do something to solve your problem, Lieutenant," McCoy said, and then added, "I don't understand, Teddy."

"He went after one of his DIs, was going to break his arm."

"Sounds like my kind of guy," Moore said.

Osgood looked at him and smiled. "The word is that the DI, an assistant DI, is a real asshole."

"And this guy broke his arm?" McCoy asked.

"No. The platoon DI saw what he was up to and stopped him. He said the guy really knows how to use a knife. If he had wanted to cut the DI, kill him, he would be dead, the DI said. But all he wanted to do was break his arm. I guess he figured he could get away with that."

"They court-martial him?"

"No. For what? The DI said, 'Try to kill me.' The guy was just obeying orders. The platoon DI came to me and explained the situation, and I transferred the guy to another platoon."

"Is this guy a sleaze, Teddy?" McCoy asked.

"What do you mean?"

"I mean, what does he look like, what does he act like?"

"I don't know. I never actually seen him. His platoon DI's a friend of mine, and he must have sort of liked this guy or he wouldn't have come to me about him."

"Or, like you said, the assistant DI is an asshole and he figured he deserved a broken arm. I want to see him, Teddy. Can you arrange that?"

"No problem," Osgood said. "I'll have him there with the others."

"You want another one of these?" McCoy asked, extending the pint of scotch to Moore. He suspected, correctly, that Moore was both exhausted by their trip and in pain.

"Please," Moore said, taking the bottle.

"What about now?" McCoy said. "Let's see how he reacts to getting up in the middle of the night."

"You're serious, aren't you?" Osgood asked.

"Yeah, I'm serious," McCoy said. He looked at Moore. "After I talked to your new boss, I talked to Captain Sessions. He said I should also ask about getting your new boss an orderly, or a driver, but really somebody to pick up the papers he leaves lying around when he's not supposed to."

"Oh," Moore said.

"He also used the word 'bodyguard,' but said we shouldn't say it around your boss."

"Yeah," Moore said, understanding.

"Why not?" Sergeant Major Osgood said. "Everybody knows people in the supply business need bodyguards. Who is your boss, anyway?"

"None of your fucking business," McCoy said. "Since you asked."

The sergeant major chuckled. He went to the bedside table, pulled open a drawer, took out a mimeographed telephone directory, found the number he was looking for, and dialed it.

"This is the sergeant major," he said. "Roll Private Hart, George F., out of the sack. Have him standing by in full field gear in five minutes. I'll send a vehicle for him."

Private Hart was not surprised when the lights in the squad bay came on in the middle of the night. That happened all the time. Nor was he particularly surprised when the drill instructor marched down the aisle between the rows of double bunks, his heels crashing against the wooden, washed-nearly-white flooring, and stopped at his bunk.

At least I'm out of the sack and at attention, he thought, taking some small solace from the situation.

It was not the first time since he had been transferred to his new platoon that he'd been singled out for what was euphemistically called "extra training." This most often consisted of an order to get dressed and take a couple of double-time laps around the barracks area with his rifle held over his head. But a couple of times they woke him at two in the morning to practice "basic elements of field fortification." That meant digging a man-sized hole with his entrenching tool and filling it up again. Then they let him shower and get back in the sack.

He understood now why they'd done those things. His new DI and his assistants wanted to make sure he was not a wiseass who had to be broken to fit the Marine mold. Although what he had almost done to Corporal Clayton C. Warren, USMC, had not officially happened and was supposed to be kept as quiet as possible to protect the dignity of the DI Corps, they knew about it, obviously, and so they wanted to make sure about him.

For his part, he'd obeyed their orders without complaint and to the best of his ability. And the DI here and his assistants, while they were a stiff-necked bunch of bastards, were at least a reasonably fair trio of stiff-necked bastards—a marvelous improvement over Corporal Clayton C. Warren, USMC.

It was against Holy Writ to meet the eyes of a DI; one was required to stare off into space. So it was a moment before Private Hart became aware that the DI whose face was an inch and a half from his was *the* DI, Staff Sergeant Homer Hungleberry, USMC, and that Staff Sergeant Hungleberry was attired in his boondockers and skivvies only.

"Caught you with your cock in your hand, did I, Hart?"

"Sir, no, Sir."

"What have you done that I don't know about, Hart?"

What the fuck is he talking about?

"Sir, I don't know."

"When I find out, and I *will* find out, I will have your ass twice. Once for doing something I don't know about and once for lying to me about it."

"Sir, yes, Sir."

"So there is something?"

"Sir, no, Sir."

"Utilities, full field gear, helmet, piece, in five minutes!"

"Sir, aye, aye, Sir."

Staff Sergeant Hungleberry withdrew his face from Private Hart's, did a left-face, and marched back down the aisle between the rows of double bunks. When he reached the light switch, he turned off the lights.

Private Hart, in the dark, located a set of utilities, his socks, boondockers, field equipment, and helmet and carried them down the aisle toward the head, where one 40-watt bulb (the others were ritually unscrewed from their sockets) was allowed to burn all night.

The firewatch, a boot required to stay awake all night, was in the head.

"What the fuck did you do now?" he inquired.

"Does it fucking matter?" Hart replied as he hastily pulled on his utilities, the field equipment, his socks, and shoved his feet into his boondockers and tied them.

"You did something," the firewatch said helpfully. "And he *knows.*"

"Fuck you," Private Hart said as he put his helmet on his head.

How the hell am I going to get my piece? My fucking piece is in the fucking arms rack, and the fucking arms rack is locked.

The answer came: *When he comes out of his room, he will find me standing at fucking attention by the arms rack waiting for him to unlock the sonofabitch.*

Staff Sergeant Hungleberry, now fully dressed, appeared. He examined Private Hart, who was standing at rigid attention.

"You have hearing problems, Hart?"

"Sir, no, Sir."

"Do I speak indistinctly? Or was I maybe talking in Chinese?"

"Sir, no, Sir."

"Then you did understand me to say, 'Utilities, full field gear, helmet, and piece in five minutes'?"

"Sir, yes, Sir."

"Then where is your fucking piece?"

"Sir, in the arms rack, Sir, and the arms rack, Sir, is locked, Sir."

"Do you really think I would ask you to take your piece from a locked arms rack?"

"Sir, no, Sir."

"Then get your fucking piece from the arms rack!"

The sonofabitch unlocked the fucking rack before he came storming down the aisle!

"Sir, aye, aye, Sir!"

He retrieved his piece, U.S. Rifle, Springfield, Model of 1903, Serial Number 2456577, from its assigned place, third from the right on the squad bay side, worked the action to ensure that it was empty, and came to attention again.

"You are still telling me that you have no idea why the sergeant major wants to see you?"

The sergeant major? What the fuck does the sergeant major want with me at midnight?

"Sir, yes, Sir. I don't know why the sergeant major wants to see me, Sir."

" 'Ten-HUT! Right SHOULDER, Harms! Right Face! Foh-wud, Harch! Open the door when you get to it!"

Private Hart marched off, opened the door when he came to it, marched through it, down the shallow stairs and toward the next barracks.

"Detail, HALT!"

After approximately two minutes, which seemed like much longer, the headlights of a Chevrolet pickup truck illuminated the area, and then the truck stopped about eight inches from Private Hart.

He could faintly but clearly hear the conversation between his DI and the corporal driving the truck.

"What the fuck is going on here?"

"Beats the shit out of me. All I know is I was told to come here and get some boot named Hart and take him to the BOQ."

"The BOQ? I thought the sergeant major sent for him."

"*To* the sergeant major at the BOQ," the corporal clarified.

"Shit!"

"That's all I know, Sergeant," the corporal said righteously. "You coming, or just him? That *is* him?"

"Hart, get in the fucking truck!"

"Sir, aye, aye, Sir."

The opening and then slamming of the passenger door told Private Hart that his DI had decided his duty required him to accompany him to the sergeant major at the BOQ.

The sergeant major at the BOQ? What the hell is going on?

Ten minutes later the pickup stopped in front of a two-story frame building in a part of Parris Island Private Hart had never been to.

He saw a man he had never seen before. But to judge by the stripes on his sleeves and his assured manner as he approached the truck, he was certainly the sergeant major.

"Who are you?"

"Hungleberry, Sergeant Major."

"That Hart?"

"Yes, Sergeant Major."

"What took you so long?"

"We was ready when the truck got there," Staff Sergeant Hungleberry said righteously.

"Get him out of the truck and march him to room twelve. Left corridor, last door on the right. Report to the officers."

"Right," Sergeant Hungleberry replied. Then he raised his voice: "Out of the truck, Hart!"

Hart got out of the truck.

" 'Ten-HUT! PORT, Harms! Lu-eft, FACE! Foh-wud, HARCH! Up the stairs and into the building."

When Private Hart passed the sergeant major, the sergeant major leaned forward to get a good look at Private Hart. Private Hart could smell his breath; he had been in enough bars to recognize the smell of whiskey there. Indeed, his experience as a vice squad detective had given him the expertise to make a professional judgment: The sergeant major had been drinking scotch, and in quantities sufficient to place in grave doubt his ability to walk a straight line or to close his eyes and touch his nose with his finger.

Jesus Christ, now what? What the fuck is this all about? I've heard they take people out behind barracks and beat the shit out of them. Is that why nothing happened to me for trying to break that asshole's arm? They were saving me for this? Are the sergeant major, drunk—and maybe a couple of drunken officers— really going to teach me that they just won't tolerate trying to break a DI's arm?

Staff Sergeant Hungleberry marched Private Hart to the door to room 12, then barked, "De-tail, HALT!" and knocked at the door.

"Come!"

Staff Sergeant Hungleberry marched Private Hart into the room, again ordered, "De-tail, HALT!" and then barked, "Sir, Staff Sergeant Hungleberry reporting to the Lieutenant with a detail of one, Sir!"

"Put your detail at ease, Sergeant," the officer ordered conversationally.

"Aww-duh, HARMS! Puh-rade, REST!"

"I said, 'at ease,' Sergeant," the officer said.

"At EASE!"

After Private Hart complied, he dared to look around the room. There were two officers, both young. One was a second lieutenant, sprawled on a bed, a whiskey glass resting on his chest. He was wearing khakis. His field scarf was pulled down and the top three buttons of his shirt were open.

Hart recognized the Purple Heart among the ribbons pinned to the shirt.

The other officer was a first lieutenant, and he too had ribbons pinned to his shirt, including the Purple Heart. In the fleeting instant when their eyes met, Private Hart's professional experience told him, *this guy can be one mean sonofabitch.*

"You're his DI?" the mean-looking officer asked.

"Yes, Sir. Staff Sergeant Hungleberry, Sir."

"OK, Sergeant. Tell me, is this guy going to be a Marine or not?"

The question surprised Hungleberry. It was a moment before he replied: "I guess he'll be all right, Sir."

That's the nicest thing anybody has said about me since I came to this fucking hellhole.

"I didn't ask for a guess, Sergeant. I asked whether this guy will make a Marine or not?"

The hesitation this time was longer.

"Yes, Sir, in my opinion, he'll be all right."

"Thank you," the officer said. He turned to the dresser behind him and picked up a pint of scotch. "Sorry to keep you out of the sack at this time of night, but we want to talk to him."

He tossed the pint to the sergeant major, who had come into the room.

"Take the sergeant someplace and give him a little taste, Teddy, would you, please?" the officer said.

"Aye, aye, Sir," the sergeant major said. In a moment Hart heard the door close.

"My name is McCoy," the officer said. "That's Lieutenant Moore."

"Yes, Sir."

"I understand you're a tough guy," McCoy said.

Hart could not think of a proper reply to that. He did not answer.

"I understand you tried to break your DI's arm. Yes or no?"

"Yes, Sir."

"I also understand you know how to use a knife?"

"Yes, Sir."

"Why didn't you kill the DI? Everybody seems agreed that he's an asshole."

"I didn't want to go to Portsmouth, Sir."

"Good reason," McCoy said. "I asked you a question before. Are you a tough guy or not?"

"I used to be a cop, Lieutenant," Hart said. "I suppose I'm as tough as most cops."

"Tougher than some?"

"Yes, Sir."

"You look like you could use a drink," McCoy said. "Lean your piece against the wall."

The offer completely surprised Hart. McCoy saw his hesitation and laughed.

"Go ahead," he said. "You're not the first guy to go through here, including me, who wanted to kill his DI. You're the first sane one I've met who actually tried to."

He walked to Hart, took his rifle from him, and motioned him into a chair. He leaned the rifle against a wall, and then he poured whiskey into a glass and handed it to him.

"You want some water?"

"No, thank you, Sir."

"Why did you want to be a cop?"

"My whole family is cops."

"When you were a cop, did you ever use your weapon? Kill somebody? Or try to?"

"Yes, Sir."

Hart took a sip of the whiskey. For the first time he saw Moore's cane.

"Which? Tried to? Or did?"

"I had to kill a couple of people, Sir, when I was a cop."

"Is that why you joined the crotch?" Moore asked somewhat thickly. "To kill people?"

What did he say? The crotch?

Hart saw McCoy flash Moore an angry look, but then he turned to Hart: "Answer the question."

"A goddamn recruiter lied to me," Hart blurted.

"No shit?" McCoy replied sarcastically. "I thought a cop would be smarter than that."

"This was a clever sonofabitch," Hart said, and a split second later remembered to append, "Sir."

"What did he tell you?" McCoy asked.

"That The Corps wanted guys who had been cops to be sort of cops for The Corps, Sir."

"And you believed him?"

"*I* believed the sonofabitch who told me I'd get a commission when I got through here," Moore said.

He's drunk, Hart realized.

"You have a commission." McCoy chuckled.

"Yeah, now."

"You're plastered," McCoy added, still chuckling, as if the realization pleased him. "You've been an officer forty-eight hours and already you're guilty of conduct unbecoming an officer and a gentleman. Try not to fall out of bed."

"Fuck you, McCoy."

McCoy shook his head and turned to Hart.

"You know what a full background investigation is?"

"Yes, Sir."

"I want straight answers now. Don't try to be clever. If we ran one on you, what would it turn up?"

Hart considered the question. Before he had formed a reply, McCoy went on.

"You're German, right? You or anybody in your family ever been involved with the German-American Bund? Anything like that?"

"No, Sir."

"How about the Communist Party? You, or anybody close, family, friends, ever been involved with that? Maybe the Abraham Lincoln Brigade?"

"No, Sir."

"Now don't get hot under the collar, but you're not a secret faggot, are you?"

"Jesus Christ, McCoy!" Moore complained.

"Are you?"

"No, Sir."

"How do you feel about rich people?"

"Excuse me?"

"How do you feel about rich people. I mean, really rich people?"

"I never met any," Hart replied, hesitated, and added, "Sir."

"The Lieutenant is asking," Moore explained, carefully pronouncing each syllable, "if you would be comfortable working with someone who is enormously wealthy, or whether you would disgrace the crotch by pissing in the potted palms."

What the fuck is this all about?

McCoy laughed.

"He doesn't usually get this pissed on a couple of drinks. I'm beginning to be sorry I brought you down here with me."

"I'm not pissed," Moore said. "How could I possibly be pissed? I've only had two or three little nips."

"You answer the question," McCoy said. "How do you think . . . could he work with the General?"

"I think the General would like him," Moore said. "But then, I have been wrong before."

"Hart, what we're looking for is someone to be a bodyguard for a general. The General is not going to like the idea of having a bodyguard. Could you handle something like that?"

"I didn't know generals had bodyguards," Hart blurted.

"Most of them don't. This one needs one."

"I really don't know."

"Your other option is taking your piece on a ship and going to a line company in someplace like Guadalcanal," Moore said. "They shoot people on Guadalcanal. It smarts when they shoot you."

"You've gone too far," McCoy flared. "Shut your fucking mouth!"

"Aye, aye, Sir," Moore said and threw McCoy an insulting mockery of a salute.

"The other qualification is the ability to keep your mouth shut," McCoy said to Hart.

"I think I could do that," Hart said.

"Yeah, so do I," McCoy said. "OK. Decision made. If you don't get along with . . . the officer we're talking about, we'll find something else for you to do. But one last time, if a CBI turns up something you're concealing from me, I will personally guarantee that you'll spend the rest of the war in an infantry line company."

"No, Sir. I know there's nothing in my background that would keep me from getting a security clearance. That's what you're talking about, isn't it? A Secret Clearance?"

"No," McCoy said. "Not Secret. We start with Secret and go up from there. Go find the sergeant major, would you, and ask him to come in here?"

"Aye, aye, Sir."

It took Hart several minutes to find Sergeant Major Osgood and Staff Sergeant Hungleberry. When they went back to the room, Lieutenant Moore was throwing up into a wastebasket.

"Jesus!" Sergeant Major Osgood said.

"I took him out of the Naval Hospital in Philadelphia, Teddy," McCoy explained. "That was dumb. He's not nearly as healthy as he thinks he is. He took some nasty mortar hits on the 'Canal."

"He going to be all right?"

"Hung over," McCoy said. "Teddy, we'll be taking Hart with us. Same deal as before, with Moore. I want him to disappear from his company and I don't want anybody talking about it."

"You got it, Ken."

"I don't know what's going on," Staff Sergeant Hungleberry said.

"That's right, you don't," Sergeant Major Osgood said. "What you're going to do now is take Hart to collect his stuff and then bring him back here. If anybody asks any questions tonight, refer them to me. I'll fix things with the brass in the morning."

"OK," Hungleberry said, doubtfully.

"What about the other guys, Ken?"

"I'll make my manners with the G-2 first thing in the morning, and I want to see them as soon as possible after that."

"Aye, aye, Sir. You going to need any help with him?"

"I was thinking of giving him a cold shower," McCoy said.

"Fuck your cold shower," Lieutenant John Marston Moore said. And then he was nauseated again.

(THREE)
Tasimboko, Guadalcanal
0530 Hours 8 September 1942

In early September, intelligence from Native Scouts attached to the First Marine Division reported several thousand Japanese in the vicinity of the village of Tasimboko, twenty miles down the coast from Henderson. Previous intelligence had placed the Japanese strength at no more than three hundred.

The inclination was to disbelieve this report, since it had not come from an established source and there were no confirming data from other sources. But arguing for it was the reputation of the Native Scouts. They had originally been part of the Royal Australian Navy Coastwatcher Establishment. Not only were they men of incredible courage, they had never been wrong before.

On 6 September 1942, an operations order was issued by Headquarters, First Marine Division, ordering the formation of a provisional battalion. After formation it would proceed by sea from Lunga Point to a beach near Taivu Point, from where it would stage a raid on the village of Tasimboko. The primary purpose of the raid was to confirm or deny the presence of several thousand Japanese and to destroy whatever Japanese matériel came into their hands.

The provisional battalion consisted of elements of the 1st Raider Battalion and the 1st Parachute Battalion. These "elements" were all that was left of them after the invasion. The parachute battalion had taken severe losses.

Lieutenant Colonel "Red Mike" Edson was senior to the 1st Parachute Battalion commander, and thus he was placed in command.

Transport from the port of departure (the beach near First Marine Division headquarters) to the raid site was to be by high-speed transport. This was something of a misnomer. High-speed transports were World War I destroyers with half their boilers removed; the space was converted to troop berthing. Removal of the boilers had lowered the vessels' speed to approximately that of an ordinary transport, but the ex-destroyers had retained most of their armament.

When the high-speed transports appeared offshore, it was immediately evident that there were not enough of them to carry the entire provisional battalion. And so hasty amendments were made to the operations order. These called for the 1st Raider Battalion to board the transports, invest and secure the beach near Tasimboko, and then hold in place until the transports could return to Lunga Point, board the 1st Parachute Battalion, and transport them to the raid area.

The Raiders began to land east of Tasimboko at dawn.

* * *

Largely because Gunnery Sergeant Joseph J. Johnston took one glance at him and decided that the large, muscular, mean-looking sonofabitch was just what he needed, Sergeant Thomas McCoy's reception at Company A, 1st Raider Battalion, was considerably warmer than it had been at Headquarters, 21st Marine Air Group.

For one thing, Able Company was considerably understrength. It took losses during the initial invasion a month before when the 1st Raider Battalion, under Lieutenant Colonel "Red Mike" Edson, landed near Lunga Point on Tulagi, a small island twenty-odd miles across SeaLark Channel from Guadalcanal.

And they'd gotten no replacements. Like every other Marine on Guadalcanal, Sergeant Johnston was very much aware that the goddamn Navy sailed away from the beaches with a hell of a lot of Marines, equipment, ammunition, and heavy artillery still in the holds of the transports. And even if some available bodies were ashore, it was unlikely that Colonel Edson would have asked for them: They would have been bodies, not Raiders. Raiders were special to begin with, and they'd been molded into something really special by their training and their first combat.

There had been additional losses since the invasion, most of them due to what The Corps called "noncombat causes." That translated to mean there were a great many very sick Raiders, brought down by tropical disease, mostly malaria, but including some diseases the surgeons and corpsmen had never heard of, much less seen before.

In Sergeant Johnston's opinion, the "rest" they gave the 1st Raiders before they were brought across SeaLark Channel to Guadalcanal had not restored them to what they were before. What it did was keep a great many more people from getting sick.

So Company A—for that matter, the entire 1st Raider Battalion—was understrength. And the available Marines were on the edge of sickness or near exhaustion (or both) from the lousy chow, the high heat and humidity, and all the necessary manual labor they had to perform.

But there was one particular personnel shortage Sergeant Johnston was especially aware of. He was a great admirer of one particular weapon in The Marine Corps arsenal, the Browning Automatic Rifle—a combination rifle and a machine gun that fired the same .30-06 cartridge.

The weapon, known as the BAR, was considerably lighter than the standard .30 caliber Browning machine gun; but like a machine gun, it was capable of full automatic fire: As long as you held the trigger back and there were cartridges in the magazine, the weapon would continue to fire.

Cartridges were held in a 20-round magazine that was quickly replaceable when emptied. In fact, it was easier and quicker to change a BAR's 20-round magazine than it was to recharge with a stripper clip the nonreplaceable five-shot magazine of a Springfield rifle.

The BAR was commonly equipped with a bipod, two metal legs fixed to the barrel near the muzzle. They permitted accurate fire at great distance. And it had a well-earned reputation for reliability. The trouble was that at about sixteen pounds, it was twice as heavy as the Springfield rifle. The heavy weight, coupled with the recoil, meant that few men indeed could fire the BAR from the shoulder. Sergeant Johnston was one of them; and when he saw Sergeant Thomas McCoy, one of his first thoughts was that he was looking at somebody else who just might be able to do it.

"Your jacket says you made the Makin Island raid."

"I made the fucker, Sergeant."

"What'd you do?"

"I had a Boys."

The Boys Rifle was developed by the Royal Army after World War I as an antitank weapon. It was a .55 caliber bolt-action rifle, which in size—it weighed thirty-six pounds—was to the BAR what the BAR was to the Springfield. It was a weapon Sergeant Johnston admired as other men might admire a Rolls-Royce or a Renoir.

"You had a Boys? We're talking about the same weapon? A British .55 caliber Boys?"

"I had a fucking Boys," Sergeant McCoy said with quiet pride.

Sergeant Johnston had heard that Lieutenant Colonel Evans Carlson, who commanded the 2nd Raider Battalion, had authorized his men to arm themselves with any weapon they wished. This was the first proof he'd had of that.

"You do any good with it?"

"I shot up a fucking Jap airplane," McCoy replied. "Put a dozen rounds in the sonofabitch. It tried to take off, got fifty feet in the air, and fucking blew up."

That would explain the Bronze Star for valor that Sergeant McCoy's records recorded, Sergeant Johnston realized. *There was no mention of any specific act, but there wouldn't be if he had shot down an airplane with a Boys.*

"I guess you can use a BAR all right, huh?"

"Yeah, sure."

"Off hand?"

Very few men could fire the BAR off hand—in other words, standing up and holding the BAR like a Springfield.

"Yeah, sure."

"Tell you what, McCoy," Sergeant Johnston said. "I got what you might call a provisional heavy weapons squad I think might be just the place for you."

"What's a provisional heavy weapons squad?"

"Twelve guys instead of eight. Two BARs. Two guys with Springfields. The rest carry Thompsons and ammo bandoliers for the BARs."

"Yeah, maybe. I think I'd like that," McCoy replied.

Sergeant Johnston did not, however, take Sergeant McCoy at his word. He checked his knowledge of the BAR, which proved to be adequate, and then he tested his marksmanship with it. Sergeant McCoy turned out to be a fucking artist firing the BAR.

When Sergeant Johnston saw Sergeant McCoy walking across the beach at Tasimboko, his BAR suspended at waist height from his shoulder, trailed by two Marines loaded down with BAR magazines, firing the sonofabitch in two- and three-shot bursts with all the finesse of a fucking violin player, he began to suspect that giving the provisional heavy weapons squad to Sergeant McCoy had been a correct command decision.

Twenty minutes later, when one of the ammo bearers returned in the dual role of ammunition replenishment and runner, there was proof positive:

"Sergeant McCoy took out a Jap outpost," the guy said, "and then we took a Jap artillery battery. He wants to know what you want him to do now."

"Get your ass back up there and tell him to dig in. We're about to get some air support."

Five minutes later the air support arrived. It consisted of those funny-looking Army Air Corps P-400 fighters, accompanied by Marine SBD bombers.

By the time the bombing and strafing ended, the transports had returned and landed the elements of the 1st Parachute Battalion. And so a general advance on the village was ordered.

It was necessary to ask for additional air support to drive the defenders from the village, but by quarter to ten it was secure.

The intelligence report of the ex–Coastwatcher Establishment Native Scouts proved to be accurate.

The Marines of the provisional battalion spent almost two hours destroying Japanese matériel, almost certainly recently landed. It included several landing craft, one 37mm cannon (McCoy had captured it early on), four 75mm cannon, radios, and large stocks of ammunition and medical supplies.

At 1230 hours, the Marines were ordered to return to the beach to reboard the transports. They took with them two of their own dead and six wounded. They left behind twenty-seven dead Japanese and an uncounted number of Japanese wounded.

Lieutenant Colonel "Red Mike" Edson stood at the sandbagged entrance to the command post of the Commanding General, First Marine Division, until General Alexander Archer Vandergrift sensed his presence. When Vandergrift looked at him, Edson saluted, and then went into the CP.

"How did it go, Mike?"

"Two KIA, six WIA, two seriously."

"I'm sorry."

"The Native Scouts were right, Sir."

"They usually are."

"We destroyed a large amount of matériel. Here's a list, Sir."

He handed the list to Vandergrift, who read it and then looked at him.

"Large quantities of medical supplies would seem to indicate a large force, wouldn't you say?"

"Yes, Sir. And that much ammo translates to a lot of weapons, too, Sir. I took what documentation I could find to G-2 to get it translated, but there's no question in my mind that what we captured was not what the Japanese here took with them into the boondocks when we landed."

Vandergrift nodded but did not reply.

"There's several thousand Japs in that area, General. What I don't understand is why they didn't attack us."

"Conservation of force for future action is often a wise choice," Vandergrift said. "I would guess that after he saw how you landed your force in two segments, the Japanese commander decided that you didn't intend to stay. Therefore there was no point in expending assets to throw you back in the sea."

"Yes, Sir."

"He can better use those assets here," Vandergrift said, pointing to the map. "Either trying to knock Henderson Field out of operation, or even taking it. I don't like those 75mm cannon. If you captured four, I think we better count on a lot more."

"Yes, Sir. I thought about that."

"Take a look at this, Mike," Vandergrift said, and handed him a sheet of paper with TOP SECRET stamped on it top and bottom.

" 'The operation to surround and recapture Guadalcanal will truly decide the fate of the control of the entire Pacific,' " Edson read aloud.

"From Lieutenant General Harukichi Hyakutake to the 17th Army," Vandergrift said. "Odd how the minds of brilliant men run in the same paths, isn't it, Mike?"

"May I ask where you got this, Sir?"

"No, you may not."

"General, there's a rumor going around that we've broken the Japanese codes."

"Mike, you've got a major flaw," Vandergrift said coldly. "You don't know how to take no for an answer."

"Yes, Sir. Sorry, Sir."

"You can consider this an order, Colonel. You will tell no one, repeat, no one, that I showed you that document."

"Aye, aye, Sir."

Vandergrift met Edson's eyes long enough to convince him that he had made his point, paused long enough to curse himself for showing him the MAGIC intercept in the first place, and then allowed his facial muscles to relax.

"So how were the men?"

"They're tired, General, and I think undernourished."

Vandergrift nodded.

"Are you putting anyone in for a decoration?"

"No, Sir," Edson said. "There were no 'conspicuous acts of gallantry' that I know about. Maybe later. But I *am* going to make one buck sergeant a staff sergeant."

"What did he do?"

"Well, I was up pretty close to the line when we got our air support—which was right on the money, General—"

"I'm glad to hear that."

"—and when the strafing and bombing lifted, I looked around, and marching down this little path in the boondocks was this great big guy with a BAR. He had it suspended from his neck and was firing it from the hip. He had two Marines with spare magazines running to keep up with him. And he was smiling from ear to ear. It looked like a World War One movie with Douglas Fairbanks."

"Really?"

"I figure any man who can smile when he's hauling a BAR around deserves to be a staff sergeant."

"I concur, Colonel," Vandergrift said with a smile.

(FOUR)
The Foster Lafayette Hotel
Washington, D.C.
0755 Hours 9 September 1942

Captain Edward L. Sessions, USMC, was standing inside the lobby of the hotel when the LaSalle convertible pulled up at the curb.

He quickly put his brimmed cap on and walked to the curb, reaching it just as the doorman pulled the car door open.

"Good morning," he said. "Let me get in the back."

There were three people in the front seat, two of whom he knew, Lieutenants McCoy and Moore. The man he had come to see, Private George Hart, was at the wheel.

McCoy slid forward on the seat, permitting Sessions to squeeze into the back.

All three of them looked as if they had driven through the night, which was of course the case.

"Let's go somewhere and get a cup of coffee," Sessions said, sitting on the forward edge of the rear seat, trying to get a better look at Hart.

"Turn right on Pennsylvania Avenue," McCoy ordered. "There's a place we can go a couple of blocks away."

"Aye, aye, Sir," Hart replied.

He was very much aware that in the normal course of events he should have been on the drill field at Parris Island at this hour, not at the wheel of a LaSalle convertible, driving past the White House.

"Long ride?" Sessions asked.

"You said it," McCoy said, "and we ran into a patriotic Virginia highway cop who took this new 35-mph speed limit very seriously. He said he was really surprised that Marines—of all people, they should know better—would be speeding."

"Get a ticket?"

"No." McCoy chuckled. "Hart still had his badge. Professional courtesy. He let us go."

"You were a detective, I understand, Hart?"

"Yes, Sir."

"How are you, Moore?"

"Fine, Sir."

"He is not," McCoy said. "I should not have let him talk me into taking him out of the hospital."

"I'm all right, Sir," Moore said.

"Congratulations on the gold bar," Sessions said.

"Thank you," Moore said. "We got you a linguist, Captain. Just one."

"I thought there were supposed to be three?"

"Two didn't speak a word of Japanese," McCoy said.

"Anybody else?"

"Couple of radio operators. The trip was really a waste of time."

"Are you including Private Hart in that?"

"Isn't that why you wanted to meet us? To make that decision?" McCoy asked.

"I thought it would be a good idea to talk to Hart before we take him to see General Pickering," Sessions said. "I wasn't questioning your judgment, Ken, I just thought it would be a good idea for me—"

"I know, to talk to him," McCoy said.

"Are you going to tell me why I am annoying you, or am I supposed to just sit here and suffer in silence?" Sessions said sharply.

"I'm pissed at me, Captain," McCoy said. "When Moore got out of bed this morning—correction: yesterday morning—he passed out."

"I told you, I slipped," Moore interrupted.

"He passed out and fell down . . . hit his leg on a dresser drawer and opened his goddamned wound. And when they took a look at him at the dispensary, they wanted to keep him. I had a hell of a time getting him out."

"I'm all right," Moore insisted.

"Do you think we should take him to Bethesda?" Sessions asked.

"Sir, I would prefer to go back to Philadelphia," Moore said.

"I should never have taken you out of Philadelphia," McCoy said.

"OK," Sessions said. "Lieutenant Moore, you will return to the Naval Hospital at Philadelphia and you will stay there until properly discharged by competent medical authority. Understand?"

Moore nodded.

"Lieutenant, when an officer receives an order from a superior officer, the expected response is, 'Aye, aye, Sir.'"

"Aye, aye, Sir."

"What the hell's the matter with you, John? You were seriously wounded," Sessions said, far more gently.

"Sir, I'm all right. I'm a little weak, that's all."

"You up to driving to Philadelphia? Or should I make other arrangements?"

"I can ride in a car, Sir."

"There it is," McCoy said. "Make the next right, Hart."

"You guys have your breakfast?" Sessions asked.

"We stopped in Richmond," McCoy said. "But I could have something. Coffee and a doughnut anyway."

"I called General Pickering after you called me yesterday," Sessions said. "He said we could bring Hart by at eight this morning. But when I called from the lobby, there was no answer. I guess he's still asleep. If it makes you feel any better, Lieutenant Moore, neither one of you should be out of the hospital."

"Yes, Sir."

"So there will be time for me to talk a little to Private Hart, and then we'll go see the General. Give him another hour in bed."

An hour later, when Captain Sessions called on the house phone in the lobby of the Foster Lafayette Hotel, there was no answer from Senator Richmond F. Fowler's suite.

"Wait here," Sessions ordered, and then modified that. "You go sit down, Moore, over there. I'm going to check with the desk and see if he left a message."

There was no message at the desk.

"I don't like this," Sessions said to McCoy. "I think we'd better see if we can get somebody to let us into the suite."

"Sir," Private Hart said, "I've got a sort of master key for hotel rooms, if you'd like me to try."

"I told you," McCoy said, smiling, "that Hart would be useful."

"Let's see if your key works, Hart," Sessions said.

There was a Do Not Disturb card hanging from the doorknob of the Fowler suite.

"Fowler's in Chicago," Sessions said. "Pickering told me when I called him."

Hart pushed the Do Not Disturb card out of the way and applied his "key"— the blade of a pocketknife ground square and flat—to the crack in the door. He then pushed the door open and stood back to let Sessions enter.

In the sitting room were the remnants of Fleming Pickering's room service dinner, including the wheeled cart and an empty quart of scotch.

Sessions, with McCoy on his heels, went quickly to Pickering's bedroom.

When they opened the door, the foul smell of human waste met them.

Fleming Pickering, wearing only a sleeveless undershirt, made a failed attempt to pull a sheet over him.

"My God!" Sessions said.

"I seem to be a little under the weather," Fleming Pickering said weakly.

McCoy went to the bed and made an instant diagnosis: "Malaria," he said.

"You think that's what it is, Ken?" Pickering asked.

"Sweating, freezing? You can't control your bowels?" McCoy asked.

"Yes. Made a hell of a mess, haven't I?"

"We've got to get him out of that bed," Hart said matter-of-factly. "In addition to the mess he's made, it's soaking wet."

"There's at least one more bedroom," Sessions said.

"You two get him on his feet," Hart ordered, "and I'll clean him up. Then we'll move him."

"Moore," Sessions ordered, "get on the horn and get the house physician up here. And then call the dispensary at Eighth and Eye and have them send an ambulance over here. An ambulance and a doctor."

"The dispensary where?" Moore asked.

"At Marine Barracks. The number will be in the phone book," Sessions said.

"No," Pickering said, as McCoy and Sessions bent over the bed to pick him up. "Moore, don't call the dispensary. Just the house doctor. His name is Selleres. He can take care of me."

"Call the dispensary, Moore," Sessions ordered.

"Goddamn it, Captain," Pickering said furiously. "I said no."

"Do what the General says, Moore," Sessions said after a moment's hesitation.

Hart came out of the bathroom with wet towels and wiped the waste from Pickering's groin area and from his legs.

"God, that's disgusting, something like this," Pickering said.

"Don't be silly, General," Hart said. "Women do it to their babies three, four times a day."

"Christ!" Pickering said.

"Where's the other bedroom?" Hart asked.

"Down the corridor somewhere, I suppose," Sessions said. Then, with Pickering suspended between them, he and McCoy carried Pickering out of the room.

Hart went ahead of them into the other bedroom and had the covers ripped off one of its twin beds before they dragged Pickering in.

"We've got to get some fluid in him," McCoy said. "He's dehydrated."

"Do you know what you're doing, McCoy?" Sessions asked.

"This isn't the first malaria I've seen."

They lowered Pickering into the bed. Hart covered him with a blanket.

"A minute ago I was sweating," Pickering said. "Now, goddamn it, I'm freezing!"

His body shook with shivering under the blanket. Hart ripped the bedspread and a blanket from the other twin bed and laid it over him.

"Doctor Sellers is on his way," Moore announced from the door.

"Seller*es*," Pickering corrected him. His teeth chattered.

"Yes, Sir," Moore said.

"What the hell are you doing out of the hospital?" Pickering demanded.

"About the same thing you are, General," McCoy said. "Making things a hell of a lot worse."

Dr. Selleres appeared a minute or two later, and immediately confirmed McCoy's diagnosis and immediate treatment.

"Somebody get General Pickering a glass of water," he ordered.

"The water here is undrinkable," Pickering said. "There should be some ginger ale."

"OK, ginger ale. Have you been nauseous?"

"No, but I have had a first-class display of diarrhea."

"The ginger ale may make you nauseous."

"I'll take my chances, thank you," Pickering said. "And aside from ginger ale, what can you do for me?"

"Well, the first thing we do is get you into an ambulance and into a hospital."

"No."

"You have to go to the hospital, General. Period. No argument."

"Jesus Christ! Why can't you do what you have to do here?"

"Well, for one thing, Fleming, we don't have facilities to conduct an autopsy here, and unless you start behaving, that's the next medical procedure you'll need."

"Bullshit."

"No. No bullshit. The facts. How long have you been experiencing symptoms like these?"

"The diarrhea's new. And the goddamned weakness. But the hot and cold spells, a couple of days. Three maybe. Maybe four."

"And you've been treating yourself with aspirin and scotch, right?"

"I thought the scotch had given me the runs," Pickering said.

Hart appeared with a bottle of ginger ale and two glasses, one empty and one with ice.

"Here you are, Sir."

"That's liable to make you sick, Fleming," Dr. Selleres said.

"So you said," Pickering snapped, and then, "I don't have the goddamn strength to sit up."

Hart went to him and held him in a sitting position. McCoy held the glass to his lips.

Sessions went into the sitting room and dialed a number from memory. When Colonel Rickabee came on the line, he told him what was going on. Then he went back into the bedroom.

"An ambulance is on the way," he said, "with a doctor and corpsmen. The General will be taken to Walter Reed Army Hospital, which has the best malaria treatment facilities in the area."

"You really think I need hospitalization, Emilio?" Pickering asked.

"Only if you want to live, Fleming," Dr. Selleres said.

"Hell!" Pickering said, and then shrugged. He looked at the people standing around his bed. "If I'm going back in the hospital, John, so are you. Can you arrange that, Sessions?"

"It's already been arranged, Sir. He's going in your ambulance."

"McCoy, will you telephone Mrs. Pickering and make sure she doesn't get hysterical when she hears about this?"

"Yes, Sir, if you want me to."

"I'll call her, Fleming," Dr. Selleres said. "If I don't, she'll call me."

Pickering ignored him. He looked at Private George Hart.

"You've just had one hell of an introduction to a prospective boss, son. I would certainly understand why you wouldn't want to work for me."

"Do I have a choice, Sir?"

"Yes, of course, you do."

"I think I'd like very much to work for you, Sir."

Pickering didn't reply for a moment. Then he said, "Sessions, Moore told me that when you snatched him out of Parris Island you made him an overnight sergeant. And he didn't even have to wipe an officer's ass. Can you do as much for this young man?"

"Yes, Sir. If that is the General's desire, Private Hart will be a sergeant before noon."

"That is the General's desire," Pickering said. Then he looked at Dr. Emilio Selleres. "I hate to admit this, but you're right, you sonofabitch. I'm about to throw up."

"Roll over on your side, Fleming," Selleres said.

Outside, there was the wail of a siren.

"Do you suppose that's for me?" Pickering asked. "Or is that Roosevelt out for a morning drive?"

And then he was shaken with chills and nausea.

VIII

"We could have eaten downstairs, you know," Andrew Foster said as he transferred two kippers from a crystal platter to his grandson's plate with all the skill and élan of any of his first-class waiters. Foster was in his sixties, tall and distinguished-looking, with elegantly cut silver hair.

"The service isn't nearly as nice downstairs," Second Lieutenant Malcolm S. Pickering replied, adding, "thank you."

"But on the other hand, I'm not nearly as pretty as any of the half-dozen young women I'm sure you would have found down there."

They were sitting at a glass-topped cast-iron table on the tiled terrace of the penthouse. A striped awning had been lowered enough to shade them from the morning sun, and mottled glass panels in steel frames had been rolled into place to shield them from the wind.

"But they couldn't possibly smell as good as you do," Pick said. "What is that you're wearing?"

"Something your mother gave me. I thought she might come with you, so I bit the bullet and sprayed some on."

"Very nice."

"Perhaps for a French gigolo," Foster said.

"Maybe a little strong." Pick chuckled.

"The last time I had some on, a gentleman of exquisite grace, inhaling rapturously, followed me across the lobby," the old man said, "thinking he'd found the love of his life."

Pick laughed. "It's not that bad."

"I'd be happy to give you what's left of the bottle."

"Thank you, but no thank you," Pick said.

A waiter came to the table and picked up a silver-collar orange juice pitcher.

"More juice, Mr. Pickering?"

"No, thank you," Pick said.

"Have some more," the old man said. "I rather doubt where you're going that freshly squeezed orange juice will be on the menu."

"Point well taken, Sir," Pick said. "Yes, please, Fred."

"Speaking of where you're going, you haven't said where or when?"

"I report to Mare Island on the thirteenth. I'm headed for VMF-229. I'm not supposed to know, but I do. It's on Guadalcanal."

"What is . . . what you said?"

"VMF-229. It's a fighter squadron."

"Do you feel qualified to go, Pick?"

"I think I'm a pretty good pilot."

"I'm sure you are."

"On the other hand, I sometimes think my ego is running away with me," Pick confessed. "I guess I'll just have to wait and see."

"I had an interesting chat, a while back, with a Marine pilot."

"There must be fifteen or twenty in the bar every night," Pick said.

"This was an interesting chap. I had him and his lady to dinner up here. With your mother."

"His 'lady'?"

"Well, she *was* a lady. I liked her and so did your mother, but it came out that their relationship had not yet culminated in holy matrimony."

"Illicit cohabitation? In the Andrew Foster? Shocking! And the innkeeper had them to dinner? With my mother?"

"Yes, and the innkeeper was very glad that he did. He told me all about your training. I understood at least twenty percent of what he told me. And I think he managed to alleviate some of your mother's concerns—"

"Which is why you had him to dinner, right?"

"Certainly. He was a very impressive man. On his way to the Pacific. Galloway was his name. He said he was to be a squadron commander."

"I don't know the name," Pick said.

"He didn't know yours, either," the old man said. "I asked."

The telephone rang.

"Take that, Fred, will you, please?" the old man said. "And remind the operator that I said I didn't want any calls."

The waiter went inside, and Pick could hear him speaking softly on the phone. Then, to his surprise, he reappeared on the terrace, telephone in hand. He plugged it in and handed it to Andrew Foster.

"The inn better be on fire, Fred," the old man said as he took the telephone.

"I thought you had better take it, Mr. Foster."

"This is Andrew Foster.

"No, Mrs. Pickering is not here.

"I'm afraid I have no idea where she is."

"She said she would be at the office from about eleven," Pick said. "What is that?"

The old man handed him the phone.

"Who is this, please?" Pick asked.

"My name is McCoy, Sir. I'm a Marine officer."

"From what I hear, you're a flaming disgrace to the goddamn Marine Corps," Pick said cheerfully.

There was a moment's hesitation, then the caller asked, "Is that you, Pick?"

"How the hell are you, you ugly bastard?"

"Pick, I'm calling from Walter Reed. Your dad's in here."

"Jesus, now what?"

"He's going to be all right. I waited until they gave him a . . . Colonel Rickabee just got the word from the doctors."

"Who's he?"

"He works for your father."

"So what's going on?"

"Your father has malaria. I went to his room in the hotel this morning and found him too weak to even sit up. He's been treating himself with scotch and aspirin. But he's going to be all right. He made me promise to call your mother and see what I could do to calm her down. I called all over, and finally somebody at your house—Talbot, something like that—gave me this number."

"Mother's butler," Pick said. "It's my grandfather's number. That was him on the phone before."

"OK. So what I know is this: He has malaria. There's two kinds, intestinal, and—
I forget what they call it, in the brain. That's really bad news. He has intestinal.
That's not as bad. What it does is give you chills and fever, and you lose control
of your bowels, and you throw up a lot."

"That's not bad, huh?"

"It dehydrates you. He was in pretty bad shape when we found him. But we got
him in the hospital, and they're giving him stuff to kill the malaria, and they're
putting fluid in him. He's going to be all right."

"Define 'all right,' " Pick said.

"He's sick. He's weak, and embarrassed."

"What do you mean, embarrassed? What the hell's he got to be embarrassed
about?"

"He . . . shit his bed. We had to wash him like a baby."

"God!"

"He said I was to tell your mother there was no need for her to do anything
foolish, like come to Washington."

"Which means she will be on the next plane. *We* will be on the first plane."

"You better think about that," McCoy said. "You're supposed to be at Mare
Island on the thirteenth."

"How do you know that?"

"I checked. Actually, you're supposed to be in Pensacola. What was that all
about?"

"I had originally . . ." Pick said, and stopped. "What the hell does it matter?"

"I called all over Pensacola for you. I finally got some Admiral's wife on the
phone, and she told me you were on your way to San Francisco."

The Admiral's wife was Mrs. Richard B. Sayre, mother to Mrs. Martha Sayre
Culhane. Upon learning that Lieutenant Pickering was headed for the Pacific, Martha
had been even more determined than ever not to marry him. Martha had said it so
often he had no choice but to believe her: She could not go through again what
she'd already gone through. She couldn't wait around for the inevitable telegram
from the Secretary of the Navy expressing his deep regret that her husband had
been lost in aerial combat against the forces of the Empire of Japan.

"There's no way you could come here and get back out there by the thirteenth,"
McCoy said.

"I could get an emergency leave," Pick said.

"Yeah, *you* probably could," McCoy said. There was a hint of disgust in his
voice.

"Meaning what?"

"Meaning you're a Marine officer, and you have your orders. There's nothing
you could do for your father here except embarrass him by showing up."

"Fuck you, Ken!" Pick flared, but then immediately: "Shit. I'm sorry. You're
right, of course."

"Look, he's sick, but in a couple of weeks, a month, he's going to be all right,
OK?"

"That's the straight poop?"

"That's straight."

"You going to see him?"

"Yeah, sure."

"Tell him . . . You know what to tell him."

"Yeah. Sure. You'll tell your mother?"

"I'll tell her and she'll come."

"He won't like that."

"Yes, he will, and besides, there's nothing he can do about it."

"OK."

"Thanks for . . . everything, I guess, Ken."

"Take care of yourself, pal."

"You, too."

The line went dead.

Pick held the phone in his hand for a long moment before dropping it into the cradle. Then he raised his eyes and found his grandfather's eyes on him.

"That was Ken McCoy. We went to OCS at Quantico together."

The old man nodded.

"You understood what that was all about?"

"Some of it."

"Dad's in Walter Reed Hospital with malaria. He's apparently pretty sick, but in no danger."

"I gather we should see about getting your mother on an airplane?"

"Just Mother. It was just pointed out to me that I do not have time to go to see him."

"I will take your mother to see him and tell him why you couldn't be there. Is there anything else I can do, Pick?"

Pick raised both hands helplessly.

"What?" he asked.

(TWO)
Temporary Building T-2032
The Mall
Washington, D.C.
1630 Hours 9 September 1942

When First Lieutenant Kenneth R. McCoy pushed open the outer door of the two-story frame building, he noticed a new sign, USMC OFFICE OF MANAGEMENT ANALYSIS, nailed to the side of the building. Previously, there had been no sign at all. Since that made Building T-2032 even more anonymous among the other identical "temporary" frame buildings—they had been there since the First World War—he wondered why Colonel Rickabee had decided to hang a sign.

As he took the stairs to the second floor two at a time, he decided that some brass hat with nothing better to do had probably issued an edict that all buildings would be properly labeled.

It had probably occupied the better part of his time for a month, McCoy mused, *first coming up with the idea, and then deciding in precise detail the size of the sign, and of its lettering, and its color.*

As he reached the second floor, he remembered that a bird colonel and his entourage had been sharing the building.

He was charged with coordinating enlisted morale projects with the Army and Navy, or some such bullshit. I wonder why he doesn't have a sign?

At the top of the stairwell was a small foyer. Access to the rest of the building was barred by a counter; wire mesh went from the countertop to the ceiling.

McCoy recognized one of the two staff noncoms behind the barrier.

"Open up, Rutterman," he said.

Technical Sergeant Harry Rutterman, who had first come to know Lieutenant McCoy as a just-graduated-from-Quantico second lieutenant, threw up his hands in horror.

"Sir, these are classified premises," he said. "Will you please state the nature of your business and show me your identification?"

"You're kidding."

"Not at all, Sir. Less than an hour ago, our beloved commanding officer passed through these portals without challenge, and then ate my ass out for letting *him* in."

"Really?"

"I think you are next on his menu, Lieutenant, if you don't mind my saying so," Rutterman said. "He left word that he wants to see you as soon as you came in."

McCoy extended his identification, a leather folder holding a badge and a photo identification card.

"Pass, friend," Rutterman said, as he pushed a button which operated a solenoid that unlocked a wire mesh door. "And good luck!"

"If I wasn't an officer and a gentleman, Harry, I'd tell you to take a flying fuck at a rolling doughnut," McCoy said as he walked past him.

Colonel F. L. Rickabee's office was at the corner of the far end of the building. Its door was closed. McCoy knocked and said, "McCoy, Sir."

"Come!"

McCoy opened the door, marched in, and stood to attention before Rickabee's desk, even though Rickabee was in civilian clothing.

"Moore?" Rickabee asked.

"He's all right, Sir. It was exhaustion more than anything else."

"Taking him out of the hospital was stupid, McCoy."

"Yes, Sir. No excuse, Sir."

"Sessions told me that General Pickering ordered you to get in touch with his wife." It was a question more than a statement.

"Yes, Sir. I was unable to reach Mrs. Pickering, but I spoke with his son, Sir."

"That's right, you know him, don't you?"

"We were in OCS together, Sir."

"Where's this man Hart?"

"At the hotel, Sir. I didn't know what to do with him. I was going to ask if you wanted to see him."

"I'll have to go on what Sessions and you feel," Rickabee said. "I'll want to see him when he comes back."

"Sir?"

Rickabee handed him a large manila envelope. McCoy opened it. It contained airline tickets and a sheaf of mimeographed orders.

HEADQUARTERS
UNITED STATES MARINE CORPS
WASHINGTON, D.C.

9 September 1942

LETTER ORDERS:

To: SGT Hart, George F 386751, USMCR
Company "A"
Marine Barracks
Washington, DC

1. You will proceed this date to San Francisco, Cal., St. Louis, Mo., and such other destinations as may be necessary in carrying out the mission assigned to you by the Office of Management Analysis, Hq USMC.

2. Travel by government and civilian rail, motor and air transportation is authorized. Priority AAA.

3. A five (5) day delay en route leave is authorized in connection with these orders.

BY DIRECTION OF BRIG GEN F. PICKERING:

F. L. Rickabee, Col, USMC
Executive Officer, Office of Management Analysis

I'll be damned. He's sending Hart out there to tell Pick his father'll be all right, McCoy thought.

He blurted what popped into his mind: "That was very nice of you, Sir."

" 'Nice' is not one of my character traits, McCoy," Colonel Rickabee said. "One: I think it important that your man Hart understand just who he will be working for. His initial introduction to the General was something less than inspiring. Seeing what he did in civilian life, who he was, will be instructional. Two: I think it is important that General Pickering knows that we think of him as one of our own. Three: Sergeant Hart is entitled to an end of boot-camp leave; and he won't be needed around here anyway for ten days, possibly more."

Bullshit—that was nice of you!

"Yes, Sir. Sorry, Sir. I know that, Sir."

"I would hate to think you were being sarcastic, McCoy."

"Not me, Sir."

"Sessions tells me you told him Mrs. Pickering will be coming to Washington."

"Yes, Sir. I think she will."

"Keep me advised of her schedule. I'd like to meet her plane, or train, whatever."

"Yes, Sir."

"General Pickering, McCoy, can be very valuable to us around here. It thus behooves us to do whatever we can for him."

Bullshit again, Colonel. You like Pickering. You're two of a kind.

"Yes, Sir."

"Get out of here, McCoy."

"Yes, Sir."

(THREE)
Municipal Airport
San Francisco, California
1530 Hours 11 September 1942

When Hart entered the terminal after leaving the Transcontinental and Western (TWA) DC-3 that brought him from Chicago, with a stop at Salt Lake City, two shore patrolmen were standing in the middle of the airport aisle. One was a sailor armed with a billy club, and the other was a Marine sergeant, wearing a .45 suspended from a white web belt.

Neither of them looks like much of a cop, former Detective George Hart decided, and then dismissed them from his mind as he headed for a row of telephone booths.

Lieutenant McCoy had given him four telephone numbers for Lieutenant Pickering: the Pickering home, in Marin County; the offices of Pacific & Far East Shipping, in San Francisco; the San Francisco apartment of Mrs. Fleming Pickering; and the Andrew Foster Hotel. If he called the last number, he was instructed to ask for Mr. Andrew Foster, stating he was a friend of Lieutenant Pickering.

His orders were to tell Lieutenant Pickering, without any bullshit, General Pickering's condition when they went into the bedroom of the Foster Lafayette Hotel, and then to tell him that the prognosis was good and that his coming to Washington would have only embarrassed his father.

"Tell Lieutenant Pickering he's doing the right thing by not coming," Lieutenant McCoy said. "And, if you have to, that I wouldn't lie to him. And tell him to call me just before he gets on his plane, and I'll give him the latest poop."

Hart had just taken the list of telephone numbers from his pocket and was about to drop a nickel in the pay phone slot, when there was a sharp rap on the telephone booth window.

It was the sailor shore patrolman. He made a sign with his index finger for Hart to come out of the booth.

"What can I do for you?" Hart asked.

"For one thing, you can show us your orders," the Marine sergeant said.

Hart produced a copy of the orders from the breast pocket of his tunic and handed them over.

The MP read them and showed them to the sailor.

"Anybody with a mimeograph machine could have made these up," he said. "There's no stamp or seal or nothing."

"That thought occurred to me on the way out here," Hart said.

"Where did you get that haircut, *Sergeant*?" the Marine asked.

"Parris Island."

"Boots' hair usually grows back in before they make sergeant," the Marine said. "I think, *Sergeant,* that you better come with us until we can check out these orders."

I was wrong. This guy's not as dumb as he looks. He picked up on the Parris Island haircut.

"How about this, Sergeant?" Hart said, and handed him the leather folder holding the badge identifying him as a Special Agent of the Office of Naval Intelligence and the accompanying photo identification card.

"I'll be damned," the sergeant said. "Sorry."

"No problem. It was the haircut, right?"

"Yeah, and there's two inspection stickers hanging out on the back of your jacket," the Marine said. "So I checked."

"I understand."

"Could I ask you a question?"

"Sure."

"How do you get a billet like that? It would sure be better than standing around an airport all day looking for AWOLs and drunks."

"I really don't know," Hart replied. "That's where they sent me when I got out of Parris Island. I used to be a cop. But I didn't apply for it or anything like that."

"It would sure beat standing around this fucking airport," the Marine repeated, and then smiled and walked off.

Hart went back into the telephone booth and struck out with the first three numbers. After three intermediate people came on the line, the fourth call was finally answered:

"Andrew Foster."

Jesus, I'm actually talking to the guy who owns all those hotels!

"Mr. Foster, my name is Sergeant Hart. I'm trying to locate Lieutenant Malcolm S. Pickering."

"Perhaps I could help you."

"Sir, I really would like to speak to Lieutenant Pickering. It's about his father."

"Is this bad news, Sergeant?"

"No, Sir. The opposite. I was with General Pickering when . . . just before we took him to the hospital. I've been asked to tell Lieutenant Pickering about that. And how the General is doing now."

"I'd be very much interested in hearing what you have to say, Sergeant," Andrew Foster said, "if that's possible. General Pickering is my son-in-law."

After a moment's hesitation, Hart delivered a slightly laundered report of the events in the hotel room, and then the prognosis the doctors at Walter Reed had offered—complete recovery after three to six weeks of rest in the hospital.

"I'm sure my grandson will be delighted to hear this, Sergeant. He's been climbing the walls around here the last couple of days. The problem would seem to be getting you together. Where are you?"

"At the airport, Sir."

"At the passenger terminal?"

"Yes, Sir."

"Across the field from the passenger terminal is Hangar 103," Andrew Foster said. "It says 'Lewis Flying Services' on it. My grandson should be there. He should be somewhere around my airplane. If he is not, call me back here. I'll either know where he is by then, or we can launch a manhunt together."

"Yes, Sir. Thank you very much."

"Sergeant, am I permitted to ask your connection with General Pickering?"

After a brief hesitation, Hart decided to answer this question, too.

"Sir, I've been assigned to look after General Pickering."

"Somehow I don't think that means you're his valet, or orderly, or whatever they call it."

"No, Sir."

"If my grandson's not there, call me, Sergeant."

"Yes, Sir."

There was little activity inside Hangar 103, and no one in Marine uniform. But a young man with a bored look was leaning against the hangar wall next to a battery charger. He was wearing oil-stained khaki trousers and an oil-stained T-shirt under a cotton zipper jacket. His tan and his haircut suggested he was no stranger to military service.

Me and Sherlock Holmes in the airport.

"Excuse me, Sir," Hart said. "I'm looking for Lieutenant Pickering."

"You found him," Pick said.

Hart saluted. "Sergeant Hart, Sir. I work for Lieutenant McCoy, Sir."

Pick did not return the salute.

"OK," he said, his voice even but tense. "No beating around the bush. Let's have it."

"Your father will be all right. They will keep him in the hospital for three to six weeks of rest and treatment. From what I have seen of your father, I'd bet on three weeks."

"Jesus Christ, that's a relief! When you said McCoy had sent you, I was really worried."

"My orders, Sir, are to tell you exactly what happened."

"Go ahead."

When he had finished, Pick said, "Thank you, Sergeant."

There was a moment's silence, and then Pick asked, "They sent you all the way out here to tell me this?"

"Yes, Sir."

"What's your connection with my father?"

"I work for him, Sir."

"Doing what?"

"Whatever he tells me to do, Sir."

"In other words you're not going to tell me. But since you *have* told me you work for McCoy, it wouldn't be unreasonable for me to assume, would it, that you're also involved—suitably draped in a cape—in all those mysterious things McCoy does but won't talk about?"

Hart didn't reply. When it was evident to Pick that he wasn't going to reply, he went on, "I'll rephrase, Sergeant. Would it be unreasonable of me to assume that you are not my father's orderly?"

"I'm not your father's orderly, Sir."

"OK, we'll leave it at that. So what are you going to do now?"

"I have a plane reservation for tomorrow afternoon, Sir."

"Nothing to do right now? How about a hotel reservation?"

"No, Sir."

"Well, we can take care of that, the hotel, I mean."

"That's not necessary, Sir."

"I'll make you a deal, Sergeant. You do two things for me, and I will take care of the hotel and throw in dinner and all the booze you can handle."

"My orders are to do whatever you ask me to do, Sir."

"Great. The first thing is, stop calling me 'Sir.' The second thing is, help me get this heavy fucking battery back in the airplane. I almost ruptured myself taking it out."

Hart knew very little about airplanes, but when he had walked across the hangar floor to meet Lieutenant Pickering, he noticed a single-engine biplane he recognized as a Stagger Wing Beechcraft. A compartment hatch in the fuselage was open.

Obviously, the battery Pickering was now disconnecting from the battery charger had come out of it.

"Why did you take the battery out?"

Pickering looked at him with amusement in his eyes.

"It was dead, Sergeant," he said. "One recharges dead batteries. It *resurrects* them, so to speak."

"I meant, why recharge it, Sir."

"You've agreed not to call me Sir," Pick said. "Which brings us to what do I call you?"

"My name is George."

"Well, George, the reason I am recharging the battery is that this is my grandpa's airplane. Most light civilian aircraft like this one have been taken over by the armed forces, for reasons I can't imagine. This one, however, Grandpa got to keep because it was essential to his business. Or at least he got our Senator to tell the Air Corps it was essential to his business. He and our Senator, by happy coincidence, are old pals. By the time they had gone through all this, the pilots had gone into the Army Air Corps. You following all this?"

"More or less," Hart said, smiling.

"More or less, *Pick,*" Pick corrected him. "You will call me Pick. That is an order."

"Yes, Pick."

"Which left the airplane here unattended, so to speak. Airplanes which are left uncared for tend to deteriorate. The batteries, for example, go dead, and the tires go flat, et cetera. Still with me, George?"

"Yes, Pick," Hart said.

"Better. So Grandpa, who is a master, by the way, of getting people to do things for him, remembered that the U.S. Navy, at enormous expense, had turned his grandchild into a Naval Aviator. Naval Aviators, Grandpa reasoned, know something about airplanes."

"And he said, 'Go check on my airplane,' right?"

"Right. And so I pumped up the tires and took the water that had condensed in the fuel tanks out of the fuel tanks, and pulled the engine around to remove the oil that had accumulated in the cylinders. It was my intention to run up the engine, you see. Running up the engine is something one does when one's airplane has been sitting around.''

"And the battery was dead," Hart said.

"And the battery was dead. George, you are a clever fellow, indeed."

"Yes, Pick."

Pick laughed.

"Give me a hand with this, will you?"

The battery wasn't all that heavy, but putting it in its battery compartment was awkward. Hart wondered how Pickering had managed to take it out. Finally it was in place, and connected.

"Now we will open the hangar doors and push the airplane outside," Pick announced.

The huge doors of the hangar moved with an ease that surprised Hart. Pushing the Stagger Wing Beechcraft was easier than he would have thought, too, but obviously one man couldn't do it.

"What were you going to do if I hadn't turned up? You couldn't push it by yourself."

"Run it up in the hangar, of course," Pick said.

"Wouldn't the—wind from the propeller—"

"We Naval Aviators call that 'prop blast,'" Pick furnished helpfully.

"—*prop blast* have blown things around the hangar?"

"I don't know," Pick said. "I never ran an engine up in a hangar."

This guy is a cheerful idiot, Hart decided. And then modified that: *a nice cheerful idiot.*

When the airplane was outside and turned at right angles to the hangar, Pickering opened another compartment in the fuselage and took out a fire extinguisher.

"You know how to work one of these?" he asked. Hart nodded. "Maybe we will be lucky," Pick went on, "but if there is a cloud of smoke and flames, you will extinguish them using this clever device. Think you can remember that?"

"Right, Pick."

"Do not stand where the propeller turns," Pick ordered solemnly. "Getting whacked with a propeller stings."

"Right, Pick."

Pickering pulled the engine through several times and then climbed into the cockpit. Hart saw him moving around inside, but he had no idea what he was doing.

The window beside Pickering opened.

"Clear!" he shouted, and now he sounded very professional.

Hart picked up the fire extinguisher, wondering if he would have to use it.

There was a whining sound, and then the propeller began to turn, very slowly. The engine coughed and stopped. A small cloud of dark smoke came out of the exhaust ports.

The whining of the starter began again, and then the propeller moved through several rotations as the engine coughed, burped smoke and died again.

It is not going to start, Hart decided, as he watched Pickering's head disappear as he moved around the cockpit.

The whining started again, the propeller turned, the engine coughed, coughed again, discharged an enormous cloud of smoke, and then caught with a mighty roar and began to run.

Hart could see a delighted smile on Pickering's face.

After a few moments the roughness disappeared.

I wonder how long it takes to—what did he say?—run up an engine?

He set the fire extinguisher on the ground and looked up at the cockpit.

Pickering was shaking his head and making gestures. After a moment Hart understood them: he was not to put the fire extinguisher down, but to get into the airplane with it.

Hart made a wide sweep around the wing and went to the fuselage door. It was closed.

The wind—the prop blast—*blew it closed.*

With some effort, he forced it open against the prop blast, laid the fire extinguisher on the floor, and then climbed aboard. The prop blast slammed the door closed. He looked at the door, saw a handle that locked the door, and turned it.

Then he walked to the cockpit. He was surprised at how much room the airplane had—there were four passenger seats—and how plush it was. The seats were upholstered in light-brown leather, and the walls and ceiling were covered with it.

Pickering motioned for him to sit in the second seat in the cockpit. It was George Hart's first visit to a cockpit and he found the array of dials and levers and controls both fascinating and intimidating.

Pickering showed him how to fasten the lap and shoulder harness, and then handed him a set of earphones.

"The intercom button, I just found out," Pickering's metallic voice came over the earphones, "is that little button on the side of the microphone. Can you hear me?"

Hart looked at Pickering and saw he had a microphone in his hand. And then Pickering pointed to a second microphone beside Hart. Hart had finally found something recognizable. The microphone was essentially identical to the ones in Saint Louis police cars.

"What do you mean, you just found out?"

"I never sat up here before," Pickering said.

Bullshit!

There was a popping sound, and then Pickering's voice.

"Frisco Ground Control, Beech Two Oh Oh on the Lewis ramp."

"Beech Two Oh Oh, go ahead."

"Request taxi instructions to box my compass."

What the hell does that mean?

"Beech Two Oh Oh is cleared via taxiway one three right to the threshold area of runway one three."

"Roger, thank you," Pickering's voice came over the earphones. "Understand threshold area of one three. One three moving and clear."

Hart watched with fascination as Pickering released the brakes, advanced the throttle, and the airplane began to move.

He pressed his mike button.

"Where are we going?"

There was another pop in the earphones.

"Aircraft calling Ground Control, say again."

"George," Pickering said, "don't talk into the intercom until I tell you you can. You are worrying Ground Control."

Hart nodded. He had just revealed his enormous ignorance, and it humiliated him.

They taxied a long way to the end of the field. As they neared it, a United Airlines DC-3 came in for a landing. Hart found that fascinating.

He also found Pickering's next act fascinating. He moved the airplane to the center of a large concrete area and carefully jockeyed it into position. He then fiddled somehow with the compass. Then he moved the airplane again, and fiddled with the compass again, and then repeated the process.

"As you can see, I have now boxed the compass," he said.

Hart didn't reply.

"You may express your admiration, we're on intercom," Pickering said.

"I'm impressed. Now what?"

"I am debating whether or not I can fly this thing," Pickering said. "How would you like a little ride, George?"

"What do you mean, whether or not you can fly this thing?"

"I told you. This is my first time sitting up here."

Bullshit. He's pulling my leg.

"I have faith in a fellow Marine," Hart replied.

"How can I resist a challenge like that? Now shut up, George. We are going to talk to the tower." There was another pop in the earphones.

"Frisco tower, Beech Two Oh Oh on the threshold of one three for takeoff."

Jesus, he is going to take me for a ride!

"Beech Two Oh Oh, what is your destination?"

"Couple of times around the pattern. Test flight."

"Beech Two Oh Oh, you are advised you are required to have a departure authorization."

"It's supposed to be there. You don't have it?"

There was a long break.

"Beech Two Oh Oh. You are cleared as number one to take off on one three. The altimeter is two niner niner niner. Winds are negligible."

"Roger, Two Oh Oh rolling," Pickering said and moved the throttle forward.

He lined the airplane up with the center of the runway and pushed the throttle all the way forward.

The Beech quickly picked up speed, and a moment later the rumbling of the landing gear disappeared.

"Beech Two Oh Oh. We don't have your departure clearance."

"Frisco, say again, you are garbled."

"Beech Two Oh Oh, we do not, I say again, we do not have a departure clearance. You are directed to land immediately. You are cleared as number one to land on runway one three."

"Frisco, say again, you are garbled."

There was another pop in the earphones.

"George, you may now express your admiration for that splendid virginal take-off."

"What the hell was the tower saying to you?"

"Essentially, it means I don't think we ought to go back there," Pickering said. "I think they take their departure clearances, whatever the hell that means, very seriously."

"Meaning you don't have one?"

"What are they going to do to me?" Pickering said. "Send me to Guadalcanal?"

"Jesus Christ, you're crazy!"

"I always wanted to fly this thing," Pickering said. "The temptation was too much. I have a very weak character."

"We're at war, for Christ's sake. They're going to shoot you down. *Us* down."

"I thought about that," Pickering replied. "By the time they get their act together and decide to report this to the military, at least fifteen minutes will have passed. By the time the Army or the Navy gets its act in gear and decides which one will get the honor of shooting down an unarmed civilian airplane, another twenty minutes or so will have passed. And then it will take them five minutes to get in the air and another ten minutes to find us. We've got damned near an hour."

"You are really out of your gourd!"

"And then it would take a real prick of a pilot to shoot down something as pretty as this airplane. I certainly wouldn't do it."

"Holy Christ!"

"That long thin thing down there over the mouth of the bay is the Golden Gate Bridge," Pickering said, pointing. Hart looked where he was pointing. "What I think we will do is fly very low over thataway, then fly under the bridge—something I have always wanted to do—and then we will find home, sweet home."

"You have to be kidding."

"I am a Marine officer and a Naval Aviator. We never kid about important things."

"When you land this thing, they are going to put you in jail."

"First they have to catch me."

"I'm dead goddamn serious."

"So'm I," Pick said with a smile. "Relax and enjoy the ride."

In addition of course to flying under the Golden Gate Bridge in the first place, what surprised Sergeant Hart about their flight was that he wasn't nearly as terrified as he expected to be. There was plenty of room under the bridge. And Pick didn't seem nervous.

In fact, looking up out of the cockpit at the massive structure as it flashed overhead was both interesting and stimulating.

He was far more afraid five minutes later when it became apparent that Pickering was about to land the airplane on what was obviously not an airfield. It was a field, or an enormous lawn, but it was definitely not an airfield.

But there, goddammit, is one of those dunce caps on a pole. What do they call them? Wind socks. Airports have wind socks. This must be an airport.

A moment later the Beech touched down.

"Where the hell are we?"

"Home sweet home, my son," Pickering said solemnly. "As you may have noticed, we have cheated death again."

"Where the hell are we?"

"This is my parents' place."

"You have your own goddamned airport?"

"Plus a barn that can be used as a hangar," Pick said. "And into which, I devoutly hope, we can get this thing before the military spots us from the air."

"You better hope we can."

"I am always a pessimist," Pickering said. "But I think we got away with it this time, George."

"They're going to catch you eventually," Hart said.

"By then I'll be on Guadalcanal," Pickering said softly. "And even if they do catch me, I will swear that I was alone. So relax, George."

Three minutes later they were closing the doors of a large barn.

(FOUR)
The Men's Bar
The Andrew Foster Hotel
San Francisco, California
1930 Hours 11 September 1942

Wearing a superbly tailored double-breasted blue pinstripe suit with a rosebud pinned to his lapel, Andrew Foster walked into the bar and found what he was looking for, two young men in tweed sports coats, gray flannel slacks, white button-down-collar shirts, and loafers. He walked to them.

"Good evening, gentlemen," he said. "I wondered if you had an opportunity to see the newspaper."

He laid *The San Francisco Chronicle* on the bar.

"Good evening, Grandfather," Malcolm S. Pickering said. "I know you've talked to George on the telephone, but I don't think you've actually met, have you? George, this is my grandfather."

"How do you do, Sir?" George Hart said with a weak smile. He'd just seen the headline—MYSTERY AIRPLANE FLIES UNDER GG BRIDGE. It was accompanied by a somewhat-out-of-focus photograph of a Stagger Wing Beech flying up the Golden Gate no more than a hundred feet off the water.

"How do you do, Sergeant?" Andrew Foster said—causing the heads of half a dozen Navy and Marine officers, three of them wearing Naval Aviator's wings, to turn in curiosity. The men's bar of the Andrew Foster was not often frequented by enlisted men.

The bartender quickly appeared.

"What can I get you, Mr. Foster?"

The name intensified the curiosity of the officers. They had heard that the old man sometimes showed up in the men's bar and bought the next round for anyone in uniform.

And here he was.

"A little Famous Grouse, Tony, please," the old man said, and then changed his mind. "Bring the bottle."

"Yes, Sir."

"I've been wondering what happened to you," Andrew Foster said. "I understand you have had a very interesting afternoon."

"Fascinating," Pick agreed. "Well, we went out to the house, Grandfather."

"You had no trouble getting there?"

"Not a bit, Sir."

"Nothing's broken, or anything like that?"

"No, Sir."

"I just had a talk with Richmond Fowler," Andrew Foster said. "He said to tell you that he would do what he could, because of your father; but he could make no promises."

"I see."

The waiter delivered a quart bottle of Famous Grouse, held it over a glass, and poured. It was nearly full before Andrew Foster said, "Thank you."

He took a large swallow, then turned to his grandson.

"Pick, damn it, I've covered for you before, but this! My God, even for you, this is spectacular!"

"Yes," Pick said, wholly unrepentant. "I rather thought it was myself."

"Why?"

"It seemed like a marvelous idea at the time, didn't it, George?"

"No, it didn't," George said.

"Did it pass through your mind what your father's reaction to this is going to be when he finds out about it?"

"No. But on the other hand, Dad's in no position to say anything to me about it."

"Meaning what?" the old man snapped.

"Meaning that Dad *swam* the Golden Gate. That was considerably more dangerous than flying *up* it and *under* the bridge."

"Christ, will you shut up!" Hart said, aware that their conversation was now the subject of a good deal of attention.

Almost immediately, he was sure that there was reason for his concern. A lieutenant, in greens and wearing wings, walked up to them.

"Lieutenant Pickering, I believe?" he said.

"Well, if it isn't Lieutenant Stecker, the pride of Marine Aviation. I didn't expect you until tomorrow."

"I came out a day early," Lieutenant Stecker said. "I'll tell you about it later."

Hart sensed the question had made Stecker uncomfortable. The proof came when Stecker pulled the newspaper to him, visibly glad for a chance to change the subject.

"I saw this in the airport," he said. "What kind of an idiot would do something like that?"

"As George Washington said to his daddy," Pick said happily, "I cannot tell a lie."

"Will you shut the hell up!" Hart snapped.

"Holy Christ! Really?" Stecker said.

"He's kidding, of course," Hart said.

"He kiddeth not. Oh, excuse me. Lieutenant Stecker, may I present my grandfather, Mr. Foster? And Sergeant Hart?"

"How do you do, Lieutenant?" Andrew Foster said.

"I think we ought to get out of here," Hart said.

"I think the sergeant is right," Andrew Foster said.

"I'm having a fine time right where I am," Pick said.

"Listen to me, you jackass," Stecker flared. "You will either leave here under your own power or I will coldcock you and carry you out."

Pick looked at him a moment.

"For some strange reason, I think you're serious."

"I'm serious."

"Thank you, Lieutenant," Hart said.

"Let's go," Stecker said.

Pick met his eyes for a moment and then shrugged. "I'm outnumbered."

They walked out of the bar.

Halfway across the lobby, Andrew Foster said, "I think you had better either get out of the hotel or go to Sergeant Hart's room. In case someone is looking for you."

"They won't know where to even start looking for me until sometime tomorrow."

"Where's your room, Sergeant?" Stecker asked.

Hart pulled the key from his pocket.

"Eleven-fifteen," he said.

"Let's go," Stecker said, and took Pick's arm and propelled him toward the bank of elevators.

"I don't know why you're pissed," Pick said to Stecker in Hart's room—a three-bedroom-plus-sitting-room suite. "You weren't there. Even if they catch me and stand me before a firing squad, you're not involved."

"You had no goddamned right to involve the sergeant in this," Stecker said. "Jesus Christ, it's a court-martial offense to be wearing civilian clothing! Not to mention the insanity of your flight under the goddamned bridge!"

"George, we have just heard from the Long Grey Line," Pick said.

"The what?"

"Lieutenant Stecker is not only a professional officer and gentleman, but a *West Pointer*. They believe, as a matter of faith, that enlisted men have no brains and have to be cared for like children."

"Oh, fuck you, Pick!" Stecker flared. "I was raised as the dependent of an enlisted man."

"George is not going to get into any trouble," Pick said.

"Says you," Stecker said. "Sergeant, where did you meet this . . . child in an officer's uniform?"

"Lieutenant," Hart said. When he had his attention, he handed him his credentials. "Even if anybody asks, there's no problem about the civilian clothing. This says I can wear it."

Stecker looked carefully at the credentials.

"Are you on duty now?" he asked.

"More or less."

"What does that mean?"

"It means he works for my father, and he came out here to reassure me."

"Reassure you about what?"

"Dad's in the Army Hospital in Washington, with malaria, exhaustion, and Christ only knows what else."

"Why didn't you let me know?"

"I didn't want to worry you."

"How is he?"

"He'll be all right," Hart answered.

"And that's what caused this insanity? Relief that your father's going to be all right?"

"What insanity?" Pickering asked innocently. "I was under the impression that any red-blooded Marine Aviator would jump at the chance to fly under that bridge. What are you, Stecker, some kind of a pansy?"

Stecker looked at him. Finally he shook his head.

"Hand me the bottle," he said. "I think I will get stinko."

"Not until you tell me why you're out here a day early," Pickering said. "Is there some angry Pennsylvania Dutch farmer looking for you with a knocked-up daughter in tow?"

"Give me the goddamned bottle," Stecker said.

Pickering gave it to him.

"My mother was driving me nuts," he said, finally, after he'd taken a pull from the neck. "It wasn't her fault, of course. . . . Fuck it. It doesn't matter."

"What?" Pickering asked softly.

"She's already lost one son in this fucking war. My father's on goddamned Guadalcanal, and now I'm going there. I couldn't stand the way she looked at me. So I came out early. I suppose that makes me the candidate for prick of the year."

"I'm sorry," Pickering said.

"I'll tell you what," Stecker said. "I did not come out here to—"

"To what?"

"You really flew under the bridge?"

"I really flew under the bridge."

"You had enough time in that airplane to feel that confident?"

"Yeah, sure I did. How long were we up there, would you say, George, before we went under the bridge?"

"About twenty-five minutes."

"How much *total* time is what I'm asking."

"Twenty-five minutes. I just told you."

Hart could tell from the look on Pickering's face that he was telling the truth.

"Lieutenant," he said, "can I have that bottle, please?"

"If he gives you the bottle, George, the next thing you know you'll want to go out chasing fast women."

"I know you disapprove, that you will be faithful until death to Saint Martha, the virtuous widow, but what's wrong with that for Hart and me?" Stecker said.

"Now that I think about it," Pickering said, "nothing. Not for any of us."

"Really?" Stecker asked. "What about the sainted widow?"

"Live today, for tomorrow we die, right?"

"Oh, Jesus!" Stecker said.

"Or go to jail," Hart said. "Whichever comes first."

"You guys want me to call some women or not?"

Stecker handed him the telephone.

"Do you want fast women, or *fast* fast women?" Pickering asked.

"Just as long as they don't talk too much before they take off their clothes," Stecker said.

"I know just the girls," Pickering said, and told the operator to give him an outside line.

(FIVE)
Headquarters
First Marine Division
Guadalcanal
12 September 1942

When Lieutenant Colonel "Red Mike" Edson returned from the Tasimboko raid on 8 September, his professional assessment then was that several thousand Japanese were in the area, probably newly arrived and well equipped. This was confirmed on the afternoon of 12 September.

Lieutenant Colonel Sam Griffith picked up a Springfield rifle and led two volunteer riflemen on a patrol into the rain forest and up the ridge inland from Henderson Field. Griffith's first combat experience in the war had been with the British Commandos, to whom he had been attached as an "observer."

Griffith returned to report that a large force of Japanese was approaching, almost certainly several thousand of them. It was unsettling news. But worse, the force was both well led and in excellent physical condition: This was almost certainly the group that had elected not to attack Edson's battalion at Tasimboko. And now they were nearby. Only a well-led force in excellent physical condition could have moved through the rain forest and across the steep ridges from Tasimboko in less than four days.

Edson recalled General Vandergrift's words to him after the Tasimboko raid: "Conservation of force for future action is often a wise choice."

That translated to mean they were facing a fellow professional, rather than what they had been facing before, an officer whose rank let him assume command of a motley force of hungry, demoralized, and poorly equipped troops.

Edson also remembered the message General Vandergrift had shown him from Lieutenant General Harukichi Hyakutake to the 17th Army.

"The operation to surround and recapture Guadalcanal will truly decide the fate of the control of the entire Pacific."

The Japanese, Edson and Griffith concluded, were about to go into action on Guadalcanal.

It was later learned that the forces that landed in the vicinity of Tasimboko (an advance element of 750 officers and men during the night of 31 August was followed the next night by 1200 officers and men) were elements of the 124th Infantry Regiment. Following the Imperial Japanese Army custom of naming an elite force after its commander, the unit was designated the *Kawaguchi Butai.* Its commander was Major General Kiotake Kawaguchi. Guadalcanal was not to be General Kawaguchi's first encounter with Americans. He and *Kawaguchi Butai* had spent April mopping up the last remnants of American resistance on the island of Mindanao in the Philippines.

General Kawaguchi's orders from General Hyakutake were to retake the airstrip (Henderson Field) as a first priority. Once that was accomplished, the Americans could no longer send aircraft aloft to intercept Japanese aviation and Naval forces. Then throwing them back into the sea would be a relatively easy matter.

On 12 September, of course, Edson had no way of knowing about any of this. His only information was what he'd suspected—which Griffith now confirmed— that he was about to get involved in a battle with several thousand fresh and probably well-led Japanese troops.

He did what experience had taught him. He ordered several strong patrols to set out at first light to gather more information about the enemy; and he summoned an officer's call to explain the situation to his command.

Edson's situation map showed the disposition of his forces along a T-shaped ridge about a mile south of the Henderson Field runway. The cross of the T was clear, broken ground with four spurs, two on each side of the ridge that formed the 1000-yard-long base.

Baker and Charley companies of the Raiders were on the line. Able and Dog companies were in reserve, close to the line. Raider headquarters and elements of Easy Company (Heavy Weapons) were several hundred yards back from the front, on the base of the T.

Remnants of the badly hurt Parachute Battalion were mixed in with the Raiders. Baker Company, Parachutists, down to seventy men, was next to Baker Company, Raiders. The parachutists of Able and Charley companies were in the wooded area near the bottom of the base of the T. And what was left of the Parachute Battalion command post was near Edson's CP.

It was generally agreed that the Japanese would probably attack toward Henderson Field from their positions south of the ridge down the long axis of the base of the T.

Marine fields of fire were discussed. It was finally concluded that given the limited resources, all that could be done had been done. They would just have to wait until morning and see what happened.

At about 2100, just as Colonel Edson was about to dismiss his officers, the Japanese attacked. Japanese artillery located east of Alligator Creek opened fire. A moment later a parachute flare burst in light over the south end of Henderson Field. Moments after that, Japanese Naval gunfire began to land on the ridge.

By morning, what had been somewhat impersonally identified as "the ridge" would be forever known as "Bloody Ridge."

IX

Lieutenant Colonel Merritt "Red Mike" Edson was staring closely at a map of Guadalcanal that covered the small, folding wooden table where he'd spread it. The Japanese had attacked hard last night, and he was trying to make some sense of their movements.

When Colonel Edson glanced up from the map, another Marine was standing beside the table looking down at the map with great interest. He had not been there three minutes before, and he was not a member of the 1st USMC Raider Battalion.

I'm annoyed for some reason, Edson thought. *I wonder why?*

"Good morning, Jack," Edson said. "I didn't see you come in."

"Good morning, Sir," the Marine said crisply, almost coming to attention.

He would have come to attention, Edson thought, *if he wasn't cradling that Mickey Mouse rifle of his in his arms like a deer hunter.*

Major Jack (NMI) Stecker, USMCR, Commanding Officer, 2nd Battalion, Fifth Marines, was one of the very few people on Guadalcanal armed with the U.S. Rifle, Caliber .30-06, M1, known after its inventor as the Garand.

Most of The Marine Corps (including Lieutenant Colonel Edson) believed that compared to the U.S. Rifle, Springfield, Caliber .30-06, Model 1903, the Garand was a piece of shit.

Major Jack (NMI) Stecker was sure these people were wrong. Not only could the eight-shot, semiautomatic Garand be fired far more rapidly than the five-shot, bolt-operated Springfield, but it was also his professional judgment that the Garand was every bit as reliable as the Springfield (minor Marine Corps heresy) and more accurate (major Marine Corps heresy).

Before the war, when he was Master Gunnery Sergeant Stecker, he represented The Corps at the testing of the new rifle at Fort Benning, Georgia. After that, he regularly and frequently augmented his income by putting his money where his mouth was when other senior staff noncommissioned officers questioned the accuracy of the Garand.

On 7 December 1941, Stecker was the senior noncommissioned officer at Quantico. Shortly afterward he was called to active duty as a captain, and a short time after that, he was promoted to major.

Though it was rarely put into words, professional Marine officers often felt a certain ambivalence about Mustang officers. On the one hand, obviously, The Corps needed more officers than were available; and just as obviously it made more sense to put officers' insignia on veteran senior noncommissioned officers than to commission men directly from civilian life.

On the other hand, there was no substitute for experience. In the case of Major Jack (NMI) Stecker, for instance, his first command was his present command, 2nd Battalion, Fifth Marines. Previous to that assignment he had never commanded a platoon or served as a company executive officer, company commander, battalion staff officer, or battalion executive officer.

In the minds of many officers, including many who honestly regarded him as one of the best master gunnery sergeants in The Corps, Jack (NMI) Stecker had not actually earned either his promotion to major or his command of 2nd Battalion, Fifth Marines. As they saw it, he got his promotion and his command (over a dozen or so regular officers) largely because he was a lifelong friend of Brigadier General Lewis T. "Lucky Lew" Harris, now assistant First Marine Division commander.

Harris first met Stecker in World War I. Second Lieutenant Lewis T. Harris had been Corporal Jack (NMI) Stecker's platoon leader during an engagement that caused Corporal Stecker to stand out from other Marines, officer or enlisted. In recognition of the conspicuous part he played in that engagement, he was awarded his nation's highest award for valor and gallantry. He was rarely seen wearing it, but he was entitled to top his rows of medals and campaign ribbons with a blue ribbon dotted with white stars which signified that the President of the United States, on behalf of the U.S. Congress, had awarded him the Medal of Honor.

Second Lieutenant Harris was one of the two dozen Marines "whose lives," in the words of the award citation, "had been saved by Corporal Stecker's utter disregard of his own personal safety and painful wounds while manifesting extraordinary courage above and beyond the call of duty in the face of apparently overwhelming enemy force, such actions reflecting great credit upon himself, the U.S. Marine Corps, and the Naval Service of the United States."

"I don't suppose you're here, Jack," Edson said to Stecker, "to tell me we're being relieved by Second of the Fifth?"

It was a remark made in jest. But Stecker did not take it that way.

"No, Sir. But I wouldn't be surprised if we were sent up here to reinforce. I thought I should make the time to come up and look around."

Yes, Edson thought, *of course you did. You may be Lew Harris' lifelong friend, and you do have The Medal, but that's not why they gave you the 2nd of the Fifth. They gave it to you because you are one hell of a good Marine officer, which you proved beyond any question on Tulagi, and again just now, by anticipating the orders you'll probably receive, and by preparing yourself and your battalion for them.*

"Would you like me to . . . ?" Edson asked, gesturing at the map.

"I'd be grateful, Sir, if you could spare the time."

"We had listening posts, here, here, and here," Edson said, pointing to the map. "They went under in the first couple of minutes." He looked up at Stecker, saw him nod understanding, and then went on: "The main thrust of the attack hit here, where my Baker and Charley companies met. I'm sure it was by accident, but they hit one platoon from Baker and one from Charley."

Stecker nodded again. He knew what that meant. It had caused a command and communication problem that would not have existed had the Japanese attack struck two platoons of one company.

"They used firecrackers. Very lifelike sounds. That caused some confusion," Edson went on. "And then—this was smart—here, here, and here, they cut fire lanes and fired down them. They took us by surprise, Jack. Hell, I didn't expect them to attack at all last night. I was going to send out patrols this morning, right about now, to see what they were up to."

Stecker grunted and nodded, but didn't say anything.

"Then they breached the line between Baker and Charley companies," Edson went on, pointing. "Mass attack. Hundreds of them. Screaming. Unnerving. Charley Company had to withdraw to here," he pointed again, "which made Baker's positions untenable, so they had to pull back—actually, they had to fight their way back—to here."

"Why didn't they pursue the attack," Stecker asked, "since Baker was pulling back?"

"Because the people who couldn't make it back were—are—still fighting. In small groups, as individuals."

Stecker grunted again.

"I have the feeling, Jack," Edson said softly, "that the Japanese didn't quite expect the resistance they got."

Stecker looked at him with a question in his eyes.

"There was no second attack," Edson explained. "There've been skirmishes all night . . . in other words, they have not only the means—though God knows we have killed a lot of them—but the will. But no planned, coordinated, second attack. And they stopped their naval artillery, I thought, before I would have stopped it."

"That means they thought they were going to go right through your lines. The artillery was lifted because they believed *they* would be holding the positions by then."

"That's how I read it."

"They'll be back, Colonel," Stecker said.

"And so I hope, Jack, will you. I've got about four hundred—maybe four hundred and twenty—effectives, and an 1800-yard line to hold."

"What about the Parachute Battalion?"

"They're even more understrength than we are."

"We're all understrength," Stecker said.

"What shape are you in, Jack?"

"I've lost more men to sickness than to the enemy," Stecker said. "But, Jesus Christ, for some reason their morale is higher than I have any reason to think it should be. They'll do all right."

That obviously has something to do with the quality of the officers leading them, Edson thought.

He said: "They're Marines, Jack."

"Yes, Sir. Thank you for your time, Sir. I better go back and try to make myself useful."

(TWO)
VMF-229
Henderson Field
Guadalcanal, Solomon Islands
0605 Hours 13 September 1942

Compared with the pilots of VMF-229, the half-dozen Naval Aviators gathered in the sandbag wall tent that served as the squadron office of VMF-229 looked neat and clean enough to march in a parade at Pensacola. This was so despite their recent takeoff from a carrier at sea, a flight of approximately two hundred miles in a tightly packed cockpit, and the faint coating of oil mist that often settled on F4F Wildcat pilots.

They were freshly shaven. Their hair was neatly trimmed. Their khaki flight suits, although sweat-stained under the arms and down the back, had recently passed through a washing machine. The undershirts that showed through the lowered zippers of their flight suits were as blinding white as any dress uniform. The shoulder holsters which held their Smith & Wesson .38 Special revolvers looked as if they had been issued that morning. Even their shoes were shined.

The Commanding Officer of VMF-229, by contrast, needed a haircut. He had obviously not shaved in twenty-four hours. The skin of his nose was sunburned raw. There were deep rings under his eyes. And his hands were dirty. His flight suit (no underwear of any kind was beneath it) was soiled with grease and sweat, and his feet were in battered boondockers. The leather holster that carried his .45 Colt automatic was green with mold.

Two of the office's three chairs were occupied by Captain Charles Galloway and his squadron clerk. The third held a stainless steel pot containing a green-colored liquid that tasted as foul as it looked. Captain Galloway had developed a theory that mixing lime-flavored powder with their water would kill the taste of the chlorine. His theory had proved to be wishful thinking.

The Navy pilots were from the carrier USS *Hornet;* they'd come to transfer to VMF-229 six F4F Wildcats. As Captain Galloway carefully examined the documentation accompanying the aircraft, they stood around uneasily; for he had a number of pointed questions about reported malfunctions that had been ostensibly repaired.

But he was a happy man. As of that morning, VMF-229 was down to three operational aircraft. And six nearly brand-new aircraft, splendidly set up by skilled mechanics in the well-equipped shops aboard *Hornet,* had just arrived.

"You checked the guns?" he asked finally, looking at the full Lieutenant, the most senior of the Navy pilots.

"Our SOP is to check weapons just before entering a threatening, or combat, situation."

"In other words, you haven't checked the guns?"

"No."

"I nevertheless thank you from the bottom of my heart," said Galloway. "We were just about out of airplanes."

"You're welcome," the Lieutenant said somewhat awkwardly.

A small, thin, blond-haired First Lieutenant of Marines, attired in a flight suit quite as filthy as Captain Galloway's, staggered into the tent. He was loaded down with three Springfield rifles, three steel helmets, and three sets of web equipment, each consisting of a cartridge belt, a canteen, a first-aid pouch, and a bayonet in a scabbard. He was trailed by his crew chief, similarly loaded down.

"Sir!" he said.

"Gentlemen, my executive officer, Lieutenant Dunn," Captain Galloway said.

"Sir, the skipper said there's some question of the R4D being able to make it in to take these gentlemen out," Bill Dunn said.

"Really?" Galloway said.

"Yes, Sir," Dunn said seriously. "And in view of the ground situation, he thought these gentlemen should be equipped so they can fight as infantry, if that should be required. I personally don't think that will be necessary."

"But apparently the skipper does?"

"Yes, Sir, but maybe he's just being careful."

Dunn began to pass out the rifles to the Navy pilots. There was little question in Galloway's mind that the last time any of them had touched a rifle was before they'd gone to flight school.

"And are they supposed to wait here until we know whether they'll be needed or not?"

"No, Sir. The skipper seems concerned that Japanese infiltrators may sneak through the lines and attempt to damage our aircraft in their revetments. Unless the situation gets worse, he wants these officers to be placed in the revetments."

"Lieutenant," the Navy pilot said, "what exactly was the word about the R4D?"

"Essentially, Sir, that they don't wish to risk the loss of the aircraft if the Japanese break through our lines, and/or damage the runway with artillery. The aircraft will not be sent until they see how the ground situation develops."

"I see," the Navy Lieutenant said solemnly.

There have been just about enough rounds landing around here to make that credible, Galloway decided. *And there's enough noise from the small arms and mortars a mile away to be scary as hell unless you know what it is.*

"Dunn, is there enough time to have these gentlemen fed before they go to the revetments?"

"There's time, Sir, but Japanese Naval artillery has taken out the mess, Sir. I will get them some C rations, Sir."

"Sorry about that, gentlemen," Galloway said. "And thank you once again, in case I don't see you again, for the aircraft."

"Our pleasure, Captain," the Navy Lieutenant said with a weak smile as he adjusted the interior straps of his helmet.

"Bill, that was a rotten fucking thing to do to those sailors," Galloway said, when Lieutenant Dunn, wearing a very-pleased-with-myself grin, walked back in the tent ten minutes later.

"Yeah, wasn't it?" Dunn replied. "But it will give them something to talk about when they get back to their air-conditioned wardroom. How they personally repelled mass attacks of sword-wielding Japanese."

"After they have a nice shower and a nice shave and have put on nice clean clothes," Galloway said.

The telephone rang.

"Greengiant," Galloway answered it.

"Yes, Sir. They're being serviced. They're brand new, Colonel. Somebody in the Navy must have screwed up.

"I'll pass the word, Sir. Thank you."

He put the field telephone back into its leather case.

"That was the skipper. The ETA on the R4D to take those guys out of here is fourteen hundred."

"They'll be glad to hear that," Dunn said.

"They would be even gladder if you told them at, say, thirteen fifty-five."

"Has anyone ever told you, Skipper, that you can be just as much a prick as any of us?"

The telephone rang again.

"Greengiant.

"Yes, Sir.

"I'll send the three remaining aircraft, Sir, and with your permission, Dunn and I will take two of the new aircraft. That'll let us kill two birds with one stone. I don't want to turn them over to somebody else without a test flight.

"Aye, aye, Sir."

He put the phone back in its leather case.

"Coastwatchers report a flight of three twin-engine bombers from Rabaul. Destination unknown, but where else than here?"

"I heard," Dunn said. "It will be a pleasure flying an airplane fresh from the showroom floor."

"Just don't break it," Galloway said as he got up from his chair. "I don't think there's any more where these came from."

When they reached their plane revetments, they found Navy pilots guarding them. Each wore a helmet and firmly clutched a Springfield, as he peered warily over the sandbags toward the general direction of the sound of the small arms and mortar fire.

Three minutes after that, Dunn and Galloway were airborne, climbing slowly, so as to conserve fuel, to a final altitude of 25,000 feet.

No Japanese aircraft appeared.

When their fuel was gone and they were making their descent to Henderson, they encountered a large flight of mixed Navy and Marine F4Fs climbing upward.

"Cactus Fighter leader, Galloway."

"Go ahead, Galloway."

"What's up?"

"There's supposed to be three recon aircraft and twenty Zeroes up here some-place."

"Haven't seen a thing."

"Lucky you."

Galloway pushed the nose of the Wildcat over and down. If there were twenty Zeroes in the air—and if the Coastwatchers said there were, you could bank on it—the worst situation to be in was nearly out of gas and trying to get on the ground.

He allowed the airspeed indicator to come close to the red line before retarding the throttle. When he glanced out the window he could see Bill Dunn.

Dunn—apparently holding the stick with his knees—had both hands free to mimic some guy holding a Springfield rifle to his shoulder and wincing in pain and surprise at the recoil.

Galloway, smiling, shook his head.

(THREE)
Headquarters, First Marine Division
Guadalcanal, Solomon Islands
1605 Hours 13 September 1942

Looking something like a schoolteacher, Major General Archer Vandergrift, com-manding the First Marine Division, stood with an eighteen-inch ruler in his hand in front of the situation map in the G-3 Section. A technical sergeant was nearby, armed with a piece of cloth and a red and black grease pencil, prepared to make corrections to the map as necessary.

The "students" were the general staff: the G-1 (Personnel), the G-2 (Intelligence), the G-3 (Plans & Operations), the G-4 (Supply), plus Lieutenant Colonel William Whaling, executive officer of the Fifth Marines; Lieutenant Colonel Hayden Price, commanding 5th Battalion, Eleventh Marines (the artillery); and Lieutenant Colonel Merritt Edson, commanding 1st Raider Battalion.

"I realize you all would rather be with your units, so I'll make this as quick as I can," General Vandergrift said. "I just want to make absolutely sure the left hand knows what the right hand is doing."

He turned to the map.

"Red Mike sent his people out at sunrise to recover what he had lost during the night," he said, using the pointer. "There was not much resistance, and they were able to regain their fighting positions. When the Raiders withdrew last night, they had to leave the food they took from the Japanese at Tasimboko. The Japanese now have it back."

He moved the pointer. "The Parachute Battalion's Able Company, which was here, had no contact with the Japanese last night. We moved it down here, to the level area, so they could support the Raiders when they went out to take back their positions. They got this far when they were taken under fire from concealed positions. The company commander . . . who was that, Mike?"

"McKennan, General. Captain William."

"Right. Good man. He made the correct decision not to get into a major scrap on what was a very narrow front. So he moved around here, got some artillery support, and this time only ran into some sniper opposition. He was where he was supposed to be by about 1500.

"Charley Company of the Raiders was pretty badly hurt last night, here on the right. They were withdrawn and replaced by Able Company, plus what was left of Dog Company, which we have disbanded.

"Edson has pulled his line back about one hundred yards, to here," Vandergrift said. "That shortened it, and it will force the Japanese to attack the open ground here. We have moved the machine guns around to take advantage of that field of fire, and the rifle positions have been built up all along that area.

"I called Mike about three o'clock and told him that I was going to send in the 2nd of the Fifth to back him up, and that as soon as I could find Jack Stecker, I was going to send him up there to look around. He told me that Jack was up there first thing this morning. Why wasn't I surprised?"

There was dutiful laughter.

"The problem of getting 2nd of the Fifth into position is that they have to cross the Henderson runway to get there," Vandergrift continued. "And the runway, obviously, has been about as busy as it can get. Whaling, have you got an estimate from Jack Stecker about when he'll be in position?"

Colonel Whaling stood up. He did not appear happy.

"Sir, I talked to him a few minutes ago. He says it will be long after dark."

"Can't be helped," Vandergrift said. "Jack will do the best he can." He turned to the map and used the ruler as a pointer again.

"Price has moved his 105s out of the woods here and into firing positions here south of the Henderson runway. Are your guns laid in, Price?" Since the Division's 155mm cannon had not been off-loaded during the invasion, the 105mm howitzer was the largest artillery piece available.

Colonel Price stood up.

"If they're not, Sir, they will be within minutes."

"OK. As soon as that happens, everybody but the gunners will move back to about here," Vandergrift said, pointing, "where they will form a secondary line in case the Japanese get through the Raiders and the Parachutists. If that happens, gentlemen, the artillery will be lost, and there won't be very much to keep the Japanese from taking Henderson."

There was no response.

"Are there any additions, corrections, or observations that anyone wishes to make?" Vandergrift asked politely.

There were none.

"That will be all, gentlemen, thank you," General Vandergrift said.

The Japanese attacked at 1830. They directed their major effort to the right of the Raider defense line at almost exactly the point where they'd attacked the previous night.

(FOUR)
Police Headquarters
Saint Louis, Missouri
1405 Hours 15 September 1942

When the knock on the frosted glass panel of his office door destroyed his concentration, Captain Karl Hart, commanding officer of the Homicide Bureau, was trying to make sense of a police officer's report of a death the previous evening by gas asphyxiation.

He had just concluded that the reporting officer was not only a functional illiterate, but a genuine goddamn moron to boot.

He ignored the knock and tried to make sense of a sentence that read, so far as he could make out, "body dispozd by coronary's office."

Coronary's *obviously was supposed to mean* Coroner's, *but what the hell was* dispozd?

There was another knock on the frosted glass panel of his door, this time an impatient knock.

"Wait a goddamned minute!"

He reached for his telephone and placed it on his shoulder. Holding it in place with his chin, he started to dial a number.

The doorknob turned, followed by the faint rattling noise it always made when it was being opened. In fury, he turned to face it.

Goddamn it, I said to wait a goddamned minute!

"Is this where I go to have somebody homicided?" Sergeant George Hart asked innocently.

"George," Captain Hart said.

"Hi, Pop."

"George," Captain Hart repeated, and then got up and walked around the desk and put out his hand.

His son shook it.

"Damn," Captain Hart said. "You could have let us know you were coming."

No, I couldn't. That would have required explanations.

"You been out to the house? Seen your mother?"

"I went there from the airport."

"What did she say?"

"She asked was I here, and had I seen you," George reported truthfully.

"Jesus H. Christ!" Captain Hart said. And then, though it had been a long, long time since he'd done it: *What the hell, why not?* he asked himself as he put his arms around his son and hugged him. "Damn, it's good to see you!"

It's the first time in God knows how long, George realized, *since I was a kid, that Pop's hugged me.*

He felt his eyes water, and that surprised him.

"How much leave they give you?"

"Five days."

"That's all?"

"That's all they give you."

"Jesus, you can hardly get from down there and back in five days," his father said. Then he saw the chevrons on George's tunic.

"You're a sergeant? Jesus, that was quick."

"The Marines recognize good men when they see one," George said.

"Look," his father said, "I got a report on a citizen stuck his head in the oven that's so bad I don't even believe it."

"Since when do you handle suicides?"

"When the guy's brother's a Monsignor and the Commissioner told me he don't want to hear the word suicide. You know the Catholics, they won't bury a suicide in holy ground—"

"*Consecrated,*" George corrected him automatically.

"Consecrated, holy, whatever. I got to talk to the cop—I can't believe this guy, he's so dumb—and then talk to the coroner, and then report to the Commissioner."

"Just out of idle curiosity, what are you going to find out really happened?"

"He slipped on a wet kitchen floor as he was about to light the oven," Captain Hart said, "bumped his head and knocked himself out. And then the gas got him."

"Brilliant." George laughed.

"It was all I could think of," Captain Hart admitted. "Anyway, you don't want to hang around here. I'll meet you in Mooney's in thirty minutes."

"OK."

"Maybe you better call your mother and ask her does she want to eat out someplace?"

"She said she was going to make a pot roast, and I was to bring you home no later than half past six."

"OK. So we'll have a couple of snorts and go home."

"OK, Pop."

"You got some money?"

"Yeah, sure."

"You said you went home from the airport. So what did an airplane ticket cost you? Where'd you get the money?" Captain Hart said, as he took a wad of bills from his pocket and peeled off two five-dollar bills. "Don't argue with me, I'm your father."

"OK, Pop. Thank you."

"Thirty minutes, George," Captain Hart said, and then there was another unexpected gesture of affection. He rubbed his hand over his son's head, but masked the affection by saying, "Jesus, I love your haircut."

Mooney's was crowded. Cops who had come off the four-in-the-afternoon shift change mingled with courthouse people who seldom waited until the clock said five before closing up.

George smiled at familiar faces and even shook a couple of hands, but there was no one in the bar he knew well enough to sit down with.

He found a stool toward the back of the room, near the Wurlitzer jukebox. Before he sat down, he reached behind the Wurlitzer and turned the volume control way down.

"Welcome home, George," Jerry the bartender said, offering his hand. He was a plump young man wearing a black vest and an immaculate white shirt with the cuffs turned up. "Your Uncle George was in a while ago, and Ramirez just left."

"I'll be around a while. My father's coming in."

"Seagram's & Seven? Or a beer?"

"Jerry, you got any Famous Grouse?"

"What the hell is that?"

"Scotch."

The bartender shook his head, no. "I got some Dewar's and there's some . . ." He turned, searched the array of bottles against the mirror and put a bottle of Haig & Haig Pinch Bottle on the bar. ". . . of this."

"That. Straight. Water on the side."

"When'd you start drinking that?" Jerry the bartender asked as he poured a very generous shot in a small, round glass.

"As soon as I found out about it," George said. He took out his wallet and laid a ten-dollar bill on the bar.

"Put that away," Jerry said. "Your money's no good in here."

"Thanks, Jerry," George said, and started to put the twenty back in his wallet. Then he remembered the two fives his father had given him, and took them from his pocket.

The truth of the matter, Jerry, is that I was having a couple of drinks with my pal Pick Pickering—you know, the guy whose grandfather owns Saint Louis' snootiest hotel, the Foster Pierre Marquette, and forty other hotels—right after we flew under the Golden Gate Bridge in his grandfather's airplane; and Ol' Pick said, "George, if we're going to drink as much as I think we are, you better get off that Seagram's & Seven and onto The Bird." So I got onto The Bird, which is what my pal Pick calls Famous Grouse; and I got to like it, right from the first.

Would I bullshit you, Jerry?

He took a swallow of the water on the side and then poured scotch into it.

"My God," Pick said, *"you were a vice cop and I have to teach you about booze? Upon my word as an officer and a gentleman, Sergeant Hart, the way one drinks whiskey—and by whiskey, I mean scotch whiskey—is to mix it in equal portions with just a little bit of ice."*

I wonder why I used to think scotch tasted like medicine? George thought after he'd taken a sip of his drink. *Well, what the hell, when I was a little kid and Pop ate oysters, I used to want to throw up. And now I love them. They're what they call an acquired taste.*

He turned on his stool and caught the arm of a waitress.

"Hey, George," she said, "I thought that was you. You look real nice in your uniform."

"Hazel, could you get me a dozen oysters?"

"You bet your life I could, honey."

When he turned back to the bar, Jerry handed him a newspaper.

"Seen the paper?"

"No, I haven't. Thank you."

He unfolded the paper and spread it on the bar. There was a four-column picture of an aircraft carrier, and below it the headline: AIRCRAFT CARRIER "WASP" SUNK IN PACIFIC.

He read the story:

> Washington, DC Sept 15 (AP)—In a terse announcement this afternoon, the Navy announced that the aircraft carrier USS 'Wasp' was lost at sea yesterday (Sept 14), with heavy loss of life, while operating in the Solomon Islands area.
>
> The Navy said that initial reports indicate the 'Wasp' was struck by at least three Japanese torpedoes from a submarine in an action which also saw a destroyer sunk, and serious, but not fatal, damage caused to the battleship USS 'North Carolina.'

There was other war news, some of it accompanied by photographs:

> In North Africa, German airfields at Benghazi have been attacked by units of the British Long Range Desert Group, and severe damage is reported.
>
> American bombers have attacked Japanese bases in the Aleutian Islands.
>
> The Russian forces defending Stalingrad are in desperate shape. The defense perimeter has been reduced to a thirty-mile area. The German High Command has predicted the fall of the city within a matter of days.

Word has reached London that the Cunard liner 'Laconia,' carrying British military dependent families and Italian prisoners of war, has been sunk off the Cape of Good Hope by the German submarine U-156.

On Guadalcanal, in the Solomon Islands, the Marines have succeeded in turning back a Japanese attack on 'Bloody Ridge' near the American air base, Henderson Field. Severe Japanese losses were reported.

Jesus Christ, Pick and Dick Stecker are on their way to Guadalcanal! It doesn't seem so fucking impersonal if you know people.

An elbow jabbed Hart in the ribs. He turned and saw that he'd been joined by a fellow noncommissioned officer of The United States Marine Corps, Staff Sergeant Howard H. Wertz, USMC, the miserable, lying cocksucker who conned him into joining the crotch by telling him he could be sort of a Marine detective.

Sliding his beer glass around in a little puddle on the bar, Wertz gave him a smirking smile.

"You look good, kid," he said. "Parris Island must have been good for you."

"Yeah, all that fresh air," Hart said. "Still scrounging up all the warm bodies you can for the crotch, are you, Sergeant?"

"You know how it is, kid. You're in The Corps, you do what they tell you."

I don't really want to stick his head in the spittoon or knock his teeth down his throat. How come? Christ knows, I thought about doing just that by the goddamned hour.

"I guess so," Hart said.

"You know what I wondered when I saw you, Hart?"

"Haven't the faintest fucking idea, Sergeant."

"I wondered where you got those chevrons on your sleeve."

"Oh, you wondered about that, huh?"

"Yeah, I mean, what the hell. I'm not normally a suspicious person, but what is it now, eight weeks since you went off to Parris Island?"

Hart did the arithmetic in his head.

"Closer to ten, actually."

"OK, ten, then. You don't get to be a Sergeant in The Corps in ten fucking weeks."

"Some people do."

"You know what I think, Hart? And I'm really disappointed. I think you sewed those stripes on to impress broads."

"Well, I admit it works. Some girls think Marine sergeants are really hot shit."

"Yeah, well, assholes like you wearing stripes they haven't earned really piss me off. You better have some orders to go with them stripes."

He held out his hand.

"No orders, Sergeant," Hart said. "Sorry."

He reached into the breast pocket of his tunic and took out his leather identification folder. He handed it to Wertz.

Wertz examined with great care the credentials of Special Agent George F. Hart of the Office of Naval Investigation.

"Go fuck yourself, Wertz," Hart said, taking them back.

"I'm not sure I believe that," Wertz said.

"Call me on it, you sonofabitch! Call the MPs and tell them you don't believe it. If I report that I showed you those credentials and told you to get out of my way, and you didn't, you'll be out of Saint Louis on your way to a rifle company so quick your asshole won't catch up with you for a month."

Staff Sergeant Wertz made a decision.

"OK. So I'm sorry."

"Get the fuck out of my sight," Hart said. "I don't want to see you in here again as long as I'm in Saint Louis."

Staff Sergeant Wertz slid off his stool and walked out of Mooney's bar.

"What the hell was that all about?" Jerry the bartender asked.

"Nothing," Hart said. "Forget it."

"You want another one of these?" Jerry asked, holding up the Haig & Haig.

"Yeah, Jerry, please."

I don't feel good about Wertz. Why not?

"Why do I have this feeling that you liked it as well as I did?" Elizabeth "Beth" Lathrop asked, in his bedroom in the suite in the Andrew Foster. When she spoke, neither Beth Lathrop nor George Hart was wearing clothes. And they were both sprawled in more or less close proximity across his bed.

"Cut the bullshit," he said, and swung his legs out of bed and went to the bottle of scotch on the dresser.

When Elizabeth "Beth" Lathrop came into the suite, she was wearing a blue cotton dress he would remember the rest of his life. As he would remember the rest of her, the long blond hair parted in the middle and held in place with a bow in back. And the smell of her perfume. And her blue eyes (matching her dress) and her long delicate fingers.

And now her perfect, pink-tipped breasts and the delicate tuft of blond hair at her crotch and the incredible warm softness within.

"Meaning what?"

"Meaning you did what you were paid to do. Leave it at that, for Christ's sake. Skip the bullshit."

He watched her face in the mirror over the dresser. It tightened, and then she shrugged.

Don't tell me I hurt your feelings, honey. You didn't really expect me to believe that "it was good for me, too" bullshit, did you?

He poured scotch into a glass and glanced over at the bed. She pulled the sheet over her. He lifted the glass toward her and caught her eye.

"Yes, thank you, I will," she said.

He walked to the bed.

"How did a nice girl like you get into this?" he asked. What a damn fool silly question for a vice cop to ask, *he thought as he asked it.*

"You know the rules," she said. "That's one of the questions you're not supposed to ask."

She pushed herself up against the headboard, pulled the sheet over her chest, and then reached for the glass.

"Thank you," she said, politely.

"Professional curiosity," he said over his shoulder as he went to make himself a drink. "What was it? Your husband threw you out? There's a kid somewhere, and this is the only way you can feed it? I think you're too smart to get under a pimp."

"No husband. No kid. No pimp. What did you mean, 'professional curiosity'?"

"I've heard a lot of stories . . ."

"I'll bet you have. I bet you ask all the girls, right?"

"I'm a cop. Or was. A vice squad detective."

"Oddly enough, I believe that," she said. "You said 'was'?"

"Now I'm in The Marine Corps."

"I wondered about that," she said. "Pick said you were an old pal from Saint Louis."

"I'm from Saint Louis."

"But you're not old pals?"

He shook his head, no.

"I work for his father."

"Oh, that's right, his father is a captain in the Navy."

"A general in The Marine Corps," he corrected her, laughing. "In Washington."

"Close," she said, and smiled.

He shook his head.

"So that wasn't a threat to make trouble for me?" she asked.

"No. Of course not."

"I've never had any trouble . . . been arrested."

"That's simply a question of time. Maybe it would be good for you. Twenty-four hours in the slam with a dozen girls off the street might make you understand what the hell you're doing to yourself."

"What have we got here, a Marine who used to be a vice detective? With morals?"

"You're so goddamned beautiful! You don't have to fuck every man who comes along!"

"Thank you," she said, "but I don't fuck every man who comes along. The only reason I fucked you was that I couldn't find a third girl for the job."

"You're running a string?" he asked, genuinely surprised. The madams of his acquaintance, and he knew half a dozen, were not at all like this girl. Most were fat and middle-aged, and all were hard as nails, with cold eyes.

"I'm a photographer," she said.

"That's a new one."

"You asked."

"Go on."

"An advertising photographer, nothing special, mostly for catalogs and brochures. The way you get commissions is to be nice to art directors. Then they started asking me if I had friends who might like to earn a little pocket money. Somebody once said that the way to get rich is to identify a need and then fill it. So I provide a service. I have associates. Do we have to keep this up?"

"Pickering's paying for this?"

"Do you have any idea how much housekeeping supplies this hotel uses? Not to mention how many Foster hotels there are? Keeping the heir apparent happy is just good business. They take it off their income tax as 'client relations.'"

"But he knows?" he asked, but it was more of a statement.

"Of course he knows. Pick's a very good-looking fellow, but he's not that good-looking. I shouldn't have to tell you this, but there's no such thing as a free lunch."

He shook his head.

"Did you ever hear that you shouldn't look a gift horse in the mouth?" Beth asked.

"You're so goddamned beautiful! You shouldn't be doing this! You don't have to do this!"

"There's another rule," Beth said. "Clients are not supposed to worry about the girls."

"Fuck you!"

"That's all you're supposed to do," Beth said. "Let's leave it at that. And this time I won't tell you how much I liked it."

He met her eyes, and then looked quickly away. Beth made him very uncomfortable.

"Have you got a girl back in Saint Louis? Is that it? You're consumed with guilt?"

"No girl back in Saint Louis. No girl anywhere."

"I'm surprised," she said.

"Why should you be surprised?"

"Because you strike me as a nice guy," Beth said.

"You know what's really strange?" George said. "I really did like doing it with you. I never liked it so much before."

"I'm pleased."

"So laugh."

"Sorry."

"Goddamn you!"

"I really am pleased," she said. "I probably shouldn't tell you this, but every once in a while . . . it's not just business."

"Am I supposed to believe that?"

"Believe whatever you goddamn please!"

Their eyes met.

After a moment she said, "Why not? It's already paid for."

"Just for the hell of it, how much?"

"For the three of us, three hundred dollars."

"You could hire every whore in Saint Louis for three hundred dollars."

"Come on," Beth said, making a gesture at his midsection. "Obviously, you want to."

He'd never wanted to sink himself in any woman half as desperately as he wanted to be in this one again.

It's all the fucking booze, *he thought, as he walked to the bed and pulled the sheet off her.* The booze, and that insane goddamn airplane ride under the bridge. All of it. I'm a little crazy, that's all. I'm too smart to fall for a whore, even one as beautiful, and nice, as this one.

"What the hell is that you're drinking?" Captain Karl Hart asked his son.

"Scotch. They make it in Scotland."

"Jerry, give me some real whiskey, and give him another of those. When did you start drinking scotch?"

"I don't know. How's the suicide?"

"Accident victim, accident victim," Captain Hart said. "I just checked. The undertaker got the lipstick and rouge off him, and the women's underwear, and I talked to the cop on the scene, and there's no further problem."

Hart had one final thought about Beth Lathrop: *There's one thing you have to say about her, she's not the kind of girl you could bring home to meet the folks.*

(FIVE)
Ferdinand Six
Buka, Solomon Islands
15 September 1942

They decided to move out. They were out of choices.

For one thing they had to eat.

They'd started with more smoked pig than the ten pounds or so Sergeant Steve Koffler found on the morning he thought everybody had taken off and left him: At Ian's orders, Patience had taken twice that much more and hidden it in the rocks by the stream, in a small cave that could be sealed with rocks and protected from wildlife and insects.

And then Ian stalked another wild pig and impaled it on his MACHETE, SUBSTITUTE STANDARD, and for two days the three of them feasted on roast pig. Ian didn't want to risk smoking it, because of the smoke, and Steve figured there was no point in arguing with him. So they roasted it over the last of their dry wood, which was smokeless. The pig was pretty good, even without salt.

But now just about everything was gone. And the men had not returned from looking for Lieutenant Reeves and Lieutenant Howard. In fact, they hadn't even sent a messenger back—suggesting the unpleasant possibility that they had run into the Japs and would not be returning.

So they took their small arms and ammunition (the British Lee-Enfield rifles and their .303 ammunition) into the jungle and buried them. The rifles in one place, their bolts in another, and the ammunition in still another.

Steve thought that was mostly bullshit. The Japanese were not going to wander around in the jungle looking for rifles and ammo. Nor was he, Ian, or anyone else going to come back and dig them up. They could just as easily have left them in the hut with the radio for the Japs to find.

As he was spreading a layer of dirt on his rifle, he wondered what he should do about reporting in. Should he get on the air and tell Townsville or Pearl Harbor that FRD6 was leaving the net for an indefinite period?

He decided against that. It just might happen that he could come back; but if he had signed off the net, those by-the-book assholes would give him all sorts of static about coming back on.

Though he recognized it as whistling in the dark, the hope that he might get back on the air later almost made him feel comfortable about leaving the Hallicrafters intact. The rotten thing about that was the Japs would probably find it. If he was absolutely certain that the Japs would actually get it, he would have smashed the sonofabitch. But he wasn't certain of that. So in the end he compromised. He took all but one of the crystals that controlled the frequencies, wrapped them in the last remnant of his skivvy shirt, and put them in the pocket of his utility jacket.

He made one last report, this time to Townsville, for the atmospherics were such that he couldn't reach Pearl Harbor. And then he signaled Patience to stop pedaling the generator.

Feeling a strange mixture of sadness and blind rage, he left the hut for what he thought would be the last time.

When he got outside, Edward James and Lieutenant Reeves were in the clearing. Reeves looked like a walking corpse, and the clothes he had on him were rags.

"What about Lieutenant Howard?" Steve blurted.

"I'm delighted to see you too, old chap," Reeves said. "I appreciate the warmth of your reception."

"We thought you were all dead," Steve blurted.

"We sodding well should be," Reeves said. "Mother did not raise me to be a sodding pack mule."

"What?"

"We struck gold," Reeves reported. "A sodding Nip truck all alone on a ration run."

"No shit?"

"Which we have carried up and down every sodding hill on this sodding island."

"Anybody get hurt?"

"Your lieutenant sprained his ankle. The chaps are carrying him in."

"That's all?"

Reeves nodded.

Sergeant Steve Koffler felt like crying.

(SIX)
The Foster Lafayette Hotel
Washington, D.C.
1630 Hours 19 September 1942

Just after he knocked on the door to Senator Richmond Fowler's suite, Sergeant George Hart noticed a doorbell button nearly hidden in the framework of the door. He had just put his finger out to it when the door opened.

A tall, trim, silver-haired woman in a cotton skirt and fluffy blouse smiled at him.

She really must have been a looker when she was young.

"Sergeant Hart, right?" she asked. "Colonel Rickabee said you were coming over."

"Yes, Ma'am."

She gave him her hand. A wedding ring was her only jewelry, but pinned to her blouse was a cheap metal pin, two blue stars on a white shield background. It signified that she had two members of her immediate family serving in the Armed Forces. George's mother had been wearing one, with one star, when he'd gone to the house from the airport.

"I'm Patricia Pickering," she said, "but I suppose that a detective like you will have already deduced that, right?"

"Yes, Ma'am."

"I'd like to apologize for what my idiot son did to you, Sergeant," she said. "To put that behind us."

"Lieutenant Pickering was very nice to me, Ma'am."

"Was that before or after he flew you under the Golden Gate Bridge?" she responded, gently sarcastic. "That was inexcusable! Stupid enough on his part, and *inexcusable* to take you with him."

He had been following her into the sitting room.

"Dick, this is Sergeant Hart," she said. "Sergeant, this is Senator Fowler."

Jesus Christ, a United States Senator is actually getting out of his chair to shake my hand!

"How do you do, Sergeant?" Fowler said. "I've been hearing a good deal about you lately, all of it good. I'm quite an admirer of your commanding officer."

"Yes, Sir."

"Correction," Senator Fowler said, "I'm quite an admirer of *Colonel Rickabee*. I'm very fond of your commanding officer, but as Mrs. Pickering and I were just saying, he does need a keeper; and according to Rickabee, you're just the man for the job."

"You're putting the sergeant on a spot, Dick," Patricia Pickering said.

"I certainly didn't mean to," Fowler said. "I meant to make the sergeant welcome."

"Thank you, Sir."

"Where are your things, Sergeant?" Patricia Pickering asked.

"Ma'am?"

"Your uniforms. Your clothing."

"Oh. Captain Sessions arranged for me to share an apartment. It's a couple of blocks away. I went there first."

"We were just talking about that, too," Fowler said. "We think it would be better for you and Lieutenant Moore to be in here with the General. Would that pose a problem for you?''

''Sir, I go where I'm told to go. But I don't know what Colonel Rickabee would say. Or General Pickering. Or, for that matter, Lieutenant Moore.''

''I don't think Colonel Rickabee will have any objection,'' Fowler said. ''I'll have a word with him. And that should take care of any objections Lieutenant Moore might have. You know him, I gather?''

''Yes, Sir.''

''And *General* Pickering's vote doesn't count,'' Patricia Pickering said firmly. ''There's a small suite next door,'' she went on, gesturing toward the wall behind Hart. ''I've asked them to put a door in. It should be there by the time Lieutenant Moore gets out of the hospital. With a little luck, that will be before my husband does.''

''For the time being you can stay in the spare bedroom,'' Fowler said. ''Is that all right with you?''

''Sir, I do what I'm told.''

Well, I guess if your father owns the hotel, and you want a door put in, they put a door in.

''There's one more thing, Sergeant,'' Patricia Pickering said. ''One of our stewards, a fine old fellow named Matthew Howe, is retired here in Washington—''

What the hell is she talking about?

''—and he is willing—actually, he seemed delighted when I asked him—to look after my husband. He'll be coming in every day to take care of him.''

''What Mrs. Pickering is saying, Sergeant,'' Senator Fowler explained, ''is that Howe will take care of General Pickering's linen and pass the canapés, leaving you and Lieutenant Moore free to take care of him in other ways.''

''Yes, Sir.''

''Our first priority, *your* first priority, is to see that General Pickering does nothing that might hinder his recovery,'' Senator Fowler said. ''Obviously, Mrs. Pickering and I have a personal interest in that. But I would also strongly suggest to you, Sergeant, that he's not going to be much use to The Marine Corps, for that matter to the country, if he winds up back in the hospital. Do I make my point?''

''Yes, Sir.''

''And finally,'' Fowler said, with a vague gesture toward Pick's mother, ''Mrs. Pickering is a little concerned that both you and Lieutenant Moore are armed. I have told her that J. Edgar Hoover and the FBI have done their job, and that there is absolutely no danger to General Pickering from the enemy here in Washington.''

''Then why do they need guns?'' Patricia Fleming asked quickly, rising to the moment. ''My God, Dick, Fleming has his old Marine Corps .45 in there in his dresser!''

She pointed toward the bedroom.

''Mrs. Pickering,'' Hart said, ''every cop carries a gun. Ninety-five percent of cops never take them out of their holsters from the time they join the force until they retire.''

Fowler looked at him with approval; Patricia Fleming looked at him dubiously.

''Have you ever had to take yours from its holster?'' she asked.

I can't lie to this woman.

''Yes, Ma'am, I've had to do that twice.''

''That's why Rickabee assigned him to Fleming, Patricia,'' Fowler said. ''You should find that reassuring.''

''I find Sergeant Hart very reassuring,'' she said. ''Everybody carrying a gun disturbs me.''

''Speaking of the FBI, Sergeant,'' Senator Fowler said, ''I had a chat with Mr.

Hoover this morning. He tells me that since they've come up with very little information about the lunatic who flew his airplane under the Golden Gate Bridge, and since no damage was done, and since the FBI has more important cases to work on, the FBI in San Francisco has been instructed to put that investigation on the back burner."

Hart saw a faint smile in Fowler's eyes and on his lips.

Jesus Christ, Hart thought, remembering the suicide in women's underwear his father had been dealing with back home, *I guess the fix is in everywhere.*

"I would be very surprised if that lunatic was ever hauled before the bar of justice," Fowler added. "You know how these things are."

"Yes, Sir."

"And thank you, Sergeant," Patricia Pickering said, "before I forget it, for getting the lunatic off to war before he got in any more trouble."

She met his eyes and smiled.

"I'm on an Eastern Airlines flight out of here at 9:30 tomorrow morning. My husband pointed out to me this afternoon that I really should get back to San Francisco. After all, you're here to take care of him, and I have a shipping company to run."

"Yes, Ma'am."

"Over his objections, I am going to the hospital to say goodbye before I leave. I'd be grateful if you would go with me."

"Yes, Ma'am."

"It is my intention, Sergeant, to tell my husband that the Secretary of the Navy personally ordered you to report to him the very first time my husband does something stupid."

"Yes, Ma'am."

"I told Frank Knox," Senator Fowler said, "that I would relay that order to you."

"Yes, Sir."

"I was about to ask you," Patricia Fleming said, "to meet me here about half past seven in the morning. But I just had a better idea: Why don't you take the car and go get your things and bring them back? Move in now, in other words? That way we'd both be here in the morning."

"Yes, Ma'am. What car?"

"It's a Buick my husband bought when he first came here. It's parked out in front. The doorman should have the keys."

You didn't really think this woman would have her car parked anywhere else, did you?

"Yes, Ma'am."

"And then we'll all have dinner. Considering what you've already done for me, and what my husband is certain to do to you, that's the very least I can do."

X

When Major Jake Dillon, USMCR, debarked from the aircraft at Anacostia Naval Air Station at 2100 the previous evening, a message for him stated that a room at the Anacostia Bachelor Officer Quarters had been reserved for him, and that Brigadier General J. J. Stewart, Director, Public Affairs Division, Headquarters, USMC, would see him in his office at 0745 the next morning.

Although Major Dillon was fully aware of the penalties provided for a Marine who failed to appear at the proper time and the proper place in the properly appointed uniform—which was the definition for Absence With Out Leave—it took him no longer than five seconds to put himself at risk of those penalties. *Fuck him,* he thought, *I'm entitled to a good night's sleep and a good breakfast.*

Instead of cheerfully and willingly complying with his lawful orders, Major Dillon caught a cab to the Willard Hotel and obtained the key to the suite Metro-Magnum Studios maintained in the Washington landmark.

He took a long hot shower, sent his uniform to the valet service for an emergency cleaning and pressing, and consumed about half a bottle of Haig & Haig Pinch Bottle scotch, while enjoying his room service dinner of filet mignon with *pommes frites,* topped off with a strawberry shortcake dessert.

In the morning, he rose at eight, had another long hot shower, and then ate a room service breakfast of freshly squeezed orange juice, milk, breakfast steak, two eggs sunny side up, rye toast, and a pot of coffee. He then read *The Washington Star* from cover to cover, excepting only the classified advertisements.

Even in the fresh light of day, his conscience did not bother him vis-à-vis his AWOL status, nor was he concerned about the consequences of his act. *What can they do to me? Send me back to Guadalcanal?* This was not the first time he had been AWOL, and more than likely it would not be the last. And this time he had some justification:

He had just gone through a rough two weeks.

What he—privately, of course—thought of as the road company of *Dillon's Heroes* had made it from Melbourne to Pearl Harbor without any problems. Unfortunately, they arrived in Pearl a day after a hospital ship had come in. For a number of valid reasons, both Army and Naval medical authorities in Hawaii were anxious to send those requiring long-term care home to the States. It obviously made more sense to give the badly wounded priority over Dillon's war bond tour heroes.

And so they had been bumped from available airspace to the States.

At first Jake thought this was probably a stroke of good luck. Compared to the healthy, well-nourished people at Pearl, Dillon's undernourished, wan, and battered heroes looked like death warmed over.

And so he decided to arrange rooms for them in the Royal Hawaiian. Three or four days' rest on the beach and some good food would do them wonders. (He would even look into getting them better-fitting uniforms.)

While they were basking on the beach, he'd go out to Fort Shafter. A former Metro-Magnum Studios lab guy, now commissioned into the Army Signal Corps, was running a photographic laboratory there. For auld lang syne—if not the war effort—he would soup the undeveloped film Jake had carried from Henderson Field in the "borrowed" whole-blood container. The sooner it was souped, the better. Christ only knew what damage the heat and humidity had already done.

He had no sooner explained the change in plans to the cast of *Dillon's Heroes*—there was no objection, save from Lieutenant R. B. Macklin, who clearly saw himself as the star of the troupe and could not wait to get onstage—than they encountered Pearl Harbor Standard Operating Procedure.

In order to keep those returning from exotic areas from infecting the natives with exotic diseases, returnees were required to submit to a medical examination. Once they had successfully passed medical muster, they would be permitted to leave the base and enter the real world.

The Navy doctors took one look at *Dillon's Heroes* and decided that entry into the real world was out of the question: All of them—Major Jake Dillon included—would be admitted to the hospital for more complete physical examinations and treatment.

It took six days before pressure from Washington forced the Navy Hospital, reluctantly, to discharge them from the hospital—only on condition that they fly immediately to San Diego for admittance to the U.S. Navy Hospital there.

Because of all this, Jake was unable to get the Guadalcanal combat footage souped. And worse, the doctors took away the whole-blood container, promising to inform his superiors of his blatant misappropriation of Navy Medical Corps property.

After Jake Dillon's failure to bring them anywhere near the Royal Hawaiian Hotel or the world-famous beach at Waikiki—not to mention his ineptitude in dealing with the medical bureaucracy—*Dillon's Heroes* concluded they were in the care of a world-class incompetent.

And to judge by his URGENT radio messages to Dillon, Brigadier General J. J. Stewart, Director, Public Affairs Division, Headquarters, USMC, held a like opinion. He was absolutely unable to understand how a major could fuck up so simple a task as bringing eight people from Melbourne—especially since Brigadier General J. J. Stewart himself had arranged for their travel.

San Diego turned out to be slightly less a pain in the ass—only because Jake was able to get the film souped. But that was just good luck: Jake ran into Tyrone Power in the hospital coffee shop. The actor was taking a precommissioning physical, and then he was driving back to L.A. The two men chatted awhile, and one thing led to another. And so, even though it was now packaged in an ice-filled garbage can, Power carried Jake's film back to Los Angeles in his Packard 220 roadster and dropped it off at the Metro-Magnum Film Laboratory.

The Navy, meanwhile, amazed that any hospital could have discharged *Dillon's Heroes,* wanted to keep them until they were fully recovered. It took four days and several telephone calls from General Stewart to get them released. And it took yet another day to talk the local Marine bureaucrats into issuing them leave orders.

During each of his many icy telephone conversations with Major Dillon, General Stewart not only pointed out that the whole operation was ten days behind schedule, but that he failed to see why the Heroes could not have waited until the end of the war bond tour before taking their leaves.

In short, Jake Dillon was in no great rush to make his 0745 appointment with Brigadier General J. J. Stewart, Director, Public Affairs Division, Headquarters, USMC.

* * *

When Major Dillon examined himself in the full-length mirror in his bathroom, his tailor-made uniform now seemed sewn for a bigger brother, and he himself looked like hell. His face was drained of color, his eyes were sunken, and there were bags under them.

It wasn't that bottle of Pinch last night, either, or even the bullshit of the last two weeks. That goddamned Guadalcanal did this to me.

He had a quick image of Guadalcanal—of men standing around in sweat-soaked utilities, weak with malaria or some other goddamned tropical disease, their skin spotted with festering sores.

He forced the image from his mind, adjusted his cover at an angle appropriate to a field-grade Marine feather merchant, and left the Metro-Magnum suite.

"The General will see you now," Brigadier General J. J. Stewart's staff sergeant clerk said.

Dillon tucked his cover under his left arm and marched into the General's office. "Major Dillon reporting, Sir."

When Stewart raised his eyes, Dillon saw disapproval in them. He was familiar with the look.

I am now going to have my ass chewed. Fuck him.

"My God, Dillon, you look awful!" General Stewart said. "Are you all right?"

"I'm a little tired, Sir."

"You were ill, too, weren't you, Dillon?" General Stewart accused. "You just didn't think you should say so, am I right?"

"Everyone on the island is a little sick, General. I'll be all right."

"Damn it, Major! You've got to take care of yourself. What the hell would I do without you?"

"Probably very well, Sir."

"Under other circumstances, Major, I would *order* you to the dispensary. But we have our mission, don't we? And the mission comes first."

"Yes, Sir."

"Where's your film?"

"I think . . . I hope . . . it will be here today, Sir."

"You didn't bring it with you?"

"No, Sir. I arranged to have it souped on the West Coast."

"At San Diego?"

"No, Sir. At Metro-Magnum."

"I'm not entirely sure that was wise. As a matter of fact, I think it was unwise. Certainly, now that I think of it, there must be footage that we wouldn't want to get into the wrong hands. What were you thinking about?"

"Sir, I was very concerned about possible damage to the raw film from heat and humidity. I know the capabilities of the Metro-Magnum lab. I decided the film was so important that it should get the best possible lab work. That meant Metro-Magnum."

General Stewart grunted.

"You don't think it might get into the wrong hands?"

"No, Sir. I'm sure it won't."

Jesus, I didn't think about that. Morty Cohen probably made a duplicate to show his friends. Are those the wrong hands? Morty will be careful who he shows it to. And what the fuck does "wrong hands" mean anyway? There should be a film record somewhere of those kids crumpled up dead, even if it's lousy public relations.

"And it's being sent here? How?"

"It'll probably come in by air, Sir, to the Metro-Magnum suite at the Willard. I thought that would be safest."

"Well, you're the expert, Dillon. But as soon as possible, I'd like to screen that footage."

"As soon as it gets here, I'll set up a screening for you."

"Good. I'm looking forward to it. And in the meantime have a look at this." He handed Dillon a manila folder. Then he suddenly seemed to remember that Jake was standing with his cover under his arm and his right hand in the small of his back—the position officially described as "at ease." "My God, Dillon, sit down," he added.

"Thank you, Sir."

He opened the folder. The pages inside were fastened with a metal clip. The first of these was a newspaper clipping neatly glued to a sheet of paper.

"MACHINE GUN" McCOY HERO OF BLOODY RIDGE

By Robert McCandless
INS War Correspondent

With The First Marine Division Sept 14 (Delayed)—"What we expected to find was his body, but what we found was Japanese bodies stacked like cordwood in front of his position, and McCoy, despite his wounds, ready to take on the rest of the Japanese Army," said Marine First Lieutenant Jonathan S. Swain, of Butte, Montana, and the 1st Raider Battalion, describing what he found when he led a counterattack to retake positions lost in the early stages of the battle for Bloody Ridge.

Staff Sergeant Thomas M. McCoy, 21, of Norristown, Pa., and a veteran of the Marine Raider attack on Makin Island, had been placed in charge of three listening posts in front of the Marine Raider line on Bloody Ridge. Two of the listening posts were wiped out in the first thirty minutes of the Japanese attack, and the two Marines with McCoy in his position were seriously wounded.

This left McCoy in the center of the Japanese attack with a .30 caliber machine gun, plus his personal weapon, a Browning Automatic Rifle.

His orders were to try to fight his way back to the main Marine Raider Line, if it became apparent that he could not hold his position in the face of overwhelming enemy force.

"I couldn't do that," McCoy, a stocky, barrel-chested young man who was a steelworker before becoming a Marine, told this reporter. "Marines don't leave their wounded and run."

So he stayed, using brief interludes in the fierce fighting to render what first aid he could to the men with him, and to recharge the magazines of his Browning Automatic Rifle.

"I had plenty of ammo," McCoy reported, "so all I had to worry about was the machine gun getting so hot it would either jam, or cook off rounds."

(When a great many rounds are fired through the air-cooled Browning Machine Gun, the weapon becomes hot enough to cause cartridges to fire as soon as they enter the action.)

When that happened, McCoy would pick up his Browning Automatic Rifle and fire that until his machine gun cooled enough to fire reliably again.

"There were at least forty Japanese within yards of his position," Lieutenant Swain reported. "There's no telling how many others he killed in the jungle on the other side of the clearing."

McCoy was painfully wounded during his ordeal, once when a Japanese rifle bullet grazed his upper right leg, and several times more when he was struck on the face and chest by Japanese mortar and hand grenade fragments. His hands were blistered from the heat of the machine gun, and bloody from his frantic recharging of automatic rifle magazines.

"I had to order him out of his position," Lieutenant Swain said. "He didn't want to leave until he was sure the wounded men with him had made it to safety."

When he finished the story, Jake raised his eyes to General Stewart.
"One hell of a Marine, wouldn't you agree?" the General said.
"Yes, Sir."
"Take a look at the radio, it's under the news story."
Jake turned the page in the manila folder and found the radio.

URGENT
HQ USMC WASHINGTON DC 1135 20SEP42

COMMANDING GENERAL
FIRST MARINE DIVISION
VIA CINCPAC

1. REFERENCE IS MADE TO THE NEWS STORY BY MR. ROBERT MCCANDLESS, INTERNATIONAL NEWS SERVICE, OF 14SEPT42 DEALING WITH THE EXPLOITS OF SSGT THOMAS M. MCCOY WHICH HAS RECEIVED WIDE DISTRIBUTION THROUGHOUT THE UNITED STATES.

2. IF THE FACTS PRESENTED BY MR. MCCANDLESS ARE TRUE, IT WOULD SEEM THAT SSGT MCCOY SHOULD BE CITED FOR VALOR IN ACTION ABOVE AND BEYOND THE CALL OF DUTY. IF THIS IS THE INTENTION OF YOUR COMMAND, PLEASE ADVISE BY URGENT RADIO THE DECORATION, INCLUDING THE PROPOSED CITATION THEREOF, TO BE RECOMMENDED.

3. SSGT MCCOY, AS SOON AS HIS PHYSICAL CONDITION PERMITS, IS TO BE DETACHED FROM 1ST RAIDER BN AND PLACED ON TEMPORARY DUTY WITH PUBLIC AFFAIRS DIVISION, HQ USMC, WASH DC IN CONNECTION WITH WAR BOND TOUR BEING CONDUCTED BY THIS OFFICE. AN AIR PRIORITY OF AAAA IS ASSIGNED. PAD HQ USMC, ATTN: SPECIAL PROJECTS WILL BE ADVISED BY URGENT RADIO OF DATE AND TIME OF SSGT MCCOY'S DEPARTURE FROM 1ST MARDIV, AND HIS ROUTING, TO INCLUDE ETA PEARL HARBOR HAWAII AND SAN DIEGO CAL.

4. IN CONNECTION WITH THE ABOVE, IT IS SUGGESTED THAT SSGT MCCOY NOT REPEAT NOT BE AWARDED ANY DECORATION FOR VALOR, INCLUDING THE PURPLE HEART MEDAL(S) FOR WOUNDS SUFFERED UNTIL HE IS RETURNED TO THE UNITED STATES. IT IS

CONTEMPLATED THAT A SENIOR USMC OFFICER OR A HIGH RANK-
ING GOVERNMENT OFFICIAL WILL MAKE SUCH AWARD(S).

BY DIRECTION OF THE COMMANDANT:

J. J. STEWART, BRIG GEN, USMC
DIRECTOR, PUBLIC AFFAIRS DIVISION
HQ USMC

"If that story is true, and I have no reason to believe it is not, that sergeant is
going to get the Distinguished Service Cross. Possibly even the Medal of Honor."

"Yes, Sir."

"I am going to recommend to the Commandant the Medal of Honor," General
Stewart said. "But in any event, obviously, the sergeant belongs on your war bond
tour."

"Yes, Sir."

"Do you think it likely that he will encounter on his way home the same kind
of difficulty you did?"

"Yes, Sir. I think he probably will."

"OK. I'll take steps to see that doesn't happen," General Stewart said firmly.
"As soon as I have word on when he's due here, I'll let you know."

"Yes, Sir."

"I had his records checked. He has a sister in Norristown and a brother in The
Corps. An officer. A first lieutenant. Here."

"Sir?"

"I thought it would make a very nice human interest photograph. A Marine officer
welcoming his brother, a sergeant and a hero, home."

"Yes, Sir."

"His brother is assigned here to headquarters. The Office of Management Analysis,
whatever the hell that is. It's in Building T-2032 on the Mall. You know where that
is?"

"Yes, Sir."

"Good, because I want you to go over there and see him. I had one of my people
call over there and they got the runaround. They said they never heard of Lieutenant
K. R. McCoy. I want you to go over there, Jake, and lay your hands on him, tell
him—more importantly tell his superiors—that we need him."

"Aye, aye, Sir. Sir?"

"Yes?"

"Sir, would that wait until tomorrow? I really feel a little bushed. I'd sort of like
to take it easy today."

"Absolutely," General Stewart said after a moment's hesitation. "First thing
tomorrow morning would be fine. Perhaps by then your film will be in from the
West Coast, right?"

"Yes, Sir. It should be."

"You take the day off, Jake," General Stewart said magnanimously. "You've
earned it."

"Yes, Sir. Thank you, General."

(TWO)
Temporary Building T-2032
The Mall
Washington, D.C.
0845 Hours 21 September 1942

Major Jake Dillon had little trouble finding Building T-2032 among its many twins on the Mall; but because he was more than a little hung over and in a foul mood, he grew rapidly annoyed when there was no answer to his repeated knocking on what seemed to be the building's main door.

"What the fuck are these feather merchants up to?" he inquired aloud.

Then he spotted a less imposing door to the left. And when he tried it, it opened. Inside he discovered a set of interior stairs, which he then climbed. At the top of the stairs, he found himself facing a counter. Above the counter, wire mesh rose to the ceiling. A staff sergeant and a civilian examined him curiously from behind the counter.

"Is this the Office of Management whatever?"

"The Office of Management Analysis, yes, Sir," the staff sergeant said.

"I'm looking for First Lieutenant K. R. McCoy," Dillon said, taking a note from his pocket.

"I'm sorry, Sir," the staff sergeant said immediately. "We have no officer by that name, Sir."

"Then you better tell Eighth and Eye," Dillon said, just the near side of nasty. "They say you do."

"I'm sorry, Sir," the sergeant said. "We have no officer by that name."

Dillon became aware of movement behind him. He glanced and saw a second lieutenant, then turned back to the sergeant.

"I want to see the officer in charge of this outfit, please," Dillon said. "Who would that be?"

"That would be General Pickering, Sir."

There was the buzzing sound of a solenoid; a gate in the wire mesh opened and the Second Lieutenant went through it.

"Would you get word to him that Major Dillon of the Public Affairs Office, USMC, would like to see him?"

"General Pickering will not be in today, Sir. Sorry," the staff sergeant said.

"Well, then, goddamn it, Sergeant, tell whoever is in charge here that I want to talk to him."

"Major Dillon!" the Second Lieutenant said.

Dillon looked at him. There was no recognition.

"Do I know you, Lieutenant? More to the point, do you work here?"

"Yes, Sir," the Lieutenant said. "My name is Moore, Sir. We met in Australia."

"In Australia?" Dillon asked, searching his memory.

"You know this officer, Lieutenant? He's been asking for Lieutenant McCoy."

Recognition came to Dillon.

"You were Fleming Pickering's orderly," Dillon accused. And then associations came. The Lieutenant was wearing the woven gold rope worn by aides-de-camp to General Officers. *"General Pickering will not be in today, Sir."*

The kid's name is Moore. He was a buck sergeant at Pickering's house when I went there from New Zealand with Whatsisname, the First MarDiv G-2 who got himself killed right after we landed on the 'Canal.

"Yes, Sir," Second Lieutenant John Marston Moore, USMCR, replied. "More or less."

"What the hell is going on here, Moore?" Dillon demanded.

General Pickering? What the fuck is that all about?

"Is the Colonel back there?" Moore asked.

"Yes, Sir," the civilian behind the counter replied.

"Open the gate, Sergeant, please," Moore said. "Major Dillon, will you come with me, please?"

The solenoid buzzed. Moore put his hand to the gate and pulled it inward.

"This way, please, Major."

"Lieutenant, what about the log?" the staff sergeant asked.

"Log him in on my authority," Moore said.

Dillon followed him through a door, and then down a corridor. He noticed that Moore was walking awkwardly, limping.

"What did you do to your leg?" he asked.

Moore did not reply.

They came to an office at the end of the corridor. Through a partially opened door Dillon saw a skinny civilian sitting at a desk. He had taken off his suit coat. His trousers were held up by a pair of well-worn suspenders.

He glanced up from his desk and saw Moore.

"You want to see me, Moore?"

"Yes, Sir. I think it's important."

The civilian gestured for Moore to enter. Moore motioned for Dillon to precede him.

"This is Major Dillon, Sir," Moore said.

"Who is Major Dillon?" the civilian asked.

"The question in my mind is who the hell are you to ask who I am?" Dillon flared.

The civilian looked at him.

"I think we need some ground rules in here," he said. "Major, I am a colonel in the USMC. If you insist, I will show you an identification card. For the time being, however, I suggest you stand there, at attention and with your mouth shut, until I find out what's going on here."

There was an unmistakable tone of *I-Will-Be-Obeyed* authority in the civilian's voice.

Jake Dillon came to attention, wondering, *If he's a colonel, how come the civilian clothes?*

"OK, John, who is this officer?" Colonel F. L. Rickabee asked.

"He's Major Dillon, Sir. He has something to do with Public Relations."

"Fascinating! And what's he doing here?"

"He's looking for Lieutenant McCoy, Sir. I overheard that as I came through the gate."

Rickabee looked at Dillon.

"If you find this officer—Lieutenant McCoy, you said?—what will you do with him, Major?"

"Colonel, Lieutenant McCoy's brother behaved very heroically on Guadalcanal; he is being returned from Guadalcanal to receive a high decoration."

"And you wanted to tell him about that?"

"No, Sir. General Stewart—"

"Who the hell is General Stewart?"

"Public Affairs, Sir. At Eighth and Eye?"

Rickabee nodded. "Go on."

"General Stewart thinks Lieutenant McCoy would be helpful in connection with getting The Corps some good publicity."

"That's out of the question," Rickabee said. "Forget it. Can you relay that to General Stewart or will I have to do it?"

"I think it would be helpful if you spoke with the General, Sir," Dillon said.

"Sir, there's more," Moore said.

"What would that be?"

"Major Dillon and General Pickering are friends."

"Is that so, Major?"

"If we're talking about Fleming Pickering, yes, Sir. We're old friends."

"Sir, Major Dillon is a friend of Major Banning's too. I don't know if—"

"Do you know what Major Banning's doing for a living these days, Major?" Rickabee interrupted him.

"Yes, Sir, I do."

"Damn!" Rickabee said. "But, now that I think of it, maybe you don't. You tell me what you think Banning's doing."

"Colonel, I don't know who you are," Dillon said. "I'm sure what Banning is doing is classified, and I'm not sure you have the Need to Know."

"Show him your badge, Moore," Rickabee ordered. Moore took his credentials from his pocket and showed them to Dillon.

Jesus Christ, what the hell is this? The last time I see this kid, he's a sergeant passing canapés for Pickering, and now he's a Special Agent of the Office of Naval Intelligence!

"That's his Need to Know. And I'm his boss," Rickabee said. "Good enough?"

"Yes, Sir," Dillon said. "Sir—"

"Close the door, John," Rickabee interrupted him. "And you can pull up a chair, Major. If you're a friend of General Pickering, you're obviously not the asshole of a public relations feather merchant I first thought you were."

Colonel Rickabee was just about finished explaining to Major Dillon the change in Fleming Pickering's military status when there was a knock at his door.

"Come!"

"Colonel," Captain Ed Sessions said, putting his head in the door. "There's an Army officer out here asking for General Pickering."

"Tell him the General will not be in today and ask him what he wants."

"I did, Sir. He said he's a liaison officer for General MacArthur. I think maybe you had better see him."

"Douglas MacArthur?"

"Yes, Sir."

"Jesus Christ! Well, go fetch him."

The door closed and then a minute later, reopened.

"Colonel Rickabee," Captain Sessions announced formally, "Colonel DePress."

A lieutenant colonel marched into Rickabee's office. He was in Army Pink and Green uniform, the lapels decorated with the insignia of the General Staff Corps, his brimmed cap tucked under his arm; and he was carrying a leather briefcase chained to his wrist. He saluted crisply before he seemed to notice the man behind the desk was not in uniform.

Rickabee made a vague gesture in the direction of his forehead; the gesture could be loosely defined as a salute.

"I'm afraid General Pickering is not available right now, Colonel," he said. "I'm his deputy. Maybe I could help you somehow?"

"Sir, I have a Personal from General MacArthur to General Pickering."

"I'll see that he gets it," Rickabee said, holding his hand out.

"Sir, my orders from General MacArthur are to personally deliver the Personal."

Rickabee considered that a moment. While they were talking, Rickabee gave the Army Lieutenant Colonel a quick once-over. *He may be a Doggie Feather Merchant,* he decided, *but he wasn't always one.*

On his right sleeve, Lieutenant Colonel DePress was wearing the insignia of the 26th Cavalry, Philippine Scouts, signifying that he had served in combat with that unit. And topping the I-Was-There fruit salad on his breast were ribbons representing the Silver Star and the Third Award of the Purple Heart.

"Colonel," Rickabee said, "not for dissemination, General Pickering is in the hospital."

"I'm sorry to hear that, Sir."

"I'm about to visit him. Would you have the time to come along?"

"Yes, Sir. I would appreciate that, Sir."

"Sessions, is there a car available?" Rickabee asked.

"I'll check, Sir."

"Colonel," Lieutenant Moore said, "I've got General Pickering's car. If you wanted to use that, Sergeant Hart could bring you back."

"OK, done," Rickabee said. "You have the material Sessions packed up for the General, Moore?"

"No, Sir."

"It's on my desk, Sir," Sessions said.

(THREE)
Walter Reed Army General Hospital
Washington, D.C.
1015 Hours 21 September 1942

Brigadier General Fleming Pickering, USMCR, had been assigned a three-room VIP suite in the Army Hospital. His rank would have entitled him to a private room in any case, but the hospital authorities had decided that since a VIP suite was available, who was better qualified to occupy it than a man who was not only a brigadier general, but "an old and close friend of the President," according to *The Washington Star*?

The suite was on the third floor. It consisted of a fully equipped hospital room and a sitting room, furnished with a sofa, a pair of upholstered chairs, and a four-place dining table set. These rooms were connected by a smaller room that held a refrigerator and a desk.

When Colonel Rickabee and party entered the suite, they found General Pickering in the small connecting room playing gin rummy on the desk top with Sergeant Hart. Pickering was wearing a silk bathrobe, and Sergeant Hart was in civilian clothing; his shoulder holster and pistol were on top of the refrigerator.

Hart stood up.

"Good morning, General," Rickabee said, and then, "as you were, Sergeant."

"Where he was was about to take me for twenty dollars," Pickering said. "I didn't expect to see you here this morning, Rickabee. And who is that ugly Marine tagging along behind you?"

"How the hell are you, Fleming?" Dillon inquired, walking to Pickering and shaking his hand.

"General," Rickabee said, "this officer has a Personal for you from General MacArthur."

Lieutenant Colonel DePress saluted.

"Good morning, General," he said.

"Good morning," Pickering said.

"May I inquire as to the General's health?"

"You may," Pickering said. "The General's health is a hell of a lot better than I can convince anybody around here that it is."

"I'm glad to hear that, Sir," Colonel DePress said.

"What, Colonel? That my health is better? Or that I can't convince the doctors that it is?"

Colonel DePress, looking uncomfortable, finally managed, "I'm glad to hear the General is feeling better, Sir," and then, somewhat awkwardly—because it was chained to his wrist—opened his briefcase and handed Pickering a large manila envelope.

A signature had been scrawled across the flap and then covered with transparent tape. The signature was General Douglas MacArthur's.

Pickering tore open the manila envelope and took from it a smaller, squarish envelope. A red blob was on its flap.

I'll be damned, Rickabee thought. *Didn't sealing wax go out with the nineteenth century?*

Pickering opened the second envelope and read the letter it contained.

"Will there be a reply, General?" Colonel DePress asked.

"Will you be seeing General MacArthur anytime soon?"

"Yes, Sir. I'll be returning in two or three days, Sir."

"Please tell General MacArthur"—Pickering began and then interrupted himself—"could I send a letter back with you?"

"Of course, General."

"I'll try to do that. If something goes wrong, please tell General MacArthur that I am very grateful for his gracious courtesy, and ask him to offer my best wishes to Mrs. MacArthur."

"I'll be happy to do that, General. And I will check with you before I leave to see if the General has a Personal for the General."

"I'd appreciate that," Pickering said. "Thank you very much, Colonel."

"My pleasure, Sir. With your permission, Sir?"

To judge by the look on his face, General Pickering was baffled by the question. Rickabee knew why: The Army officer was asking ritual permission to leave the Marine general's presence, and Pickering was unfamiliar with the ritual.

"Colonel," Rickabee said, doing his best to finesse the situation, "Sergeant Hart will take you wherever you need to go. And with General Pickering's permission, he'll stay with you as long as you need him."

"Very kind of you, Sir. Just to General Marshall's office would be a great help."

"On your way, Sergeant Hart," Pickering said.

"Aye, aye, Sir," Hart said.

Colonel DePress saluted again. This time Pickering returned it.

When the door had closed on them, Jake Dillon asked, "What the hell was that all about?"

"Goddamn it, Jake," Pickering said. "You're just a lousy major. How about a little respect for a goddamned general?"

"Yes, Sir, Goddamned General. What the hell was that all about?"

Pickering chuckled and tossed him the small envelope from General MacArthur.

So they really are close friends, Rickabee decided. *Dillon isn't just another one of Pickering's suck-up acquaintances.*

"I'll be damned," Dillon said, when he had read the letter.

"Show it to Rickabee and Moore," Pickering said.

Dillon handed it to Rickabee.

OFFICE OF THE SUPREME COMMANDER
GENERAL HEADQUARTERS
SOUTHWEST PACIFIC OCEAN AREAS

13th September 1942
Brigadier General Fleming Pickering, USMC
By Hand of Officer Courier

My Dear Fleming,

I shall probably be among the last to offer my congratulations upon your appointment to flag rank. But you of all people, with your deep understanding of the communications problems in this theater of war, will understand why the news reached here so belatedly; and as a cherished friend and comrade in arms you will believe me when I say that had I known sooner, I would sooner have written to say with what great joy Mrs. MacArthur and I received the news.

Please believe me further that had it been within my power, that is to say if you had been under my command during your distinguished and sorely missed service here, you would long ago have been given rank commensurate with your proven ability and valor in combat.

Mrs. MacArthur joins me in extending every wish for your continued success in the future, and our warmest personal good wishes,

Yours,

Douglas

Pickering waited until Rickabee finished reading, then said, "That's what's known as the old el softo soapo, of which the General is a master, Rickabee."

"I don't think so," Dillon said.

"Neither do I," Rickabee said, thinking aloud. "Those references to his wife made it personal. I think he really likes you."

"The staff over there hated your ass, Flem," Dillon said, "which is the proof of that pudding."

"So what brings you here, Jake, to change the subject?"

"You mean to the States, or here, here and now?"

"Both."

"Well, I am about to win the war by running a war bond tour. I brought eight heroes here from the 'Canal—really seven, plus one asshole who managed to get himself shot and looks like a hero."

"Straight from Guadalcanal or via Australia?"

"I saw Feldt and Ed Banning, if that's what you're asking. And I saw the girls in Melbourne, Howard's and that kid sergeant's."

"That's what I was asking. And Howard and Koffler are still on Buka?"

"That's an unpleasant story, Fleming. They're really up shit creek."

"Damn," Pickering said. "Banning was trying to come up with some way to relieve them."

"I don't think that's going to happen," Dillon said. "Not that Banning wouldn't swap his left nut to get them out of there."

"You understand what we're talking about, Rickabee?"

"Yes, Sir," Rickabee said. "We had a back-channel from Banning this morning—you'll find a carbon of it in that material I had Sessions put together for you—and Ferdinand Six was still operational as of—what?—thirty hours ago."

"When they do go down," Dillon said softly, "Feldt and Banning are going to drop in one team after another until one makes it. So far they have four teams ready to go—two Aussies and two Marines."

"Banning should not have told you that," Rickabee said.

"Banning took his lead from me," Pickering said a little sharply. "I don't think Major Dillon is a Japanese spy or has a loose mouth."

"With respect, Sir," Rickabee said, "there is an absolute correlation between the number of people privy to a secret and the time it takes for that secret to be compromised."

"That may well be, Colonel," Pickering said icily, reminding Jake Dillon that Fleming Pickering was not accustomed to being corrected, and didn't like it at all. "But in this circumstance, I believe I have the authority to decide who gets told what."

"Yes, Sir. That is correct, Sir." Rickabee said. In Dillon's judgment—looking at Rickabee's tight lips and white face—Rickabee's temper was at the breaking point. Career Marine Colonels are not fond of reservists, period, but they go into a cold, consuming rage when reservists who outrank them bring them up sharp.

"And I brought some film from the 'Canal," Jake said, hoping to change the subject. "From Hawaii to the West Coast in an ice-filled garbage can."

"What did you say?" Pickering asked after a moment, after he had stared Rickabee down. "An ice-filled garbage can?"

"I got one of those insulated whole-blood containers from the medics on the 'Canal," Jake explained. "They took it away from me at Pearl Harbor. So I got a garbage can and put the film in, packed in ice."

"What kind of film?" Pickering asked.

"Combat footage, from the 'Canal. I'm going to make up a newsreel feature. Maybe, if the film is any good, and if there's enough usable footage, a short."

"I'd like to see that," Pickering said. "Where is it?"

"So would I," Rickabee said.

"I had it souped at Metro-Magnum," Jake replied, adding, "Hell, now that I think about it, it may be at the Willard now."

"Find out," Pickering ordered.

"Yes, Sir, General," Dillon said.

"Don't push your luck, Jake," Pickering said.

Jake had no idea if Pickering was kidding or not. He picked up the telephone and called the Willard. He was told that an air freight package had arrived for him thirty minutes before.

"It's there," he said. "I'll get in a cab and go get it."

"If I sent someone to get it, would they give it to him?"

"Probably not. It's probably in a Metro-Magnum can and they guard those like Fort Knox."

"What kind, what size, film is it?"

"Sixteen millimeter."

Rickabee picked up the telephone and asked for the office of the hospital commander.

"Good morning, Sir. Colonel Rickabee, General Pickering's Deputy. The General needs a staff car to transport Major Dillon into Washington and return. And the General will require that a 16mm projector and screen be set up in his sitting room right away.

"No, Sir. The General will not require a projectionist. Just the camera and screen. Plus, of course, the car.

"Thank you, Sir."

He hung up and turned to Dillon.

"There will be a staff car waiting at the main entrance, Major."

"Thank you, Sir."

"I trust you are suitably awed by my power as a general, Jake," Pickering said.

"Yes, Sir, Goddamn General, I am truly awed."

Rickabee and Pickering laughed.

Well, at least I got them laughing. For a moment there, it looked like it was going to get goddamned unpleasant.

(FOUR)

"Interesting man," Rickabee said after Dillon left . . . and after sending Moore to get a pot of coffee he didn't really want. "I think there's more there than meets the eye."

"He was—I suppose still is—Vice President for Publicity for Metro-Magnum Studios. I don't think they'd pay him the kind of money they did unless he was worth it. Clark Gable told me once that Jake's real value came when movies were in production. He could tell whether the public would like them or not, just from looking at rushes. And he knew how to fix them."

"I wasn't aware you . . . I guess the phrase is 'traveled in those circles'?"

"Oh, no. I never did. I was a skeet shooter. There were some movie people, Gable, Bob Stack, people like that, and Jake, who shot skeet. That's how I met him. Marines can smell each other. Jake was a China Marine, a sergeant, before he went Hollywood. He was a better shot with a sixty-nine-dollar Winchester Model 12 from Sears, Roebuck than Gable was with his thousand-dollar English shotguns."

"What did you shoot, General?" Rickabee asked.

"When my wife was watching, one of the pair of Purdys she gave me for my thirtieth birthday," Pickering said. "When she wasn't, a Model 12. I don't think a better shotgun was ever made."

Rickabee was not surprised.

"I still don't know how you and Jake managed to show up here together," Pickering said.

"He came to the office looking for Lieutenant McCoy."

"What did he want with the Killer?"

"He doesn't like to be called that," Rickabee said.

"To hell with him, I'm a general, I'll call him whatever I want to," Pickering said. "Besides, I am literally old enough to be his father."

"McCoy's brother apparently was quite a hero on Bloody Ridge. An INS reporter has dubbed him 'Machine Gun McCoy.' Dillon's boss, a Brigadier General named Stewart, in Public Relations at Eighth and Eye, found out about our McCoy and wants to make public relations about him. When they started asking us questions, we gave them the runaround, and General Stewart sent Dillon to straighten us out. Moore recognized Dillon—"

"Jake met him at my house in Australia," Pickering interrupted.

"—and brought him into my office."

"So what do we do about McCoy? You want me to call this General—Stewart, you said?—and get him off our back?"

"I thought perhaps you would be willing to call General Forrest. That would keep us out of it entirely. And it would give you a chance to talk to him."

Major General Horace W. T. Forrest was Assistant Chief of Staff, Intelligence, Headquarters, USMC.

"Why do I suspect an ulterior motive, Rickabee? Why didn't *you* just call Forrest?"

"I thought it might be of value, General, to remind General Forrest that you are not just a nightmare of his."

"You really think it's that bad?"

"My job is to see things as they are, General. Let me put it this way: I suspect that General Forrest secretly hopes that your recovery will take some time, maybe until the war is over. He has not come to see you, you may have noticed, or even had his aide call your aide to ask about your condition."

"In that case, get the sonofabitch on the phone," Pickering said. "After you tell me what to say to him."

"The General has been made aware of the problem, Sir. Another general officer, who has no need to know why, has to be discouraged from asking about one of your officers. I'm sure the General will know how to deal with the situation."

"I haven't the foggiest idea ..." Pickering said, and stopped. Rickabee was already picking up the telephone.

"General Pickering for General Forrest," Rickabee said, and then handed Pickering the telephone.

"Forrest."

"Pickering, General."

"Well, what a pleasant surprise, General. I understand you've been a little under the weather."

"I'm feeling much better, General."

"Ready for duty, General?"

"I've placed myself on limited duty, General, until I can get the doctors to agree with my prognosis."

"Well, General, you really don't want to rush things. You'd better listen to the doctors."

"I have a little problem, General. I thought I could ask your help with it."

"Anything within my power, General."

"It has to do with General Stewart—"

"Public relations type, that Stewart?"

"That's right, General."

"Well, you and I, General, are really not in the public relations business, are we?"

"That's precisely the problem, General. General Stewart apparently has an interest in putting one of my officers into the public eye."

"Who would that be, General?"

"Lieutenant McCoy, General."

"Oh, yes. I know McCoy. What the hell does Stewart want with him?"

"It seems that McCoy's brother did something spectacular on Guadalcanal, General. General Stewart is having him returned for publicity purposes. He found out that Sergeant McCoy's brother is my McCoy and wants to involve him."

"Give him the runaround, General."

"General Stewart is a determined man, General. He sent a major to see Colonel Rickabee."

"Give the major the runaround. I was under the impression that Rickabee was pretty good at that sort of thing."

"Colonel Rickabee is, General. But the Major is about as determined as General Stewart. Which is why I'm asking for your help, General."

"I'll deal with General Stewart, General. Put it out of your mind."

"Thank you very much, General."

"As soon as you feel up to it, General, have your aide call mine and we'll set something up. You and I really have to sit down and have a long talk."

"That's very kind of you, General. I'll do that."

"Good to finally have the chance to talk to you, Pickering," General Forrest said, and the line went dead.

Pickering put the telephone back in its cradle and looked at Rickabee.

"How'd I do?"

"General officers are expected to do very well, General. You didn't let the side down."

"If I were Forrest, I wouldn't like me either," Pickering said. "I wouldn't like it a goddamn bit if somebody I never heard of, who got his commission in a damned strange way, showed up as one of my senior subordinates."

"General, President Roosevelt is the Commander in Chief. There should be no questioning of his orders by a Marine."

"I don't think Forrest is questioning the legality of the order, but I suspect he has some question about its wisdom."

"Who was it, General—Churchill?—who said, 'War is too important a matter to leave to the generals'?"

"I think it was Churchill," Pickering said. "But that leaves me sort of in limbo, doesn't it? As a general who really shouldn't be a general?"

"That question, General, is moot. And who was it that said, 'Yours not to reason why, et cetera, et cetera'?"

"I have no idea, but I take your point."

There was a knock at the door. And then three Army enlisted men in hospital garb appeared. Two of them were pushing a table with a Bell & Howell motion picture projector on it and the third was carrying a screen.

"I believe the General wishes that set up in the sitting room," Rickabee said. "Is that correct, General?"

"That is correct, Colonel," General Pickering said.

(FIVE)

When Sergeant George S. Hart entered The Corps, he brought one thing with him that few of his fellows had when they joined—a familiarity with violent death.

As a cop, he'd seen—and grown accustomed to—all sorts of sights that turned civilians' stomachs, civilians being defined by cops as anyone not a cop. He'd seen bridge jumpers after they'd been pulled from the Mississippi; people whose dismembered bodies had to be pried from the twisted wreckage of their automobiles; every kind of suicide; people whose time on earth had been ended by axes, by lead pipes, by rifle shots, pistol shots, shotguns.

Even before he joined the force, he'd been present in the Medical Examiner's office while the coroner removed hearts, lungs, and other vital organs from open-eyed cadavers and dropped them like so much hamburger into the stainless-steel scale hanging over the dissection table. All the while, the coroner would exchange jokes with Hart's father.

But none of this had prepared him for the motion picture film Major Jake Dillon brought with him from Guadalcanal.

There were five large reels of film.

"You understand, Fleming," Dillon said to The General (for that was how Hart had begun to look at Fleming Pickering—The General, not the General), "that this is a really rough cut. All my lab guys did was soup it and splice the short takes together. This is the first time anyone has had a look at it."

After Major Dillon told him to kill the lights in The General's sitting room and started to run the film, it was sort of like being in a newsreel theater with the sound off.

The film began with a picture of a small slate blackboard on which the cameraman had written the date, the time, the location, the subject matter, and his name.

For example:

> 5 August 1942 1540
> Aboard USS Calhoun
> En route to Guadalcanal
> 1st Para Bn Prepares for invasion
> Cpl H.A. Simpson, USMCR

Then there were Marines; most of them were smiling. They were standing or sitting around, cleaning their weapons, sharpening knives, working ammunition-linking machines for machine gun belts, or writing letters home, stuff like that.

George was getting just a little bored with this when the content changed. They were at the invasion beach.

> 7 August 1942 0415
> Tulagi
> First Wave, 1st Raider Bn
> Cpl H.A. Simpson, USMCR

The cameraman was in an invasion barge. You could see Marines with all their gear, hunched down, waiting for the boat to touch shore. They were no longer smiling.

Then you could see the beach, a landing pier, burning Japanese seaplanes, and shellfire, and lots of smoke.

And then guys were climbing over the sides of the barge. Then the camera was out of the barge and on top of the pier; parts of the pier had been destroyed.

And then you started to see bodies. The first body was just lying there, with arterial blood pumping out his back. The camera was on that for maybe ten seconds; it seemed a lot longer.

And then you saw two Marines running along the pier. Both of them, at the same time, just fell down. Not like in the movies, where people clutch their chests or their throats and spin around before they fall. These Marines just stopped in midstride, fell down, and were dead.

There was a lot that was out of focus, and a lot of gray space, with no images; and then there were more bodies. Some of them now were Japanese.

"I'd like a drink, please," The General said.

"General," Lieutenant Moore said, "you said to remind you when you'd already had the day's ration."

"Lieutenant, ask Sergeant Hart to get me an inch and a half of scotch, please."

"Aye, aye, Sir. Hart?"

"Aye, aye, Sir."

"Help yourself, George, if you like," The General said. "You, too, John."

There was a shot of some Japanese, in pieces, around a small hole in the ground.

After a moment Hart decided it had been caused by the impact of a Naval artillery shell.

There was a shot of a Marine lying on his back with his face blown off.

Bodies. Bodies. Bodies.

There was a shot of some Marine with more balls than brains standing up in the open and firing his rifle off hand, like he was on the goddamned rifle range at Parris Island, sling in the proper place and everything.

And then a shot of a couple of Japanese with the tops of their heads blown off, and then a shot of the Marine with the rifle, closer up now, so close that Hart could see that he was an older guy, an officer, a major. He was gesturing angrily at the cameraman and Hart could tell that he was really pissed that the cameraman was taking his picture.

It went on and on and on, Marines running and shooting their weapons, Marines down, with corpsmen bending over them; even a shot of a guy with blood on his face clinging for dear life to one of the supports of the pier, looking like he was hysterical. There was time enough for The General to ask for three more drinks. Hart made them, and two more for himself. The last two he made for The General were an inch and a half, straight up.

Finally it was over; and Major Dillon told Hart to turn the lights on.

"Your people did a fine job, Jake," The General said.

"Yeah," Dillon said. "But there's not much I can put in newsreel theaters, is there?"

"I'd like a copy of that," Colonel Rickabee said.

"Colonel, that would be hard—" Major Dillon said.

"Why, Rickabee?" The General interrupted.

"I want to show it to my people—our people."

"Get him a copy, Jake," The General ordered.

"General Stewart wants to look at this right away."

"Fuck General Stewart," The General said. "He'll have to wait until you get a copy of that for Rickabee."

"OK, Flem. Whatever you say."

"The Navy has a pretty good photo lab at Anacostia, Dillon," Rickabee said. "But I don't know if they can copy motion picture film."

"I've got a pal, used to work in the Metro-Magnum lab," Dillon replied, "who's running the Army lab at the Astoria Studios on Long Island. I know he won't fuck it up, and he could do a quick edit and get rid of the garbage."

"Call him," Fleming Pickering ordered. "See if he can—will—do it. If he will, we can send George to New York."

Hart could see that Colonel Rickabee didn't like that. But he was not surprised that he didn't raise an objection. He had already learned that arguing with The General was usually a waste of breath.

XI

Sergeant George Hart let himself as quietly as possible into the small suite he shared with Lieutenant John Marston Moore. But as he walked on his toes into the bedroom, the lights came on. And when he opened the door, Moore was awake, holding himself up on his elbows.

"I tried not to wake you, Lieutenant."

Moore shook his head, signifying it didn't matter.

"Everything go OK?"

Moore held up a large film can.

"I just dropped off the original with Major Dillon at the Willard," he said. "This is two copies."

"Two?"

"They asked me how many copies I wanted, so I said two."

"Good man," Moore said. "I think The General wants one."

Despite the differences in their ranks and backgrounds, Hart had come to think of Moore as a friend. And his story was too good to just keep, particularly since Moore was one of the very few people in the world who would believe it.

"Veronica Wood has nipples the size of silver dollars," he announced.

Veronica Wood was a motion picture actress. A photograph, showing her in a translucent negligee, her long blond hair hanging down to her waist, was pinned up on barracks walls around the world.

"I'm sure you're going to tell me how you know that," Moore said.

"She was in bed with Major Dillon," Hart said. "I knocked at the door, and he said come in, and I did, and there she was. She said 'Hi!' and smiled at me. She didn't even try to cover herself. They were both stinko."

"I would say that Major Dillon is entitled, wouldn't you?"

"Yeah. Jesus, those movies!"

"They were pretty awful, weren't they?" Moore said, and then added: "But you understand, George, that all they shot was . . . what you saw. It really wasn't all that bad."

"Yeah, and that's why you walk around with a cane, right?"

"Speaking of dollar-sized nipples, Sergeant," Moore said, "you had a telephone call from a lady."

"I did?"

"You did. At midnight. I answered the phone, and she said, in a very nice voice, 'George?' and I said, 'Sorry, he's not here right now, can I take a message?' and she said, no, she'd call back."

"You're probably talking about my mother," George said.

"I really don't think so. This lady didn't sound like a mother. And wouldn't your mother have said, 'Tell him his mother called'?"

"I have no idea—"

"Maybe it was Captain Sessions' secretary," Moore said innocently. "I've noticed the way she looks at you."

"Thanks a lot, Lieutenant."

Captain Sessions' secretary was at least thirty-five, weighed more than a hundred fifty pounds, and had a mustache.

"Consumed with unrequited passion in the wee hours of the morning," Moore went on. "Yearning for the feel of your strong arms around her—"

"My arms wouldn't fit around her," George said. "Beats the hell out of me. The only person I gave this number to is my mother."

"Jesus, George. If it was your mother, I'm sorry—"

"I don't think it was my mother," George said. "She would have asked where I was at midnight."

"Speaking of midnight, the wee hours," Moore said, "The General called about ten. I am instructed to inform you that he doesn't want to see you before thirteen hundred tomorrow."

"What?"

"You have the morning off. The General also said to remind you that you are not to waste your money eating at the Waffle House or Crystal Burger."

"What does that mean?"

"We are to take full advantage of hotel services. Booze, chow, laundry, whatever. He said I was to consider that an order."

"That's nice," George said.

"I think it's more than nice," Moore said. "I think it's important to him. You took care of his idiot son and now he wants to repay the favor."

"You ever meet him?"

Moore shook his head, no.

"He's a really nice guy," Hart said. "A little wild, but a nice guy."

"Somehow, when I heard he'd flown under the Golden Gate, I suspected he was not a shrinking violet," Moore said. "Where's the car?"

"Out in front. Just about out of gas. I couldn't find an open station."

"Well, then, I'll take a cab to the hospital in the morning, and you get it gassed up before you come."

He let himself fall back on the bed, and rolled on his side.

"Turn out the light when you're finished," he said.

(TWO)
Henderson Field
Guadalcanal, Solomon Islands
1515 Hours 23 September 1942

Lieutenant Colonel Clyde W. Dawkins had informed Captain Charles M. Galloway that part of a squadron of dive bombers was on its way—half a dozen of them, of VMSB-141s. These were under Lieutenant Colonel Cooley, an officer Galloway admired; he'd flown with Cooley years before.

So Galloway was not surprised when he heard odd noises overhead. He was familiar with the peculiar sound made by half a dozen thousand-horsepower Wright R-1820-52 engined Douglas Dauntlesses. What did surprise him, when he stepped out of VMF-229's sandbag tent squadron office, was the sight of two Grumman Wildcats about to touch down ahead of the SBDs.

He could tell that they, too, were replacement aircraft. Their fuselages glistened, unmarked by the mud carried by every airplane that landed at Henderson.

Seeing them there—so new and fresh—should have pleased him. In fact, he wasn't at all pleased, he was hugely annoyed—on two counts: First, nobody had told him two new Wildcats were coming—thus denying him the chance to plead for them for VMF-229. Second, they came in with the SBDs. And that meant the Navy had fucked up again. . . . The SBDs were brought in toward Guadalcanal aboard one of the escort carriers. In order to protect the carrier from Japanese aviation and to permit it to return to other duties as quickly as possible, the SBDs took off for Guadalcanal at the farthest point possible from Henderson—after due consideration of the weather and reserve fuel requirements.

Since the Dauntlesses had a much greater range than the Wildcats, and since the Dauntlesses and the Wildcats had obviously been launched from the same carrier, one of two things had happened: Either the Dauntlesses had been launched within Wildcat range of Henderson, thus endangering the escort carrier that much longer. Or—more likely—the Wildcats had been launched at Dauntless range and were landing with near-empty tanks.

Wildcats that ran out of fuel and ditched in the ocean were no different from Wildcats lost in action.

Captain Galloway was again reminded that a lot of really stupid people were running around with a lot of rank on their collar points. There was nothing he could do about that, of course, but there was a chance he could talk Dawkins into giving VMF-229 the two new Wildcats.

He took off at a trot for the sandbagged headquarters of MAG-21.

When he walked into the MAG-21 office, Charley learned that Lieutenant Colonel Dawkins was in the air, taking his turn on patrol. Since the Coastwatchers couldn't always give them warning that Japanese planes were coming, one- and two-plane patrols were always overhead.

The two pilots of the new Wildcats came into the MAG-21 tent a few minutes after Charley Galloway got there. In Charley's judgment, they looked as if they'd graduated from Pensacola last week.

One was wearing a ring knocker ring, Charley noticed without any special glee. The other looked like a troublemaker: Charley saw the spark of intelligence in his eyes . . . but also the far side of mischievousness.

"I'm Captain Galloway," Charley said, putting out his hand. "I've got VMF-229. That was you two coming in in the Wildcats just now?"

The ring knocker came to attention and saluted. This did not surprise Charley.

"Yes, Sir. Lieutenant Stecker, Sir. Reporting aboard, Sir. With Lieutenant Pickering."

"To MAG-21, you mean, Mister?" Charley asked as he returned the salute.

"No, Sir. We're on orders to VMF-229."

He opened his canvas flight bag and handed Galloway a set of their orders. Galloway read them; they were indeed assigned to VMF-229. He managed to conceal his delight fairly successfully.

Since they flew those airplanes in, and they're assigned to me, if I just take these guys—and the airplanes—to the squadron, I stand a much better chance of keeping the airplanes, too. Possession is nine-tenths of the law.

"Welcome aboard, gentlemen," Charley said. "Will you come with me, please?"

Lady Luck smiled on him. Fifty yards from MAG-21, he encountered Technical Sergeant Oblensky.

"Sergeant Oblensky, these officers just delivered two F4F aircraft. As your first priority, will you see that those aircraft are moved to our squadron area? I'd like to have that accomplished before Colonel Dawkins returns from patrol."

"Aye, aye, Sir," Big Steve said. "I'll do that immediately, Sir."

Lieutenant Bill Dunn was in the squadron office when Galloway walked in. He looked with interest at the neat and shiny newcomers.

"Lieutenant Dunn," Captain Galloway said, "these two officers just arrived for duty with us. In new Wildcats. Sergeant Oblensky is moving one of them to our area. Would you please go move the other one, right now?"

"Your wish is my command, Skipper," Dunn said, and quickly left the tent.

Galloway waited until Dunn left the tent, then said, "Lieutenant Dunn is working on being a double ace. He's my executive officer."

He saw increased interest in the eyes of both of his new officers.

"Stecker, you said?"

"Yes, Sir."

"You're an Annapolis man, I see, Mister Stecker?"

"No, Sir. West Point."

West Point? You don't see many of those in The Corps.

"And you, Mr.—"

"Pickering, Sir."

"*—Pickering.* Where did you get your commission?"

"Quantico, Sir. Officer Candidate School."

"And your flight training?"

"P'Cola, Sir. Both of us."

"And how many hours do you have? You first, Mr. Pickering."

"Four hundred sixty-eight, Sir."

That was a good deal more than Charley expected to hear. The last half-dozen replacements to VMF-229 had averaged about 250 hours total time, very little of that in Wildcats.

"How much in Wildcats?"

"Two twenty-eight, Sir."

"This is not, then, your first squadron assignment?"

"Yes, Sir, it is."

"How did you get so much time in Wildcats, then?"

"They had us ferrying them, Sir, from Bethpage all over the country."

"Both of you, you mean?"

"Yes, Sir."

"You answer this, Mr. Stecker. I want a straight answer: What was your last thought when you took off from the escort carrier?"

"Sir," Stecker hesitated a moment, and then blurted, "that I had better run the engine as lean as possible, Sir, or prepare to take a swim."

"How much fuel remaining when you touched down?"

"About fifteen minutes, Sir."

"You, Pickering?"

"My fuel warning light was lit, Sir."

"And what was your reaction to that?"

"I was scared shitless," Pick said, remembering a moment later to add, "Sir."

"In other words, you're telling me that you knowingly took off with inadequate fuel?"

"It didn't turn out to be inadequate, Sir."

"You're not being flip, are you, Pickering?"

"Sir," Stecker said, "Mr. Pickering raised the question of fuel just before we were to launch and was told to man his aircraft."

"Sir, I think it was a question of getting the carrier turned around as quickly as possible."

In other words, I was right, there was an asshole on that escort carrier, probably wearing commander's boards.

"Where are you from, Pickering? Are you married?"

"San Francisco, Sir. No, Sir, I'm not married."

Galloway looked at Stecker.

"No, Sir. I'm not married. I'm from eastern Pennsylvania, Sir."

"Philadelphia?"

"About seventy miles north of Philadelphia, Sir."

"My girl's from Philadelphia," Galloway said.

Why the hell did I offer that information?

"Yes, Sir," Stecker said.

"And just before I came over here, I was in San Francisco," Galloway said. A quick, entirely pleasant memory of Caroline came into his mind. They'd spent a fair amount of time together in their marble-walled, multiple-showerhead bath. "Had a hell of a time in the Andrew Foster Hotel. You know it?"

"Yes, Sir," Pick said. "We've been there."

Galloway picked up on a look the two of them exchanged.

The Andrew Foster Hotel touched a nerve, he decided. *They probably got really shitfaced there. In due course a report of conduct unbecoming officers and gentlemen will be forwarded through channels for my attention. I hope they had a good time.*

"What we do here is try to protect the field and the area around it from the Japanese," Galloway explained. "Most of the time—nine times out of ten—we have advance knowledge that they're coming. When we do get it, we get in the air as fast as we can and try to intercept them as far from here as we can."

"May I ask how we get the advance knowledge, Sir?" Stecker asked.

"Primarily from the Coastwatchers. They're Australians who stayed behind when the Japs occupied the islands to the north of us. Guys with real big balls. They radio Pearl Harbor and it's relayed to us here. Other times we get word from our own patrolling aircraft or from carrier-launched patrols. But mostly it's the Coastwatchers who alert us."

"What are those funny-looking airplanes I saw when I sat down?" Pick asked. "The ones with alligator teeth painted on them?"

He didn't say "Sir"; he should know what a Bell fighter is; and those are shark teeth, not alligator teeth. But there's something about this kid I like.

"Those are *shark* teeth, Mr. Pickering," Galloway said. "The aircraft are Army P-400 fighters, and the pilots who man them are as good as any I've ever known. Any further questions?"

"Yes, Sir. When will we go up for the first time?"

"Anxious to get into combat, are you?"

"No, Sir. I was just curious, that's all."

Hell, I'd ask the same question.

"Well, we'll get you a place to sleep and show you the mess. In the morning either Lieutenant Dunn or myself will take you for a little ride and see how well you can fly. If that goes well, you'll go up for real very soon after that. If it doesn't go well, we'll wait until we're sure you won't kill yourself or somebody else."

"Yes, Sir. Thank you, Sir."

Lieutenant Bill Dunn came into the tent.

"Sir, I took the liberty of asking Big Steve to put our squadron numbers on those airplanes."

"Good boy, Bill," Galloway said, and then introduced the newcomers to Dunn.

"Find them a place to sleep and get them settled for this afternoon," Galloway said. "I told them we'll give them an area check ride in the morning."

"Aye, aye, Sir."

"Unless you have a question, Stecker?"

"Sir, more on the order of a request."

"Shoot."

"If we're to have a couple of hours free, would there be time for me to go to 2nd of the Fifth?"

"Second Battalion, Fifth Marines?" Galloway asked. "Why do you want to go there? A buddy's with 2nd of the Fifth?"

"My father, Sir."

There was silence for a moment.

"You don't happen to be Jack (NMI) Stecker's boy, do you, Mr. Stecker?"

"Yes, Sir."

Well, that explains West Point. If they hang the Medal of Honor around your neck, your kids get to go to the Service Academy of their choice.

He then remembered hearing that Major Jack (NMI) Stecker's son, an Annapolis graduate, a Navy ensign, had been killed aboard the battleship *Arizona* at Pearl Harbor on December 7th.

Major Jack (NMI) Stecker is going to be something less than overjoyed to find his other son on this fucking goddamned island as a fighter pilot.

"Find somebody to drive him up there in my jeep, please, Bill," Galloway said.

"Aye, aye, Sir."

(THREE)
The Foster Lafayette Hotel
Washington, D.C.
0915 Hours 22 September 1942

A discreet knock at the door came shortly after a room service waiter rolled in a tray carrying ham and eggs, toast, coffee, a pitcher of freshly squeezed orange juice, a copy of *The Washington Star,* and a rose in a tiny vase.

"Come in," Sergeant George Hart called cheerfully.

The door opened and a man in a paint-stained smock stuck his head in.

"Sorry to disturb you, Sir," he said. "If you'll tell me when it's convenient, I'll come back and finish painting the door."

He pointed at the wall that separated the suite Hart shared with Moore from the one Senator Richmond F. Fowler shared with Brigadier General Fleming Pickering. A tarpaulin concealed the newly installed door.

"Come ahead," George said. "Watching other people work has never bothered me."

The witticism was lost on the painter.

"I'll come back when you've left, Sir."

"I don't plan to leave. Come on in and paint the door."

"Yes, Sir."

George turned his attention to *The Washington Star.*

According to Reuters News Service, there was heavy fighting between the Germans and the Russians on Mamayec Kurgan Hill, outside Stalingrad. Casualties on both sides were described as severe.

British troops had landed at Tamatave on the east coast of Madagascar, with the apparent intention of taking the capital, Tananarive. This was held by reportedly "very strong" Vichy French forces. There was a map, with arrows. George knew who the Vichy French were, they were the ones who'd made peace with the Germans. But he had no idea where Madagascar was. The map was no help.

In the Pacific, the Commander in Chief, Pacific, had announced that six transports, under heavy escort, had made it safely to Guadalcanal, where they successfully delivered the Seventh Marines (to reinforce the First Marine Division), and a "substantial amount" of supplies. There was a map here, too; and George studied this one with interest.

Until he'd seen Major Dillon's movies yesterday, he really hadn't been all that interested in Guadalcanal.

He was reading the comic strips when the telephone rang. Not the one in his suite, one of the telephones in The General's.

He carefully squeezed past the painter working on the door and picked it up. It was The General's phone, not the Senator's. He knew the drill:

"General Pickering's quarters, Sergeant Hart speaking, Sir."

He would then tell them The General was not available at the moment and could he take a message?

"George?"

His heart jumped.

"Jesus Christ!"

"I called last night when I got here," Elizabeth Lathrop said. "Some officer answered and said you would be late."

He could feel her fingernails on his back, smell the soap in her hair, taste the skin of her neck.

"How the hell did you get this number?"

"Where else would Pick's father stay in Washington?"

"What do you want?"

He could tell from her tone that the question hurt.

Jesus Christ, I didn't want to hurt her feelings!

"Well, I happened to be in the neighborhood," she said, more coldly, "and I thought I would just call up and say hi."

"You're in Washington?"

"Yes," she said. "And I thought maybe you'd want to see me."

He thought: *I would kill to be inside you again, with your breasts soft and warm against my chest.*

Detective George Hart of the Saint Louis Vice Squad answered for him without thinking: "Honey, I can't afford you."

The telephone made a clicking noise, then hummed, and then after a moment, there came the dial tone.

"Shit!" Hart said, loudly and bitterly. He slammed the handset into the cradle and said "shit!" again.

The man painting the door looked at him with open curiosity. George glowered at him and the painter looked away.

How the hell can I find her? Call the local cops and ask them as a professional service to a brother vice detective if they have an address or known associates of a high-class whore named Lathrop, Elizabeth, white female, approximately five three, approximately twenty-two or twenty-three, approximately one hundred five pounds, blue eyes, blond hair, no distinguishing scars or bodily blemishes?

That's probably not even her fucking name. That's her professional name. Her real name is probably Agnes Kutcharsky or some shit.

He had just squeezed past the painter when the telephone rang again.

"General Pickering's quarters, Sergeant Hart speaking, Sir."

"Don't you think I know you don't have any goddamned money?"

"Baby!"

"You sonofabitch!"

"I'm sorry. That just . . . I don't know why I said that."

There was a long silence.

"I said I was sorry."

"OK."

"Where are you?"

"The Hotel Washington."

I've seen that marquee. It's around here someplace. Hell, yes, right down the street, a block down from Pennsylvania Avenue, around the corner from the movie theater.

"That's right around the corner."

"Yeah, I know. Do they give you any time off?"

"I'm off now."

"Would you like to come here? And have a drink or something?"

A drink, at half past nine in the morning? Or something?

"Or something," George said.

"I'm in 805," Elizabeth Lathrop said. The phone clicked again before he could open his mouth to say, "I'll be there in a couple of minutes."

It was beautiful outside. The sun was shining and the temperature was just right. *Indian summer,* he thought, as he walked—almost trotted—past the White House. *It's sort of like a dream,* he thought, *walking past the White House, on my way to be with Elizabeth.*

The Washington Theater was showing *Eagle Squadron;* Tyrone Power was playing an American who went to fly for the English. Hart remembered hearing someplace that Tyrone Power was joining The Corps. *From Major Dillon, that's it,* he remembered; he'd heard him tell The General. He wondered if they would send him to Parris Island. It was strange to think of Tyrone Power with all his hair cut off getting screamed at by some asshole like Corporal Clayton C. Warren.

The Hotel Washington was just where his memory placed it. He pushed his way through the revolving door, walked across the lobby to the bank of elevators, and rode up to the eighth floor; 805 was the third door to the left.

When Beth opened the door, she was wearing a white blouse, an unbuttoned sweater, and a tweed skirt. And she wouldn't look at him.

"Hi! Come on in."

"I'm sorry about what I said on the telephone."

She nodded but didn't reply.

"It's only a couple of blocks from the Foster Lafayette to here."

She nodded again.

"So what brings you to Washington?"

Now she looked at him, and there was pain in her eyes again.

"Oh, Jesus!" Hart said, almost moaning.

"Stupid of me, right?" Elizabeth said. "But I decided, what the hell . . ."

He reached out and touched her face; and her hand came up and touched his. Then all of a sudden he was holding her in his arms as tight as he had ever held anybody. He didn't kiss her, he just clung to her, his face buried in her hair. And she was hanging on to him, too, and she was weeping a little, and he realized he felt a little like crying too.

And then he became aware of the warmth of her legs against his, and the softness of her breasts against him, and he grew erect. He pulled his middle away from her.

She pulled her head back and looked at him, and he was right, she had been crying; tears were making a path down her cheeks through her makeup.

"It's all right," she said, sort of laughing. "I would have been disappointed . . ."

She put her hand on his cheek.

There was an imperious rapping at the door.

"Who's there?"

"Assistant manager, Miss Lathrop. Please open the door."

She freed herself from George's arms. Rubbing at her eyes with her knuckles, she went to the door and opened it.

A middle-aged man in a business suit entered without being invited.

Assistant manager, my ass. That's a house detective. I've seen enough of them to know one when I see one.

"You're not allowed up here, Sergeant. The Washington is not that kind of hotel. And, Miss Lathrop, we would appreciate it if you would check out as soon as possible."

As he walked quickly to the ruddy-faced house detective, George took his credentials from his tunic pocket.

"What's going on in here is none of your business," he said.

The house detective took a long look at the credentials and then looked at Hart.

"Take a walk," Hart said. "And don't come back. And the lady will not be checking out. Got it?"

Without a word, the house detective turned and pulled the door open and went through it.

What was that all about? Did he just add up a Marine sergeant going to a hotel room as a guy about to pay for a piece of ass? Or did he take one look at Elizabeth and decide she was a whore? Jesus, she doesn't look like a whore or act like one.

He turned and looked at her.

"Well," she said.

Hart shrugged.

"What was that you showed him?"

"I've got sort of a Marine Corps badge."

"I thought maybe you showed him your vice detective badge," Beth said. There were tears in her eyes again.

"He's gone. He won't be back."

"Would you just put your arms around me again?" Beth asked softly, looking into his eyes. "And just hold me?"

He held his arms open and she took the few steps to him. When he put his arms around her, she started to cry again. He ran his hands over her back and against her hair and made soothing noises.

And then the warmth of her legs and the softness of her breasts got to him again; and the erection returned. When he tried to pull away from her, she followed him. And then she tilted her head back again and looked into his eyes for a moment. And then her mouth was on his, hungrily, and she dragged him backward onto the bed.

(FOUR)
**Walter Reed Army General Hospital
Washington, D.C.
1145 Hours 22 September 1942**

At quarter past ten, Technical Sergeant Harry N. Rutterman put his head in Colonel F. L. Rickabee's office and told him that General Pickering was on the line.

The conversation was a short one:

"There's something we have to talk about, Rickabee," General Pickering said. "Is there some reason you can't come over here, say at quarter to twelve?"

"No, Sir," he said, though he was not telling the precise truth when he said it.

His work schedule was a god-awful mess. Adding a meeting with The General would only make it worse. On the other hand, a general's wish was a colonel's command. . . .

"Thank you," Pickering said, and hung up.

When Colonel F. L. Rickabee, at precisely the appointed hour, walked into the sitting room of Brigadier General Fleming Pickering's VIP suite, he found a table set for two. And The General was dressed in uniform—or part of one—and not in a bathrobe and pajamas. Though he wasn't wearing his blouse or a field scarf, there was a silver star on the collar points of his khaki shirt. Rickabee decided that Pickering had a purpose when he pinned on the insignia of his rank.

Otherwise why bother? He's not going anyplace. On the other hand, maybe someone's coming to see him—maybe General Forrest—and he's putting his uniform on for that. And wants some advice from me before he meets him?

"Good morning, General."

"Sorry to drag you away from your office, but I suspect I would have made waves if I had come to you."

"My time is your time, General," Rickabee said. "And I thought you would be interested in this, Sir. It was delivered by messenger yesterday afternoon."

He took a sheet of paper from his inside pocket and handed it to Pickering.

INTEROFFICE MEMORANDUM

DATE: 21 September 1942

FROM: Assistant Chief of Staff, Personnel

TO: Director
           Public Affairs Office
           Hq, USMC

HAND CARRY

SUBJECT: Office of Management Analysis
           Hq, USMC

1. Effective immediately, no, repeat no, public relations activity of any kind will involve the Office of Management Analysis, or any personnel assigned thereto.

2. The Public Affairs Office is forbidden to contact the Office of Management Analysis for any purpose without the specific permission of the undersigned.

3. Discussion of this policy, or requests for waivers thereto, is not desired.

BY DIRECTION OF THE COMMANDANT:

Alfred J. Kennedy
Major General, USMC
Assistant Chief of Staff, G-1

Pickering read it and snorted, then handed it back.

"I suppose that will keep them off our backs. Being a general officer does seem to carry with it the means to get things done, doesn't it?"

"Yes, Sir, it does seem to, General."

"I thought we could save time by having lunch," Pickering said. "I asked them to serve at twelve."

"Very kind of you, Sir."

"You better hold the thanks until you see what they give us. Now that I think of it, I should have ordered some emergency rations."

"Sir?"

"I sometimes have the hotel send over a platter of hors d'oeuvres against the likelihood that lunch or dinner will be inedible."

"I see."

"I am medically restricted to four drinks a day," Pickering said. "I am about to have my second. Would you care to join me?"

You are medically restricted to no more than two drinks a day, General, not four. And somehow I suspect that the drink you are about to have is going to be Number Three or Number Four, not Number Two.

"Yes, Sir. I would. Thank you."

"Scotch all right?"

"Scotch is fine, Sir."

Pickering went into the small room between the sitting room and the bedroom. He returned in a moment with a nearly empty bottle of Famous Grouse.

"My supply of this is running a little low," he said.

"No problem, Sir, I don't have to have scotch."

"Oh, no. There's a couple of bottles left here, and if Hart and Moore haven't been at them, several more in the hotel. But the stock is running low. I have a hell of a stock, however, a hundred cases or more, in San Francisco. Most of it came off my *Pacific Princess* when I chartered her to the Navy."

"Well, they have a rule, no liquor aboard Navy vessels."

What the hell is this all about?

"We have people running back and forth between the West Coast and here all the time, don't we, Rickabee?"

"Yes, Sir."

"Do you suppose it would be possible for one of them to bring a couple of cases of this back here for me?"

"Certainly, Sir. No problem at all, Sir. Captain Lee is at Mare Island right now, Sir. I'll just call him and that'll take care of it. He's leaving tonight, that should get him in here the day after tomorrow."

"One of the little privileges that goes with being a general, right? Being able to get a Marine officer to haul a couple of cases of booze cross country for you?"

Jesus, I don't like this. What the hell is he leading up to?

"If you will call your people in San Francisco, General, and tell them Captain Lee will be coming by?"

The question was directed to Pickering's back. He had turned and walked out of the room again, and he didn't reply.

He returned in a moment with two glasses dark with whiskey. He handed one to Rickabee.

"Here you are, Rickabee."

"Thank you, Sir."

"Who shall we drink to?"

"How about The Corps, Sir?"

"How about those two Marines on Buka?" Pickering said.

"The Marines on Buka," Rickabee said, raising his glass.

"They have names," Pickering said. "Lieutenant Joe Howard and Sergeant Steve Koffler."

He's really pissed about something. Or is he drunk?

"Lieutenant Howard and Sergeant Koffler," Rickabee said.

"Joe and Steve," Pickering said, and took a healthy swallow from his drink. "Did you know, Rickabee, that I made Koffler a buck sergeant?"

"No, Sir, I did not."

"He's only a kid. A long way from being old enough to vote. But I figured that any Marine who volunteers to do what he is doing should be at least a buck sergeant. So I told Banning to arrange it."

"I didn't know that, General."

"Joe Howard's a Mustang," Pickering said. "An old pal of mine, a Marine I served with in France—he was a sergeant and I was a corporal, fellow named Jack (NMI) Stecker—thought that Sergeant Howard would make a pretty good officer and got him a direct commission."

"Yes, Sir. I know Major Stecker, Sir. I knew him when he was a master gunny at Quantico."

"One hell of a Marine, Jack (NMI) Stecker," Rickabee said.

"Yes, Sir, he is."

He is drunk. Otherwise why this trip down Marine Corps Memory Lane?

Further evidence of that came when General Pickering went back into the small room, returned with the bottle of Famous Grouse, and killed it freshening their glasses.

"No problem, I just checked. There's two more bottles where that came from. And then, of course, as a courtesy to a Marine General, Captain Lee is going to bring me some more, isn't he?"

"Yes, Sir."

"Sergeant Hart had two copies of Dillon's movies made," Pickering said. "Did you know that, Rickabee?"

"Yes, Sir. Lieutenant Moore told me."

"Clever fellow, that Hart."

"Yes, Sir."

"There's more to Moore than you might judge the first time you met him," Pickering said.

"Yes, Sir."

"Dillon's movies were very interesting, weren't they, Rickabee?"

"Yes, Sir. They were."

"Perhaps 'disturbing' would be a more accurate word."

"Disturbing *and* interesting, General."

"I lay awake a long time thinking about those movies," Pickering said. "And this morning, when Moore brought me the second copy Hart had made, I had the hospital send the projector back and watched them again. The projectionist got sick to his stomach."

"Really?"

"Well, what the hell do you expect, Rickabee? He was only a soldier, and we're *Marines*, right?"

Jesus Christ, he is about to get out of hand!

"That's when I called you," Pickering went on, "and asked you to come over here ... when the soldier was being sick."

"Yes, Sir."

"Those movies triggered a lot of thoughts in my mind, Rickabee. When I saw the shots of Henderson Field, it occurred to me that my son and Jack (NMI) Stecker's son are soon to be among the pilots there ... if they're not there already."

"Yes, Sir."

"And then I went back a long time, to when Jack and I were going through Parris Island. You go through Parris Island, Rickabee?"

"No, Sir. I came into The Corps as an officer."

"You know, a lot of people think that everybody in The Corps should go through Parris Island. I mean officers, too."

"It would probably be a good idea, General."

"Banning didn't go through Parris Island, either, did he?"

"No, Sir. I believe Major Banning came into The Corps as an officer, Sir."

"Good man, Banning," Pickering said.

"Yes, Sir."

"You know what they teach you as a boot at Parris Island, Rickabee? What they taught me, and Jack Stecker?"

"I don't take The General's point, Sir."

"They taught Jack and me that one of the things that makes Marines special, makes them different, better, than soldiers is that Marines don't leave their wounded, or their dead, on the battlefield."

"Yes, Sir."

"Do you think they still teach that, Rickabee? Or was that something just from the olden days of World War One?"

"No, Sir. I don't think it is."

"You think they taught that to Lieutenant Moore and Sergeant Hart, for example, when they went through Parris Island?"

"Yes, Sir. I'm sure they did."

"And they went back for Moore, didn't they, on Guadalcanal, when he was hit? A couple of Marines with balls went out there and got Moore and the Marines with him because they knew they were either dead or wounded, and Marines don't leave their dead or wounded, right?"

Where the hell is this conversation going?

"Yes, Sir. That's probably just what happened."

There was a knock at the door and two Army medics pushed a rolling cart into the room.

I hope the food sobers him up.

Lunch was vegetable soup, fried chicken, macaroni and noodles, a slice of bread, a banana custard, and a pot of tea.

"Please bring me some coffee," General Pickering said, and then changed his mind. "No. Belay that. I don't want any coffee. Thank you very much."

He took instead another swallow of Famous Grouse. Then he carefully cut a piece of chicken from the breast on his plate and put it in his mouth.

I hope that tastes terrible and he will divert the anger that's inside him to eating out the mess officer.

"Well, the mess sergeant must be drunk," General Pickering said. "That's really good."

"I'm pleased, Sir."

"I wonder what Joe Howard and Steve Koffler are eating on Buka?"

"I'm afraid they're not eating this well, General."

"More to the point, Rickabee," General Pickering asked conversationally, "when did we kick them out of The Corps?"

What the hell does that mean?

"Sir?"

"Well, I would call their physical condition pretty much the same as being wounded, and that's presuming they're still alive. If they were Marines, we'd go get them, wouldn't we? Marines don't get left on their battlefield when they're wounded. Or dead. So that means they're not Marines, right?"

"General, if Major Banning could relieve them, he would."

"Wrong. Major Banning has written them off. You were here when Dillon told me that. As far as Banning is concerned, as far as anybody is concerned, they're dead."

"I'm afraid that's true, Sir. There's absolutely nothing that can be done, given the circumstances."

"I'm going to tell you something, Colonel Rickabee," General Pickering said, just this side of nastily. "This Marine is going to try."

"I'm not sure I take The General's meaning, Sir."

"You can knock off that 'The General this' and 'The General that' crap, Rickabee. And you know damned well what I mean. You just don't want to hear it."

"May I speak bluntly, Sir?"

"You better. Bullshit time is over."

"There's nothing you can do, Sir."

"Maybe not. But I am damned sure going to try. If I have the power to have some captain deliver overnight two cases of booze to me from the West Coast, I ought to be able to divert a little of it to getting those two kids off of Buka."

"Trying to reinforce them would endanger their safety."

"What safety, for Christ's sake? Feldt and Banning are sitting around in Townsville with their thumbs up their ass waiting to hear they're dead."

"I'm sorry to hear that you have lost your confidence in Major Banning."

"I was sorry to lose it. What's happened is that he's forgotten he's a Marine and fallen under Feldt's goddamned British philosophy that no sacrifice is too great for King and Country."

"I can't believe that Ed Banning is capable of forgetting he's a Marine," Rickabee said, aware that he was on the edge of losing his temper.

"Then why is he sitting around waiting for those two kids to get killed?"

I'll be a sonofabitch. Touché, General.

"General, I wouldn't know where to start. I'm exceedingly reluctant to sit here in Washington and second-guess what Banning is doing, the decisions he is forced to make."

"I'm not," Pickering said simply. "And, for a place to start, I want to see McCoy."

"McCoy?"

"Is there some reason that's impossible?"

"Sir, there is an operation in the planning stages—"

"What kind of an operation?"

"We're going to set up a weather observation station in Mongolia, General. The mission was laid on The Corps by the Joint Chiefs. The station will be required later in the war for long-range bombing raids. McCoy is singularly well qualified to take a major role."

"Mongolia?" Pickering asked dubiously, and then: "When does this operation get under way?"

"In about four months, Sir. They're trying to decide the best way to get the people into Mongolia."

"I'm planning to get Howard and Koffler off Buka in the next month, Rickabee. Send for McCoy. I have the feeling there's a very good reason they call him 'Killer.' And in any event, he's a simple ex–enlisted man like me who believes that Marines don't leave their dead and wounded on the battlefield."

"There are a number of professional officers, General, including this one, who don't think so either."

"I've angered you, Rickabee, haven't I?"

What you've done is made me a little ashamed of myself.

"No, Sir. Not at all, Sir. I'll have McCoy here in the morning, and I'll give this some thought."

(FIVE)
The Foster Lafayette Hotel
Washington, D.C.
1910 Hours 22 September 1942

"May I help you, Miss?" the desk clerk said to the striking young woman with jet-black, pageboy-cut hair.

"May I have the key to 614, please?" she asked.

Although every effort had been made to prepare him for every possible contingency, the request posed certain problems for the desk clerk.

For one thing, he had no idea who this woman was. For another, 614 was a three-room suite maintained year-round by American Personal Pharmaceuticals, Inc., for the convenience of corporate executives who had business in Washington. For another, the desk clerk was aware that the Chairman of the Board of American Personal Pharmaceuticals, Inc., and his wife had a personal relationship with the Foster family: Mrs. Elaine Sage had been the college roommate of Mrs. Patricia Pickering, Andrew Foster's only child.

A quick look at the key board confirmed the desk clerk's recollection that 614 was not occupied at the moment.

The stunning young woman in the pageboy was obviously not Mrs. Elaine Sage. She was not even married; there was no ring on her finger. Neither was there a ring on the third finger of the left hand of the uncomfortable-looking young Marine officer standing behind her.

"Six-fourteen, Miss?"

"Please. I'm Ernestine Sage."

"Just a moment, please," the desk clerk said and walked quickly to the small office occupied by the assistant manager on duty.

"There is a young woman at the counter—a real looker, in bangs—who wants the key to 614. She says her name is Sage."

"A looker with bangs? Give it to her. That's Ernest Sage's daughter."

"She's got a Marine with her," the desk clerk said.

"Really?" the assistant manager said, and got up and walked through the door to the counter.

"Hello, Miss Sage," he said. Then, in one smooth move, he snatched the key from the key board, handed it to her, and tinkled the bell for a bellboy. "Nice to have you in the house again. And you too, Lieutenant McCoy."

"How are you," Ken McCoy responded, running the words together and flashing a brief uncomfortable smile.

"Thank you, it's nice to see you," Ernie Sage said, and turned to follow the bellboy with their luggage to the elevators.

The assistant manager picked up the telephone and asked for room service.

"Send flowers, fruit, and a bottle of champagne, Moet, to six fourteen," he ordered. After he hung up, he turned to the desk clerk. "That was indeed Miss Ernestine Sage. The gentleman with her is Lieutenant K. R. McCoy. Lieutenant Malcolm S. Pickering—who was once the bell captain here, by the way, did you know that?"

"No, I didn't."

"—Lieutenant Pickering once told me that Lieutenant McCoy was his best friend. He asked me as a personal favor to him to take very good care of Lieutenant McCoy whenever he was in the house. Is everything clear now, Tom?"

"Crystal clear."

* * *

In the elevator, oblivious to the presence of the operator, the bellboy, and a well-dressed couple in their fifties, Ernie Sage said, "Don't you *dare* look embarrassed! *I'm* not the one who doesn't want to get married."

"Jesus, Ernie!" McCoy said, flushing.

"*I* have no objection to becoming an honest woman," Ernie said, enjoying herself. "*You're* the one who insists on living in sin."

McCoy rushed off the elevator before the doors were fully open and hurried down the corridor. Ernie smiled warmly at the well-dressed middle-aged couple before following the bellboy.

Once the door was open, McCoy headed for the couch in the sitting room and picked up the telephone from the coffee table in front of it. He gave the operator a number.

"Give me the watch officer, please.

"Lieutenant McCoy, Sir. The Colonel told me to check in when I got to Washington.

"No, Sir. I'm in the Foster Lafayette Hotel. Room 614.

"Thank you, Sir."

Ernie, meanwhile, had led the bellboy into the largest bedroom, tipped him, and then watched him leave. By the time McCoy was done with the phone, she had removed all her clothing but her underwear. She was now standing in the bedroom doorway with her hip thrust out provocatively. Her arm was behind her head and a rose was in her teeth.

"Hi, Marine! Looking for a good time?"

"You're nuts, you know that?"

"I don't know about you, but I find it terribly sexy to be in a hotel room with someone I'm not married to."

"You're going to keep that up, are you?"

There was not time for her to reply. There was a knock at the door. After she closed the bedroom door, McCoy opened the corridor door to a waiter delivering a rolling cart with champagne, fruit, cut flowers, and a copy of *The Washington Post.*

The bellman refused the two dollars McCoy extended to him.

"No, Sir. Professional courtesy. Pick and I used to run bells together. Any friend of Pick's—"

"Thanks," McCoy said.

As soon as the door had closed behind the bellboy, the bedroom door opened.

"Isn't that nice?" Ernie said. "Why don't you just roll that in here?"

"I've had worse offers," McCoy said.

The telephone rang. Ernie picked up the phone on the bedside table.

"Hello?" she said, and then extended it to McCoy.

"Lieutenant McCoy.

"Yes, Sir. I'll be there.

"Sir, I have someone with me. A friend of General Pickering's. She would like to visit with him. Would that be possible?"

"Try to keep me away! I'm not in the goddamned Marines!" Ernie announced.

"Yes, Sir. I understand. Thank you, Sir.

"Whichever would be easier, Sir. I'll be here. Yes, Sir. Good night, Sir."

"You understand what?" Ernie said when he put the telephone down.

"You can see him for thirty minutes at half past seven in the morning."

"Oh, I'm so grateful!"

"Hey, I told you this was duty."

"What's it all about?"

"I don't know. I'm—which does *not* mean 'you'—about to find out. Captain Sessions is coming over here."

"Great!" Ernie said sarcastically.

"He could have made me go to the office. You're getting to be a pain in the ass, Ernie."

Her face tightened. She opened her mouth to reply, then visibly changed her mind.

"Sorry," she said.

"I'm sorry I said that," McCoy said, genuinely contrite.

She waved her hand, signifying it didn't matter.

"When's Ed Sessions coming?"

"It'll probably take him thirty minutes, maybe forty-five. He's got some stuff the Colonel wants me to read before we see General Pickering."

"I don't know about you, baby," Ernie said, "but on general principles, I have nothing against a quickie."

When Captain Edward Sessions walked into suite 614, Lieutenant K. R. McCoy and Miss Ernestine Sage, fully clothed, were sitting on the couch in the sitting room, working on an enormous platter of shrimp and oysters. It did not escape his attention, however, that despite the early hour, the bed he could see through a partially opened door seemed to have been slept in.

"Good to see you, Ernie," he said, and she stood on her tiptoes and kissed his cheek.

"Would you be crushed, Ed, if I told you I suspect something is about to happen that I'm not going to like at all?"

"No," he said.

He fumbled in his pocket for the key to the handcuff which chained his briefcase to his wrist, freed his wrist, and handed the briefcase to McCoy.

"If some kind soul were to offer me a drink and an oyster, I could occupy myself while you read that, Ken," Sessions said.

"We just had a bottle of champagne," Ernie said. "I would order another, but I don't think we have anything to celebrate. Scotch, Ed?"

"Please," he said.

McCoy settled himself in a corner of the couch and opened the briefcase. Before she made Sessions' drink, Ernie looked long enough to see TOP SECRET cover sheets on the manila folder he took from the briefcase. After a moment's thought she made one for herself.

She glanced at Ken. She recognized the look of absolute concentration on his face. She knew he would be annoyed if she offered him a drink or even handed him one.

She gave Ed Sessions his drink.

"How's Jeanne, Ed?"

"Great. If she knew you were here, she would have come. She'll be sorry to have missed you."

Five minutes later McCoy raised his eyes from the stack of folders on his lap.

"OK. I gave it a quick once-over. What's this got to do with me?"

"All I know is that General Pickering told the Colonel to send for you," Sessions said.

"Is Banning behind that?" McCoy asked.

Sessions shrugged his shoulders.

"I don't know. All I know is that the Colonel wants you 'conversant' with that stuff before we see The General in the morning."

"We who?"

"The Colonel, me, and you," Sessions said.

"I can't memorize all this by morning."

"He said 'conversant,' not 'memorize.'"

McCoy nodded and returned his attention to the folders with their TOP SECRET cover sheets. Finally he stuffed everything back into the briefcase.

"I didn't know until just now that Marines were involved in that operation."

Sessions grunted.

"I'm sorry you had to come over here," McCoy said. "I could have gone to the office."

"They don't have oysters and good whiskey in the office. Anyway, I got to see Ernie," Sessions said as he picked up the briefcase and handcuffed it to his wrist.

"Give Jeanne my love," Ernie said.

"Maybe we can get together while you're here."

"How long will we be here?"

"I guess we'll find that out in the morning," Sessions said. He shook hands with McCoy, kissed Ernie, and left.

McCoy got off the couch and made himself a drink.

"You're not going to tell me what that was all about, right?" Ernie asked.

"I don't know what it's all about," McCoy said. And then, obviously to change the subject, "Well, what should we do now?"

"I've never had any problem with 'early to bed and early to rise,'" Ernie said, and then added, "You know what I'd really like to do? Take a walk."

"A *walk*?" he asked incredulously.

"A walk. One foot after the other. It's beautiful out. Past the White House. Take a look in the windows of the department stores."

McCoy shrugged. "Why not?"

They'd stopped outside the Washington Theater to scan the posters showing Flight Lieutenant Tyrone Power of the Eagle Squadron about to climb in the cockpit of his Spitfire when the doors opened and a Marine sergeant and his girl came out.

The Marine sergeant spotted the officer's bars on McCoy's shoulders and saluted before he recognized McCoy.

"How are you, Hart?" McCoy said.

"Can't complain, Sir."

"I'm Ernie Sage, Sergeant," Ernie said, "since I doubt if the Lieutenant will introduce us."

"Ernie, this is Sergeant George Hart. He works for General Pickering," McCoy said.

"How is he?" Ernie demanded. "And a straight answer, please?"

"You can tell her," McCoy said. "She's going to see him in the morning anyway."

"He's much better. He's not nearly as strong as he thinks he is."

"Since I doubt if Sergeant Hart is going to introduce us, Miss, my name is McCoy."

"Wise guy!" Ernie said.

"Elizabeth—they call me Beth—Lathrop."

"And I'm Ernie, and I'm Ken's girlfriend, and I just decided that we should all go somewhere for a drink."

"You can't do that in public," McCoy said uncomfortably. "It's against regulations for officers to drink with enlisted Marines."

"Well, then, we'll go to the hotel," Ernie said. "Sergeant, that's not as snobbish as it sounded. When the Lieutenant was a corporal, he was just as much a by-the-book Marine."

"I don't want to—" Hart protested.

"Nonsense," Ernie said. "I want to hear more about Uncle Fleming."

"The hotel and a drink's a good idea," McCoy said. "I've had enough walking for the night."

"I know who you are," Beth said. "You're Pick's friend."

"You know Pick?" Ernie asked delightedly.

"I know him," Beth said.

There was a strange note in her voice. Ernie concluded from it that this was one of Pick Pickering's discards. Their number was legion.

"Well, then, you have to come," Ernie said. "We can swap nasty stories about him."

McCoy, too, picked up on her uneasiness, and Hart's—his reluctance to come with them.

It's either that I'm an officer, he decided, *or more likely, that he wanted to go off with the dame and get a little and is afraid this will screw that up.*

Tough luck, if that's what Ernie wants, that's what she'll get.

XII

"Ernie, I hate to run you off, but we have to shuffle some paper," General Pickering said. "I'll have Sergeant Hart run you back to the hotel."

"We drove up, Uncle Fleming," Ernie said. "We have our car. You behave, you understand?"

"You call my wife and make a valiant effort to convince her that I am really in prime health, and I will behave. Deal?"

"Deal," she said, and kissed him. "You take care of Ken, too."

"I'll do my best," Pickering said. "Make sure you give your mother and dad my best."

She smiled and then turned to McCoy. "I will see you at the hotel, right?"

"I just don't know," McCoy said. "I'll call if—"

"You'll see him at the hotel," Pickering interrupted. "Now get out of here."

She blew him a kiss and left.

Pickering looked at McCoy.

" '*We* drove up'?" he quoted. " '*I* have *our* car'?" When McCoy didn't answer, Pickering went on. "You could do a hell of a lot worse than that girl, Ken. I always hoped she'd marry Pick."

"Yes, Sir. She told me. So did her father."

"Her family scare you? Their money?"

"I don't think people who earn their living the way I do should get married," McCoy said.

"I just heard about the Mongolian Operation yesterday. Is that it?"

"That's part of it, General."

"Well, since it's none of my business, I think you're wrong. Take what you can when you can get it, Ken. Life is no rehearsal."

"Yes, Sir."

"I admitted it was none of my business," Pickering said. "Maybe I'd feel the same way you do."

There was a knock at the door and Sergeant Hart came in.

"Colonel Rickabee and the others are here, Sir."

"Major Dillon, too?"

"Yes, Sir."

Pickering waved his hand, signaling Hart to bring them in.

"Thank you for coming, Jake," Pickering said. "I think it's important. Is this going to get you in hot water with General—Whatsisname?—Stewart?"

"I sent word that I was sick," Dillon replied, "and sent the film over there by messenger. It'll be all right."

"General, I can call General Stewart," Rickabee volunteered.

"Hold off on doing that awhile," Pickering said.

"Jake, you don't know McCoy, do you?"

"Only by reputation. Killer McCoy, right?"

"He doesn't like that, don't call him that again," Pickering said, giving him a hard look.

"Sorry, Lieutenant," Dillon said, shaking McCoy's hand. "No offense."

"None taken, Sir," McCoy said, not entirely convincingly.

"I guess you've seen this?" Dillon said, taking a copy of the INS story about Machine Gun McCoy from his pocket and handing it to him with a smile.

"Yes, Sir, I've seen it."

"This one came by messenger this morning," Dillon said. "There's talk about making a flick about him."

"I heard they're thinking about making a movie about the Makin raid," McCoy said.

"Not thinking. They approved the treatment, a screenplay is in the works, and they signed Randolph Scott to play Colonel Carlson."

"Jesus Christ," McCoy said disgustedly. "Why not Errol Flynn?"

"Sir, does The General want Lieutenant Moore and Sergeant Hart in on this?" Colonel Rickabee asked.

"I told you to knock off that 'The General' crap," Pickering said sharply, which Rickabee correctly interpreted to mean that The General was at least slightly hung over and in a nasty mood. "And, yeah, I think so," Pickering went on. "Does that pose a security clearance problem for you?"

"No, Sir. Sergeant Hart is cleared to TOP SECRET. And no problem, of course, with Moore."

"OK, then. They stay," Pickering ordered. "I think they're going to be involved in this anyway, to one degree or another."

"Yes, Sir."

"On the security business, what is said in this room, for reasons that will become obvious, is classified TOP SECRET," Pickering said. "Everybody understand that?"

There was a chorus of "Yes, Sir."

"Let me state the problem, then," Pickering said. "Our first priority is to keep Ferdinand Six up and running. Our second priority is to get Howard and Koffler off Buka—and Reeves too, probably. Just as soon as I can get out of here, my intention is to go back to Australia and get our people to do whatever is necessary to bring Howard and Koffler back. For reasons I don't want to get into, they seem to have just written them off."

"No, Sir," Colonel Rickabee said, flatly.

"I beg your pardon?"

"You can't go back over there, General. That's out of the question," Rickabee said.

Pickering looked at him coldly. There was a long and awkward silence. When Pickering finally spoke, it was not in response to Rickabee.

"Hart has no idea what the rest of us will be talking about," he said. "And I really don't know how much McCoy knows."

"I read the file last night, Sir," McCoy said.

"Sessions has it with him, Sir," Rickabee said.

"See that Hart reads it," Pickering said. "How complete is it?"

"Enough to give him the picture, General," McCoy said.

"OK. So we'll start with you, McCoy. If you were God, more to the point, if you were a general officer, how would you go about getting those people out . . . while at the same time keeping Ferdinand Six up?"

"General," McCoy said, uncomfortably, "if Major Banning can't do that, I don't know—"

"I'll rephrase the question. If you were Major Banning, what would you do if you were *ordered* to get Howard and Koffler off Buka?"

"It wouldn't be easy," McCoy said. "Even if keeping the radio station in operation wasn't a consideration."

"You'll notice, Rickabee," Pickering said, "that he didn't say 'impossible.'"

"Maybe I should have," McCoy said.

"OK. Explain that," Pickering said. "But don't quote Banning to me. Tell me why you think it would be 'not easy' to 'impossible.'"

"Yes, Sir," McCoy said in a reflex reply. "Well, my first thought was that getting them out by air *would* be impossible. There's no airfield. So that left getting them out by water. We cannot send surface ships, even native boats, because the waters are heavily patrolled. That leaves submarines—"

Pickering interrupted him. "What's wrong with submarines?"

"Several things," McCoy said. "First of all, I doubt if we could get one."

"Let's say we can get one," Pickering said, "and take it from there."

"We probably could not get one to—" Rickabee said, and was interrupted by Pickering.

"Two things, Rickabee. One, McCoy has the floor, and, two, I told him to go ahead on the presumption that he can get a submarine."

"—make an *extraction,* Sir," Rickabee went on, ignoring him. "But, since Ferdinand Six is of great value to the Navy, they probably would give us one to insert a Coastwatcher team."

"You have a point," Pickering said, not at all graciously. "Go on, McCoy."

"A submarine could be used to land a replacement team and to take out the team that's there," McCoy said. "At least that was my first thought."

"Psychologically speaking, I think it would be a good idea," Pickering announced, "to refer to the Marines on Buka by their names. Their names are Lieutenant Joe Howard and Sergeant Steve Koffler. We're not talking about a navigation buoy we left floating around an atoll someplace."

"Yes, Sir," McCoy said.

"You were about to tell us what's wrong with a submarine," Pickering said.

"One, it would have to surface offshore someplace, obviously. That means it would have to do so at night, to lower the chances that Japanese ships, aircraft, or *Japanese* coastwatchers would see it."

"'*Japanese* coastwatchers'?" Pickering parroted.

"The Makin raid has taught the Japanese some lessons. For one, they're now afraid there'll be other raids. They are watching all their beaches."

"They don't have the manpower to watch all their coastline," Pickering argued.

"They probably have enough to watch the beaches where you could put rubber boats ashore. And rubber boats is something else."

"Explain that," Pickering ordered.

"We had trouble getting onto the beach at Makin," McCoy said. "And we damned near didn't get off. You want me to talk about putting a replacement team in by submarine?"

"Please."

"We could probably find enough people in the 2nd Raider Battalion to handle the rubber boats—"

"Why couldn't the replacement team paddle their own boats?" Rickabee asked.

"Because it's a hell of lot harder than it looks, a hell of a lot harder than Colonel Carlson and Captain Roosevelt, or me, thought it would be," McCoy said simply. "It requires both skill and a lot of muscle. I just said we damned near didn't get off the beach. Seven of us didn't."

George Hart stared for a time at Lieutenant McCoy, for he found it hard to really accept it that the man now sitting across the room from him in an immaculate uniform, not even wearing any ribbons, holding a cup of coffee, the man who had entertained him and Beth the night before with stories of the trouble he'd had getting Pick Pickering through Officer Candidate School, had been one of the Marine Raiders who struck Makin Island.

"Ken," Captain Sessions asked, speaking for the first time, "you're saying you don't think we could train our people to handle rubber boats?"

"No, I don't think so. And even if we could, what about the—Lieutenant Whatsis-name and the sergeant?"

"Howard and Koffler," Pickering furnished evenly.

"Yes, Sir. Howard and Koffler. They would have to be rowed back through the surf to the submarine. They sure couldn't do it themselves. The replacement team would be exhausted from rowing to shore. It's a lot harder, that sort of crap, than anyone understands until they've tried it."

"OK," Pickering said.

"Let me kill the idea, please, Sir," McCoy said. "The replacement team would be taking a radio, radios, in with them."

"*Two* radios," Rickabee said. "A replacement and a spare."

"Each weighing about a hundred pounds?"

"That's right."

"Then, Sir, based on our experience at Makin, you would have to send in *four* radios, to make sure *two* made it to the beach. And we didn't try to off-load anything that heavy from the submarines into the rubber boats. The heaviest thing we carried ashore was a Browning .50. And that was a bitch. We lost two I know about. Maybe, probably, more."

"You sound as negative about this as Banning, McCoy," Pickering said.

Although his tone was conversational, it was clear that General Pickering was both angry and disappointed.

"But just for the hell of it," McCoy went on, "let's suppose we could somehow get around the rubber boat problem. How would we get word to"—he searched his memory and came up with the names—"Koffler and Howard to meet up with the submarine?"

"We are in radio contact," Pickering said.

"I think we have to presume that the Japs are monitoring their transmissions, and that they have broken the code," McCoy said. "They are not stupid."

Rickabee remembered again that Corporal McCoy had not applied for OCS. A report he had written about Japanese troop movements when he worked for Captain Ed Banning in the Fourth Marines in China had come to the attention of General Forrest. Forrest's reaction had been blunt and to the point. *"I think we ought to put bars on that corporal's shoulders. Right now he and I are the only two people in The Marine Corps who don't seem to devoutly believe that all Japs are five feet two, wear thick glasses, and that we can whip them with one hand tied behind our backs."*

Captain Ed Sessions had marched a very reluctant Corporal McCoy before an officer candidate selection board. Before he did that, Captain Sessions had informed the president of the board that if he found reason to reject Corporal McCoy as suitable officer material, he better be prepared to defend that to General Forrest.

"Going off at a tangent, McCoy, accepting what you just said," Rickabee asked, "why do you think the Japanese haven't located and taken out Ferdinand Six?"

"Yeah," Pickering said thoughtfully.

"They know where they are within a mile or so. So the question is really, why haven't they taken them out?"

"OK."

"That's rough terrain. Steep hills, thick jungle. Which also explains why they don't try to take them out with aircraft; it would be a waste of effort. They can't see them from the air, and even if they did, bombing or strafing them would be a waste of effort.

And by the time they got within a couple of miles on the ground, the Coastwatchers would know about it. The Coastwatchers have natives who know the terrain. They can keep out of the Japs' way. And the Japs know that. They're *not* stupid."

"They must know what Ferdinand Six is costing them," Pickering said.

"Yes, Sir. But they also know that radios don't function forever in the jungle, and that white men can't live there for any length of time. They're patient; the problem will solve itself."

"You were saying that you think the Japanese have broken the code?"

"What are they using?" McCoy asked, looking at Captain Sessions.

"An old SOI," Sessions offered, meaning *S*ignal *O*perating *I*nstruction. "When they repeat it, they jump ahead, using Howard's serial number. I think you're right. They've broken it."

"I have no idea what you're talking about," Pickering said.

"General, they have a code book with a different code for each of thirty days," Sessions explained. "When they run past thirty days, they start over again from the beginning. But not in the same sequence this time—not one, two, three. This time, say, if Howard's serial was 56789, they use the code for the fifth day; and the day after that, they count ahead six days, the second number of his serial number. You understand how it works, General?"

"I do now."

"So what I was saying," McCoy went on, "was that even if we got a submarine, found a beach which would take rubber boats, and managed to get the replacement team and their hundred-pound radios ashore, it wouldn't do us any good, because we have no way of letting—*Howard and Koffler*—know when and where to meet the submarine. If we tried to tell them, we have to assume the Japanese would intercept the message. The Japs would then ambush them on their way to the beach. And they'd be waiting for the submarine to surface."

Colonel F. L. Rickabee was very impressed with Lieutenant K. R. McCoy. Having placed a great deal of confidence in Major Ed Banning's ability, he had not given a great deal of thought to the problems of extracting the—*Howard and Koffler*—from Buka . . . until his somewhat strained luncheon the previous afternoon with a somewhat intoxicated and very upset Brigadier General Fleming Pickering.

After giving the problem some hard thought, he had come up with very much the same conclusion that Banning had obviously reached in Australia—that getting those two guys out was impossible. It seemed pretty clear that McCoy had reached the same conclusion now that the facts were available to him.

This should shut Pickering up, Rickabee thought with a great sense of relief. *As a veteran of the Makin raid, McCoy was obviously an expert in rubber boat landings. Pickering would accept his judgment. And McCoy was a Mustang: A former enlisted Marine would not decide they couldn't go and pick up the dead and wounded unless it was really impossible.*

Better he should get this painful truth from McCoy than from me again.

"I gather that you and Major Banning are in agreement, then, McCoy, that there is absolutely nothing we can do for Joe Howard and Steve Koffler?" General Pickering asked, his voice now sounding very tired.

"No, Sir," McCoy said. "I didn't say that."

"Well then, goddamn it, let's have it!"

"I thought of two ways we might be able to carry this off," McCoy said. "One's kind of wild."

"Let's hear it, McCoy."

"I started out with the submarine idea," McCoy said. "Christ, there's so much I don't know!"

"We can get answers. Go ahead," Pickering said.

"Yes, Sir. OK. Step one. We find a beach that will take boats. Depending on what the surf and the beach are like when we get there, we put ashore the radios, the replacement Marines, and an Australian Coastwatcher. We'll also bring one, or better, two natives who know the island and can find Ferdinand Six. If the surf is bad, we just put the natives ashore. We don't try to land the radios and the replacement team. Then the natives find Ferdinand Six and tell them where the submarine will be—probably a different beach. Maybe with a little bit of luck, there would be native boats to go out to the submarine—"

"I like it," General Pickering said, looking triumphantly at Colonel Rickabee.

Oh, shit! Rickabee thought.

"Then," McCoy went on, "as I was thinking about that, I had a wild hare."

And how, Lieutenant McCoy, Rickabee wondered, *would you describe your previous "Errol Flynn Fights the Nasty Nips" idea as a tame hare?*

"Well?"

"Use an R4D, just go in, off-load the replacement team and radios, and pick up the guys that are there," McCoy said.

"I thought it was pretty well established that there was no airfield."

"There's beaches," McCoy said. "Maybe there's the right kind of sand, packed so it will take an R4D."

"I don't think so," Sessions said.

"You're talking about landing an R4D on a beach?" Rickabee asked incredulously. "It would just sink in."

"I've been nosing around for the Mongolian Operation," McCoy said. "We can make that flight only one time. If the Japs see the plane, we have to hope they think it was some guy just got lost. But if two planes got lost, they would be very suspicious. So we're going to have to take everything we'll need in with us and get it safely on the ground. And it's a one-way ride; there's no way the plane can get out again. So the question came up—they're still talking about it—of what to do with the airplane."

"I have no idea what you're talking about, McCoy," Pickering said.

"General, I'll have the Mongolia file in your hands this afternoon," Rickabee said.

"I want to hear about it now."

"General, we're getting into Need to Know," Rickabee said, gesturing toward Dillon and Hart.

"I'll decide who needs to know what," Pickering said icily. "Go on, McCoy."

"Sir, we're setting up a weather observation station in the Mongolian desert. The only way we can get in is by air. So they're going to add auxiliary fuel tanks to an R4D that will give us the necessary range from the Aleutian Islands—"

"The Japanese hold Attu in the Aleutians," Pickering interrupted.

"Yes, Sir. That's one of the problems. Anyway, we can probably get enough range to make it in. The original idea was to parachute the team in and then leave the airplane on automatic pilot and let it crash when it ran out of fuel. But they were still cutting the fuel supply so tight, they were afraid it would run out too close to the drop site. So then they thought if they didn't use parachutes and the packing necessary for the equipment, they could carry that much more fuel. So they've been wondering how they land the plane in the desert. Maybe just land it and bury it in sand. Or maybe land it, unload it, and then take off again and put it on autopilot. Anyway, they're working on how to land it on sand. I don't know whether that will work, or if it does, whether it would work on a beach in Buka, but it would sure solve a lot of problems."

"The plane that dropped Howard and Koffler on Buka was shot down on its way home," Rickabee said.

This Mongolian Operation, obviously, is just about as risky for the people involved as Ferdinand Six, Pickering thought. *And one of the reasons McCoy is so matter-of-factly willing to go on it is that he believes, as a matter of faith, that if he gets in trouble, somebody else in The Corps will do all that's humanly possible to get him out.*

I'm right about this! *Even if Rickabee, and probably Sessions, think I'm a goddamned fool.*

"We could solve that problem, too," Pickering said. "Who's 'they,' McCoy? Where are they working on this land-on-sand business?"

"At an Army Air Corps airfield in Florida, General. On the Florida panhandle, up near the Alabama border."

"That's where Jimmy Doolittle trained for his B-25 Shangri-la mission on Tokyo," Pickering thought aloud.

"Eglin Field, I think, Sir," McCoy said.

"No. It's probably an auxiliary field, between Eglin and Pensacola. I was there a while back. Is there any reason you can't go down there and find out something for sure?"

"I can go down there, yes, Sir."

"Then go."

"General, if I could have Lieutenant Moore and Sergeant Hart . . . having them with me might be helpful."

"OK. Whatever you think you need," Pickering said, and went on: "We have concluded that the extraction of Joe Howard and Steve Koffler is not impossible . . ."

You have the fantasy that it's not impossible, Rickabee thought. *Jesus Christ, landing an airliner on a beach, right under the nose of the Japanese! Fifty, sixty miles from a Japanese fighter base!*

"We will now deal with your statement, Colonel, that my going to Australia is 'out of the question.'"

"Admiral Leahy would not give you permission, General," Rickabee said. And then, anticipating Pickering's response to that, he went on. "And if you were to go without permission, he would order you home as soon as he heard about it. Among other things, that would serve to call attention to this operation, which is the last thing you want to happen."

"Jesus!" Pickering said bitterly.

It was clear to Rickabee that he had made his point. "Lieutenant McCoy," he said, "carrying a letter of instructions from you, General, to Major Banning, would, I suggest, be all that's needed."

"I don't think so," Pickering said. "McCoy is a lieutenant, Banning a major. What I have been thinking is that Jake outranks Banning."

Goddamn it, I should have known he would pick up on that, Rickabee thought. *Dillon came back into The Corps as a major while Banning was still in the Philippines as a captain.*

"Flem, for Christ's sake," Jake Dillon said uncomfortably, "I'm a press agent wearing a major's uniform. I don't know anything about this sort of thing."

"You're a Marine, Jake," Pickering said. "And all you have to do is go there and report to me that Banning is or is not doing what you tell him to do. And what you tell him to do is what McCoy tells you he wants done."

"General, that puts me in a hell of a spot," McCoy said.

"There is a limited access communications channel available to us. Moore is familiar with it . . ." Pickering said.

Jesus, he's talking about the MAGIC channel, Rickabee thought. *He shouldn't*

even think of using that for this harebrained scheme of his! But Jesus, except for
Admiral Leahy or the President himself, there's no one to tell him he can't.

"We will utilize that to keep in touch with day-to-day developments. As Rickabee
just pointed out, the less attention paid to this operation, the better. The question,
John, is whether you feel up to going back to Australia."

"Yes, Sir. I feel fine."

"General, he's walking around with a cane!" Rickabee protested.

"You're sure?" Pickering asked Moore.

"Yes, Sir, I'm sure," Lieutenant Moore said.

"OK. We're under way," Pickering said. "Now we start with the administrative
details. I've got some letters to write. Can I have a typewriter sent over here,
Rickabee?"

"I'll send you a secretary, Sir."

"I asked for a typewriter," Pickering said.

"Aye, aye, Sir."

"You can start on getting orders cut," Pickering said. "And McCoy and Moore
and Hart will need plane tickets right away."

"Sir," Lieutenant McCoy said, "the overnight train to Miami—'Seacoast Airline'
they call it for some reason I never understood—comes through Washington at half
past six. If we could get on that, we could get a good night's sleep. We could get
off in Tallahassee and catch the Greyhound bus to Eglin."

"See if you can get them a compartment—compartments—on the train," Pickering ordered. "And see if you can't arrange to have somebody from Eglin pick them
up at Tallahassee."

"Aye, Aye, Sir," Sessions said. "No problem, we have an officer there in connection with Operation CHINA SUN."

In the car on the way back to the Mall and Temporary Building T-2032, Captain
Edward Sessions turned to Colonel F. L. Rickabee and asked, "Do you think they'll
be able to pull this off, Colonel?"

"It isn't my place to think about my orders, Captain. I'm a Marine officer; when
I am given an order, I do my best to carry it out. But since you asked, no, I don't
think so. Do I hope they can? Yes, I do."

"Why do you suppose McCoy wanted to take Moore and Hart with him to
Florida?"

"I have absolutely no idea," Rickabee said, "my mind being otherwise occupied
with such mundane questions as under what authority we are going to be able to
transport Major Dillon to Australia. He is assigned to Public Affairs, after all. . . .
And on the subject of Major Dillon, did it occur to you that Dillon has been made
privy to Operation CHINA SUN?"

"I think Dillon can be trusted to keep his mouth shut, Colonel."

"I hope so," Rickabee said. "Jesus Christ, I hope so!"

Second Lieutenant John Marston Moore waited until they were in suite 614 of the
Foster Lafayette Hotel before asking the question Captain Sessions asked: "Exactly
what are we going to do in Florida, McCoy?"

"I'm going to talk to an Air Corps guy I met down there. He knows all about the
kind of sand you need to land airplanes on. And, more important, he invented a gimmick
. . . you stick a cone, sort of, just far enough into the sand to make it stand up. Then
you drop a ten-pound weight on it from exactly twenty-four inches. How far that drives
the cone into the ground tells you how much weight the sand will support."

"Fascinating," Moore said.

"I want to talk to him and talk him out of a couple of the cone things—as many as he'll give me," McCoy said. "That'll probably take the better part of an hour. Two hours if he buys us lunch in their officer's club. That reminds me, Hart, you're going to have to wear civilian clothes."

"Yes, Sir," Hart said.

"And what else?"

"The beach along the Gulf Coast there is as pretty as any in Hawaii," McCoy said. "And the seafood is great. With a little bit of luck, we'll have twenty-four hours, maybe thirty-six, before Sessions gets us seats on the courier plane out of Pensacola back here."

"What do you need us along for?" Hart asked.

"Beth said she was on vacation," McCoy said. "Don't you think she'd like a day or two on the beach in Florida? And a romantic dinner on a train? I know damned well Ernie will."

"Who's Beth?" Moore asked.

"Hart's girlfriend," McCoy said. "She came to Washington to see him."

"That was the mysterious telephone call?" Moore asked.

Hart nodded.

Jesus, what the hell will happen if they find out what Beth does for a living? Hart asked himself.

It took Hart a moment to decide that McCoy was perfectly serious.

McCoy saw the look on his face, and on Moore's.

"Would you two like a few words of wisdom from an old Marine?" he asked, and went on without waiting for a reply. "In case you haven't figured this out yet, we're about to get shipped out. The way Pickering is pushing Rickabee, we're going just as soon as they can cut orders. When Pickering said he wanted me to find out about landing an R4D on sand, the first thing I thought was that I would call this Air Corps guy, tell him the problem, then send Hart down there to get the gimmicks to test the sand. *Then* I thought that if I hung around here waiting for him to come back, Rickabee and Sessions would find things for me to do. *Then* I decided that I would have to go myself, even though that's a sacrifice. *Then* I decided that it would not be fair to a wounded hero—such as yourself, Lieutenant Moore—to leave you behind to run errands while Sergeant Hart and myself and our girlfriends are riding on a luxury train and lying on a Florida beach. Am I getting through to you two?"

Moore laughed. "It sounds like we'll be busy!" he said.

"As General Pickering said to me just this morning," McCoy said, " 'Take what you can, when you can get it.' Who am I to argue with a general?" Then he saw the look on Hart's face. "What's the matter with you? Don't you think Beth will want to go?"

"I'm sure she'll want to go," Hart said.

I'm not sure I should take her. Jesus, why did she have to be a whore?

"Then you better get your ass over to Union Station and get tickets for the girls on the Seacoast Airline Limited or whatever the hell they call it. You got any money?" he asked, as he took a sheaf of bills from his pocket.

"Pity you don't have a girl, Moore," McCoy said. "But maybe you'll get lucky in the club car."

When Major Jake Dillon walked into the Metro-Magnum Studios suite in the Willard Hotel, Veronica Wood was preparing herself for *her* day's work: Her long blond hair was pulled tightly back against her head, and she had converted the coffee table in the sitting room to a makeup table. She was wearing a really ugly brown cotton bathrobe.

"Where the hell have you been?" she asked, looking up at him. The bathrobe was hanging open.

Fantastic teats!

"I had work to do," Jake said.

"You think those cheap bastards would put a decent goddamned dressing room in here," Veronica said. "I've got an interview with that bitch from the *Post* at noon. I'm going to look like shit."

"This is Seymour's apartment," Dillon said, referring to the Chairman of the Board and Chief Executive Officer of Metro-Magnum Studios. "He doesn't like to look at himself in mirrors."

She chuckled and smiled at him.

"You had a telephone call," she said. "Couple of them. Same guy. Name of Stewart. He's pissed at something."

"Did he say he was 'General' Stewart?"

Veronica thought about that a moment, and then nodded. "Yeah. He did."

"Oh, shit."

"He said you were supposed to call him the minute you got in."

"OK, thank you, sweetheart."

"You're going to be with me at lunch, right?"

"I don't think that's possible, honey."

"Goddamn, Jake, you know I can't deal with that goddamned dyke!"

"Bobby O'Hara will be there," Jake said. "I'll call him."

"I want *you* there, *goddamn it,* Jake!"

"Bobby is very good with her," Dillon said. "They're both Irish."

He picked up the telephone and made two calls. The first was to Mr. Robert T. O'Hara, of the Washington office of Metro-Magnum Studios, Inc., to remind him he had a luncheon engagement with Miss Veronica Wood. The call lasted about sixty seconds.

The second, to Colonel F. L. Rickabee of the Office of Management Analysis, was even more brief.

"Colonel, Jake Dillon. General Stewart has been looking for me. I'm supposed to call him."

"Don't call him. Don't go near him. I'll take care of it," Rickabee said, and then the line went dead.

"*Please,* Jake!" Veronica Wood asked. "Come with me? *I* was nice to *you.*"

"That was last night. What have you done for me today?"

"You sonofabitch!" Veronica said delightedly. "That's why I love you. You're a prick but you admit it."

"If I go to lunch with you, will you promise not to say 'prick'? I don't think Whatsername from the *Post* likes that word."

The telephone rang again. Dillon picked it up. As he spoke his name, he realized that was pretty dumb. It was probably General Stewart, shitting a brick about something.

"Hey, Jake. Charley Stevens. How the hell are you?"

Charley Stevens was a screenwriter.

"How are you, Charley?"

"Got a question, Jake. I'm doing the first rewrite of the *Wake Island* script. Got a question, figured you were a Marine and could answer it. Need some love interest. Please tell me, there were nurses on Wake Island?"

"No nurses on Wake Island, Charley, sorry."

"Shit!" Charley Stevens said.

"You'll think of something, Charley," Jake said and hung up.

(TWO)
Office of the Director
Public Affairs Office
Headquarters, U.S. Marine Corps
Washington, D.C.
1530 Hours 22 September 1942

Brigadier General J. J. Stewart summoned his deputy into his office and handed him a sheet of green paper.

"Take a look at this, will you?" he fumed.

INTEROFFICE MEMORANDUM

DATE: 22 September 1942

FROM: Assistant Chief of Staff, Personnel

TO: Director
             Public Affairs Office
             Hq, USMC

HAND CARRY

SUBJECT: Dillon, Major Homer J., USMCR,
             Temporary Assignment Of

   1. Effective immediately, subject officer is placed on temporary duty for an indefinite period with the Office of Management Analysis, Hq USMC.
   2. All records of subject officer now under the control of the Public Affairs Division will be hand-carried to the Office of Management within twenty-four (24) hours.
   3. Discussion of this assignment or requests for reconsideration thereof is not desired.

BY DIRECTION OF THE COMMANDANT:

Alfred J. Kennedy
Major General, USMC
Assistant Chief of Staff, G-1

After General Stewart's deputy read the memorandum, he looked at General Stewart, but he didn't say anything.

"How the hell they expect me to do my job if they keep stealing my officers, I don't know," General Stewart said. "Who the hell am I going to get to run the war bond tour? I've got a goddamned good mind to take this to the Commandant!"

In the end, of course, he did not. He was a good Marine officer, and good Marine officers accept the orders they are given without question or complaint.

(THREE)
Sea Breeze Motel
Mary Esther, Florida
24 September 1942

Lieutenant K. R. McCoy, in a T-shirt and swimming trunks, opened the door to room 17 in response to an imperious knock. He found himself facing a stout woman in her late forties, wearing flowered shorts and a matching blouse under a transparent raincoat. On her head she had a World War I–style steel helmet, painted white, bearing an insignia consisting of the letters CD within a triangle. A brassard around her right arm had a similar insignia, and she was armed with a policeman's nightstick, painted white.

While McCoy was reacting to the sudden appearance of the CD lady, she pushed past him into room 17 and slammed the door behind her. Before returning to his room, he had spent three hours on the beach doing his share of the damage to a case of PX beer. After that, he attended a steak broil at the Hurlburtt Field Officer's club; each table there had come furnished with four bottles of California Cabernet Sauvignon.

"I could see light!" the lady announced in righteous indignation. "Your drapes permitted light to escape!"

"Sorry," McCoy said.

"There are German submarines out there!" the lady declared. "Don't you people know there's a war on?"

"Where do you think it went when it escaped?" Lieutenant John Marston Moore, USMCR, asked from the bed where he was resting. "The light, I mean?"

His voice was somewhat slurred, as if he had partaken of a considerable quantity of intoxicants.

"Shut up, Johnny," Miss Ernestine Sage said. She was wearing a bathing suit and a T-shirt. In three-inch-high red letters, US MARINES was stretched taut across her bosom.

The pride of the Mary Esther, Florida, Civil Defense Force stared at her; and then she looked around the room. Also in the room were Miss Elizabeth Lathrop, in a swimsuit and T-shirt reading US ARMY AIR CORPS, Sergeant George Hart, and two galvanized iron buckets filled with iced beer and several bottles of liquor.

"You girls should be ashamed of yourselves!"

" 'Let he who is without sin cast the first stone,' " Lieutenant John Marston Moore announced sonorously, "as our blessed Lord and Saviour said on the road to Samara."

Ernie Sage began to giggle.

"You keep those drapes drawn or I'll write you up!" the Civil Defense lady ordered furiously. "I mean it!"

"Yes, Ma'am," McCoy said. "We're sorry."

He turned off the lights. The Civil Defense lady left the room to return to her appointed rounds. McCoy closed the door, locked it, and then turned the lights on again.

"You're really the life of the party, aren't you?" McCoy said to Moore, misquoting *Where do you think the light went when it escaped?* "The one thing we don't need is to get hauled off to the local police station."

"Yes, Sir," Moore said, sounding not at all remorseful. "Sorry, Lieutenant, Sir."

"Are there really German submarines out there?" Ernie asked.

"Probably," McCoy replied. "They try to sink the oil tankers coming out of the

Texas Gulf ports and whatever sails from New Orleans. But I don't think they're in this close to shore. There's just too many airfields along here. There was a story going around that they caught half a dozen Germans near the mouth of Mobile Bay. They were supposedly landed from a sub."

"Isn't *that* interesting?" Moore said.

McCoy flashed a cold look at him and Ernie saw it. Without a good deal of effort, she had already concluded that whatever Ken and the other two were doing down here had something to do with beaches.

When they were on the beach this afternoon, Moore and Hart had a steel cone and a square block of lead. They went up and down the beach, pounding the cone into the sand. And then at the Officer's Club Steak Broil—the club was right on the beach—Ken left the party for a "walk on the beach" with Lieutenant Mainwaring, the Marine officer who picked them up at the train station in Tallahassee and drove them here, and the Army Air Corps guy who gave Beth the T-shirt. They took the cone and lead block with them. They were gone forty-five minutes.

It does not take a wild imagination, Ernie Sage thought, *to put that cone, whatever the hell it's for, together with Johnny's dry crack after Ken's story about Germans caught coming ashore from a submarine, and come up with a studied guess that what they're about to do involves a submarine and a beach. And not a beach in Florida, either.*

Oh, God!

"Mademoiselle," Johnny Moore interrupted her chain of thought by handing her his empty bottle of beer, "if you would be so kind?"

"Avec grand plaisir, mon cher," Ernie said, and went to the beer buckets and got him one.

"What did they do to the Germans?" Beth asked. "The ones they caught from the submarine?"

"I don't know," McCoy said. "I didn't see the file, just heard the scuttlebutt. If they were in uniform, they were just put in a POW cage. If they were in civilian clothing, that makes them spies. Then they could be shot. Or maybe hung."

"What would the Japanese do if they caught Americans?" Ernie asked.

"How did we get onto this subject?" McCoy said.

That means, Ernie decided, *that the Japanese would do nothing quite as civilized as shooting someone they caught trying to land somewhere from a submarine—these three, for example.*

There was a knock at the door. Not nearly as imperious as the previous knock. This one, in fact, was somehow furtive.

"Do you think the guardian of the beach has summoned the local vice cops?" Moore asked.

"I hope not," McCoy said as he turned the lights off, unlocked the door, and opened it.

When the lights came back on, Lieutenant Mainwaring and Captain Al Stein, the Army Air Corps officer—now that she saw him, Ernie remembered his name—and two Air Corps enlisted men were entering the small room. They had two wooden crates with them, rolling them on what Ernie thought of as a furniture man's dolly.

"Room service," Stein said.

"Why did you bring them here?" McCoy asked.

Ernie tried to read what was stenciled on the crates. Whatever had been stenciled there had been obliterated, and very recently, for the paint was still wet.

"Because I don't have the faith everybody else seems to have in this colonel of yours to fix this."

"Everything will be all right, Al," Mainwaring said.

"He said as Stein was led off in irons, destination Leavenworth U.S. Army prison."

"Help yourself to a beer," McCoy said to the Air Corps sergeants. "Or there's booze if you'd rather."

"I think maybe we'd better get the truck back," the older of the two Air Corps sergeants said.

"Have a beer," Stein ordered.

"OK, Captain, thank you."

"Have all the beer you want," McCoy said. "We really appreciate this."

"Ah, what the hell, Lieutenant," the sergeant said.

"I am sure, Captain Stein," Moore said, propping himself up against the headboard, "that an officer of your demonstrated logistical genius is aware that these crates won't fit in that Chevrolet staff car?"

Stein looked at Moore and laughed.

"I'm surprised that you're still able to talk."

"Hell, he's been quoting the Bible to us," McCoy said. "An amazing man is our Lieutenant Moore."

"We'll bring the truck back at oh six hundred, Lieutenant," the Air Corps sergeant said. "That'll give us just over an hour to make it to Pensacola. Plenty of time. We just didn't want to try to get these crates through the gate at the field in the morning."

"You have three seats on the seven A.M. courier flight and authorization for six hundred pounds of accompanied baggage," Lieutenant Mainwaring said.

"That's what these weigh?"

"Pray they don't weigh them," Stein said.

"What about the extra cone sets?"

"I've got those in the car," Mainwaring said. "All I could get you was three."

"Plus the one we have?" McCoy asked.

"*Including* the one you have," Stein said.

"Beggars can't be choosers," McCoy said. "Thank you."

"I won't see you in the morning, McCoy," Stein said. "So I'll say this now. In no more than seventy-two hours—probably within forty-eight—somebody's going to miss this stuff. I would deeply appreciate it if you will do whatever you can to keep Mrs. Stein's little boy from ending his Air Corps career making little rocks out of big ones at Leavenworth."

"Did you talk to the Colonel, Mainwaring?" McCoy asked.

Mainwaring nodded.

"There's supposed to be TWX on the way down here."

"That ought to do it, Stein," McCoy said. "But I'll check on it myself as soon as we get to Washington."

"Good enough," Captain Stein said. He looked at his two sergeants. "Take enough of those bottles to sustain you throughout the journey, gentlemen, and then let us be on our way."

"Thanks, Stein," McCoy said. "We owe you one."

"You owe me a good deal more than one," Stein said, putting out his hand. "Good luck, McCoy. Be careful. You two, too," he said, waving at Hart and Moore.

"May the peace of God which passeth all understanding," Moore proclaimed from the bed, "go with you and yours."

"Oh, shit!" Stein said, laughing, and snapped off the lights. Just before the door slammed shut after them, Stein called out, "Mazeltov, you all!"

"Why do you think Moore got so drunk?" Ernie asked as she made a halfhearted attempt to clean up the room when the others had gone.

"I think he was in pain," McCoy said.

"What kind of pain?"

"I think it started when he went in the water and got salt water in his wounds," McCoy answered matter-of-factly. "And then I think he hurt his legs, either in the water, or maybe walking in the sand."

"So why didn't you do something about it?"

"Getting drunk worked as good as anything from the dispensary," McCoy said. "And if we had taken him there, they probably would have wanted to keep him."

"That's pretty damned callous!"

"He's a big boy, baby. He wanted to come down here."

"And he wants to do whatever it is you're about to do, right?"

"Right."

"And you're not going to tell me what that is, right?"

"Right."

"How about how Beth and me are supposed to get back to Washington?"

"The way Mainwaring was looking at you, I thought maybe you'd want to stay."

"Go to hell!"

"After Mainwaring drops us at Pensacola—I'm not sure we can get you on the base without a lot of hassle; you may have to wait outside the gate—he'll take you to Mobile. That's another forty miles or so. You catch a train there to Montgomery and connect with the Crescent from New Orleans to Washington."

"And by the time I get to Washington, are you still going to be there?"

"Baby, I don't know."

"In other words, I may not see you after tomorrow morning?"

He didn't reply.

"For how long?"

He shrugged.

"And if I hadn't asked, you were just going to get on that goddamned airplane tomorrow without even saying goodbye?"

"Saying goodbye to you is hard for me, baby."

"How about saying, 'I love you, Ernie'? Is that hard for you, Ken?"

"I love you, Ernie," McCoy said.

"If you love me, you sonofabitch, why won't you marry me?" she said. But she didn't expect a reply or wait for one. She walked quickly to him and waited for him to put his arms around her. When he did, she told him she loved him, too.

Two rooms down, Beth Lathrop also asked what was going to happen to her and to Ernie the next day. When she asked it, she was standing in the door to the bathroom, wrapped in a towel.

"Mainwaring is going to take both of you to Mobile to catch a train."

"Do you think she means it when she says she can get me assignments as a photographer?"

"I'm sure she does."

She doesn't know you're a whore. Maybe if she knew that, she wouldn't.

"You don't think she's just saying that?"

"You better be able to produce, Beth."

"What does that mean?"

"It better not be bullshit, you being a photographer."

"You bastard! Is that what you think?"

"All I'm saying is that if you're not a photographer, now is the time to say so. Don't make a fool of her. She's a nice girl."

"You think I've been lying all the time, don't you?"

"I don't know what the hell to think."

"That's not all. Say what you're thinking!"

"She knows Pick. He knows you. What is he going to tell her about you?"

"I didn't think about that," Beth said. "Oh, Jesus!"

"Shit," George said, and went to the dresser and opened the bottle of beer he'd brought from McCoy's and Ernie's room.

"OK," Beth said, "so what I'll do is tell her thanks but no thanks."

"No," Hart said. "No, you won't. If she says she can get you a job, you'll take it."

"What about Pick?"

"She won't be seeing him anytime soon," Hart said. "Maybe ever."

"My God, what a rotten thing to even think!"

"And anyway, what he tells her about you has nothing to do with you and me."

"Meaning what?"

"Meaning I don't give a good goddamn what anyone knows, or thinks."

That's true, goddamn it, he thought. *I don't even give a good goddamn what my father would say if he found out.*

"You say that but you don't mean it," Beth said.

"Goddamn it, I mean it."

"I mean it, George, when I say I love you," Beth said.

"Yeah, me, too," George said.

"I'll do whatever you tell me to do," Beth said.

"Whatever I tell you?"

"Whatever you tell me, honey."

"Take off the damned towel."

(FOUR)
Walter Reed Army General Hospital
Washington, D.C.
1005 Hours 25 September 1942

Colonel F. L. Rickabee was in uniform when he knocked on Brigadier General Fleming Pickering's hospital room. He entered without waiting.

"Good morning, General," he said.

Christ, Pickering thought, *clothes* do *make the man! He is far more impressive in his uniform than in those off-the-rack Sears, Roebuck suits he usually wears.*

"Good morning, Rickabee."

"Sorry to be late, Sir. I went to the Friday Morning."

"You went to the what?"

"The Friday Morning Intelligence Summary at ONI," Rickabee explained. ONI was the *O*ffice of *N*aval *I*ntelligence.

"That's why you're in uniform?"

"Yes, Sir. That saves the usual two minutes of Naval humor when I show up in mufti."

Pickering chuckled.

"Hear anything interesting?"

"Yes, Sir. The Naval attaché in London sent an URGENT radio that he had just heard a reliable report from the English that on the twenty-third, General Rommel was flown to Germany from North Africa, ostensibly for medical treatment, and that yesterday General Halder was relieved and replaced by a man named Zeitler."

"Who's General Halder?" Pickering asked.

"He was Chief of Staff OKH—*Oberkommando* Heeres, Ground Forces Headquarters—which has *de facto* responsibility for the Russian Front. There's some thought that Hitler may send Rommel to Russia. Interesting."

"Yes," Pickering agreed.

Proving again, Brigadier General Pickering, Pickering thought, *that your total knowledge of the global war can be written inside a matchbook with a grease pencil. The only name you recognized was Rommel's.*

"And just as we were breaking up there was an OPERATIONAL IMMEDIATE in from CINCPAC that there was confirmed damage to two Japanese destroyers and a cruiser making a supply run to Guadalcanal."

"Sea or air?"

"Sea, Sir."

"I don't think you came all the way over here to report on the—what did you call it?—the Friday Morning."

"No, Sir."

"Well, let's have it."

"Sir, I have certain obligations as your deputy—"

"Cut the crap," Pickering interrupted. "Get to the point."

Rickabee's face tightened.

"I consider it my duty, General, to make it clear to you that in my professional judgment, your intended operation to relieve the men at Buka is ill-advised; it has very little chance of success; it will require the expenditure of assets, personnel, and matériel that are needed elsewhere; and it is of questionable legality."

After a moment Pickering asked, "Anything else?"

"Yes, Sir. There is a very good chance that when word of it gets out, you will be relieved as Director of the Office of Management Analysis. I would hate to see that happen, Sir, for both selfish and personal reasons."

"Selfish?"

"Yes, Sir. We need somebody who can go to Admiral Leahy directly when we need something."

Pickering poured a cup of coffee for himself. He held the pot up as an offer to Rickabee, who shook his head, no. And then he put the cup to his lip.

He lowered it without taking a sip.

"The operation goes," he said. "I appreciate your candor, Rickabee."

"Aye, aye, Sir. I thought that would be The General's reaction."

"We're back to 'The General,' are we?" Pickering asked.

Rickabee ignored the remark. He reached into the lower, bellows pocket of his blouse and took out an envelope.

"I had Sessions make this up last night, Sir," he said. "There are copies for Dillon, that's his; and for McCoy, Moore, and Sergeant Hart. They will be on the courier plane from Pensacola arriving at Anacostia about seventeen hundred."

Pickering took what Rickabee handed him and read it.

"You'll have to sign the endorsement, General. That's just to show you what it will look like when we're done. I thought about getting Major Dillon a set of ONI Special Agent credentials—McCoy, Moore, and Hart already have them, of course—but I thought that might cause people to ask questions we don't want asked."

Pickering's original orders on White House stationery, signed by Admiral Leahy, had been photographed and reduced in size by half, printed, and placed within sheets of cellophane, stapled shut.

THE WHITE HOUSE
Washington, D.C.

3 September 1942

Brigadier General Fleming W. Pickering, USMCR, Headquarters, USMC, will proceed by military and/or civilian
rail, road, sea and air transportation (Priority AAAAA-1) to
such points as he deems necessary in carrying out the mission
assigned to him by the undersigned.

United States Armed Forces commands are directed to
provide him with such support as he may request. General
Pickering is to be considered the personal representative of
the undersigned.

General Pickering has unrestricted TOP SECRET security
clearance. Any questions regarding his mission will be directed to the undersigned.

W. D. Leahy, Admiral, USN
Chief of Staff to the President

''Turn it over, General,'' Rickabee said. Pickering did so.

TOP SECRET

OFFICE OF THE CHIEF OF STAFF TO THE PRESIDENT
Washington, D.C. 24 September 1942
1st Endorsement

1. The following personnel of my personal staff are engaged in carrying out the mission
assigned to the undersigned by the Chief of Staff to The President.

Dillon, Major Homer J USMCR 17724
McCoy, 1st Lt Kenneth R USMCR 489657
Moore, 2nd Lt John M USMCR 20043
Hart, Sgt George F USMCR 2307887

2. All provisions regarding travel priorities, logistical support and access to classified
matériel specified in the basic order apply to the personnel listed hereon.

3. Any questions regarding the listed personnel or their mission will be referred to the undersigned.

Fleming Pickering
Brigadier General, USMCR

‖ **TOP SECRET** ‖

"Very impressive, Rickabee," Pickering said. "You think this will do it, so far as getting them on airplanes, et cetera?"

Rickabee handed Pickering a typewritten copy of the endorsement and a fountain pen.

"When you sign that endorsement, General," Rickabee said, "we'll photograph it, reduce it, and heat-seal the whole thing in plastic, like an ID card. With that White House stationery, it should be a very impressive document. In any event, it's my best shot at getting done what has to be done without people all over Washington asking questions."

Pickering signed it and handed it back.

"Thank you," Pickering said. "Considering your overall objections to the whole idea, I'm grateful to you."

"General, *your deputy* felt obliged to make you aware of his best judgment," Rickabee said. "This *Marine* hopes you get away with it."

XIII

(ONE)
Supreme Headquarters
South West Pacific Ocean Area
(Formerly, Commerce Hotel)
Brisbane, Australia
27 September 1942

Five people in Australia were cleared for material classified TOP SECRET—MAGIC: the code name assigned to what was then regarded as the most important secret of the war. Navy cryptographers at Pearl Harbor had broken some—but not all—of the codes used by the Imperial General Staff to communicate with the Imperial Japanese Army and Navy.

In theory, of those at SWPOA, only General Douglas MacArthur and his intelligence officer, Brigadier General Charles A. Willoughby, were authorized access to MAGIC messages.

Neither General MacArthur nor General Willoughby, however, had the cryptographic training or the time to decode such messages. Consequently, two others at SWPOA administered the MAGIC program. After Navy cryptographers at Pearl Harbor had decoded and analyzed an intercepted Japanese message, both the message and its analysis were encrypted using an American code (which was restricted to MAGIC) and transmitted to SWPOA. There the analysis and message were decoded and placed before General MacArthur and General Willoughby.

The people who did this were First Lieutenant Hon Song Do, Signal Corps, U.S. Army Reserve, and Mrs. Ellen Feller, a civilian employee of the Navy Department who was accorded the assimilated rank of a lieutenant commander. In addition, Major Edward F. Banning, USMC, Commanding Officer of USMC Special Detachment 14, was cleared for access to MAGIC. Banning knew enough about cryptography to operate the cryptographic machine.

"Pluto" Hon, as he was known, was a very smart young man. He held a Ph.D. in mathematics from MIT and he was a trained cryptographer. That is to say, he was familiar with the esoteric theories of that craft and not just a man who knew how to work the code machine. That wasn't all that made Lieutenant Hon impressive: Hon, whose ancestry was Korean, read and spoke Japanese fluently, and understood Japanese culture better than practically anyone else you were likely to find in the United States Armed Forces. And he was as good an analyst and cryptographer as anyone you were likely to meet at Pearl Harbor. Indeed, he'd been stationed there before being sent to General MacArthur's headquarters.

Another of the best-kept secrets of Supreme Headquarters, SWPOA, was that Hon was a regular at General and Mrs. MacArthur's after-dinner bridge parties. Most often Hon and General MacArthur were partners. The General liked to win.

Of the three people who administered the MAGIC program at SWPOA—Banning, Feller, and Hon—Major Banning was senior. He was of course senior in grade to Lieutenant Hon. And as a serving officer of equivalent grade, he was senior to Mrs. Feller. All the same, Major Banning was very much aware that the one person of the three who really knew what he was doing was Lieutenant Hon. In other words—

and the irony wasn't lost on Banning—the one real expert was the lowest-ranking member according to military hierarchy.

This rarely posed problems for him or for Lieutenant Hon. Or rather, this rarely posed problems *between* them. The problems were caused by the third member of the team, Mrs. Ellen Feller.

Mrs. Feller rather liked her role as a senior civilian.

Mrs. Feller came to Australia over a long and convoluted route. Her husband was the Reverend Glen T. Feller, of the Christian & Missionary Alliance. Before the war Reverend Feller had brought Jesus to the heathen of China and Japan. As a result of this experience, Mrs. Feller spoke Japanese and Chinese—though not nearly as well as she believed she did. When the Reverend Feller decided to pass the war years bringing the word of Jesus to Native American Heathen in the American Southwest, Mrs. Feller (who didn't like her husband very much) sought and found employment as an Oriental Languages Translator in the Navy Department in Washington.

When Fleming Pickering was commissioned into the Navy as a captain, he needed a secretary with the necessary clearances, and Mrs. Feller proved acceptable to him. Later, shortly after the fall of Corregidor, Pickering came to Australia. Once there, he realized that Lieutenant Pluto Hon, as brilliant and competent as he was, couldn't handle the tremendous work load on his own. As a result, he dispatched an URGENT radio to Secretary of the Navy Frank Knox requesting immediate reinforcement. Secretary Knox dispatched Pickering's former secretary.

It didn't take Major Ed Banning and Lieutenant Pluto Hon long to learn to detest Mrs. Feller, though of course each man kept his opinion private. The lady was a three-star bitch . . . no, a four-star bitch. Of that neither had any doubt.

In fact, she was worse than that; she was dangerous—and they had little doubt of that either.

For one thing, as far as Lieutenant Hon was concerned, virtually all of Mrs. Feller's analyses of MAGIC intercepts failed to catch the point of the Japanese originals. Hon credited this failure to her remarkably shallow knowledge of Japanese culture and modes of thought. Though she was shallow, that didn't mean she wasn't clever. She was as aware as Hon was that her work was weak. So she simply used his, much of the time. Often, when his own analyses disagreed in one way or another with the ones from Pearl Harbor, she "appropriated" Hon's and passed them off as her own. Thus, the analyses Mrs. Feller brought to the attention of Generals MacArthur and Willoughby were frequently not hers but his. Indeed, she had General Willoughby convinced that she was not only a very attractive lady, indeed, but a brilliant one.

It didn't take Major Banning long to pick up on Mrs. Feller's dishonesty; his contempt for the lady had its source there. But his contempt went further than that. When Captain Fleming Pickering was in Australia, he showed an outrageous disdain for the proper security of classified documents. He left them lying all over the houses he rented.

In consequence, Banning arranged for agents of the Army's Counterintelligence Corps to sweep Captain Pickering's quarters whenever he left them. Since he didn't trust Mrs. Feller on general principles, he kept the sweep in operation after Captain Pickering's departure.

At the end of his stay in Brisbane, Pickering rented a house near the racetrack called Water Lily Cottage. After Pickering left Australia, Mrs. Feller and Sergeant John Marston Moore occupied the cottage.

Sergeant Moore, also the son of missionaries, had been sent to Special Detachment 14 as a Japanese linguist. Because of Moore's profound understanding of Japanese language and culture, Hon attempted to enlist Moore in the MAGIC analysis process

without letting him know about MAGIC itself. The attempt—encouraged by Pickering, energetically opposed by Banning—was a failure . . . at least if anybody hoped
to keep Moore from learning about MAGIC. It took him about two days to figure
out that the documents he was analyzing had to have come from intercepted and
decoded Japanese messages.

Pickering's solution to that was to add Moore to the MAGIC list—on his own
highly questionable authority. Pickering's decision caused Banning not a few problems, especially after Pickering left Australia. For instance, because the First Sergeant
and Company Commander of the Headquarters Company could not be told that
Moore was analyzing intercepted Japanese messages for the Supreme Commander,
these men often decided that Sergeant Moore's contribution to the war effort should
be as Charge of Quarters or Sergeant of the Guard. To spare Moore from these
tasks, and to get him as far as possible out-of-sight-out-of-mind, Banning moved
Moore into Water Lily Cottage.

It took the thorough agents of the CIC only a few days to learn that Mrs. Feller
was taking Sergeant Moore into her bed. Indeed, the agents were aware that she
had taught him sexual acts that were specifically proscribed by military regulation.

When CIC informed Banning of this illicit relationship, he did nothing to end it.
For one thing, it didn't surprise him. For another, maybe getting a little would
improve the bitch's personality. For another, calling her attention to it would make
it obvious to her that she was under CIC surveillance. For another—and this was
the deciding factor: Mrs. Feller arrived in Australia on the same day Captain Pickering
left for Guadalcanal. According to CIC, on that day Mrs. Feller went straight from
the airport into Captain Pickering's bed. After learning this, Banning realized that
his hands were tied where Mrs. Ellen Feller was concerned. He could complain to
only one person about her, and that person was Fleming Pickering, and that was a
hornet's nest he decided not to disturb. He told this to no one, not even Pluto.

It didn't take Mrs. Feller long to prove that she was not only very skilled in
protecting her ass, but dangerously ruthless in doing so.

Shortly after the Guadalcanal invasion, the First Marine Division G-2 and most
of the Japanese-language interpreters of the division were killed in action. The
Marine Corps liaison officer at SWPOA received orders to go to Guadalcanal as
the G-2's replacement. Because he was a Japanese linguist, similar orders went to
Sergeant John Marston Moore. No one in Headquarters, USMC, knew that he was
privy to MAGIC and should be kept far away from any place where there was the
slightest risk of his falling into enemy hands.

Mrs. Feller, meanwhile, saw in his sudden transfer the chance to end a potentially
sticky situation. As nice a boy as he was, John was only a sergeant; and senior
civilian employees with the assimilated rank of lieutenant commander should really
not be cavorting in bed with common enlisted men. She was only too aware that
eventually someone would find out.

Knowing full well that Moore should not be sent anywhere near Guadalcanal,
Mrs. Ellen Feller not only kept her mouth shut about his MAGIC access, but ordered
Moore to say nothing about it either. By the time Pluto Hon and Banning (who was
in Townsville with Commander Feldt) learned what was going on, Moore was on
a plane for Guadalcanal. And by the time Moore could be ordered off Guadalcanal,
he'd been seriously wounded.

That was bad enough. But in Banning's view, this very bad situation just missed
becoming a disaster. If Moore had been captured, MAGIC would have been compromised and shut down.

When it was over, Banning fully expected to be relieved or even court-martialed.
He was the senior officer of the Office of Management Analysis in Australia, and
the responsibility for the failure was clearly his. But Colonel Rickabee had apparently

determined that since Moore's transfer was a fluke and that MAGIC was not compromised, he would leave things the way they were.

After the Moore fiasco, Pluto Hon and Ed Banning devised a system for dealing with Mrs. Feller: Her responsibility would now include only the delivery of MAGIC material to MacArthur and Willoughby. She would no longer work the decoding machine or produce analyses of MAGIC intercepts. That suited her fine. The cryptographic facilities, known as the dungeon, were in the basement of the Commerce Hotel. She didn't like it down there, anyway. And she could still present Hon's analyses as her own and thus bask in General Willoughby's appreciation of her genius.

If anything came up that Banning or Hon thought should be delivered to MacArthur personally, they did so. Usually Pluto would slip whatever it was to MacArthur before or after a bridge game.

The message from KCY to HWS came in like any other:

HWS, KCY. HWS, KCY. SB CODE.
SWPOA Radio, this is CINCPAC Radio. Stand by to copy an encoded message.

The high-speed operator, an Army staff sergeant, reached for his telegraph key and tapped out KCY, HWS, GA.

CINCPAC Radio, Tthis is SWPOA Radio, go ahead.

He then turned from the radio equipment on the table before him to a fairly large, black device equipped with a typewriter keyboard and put his fingers on the keys.

As the message came in, in five-character blocks, he typed it out. The five-character blocks made no sense at all; and the next stage in the process was equally odd; for his typing did not form letters on a sheet of paper. Rather it made perforations, like Braille, on a narrow strip of paper. This fed out of the side of the machine into an olive-drab wastebasket.

Finally the message was finished.

The SWPOA operator turned back to his key and tapped out:

KCY, HWS, UR 09x27x34 AK.
CINCPAC Radio, SWPOA Radio acknowledges receipt of your message number 34 of 27 September.

Pearl Harbor immediately replied: HWS, KCY, SB CODE.
Pearl Harbor had another coded message to transmit.
The operator tapped: KCY, HWS, H1.

CINCPAC, SWPOA, hold one moment, please.

"Charley," the high-speed operator called to another high-speed operator, "can you take KCY Code on Six?"

The other operator checked his equipment, called out, "Got it," and tapped out, KCY, HWS, GA on his key, and then turned to the tape device by his side.

The staff sergeant who had taken Message 09×27×34 left his chair, retrieved the perforated tape from the wastebasket, walked across the room to another machine, turned it on, and fed the tape into a slot in the side of the device.

This device was something like a Teletype machine. It had a roll of paper feeding onto a platen, and the keys (but not the keyboard) of a typewriter. After a moment, with a clatter, the decoded message began to appear on the paper.

FROM CINCPAC RADIO PEARL HARBOR
TO SWPOA RADIO BRISBANE
27SEP42 NUMBER 34
TOP-SECRET PKFDD DSDTS HSJS POWST
MNCOI SCHRE

"Shit!" the staff sergeant said softly, and then reached up and pushed the BREAK key. The machine stopped clattering. He pushed the EJECT TAPE button, and the strip of perforated paper began to back out of the device.

He walked to the desk of the officer on duty.

"Sir, I've got a MAGIC," he said.

The officer, a Signal Corps captain, nodded and looked around the room.

"I don't know where the hell Swift is," he thought aloud. "Can you run it down?"

"Yes, Sir," the staff sergeant said. Actually he was glad that PFC Swift, the messenger, was fucking off someplace. It gave him an excuse to get out of the radio room for a few minutes, if only down to the dungeon.

He walked to the steel door of the radio room, took from a peg a .45 in a leather holster on a web belt, strapped it on, and then left.

The radio room was on the roof of what had been the Commerce Hotel. It was necessary to walk down a flight of stairs to reach the elevators. When an elevator came, he rode it to the basement. After that, he went down a long, brick-walled corridor until he reached another steel door. This one was guarded by two soldiers armed with .45 pistols and submachine guns.

"Lieutenant Hon in there?" he asked, jerking his thumb toward the steel door.

"Yeah," the guard said and reached for a telephone. It was a direct line. When he picked it up, the other end—in the cryptographic room behind two more steel doors—rang.

"Lieutenant, there's something out here for you," the guard said, adding "Yes, Sir," and then hanging up. "He'll be right out."

Ninety seconds later, a first lieutenant of the Army Signal Corps, a tall, muscular, heavyset Oriental, came through the door. His sleeves were rolled up and his tie was pulled down.

"Hey, Sergeant," he said in a thick Boston accent, "when did they turn you into an errand boy?"

"When they couldn't find Swifty, Lieutenant," the staff sergeant said.

"Swifty is probably out spreading goodwill, or maybe pollen, among the indigenous population," Lieutenant Hon said. The staff sergeant and the guard laughed.

Lieutenant Hon took the tape, said "Thank you," and went back behind the steel door.

Lieutenant Hon passed through the second of the steel doors, closed and locked it behind him; and then, after setting it up for MAGIC, he fed the tape into his code machine. When it began to clatter, he read the message that came out:

FROM CINCPAC RADIO PEARL HARBOR
TO SWPOA RADIO BRISBANE
27SEP42 NUMBER 34

TOP SECRET-MAGIC
FOLLOWING NON LOG SERVICE MESSAGE FROM RICKABEE WASHINGTON FOR BANNING BRISBANE

X START X THREE OFFICER ONE ENLISTED SPECIAL DETACHMENT 14 AUGMENTATION TEAM DEPARTED SAN DIEGO BY AIR WITH 800 POUNDS SPECIAL EQUIPMENT 0730 27SEPT42 X ADVISE ARRIVAL YOUR STATION X REGARDS FROM BRIG GEN PICKERING X BANNING X END

Lieutenant Pluto Hon wondered idly why Banning was getting three more officers. What will he do with them? he asked himself. And what's the 800 pounds of special equipment? At the same time he was pleased to see the regards from Brigadier General Pickering.

General Pickering. He'd heard a rumor about that. He found it hard to understand how Pickering would get a commission in the Marines. Then he put all that from his mind.

Because it was a Service message, it didn't have to be logged in. Instead, he put a match to it, and the tape, and watched them burn. Banning would certainly call within the next twenty-four hours. When he did, Hon could tell him then that he was getting three officers and a Marine.

The four men and their equipment would probably arrive on either the twenty-ninth or thirtieth. So he called the motor pool and ordered a staff car and a three-quarter-ton truck for those days. Next he decided to put them up at Water Lily Cottage for as long as they were in Brisbane. If Ellen Feller didn't like it—in that marvelous Army phrase—she could go fuck herself.

It did not enter his mind to inform Mrs. Feller herself about the message.

Even though he was a lowly lieutenant floating around in a sea of colonels and generals, all needing wheels, the motor pool gave him no trouble about the vehicles. Three weeks before, he was late for a bridge game with General MacArthur. When he arrived, he apologized, saying that the motor pool had been unable to give him transportation.

"Dick," the Supreme Commander said to Colonel Richard Sutherland, his aide-de-camp, "make sure that doesn't happen to Pluto again."

Lieutenant Pluto Hon didn't think it would. As the man said, when you are a first-rate bridge player you fall heir to a number of social advantages.

(TWO)
U.S. Army Air Transport Command Passenger Terminal
Brisbane, Australia
1615 Hours 29 September 1942

It took some time for the SWPOA telephone operator to even admit to the existence of Lieutenant Hon Song Do; and it took another minute before Hon came on the line.

"Pluto, this is John Moore," Moore said into the phone. He was standing in the passenger terminal next to a counter. The telephone was on the counter.

"John Moore?" Pluto asked incredulously. "Johnny, my God! Where are you?"

"At the ATC passenger terminal."

"We heard you were hurt and sent back to the States—"

"Can you get us some wheels? We'll need a truck, or a jeep with trailer."

It came together in Pluto's mind. Johnny Moore was the Marine in the Special Detachment Augmentation Team that the message from Rickabee mentioned.

"I just checked an hour ago," Pluto said. "There was no plane due from Pearl."

"We went into Melbourne on a Navy PB2Y," Moore replied. "The Army flew us up here on a C-46."

The PB2Y was the Consolidated Aircraft Coronado, a four-engine amphibian Navy transport, while the C-46 was the Curtiss-Wright Commando, a twin-engine, thirty-six-passenger transport taken into the Army as the C-46 and by the Navy as the R5C.

"I turned the vehicles loose," Pluto said. "Can you catch a cab to the cottage? Banning said to put you up there."

"We've got a bunch of stuff with us," Moore said, and then added, "Hold it a minute." There was a pause, and then Moore asked, "Where's Major Banning? Didn't he know we were coming?"

"He's probably at the club; we were going to have dinner there."

"Major Dillon says to tell you to ask him to meet us at the cottage."

Who the hell is Major Dillon?

"I'll get a truck started on its way over there and I'll go by the club and find Banning. Can you all get in the truck or should I come out there and get you?"

"Wait one," Moore said. And then came back on the line. "Major Dillon says he'll get wheels here to take him to the cottage, but we're going to need a truck."

"I'll have one there in twenty minutes," Pluto said. "God, boy, it's good to hear your voice. See you in a little while."

Lieutenant Hon tried to telephone Mrs. Ellen Feller to tell her there would be guests in Water Lily Cottage. But she was not in the office General Willoughby had provided for her in the SWPOA G-2 Section, and there was no answer at the cottage.

He did manage to reach Major Banning at the bar of the Officer's Club.

"Dillon? The only Dillon I know is a Hollywood press agent, and he's in the States running a war bond tour."

"I didn't speak to him, Sir. Just to Sergeant Moore."

"Well, he can't have been hurt as badly as we heard, otherwise they wouldn't have sent him back over here," Banning said. "You be waiting out front, Pluto, I'll be there in ten minutes."

At the time Lieutenant Hon was trying to reach her, Mrs. Ellen Feller was at the Officer's Class Six Store. She had charmed the sergeant in charge there to allow her to exchange the two bottles on her ration of "Spirits, Domestic" (the Army's term for gin, bourbon, or blended whiskey) to "Spirits, Foreign" (brandy, cognac, or similar). The sergeant didn't mind; there was a greater demand for bourbon than for cognac, and Mrs. Feller was one of his very few customers with a great pair of teats.

She went from the Class Six Store to the PX, where she obtained her weekly ration of Chesterfield cigarettes (twelve packs), Hershey bars (a dozen), and Lux bath soap (three bars). Then she went back to where they were waiting for her in the Chevrolet staff car.

She'd had to beg a ride from the motor pool. Because that bastard Banning was in town, he'd claimed the Studebaker President sedan that was assigned to them.

They dropped her off at Water Lily Cottage about ninety seconds before a staff car pulled into the driveway. When the car drove up, she was on the wide stairs leading to the porch of the large, open, single-floor house. When she saw it, she stopped, turned, and went back down.

A Marine major stepped out of the car.

"May I help you?"

"You're Ellen Feller, right?"

"That's correct."

He put out his hand. "I'm Jake Dillon."

"And how may I help you, Major Dillon?"

"Well, we're going to be staying here for a while," he said. "I hope that won't be too much of an inconvenience."

"Staying here?" she parroted. "I don't think so. These are my quarters."

There was somebody else in the car, getting out of it with difficulty. It was another Marine officer, this one a second lieutenant. The driver had to pull him to his feet.

Banning is obviously behind this. I'll be damned if I will permit that man to turn my quarters into a transient BOQ for every Marine officer who passes through town.

"That's not the way I heard it," Jake Dillon said. There was neither sympathy nor kindness in his voice. He was tired from a practically nonstop flight halfway around the world, and his considerable experience with the opposite sex had permitted him to make an instant assessment of Mrs. Ellen Feller: She was a bitch.

"Oh? And how did you hear it?"

My God, that's Johnny Moore! What is he doing back here?

"Flem Pickering told me he's renting this place," Dillon said. "More to the point, he told me to use it while we're here."

She looked at him and flashed him a bitchy smile. "There must be some misunderstanding," she said. Then she walked to meet John Marston Moore. Moore was rounding the front of the staff car, supporting himself on a cane.

He smiled when he saw her. It was almost a smile of anticipation.

The last time she'd seen him was the day he'd gone off to Guadalcanal. She'd given him a farewell present in Water Lily Cottage that was as good for her as it had been for him.

She watched him closely, wondering if he blamed his going to Guadalcanal on her.

That expression on his face is not sarcastic, or angry. He remembers what we did here together. But my God, he looks awful! And he's even having trouble walking.

"You all right, Moore?" Jake asked. "Need some help?"

"I'm fine, Sir," he said. "Hello, Ellen."

"John, I'm so *glad* to see you!" She wrapped her arms around him and gave him a hug. "What are you doing here?"

"Is Major Banning around, Mrs. Feller?" Jake asked, shutting off any answer Moore might have made.

"I don't know," Ellen said. "I just came home. I don't think so. I don't see the car."

"I guess there's a phone in there?" Dillon asked.

"Yes, of course," Ellen said, smiling at him. "Come in and I'll show you."

"Can you handle the stairs, kid?" Dillon asked.

"I'm fine, Sir."

In a pig's ass you are. You look like hell.

"Is there any booze in the house?" Dillon asked. "You want a drink, Moore?"

"I wouldn't mind a little nip."

"I just happened to buy some brandy," Ellen said. "I like to have it around the house."

They watched as Moore somewhat awkwardly negotiated the steps. And then they followed him into the house.

"Be it ever so plush," Moore said, settling himself on the couch and gesturing around at the luxurious furnishings, "there's no place like home."

Ellen laughed dutifully.

"How many of you will there be, Major . . . Dillon, you said?"

"Two more."

"Things will be a little crowded, then," Ellen said. "But I'm sure we can manage."

Ellen went into the kitchen and put her packages on the sink. She was taking a glass from the cupboard when she heard the telephone being dialed.

"Admiral Soames-Haley, please," she heard Dillon say. "My name is Dillon. I'm a major in The U.S. Marine Corps."

Rear Admiral Keith Soames-Haley, RAN, Ellen knew, had been a shipping-business friend of Fleming Pickering's before the war. Now he was high up in the hierarchy of the Australian Navy. So Dillon's words to the Admiral did not bother her—initially:

"Admiral, my name is Jake Dillon. I'm just in from the States. I have a letter for you from our mutual friend, Flem Pickering.

"Yes, that's right, Sir. It's General Pickering now. He's pretty much recovered. But knowing what he's like, they're reluctant to let him out of the hospital until he is absolutely fit.

"No, Sir. If you don't mind, General Pickering asked me to deliver the letter personally, Sir, and he hoped that you could give me thirty minutes of your time.

"I understand, Sir. Tomorrow morning would be fine. I'll be at your office at half past eight. Thank you, Admiral. Goodbye, Sir."

But then Ellen had questions: *Why does Fleming Pickering need to use this man Dillon to send a letter to Admiral Soames-Haley? If he wanted to send Soames-Haley a letter, he could have just mailed it. Or sent it via officer courier. And why did Dillon want half an hour of Soames-Haley's time? Not to discuss Pickering's physical condition. What in the world is going on here?*

She put three glasses and one of the brandy bottles onto a tray and carried it into the living room. The brandy was from Argentina, of all places, but surprisingly good.

She heard a door close, and then the unmistakable sound of Jake Dillon voiding his bladder. She put the tray on the table in front of the couch and sat down beside John Marston Moore.

"I'm so glad to see you," she said in almost a whisper. "What's going on?"

He shrugged.

She leaned toward him and kissed him, first on the cheek and then on the mouth. When she did that, she gave him just a little touch of her tongue. But when he tried to pull her closer, she pulled away, gestured toward the sound of the voiding water, and whispered, "Not now. Behave."

All the same, she let her hand run up his leg. She'd concluded that whatever was going on, having Moore on her side was a good idea.

"When did you become an officer?" she asked. Her hand was still on his leg.

"A couple of weeks ago," he said.

"I'm surprised that they sent you back—because of the cane, I mean."

He shrugged again.

Damn, he's not going to tell me anything. Not without a little encouragement, anyway.

She stood up and opened the bottle of Argentinian brandy, poured a good half inch of it into a snifter, and handed it to Moore.

He drank it hungrily, surprising her.

"That was medicinal," he said. "Now I'll have a social one if you don't mind."

"Are you in pain?"

"No," he lied. "It was a long ride in those airplanes," he said. "I'll be all right."

"Poor baby," she said, and poured more brandy into his glass.

When Jake Dillon came into the room, she was sitting with her legs modestly crossed in an armchair across from the couch.

"Help yourself, if you don't mind, Major," she said.

"Thank you," he said, and poured a healthy snort into his snifter.

"How's the leg?" he asked Moore.

"Legs, plural," Moore said. "I'm damned glad to get off them."

As he spoke they heard the sound of tires on the gravel of the driveway. After that, a car door slammed, and then they heard feet crossing the porch.

Banning saw Dillon before Dillon saw him.

"I thought you were supposed to be selling war bonds," he said, and then he saw Moore. "I will be double damned! Moore! *Lieutenant* Moore. How are you, John?"

Banning walked quickly to the couch and held out his hand.

"I'm doing just fine, Sir," Moore said. "It's good to see you, Sir. Hey, Pluto!"

Dillon waited until Hon had shaken Moore's hand, and then he said, "He is not fine. He can barely stagger around with a cane."

"Then why is he here?" Banning asked.

"Because he told Brigadier General Pickering that he wanted to come, and Brigadier General Pickering said, 'Good boy.'"

"What the hell is this all about, Jake?"

"Why don't we wait until the other two get here, and we can get it all over at once?"

"Who's the other two?"

"Your friend Killer McCoy and a sergeant named Hart."

Ellen Feller was acquainted with Ken McCoy. And she was not happy to learn that he was on his way.

Oh, my God! I thought I'd seen the last of Ken McCoy for a while. Forever. When I woke up this morning, everything was going just fine. I've even got Willoughby just about convinced that the G-2 of SWPOA needs his own Intercept Analysis section, and that I'm obviously the person to run it. But then Moore, and now McCoy! It never rains but it pours!

During the last days that the Marines were in China, Corporal Kenneth R. McCoy was a member of the detachment of the Fourth Marines dispatched to escort the personnel and baggage of the Christian & Missionary Alliance Mission from Nanking to their evacuation ship in Tientsin.

It turned out that Corporal McCoy was a very unusual Marine enlisted man. For one thing, Mrs. Ellen Feller found that Corporal McCoy was really very sexy. For another, she was all too aware that he could be very dangerous. This was especially apparent when he discovered that the luggage of the Rev. and Mrs. Glen T. Feller contained a considerable quantity of jade artifacts and jewelry. The export from China of such artifacts was forbidden.

Mrs. Feller defused the situation by taking McCoy into her bed.

Unfortunately, the affair almost got out of hand; the damned fool fancied he was in love with her. The result was an unpleasant scene on the ship just before it sailed. Afterward, she worried for a long time that he would take revenge and turn her in over the jade. But when the Fourth Marines were transferred to the Philippines, her fear vanished—forever, she thought. There was no way they were going to get out of the Philippines, not with the Japanese there. And even if he survived the war, no one would care about jade removed illegally from China in 1941.

The trouble was that McCoy seemed to have nine lives. He got out of the Philippines somehow and showed up in Washington, as a fresh-from-OCS second lieutenant. The last she heard of him he was in the 2nd Raider Battalion. He survived the Makin Island raid, too, just as he'd survived the Philippines.

The bastard has more lives than a cat!

And what is he . . . what are all of them doing here now?

"Who's the sergeant with McCoy?" Banning asked.

"Interesting guy," Dillon said. "He used to be a detective on the vice squad in St. Louis. Rickabee plucked him out of Parris Island and made him Pickering's bodyguard."

"What's he doing here?" Banning asked.

"He's here because he told Brigadier General Pickering that he wanted to come," he said, using the line he'd used for Moore, "and Brigadier General Pickering said, 'Good boy.'"

"In other words, you're not going to tell me?"

"Not until McCoy and Hart get here, and Mrs. Feller goes shopping or something," Dillon said.

"Major Dillon," Ellen Feller said coldly, "I don't know if you're aware of this or not, but I hold the same security clearances as Major Banning."

"I didn't know that, Mrs. Feller," Jake said. "But what I do know is that General Pickering told me that the less you know about this the better."

"You won't mind, will you, Major," she said, "if I verify that with General Pickering?"

"I wish you would," Dillon said calmly. "But for the moment, I'd be grateful if you could find something else to do for an hour or two. Here comes a truck. I suspect McCoy and Hart are on it."

"How am I supposed to do my job if I am denied access to . . . whatever is going on around here?"

"Mrs. Feller, I'm just a simple Marine," Jake Dillon said. "General Pickering gave me an order and I'm going to carry it out. He said that the less you know about this, the better."

She stood up, her face white.

Whatever you do now, don't lose your temper! Just get out of here, calm down, and think this through. There is absolutely no reason to think you won't be able to deal with this offensive bastard.

"Major Banning, may I use the Studebaker?" Ellen asked.

"Are we going to need wheels, Jake?"

"Possibly," Dillon said. "Can't you call and get a staff car?"

"You can't get a staff car this time of night, and you know it!"

Careful, Ellen! They would love it if you lost your temper!

"I think I can get you one, Mrs. Feller," Lieutenant Pluto Hon said, and walked to the telephone.

(THREE)
Ladies' Bar
McShay's Saloon & Cafe
Brisbane, Australia
2005 Hours 29 September 1942

"What are we doing in here?" Major Ed Banning asked Lieutenant Ken McCoy as McCoy led him into the room and to a table.

"There aren't as many people in here as in the other bar," McCoy said. "I looked through the window."

A waitress came to the table. She stood about five feet tall and measured nearly that distance around.

"And what can I get for the Yanks?"

"I want a beer, please," McCoy said. "And how about something to eat?"

"What would you like, love?"

"I would like a steak about that thick," he said, holding his thumb and index finger an inch and a half apart. "Medium."

The waitress laughed. "But you'd settle, right, for fish and chips?"

"How about scrambled eggs and chips?"

The waitress nodded.

"And for you, love?"

"Just the beer, please," Banning said. He waited until she was out of earshot, then asked, "Is that why we left the house? You were hungry?"

"I got you out of there because you were about to get into it with Dillon and say something you would regret," McCoy said. "And because I'm starved."

"You understand," Banning said, "that I will have to ask to be relieved?"

"Shit," McCoy said.

"What the hell is that supposed to mean?"

"That I was right in getting you out of there," McCoy said.

The beer was delivered in two enormous, foamy mugs. McCoy took a swallow of his and made a face.

"It's warm," he said.

"The Aussies like it that way," Banning said.

"Jesus!"

"They get that from the English," Banning said, and then returned to his original topic. "It has been made perfectly clear that there is considerable doubt in my ability to perform my assigned duties. Under the circumstances I have no choice but to request to be relieved. Can't you see that?"

"Drink your beer," McCoy said.

"I can't understand your reaction to Pickering's idiotic idea," Banning said. "You actually seem to think it can be carried off."

"One, I'm just a simple Mustang who does what he's ordered to do. And, two, yeah, I think it can be carried off."

"Not by me!"

" 'If you're not going to play by my rules, I'm going to take my ball and go home, and fuck all of you!' Right?"

"McCoy, we've been friends for a long time, but don't push it! I'm not a child, and this is not a goddamned game!"

"It really hasn't been a long time, but it does seem like fucking forever, doesn't it?" McCoy said. "My ambition in Shanghai was maybe to make staff sergeant before I retired."

"It's hard to believe all that's happened in the last year, eighteen months."

"I wonder what's happening in Shanghai tonight?"

"Some Jap sonofabitch is driving my Pontiac down the Bund," Banning said, chuckling. "And will probably get laid in my bed later on."

"You never heard anything about Mrs. Banning?"

"No," Banning said softly, flatly.

"White Russians seem able to deal with bad situations," McCoy said.

"What do they call that, 'Whistling in the dark'?"

"She made it from Russia to Shanghai," McCoy said. "That took some doing."

"You don't think Shanghai, under the Japs, would be worse for a white woman?"

"Was that a question or what?"

"A question."

"I don't think the Japs are standing every white face they see against a wall, which is what the communists did to the White Russians. For all you know, she's just in some internment camp with other Americans."

"She's not an American."

"She's an American officer's wife. She can say she lost her passport and her other identification. I think that's what she probably tried to do, and I think she can probably get away with it."

Banning held his empty beer mug over his head.

"Right you are, love," the waitress bellowed.

"I am going to request that I be relieved," Banning said. "Can't you see that I have to?"

"We need you for this goddamned operation, don't be silly."

"That's why Pickering sent Dillon over here, right?"

"Pickering thinks you became too professional, too cold-blooded, and fell under the evil influence of the Australian swabbie."

"What the hell does that mean?"

"What's his name?"

"Feldt, Lieutenant Commander Eric Feldt, and I would appreciate it if you didn't call him an Australian swabbie."

"Pickering thinks that Feldt is too willing to write these guys off. Pickering is thinking like he's still a corporal in France, running around no-man's-land picking up the wounded. The difference, the important difference, is that Pickering has the influence. He's a general."

"What's influence got to do with it?"

"If your man Feldt gets in the way, he's going to get run over."

"That would really be the cherry on the cake," Banning said. "If it wasn't for Feldt there wouldn't be a Coastwatcher Establishment. If they relieve him, it would collapse."

"Then you better tell him not to cross Dillon, because that's the same as crossing Pickering. If he does, he's out on his ass. Your man Feldt works for the Australian Admiral with two names—"

"Soames-Haley," Banning furnished. "Vice Admiral Keith Soames-Haley."

"Right. Who is an old buddy of Pickering's. Dillon's going to see him first thing tomorrow morning, with a letter from Pickering. If it comes to Soames-Haley having to make a choice between Pickering and Feldt, who do you think it will be?"

"Sonofabitch!"

"What you better do is stop insisting this can't be done and start thinking about how it can be."

Banning looked at him for a long moment before replying.

"As you were saying, McCoy, it seems only yesterday that you were a corporal I was defending on a murder charge."

"Yeah, and you wanted me to throw myself on the mercy of the court and take my chances on getting no more than six months or a year in Portsmouth. You didn't even ask me if I was guilty."

Banning's face tightened.

"That was below the belt, don't you think?"

"It's the truth. The Colonel wanted to stay on the right side of the American Consul General and the Italians, and if that meant a corporal had to go to Portsmouth, tough luck for him. And you went along with him."

The reason I'm so goddamned mad, Banning thought, *is that it is the unvarnished truth.*

"I thought you accepted my apology for that," Banning said.

McCoy shrugged. "You brought it up. I was willing to forget it."

The waitress appeared suddenly. In one hand she held two beer mugs. In the other was a plate heaped high with french fried potatoes and scrambled eggs, topped with two slices of toast.

"In other words, you're in agreement with Pickering that I haven't done enough to try to get those two off Buka? Maybe because I don't want to make waves? Because not doing more than I have was the easiest thing to do?''

"I'm very impressed with Pickering," McCoy said.

"That doesn't answer the question."

"OK. Yeah, I am."

"That brings us back to square one. I have to ask to be relieved."

"Who are you going to ask? Rickabee?"

"He's my immediate superior."

"He works for Pickering."

"That whole thing is a sick joke. Pickering has no more right to be a brigadier general than—"

"Than what? Than Jake Dillon has to be a major? Than me to be a lieutenant? Is that what's really bothering you? You think we're all a bunch of amateur Marine officers, ex–enlisted men, who should defer to your *professional* officer-type thinking?"

"Now you've gone too far," Banning said coldly.

"Not quite," McCoy said. "Let me go all the way. Let me tell you *my* orders. From Rickabee, not Pickering. I am to advise him within forty-eight hours of my arrival here whether or not I think you're going to be in the way. If I decide you will be in the way, you'll be on the next plane out of here and you'll spend the rest of the war counting mess kits in Barstow." The Marine Corps operated a large supply depot at Barstow, California.

Banning looked at him as if he could not believe what he just heard.

"I find that hard to believe," he said finally.

"Believe it. They sent me to the 2nd Raider Battalion to see if Colonel Evans Carlson was a communist and needed to be gotten rid of. You're only a major. You're not even in the same league."

"Apparently," Banning replied sarcastically, "you decided Carlson was not a communist."

McCoy ignored him.

"Sessions has his bags packed. He's got that MAGIC clearance that I'm not supposed to know about. You wanted to know why Moore was sent here still using a cane: Moore will fill in for you doing whatever this MAGIC crap is. You want to get relieved, stay on your high horse and Sessions will be on his way here in seventy-two hours."

Banning picked up his beer mug, took a long pull at it, and then burped.

"Well, Lieutenant McCoy, I am relieved to learn that Jake Dillon's not really in charge."

"Don't underestimate Major Dillon, Major Banning," McCoy said.

"I don't want to count mess kits," Banning said.

"That's up to you," McCoy said. "I hope both you and Feldt are around to help while we do this."

"He's not going to like it," Banning said.

"The idea itself, or the challenge to his authority?"

"Either. Both."

"Then you better talk to him."

Banning nodded.

"What do you want from me, McCoy?"

"I want you to punch holes in the plan and then I want solutions to the problems you find."

Banning nodded.

"Ellen Feller's liable to pose problems," Banning said. "The way Dillon ran her off was stupid. He didn't have to tell her to butt out; he didn't have to get her ego involved. She'll be on the back channel to Pickering by morning. If she hasn't already radioed to tell him to tell us to let her in on this."

"He won't," McCoy said. "He doesn't want her to get splattered if the shit hits the fan."

"Did you know that your sainted General Pickering was fucking her?"

"No," McCoy admitted, visibly surprised. "You're sure?"

Banning nodded.

"And Lieutenant Moore has enjoyed the privilege of her bed."

"No kidding?"

"Everybody, apparently, but you and me," Banning said, and smiled.

"Everybody but you and Dillon," McCoy said. "But that was as of an hour ago."

"You, too?"

McCoy didn't respond to the question.

"Dillon's quite a swordsman," he said admiringly. "Hart told me he had Veronica Wood in the sack in Washington. He saw them."

"Veronica Wood?" Banning said. "Maybe there *is* more to Dillon than meets the eye."

Their eyes met for a moment, long enough for them both to understand that they'd resolved the problem between them.

"Speaking of women," McCoy said, "do you happen to know if our Lieutenant Howard had a girlfriend over here?"

"Yeah, as a matter of fact, he did. Does. Why?"

"Well, he's like me. No family. His home address is care of USMC, Washington, D.C. We need some really personal details about this girlfriend."

"What for?"

"Radio code, before we go in. Where is this girl? Who is she?"

"She's a Navy nurse, assigned to the 4th General Hospital in Melbourne."

"I want to talk to her," McCoy said. "Right away."

"She knows where he is, incidentally. And so does Steve Koffler's girl. She's in the RAN. I can have both of them here by tomorrow afternoon. I'll have to find a phone."

"It'll wait until after I eat," McCoy said. "You're sure you don't want some of this?"

"If you *insist,* Ken," Banning said, reaching for a french fry.

"I'm glad we're back to 'Ken,'" McCoy said. "Let's keep it that way."

Banning met his eyes and nodded.

(FOUR)
Water Lily Cottage
Manchester Avenue
Brisbane, Australia
1530 Hours 30 September 1942

Lieutenant John Marston Moore was lying on the couch with his legs elevated on two pillows.

"It says here," he said, lowering *The Brisbane Dispatch* and reaching for a bottle of beer on the coffee table, "that they made 488 cargo ships last year."

"Who's 'they'?" Lieutenant K. R. McCoy asked. He was sitting at a table with Lieutenant Hon Song Do, having just taught General MacArthur's favorite bridge partner the favorite game of Marine enlisted men, Acey-Deucy.

"Us, for Christ's sake!" Moore said.

"I wonder how many they sank?" McCoy asked innocently. " 'They' meaning the Japs and the Germans."

"You mean despite the Air Raid Warning lady's best efforts?" Moore asked.

McCoy laughed. When he saw the look of confusion on Hon's face, he said, "Private joke, Pluto. And you go easy on the suds, Moore."

"Aye, aye, Sir," Moore said, raising the bottle to his lips.

There was the sound of gravel crunching beneath tire wheels. A minute later the door opened and two Navy nurses walked into the room. They were followed by Major Jake Dillon.

"Ladies, these gentlemen—using the word loosely—are Lieutenants Hon, Mc-Coy, and Moore," Dillon said.

"Banning told me one of them was Australian," McCoy said.

"And these ladies, gentlemen," Dillon said, "are Lieutenant Barbara Cotter and her friend Lieutenant Joanne Miller. They came together from Melbourne."

"Whose stupid idea was that?" McCoy said unpleasantly. "There was only supposed to be Howard's girl."

"Jesus, McCoy!" Moore said.

"It was mine, Lieutenant," Barbara said. "I thought they were bringing me here to get some bad news, and I asked her to come with me."

"I don't see any problem, McCoy," Dillon said. They locked eyes for a moment, and then Dillon said, "I was able to tell Barbara that we heard from Joe Howard at eight this morning."

"My name is Hon," Hon said, getting up from the table. "They call me Pluto."

"Barbara," Lieutenant Cotter said.

"Barbara," McCoy said, still unpleasantly, "how much does the other one—"

"Joanne," Lieutenant Miller furnished just as unpleasantly.

"—know about your boyfriend?"

"She knows he's off somewhere I can't tell her, doing something I can't tell her. I am not a fool, Lieutenant."

McCoy looked at Joanne Miller.

"Lieutenant . . . oh shit!"

"Actually, it's Miller," Joanne said.

"What the hell is your problem, McCoy?" Dillon asked.

"They call it 'military security,' Major," McCoy said. "Lieutenant, take this as an order. Everything you know about anything your friend has told you, anything you hear here, anything you might guess here, is TOP SECRET."

"It may come as a big surprise to you, Lieutenant," Joanne Miller said, "but I had actually figured that out myself."

"I didn't mean to jump on you," McCoy said.

"Really?" Joanne Miller asked.

"You come sit by me, Joanne," Moore said, "and I'll be nice to you."

She looked at him and smiled. And then she walked to the couch and sat on the edge of it.

"Jake didn't say what all this was about," Barbara said.

"We need some details," Pluto said. "Personal details, that only you and Lieutenant Howard would know, about your personal relationship."

"Why?" Barbara asked.

"We need a new code," Pluto said. "We have to assume that the code Howard's using now has been broken by the Japanese."

"I don't understand," Barbara said.

"Does he have a private name for you? Or do you have one for him?"

"You mean something like 'Baby' or 'Darling'?"

"Yes, but not those words. They're too general. How about 'Cutesy-poo'? 'Precious Doll'? Something like that?"

"Joe doesn't talk like that," Barbara said.

"I'm surprised," Moore said. "I can think of a dozen unusual terms of endearment I would use if you were my girl."

"That's the end of your beer," McCoy said. "If you can't handle the sauce, leave it alone!"

"Aye, aye, Sir," Moore said and smiled at Joanne Miller.

She surprised him by laying her hand on his forehead.

"How long have you had malaria?" she asked.

"I don't have malaria," he said.

"The hell you don't," she said. "Glassy eyes, high temperature." She looked at Major Dillon. "He has malaria and he belongs in a hospital! Doesn't anybody give a damn?"

"Shit," McCoy said.

"I'm sorry you find that inconvenient, Lieutenant," Joanne Miller said icily.

"Putting him in a hospital right now would be inconvenient."

"People die of malaria, you damned fool!"

"What would they do for him in a hospital that can't be done here?" McCoy asked.

"Well, they would put him on quinine, or a quinine substitute, for one thing. And put him in bed. And they wouldn't give him anything to drink."

"Is there any reason that couldn't be done here? Is there anything else?"

"Well, for one thing, where are you going to get the quinine? And who would take care of him?"

"Nobody's listening to me," Moore said. "I'm all right."

"Major, why don't you take the Lieutenant to the hospital and see that they give her whatever she needs? Maybe you better get a doctor over here to look at him."

Dillon considered that a moment and then nodded.

"You'd better bring a nurse, too," Joanne Miller said.

"We already have two nurses," McCoy said.

She looked at him and decided he was perfectly serious.

"I'm on a seventy-two-hour pass. I can't stay here."

"You've just been placed on temporary duty," McCoy said.

"On whose authority?"

"It can be arranged," Dillon said. "Would you mind coming with me, Lieutenant?"

"I see this," Lieutenant John Marston Moore announced, "as the beginning of a great romance."

"You're a damned fool, you know that?" Joanne said, but when she stood up and looked down at him and saw him smiling, she found herself unable not to smile back.

"Getting back to business," Pluto said, the moment the door had closed after Joanne and Dillon. "There has to be something. Maybe a place. Where did you meet? Under what circumstances? Did you ever"—he hesitated, and then went on—"go to a hotel or something?"

Barbara Cotter smiled, and Pluto thought he saw a suggestion of a blush.

"What was the name of the hotel? Did anything special happen there?"

"The first time I met Joe," Barbara said, half uncomfortably, half amused, "he was sent to me for a blood test. For syphilis. Hell of a way to start a romance, isn't it?" She looked at Pluto. "Is this the sort of thing you want?"

"I think maybe," Pluto said. "Tell me about it."

XIV

Major Jake Dillon returned from the local military hospital with everything necessary to treat a malaria patient, including a doctor. The only thing he didn't have with him was a hospital bed.

"I appreciate your coming over here, Sir," Major Banning greeted the doctor, a Lieutenant Colonel.

The doctor's bearing, haircut, and ribbon-laden tunic told Lieutenant (J.G.) Joanne Miller, NNC, that he had not been recently commissioned into military service from civilian life.

The doctor grunted at Banning and walked to the couch where Second Lieutenant John Marston Moore, USMCR, was resting.

"How do you feel, son?"

"I feel fine, Doctor," Moore said.

"Bullshit," the Colonel said. His ready use of the word confirmed Joanne's guess that this physician's patients over the years had not been in a position to complain about his bedside manner.

He examined Moore quickly but carefully.

"When did you stop taking Atabrine?"

Moore thought a moment. "About six days ago, Sir."

"Why? Did you really think they were giving it to you just so they could watch you turn yellow?"

"It was . . . inconvenient . . . for me to get more, Sir."

"Yeah, well, you see where that led us. It was inconvenient for me to come over here tonight, and it will be inconvenient to treat you here. You belong in a hospital."

"Colonel," Banning said, "did Major Dillon explain why that—"

"I've seen your orders, Major. I am suitably impressed. I said it would be inconvenient to treat him here, not that it couldn't be done."

"Yes, Sir," Banning said.

"So far as the malaria is concerned, the reason he relapsed is that he interrupted his Atabrine regimen. We put him back on Atabrine and he'll start feeling better by tomorrow morning. Now, what's wrong with your legs?"

"They're all right, Sir."

"Bullshit. You nearly jumped out of your skin when I touched them. Take your pants off."

When Moore hesitated, the Colonel said, "That wasn't a suggestion, Lieutenant. And these ladies are nurses, they've seen men with their pants off before."

Moore started to push his trousers down.

"I don't *know* that, come to think of it," the Colonel said. He looked at Joanne Miller. "You *are* an RN, right? Any specialty?"

"I'm a nurse-anesthesiologist, Doctor."

He grunted and looked at Barbara Cotter. "What about you?"

"I'm a psychiatric nurse, Doctor."

"That probably comes in handy around here," the Colonel said, and then looked at Moore's legs. "Mary, Mother of God! What moron discharged you from a hospital?"

He probed the legs knowledgeably with his fingers. Moore winced.

"Believe it or not, before I became a member of the Palace Guard, I thought I was an orthopedic surgeon. What did that, a grenade?"

"A grenade or a mortar round."

"Well, there's no sign of infection, but you really need some physical therapy." He looked at the nurses. "Make him walk around, if nothing else. Put him on his belly and force the legs back until the threshold of pain. Fifteen, twenty movements, each leg, four times a day. Got it?"

"Yes, Doctor," they said, almost in unison.

"When I said 'walk him around,' I didn't mean he's to get out of bed or off the couch for more than thirty minutes at a time unless there's a reason. Give him all he wants to eat, aspirin for the pain, and Atabrine every two hours until tomorrow morning, when every four hours will be enough. I'll come back tomorrow. Got it?"

"Yes, Doctor," Barbara said.

"Alcohol, Doctor?" Joanne asked.

"A couple of drinks won't hurt him. Don't let him get fall-down drunk."

Why did I ask that? Joanne wondered.

"Speaking of which, if someone were to offer me some of that Famous Grouse, I wouldn't turn it down," the Colonel said.

"Certainly," Banning said. "I could use one myself. Would you be offended, Sir, if I offered you a bottle of it?"

"Offended? Jesus, how dumb do I look?"

"Just don't tell anyone where you got it, please, Doctor," Banning said.

"If you were trying to be subtle, Major, and trying to tell me to keep my mouth shut about tonight, save your breath. I don't even want to know what you and your people are up to, and I have been around the Service long enough to know what things you talk about and what things you don't."

Thirty minutes after the doctor left, the telephone rang. Banning answered it, and then a moment later announced, "The weather's clearing at Townsville. We can go."

He looked at Pluto Hon. "I just had an unpleasant thought. Will Moore be able to get into the dungeon?"

What in the world, Joanne Miller wondered, *is the dungeon?*

"With a little bit of luck, he won't have to," Hon said. "But yes, Sir. I took care of it."

"And what about the truck and the car?"

"They're supposed to be here," he looked at his wristwatch, "in ten minutes, Sir."

"Let's get Dillon's skis outside, on the porch, so they won't have to come in here," Banning said.

Dillon's skis? Joanne wondered. *Is that what he said, "Dillon's skis"?*

Two large wooden crates were manhandled through the living room and out the door.

"Pluto will come back as soon we find out if that substitution code works—or come up with something that does," Banning said to Moore. "With you sick, I hate to take him. There's no other way."

"I'm all right," Moore said.

"Yeah, sure you are," Joanne heard herself say.

"We're leaving the car for you," Banning said. "You are not, repeat not, to give it to Mrs. Feller under any circumstances."

"Aye, aye, Sir," Moore said.

Banning looked at Joanne Miller. "When Hon comes back, one of you can pick him up at the airport."

Lieutenant (J.G.) Miller decided she did not like Major Ed Banning.

"Aye, aye, Sir," she said, as sarcastically salty as she could manage. As she said it, she came to attention.

Her sarcasm went right over his head.

"Good girl," he said, and smiled and left.

Two minutes later, Lieutenants Miller and Cotter were alone in Water Lily Cottage with their patient.

(TWO)
Billeting Office
Office of the Headquarters Commandant
Supreme Headquarters
South West Pacific Ocean Area
Brisbane, Australia
1905 Hours 30 September 1942

There were only two female field-grade officers, a major and a lieutenant colonel, assigned to Supreme Headquarters, South West Pacific Ocean Area. Both of them were nurses. The Lieutenant Colonel was on the staff of the senior medical officer, and she was in charge of whatever concerned Army nurses. The Major was on the staff of the Assistant Chief of Staff, G-4 (Matériel), as the resident expert on medical supplies. Both had elected to live in the Female Bachelor Officer's Quarters provided for the nurses assigned to what was known as Mercy Forward. Mercy Forward was in fact a detachment of the Fourth U.S. Army General Hospital (code name, Mercy) sent to Brisbane from Melbourne to provide medical service for MacArthur's headquarters.

Major R. James Tourtillott, the SWPOA Deputy Headquarters Commandant, explained all this in some detail to Mrs. Ellen Feller, Department of the Navy Civilian Professional Employee (Assimilated Grade: Lieutenant Commander), to explain why there was no Female Field Grade Bachelor Officer's Quarters he could move her into.

"Where have you been living, Mrs. Feller?" Major Tourtillott asked. "Is there some reason you can't just stay there?"

Yes, there is a goddamned reason! Major Ed Banning, that bastard, has turned Water Lily Cottage into a goddamned hospital, complete with two nurses: "Sorry, Mrs. Feller, you'll have to move into a BOQ until this is over. We just have to have your room."

Obviously, there is no reason, no reason at all, why Johnny Moore could not be treated for his malaria—if he really has malaria, he looks perfectly healthy to me—in Mercy Forward. And even if there is some "security reason," as Banning said, for keeping him out of the hospital, there is no reason at all why those two Navy nurses couldn't live in the Nurse's BOQ at Mercy Forward. They're only junior-grade lieutenants, after all, and I'm an assimilated Lieutenant Commander.

"There's a project, Major Tourtillott, a classified project that I can't talk about, that seems to have evicted me."

"I could call Mercy Forward and see if they could put you up with the nurses."

"I don't want to move in with the nurses, for one thing, and for another, I have to be somewhere close to Supreme Headquarters. I'm on twenty-four-hour call."

"I'm sure something can be worked out, Mrs. Feller," Tourtillott said, thinking that the best solution for housing this lame-duck female—*I wonder what the hell she does? As an assimilated Lieutenant Commander, she's no secretary*—would probably be to move her into the Devonshire, a small, luxurious hotel requisitioned to house full colonels and one-star generals; but he couldn't do that without the OK of the Headquarters Commandant. "But not today."

"You don't seem to understand," Ellen Feller said. "I don't have a place to sleep."

Major Tourtillott handed her a printed form.

"This is a billeting voucher on Mason's Hotel," he said. "They'll put you up overnight, and if you'll come back, say at oh nine hundred, oh nine thirty, I'll have you fixed up by then."

"Where is Mason's Hotel?"

"Not far," Major Tourtillott said. "It's the best I can do right now."

The reason I am being humiliated like this is because Banning hates me, has been waiting for an opportunity to humiliate me, and now he's found it in spades. Not only is he denying me access to whatever he and that offensive Major Jake Dillon are up to, but he is rubbing that humiliation in my face by ordering me out of Water Lily Cottage.

He thinks he can just order me around like I'm one of his Marines.

And he thinks there is absolutely nothing I can do about it, because he's the senior Office of Management Analysis officer . . . even if my assimilated rank is equal to his.

Well, we'll see about that! Fleming Pickering won't let him get away with this, once he hears about it!

Room 6 of Mason's Hotel turned out to be a small, more or less square room on the upper floor of a fifty-year-old, wood-framed, tin-roofed, two-story building.

There was a bed with a visibly sagging mattress; a chest of drawers; a mirror which had lost at least half of its silver backing; a table against a wall; a straight-backed chair; a bedside table with a 25-watt lamp on it; and a bare 100-watt bulb hanging from the ceiling. There was a sink; and behind a curtain there was a tin-walled cubicle with a showerhead and concrete floor. The toilet was down the corridor.

Mrs. Ellen Feller moved the 25-watt lamp from the bedside table to the table against the wall, pulled the chair up to it, and spent the next two hours composing a message to Brigadier General Fleming Pickering. It would go out that very night over the MAGIC channel, she decided, even if that meant she would have to pay for a taxi all the way out to the Supreme Headquarters, SWPOA building, spend thirty minutes in Pluto Hon's damned damp dungeon, and then either beg a ride back here from the staff duty officer or pay for another damned taxi.

Putting her thoughts on paper, however, turned out to be much more difficult than she initially imagined. Her first draft, quickly balled up and tossed on the floor, sounded like whining. And that wouldn't do. To win her point, she had to paint herself as a member of the team who had been unjustly excluded from team activities.

Neither was Fleming Pickering going to be automatically sympathetic to her eviction from Water Lily Cottage, she realized. Banning would just tell him that John Moore's nurses needed her room.

Maybe Johnny Moore really has malaria.

And then, slowly, as her fury waned, she saw other problems. For instance, she wasn't entirely sure that Fleming Pickering would even get her carefully worded message. It would have to pass over Rickabee's desk. And Colonel Rickabee and that bastard Banning were not only brother Marine officers, but personally close. Even if she sent it EYES ONLY PICKERING, Rickabee would see it. He would be prepared to argue Banning's case by the time he handed it to Pickering.

And she couldn't send it EYES ONLY PICKERING and still look like a member of the team registering a justified complaint. Rickabee was Banning's immediate superior, not Pickering. Any complaints should be directed to him.

And finally, of course, that rude bastard Dillon just might have been telling the truth. Pickering himself just might have told him to keep Ellen Feller out of whatever it was they were doing.

Finally, she gave up. She retrieved all the crumpled-up balls of paper and put a match to them.

There were more than two ways to skin a cat.

General Willoughby was proud and sensitive about his role as MacArthur's intelligence officer. He would not be at all pleased to learn that a clandestine intelligence operation, directed from Washington, was being conducted right under his nose.

Let Willoughby send an EYES ONLY to Washington—either on his own or at MacArthur's direction.

It wouldn't be hard for Willoughby to "find out." She'd go to the dungeon in the morning, and she would personally carry to General Willoughby the first MAGIC that came through. Willoughby almost always wanted to chat a little. He'd offer her a cup of coffee and she'd accept it, of course.

She would, she decided, wear the white cotton see-through blouse Willoughby always seemed to find so fascinating.

On that happy note, Mrs. Ellen Feller (Assimilated Grade: Lieutenant Commander) took off her clothing, climbed into the bed with the sagging mattress, and went to sleep.

(THREE)

At half past nine, Lieutenant (J.G.) Joanne Miller, NNC, came back into the living room. Second Lieutenant John Marston Moore, USMCR, was regally established there in a high-backed armchair, his feet on its matching footstool. He was wearing a hospital bathrobe, pajamas, and slippers. A card table had been arranged so that Joanne could sit on one side and Lieutenant (J.G.) Barbara Cotter on the other. The three of them had been playing gin rummy.

Joanne had gone into the kitchen to make a fresh pot of tea and to get Lieutenant Moore's Atabrine. She had refused his request for another beer, and he had somewhat surprised her by not giving her an argument. Usually, when he asked for a beer and she turned him down, he gave her an argument. And that was beginning to get to her. But then he began to annoy her in a different way. Every time she glanced at him, she saw that he was looking at her.

He's just a kid, a horny kid, she thought. *If I ignore him, he'll stop.*

He swallowed the Atabrine, washing it down with a swallow of Coca-Cola.

"How old are you?" she heard herself asking.

"Twenty-two," he said.

"You don't look it."

She saw the strange look on Barbara's face.

"Did I do something wrong, or what?" Moore asked.

I'm twenty-four. What right have I got to think of him as a kid?

"That just slipped out. Sorry."

"I thought you were going to tell me it was past my bedtime or something," he said.

"It is."

He looked at his watch.

"Please, Mommy," he said. "It's only half past nine. Can't I stay up till ten?"

"I said I was sorry," she said. "I really don't give a damn if you stay up all night. I'm going to bed."

Barbara flashed her another *what's-wrong-with-you?* look.

"Just a couple more hands, John," Barbara said. "It's been a long day for me, too."

Joanne went into the bedroom recently vacated by Ellen Feller and started to prepare for bed. She had just emerged from the shower when she heard the telephone ring. A minute later Barbara called her name.

Joanne put on her bathrobe and went into the living room in time to see John Moore walking awkwardly across the room to the couch. He picked up his cane and then went into his bedroom.

"He says he has to go out," Barbara said, and gestured toward the telephone.

"Like hell he's going out!"

She pushed the door to his bedroom open. Moore was pulling his pajama top over his head.

"What do you think you're doing?"

"I've got to go to the dungeon," he said. "I'd be grateful if one of you would drive me."

"You're not going anywhere."

"Hey," he said, almost nastily, "enough of this 'me Mommy and you Little Boy' bullshit. I have to go to the dungeon. They called. I'm going."

"What the hell is the dungeon?"

He didn't answer her. He found a T-shirt and pulled it over his head. After he stuck his arms in the sleeves of a shirt, he looked at her.

"The dungeon is what they call the cryptographic room. It's in the SWPOA basement. A message there has to be decoded."

"And they don't have a cryptographic officer on duty? Why do you have to go?"

Again, he didn't reply. He turned his back to her and dropped his pajama trousers. She could see the scars on his legs. He almost fell over putting his undershorts on. When he reached for his trousers, she went to him.

"Let me help you," she said, much more fiercely than she intended. "I don't want you breaking your leg."

He sat on the bed. She dropped to her knees, picked up his pants, and worked them up his calves. When she looked up at him, she saw him staring down the front of her bathrobe.

She flushed and angrily put her hand to the opening, closed the robe, quickly got to her feet, and turned around.

"I hope you got an eyeful!" she snapped.

She could see him in the mirror over the chest of drawers.

He pushed himself off the bed, stood up, and pulled his trousers up. He had an erection. It stood there defiantly until he had tucked his shirt in and buttoned his waistband. As he pushed himself inside his fly and zipped himself up, he said, "If you didn't want me to look, why did you come in here dressed like that?"

A wave of anger swept through her. She spun around and slapped him as hard as she could, so hard that he fell backward onto the bed.

"You *bastard!*" she hissed.

And then, as quickly as it came, the anger passed and she realized what she had done.

"Jesus!" he said, shaking his head.

Joanne fled the bedroom, crossed the living room without looking at Barbara, went into their bedroom, and slammed the door.

She leaned against the bedroom door, breathing heavily.

A moment later she heard him ask, "Where's the keys to the Studebaker?"

"You shouldn't be going out," Barbara said.

"Give me the damned keys!" he said.

"I'll drive you," Joanne heard Barbara say. She heard the front door close. After that, the engine started, and then the headlights swept across the window curtains.

She pushed herself off the wall and went and sat on the edge of her bed.

"It's all right, I'm awake," Joanne said when Barbara came into their room without turning on the light. They had been gone two hours.

Barbara turned the lights on and started to get undressed.

"Is he all right?"

"I just gave him his eleven-thirty Atabrine," Barbara said.

"What was that all about?" Joanne asked. "Did you get to see the dungeon?"

"No. They wouldn't let me in there. Whatever it is, it's in the basement of the SWPOA headquarters building. But I did get to see General MacArthur."

"*MacArthur?* Really?"

"Yeah. In the flesh. First we went down in the basement. They made me wait outside—"

"Who made you wait?"

"A couple of sergeants with submachine guns made me wait outside a steel door. John went inside, he was in there I guess almost an hour, and then he came back out. Then we got back on the elevator, and he said, 'Now you'll get a chance to see how the other half lives,' and we rode up to the seventh floor. More sergeants with submachine guns.

"One of them said, 'The Supreme Commander is expecting you, Lieutenant.'"

"Really?"

"And the sergeant opened a door, and John said, 'I'll be right out,' and went in. MacArthur was standing right inside, walking around with a cup of coffee."

"And?"

"John said, 'Good evening, General.' And MacArthur said, 'Where's Pluto?' and John said, 'He had to go to Townsville, Sir,' and handed him a folder with a TOP SECRET cover sheet. MacArthur read it and grunted. Then he asked, 'Has General Willoughby seen this?' and John said, 'No, Sir. I just decoded it,' and MacArthur said, 'I'll see that he gets it.' And then he said, 'Have I met you before, Lieutenant?' and John said, 'I was stationed here before, Sir, as a sergeant.' And MacArthur said, 'Yes, of course, you're the fellow they sent to Guadalcanal by mistake. I'm glad to see you're recovered.'"

"Recovered, in a pig's eye!" Joanne interrupted.

"You want to hear what happened or not?" Barbara asked.

"Go on."

"So then MacArthur laid his hand on John's shoulder, sort of patted him, and said, 'I'm sorry you had to come here this late at night. When did you say Pluto will be back?' and John said, 'Probably tomorrow, Sir,' and MacArthur grunted and walked him to the door. 'Good night, son. Thank you,' he said, and then he saw me and smiled and nodded. What do you think about that?"

"I hope you're not making it all up," Joanne said.

"Well, you can go to hell!" Barbara said. She went into the bathroom.

"I'll give him his one-thirty," Joanne called after her, then rolled on her side and stretched her arm out for the alarm clock so she could set it.

* * *

Joanne pushed open the door to John Marston Moore's room and walked to the side of his bed, using her flashlight.

"Pill time," she said. "Shield your eyes, I'm going to turn the light on."

"I'm not asleep. Turn it on."

She turned the bedside table lamp on. He pushed himself up against the headboard.

"Trouble sleeping?" she asked.

She dumped two Atabrine pills from the bottle, handed them to him, and then handed him a glass of water.

"Yeah," he said after he swallowed the Atabrine.

She sat down on the bed, stuck a thermometer in his mouth, and started to take his pulse.

He smelled of soap. She remembered hearing the sound of running water half an hour after Barbara finished her shower and climbed in bed. She almost got up then to make sure he didn't fall down and hurt himself. But it occurred to her that he had been managing showers by himself with no trouble before Joanne Miller, RN, started taking a professional interest in his physical welfare. She realized he didn't need her help now.

That kept her from making a fool of herself. She did not get out of bed. She lay there, with a clear image of him in the shower. The scars on his leg. His legs. His chest. His rear end. What he had to tuck in his pants just before she slapped him for looking down her robe at her breasts. As a nurse, that word—for what he stuck inside his pants—meant nothing much to her. As a nurse, she used it easily, professionally. But now was something else . . . "What's the matter?" she asked. "Why can't you sleep?"

"You are," he mumbled around the thermometer.

"Ssssh," she said. She wondered if her face was really flushed, or whether it just felt that way.

There was nothing wrong with his heartbeat. And when she took the thermometer from his mouth, she saw that his temperature was only slightly elevated.

"Your temperature has dropped," she said.

"That's surprising," he said.

She gave him a professional smile and then looked at his eyes to see if the pupils were dilated.

That was a mistake. I didn't assess the diameter of his pupils. I fell in.

"I'd like to apologize for . . . before. I shouldn't have slapped you."

His hand is on my cheek. Why don't I push it away? Or get up?

"Jesus, you're beautiful!"

"You shouldn't be doing that," Joanne said. "I shouldn't let you do that."

"Look at me again," he said.

"No!"

"Look at me again!"

I knew if I did that, this would happen! Joanne thought as she felt his hands on her back, pulling her to him.

She felt her heart jump when their lips touched. And she felt a weakness in her middle. And she barely had the strength to push away from him.

"This is absolutely insane!"

"Yeah, isn't it?"

His lips were now on her neck.

"We have to stop!"

"Why?"

He's pushing my robe open!

"Barbara! She'll hear us."

He touched her nipple with his tongue, and then looked up at her and smiled.

"She's probably asleep," John said.

Oh, God, I hope she is, Joanne thought as she reached down and pushed John's head back where it had been.

(FOUR)
Ferdinand Six
Buka, Solomon Islands
1 October 1942

It's either hotter than usual, Sergeant Steve Koffler thought, *or Ian Bruce is getting sick or something, because he's really wheezing as he pumps the pedals of the generator.*

FRD6.KCY. FRD6.KCY AK. KCY CLR.

Detachment A of Special Marine Corps Detachment 14, this is the United States Pacific Fleet Radio. Receipt of your transmission is acknowledged. Our exchange of messages is concluded.

Steve did not follow the prescribed procedure, which was to tap out FRD6 CLR before shutting down. It was a waste of goddamned time, and Ian Bruce looked worn out.

He reached for the ON/OFF switch and then stopped.

FRD6, FRD1. FRD6, FRD1. SB CODE.

Detachment A of Special Marine Corps Detachment 14, this is Coastwatcher Radio. Stand by to receive an encoded message.

What the fuck do they want?

He glanced at Ian Bruce. Ian was looking at him, waiting for the signal to stop pumping. Steve shook his head, made a keep-it-up gesture and replied to Townsville.

FRD1, FRD6. GA.

Go ahead, Townsville.

The message was not unusually long, maybe fifteen five-character blocks, but after Steve sent the usual, FRD1, FRD6. AK, Townsville came right back: FRD6, FRD1. FRD1 SB. FRD1 SB.

Townsville was standing by, waiting for an answer to their message.

Steve made a cutting motion across his throat. It would take him a couple of minutes, at least, to decode the message. Ian Bruce needed a break.

And a bath. I can smell him from here.

"Bloody hell!" Ian Bruce said.

"See if you can find Lieutenant Howard, will you?"

"Right you are."

Both Lieutenant Howard and Sub-Lieutenant Reeves came into the hut before Steve finished decoding the message.

"What the hell is this?" he asked, giving the decoded message to Howard.

USE AS SIMPLE SUBSTITUTION X JULIETS NAME X ROMEOS NAME
X WHAT SHE THOUGHT HE HAD WHEN THEY MET X NAME OF TEST
X RESULT OF TEST X

> 18×19×09×37×11
> 15×23×08×09×11
> 01×02×03×04×05
> 06×07×23×31×05

"They've gone sodding bonkers," Sub-Lieutenant Reeves said, and then added
an unpleasant afterthought. "You don't think this could be from our Nipponese
chums, do you?"

Steve shook his head. "No," he said. "I recognized his hand."

"I know what simple substitution is," Joe Howard said, "and so should you.
But who the hell is Romeo?"

"It would have to be our lad, here," Reeves said. "Neither you nor I are romantically involved at the moment."

"Lay off him," Howard said.

"No offense, Steve, my lad."

"Go fuck yourself," Steve said. "What does that 'what she thought he had when
they met' mean?"

"I think I know," Howard said.

He dropped to the dirt floor. They had two pads of message paper left. He picked
up one of them. Holding it on his knees, he wrote:

BarbaraJosephSyphilisWassermanNegative

"My girl's name is Barbara," he said. "Mine is Joseph. I was taking my precommissioning physical in San Diego, and the doctor thought I was lying when I
told him I'd never had VD. He sent me to the VD ward for a Wasserman."

"I have the oddest feeling that he actually believes he knows what he's doing,"
Lieutenant Reeves said.

"Barbara was the nurse on duty," Joe added.

Very carefully, he wrote numbers under the letters. When he finished, it looked
like this:

BarbaraJosephSyphilisWassermanNegative

12345678901234567890123456789012345678

Then he recopied the numbers so there was space beneath them, and made the
translation.

> 18×19×09×37×11
> I   l   o   v   e
> 15×23×08×09×11
> y   a   j   o   e
> 01×02×03×04×05
> b   a   r   b   a
> 06×07×23×31×05
> r   a   a   n   a

"Does that say anything?" Reeves asked.

"Yeah," Joe Howard whispered.

He wrote out two five-character blocks of numbers and handed them to Steve.

"You up?"

"No."

"I'll pump the goddamned bicycle. You get on the air and send that."

"What the hell does it say?" Reeves asked.

"What *they* sent says, 'I love ya, Joe Barbara,'" Steve Koffler said. "The last three letters are fillers, to fill the five-character block. What *he's* replying is none of your business."

The dials came to life. Steve's hand worked the key.

FRD1, FRD6. FRD1, FRD6.
Coastwatcher Radio, this is Ferdinand Six.

FRD6, FRD1, GA.
Ferdinand Six, go ahead.

Steve sent the reply, and then showed it to Reeves.

28×38×25×10×10
M   e   T   o   o
01×02×04×15×05
B   a   b   y   a

Townsville came right back:

FRD6, FRD1. AK

10×23×28×32×10
35×38×37×38×01
02×12×13×30×38
END

FRD1, FRD6. AK. SB.
Coastwatcher Radio, acknowledged. Standing by.

"Go pump the bike," Steve said. "Let him decode this. Maybe there's more."
There was:

30×02×35×13×07
31×17×11×19×22
17×19×19×10×22
26×16×23×26×11
38×31×14×11×24
09×09×31×02×07
END

Steven sent the reply: FRD1, FRD6. AK. MORE??

The reply came immediately: FRD1. CLR.

"That's it," Steve said as he made the cutting motion across his throat. Reeves stopped pumping.

Steve turned the radio off, stood up, and handed the last message to Howard.

After that he hovered over Howard, watching him as he finished decoding the previous message.

10×23×28×32×10
S   A   M   E   S
35×38×37×38×01
T   E   V   E   B
02×12×13×30×38
A   P   H   N   E

"What the hell does that say?"

" 'Same Steve, signed Daphne,' " Howard said.

"Daphne is spelled with a 'D,' not a 'B,' " Steve said.

"There's no 'B' in the substitution, Steve," Howard said. "What sounds closest?" He started working on the final block of numbers and finally handed that to Steve.

"Take a look at that, Jacob," Howard said. "What do you make of it?"

30×02×35×13×07
N   A   T   H   A
31×17×11×19×22
N   I   E   L   W
17×19×19×10×22
I   L   L   S   E
26×16×23×26×11
E   P   A   T   I
38×31×14×11×24
E   N   S   E   S
09×09×31×02×07
O   O   N   A   A

"Nathaniel Willseep At?" Reeves asked. "What the bloody hell is 'ienses'?"

"Nathaniel will see Patience soon," Howard said.

"There's no 'C' in Patience," Steve said.

"Same thing. You use what you have, in this case an 'S.' The question is, who is Nathaniel? And what the hell does it mean?"

They found Miss Patience Witherspoon washing Steve's spare utility trousers on a rock in the stream. Nathaniel Wallace turned out to be one of her friends when she was at the Mission School.

"Do you know where he is now?" Reeves asked.

"Yes, Sir. He was sent to Australia just before the war to enroll in King's College. Nathaniel is very intelligent. He did very well in school."

"And did Nathaniel know you were going into the bush with me?" Reeves asked very carefully.

"I sent him a note with the *St. James,*" Patience said. "Asking him to pray for us."

"What?" Howard asked.

"The *St. James* was the last ship to leave here before the Japanese came," Reeves said. "It wasn't a ship, really, more like a powered launch."

"Bingo," Howard said. "We are about to be reinforced."

He'd caught himself just in time. He was about to say "relieved."

"Is that what you think?" Reeves asked.

"They must know our radio is on its last legs," Howard said. "And that we need supplies."

"But why take the risk of letting us know someone's coming?"

"So we'll be on the lookout for parachutes, prepared to receive them."

"You think they'd do that again?"

"There's no other way."

"And the Japs know it," Reeves said. "And they're looking for parachutes. And when they break that child's code of yours, they'll really be looking."

"That child's code isn't going to be as easy to break as you think," Howard said. "It'll take them a couple of days . . . when they start on it. And then they have to guess the meaning."

"Submarine," Steve Koffler said. "They could send people in by submarine."

"I don't think so, Steve," Howard said. "I think we should start looking for an airplane, and parachutes. Even if they could talk the Navy out of a submarine, and they managed to land somebody safely, how could he get here? Especially carrying replacement radios and equipment?"

"He's from here," Steve said. "This Nathaniel is."

"Nathaniel is very intelligent," Miss Patience Witherspoon said. "And very strong."

(FIVE)
Royal Australian Navy Coastwatcher Establishment
Townsville, Queensland
1 October 1942

"We'll get into specific details later," Major Edward F. Banning said to open the first briefing session for Operation PICKLE, "so please don't start asking questions until I'm finished."

Just over twenty people were sitting around the tables of the mess hall, Australians of the Coastwatcher Establishment and Marines of Special Detachment 14. Some were drinking coffee and eating doughnuts. The majority were drinking beer.

"The RAN is going to provide us with a submarine, HMAS *Pelican*. It will take a replacement team to this beach. . . ." He turned and pointed to a map of Buka with an eighteen-inch ruler.

". . . According to Chief Wallace, it's approximately fifty yards wide at low tide and has a relatively gradual slope. And again according to Chief Wallace, it is a twenty-four- to thirty-six-hour march from Ferdinand Six, which is about here. I asked him to err on the side of caution. Carrying that equipment in that terrain is going to be a bitch.

"Getting it ashore in rubber boats is going to be a bitch, too. The shallow slope of the beach results in pretty heavy surf under most conditions. We won't know what those conditions are until we get there."

"We?" Sergeant George Hart thought, somewhat unkindly. *What's this we crap? We're not going. These guys are going.*

"At that time—when the *Pelican* surfaces—a decision will have to be made," Banning went on, "whether to try to land the entire team and all the equipment. If the surf or other conditions make that too risky, then we'll put just Chief Wallace and three other men ashore.

"That decision will be made by Lieutenant McCoy. Lieutenant McCoy's something of an expert on rubber-boat landings. The last one he made was on Makin Island with the Marine Raiders."

Heads turned to look at Lieutenant K. R. McCoy.

That was probably necessary, George Hart decided, *to impress these people. But McCoy sure didn't like it.*

"If it turns out we can only put four men ashore safely, two will immediately start out for Ferdinand Six. Two will remain on the beach. The two on the beach will have two missions. The first is to conduct tests of the beach, to see if the sand there will support the weight of an airplane. That information will be sent to the submarine and then relayed here. After that the submarine will immediately depart the area; it will return the following day. Their second mission will be to tell the submarine, after its return, whether or not it is safe to land the full team.

"Repeated attempts to land the replacement team and its equipment will be made until (a) they are successful or (b) the tests have indicated that the beach will take an aircraft.

"If that proves to be the case, then the aircraft will land there with the second replacement team and its equipment. That will of course solve both the insertion and extraction problems, since the aircraft will take the present team out with it, as well as the two people we insert onto the beach.

"The problem—at least in my judgment—is that the aircraft plan is not likely to work. If it doesn't, then the insertion of the replacement team and the extraction of the people now operating Ferdinand Six will be by submarine."

He looked around the room. "OK, questions?"

"Do I understand, Sir," a young Australian Sub-Lieutenant asked, "that I would be inserted regardless of surf conditions?"

"No," Lieutenant Commander Eric Feldt answered for Banning. "We will land either the entire team or none of it. Except, of course, for Chief Wallace."

"Yes, Sir."

"Question, Sir?" a buck sergeant of USMC Special Detachment 14 asked. "Shoot."

"In case of bad surf conditions, no radios will go ashore, right?"

"Right. I just said that. The whole team goes in or none of it."

"How will the two people onshore communicate with the sub?"

"The Navy—our Navy," Lieutenant McCoy answered, "has a portable, battery-powered radio. A voice radio. Two of them are being flown in here. It has enough range to reach from the beach to the sub. And about two hours' battery life. If we can't land the whole team, I'll take one of them and a spare set of batteries with me in the rubber boat."

"Yes, Sir. But what about the airplane?"

"What about the airplane?"

"How are you going to communicate with it?"

"Shit!" Lieutenant McCoy said furiously.

"I mean, Sir, if we get it."

"I know what you mean," McCoy said. "Goddamn it, I didn't think about that!"

"Lieutenant," Chief Signalman Nathaniel Wallace, Royal Australian Navy Volunteer Reserve, asked, pronouncing it Lef-tenant, "I think we could probably modify the Navy radio so it would net with the aircraft radios. When did you say they are coming?"

"As soon as they can fly them in. Probably today," McCoy replied.

"I may be wrong, of course, but those types of short-range radios often radiate in the same general area of the frequency spectrum as aircraft radios. I rather suspect that we could make it work."

"Jesus Christ, I hope so."

Chief Signalman Wallace was the ugliest single human being Sergeant George Hart, USMC, could ever remember seeing. He was also the only Navy man he had ever seen wearing a skirt.

But it wasn't possible to dismiss him as some quaint and ignorant savage out of the pages of *National Geographic* magazine. Hart had already long since realized

546 ≡ W.E.B. GRIFFIN

that his bushy head of hair and blue-black teeth, his scars and tattoos, were not all of him. On the other side of all that was a mind at least as sharp as his own.

For one thing, Nathaniel spoke fluent English—*English* English, like the announcers on the British Broadcasting Corporation's International Service. For another, of the dozen or more radio technicians (including three Marines) who ran the Coastwatcher Establishment's radio station, he probably knew the most about radios, inside and out.

Above the waist, Chief Wallace wore the prescribed uniform for Chief Petty Officers of the RAN. Just as in the American Navy, the senior enlisted rank of the RAN wore officer-type uniforms: Instead of the traditional bell-bottom trousers and a blouse with a black kerchief and flap hanging down the back, they wore a double-breasted business suit with brass buttons, and a shirt and tie. And instead of those cute little sailor hats (as George and most other Marines thought of them), Chief Petty Officers wore brimmed caps with a special Chief Petty Officer insignia pinned on them.

The white crown of Chief Wallace's brimmed cap was not quite as wide as the mass of black, crinkly hair it rode on. It was centered with almost mathematical precision at least three inches over his skull. A neatly tied black necktie was pulled with precision into the collar of his immaculate white shirt. The brass buttons of his jacket glistened, as did his black oxford shoes. Between the jacket and the shoes he wore a skirt, of blue denim, and knee-high immaculate white stockings. This served to expose incredibly ugly knees and skinny upper legs matted with crinkly hair.

"If we can't get the radio to communicate with the aircraft, McCoy, we could work out some sort of landing panel signals," Banning said.

"With respect, Sir," Chief Signalman Wallace said, "I don't think it will be a problem."

"Any other questions?" Major Banning asked.

"What are these beach tests, Sir?" a USMC Special Detachment 14 corporal asked.

"As I understand it," Major Banning said, "Sergeant Hart has a steel cone he pounds into the sand with a ten-pound weight. He then reads the markings on the cone. The theory is that it can be determined how much weight the sand will support."

"Yes, Sir."

"I'll say it again. Don't count on the airplane."

"Yes, Sir."

What that sonofabitch just said, Sergeant George Hart realized in shock, *was that I'm going to be in one of those rubber boats!*

(SIX)
Headquarters, MAG-25
Espíritu Santo
0730 Hours 2 October 1942

"Come on in, Jack," Lieutenant Colonel Stanley N. Holliman, USMC, Executive Officer of MAG-25, said, waving his hand at Major Jack Finch, USMC.

Major Finch entered the office. He was wearing a wash-faded Suit, Flying, Cotton, Tropical Areas, and he was armed with a .45 Colt automatic in a shoulder holster.

"Stan, I was on the threshold—" he began to complain, and then stopped. There was a stranger in Holliman's office, a non-aviator Marine in a rear-echelon uniform. "Good morning, Sir. You wished to see me?"

"This won't take long," Colonel Holliman said. "Dillon, this is Major Jack Finch. Jack, this is Major Homer Dillon."

"People call me Jake," Dillon said, putting out his hand.

"I think we'd save some time, Dillon," Holliman said, "if you would show Finch what you showed me."

Dillon took a stiff piece of plastic from the right bellows pocket of his jacket and extended it to Finch. He read it and then looked at Colonel Holliman.

"Read both sides, Jack," Holliman said.

"I'm impressed," Finch said. "I guess that's the idea, huh?"

"MAG-25, naturally, is going to do whatever it can for Major Dillon and the Chief of Staff to the President," Holliman said.

"Yes, Sir."

"He wants a few things from you, Jack."

"Yes, Sir?"

"Starting with the best R4D you have. It will not be available for anything else until further notice."

"Yes, Sir."

"I've told him you can install auxiliary fuel tanks in a couple of hours. Is that correct?"

"Yes, Sir. The fuel lines are already installed. All that has to be done is to reload the tanks and hook them up."

"Major Dillon has also brought with him some special equipment that will have to be installed," Holliman said.

"What kind of special equipment?"

"They're something like skis," Dillon said. "They're supposed to make it possible to land an R4D on sand."

"On sand?" Finch asked incredulously.

"Certain kinds of sand," Dillon said. "We don't know yet if our sand is the right kind; but in case it is, we want to be ready."

"I don't suppose you're going to tell me where this sand is?" Finch asked.

"You understand that all this is classified?" Dillon asked.

"I thought maybe it would be," Finch said, tempering the sarcasm with a smile.

"Just for the record, I'm telling you the classification is TOP SECRET," Jake said. "The sand is on a beach on an island called Buka."

"That's way the hell up by Rabaul!"

"Right. And there is a Japanese fighter base on Buka."

"I know," Finch said. "I've seen the maps."

"There is also a Coastwatcher station on Buka. Their equipment is about shot, and we have every reason to believe that the people are in pretty bad physical shape. What we're going to do is extract them, and replace them."

"Well, I'll be goddamned!" Finch said softly. Then he added, "I guess it's that important, isn't it?" And then he had a second thought. "Just among three Marines, how did The Corps get stuck with this mission?"

"Two of the three people to be extracted are Marines," Dillon said.

"I didn't know we had Marines with the Coastwatchers," Holliman said.

"We have these people, and there are two more on the replacement team," Dillon said.

"I'll be damned," Finch said.

"Major Dillon also wants from you the name of the best R4D pilot you know who would be willing to volunteer for this mission."

"That's easy. Finch, John James, Major."

"See if you can come up with some other names, Jack," Holliman said. "I need you as squadron commander."

"Sir, I'm the best R4D pilot. I can't really think . . . of anyone with more experience."

"You hesitated," Dillon challenged.

"I'm the most experienced R4D pilot in MAG-25," Finch said flatly.

"Who were you thinking of, Major?" Dillon pursued.

"Tell him, Jack," Holliman ordered.

"Charley Galloway, Sir," Finch said with obvious reluctance. He looked at Dillon. "Galloway's a captain. He's commanding VMF-229 on Henderson Field on Guadalcanal."

"You said you needed a volunteer, volunteers," Holliman said. "I'm not sure Galloway would. Not because he doesn't have the balls, but because he would honestly figure he is more valuable to The Corps as a squadron commander than doing something . . . like this."

"Something idiotic, maybe suicidal, like this?" Dillon asked.

"Your words, Major, not mine."

"The question is, is Galloway the pilot who could most likely carry this off?"

"He was my IP," Finch said. "He's as good as there is. I don't want to sound like I'm trying to sell him for the job, but Galloway was in on the acceptance tests of the R4D before the war. He even went through the Air Corps program on dropping parachutists."

"Then in your judgment you and Captain Galloway are the two best pilots for this. Is that what you're saying?"

"Yes, that's what I'm saying."

"Colonel, would you agree with that?"

"I could lie, I suppose," Holliman said. "Maybe I should. But I won't. Yeah, they're the best."

"Well then, the next step, obviously, is to ask Captain Galloway if he'd be willing to volunteer."

"I'm going up there this morning," Finch said. "I was about to take off when I was told to come here. I'll ask him."

"If you don't mind I'll ride along with you. I'd like to see him myself. Charley's an old friend of mine."

That announcement seemed to surprise both Holliman and Finch, but they didn't say anything.

"That would mean bumping a passenger already on my plane. Or two hundred pounds of cargo," Finch said.

"You can send whoever or whatever I bump up there on the R4D you're going to install the fuel tanks and skis on," Dillon replied. "I want that ready to go from Henderson as soon as possible."

XV

There is a smell of pain, Lieutenant (J.G.) Joanne Miller, NNC, thought. *He's sweating because of the pain I'm causing him, and the sweat smells of pain.*

"Am I hurting you?" she asked as she bent his lower leg back until it would flex no more. She pressed harder, raising his hips off the bed.

"I'm all right," John said.

"Don't be a goddamn hero," Lieutenant Colonel M. J. Godofski, MC, USA, said. "You're not going to impress Joanne with some manly bullshit about not feeling pain. If it hurts, say so."

Godofski was leaning against the bedroom wall, puffing on a cigar.

"OK, Colonel, it hurts," John said.

"Good," Godofski said. "It should hurt a little. Not to the point where you can't stand it. We're trying to make your blood vessels down there take more blood than they're used to taking. They have to be trained to replace the ones you lost. Understand?"

"Yes, Sir."

Joanne counted *thirteen, fourteen, fifteen* and stopped.

"That's fifteen, Doctor."

"Can you take five more, son?"

"Yes, Sir."

Colonel Godofski nodded.

Sixteen, seventeen, eighteen, nineteen, twenty.

Honey, I'm sorry!

"Twenty, Doctor."

Godofski went to the bed and probed John's muscles with his fingers.

"Just give him fifteen on the other leg," he said. "It was damaged more than the other one. We don't want to overdo it."

"Yes, Doctor."

"I'll see you tomorrow, son," Godofski said. He looked at Joanne. "I think he's out of the woods with the malaria. No sweats. No diarrhea. His temperatures seem constant. We'll leave him on the Atabrine regimen for a couple more days and see what happens."

"Yes, Doctor."

"They called up from Melbourne about you yesterday. Wanted to know when they can have you back. You must be a pretty good gas passer."

Joanne nodded.

"They're getting in a bunch of wounded from New Guinea," Godofski said.

"I didn't ask for this assignment," Joanne said.

"I didn't ask for mine, either," he said and walked out of the room.

"But are you sorry you came?" John asked as he picked up his ankle. "That's what it sounded like."

"Shut up," Joanne said.

One, she began to count, *two.*

She saw the sweat suddenly pop out on his forehead.

Thirteen, fourteen, fifteen.

"Jesus!" John said.

Oh, honey, I'm sorry.

She sat on the bed beside him and wiped the sweat from his face and neck.

"I like that," he said, then caught her hand and kissed it.

She slapped him on the buttocks and stood up.

"Go take a bath, you stink."

"I like *that,* too," he said.

"Will you stop? Barbara will hear you."

"You don't think she doesn't know?" John asked.

The doorbell went off; it was an old-fashioned turn-to-ring device.

"That's probably the Colonel," John said. "He's had second thoughts. He wants you to give me twenty."

He rolled onto his back. She put her hand on his cheek.

He caught it and used it for support as he pulled himself to a sitting position. Next he swung his legs out of bed; the movement made him wince.

"You're all right? You're not going to fall down in there?"

"No," he said as he made his way into the bathroom.

She was pulling the sweaty sheets from his bed when Barbara put her head in the door.

"Taking a shower," Joanne said. "If that's what you were about to ask."

Barbara, who looked upset, walked to the bathroom and opened the door.

"John, Daphne Farnsworth is here. Would you come out, please?"

"Be right there. Offer her a cup of coffee. *Tea,*" John replied.

"I've wanted to meet her," Joanne said.

Barbara didn't reply.

There were two women in the living room. One of them was obviously Daphne Farnsworth, Royal Australian Navy Women's Volunteer Reserve, and Barbara's friend. *She's not in uniform; I wonder why not,* Joanne asked herself. Though Daphne looked damned unhappy at the moment, that didn't detract from her looks; she was a pretty young woman, with light-brown hair, hazel eyes, and that soft peaches-and-cream skin English women seem to have.

Or Australian women, Joanne thought. *Same blood. I wonder why she's so unhappy? Or is that shame I see in her eyes? What's going on here?*

The other woman was wearing what looked like a man's suit with a skirt, and she was old enough to be Daphne Farnsworth's mother. But Joanne was sure that wasn't the case.

"Daphne, this is Joanne Miller," Barbara said. "I've talked about her to you."

Daphne Farnsworth, with effort, managed a smile.

"This lady is a policeman," Barbara said. "I'm sorry, I've forgotten your name."

"*Constable* Rogers," the woman said, unsmiling. "How do you do?"

"Won't you please sit down?" Barbara said. "Can we offer you something? Tea? Something to drink?"

"No, thank you," Constable Rogers said, but she sat down on the edge of the couch, her knees together, and rested her black purse on them.

That looks, Joanne thought, *like a midwife's bag.*

"Daphne, can't I get you something?" Barbara asked.

Daphne offered another weak smile and shook her head, no.

There was an awkward silence while they waited for John Moore to come in. It lasted no more than two minutes but seemed much longer. Still drying his hair with a towel, John Moore finally walked into the living room.

"Hello, Daphne!" he called cheerfully, and then he saw Constable Rogers and bit off whatever else he had intended to say.

"I'd heard you were hurt," Daphne said. "I'm glad to see you're all right."

"May I ask who you are?" Constable Rogers asked, rising to her feet.

"My name is Moore. Who are you?"

"I'm Constable Rogers—"

"Constable?"

"—and I am instructed to place Mrs. Farnsworth into the custody of Major Edward Banning, of the United States Marine Corps."

"Into the custody? What the hell are you talking about?"

"Can you tell me where I might find Major Banning? This is the address I was given."

"Major Banning is not here. I work for him. Will that do?"

"If you would, I'd like to see some identification, please," Constable Rogers said.

"Daphne, what the hell is going on here?" John asked, and then saw tears in Daphne's eyes.

He went into the bedroom and came back out holding his credentials in his hand. Constable Rogers examined them carefully.

"That will be sufficient, thank you," she said. Then she fished in her purse and came out with a form, in triplicate, with carbons, the whole thing neatly stapled together. "If you would be good enough to sign that, Sir?"

Moore took the form, glanced at it, took the fountain pen Constable Rogers extended to him, and signed his name in the block provided for SIGNATURE OF INDIVIDUAL ASSUMING CUSTODY OF DETAINEE.

Constable Rogers tore off one of the carbons and handed it to Moore.

"Thank you very much," she said as she neatly folded the rest of the form and stuffed it in her purse.

She turned to Daphne. "When you are finished here, Mrs. Farnsworth, if you will come to the Main Police Station, room 306, they will arrange for your transportation back to Melbourne."

Daphne nodded but didn't say anything. With a curl of her lips she probably thought was a smile, Constable Rogers gave a nod to Moore and then to Barbara and Joanne and walked out of the living room.

"Daphne, what the hell is this all about?" John Moore asked.

"She called you *Mrs.* Farnsworth?" Barbara said.

"Yeoman Farnsworth," Daphne said softly, looking at Barbara and then averting her eyes, "has been discharged for the good of the Service."

"What?"

"I'm pregnant," Daphne said. "About four months, they tell me."

"Oh, my God!" Barbara said. "Steve?" she asked; and then a moment later, with horror in her voice, she blurted, "I'm so sorry I asked that."

Daphne shrugged. "Steve," she said.

"What's this . . . ? Who was that terrible woman?"

"Banning said Feldt would arrange for Daphne to come here," Moore explained.

"They came to where I was working," Daphne said. "Two policemen brought Constable Rogers. Then they took me to my room and let me pack a bag. And then they took us to the railroad station and put us on the train."

*God*damn *Major Banning!* Joanne thought.

"That's outrageous!" Moore said.

And what if you're in the family way, too, Joanne Miller? You didn't think about that, did you, carried away on the wings of love? Oh, God!

"They can't do that!" Barbara said furiously. "You didn't do anything wrong!"

"Oh, yes they can," Daphne said. "They read me the appropriate passages from the Emergency War Powers Act. Any citizen may be detained for ninety-six hours when it is considered necessary in the prosecution of the war."

"Damn them!" Barbara said.

"What does Major Banning want with me?" Daphne asked. "I'm afraid to ask, but does it have something to do with Steve?"

"Yes, but he's all right, Daphne," Moore said.

"Then what?"

"We needed a new code to communicate with them," Moore explained. "Pluto Hon came up with a simple substitution code based on personal things that only Barbara and Lieutenant Howard would know. He wanted to do the same thing with you and Koffler."

"He's all right?" she asked.

"Yes, he's all right."

"Daphne," Barbara said, "I wish I was pregnant."

What the hell is the matter with you, Barbara? That's absolute idiocy! Joanne thought. *God, don't let me be pregnant!*

"It's not quite the same for you, Barbara," Daphne said.

"I believe Joe's coming back," Barbara said. "Steve will, too."

"You're in love with Joe," Daphne said.

"You're not in love with Steve?"

"How could I be in love with him? I hardly know him."

How could I be in love with Johnny? I hardly know him, either.

"You're upset," Barbara said. "Understandably."

"Actually, I think I'm thinking pretty clearly," Daphne said. "What happened—and I was with him only that one night—happened because he came to Wagga Wagga—"

"Where?" Moore blurted and was immediately sorry.

"My family has a station, Two Creeks Station, in Wagga Wagga, New South Wales," Daphne explained. "You'd call it a farm, or a ranch."

He should not be hearing this, Joanne decided. *This is between women, and none of his business.*

"Why don't you go get dressed?" Joanne snapped.

"Hey, I'm trying to help," John replied. "And I do have to get the stuff for a code from her."

"You know all about codes, too?"

"I know what Pluto told me to get from her when she showed up," Moore said. "What about . . . *Wagga Wagga?*"

Daphne smiled.

"Steve thought it was funny, too," she said. "I thought you knew all this, John?"

"I wasn't here," Moore said. "I came after Koff—Steve and Lieutenant Howard jumped into Buka."

"That's right, isn't it?" Daphne said. "I'd forgotten."

"You don't have to talk to him about this," Joanne said.

"It would be helpful if she would," Moore said coldly.

"It's all right. If it will help Steve," Daphne said.

"I'm not trying to pry," Moore said, looking at Joanne. "I just need words we can use for a code. Wagga Wagga sounds fine." He looked at Daphne. "Steve would remember that?"

"Oh, I'm sure he would. He got lost twice trying to find it," Daphne said.

"What was he doing there?"

"After I learned that my husband was killed in North Africa," Daphne said, "there was a memorial service for him. When Steve heard, he wanted to do something for me. So he drove out. In that Studebaker, I think," she said, gesturing outside. "With a box of candy and flowers and a bottle of whiskey, he didn't know what was appropriate, so he brought one of each."

"Steve's a nice kid, John," Barbara said gently.

"Yes, a nice kid," Daphne said. "And I rode back from New South Wales to Victoria with him. He had to stop at Captain Pickering's place. What was it called?"

"The Elms, in Dandenong," Barbara furnished.

"And everybody was there, and they ran you and me off, and we eavesdropped—"

"I was sent from the hospital to give them their shots," Barbara said, looking at Joanne. "I didn't even know Joe was in Australia until I walked in there. We had only the one night, too."

"—and we heard what was going to happen to them the next day," Daphne went on, "and I decided—helped along by several gins—that the two loneliest people in the world were Yeoman Farnsworth and Sergeant Koffler, and . . . I'd always heard that all it takes is once; but even that didn't seem to matter."

"Steve's in love with you," Barbara said.

"You said it, Barbara," Daphne said. "Steve is a nice kid."

So is John Moore a nice kid. You should have realized, Joanne Miller, that your maternal instincts and/or hormones were getting out of control. You should have reminded yourself that all he is is a nice kid.

"He's more than a nice kid," Moore said. "He's one hell of a man. I don't think I like that 'nice kid' crap."

Go to hell, you bastard!

"You're right," Barbara said. "I didn't mean that the way it sounded."

"He's a kid," Daphne insisted. "Even if he were here, even if he wanted to marry me, even if I wanted to marry him, I couldn't. He's a minor, and your regulations don't permit your sergeants to marry; they have to be staff sergeants or above."

"You're sure about that?" Barbara asked.

"Yes," Daphne said.

"They'd probably waive that, considering . . . the child," Moore said.

"Australian law considers the child to be my husband's," Daphne said.

"But he was in Africa," Barbara protested. "He couldn't possibly—"

"I'm telling you what the law says," Daphne interrupted.

"And you're determined to have it?" Joanne asked.

God, I hate to talk about abortion with John sitting there with a shocked look on his face! But somebody, obviously, has to start thinking practically about this.

"Oh, I thought about that," Daphne said. "How am I going to support the child?"

"But it is getting a little late for an abortion, isn't it?" Barbara said.

"Yes, it is," Daphne admitted.

"What about your family?"

"My family can count. They will want nothing to do with me or the baby when they find out. God, it was conceived the night of my husband's memorial service."

"Your family doesn't know?" Joanne asked incredulously.

"Don't worry about support," John Moore said. "That's not one of the problems. This can be worked out with The Corps."

"And if it can't?" Joanne snapped.

"There's money available," he said.

"Whose?" she demanded.

"Mine, all right?"

He actually believes that. More evidence that he's no less a child than the child who made this pathetic young woman pregnant.

"In the end I decided that God had a hand in what's happening to me," Daphne said.

"God?" Joanne asked. "What's God got to do with it?"

"I thought that maybe I was being punished for being an adulteress . . ."

"That's nonsense!" Barbara protested.

"Or that God wanted Steve to leave something behind, a new life. Anyway, I'm going to have his baby. I'll work it out."

"Not alone," Barbara said.

"Right," Moore said. "And for one thing, you're not going back to Melbourne. You're going to stay here with us."

"I've got to have a job," Daphne said.

"I told you, you don't have to worry about money."

Goddamn you! The one thing she doesn't need is false hope!

"Can we get her a job here?" Barbara asked.

"Yeah, sure," John Moore said. "Detachment 14 has authority to hire Australians. But that's not what I was talking about."

He turned to Daphne.

"I'm going to put my clothes on. Then we're going to have to take care of the *Wagga Wagga* business."

Daphne nodded.

"Won't that wait, for God's sake?" Joanne snapped.

"I don't know what the hell is the matter with you," Moore responded furiously, "but everybody else around here is breaking their ass trying to get the boyfriends off Buka."

"Is that what you're really doing, John?" Barbara asked very quietly.

Moore didn't respond. He simply turned and went into his bedroom. As he left, Daphne's eyes followed him. *God! That's admiration in those eyes of hers—awe!* Joanne thought. *As far as she's concerned Johnny Moore might as well be the Angel Gabriel, come to set all the evils of the world right.*

Barbara, meanwhile, with tears in her eyes, went to Daphne and put her arms around her.

And Joanne pursued John Marston Moore.

She found him naked, awkwardly trying to put his leg into his underpants.

He modestly turned his back to her.

"You sonofabitch!" she hissed. "You make me sick to my stomach."

"Are you going to tell me why?" he asked over his shoulder.

"You had absolutely no right to tell that poor girl you'd take care of her. That was incredibly cruel. She needs to hear the truth; she doesn't need you giving her false hope."

"You're talking about the money?"

"Of course I'm talking about the money!"

"I hadn't planned to tell you this . . ." Moore said. Instead of finishing that thought, he squatted, wincing, to pull his shorts up; and then he turned to face her, ". . . until our wedding night. But among all the worldly goods I'm going to endow you with is a lot of money. Pushing three million, to be specific."

My God, he means it!

"More than enough for you and me, and our kids, and Koffler's kid," Moore said. "OK?"

"I never said I was going to marry you," Joanne said softly.

"Well, what do you say?"

"You may have to," she said. "I'm probably pregnant."

"That would be nice," he said, and held his arms open for her.

(TWO)
154° 30″ East Longitude 8° 27″ South Latitude
The Solomon Sea
1229 Hours 4 October 1942

When Sergeant George Hart, USMC, looked out of the port waist blister of the Royal Australian Navy Consolidated PBY-5 Catalina, he saw beneath him the expanse of blue ocean—absolutely nothing but blue ocean. He'd been riding in the Catalina for four hours; for the last twenty minutes it had been flying slow, wide circles . . . It just might happen that blue ocean was all he was going to see. He found it hard to believe that the pilot up front really had any precise idea where he was.

There was no land in sight, and there hadn't been for a long time. He remembered from high school enough about the modern miracle of flight and airplanes to recall that there were such things as head winds and tail winds—and presumably side winds, too. These sped up or retarded an aircraft's passage over the Earth, and/or they pushed the aircraft away from the path the pilot wished to fly.

It was possible, he recalled, to navigate by using the known location of radio stations. This pilot was obviously not doing that, because there were obviously no useful radio stations operating anywhere near here.

What the pilot was doing was making a guess where he was by dead reckoning: He'd have worked that out by plotting how long he'd been flying at a particular compass heading at a particular speed.

That would work only if there were no head winds, tail winds, or winds blowing the airplane to one side or another.

How they expected to find a boat as small as a submarine this far from land was an operation he simply didn't understand.

Curiosity finally overcame his reluctance to reveal his ignorance.

A RAN sailor was standing beside him looking out the blister. "I don't see how you're going to find the submarine," George confessed to him with as much savoir faire as he could muster.

"For the last hour," the sailor answered, "she's been surfacing every fifteen minutes, long enough to send a signal . . . They just hold the key down for ten or fifteen seconds. You saw that round thing on top?" He gestured toward the wing above them.

George nodded.

"Radio direction finding antenna. Sparks just turns that until the signal from the sub is strongest and gives the pilot the heading."

"Yeah," George said. "That always works, huh?"

The sailor pointed down at the sea. There was now a submarine just sitting there. It looked even smaller, even farther down, than he expected.

The submarine was the HMAS *Pelican*. George knew a good deal about HMAS *Pelican*. On his desk in Townsville, Commander Feldt had a book with photographs and descriptions of every class of ship in the major navies of the world, as well as descriptions of many individual ships, too.

Since the *Pelican* was in the book, he looked it up; after all, he was going riding—correction, *diving*—in it.

It—correction, *she*—began life as HMS *Snakefish* in 1936, at the Cammell Laird

Shipyard in Scotland. In 1939 she was transferred to the Australian Navy and renamed *Pelican.*

Does the Royal Navy treat the Royal Australian Navy the way the U.S. Navy treats The U.S. Marine Corps? George wondered. *As a poor relation, only giving it equipment that's no good, or worn out? Probably,* he decided.

According to Commander Feldt's book, HMAS *Pelican* had a speed on the surface of 13.5 knots and a submerged speed of 10. Elsewhere in the book George read that Japanese destroyers could make more than 30 knots. That meant that the Japanese would have a hell of an advantage if they spotted the *Pelican* and wanted a fight. Particularly since destroyers had a bunch of cannons, of all sizes, and depth charges. And the *Pelican* had only a single four-inch cannon and a couple of machine guns.

Of course the *Pelican* had torpedoes, but this did not give George much reassurance. He didn't think it would be very easy to hit a destroyer while it was twisting and turning at 30 knots and simultaneously shooting its cannons and throwing depth charges at you.

The Catalina suddenly began to make a steep descent toward the surface of the ocean. George grabbed one of the aluminum fuselage members. A moment later he saw blood dripping down onto his utilities.

The Catalina straightened out for a time, but then it made a really steep turn, after which it dropped its nose again.

A moment later there was an enormous splash, and then another, and then another. They were on the surface of the ocean. He looked around for the *Pelican* but couldn't see it.

The crew of the Catalina opened a hatch in the side of the fuselage and tossed out two packages. In a moment these began to inflate and assume the shape of rafts.

Lieutenant McCoy, wearing utilities, scrambled through the hatch and into one of the boats. A moment later Chief Signalman Wallace, wearing his skirt and his Chief Petty Officer's cap and nothing else, dropped into the other. Then two of the other three Marine members of the replacement team, a staff sergeant named Kelly and a corporal named Godfrey, got in the rafts. That left Sergeants Doud and Hart in the Catalina. Because of their strong backs, they'd been chosen to transfer the equipment from the Catalina to the rafts.

Before they took off, Hart told McCoy that he suspected this would be a bitch of a job. And McCoy told him he thought it would be worse than a bitch of a job. He was right. One of the radios almost went in the water. And when a swell suddenly raised one end of McCoy's raft, one of the tar-paper–wrapped weapons packages did go in.

No problem, there was a spare.

Finally everything was loaded onto the rafts, and Sergeants Doud and Hart half fell, half jumped into them.

The Catalina's hatch closed and there was a cloud of black smoke as the pilot restarted his port engine. The plane swung away from them, gunned its engines, and started its takeoff.

George felt a heavy sense that he was far removed from anything friendly. And he didn't get any relief from that when he finally spotted the submarine.

The Pelican'*s crew are not waving a friendly hello,* he realized after a moment, *but gesturing angrily for us to get our asses in gear and paddle over.*

One of those thirty-knot Japanese destroyers with all those cannons and depth charges is charging this way.

Why am I not afraid?

Because this whole fucking thing is so unreal that I'm unable to believe it. What the hell am I doing paddling a little rubber boat around in the middle of the Solomon Sea?

The *Pelican* was a lot farther away than it seemed. By the time the raft bumped up against her hull, he was breathing so hard it hurt. And the saltwater stung like hell on the slash in his hand he'd got in the Catalina.

The *Pelican*'s crew threw lines down to them. These were fastened to the equipment they were taking aboard, and then the crew dragged that up to the submarine's deck. Finally, the raft paddlers crawled aboard—with considerable help from the crew.

Just before passing through a hatch into the conning tower, George took one last look around him. He was surprised to see that one of the rafts was drifting away from the *Pelican*.

Why're they loose? They were securely tied.

But then he saw that the other raft was loose, too.

And then there was a burst of machine-gun fire from above him.

Jesus Christ! They're shooting holes in the rafts! What the hell for? What are we going to use to get ashore?

They're shooting holes in the rafts because they expect one of those thirty-knot Japanese destroyers, that's why they're shooting holes in them. It would take too much time to deflate them and bring them aboard.

He went inside the conning tower and down a ladder. He was almost on the main deck, thinking, *Jesus, it stinks in here,* when a Klaxon horn went off right by his ear.

Faintly, through the squawk of the Klaxon, he heard a loudspeaker bellow, "Dive! Dive! Dive!"

(THREE)
Officer's Mess, MAG-21
Henderson Field
Guadalcanal, Solomon Islands
0730 Hours 5 October 1942

The officer's mess of Marine Air Group 21 was pretty much the same as the enlisted mess. They differed mainly in location and in size. The officer's mess (a sandbag enclosure topped by an open-walled tent) was on the north side of the communal kitchen (a sandbag enclosure topped by an open-walled tent). The enlisted mess (an open-walled enclosure topped by an open-walled tent) was about twice as large as the officer's mess, and it was on the south side of the communal kitchen.

Lieutenant Colonel Clyde W. Dawkins, USMC, in a fresh but already sweat-soaked cotton flight suit, sat on the plank seat of what looked like a six-man picnic table. Both hands were on a mug of coffee. The remnants of his breakfast tray (a steel tray holding mostly uneaten powdered eggs, bacon, toast and marmalade) were pushed to the side.

Before he spoke, Colonel Dawkins carefully considered what he intended to say.

"It's bullshit, Charley, is what I think," he finally said to Captain Charles M. Galloway, USMCR, commanding officer of VMF-229. Galloway was sitting on the other side of the picnic table.

Charley Galloway shrugged.

"And I'll tell you something else, I think your Major Dillon's orders are bullshit, too," Dawkins said.

"You don't mean phony?" Galloway asked, surprised.

"Not *forged,*" Dawkins said. "I think that there is a General Pickering, even if I never heard of him, and that he works for Admiral Leahy."

"I've got a kid named Pickering in my squadron," Galloway said. "He got two Bettys his first time out, a Zero the second."

Dawkins ignored that aside. "It's the endorsement that I think is bullshit."

"I think you mean that," Galloway said, surprised.

"Think about it," Dawkins said. "Think about two things. First ask yourself if it's reasonable that the President's Chief of Staff—Jesus, he used to be Chief of Naval Operations, and now he got promoted higher than that!—I find it hard to accept that *Admiral Leahy* is personally concerned with two guys on a tiny island he probably couldn't find on a map. He's got better things to do."

Galloway looked at him and shrugged again.

"For the second thing," Dawkins went on, "it wouldn't be the first time in the recorded annals of military history that an officer with a set of vague orders giving him lots of authority went ape shit."

Galloway did not reply.

"Did you know, for example, that just before the Spanish-American War, the American Ambassador to Spain went to the Spaniards and *ordered* them to get out of Cuba? He had absolutely no orders from Washington. Nada."

"Really?" Galloway found that fascinating.

"Really. He didn't have two cents' worth of authority; he just decided that's what he wanted to do, and did it."

"I don't think Dillon's that kind of guy. He used to be a sergeant with the Fourth Marines in China."

"And now he's a major running around with orders on White House stationery. You're making my point for me, Charley. I can easily see where that would go to an ex-sergeant's head, having orders to do just about anything he wants to do." He hesitated. "Present company excepted, of course."

"Yeah, sure," Galloway said. "I think it's just as reasonable to assume that this General Pickering . . . I agree, I doubt if Admiral Leahy knows where Buka is, or didn't—"

"I don't follow you," Dawkins interrupted.

"OK. This General Pickering. He knows (a) that we have our ass in a crack here; (b) that about the only reason the Japanese don't bomb this place into oblivion, and bomb the hell out of the supply ships coming here, is that the Coastwatchers on the islands let us know when they've launched their aircraft from Rabaul; and (c) that the Coastwatcher station on Buka is pretty fucking close to going out of business. I just thought of another one: and (d) that nobody here seems to give a damn. Maybe because the Navy thinks it's MacArthur's responsibility, since the Coastwatchers are under the Australians, and he's sort of in charge of the Australians. But MacArthur figures it's the Navy's business, since Guadalcanal and Buka are CINCPAC's concern; they're not in his SWPOA. So Pickering goes to Admiral Leahy and gives him a quick rundown, and Leahy says, 'OK, General, take care of it.'"

"That's possible, I suppose," Dawkins said reluctantly.

"I think that's more likely than what you're suggesting," Charley said.

"How about an URGENT radio from Leahy to both CINCPAC and SWPOA: 'Settle it between yourselves, but make sure Buka stays in operation. Love and Kisses, Admiral Leahy'?"

Galloway chuckled.

"All Dillon asked me to do, Colonel, is make a quick trip up there and back. And only if they can't reinforce Buka by submarine."

"In an unarmed transport, landing right under the nose of the Japanese on a beach that may or may not take the weight."

"They'll know if the beach will take the weight before I go," Galloway said.

"You and Finch, from our vast pool of qualified squadron commanders who are otherwise unoccupied," Dawkins said sarcastically.

"We have more time in the R4D than most people," Galloway said.

"Speaking of the R4D. Why the R4D?"

"You saw the skis. I think they'll work. The problem with the regular landing gear, I think, is not that the airplane might stick in the sand while it's landing or taking off. But when it's stopped. If it's not moving, it might sink. The skis will fix that, I think."

"You think," he said, and gave him a look. "But I meant, why the R4D in the first place? Specifically, why not a Catalina? It could land in the water, for one thing. For another, it has .50 calibers in the blisters and a .30 in the nose. The R4D has zero armament."

"Dillon said they considered the Catalina—"

"Who's 'they'?"

"I guess Dillon and this General Pickering."

"And?"

"Decided against it. Dillon said that getting rubber boats through the surf on the Makin Island raid wasn't as easy as it came out in the newspapers. And the Japanese don't have an airplane that looks like the Catalina. But they do have a bunch of R4Ds . . . actually, they're not R4Ds but DC-2s; Douglas licensed the Japs to make DC-2s before the war. But they look like R4Ds from a distance."

"And your General Pickering thinks the Japanese will think your R4D is one of their DC-2s and leave it alone?"

"The Japanese would *not* think a Catalina was one of theirs," Galloway said.

Colonel Dawkins decided not to argue the point. Charley Galloway had volunteered for this idiotic mission because he was gallant. There was no other word for it. That also applied to Major Jack Finch. Major Finch and Captain Galloway were both gallant. They fit the classic definition of gallant: warriors who knew goddamned well they were likely to be killed, and were willing to take that risk, (a) because the mission was important, and (b) because they might possibly save the lives of other warriors.

But as a responsible commander, Lieutenant Colonel Dawkins decided, the cold reality was that he could not indulge their gallantry. If they remained in command of their squadrons, they would ultimately be of greater value to the overall mission, and would ultimately be responsible for saving more lives, than if they soared nobly off into the wild blue yonder on an idiotic mission dreamed up by an ex–China Marine sergeant and a paper-shuffling rear-echelon brigadier general back in Washington.

He also decided it would do no good to take the matter up with either Lieutenant Colonel Stanley N. Holliman, USMC, Executive Officer of MAG-25, or Brigadier General D. G. McInerney, the senior Marine Aviator on Guadalcanal. While he had a great—in the case of General McInerney, nearly profound—professional admiration for these officers, both men were also awash in the seas of gallantry. They would not understand why Dawkins did not wish this idiotic mission to take place.

They will understand the gallantry. They will be touched by the gallantry.

If they can find the time, they will be standing at attention, saluting and humming the Marine Hymn as Galloway and Finch and their goddamned R4D on goddamned skis roar down the runway.

There is only one man who can bring this idiocy to a screeching halt, Colonel Dawkins decided, *and therefore it is my duty to go see him.*

"When are you going, Charley?" he asked Galloway.

"Whenever they send word. Here to Port Moresby, then to Buka, then back here."

"Why Moresby? It's just as close, direct from here."

"Moresby has landing lights," Galloway explained. "We want to make the leg up there in the dark."

"I see," Dawkins said. He stood up. "I've got to go see G-3 Air at the Division CP. You need a ride anywhere?"

"No, Sir. Thank you."

"Well, hello, Dawkins," Major General Alexander Archer Vandergrift, Commanding General of the First Marine Division, said when he came out of his office and saw Dawkins sitting on a folding chair. "We don't see much of you."

Colonel Dawkins rose to his feet.

"Sir, I'd hoped the General could spare me a few minutes of his time."

Vandergrift's eyebrows rose in surprise. He glanced at his watch.

"I can give you a couple of minutes right now," he said, then held open the piece of canvas tenting that served as the door to his office.

Vandergrift went to his desk (a folding wooden table holding a U.S. Field Desk, a cabinetlike affair with a number of drawers and shelves), sat down on a folding chair, crossed his legs, and looked at Dawkins.

Dawkins assumed the at-ease position. He put his feet twelve inches apart and folded his hands together in the small of his back.

The formality was not lost on Vandergrift.

"OK, Colonel, let's have it," he said.

"Sir, there's an officer visiting, Major Dillon—"

"Jake came by to make his manners," Vandergrift interrupted. "What about him?"

"Did the General happen to see Major Dillon's orders?"

"The General did," Vandergrift said dryly. "Interesting, aren't they?"

"He has laid a mission on one of my squadron commanders, and on Major Finch of MAG-25—"

"I'm familiar with it," Vandergrift said. "You obviously don't like it. So make your point, Colonel."

"That's it, Sir, I don't like it."

"Because of the risk?"

"Yes, Sir."

"I don't think you've been to see General McInerney about this, have you, Colonel?"

"No, Sir. I'm out of the chain of command."

"I won't give you the standard speech about the chain of command. You're a good Marine and you know all about it. And, in a way, since you do know the consequences of violating it, I admire your conviction in coming to see me directly."

"Sir, they have one chance in five of carrying this off."

"When he came to see me, it was General McInerney's judgment that they have one chance in ten," Vandergrift said.

"Yes, Sir. General McInerney is probably right. It borders on the suicidal, and it will deprive us of two good squadron commanders."

Raising his eyes to meet Dawkins', Vandergrift started to say something, stopped, and then went on: "After we'd accepted the obvious fact that we've gotten an order and we have no choice but to obey it, General McInerney and I also concluded that General Pickering was certainly aware of the risk and that he considers it acceptable."

"I don't know General Pickering, General. I've been searching my mind, and—"

"He and General McInerney were together in France. With Jack (NMI) Stecker, by the way. At about the same time Jack got his Medal of Honor, Pickering got the Distinguished Service Cross. I met him here. When Colonel Goettge was killed, he filled in as G-2 until they could send us a replacement. I was impressed with his brains, and his character."

"Yes, Sir."

Well, I tried and I lost.

"He was then a Navy captain," Vandergrift went on, "on the staff of the Secretary of the Navy. He showed up here the day after the invasion and told me he just couldn't sail off into the sunset with the Navy when they left us on the beach. I tell you this because . . ." He paused a moment, then began again. "While I don't know how he got to be Brigadier General of Marines, General McInerney and I both think it was a wise decision on somebody's part."

"Yes, Sir."

"Have you any other questions, Colonel?"

"No, Sir."

"I'm going to give you the benefit of the doubt, Colonel, and conclude that before you went over General McInerney's head, you gave it a lot of thought. So far as I'm concerned, this discussion never took place."

"Yes, Sir. Thank you."

"One more thing, Dawkins. One of the Wildcat pilots in VMF-229 is General Pickering's only son. I think we may presume that the lives of Marine Aviators on Guadalcanal are never out of General Pickering's mind for very long."

"General, I knew none of this."

"There's no way you could have. That's why I have decided to forget this conversation. That's all, Dawkins."

(FOUR)
The Office of the Supreme Commander
South West Pacific Ocean Area
Brisbane, Australia
1625 Hours 5 October 1942

Double doors led into the Supreme Commander's office. Master Sergeant Manuel Donat, of the Philippine Scouts, pushed open the left-hand one of these, waited until the Supreme Commander looked up, and then announced:

"Lieutenant Hon is here to see you, General."

"Ask the Lieutenant to come in, Manuel," General Douglas MacArthur said. He was slouched down in his chair, reading a typewritten document.

"Good afternoon, Sir," Pluto Hon said, saluting. He had a large manila envelope tucked under his arm.

MacArthur touched his forehead with his hand, returning the salute.

"That looks formidable," he said, pointing at the envelope Hon now extended to him.

"It's rather long, Sir."

"Manuel, get the Lieutenant a cup of coffee. Get us both one, as a matter of fact. Have a seat, Pluto. I'll be with you in just a moment."

"Thank you, Sir," Pluto said, sitting down on the edge of a nice, possibly genuine, Louis XIV chair. He was convinced the chair had been placed where it was because it was delicate and tiny by comparison to MacArthur's massive desk and high-backed leather swivel chair. Anyone sitting in it could not help but feel inadequate.

Holding a stub that was once a large black Philippine cigar between his thumb and index finger, MacArthur rested his elbow on the leather-bound desk pad and carefully read a document before him.

Finally, as Master Sergeant Donat appeared with a silver coffee service on a tray, he pulled himself out of his slouch, closed the TOP SECRET cover sheet on the document, and tossed it in his out basket. Then he looked at the cigar butt between his fingers.

"It offends Mrs. MacArthur that I smoke them so short," he said. "But of course, for a while, there will be no more of these. I have to smoke them all the way down."

"Yes, Sir," Pluto said.

"Captain ... *General* Pickering found these for me, as a matter of fact, in Melbourne. Did you know that?"

"Yes, Sir. I actually went and picked them up, Sir."

"Well, when they're gone, that's it. There will be no more." He looked at Hon and smiled. "How are you, Pluto? I understand you were out of town."

"Yes, Sir. I'm fine, thank you, Sir."

"Townsville, was it?"

"Yes, Sir."

MacArthur pulled the MAGIC material from the manila envelope. It had two parts. One was an analysis of intercepted Japanese messages; the other was the messages themselves, and their translations. He pushed the messages and translations to one side and began to read the analyses.

He read carefully. There was a good deal to read and consider.

Finally he looked at Hon.

"Very interesting," he said. "I see again—how shall I phrase this? *that there are subtle differences of shading,* how's that?—between your analyses and those of the people in Hawaii?"

" 'Subtle differences of shading' does very well, Sir. We are in general agreement with Pearl Harbor."

"We? Does that mean this is not your analysis? Mrs. Feller's perhaps?"

"Actually, Sir, *those* analyses were done by Lieutenant Moore. I'm in complete agreement with them, Sir."

"Fascinating, don't you think, that I picked up on that?" MacArthur said. "That I could tell it wasn't you?"

"You're used to my style, I suppose, Sir."

"Yes, *literary* style, one could say, right? I seem to be able to recognize yours, don't I?"

"Yes, Sir."

"Actually, a day or two ago, I paid Mrs. Feller something of a left-handed compliment," MacArthur said. "Willoughby was in here, impressed with an analysis Mrs. Feller had prepared; and I said, yes, it's quite good, it sounds like Pluto."

He knows! Why am I surprised? He's a goddamned genius!

"Yes, Sir."

"If we are to accept this analysis," MacArthur said, "plural, *these analyses,* we are forced to the conclusion that a reason—a major reason, perhaps even *the* major reason—why the Japanese have not thrown the Marines back into the sea at Guadalcanal is that there's a breakdown in communication between the Japanese Army and Navy. I find it difficult to accept that."

"Sir, why the analyses, Pearl Harbor's and ours—"

"Yours and the other lieutenant's, what's his name?"

"Moore, Sir."

"What's the condition of his health? When he was in here, he looked terrible."

"There has been a recurrence of his malaria, Sir. They have it back under control."

"He was walking with obvious discomfort, using a cane," MacArthur said. "I wonder if Pickering did the right thing sending him back over here in that condition."

"He's getting physical therapy, General."

"Good. We were talking about a breakdown in communication between the Japanese Army and Navy."

"Yes, Sir. I was saying that Pearl Harbor, Moore, and I all agree that Japanese pride got in the way of efficient operation. Neither the Navy nor the Army was willing to ask each other—or the Imperial General Staff, for that matter—for help. If they did, that would admit to some kind of inability to deal with the situation. The honor of the Army and Navy and of the individual commanders would then be open to question."

"That's what I said," MacArthur said somewhat coldly. "A breakdown in communication."

"An *absence* of communication, Sir, rather than a *breakdown.*"

MacArthur gave him a frosty look.

"I suppose that semantics are your profession, Pluto, aren't they?"

"Actually, Sir, I'm a mathematician," Pluto said.

MacArthur looked at him for a moment and then laughed. "You're also a skilled semanticist, Pluto," he said with an airy wave of his hand.

"So it is your analysis that that situation no longer prevails," he went on, "and we may now expect from the Japanese more coordinated activity, more interservice cooperation, and less prideful, selfish rivalry?"

"Yes, Sir."

"And why would you come to that conclusion? What made them, so to speak, see the light?"

"They had to go to the Emperor and confess failure, Sir. And their worlds didn't come to an end."

" 'They' being the senior officers of the Army and Navy?"

"And of the Imperial General Staff, Sir."

"They did do rather well in the opening days of this war, didn't they? Everything they set out to do, they did."

"Yes, Sir, they did."

"No confessions of failure were needed, were there?"

"No, Sir."

"And you think they led the Emperor to believe then that our Guadalcanal operation was something they could easily deal with? . . . almost certainly because they believed it themselves."

"We have the intercepts to prove that, Sir. I could get them for you if you'd like to see them."

MacArthur waved his hand grandly.

"I've seen them," he said.

The implication, Pluto thought, *is that once he's read something, he is incapable of forgetting it.*

"What I'm saying, Sir, is that the Guadalcanal landing was on 7 August. That was almost two months ago, and the Marines were not thrown back into the sea. Not only are they still there, but Henderson Field is operational. So the Japanese commanders had to confess that the American presence could not be easily dealt with. For all intents and purposes, the battle of Bloody Ridge simply wiped out *Kawaguchi Butai.* Prisoners have reported that its commander, Major General Kiotake Kawaguchi, actually committed hara-kiri—"

"Has there been confirmation of that?" MacArthur interrupted.

"No, Sir. Not as far as I know."

I wish to hell there was. MacArthur is fully aware that Kawaguchi Butai *wiped out the last American resistance on Mindanao. He'd be pleased to know that their general has disemboweled himself after a defeat by Americans who are only slightly better fed and equipped than the Americans he had such an easy time with in the Philippines.*

"It was a humiliating defeat for them, wasn't it?" MacArthur asked rhetorically.

"Yes, Sir. I think the senior people expected to be relieved, Sir. They weren't. But now they're dealing with the changed situation."

"And this assessment of their change in attitude is based on what, Pluto?"

"On the language, Sir. In our judgment, there is less intentional obfuscation. That's based on word choice, Sir. I don't know if I'm making myself clear."

"You're doing fine," MacArthur said. "Go on."

"It's as if they've decided that their mission now is to regain Guadalcanal . . . as a *national* mission, not as a task the Army or Navy can handle by itself."

"And are they going to be more difficult to deal with? Is there a chance we will be thrown off Guadalcanal? That there will be more efficient resistance to our operations on New Guinea?"

"Yes, Sir. To a degree; we'll have to wait and see to *what* degree. But, yes, I think we can expect greater naval activity against Guadalcanal. I don't think they'll be able to throw us off, though."

MacArthur nodded, spun around in his chair, and for a moment stared thoughtfully at the huge map on the wall behind his desk. Then he turned around again.

"All right, Pluto, I would now like to hear how General Pickering's clandestine operation is going."

Christ, talk about getting taken by surprise!

What do I do now, lie? You can't lie to the Supreme Commander, South West Pacific Ocean Area!

"What would you like to know, Sir?"

"General Willoughby came to me a day or so ago, agitated. He said that an impeccable source had informed him that a clandestine intelligence operation is being conducted here by people acting on Pickering's orders."

"Sir, I wouldn't define it as a clandestine intelligence operation," Pluto said. MacArthur waited for him to go on. "It's more on the order of support for the Coastwatchers."

"The Coastwatcher Establishment is an intelligence operation. General Willoughby feels that anything connected with intelligence is his responsibility."

"General Pickering is attempting to relieve the Coastwatcher detachment on Buka, to replace it with fresh men and equipment."

"And he decided that this was none of General Willoughby's business?"

"I wouldn't know how to answer that, Sir."

MacArthur tilted his head toward Pluto and examined him carefully.

"I asked how the operation is going," he said.

"An attempt to land the replacement team and equipment from a submarine will be made as soon as possible. If that fails, an attempt will be made to make the insertion and extraction by airplane."

"Show me," MacArthur ordered, pointing at the map.

Pluto outlined the operation.

"Presumably thought has been given to a diversionary attack on Japanese air bases on Buka and New Ireland?"

"It was decided, Sir, that was not feasible."

"Nonsense," MacArthur said. "An unarmed airplane will have no chance without a diversionary attack to draw their fighters off."

"Yes, Sir."

"Not feasible! Whose decision was that?" MacArthur asked. But he did not expect a reply; he was already picking up the telephone: "Get me General McKinney," he ordered. A moment later, imperiously, he said, "Then send the senior officer present in here right away."

An Army Air Corps colonel appeared a minute or so later, marched to MacArthur's desk, and saluted.

"Colonel," MacArthur said, "this officer is Lieutenant Hon. He will brief you on the details of a clandestine operation which is about to take place. In my judgment, a diversionary attack on Japanese fighter bases in the Rabaul/Buka area is essential to the success of this operation. If there is some reason General McKinney feels this is not *feasible,* please ask him to be good enough to explain this to me personally."

"Yes, Sir," the Air Corps Colonel said.

"That will be all," MacArthur said. "Lieutenant Hon will be with you in a minute."

"Yes, Sir," the Air Force Colonel said, saluted again, did an about-face, and marched out of the room.

"Would you be free, Pluto, for a little bridge tonight? Say, half past seven?"

"Yes, Sir. Of course, Sir."

"Sometime between now and then, get this off, will you?"

He handed Hon a folded sheet of paper.

"Yes, Sir," Hon said, saluted, and marched out of the office.

The Air Corps Colonel was waiting for him.

"If you're free, Lieutenant, I think it would be best to discuss this in my office."

Pluto looked at the sheet of paper MacArthur had handed him.

"Colonel, if you'll give me the room number, I'll be there in fifteen minutes. I have to go to the dungeon and get off a Personal for the Supreme Commander."

"Of course. I'm in 515."

"Thank you, Sir," Hon said.

XVI

From the very moment Sergeant George Hart stepped off the train in the middle of the night at Port Royal, S.C., and boarded the truck for transportation to The U.S. Marine Corps Recruit Depot at Parris Island; from the moment, in other words, that he realized he was *really* in The Marine Corps and would almost certainly go into battle, he had given a good deal of thought to his first time in harm's way.

In the image of himself he conjured up most often, he was pictured in utilities, with USMC and the Marine emblem stenciled on his chest. Neatly buckled under his chin, he wore a steel helmet covered with netting that bore a camouflage of twigs and leaves. He was laden down with field gear and armed with a rifle—possibly even the new one, the semiautomatic Garand—and bandoliers of ammunition and hand grenades.

He heard the roar of artillery and the rattle of machine guns. And he was led by a captain who looked like Tyrone Power and by a sergeant who looked like Ward Bond (both men had made a lot of money playing Marines in the movies). One or the other of them shouted, "Let's go, Marines! Let's go kill the dirty Japs! Semper Fidelis!" And then he blew a whistle as he jumped up and charged toward the enemy, firing a Thompson submachine gun from the hip.

In the event, that wasn't exactly what Sergeant George Hart got.

What he got was a very young-looking lieutenant who didn't look anything like Tyrone Power or Ward Bond. He was wearing swimming trunks, had black grease smeared all over him, and his call to battle was, "With just a little bit of luck, we can make it onto shore without the Japanese seeing us. I will personally castrate anybody who loads, much less shoots, his weapon unless we're fired on."

Sergeant Hart took some reassurance from his conviction that Lieutenant K. R. McCoy knew what he was doing. After all, he'd been on the Marine Raider raid on Makin Island. They hadn't been ashore on Makin more than two minutes, he'd told everybody on this expedition more than once, when some asshole accidentally fired his rifle, telling the Japanese they had visitors.

As far as Hart was concerned, Lieutenant McCoy's castration threat was not total hyperbole, either. McCoy was skilled with knives. He'd earned the "Killer McCoy" nickname, for instance, by killing people with one—several people. And at this moment Lieutenant McCoy had a non-issue, nasty-looking dagger affair adhesive-taped to his upper leg. There was no way of knowing it for sure, but Hart had a strong suspicion that it was *the* knife he'd used on the Chinese and Italians he'd killed when he was a corporal in China.

Sergeant Hart himself had a non-issue knifelike device adhesive-taped to his upper right leg. This had started life as a dull-edged bayonet for the U.S. Carbine, Caliber .30 M1, and had been converted to a kind of dagger by putting a sharp edge on both sides of the blade and then blueing the blade so it wouldn't reflect light.

Sergeant Hart was not only armed with a modified bayonet from a U.S. Carbine, but he carried the Carbine itself, as well. Compared to the .30-06 cartridge used by the Springfield and Garand rifles and the light Browning machine gun, the .30 caliber Carbine cartridge looked puny—more like a long pistol cartridge than a real rifle cartridge.

During a briefing to the members of the landing team on board the submarine, McCoy did not challenge this notion: "Think of the carbine as a pistol with a stock, not a rifle," Lieutenant McCoy had advised them. "If you make sure of your target before you fire, it will put him down."

During the briefing, all the members of the landing team showed an intense interest in the Carbine. For everybody was to be armed with one—with the exception of Chief Signalman Wallace and Lieutenant McCoy, who were armed with Australian Sten 9mm submachine guns.

"There are two reasons we're not taking anything heavier," McCoy had explained. "For one thing, a Garand would be harder to handle in the rubber boats. For another, we are not *invading* Buka, we're sneaking ashore. And with a little bit of luck, we won't even see a Japanese soldier."

There had been some grumbling about this at Townsville and on the *Pelican,* particularly from Staff Sergeant Tom Kelly, who was an expert with the Thompson submachine gun, and from Sergeant Al Doud, who wanted to bring a light Browning machine gun. But the grumbling had quickly dissipated. Not only was McCoy *a veteran of the Makin Island raid,* but he was just not the sort of officer you fucked with.

They were taking very little field equipment with them, just packs stuffed with field rations, clothing, and some first-aid equipment. And they would paddle in, McCoy had informed them, because outboard motors were unreliable and made too much noise.

In the boats, they would wear swimming trunks; paddling the rafts was easier that way; and it was hard to swim in water-soaked utilities.

The plan was now a little different from the one McCoy and Banning had first put together. Now Lieutenant McCoy, Staff Sergeant Kelly, and Corporal Harry Godfrey would go in on one raft, while Chief Signalman Wallace and Sergeants Al Doud and George Hart would be in the other.

"Yes, the boats will be unbalanced," McCoy said, in answer to a question from Staff Sergeant Kelly, "but they will also be 150 or 180 pounds lighter than if we had four people in each one. We need that weight for the radios."

When his briefing was over, McCoy required each member of the team to recite not only his own role in the landing operation, but that of each of the others. If anyone didn't know exactly what he was supposed to do, Hart thought, he really had to be stupid:

On landing, McCoy would immediately radio the *Pelican* that they had made it through the surf. After that, he and Wallace would remove the weapons from their waterproof packs, and then select from their equipment those items to be carried inland. Meanwhile, Sergeant Doud and Corporal Godfrey would deflate the rafts, and Sergeant Hart would begin to test the sand. Staff Sergeant Kelly would accompany him to provide what assistance was required.

Without changing out of their bathing suits, Sergeant Hart and Staff Sergeant Kelly would run a test every ten yards or so along the beach. While they were doing this, the others would dress; then the boats would be deflated, the weapons distributed, and the rafts, the radios, and the supplies they weren't taking to Ferdinand Six would be moved to some spot off the beach where they could be concealed.

After departure of the party going to Ferdinand Six, the party that was staying behind—that is to say, Sergeant Hart and Corporal Godfrey—would complete the concealment of the radios and supplies, put on their uniforms, and wait for the others to return. Presuming they didn't encounter Japanese en route and that Chief Signalman Wallace could really find Ferdinand Six (it was some ten or twenty or thirty miles away in the mountainous jungle), the journey would take from thirty-six to seventy-two hours.

Assuming it did not encounter a 30-knot Japanese destroyer and/or a Japanese patrol aircraft, HMAS *Pelican* would surface each morning at the same time to see how things were going on the beach. If the people from Ferdinand Six had not returned within seventy hours, it would be presumed they were not coming and Sergeant Hart and Corporal Godfrey would be free to make an attempt to paddle back through the surf to the *Pelican* for evacuation.

Even if the tests suggested the sand on the beach could take the weight, Sergeant Hart privately concluded, there would be no point in sending in the airplane if the people from Ferdinand Six weren't there to meet it. And they certainly wouldn't take the risk just to pick up a sergeant and a corporal. The Marine Corps had more important uses for an airplane like that. *Semper Fi!*

Sergeant Hart heard electrical pumps. Then he thought he sensed movement, but he wasn't sure. A moment later he decided he was wrong. There was no movement, he was just nervous—read scared shitless.

And then there were more mysterious submarine-type noises, and now he was sure he sensed movement.

An Aussie officer appeared, climbing halfway down a ladder. "We're ready for you, Mr. McCoy," he announced courteously.

Hart followed McCoy up the ladder. When he reached the level of the next deck, there was the absolutely delicious smell of fresh air.

We're on the surface, and the hatches are open, otherwise there would be no fresh air.

While he waited his turn to follow McCoy and some Aussie sailors through a hatch, the *Pelican*'s hull trembled. It was her diesel engines starting.

He stepped through a hatch onto the deck. It was light enough to see that the surface of the sea was smooth, so smooth it looked oily.

Thank God for that!

McCoy started aft. When Hart started to follow him, McCoy stopped him and gestured toward the bow of the submarine, where Aussie sailors were manhandling the radios and supplies through hatches.

Two minutes later, as he watched Staff Sergeant Kelly kneel beside one of the two rafts to inflate it, McCoy spoke in his ear.

"Just one, Kelly," McCoy said.

"Sir?"

"There's no way we can get loaded rafts through that surf," McCoy said. "The waves are ten, twelve feet, close together."

Hart felt light-headed; this was instantly followed by a sudden chill. He knew why McCoy only wanted one raft. It was because he'd decided they had to shift to Plan B. He had confided this plan only to Chief Wallace and Sergeant Hart, since they were the only ones who'd be involved in it.

If the surf was so rough that passing through it in heavily laden rafts was impossible, Plan B would be placed into effect.

They had not rehearsed Plan B as carefully as Plan A, but Plan B was a little simpler. It required only one raft to attempt making it to shore. This would contain Lieutenant McCoy, Chief Signalman Wallace, and Sergeant Hart. They would carry with them only their personal weapons, three days' supply of rations, and two of the radios Chief Signalman Wallace had modified so they could communicate with both HMAS *Pelican* and aircraft (on air-to-ground frequencies).

When they reached the beach, McCoy and Wallace would wait to see if Hart's tests of the beach sand suggested that an R4D aircraft could land successfully. The results, one way or the other, would be radioed to the *Pelican,* for relay to Townsville.

If the test results were favorable, Lieutenant McCoy and Chief Signalman Wallace would head for Ferdinand Six, while Sergeant Hart would remain on the beach, there being no good reason to subject him to the hazards of the trip through the jungle. Presuming McCoy and Wallace found Ferdinand Six, they would radio Townsville the estimated time of their return to the beach. Then they'd return there with sufficient manpower to handle the supplies which would come in with the R4D.

If the tests indicated that a safe landing could not be made, Sergeant Hart would go with Lieutenant McCoy and Chief Signalman Wallace to Ferdinand Six. And they'd all wait there until some other, better, *workable* plan to reinforce Ferdinand Six and extract its garrison could be devised.

It had to be presumed, finally, that if they couldn't land on Buka through the surf, then that was it. There was no other way in. Swimming was out of the question. Sharks.

"You're going to try it with just one rubber raft?" Staff Sergeant Kelly asked, a little confused.

"Chief Wallace, Sergeant Hart, and me," McCoy replied. "None of the equipment."

"Lieutenant, I'd like to try," Staff Sergeant Kelly said.

"You would only be another mouth to feed," McCoy said. "But thanks, Sergeant Kelly."

"I really want to go, Lieutenant," Kelly said.

"When you get that raft over the side, Sergeant, you better start getting everything else below."

"Shit!" Sergeant Kelly said.

Lieutenant McCoy did not seem to hear him.

About a hundred yards from the beach, the surf turned the rubber raft end over end, and George Hart found himself suddenly underwater, instinctively swimming toward the surface.

I am going to drown on this fucking beach!

He broke through the surface much sooner than he expected to. When he glanced around, another wave was about to fall on him; he took a quick breath and ducked under the water.

When he came up again and started treading water, he became aware that the bag containing the sand-density measuring equipment was banging against his back. He had looped the rope handle around his neck. It was a good thing he had his life preserver on, he realized. That stuff was heavy.

Then he saw McCoy. The Lieutenant was in the act of wrapping the weapons package in a life preserver, with the idea it might float in to shore. The next person he saw was a stranger. But in a moment he became recognizable; it was Chief Signalman Wallace. When Hart was previously with Wallace, his hair was a six-inch-high support for his Chief Petty Officer's brimmed cap. Now that it was soaking wet, Wallace's hair was hanging down over his face, almost to his chin. He looked like a really ugly woman.

Hart pointed at him. McCoy followed the pointing hand and laughed. Wallace at first looked surprised, and then his face clouded.

"Sod you both!" he called. Pushing the hair out of his face, he turned and started swimming toward the beach. He was towing two other packages, also hastily wrapped in life preservers.

That's all of them, then. The weapons, the radios, and our clothes.

Another wave came in and crashed over Hart. It took him so much by surprise that he breathed some water in.

He coughed and gagged a moment or two, and then he started swimming after McCoy and Wallace.

Ahead of him, he saw the rubber raft. It was now right side up, and a wave was gently depositing it on the beach.

Forty yards from the sand, treading water again, his feet touched sand. So he started walking the rest of the way ashore. He almost made it, walking in water not even waist high, when another wave took him by surprise, knocked him down, and scraped him along the bottom.

The beach turned out to be much wider than they expected, even wider and flatter than it appeared from the raft. Even so, the first thing he started to do was what they'd told him to do: He began taking measurements right down the middle.

But then he decided that they'd given him those instructions because they'd been thinking of beaches like the ones in Florida. This one was twice, three times, that wide. With a beach that wide, there was no telling where the tide would go—how far the water would come up the beach at high tide.

Instead, because the beach stopped dead in a mass of roots and trees, he stepped off from its inland side a distance that was twice the length of the wing of the Air Corps C-47 (he'd measured one in Florida). Then he looked around again, saw where he was, and stepped off that distance again. And then, after another look around, he stepped off one more wing length.

Even taking into account the foliage, there was room for at least two R4Ds to sit wingtip to wingtip between the trees and the place where he decided to pound the cone into the sand. And to seaward, there was even more sand.

Then he put the cone down and pounded it in. Next he was on his knees, bent over to read the cone's markings.

I don't believe this, George thought, *it's too good to be true!*

He picked the cone up and moved five feet closer to the water; then he stood the cone up and dropped the weight on it.

The cone went into the sand no farther than it did on the first try.

Jesus! Maybe there's clay or rocks or something here! This can't be right!

He scraped at the sand with his fingers, but could move only an inch or so away without difficulty.

He jumped to his feet and ran fifty yards down the beach and repeated the test. And then he ran a hundred yards down the beach and did it again.

He went back to where he started.

McCoy intercepted him, holding out for him a set of utilities.

"Put these on."

Amazingly cheerful, Hart replied, "Afraid I'll get sunburned?"

"For the bugs," McCoy said.

Hart was so excited he'd forgotten he'd been waving his hand in front of his face and swatting at various parts of his body. When he looked now, he was spotted all over with insect bites.

"The antibug grease is in the first-aid stuff," McCoy said, gesturing toward the *Pelican.*

Hart nodded.

"How does it look?"

"Too good to be true," Hart said. He pulled the utilities over his swimming trunks and ran farther down the beach.

Five minutes later he ran back to McCoy, who was holding the battery-powered shortwave radio.

"What do I tell them?" McCoy asked.

"Two, repeat Two, this is no mistake, Two," Hart said.

"You're sure?" McCoy said.

"I'm sure," Hart said, beaming.

McCoy put the microphone to his lips.

"Bird, this is Bird One, Over."

"Go ahead, Bird One."

"Message is Two. Repeat Two. This is not a mistake. Two. Over."

"Understand Two No Mistake Two, Over."

"The message is Two. Over."

"Good luck, you chaps. See you soon. Bird out."

McCoy and Hart smiled at each other.

"Wallace is snooping around the boondocks looking for some water for you," McCoy said.

"Good," Hart said.

What the fuck am I so cheerful about? As soon as he finds the water, he and McCoy are going to take off and leave me alone on this fucking beach.

Wallace appeared five minutes later, wearing only a loincloth. There was a compass on a thong around his neck. In one hand he held his Sten gun, and in the other was one of the funny-looking machetes Hart had seen in Townsville. His hair was now dry, and it seemed to have snapped back into place, but not to the carefully configured coiffure Hart had grown used to. Wallace did not now look like a Chief Signalman of the Royal Australian Navy Volunteer Reserve.

He looks like a fucking cannibal.

McCoy told him what Hart's tests of the beach had turned up.

"I thought it might turn out that way," Wallace said thoughtfully. "Once I saw the beach, it occurred to me that the wave action is ideal to pack the sand. And the odd large wave tends to provide the right amount of moisture to keep it from drying out."

Hart had no idea whatever what Wallace was talking about.

"I found a place where you might be comfortable," Wallace went on. "And I've been thinking, Lieutenant McCoy, that it would be a rather better idea if you stayed here with Sergeant Hart."

"Why?" McCoy asked.

"No offense, Lieutenant McCoy, but I can move faster alone."

Please God, let him agree with Wallace.

"If you think so, OK," McCoy said.

Wallace nodded.

"Well, let me help you two get settled, and then I'll be on my way."

(TWO)
Royal Australian Navy Coastwatcher Establishment
Townsville, Queensland
0555 Hours 6 October 1942

FRD1, KCY. FRD1, KCY. SB CODE OI.
Royal Australian Navy Coastwatcher Radio, this is Commander in Chief Pacific Radio. Please stand by to receive an encrypted Operational Immediate Message.

Signalman Third Class Paul W. Cahn, RANVR, threw the switch to TRANSMIT and tapped his key quickly KCY, FRD1. GA. As the message came in, in the familiar five-character blocks of gibberish, he turned to the device that made cryptographic tape and began to type.

Without stopping his typing, Signalman Cahn called out to Sergeant Vincent J. Esposito, USMC, "Vince, you better go get the brass. I think they're in the mess. Whatever this is, it's Operational Immediate."

Operational Immediate was the second-highest priority for message transmission. Sergeant Esposito put down his coffee cup and walked quickly out of the radio room.

Less than two minutes later, Signalman Cahn reached for his key, tapped out,

KCY, FRD1, AKN UR OI. CLR.
CINCPAC Radio, Coastwatcher Radio acknowledges receipt of your Operational Immediate transmission and is clearing the net at this time.

He waited for the reply, FRD1, KCY. CLR, and then took the strip of paper which had been fed out of his tape machine and fed it into the cryptographic machine. In a moment, the keys began to clatter:

FRD1, KCY.
KCY 6OCT34
OPERATIONAL IMMEDIATE
FOLLOWING RECEIVED 0545 FROM BIRD FOR RELAY
START
PART ONE
PLAN BAKER RPT BAKER EXECUTED AS OF 0530 RPT 0530
PART TWO
EGGS AND CHICKS IN NEST RPT IN NEST
PART THREE
CONDITION TWO RPT TWO THIS IS NO RPT NO MISTAKE
END

By the time Cahn removed the decrypted message from the machine, Lieutenant Commander Eric Feldt, RAN, and Major Edward Banning, USMC, had come into the radio room. Banning had a large manila envelope in his hand.

Signalman Cahn handed the message to Commander Feldt. He read it and handed it to Major Banning, who read it and handed it to Sergeant Esposito, who had been desperately trying to read it over Banning's shoulder.

"Christ, they couldn't get through the sodding surf! Or something else went wrong! Bloody hell!" Commander Feldt said.

"McCoy and Wallace are ashore," Banning said. "And Condition Two!"

McCoy's orders were to assess the condition of the sand on the beach on a scale of One to Five: One meant it was Perfect and Five meant it was Extremely Hazardous.

Banning took a sheet of paper from the manila envelope. He had prepared a number of messages beforehand to cover all the contingencies he could think of. The message he was looking for had three spaces that he'd left blank. He wrote BAKER in one of them and 0530 06OCT42 and TWO in the others. Then he handed the sheet to Cahn.

"The sooner the better, Cahn," he said.

"Aye, aye, Sir."

Cahn set the switch on the tape machine to CLEAR, then typed the message.

FOR CINCPAC RADIO
OPERATIONAL IMMEDIATE

FROM OFFICER COMMANDING RAN COASTWATCHER
ESTABLISHMENT

FOR RELAY TO COMMGENERAL 1ST MAR DIVISION

FOLLOWING FOR MAJOR HOMER DILLON USMC X PLAN BAKER
SUCCESSFULLY EXECUTED AS OF 0530 06OCT42 X CONDITION TWO
REPEAT TWO X EXECUTE PLAN VICTOR X ADVISE ONLY DELAYS
AND REASONS THEREFORE X FELDT

He then moved switches on the encryption device to ENCRYPT, fed the tape to it,
and waited for the message to appear.

Two minutes later, CINCPAC Radio acknowledged receipt of Coastwatcher Radio's encrypted Operational Immediate message. Four minutes after that, CINCPAC
sent another message.

FRD1, KCY. FYI 1STMARDIV AKN UR OI.
*Coastwatcher Radio, this is CINCPAC Radio. For Your Information, First
Marine Division Radio has acknowledged receipt of your Operational Immedi-
ate.*
KCY, FRD1. THANKS. FRD1 CLR.

"They've got it, Sir," Cahn reported.

"When do we net with Ferdinand Six?" Banning asked.

"Six-fifty, Sir," Cahn said after consulting his Signal Operating Instructions for
0001-2400 6 October 1942. "About ten minutes, Sir."

"Try them now," Commander Feldt ordered.

Cahn did so. There was no reply from Ferdinand Six. Neither was there a reply
at the appointed hour.

"Keep trying," Feldt ordered.

At 120-second intervals, Cahn tapped out FRD6, FRD1. FRD6, FRD1.

At 0710, twenty minutes late, FRD6 came on the air:

FRD1, FRD6. FRD1, FRD6.

"He's calling us, Commander," Cahn said. "Not responding to us. Maybe his
reception is bad."

"Try him again."

FRD6, FRD1. FRD6, FRD1.

FRD1, FRD6. UR 2×5.

FRD6, FRD1, SB CODE.

FRD1, FRD6. GA.

FRD6, FRD1.
USE AS SIMPLE SUBSTITUTION
FIRST NAME BELLE OF WAGGA WAGGA
SECOND NAME DITTO
MODEL RPT MODEL BANNINGS CAR

05×08×15×16×02
05×21×12×02×04
15×04×21×11×10

13×14×24×25×13
11×23×06×17×02
15×21×23×24×02

ACKNOWLEDGE UNDERSTANDING
FRD1, SB

Signalman Cahn listened carefully, making minute adjustments to his receiver for half a minute.

"I lost his carrier, Sir. He probably shut down to decode that."

"We hope," Banning said. He turned to Sergeant Esposito. "Esposito, get on the Teletype and send what we have to Brisbane. Eyes only, Lieutenant Hon."

"Aye, Aye, Sir."

"Tell him I suggest—use that word, suggest—that he relay to General Pickering on the special channel."

"Aye, aye, Sir."

"Are you sure you want to do that?" Feldt asked. "Falsely raised hopes are worse than no news at all."

"O ye of little faith," Banning said. "Send it, Esposito."

Sergeant Esposito picked up the various messages and sat down at the Teletype machine and started typing.

(THREE)
Ferdinand Six
Buka, Solomon Islands
0715 Hours 6 October 1942

"I hope you know what the hell Wagga Wagga is," Lieutenant Joe Howard, USMCR, said to Sub-Lieutenant Jakob Reeves, RANVR. "Because I don't."

"It's a backwater town in New South Wales," Reeves said.

"A town?"

Reeves nodded. "Using the term generously. And as far as I know I don't know a living soul there, much less the belle thereof."

"My girl's from Wagga Wagga," Sergeant Steve Koffler said.

"That must be it," Howard said.

"I thought your girl was down at the creek, washing your linen," Reeves said.

"I told you, goddamn it, you sonofabitch, to knock that shit off!"

"That's enough, Koffler."

"Fuck him, I told him to stop!"

"That's enough, Sergeant Koffler," Howard said firmly.

"Shit!"

"He *has* been diddling—"

"That's enough out of you, too, Reeves," Howard said.

"*You* don't give *me* orders, Lieutenant!"

With a great effort, Howard controlled his temper, although he did not flinch under Reeves' angry glare.

Eventually Reeves shrugged.

"Sergeant, I apologize," he said. "I was making a joke. Or thought I was."

"Forget it," Koffler said, sounding not at all sincere.

"For reasons I can't imagine, I think all of our tempers are on a short fuse," Howard said. "None of us can afford to let things get out of hand."

"Just for the fucking record," Koffler said, the picture of righteous indignation, "that happened just *once,* and I was drunk."

Howard had a terrible urge to laugh.

"On that beer shit that Reeves makes," Koffler said.

"Well, fuck you, Sergeant," Reeves said. "If you feel that way, you can't have any more of my beer shit."

Howard laughed out loud. Reeves looked pleased with himself.

"You just dug your own grave, Koffler," he said. "No more of Lieutenant Reeves' splendid, tasty beer for you."

"That shit sneaks up on you," Koffler said.

The flare-up seemed to have passed, Howard decided with relief.

"What do you think they mean by 'model of Banning's car'?" Reeves asked.

"Studebaker," Howard said. "Right? Or are they talking about that English car, the Jaguar, that Captain Pickering was driving?"

"It says 'model repeat model,'" Koffler said. "I think they mean 'President,' a Studebaker President. If they meant the Jaguar they would have said 'Pickering.'"

"I'm sure Steve's right," Reeves said.

"Let's try it," Howard said. It did not go unnoticed by him that Reeves had used Koffler's first name.

"Well, it's English," Howard said five minutes later, "but what the hell does it mean?"

Reeves and Koffler looked down at the sheet of paper. On it Howard had written the message in code blocks, then his interpretation of that:

```
N A T H A
N S W A N
T H I S N
O R N T O
S E E P A
T I E N S
```

Nathan Swan This Norn to See Patiens

" 'Norn' is maybe 'North'?" Koffler guessed.

"There's no 'M' in 'Daphne Farnsworth Patiens,'" Reeves said. "Make it 'swam' and 'morn.'"

"Nathan *swam* this *morn* to see Patience," Howard said. "That makes more sense, but what does it mean?"

"Nathan is obviously the Nathaniel of the first message," Reeves said. "What it could mean is that he came ashore, swam ashore, from a submarine or something."

"This morn? This *morning*?"

"Yes. If that's what it means. This morning."

"Could he do that?" Koffler said.

"He could try to do it. That's not quite the same thing. The reason there are so few ports on Buka is that the surf is so rough in most places—this time of the year especially. Presumably they know that. That means he would either have to try to make it ashore near a port, which would place him very far away, or through the surf somewhere near here. Which would be quite difficult."

"They know what shape we're in supplywise," Howard said. "Maybe they figured it was worth the risk."

"You think there's a chance he's not alone?" Steve asked.

"This could very well be wishful thinking, Steve," Reeves said. "Certainly, it is. But if I were the man in charge and were going to all the trouble of sending someone up here, I would go the extra mile and try to send in more than one person—and supplies, of course."

"Get on the air, Steve," Howard ordered. "Send, 'Message acknowledged and understood.'"

"That's all?"

"That's all. If they wanted to tell us more than they did, they would have."

"Aye, aye, Sir."

(FOUR)
**Command Post, 2nd Battalion, Fifth Marines
Guadalcanal, Solomon Islands
0830 Hours 6 October 1942**

Using his arm as a pillow, Major Jack (NMI) Stecker, USMCR, was curled up asleep on his side on the deck of the S-3 section. His Garand rifle, with two eight-round clips pinned to the strap, was hanging from a nail in the wooden frame of the situation map.

When the flyboy from Henderson Field walked into the command post asking to see the Old Man, Stecker's S-3 sergeant was reluctant to disturb him.

"He was up all goddamned night, Captain," he said. "Can this wait a couple of hours?"

Captain Charles M. Galloway, USMCR, shook his head, no, and then said it aloud: "No, it won't, Gunny."

"Aye, aye, Sir," the gunny said, and went to Stecker and knelt beside him and gently shook his shoulder.

"Sir? Sir?"

Stecker woke reluctantly, shrugging off the hand on his shoulder. But then he was suddenly wide awake, forcing himself to sit up.

"What's up, Gunny?" Stecker asked as he looked at his watch.

"An officer to see you, Sir."

Stecker searched the dark area and found Galloway.

"This better be important, Captain," Stecker said, matter-of-factly.

"Sir, my name is Galloway. I have VMF-229."

Stecker saw the look on Galloway's face.

"Give us some privacy, will you, Gunny?" he said softly.

He waited until the gunny was out of earshot and then said, "OK, let's have it."

"Your son crashed on landing about twenty-five minutes ago, Sir," Galloway said.

"You're here, that means bad news," Stecker said.

"He's pretty badly banged up, Sir, but he's alive."

"Define 'pretty badly,' would you, please?"

"Both of his legs are broken; he has a compound fracture of the right arm; his collarbone has probably been cracked. He almost certainly has broken ribs, and there are probably some internal injuries."

"Jesus Christ!" Stecker exhaled. "Is he going to live?"

"Commander Persons—I just left him—said that barring complications—"

"Persons?" Stecker interrupted. "Mean little guy?" He held his hand up to nearly his shoulder level, to indicate a runt.

"Yes, Sir."

"Barring complications, what?"

"He will recover and will probably even be able to return to flight status."

I'm telling you that because that's what Persons told me, and because I want to believe it, not because I do believe it. When they pulled him from the wreck, I was surprised that he was alive.

"I don't like to think what Mrs. Stecker will do when she gets the telegram," Stecker said. "I suppose you've already set that in motion?"

"No, Sir. I haven't. MAG-21 handles that, Sir. You could probably talk to Colonel Dawkins—"

"What happened? 'Crashed on landing'? Is that a polite way of saying it was his fault?"

"It looked to me as if his right tire was flat, Sir."

"You saw the accident?"

"Yes, Sir. I was right behind him in the pattern."

"And?"

And a second after he touched down, he started to ground loop to the right, and then he was rolling end over end down the strip; the only way it could have been worse was if there had been more gas in his tanks and it exploded.

"He was attempting to make a dead-stick landing, Sir. He was out of fuel."

"How did that happen?"

"They hit us pretty badly this morning, Major—"

"I was up earlier, I saw it."

"—and he stayed up as long as he thought he could, as long as he thought he had fuel to stay."

"You encourage that sort of thing, Captain, do you? Staying up there until you have just enough fuel to *maybe* make it back to the field?" Stecker asked nastily, and then immediately apologized. "Forgive me. That was uncalled for. And you were up there, too, weren't you, presumably doing the same thing?"

"We lost three Wildcats this morning, Sir. And the Air Corps lost two of their P400s."

"Counting my son?"

"No, Sir. Not counting him."

But including a Wildcat piloted by Major Jack Finch. Finch wouldn't have been up there if I hadn't told him he could, for auld lang syne.

"All lost? Or just shot down?"

"One of the P400 pilots made it back to the field, Sir. Just him."

"Tell me about this flat tire," Stecker said after a moment.

"He told me that he'd taken some hits. . . . Major, I didn't mention this, but he shot down two Bettys and a Zero this morning. He's an ace. That makes it six total for him."

"All I knew he had was one," Stecker said. "The flat tire?"

"He called and said he'd taken some hits, so I pulled up beside him and took a look, and there were holes in the area of his landing gear."

"And you told him this?"

"I signaled him, Sir. His radio was not working. But he understands my signal."

"Then why didn't he try to make a wheels-up landing?"

"I can only presume he thought he could make it, Sir."

"And that he wanted to save the airplane?"

"Yes, Sir. I think that probably had a lot to do with the decision he made."

"What about the Pickering boy?" Stecker asked. "Was he one of the other three you lost?"

Galloway was surprised at the question.

"No, Sir. He made it back all right. He was flying on your son's wing, Major."

And he landed three minutes before your boy—time enough for him to be walking

*away from his revetment when your boy came in, to see the crash, and to run to
the plane and listen to your boy scream for the five minutes or so it took to pry
him from the wreckage. He made it back all right, but I'm going to have trouble
with him. I know the look he had in his eyes.*

"I know his father," Stecker said.

"Yes, Sir. Major, I have a jeep—"

Stecker met his eyes.

"I've been trying to decide if I have the courage to go see him. Jesus Christ,
they ought to skip a generation between wars so that fathers don't have to see their
children torn up."

"They're going to fly him out, to Espíritu Santo, Sir."

"If I ride down there with you, can I get a ride back up here?"

"Yes, Sir. No problem."

"Squadron commanders at Henderson have their own jeeps?" Stecker asked.

"I borrowed Colonel Dawkins' jeep, Sir. I didn't think he'd mind."

Stecker pushed open the canvas flap.

"Gunny, I've got to go down the hill for a while," he said.

"Major, I'm goddamned sorry," the gunny said and glowered at Galloway as if
it were obviously his fault.

"Thank you, Gunny," Stecker said. "It is not for dissemination."

"Aye, aye, Sir."

"Hello, Pick," Major Jack (NMI) Stecker said to Second Lieutenant Malcolm S.
Pickering. "How are you?"

Pickering was on a hospital cot next to the one where Second Lieutenant Richard
J. Stecker lay. Tubing ran from Pickering's arm into Stecker's; a transfusion was
taking place.

"Jesus Christ, I'm sorry!" Pick said and sat up. There were tears in his eyes.

Stecker quickly pushed him back on the cot.

"Watch out for the tubes," he said. Then he dropped to his knees and put a firm
hand on Pick's shoulders.

"There was just too fucking many of them!" Pick said. "I just couldn't cover
him!"

"I'm sure you did the best you could, Pick," Stecker said, and then he turned
and looked at the adjacent cot.

The suit, Flying, Cotton, Tropical Climates, had been cut from Second Lieutenant
Richard J. Stecker's body. He was clothed now in undershorts and vast quantities
of bandage and adhesive tape. There were splints on both legs. He was unconscious.

Major Jack Stecker laid a very gentle hand on his son's face and held it there
for a long time.

Captain Charles M. Galloway felt like crying.

"Major, I'll go find Commander Persons," he said.

Stecker nodded.

Major Jake Dillon found Captain Galloway before Galloway found the medical
officer.

"I thought you'd be here," Dillon said.

"What the hell do you want?"

Dillon handed him a message form:

FOLLOWING FOR MAJOR HOMER DILLON USMC X PLAN BAKER
SUCCESSFULLY EXECUTED AS OF 0530 06OCT42 X CONDITION TWO
REPEAT TWO X EXECUTE PLAN VICTOR X ADVISE ONLY DELAYS
AND REASONS THEREFORE X FELDT

"Victor means go to Moresby, right?" Galloway asked.

Dillon nodded.

"What are you going to do for a copilot?" Dillon said. "Sorry to hear about Major Finch."

"The way you were supposed to say that, Jake," Galloway said nastily, "was, 'Sorry about Jack Finch,' and *then* ask what I'm going to do about a copilot."

"OK, I'm sorry. But what are you going to do about a copilot?"

"I'm going to take the other kid in there, the one giving blood to Stecker."

"What kid?"

"Pickering."

"He's not a qualified R4D pilot. What the hell are you talking about?"

"He's a pilot. And he's not a bad one. And besides, all he'll have to do is put the wheels and flaps up and down and talk on the radio. I'll be flying."

"I don't understand, Charley. There must be another guy qualified in R4Ds somewhere on Henderson."

"If Pickering stays here, he's going to fly. And in the mental condition he's in, if he flies, he's *going* to get killed. If he comes with me, he only *might* get killed."

"That doesn't make any sense. It has nothing to do with his father?"

"Don't try to tell me about flying or pilots, Jake, OK?" Galloway replied.

"Forget it, Charley. How long will it take to get going?"

"I don't know, Jake. It will have to wait until he's finished giving his buddy blood, OK? This idiot idea of yours will have to wait that long."

(FIVE)
Cryptographic Center
Supreme Headquarters, South West Pacific Ocean Area
Brisbane, Australia
0935 Hours 6 October 1942

Lieutenant Hon Song Do, Signal Corps, USA, had just about finished decryption of the Overnight MAGICs when one of the two telephones in his cubicle rang. Of these, one was a Class A switchboard line, and the other a secure Class X line that connected with only a few telephones in SHSWPOA. Brass hats too important to use the ordinary system had Class X phones—the Supreme Commander, the Chief of Staff, the four Gs (Personnel, Intelligence, Plans & Training, and Supply), and a few of the Special Staff officers, including the Provost Marshal.

"Lieutenant Hon, Sir," he said, hoping that it wasn't the Supreme Commander and that his annoyance at being disturbed did not show in his voice.

"Major Banning, please," a voice Pluto did not recognize said.

"I'm sorry, Sir, Major Banning is not available."

"When will he be available?"

"I'm not sure, Sir."

"Where can I reach him?"

"May I ask who this is?"

"Colonel Gregory."

The name did not ring a bell.

"I'm sorry, Sir, I'm not permitted to divulge Major Banning's location. May I take a message?"

"My name is not familiar to you, Lieutenant?"

"No, Sir. I'm sorry, but it's not."

The phone went dead in his ear.

"Well, fuck you, too, Colonel Whatsyourname," Pluto said and hung the telephone back on the wall.

Fifteen minutes later, a .45 automatic jammed in the small of his back, a locked leather briefcase handcuffed to his wrist, Pluto made sure that everything was turned off. And then, feeling like Bulldog Drummond, Master Detective, he rigged a thread between a pin stuck in the brick wall and one of the chairs. If anyone entered the room, he would disturb the thread.

Banning's orders.

A little melodramatic, Pluto thought, *but if Banning thought it was necessary . . .*

He locked the door and went down the corridor to the guard post.

"Make sure you feed the dragon, Sergeant," he said to the senior guard as he signed himself out. "I thought I heard his tummy rumbling."

The little joke fell flat. The sergeant gave a small, just perceptible jerk of his head down the corridor. There was an officer down the way in the gloom.

One of the MP officers, Pluto decided, *checking to see that the enlisted men are not cavorting with loose women.*

"Lieutenant Hon, I'm Colonel Gregory," the officer said. He was a small, natty man in pinks and greens. A *Lieutenant* Colonel, not a full bird, wearing the insignia of the General Staff on his lapels.

"Yes, Sir?"

"Have you got a minute, Lieutenant?"

"Actually, Sir, no," Pluto said, holding up the briefcase.

Colonel Gregory held out a leather folder to Pluto. It held a badge and a photo identification card. It was something like the ones Banning and Moore carried, identifying them as Special Agents of the Office of Naval Intelligence. The credentials Gregory held out identified him as an Agent of the U.S. Army Counterintelligence Corps.

"Yes, Sir," Pluto said.

"Ed Banning and I are sort of friends, Lieutenant. I really would like to talk to him."

"I'm sorry, Colonel, I can't help."

Gregory's eyes appraised him carefully.

"You going upstairs with that briefcase, Lieutenant? Or out to Water Lily Cottage?"

How the hell does this guy know about Water Lily Cottage? More important, what the hell does he want?

When Gregory realized that Hon was not going to answer him, he said, "No offense, Pluto, but you look more like a Japanese spy than I do, don't you think?"

How the hell does he know that people call me Pluto?

"I don't know who you are, Colonel," Pluto said.

"I really hoped to avoid using the word until we were alone, but I'm here to talk about your Buka operation," Gregory said.

Shit! We're compromised. Who the hell told him?

The first possibility that came to his mind was Mrs. Ellen Feller, but that couldn't be. Banning had gotten her out of Water Lily Cottage before anyone mentioned the word Buka.

Then who? In a moment the answer came: *That fucking Air Corps Colonel that MacArthur summoned to his office.*

"You're not compromised," Colonel Gregory said, reading his mind. "Nobody knows a thing who is not supposed to. Are you going to Water Lily Cottage?"

Pluto nodded.

"Let me ride out there with you then. We might have to get Moore involved in this anyway."

This sonofabitch knows a hell of a lot about Water Lily Cottage.

"I don't know how long I'll be out there, Colonel. How would you get back?"

"We keep the cottage under surveillance. There'll be a car there to bring me back. Shall we go?"

"I'm not going to tell you where Major Banning is, Colonel."

"You've made that perfectly clear, Pluto," Gregory said.

Gregory volunteered to drive the Studebaker. After a moment's hesitation, Pluto agreed: *He is a CIC type; he is not going to commandeer the car and take me someplace where they will stick lighted matches under my fingernails to make me tell them where Banning is. And besides, driving a car with a briefcase chained to your wrist is difficult, even dangerous.*

It soon became apparent that Gregory not only knew where Water Lily Cottage was, but the shortest route.

"I've got a question," Gregory said.

"Sir?"

"Just idle curiosity. When you gave me the hard time on the phone and I realized that I was going to have to deal with you personally, I went to look at your personnel file. You don't have one. What do they do, keep it in Pearl Harbor or Washington?"

I honestly don't know.

"What I was wondering is, how do you get paid?"

"They send me a check," Pluto said. "I take it to Finance and they cash it."

Gregory grunted. Then he changed the subject.

"I got a copy of that Transfer of Detainee form that Moore signed for Mrs. Farnsworth. The Kangaroo FBI sent it to the Provost Marshal, and he didn't know what to do with it, so he sent it to me. What the hell was that all about?"

"The Kangaroo FBI?"

"His Majesty's Royal Australian Constabulary," Gregory said. "What are you going to do with her?"

Pluto again elected not to reply.

"I know she's staying in the cottage, for Christ's sake," Gregory said. "I told you we keep it under surveillance. At Ed Banning's request."

"She's a fine young woman," Pluto said. "Her heinous crime was to get herself impregnated by one of our Marines. Banning didn't know that when he sent word we wanted to talk to her. The Kangaroo FBI, as you so aptly describe them, went overboard."

"They tend to do that," Gregory replied. He didn't speak for a moment or two. "And so she'll become one of yours, I presume?" he asked when he was ready to talk again. "As in Special Detachment 14, rather than The U.S. Marine Corps generally?"

"Right. I think we'll hire Mrs. Farnsworth."

"As soon as Banning gets back from wherever he is?"

Pluto declined to reply.

Gregory chuckled, and then remained silent until they pulled up the drive to Water Lily Cottage and stopped. As Pluto reached for the car door handle, he touched his arm.

"Do you think we could send the ladies shopping or something? I'd really rather have our little chat in private."

"Well, Lieutenant," Colonel Gregory said to Moore as soon as the Studebaker with Barbara Cotter, Joanne Miller, and Daphne Farnsworth in it had nosed out of the driveway, "you seem to have recovered from your recurrence of malaria. And congratulations on your promotion."

"You seem to know a hell of a lot about me, Colonel," Moore said.

"You provided my people with a lot of laughs when you were here the first time . . . humping Mrs. Feller," Gregory said.

"Son of a bitch!" Moore blurted.

"From the look on your face, Pluto, I don't think you knew that, did you? I guess Banning decided you didn't have the Need to Know," Gregory said.

He chuckled at Moore's flushing face.

"Your secret is—*secrets are*—safe with me. Believe it or not, I was reluctant to bring that up, but I wanted to make the point quickly that I know a good deal about you—and about what goes on here—because Ed Banning wanted me to know."

"What the hell is this all about?" Pluto asked.

"This is a very delicate situation, gentlemen," Gregory said. "One of those aberrations where people of our lowly ranks and positions have to make decisions involving our superiors."

"I have no idea what you're talking about," Pluto said.

"At his first opportunity, Colonel Armstrong went to General McKinney and told him he had been ordered by the Supreme Commander to stage diversionary air attacks in connection with a clandestine operation being conducted in or around Buka—"

"That must be the Air Corps officer who was in General MacArthur's office?" Pluto interrupted.

"Right," Gregory said, "—under the auspices of Lieutenant Hon. Or Banning, who is Hon's boss. I don't mean to sound cynical, but that sounds like bullshit to me; Ed Banning is a nice guy, but he's only a major. I'd like to know what authority, if any, there is for this operation."

Moore looked at Hon for instruction.

Without those orders for authority, Hon thought, *what we are is two pissant Lieutenants surrounded by very senior brass who are likely to fuck this whole thing up on general principles. Jesus, I wish Banning or Dillon was here!*

"Show him your orders, John," Pluto said.

Moore went into his bedroom, returned with his plastic sealed orders, and handed them to Colonel Gregory.

"Well," Gregory said after reading them and handing them back, "I suppose that operating under the auspices of the Chief of Staff to the President gives you all the authority you could ask for."

"Is that what you came to find out?" Pluto asked.

"Not exactly," Gregory said. "So General McKinney, who is not exactly on General MacArthur's fair-haired-boy list, went to General Willoughby. He did that on the reasonable presumption that as the G-2, Willoughby would know all about this clandestine operation and could tell him what was going on. But it turns out that all Willoughby knows he got from Mrs. Feller. I.e., that there's a clandestine operation he knows nothing about. He was pissed off about that—understandably, I think. But what really upset him was that MacArthur was in on the secret. Obviously, since MacArthur laid this air-raid diversion mission on McKinney."

"We didn't ask for that," Pluto said. "That was MacArthur's idea."

"That's the problem," Gregory said. "By definition, any tactical or strategic mission invented by MacArthur is brilliant. And not subject to cancellation."

"I don't know what you're talking about," Pluto said.

"Buka is not within the boundaries of South West Pacific Ocean Area," Gregory said. "It belongs to CINCPAC. MacArthur cannot order an operation in CINCPAC's area. If he does, the shit will hit the fan all the way back to Washington. The Navy is just as sensitive about its territory—about infringements thereon—as MacArthur himself."

"So there will be no diversionary air attack?" Pluto asked. "No problem. We didn't think it was feasible in the first place."

"You miss the point, Pluto," Gregory said. "There *will* be diversionary air activity; MacArthur has ordered it. It's entirely possible, I think, that he hopes it will cause the shit to hit the fan. He knows damned well where his boundaries are."

"I'm confused again," Pluto said.

"General Willoughby has a number of other virtues, I'm sure, but the one I admire most is his determination to keep his boss out of trouble. While simultaneously keeping his own ass out of trouble with MacArthur, of course. He and McKinney have come up with a possible solution. Willoughby sent me to present it to you."

"Why didn't Willoughby just call me in?" Pluto thought aloud.

"Since MacArthur never told Willoughby about his order to McKinney, he doesn't officially know about it."

"What do they want from us?" Moore asked.

"They want Hon to go back to Colonel Armstrong and request aerial reconnaissance of your operations area—in other words, of Buka. Because the only aircraft with the range to do that are bombers, B-17s, it can be described to General MacArthur as a diversionary raid. At the same time it can be described as reconnaissance activity to CINCPAC. They don't object to that. Actually, they're glad to have it. McKinney can offer daylight reconnaissance for four days."

"Why don't we just tell MacArthur that we'd rather not have any aircraft involved in this, period?" Moore asked.

"I tried that," Pluto said. "General MacArthur has decided we need a diversionary attack."

"When is this thing going to happen?" Gregory said. "And don't tell me I don't have the Need to Know."

Hon pointed to the briefcase.

"By now the R4D should be on its way to Port Moresby. Townsville sent me a copy of the message just before you called me."

"I happen to know that Colonel Armstrong is in his office right now," Gregory said, "if you have anything to say to him."

"We don't have any wheels to get back to SWPOA," Hon said.

"I told you that wouldn't be a problem," Gregory said.

He walked out on the wide porch of Water Lily Cottage and waved his arm. Thirty seconds later, a black Humber four-door sedan with a man in civilian clothing behind the wheel pulled into the driveway.

XVII

Sergeant Steve Koffler, USMC, sat on the dirt floor of his hut, carefully scraping at the rib cage of a wild pig Ian Bruce had beheaded with his MACHETE, SUBSTITUTE STANDARD. They'd roasted the pig whole over an open fire like in the movies about the South Pacific, at a luau or some such bullshit.

The difference was that the pigs they cooked in the movies were great big porkers, and this one had been about the size of a medium-sized dog. It had lasted just one meal, not counting the stew they'd made with the leftovers.

He wasn't scraping the rib cage to get food from it. There wasn't anything edible left, just some stringy shit. He was scraping the rib because there wasn't a goddamned thing else to do.

Steve had sort of hoped there would be another message for them when he'd gone on the air with a Here-They-Come report, but there hadn't been. And there hadn't been when he'd made the regular net check-in either.

So that left the bullshit message of the day before, about that guy Nathan swimming to see Patience.

And that bullshit simple substitution code with Daphne's name . . . which made him think of Daphne, practically all fucking night. That was a bitch, because there was absolutely no fucking way he was ever going to see Daphne again in his entire life, no matter how the fuck long that lasted. It didn't look like it was going to be long at all, frankly.

He was going to die on this fucking island, and the goddamned ants would pick his bones as clean as they'd picked the rib cage of Ian's fucking pig.

Better sooner than later, this shit is really getting me down.

He put his knife aside. But then he picked it up and worked the edge under one of the scabs on his legs, just prying it loose enough so he could force the pus out.

Jesus, if Daphne walked into this fucking hut right now, and saw me, she'd run away screaming. I look like I got fucking leprosy or terminal syphilis or something.

Patience Witherspoon stuck her head in the opening.

You had to show up right now, right? When I was thinking of Daphne?

"Oh, Steven, come quickly!" Patience said excitedly, holding her arm across her bosom.

"What's up?"

Jesus, maybe Ian got another pig! He hasn't been around since yesterday. Reeves had to pump the fucking bicycle.

"Oh, come quickly!" Patience said, and disappeared.

Maybe I should fuck her again. That once wasn't bad, and if I'm going to die, what the fuck difference does it make if she looks like something out of National Geographic *magazine?*

Fuck that. Don't even think that. You may be holding the shitty end of the stick in the absolute asshole of the world, but you're a white man, and a Marine, and you know better than fucking cannibals.

He rose to his feet and picked up the Thompson and left the hut.

Well, there's Ian. He doesn't have a pig. Who the fuck is that with him? I never saw that cannibal before. What is this, Cannibal Homecoming?

Patience came running back and caught his hand and pulled him to the new cannibal, slowing as they got close.

"Steven," she said shyly, "I want you to meet my old friend Nathaniel Wallace. Nathaniel, this is Steven."

"Chief Signalman Wallace, Sergeant," the cannibal said, putting out his hand. "I've been looking forward to meeting you."

"You have?"

"You have a fine hand," Wallace said. "I tried to copy your style."

"I'll be goddamned."

(TWO)
Henderson Field
Guadalcanal, Solomon Islands
1105 Hours 7 October 1942

Captain Charles M. Galloway ran the engines up, saw that all the needles were in the green, and looked back over his shoulder toward Major Jake Dillon. Dillon was standing behind the pilots' seats, wearing a headset. Galloway took the microphone from its holder and moved the switch to INTERCOM.

"Strap yourself in, Jake," Galloway ordered, jerking his thumb to show Dillon a fold-down seat behind him. "I don't want you in my lap if I have to try to stop this thing."

He looked at Second Lieutenant Malcolm S. Pickering, in the copilot's seat.

"We have twenty degrees of flaps," he said, pointing. "There's the gear control. The way we're going to do this is move onto the runway, run the engines up, remove the brakes, and see if we can get it to fly. You follow me through on the throttles. When I give you the word, you will raise the gear and then the flaps. Got it?"

Pickering took his microphone and pressed the switch.

"Got it, Skipper."

"Call the tower," Galloway said.

Pickering moved the switch to TRANSMIT.

"Cactus, this is"—he stopped, searching the control panel in vain for the aircraft's call sign—"Eastern Airlines City of San Francisco on the threshold for takeoff."

"Eastern *Airliner,* you are cleared for takeoff as number one," the Cactus tower replied. The amusement in his voice came through even over the frequency-clipping radio.

Pickering dropped his microphone in his lap and watched as Galloway moved onto the runway, lined up with its center, stopped, locked the brakes, and put his hand on the throttle quadrant. Then he put his hand over Galloway's as Galloway ran the throttles forward to TAKEOFF POWER.

The engines roared and the airplane strained against the brakes.

Galloway released them, and the R4D started to roll. He pulled his hand from under Pickering's and put it on the wheel.

Pickering picked the microphone from his lap.

"Cactus, Eastern Airlines rolling."

The aircraft slowly began to gain speed. It was over the Recommended Maximum

Gross Weight for the temperature and available runway length. And the runway was not smooth concrete but wet dirt, patched here and there with pierced steel planking.

Galloway was more than a little worried about blowing a tire, but he kept that to himself. As soon as he could, he eased forward on the wheel to get the tail wheel off the ground.

Then he kept his eye on the end of the runway, dropping his eyes every second or so to the airspeed indicator, which had come to life at 40 knots.

The speed climbed very slowly. But then Galloway sensed life in the controls. He eased back on the wheel, felt the airplane want to try to fly, and then eased the wheel back just a hair more.

The heavy rumbling of the undercarriage suddenly quit.

"Gear up!" he called.

Pickering took his hand from the throttle quadrant and dropped it to the wheel-shaped landing gear control ten inches down and to the rear. He put it in RETRACT.

The wheels took a long time coming up. On Jack Finch's orders, the pilot who had flown the airplane to Guadalcanal from Espíritu Santo had also tested and timed how long it took to get the gear up with the added weight and wind resistance of the skis. It hadn't taken appreciably longer than normal, a tribute to the strength of the hydraulic system.

A moment before he expected the GEAR UP light to go on, Galloway ordered, "Flaps Up!"

The GEAR UP light went on as Pickering moved the flap-control lever.

"Gear up," Pickering's voice came over the earphones, and then a moment later, "Flaps retarded."

The airspeed indicator needle pointed at 110. Galloway put the airplane into a shallow climb to the left and kept it there until the surf on the Guadalcanal beach passed under his wing. Then he straightened it out, retarded the throttles, and set up a shallow climb.

It was just about 900 miles in a straight line from Henderson to Port Moresby on New Guinea, but Galloway was planning for at least a thousand-mile flight, in case he ran into weather, and because he knew that flying dead reckoning, the airfield was probably not going to be where he expected it to be.

To conserve fuel, he would cruise somewhere around 8,000 to 10,000 feet and at an indicated 180 knots. A thousand miles at 180 knots translated to right at six hours. That would give them an Estimated Time of Arrival at Port Moresby of 1700, 1710. The worst possible case—if they failed to find the field for another hour or so—would still see them on the ground at 1800. Before nightfall.

There was plenty of fuel. An R4D in this configuration could officially carry twenty-eight fully loaded paratroops, or 5,600 pounds. Galloway's experience during the C47/R4D acceptance tests had taught him that was a very conservative estimate of Maximum Gross Load.

Dillon had told him five people would be going into Buka. That would be less than 1,000 pounds, because they would not be fully equipped paratroopers. But call it a thousand anyway. And they would have with them an already weighed 950 pounds of supplies. So call that a thousand pounds, too. That left 3,600 pounds of cargo lift weight available.

More than that, really. Galloway had concluded that the Maximum Gross Weight erred on the side of caution by about 20 percent (a thousand pounds). So that left him 4,600 pounds.

AvGas weighed about seven pounds a gallon. And he had auxiliary fuel tanks mounted inside the cabin over the wing root. He'd ordered these filled with 600 gallons of gasoline.

One of the Rules for Over Water Flight that Captain Galloway devoutly believed in was that as long as you could get the airplane to stagger into the air with it, there was no such thing as too much fuel aboard. If necessary, they could fly to Australia.

Galloway turned to Pickering.

"Can you hear me?"

Pickering nodded.

"You've never been in one of these before?"

"Not sitting up front," Pickering said.

"They're a very forgiving airplane," Galloway said.

"That's nice," Pickering said. "May I ask a question?"

"Shoot."

"From the movies I've seen, people are supposed to be asked to volunteer for a mission they can't be told about."

Galloway smiled.

"You volunteered the day you joined The Corps," he said. "And again when you went through P'Cola. You had two chances to say no."

"Where are we going?"

Galloway threw the map into his lap. "First stop, Port Moresby. It'll take us about six hours—"

"We have that much fuel aboard?" Pickering asked, and then realized the stupidity of his question. "I guess we do, don't we?"

"—and then—turn the chart over—Moresby to Buka and return."

"The Japanese hold Buka, right? Where are we going to land? Or *are* we going to land?"

"We're going to pick up some people and equipment at Moresby and fly to Buka. We'll land on the beach, off-load the people and their equipment, and pick up three passengers."

Pickering looked at him. "Christ, you're serious!"

Galloway nodded.

"There's something I think I should tell you, Captain," Pickering said. Charley picked up on the "Captain"; Pickering usually called him "Skipper."

"You're not Alan Ladd or Errol Flynn, right?"

"No," Pickering said. "I used to think I was a pretty good pilot."

"You are. With the Zeke you shot down this morning, that made five, you're officially an ace."

"That's not what I meant," Pickering said. "I mean, when I got my first ride in a Yellow Peril at P'Cola, the IP thought I was a wiseass—"

I can certainly understand that, Mr. Pickering.

"—and tried to make me airsick, and couldn't. So he turned it over to me and told me to take it back to the field and land it and I did; and then he was really pissed because he thought I already knew how to fly and hadn't told anybody."

"No kidding?"

"No kidding," Pickering said. "I had no trouble learning to fly the Wildcat, either, and . . . shit, just before I came over here, I took my grandfather's Stagger Wing Beech up, the first time I'd ever sat behind the wheel, buzzed Marin County, and then flew under the bridge."

"You flew under the Golden Gate Bridge?" Galloway asked incredulously.

Pickering nodded.

"Both ways, I flew in from the ocean, went under the bridge, did a one-eighty over Alcatraz, and flew back out under the bridge."

"That's a little hard to believe."

"I did it. And I wasn't scared. And I wasn't scared here until this morning."

I'll be a sonofabitch if I don't believe him about flying under the Golden Gate.

"Maybe you grew up this morning," Galloway said.

"Could be. After I saw what happened to Dick Stecker, I was about to hand you my wings and take my chances with a rifle. I don't want to end up like that."

He means that, too.

"So why didn't you?"

"Because wherever you were going was away from Henderson, from Guadalcanal," Pickering said. "I figured I could hand you my wings wherever we landed."

"You're out of luck, Pickering. At least until this mission's over," Galloway said. "You want to turn in your wings, that's your business. But not until we get back."

"You can't make me get back in this airplane once we land."

"Yes, I can. You're a goddamned Marine officer, and you'll do what you're ordered to do."

"Or what?"

"There is no 'or what,' " Galloway said. "The subject is closed, Mr. Pickering."

Pickering shrugged and folded his arms across his chest.

Galloway put his hand on the wheel and reached up and turned the automatic pilot off.

"Put your hands and feet on the controls," he ordered. Pickering looked at him. After a moment he unfolded his arms and put his left hand on the wheel.

"You have the aircraft, Mr. Pickering," Galloway said. "Maintain the present course and rate of climb until reaching nine thousand feet."

Pickering nodded.

They rode in silence for a minute or so. Galloway had enough time to judge that Pickering was telling the truth about that—the rate-of-climb and airspeed-indicator needles didn't even flicker, nor did the attitude of the aircraft change a half degree. He was one of those rare people you heard about but never actually saw: He was born with the ability to fly.

A glint of light at his left startled him. He snapped his head and looked out.

First Lieutenant William Charles Dunn, USMCR, Executive Officer—and at the moment, acting Commander—of VMF-229 waved cheerfully at him from his F4F.

Galloway furiously signaled him to return to base.

When Dunn brought the subject up before they left, Galloway expressly told him not to escort the R4D.

It would have been nice if a whole squadron of Wildcats could escort the R4D away from Guadalcanal, to protect it from Japanese bombers. They'd be delighted to shoot an R4D down if they saw it. But a whole squadron of Wildcats could not be diverted from their primary mission for that—they couldn't even divert two or three of them.

And a single Wildcat wouldn't do any good. Not only that, it would place itself in unnecessary jeopardy.

Bill Dunn continued to wave cheerfully, apparently choosing to interpret Galloway's furious signals as a friendly return of his own greeting. Galloway remembered that back at Henderson, Bill seemed to cave in to the logic of his arguments far easier than Galloway expected.

"We're at nine thousand feet, Sir," Pickering reported.

"See if you can trim it up for straight and level flight at an indicated 180 knots, Mr. Pickering, without running into Mr. Dunn."

Pickering looked at him in confusion, and then saw Dunn in the Wildcat. He took his left hand from the wheel and, smiling, waved at him.

Meanwhile, the R4D leveled off. The altimeter indicated 9,000 feet, and the rate-of-climb indicator needle stopped moving. It was right in the center of the dial.

In direct violation of a specific order to the contrary, Lieutenant Dunn remained on the wingtip of the R4D until he had only enough fuel, plus ten minutes, to return to Henderson Field.

Then he waved one more time and entered a slow 180-degree turn to the left.

When he was out of sight, Galloway unfastened his shoulder and seat belts and got up out of his seat. Pickering looked at him.

"Piss call," Galloway said. Pickering nodded.

He'll be all right, Galloway thought. *He had every reason in the world to go a little crazy. Bringing him along was the right thing to do.*

(THREE)
Royal Australian Air Force Station
Port Moresby, New Guinea
1340 Hours 7 October 1942

RAAF Moresby was located too far forward to have the most advanced cryptographic equipment. It was necessary, therefore, to decrypt both incoming and outgoing classified messages by hand.

A loose-leaf notebook kept locked up in the safe of the cryptographic officer held a number of codes printed on chemically treated paper. It would readily burn—almost explode—if a match were applied.

Each day there was a new code. But the change did not follow the calendar. Rather, it occurred upon notification from RAAF Radio, Melbourne. In other words, a code might be valid for eighteen hours, or twenty-six, or two, depending on when RAAF Radio, Melbourne, decided to change it.

The cryptographic officer's notebook also contained a number of codes for special use. A new set of these codes was sent in every two weeks by officer courier.

The RAAF Moresby Cryptographic Section consisted of a Flight Lieutenant and two Leading Aircraftsmen, RAAF. When the message came in from RAAF Radio Melbourne for Lieutenant Commander Eric Feldt, RANVR, these men were frankly annoyed. Now that action against the Japanese on New Guinea was finally getting in gear, they had enough work as it was without having to handle the classified traffic for a goddamned sailor and his motley command—four American Marines and a Bushman wearing a RAN Petty Officer's uniform.

So they decrypted the Commander's message as far as his name and address, and stopped there. It was their intention to let the rest of it wait until they'd taken care of the regular traffic. But that idea didn't work out. Air Commodore Sir Howard Teeghe, Commanding RAAF Moresby (his rank was equivalent to Brigadier, Commonwealth Ground Forces and Brigadier General, U.S. Army and Marine Corps), made the first visit anyone could remember to RAAF Moresby Cryptographic Section and informed the Lieutenant that Commander Feldt was expecting some rather important material. Whenever that came, Air Commodore Teeghe said, he'd be grateful if they got right on it.

While the Air Commodore waited, the Lieutenant himself decrypted the rest of the message and handed it to him:

MOST URGENT
MELBOURNE 1250 7TH OCTOBER NUMBER 212
FROM ADMIRALTY MELBOURNE
VIA RAAF MELBOURNE
FOR OFFICER COMMANDING RAAF MORESBY

MOST SECRET

START
PART ONE

INFORMATION TO LT COMMANDER E. FELDT RANVR
PART TWO
START FOLLOWING FROM BANNING:
SUB A
SWIMMER WITH PATIENCE AS OF 1010 7OCT
SUB B
GREYHOUND DEPARTED STATION ABLE 1110M ETA STATION BAKER
1700M RPT 1700M
SUB C STATION C COORDINATES 06 13 21 XXXX 14 16 07 RPT 06 13
21 XXXX 14 16 07
SUB D RENDEZVOUS STATION C 0550M 9 OCT RPT 0550M 9 OCT
END FROM BANNING
PART THREE
ADVISE ADMIRALTY MOST URGENT SIGNAL
SUB A ON ARRIVAL GREYHOUND
SUB B READINESS TO EFFECT SCHEDULED RENDEZVOUS
SUB C CAUSE OF AND EXPECTED TIME OF REMEDY ANY DELAY
SUB D ON DEPARTURE GREYHOUND FOR STATION C
SUB E RETURN OF GREYHOUND TO STATION B
BY AUTHORITY: SOAMES-HALEY, VICE ADM RAN
END

When the R4D with MARINES lettered along the side of its fuselage made a low approach from the sea and touched down smoothly, Lieutenant Commander Eric Feldt, RANVR, was standing outside RAAF Moresby Base Operations. It was 1655 hours (Melbourne Time).

A BSA motorcycle with a sidecar onto which a FOLLOW ME sign had been bolted led the R4D to a sandbag revetment. The driver signaled the aircraft where to shut down, then a ground crew appeared and manhandled the airplane into the revetment.

The rear door opened and a ladder was lowered. Once that was done, Major Jake Dillon climbed down.

"Hello, Jake," Feldt said. "How are you, old man?"

It was not the profane and/or obscene greeting Dillon expected.

"Can't complain, Eric. Yourself?"

Captain Charley Galloway appeared and climbed down the ladder.

"Captain Galloway, Commander Feldt," Dillon said.

Galloway saluted.

"You're the Coastwatcher commander, Commander?" Galloway asked.

Feldt nodded.

"A lot of people where I come from have a lot of respect for your people, Commander," Charley said.

Feldt looked uncomfortable.

"I hope you had a good flight," he said after a moment. Then he put out his hand to Second Lieutenant Malcolm S. Pickering as he turned from climbing down the ladder. "My name is Feldt, Lieutenant. Welcome to Port Moresby."

"Thank you, Sir."

"Is the aircraft all right, Captain?"

"It ran like a Swiss watch, Sir. I'd like to go over it before we leave, of course."

"There's plenty of time for that. You're not due at Buka until six the day after tomorrow. Major Banning sent some steaks and whiskey. The rest of the lads are guarding it from the RAAF boys. I've got a car whenever you're ready."

MOST URGENT
RAAF MORESBY 1705 7TH OCTOBER NUMBER 107
FROM OFFICER COMMANDING RAAF MORESBY
FOR ADMIRALTY MELBOURNE FOR VICE ADMIRAL SOAMES-HALEY
VIA RAAF MELBOURNE

MOST SECRET

START
PART ONE
REFERENCE YOUR 212 7 OCT PART THREE SUB A: 1655M RPT 1655M
PART TWO
REFERENCE YOUR 212 7 OCT PART THREE SUB B: NO RPT NO PROB-
LEM ANTICIPATED
END
FELDT LT COMM RANVR

(FOUR)
Flight Operations Briefing Room
Royal Australian Air Force Station
Port Moresby, New Guinea
1800 Hours 8 October 1942

The four Marines and the RANVR Signalman First who were to land on Buka, along with Major Jake Dillon, Captain Charles M. Galloway, and Lieutenant M. S. Pickering, were sprawled in chairs in the small, airless, steaming hot room. Most of them clutched beer bottles.

"I rather doubt if any of you people are sober enough to understand any of this, but permit me to go through the motions," Lieutenant Commander Feldt said.

Their laughter sounded just a bit forced.

"The last word we had from Ferdinand Six was at 9:55 this morning. Chief Wallace reports that the party that will carry the supplies up to Ferdinand Six from the beach, and the people who are being extracted, all departed at noon yesterday, that is, 7 October. Using as a guide the time it took Wallace to get from the beach to Ferdinand Six, it should take them about thirty hours to reach the beach. That means, barring any trouble, they should be getting there right about now.

"Of course they may not have been able to move as quickly as Wallace did alone. We don't know what shape Reeves, Howard, and Koffler are in. That may delay them. On the other hand, since they know where they were going, and Wallace had to look for Ferdinand Six, they may have got to the beach hours ago. Either way, we have just about twelve hours in the schedule to take care of the unexpected; the pickup is scheduled for ten minutes to six tomorrow morning.

"There are several potential problems. One is that they will run into our Nipponese friends; that could delay them beyond the twelve-hour cushion—"

"Or forever," one of the Marines said.

There was more forced laughter.

"Thank you ever so much, Sergeant, for that encouraging observation," Feldt said.

The sergeant held up his beer bottle.

"My pleasure, Commander."

"If I may continue?"

"Certainly, Sir."

"Or, as you have so cleverly deduced, Sergeant, it could well keep them from reaching the beach at all," Feldt said. "Second, since we were unable to land a Hallicrafters through the surf, the only radio now on the beach is the hand-held, battery-powered voice radio. That has a limited range and a limited battery life.

"In other words, Captain Galloway can't use that radio as a radio direction-finder; it's not powerful enough. Thus he'll have to find the beach on his own. If—and when—he finds it, he'll attempt to contact the beach, code name Greyhound Base, by radio.

"Now, if the radio is working, the officer in charge there, Lieutenant McCoy, will radio—"

"Sir, what if he's not on the beach?" another Marine sergeant asked; he sounded both very concerned and completely sober. "I thought he was supposed to go to Ferdinand Six. And you just said that they may not make it back to the beach."

"Sorry, I should have got into that. When they landed from the sub, they decided that Wallace could make better time to Ferdinand Six traveling alone. So Lieutenant McCoy stayed with Sergeant Hart."

"Did you say McCoy?" Pick Pickering asked.

"Yes, I did."

"Is he one of your people?" Pick asked.

"As a matter of fact, Lieutenant, no, he is not. He's sort of a rubber-boat expert they sent from Washington."

"Is that Killer McCoy?"

"Yes, but when you meet him, Lieutenant, I strongly suggest that you do not so address him."

"Aye, aye, Sir," Pick said.

"You know this guy?" Charley Galloway asked; they were sitting together.

"We went through OCS Quantico," Pick said.

Galloway shrugged.

"If I may continue?" Felt asked sarcastically. "As I was saying, if the battery-powered radio is working, the beach will communicate with the aircraft. If it is not working, McCoy has two signal panels, one red, meaning Do Not Attempt Landing, and one blue, meaning the beach is Safe to Land. If they display the red panel, the Hallicrafters aboard will be kicked out of the airplane into the water. If we're lucky, their packaging will float them and they will be washed ashore. The aircraft will then return here."

"I'm willing to jump in, Commander," the sober-sounding sergeant said.

"We all are," the other sergeant said, the one who obviously had had one or two more bottles of beer than his metabolism could handle.

"We considered that and decided against it," Feldt said. "You will return here so we can try this again. Clear? I don't want any heroics out there."

There was no reply.

"What I am waiting for, gentlemen, is an acknowledgment of that order."

"Aye, aye, Sir," the two sergeants said. Feldt looked at the other three members of the team and waited for them to say, "Aye, aye, Sir."

"If the green panel is displayed, the aircraft will land," Feldt said. "The radios and other supplies will be off-loaded, Reeves, Howard, and Koffler will be taken aboard, and the aircraft will depart."

"What happens to the two guys on the beach?" one of the Marines asked, "if the airplane can't land?"

"They're fucked," the drinking sergeant said.

"They will remain in position for seventy-two hours if they wish," Feldt said matter-of-factly. "In case we can restage the landing. At the end of seventy-two hours they will make their way to Ferdinand Six."

"Like I said, they're fucked," the drinking sergeant said.

"That will be quite enough, thank you, Sergeant," Feldt said. "If the people from Ferdinand Six are on the beach, they will of course lead everybody back there. If they are not there, the landing team, plus Lieutenant McCoy and Sergeant Hart, will carry one of the Hallicrafters and the equipment in bags marked with red tags and make for Ferdinand Six. The other equipment will be concealed somewhere near the beach for pickup at a later time. We've been over all this, of course, in great detail before.

"Are there any questions?"

There were none.

"There is one case of beer left, plus a few other bottles. When that's gone, that's it. My advice is try to get some sleep. We'll wake you at 0100. There will be breakfast, the rest of the steak and eggs, and then you will board the aircraft. I remind you there is only a bucket aboard the aircraft for bowel movements, and that can get messy. So try to take care of that before you get on the airplane.

"I thank you for your kind attention, and please be generous when the hat is passed."

There was more laughter. This time some of it seemed genuine.

(FIVE)
North Philadelphia Station
Pennsylvania Railroad
Philadelphia, Pennsylvania
0915 Hours 9 October 1942

"That must be him, Lieutenant," Sergeant Howard J. Doone, USMC, said to First Lieutenant J. Bailey Chambers, USMC, discreetly pointing down the platform to a Brigadier General of The U.S. Marine Corps who had just stepped from the train.

Lieutenant Chambers moved quickly down the platform, saluted, and inquired, "General Pickering, Sir?"

Fleming Pickering returned the salute.

"Admiral Ashworth's compliments, Sir," Lieutenant Chambers said.

"My compliments to the Admiral," Pickering said. "We have a car?"

"Yes, Sir."

"Do you know where to find Tatamy, Sergeant?" General Pickering asked.

"Yes, Sir. It's a small town just north of Easton. About sixty-five, seventy miles, Sir."

"Let's go, then," Pickering said. "Where's the car?"

"The General's traveling alone?"

"My aide is otherwise occupied, Lieutenant. Let's go."

"Aye, aye, Sir."

Mrs. Ellie Stecker heard the car door slam. She pushed aside the lace curtain and watched a Marine brigadier general get out of the backseat before the driver could run around the front and open it for him.

Oh, dear God, please no!

She heard footsteps on the narrow wooden porch of the row house, and then the twisting of the doorbell.

If I don't answer it, it won't be happening.

The Brigadier General had his cover tucked under his arm when she pulled the door open.

"Mrs. Ellie Stecker, please. My name is Pickering."

"I am Mrs. Stecker."

"Mrs. Stecker, I'm afraid I—"

"Dick? Or my husband?"

"Dick. He's been in a crash."

"Is he alive?"

"Yes, Ma'am," Pickering said.

Thank you, God!

"How bad?" she asked.

"He's rather badly hurt, I'm afraid," Pickering said.

"What, exactly, General, does that mean?"

Pickering reached in his pocket and handed her a sheet of paper.

URGENT

FROM HQ FIRST MARDIV 1130 6OCT42

TO COMMANDANT USMC

    WASHINGTON DC

    FOLLOWING PERSONAL FOR BRIG GEN FLEMING PICKERING USMC

    REGRET TO ADVISE THAT 2ND LT RICHARD J STECKER USMC SERIOUSLY INJURED PLANE CRASH TODAY X OFFICIAL NOTIFICATION WILL FOLLOW X IF POSSIBLE WOULD APPRECIATE YOUR RELAYING ELLIE MY DEEP REGRET AND OFFER ANY HELP NEEDED X JACK SAW HIM BEFORE AIR EVACUATION ESPIRITU SANTO THENCE NAVY HOSPITAL PEARL HARBOR X PROGNOSIS FULL RECOVERY X YOUNG STECKER AND YOUR BOY BOTH ACES AND FINE MARINES X REGARDS X VANDERGRIFT

    END PERSONAL GENERAL VANDERGRIFT TO GENERAL PICKERING

"That was very kind of General Vandergrift," Ellie Stecker said, "and of you, General, to come here with this."

"Jack and I are old friends," Pickering said. "And I'm fond of Dick, too."

"Oh, my God, I didn't put that together. You're Pick's father, of course. But I thought you were a captain in the Navy?"

"That was a mistake that was straightened out," Pickering said. "By the time you get to California, we should have more specific word for you on exactly what happened."

"I don't understand."

"Arrangements have been made to fly you to Pearl Harbor," Pickering said.

"How can that be done?" she asked.

"It's done," Pickering said. "One of my officers will have the details worked out by the time we get back to Philadelphia."

"It wouldn't be fair to the other wives and mothers—"

"The Commandant seems to feel, Ellie, that someone who has put as many years into The Corps as you have is entitled to a little special treatment."

When he telephoned Walter Reed with Vandergrift's message, the Commandant's precise words were, "You seem to have a lot of influence, Pickering. Why don't you use some of it to get Jack's wife out to Hawaii to be with her boy?"

"Oh, I don't know how I could—"

"Nonsense," Pickering said. "This won't be the first time you've picked up and gone somewhere on no notice at all."

She looked at him.

"No," she said finally, "it won't. I'll throw some things in a bag."

(SIX)

MOST URGENT
RAAF MORESBY 0410 9TH OCTOBER NUMBER 21
FROM OFFICER COMMANDING RAAF MORESBY
FOR ADMIRALTY MELBOURNE FOR VICE ADMIRAL SOAMES-HALEY
VIA RAAF MELBOURNE

MOST SECRET

START
PART ONE
REFERENCE YOUR 212 7 OCT PART THREE SUB D: 0315M RPT 0315M
END
FELDT LT COMM RANVR

It began to grow light a little after five. Captain Charles M. Galloway, who was flying, reached over and touched the sleeve of his copilot, who was dozing. His arms were folded on his chest; his head was tilted to one side.

He woke startled.

"Go back and find somebody to come up here," Galloway ordered.

Pickering nodded, unstrapped his seat and shoulder belts, and went back into the cabin. He returned with the Marine sergeant who had given the Aussie Naval officer all the trouble during the briefing. He looked—and was—more than a little hung over.

Galloway waited until Pickering had strapped himself back in.

"You have the aircraft, Mr. Pickering," he said, and then unstrapped himself and got up.

Pickering looked over his shoulder to see what Galloway was up to.

Galloway unfolded the step that let you stand and take navigational observations through the Plexiglas dome on top of the fuselage. Then he installed the hung-over sergeant on it, facing to the rear.

He returned to his seat and strapped himself back in.

"What was that all about?"

"I don't know what I'll do if it happens," Galloway said. "But if we are spotted by a curious Japanese, I think it would be nice to know it before he starts shooting."

"I'm sorry I asked," Pickering said.

(SEVEN)
Approximately 40 miles South of Cape Hanpan
Buka, Solomon Islands
0550 Hours 9 October 1942

The call came in loud and clear over Pickering's earphone; he even recognized the voice:

"Greyhound, Greyhound, this is Greyhound Base. Over."

"I'll be damned," Captain Charley Galloway said.

Pickering picked up his microphone.

"This is Greyhound. Read you five by five. Over."

"Greyhound, I have you in sight. You are approximately two miles south. Over."

"Shit!" Charley Galloway said and pushed the nose of the R4D down.

"Understand two miles. Winds, please? Over."

"The wind is from the north. About ten knots. Over."

"Understand north, ten knots. Over."

"I suppose if there was something wrong with the beach, he would have said so," Galloway said as he began to retard the throttles.

"Yeah, I think he would have," Pickering said. "But let's check."

"How's the sand down there, Killer? Over."

"Condition Two. Repeat Condition Two. Over."

"Thank you, Killer. Please make a piss call before boarding."

Galloway glanced at him and smiled before ordering, "Twenty degrees flaps. Put the wheels down."

A moment later Pickering said, "Twenty degrees flaps. Gear extended."

"OK, here goes," Galloway said.

Just before he eased back on the stick to put the tail wheel on the ground, two men with arms waving jumped out of the foliage onto the beach. By the time Charley Galloway very carefully stopped the R4D, turned it around, and taxied back to them, they had been joined by what looked like twenty others; most of them wore loincloths and had bushy hair.

Less than five minutes later, Lieutenant K. R. McCoy came into the cockpit.

"Everybody is aboard, Sir," he said to Galloway, "and the door is secure."

"How goes it, Killer?" Lieutenant Pickering asked.

"Fuck you, Pickering, you know how I feel about that Killer shit!"

"I guess you two know each other," Charley Galloway said, as he put his hand to the throttle quadrant and shoved them forward to TAKEOFF POWER.

(EIGHT)
U.S. Army Air Corps B-17E Tail Number 11354
17,500 Feet
Off West Coast, Bougainville, Solomon Islands
0805 Hours 9 October 1942

"What the hell is that down there?" Second Lieutenant Harry Aaronson, the bombardier, inquired over the intercom.

"Down where, for Christ's sake, Aaronson?" First Lieutenant Joseph Wall, the Aircraft Commander, replied.

"At maybe eight, nine thousand, two o'clock."

"I can't see it," Wall replied.

"It looks like a C-47," First Lieutenant Thomas Killian, the copilot, said.

"What the fuck would a C-47 be doing up here? That must be a Jap bomber or something."

Wall banked the airplane to the right and put the nose down so that he could see.

"That's a C-47," he pronounced with finality and straightened the airplane up.

"Then it would have to be a Japanese C-47," Killian argued. "Nobody on our side could be *that* lost. And the Japs don't *have* any C-47s."

"The Japanese have L2Ds," Lieutenant Wall announced. "They stole the C-47 blueprints and they build them in Japan."

"Bullshit," Lieutenant Harry Aaronson said. "You couldn't get all the blueprints for an airplane in a boxcar."

"Well," Lieutenant Wall said slowly, having never considered that before, "the Japs had L2Ds that are C-47s, and that's one of them."

"Let's go shoot the sonofabitch down," Lieutenant Aaronson said.

Lieutenant Wall's orders—for the flight the day before yesterday, for the flight today, and probably for the flight the day after tomorrow—were to conduct an aerial observation of the west coast of Bougainville Island. During these observations they would take aerial photographs of a list of topographic features and of any naval activity in the waters adjacent thereto. They were not carrying any bombs—which frankly struck Lieutenant Wall as a pretty goddamned silly way to make war.

On the other hand, shooting down an unarmed Japanese airplane didn't seem right. *Fuck it, Remember Pearl Harbor!*

"I don't want one shot fired until I say so, you got that?"

He put his hand to the throttle quadrant to take power off and pushed the nose of the airplane down.

"The sonofabitch *is* lost," Lieutenant Aaronson said. "That's one of ours. Shit! It says 'Marines' on the fuselage."

"I didn't know the Marines had C-47s," Lieutenant Killian said.

"They don't, that's a mirage, you asshole."

"Tom, see if you can raise them on the radio," Lieutenant Wall said to Lieutenant Killian.

"Captain," Sergeant George Hart reported, "there's a B-17 behind us."

"A *B-17?*"

"Yeah. I think. I never heard of a Japanese plane with four engines."

"*I* have," Galloway said and unstrapped himself to have a look.

"Oh, shit!" Lieutenant Pickering said.

It was not possible to establish radio communication between the two aircraft, but the navigator of the B-17 made a sign with a question mark and an arrow on it and gave it to Lieutenant Killian. He held it in the window so the pilot of the transport could read it.

He nodded, and in a moment a sign appeared in the pilot's window of the transport plane: MORESBY.

Another sign was prepared in the B-17.

ON OUR WAY. WANT COMPANY?

Whereupon the pilot of the Marine transport enthusiastically smiled and shook his head up and down in the affirmative.

(NINE)
Mercy Forward
Brisbane, Australia
1130 Hours 11 October 1942

"Hello, Steve," Daphne Farnsworth said. "How are you feeling?"
My God, he looks awful!

"I'm all right. How you doing?"

"I'm fine, thank you," Daphne said. She thrust a box of candy at him.

He's one ulcerous sore from his shoulders to his fingers!

"Thank you."

"I would have brought you some whiskey, but Barbara said they meant it; with the medicine they're giving you, it would make you sick."

"You mean the worm medicine," he furnished helpfully.

"I suppose."

"Doctor Whatsisname said—"

"Colonel Godofski?"

"Yeah. He said it was poison. That was the only way to get rid of them."

"He said you'll be well soon," Daphne said.

"So how come you're wearing a dress?"

"I'm out of the Navy," Daphne said.

"No fooling? How come?"

"It's not important," Daphne said, wanting to tell him.

"Just curious, that's all. I thought you had to join up for the Duration Plus Six Months, like you do in The Corps."

"I'm going to have a baby," Daphne said. *Well, there, it's out.*

"Oh," Steve said.

"That's why I'm out of the Navy."

"Yeah, sure. Who's the father? You married some Australian guy, right?"

"I'm not married, Steve."

"Why the hell not?"

Daphne shrugged.

"The sonofabitch won't marry you? What the hell is the matter with him? You give me a couple of days to get out of this goddamned hospital, and I'll fix his ass all right."

"He didn't know about the baby," Daphne said. "He was away."

"When did he get back?"

"Yesterday," Daphne said.

He looked at her for a long moment until she could bring herself to meet his eyes, and he saw the answer in them.

"No shit, just that once?"

"It wasn't just once," Daphne said.

"You know what I mean," Steve said. "Well, what do you know about that?"

Daphne averted her eyes.

"I don't want you to feel that you have any obligation, any responsibility," Daphne said.

There was no reply and she forced herself to look at him. He had his lower lip under his teeth, and his body was shaking, and tears ran down his cheeks.

"Steve, what's the matter?"

"I thought I was never going to get off that fucking island, and now I'm going to have a baby!"

And then the sobbing came, and she went to him and put her arms around him, and he put his arms around her, and it didn't matter that they were ulcerous from his shoulders to his wrists.

CLOSE COMBAT

I

(ONE)
Henderson Field
Guadalcanal, Solomon Islands
0515 Hours 11 October 1942

First Lieutenant William Charles Dunn, USMCR, glanced up at the Pagoda through the scarred Plexiglas windshield of his battered, mud-splattered, bullet-holed Grumman F4F4 Wildcat. The Henderson Field control tower didn't look like a pagoda, but Dunn had never heard the Japanese-built, three-story frame building called anything else.

A tanned, bare-chested Marine stepped onto the narrow balcony of the Pagoda, pointed his signal lamp at the Wildcat on the threshold of the runway, and flashed Dunn a green.

Captain Bruce Strongheart, fearless commanding officer of the Fighting Aces Squadron, carefully adjusted his silk scarf and then nodded curtly to Sergeant Archie O'Malley, his happy-go-lucky, faithful crew chief. O'Malley saluted crisply, and Captain Strongheart returned it just as crisply. Then, adjusting his goggles over his steel-blue eyes, his chin set firmly, not a hair of his mustache out of place, he pushed the throttle forward. His Spad soared off the runway into the blue. Captain Strongheart hoped that today was the day he would finally meet the Blue Baron in mortal aerial combat. The Blue Baron, Baron Eric von Hassenfeffer, was the greatest of all German aces. With a little bit of luck, he would shoot down the Blue Baron (in a fair fight, of course) and be back at the aerodrome in time to share a champagne luncheon with Nurse Helen Nightingale.

Dunn was twenty-one years old. He hadn't shaved in two days, or had a shower in three. He was wearing: a sweat-stained cloth flight helmet, with the strap unbuckled and the goggles resting on his forehead; an oil- and sweat-stained cotton Suit, Flying, Tropical Climates; a T-shirt with a torn collar; a pair of boxer shorts held in place with a safety pin (the elastic band had long ago collapsed); ankle-high boots known as "boondockers"; and a .45 Colt automatic in a shoulder holster.

Dunn, who was (Acting) Commanding Officer of USMC Fighter Squadron VMF-229, looked around to check whether all of his subordinates had made it out of the revetments to the taxi strip, or to the runway. There was a Wildcat on the runway, sitting almost parallel with him (First Lieutenant Ted Knowles, who had arrived from Espíritu Santo four days before). Five more Wildcats were on the taxiway.

Seven in all, representing one hundred percent of the available aircraft of VMF-229, were prepared to soar off into the wild blue. According to the table of organization and equipment, VMF-229 should have had fourteen F4F4s.

Dunn then looked at his faithful crew chief, Corporal Anthony Florentino, USMC—three weeks older than he was. Florentino had developed the annoying habit of crossing the taxiway and standing at the side of the runway to bid his commanding officer farewell. When Dunn's eyes caught his, he smiled and made a thumbs-up gesture.

I wish to Christ he wouldn't do that.

Tony Florentino had large expressive eyes; it wasn't hard for Dunn to see what he was thinking: *This time the Lieutenant's not coming back.*

He's not questioning my flying skill, Dunn was aware, *but he knows the laws of probability. Of the original sixteen pilots who came to Guadalcanal with VMF-229, only two are left—me and the Skipper, Captain Charles M. Galloway. Of the twenty-two replacement pilots flown in from Espíritu Santo, only nine remain.*

You can't reasonably expect to go up day after day after day and expect to survive— not against enemies who not only outnumber you, but are flying, with far greater experience, the Zero, a fighter plane that is faster and more agile than the Wildcat.

Dunn glanced at Ted Knowles and nodded, signaling that he was about to take off. Then he looked at Tony Florentino again and made an OK sign with his left hand. After that he took the brakes off and pushed the throttle forward.

For Christ's sake, Tony, please don't do that Catholic crossing-yourself-in-the-presence-of-death crap until I'm out of sight.

Lieutenant Dunn, glancing back, saw that Lieutenant Knowles was beginning his takeoff roll. Then he saw Corporal Florentino crossing himself.

He dropped his eyes to the manifold pressure gauge. He was pulling about thirty inches. The airspeed indicator jumped to life, showing an indicated sixty knots. He was pulling just over forty inches of manifold pressure when he felt the Wildcat lift into the air.

He took his right hand from the stick and grabbed the stick with the left. Then he put his free hand on the landing-gear crank to his right and started to wind it up. It took twenty-eight turns. The last dozen or so, as the wheels moved into their final stowed position, were *hard* turns. When he was finished, he was sweating.

Dunn put his right hand back on the stick and headed out over the water. In the corner of his eye, he saw Knowles slightly behind him.

When he was clear of the beach, he reached down and grabbed, in turn, each of the four charging handles for the .50 caliber Browning machine guns (these were mounted two to a wing). He reached up and flipped the protective cover from the GUNS master switch, then pulled on the stick-mounted trigger switch.

All guns fired. He was not surprised. VMF-229 had the best mechanics at Henderson. And these were under the supervision of Technical Sergeant Big Steve Oblensky, who'd been a Flying Sergeant when Bill Dunn was in kindergarten. Another Old Breed Marine, Gunnery Sergeant Ernie Zimmerman, took care of the weapons. Dunn was convinced that Zimmerman knew more about Browning machine guns than Mr. Browning did.

But he would not have been surprised either if there had been a hang-up . . . or two hang-ups, or four. This was the Cactus Air Force (from the code name in the Operations Order) of Guadalcanal, located on a tropical island where the humidity was suffocating, the mud pools were vast, and the population of insects of all sizes was awesome. Their airplanes were in large part made up of parts from other (crashed, bombed, or shot down) airplanes, and were subjected to daily stresses beyond the imaginations of their designers and builders. Flying them was more an art than a science. That anything worked at all was a minor miracle.

Reasonably sure that by now the rest of the flight was airborne, Dunn picked up his microphone and pressed the switch.

"Check your guns," he ordered. "Then check in."

It was not the correct radio procedure. Marine flight instructors back in the States would not have been pleased. Neither, for that matter, would commanding officers back at Ewa in Hawaii, or probably even at Espíritu Santo. But there was no one here to complain. Those addressed knew who was speaking, and what was required of them.

In the next few minutes, one by one, they checked in.

"Two, Skipper, I'm OK."

That was Knowles, on his wing.

"Seven, Sir, weaponry operable."

One of the new kids, thought twenty-one-year-old Bill Dunn, *yet to be corrupted by our shamefully informal behavior.*

"Three, Skipper."

"Six, OK."

"Five, Skipper."

There was a minute of silence. Dunn reached for his microphone.

"Four?"

"I've got three of them working."

"You want to abort? And try to catch up?"

"I'll go with three."

"Form on me, keep your eyes open," Dunn ordered. "And for Christ's sake watch your fuel!"

There was no response.

VMF-229 formed loosely on its commanding officer and proceeded in a northwest direction, climbing steadily. At 12,000 feet, Dunn got on the mike again.

"Oxygen time," he ordered.

(TWO)
1125 Hours 11 October 1942

Lieutenant Colonel Clyde W. Dawkins, USMC, Commanding Officer, Marine Air Group 21, set out to confer with the (acting) commanding officer of VMF-229. Dawkins was a career Marine out of Annapolis—a tanned, wiry man of thirty-five who somehow managed to look halfway crisp and military even in his sweat-soaked Suit, Flying, Tropical Climates.

He found Lieutenant Dunn engaged in his personal toilette. Dunn was standing naked under a fifty-five-gallon drum set up on two-by-fours behind the squadron office, a sandbag-walled tent. Water dribbling from holes punched in the bottom of what had been an AvGas fuel drum was not very efficiently rinsing soap from his body. Dunn's eyes were tightly closed; there was soap in them, and he was rubbing them with his knuckles.

Dunn was small and slight, five feet six or so, not more than 140 pounds; he had little body hair.

He's just a kid, Dawkins thought.

Six months before, the idea of a twenty-one-year-old not a year out of Pensacola even serving as an acting squadron commander would have seemed absurd to him.

But six months ago was before Midway, where this skinny blond kid had shot down two Japanese airplanes and then made it back home with a shot-out canopy and a face full of Plexiglas shards and metal fragments. And before Guadalcanal, where he had shot down five more Japanese.

The regulations were clear: Command of an organization was vested in the senior officer present for duty. And Bill Dunn was by no means the senior first lieutenant present for duty in VMF-229. He should not be carried on the books as executive officer (though in fact he was), much less should he have assumed command during the temporary absence of Captain Charles M. Galloway, USMCR.

But he was the best man available, not only in terms of flying skill, but as a leader. Dawkins had agreed with Galloway when the question had come up; *fuck the regulations, Dunn's the best man.*

This was the second time Dunn had assumed command of VMF-229. Six weeks before, Galloway had been shot down and presumed lost. When he heard the news, tears ran shamelessly down Dunn's cheeks. But the next morning, he led VMF-229 back into the air without complaining. If any doubt at all about the kid's ability to command VMF-229 had come up, Dawkins would have relieved him. But he did fine.

Meanwhile, Galloway's luck held . . . that time. A Patrol Torpedo boat plucked him from the sea, and he returned to duty. And then six days ago, on orders from Washington, Galloway went off on some mission that was both supersecret and—Dawkins inferred—superdangerous. It was entirely likely that he would not come back from it.

And so Dawkins was glad he had the skinny little hairless boy with the soap in his eyes to command VMF-229. He didn't look like one, but Lieutenant Bill Dunn was a fine Marine, a born leader, a warrior.

Dunn held his face up to the water dribbling from the fifty-five-gallon drum, then stepped to the side and wiped his face with a dirty towel. When he opened his eyes, he saw Colonel Dawkins.

"Be right with you, Skipper," he said.

"Take your time," Dawkins said.

Dunn pulled on a T-shirt and shorts. These didn't look appreciably cleaner than the ones he'd removed and tossed on a pile of sandbags. Then he pulled on a fresh flight suit. After that, he sat on the pile of sandbags and slipped on socks, then stuck his feet in his boondockers. Finally, he put the .45 in its shoulder holster across his chest.

When he was finished dressing, he looked at Dawkins.

"What happened to Knowles?" Dawkins asked.

"He got on the horn and said he was low on fuel, so I sent him back. Him and two others who were getting low themselves. We still had thirty, thirty-five minutes' fuel remaining."

"He almost made it," Dawkins said.

"Oblensky saw it. He told me he tried to stretch his dead-engine glide and didn't make it."

Technical Sergeant Oblensky had been a flying sergeant when Colonel Dawkins had been a second lieutenant. His professional opinion of the cause of the crash was at least as valid as anyone else's Dawkins could think of. He hadn't questioned it.

"He should have put it in the water," Dawkins said.

"He was trying to save the plane," Dunn said.

"What do we call it, 'pilot error'?"

"How about 'command failure'? I should have checked to make sure he wasn't running on the fumes."

"It wasn't your fault, Bill," Dawkins said.

Dunn met his eyes, but didn't respond directly.

"How is he?" Dunn asked. "That's why you're here, isn't it?"

"He died about five minutes ago."

"Shit! When I was over there, they told me they thought he would."

"They did everything they could for him."

"Yeah."

"What kind of shape are you in, Bill?"

"Me personally, or the squadron?"

"You personally, first, and then the squadron."

"Except for wishing Charley Galloway was here and not off Christ only knows where, playing whatever game he's playing, I'm all right."

"I'm sure it's not a game," Dawkins said, a hint of reproof in his voice. "That mission came right from Washington."

Dunn didn't reply.

"You're doing a fine job as squadron commander," Dawkins said.

"Squadron commanders write the next of kin," Dunn said. "I'm getting god-damned sick of that."

"I'll write Knowles's family. What is it, wife or parents?"

"He got married at P'Cola the day he graduated," Dunn said. "And heard last week that she's knocked up." He pressed his lips together, bitterly. "Sorry. That she's in the family way."

"I'll write her, Bill."

"No. I killed him. I'll write her."

"Damn it! You didn't kill him. He knew what the fuel gauge is for."

"And I should have known that he wouldn't turn back until he was ordered to turn back," Dunn said. "Which I would have done had I done my job and checked on his fuel."

"I'm not going to debate with you, Mr. Dunn," Dawkins said coldly, breaking the vow he made on the way from the hospital to VMF-229 to overlook Bill Dunn's habit of saying exactly what was on his mind, without regard to the niceties of military protocol.

"I will write Mrs. Knowles," Dunn said. "And since I am a coward, I will tell her that the father of her unborn child died doing his duty."

"You never know when to shut up, do you?" Dawkins flared. But he was immediately sorry for it.

Dunn met his eyes again, yet didn't reply.

"Nothing happened this morning?" Dawkins went on quickly. "You saw nothing up there?"

Dunn shook his head "no." "Dawn Patrol was a failure," he went on. "The Blue Baron declined the opportunity for a chivalrous duel in the sky."

Dawkins chuckled.

"I used to read *Flying Aces* too, when I was a kid," he said. "Who are you? Lieutenant Jack Carter?"

"Captain Bruce Strongheart," Dunn said with a smile. "Right now I'm getting dressed to have a champagne lunch with Nurse Nightingale."

"That wasn't her name," Dawkins said. "It was . . . Knight. Helen Knight."

"You *did* read *Flying Aces,* didn't you?" Dunn said, smiling.

"Yeah," Dawkins said. "I always wondered if Jack Carter ever got in her pants."

"I always thought she had the hots for Captain Strongheart. Beautiful women seldom screw the nice guy."

"Is that the voice of experience talking?"

"Unfortunately," Dunn said.

"They'll be back," Dawkins said, suddenly getting back to the here and now. "I wouldn't be surprised if in force. How's your squadron?"

"After Knowles, I'm down to five operational aircraft. By now, they should be refueled and rearmed. Tail number 107 is down with a bad engine. I don't think it will be ready anytime soon; maybe, just maybe, by tomorrow. Oblensky is switching engines. There are two in the boneyard he thinks he may be able to use."

"What happened to the engine?"

"Well, not only was it way overtime, but it really started to blow oil. I listened to it. I don't think it would make it off the runway. I redlined it for engine replacement."

"They keep promising us airplanes."

"They promised me I would travel to exotic places and implied I would get laid a lot," Dunn said. "I don't trust them anymore."

"I'm giving them the benefit of the doubt," Dawkins answered. "I believe they're trying." His mouth curled into a small smile. "You don't think Guadalcanal is 'exotic'?"

"I was young then, Skipper. I didn't know the difference between 'exotic' and 'erotic.'"

Dawkins touched his arm. "You better get something to eat."

"The minute I start to eat, the goddamned radar will go off."

"Probably," Dawkins said.

This, Dawkins thought, *is where I'm supposed to say something reassuring. Or better, inspiring. Hell of a note that a MAG commander can't think of a goddamn thing reassuring or inspiring to say to one of his squadron commanders.*

He thought of something:

"When Galloway comes back, I'll lay three to one he comes with stuff to drink."

"If he comes back," Dunn said. "What odds are you offering about that?"

"He'll be back, Bill," Dawkins said, hoping his voice carried more conviction than he felt.

(THREE)

FROM: MAG-21 1750 11OCT42

SUBJECT: AFTER-ACTION REPORT
TO; COMMANDER-IN-CHIEF, PACIFIC, PEARL HARBOR
INFO: SUPREME COMMANDER SWPOA, BRISBANE
                    COMMANDANT, USMC, WASH, DC
   1. UPON RADAR DETECTION AT 1220 11OCT42 OF TWO FLIGHTS OF UNIDENTI-
FIED AIRCRAFT APPROX 140 NAUTICAL MILES MAG-21 LAUNCHED;
       A. EIGHT (8) F4F4 VF-5
       B. FIFTEEN (15) F4F4 VMF-121
       C. SIX (6) F4F4 VMF-223
       D. FIVE (5) F4F4 VMF-224
       E. FIVE (5) F4F4 VMF-229
       F. THREE (3) P40 67TH FIGHTER SQUADRON USAAC
       G. NINE (9) P39 67TH FIGHTER SQUADRON USAAC.

   2. VF-5 AND VMF-121 NO CONTACT.

   3. DUE TO INABILITY EXCEED 19,000 FEET WITH AVAILABLE OXYGEN EQUIP-
MENT USAAC AIRCRAFT MADE NO INITIAL CONTACT.

   4. AT 1255 11OCT42 REMAINING FORCE MADE CONTACT AT 25,000 FEET WITH
34 KATE REPEAT 34 KATE BOMBERS ESCORTED BY 29 ZERO REPEAT 29 ZERO
FIGHTERS APPROXIMATE 20 NAUTICAL MILES FROM HENDERSON FIELD.

   5. ENEMY LOSSES:
       A. NINE (9) KATE
KUNTZ, CHARLES M 1/LT USMC TWO (2)
MANN, THOMAS H JR 1/Lt USMCR TWO (2)

DUNN, WILLIAM C 1/LY USMCR ONE (1)
HALLOWELL, GEORGE L 1/LT USMCR TWO (2)
KENNEDY, MATTHEW H 1/LT USMCR (2)
    B. FOUR (4) ZERO
DUNN, WILLIAM C 1/LT USMCR ONE (1)
MCNAB, HOWARD T/SGT USMC (2)
ALLEN, GEORGE F 1/LT USMCR ONE (1)
    C. IN ADDITION, SHARPSTEEN, JAMES CAPT USAAC 67 USAAC FS DOWNED
ONE (1) KATE STRAGGLER.

   6. MAG-21 LOSSES:
    A. ONE (1) F4F4 CRASHED AT SEA. PILOT RECOVERED.
    B. ONE (1) F4F4 CRASHED ON LANDING, DESTROYED.
    C. THREE (3) F4F4 SLIGHTLY DAMAGED, REPAIRABLE.

   7. DUE TO CLOUD COVER REMAINING ENEMY FORCE COULD NOT SEE HENDER-
SON FIELD, BOMB LOAD DROPPED APPROXIMATELY FOUR NAUTICAL MILES TO
WEST. NO DAMAGE TO FIELD OR EQUIPMENT.

DAWKINS, CLYDE W LTCOL USMC COMMANDING

SECRET

(FOUR)
Henderson Field
Guadalcanal, Solomon Islands
0615 Hours 12 October 1942

As the Douglas R4D (the Navy/Marine Corps version of the twin-engine Douglas
DC-3) turned smoothly onto its final approach, the pilot, who had been both carefully
scanning the sky and taking a careful look at the airfield itself, suddenly put his
left hand on the control wheel and gestured with his right to the copilot to relinquish
control.

The lanky and (like nearly everyone else in that part of the world) tanned pilot
of the R4D was twenty-eight-year-old Captain Charles M. Galloway, USMCR—
known to his subordinates as either "The Skipper" or "The Old Man."

The copilot was a twenty-two-year-old Marine Corps second lieutenant whose
name was Malcolm S. Pickering. Everyone called him "Pick."

As Pick Pickering took his feet off the rudder pedals, he took his left hand from
the wheel and held both hands up in front of him, fingers extended, a gesture
indicating, *You've got it.*

I didn't have to take it away from him, Charley Galloway thought as he moved
his hand to the throttle quadrant. *His many other flaws notwithstanding, Pickering
is a first-rate pilot. More than that, he's that rare creature, a natural pilot.*

*So why did I take it away from him? Because no pilot believes any other pilot
can fly as well as he can? Or because I am functioning as a responsible commander,
aware that high on the long list of critically short matériel of war on Guadalcanal
are R4D airplanes. And consequently I am obliged to do whatever I can to make
sure nobody dumps one of them?*

He glanced over at Pickering to see if he could detect any signs on his face of a bruised ego. There were none.

Is that because he accepts the unquestioned right of pilots-in-command to fly the airplane, and that copilots can drive only at the pleasure of the pilot?

Or because he is a fighter pilot, and doesn't give a damn who flies an aerial truck, all aerial truck drivers being inferior to all fighter pilots?

Galloway made a last-second minor correction to line up with the center of the runway, then flared perfectly and touched down smoothly. The runway was rough. The landing roll took them past the Pagoda, the Japanese-built control tower, and then past the graveyard. There the hulks of shot-up, crashed, burned, and otherwise irreparably damaged airplanes waited until usable parts could be salvaged from them to keep other planes flying.

Where, Galloway thought, *Pickering can see the pile of crushed and burned aluminum that used to be the Grumman Wildcat, his buddy, First Lieutenant Dick Stecker, dumped on landing . . . and almost literally broke every bone in his body.*

Galloway carefully braked the aircraft to a stop, then turned it around and started to taxi back down the runway.

"You still want to turn your wings in for a rifle?" Galloway asked.

Pickering turned to look at him.

He didn't reply at first, taking so long that Galloway was suddenly worried what his answer might be.

"I was upset," Pickering said, meeting his eyes, "when I saw Stecker crash. If I can, I'd like to take back what I said then."

"Done," Galloway said, nodding his head. "It was never said."

"I did say it, Skipper," Pickering answered softly. "But I want to take it back."

"Pickering, they're short of R4D pilots. I'm an R4D IP"—an Instructor Pilot, with the authority to classify another pilot as competent to fly an R4D. "As far as I'm concerned, you're checked out in one of these. I'm sure there'd be a billet for you on Espíritu Santo."

"If that's my option, Captain," Pickering said, "then I will take the rifle. I'm a fighter pilot."

"It takes as much balls to fly this as it does a Wildcat," Galloway said.

"More. These things don't get to shoot back," Pickering said.

Galloway chuckled, then said, "Just to make sure you understand: I wasn't trying to get rid of you."

Pickering met his eyes again for a long moment.

"Thank you, Sir," he said.

(FIVE)

Corporal Robert F. Easterbrook, USMCR, was nineteen years old, five feet ten inches tall, and weighed 132 pounds (he'd weighed 146 when he came ashore on Guadalcanal two months and two days earlier). And he was pink skinned—thus perhaps understandably known to his peers as "Easterbunny." Easterbrook was sitting in the shade of the Henderson Field control tower, the Pagoda, when the weird R4D came in for a landing. It had normal landing gears, with wheels; but attached to all that was what looked like large skis. None of the other Marine and Navy R4Ds that flew into Henderson were so equipped.

"Holy shit!" he said to himself, and he thought: *That damned thing is back! I've got to get pictures of that sonofabitch.*

Twelve months before, Corporal Easterbrook had been a freshman at the University of Missouri, enrolled in courses known informally as "Pre-Journalism."

It had been his intention then to work hard and attain a high enough undergraduate grade-point average to ensure his acceptance into the University of Missouri Graduate School of Journalism. Later, with a Missouri J School diploma behind him, he could get his foot on the first rung of the ladder leading to a career as a photojournalist (or at least he'd hoped so).

He would have to start out on a small weekly somewhere and work himself up to a daily paper. Later—much later—after acquiring enough experience, he might be able to find employment on a national magazine ... maybe *Collier's* or the *Saturday Evening Post,* or maybe even *Look.* It was too much to hope that he would ever see his work in *Life* or *Time*—at least before he was old, say thirty or thirty-five. As the unquestioned best of their genre, these two magazines published only the work of the very finest photojournalists in the world.

On December 8, 1941, the day after the Japanese attack on Pearl Harbor, Bobby Easterbrook had gone down to the post office and enlisted in the United States Marine Corps Reserve for the Duration of the War Plus Six Months. He now regarded that as the dumbest one fucking thing he had ever done in his life,

Even though his photographic images had appeared in the past two months not only within the pages, but on the covers, of *Look* and *Time* and several dozen major newspapers, that success had not caused him to modify his belief that enlisting in The Crotch was the dumbest one fucking thing he had ever done in his life.

In fact, he'd concluded that the price of his photojournalistic success and minor fame—he'd been given credit a couple of times, USMC PHOTOGRAPH BY CPL R. F. EASTERBROOK, USMC COMBAT CORRESPONDENT—was going to be very high. Specifically, he was going to get killed.

There was reason to support this belief. Of the seven combat correspondents who had made the invasion, two were dead and three had been badly wounded.

In June 1942, the horror of boot camp at Parris Island still a fresh and painful memory, the Easterbunny had been a clerk in a supply room at the Marine Base at Quantico, Virginia.

He'd got that job after telling a personnel clerk that he had worked for the *Conner Courier.* That was true. During his last two years of high school, he'd worked afternoons and as long as it took on Fridays to get the *Courier* out.

When he talked with the personnel clerk, he implied that he'd been a reporter/photographer for the *Conner Courier.* That was not exactly true. Ninety-five percent of the photographic and editorial work on the *Conner Courier* (weekly, circ. 11,200) was performed by the owner and his wife. But Mr. Greene had shown Bobby how to work the *Courier's* Speed Graphic camera, and how to develop its sheet film, and how to print from the resultant negatives.

Still, the only words he wrote that actually appeared in print were classified ads taken over the telephone, and rewrites of Miss Harriet Comb's "Social Notes." Miss Combs knew everything and everyone worth knowing in Conner County, but she had some difficulty writing any of it down for publication. Complete sentences were not one of her journalistic strengths.

The personnel corporal appeared bored hearing about the Easterbunny's journalistic career ... until it occurred to him to ask if Private Easterbrook could type.

"Sure."

That pleased the corporal. The Corps did not at the moment need journalists, he told Private Easterbrook, but he would make note of that talent—a "secondary specialty"—on his records. What The Corps did need was people who could type.

Private Easterbrook was given a typing test, and then a "primary specialty" classification of clerk/typist.

Becoming a clerk/typist at least got him out of being a rifleman, Private Easterbrook reasoned—his burning desire to personally avenge Pearl Harbor having diminished to the point of extinction while he was at Parris Island.

He'd been kind of looking forward to a Marine Corps career as a supply man—with a little bit of luck, maybe eventually he'd make supply sergeant—when, out of the clear blue sky, at four o'clock one afternoon, he'd been told to pack his seabag and clear the company. He was being sent overseas. It wasn't until he was en route to Wellington, N.Z., aboard a U.S. Navy Martin Mariner, a huge, four-engine seaplane headed for Pearl Harbor, that he was able to begin to sort out what was happening to him.

He learned then that the Marine Corps had formed a team of still and motion picture photographers recruited from Hollywood and the wire services. They were to cover the invasion of a yet unspecified Japanese-occupied island. Just before they were scheduled to depart for the Pacific, one of the still photographers had broken his arm. Somehow Easterbrook's name—more precisely, his "secondary specialty"—had come to the attention of those seeking an immediate replacement for the sergeant with the broken arm. And he had been ordered to San Diego.

The team was under the command of former Hollywood press agent Jake Dillon—now Major Dillon, USMCR, a pretty good guy in Easterbrook's view. Genuinely sorry that the Easterbunny was not able to take the ordinary five-day leave prior to overseas movement, Major Dillon had thrown him a bone in the form of corporal's stripes.

Aboard the attack transport, the eight-man team (nine, counting Major Dillon) learned the names of the islands they were invading: Guadalcanal, Tulagi, and Gavutu, in the Solomons. No one else had ever heard of them before, either.

Major Dillon and Staff Sergeant Marv Kaplan, a Hollywood cinematographer Dillon had recruited, went in with the 1st Raider Battalion, in the first wave of landing craft to attack Tulagi. At about the same time, Corporal Easterbrook landed with the 1st Marine Parachute Battalion on Gavutu, two miles away.

The Marine parachutists didn't come in by air. They landed from the sea and fought as infantry, suffering ten percent casualties. After Gavutu was secured, the Easterbunny went to Tulagi. There Major Dillon handed him Staff Sergeant Kaplan's EyeMo 16mm motion picture camera and announced tersely that Kaplan had been evacuated after taking two rounds in his legs, and that Easterbrook was now a Still & Motion Picture Combat Correspondent.

He also relieved Easterbrook of the film he had shot on Gavutu. One of the pictures he took there—of a Marine paratrooper firing a Browning Automatic Rifle with blood running down his chest—was published nationwide.

Three days later, he crossed the channel with Dillon to Lunga Point on Guadalcanal, where the bulk of the First Marines had landed. There they learned that one of the two officers and two of the six enlisted combat correspondents had been wounded.

Shortly afterward, Dillon left Guadalcanal to personally carry the exposed still and motion film to Washington. Easterbrook hadn't heard news of him since then, though there was some scuttlebutt that he'd been seen on the island a couple of days ago. But the Easterbunny discredited that. If Dillon was on Guadalcanal again, he certainly would have made an effort to see who was left of the original team. That meant Lieutenant Graves, Technical Sergeant Petersen, and Corporal Easterbrook. In the two months since the invasion, everybody else had been killed or seriously wounded.

Looking at those numbers, Bobby Easterbrook had concluded a month or so ago that it was clearly not a question of if he would get hit, but when, and how seriously.

He had further concluded that when he did get hit, he'd probably be hit bad. Although it had been close more times than he liked to remember, so far he hadn't been scratched. The odds would certainly catch up with him.

All the same, since getting hit was beyond his control, he didn't dwell on it. Or tried not to dwell on it. . . . He kept imagining three, four, five—something like that—scenes where he'd get it. Sometimes, he could keep one or another of these out of his mind for as much as an hour.

He looked again at the weird R4D, glad at the moment for the diversion. "Holy shit!" he said again.

When the airplane first came to Henderson, he asked Technical Sergeant Big Steve Oblensky about it. The maintenance sergeant of VMF-229 was usually a pretty good guy; but that time Oblensky's face got hard and his eyes got cold, and he told him to butt the fuck out; if The Corps wanted to tell him about the airplane, they would send him a letter.

The Easterbunny pushed himself to his feet as the weird R4D, its unusual landing gear extended, turned on its final approach. He shot a quick glance at the sky, then held his hand out and studied the back of it. He'd come ashore with a Weston exposure meter, but that was long gone.

He set the exposure and shutter speed on his Leica 35mm camera to f11 at 1/100th second. He'd also come ashore with a Speed Graphic 4 × 5-inch view camera, but that too was long gone.

He shrugged his shoulder to seat the strap of his Thompson .45 ACP caliber submachine gun, so it wouldn't fall off, and took two exposures of the R4D as it landed and rolled past the Pagoda, and then another as it taxied back to it.

As he walked toward the aircraft, he noticed Big Steve Oblensky driving up in a jeep. Jeeps, like everything else on Guadalcanal, were in short supply. How Oblensky managed to get one—more mysteriously, how he managed to keep it—could only be explained by placing Oblensky in that category of Marine known as The Old Breed—i.e., pre-war Marines with twenty years or more of service. They operated by their own rules.

For instance, Bobby Easterbrook had taken at least a hundred photos of Old Breed Marines wearing wide-brimmed felt campaign hats in lieu of the prescribed steel helmet. None of the brass, apparently, felt it worthwhile to comment on the headgear, some of which the Easterbunny was sure was older than he was.

Another sergeant was in the jeep with Oblensky, a gunnery sergeant, a short, barrel-chested man in his late twenties; another Old Breed Marine, even though he was wearing a steel helmet. Oblensky was coverless (in The Corps, the Easterbunny had learned, headgear of all types was called a "cover") and bare-chested, except for a .45 ACP in an aviator's shoulder holster.

"Why don't you go someplace, Easterbunny, and do something useful?" Technical Sergeant Oblensky greeted him.

"Let me do my job, Sergeant, OK?"

Three months ago, I would never have dreamed of talking to a sergeant like that.

"You know this feather merchant, Ernie?" Technical Sergeant Oblensky inquired.

"Seen him around."

"Easterbunny, say hello to Gunny Zimmerman."

"Gunny."

"What do you say, kid?"

"Except that he keeps showing up where he ain't wanted, the Easterbunny's not as much of a candy-ass as he looks."

I have just been paid a compliment; or what for Big Steve Oblensky is as close to a compliment as I could hope for.

The rear door of the R4D started to open. Bobby Easterbrook put the Leica to his eye and waited for a shot.

First man out was a second lieutenant, whom the Easterbunny recognized as one of the VMF-229 Wildcat pilots. He was wearing a tropical-weight flight suit. It was sweat stained, but it looked clean. Even new.

That's unusual, the Easterbunny thought. *But what's really unusual is that an R4D like this is being flown by pilots from VMF-229, which is a fighter squadron. Why?*

Neither of the Old Breed sergeants in the jeep saluted, although the gunny did get out of the jeep.

"We got some stuff for the squadron," the Second Lieutenant said. "Get it out of sight before somebody sees it."

That put Oblensky into action. He started the jeep's engine and quickly backed it up to the airplane door. He took a sheet of canvas, the remnants of a tent, from the floor of the jeep, set it aside, and then climbed into the airplane. A moment later, he started handing crates to Zimmerman.

Very quickly, the jeep was loaded—overloaded—with crates of food. One, now leaking blood, was marked BEEF, FOR STEAKS 100 LBS KEEP FROZEN. And there were four cases of quart bottles of Australian beer and two cases of whiskey.

Oblensky and Zimmerman covered all this with the sheet of canvas, and then Oblensky got behind the wheel and drove quickly away.

Another officer, this one a first lieutenant, climbed down from the cargo door of the airplane; and he was immediately followed by a buck sergeant. They were wearing khakis, and web belts with holstered pistols, and both had Thompson submachine guns slung from their shoulders.

Gunny Zimmerman walked up and saluted. The Easterbunny got a shot of that, too. When the Lieutenant heard the click of the shutter, he turned to give him a dirty look with cold eyes.

Fuck you, Lieutenant. When you've been here a couple of days, you'll understand this isn't Parris Island, and we don't do much saluting around here.

The Lieutenant returned Gunny Zimmerman's salute, and then shook his hand.

"Still alive, Ernie?" the Lieutenant asked.

"So far," Gunny Zimmerman replied.

"Say hello to George Hart," the Lieutenant said, and then turned to the sergeant. "Zimmerman and I were in the 4th Marines, in Shanghai, before the war."

"Gunny," Sergeant Hart said, shaking hands.

"You were in on this?" Zimmerman asked, with a nod in the direction of the weird airplane.

"I couldn't think of a way to get out of it," Sergeant Hart said.

The Lieutenant chuckled.

"I volunteered him, Ernie," he said.

"You do that to people," the gunny said. "Lots of people think you're dangerous."

"Dangerous is something of an understatement, Gunny," Sergeant Hart said.

The Lieutenant put up both hands in a mock gesture of surrender.

I read this lieutenant wrong. If he was a prick, like I thought, he wouldn't let either of them talk like that to him. And what's this "4th Marines in Shanghai before the war" business? He doesn't look old enough to have been anywhere before the war.

Now a major climbed down the ladder from the airplane. He was dressed in khakis like the Lieutenant, and he was wearing a pistol. The Easterbunny took his picture, too, and got another dirty look from cold eyes.

And then Major Jake Dillon climbed down. He was also in khakis, but he carried a Thompson, not a pistol; and he smiled when he saw him.

"Jake," the first Major said, and pointed to Corporal Easterbrook.

"Give me that film, Easterbrook," Major Dillon ordered.

The Easterbunny rewound the film into the cassette, then opened the Leica, took it out, and handed it to Major Dillon. Dillon surprised him by pulling the film from the cassette, exposing it, ruining it.

"This we don't want pictures of," Dillon said conversationally, then asked, "Where'd you get the Leica?"

"It's Sergeant Lomax's," Easterbrook replied. "It *was* Sergeant Lomax's. Lieutenant Hale took it when he got killed, and I took it from Hale when he got killed."

Major Dillon nodded.

"There's some 35mm film, color and black-and-white, in an insulated container on there," he went on, gesturing toward the airplane. "And some more film, and some other stuff. Take what you think you're going to need, and then give the rest to the Division's public relations people."

"Aye, aye, Sir."

"I want to talk to you, to everybody, but not right now. Where do you usually hang out?"

"With VMF-229, Sir."

"OK. See if you can locate the others, and don't get far away."

"Aye, aye, Sir."

Technical Sergeant Big Steve Oblensky came up in the now empty jeep.

Another face appeared in the door of the R4D. It was another one the Easterbunny recognized, the skipper of VMF-229, Captain Charles Galloway.

"Ski," he ordered, "take these officers to the Division CP, and then come back. There's stuff in here to be unloaded, and I want this serviced as soon as you can."

"Aye, aye, Sir," Tech Sergeant Oblensky said.

The two Majors and the Lieutenant with the cold eyes climbed into the jeep and it drove away.

Captain Galloway looked at Easterbrook, then asked conversationally (it was not, in other words, an order), "You doing anything important, Easterbunny, or can you lend us a hand unloading the airplane?"

"Aye, aye, Sir."

"You, too, Hart," Galloway said.

Captain Galloway and the other VMF-229 pilot, the Second Lieutenant, started to unload the airplane. His name, the Easterbunny now remembered, was Pickering.

II

When the jeep driven by Technical Sergeant Big Steve Oblensky drove up, Major General Alexander Archer Vandergrift was about to climb into his own jeep.

Vandergrift, the commanding general of the First Marine Division, and as such the senior American on Guadalcanal, was a tall, distinguished-looking man just starting to develop jowls. He was wearing mussed and sweat-stained utilities, boondockers, a steel helmet, and had a web belt with a holstered .45 1911A1 Colt pistol around his waist.

The three officers in the jeep stepped out quickly, and one by one rendered a salute. Vandergrift, who had placed his hand on the windshield of his jeep and was about to lift himself up, paused a moment until they were through saluting, then returned it. Then, almost visibly making up his mind not to get in his jeep and to delay whatever he intended to do, he walked toward them.

"Oblensky," General Vandergrift ordered conversationally, "get a helmet. Wear it."

"Aye, aye, Sir," Technical Sergeant Oblensky replied.

"Hello, Dillon."

"Good morning, Sir."

"Your operation go OK?"

"Yes, Sir."

"Can I interpret that to mean we can count on that team of Coastwatchers?"

"Yes, Sir. They're operational, with a new radio and a spare."

"And the men that were there?"

"Exhaustion and malnutrition, Sir. But they'll be all right."

"Is that what you wanted to see me about?"

"Yes, Sir. And Major Banning hoped you would have time for him."

Vandergrift looked closely and curiously at Major Edward J. Banning, concluding that there was something familiar about the stocky, erect officer, and that also suggested he was a professional. He offered his hand.

"I have the feeling we've met, Major. Is that so?"

"Yes, Sir. When you were in Shanghai before the war."

"Right," Vandergrift said, remembering: "You were the intelligence officer of the Fourth Marines, right?"

"Yes, Sir."

"What can I do for you, Major?"

"Sir, I'm here at the direction of General Pickering. Is there someplace . . . ?"

"We can go inside," Vandergrift said.

"Sir, you're not going to need me for this, are you?" the Lieutenant asked.

"No," Major Banning replied.

"I'd like to go see my brother," the Lieutenant said.

"Go ahead," Banning said.

"Where is your brother, Lieutenant?" Vandergrift asked.

"With the 1st Raider Battalion, Sir."

"My driver will take you," Vandergrift said. "But you can't keep the jeep."

"Thank you, Sir. No problem, I can get back on my own."

The Lieutenant saluted, and walked toward the jeep. Vandergrift gestured toward his command post, then led the others inside to what passed, in the circumstances, for his private office.

A sheet of tentage hung much like a shower curtain provided what privacy there was. Inside the curtained area was a U.S. Army Field Desk, a four-foot-square plywood box with interior shelves and compartments; its front opened to form a writing surface. It sat on a wooden crate with Japanese markings.

"One of your officers, Dillon?" Vandergrift asked as he pulled the canvas in place and waved them into two folding wooden chairs. He was obviously referring to the Lieutenant he'd just lent his jeep to. "I heard about Lieutenant Hale being killed. I thought there would be a replacement for him."

"One of General Pickering's officers, Sir," Banning replied.

"That's Killer McCoy, General," Major Dillon said.

"*That's* Killer McCoy?" Vandergrift replied, surprised. "I would have expected someone more on the order of Sergeant Oblensky."

"That's the Killer, Sir," Dillon said.

"I wish I'd known who he was," Vandergrift said. "I could have saved him a trip to the Raiders."

"Sir?" Banning asked, obviously concerned.

"If his brother is who I think he is, he was flown out of here the day before yesterday," Vandergrift said. When he saw the looks on their faces, he hastily added: "In near-perfect health. I'm surprised you don't know, Dillon. *Sergeant Thomas J. McCoy* was ordered back to the States by the Director of Public Affairs. They seem to think he can boost enlistments and sell war bonds. The press is calling him 'Machine Gun McCoy.'"

"I'd heard about that, Sir. It just slipped my mind."

"I could understand Sergeant McCoy being called 'Killer,'" Vandergrift said, shaking his head in a mixture of surprise and amusement. "Not only did I recommend him for the Navy Cross, for what he did on Edson's Ridge with his machine gun, but he's built like a tank and looks like he can chew nails. But that young man . . ."

"In his case, Sir, the Killer's looks can be deceiving," Banning said.

"What's he doing here?"

"I don't know how familiar you are with the Buka Operation, General?"

"The Marines operating the Buka Coastwatcher station were at the end of their rope, and you went in and replaced them?"

"Yes, Sir," Banning said. "McCoy set up the Buka operation for General Pickering. And went in with it. He went ashore from the sub before the plane got there. That was his second rubber-boat landing. He was on the Raider raid on Makin."

"He gets around, apparently," Vandergrift said, and then asked, "What's he going to do here?"

"He's returning to the States, Sir, via Espíritu Santo."

Vandergrift nodded, then, ending the casual conversation, said, "You say General Pickering sent you to see me, Major?"

"Yes, Sir," Banning said, then turned to Major Dillon. "Jake, will you excuse us, please?"

Dillon nodded, then pushed the canvas aside and left them alone.

General Vandergrift looked at Banning.

Banning took a sheet of flimsy paper from his shirt pocket and handed it to the General.

NOT LOGGED
ONE COPY ONLY
DUPLICATION FORBIDDEN
FOLLOWING IS DECRYPTION OF MSG 220107 RECEIVED 090942 2105 GREENWICH
FROM SECNAV WASHINGTON DC
TO SUPREME COMMANDER SWPOA
EYES ONLY MAJOR EDWARD BANNING USMC
SECNAV DESIRES THAT MAJOR BANNING
   [1] PREPARE AN ANALYSIS OF JAPANESE INTENTIONS AND CAPABILITIES RE-
GARDING GUADALCANAL BASED ON ALL INTELLIGENCE AVAILABLE TO HIM AND
HIS STAFF
   [2] PERSONALLY OBTAIN FROM COMGEN 1ST MARINE DIVISION HIS EVALUA-
TION OF HIS CAPABILITIES TO COUNTER THREAT, YOU ARE DIRECTED TO MAKE
YOUR ANALAYSIS[[1] ABOVE] AVAILABLE TO COMGEN 1ST MARDIV.
   [3] PROCEED TO PEARL HARBOR T.H. WHERE BOTH ANALYSES WILL BE TRANS-
MITTED VIA SPECIAL TRANSMISSION FACILITIES TO SECNAV EYES ONLY BRIG
GEN FLEMING PICKERING USMCR WHO WILL BRIEF SECNAV
   [4] BE PREPARED, IF SO ORDERED, TO PROCEED FROM PEARL HARBOR, T.H.,
TO WASHINGTON DC TO PERSONALLY BRIEF SECNAV.
   [5] SECNAV ND GEN FLEMING WISH TO STATE THEIR UNDERSTANDING OF
SENSITIVITY OF THIS ASSIGNMENT AND TO EXPRESS COMPLETE CONFIDENCE
IN GENERAL VANDEGRIFTS AND MAJOR BANNINGS DISCRETION

BY DIRECTION SECNAV
HAUGHTON, CAPT USN
EXECUTIVE ASSISTANT TO SECNAV

General Vandergrift read the message, looked at Banning, then read the message again.

"Very interesting," he said. When Banning didn't reply, Vandergrift added, "Are you going to tell me what this is all about, Banning?"

Banning looked uncomfortable.

"Sir, I think it's right there. I don't like to speculate. . . ."

"Speculate," Vandergrift ordered, softly but sharply.

"Sir, is the General aware of General Pickering's mission when he was here before?"

"You mean, here on Guadalcanal? Or in the Pacific?"

"In the Pacific, Sir."

"It was bandied about that Pickering was Frank Knox's personal spy."

"Sir, it is my understanding that General Pickering was dispatched to the Pacific to obtain for Secretary Knox information that Secretary Knox felt he was not getting through standard Navy channels."

"You're a regular, Banning," Vandergrift said. "I shouldn't have to tell you about going out of channels." He paused. "About my personal repugnance to going out of channels."

"Sir, may I speak frankly?"

"I expect you to, Major."

"Sir, with respect, you don't have any choice. I am here at the direction of the Secretary of the Navy. I respectfully suggest, Sir, that if the Secretary of the Navy elects to move outside the established chain of command, he has that prerogative."

"Would you say, then, Major, that the contents of this message are not known to the Commander-in-Chief, Pacific?"

"I would be very surprised if it was, Sir."

"And the reference . . ." Vandergrift said, then paused and looked at the message again, ". . . the reference to their confidence in my discretion, and yours, means that we are not expected to tell them about it?"

"I would put that interpretation on that, Sir," Banning said.

"When this comes out, Banning, as it inevitably will, my superiors will conclude that I went over their heads. I would draw the same conclusion."

"Sir, I can only respectfully repeat that we have received an order from the Secretary of the Navy."

"In which I see the hand of Fleming Pickering," Vandergrift said. "I think this was Pickering's idea, not Mr. Knox's."

Banning didn't reply for a moment. There was no doubt in his mind that the whole thing was Fleming Pickering's idea. For one thing, the Secretary of the Navy almost certainly had no idea who one obscure major named Edward Banning was.

"Sir, I respectfully suggest—"

"I know," Vandergrift interrupted him. "It doesn't matter whose idea it was, Knox has signed on to it. Right? And we have our orders, right?"

"Yes, Sir," Banning said, uncomfortably.

"The reference . . ." Vandergrift began, and again stopped to look at the message in his hand, ". . . to 'all intelligence available to you and your staff.' I presume that includes MAGIC intercepts?"

"Sir," Banning said, now very uncomfortable. "I'm not at liberty . . ."

"Pickering was here, as you know. I know about MAGIC."

"Sir—"

Vandergrift held up his hand, shutting him off, and then went on, ". . . and thus I should have known better than to put that question to you. Consider it withdrawn."

Banning was visibly relieved.

"General," he said, "I have access to certain intelligence information, the source of which I am not at liberty to disclose. More important, not compromising this source of intelligence is of such importance—"

Vandergrift held up his hand again, silencing him. Banning stopped and waited as Vandergrift visibly chose the words he would now use.

"Let's go off at a tangent," he said. "The last time I was in Washington, I had a private talk with General Forrest. Perhaps he was out of school and shouldn't have told me this, but we're very old friends, and I flatter myself to think he trusts my discretion. . . ."

Jesus Christ, did Forrest tell him about MAGIC? I find that hard to believe!

Major General Horace W. T. Forrest was Assistant Chief of Staff, G-2 (Intelligence), of The Marine Corps.

"Anyway, General Forrest told me a story about the British being in possession of a coding machine . . ."

The Enigma machine. I can't believe Forrest told him about that, either.

". . . which permitted them to decode certain German codes . . ."

I'll be damned, he did!

". . . and that one of the German messages intercepted and decoded was the order from Berlin to the Luftwaffe to destroy Coventry," Vandergrift went on. "Which posed to Prime Minister Churchill the difficult question, 'Do I order the Royal Air Force to prepare to defend Coventry? Which will probably save Coventry, and a large number of human lives, civilian lives. But which will also certainly let the Germans know we have access to their encoded material. Or do I let them destroy Coventry and preserve the secret that we are reading their top-secret operational orders?'"

"I'm familiar with the story, Sir."

"Yes, I thought you might be," Vandergrift said. "Coventry, you will recall, was leveled by the Luftwaffe, with a terrible loss of life. I presume the English are still reading German operational orders, and that the Germans do not suspect that they are."

"Yes, Sir."

"I believe Churchill made the correct decision. Do I make my point, Major?"

"Yes, Sir."

"I will not inquire into the source of your intelligence, nor will I act upon anything you tell me."

"Yes, Sir," Banning said.

"Go on, please, Major," Vandergrift said.

"Lieutenant General Harukichi Hyakutake has assumed command of Japanese operations on Guadalcanal," Banning said.

Hyakutake commanded the Japanese Seventeeth Army.

Vandergrift looked surprised.

"I was about to say, I know that. But you mean he's here, don't you? Physically present on Guadalcanal?"

"Yes, Sir. He arrived 9 October."

"He's a good man," Vandergrift said, almost to himself. It was not an opinion of Hyakutake's character. Rather, it was one professional officer's judgment of the professional skill of another.

"Sir, would it be a waste of your time if I recapped the situation as I understand it?"

"No," Vandergrift said. "Go ahead."

"It is our belief, Sir, that until very recently, neither the Japanese Imperial General Staff itself, nor the Army General Staff, nor the Japanese Navy, has taken seriously our position on Guadalcanal. This is almost certainly because of a nearly incredible lack of communication between their Army and their Navy. For example, Sir, we have learned that until we landed, the Japanese Army was not aware that their Navy was building an airfield here."

"That's hard to believe," Vandergrift said. "But on the other hand, sometimes our Army doesn't talk to our Navy, either."

"As bad as that gets, Sir, it's nothing like the Japanese," Banning said. "Neither, Sir, was the Japanese Army made aware of the extent of Japanese Navy losses at Midway, not until about two weeks ago. Because they presumed that their Naval losses there were negligible, the Japanese Army concluded that we would not be able to launch any sort of counteroffensive until the latter half of 1943."

"And then we landed here," Vandergrift said.

"Yes, Sir. And even when we did, they were unwilling or unable to believe that it was anything more than a large-scale raid. The Makin Island raid times ten, or times twenty, so to speak. This misconception was reinforced when Admiral Fletcher elected to withdraw the invasion fleet earlier than was anticipated."

"Admiral Fletcher," Vandergrift said evenly, "apparently believed that he could not justify the loss of his ships in a Japanese counterattack."

"The Japanese interpretation, Sir, was that following the Battle of Savo Island, and our loss of the cruisers *Vincennes* and *Quincy*—"

"And the Australian *Canberra . . .*"

"—and the *Canberra,* that the Marines were abandoned here."

"There were people here who thought the same thing," Vandergrift said.

"Yes, Sir," Banning said. "General Pickering among them."

"Go on, Banning."

"And then Japanese intelligence, as reported to and accepted by the Imperial General Staff, was faulty," Banning said. "Remarkably so. Their estimate of Marines ashore was two thousand men, for instance. And they claimed our morale was low, and that deserters were attempting to escape to Tulagi."

"Really?" Vandergrift asked. "I hadn't heard that."

"Based, apparently, on this flawed intelligence, the IJGS made the decision that recapture of Guadalcanal would not be difficult. And because the airfield would be of value to them when they completed it, they decided that the recapture should be undertaken without delay. Initially, in other words, they didn't consider the possibility that we had the capability to make the airfield operational."

"I find it hard to accept they could be so inept," Vandergrift said.

"Yes, Sir, so did we. But that, beyond question, seems to be the case. In any event, at that point, General Hyakutake was given responsibility for the recapture of Guadalcanal. He decided that six thousand troops would be necessary to do so, and that he could assemble such a force from his assets without hurting Japanese operations on New Guinea and elsewhere.

"He then dispatched an advance force, approximately a thousand men under Colonel Ichiki Kiyono, which landed here on 18 August at Taivu. Again, presumably because of the intelligence which reported your forces as two thousand men, with low morale, and attempting to escape to Tulagi, Kiyono launched his attack along the Ilu River. . . ."

"And Kiyono's force was annihilated," Vandergrift said.

"Yes, Sir. Which caused the Japanese to do some second thinking. The Army and the Navy, at that point, Sir, were not admitting to one another the extent of their own losses. Nor—presuming either had learned them—the strength of the First Marine Division or the capabilities of Henderson Field.

"Their next step was greater reinforcement of their troops here. By the end of August, they had landed approximately six thousand men under Major General Kiyotake Kawaguchi. At the same time, finally, they realized that they could not logistically support both their operations here and in New Guinea. IJGS radioed General Horii, who had almost reached Port Moresby, and ordered him to halt his advance and dig in. Troops and matériel intended for Papua were ordered redirected here. It was at about this point, Sir, that they gave evidence of a much changed attitude toward Guadalcanal. It was phrased in several ways, but in essence, they concluded that 'Guadalcanal has now become the pivotal point of operational guidance.'"

Vandergrift grunted.

"General Kawaguchi's orders were to reconnoiter your positions, to determine whether with his existing forces he could break through them, capture Henderson Field, and ultimately push you into the sea. Or whether the attack should be delayed until he had additional troops and matériel. He elected to attack, possibly still relying on erroneous data about your strength, or possibly because he had come to believe what General Hyakutaka had been saying for some time, and thus the risk was justified."

"Excuse me?" Vandergrift asked.

"In September, Sir, we broke an intercept from General Hyakutake to the 17th Army, in which he said, 'The operation to surround and recapture Guadalcanal will truly decide the fate of the control of the entire Pacific.' At that time, Sir, that line of thinking was almost heretical."

"Well, he's right," Vandergrift said. "And now he's here, and in command."

"Yes, Sir. In any event, Kawaguchi attacked what we now call 'Bloody Ridge.'"

"And, by the skin of our teeth, of Merritt Edson's teeth, of the Raider and Parachutists' teeth, we held," Vandergrift said. "Your Lieutenant McCoy's brother stood up with an air-cooled .30 caliber Browning in his hands and killed thirty-odd Japanese. And he was by no means the only Marine who did more than anyone could reasonably, or unreasonably, expect of them."

"Yes, Sir. We've heard. They may have to rewrite the hymn."

"What?"

"From the Halls of Montezuma to the hills of Bloody Ridge."

"Now *that's* heresy, Major," Vandergrift said. "But maybe we'll need another verse." He smiled at Banning, then went on: "I'm glad we've talked, you and I. It's cleared my mind about several things." He paused. "You people have really been doing your homework, haven't you?"

Banning didn't reply.

"I don't suppose you know—or if you know, that you can tell me—what Hyakutake's plans are now?"

"I believe that is why I was sent here, Sir, to tell you what we think, and to get your evaluation of that for General Pickering."

Vandergrift looked at him, waiting.

"It is our belief, Sir, that as soon as General Hyakutake has ashore what he considers to be an adequate force, he intends to launch an attack on your lines with the objective of taking Henderson Field. We believe that the attack will be three-pronged, from the west and south. The 2nd Division, under Major General Maruyama, will attack from the south, in concert with troops under Major General Sumiyoshi Tadashi attacking from the west. The combined fleet will stand offshore in support, and to turn away any of our reinforcements."

"How soon is this going to happen?"

"I have no idea, Sir. But I think it is significant that General Hyakutake is physically present."

"And we are supposed to hold? Does anyone really think we can, with what we have?"

"General Harmon does not, Sir. He has been pressing very hard to get you reinforced in every way."

Major General Millard Harmon, USA, was a member of Admiral Fletcher's staff, his ground force expert.

Vandergrift was silent a moment.

"I will give you specifics for your report to General Pickering, Major, because I think he expects them. But what they add up to is that unless we get significant reinforcements, ground and air, we are going to reach the point where even extraordinary courage will be overwhelmed by fatigue and malnutrition."

"The Army's 164th Infantry has sailed, Sir, to reinforce you. They should be here shortly."

"That I'd heard," Vandergrift said. "But one regiment is not going to be enough."

"Yes, Sir."

"Get yourself a cup of coffee. I want to organize my thinking for General Pickering on paper."

"Aye, aye, Sir."

(TWO)
The Presidential Apartment
The White House
Washington, D.C.
0830 Hours 12 October 1942

"Frank," the President of the United States began, but interrupted himself to fit a cigarette into a long silver-and-ivory holder and to wait until a black, white-jacketed Navy steward had produced a silver Ronson table lighter.

The Honorable Frank Knox, Secretary of the Navy, a dignified, modestly portly gentleman wearing pince-nez spectacles, raised his eyes to the President and waited, his jaws moving slowly as he masticated an unexpectedly stringy piece of ham.

They were taking breakfast alone, at a small table in a sitting room opening onto Pennsylvania Avenue. Roosevelt was wearing a silk dressing gown over a white shirt open at the collar. Knox was wearing a banker's gray pin-striped suit.

"Frank," the President resumed, "just between you, me, and the lamppost, would you say that Bill Donovan is paranoid?" William J. Donovan, a World War I hero, a law school classmate of Roosevelt's, and a very successful Wall Street lawyer, had been recruited by Roosevelt to head the Office of Information. This later evolved into the Office of Strategic Services, and ultimately into the Central Intelligence Agency.

"I respectfully decline to answer, Mr. President," Knox said, straight-faced, "on the grounds that any answer I might give to that question would certainly incriminate me."

Roosevelt chuckled.

"He came to see me last night. First, I got the to-be-expected complaints about Edgar getting in his way."

The reference was clearly to J. Edgar Hoover, Director of the Federal Bureau of Investigation. Hoover, who jealously guarded the prerogatives of the FBI, saw in Donovan's intelligence-gathering mission a threat to his conviction that the FBI had primary responsibility for intelligence and counterintelligence operations in the Western Hemisphere.

"Far be it from me, Mr. President," Knox said, alluding to that sore point, "to suggest to you that you may not have made the delineation of their respective responsibilities crystal clear."

Roosevelt chuckled again, gestured to the steward that he would like more coffee, and then asked innocently, "Frank, have you never considered that two heads are better than one?"

"Even two granite heads?" Knox asked.

"Even two granite heads," Roosevelt said. "And then, after a rather emotional summation of his position vis-à-vis Edgar, Bill dropped his oh-so-subtle venom in the direction of Douglas MacArthur."

"Oh? What did MacArthur do to him?"

"The worst possible thing he could do to Bill," Roosevelt replied. "He's ignoring him."

"I don't quite follow you, Mr. President."

"Bill sent a team to Australia. And there they are sitting, with very little to do. For it has been made perfectly clear to them that they are considered interlopers, and that MacArthur intends to ignore them. Donovan's top man can't even get an audience with the Supreme Commander."

"I don't see, Mr. President, where this has anything to do with me. MacArthur doesn't work for me."

"I sometimes wonder if Douglas understands that he works for me, either. I suspect he believes the next man up in his chain of command is God," Roosevelt said. "But that isn't the point. Donovan believes that MacArthur has been poisoned regarding both him personally, and the Office of Strategic Services generally—"

"The what?" Knox interrupted.

"The Office of Strategic Services. We have renamed the Office of Information. Didn't you hear?"

"I heard something about it," Knox said, and then picked up his coffee cup.

"As I was saying," Roosevelt went on. "Donovan believes that the reason his people are being snubbed is that when Fleming Pickering was over there, he whispered unkind slanders in the porches of Douglas MacArthur's ear. And General Pickering *does* work for you."

"I don't believe that Pickering would do that kind of thing," Knox said, after a moment.

"I would rather not believe it myself," Roosevelt said. "But I thought you could tell me what the friction is between Donovan and Pickering."

Knox took another sip of his coffee before replying.

"I'm tempted to be flip and say it's simply a case of the irresistible force meeting the immovable object. There was some bad feeling between them before the war. Donovan represented Pickering's shipping company in a maritime case. Pickering thought Donovan's bill was out of line, and told him so in somewhat pungent terms."

"I hadn't heard that," Roosevelt said.

"And then Donovan tried to recruit Pickering for the Office of Information. Pickering assumed, and I think reasonably, that he was being asked to become one of the Twelve Disciples." When formed, the mission of the Office of Information was to analyze intelligence gathered by all U.S. intelligence agencies. Ultimately, data would be reviewed by a panel of twelve men, the Disciples, drawn from the upper echelons of American business, science, and academia, who would then recommend the use to be made of the intelligence gathered.

Knox looked at his coffee cup but decided not to take another sip. "When he got to Washington," he resumed, "Donovan kept Pickering cooling his heels waiting to see him for a couple of hours, and then informed him that he would be working *under* one of the Disciples. This man just happened to be a New York banker with whom Pickering had crossed swords in the past."

"So there's more than one monumental ego involved?"

"I rather sympathized with Pickering about that," Knox said. "Pickering himself is a remarkable man. I understand why he turned Donovan down. He believed he would be of greater value running his shipping company—Pacific & Far East Shipping is, as you know, enormous—than as a second-level bureaucrat here."

"And then you recruited him?"

"Yes. And as you know, he did one hell of a job for me."

"In the process enraging two of every three admirals in the Navy," Roosevelt said softly.

"I sent him to the Pacific to get information I was not getting via the Annapolis Protection Society," Knox said. "He did what I asked him to do. And he's doing a good job now."

"Donovan says that he cannot get the men he needs from The Marine Corps, because Pickering is the man who must approve the transfers."

"And Marine Corps personnel officers have complained to the Commandant that

Pickering is sending to Donovan too many good officers that The Marine Corps needs," Knox replied.

"You don't think Pickering whispered slanders in MacArthur's ear when he was over there?"

"He doesn't whisper slanders," Knox said. "Flem Pickering doesn't stab you in the back, he stabs you in the front. The first time I met him, he told me I should have resigned after Pearl Harbor."

Roosevelt's eyebrows went up. But he seemed more amused than shocked or outraged.

"Was that before or after you recruited him?" he asked, with a smile.

"Before. But, to be as objective as I can, I think it is altogether possible that when he and MacArthur were together, Bill Donovan's name came up. If that happened, and if MacArthur asked about him, Pickering would surely have given his unvarnished opinion of Donovan; that opinion would not be very flattering."

"Donovan wants his head," Roosevelt said.

"I would protest that in the strongest possible terms, Mr. President. And I would further suggest, present personalities aside, that giving in to Donovan on something like this would set a very bad precedent."

"Frank, I like Fleming Pickering. We have something in common, you know. Both of us have sons over there, actually fighting this war. And I am aware that the Commander-in-Chief tells Bill Donovan what to do, not the reverse."

Knox looked at him. "But?"

"I would like to get Pickering out of sight for a few weeks. Is he up to travel?"

"If you asked him, he would gladly go. But he was badly wounded, and he had a bad bout with malaria. Where do you want me to send him?"

"Let's decide that after we decide what shape he's in. Are you free for lunch?"

"I'm at your call, Mr. President."

"You, Richardson Fowler, Admiral Leahy, and General Pickering. If nothing else, presuming he doesn't have a wiretap in this room, Bill Donovan could really presume we've called Pickering on the carpet, couldn't he?"

Knox didn't reply. He gestured to the steward for more coffee.

(THREE)
The Foster Lafayette Hotel
Washington, D.C.
1150 Hours 12 October 1942

It had suddenly begun to rain, hard, as the 1940 Buick Limited convertible sedan passed the Hotel Washington and continued down Pennsylvania Avenue toward the White House.

"This goddamn town has the worst weather in the world," the driver, alone in the car, observed aloud.

He was a tall, distinguished-looking man in his early forties, wearing a superbly tailored United States Marine Corps brigadier general's uniform.

He passed the White House, made a right turn, then a U-turn, and pulled up before the marquee of the Foster Lafayette Hotel, arguably the most luxurious hotel in the capital. Beyond question, it was the most expensive.

The ornately uniformed doorman pulled open the passenger-side door.

"Your choice," Brigadier General Fleming Pickering said, "you park this or loan me your umbrella."

"I think the Senator's going with you, General," the doorman said, with a smile.

At that moment, Senator Richardson K. Fowler (R., Cal.), a tall, silver-haired, regal-looking sixty-two-year-old, appeared at the car and slipped into the passenger seat. He had been waiting for the Buick to appear, standing just inside the lobby, looking out through the plate glass next to the bellboy-attended revolving door.

"You made good time, Flem," he said.

The doorman closed the door after him.

"Let's have it," Pickering replied curtly.

"Let's have what?"

"You said, quote, 'as soon as possible.' "

"We're having lunch with the President and Frank Knox," Fowler said. "And, I think, Admiral Leahy."

"That's all?" Pickering asked suspiciously.

"Most people in this town would be all aflutter at the prospect of a private luncheon with the President, his Chief of Staff, and the Secretary of the Navy," Fowler began, and then saw something in Pickering's eyes. "What did you think it was, Flem?"

"You know damned well what I thought it was," Pickering said.

"Pick's going to be all right, Flem," Fowler said gently. "He's a Pickering. Pickerings walk through raindrops."

The last time General Pickering heard, his only son, Second Lieutenant Malcolm S. "Pick" Pickering, USMCR, was flying an F4F4 Wildcat off Henderson Field on Guadalcanal.

"Get out," Pickering said. "Open the door."

"We're due at the White House in twenty minutes," Fowler said, looking at his watch.

"That's plenty of time," Pickering said. "It's right across the street. All I want is a quick drink." He met Fowler's eyes, and confessed, "I've been frightened sick ever since you called. You sonofabitch. You should have told me that it was lunch with Roosevelt."

"I'm sorry, Flem," Fowler said, genuinely contrite.

Fowler opened his door, and Pickering slid across the seat to follow him.

"Don't bury it," Pickering said to the doorman, who hurried back to the car. "We'll be out in a minute."

The doorman walked around the front of the Buick, got in, and drove it fifteen yards. He parked it by a sign proclaiming, NO PARKING AT ANY TIME, then walked back to his post.

General Pickering was always well treated by the staff of the Foster Lafayette. For one thing, he occupied a five-room suite on the sixth floor, adjacent to Senator Fowler's somewhat larger suite. More important, Pickering's wife, Patricia, was the only child of Andrew Foster, the owner of the Foster Lafayette and forty-one other Foster hotels.

Inside the lobby, Fowler turned to Pickering and asked, "You want to go upstairs?"

In reply, Pickering pointed toward the door of the Oak Grill. There a line of people waited behind the maître d'hôtel's lectern and a velvet rope for their turn to enter the smaller and more exclusive of the Lafayette's two restaurants.

Fowler shrugged and followed Pickering.

The maître d'hôtel saw them coming. Smiling as he unhooked the velvet rope, he greeted them:

"General, Senator, your table is ready."

That was not the unvarnished truth. The Oak Grill customarily placed brass RESERVED signs on a few tables more than were actually reserved. Such tables were required for those people who came without reservations and were too important to stand in line. Before General Pickering had taken up residence in the Lafayette, Senator Fowler's name had headed the list of those who got tables before anyone else, reservation or no. Now Fleming Pickering's name was at the top.

A waiter appeared before Pickering and Fowler had time to slide onto the leather-cushioned banquette seats.

"Luncheon, gentlemen?"

"No, thank you," Pickering said. "What we need desperately is a quick drink."

"Don't bring the bottle," Senator Fowler said.

The management of the Oak Grill was aware that when General Pickering asked for a drink, he was actually requesting a glass, a bowl of ice, a pitcher of water, and a bottle of Famous Grouse scotch. Two of these, from the General's private stock, were kept out of sight under the bar.

The waiter looked to Pickering for guidance.

"Just the drinks, please," Pickering ordered. When the waiter was gone he added, "I really hadn't planned to get plastered."

"There are those, you know, who would be reluctant to show up across the street reeking of booze."

"You don't say?"

"And, you know, most general officers ride in the backseat, beside their aides, while their sergeant drives."

"My aide and my sergeant have more important things to do," Pickering said, and then added, "Speaking of which . . ."

He took a thin sheet of paper from the left bellows pocket of his tunic and handed it to Fowler.

NOT LOGGED
ONE COPY ONLY
DUPLICATION FORBIDDEN
FOLLOWING IS DECRYPTION OF MSG 234707 RECEIVED 091142 1105 GREENWICH
FROM SUPREME COMMANDER SWPOA
091142 1325 GREENWICH VIA PEARL HARBOR
FOR SECNAV WASHINGTON DC
EYES ONLY BRIG GEN FLEMING PICKERING USMCR
OFFICE MANAGEMENT ANALYSIS HQ USMC
GREYHOUND RETURNED SAFELY TO KENNEL XXX PUPS A LITTLE WORSE FOR
WEAR BUT HEALTHY XXX
BEST PERSONAL REGARDS FROM ALL HANDS XXX SIGNATURE BANNING

Senator Fowler read it and handed it back to Pickering.

"Aside from recognizing the somewhat grandiose title Douglas MacArthur has given himself, I haven't the foggiest idea what I just read," he said. "But are you supposed to carry something marked 'Secret' around in your pocket so casually?"

Pickering looked at him and smiled.

"Watch this," he said.

He crumpled the sheet of paper and put it in the ashtray. Then he took a gold Dunhill lighter from his pocket, got it working, and touched the flame to the crumpled paper. There was a flash of light, and the paper disappeared in a small cloud of white smoke.

"Christ!" Fowler said, surprised.

Heads elsewhere in the Oak Grill turned, startled by the light.

"They treat it chemically somehow," Pickering said, pleased. "The coal on a cigarette will set it off. You don't need a flame."

"How clever," Fowler said drolly as the waiter delivered the drinks. He picked up his and raised it. "To Pick, Flem. May God protect him."

Pickering met his eyes and then touched glasses.

"That came in a moment before you called," he said. "We put a couple of Marines—precisely, *I* put a couple of Marines—onto an island called Buka, not far from the Japanese base at Rabaul. The Australians left people behind when the Japanese occupied it—"

"You put somebody onto a Japanese-occupied island?" Fowler interrupted.

Pickering nodded. "They call these people Coastwatchers. They have radios, and provide our people with early warning of Japanese movement, air and ship. This fellow's radio went out, so we sent him a new one, a Hallicrafters—"

"'You' or 'we,' which?" Fowler interrupted again.

"Me," Pickering said. *"I* asked a couple of Marines to volunteer to parachute onto Buka with a new radio. Then I found out that the Australians were infected with the British notion that no sacrifice is too great for King and Country ..."

"Meaning what?"

"That they were going to leave my Marines there until they were either killed by the Japanese or died of disease or starvation. Goddamn them!"

"So you got them out? The greyhound and the pups? That's what they meant?"

Pickering nodded. "We replaced them. Took the first Marines out and sent some others in. I was worried about it; it was a hairy operation. And the moment after the courier handed me Banning's message and I could exhale, I got your 'come as soon as possible' message. I thought that Pick ... I thought the other shoe had dropped. I stuffed that in my pocket without thinking."

"Pick, like his old man, will walk between raindrops," Fowler said. "To quote myself."

Pickering looked at him for a moment, then raised his glass.

"I could use another one of these."

"No," Fowler said, then repeated it. "No, Flem."

Pickering shrugged.

Fowler's 1941 Cadillac limousine was at the curb when they came out of the lobby.

"I gather it's beneath the dignity of a United States senator to arrive at the White House in anything less than a limousine?" Pickering asked as he started to get in.

"It is beneath this United States senator's dignity to call upon the President soaked to the skin," Fowler replied. "They would make you park your car yourself if you drove over there. And, you may have noticed, it's raining."

Pickering didn't reply.

"How are you, Fred?" he cheerfully asked Fowler's chauffeur.

"Just fine, General, thank you."

The limousine was stopped at the gate. Before passing them onto the White House grounds, a muscular man in a snap-brim hat and a rain-soaked trench coat scanned their personal identification, then checked their names against a list on a clipboard.

A Marine sergeant opened the limousine door when they stopped under the White House portico, then saluted when Pickering got out.

Pickering returned the salute. "How are you, Sergeant?" he asked.

The sergeant seemed surprised at being spoken to. "Just fine, Sir."

A White House butler opened the door as they approached it.

"Senator, General. If you'll follow me, please?"

He took them via an elevator to the second floor, where another muscular man in civilian clothing examined them carefully before stepping aside.

The butler knocked at a double door, then opened it without waiting for an order.

"Mr. President," he announced, "Senator Fowler and General Pickering."

Franklin Delano Roosevelt rolled his wheelchair toward the door.

"My two favorite members of the loyal opposition," he said, beaming. "Thank you for coming."

"Mr. President," Fowler and Pickering said, almost in unison.

"Fleming, how are you?" Roosevelt asked as he offered his hand.

"Very well, thank you, Sir."

Pickering thought he detected an inflection in the President's voice that made it a real question, not a *pro forma* one. There came immediate proof.

"Malaria's all cleared up?" the President pursued. "Your wounds have healed?"

"I'm in fine shape, Sir."

"Then I can safely offer you a drink? Without invoking the rage of the Navy's surgeon general?"

"It is never safe to offer General Pickering a drink, Mr. President," Senator Fowler said.

"Well, I think I'll just take the chance, anyway," Roosevelt said.

A black steward in a white jacket appeared carrying a tray with two glasses on it.

"Frank and I started without you," Roosevelt said, spinning the wheelchair around and rolling it into the next room. Fowler and Pickering followed him.

As they entered, Knox rose from one of two matching leather armchairs. He had a drink in his hand. Admiral William D. Leahy rose from the other chair. He was a tall, lanky, sad-faced man whose title was Chief of Staff of the President. There was a coffee cup on the table beside him.

The men shook hands.

"How are you, General?" Admiral Leahy asked, and again Pickering sensed it was a real, rather than *pro forma,* question.

"I'm very well, thank you, Admiral," Pickering said.

"I already asked him, Admiral," Roosevelt said. "We apparently have standing before us a tribute to the efficacy of military medicine. As badly as he was wounded, as sick as he was with malaria, I am awed." He turned to Pickering, Knox, and Fowler, smiled, and went on: "The Admiral and I have had our schedule changed. You will be spared taking lunch with us."

"I'm sorry to hear that, Mr. President," Senator Fowler said.

"Oh, no you're not," Roosevelt said. "With me gone, you three political crustaceans can sit here in my apartment and say unkind things about me."

There was the expected dutiful laughter.

"I hear laughter but no denials," Roosevelt said. "But before I leave you, I'd like to ask a favor of you, Fleming."

"Anything within my power, Mr. President," Pickering said.

"Could you find it in your heart to make peace with Bill Donovan?"

Is that what this is all about? Did that sonofabitch actually go to the President of the United States to complain about me?

"I wasn't aware that Mr. Donovan was displeased with me, Mr. President."

"It has come to his attention that you said unkind things about him to our friend Douglas MacArthur," Roosevelt said.

"Mr. President," Pickering said, softly but firmly, "to the best of my recollection, I have never discussed Mr. Donovan with General MacArthur."

Frank Knox coughed.

"Then tell me this, Fleming," the President said. "If I asked you to say something nice to Douglas MacArthur about Bill Donovan, would you?"

"I'm not sure I understand you, Mr. President."

"Frank will explain everything," Roosevelt said. "And when you see Douglas, give him my very best regards, won't you?"

The President rolled himself away before Pickering could say another word.

III

(ONE)
Guadalcanal
Solomon Islands
0450 Hours 13 October 1942

Major Jack (NMI) Stecker, USMCR, commanding officer of 2nd Battalion, Fifth Marines, woke at the first hint of morning light. He was a large, tall, straight-backed man who could look like a Marine even in sweat-soaked utilities—as the Commanding General of the 1st Marine Division recently noted privately to his Sergeant Major. The rest of the Division, including himself, the General went on to observe, looked like AWOLs from the Civilian Conservation Corps.

Major Stecker had been sleeping on a steel bed and mattress, formerly the property of the Imperial Japanese Army. A wooden crate served as Stecker's bedside table; it once contained canned smoked oysters intended for the Japanese garrison on Guadalcanal.

The "tabletop" held a Coleman lantern; a flashlight; an empty can of Planter's peanuts converted to an ashtray; a package of Chesterfield cigarettes; a Zippo lighter; and a U.S. Pistol, Caliber .45 ACP, Model 1911, with the hammer in the cocked position and the safety on.

On waking, Major Stecker sat up and reached for the pistol. He removed the magazine, worked the action to eject the chambered cartridge, and then loaded it back into the magazine. He let the slide go forward, lowered the hammer by pulling the trigger, and then reinserted the magazine into the pistol.

It was one thing, in Major Stecker's judgment, to have a pistol in the cocked and locked position when there was a good chance you might need it in a hurry, and quite another to carry a weapon that way when you were walking around wide awake.

Before retiring, he had removed his high-topped shoes—called boondockers—and his socks. Now he pulled on a fresh pair of socks—fresh in the sense that he had rinsed them, if not actually washed them in soap and water—and then the boondockers, carefully double-knotting their laces so they would not come undone. When he was satisfied with that, he slipped the Colt into its holster and then buckled his pistol belt around his waist.

He pushed aside the shelter-half that separated his sleeping quarters from the Battalion Command Post.

The Battalion S-3 (Plans & Training) Sergeant, who was sitting on a folding chair (Japanese) next to a folding table (Japanese) on which sat a Field Desk (U.S. Army), started to get to his feet. Stecker waved him back to his chair.

"Good morning, Sir."

"Good morning," Stecker said with a smile, then walked out of the CP and relieved himself against a palm tree. He went back into the CP, picked up a five-gallon water can, and poured from it two inches of water into a washbasin—a steel helmet inverted in a rough wooden frame.

He moved to his bedside table and reached inside for his toilet kit, a battered leather bag with mold growing green around the zipper. He lifted out shaving cream and a Gillette razor. Then he went back to the helmet washbasin, wet his face, and shaved himself as well as he could using a pocket-size, polished-metal mirror. He had come ashore with a small glass mirror, but the concussion from an incoming Japanese mortar round had shattered it.

He carried the helmet outside, tossed the water away, and returned to his bedside table. He reached inside for a towel, then wiped the vestiges of the shaving cream from his face.

His morning toilette completed, he picked up a U.S. Rifle, Caliber .30-06, M1 that was beside his bed (one of the few M1s on Guadalcanal). It had a leather strap, and the strap had two spare eight-round clips attached to it.

The M1 rifle (called the Garand, after its inventor) was viewed by most Marines as a Mickey Mouse piece of shit, inferior in every way to the U.S. Rifle, Caliber. .30-06, M1903 (called the Springfield, after the U.S. Army Arsenal where it was manufactured). Every Marine had been trained with a Springfield at either Parris Island or San Diego.

Major Stecker disagreed. In his professional judgment, the Garand was the finest military rifle yet developed.

Before the war, as Sergeant Major Stecker, he participated in the testing of the weapon at the Army's Infantry Center at Fort Benning, Georgia. And he concluded then that if he ever had to go to war again, he would arm himself with the Garand. Not only was it at least as accurate as the Springfield, but it was self-loading. You could fire the eight cartridges in its *en bloc* clip as fast as you could pull the trigger. And then, when the clip was empty, the weapon automatically ejected it and left the action open for the rapid insertion of a fresh one. The Marine Corps' beloved Springfield required the manipulation of its bolt after each shot, and its magazine held only five cartridges.

Although there were in those days fewer than two hundred Garands in Marine Corps stocks, it had not been difficult for the sergeant major of the U.S. Marine Corps Schools at Quantico, Virginia, to arrange to have one assigned to him. For one thing, he was the power behind the U.S. Marine Corps Rifle Team, and for another, sergeants major of the pre-war Marine Corps generally got whatever they thought they needed, no questions asked.

When Sergeant Major Stecker was called to active duty as a Captain, USMC Reserve, he briefly considered turning the Garand in. . . . He decided against it. If he turned the Garand in, he reasoned, it would almost certainly spend the war in a rifle rack at Quantico. If he kept it, the odds were that it would be put to its intended use—bringing accurate fire to bear upon the enemy.

By the time the 1st Marine Division reached the South Pacific, Jack (NMI) Stecker was a major. . . . He had in no way changed his opinion about the Garand rifle— far to the contrary. Although there were few in the 1st Marines who felt safe teasing Major Stecker about anything, three or four brave souls felt bold enough to tease him about his rifle. The last man to do it was Brigadier General Lewis T. Harris, the Assistant Division Commander. They were then on the transport en route to Guadalcanal.

General Harris was a second lieutenant in France in 1917 at the time Sergeant Stecker, then nineteen, earned the Medal of Honor. And they had remained friends since. General Harris, for instance, was the man who talked Stecker into accepting a reserve commission in the first place. And it was Harris who later arranged his promotion to major and his being given command of Second of the Fifth—against a good deal of pressure from the regular officer corps, who believed that while there was a place for commissioned ex–enlisted men in the wartime Corps, it was not in positions of command.

On the transport, General Harris looked at Stecker and observed solemnly: "I'm willing to close my eyes to officers who prefer to carry a rifle in addition to the prescribed arm," which was the .45 Colt pistol, "but I'm having trouble overlooking an officer who arms himself with a Mickey Mouse piece that will probably fall apart the first time it's fired."

Stecker raised his eyes to meet the General's. "May the Major respectfully suggest that the General go fuck himself?"

They were alone in the General's cabin, and they went back together a long way. The General laughed and offered Stecker another sample of what the bottle's label described as prescription mouthwash.

The comments about Jack (NMI) Stecker's Mickey Mouse rifle died out after the 2nd Battalion of the Fifth Marines went ashore on Tulagi (at about the same time the bulk of the Division was going ashore on Guadalcanal, twenty miles away). The word spread that the 2nd Battalion's commanding officer, standing in the open and firing offhand, had put rounds in the heads of two Japanese two hundred yards away.

Jack Stecker put his helmet on his head and slung the Garand over his shoulder.

"I'm going to have a look around," he said to the G-3 sergeant.

The field telephone rang as he crossed the room. As Stecker reached the entrance, the G-3 sergeant called his name. When Stecker turned, he held out the telephone to him.

Stecker took the telephone, pushed the butterfly switch, and spoke his name.

"Yes, Sir," he said, and then "No, Sir," and then "Thank you, Sir, I'll be waiting."

He handed the telephone back to the sergeant.

"The look around will have to wait. I'm having breakfast with The General. He's sending his jeep for me."

There were several general officers on the island of Guadalcanal, but The General was Major General Alexander Archer Vandergrift, who commanded the First Marine Division.

"Whatever it is, Sir," the G-3 sergeant said, "we didn't do it."

"I don't think The General would believe that, Sergeant, whatever it is," Stecker said, and walked out of the command post.

(TWO)

The 1st and 3rd Battalions of the Fifth Marines, First Marine Division, had come ashore near Lunga Point on Guadalcanal, in the Solomon Islands, on 7 August. Simultaneously, the 1st Marine Raider Battalion and the 2nd Battalion of the Fifth Marines had landed on Tulagi Island, twenty miles away; and the 1st Marine Parachute Battalion on the tiny island of Gavutu, two miles from Tulagi.

This operation was less the first American counterattack against the Japanese— since that would have meant the establishment on Guadalcanal of a force that could reasonably be expected to overwhelm the Japanese there—than an act of desperation.

From a variety of sources, Intelligence had learned that the Japanese would in the near future complete the construction of an airfield near Lunga Point on the north side of the island. If it became operational, Japanese aircraft would dominate the area: New Guinea would almost certainly fall. And an invasion of Australia would become likely.

On the other hand, if the Japanese airfield were to fall into American hands, the situation would be reversed. For American aircraft could then strike at Japanese shipping lanes, and at Japanese bases, especially those at Rabaul, on the island of New Britain. A Japanese invasion of Australia would be rendered impossible, all of New Guinea could be retaken, and the first step would be made on what publicists were already calling "The March to Japan."

General Douglas MacArthur, Supreme Commander, South West Pacific Ocean Area, and Admiral Chester W. Nimitz, Commander-in-Chief, Pacific, very seldom agreed on anything; but they agreed on this: that the risks involved in taking Guadalcanal had to be accepted. And so the decision to go ahead with the attack was made.

The First Division was by then in New Zealand, having been told it would not be sent into combat until early in 1943. Nevertheless, it was given the task. It was transported to Guadalcanal and Tulagi/Gavutu in a Naval Task Force commanded by Vice Admiral Frank Jack Fletcher.

The initial amphibious invasion, on Friday, 7 August 1942, went better than anyone thought possible. Although the 1st Marine Parachute Battalion on Gavutu was almost literally decimated, both Gavutu and Tulagi fell swiftly and with relatively few American casualties. And there was little effective resistance as the Marines went ashore on Guadalcanal.

But then Admiral Fletcher decided that he could not risk the loss of his fleet by remaining off the Guadalcanal beachhead. His thinking was perhaps colored by the awesome losses the Navy had suffered at Pearl Harbor on 7 December 1941. And so he assumed—not completely without reason—that the Japanese would launch a massive attack on his ships as soon as they realized what was happening.

Admiral Fletcher summoned General Vandergrift to the command ship USS *McCawley* on Saturday, 8 August. There he informed him that he intended to withdraw from Guadalcanal starting at three the next afternoon.

Vandergrift argued that he could have the Japanese airfield ready to take American fighters within forty-eight hours, and that he desperately needed the men, and especially the supplies, still aboard the transports. He argued in vain.

The next morning, Sunday, 9 August, Fletcher's fears seemed to be confirmed. In what became known as the Battle of Savo Island, the U.S. Navy took another whipping: the cruisers USS *Vincennes* and USS *Quincy* were both sunk within an hour. The Australian cruiser HMAS *Canberra* was set on fire, and then torpedoed and sunk by an American submarine to save it from capture. A third American cruiser, USS *Astoria,* was sunk at noon.

At 1500 that afternoon, ten transports, one cruiser, four destroyers, and a minesweeper of the invasion fleet left the beachhead for Noumea. At 1830, the rest of ships sailed away. On board were a vast stock of weapons and equipment, including all the heavy artillery and virtually all of the engineer equipment, plus rations, ammunition, and personnel.

If it had not been for captured stocks of Japanese rations, the Marines would have starved. If it had not been for captured Japanese trucks, bulldozers, and other engineer equipment (and American ingenuity in making them run) the airfield could not have been completed.

And it was not a question of if the Japanese would launch a major counterattack to throw the Marines back into the sea, but when.

In Jack Stecker's view, the next few days were going to be a close thing for the Marines on Guadalcanal. For a number of reasons. For one, he had been a longtime observer of the Japanese military. Before the war, he did a tour with the 4th Marines in Shanghai, where he soon realized that the Japanese were not small, trollish men wearing thick glasses whom the United States could defeat with one hand tied behind them; that they were in fact well trained, well disciplined, and well armed.

And so Stecker was not at all surprised after the war started to see the Japanese winning victory after victory. What surprised him was how long it was taking them to mount a massive counterattack on Guadalcanal. Control of the Guadalcanal airfield (now named Henderson Field, after a Marine Aviator who had been killed in the Battle of Midway) was as important to them as it was to the Americans. And unlike the Americans, the Japanese had enormous resources of ships, aircraft, and men to throw into a counterattack.

For instance, when the American invasion fleet sailed off into the sunset, it carried with it the heavy (155mm) artillery of the First Marine Division. That meant the Japanese could bombard the airfield and Marine positions with their heavy artillery, without fear of counterbattery fire from the Americans, whose most powerful cannon was the 105mm howitzer.

And meanwhile, Guadalcanal was a tropical island, infested with malaria and a long list of other debilitating tropical diseases. These weakened the physical strength of the Marines from the moment they landed. That situation, made worse by short rations and the strain of heat and humidity, could easily get desperate. Already Stecker's Marines were sick and exhausted.

As for the reason they were on the island in the first place, Henderson Field was operational and a second auxiliary airstrip had been bulldozed not far away, yet there had been no massive buildup of American air power. As soon as aircraft were flown in, they entered combat. Although Japanese losses were much heavier than American, the attrition of U.S. warplanes seemed to Stecker to have overwhelmed available reinforcements.

Stecker had a personal interest in Marine Aviation. His son, a Marine Aviator on VFM-229, had barely survived a crash landing in an F4F4 Wildcat. He had left the island a high-priority medical evacuee, covered in plaster and bandages. Despite all the painkilling narcotics the doctors thought he could handle, he was moaning in agony.

The prognosis was, eventually, full recovery. Stecker had his doubts.

A mud-splattered jeep came up to him.

"Major Stecker?" the driver asked.

The driver looked to be fifteen, Stecker thought, and was certainly no older than eighteen.

"Right," Stecker said, and got in the front seat.

"Sorry to be late, Sir. I got stuck in the mud."

Late? What does he mean, "late"? How long have I been standing there?

"It happens," Stecker said.

(THREE)

There was no General's Mess. Instead there was was a plank table under a canvas fly, set with three places. Each place held a china plate and a china mug ("borrowed," Stecker was sure, from the transport), and was laid out with the flatware that came with a mess kit: a knife, a fork, and a large spoon. Stecker wondered why the mess cook hadn't "borrowed" some better tableware. But then it occurred to him that somewhere in the hold of one of the ships that sailed off into the sunset the day after they landed there was a crate marked HQ CO OFFICERS' MESS filled with some decent plates and flatware.

He stood at the end of the table and waited for the Division Commander to arrive.

Vandergrift appeared a minute later, trailed by Brigadier General Lucky Lew Harris, who was shorter and stockier than his superior. Vandergrift was wearing utilities; Harris wore mussed and sweat-stained khakis.

Stecker came to attention.

"Good morning, Sir."

"Good morning, Jack."

"General," Stecker said, nodding to Harris.

"Colonel," Harris said.

Christ, Lew's going over the edge, too. He called me "Colonel"; he, of all people, knows better than that.

A mess cook appeared. He was trying, without much success, to look as neat and crisp as a cook-for-a-general should look. He carried a stainless-steel pitcher and a can of condensed milk. He put the pitcher and the can of condensed milk on the table. And then he opened the can by piercing the top in two places with a K-Bar knife.

"Thank you," General Vandergrift said. "I can use some coffee."

"Sir, I can give you powdered eggs and bacon, or corned beef."

"Corned beef for me, please," General Vandergrift said. He picked up the coffee pitcher and poured coffee for himself and the others.

"Please be seated, gentlemen," the General said.

Stecker and Harris sat down. The cook looked at them. Both nodded. The General had ordered corned beef; they would have corned beef.

The General raised his eyes to the cook.

"Is there any of the Japanese orange segments?"

"Yes, Sir. I was going to bring you some, Sir."

Vandergrift nodded.

"Thank God for the Japanese," Vandergrift said. He turned to look at Stecker.

"I suppose if you had something unusual to report, Jack, you would have already said what it is."

"Fairly quiet night, Sir."

Vandergrift nodded.

"Jack, we got a radio about a week ago asking us to recommend outstanding people for promotion. Officers and enlisted. We're going to have to staff entire divisions, and apparently someone at Eighth and I thinks the cadre should be people who have been in combat." (Headquarters, USMC, is at Eighth and I Streets in Washington, D.C.)

"Yes, Sir. I agree. Are you asking me for recommendations, Sir?"

"I wasn't, but go ahead."

"Sir, I have an outstanding company commander in mind, Joe Fortin, and my G-3 sergeant is really a first-class Marine. Are you talking about direct commissions, Sir?"

"Before you leave," Vandergrift said, not replying directly, "give those names to General Harris."

"Aye, aye, Sir."

"What Eighth and I wanted, Jack, was the names of field-grade officers, for promotion"—majors, lieutenant colonels, and colonels—"and staff NCOs for either direct commissions or for Officer Candidate School." (Staff NCOs were enlisted men of the three senior grades.)

"Yes, Sir."

He already told me that. And he's certainly not asking me to offer my opinion of field-grade officers. If I'm not the junior major on this island, I don't know who is. What's he leading up to?

"A couple of names came immediately to mind, and we fired off a radio," General Vandergrift went on. "And for once Eighth and I did something in less than sixty days."

"Yes, Sir?"

The cook arrived with a plate of corned beef hash and three coffee cups, each of which held several spoonfuls of canned orange segments, courtesy of the Imperial Japanese Army.

He served the corned beef hash, left, and returned with another plate, this one holding bread that had apparently been "toasted" in a frying pan.

"General, we don't have any jam except plum," the cook said, laying a plate of jam on the table.

"Plum will be fine, thank you," General Vandergrift said.

General Harris spread his toast with the jam, and took a bite.

"This must be American," he said. "It's awful."

"Did you send for a photographer, Lew?" General Vandergrift asked.

"Yes, Sir. He's standing by."

"Well, let's get him in here and get this over with."

"Aye, aye, Sir," General Harris said. He rose and walked out from under the canvas fly, returning a minute later with a Marine in sweat-stained, tattered utilities. He had a shoulder holster holding a .45 Colt across his chest, a Thompson submachine gun hanging from his right shoulder, and a musette bag slung over the left. He carried a small 35mm Leica camera.

"Good morning," General Vandergrift said.

"Good morning, Sir," Corporal Easterbrook replied.

"Will you stand up, please, Jack?" Vandergrift said as he got to his feet.

Now what the hell?

"You want to take off those major's leaves, please, Jack?" Vandergrift said.

"Sir?"

"You heard the General, Colonel, take off those major's leaves," General Harris said.

I don't believe this.

"Pursuant to directions from the Commandant of the Marine Corps, I announce that Major Jack (NMI) Stecker, USMCR, is promoted Lieutenant Colonel, USMCR, effective this date," General Vandergrift said. "How do you want to do this, Corporal? Me pinning on the insignia, or shaking Colonel Stecker's hand?"

"I'd like one of each, Sir," Corporal Easterbrook said.

"Very well, one of each," General Vandergrift said.

When they shook hands, General Vandergrift met Lieutenant Colonel Stecker's eyes for the first time. "Congratulations, Jack. The promotion is well deserved."

"Jesus!" Stecker blurted.

"I would hate to think that your first act as a lieutenant colonel was to question a general officer's recommendation," Vandergrift said. Then he looked at Corporal Easterbrook. "Is this all right, Corporal?"

"Colonel, if you would look this way, please?" Easterbrook said. When Stecker did that, he tripped the shutter.

(FOUR)
The Beach
Guadalcanal, Solomon Islands
0805 Hours 13 October 1942

Lieutenant Colonel Jack (NMI) Stecker was standing out of the way, on the highest ground (an undisturbed dune) he could find, watching the lines of landing craft moving between the beach and the transports standing offshore.

They were being reinforced.

After they waded the last few yards ashore, soldiers of the 164th Infantry Regiment were being formed up on the beach by their noncoms to be marched inland. At first, General Vandergrift had said at breakfast, these men would not be placed in the line as a unit. Rather, they were to be distributed among the Marine units already there; for they were desperately needed as reinforcements. At the same time, the Marines could guide them through their first experience under fire.

They're not going to be much help, he thought. *They're not even soldiers, but National Guardsmen. Still, it's a regiment of armed men, presumably in better physical shape than anyone here.*

And armed with the Garand. Goddamn it! Why is The Marine Corps at the bottom of the list when it comes to good equipment?

As the soldiers in their clean fatigue uniforms waited to move inland, Marines in their torn and soiled dungarees came down to the beach to do business with them. Word had quickly spread that the soldiers had come well supplied with Hershey bars and other pogie bait. Though the Marines had no Hershey bars or other pogie bait, they did have various souvenirs: Japanese helmets, pistols, flags, and the like. In a spirit of interservice cooperation, they would be willing to barter these things for Hershey bars.

Stecker smiled. He was aware that at least fifty percent of the highly desirable Japanese battle flags being bartered had been turned out by bearded, bare-chested Marine Corps seamstresses on captured Japanese sewing machines.

"Good morning, Sir," a lieutenant said, startling Stecker. He turned and saw a young officer in utilities and boondockers, armed with only a .45 hanging from a belt holster. He was wearing a soft-brimmed cap, not a steel helmet.

The Lieutenant saluted. Stecker returned it.

The utilities are clean. He doesn't look like he's hungry or suffering from malaria. Therefore, he probably just got here. Maybe with these ships, they're sending us a few individual replacements. He will learn soon enough to get a rifle to go with that pistol. And a helmet. But it's not my job to tell him.

"Look at all the dogfaces with Garands," the Lieutenant said. "Boy, the Army is dumb. They don't know the Garand is a Mickey Mouse piece of shit."

Well, I can't let that pass.

"Lieutenant, for your general fund of military knowledge, the Garand—"

Lieutenant Colonel Stecker stopped. The Lieutenant was smiling at him.

Hell, I know him. From where?

"Ken McCoy, Colonel," the Lieutenant said. "They told me I could probably find you here."

"Killer McCoy," Stecker said, remembering. "I'll be damned. I didn't expect to see you here." He put his hand out. "And I'm sorry, you don't like to be called 'Killer,' do you?"

Stecker remembered the first time he met McCoy. Before the war. He was then Sergeant Major Stecker of the Marine Corps base at Quantico, Virginia. McCoy was a corporal, a China Marine just back from the 4th Marines in Shanghai. He was reporting in to the Officer Candidate School.

Almost all officer candidates were nice young men just out of college. But as a test—for which few Marines, including Sergeant Major Stecker, had high hopes— a small number of really outstanding enlisted Marines were to be given a chance for a commission. It was a bright opportunity for these young men. So Stecker was surprised, when he first met him, that McCoy was not wildly eager to become an officer and a gentleman.

Soon after that, he found out that McCoy was in OCS largely because the Assistant Chief of Staff, Intelligence, of the Marine Corps had let it be known that The Corps should put bars on McCoy's twenty-one-year-old shoulders as soon as possible.

McCoy had an unusual flair for languages: He was fluent in several kinds of Chinese and Japanese and several European languages.

That wasn't all he had a flair for.

While his sources didn't have all the details, Stecker learned that McCoy was known in China as "Killer" McCoy—not for his success with the ladies, but because of two incidents where men had died. In one, three Italian Marines of the International Garrison attacked him; he killed two with his Fairbairn knife and seriously injured the third. In the second, he was in the interior of China on an intelligence-gathering mission, when "bandits" attacked his convoy (the "bandits" were actually in the employ of the Japanese secret police, the Kempe Tai). Firing Thompson submachine guns, McCoy and another Marine killed twenty-two of the "bandits."

At Quantico, the lieutenants-to-be were trained on the Garand. When it came to Sergeant Major Stecker's attention that Officer Candidate McCoy had not qualified when firing for record, he went down to have a look; for McCoy should have qualified. And so there had to be a reason why he didn't. And Stecker found it: him. He was an officer who knew McCoy in China. . . . What was that sonofabitch's name? *Macklin.* Lieutenant R. B. Macklin. . . . Macklin had something against Candidate McCoy; and it was more than just the generally held belief that commissioning enlisted men without college degrees would be the ruination of the officer corps.

Macklin actively disliked McCoy . . . more than that, he despised him. A small measure of his hostility could be gleaned at the bar of the officers' club, where from time to time he passed the word that "Killer" McCoy was so called with good reason. He did not belong at Quantico about to be officially decreed an officer and a gentleman; he belonged in the Portsmouth Naval Prison.

Sergeant Major Stecker had no trouble finding two ex–China Marines who told him more about Lieutenant Macklin than he would like to know:

In China, in order to cover his own responsibility for a failed operation, Macklin tried to lay the blame on Corporal McCoy. The 4th Marines' Intelligence Officer, Captain Ed Banning (Stecker remembered him as a good officer and a good Marine), investigated, found Macklin to be a liar, and wrote an efficiency report on him that would have seen him booted out of The Corps had it not been for the war. Instead, he wound up at Quantico.

. . . where the sonofabitch was determined to get McCoy kicked out of OCS. One of his first steps was to see that McCoy didn't qualify on the range. And if that wasn't enough, he was also writing McCoy up for inefficiency, for a bad attitude, and for violations of regulations he hadn't committed.

And he actually went into the pits to personally score McCoy's bull's-eyes as Maggie's drawers. *Then I got in the act, and refired McCoy for record. The second time, with me calling his shots through a spotter scope, he scored High Expert. And that night all those disqualifying reports mysteriously vanished from his file.*

Candidate McCoy graduated with his class and was commissioned. And then he dropped out of sight. Stecker heard that he was working for G-2 in Washington; but later he heard that McCoy had been with the 2nd Raider Battalion on the Makin Island raid.

I wonder whatever happened to that sonofabitch Macklin?

"Congratulations on your promotion," Colonel," McCoy said, without responding to the apology for being called "Killer."

"I'm still in shock," Stecker confessed. "It just happened. How did you find out?"

"General Vandergrift told me," McCoy said. "He also told me what happened to your son. I was sorry to hear that."

"What were you doing with the General?" Stecker wondered aloud. Lieutenants seldom hold conversations with general officers, much less obtain personal data from them about field-grade officers.

"I'm on my way to the States," McCoy said. "I was told to see if my boss can do anything for him in the States."

"Your boss is?"

"General Pickering."

"What have you been doing here?"

"We replaced the Coastwatcher detachment on Buka," McCoy said matter-of-factly.

Stecker had heard about that operation; and he was not surprised to hear that McCoy was involved, or that he was working for Fleming Pickering. "It went off all right, I guess?" Colonel Stecker asked.

"It went so smoothly, it scared me. Colonel—"

"I'm going to have trouble getting used to that title," Stecker interrupted.

"It took a while, but I'm now used to being called 'lieutenant,'" McCoy said. "I never thought that would happen. They wouldn't have promoted you if they didn't think you could handle it."

"Or unless they've reached the bottom of the barrel so far as officers are concerned. One or the other."

"What I started to say was that I'm going home via Pearl. Pick Pickering asked me to go by the Naval Hospital to see your son. I thought maybe you'd want me to tell him something, or . . ."

"I expect they're doing all they can for him," Stecker said. "You could tell him . . . Tell him you saw me, and that I'm proud of him."

"Yes, Sir."

Colonel Stecker was aware that he had just done something he rarely did, let his emotions show.

"What can I do for you, McCoy?" he asked.

"That's my question, Sir. General Pickering told me to look you up and see what he could do for you. Or what I could."

"That's very kind of the General . . ." Stecker said, and then paused. "We were in France together, in the last war, did you know that?"

"Yes, Sir."

"I was a buck sergeant, and he was a corporal. We were as close as Pick and my son Dick are."

"Yes, Sir. He told me."

"So please tell him, McCoy, that I appreciate the gesture, but I can't think of a damned thing I need."

"Aye, aye, Sir."

"When are you going to Pearl?"

"We were supposed to go today, but when the R4D pilots came in from Espíritu Santo, they found something wrong with the airplane. They're fixing it now, so I guess in the morning."

Stecker put out his hand.

"It was good to see you, McCoy. And thank you. But now I have to get back to my battalion."

"Could I tag along with you, Sir?"

"Why would you want to do that?"

"I feel like a feather merchant just hanging around waiting to be flown out of here," McCoy said simply. "Maybe I could be useful."

"I don't think anyone thinks of you as a feather merchant, McCoy," Stecker said. "But come along, if you like."

(FIVE)
VMF-229
Henderson Field
0930 Hours 13 October 1942

"Well, look who's come home," First Lieutenant William C. Dunn, USMCR, said to First Lieutenant Malcolm S. Pickering, USMCR. When he walked into the tent, Dunn found Pickering sitting on his bunk.

Pickering reached around and picked up from the bunk a small cloth bundle tied with string. With both hands, he shot it like a basketball at Dunn.

"Don't say I never gave you anything," Pickering said.

The package was heavier than it looked; Dunn almost dropped it.

"Bribery of superior officers is encouraged," Dunn said. "What is it?"

"Royal Australian Air Force Rompers and booze," Pickering said. "From Port Moresby."

Dunn took a K-Bar knife from a sheath and slit the cord. Then he carefully removed a pair of quart bottles of Johnny Walker scotch from the two cotton flying suits they were wrapped in and put them in the Japanese shipping crate that served as his bedside table.

"Thanks, Pick," Dunn said.

"I figured even an unreconstructed Rebel like you would rather drink scotch than not drink at all," Pick said.

"Kicking the gift horse right in the teeth, what I really need is underpants," Dunn said. "I don't suppose there's . . ."

"Shit, I didn't even think of skivvies," Pickering said. "When I saw the booze and the flight suits . . ."

"All contributions gratefully received," Dunn said. He proved it by stripping out of the sweat-soaked flight suit he was wearing; and then, standing naked except for his held-together-with-a-safety-pin shorts, he began tearing off the labels from one of the flying suits.

He looked at Pickering.

"So tell me all about the great secret mission."

"Not much to tell. It went like clockwork."

"Where did you learn to fly an R4D?"

"On the way to New Guinea," Pick replied.

Dunn looked at him curiously, then saw he was serious.

"Then how come . . . ?"

"I was about to go over the edge," Pick said. "Galloway saw it and took me along, just to work the radios, to get me out of here."

"Because of Dick Stecker?" Dunn asked quietly.

"I was about to turn in my wings of gold for a rifle," Pick said.

"Same thing happened yesterday as happened to Dick. Or nearly the same thing. Ted Knowles ran out of gas and crashed. Did you get to meet him before you left?"

Pickering shook his head, no.

"He was making a dead-stick approach. According to Oblensky, he tried to stretch his glide and didn't make it. He rolled it end over end. When I went to see him, all you could see was gauze."

"Did he come through it?"

Dunn shook his head, no. "Nice guy. My fault. I didn't check the flight about remaining fuel, and he didn't want to look like he was anything less than a heroic Marine Aviator, so he tried to fly it on the fumes."

"That's not your fault," Pickering said.

"So Colonel Dawkins says," Dunn said as he started pulling on the new flight suit. "Personally, your notion about turning in the wings for a rifle seems tempting."

"You don't mean that."

"I don't know if I do or not," Dunn said. "Galloway talked you out of it?"

"No. I talked myself out of it. I'd make a lousy platoon leader. And so would you. But we do know how to fly airplanes. Ye old round pegs in ye old round holes, so to speak."

Dunn zipped the zipper of the new flying suit up and down, and admired himself.

"Thanks, Pick," he said, and started to transfer the contents of the discarded flying suit into the new one.

Captain Charles M. Galloway entered the tent. He saw Dunn's new RAAF flight suit.

"Where'd you get that?"

"They had many too many flight suits at Moresby," Pickering said. "They probably won't even miss the ones I stole."

"And what if you have to go back there?"

"What if I don't?" Pickering replied.

Galloway shook his head in resignation.

"Oblensky redlined the R4D for a fuel-transfer pump," Galloway said. "They're going to have to fly it up from Espíritu Santo. It'll be tomorrow before your pal The Killer and his friends can leave, in other words."

"His pal 'The Killer'?" Dunn said. "That sounds interesting."

"He's a very interesting guy, as a matter of fact," Galloway said, and then looked directly at Pickering. "You feel up to flying?" he asked. When there was no immediate response, he went on: "The Skipper wants a search of the Southeast."

"And you volunteered me?"

"I volunteered me," Galloway said. "You want to go along with me? Or do you want to go to Espíritu Santo?"

"I told you on the airplane I'm a fighter pilot, not a truck driver," Pickering said. "Or are you having second thoughts?"

"Just checking, Mr. Pickering, just checking. Five minutes."

He turned and left the tent.

"What was that 'do you want to go to Espíritu Santo' remark about?" Dunn asked.

"We had some time to kill in Port Moresby. Galloway put me in the left seat of the R4D and I shot a dozen touch-and-goes. Since he is an R4D IP, he signed me off on it. I am now officially a dual-engine-qualified Naval Aviator checked out in the R4D. They're easy to fly; a very forgiving airplane."

"That's not what I asked, Pick."

"He said I could go to Espíritu Santo and fly R4Ds for them, if I wanted."

"I think I would have gone."

"You weren't listening, Mr. Dunn, Sir. I am a fighter pilot, Sir, not a truck driver," Pickering said, and pushed himself off the bunk and walked out of the tent.

(SIX)
28,000 Feet above Savo Island
Solomon Islands
1135 Hours 13 October 1942

Pick Pickering was more than a little embarrassed when he saw that he was flying just off Charley Galloway's right wing. He was supposed to be at least a hundred feet to his rear and a hundred feet above him.

You have been woolgathering, again, Pickering! he thought.

That put him back in boarding school: Mr. Whatsisname, the shriveled little guy with the bow ties and the ragged-sleeved tweed jackets, used to bring him back to the here and now by slamming a book on his desk. Obviously guilty as charged, presuming one understood that woolgathering meant not paying attention, day-dreaming.

But what the hell was woolgathering? Where did that come from? You cut the wool off live, kicking sheep. If you didn't pay attention to what you were doing, you'd either lose your fingers or the sheep.

He was cold. Despite the horsehide Jacket, Leather, Aviators, with the fur collar up and snapped in place, and the fine calfskin Gloves, Aviators, it was cold at 28,000 feet. And the cold was made worse because the sweat-soaked flight suit was still moist and clammy.

The oxygen mask irritated his face—he needed a shave—and the oxygen itself seemed colder than normal.

When he glanced again at Galloway, he saw that Galloway, his features hidden behind his oxygen mask, was looking at him.

You have been caught woolgathering, Mr. Pickering. You will be chastised for not paying attention and for not being where you are supposed to be.

Both of Galloway's hands, held palm upward, appeared in the canopy.

Christ, he thinks I crept up to him on purpose, to subtly remind him we are running a little low on fuel: Perhaps, Captain, Sir, you will consider returning to the base before we have to swim back?

Or perhaps I should try to stretch the glide of a dead-stick landing, and do an end-over-end down the runway like Dick and that guy of Dunn's that I didn't know?

A gesture of helplessness, of futility, the palms-up business. The Japanese having elected not to come out and fight, or at least not to come out where we can see them.

Pickering held up both of his hands in the same gesture. Galloway's left hand disappeared from sight, presumably to return to the stick. His right gloved hand, index finger extended, signaled that they should start their descent. Pickering nodded, exaggeratedly, signaling his understanding.

Galloway's Wildcat's nose dropped a couple of degrees and he entered a wide, shallow descending turn. Pickering retarded his throttle, so that as he followed him he would be on Galloway's wing, where he knew Galloway expected him to be.

That lasted almost precisely two minutes, Captain Galloway being highly skilled in making very accurate, two-minute 360-degree turns.

Or, for that matter, one-minute 360-degree turns. Or, for that matter, any-time, any-degree turns. The sonofabitch can really fly an airplane.

Oh, shit! Where did they come from?

There were airplanes down there, a lot of airplanes, Kates and Vals. A dozen of each.

Kates were Nakajima B5N1 torpedo bombers, single-engine, low-wing monoplanes. They could carry bombs or torpedoes. Now obviously bombs, since you can't torpedo an airfield.

Vals were Aichi D3A1 Navy Type 99 carrier bombers, probably not today flying off a carrier, but from the Japanese base at Rabaul. Vals had fixed landing gear, the wheels covered with pants. They looked old-fashioned, but they were good, tough airplanes.

How the hell could we have missed them?

And where Kates and Vals are found, so almost certainly there are Zeroes.

Where the hell are the Zeroes? Above us, for Christ's sake?

Pickering touched the throttle and started to pull alongside Galloway again, but that didn't happen. Galloway came out of the turn and pushed the nose of his Wildcat down.

Pickering followed him. His eyes dropped to the instrument panel and he made the calculation mentally.

I have thirty, thirty-five minutes' fuel remaining. Galloway probably has another five minutes over that; he can coax extra minutes of fuel from an engine. Cut that time considerably by running it at full throttle, or Emergency Military Power.

We're going to have time for one pass, that's all. Knock down what we can in one pass and then head for the barn.

Where the hell is the rest of the Cactus Air Force? They were supposed to take off at 11:15. Earlier, obviously, if there had been a warning from Buka, or from another Coastwatcher station, or even from the radar. As close as these Japanese are to Henderson, they should have spotted them with the radar.

Jesus Christ! Did we break our ass to make sure Buka stayed on the air and now something has happened to them?

An alert Kate tail gunner spotted them and opened fire. His tracers made an arc in the air before they burned out.

At too great a distance, you stupid bastard!

But as they grew closer, they came in range, and other tail gunners opened fire. And now the tracers were closer and there were a hell of a lot more of them.

Pickering depressed the trigger on the stick.

Jesus Christ, what's the matter with me, I'm not even close to him?

He edged back on the stick, and then again.

The tracer stream moved into the fuselage of the Kate, just forward of the horizontal stabilizer, and then, as if with a mind of its own, seemed to walk up the fuselage toward the engine.

There goes a piece of the cowling!

And then smoke suddenly appeared, and the Kate fell off to the left. Before it flashed out of sight, the smoke burst into an orange glow.

Got him! Where the hell is Galloway?

He saw Galloway already below the formation of Kates, almost into the formation of Vals. There was a Zero on his tail, gaining rapidly as Galloway decreased the angle of his dive.

Sonofabitch!

Pickering grabbed the microphone.

"Charley, behind you!"

Pickering threw the stick to the left and shoved the throttle to FULL EMERGENCY POWER. It didn't seem to be working; it took forever to get behind the Zero, and by then he was firing at Galloway.

Pickering depressed his trigger.

Galloway turned sharply to the right, increasing the angle of his dive.

The Zero, trying to follow him, flew into Pickering's tracer stream. He came apart.

There was smoke coming from Galloway's engine.

Oh, shit! No!

Galloway continued his dive toward the sea. Pickering followed him.

The Cactus Air Force—whatever airplanes could get into the air—appeared, climbing toward the Japanese.

Too goddamn late!

The Japanese were over Henderson.

Galloway's engine was no longer smoking.

Jesus Christ, what did he do, shut it down?

Pickering looked behind him. He could see bombs falling from the Vals.

Galloway was almost on the deck.

Oh, shit, he's going in!

Galloway leveled off at no more than 200 feet over the sea and began a straight-in approach to Henderson.

As Pickering started to level off to follow him, he saw bombs landing on the dirt fighter strip. He looked at his gas gauge. He had five, six minutes remaining.

He moved the landing-gear switch to LOWER and pulled the Wildcat up sharply. The crank spun furiously as gravity pulled the gear down.

Twenty seconds later, his wheels touched down. Five seconds later, he felt the Wildcat lurch to the right.

Oh, not that! God, I don't want to die that way!

It straightened out a little, and then he went off the runway into a section of pierced steel planking and spun around, once, twice . . . The gear collapsed in the turns. The propeller hit the dirt, and the engine screamed and stopped.

Am I still moving?

No. This sonofabitch isn't going anywhere. . . .

He unfastened his harness and scrambled as quickly as he could out of the cockpit. He ran twenty-five yards and then threw himself down on the ground, waiting for the Wildcat to explode.

It didn't.

There were explosions, but those were bombs landing on the airfield.

He raised his head to look at the field. There was a huge orange glow and dense black smoke. The Japanese had put at least one bomb in the fuel dump.

He saw a jeep coming across the field to him through the smoke and the detonations of the Japanese bombs.

It slid to a stop beside him. A Corpsman jumped out.

"You OK?" the Corpsman asked.

"I'm fine," Pickering replied.

The Corpsman lay down beside him.

"I think we're better staying where we are," he said matter-of-factly. "Look at that fucking gasoline burn!"

IV

SECRET

FROM: COM GEN 1ST MAR DIV 1305 13OCT42

SUBJECT: AFTER-ACTION REPORT

TO: COMMANDER-IN-CHIEF, PACIFIC, PEARL HARBOR
INFO: SUPREME COMMANDER SWPOA, BRISBANE
                        COMMANDANT, USMC, WASH, DC

   1. AT 1140 13OCT42 A TWO (2) F4F4 PATROL OF VMF-229 INTERCEPTED A PRE-
VIOUSLY UNDETECTED JAPANESE FORCE CONSISTING ESTIMATED AS TWELVE
(12) VAL; TWELVE (12) KATE AND FIFTEEN (15) ZERO AND ENGAGED.
   2. ENEMY LOSSES:
     A. TWO (2) KATE
       GALLOWAY, CHARLES M CAPT USMCR ONE (1)
       PICKERING, MALCOLM S 1/LT USMCR ONE (1)
     B. ONE (1) ZERO
       PICKERING, MALCOLM S 1/LT USMCR ONE (1)
   3. VMF-229 LOSSES:
     A. ONE (1) F4F4 DAMAGED, REPAIRABLE.
     B. ONE (1) F4F4 CRASHED ON LANDING, DESTROYED.
     C. VMF-229 LOSSES REDUCE OPERATIONAL AIRCRAFT AVAILABLE TO VMF-
229 TO THREE (3) F4F4. PLUS TWO (2) POSSIBLY REPAIRABLE F4F4.
   4. MAG-21 LOSSES:
     A. HENDERSON AND FIGHTER ONE RUNWAYS CRATERED BY ENEMY BOMBS.
REPAIRS UNDERWAY.
     B. AVGAS FUEL DUMP STRUCK BY ENEMY BOMBS AND SET AFIRE. ESTIMATED
LOSS OF AVGAS FIVE THOUSAND FIVE HUNDRED (5500) GALLONS.
     C. LIGHT TO SEVERE DAMAGE, EXTENT NOT YET DETERMINED, TO ELEVEN
(11) USN, USMC AND USAAC AIRCRAFT ON HENDERSON FIELD.
   5. THE UNDERSIGNED HAS, ON THE RECOMMENDATION OF CO, MAG-21, AU-
THORIZED THE EVACUATION OF USAAC B-17 AIRCRAFT FROM HENDERSON TO
ESPIRITU SANTO UNTIL SUCH TIME AS STOCKS OF AVGAS AND SPARE PARTS,
NOW ESSENTIALLY EXHAUSTED, CAN BE REPLENISHED. ALL REMAINING STOCKS
OF AVGAS NEEDED FOR F4F4 AND P39 AND P40 AIRCRAFT. B17 AIRCRAFT WILL
DEPART AS SOON AS REPAIRS TO RUNWAY ARE ACCOMPLISHED.

VANDEGRIFT MAJ GEN USMC COMMANDING

SECRET

(TWO)
VMF-229
Henderson Field
1330 Hours 13 October 1942

"You had a blowout is what it looks like, Mr. Pickering," Technical Sergeant Oblensky said.

They were in a maintenance revetment, an area large enough to hold two Wildcats. It was bordered on three sides by sandbag walls. Sheets of canvas, once part of wall tents, had been hung over it to provide some relief from the heat of the sun, and from the rain.

"A blowout?" Pickering asked bitterly.

"If I had to guess, I'd guess you run into a bent-up piece of pierced steel planking. But maybe a piece of bomb casing or something."

"Jesus Christ!"

"Put you out of control. And then the gear collapsed. It won't handle that kind of stress, like that. You're lucky it wasn't worse."

"The airplane's totaled, right?"

"Yeah. Not only the gear. When that went, there was structural damage, hard to fix. And then the engine was sudden-stop. Probably not even worth trying to rebuild, even if we had the stuff to do it with. I'll pull the guns and the radios and the instruments and whatever else I can out of it and have it dragged to the boneyard."

"How many aircraft does that leave us with?"

"Three. Plus I think I can fix what Captain Galloway was flying. He lost an oil line, but he shut it right down, maybe before it had a chance to lock up. I'll have to see."

Galloway at that moment walked in.

"I blew a tire," Pickering said.

"Blew the shit out of it," Oblensky confirmed. "Have a look."

"Thank you, Mr. Pickering," Galloway said.

"Thank me for what?"

"You know for what. I couldn't have gotten away from that Zero."

"You were doing all right," Pickering said.

"When I say 'thank you,' you say 'you're welcome.'"

Pickering met his eyes. "You're welcome, Skipper."

"I just saw Colonel Dawkins. There were witnesses to both of yours. Both confirmed. What does that make, seven?"

"Eight. I'll confirm yours. I saw it go down."

"They confirmed that, too," Galloway said, and turned to Oblensky. "Did you have a chance to look at that engine?"

"I'm going to pull an oil line from this," Oblensky said, gesturing at Pickering's F4F4, "and put it on yours and then run it up and see what happens. You said you shut it down right away."

"I don't want anyone flying it but me, understand?"

"If I didn't think it was safe, I wouldn't let anybody fly it."

"Just say 'aye, aye, sir,' for Christ's sake, Steve," Galloway said.

"What happens now, Skipper?" Pickering asked.

"What you do now is run down all your friends—they're scattered all over— and bring them here. As soon as the runways are fixed, they're flying the B17s off to Espíritu Santo. They can go with them."

"What about the R4D?"

"It took a hundred-pound bomb through the wing. It didn't explode, but that airplane's not going anywhere. Mr. Pickering will need your jeep, Steve."

"It was over by the AvGas dump when that went up," Oblensky said. "No jeep, Skipper."

"Well, Mr. Pickering, you said you were thinking of joining the infantry. The infantry walks, so that should be no problem for you."

For a moment Lieutenant Pickering looked as if he was about to say something obscene. But he thought about it, and what he said was, "Aye, aye, Sir."

(THREE)
VMF-229
Henderson Field
1535 Hours 13 October 1942

When Captain Charles M. Galloway walked in, Majors Ed Banning and Jake Dillon, Lieutenant Ken McCoy, Sergeant George Hart, and Corporal Robert F. Easterbrook were sitting on the bunks and wooden crates of the Bachelor Officers' Quarters— a tent with sandbag walls. Galloway was trailed by Lieutenant Bill Dunn.

Galloway looked at Banning.

"Major, the B-17s can't get off today. That last raid cratered the runway again."

There had been a second Japanese bombing attack at 1350, a dozen or so Kates and slightly fewer Zeroes.

"I saw fighters take off," Banning replied. It was a question, not a challenge.

"You saw two fighters get off," Galloway replied. "Joe Foss and somebody else. They took a hell of a chance; dodged the craters and debris."

"I saw one Japanese plane go down," Major Dillon said.

"Foss again," Galloway said. "He got a Zero. But that was all the damage we did."

"What the hell happened to the Coastwatchers?" McCoy asked.

Galloway looked at him. He had not yet got a fix on this semilegendary Marine. A lot of what he'd heard about Killer McCoy had to be bullshit, yet he'd also noticed that Major Ed Banning (a good professional Marine, in his view) treated McCoy with serious respect.

"According to what I heard, McCoy, there was a transmission delay between Pearl Harbor and here. You know what atmospherics are?"

McCoy nodded. Galloway noticed that the nod was all he got, not a "Yes, Sir."

"Well, we monitor Coastwatcher radio. Sometimes we can hear them, sometimes we can't. This time we couldn't. So the warning had to go through CINCPAC radio at Pearl" (*Commander-In-Chief, Pac*ific headquarters at Pearl Harbor, T.H.). "There was a delay in them getting through to here. They said atmospherics. We were refueling our fighters when we finally got the warning. By that time the Japanese were over the field."

"Buka's operational, Ken," Banning said. "These things happen."

"So what happens now?" Dillon said.

"The Seventeens can't dodge runway craters. And they don't think they can fill them before it gets dark. So the Seventeens will have to wait until first light. You'll leave then."

"Unless the Japs come back again," Dillon said.

"Unless the Japs come back again," Galloway parroted. "I'm sorry, it's out of my control."

"If the Seventeens can't get off in the morning, is there any other way I can get to Espíritu Santo?" Banning asked.

Interesting question, Galloway thought. *He doesn't want out of here to save his skin. If he did, he wouldn't talk openly about going the way he just did. And why did he ask how "I" can get to Espíritu, not "we"? What business does he alone have to take care of?*

Galloway seemed to be reading his mind.

"Galloway, I'm going to have to claim a priority to get to Espíritu, if it comes to that."

"There will probably—almost certainly—be an R4D, or several of them, who will try to land here at first light. Bringing AvGas in. They carry as many wounded as they can when they leave."

"If it comes down to that, and the B-17s aren't flying ..." Banning said, ". . . what I was hoping was maybe catching a ride in an SPD or a TBF."

The Douglas SPD-3 "Dauntless" was a single-engine, low-wing monoplane, two-place dive-bomber. It was powered by a Pratt & Whitney 1000-horsepower R-1820-52 engine. The Grumman TBF "Avenger" was a three-place, single-engine, low-wing monoplane torpedo bomber, powered by a 1700-horsepower Wright R-2600-8 "Cyclone" engine. Both aircraft were used by both the U.S. Navy and the USMC.

"I'll ask," Galloway answered, "but I don't think that's going to happen."

"I wouldn't ask if it wasn't necessary," Banning said.

Galloway was now uncomfortable.

"Dunn's found some cots for you to sleep on. But we lost our jeep, so they'll have to be carried. How about you, Sergeant?" he asked, and looked at George Hart. "And you, Easterbunny?"

Corporal Easterbrook looked unhappy.

"You have something else to do?" Galloway said.

"Captain, if I'm going to spend the night with the Raiders," Easterbrook said. "I'm going to have to start up there now."

"Go ahead, Easterbrook," Lieutenant McCoy said. "We can carry our own cots. We only look like feather merchants."

He was talking to me, goddamn it, not you, McCoy, Galloway thought. And then he wondered why that made him so angry.

"Thank you, Sir," Easterbrook said, and left the tent.

"I wasn't picking on him, McCoy," Galloway heard himself say. "He's a pretty good kid. I try to keep an eye out for him."

"Somebody should," McCoy said. "He's about to go over the edge."

"Meaning what, McCoy?" Dillon broke in, an inch short of unpleasantly.

"Meaning he's about to go over the edge. Did you see him during the last raid? Take a good look at his eyes."

"Oh, bullshit!" Dillon flared. "Nobody likes to get bombed. He's a Marine, for Christ's sake."

"He's a Marine about to go over the edge," McCoy said.

"You're a fucking expert, are you?" Dillon said, now unabashedly unpleasant. "You have a lot of experience in that area?"

"Yes, Jake," Banning said, calmly but firmly, "he does. In the Philippines, for example."

"You were in the Philippines?" Bill Dunn blurted. "How did you get out?"

"Like I hope to get out of here tomorrow," McCoy replied. "On a B-17." He stood up. "Come on, George, you and I will go carry cots for these field-grade feather merchants."

Banning laughed, and stood up.

"To hell with you, McCoy, I won't let you get away with that. Off your ass, Jake. If I can carry my own cot, so can you."

Dillon, not moving, looked up at Banning.

"Off your ass, Jake," Banning repeated. His tone was conversational, but there was no mistaking it for a friendly suggestion. It was an order.

(FOUR)

SECRET

FROM: COM GEN 1ST MAR DIV 0845 14OCT42

SUBJECT: AFTER-ACTION REPORT

TO: COMMANDER-IN-CHIEF, PACIFIC, PEARL HARBOR
INFO: SUPREME COMMANDER SWPOA, BRISBANE
                    COMMANDANT, USMC, WASH, DC

1. AT APPROXIMATELY 1830 13OCT42 HEAVY JAPANESE ARTILLERY BARRAGE WITH IMPACT WESTERN END OF HENDERSON FIELD COMMENCED. IT IS BELIEVED THAT WEAPONRY INVOLVED IS 150-MM REPEAT 150-MM NOT PREVIOUSLY ENCOUNTERED. IT IS POSSIBLE THAT THIS ARTILLERY IS NEWLY ARRIVED ON GUADALCANAL.

2. INASMUCH AS 1ST MARDIV DOES NOT POSSESS ANY COUNTERFIRE RANGING CAPABILITY, 5-INCH SEACOAST ARTILLERY OF 3RD USMC DEFENSE BATTALION AND 105-MM HOWITZERS OF 11TH MARINES WERE INEFFECTIVE IN COUNTERBATTERY FIRE.

3. AT APPROXIMATELY 0140 14OCT42 HENDERSON FIELD WAS MARKED WITH FLARES BY JAPANESE AIRCRAFT. IMMEDIATELY THEREAFTER INTENSIVE ENEMY NAVAL GUNFIRE FIRE COMMENCED AND LASTED FOR A PERIOD OF NINETY-SEVEN (97) MINUTES.

4. A MINIMUM OF EIGHT HUNDRED (800) AND POSSIBLY AS MANY AS ONE THOUSAND (1000) ROUNDS ARMOR PIERCING AND HIGH EXPLOSIVE FELL ON HENDERSON FIELD AND IMMEDIATELY ADJACENT AREAS. FROM THE NATURE OF THE DAMAGE CAUSED, IT IS BELIEVED NAVAL FOURTEEN (14) INCH CANNON WERE INVOLVED, MOST LIKELY FROM A JAPANESE BATTLESHIP OR BATTLESHIPS.

5. ENEMY LOSSES:
    NEGLIGIBLE, IF ANY. MAIN NAVAL GUNFIRE CAME FROM WARSHIPS BEYOND THE RANGE OF 5-INCH SEACOAST CANNON OF 3RD MARDEFBN. ACCOMPANYING SMALLER VESSELS, PRESUMABLY DESTROYERS, WERE ENGAGED WITHOUT VISIBLE RESULT.

6. US LOSSES:
    A. FIELD GRADE OFFICER KIA ONE (1)
    B. FIELD GRADE OFFICER WIA ONE (1)
    C. COMPANY GRADE OFFICER KIA FIFTEEN (15)
    D. COMPANY GRADE OFFICER WIA ELEVEN (11)
    E. ENLISTED KIA THIRTY-NINE (39)
    F. ENLISTED WIA SEVENTY-NINE (79)
    G. MISSING IN ACTION: TO BE DETERMINED

H. SEVERE DAMAGE TO HENDERSON FIELD RUNWAY, CONTROL TOWER, RE-VETMENTS AND SUPPLY STORAGE AREAS. REMAINING AVGAS SUPPLY CRITICAL.

I. EXTENT OF DAMAGE TO AIRCRAFT NOT YET FULLY DETERMINED. IT IS OBVIOUSLY SEVERE. FOR EXAMPLE OF THIRTY-NINE (39) SPD AIRCRAFT AVAIL-ABLE AS OF YESTERDAY, FOUR (4) ARE AVAILABLE AT THIS TIME, AND TWO (2) OF EIGHT (8) B17 AIRCRAFT WERE TOTALLY DESTROYED.

7. AS SOON AS RUNWAY REPAIRS PERMIT REMAINING B17 AIRCRAFT WILL WITHDRAW TO ESPIRITU SANTO.

8. MOST CRITICAL NEED OF THIS COMMAND IS RESUPPLY OF AVGAS. UR-GENTLY REQUEST RESUPPLY BY ANY MEANS AVAILABLE. RECOMMEND NO RE-PEAT NO REPLENISHMENT OF AIRCRAFT UNTIL SUFFICIENT AVGAS AVAILABLE HENDERSON FIELD FOR FUELING.

VANDEGRIFT MAJ GEN USMC COMMANDING

(FIVE)
MAG-21
Henderson Field

"Colonel," Captain Samuel M. Davidson, U.S. Army Air Corps, said to Lieutenant Colonel Clyde W. Dawkins, "I'm not sure I like this. As a matter of fact, the more I think about it, I don't like it at all."

"You don't have any choice in the matter, Sam," Dawkins said. "These people are going with you, period."

"Who the hell are they?"

"Two majors, a lieutenant, and a sergeant. I told you."

"I told my people they're going out with us."

"I'll find something constructive for them to do," Dawkins said. "And just as soon as I can find space for them, I'll get them out of here."

"And what if . . . ?" He paused a moment and then began again: "I really don't mean to sound insubordinate, but the first obligation of an officer is to take care of his men. What if I simply say 'with all respect, Sir, no'?"

"I said no way, Sam. I was shown a set of orders on White House stationery, signed by Admiral Leahy, the President's Chief of Staff. To repeat myself, you don't have any choice in the matter."

"How did they get here?"

"In an R4D. It took a bomb through the wing."

"The one with that funny landing gear?"

Dawkins nodded.

"You want to tell me what that was all about? It looked like skis."

"Sorry, Sam. I couldn't tell you if I knew, and I don't. I really don't. But if it makes you feel any better, I was in the Division Command Post, and I saw General Vandergrift shake one of the Major's hands and thank him. They're not tourists."

There was a loud, frightening crash, a long one, along with the scream of timbers being ripped apart.

"What the hell was that?" Captain Davidson asked.

"That was the Pagoda," Dawkins said. "General Geiger decided that the Japanese were using it as an artillery aiming point. They bulldozed it, I guess."

"Why didn't they just blow it up?"

"Probably because there's a shortage of dynamite, in addition to everything else," Dawkins said.

"Where are these people, then?" Captain Davidson asked.

"Bill Dunn, Charley Galloway's exec, has been told to take them to your plane."

"You know, I've only got three functioning engines."

"That shouldn't bother the Army Air Corps."

"I feel like I'm running away, Colonel. I don't like that feeling, either."

"You'll be back," Dawkins said. He stood up and put out his hand. "Have a nice flight, Sam. It's been good knowing you."

"What's going to happen to you?"

"Who knows? Sooner or later, one side is going to run completely out of airplanes."

Davidson met his eyes for a minute. Then he brought himself to a position of attention worthy of the parade ground at West Point, and saluted.

"Serving with you has been a privilege, Sir," he said.

"Thank you, Sam," Dawkins said after a moment, as he returned the salute. "For a dog-faced soldier, you're not too bad an airplane driver."

Davidson did a precise about-face and marched out of the sandbag-walled tent that served as the headquarters of Marine Air Group 21.

Corporal Robert F. Easterbrook ran up to the B-17 as it stood, second in line, for takeoff. The prop blast from its idling engines blew his helmet off.

He glanced at the helmet, then went up to the airplane and banged on the fuselage. After a moment, the door in the fuselage opened and an Army Air Corps staff sergeant peered out.

"Major Dillon! Major Dillon!" the Easterbunny shouted over the roar of the engines.

The staff sergeant disappeared, and a moment later Major Dillon showed up in the door.

Easterbrook handed Dillon a canvas bag.

"Still and motion picture film of the Raiders last night," he shouted. "And a couple of reels of this fucking mess."

Dillon took the bag and nodded.

Easterbrook stood back and the door closed.

Easterbrook waved at the nice lieutenant who'd kept him from having to carry cots the day before.

The door opened again. Major Dillon motioned for Easterbrook to come closer. When he did, he extended his hand.

Easterbrook thought it was nice that the Major wanted to shake his hand.

Major Dillon took Corporal Easterbrook's wrist, not his hand. With a mighty jerk, he pulled Corporal Easterbrook into the airplane. The door closed.

The pilot advanced the throttles. The B-17 started to roll. He turned onto the runway and shoved the throttles to FULL MILITARY POWER. It began to accelerate very slowly, and for a moment Captain Davidson thought that with only three engines working, there was a very good chance they weren't going to make it.

But then he felt life come into the controls. He edged the wheel back very, very carefully.

The rumble of the landing gear on the battered runway died.

"Wheels up!" Captain Davidson ordered.

(SIX)
United States Naval Base
Espíritu Santo
1715 Hours 14 October 1942

While Rear Admiral Daniel J. Wagam, USN, of the CINCPAC Staff, was not a cowardly man, or even an unusually nervous one, he was enough of a sailor to know that the greater the speed of a hull moving through the water, the greater the stresses applied to that hull.

He could see no reason why this basic principle of marine physics should be invalidated simply because the hull belonged to a flying boat. Flying boats, moreover, were constructed not of heavily reinforced steel plate, but of thin aluminum.

Consequently, Admiral Wagam was not at all embarrassed to feel a bit uncomfortable whenever his duties required him to take off or land in a flying boat. Each required the flying boat's hull to move through the water at a speed two or three times greater than a battleship's hull would ever be subjected to, or even a destroyer's.

The twin engines of the PBM-3R "Mariner" made a deeper, louder sound, and the Admiral glanced out of the window beside him. They were moving; the water was just starting to slide by. (The PBM-3R Martin "Mariner" seaplane was a variant of the Martin PBM-series maritime reconnaissance aircraft. Powered by the same two Wright R-2600-22 1900-horsepower "Cyclone" engines, but stripped of armament, the -3R aircraft were employed as transports, capable of carrying 20 passengers or an equivalent weight of cargo.)

When the Mariner began its takeoff, he tried, of course, not to show his concern: He turned to speak to his aide, Lieutenant (Junior Grade) Chambers D. Lewis III. Lewis's father, Admiral Lewis, had been Admiral Wagam's classmate at Annapolis.

His mouth was barely open, however, when the roar of the Mariner's engines died and the seaplane lurched to a stop.

"I wonder what the hell that is?" Admiral Wagam said aloud.

The seaplane now rocked side to side in the sea, reminding the Admiral that they were not in a bona fide vessel, but rather in an aircraft that happened to float.

The pilot appeared in the aisle between the two rows of seats. When he passed Admiral Wagam, the Admiral held up his hand.

"Is there some problem?"

"Sir, I was told to abort the takeoff and hold for a whaleboat," the pilot replied. Admiral Wagam nodded, and turned back to his aide.

"Probably some mail they didn't have prepared in time," he said. "Some people don't know the importance of meeting a posted schedule."

"That's true, Sir," Lieutenant Lewis agreed.

Admiral Wagam paid no attention to the activity aft, where there was a port in the hull, until Captain J.H.L. McNish, USN, of his staff, appeared by his seat, knelt, and said, "Admiral, I'm being bumped."

"What do you mean, you're being bumped?" Admiral Wagam asked, both incredulous and annoyed.

This aircraft was not part of the Naval Air Transport command. It had been assigned to Admiral Wagam, more or less personally, to take his staff to Espíritu for a very important conference: Guadalcanal was in trouble. Extraordinary measures would be necessary to keep the Marines there from being pushed off their precarious toehold. Wagam personally didn't give them much hope; the necessary logistics simply weren't available. Indeed, in his professional opinion—and he'd said so— the whole operation had been attempted prematurely. But he was going to do the very best he could with what he had to work with. And that meant flying here from Pearl to see the situation with his own eyes; and bringing his staff, to give them the absolutely essential hands-on experience.

But getting them back to Pearl quickly was just as important as bringing them here. They had to get to work. One of the reasons he had gone all the way to the top—to CINCPAC himself—to have an airplane assigned to his team was to make sure the team stayed together.

CINCPAC had agreed with his reasoning, and authorized the special flight. Admiral Wagam certainly would have no objections to carrying other personnel, or mail or cargo, if there was room, but he had no intention of standing idly by while one of his staff was bumped.

If there was a priority, he had it. From CINCPAC himself.

"I'm being bumped, Sir," Captain McNish repeated.

"I'll deal with this, Mac," Admiral Wagam said, and unfastened his seat belt and made his way aft. Standing by the pilot were a commander he remembered meeting on the island and a Marine major in a rather badly mussed uniform.

"Commander," Admiral Wagam said, "just what's going on here?"

"Sir, I'm going to have to bump one of your people. Captain McNish is junior—"

"No one's going to bump any of my people," the Admiral declared. "This is not a Transport Command aircraft. It is, so to speak, mine. I decide who comes aboard."

"I'm sorry about this, Admiral," the Marine Major said.

"Well, Major, I don't think it's your fault. The Commander here should have known the situation."

"Admiral, I have to get to Pearl. This is the aircraft going there first," the Major said.

"A lot of people have to get to Pearl," the Admiral snapped. "But I'm sorry, you're not going on this aircraft."

"I'm sorry, Sir," the Major said. "I am."

"Did you just hear what I said, Major?" the Admiral replied. "I said you're not getting on this aircraft!"

"With respect, Sir, may I show you my priority?"

"I don't give a good goddamn about your priority," the Admiral said, his patience exhausted. "Mine came from CINCPAC."

"Yes, Sir," the Major said. "The Commander told me. Sir, may I show you my orders?"

"I'm not interested in your goddamn orders," the Admiral said.

"Sir, I suggest you take a look at them," the Commander said.

The Admiral was aware that he had lost his temper. He didn't like to do that.

"Very well," he said, and held out his hand. He expected a sheaf of mimeographed paper. He was handed, instead, a document cased in plastic. On casual first glance, he noted that it was a photographically reduced copy of a letter. He took a much closer look.

THE WHITE HOUSE
Washington, D.C.

3 September 1942

By direction of the President of the United States, Brigadier General Fleming W. Pickering, USMCR, Headquarters, USMC, will proceed by military and/or civilian rail, road, sea and air transportation (Priority AAAAA-1) to such points as he deems necessary in carrying out the missions assigned to him.

United States Armed Forces commands are directed to provide him with such support as he may request. General Pickering is to be considered the personal representative of The President.

General Pickering has unrestricted TOP SECRET security clearance. Any questions regarding his mission will be directed to the undersigned.

W.D. Leahy, Admiral, USN
Chief of Staff to The President

When he saw that the Admiral had read the document, Major Edward F. Banning, USMC, said, "Sir, may I ask the Admiral to turn that over and read the other side?" Admiral Wagam did so.

OFFICE OF THE CHIEF OF STAFF TO THE PRESIDENT
Washington, D.C. 24 September 1942

1st Endorsement

1. Major Edward F. Banning, USMC, is attached to the personal staff of Brigadier General Fleming Pickering, USMCR for the performance of such duties as may be assigned.

2. While engaged in carrying out any mission assigned, Major Banning will be accorded the same level of travel priorities, logistical support and access to classified matériel authorized for Brigadier General Pickering in the basic Presidential order.

3. Any questions regarding Major Banning's mission(s) will be referred to the undersigned.

W.D. Leahy, Admiral, USN
Chief of Staff to The President

Admiral Wagam looked at Major Banning.
"You are, I gather, Major Banning?"
"Yes, Sir."
"Well, I can only hope, Major, that whatever it is you have to do in Pearl Harbor is more valuable to the war effort than what Captain McNish would have contributed."

"I wouldn't have bumped the Captain, Admiral," Banning said, "if I didn't think it was."

The Admiral nodded, turned, and went back up the aisle to tell Mac that he was sorry, there was nothing he could do about it, he was going to have to go ashore in the whaleboat.

(SEVEN)
USN Photographic Facility Laboratory
Headquarters, CINCPAC
Pearl Harbor, T.H.
0735 Hours 15 October 1942

"Ah-ten-HUT!" a plump, balding chief photographer's mate called, and all but one man, a Marine major, popped to attention.

"As you were," Brigadier General Fleming Pickering, USMCR, said. As he spoke, he walked past one of the junior aides to CINCPAC. The aide's orders were to take very good care of General Pickering; that meant that at the moment he was holding the door open for him. "I'm looking for Major Banning," Pickering continued.

"Over here, Sir," Banning called.

Pickering was the last person in the world Banning expected to see here. But then, he thought, Pickering could almost be counted on to do the unexpected.

Pickering walked over to him, his hand extended.

"Good to see you, Ed. I heard an hour ago you were here. I had a hell of a time finding you. What are you doing here?"

"Good to see you, General," he said. He held up a roll of developed 35mm film. "Having a look at this. One of Jake Dillon's photographers shot it just before we left Guadalcanal."

Pickering took it from him and held it up to the light.

"What am I looking at?"

"That roll is what Henderson Field looked like just before we left," Banning said. "If it came out, I thought I'd try to figure some way to get it to you in Washington in time for your briefing."

Two men walked up: the chief photographer's mate, and an officer in whites wearing lieutenant commander's shoulder boards.

"Lieutenant Commander Bachman, Sir. Is there some way we may help the General, Sir?"

"Two ways, Commander," Pickering said. "I want two copies, eight-by-tens, of each frame of this, and any other film Major Banning has. And I would kill for a cup of coffee."

"Sir, the coffee's no problem. But I'm sure the General will understand we have priorities. It may be some time before we can—"

"This is your first priority, Commander," Pickering interrupted. "You can either take my word for that, or the Lieutenant here will call Admiral Nimitz for me."

"Sir," Admiral Nimitz's aide said, "my orders are that General Pickering is to have whatever CINCPAC can give him."

"You heard that, Chief," Commander Bachman said.

"Aye, aye, Sir."

"Sir," Banning said. "I've also got eight rolls of 16mm motion picture film. There was a problem getting that developed. . . ."

"Is there still a problem with that, Commander?"

"No, Sir," Commander Bachman said.

"How about making a copy of it?"

"That's rather time consuming, Sir, but we can do it, Sir."

"Get it developed first," Pickering said, looking at his watch. "We'll see about the time."

"Where will the General be, Sir?"

"I need a secure place to talk to Major Banning. Have you got one here? Or I can go—"

"My office is secure, Sir."

"Good, then what we need is your office, and that coffee," Pickering said. He turned to Admiral Nimitz's aide. "Son, I know your orders, but I'm afraid you're going to have to let me out of your sight; Major Banning here is a stickler for security."

"Aye, aye, Sir," the aide said, smiling. Pickering had obviously heard Admiral Nimitz's order: "Don't let him out of your sight, Gerry. And be prepared to tell me who he talked to, and what was said."

A photographer's mate third class came in with a tray holding a stainless-steel pitcher of coffee, two china mugs, and a plate of doughnuts. He laid the tray on Major Bachman's desk and then left, closing a steel door after him.

"I never thought I'd have to say this to you, Ed," Pickering said with a smile, "but you need a shave, Major."

Banning smiled back. "A question of priorities, Sir. I figured I could shave once I got this stuff on its way to you."

"Did you get to see General Vandergrift? Was he cooperative?"

"Cooperative, yes. But uncomfortable. He thought it was violating the chain of command."

"Couldn't be helped," Pickering said. "All right, let's have it."

"Christ, it's worse than I thought," Pickering said after Banning finished reporting Vandergrift's assessment of his situation, along with his own and the other code-breaker's analysis of Japanese intentions and capabilities.

"It's not a pretty picture, Sir."

"Goddamn it, we can't lose Guadalcanal!"

"We may have to consider that possibility, Sir."

Pickering exhaled audibly, then looked at Banning.

"I don't suppose you had a chance to see my son?"

"Yes, Sir. I spent a good deal of time with him. He was the copilot on the R4D."

"He was in on the operation? How did that happen? I didn't know he could fly an R4D."

"I think it was a question of the best man for the job, Sir. He was picked by the pilot, Sir. Jake Dillon was a little uncomfortable when he saw him at Port Moresby."

Major Banning had learned the real story behind Lieutenant Pickering's role as the R4D copilot: that Pick Pickering had almost gone over the edge after his buddy was terribly injured, and that Galloway ordered him into the plane for what could be accurately described as psychiatric therapy. But there was no point in telling his father this.

"I'll be damned," Pickering said.

"And the day before yesterday, he shot down another two Japanese planes. A Zero and a bomber. That makes eight. He's a fine young man, General."

"In a fighter squadron which is down to three airplanes, according to what you just told me. You ever hear of the laws of probability, Ed?"

"His squadron commander, Captain Galloway—the man who flew the R4D, a very experienced pilot—told me, Sir, that Pick is that rare bird, a natural aviator. He's good at what he does, Sir. Very good."

"Jack Stecker's boy is an ace, plus one. He was obviously pretty good at what he did, too. He's over at the hospital wrapped up like a mummy. They feed him and drain him with rubber tubes."

"I heard about that, Sir. McCoy saw Colonel Stecker on the 'Canal. You heard he was promoted?"

"I heard. Getting him promoted pitted Vandergrift and me against most of the rest of the officer corps," Pickering replied bitterly, adding: "Christ, Jack ought to be wearing this star, not me."

"You wear it very well, Sir," Banning said without thinking.

Pickering looked at him but did not reply.

"Speaking of McCoy . . . where are the others?"

"Probably in the air by now, Sir. I came ahead. I thought that was what you wanted. I bumped a Navy captain from some admiral's private airplane."

Pickering chuckled. "Wagam. Rear Admiral. I know. I was in Nimitz's office when he reported back in. Complaining."

"I hope it wasn't awkward for you, Sir."

"Not for me. For him. He didn't know who I was. Just some Marine. When he was finished complaining about some Washington paper-pusher Marine running roughshod over CINCPAC procedures, Nimitz introduced him to me. 'Admiral,' Nimitz said, 'I don't believe you know General Pickering, do you?'"

Banning chuckled. "I didn't expect to see you here, either, General."

"I didn't expect to be here," Pickering said. "Dillon and company must be on the plane I'm waiting for."

"It's going on to Washington, Sir?"

"No. As soon as they service it, it's going to Australia."

"You're going to Australia, Sir?" Banning asked, surprised.

"Yes, I am," Pickering said, his tone making it clear that he wasn't happy about it.

"Then who's going to brief Secretary Knox?"

"You are," Pickering said. "You've got a seat on a Pan American clipper leaving here at 4:45. Which means we have to get you to the terminal by 3:45."

Banning looked uncomfortable.

"Ed, just give a repeat performance of what you did just now for me," Pickering went on. "Frank Knox puts on his pants like everybody does. Actually, I've grown to rather like him."

"Sir, my going to Washington is going to pose problems in Brisbane."

"About MAGIC, you mean? Pluto and Moore and Mrs. Feller should be able to handle it; they've been holding down the fort pretty well as it is, with all the time you've been spending in Townesville with the Coastwatchers."

Banning looked even more uncomfortable.

"All right, Ed, what is it?"

"Sir, between the three of us, we have been pretty much keeping Mrs. Feller out of things."

"You have? Obviously, you have a reason?"

"I am reluctant to get into this, Sir."

"That's pretty damned obvious. Out with it, Ed."

"General, I don't want to sound like a prude, but when we're dealing with intelligence at this level—at this level of sensitivity—people's personal lives are a factor. They have to be."

"What are you suggesting, Ed, that Ellen Feller is a secret drinker? For God's sake, she was a missionary!"

"She sleeps around, Sir."

"You know that for a fact? You have names?"

"General," Banning said, hesitated, and then plunged ahead. "I considered it my responsibility to make sure that you didn't leave any classified material in your quarters."

"I never did that!"

"Yes, Sir. You did."

"Jesus! You're serious about this, aren't you?"

"Yes, Sir. Sir, I arranged with the Army to keep Water Lily Cottage under security surveillance. They assigned agents of their Counterintelligence Corps to do so. They reported daily to me."

"What's that got to do with Mrs. Feller?"

"They were very thorough, Sir. They reported all activity within the Cottage. On a twenty-four-hour basis."

Now Pickering looked uncomfortable.

"Jesus," he said softly, and then he met Banning's eyes. "Ed, just because, in a moment of weakness, I got a little drunk and did something I'm certainly not proud of, that does not mean that Ellen Feller can't be trusted with classified information. Christ, it only happened once. Those things happen."

"It wasn't only you, General," Banning said.

"Who else?" Pickering asked.

"Moore, Sir. Before he went to Guadalcanal."

"Moore?" Pickering asked incredulously.

John Marston Moore, who was twenty-two, was raised in Japan, where his parents were missionaries. With that background, he was assigned to Pickering as a linguist, which led to his becoming a MAGIC analyst. Later, he was seriously wounded on Guadalcanal, after which Pickering arranged to have him commissioned.

"And, Sir, Mrs. Feller could have prevented Moore from going to Guadalcanal. As she should have."

"That's a pretty goddamn serious charge. Why the hell didn't you report this to me?" Pickering flared.

"And she's slept with several officers of SWPOA, Sir," Banning continued, calmly but firmly. "Two of General Willoughby's intelligence staff, and a Military Police officer."

"The answer to my question, obviously, is that you never reported this to me because it would be embarrassing."

"I didn't know what your reaction would be, Sir. And we've had the situation under control."

"Now for that, goddamn it, you owe me an apology. I may be an old fool, but not that much of a fool. You should have come to me, Ed, and you know it!"

Banning didn't reply.

"Does she know that you know?"

"Yes, Sir. When I found out she stood idly by when they sent Moore to Guadalcanal, I lost my temper and it slipped out."

"You lost your temper?"

"She was more worried about getting caught with Moore in her bed than she was about MAGIC. Yes, Sir, I was mad; I lost my temper. I told her what I thought of her."

Pickering looked at him for a moment, and then laughed.

"I can't tell you how glad I am to hear that," he said. "You have been a thorn in my side for a long time, Banning. I find it very comforting to learn that you, the perfect Marine, the perfect intelligence officer, can lose your temper and do something dumb."

"General, if an apology is in or—"

"The subject is closed, Ed," Pickering interrupted. "I will deal with Mrs. Feller when I get to Brisbane."

"I'm sorry I had to get into this—"

Pickering interrupted him again: "Looking at your face just now, I would never have guessed that." He touched Banning's shoulder. "Let's see how many photos we have, Ed. And then we'll see about getting you a shower and a shave before you catch your plane."

He went to the door and then stopped.

"Curiosity overwhelms me. Not you, too?"

"No, Sir," Banning said after hesitating. "But there were what could have been offers."

"And now you'll never know what you missed, Ed. The price of perfection is high."

(EIGHT)
Muku Muku
Oahu, Territory of Hawaii
1645 Hours 15 October 1942

Wearing a red knit polo shirt and a pair of light-blue golf pants, Brigadier General Fleming Pickering walked out onto the shaded flagstone patio of a sprawling house on the coast. Five hundred yards down the steep, lush slope, large waves crashed onto a wide white sand beach.

Major Jake Dillon, USMCR, was sitting on a stool. A glass dark with whiskey was in his hand; a barber's drape covered his body. He was having his hair cut by a silver-haired black man in a white jacket.

"You find enough hair to cut, Denny?" Pickering asked.

"He's got more than enough around the neck, Captain," the black man said to Pickering with a smile. "Excuse me, General," he corrected himself; to his mind Pickering would always be Captain of his merchant fleet. "We just won't mention the top."

"If you didn't have that razor in your hand," Dillon said, "I'd tell you to go to hell."

Denny laughed.

"Very nice, General," Jake Dillon teased. "What is this place?"

"This is Muku Muku, Major," the black man said. "Pretty famous around the Pacific."

"What the hell is it?"

"My grandfather bought this, all of it," Pickering said and made a sweeping gesture, "years ago. Now they've turned it into Beverly Hills."

Dillon laughed. "You make Beverly Hills sound like a slum, the way you said that."

"What I meant was very large houses on very small lots," Pickering said. "I can't understand why people do that."

Another elderly-looking black man in a white jacket opened one of a long line of sliding plate-glass doors onto the patio. Lieutenant Kenneth R. McCoy walked outside. He was wearing obviously brand-new khakis.

"You find everything you need, Ken?" Pickering asked.

"Yes, Sir," McCoy said. "Thank you."

"Can I offer you something to drink, Lieutenant?" the black man said. "You, Captain?"

"I'll have whatever the balding man is having," Pickering said.

"That's fine," McCoy said. "General, what is this place?"

"It's Muku Muku," Dillon said. "I got that far."

"My grandfather bought it," Pickering said. "As sort of a rest camp for our masters, and our chief engineers, when they made the Islands . . . the Sandwich Islands then. In the old days, the sailing days, they were at sea for months at a time."

"I sailed under the Commodore, the Captain's grandfather," the black man working on Dillon said. "The *Genevieve*. The last of our four-masters. Went around the Horn on her."

"That's right, isn't it?" Pickering said. "I'd forgotten that, Denny."

"And I retired off the *Pacific Endeavour*," Denny said. "From sail to air-conditioning." He looked over at McCoy. "Just as soon as I'm through with this gentleman, Sir, I'll be ready for you."

"And then my father started sending masters' and chief engineers' families out here from the States, to give them a week or two—or a month's—vacation. And then he tore it down, in the late twenties . . ."

"Nineteen thirty-one, Captain," Denny corrected him.

"I stand corrected," Pickering said. "He tore down the original house—it was a Victorian monstrosity—and built this place. And to get the money, he sold off some of the land."

"Turning it into a slum," Dillon said.

"I didn't say 'slum,' I said 'Beverly Hills,' " Pickering answered. "He always said he was going to retire here. But then he dropped dead."

The second black man appeared with two whiskey glasses on a silver tray.

Pickering picked his up and raised it.

"Welcome home, gentlemen," he said. "Welcome to Muku Muku."

"After all I've been through," Dillon said, "I frankly expected more than this fleabag."

"Oh, Jesus," McCoy groaned. Pickering laughed delightedly.

There was the sound of aircraft engines. They looked out to sea. A white four-engine seaplane came into view. It was making a slow, climbing turn to the left.

"There goes Banning," Pickering said. "That's the Pan American flight to San Francisco."

"I wondered where he was," Dillon said as he was being brushed off by Denny.

"He's going to brief Frank Knox on Guadalcanal," Pickering said. "That film your man made was valuable, Jake."

"I'm glad to hear that," Dillon said. "So what happens to us now, Flem?"

"You'll spend tomorrow here, and maybe the day after tomorrow. I fed the four of you into the regular air transport priority system. With an AAAA priority, they say it generally takes a day or two to find a seat."

"What I meant is what happens to me? Am I still working for you?"

McCoy took Dillon's place on the stool. Denny draped the cloth around him.

"Jake, I want you to understand that I appreciate the job you did for me, but . . ."

"No apologies required, Flem. I was out of my depth in that whole operation. McCoy ran it. I'm ready to go back to being a simple flack."

"Don't get too comfortable doing that," Pickering said. "We may call on you again."

"General," McCoy said. "I promised Colonel Stecker and Pick that I would see Stecker while I was here. . . ."

"My plane leaves Pearl Harbor at eight in the morning," Pickering said. "I'd like to have you around until it leaves. Then you can go to the Naval Hospital. Be prepared for it; he's really in bad shape."

"Thank you, Sir."

"I sent a message to Colonel Rickabee, primarily to warn him that Banning will need a shave and a haircut and a decent uniform when he arrives . . . before he goes to see Frank Knox. But I also asked him to call Ernie Sage and tell her you're here, and on your way to the States."

Colonel F. L. Rickabee, a career Marine intelligence officer, was Pickering's deputy at the Office of Management Analysis in Washington. Ernestine "Ernie" Sage was McCoy's girlfriend, the daughter of the college roommate of Pickering's wife.

"Thank you, Sir," McCoy said.

"Tell me, McCoy," Pickering asked. "What do you think of George Hart? How is he under pressure?"

McCoy laughed.

"He was the maddest one sonofabitch I ever saw in my life on the beach at Buka," McCoy said. "First, the rubber boat got turned over and he had a hell of a hard time getting ashore. And then I told him he was going to have to wait there—alone, overnight at least—while the native radio operator and I went looking for Howard and Koffler."

"But he did what he was expected to?"

"Oh, yes, Sir. He's a good Marine, General."

"I thought he might turn out to be," Pickering said.

(NINE)
Marine Barracks
U.S. Naval Station
Pearl Harbor, T.H.
1715 Hours 15 October 1942

Sergeant George F. Hart, USMCR, and Corporal Robert F. Easterbrook, USMCR, came out of the basement of Headquarters Company unshaved, unwashed, and wearing the utilities they had put on at Guadalcanal. Each was carrying a large, stuffed-full seabag.

"What now, Sergeant?" Sergeant Hart asked the freshly shaved, freshly bathed, and impeccably shined and uniformed staff sergeant who was their escort since the plane from Espíritu Santo landed.

"I was told to get you issued a clothing issue," the staff sergeant replied. "I done that. You been issued. I guess you wait to see what happens next."

At that moment, a corporal, who was just as impeccably turned out as the staff sergeant, pushed open the door and marched down the highly polished linoleum toward them.

"I'm looking for a Sergeant Hart and a Corporal Eastersomething," he announced.

"You found them," the staff sergeant announced. "Ain't you the Colonel's driver?"

"Yeah. You want to come with me, you two?"

"Where are we going?" Sergeant Hart asked.

The corporal ignored the question, but did hold the door open for them as they staggered through it under the weight of their seabags. Corporal Easterbrook was carrying additionally a Thompson .45 ACP caliber submachine gun, an EyeMo

16mm motion picture camera, and a Leica 35mm still camera, plus a canvas musette bag.

Parked at the curb was a glistening 1941 Plymouth sedan, painted Marine green— including its chromium-plated bumpers, grille, and other shiny parts. The corporal opened the trunk and the seabags were dropped inside.

"You taking the Thompson with you?" the corporal asked.

"Yes, I am," Easterbrook replied.

"You're not supposed to take weapons off the base," the corporal said. "But I guess this is different."

" 'Off the base'?" Sergeant Hart asked. "Where are we going?"

The corporal did not reply until they were in the car. Once they were inside, he consulted a clipboard that was attached to the dashboard.

"Some place in the hills," he said. "Muku Muku. They gave me a map."

"What the hell is Muku Muku?" Sergeant Hart asked.

"Beats the shit out of me, Sergeant. It's where I was told to take you."

"There it is," the corporal said. "There's a sign."

Sergeant Hart looked where he pointed. A bronze sign reading "Muku Muku" was set into one of the brick pillars supporting a steel gate.

The corporal drove the Plymouth five or six hundred yards down a narrow macadam road lined with exotic vegetation. The road suddenly widened and became a paved area in front of a large, sprawling house.

That's a mansion, Sergeant George Hart thought, *not a house. Must be Pickering's. There's no other logical explanation.*

"What the hell is this?" Easterbrook asked.

"It must be our transient barracks," Hart replied.

Fleming Pickering opened the passenger door and put out his hand.

"Welcome home, George," he said.

"Thank you, Sir," Hart said. "I didn't expect to see you here, General."

"I didn't expect to be here," Pickering replied. "Get yourself cleaned up, have a drink, and I'll explain it all to you." He leaned over the front seat and offered his hand to Easterbrook.

"I'm General Pickering," he said. "You're Easterbrook, right?"

"Yes, Sir."

"Those pictures you took, and the motion picture film you shot, were just what I needed. Come on in the house, and I'll try to show you my gratitude."

When Fleming Pickering knocked on the door, Sergeant Hart and Corporal Easter-brook were sitting in a large room furnished with two double beds. They were showered and shaved and wearing new skivvies. A moment later Pickering walked in, a freshly pressed uniform over his arm.

"This is Easterbrook's," he said, handing it to him. "Yours will be along in minute, George."

"Yes, Sir."

"You don't have a drink?" Pickering said. "I thought the refrigerator would need restocking by now."

He slid open a closet door. Behind it was a small refrigerator, full of beer and soft drinks.

"And there's whiskey in that cabinet," he said, pointing. "If you'd rather."

"I'll have a beer, please, Sir," Hart said, and walked to him.

Pickering opened a beer, then walked to Easterbrook and handed it to him.

"Son, why don't you put on a shirt and trousers, that's all you'll need, and then go down and sit with McCoy on the patio. I need a word with Sergeant Hart."

"Yes, Sir," Easterbrook replied, and hastily put on a khaki shirt and pants.

Pickering made himself a drink of scotch, and waited until Easterbrook was gone before he spoke.

"You were just paid a pretty good compliment, George," Pickering said. "McCoy said of you, quote, 'He's a good Marine, General.'"

"I'm flattered," Hart said. "If only half the things they say about him are true, he's a hell of a Marine."

"I'm on my way to Australia, George. Tomorrow morning. In a day or two, they'll find you a seat on a plane to the States. Show your orders in San Francisco and tell them to route you via St. Louis on your way to Washington. Take a week to see your folks, and then go to Washington. Then pack your bags again. I don't think I'll be coming back there anytime soon—that may change, of course—but I'd like to have you with me in Australia."

"Aye, aye, Sir," Hart said, and then: "May I ask a question, Sir?"

"Certainly."

"Wouldn't it make more sense if I went to Australia from here?"

"It would, but I didn't want to ask you to do that. I mean, after a man gets tossed out of a rubber boat . . ."

"McCoy told you about that?"

". . . in the surf off an enemy-held island, he's entitled to a leave. I can do without you for two or three weeks, George."

"Easterbrook deserves to go home. Major Dillon and McCoy have things to do in the States. I don't. I'll go with you, Sir, if that would be all right."

"Strange, I thought that would be your reaction," Pickering said. "And I can use you, George."

There was a knock at the door, and a white-jacketed black man walked in with a freshly pressed set of new khakis.

"Finish your beer," Pickering said. "And then come down to the patio."

"Aye, aye, Sir."

Corporal Robert F. Easterbrook, carrying a bottle of beer, slid open a plate-glass door and walked uneasily onto the patio.

"They take care of you all right at the Marine Barracks, Easterbrook?" Lieutenant McCoy asked.

"Yes, Sir."

"Pull up a chair, take a load off," Major Dillon said, smiling, trying to be as charming as he could.

He thought: *Well, now that I've got you off Guadalcanal, what the hell am I going to do with you?*

V

(ONE)
Pan American Airlines Terminal
San Francisco, California
0700 Hours 16 October 1942

Almost all the passengers on Pan American Flight 203 from Hawaii were in uniform, Army, Navy, and Marine. And all the uniforms were in far better shape than his, Major Edward Banning noted. He was sure, too, that no one on the airplane was traveling without a military priority. But it was a civilian airliner, and Pan American provided the amenities it offered before the war.

The food was first class, served by neatly uniformed stewards. It was preceded by hors d'oeuvres and a cocktail, accompanied by wine, and trailed by a cognac. Banning had three post-dinner cognacs, knowing they would put him to sleep, which was the best way he knew to pass a long flight.

For breakfast, there were ham and eggs, light, buttery rolls, along with freshly brewed coffee; he wasn't about to complain when the yolks of the eggs were cooked hard.

We all have to be prepared to make sacrifices for the war effort, he thought, smiling to himself. He was pleased with his wit—until it occurred to him he still might be feeling the effects from the night before of the pair of double bourbons, the bottle of wine, and the cognacs.

After breakfast, the steward handed him a little package containing a comb; a toothbrush and toothpaste; a safety razor; shaving cream; and even a tiny bottle of Mennen after-shave. Armed with all that, he went back to the washroom and tried to repair the havoc that days of neglect had done to his appearance.

Brushing his teeth made his mouth feel a great deal better, and a fresh shave was pleasant. But the face that looked back at him in the mirror did not show a neatly turned out Marine officer. It showed a man with bloodshot eyes—not completely due, he decided, to all the drinks he let himself have last night. His skin was an unhealthy color. And he was wearing a shirt that smelled of harsh Australian soap mixed with the chemicals of the Pearl Harbor photo lab.

I need a shower, eight hours in a bed, and then some clean uniforms. I wonder how long it will take them in San Francisco to get me a seat on an airplane. Maybe enough time to go to an officers' sales store and get at least a couple of new shirts. Maybe even enough to get some sleep.

The United States Customs Service was still functioning normally, randomly looking inside bags. And the Shore Patrol was in place, maintaining high disciplinary standards among transient Navy Department personnel. There was even an SP officer, wearing the stripes of a full lieutenant along with an SP brassard and a white pistol belt.

The Shore Patrol officer walked purposefully over to Banning.

What is this? "Major, the shape of your uniform, and the length of your hair is a disgrace to the U.S. Naval Service generally, and The Marine Corps specifically. You will have to come with me!"

"Major Banning?" the Lieutenant asked.

"My name is Banning."

"Will you come with me, please, Sir?"

"I'm not through Customs."

"I wouldn't worry about that, Sir. Would you come with me, please? Can I help you carry anything?"

"Where are we going?"

"To the airport, Sir. There's a plane waiting for you."

"I just got off an airplane!"

"Right this way, please, Major," the Shore Patrol lieutenant said, already starting to lead the way to a Navy gray Plymouth sedan with a chrome siren on the fender and SHORE PATROL lettered on its doors.

The Army Air Corps major saluted as Banning got out of the Plymouth.

"Major Banning, we're ready anytime you are," he said.

"Is there a head, *a men's room,* anyplace convenient?"

"Right inside, Major, I'll show you," the Major said. "Major, we have a seven-place aircraft . . ."

"What kind of an aircraft?"

"A B-25, Sir. General Kellso's personal aircraft. Would you have any objection if we took some people with us?"

"Wouldn't that be up to you?" Banning said. "Or General Kellso? You said it was his airplane."

"Right now, it's the Secretary of the Navy's, Major, with the mission of taking you to Washington."

"Load it up, Major. Where did you say the bathroom is?"

"Right over there."

The rest room was chrome and tile and spotless. It even smelled clean.

Banning entered a stall and closed the door and sat down.

There was a copy of *Life* magazine in a rack on the back of the door. A picture of Admiral William D. Leahy, in whites, was on the cover.

Banning took it from the rack.

In the shape my digestive tract is in, I may be here all day. The human body is not designed to fly halfway around the world in airplanes.

He started to flip through the magazine.

There was a picture of an Army sergeant kissing his bride, a Canadian Women's Army Corps corporal.

There was a Westinghouse advertisement, proudly announcing that it had won an Army-Navy E for Excellence award for producing four thousand carloads of war matériels a month—enough to fill a freight train thirty-seven miles long.

How come none of it seems to have reached Guadalcanal?

There was a series of photographs of Army officers in an English castle. The censor had obliterated from the photographs anything that could identify the castle. The American officers all looked well fed.

And their trousers, unlike yours, Banning, are all neatly pressed.

There was an advertisement from Budweiser, announcing what they were doing for the war effort—from baby foods to peanut butter to flashlights, carpet, and twine. Beer wasn't mentioned.

There was a series of photographs recording Wendell Willkie's travels to Egypt. He was described as the "leader of President Roosevelt's Friendly Opposition."

Another series of photographs showed the aircraft carrier USS *Yorktown*'s final moments in the Battle of Midway. Another showed the Army Air Corps in the

Aleutian Islands. Another, a nice-looking woman named Love, who was married to an Air Corps light colonel. She was about to head up an organization of women pilots who would ferry airplanes from the factories. Another, a huge new British four-engine bomber called the Lancaster; the monster could carry eight tons of bombs.

I'll bet not one of them ever gets sent to New Guinea or the Solomons. Or at least not until after the Japanese have reoccupied Guadalcanal and captured all of New Guinea.

What really caught his attention was the Armour & Company full-page advertisement, showing in color what the "typical" soldier, sailor, and Marine was being fed this week: roast chicken, frankfurters, barbecued spareribs, baked corned beef, Swiss steak, baked fish, and roast beef. Servicemen could have second helpings of anything on the menus, it claimed.

Jesus H. Christ! If there'd been ten pounds of roast chicken or roast beef on Guadalcanal, the war against the Japs would have been called off while the Marines fought over it.

Surprising him, his bowels moved. He put *Life* back in the rack on the door, looked again at Admiral Leahy's photograph, and had one final unkind thought: *The Chief of Staff to the Commander-in-Chief needs a haircut himself; it's hanging over his collar in the back. And I have seen better pressed white uniforms on ensigns.*

"Sorry to keep you waiting," Banning said as he washed his hands and saw the Air Corps Major's reflection in the mirror over the sink.

"It's your airplane, Major," the Air Corps Major said. "Take your time."

(TWO)
Office of the Assistant Chief of Staff G-1
Headquarters, United States Marine Corps
Eighth and I Streets, NW
Washington, D.C.
0825 Hours 16 October 1942

Colonel David M. Wilson, USMC, Deputy Assistant Chief of Staff G-1 for Officer Personnel, had no idea what Brigadier General J. J. Stewart, USMC, Director, Public Affairs Office, Headquarters USMC, had in mind vis-à-vis First Lieutenant R. B. Macklin, USMC, but he suspected he wasn't going to like it.

General Stewart had requested an appointment with the Assistant Chief of Staff, Personnel, himself, but the General had regrettably been unable to fit him into his busy schedule.

"You deal with him, Dave. Find out who this Lieutenant Macklin is, and see what Stewart thinks we should do for him. I'll back you up whatever you decide. Just keep him away from me."

Colonel Wilson was a good Marine officer. Even when given an order he'd rather not receive, he said, "Aye, aye, Sir," and carried it out to the best of his ability.

He obtained Lieutenant Macklin's service record and studied it carefully. What he saw failed to impress him. Macklin was a career Marine out of Annapolis. Though Colonel Wilson was himself an Annapolis graduate, he was prepared to admit—if not proclaim—that Annapolis had delivered its fair share of mediocre to poor people into the officer corps.

He quickly came to the conclusion that Macklin was one of these.

Macklin had been with the 4th Marines in Shanghai before the war. He came out of that assignment with a truly devastating efficiency report.

One entry caught Wilson's particular notice: "Lieutenant Macklin," it said, was "prone to submit official reports that not only omitted pertinent facts that might tend to reflect adversely upon himself, but to present other material clearly designed to magnify his own contributions to the accomplishment of an assigned mission."

In other words, he was a liar.

Even worse: "Lieutenant Macklin," the report went on to say, "could not be honestly recommended for the command of a company or larger tactical unit."

Politely calling him a liar would have kept him from getting a command anyway, but his rating officer apparently wanted to drive a wooden stake through his heart by spelling it out.

And that could not be passed off as simply bad blood between Macklin and his rating officer. For the reviewing officer clearly agreed with the rating officer: "The undersigned concurs in this evaluation of this officer." And it wasn't just any reviewing officer, either. It was Lewis B. "Chesty" Puller, then a major, now a lieutenant colonel on Guadalcanal.

Colonel Wilson had served several times with Chesty Puller and held him in the highest possible regard.

After Macklin came home from Shanghai, The Corps sent him to Quantico, as a training officer at the Officer Candidate School. He got out of that by volunteering to become a parachutist.

It was Colonel Wilson's considered (if more or less private) opinion that Marine parachutists ranked high on the list of The Corps' really dumb mistakes in recent years. While there might well be some merit to "The Theory of Vertical Envelopment" (as the Army called it), it made no sense at all to apply that theory to The Marine Corps.

For one thing, nothing he'd seen suggested that parachute operations would have any application at all in the war The Marine Corps was going to have to fight in the Pacific. A minimum of 120 R4D aircraft would be required to drop a single battalion of troops. In Colonel Wilson's opinion, it would be a long time before The Corps would get that many R4Ds at all, much less that many for a single battalion. In his view, it was a bit more likely that he himself would be lifted bodily into heaven to sit at the right hand of God.

For another, Colonel Wilson (along with a number of other thoughtful senior Marine officers) had serious philosophical questions about the formation of Marine parachutists: Since The Corps itself was already an elite organization, creating a parachutist elite within the elite was just short of madness.

He was not a fan of that other elite-within-the-elite, either: the Marine Raiders. But the parachutists and the Raiders were horses of different colors. For one thing, the order to form the Raiders came directly from President Roosevelt himself; and there was nothing anyone in The Corps could do about it, not even the Commandant.

And for another, so far the Raiders had done well. They'd staged a successful raid on Makin Island, and they'd done a splendid job on Guadalcanal.

Viewed coldly and professionally, the parachutists' record was not nearly as impressive: After their very expensive training, there were no aircraft available to transport them (surprising Colonel Wilson not at all), and so they were committed as infantry to the Guadalcanal operation, charged with making an amphibious assault on a tiny island called Gavutu. They fought courageously, if not very efficiently; and the island fell. Later, Wilson heard credible scuttlebutt that their fire discipline was practically nonexistent. And the numbers seemed to confirm this: The parachute battalion was literally decimated in the first twenty-four hours. And after the invasion, they continued to suffer disproportionate losses.

Macklin was with the parachutists in the invasion of Gavutu; but he went in as a supernumerary. Which meant that he was a spare officer; he'd be given a job only after an officer commanding a platoon, or whatever, was killed or wounded.

Macklin never reached the beach. He managed to get himself shot in the calf and face and was evacuated.

Colonel Wilson had been a Marine a long time. He'd been in France in the First War, and he'd passed the "peacetime years" in the Banana Wars in Latin America. He had enough experience with weaponry fired in anger to know that getting shot only meant that you were unlucky; there was no valor or heroism connected with it.

According to his service record, Macklin was in the Army General Hospital in Melbourne, Australia, recovering from his wounds, when he was sent to the States to participate in a war bonds tour of the West Coast. That was where he was now.

Colonel Wilson thought he remembered something about that last business. And a moment later a few details came up from the recesses of his mind: In a move that at the time didn't have Colonel Wilson's full and wholehearted approval, the Assistant Commandant of The Marine Corps arranged to have an ex–4th Marines sergeant commissioned as a major, for duty with Public Affairs. The Assistant Commandant's reasoning was that The Corps was going to need some good publicity, and that the way to do it was to bring in a professional. The man he was thinking of was then Vice President, Publicity, of Metro-Magnum Studios, Hollywood, California (who just happened to earn more money than the Commandant or, for that matter, than the President of the United States). *And wasn't it fortuitous that he'd been a China Marine, and—Once a Marine, Always a Marine—was willing to come back into The Corps?*

Major Jake Dillon, Colonel Wilson was willing to admit, did not turn out to be the unmitigated disaster he feared. He'd led a crew of photographers and writers in the first wave of the invasion of Tulagi, for instance, and there was no question that they'd done their job well.

Dillon was responsible for having Lieutenant Macklin sent home from Australia for the war bond tour.

Why did Dillon do that? Colonel Wilson wondered.

And then some other strange facts surfaced out of his memory: Dillon was somehow involved with the Office of Management Analysis. Colonel Wilson was not very familiar with that organization. But he knew it had nothing to do with Management Analysis, that it was directly under the Commandant, and that you were not supposed to ask questions about it, or about what it did.

It didn't take a lot of brains to see what it did do.

The Office of Management Analysis, anyhow, had a new commander, another commissioned civilian, Brigadier General Fleming Pickering. Pickering was put in over Lieutenant Colonel F. L. Rickabee, whose Marine career had been almost entirely in intelligence. And it was said that Pickering reported directly to the Secretary of the Navy. Or, depending on which scuttlebutt you heard, to Admiral Leahy, the President's Chief of Staff.

There was surprisingly little scuttlebutt about what Dillon was doing for the Office of Management Analysis.

Meanwhile, Colonel Wilson ran into newly promoted Colonel Rickabee at the Army-Navy Country Club, but carefully tactful questioning about his job and his new boss produced only the information that General Pickering shouldn't really be described as a commissioned civilian. He'd earned the Distinguished Service Cross as a Marine corporal in France about the time Sergeant (now Lieutenant Colonel) Jack (NMI) Stecker had won his Medal of Honor.

* * *

At precisely 0830, the intercom box on Colonel Wilson's desk announced the arrival of Brigadier General J. J. Stewart.

"Ask the General to come in, please," Colonel Wilson said, as he slid the Service Record of First Lieutenant R. B. Macklin into a desk drawer and stood up.

He crossed the room and was almost at the door when General Stewart walked in.

"Good morning, General," he said. "May I offer the General the General's regrets for not being able to be here. A previously scheduled conference at which his presence was mandatory . . ."

"Please tell the General that I understand," General Stewart said. "There are simply not enough hours in the day, are there?"

"No, Sir. There don't seem to be. May I offer the General some coffee? A piece of pastry?"

"Very kind. Coffee. Black. Belay the pastry."

"Aye, aye, Sir," Colonel Wilson said, then stepped to the door and told his sergeant to bring black coffee.

General Stewart arranged himself comfortably on a couch against the wall.

"How may I be of service, General?"

"I've got sort of an unusual personnel request, Colonel," General Stewart said. "I am certainly the last one to try to tell you how I think you should run your shop, or effect personnel allocation decisions, but this is a really unusual circumstance. . . ."

"If the General will give me some specifics, I assure you we'll do our very best to accommodate you."

"The officer in question is a young lieutenant named Macklin, Colonel. He was wounded with the first wave landing at Gavutu."

I wonder who shot him. Our side or theirs?

"Yes, Sir?"

"Parachutist," General Stewart said. "He was evacuated to Australia. Fortunately, his wound—wounds, there were two—were not serious. He was selected—"

General Stewart interrupted himself as the coffee was delivered.

"The General was saying?"

"Oh, yes. Are you familiar, by any chance, with the name—or, for that matter, with the man—Major Homer C. Dillon?"

"By reputation, Sir. I've never actually . . ."

"Interesting man, Colonel. He was Vice President of Metro-Magnum Studios in Hollywood. I don't like to think of the pay cut he took to come back in The Corps. Anyway, Major Dillon was in Australia, in the hospital, and met Lieutenant Macklin. It didn't take him long to have him shipped home to participate in the war bond tour on the West Coast."

"I see."

"It was a splendid choice. Lieutenant Macklin is a splendid-looking officer. Looks like a recruiting poster. First-class public speaker. Makes The Corps look good, really good, if you understand me."

There is no reason, I suppose, why a lying asshole has to look *like a lying asshole.*

"I take your point, Sir."

"Well, the war bond tour, *that* war bond tour, is about over. We're bringing some other people back from the Pacific. This time for a national tour. Machine Gun McCoy, among others."

"Excuse me, Sir?"

"Sergeant Thomas McCoy, of the 2nd Raiders. Distinguished himself on Bloody Ridge. They call him 'Machine Gun' McCoy."

"I see."

"And some of the pilots from Henderson Field, we're trying to get all the aces."

"I see, Sir. I'm sure the tour will be successful."

"A lot of that will depend on how well the tour is organized and carried out," General Stewart said, significantly.

"Yes, Sir," Colonel Wilson agreed.

"Which brings us to Lieutenant Macklin," General Stewart said. "With the exception of a slight limp, he is now fully recovered from his wounds . . ."

"I'm glad to hear that, General."

". . . and is obviously up for reassignment."

After a moment, Colonel Wilson became aware that General Stewart was waiting for a reply from him.

"I don't believe any assignment has yet been made for Lieutenant Macklin," he said.

But I will do my best to find a rock to hide him under.

"What I was going to suggest, Colonel . . . what, to put a point on it, I am requesting, is that Macklin be assigned to my shop."

What's this "shop" crap? You sound like you're making dog kennels.

"I see."

"My thinking, Colonel, is that nothing succeeds like success. And Macklin, having completed a very, very successful war bond tour, is just the man to set up and run the next one. And then, of course, there is sort of a built-in bonus: Our heroes, Machine Gun McCoy and the flyboys, would be introduced to the public by a Marine officer who is himself a wounded hero."

"General, I think that's a splendid idea," Colonel Wilson said. "I'll have his orders cut by sixteen hundred hours."

I was wrong. This has been a gift from heaven. I get rid of Macklin in a job where he can't hurt The Corps; and the General here thinks I am a splendid fellow.

"Well, I frankly thought I would have to sell you more on the idea, Colonel."

"General, if I may say so, a good idea is a good idea. Is there anything else I can try to do for you?"

General Stewart looked a little uncomfortable.

"There are two things," he said, finally. "Both a little delicate."

"Please go on, Sir."

"I certainly don't mean to suggest that you're not up to the line in your operation . . ."

But?

". . . but, maybe a piece of paper got lost or something. Lieutenant Macklin is long overdue for promotion."

With what Chesty Puller had to say about the sonofabitch, the only reason he wasn't asked for his resignation from The Corps is that there's a war on.

"I'll look into that myself, General, and personally bring it to the attention of the G-1."

"I couldn't ask for more than that, could I? Thank you, Colonel."

"No thanks necessary, Sir," Wilson said. "You said there were two things?"

"And—to repeat—both a little delicate," General Stewart said.

"Perhaps I can help, Sir."

"I mentioned Major Dillon," General Stewart said.

"Yes, Sir?"

"I don't know if you know this or not, Colonel, but Major Dillon has been placed on temporary duty with the Office of Management Analysis."

"The Office of Management Analysis, Sir?"

"Don't be embarrassed. I had to ask a lot of questions before I found anyone who even knows it exists," General Stewart said. "But I think it can be safely said that it deals with classified matters."

"I see," Colonel Wilson said solemnly.

"The thing is, Colonel, I'm carrying Major Dillon on my manning table. So long as he is on temporary duty, I can't replace him. You understand?"

"Yes, Sir."

"Do you think you could have him transferred, taken off my manning table?"

"I will bring that to the attention of the G-1, Sir. And if anything can be done, I'm sure the General will see that it is."

"Splendid!" General Stewart said as he stood up and put out his hand. "Colonel, I really appreciate your cooperation."

"Anything for the good of the Corps, Sir."

"Indeed! Thank you, Colonel. And if there's ever any way in which Public Affairs can be of service . . ."

"That's very good of you, Sir. I almost certainly will take you up on that."

(THREE)
Anacostia Naval Air Station
Washington, D.C.
2055 Hours 16 October 1942

As the B-25 was taxiing from the runway to the Transient Aircraft Ramp, the pilot came out of the cockpit and walked back to Banning, who was seated in the front of the fuselage, in a surprisingly comfortable airline-type seat.

"A car's going to meet you where we park," he said.

"Thank you," Banning said.

He had a headache. His mouth was dry. He'd been sleeping fitfully until his ears popped painfully as they made their descent and approach.

They'd stopped at St. Louis for fuel. And he had a fried-egg sandwich and a cup of coffee there. The mayonnaise and the slice of raw onion on the sandwich had given him heartburn.

He belched painfully.

It was raining, steadily, and a chilling wind was blowing across the field. And there was no car in sight. He'd just about decided that the pilot had the wrong information, or that the plane was parked in the wrong place, when a 1940 Buick convertible sedan rolled up. The Buick was preceded by a pickup truck painted in a checkerboard pattern and flying a checkered flag.

The rear door of the Buick opened.

"Will the Major please get in so the Captain will not get drowned?" a voice called.

Banning quickly stepped into the backseat and put out his hand.

"How are you, Ed?" he said. "Good to see you."

"Take us to the hotel, Jerry," Captain Edward Sessions, USMC, ordered, and then turned to Banning. "It's good to see you, Sir," he said. He was a tall, not quite handsome twenty-seven-year-old in a trench coat. A plastic rain cover was fastened over the cover of his billed cap.

"I didn't want to get my best uniform soaked," he went on. "There's a good chance I will be in the very presence of the Secretary of the Navy himself.

"We will be."

"Tonight?" Banning asked, surprised.

"Very possibly. The Colonel's at the hotel; that's where we're going. He should know by the time we get there."

"What hotel?"

"The Foster Lafayette," Sessions said. "Your hotel, Sir. By order of General Pickering. He sent a radio from Pearl Harbor." He made a gesture with his hand. "The car, too. He said we were to give you the keys."

"Jesus," Banning said.

"And this, I thought, would give you a laugh," Sessions said, and thrust a newspaper at Banning. "There's a light back here somewhere. . . . Ah, there it is."

A pair of lights came on, providing just enough illumination to read the newspaper. It was *The Washington Star.*

"What am I looking at?"

Sessions pointed at a photograph of a Marine officer in dress blues. He was standing at a microphone mounted on a lectern on a stage somewhere.

There was a headline over the photograph:

PACIFIC HEROES COMPLETE WAR BOND TOUR; 'BACK TO THE JOB WE HAVE TO DO' SAYS PURPLE HEART HERO OF GUADALCANAL.

"So?" Banning asked.

"Take a good look at the hero," Session said.

"Macklin! I'll be damned."

"I thought that would amuse you," Sessions said.

"Nauseate me is the word you're looking for," Banning said. And then something else caught his eye.

NAVY SECRETARY KNOX 'EXPECTS GUADALCANAL CAN BE HELD'

By Charles E. Whaley

Washington Oct 16—Secretary of the Navy Frank Knox, at a press conference this afternoon, responded with guarded optimism to the question, by this reporter, "Can Guadalcanal be held?"

"I certainly hope so," the Secretary said. "I expect so. I don't want to make any predictions, but every man out there, ashore or afloat, will give a good account of himself."

The response called to mind the classic phrase, "England expects every man to do his duty," but could not be interpreted as more than a hope on Knox's part.

One highly placed and knowledgeable military expert has, on condition of anonymity, told this reporter that the "odds that we can stay on Guadalcanal are no better than fifty-fifty." He cited the great difficulty of supplying the twenty-odd thousand Marines on the island, which is not only far from U.S. bases, but very close to Japanese bases from which air and naval attacks can be launched on both the troops and on the vessels and aircraft attempting to provide them with war matériel.

"What are you reading?"

"Some expert, who doesn't want his name mentioned, told the *Star* it's fifty-fifty whether we can stay on Guadalcanal."

"You think he's wrong?"

"It's pretty bad over there, Ed," Banning said. "I don't even think it's fifty-fifty. The night before we left, they were shelling Henderson Field with fourteen-inch battleship cannon. Nobody can stand up under that for long."

"Is that what you're going to tell Secretary Knox?"

"I'm going to tell him what Vandergrift thinks."

"Which is?"

"That unless he gets reinforced, and unless they can somehow keep the Japs from reinforcing, we're going to get pushed back into the sea."

"Jesus."

Captain Sessions unlocked the door, removed the key, and then handed it to Banning. After that, he pushed open the door and motioned him to go in.

"I realize that this isn't what you're accustomed to, but I understand roughing it once in a while is good for the soul."

"I just hope there's hot water," Banning said, and then, suddenly formal: "Good evening, Sir."

"Hello, Banning, how are you?" a slight, pale-skinned man in an ill-fitting suit said. He was Colonel F. L. Rickabee, of the Office of Management Analysis.

Rickabee was standing in a corridor that led to a large sitting room furnished with what looked like museum-quality antiques. Rickabee waved him toward it. Banning saw a Navy captain and wondered who he was.

"Gentlemen," Rickabee announced, "Major Edward F. Banning."

Banning nodded at the Navy captain. A stocky man in a superbly tailored blue pin-stripe suit walked up, removing his pince-nez as he did, and offered his hand.

"I'm Frank Knox, Major. How do you do?"

"Mr. Secretary."

"Do you know Captain Haughton, my assistant?" Knox asked.

No. But I've seen the name enough. "By Direction of the Secretary of the Navy. David Haughton, Captain, USN, Administrative Assistant."

"No, Sir."

"How are you, Major?" Haughton said. "I'm glad to finally meet you."

"My name is Fowler, Major," another superbly tailored older man said. "Welcome home."

"Senator," Banning said. "How do you do, Sir?"

"Right now, not very well, and from what Fleming Pickering said on the phone, what you have to tell us isn't going to make us feel any better."

"Major, you look like you could use a drink," Frank Knox said. "What'll you have?"

"No, thank you, Sir."

"Don't argue with me, I'm the Secretary of the Navy."

"Then scotch, Sir, a weak one."

"Make him a stiff scotch, Rickabee," Knox ordered, "while your captain loads the projector."

"Yes, Sir, Mr. Secretary," Colonel Rickabee said, smiling.

"Sir, I had hoped to have a little time to organize my thoughts," Banning said.

"Fleming Pickering told me I should tell you to deliver the same briefing you gave him in Hawaii," Senator Fowler said. "And I thought the best place to do that would be here, rather than in Mr. Knox's office or mine."

Banning looked uncomfortable.

"You're worried about classified material?" Captain Haughton asked. "Specifically, about MAGIC?"

"Yes, Sir."

Haughton looked significantly at Secretary Knox, very obviously putting the question to him.

"Senator Fowler does not have a MAGIC clearance," Knox said. "That's so the President and I can look *any* senator in the eye and tell him that no senator has a MAGIC clearance. But I can't think of a secret this country has I wouldn't trust Senator Fowler with. Do you take my meaning, Major?"

"Yes, Sir."

Rickabee handed Banning a drink.

Banning set it down and took the photographs and the two cans of 16mm film from his bag. He handed the film cans to Sessions and the envelope of photographs to Secretary Knox.

"We brought these with us when we left Guadalcanal. The photographer handed them to Major Dillon literally at the last minute, as we were preparing to take off."

"My God!" Frank Knox said after examining the first two photographs. "This is Henderson Field?"

"Yes, Sir."

"It looks like no-man's-land in France in 1917."

"General Vandergrift believes the fire came from fourteen-inch Naval cannon. Battleships, Sir."

"I saw the After-Action Report," Knox said. It was not a reprimand.

Banning took a sip of his drink. He looked across the room to where Sessions was threading the motion picture film into a projector. A screen on a tripod was already in place.

"Anytime you're ready, Sir," Sessions reported.

"OK, Major," Frank Knox said. "Let's have it."

"Just one or two questions, Major, if I may," Frank Knox said after Banning's briefing was finished.

"Yes, Sir."

"You're pretty sure of these Japanese unit designations, I gather? And the identities of the Jap commanders?"

"Yes, Sir."

"They conform to what we've been getting from the MAGIC people in Hawaii. But there is a difference between your analyses of Japanese intercepts and theirs. Subtle sometimes, but significant, I think. Why is that?"

"Sir, I don't think two analysts ever completely agree. . . ."

"Just who are your analysts?"

"Primarily two, Sir. Both junior officers, but rather unusual junior officers. One of them is a Korean-American from Hawaii. He holds a Ph.D. in Mathematics from MIT, and was first involved as a cryptographer—a code-breaker, not an analyst. He placed . . . a different interpretation . . . on certain intercepts than did Hawaii; and more often than not, time proved him correct. So he was made an analyst. The second spent most of his life in Japan. His parents are missionaries. He speaks the language as well as he speaks English, and studied at the University of Tokyo. You understand, Sir, the importance of understanding the Japanese culture, the Japanese mind-set . . ."

"Yes, yes," Knox said impatiently. "So your position is that the Hawaiian analysts are wrong more often than not, and your two are right more often than not?"

"No, Sir. There's rarely a disagreement. The relationship between Hon—"

"What?"

"The Korean-American, Sir. His name is Hon. His relationship with Hawaii—and Lieutenant Moore's—is not at all competitive. When they see things differently, they talk about it, not argue."

"I wonder if we can make that contagious," Senator Fowler said. "From what I hear, most of our people in the Pacific don't even talk to each other."

"I wanted to get that straight before we go across the street," Knox said.

"Sir?" Banning asked.

"We're going across the street?" Senator Fowler asked.

"Don't you think we should?" Knox replied.

"Yes, as a matter of fact, I think we should. Can we?"

What the hell are they talking about, "going across the street"? Banning wondered. The only thing across the street from here is another hotel, an office building, and the White House.

"There's one way to find out," Knox said. He walked to one of the two telephones on the coffee table and dialed a number from memory.

"Alice, this is Frank Knox. May I speak to him, please?" There was a brief pause, and then Knox continued. "Sorry to disturb you at this hour, but there is something I think you should see, and hear. And now."

Who the hell is Alice? Who the hell is "him"?

Frank Knox put the telephone in its cradle and turned to face them.

"Gentlemen, the President will receive us in fifteen minutes," he said. "Us meaning the Senator, Major Banning, and me. Plus someone to set up and run the projector."

"Sessions," Colonel Rickabee said.

"Aye, aye, Sir," Captain Sessions said.

"Thank you very much, Major . . . Banning, is it?" Franklin Delano Roosevelt said.

"Yes, Sir."

". . . Major *Banning*. That was very edifying. Or should I say alarming? In any event, thank you very much. I think that will be all . . . unless you have any questions for the Major, Admiral Leahy?"

"I have no questions, Sir," Admiral Leahy said.

"Frank, I'd like to see you for a moment," the President said.

"With your permission, Mr. President?" Senator Fowler said.

"Richardson, thank you for coming," Roosevelt said, flashing him a dazzling smile and dismissing him.

"Captain, you can just leave the projector and the screen," Knox ordered. "Would you like to have the film and photographs, Mr. President?"

"I don't think I have to look at it again," Roosevelt said. "I certainly don't want to. Admiral?"

Leahy shook his head, no.

Sessions took the film from the projector. Banning collected the photographs and put them back into their envelope. A very large black steward in a white jacket opened the door to the upstairs corridor and held it while Banning and Sessions passed through.

Roosevelt waited to speak until the steward was himself out of the room and the door was closed behind him.

"Well, question one," he said. "Are things as bad as Major Banning paints them?"

"It's not only the Major," Admiral Leahy said. "This came in as I was leaving my office."

He handed the President a sheet of Teletype paper.

"What is that?" Knox asked.

"A radio from Admiral Ghormley to Admiral Nimitz," Admiral Leahy said.

"I'm the Secretary of the Navy, Admiral. You can tell me what Admiral Ghormley said," Knox said, smiling, but with a perceptible sharpness in his tone.

Roosevelt looked up from the paper in his hands, and his eyes took in the two of them.

"Admiral Ghormley has learned of a Japanese aircraft carrier, and its supporting vessels, off the Santa Cruz Islands," Roosevelt said, and then dropped his eyes again to the paper. "He says, 'This appears to be all-out enemy effort against Guadalcanal. My forces totally inadequate to meet situation. Urgently request all aviation reinforcements possible.' End quote."

"That's a little redundant, isn't it?" Knox asked. " 'Totally inadequate'? Is there such a thing as 'partially inadequate'?"

"I think the Admiral made his point, Frank," the President said. "Which brings us to question two, what do we do about it?"

"I'm confident, Mr. President, and I'm sure Secretary Knox agrees with me, that Admiral Nimitz is doing everything that can be done."

"And General MacArthur?" the President asked.

"And General MacArthur," Admiral Leahy said. "The loss of Guadalcanal would be catastrophic for him. The rest of New Guinea would certainly fall, and then quite possibly Australia. MacArthur knows that."

"There is always something else that can be done," Roosevelt said. "Isn't there?"

"Not by the people on Guadalcanal," Knox said. "They are doing all they can do."

"You're suggesting Nimitz can do more?" Admiral Leahy said.

"Nimitz and MacArthur," Knox said.

"For the President to suggest that . . . to order it . . . would suggest he has less than full confidence in them," Leahy said.

"Yes," Roosevelt said, thoughtfully.

"I don't agree with that," Knox said. "Not a whit of it. Mr. President, you're the Commander-in-Chief."

"I know. And I also know that the first principle of good leadership is to give your subordinates their mission, and then get out of their way."

"I'm talking about guidance, Mr. President, not an order. I myself am always pleased to know what you want of me. . . ."

Roosevelt looked at the two of them again.

"Admiral, you're right. I can't afford to lose the goodwill of either Admiral Nimitz or General MacArthur; but on the other hand, the country cannot afford to lose Guadalcanal."

He spun around in his wheelchair and picked up a telephone from a chair-side table.

"Who's this?" he asked, surprised and annoyed when a strange voice answered. "Good God, is it after midnight already? Well, would you bring your pad in please, Sergeant?"

He hung up and turned back to Knox and Leahy.

"Alice has gone home. There's an Army sergeant on standby."

There was a discreet knock at an interior door, and without waiting for permission, a scholarly-looking master sergeant carrying a stenographer's pad came in.

"Yes, Mr. President?"

"I want you to take a note to the Joint Chiefs of Staff," the President said. "I want it delivered tonight."

"Yes, Mr. President."

"And make an extra copy, and have that delivered to Senator Richardson Fowler. Across the street. At his hotel. Have him awakened if necessary."

"Yes, Mr. President."

The President looked at Admiral Leahy and Secretary Knox.

"I don't think Richardson liked being sent home," he said, smiling wickedly. "Maybe this will make it up to him." He turned back to the Army stenographer. "Ready, Sergeant?"

"Yes, Mr. President."

Ten minutes before, room service delivered hamburgers and two wine coolers full of iced beer.

After Banning wolfed his down, he was embarrassed to see that no one else was so ravenous. Captain Haughton, he saw, had hardly touched his.

"There's another under the cover," Senator Fowler said. "I ordered it for you. I didn't think you'd have a hell of a lot to eat on the way from San Francisco."

"I'm a little embarrassed," Banning said, but lifted the silver cover and took the extra hamburger.

"Don't be silly," Fowler said.

There was a rap at the door.

"Come in," Senator Fowler called. "It's unlocked."

The door opened. A neatly dressed man in his early thirties stepped inside.

"Senator Fowler?"

"Right."

"I'm from the White House, Senator. I have a Presidential document for you."

"Let's have it," the Senator said.

"Sir, may I see some identification?"

"Christ!" Fowler said, but went to the chair where he had tossed his suit jacket and came up with an identification card.

"Thank you, Sir," the man said, and handed him a large manila envelope.

"Do I have to sign for it?"

"That won't be necessary, Sir," the courier said, nodded, and walked out.

Fowler ripped open the envelope, took out a single sheet of paper, read it, and grunted. Then he handed it to Captain Haughton, who was holding an almost untouched glass of beer.

"Pass it around when you're through," Fowler said.

THE WHITE HOUSE
Washington, D.C.

17 October 1942

To the Joint Chiefs of Staff:

My anxiety about the Southwest Pacific is to make sure that every possible weapon gets into that area to hold Guadalcanal.

Franklin D. Roosevelt

"I don't know what this means," Banning said, a little thickly, when he'd read it and passed it to Sessions.

"It means that if either Nimitz or MacArthur is holding anything back for their own agendas, if they are smart, they will now send it to Guadalcanal," Fowler said.

Banning grunted.

"Major, if you were God, what would you send to Guadalcanal?"

"Everything," Banning said.

"In what priority?"

"I don't really know," Banning said. "I suppose the most important thing would be to keep the Japanese from building up their forces on the island. And I suppose that means reinforcing the Cactus Air Force."

"I think they can do that," Fowler said. "God, I hope they can."

He poured a little more beer in his glass, then smiled. "Another question?"

"Yes, Sir?"

"What was Jake Dillon doing on that hush-hush mission Pickering set up?"

"I don't think I understand the question, Sir."

"I've known Jake a long time," Fowler said. "Don't misunderstand me. I like him. But Jake is a press agent. A two-fisted drinker. And one hell of a ladies' man. But I'm having trouble picturing him doing anything serious."

"I think you underestimate him, Senator," Banning said, aware that Fowler's question angered him. "That mission wouldn't have gone off as well as it did, if it hadn't been for Dillon. Perhaps it wouldn't have gone off at all."

"Really?" Captain Haughton asked, surprised.

"Yes, Sir," Banning said.

"You want to explain that?" Fowler asked.

How the hell did I get involved in this?

"Major Dillon can get people to do things they would rather not do," Banning said.

"With Dillon on orders signed by Admiral Leahy, it wasn't a question of whether anyone wanted to do what he asked them to do, was it?" Captain Haughton argued.

"Even though Commander Feldt of the Coastwatchers is, kindly, often difficult to deal with," Banning said quietly, "Dillon got Feldt to send his best native into Buka. Even though they were understandably reluctant to have one of their very few submarines hang around Buka a moment longer than necessary, he got the Australian Navy to let that sub lie offshore for three days in case they had to try to get our people off the beach. He got MAG-21, the Cactus Air Force, to loan the best R4D pilot around to fly the R4D that made the landing, even though he was one of their fighter squadron commanders."

"As opposed to what?" Senator Fowler asked.

"As opposed to having sacrificial lambs sent in. Nobody thought the operation was going to work. Dillon convinced them it would. There are ways to get around orders, even orders signed by Admiral Leahy."

"I'm surprised," Senator Fowler said. "I'd never thought of Jake as a heavy-weight."

"He's a heavyweight, Senator," Banning said flatly. "I was going to—I got busy at Pearl, and didn't get around to it—to recommend to General Pickering that he be assigned to Management Analysis."

"We've already returned him to Public Affairs," Sessions said. "Effective on his arrival in the States."

"If something comes up, Banning," Colonel Rickabee said. "We can get him back."

Then Rickabee stood up.

"I've got some orders for you, Banning. Take a week off. At General Pickering's orders, you will stay here. That doesn't mean you can't leave town, but I don't want it to get back to General Pickering that you've moved into a BOQ. A week from tomorrow morning, not a second sooner, I'll see you in the office." He paused. "Now get some sleep. And a haircut. You look like hell."

VI

The bay was choppy. Landing was a series of more or less controlled crashes against the water. Brigadier General Fleming Pickering was almost surprised these didn't jar parts—large parts, such as engines—off the Mariner.

Maneuvering from the Mariner into the powerboat sent out to meet it was difficult, and the ride to shore was not pleasant.

The tide was out, which explained to Pickering the chop (a function of shallow water). It also made climbing from the powerboat onto the ladder up the side of the wharf a little dicey. Halfway up the ladder, behind a rear admiral who was obviously a very cautious man, it occurred to Pickering that he had failed to send a message ahead that he was arriving.

Not only would he have to find wheels someplace, but he didn't really know where to go. It was probable that Ellen Feller would be in Water Lily Cottage. And he did not want to deal with her just yet.

The admiral finally made it onto the wharf, and Pickering raised his head above it.

"Ten-hut," an Army Signal Corps lieutenant called out. "Pre-sent, H-arms!"

Two Marine lieutenants and a Marine sergeant, forming a small line, saluted. The rear admiral, looking a little confused, returned the salute.

That's not for you, you jackass.

Pickering climbed onto the wharf and returned the salute.

"How are you, Pluto?" he said to First Lieutenant Hon Song Do, Signal Corps, U.S. Army, and put out his hand.

"Welcome home, General," Pluto said, smiling broadly.

Pickering turned to a tall, thin, pale Marine second lieutenant, and touched his shoulder.

"Hello, John," he said. And then, turning to the other lieutenant and the sergeant standing beside him, he added, "And look who that is! You two all right?" Pickering asked as he shook their hands.

"They let us out of the hospital yesterday, Sir," Sergeant Stephen M. Koffler, USMCR, said. Koffler's eyes were sunken . . . and extraordinarily bright. His face was blotched with sores. His uniform hung loosely on a skeletal frame.

That was obviously a mistake. You look like death warmed over.

"We're fine, Sir," First Lieutenant Joseph L. Howard, USMCR, said.

Like hell you are. You look as bad as Koffler.

"I'm going to have a baby," Sergeant Koffler said.

"Damn it," Lieutenant Howard said. "I told you to wait with that!"

"Funny, you don't look pregnant," Pickering said.

"I mean, my girl. My fiancée," Koffler said, and blushed.

"Koffler, damn it!" Lieutenant Howard said.

Pickering looked back at Second Lieutenant John Marston Moore, USMCR, and asked, "What's that rope hanging from your shoulder, John?"

"That's what we general officer's aides wear, General," Moore said.

You don't look as bad as these two, but you look like hell, too, John. God, what have I done to these kids?

"And you will note the suitably adorned automobile," Hon said.

Not far away was a Studebaker President, with USMC lettered on the hood. A red flag with a silver star was hanging from a small pole mounted on the right fender.

"I'm impressed," Pickering said. "How'd you know I was coming?"

"McCoy sent a radio," Hon said.

"Have you got any luggage, Sir?" Koffler asked.

"Yes, I do, and you keep your hands off it. Hart'll bring it." He looked at Hon. "Where are we going, Pluto?"

"Water Lily Cottage, Sir," Hon replied, as if the question surprised him. "I thought . . ."

"Who's living there now?"

"Moore, Howard, and me. We found Koffler an apartment, so called, a couple of blocks away."

"And Mrs. Feller?"

"She's in a BOQ," Pluto Hon said uncomfortably. "General, when we have a minute, there's something I've got to talk to you about—"

"Major Banning already has," Pickering said, cutting him off, then changed the subject. "We're all not going to fit in the Studebaker."

"We have a little truck, Sir," Moore said, pointing.

"OK. Koffler: You wait until Sergeant Hart comes ashore with the luggage and then show him how to find the cottage."

"Aye, aye, Sir."

"I'll see you there. I want to hear all about Buka."

Pluto Hon slipped behind the wheel, and Howard moved in beside him. Moore got in the back beside Pickering—somewhat awkwardly, Pickering noticed, as if the movement were painful.

Howard turned. "General, I'm sorry about Koffler. I told him not to say anything. . . ."

"Well, if I was going to have a baby, I think I'd want to tell people. What was that all about, anyway?"

"It'll keep, Sir," Moore said. "We have it under control."

"I want to hear about it."

"You remember the last night, Sir, in the big house? Before we went to Buka?" Howard said.

"The Elms, you mean?" Pickering asked.

When MacArthur had his headquarters in Melbourne, Pickering rented a large house, The Elms, in the Melbourne suburbs. After MacArthur moved his headquarters to Brisbane, Pickering rented a smaller house, Water Lily Cottage, near the Brisbane racetrack.

"Yes, Sir. And you remember the Australian girl, Daphne Farnsworth?"

"*Yeoman* Farnsworth, Royal Australian Navy Women's Reserve," Pickering said. "Yes, I do. Beautiful girl."

"Has a weakness for Marines, I'm sorry to say," Pluto said. "I can't imagine why."

"The lady is in the family way, General," Moore said, not amused. "It apparently happened that last night at The Elms."

"How do you know that?" Pickering asked, smiling.

"It was the only time they were together," Pluto said.

"Well, Pluto, after all, he *is* a *Marine*," Pickering said. "What? Is there some kind of problem?"

"Several. For one thing, they threw her out of the Navy in something like disgrace."

"Well, to judge by the look on his face, making an honest woman of her is high on Koffler's list of things to do."

"She's a widow," Moore went on. "Her husband was killed in North Africa. They had his memorial service the day before she and Koffler . . ."

"What are you saying? That Koffler has been sucked in by a designing woman?"

"No, Sir. Not at all. She's been disowned by her family, if that's the word."

"And meanwhile, Koffler was on Buka?"

"Yes, Sir."

"How is she living?"

"Well, she had a job. But she lost that."

"I hired her, Sir, to work for us," Moore said.

"Good idea. But what's the problem? Koffler's back. He wants to marry her . . ."

"We're having a problem with that, Sir. The SWPOA Command Policy is to discourage marriages between Australians and Americans. They throw all sorts of roadblocks up. For all practical purposes, marriages between Australians and lower-grade enlisted men, below staff sergeant, are forbidden." (SWPOA was the abbreviation for the *South West Pacific Ocean Area*, which was MacArthur's area of responsibility in the Pacific.)

"No problem. We'll make Koffler a staff sergeant."

"There's more, Sir."

"I'll deal with it," Pickering said. "Tell Koffler to relax."

How I don't know. But certainly, someone who has been flown across the world at the direct order of the President of the United States to arrange a peace between the chief of American espionage and the Supreme Commander of the South West Pacific Ocean Area should be able to deal with the problem of a Marine buck sergeant who has knocked up his girlfriend.

"Does General MacArthur know I'm back?"

"I can't see how he could, Sir."

"I thought perhaps they'd sent word from Washington."

"I don't think so, Sir. Wouldn't that have been a 'personal for General MacArthur'?"

"Probably. Almost certainly."

"I keep pretty well up on that file, Sir," Pluto Hon said. "There hasn't been anything."

"Well, that at least gives me today. I need a bath, a couple of drinks, and a long nap. I'll call over there at five o'clock or so and ask for an appointment in the morning."

"There's a couple of things I think you should see, Sir," Pluto said.

"This morning?" Pickering asked.

"Yes, Sir."

When Pickering came out of his bedroom into the living room of Water Lily Cottage, Pluto Hon and John Marston Moore were waiting for him. Pickering was wearing a terry-cloth bathrobe over nothing at all, and he was feeling—and looking—fresh from a long hot shower.

In the middle of room, they'd set up a map board—a sheet of plywood placed on an artist's tripod. Maps (and other large documents) were tacked onto the plywood. A sheet of oilcloth covered the maps and documents; it could be lifted to expose them.

An upholstered chair, obviously intended for him, had been moved from its usual place against the wall so that it squarely faced the map board.

"Very professional," Pickering said.

"We practice our briefings here," Pluto said seriously. "It's a waste of time, but General Willoughby's big on briefing the Supreme Commander with maps and charts."

"You don't work for Willoughby," Pickering said. "And you don't have time to waste."

Pluto didn't reply. Pickering knew that his silence was an answer in itself.

"How bad has it been, Pluto? Let's have it."

"I don't want to sound like I'm whining, Sir."

"Let's have it, Pluto."

"The point has been made to me, Sir, by various senior officers, that I am a first lieutenant, and that first lieutenants do what they're told."

"You're talking about MAGIC intercept briefings, right?" Pickering asked.

"Yes, Sir. I believe it is General Willoughby's rationale that since he has no one on his staff cleared for MAGIC, he can't have them prepare MAGIC briefings for the Supreme Commander. That leaves us."

"*Left* you. Past tense," Pickering said. "For one thing, MacArthur doesn't need kindergarten-level briefings; he has an encyclopedic memory. For another, I can't afford to have either of you wasting your time playing brass-hat games. The next time Willoughby calls, your reply is, quote, 'Sir, General Pickering doesn't believe that a formal briefing is necessary.' Unquote. If he has any questions, tell him to call me."

"General, as I said on the wharf, General, Sir, welcome home!" Pluto said.

"But since you've already gone to all this trouble, Pluto, brief me."

"Yes, Sir," Pluto said. Moore walked to the map board—*limped,* Pickering thought; *limped painfully; his legs are nowhere near healed*—and flipped the oilcloth cover off, revealing a map of the Solomon Islands.

There was something out of the ordinary about it. After a moment, he knew what it was.

"Don't tell me that map's not classified?"

"Sir, that's another decision I took on my own," Pluto said. "We start with MacArthur's situation map. Maps. Actually three. MacArthur had one; Willoughby had a second; and G-3 had a third. All classified TOP SECRET. For our purposes, before Willoughby started the briefing business, we used to just go to G-3 with an overlay. Nothing on the overlay but MAGIC information. No problem, in other words. We just locked the door, did our thing on the overlay with our MAGIC intelligence, and then took the overlay back to the dungeon with us. But when we started having to take a map with us to brief MacArthur . . ."

"What I'm looking at is a TOP SECRET situation map, to which MAGIC intelligence has been added?"

"Yes, Sir. General Willoughby said the Supreme Commander doesn't like overlays."

"And," Pickering said, "because you thought there was a possibility that this map might get out of your hands—with MAGIC intelligence on it—you decided not to stamp it TOP SECRET. . . ."

"Yes, Sir. We don't let this map out of our hands. It's been chemically treated, so it practically explodes when you put a match to it—"

"Finish your briefing," Pickering interrupted. "Take the MAGIC data off onto an overlay, and burn the map."

"Yes, Sir," Pluto said. "Sir, how much of a briefing did you get from Major Banning in Hawaii?"

"A damned good one. I presume you know what he told me? How much of it is still valid?"

"Would you mind, Sir?"

Good for you, Son. Don't leave anything to chance.

"General Hyakutake is ashore," Pickering summarized. "As soon as he believes he has an adequate force, he will start an attack on three fronts, counting the combined fleet as a front. I forget the names of the Japanese generals—"

"Major Generals Maruyama and Tadashi," Pluto interrupted him. "Did he have a date?"

"No."

"We have new intercepts indicating 18 October. Tomorrow."

Pickering grunted.

"Did Major Banning get into Japanese naval strength?"

"He did, but let's have it again."

"On 11 October," Moore began, "Admiral Yamamoto sent from Truk a force consisting of five battleships, five aircraft carriers, four cruisers, forty-four destroyers, and a flock of support vessels." He paused for a moment. "We don't know if Yamamoto himself is aboard; they're not quite under radio silence, but nearly."

"My God!"

"The Japanese do not commit their entire available force at one time," Pluto said. "Or so far haven't done that. It is reasonable to assume that they will commit this force piecemeal, as well."

"Even a piece of that size force is more than we have," Pickering thought aloud.

" 'My forces totally inadequate to meet situation,' " Moore said, obviously quoting.

"Who said that?" Pickering asked.

"Admiral Ghormley, in a radio yesterday to Nimitz," Pluto said.

"And there was a follow-up about an hour ago," Moore said, and started to read from a sheet of paper. "Ghormley wants all of MacArthur's submarines; all the cruisers and destroyers now in the Aleutians Islands/Alaska area; all the PT boats in the Pacific, except those at Midway; and he wants the assignment of destroyers in the Atlantic 'reviewed.' "

"They're not going to give him that," Pickering said. "And there wouldn't be time to send destroyers from the Atlantic, if they wanted to. Or cruisers from Alaska, for that matter."

Pluto shrugged, but said nothing.

"He also wants ninety heavy bombers; eighty medium bombers; sixty dive-bombers; and two fighter groups, preferably P38s."

"In other words," Hon said. "Essentially all of MacArthur's air power, plus a large chunk of what the Navy hasn't already sent to the area."

Pickering opened his mouth to speak, then changed his mind, stopping himself from saying, *He sounds pretty goddamn desperate.*

Why did I stop myself? Am I starting to believe that I'm really a general? And generals do not say anything derogatory about other generals or admirals in the presence of people who are not generals or admirals. Like two young lieutenants, for example.

"He sounds pretty goddamn desperate," Pickering said. "Is he justified?"

"I don't think so, Sir," Pluto said. "My thought when I read that—in particular, the phrase 'totally inadequate,' and his obviously unrealistic requests for air support (I don't think there are ninety operational B17s over here, for example)—is that it's going to raise some unpleasant questions in the minds of Admiral Nimitz and his staff."

"Yeah," Pickering said.

"That's all I have, Sir, unless you've got some questions. Would you like to take a look at the map?"

"No. I've sailed those waters," Pickering said. "And I was on the 'Canal. Burn it."

"Yes, Sir."

The telephone rang. Moore limped quickly across the room to pick it up.

Instead of "hello," he recited the number. Then he smiled. "One moment, please," he said, and covered the mouthpiece with his hand. "Colonel Huff for General Pickering," he said. "Is the General available?"

Colonel Sidney Huff was aide-de-camp to the Supreme Commander, South West Pacific Ocean Area.

Pickering pushed himself out of the chair, went to Moore, and took the telephone from him.

"Hello, Sid," he said. "How are you?"

"The Supreme Commander's compliments, General Pickering," Huff said very formally.

"My compliments to the General," Pickering said, smiling at Moore.

"General MacArthur hopes that General Pickering will be able to join him and Mrs. MacArthur at luncheon."

"What time, Sid?"

"If it would be convenient for the General, the Supreme Commander customarily takes his luncheon at one, in his quarters."

"I'll be there, Sid. Thanks."

"Thank you, General."

The phone went dead.

Pickering hung up and looked at Hon.

"Sometimes I have the feeling that Colonel Huff doesn't approve of me," he said. "He didn't welcome me back to Australia."

"I wonder how he knew you were back, and here?" Moore wondered aloud.

"I think he likes you all right," Hon said. "It's that star you're wearing that's a burr under his brass hat."

"Why, Lieutenant Hon. How cynical of you!"

"That's what I'm being paid for, to be cynical," Hon said.

(TWO)
Lennon's Hotel
Brisbane, Australia
1255 Hours 17 October 1942

When Pickering arrived, with Sergeant George Hart at the wheel of the Studebaker President, MacArthur's Cadillac limousine was parked in front of the hotel.

"We're putting a show on, George," Pickering said. "Stop in front and then rush around and open the door for me."

"I already got the word from Lieutenant Hon, General," Hart said, smiling at Pickering's reflection in the rearview mirror.

Colonel Sidney Huff was waiting on the veranda of the sprawling Victorian building. He watched as Hart opened the door and Pickering stepped out; then he waited for Pickering to start up the walk before moving to join him.

He saluted. Pickering returned it and put out his hand.

"Good to see you, Sid," Pickering said.

"It's good to see you again, too, Sir," Huff said. "If you'll come with me, please, General?"

He led Pickering across the lobby to a waiting elevator. When MacArthur had his headquarters in the Menzies Hotel in Melbourne, Pickering remembered, one of the elevators was reserved for his personal use; it had a sign. This one had no sign, and was presumably available to commoners.

When the elevator door opened on the third floor, a nattily dressed MP staff sergeant rose quickly and came to attention. The chair he was sitting in didn't seem substantial enough to support his bulk.

Huff led him down the corridor to the door to MacArthur's suite and pushed it open. Pickering walked through.

"Fleming, my dear fellow," said the Supreme Commander, South West Pacific Ocean Area, holding his arms wide.

He was in khakis, without a tie. He had a thin, black cigar in his hand. The corncob pipe generally disappeared in the absence of photographers.

"General, it's good to see you, Sir," Pickering said, and handed him a package. "They're not Filipino. Cuban. But I thought you could make do with them."

"This is absolutely unnecessary, but deeply appreciated," MacArthur said, sounding genuinely pleased. "What was it the fellow said, 'a woman is only a woman, but a good cigar is a smoke'?"

"I believe he said that out of the hearing of his wife," Pickering said.

"Speaking of which, Mrs. MacArthur, *Jean*, sends her regrets. She will be unable to join us. But she said she looks forward to seeing you at dinner. You did tell him about dinner, Sid?"

"No, Sir, I didn't have the chance."

"A small dinner, *en famille*, so to speak. And then some bridge. Does that fit in with your schedule?"

He did not wait for a reply. He handed Colonel Huff the cigars. "Unpack these carefully, Sid, they're worth their weight in gold. And put them in a refrigerator. And then get yourself some lunch."

"Yes, Sir."

Huff left the room.

"What is your schedule, Fleming?" MacArthur asked.

"I gratefully accept Mrs. MacArthur's kind invitation to dinner, General."

"'Jean,' please. She considers you, as I do, a friend. But that's not the schedule I was talking about."

"You mean, what am I doing here?"

"To put a point on it, yes," MacArthur said. "But let me offer you something to drink. What will you have?"

"I always feel depraved when I drink alone at lunch," Pickering said.

"Then we will be depraved together," MacArthur said. "Scotch whiskey, I seem to recall?"

"Yes, thank you."

Almost instantly, a Filipino in a white jacket rolled in a table with whiskey, ice, water, and glasses.

As the steward, whose actions were obviously choreographed, made the drinks, MacArthur said, "Churchill, I am reliably told, begins his day with a healthy hooker of cognac. I like a little nip before lunch. But, unless it's something like this—a close friend, no strangers—I don't like to set a bad example."

"I'm flattered to be considered a close friend, General," Pickering said.

"It should come as no surprise," MacArthur said, and took a squat glass from the steward and handed it to Pickering. "There we are," he said, and took a second glass and raised it. "Welcome back, Fleming. I can't tell you how glad I am to see you."

"Thank you, Sir," Pickering said.

"And to look at you, you're in splendid health. Is that the case?"

"I'm in good health, Sir."

"I had a report to the contrary from Colonel DePress ..."

From who? Who the hell is Colonel DePress?

"... who told me that when he saw you in Walter Reed, you were debilitated by malaria, and in considerable pain from your wound. I was disturbed, and so was Jean."

Pickering remembered Colonel DePress now. He was one of MacArthur's officer couriers, a light colonel, wearing the insignia of the 26th Cavalry, Philippine Scouts. He'd delivered a letter from MacArthur congratulating him on his promotion to brigadier general.

"I like your Colonel DePress," Pickering said. "I hate to accuse him of exaggerating."

"I don't think he was. But no pain now? And the malaria is under control?"

"No pain, Sir, and the malaria is under control."

"Good, good," MacArthur said cheerfully, and then, instantly, "You were telling me what you're up to here, Fleming."

Second Principle of Interrogation, Pickering thought: *Put the person being questioned at ease, and then hit him with a zinger.*

"I'm here on a peacemaking expedition, General," Pickering said.

"Sent by whom?"

"The President, Sir."

"You may assure the President, General," MacArthur laughed, "that the tales of friction between myself and Admiral Nimitz, like the tales of the demise of Mark Twain, are greatly exaggerated. I hold the Admiral in the highest possible esteem, and flatter myself to think that he considers me, for a lowly soldier, to be a fairly competent fellow."

"The President had in mind Mr. Donovan, Sir," Pickering said.

"Donovan? Donovan? I don't know who you mean."

"Mr. William Donovan, Sir, of the OSS."

"I know him only by reputation. He had a distinguished record in the First War. But then, so did you and I, Fleming. Whatever gave the President the idea that we are at swords' points?"

"I believe the President is concerned about what he—or at least Mr. Donovan—perceives to be a lack of cooperation on the part of SWPOA with regard to Mr. Donovan's mission to you."

"Oh," MacArthur said, and then he laughed. "Franklin Roosevelt is truly Machiavellian, isn't he? Sending you to me, to plead Donovan's case? You've had serious trouble with Mr. Donovan, have you not, Fleming?"

How the hell does he know I can't stand the sonofabitch? Or about my trouble with him?

"And were you dispatched to see Admiral Nimitz, with the same mission?"

"No, Sir. I saw Admiral Nimitz, but not about Mr. Donovan."

"How to deal with Mr. Donovan is just one item on a long list about which Admiral Nimitz and I are in total agreement," MacArthur said. "We are agreed to ignore him, in the hope that he will go away. Neither of us can see where any possible good he or his people can do us can possibly be worth the trouble he or his people are likely to cause."

"Mr. Donovan is held in high esteem by the President, General."

"Is he? And that's why he sent you, of all people, to plead his case? The word—and certainly no disrespect to the Commander-in-Chief is intended—is *Machiavellian.*"

MacArthur shook his head, smiling, and took a healthy sip of his drink.

"You may report to the President, General, that you brought the matter of the OSS to my attention, and I assured you that I have every intention of offering the OSS every possible support from the limited assets available to SWPOA."

"Yes, Sir."

"As a friend, Fleming, I will tell you that I have a guerrilla operation going in the Philippines. I have high hopes for it, and a high regard for the men there who daily face death. I have no intention . . . no intention . . . of having Wild Bill Donovan get his nose under that tent!"

He looked at Pickering, as if expecting an argument. When there was none, he went on.

"I understand your people carried off the Buka operation splendidly, without a hitch," he said.

"It went well, Sir. I just saw the two men we took out."

"They should be decorated. Have you thought about that?"

"No, Sir," Pickering confessed, somewhat embarrassed. "I have not."

"Recognition of valor is important, Fleming," MacArthur said. "I have found it interesting, in my career, that I have the most difficulty convincing of that truth those men who have been highly decorated themselves. You, apparently, are a case in point."

The subject of Bill Donovan's people, obviously, is now closed.

"It may well be," MacArthur went on, "that many people who have been given high awards, myself included, feel that they were not justified."

A swinging door opened.

"General," MacArthur's Filipino steward announced, "luncheon is served."

MacArthur turned to Pickering and said, smiling broadly, "Just in time. I was about to violate my rule that one drink at lunch is enough. Shall we go in?"

(THREE)

EYES ONLY—THE SECRETARY OF THE NAVY
DUPLICATION FORBIDDEN
ORIGINAL TO BE DESTROYED AFTER
ENCRYPTION AND TRANSMITTAL TO SECNAV

Brisbane, Australia
Saturday 17 October 1942

Dear Frank:

I arrived here without incident from Pearl Harbor. Presumably, Major Ed Banning is by now in Washington and you have had a chance to hear what he had to say, and to have had a look at the photographs and film.

Within an hour of what I thought was my unheralded arrival, I was summoned to a private—really private, only El Supremo and me—luncheon. He also had a skewed idea why I was sent here. He thought I was supposed to make peace between him and Admiral

Nimitz. He assured me that he and Nimitz are great pals, which I think, after talking with Nimitz at Pearl Harbor, is almost true.

When I brought up Donovan's OSS people, a wall came down. He tells me he has no intention of letting "Donovan get his camel's nose under the tent" and volunteered that Nimitz feels the same way. (I didn't even mention Donovan to Nimitz.) I also suspect this is true. I will keep trying, of course, both because I consider myself under orders to do so, and because I think that MacA is wrong and Donovan's people would be very useful, but I don't think I will be successful.

The best information here, which I presume you will also have seen by now, is that the Japanese will launch their attack tomorrow.

Admiral Ghormley sent two radios (16 and 17 October) saying his forces are "totally inadequate" to resist a major Japanese attack, and making what seems to me unreasonable demands on available Naval and aviation resources. I detected a certain lack of confidence in him, on MacA's part. I have no opinion, and certainly would make no recommendations vis-a-vis Ghormley if I had one, but thought I should pass this on.

A problem here, which will certainly grow, is in the junior (very junior) rank of Lieutenant Hon Song Do, the Army cryptographer/analyst, who is considered by a horde of Army and Marine colonels and Navy captains, who aren't doing anything nearly so important, as . . . a first lieutenant. Is there anything you can do to have the Army promote him? The same is true, to a slightly lesser degree, of Lieutenant John Moore, but Moore, at least (he is on the books as my aide-de-camp) can hide behind my skirts. As far as anyone but MacA and Willoughby know, Hon is just one more code-machine lieutenant working in the aptly named dungeon in MacA's headquarters basement.

Finally, MacA firmly suggested that I decorate Lieutenant Joe Howard and Sergeant Steven Koffler, who we took off Buka. God knows, they deserve a medal for what they did . . . they met me at the airplane, and they look like those photographs in Life magazine of starving Russian prisoners on the Eastern Front . . . but I don't know how to go about this. Please advise.

More soon.

Best regards,

Fleming Pickering, Brigadier General, USMCR

Brisbane, Australia
Saturday 17 October 1942

Dear Fritz:

At lunch with MacA yesterday, he justified his snubbing of Donovan's people here by saying that he has a guerrilla operation up and running in the Philippines.

At cocktails-before-dinner earlier tonight, I tried to pump General Willoughby about this, and got a very cold shoulder; he made it plain that whatever guerrilla activity going on there is insignificant. After dinner, I got with Lt Col Philip DePress—he is the officer courier you brought to Walter Reed Hospital to see me when he had a letter from MacA for me. He's a hell of a soldier who somehow got out of the Philippines before they fell.

After feeding him a lot of liquor, I got out of him this version: An Army reserve captain named Wendell Fertig refused to surrender and went into the hills of Mindanao where he gathered around him a group of others, including a number of Marines from the 4th Marines, who escaped from Luzon and Corregidor, and started to set up a guerrilla operation.

He has promoted himself to Brigadier General, and appointed himself "Commanding General, US Forces in the Philippines." I understand (and so does Phil DePress) why he did this. The Filipinos would pay absolutely no attention to a lowly captain. This has, of course, enraged the rank-conscious Palace Guard here at the Palace. But from what DePress tells me, Fertig has a lot of potential.

See what you can find out, and advise me. And tell me if I'm wrong in thinking that if there are Marines with Fertig, then it becomes our business.

Finally, with me here, Moore, who is on the books as my aide-de-camp, is going to raise questions if he spends most of his time, as he has to, in the dungeon, instead of holding doors for me and serving my canapes. Is there some way we can get Sergeant Hart a commission? He is, in faithful obedience to what I'm sure are your orders, never more than fifty feet away from me anyway.

I would appreciate it if you would call my wife, and tell her that I am safe on the bridge and canape circuit in Water Lily Cottage in Beautiful Brisbane on the Sea.

Regards,

Fleming Pickering, Brigadier General, USMCR

TOP SECRET

(FOUR)
Office of the Brig Commander
US Naval Base, San Diego, California
0815 Hours 18 October 1942

There was, of course, an established procedure to deal with those members of the Naval Service whose behavior in contravention of good order and discipline attracted the official attention of the Shore Patrol.

Malefactors were transported from the scene of the alleged violation to the Brig.

Once there, commissioned officers were separated from enlisted men and provided with cells befitting their rank.

As soon as they reached a condition approaching partial sobriety, most of these gentlemen were released on their own recognizance and informed by the Shore Patrol duty officer that an official report of the incident would be transmitted via official channels to their commanding officers. They were further informed that it behooved them to return immediately and directly to their ship or shore station.

The enlisted personnel were first segregated by service: sailors in one holding cell, Marines in another, and the odd soldier or two who'd somehow wound up in San Diego, in a third.

Then a further segregation took place, dividing those sailors and Marines whose offense was simply gross intoxication from those whose offenses were considered more serious.

In the case of the minor offenders, telephone calls would be made to Camp Pendleton, or to the various ships or shore-based units to which they were assigned, informing the appropriate person of their arrest. In due course, buses or trucks would be sent to the Brig to bring them (so to speak) home, where their commanding officers would deal with them.

Those charged with more serious offenses could count on spending the night in the Brig. Such offenses ran from resisting arrest through using provoking language to a noncommissioned, or commissioned, officer in the execution of his office, to destruction of private property (most often the furnishings of a saloon or "boarding-house"), to assault with a deadly weapon.

In the morning, when they were more or less sober and, it was hoped, repentant, they were brought, unofficially, before an officer. He would decide whether the offender's offense and attitude should see him brought before a court-martial.

A court-martial could mete out punishment ranging from a reprimand to life in a Naval prison.

Although none of the malefactors brought before him believed this, Lieutenant Max Krinski, USNR, most often tilted his scale of justice on the side of leniency. This was not because Lieutenant Krinski believed that there was no such thing as a bad sailor (or Marine), but rather that he believed his basic responsibility was to make his decisions on the basis of what was or was not good for the service.

Lieutenant Krinski, a bald-headed, barrel-chested, formidable-appearing gentleman of thirty-eight, had himself once been a Marine. In his youth, he served as a guard at the U.S. Naval Prison at Portsmouth. He did not, however, join the Marines to be a guard. More to the point, he quickly discovered that all the horror stories were true: Prisoners at Portsmouth were treated with inhuman brutality and sadism.

Although he was offered a promotion to corporal if he reenlisted, he turned it down, left the service, and returned to his home in upstate New York. After trying and failing to gain success in any number of careers (mostly involving sales), he took and passed the civil service examination for "Correctional Officers" in the Department of Corrections of the State of New York.

His intention was to go to college at night and get the hell out of the prison business; but that didn't work out. On the other hand, as he rose through the ranks of prison guards (ultimately to captain), the work became less and less distasteful.

In 1940, a Marine Corps major approached him and asked if he was interested in a reserve commission. As he knew, Marines guarded the Portsmouth Naval Prison; but the major made that point specific. This made it quite clear to Krinski that The Marine Corps was seeking Captain Krinski of the Department of Corrections, rather than former PFC Krinski of the Marine Detachment, Portsmouth Naval Prison. He declined the Marine major's kind offer.

But if war came, he realized, he could not sit it out at Sing Sing. He approached the Army, but they were not interested in his services. (He still hadn't figured out why not.) And so when he approached the Navy, it was without much hope. . . . Yet they immediately responded with an offer of a commission as a lieutenant (junior grade), USNR, and an immediate call to active duty.

If war should come, the Navy explained to him, they would be assigned responsibility for guarding prisoners of war, and they had few suitably qualified officers to supervise such an operation.

But shortly after he entered active duty, it was decided that prisoners of war would be primarily an Army responsibility. Not knowing what to do with him, the Navy sent him to San Diego to work in the Brig. Three months later, he was named Officer-In-Charge. And two months after that, just as the war came, he was promoted to full lieutenant.

In Lieutenant Krinski's judgment, there were a few bad apples who deserved to be sent to the horrors of Portsmouth. But most of the kids who came before him would not be helped at all by Portsmouth discipline. And sending them there would not only fuck up their lives, but deprive the fleet or The Marine Corps of a healthy young man whose only crime against humanity was, for example, to grow wild with indignation when he discovered that the blonde with the splendid teats was not (presexual union) going down the boardinghouse corridor to get a package of cigarettes (to better savor her postsexual consummation time with him), but off in search of another Iowa farm boy . . . taking his four months' pay with her.

Instead of delivering them to confinement pending court-martial, Lieutenant Krinski would counsel these kids (eleven years spent counseling murderers, rapists, armed robbers, and others of this ilk had given him a certain expertise) and send them back to their units.

This morning, unhappily, he realized he had a different kind of case entirely. And that didn't please him. Handcuffed to one of the steel-plank cots in the detention facility, he had a twenty-year-old Marine whose deviation from the conduct demanded of Marines on liberty could in no way be swept (so to speak) under the rug. This was one mean sonofabitch . . . or at least as long as you took at face value the report of the arresting Shore Patrolmen (augmented by the reports of their fellow law enforcement officers of the San Diego Police Department). Krinski had no reason to doubt any of these.

Though the Marine was obviously drunk when the alleged incidents occurred, that was no excuse.

At any rate, according to the documents Krinski had before him, this character began the evening by offering his apparently unflattering, and certainly unwelcome, opinion of a lady of the evening. She was at the time chatting with a gunnery sergeant in one of the bars favored by Marine noncommissioned officers.

The discussion moved to the alley behind the bar, where the gunnery sergeant suffered the loss of several teeth, a broken nose, and several broken ribs, the latter injury allegedly having been caused by a thrown garbage can.

That was incident one. Incident two occurred several hours later when a pair of Shore Patrolmen finally caught up with him. At that time, he took the night stick away from one of them and used it to strike both Shore Patrolmen about the head and chest, rendering them *hors de combat.*

Incident three took place an hour or so after that in the Ocean Shores Hotel. This was an establishment where it was alleged that money could be exchanged for sexual favors. There was apparently some misunderstanding about the price arrangement, and the Marine showed his extreme displeasure by causing severe damage to the furniture and fittings of the room he had "taken" for the night. Mr. J. D. Karnoff, an employee of the establishment, known to many (including Lieutenant

Krinski) as "Big Jake," went to the room to inform the Marine that such behavior was not tolerated on the premises and that he would have to leave. When Big Jake tried to show this upstanding Marine to the door, he was thrown down the stairs, and suffered a broken arm and sundry other injuries.

Incident four occurred when six Shore Patrolmen, under the command of an ensign, came to the Ocean Shores. These men were accompanied by two officers of the San Diego Police Department. This force ultimately subdued the Marine and placed him under arrest, but not before he kicked one of the civilian law enforcement officers in the mouth, causing the loss of several teeth, and accused the ensign of having unlawful carnal knowledge of his mother.

It was Lieutenant Krinski's judgment that Marine staff sergeants should know better than to beat up gunnery sergeants; assault Shore Patrolmen with their own nightsticks; throw bouncers down stairs; kick civilian policemen in the mouth; and accuse commissioned officers of unspeakable perversions—especially while they were engaged in the execution of their office.

Having completed his unofficial review of the case, Lieutenant Krinski shifted into his official function. He called in his yeoman and told him to prepare the necessary documents to bring the staff sergeant before a General Court-Martial.

"Charge this bastard with everything," Lieutenant Krinski ordered. "And do it right. I don't want him walking because we didn't cross all the 't's or dot all the 'i's."

An hour later, Lieutenant Krinski's yeoman told him that he had a call from some Marine captain in Public Affairs.

"What does he want?"

"He didn't say, Sir."

"Lieutenant Krinski," he growled into the telephone.

"I'm Captain Jellner, Lieutenant, from Marine Corps San Diego Public Affairs."

"What can I do for you?"

"I'm looking for someone."

"This is the Brig, Captain."

"I know. I've looked everyplace else. I'm clutching at straws, so to speak."

"You have a name?"

"McCoy, Thomas J., Staff Sergeant."

"I've got him, and I'm going to keep him."

"Excuse me?"

"He's going up for a General Court-Martial, Captain. I hope they put him away for twenty years."

"McCoy, Thomas J., Staff Sergeant?" Captain Jellner asked incredulously.

"That's right."

"Good God!"

"You know this guy?"

"Yes, I do. And he's on his way to Washington, Lieutenant. To receive the Medal of Honor."

"He was. Now he's on his way to Portsmouth."

"Did you hear what I just said? About the Medal of Honor?"

"Yes I did, Captain. Did you?"

"I strongly suspect that someone senior to myself will be in touch with you shortly, Lieutenant. In the meantime, I would suggest that you—"

"This sonofabitch is going to get a General Court-Martial. I don't give a good goddamn who calls me," Lieutenant Krinski said, and hung up.

VII

The Admiral's Barge is the boat that transports naval flag officers from shore to ship, from ship to shore, or between men-of-war. The traditions connected with it—its near-sacred rituals—predate aircraft by centuries.

Originally, flag officers were thought to possess a close-to-regal dignity ("Admiral" comes from the Spanish phrase "Prince of the Sea"). Such dignity required that they be able to descend from the deck of a man-of-war to an absolutely immaculate boat manned by impeccably uniformed sailors.

Today, an Admiral was arriving at Noumea by aircraft. Unhappily, it was going to be impossible to provide this Admiral anything like a dignified exit from his aircraft via Admiral's Barge. For one thing, there was no *real* Admiral's Barge available, only a fairly ordinary whaleboat. For another, the weather was turning bad, the bay was choppy, and the huge four-engined PB2-Y was rocking nervously in the waves.

But tradition dies hard in the U.S. Navy, and this was a three-star Vice Admiral arriving on an inspection tour. And so an effort had to be made. Before boarding the whaleboat at the wharf, the two greeting officers had changed from tieless open khaki shirts and trousers into white uniforms. And the crew had been ordered to change from blue work uniforms into their whites. And then when the only three-star Vice Admiral's flag available was found to be too large for the flagstaff on the whaleboat, a suitably taller staff had to be jury-rigged.

It could only be hoped that the Admiral would understand their problems and not let the absence of the honors he was entitled to color his judgment of their entire operation.

The door in the fuselage swung out, and a muscular young lieutenant commander in khakis stepped into the opening. The coxswain carefully edged the whaleboat closer to the door; it wouldn't take much to ram a hole in the aluminum skin of the PB2-Y.

The Lieutenant Commander jumped into the whaleboat. And as he landed, he lost his footing; but, with the help of two boat crewmen, he quickly regained it.

A pair of leather briefcases, four larger pieces of luggage, and a long, cylindrical, leather chart case were tossed aboard the whaleboat by a hatless gray-haired man who was also wearing khakis. Then he, too, jumped aboard. He did not lose his footing.

It was at that point that both dress white–uniformed greeting officers noticed the three silver stars on each collar of the gray-haired man's open-necked khaki shirt.

"Welcome to Noumea, Admiral," the senior officer, a captain, said.

"Thank you," the Admiral said.

"Admiral, the Admiral instructed me to give you this immediately," the Captain said, handing the Admiral a manila envelope.

"Thank you," the Admiral repeated as he sat down in the whaleboat. He tore the envelope open, took out a sheet of paper, read it, and then handed it to the muscular Lieutenant Commander.

The Lieutenant Commander read it.

URGENT
UNCLASSIFIED
FROM: CINCPAC 0545 18OCT42
TO: CHIEF OF NAVAL OPERATIONS WASH DC
    COMMANDER, SOUTH PACIFIC AREA,
    AUCKLAND, NEW ZEALAND
    SUPREME COMMANDER SWPOA, BRISBANE,
    AUSTRALIA

INFO: ALL SHIPS AND STATIONS, USNAVY PACIFIC

   EFFECTIVE IMMEDIATELY, VICE ADMIRAL WIL-
LIAM F. HALSEY, USN, IS ANNOUNCED AS COM-
MANDER, US NAVY FORCES, SOUTH PACIFIC, VICE
ADMIRAL ROBERT L. GHORMLEY, USN, RELIEVED.

CHESTER W. NIMITZ, ADMIRAL, USN, CINCPAC.

"I'll be damned," the Lieutenant Commander said. He handed the sheet of paper back.

Vice Admiral William F. Halsey jammed it in his trousers pocket. "I was thinking the same thing," he said.

(TWO)
Personnel Office
Marine Corps Recruit Depot
San Diego, California
1550 Hours 18 October 1942

"Major, there's just nothing I can do for the corporal," the major in charge of the personnel office said to Major Jake Dillon. "If I could, I would, believe me."

"Welcome home, Easterbunny," First Lieutenant Kenneth R. McCoy said bitterly.

"You said something, Lieutenant?" the Major snapped. He did not like the attitude of the young officer, and wondered just who he was.

"I was just thinking out loud, Major," McCoy said. "So what happens to him now?"

"We'll send him over to the casual barracks until we receive orders on him, locate his service records. . . ."

"I'm prepared to sign a sworn statement that his records were lost in combat," Dillon said. "How about that?"

"In that case, we would begin reconstructing his records."

"How long would that take?" Dillon asked.

"It depends. Perhaps a month, perhaps a little less, perhaps a little longer."

"And in the meantime, Sir," McCoy said, ". . . until you can reconstruct his records . . . the corporal would be pulling details in the casual barracks, without any money? Is that about it?"

"That's about it, Lieutenant. And I don't like the tone of your voice."

"With respect, Sir," McCoy said sarcastically, "isn't that a pretty shitty way to treat a kid who's just back from Guadalcanal?"

"That did it, Lieutenant," the Major snapped. "I won't be talked to like that. May I have your identity card, please?"

"What for?" Dillon asked.

"So that I can put him on report to his commanding officer for insolent disrespect."

"I'm his commanding officer," Dillon said. "I heard what he said. I agree with him."

"And who is your commanding officer, Major?"

"I don't think you're cleared to know who my commanding officer is," Dillon said. "Come on, McCoy."

"I asked you who your commanding officer is, Major!"

"Go fuck yourself, Major," Dillon said, and with McCoy on his heels, marched out of the office.

As they walked off the steps of the frame building and turned toward Corporal Robert F. Easterbrook, USMC, who was sitting on his seabag waiting for them, McCoy said softly, "Do you think we'll get arrested now, or as we try to get off the base?"

"Is that sonofabitch in the same Marine Corps as you and me?" Dillon asked bitterly, still angry. "Sonofabitch!"

Easterbrook rose to his feet.

"We ran into a little trouble, Easterbrook," Dillon said.

"Nothing to worry about," McCoy said.

"What happens now?" Easterbrook asked.

"You and I are going to stay here, Corporal, while Lieutenant McCoy goes to the motor pool and gets us some wheels, and then we're all going to Los Angeles."

"I've got to get to Washington," McCoy said.

"They have an airport in Los Angeles," Dillon said. "I'd like to buy you guys a steak."

"Aye, aye, Sir," McCoy said.

Twenty minutes later, they were out of the U.S. Marine Recruit Depot, San Diego, and headed up the Pacific Highway toward Los Angeles in a Marine Corps 1941 Plymouth staff car that was driven by a PFC who looked as old as Major Dillon.

"I didn't ask. How did you get the staff car?" Dillon asked.

"I told them that I was an assistant to Major Dillon of Marine Corps Headquarters Public Relations," McCoy said, "and the Major needed a ride to Hollywood, so that the Major could ask Lana Turner to come to a party at the officers' club."

"I thought maybe you waved that fancy ID card of yours at the motor officer."

"I was saving that for the MPs at the gate when they started to arrest you for telling that feather-merchant major in personnel to go fuck himself."

"I should have let him write you up," Dillon said. "You can be a sarcastic sonofabitch, McCoy, in case nobody ever told you."

"Excuse me, Sir," Corporal Easterbrook said, turning around in the front seat, his voice suddenly weak and shaky, "but I have to go to the head."

"Christ, why didn't you go at 'Diego?" McCoy asked. But then he looked closer at Easterbrook and said, "Oh, shit!"

"Meaning what?" Dillon asked.

"Meaning he's got malaria," McCoy said. "Look at him." He leaned forward and laid his hand on Easterbrook's forehead. "Yeah," he said, "he's burning up. He's got it, all right."

"Goddamn," Dillon said.

"Sir, I got to go right now," Easterbrook said.

"Find someplace," McCoy snapped at the driver. "Pull off the road if you have to."

The driver started to slow the car, but then put his foot to the floor when he saw a roadside restaurant several hundred yards away.

With a squeal of tires, the PFC pulled into the parking lot, stopped in front of the door, then went quickly around the front of the car, pulled the passenger door open, and helped Easterbrook out.

"He's dizzy, Lieutenant," the PFC said. "He's got it, all right."

"Let's get him to the toilet," McCoy said.

"Shit!" Major Dillon said.

"Hey, he's not doing this to piss you off," McCoy said.

Supported by McCoy and the PFC, Easterbrook managed to make it to a stall in the men's room before losing control of his bowels. Then he became nauseous.

"Let me handle him, Lieutenant," the PFC said.

"Sir, I'm sorry to cause all this trouble," Easterbrook said.

"Never apologize for something you can't control," McCoy said. "I'll be outside."

Major Dillon was waiting on the other side of the men's room door.

"Well?"

"He's got malaria. Half the people on the 'Canal have malaria," McCoy replied.

"What do we do with him?"

"He needs a doctor," McCoy said.

"You want to take him back to 'Diego and put him in the hospital?"

"I said a doctor," McCoy said. "General Pickering told me you know everybody in Hollywood. No doctors?"

"You mean treat him ourselves?"

"Why not? All they do for them in a hospital is give them quinine, or that new stuff . . ."

"Atabrine," Dillon furnished, without thinking.

". . . Atabrine," McCoy went on. "And rest. If we put him in the hospital, they'll just lose him. Christ, he probably couldn't get into the hospital. . . . How's he going to prove he's a Marine without a service record?"

"I'm not at all sure—" Dillon began and then interrupted himself: "I think they'd take my word he's a Marine, even if those personnel feather merchants won't pay him."

"Have you got someplace we can take him, or not? He'll be out of there in a minute."

"Goddamn you, McCoy. Why did you have to tell me he was about to go over the edge?"

"Because he was."

"Dr. Barthelmy's office," Dawn Morris said into the telephone receiver. Miss Morris, who was Dr. Harald Barthelmy's receptionist, was a raven-haired, splendidly bosomed, long-legged young woman. Though she was dressed like a nurse, she had no medical training whatever.

"Dr. Barthelmy, please. My name is Dillon."

"I'm sorry, Sir, the doctor is with a patient. May I have him return your call?"

"Honey, you go tell him Jake Dillon is on the phone."

Dawn Morris knew who Jake Dillon was. He was vice president of publicity for Metro-Magnum Studios . . . the kind of man who could open doors for her. The kind of man she'd planned to meet when she took a job as receptionist for the man *Photoplay* magazine called the "Physician to the Stars."

"Mr. Dillon," Dawn Morris cooed. "Let me check. I'm sure the doctor would like to talk to you if it's at all possible."

"Thank you," Jake Dillon said.

She left her desk and walked down a corridor into a suite of rooms that Dr. Barthelmy liked to refer to as his "surgery."

After his undergraduate years at the University of Iowa, and before completing his medical training at Tulane in New Orleans, Dr. Barthelmy spent a year at Oxford as a Rhodes scholar. As a result, he'd cultivated a certain British manner: He'd grown a pencil-line mustache, and acquired a collection of massive pipes and a wardrobe heavy with tweed jackets with leather elbow patches. And he now spelled his Christian name with two 'a's and addressed most females as "dear girl" and most males as "old sport."

The surgery was half a dozen consulting rooms, opening off a thickly carpeted corridor furnished with leather armchairs and turn-of-the-century lithographs of Englishmen shooting pheasants and riding to hounds.

Dawn knew immediately where to find Dr. Barthelmy. One of his nurses, a real one, an old blue-haired battle-ax, was standing outside one of the consulting cubicles. This was standard procedure whenever Dr. Barthelmy had to ask a female patient to take off her clothes. A woman had once accused Dr. Barthelmy of getting fresh while he was examining her; he was determined this would never happen again.

"I have to see the doctor right away," Dawn said to the nurse.

"He's with a patient," the nurse said.

"This is an emergency," Dawn said firmly.

The nurse rapped on the consulting-room door with her knuckles.

"Not now, if you please!" a deep male voice replied in annoyance.

"Doctor, it's Mr. Jake Dillon," Dawn called. "He said it's very important."

There was a long silence, and then the door opened. Dr. Barthelmy looked at her.

"Mr. Dillon said it's very important, Doctor," Dawn said. "I thought I should tell you."

"Would you ask Mr. Dillon to hold, my girl?" Dr. Barthelmy said. "I'll be with him in half a mo."

"Yes, Doctor," Dawn said.

The consulting-room door closed.

"He's on line five, Doctor," Dawn called through it, and then went quickly back to her desk.

She picked up the telephone.

"Mr. Dillon, Dr. Barthelmy will be with you in just a moment. Would you hold, please?"

"Yeah, I'll hold," Dillon replied. "Thanks, honey, but you stay on the line."

"Yes, of course, Mr. Dillon."

"Jake, old sport, how good to hear your voice."

"Harry, what do you know about malaria?"

"Very little, thank God."

"Harry, goddamn it, I'm serious."

"It is transmitted by mosquitoes, and the treatment is quinine, or some new medicine the name of which at the moment escapes me. You have malaria, old boy?"

"A friend of mine does."

"And you want me to see your friend? Of course, dear boy."

"I'm twenty minutes out of San Diego. By the time I get to my house, I want you there with the new medicine (it's called Atabrine, by the way), a nurse, or nurses, and whatever else you need."

There was a just-perceptible pause before Dr. Barthelmy replied: "That sounded like an order, old sport. *I'm* not in the Marine Corps, as you may have noticed."

"Harry, goddamn it . . ."

"Which house, old boy? Holmby Hills or Malibu?"

"Malibu. I leased the Holmby Hills place to Metro-Magnum for the duration."

"Your contribution to the war effort, I gather?"

"Fuck you, Harry. Just be there," Dillon said, and hung up.

Dawn waited until she heard the click when Dr. Barthelmy hung up, and then hung up herself.

There are not many people, she thought, *who would dare talk to Dr. Harald Barthelmy that way. Or, for that matter, call him "Harry." Only someone with a lot of power. And getting to know someone with a lot of power is what I have been looking for all along. The question is, how am I going to get to meet Jake Dillon?*

Dr. Harald Barthelmy himself answered the question five minutes later. He came into the reception area, smiled at waiting patients, and said, "May I speak to you a moment, Miss Morris?"

"Yes, of course, Doctor," Dawn said, rising up from behind her desk and stepping into the surgery corridor with him. He motioned her into one of the consulting rooms.

There was, she noticed, an open book facedown on the examination table. The spine read, "Basic Principles of Diagnosis and Treatment."

I'll bet, Dawn thought, *that that's open to "Malaria."*

"If memory serves, Miss Morris, you told me you had accepted the receptionist position as a temporary sort of thing, until you can get your motion picture career on the tracks, so to speak?"

"Yes, Doctor. That's true."

"Something a bit out of the ordinary has come up. I don't suppose you . . . monitored . . . my conversation with Mr. Dillon? *Major* Dillon?"

"Oh, of course not, Doctor."

"I'd rather hoped you would have. No matter. You do know who Major Dillon is?"

"I think so, Doctor."

"He is a quite powerful man in the motion picture community. He rushed to the colors, so to speak, the Marine Corps, of all things, when the trumpet sounded. But that has not diminished at all his importance in the film industry. Do you take my meaning?"

"Yes, Doctor, I think so."

"To put a point on it, my girl, he could be very useful to someone in your position."

"I don't quite understand . . ."

"Mr. . . . *Major* Dillon—who is a dear friend, of long standing—has come to me asking a special favor. One of his friends—I don't know who—is apparently suffering from malaria, and for some reason doesn't want to enter a hospital. I can think of a number of reasons for that. He, or she, for example, may be under consideration for a part, for example, and does not want it known that he, or she, is not in perfect health. You understand?"

"Yes, I do."

"As a special favor to Mr. Dillon, I have agreed to treat this patient at Mr. Dillon's beach house in Malibu. Malaria is not contagious. The regimen is a drug called Atabrine and bed rest. Mr. ... *Major* Dillon has at his house a Mexican couple who would be perfectly capable of dispensing the Atabrine, but he would feel more comfortable if a nurse were present.''

''I understand.''

''Dear girl, do you think you could portray a nurse convincingly?'' Dr. Barthelmy asked. ''It would make things so much easier for me. God knows, I haven't a clue where I could get a special-duty nurse on such short order.''

''I'm sure I could.''

''I would be most grateful; and so, I am sure, would Major Dillon,'' Dr. Barthelmy said. ''I'll have the agency send someone over to fill in for you straightaway.''

He turned from her, took a prescription pad from a cabinet drawer, and began to write. He handed her four prescriptions.

''These should do it,'' he said. ''As soon as your replacement shows up, have them filled and charged to my account at the chemist's, and then let me know and we'll run over to Malibu.''

''Yes, Doctor.''

''Good girl!''

When Dawn Morris slid open the glass door and walked out to them, Jake Dillon and Ken McCoy were sitting on chaise lounges on the balcony of the beach house. Beside them lay the remnants of a hamburger and french fries meal. Beer bottles were in their hands.

''The patient,'' Dawn announced, ''has had his medicine and is resting comfortably. I thought it best to leave him alone. Where would you suggest I wait?''

'' 'Resting comfortably'?'' Dillon replied. ''I doubt that.''

''I beg your pardon, Major Dillon?''

''He may be a sick kid, but he's not that sick. If you leaned over him to give him the Atabrine, the one thing he's not doing is resting comfortably.''

McCoy laughed. ''Jesus, Jake!''

''I beg your pardon?'' Dawn asked, trying for a mixture of indignation and confusion.

''Honey, if you're a nurse, I'm an obstetrician,'' Dillon said. ''Where did Harry get you, Central Casting?''

Dawn hesitated only a moment.

''I'm Doctor Barthelmy's receptionist.''

Dillon nodded.

''Would you like me to go?'' Dawn asked.

''Hell, no. I just wanted to be sure that we understood each other. What did Harry tell you, that I could get you a screen test?''

''He was more subtle than that,'' Dawn said.

''I have to go to Washington in the morning,'' Dillon said, glanced at McCoy, and corrected himself: ''*We* have to go to Washington. When I come back, if I see that you've taken good care of the Easterbunny ... if you've seen to it that he's taken the Atabrine when he should, that he's been given everything he wants to eat, and that you have made him happy in every way you can think of—and yes, I mean what you think I mean—I'll make a couple of calls for you, tell a couple of producers who owe me favors that I owe you one. Your tests may turn out to be bombs. Most screen tests do. But on the other hand, they may not. What's your name?''

''Dawn Morris.''

''What's your real name?''

''Doris Morrison.''

Dillon thought that over a moment. ''Dawn Morris isn't bad,'' he decided. ''Do we understand each other, *Dawn Morris?*''

"Yes, Mr. Dillon, we do."

"It's *Major* Dillon," he said. "This is Lieutenant Ken McCoy. You can call us Jake and Killer."

"Screw you!" McCoy flared disgustedly. "Goddamn, Dillon!"

"You can call us Jake and Lieutenant," Dillon said, not chagrined. "Sit down, Dawn. Can I have Maria-Theresa fix you something to eat?"

"I am a little hungry," Dawn confessed.

(THREE)
Supreme Headquarters
South West Pacific Ocean Area
Brisbane, Australia
1910 Hours 18 October 1942

General Douglas MacArthur's Philippine Scout orderly pushed open the door to MacArthur's sitting room and announced, "General MacArthur, it is General Pickering." The orderly was a portly, dark-skinned master sergeant, and Fleming Pickering could never remember seeing a smile on him. He was not smiling now.

"Thank you, Juan," MacArthur said, and rose from an armchair to extend his hand. "Fleming, I'm glad they were able to find you."

"I was in the dungeon, Sir," Pickering replied, and nodded at Mrs. MacArthur. "Good evening, Mrs. MacArthur."

"Oh, Fleming, I've told you time and again that we're friends, and to please call me Jean."

"Well then, good evening, Jean," Pickering said.

"Do you have to go back to your 'dungeon,'" MacArthur asked, "or can I offer you something?" He turned to his wife. "The 'dungeon,' Jean darling, is the cryptographic room in the basement."

"Deep in the basement," Pickering added, "and yes, Sir, I have to go back. And yes, Sir, I would be very grateful if you offered me something."

"Good, because I have one thing to tell you which I think will please you, and another thing to tell you I hope ultimately will be cause for celebration."

"Sir?"

"Where the hell is he?" MacArthur asked impatiently. "I am about to wear this bell out!"

Pickering saw for the first time that MacArthur was tapping his foot on what looked like a doorbell button under the coffee table.

The Filipino orderly appeared.

"Ah, there you are, Juan!" MacArthur said warmly, without a hint of displeasure in his voice. "Would you please get General Pickering something to drink? And while you're at it, would you refreshen this, please? Jean, darling?"

"Nothing for me, thank you, Juan," she replied.

"The General drinks scotch-soda, small ice, is correct?" Juan asked.

"That's right, thank you," Pickering said.

"Why do you call it the 'dungeon'?" Mrs. MacArthur asked. "Because it's in the basement?"

"Because the walls run with water, and there is a steel door which creaks like a Boris Karloff movie," Pickering said.

"I don't think I have ever been down there," she said.

"I don't think they'd let you in, dear," MacArthur said. "Willoughby has to have written permission from Fleming before he can get inside the steel door."

"That's not true, Sir," Pickering said. "He would need a note from you."

"The security is necessarily quite rigid, Jean," MacArthur lectured. "It is in the dungeon that Fleming and Pluto and the boy . . . I shouldn't say 'boy' . . . and the *young officer* who was raised in Japan, Moore, analyze intercepted Japanese messages. Only three people here—myself, Willoughby, and Fleming—are authorized access to that material. Or, for that matter, are even authorized to know what MAGIC means."

"I see," she said.

Except of course, you, Jean, Pickering thought. *The most serious violation of security vis-à-vis MAGIC is committed by the Supreme Commander.*

Or are you being holier than thou? If Patricia were here, would you talk to her, secure in the knowledge that it would go no further?

Juan handed Pickering a stiff drink.

"Thank you, Juan."

"There was a radio from CINCPAC an hour or so ago," MacArthur said. "Actually two, but the important one to you first. That's when I asked if you could be located."

"Yes, Sir?"

"After distinguishing itself almost beyond words in the air war over Guadalcanal, VMF-229 has been withdrawn from combat," MacArthur announced. "I sent a personal radio to General Vandergrift, to which there was an immediate reply. Lieutenant Malcolm Pickering, I am delighted to inform you, is one of the officers who survived."

My God, he came through! Pick's all right!

Pickering's physical response came as a total shock to him. His throat tightened. His eyes watered. He was able to keep from sobbing only by an act of massive willpower.

"Fleming's son, Jean, has eight times been the victor in aerial combat," MacArthur announced. "A warrior in his father's mold!"

"You must be so proud of him!" she said.

"I am," Pickering said, surprised that he could speak.

And so goddamned relieved! Thank you, God!

"General Vandergrift did not say to where they have been withdrawn," MacArthur said. "I suppose I should have asked. Perhaps Espíritu Santo, or Noumea, or here, or New Zealand. Should I send another personal radio?"

"No, Sir. That won't be necessary. Pluto will either know or can quickly find out."

And why should I be able to have access to scarce communications facilities when ten thousand other fathers will have to wait until the services in their own good time get around to telling them whether their sons are dead or alive?

Don't get carried away, Pickering, and kick the goddamn gift horse in the goddamn mouth!

"You said there were two things, General?" Pickering asked.

"Yes, there are," MacArthur said, and reached to the table beside him and came up with a radio message. "This came in at the same time the other did."

MacArthur handed him the CINCPAC radio message announcing that Nimitz had relieved Ghormley and appointed Halsey to replace him.

"You saw Admiral Nimitz on your way here," MacArthur said. "Did he tell you he was thinking about doing something like this?"

It was, Pickering understood, more than a matter of curiosity. MacArthur wanted to know if Pickering had information that he had not chosen to share with him.

"No, Sir," Pickering said, meeting MacArthur's eyes. "He didn't."

"Does this surprise you?"

"Admiral Nimitz gave me no indication that he was . . . dissatisfied . . . with Admiral Ghormley," Pickering said.

"But?"

"But Ghormley seemed . . . General, you're putting me on the spot. I dislike criticizing officers who know vastly more about waging war than I do."

"Entre nous, Fleming," MacArthur said. "We are friends."

That was a command, not a request. He wants a reply and I will have to give him one.

And when in doubt, tell the truth.

"General, in the belief it would go no further, Pluto Hon said to me that Admiral Ghormley's radios of 16 and 17 October were unreasonable, and sounded a little desperate . . . the ones in which he claimed his forces were totally inadequate and requested tremendous new levels of support. I thought so, too."

"Absolutely!" MacArthur agreed. "The one thing a commander simply cannot do is appear unsure of himself. Nimitz saw this. He had no choice but to relieve Ghormley; Ghormley gave him none."

Pickering looked at him but did not reply.

"Relieving an officer, especially if he is someone you have served with and think of as a friend, is one of the most painful responsibilities of command," MacArthur declared. "It must have been very distressing for Admiral Nimitz."

He looked for a moment as if he was listening to his own words, and upon hearing them, agreeing with them. He nodded, then smiled.

"But at least he picked the right man," he said.

"You know Admiral Halsey, Sir?"

"I've met him. I know his reputation. But he is apparently someone who immediately takes charge. He has called a conference for the day after tomorrow at Noumea. Vandergrift will be there. And Harmon. And Patch. The Admiral is apparently one of those rare sailors who thinks that sometimes soldiers and Marines may have something to say worth listening to."

"Douglas!" Jean MacArthur chided. "That's unkind!"

MacArthur ignored her.

"In the belief that you would find this conference interesting, Fleming, I've arranged for a plane to take you there."

"That's very kind of you," Pickering said.

He suddenly understood: MacArthur had not been invited to Admiral Halsey's conference.

Prince Machiavelli knows that while I would be no more welcome there than he would, or any of his palace guard (Willoughby, for example), they can't keep me out. And, since we are friends, it is to be expected that on my return, I will report what happened. The wily old sonofabitch!

"But my mission here, Sir, is to convince you that Mr. Donovan's people would be of greater value than harm. I'm not sure I should go to Admiral Halsey's conference with that hanging in the air."

"We can talk about Wild Bill Donovan when you return," MacArthur said.

That could be interpreted to mean tit-for-tat; I go to the conference and tell you what they said, and you let Donovan's people in. But I know you better than that. When I return we will talk about Donovan again and you will tell me of another reason you don't want his camel's nose under your tent.

"General, you have again put me on the spot," Pickering said, draining his scotch. "Ethically. If I go to Halsey's conference, there is a good chance I will be made privy to things the Navy wouldn't wish you to know."

"My dear Fleming," MacArthur said. "I understand completely. But it is a moot point. If anything transpires at that conference that I should know, Admiral Nimitz will see to it that I do."

I believe that. I also believe that somewhere in the hills of Tennessee there is a pig that really can whistle.

"And anyway," MacArthur said, tapping his foot on the floor-mounted button again, and smiling at Pickering. "When they see you at the conference, they won't say anything they don't want me to hear. They know how close we are."

(FOUR)
Office of the Director of Public Affairs
Headquarters, U.S. Marine Corps
Eighth and I Streets, N.W.
Washington, D.C.
0945 Hours 20 October 1942

Brigadier General J. J. Stewart, USMC, a ruddy-faced, stocky, pleasant-looking officer of not-quite-fifty, had received by hand the square envelope he was now holding. In theory, every item delivered into the Navy Department message center system was treated like every other: It would gradually wend its way through the system until it ultimately arrived at its destination.

There were exceptions to every standard operating procedure, however, and the item General Stewart held in his hand headed the list of exceptions. The return address read: "The Secretary of the Navy, Washington, D.C."

General Stewart carefully opened the envelope by lifting the flap. His usual custom was to stab the envelope with his letter opener, a miniature Marine Officer's Sword given to him by his wife. But such an act felt too much like a—well, minor desecration. He extracted the single sheet of paper and read it carefully.

The Secretary of the Navy
Washington, D.C.

October 19, 1942

Brigadier General J. J. Stewart
Director, Public Affairs
Headquarters, U.S. Marine Corps
Washington, D.C.

The Secretary wishes it known, upon the release of Major Homer C. Dillon, USMCR, from temporary duty with the Office of Management Analysis, that he is cognizant of, and deeply appreciative of, the extraordinary performance of duty by Major Dillon in the conduct of a classified mission of great importance.

The Secretary additionally wishes to express his appreciation of the professional skill and extraordinary devotion to duty, at what was obviously great personal risk, of Corporal Robert F. Easterbrook, USMC. Corporal Easterbrook's still and motion picture photography, when viewed by the President, the Secretary and certain members of the U.S. Senate, provided an insight into activities on Guadalcanal which would not have otherwise been available.

By Direction:

DAVID W. HAUGHTON
Captain, U.S. Navy
Administrative Assistant to the Secretary

General Stewart's first thought was that what he was reading had been written the day before. Probably late in the afternoon, or even at night. Otherwise it would have been delivered before this.

Then he began to try to understand what the words meant.

Though he could not be considered an actual thorn in General Stewart's side, Major Homer C. Dillon was the sort of officer who made General Stewart uncomfortable. He didn't fit into the system. He knew too many important people.

As for the "classified mission of great importance" Dillon had been involved in, General Stewart had no idea what it was all about. He'd been told at the time, and rather bluntly, that Major Dillon was being placed on temporary duty for an indefinite period with the Office of Management Analysis. He'd never previously heard of that organization. Yet when he quite naturally asked about it, he'd even more bluntly been told that his curiosity was unwelcome.

He'd made additional, very discreet inquiries, and learned that the Office of Management Analysis had virtually nothing to do with either management or analysis. That information did not surprise him; for he also learned that the number-two man at the Office of Management Analysis was Colonel F. L. Rickabee, whom General Stewart knew by reputation—the reputation being that he'd been involved in intelligence matters since he was a first lieutenant. The number-one man at Management Analysis was Brigadier General Fleming Pickering, a reservist. *The Washington Post* had described Pickering as a close personal friend of the President, and scuttlebutt had it that he was Secretary of the Navy Frank Knox's personal spy in the Pacific.

Dillon had obviously been doing something for the Office of Management Analysis. . . . Exactly what he was doing there, General Stewart suspected he would never know. But he'd done it well, witness the letter. And so now he was being returned to Public Affairs for duty, with the official thanks of the Secretary of the Navy.

But who the hell is this corporal?

"Sergeant Sawyer!" General Stewart called; and in a moment, Technical Sergeant Richard Sawyer, USMC, a lean, crisp Marine in his middle thirties, put his head in the door. General Stewart motioned him inside and Sergeant Sawyer closed the door behind him.

"Sawyer, were you aware that Major Dillon is being returned to us?"

"Yes, Sir. There was a call yesterday afternoon. The Major is apparently on his way here—by now, he's probably arrived—from the West Coast. I arranged for a BOQ for him."

"Good man," General Stewart said. "Does the name Easterbrook, Corporal Robert F., ring a bell with you?"

Sergeant Sawyer considered the question a moment, and then shook his head, no.

"No, Sir."

"See if you can find out who he is, will you?"

"Aye, aye, Sir," Sergeant Sawyer said, and then an idea came to him. "General, he may be one of the combat correspondents Major Dillon took with him when he went over there the first time, for the Guadalcanal invasion. I'll check."

"When he 'went over for the first time'? Sawyer," Stewart asked, picking up on that. "Are you saying that Major Dillon went overseas more than once? Has he been over there again?"

"Yes, Sir. I presume so. The call I had—"

"Who was that from?"

"Sir, from a Captain Sessions in the Office of Management Analysis. The Captain said, Sir, that Major Dillon had just arrived from Pearl Harbor."

"Thank you, Sergeant. See what you can turn up about the Corporal, will you?"

"Aye, aye, Sir. There's a copy of their orders around here someplace."

Five minutes later, Sergeant Sawyer returned to confirm that Corporal Robert F. Easterbrook was indeed a member of the team of combat correspondents Major Homer C. Dillon had taken to the Pacific for the invasion of Guadalcanal.

At 1015 Major Jake Dillon walked into the Public Affairs Division office and went up to the sergeant's desk just inside the door. Dillon was wearing an impeccably tailored uniform, and still smelling faintly of the after-shave applied by the barber in the Willard Hotel.

The sergeant stood up.

"May I help the Major?"

"I guess I'm reporting for duty, Sergeant. My name is Dillon."

The sergeant smiled. "Yes, Sir. We've been expecting you." He flipped a lever on a wooden intercom box on his desk. "General, Major Dillon is here."

"Splendid!" Stewart's voice replied metallically. "Please ask the Major to come in."

"If you'll come with me, please, Major?" the sergeant said, then led Dillon deep into the office, finally stopping before the desk of Technical Sergeant Sawyer.

"Major Dillon to see the General," he announced.

"Yes, Sir," Sergeant Sawyer said, and then went to a door, held it open, and announced, "Major Dillon, Sir."

Dillon stepped in. Brigadier General J. J. Stewart walked across the room to him, smiling, his hand extended.

"Welcome home, Major Dillon," he said. "It's good to see you back."

"Thank you, Sir," Dillon said. It was not quite the reception he had anticipated. He'd heard that Brigadier General J. J. Stewart had asked rather persistent questions about what he was doing for Fleming Pickering, and that the General had been bluntly told to butt out.

"They take care of you all right? Your quarters are satisfactory?"

"Sir," Dillon said carefully, "I'm in the Willard."

General Stewart remembered now that Metro-Magnum Studios, Major Dillon's pre-war employers, maintained two suites in the Willard for the use of its executives and stars. He also remembered hearing that as a gesture of their support for The Boys In Uniform, Metro-Magnum had kept Dillon on their payroll. There was nothing *wrong* with that, of course, but it was a little unsettling to have a major on your staff who took home more money than the Commandant of The Marine Corps. And who didn't live in a BOQ because there was a suite in the Willard Hotel available to him.

"Oh, yes," General Stewart said. "I wish I'd remembered that. It would have saved me the trouble of having the red carpet, so to speak, rolled out for you at the Bachelor Officer's Quarters."

He smiled at Dillon. "Would you like some coffee, Dillon?"

"Yes, Sir, thank you very much."

"And then I'd like to hear about Corporal Easterbrook."

"I'd planned to talk to you about him, General."

"Oh, really?"

"God only knows where his service records are, Sir. They're lost somewhere. He can't get paid."

"Where is he, Dillon?" If the corporal needed money, General Stewart reasoned, he was no longer on Guadalcanal.

"On the West Coast, Sir."

"San Diego?"

"Actually, Sir, he's at my place, outside Los Angeles. I didn't want to leave him at 'Diego without any money and records."

"How did he get to the United States?"

"I brought him with me, Sir. He had taken some film . . . General, I'm not sure I should get into this."

"I understand," General Stewart said. "And I have been informed how valuable the corporal's photography has been to some very important people. Specifically, there has been a letter to that effect from Secretary Knox."

"Easterbrook is a good man, General," Dillon said.

"That being so, Dillon, why is it that he's only a corporal?"

Because he's nineteen years old, still soaking wet behind the ears, and has been in The Corps about eight months.

Goddamn it. He's also been on the 'Canal since we landed. And doing the work of the others, the ones who were killed and wounded. He is no longer a kid.

"It was my intention, General, to recommend that he be promoted," Dillon said. "He's been doing the work of the two lieutenants I lost over there."

"We can . . . what is it they say? . . . get his lost records reconstructed here. I'll speak to the G-1 myself."

"Thank you, Sir."

"And while we're doing that, Dillon, I don't see why we can't see that he is promoted. To sergeant, certainly. If you think it's justified, to staff sergeant."

Why the hell not? He's been doing staff sergeant's work, lieutenant's work. And if you're a major, Dillon, you're in no position to say that anybody who's gone through what the Easterbunny has doesn't deserve a couple of more stripes.

"Easterbrook has certainly earned the right to be a staff sergeant, Sir."

"I've got a very good sergeant here in the shop, Dillon. He'll know how to arrange it."

"Sir, I think that's a very good idea. Thank you."

"And now we get to you, Dillon, now that you're back with us. But, I have to ask, are you back with us? Or will there be more . . . temporary duty?"

"I don't think so, Sir. That was a special situation."

"Well, then, let me bring you up to date on what has happened since you've been gone. For one thing, the war bond tour was a great success. I think it will be a continuing function. Not only do the tours sell war bonds, but they are good for civilian morale and for recruitment. I have heard some very interesting figures about how many people show up at Marine Recruiting Stations immediately after a war bond presentation."

"I'm glad to hear that worked out, General," Dillon said.

"We are already forming the second tour. This one will feature Marine aces, plus some other heroes, from Guadalcanal. Sergeant Machine Gun McCoy, for example. You're familiar with him?"

"Yes, Sir."

"It's just about firmed up—not for release, of course—that McCoy is going to be given the Medal of Honor."

"From what I've heard about what he did at Bloody Ridge, I think that's justified."

"There was an officer on the first tour, wounded with the parachutists during the first wave to hit Gavutu," General Stewart went on. "A chap by the name of Macklin. First Lieutenant R. B. Macklin. Ring a bell?"

"Yes, Sir. If it's the same man, I sent him home for the tour when he was in the hospital in Australia."

Who else would it be but that sonofabitch? I cast him for the role of hero because I needed a handsome hero—even though I knew the story about the lieutenant with only a minor shrapnel wound to his leg who had to be pried from a piling at Gavutu ... screaming hysterically for a corpsman. I knew it had to be Macklin.

"I'm sure it's him, then. Good-looking chap. He was very effective on the tour, and I talked G-1 into letting us have him permanently."

"Sir?"

"I arranged with G-1—with the same fellow, by the way, who will help us see Easterbrook get his promotion—to have Macklin assigned to us for the war bond tours."

"I see."

"And there has been one other development while you were away. The Assistant Commandant was very pleased ... *very* pleased ... with the performance of your people on Guadalcanal. The picture of the Marine parachutist on Gavutu—the one firing the BAR with the blood running down his chest—"

"Easterbrook took that picture, General," Dillon interrupted.

"Yes," General Stewart said. "Of course! I should have remembered! Well, anyway, that was on the front page of every important newspaper in the country."

"*Life,* too," Dillon interjected.

General Stewart did not like to be interrupted; it was evident in his tone of voice as he went on: "Yes, *Life,* too. And since the concept of combat correspondents obviously worked so well, the Assistant Commandant decided to formalize. Do you know Colonel Denig, by any chance?"

Dillon shook his head, no.

"Well, we'll have to arrange for you to meet. Splendid officer. Anyway, Denig is recruiting suitable people to be combat correspondents, officer and enlisted. Metro-Goldwyn-Mayer has offered to give them training in motion picture photography; various newspapers will do the same thing, et cetera, et cetera. The operation, for the time being, will be located on the West Coast."

"Sounds like a good idea," Dillon said.

"Homer," General Stewart chided, "whatever ideas the Assistant Commandant might have are good ideas, don't you agree?"

Well, he was the one who hung these major's leaves on me. That wasn't such a good idea. And what is this "Homer" crap? Are we now pals, General?

"Absolutely," Dillon said.

"Now that you're back with us, Homer, what I've been thinking about for you is sending you back to California to take charge of the whole thing—the war bond tours and the training of combat correspondents at the Hollywood studios. It seems to me to be right down your alley. How does that strike you?"

We're both supposed to be Marines. You outrank the hell out of me. You're supposed to say "do this" and I'm supposed to say "aye, aye, Sir." What is this "how does that strike you?" crap?

"Wherever you think I'd be of the most use to The Corps, Sir," Dillon said.

"Good man!" General Stewart said. "Now is there any reason why you couldn't get right on this? Any reason I don't know and you can't talk about?"

Well, for one thing, General, when it comes to getting a new set of records for the Easterbunny, I don't trust you as far as I can throw you. I think I'll stick around and make sure that's done.

"I think it would be best, Sir," Dillon said, "if I made myself available here for the next two or three days."

"Certainly. I understand fully. Whenever you feel comfortable going back out there, you just call Sergeant Sawyer about transportation. This is important. I don't see any reason why we can't get you a high enough priority to fly out there."

"That's very kind of you, Sir."

"Macklin is temporarily set up in the Post Office Building in Los Angeles. I'll have my sergeant send a telegram telling him you're coming."

"Yes, Sir."

"Well, I don't want to give you the impression, Homer, that I'm running you off," General Stewart said. "But just take a look at this desk!"

"Thank you very much for your time, General," Dillon said formally, and then stood up and came to attention. "By your leave, Sir?"

"That will be all, thank you, Major Dillon," General Stewart replied, as formally.

VIII

"So far as I can tell, gentlemen," Lieutenant Commander Warren W. Warbasse, Medical Corps, USNR, said, "you are all far healthier than you look, or frankly should be."

"Doctor, I don't know about these two, but in *my* case that is obviously due to the fact that I am pure in heart," First Lieutenant Malcolm S. Pickering, USMCR, said solemnly. "I did not run around the tropical islands chasing bare-breasted maidens in grass skirts."

Dr. Warbasse smiled. He was thirty-five or so, tall and curly haired, with a mildly aesthetic look. Despite this last, he had instincts that were solidly down to earth. These told him that the young officer was well on his way to being plastered. He wondered how he managed to find the liquor; the three of them had been brought by station wagon directly to the hospital from the seaplane base at Pearl.

It was a standard procedure for those returning from Guadalcanal. The percentage of returnees with malaria was mind-boggling.

"I'd like to keep you in that pure state, Lieutenant," Dr. Warbasse said. "Have they told you where you're going from here?"

"Ewa, Commander," Captain Charles M. Galloway, USMCR, said. "The squadron has been ordered there for refitting."

"The other squadron officers will follow?" Dr. Warbasse asked.

"Sir," First Lieutenant William C. Dunn said, a little thickly. "You are looking at the officers of VMF-229. Our noble skipper, his devoted executive, and this disgrace to The Marine Corps."

My God, that's all the officers out of the squadron? Three out of how many? Twenty, anyway, probably twenty-five.

"Have you been at the sauce, too, Captain?" Dr. Warbasse asked. "Or can I talk sensibly with you?"

"I didn't even know they had any until he breathed on me in there," Galloway said.

"Ordinarily, I would order you into the hospital for a couple of days' bed rest," Dr. Warbasse said. "But since you're going to Ewa, maybe I could waive that, if I had some assurance that these two wouldn't try to drink the islands dry."

"I'll keep an eye on them, Doctor," Galloway said.

"I hope so," Dr. Warbasse said. "It would really be a shame to have to scrape you off a tree, or shovel you out of a Honolulu gutter, after all you have gone through."

"I'll keep my eye on them, Commander," Galloway repeated.

"OK. You're free to go."

"Commander, do you happen to know where I could find Commander Kocharski?" Galloway asked.

"Who is that?" Pickering asked. "The Polish chaplain?"

"Shut up, Pick. You are not amusing," Galloway said.

"The nurse?" Dr. Warbasse asked.

"The *nurse*?" Pickering asked delightedly. "And who is going to keep an eye on our keeper while he's off chasing a nurse, I wonder."

"One more word, Pick, and you're in here for as long as they'll keep you," Galloway said, not quite succeeding in restraining a smile. He looked at Dr. Warbasse. "She's an old friend of mine."

"Commander Kocharski is the chief surgical nurse," Dr. Warbasse said. "Seven C."

"Thank you, Sir," Galloway said. "Out, you two!"

Commander Warbasse's curiosity got the best of him. "I'd like a word, Captain."

"You two better be here when I come out," Galloway said, then closed the door after them and turned to face Dr. Warbasse.

"Did I hear him correctly? You're all that's left of VFM-229?"

"All the officers, yes, Sir."

"Welcome home, Captain," Dr. Warbasse said. "One more thing, there's been some scuttlebutt that they're sending the Guadalcanal Marine and Navy aces home for a war bond tour, after they've gone through here. Is that who I'm looking at? Those boys are aces?"

Galloway hesitated a moment before deciding that the doctor had not meant anything out of line, that he probably thought of every serviceman who passed his way as a "boy." But there was still a little ice in his voice when he finally replied.

"I don't know anything about a war bond tour, Doctor, but the blond *boy,* who is my executive officer, is a double ace. The other *boy,* the *boy* with the big mouth, has eight kills."

"And you, Captain? Or am I being offensive?"

"Six," Galloway said. "Is that all, Doctor?"

"Except to repeat, welcome home, yes, that's all."

"Is this important, Captain?" the nurse in Ward 7C's glass-walled office asked. "Commander Kocharski has been in the operating room all morning. She's taking a nap, and I really hate to disturb her."

"Please tell her it's Charley Galloway," Galloway said.

"I think I'm in love with you, Lieutenant," Lieutenant Dunn said. "What did you say your name was?"

"Shut up, Bill!" Galloway snapped.

"Just a moment, please," the nurse said.

A minute later, a large woman in her forties appeared in the office. She wore no makeup, her pale-blond hair was cut very short, and she was in a fresh set of surgical whites.

"Hello, Charley," she said, very softly.

"Hiya, Flo," Galloway said.

"My God, I hope this isn't what I think it is."

"That ugly friend of yours was last seen boarding a transport for Pearl via Noumea," Galloway said. "He asked me to say hello."

With astonishing speed for her bulk, Lieutenant Commander Kocharski moved across the office to Captain Galloway. She wrapped her arms around him, then put her face on his chest and sobbed.

"Oh, Charley, thank God!" she said. "The sonofabitch never writes, and I've been nearly out of my mind."

The other nurse looked at Lieutenant William C. Dunn to see his reaction to this. Dunn winked at her, and she snapped her head away.

"He's all right, Flo," Galloway said, somewhat awkwardly patting Commander Kocharski on the back. "And he'll be stationed here. We're refitting at Ewa."

Commander Kocharski regained control of her emotions.

"Jesus Christ, look at me!" she said, wiping the tears from her cheeks.

"You look good, Flo," Galloway said.

Commander Kocharski looked at Dunn.

"I know who you are," she announced. "You're Billy Dunn. Steve wrote me about you. He said even if you look like a high school cheerleader, you're the best pilot he ever saw."

The nurse lieutenant looked at Dunn just in time to hear Commander Kocharski add, "Carol, he's shot down eight Japs."

"Actually, ten," Lieutenant Pickering interjected, and added: "I have just had a divine revelation: The lady's referring to *Big* Steve."

"Which one are you?" Commander Kocharski asked, turning to him.

"Pickering is my name," Pick said.

"Dick Stecker's buddy," Commander Kocharski immediately identified him. "He's much better. Or have you seen him?"

"That's our next stop," Galloway said.

"He's in Nine Dog," Commander Kocharski said. "I better go with you, to make sure they let you see him."

"I gather you and Big Steve are good friends?" Pickering asked.

"Friends, hell. We're married," Commander Kocharski said. "We had our time in, we were going to retire, so we got married, and then this goddamned war came along."

"Lieutenant," Galloway said to the other nurse, deadly serious, "if what the Commander just said gets any further than these four walls, there are three officers here who will swear nothing like that was ever said."

"She's told me," the nurse said. "And I didn't hear what she said, anyway."

"Thank you," Galloway said.

"Big Steve never told me he was married," Pickering said.

"I'll tell you about it later," Galloway said.

"Charley, I can get off; can we go somewhere for a drink? Jesus, there's no place private, unless I sneak you into the nurses' quarters . . ."

"By an odd coincidence, I know a place where we could have a drink in private," Pick said. "But we'd need wheels to get there."

"I think the two of you have all the sauce you can handle," Commander Kocharski said, and then asked suspiciously, "What kind of a place?"

"My father's got a house here," Pickering said. "I can use it."

"We have wheels," Flo said. "Your car, Charley. I've been driving it."

"Then the problem is solved," Pickering said.

"You can sit on my lap," Dunn said to the nurse.

"Of all the nerve! What makes you think I'd go anywhere with you?"

"I wish you would come with us, Carol," Flo said.

"Well, all right," Carol said.

"She didn't take a hell of a lot of convincing, did she?" Pick asked.

"Steve said you had a big mouth, young man," Commander Kocharski said. "If you're smart, you'll keep it shut around me and my friends."

"Yes, Ma'am," Lieutenant Pickering said very politely.

(TWO)
Muku Muku
1555 Hours 20 October 1942

"Dawkins," Lieutenant Colonel Clyde W. Dawkins answered the telephone at Ewa. Galloway thought he sounded very tired.

"Galloway, Sir. We just got in. Dunn, Pickering, and me."

"Welcome to the Pearl of the Pacific, Charley. What they're going to do is run you through the hospital, primarily to check for malaria. . . ."

"Sir, we've already been through that."

"OK. I'll send a car for you. It'll take thirty minutes. Wait just inside the main entrance to the hospital. . . ."

"Sir, that won't be necessary."

"What does that mean?"

"Sir, I decided that the officers of VMF-299 needed a seventy-two-hour liberty, and I granted them one."

There was a long pause before Dawkins asked, "I gather you're not at Pearl Harbor, Charley?"

"No, Sir."

"Where are you?"

"It's a place called Muku Muku, Sir."

"What the hell is that, Galloway? A brothel?"

Galloway glanced around the flagstone patio overlooking the crashing surf. Commander Kocharski and Lieutenant Pickering were sitting each to one side of a table entirely occupied by a large silver platter of hors d'oeuvres. A white-jacketed, silver-haired black man stood off nearby. Lieutenant Carol Ursery, Nurse Corps, USN, and First Lieutenant William C. Dunn, USMCR, were dancing (so slowly that Galloway found it pleasantly erotic) to phonograph music.

"No, Sir, it is not," Galloway said.

"Goddamn it, Galloway, I'm tired. Don't play with me."

"It's a private home, Sir. On the coast. It belongs to Pickering's family."

"Charley, I'm sorry, but you're going to have to come out here, and now."

"Sir, with respect, won't it wait until the morning? It's 1600 . . ."

There was another long pause.

"Where is this place, Charley? How do I get there?"

"You want to come here, Sir?"

"Either way, Galloway," Dawkins said. "I come there, or the three of you come out here."

"Hold one, Sir," Charley said, and covered the microphone with his hand. "Pickering, get on the horn and tell the Skipper how to get here from Ewa."

"Welcome to Muku Muku, Colonel," the silver-haired black man said as he opened the door of Dawkins' 1941 Plymouth staff car. "I'm Dennis, the chief steward. Mr. Pickering and his guests are on the patio. If you'll come with me, please?"

"What the hell is this place?" Dawkins asked as he looked around.

"Officially, Colonel, it is the Pacific & Far East Shipping Corporation's Guest House for Visiting Masters & Chief Engineers," Denny said. "But everybody calls it Muku Muku."

Dawkins followed Denny through the elegantly furnished house to the patio. A very large Polish woman in a gloriously flowered Muumuu saw him first and stood up. When she rose, so did Lieutenant Pickering. Lieutenant Dunn and a nurse a good six inches taller than he was were dancing to Glenn Miller records on a phonograph. They stopped dancing when they saw him, but they did not, Dawkins noticed, let go of each other's hands.

"Good evening, Sir," Pickering said. "Welcome to Muku Muku. Can Denny get you something to drink?"

"Where is Captain Galloway?" Dawkins said.

"He just went inside for a moment," Pickering said. "Excuse me, Sir. May I present Commander Kocharski and Lieutenant Ursery?"

Why am I not surprised? What did I think Commander Kocharski would look like? Lana Turner?

"Commander," Dawkins said, taking her hand; it was larger than his, he noticed. "I have the odd feeling that you would be interested to hear that I have just learned that the Commandant of The Marine Corps has just approved the promotion of Technical Sergeant Oblensky to master gunner."

Master gunners, who rank between noncommissioned and commissioned officers, are the Marine Corps equivalent of Warrant Officers in the Army. They are entitled to be saluted by enlisted men, and are afforded other commissioned officers' privileges.

"Oh, that's wonderful news!" Flo said.

"You've heard, I guess, he's on his way here?"

"Galloway told me, Colonel," Flo said.

"Apropos of nothing whatever," Dawkins said, "I have been informed that there is no bar to marriage between master gunners and officers of the Naval service."

"Is that so?" Flo said. "Isn't that fascinating?"

"Good evening, Sir," Galloway said, coming onto the patio.

"Captain," Dawkins said.

"Steve's got his master gunner, Charley," Flo said. "The Colonel just told me."

"Thank you, Skipper," Galloway said.

"Thank General Vandergrift," Dawkins said. "He wrote the Commandant."

"I repeat, Sir," Galloway said. "Thank you, Skipper."

"Well, that's the good news," Dawkins said, and reached in his pocket and handed Galloway a folded radio message. "This is the bad."

PRIORITY
HEADQUARTERS USMC
WASHINGTON DC 0905 18OCT42

TO: COMMANDING OFFICER MAG-21
    VIA CINCPAC

1. FOLLOWING OFFICERS VMF-229 ARE DE-TACHED FOR A PERIOD OF NINETY (90) DAYS AND PLACED ON TEMPORARY DUTY WITH USMC PUB-LIC AFFAIRS DETACHMENT, US POST OFFICE BUILDING, LOS ANGELES, CAL. FOR THE PURPOSE OF PARTICIPATING IN WAR BOND TOUR NUMBER TWO.

GALLOWAY, CHARLES M CAPT USMCR
DUNN, WILLIAM C 1/Lt USMCR
PICKERING, MALCOLM S 1/Lt USMCR

2. SUBJECT OFFICERS WILL PROCEED IMMEDI-
ATELY BY MILITARY OR CIVILIAN AIR TRANSPOR-
TATION (PRIORITY AAA-2) FROM PRESENT STATION
TO LOS ANGELES, CAL., REPORTING UPON ARRIVAL
THEREAT TO OFFICER-IN-CHARGE USMC PUBLIC
AFFAIRS DETACHMENT. IF TIME SCHEDULE OF
WAR BOND TOUR NUMBER TWO PERMITS, A TEN
(10) DAY ADMINISTRATIVE DELAY EN ROUTE
LEAVE IS AUTHORIZED.

3. DIRECTOR, PUBLIC AFFAIRS, HQ USMC AND
OFFICER-IN-CHARGE USMC PUBLIC AFFAIRS DE-
TACHMENT LOS ANGELES, CAL. WILL BE IN-
FORMED BY PRIORITY RADIO OF DATE, TIME, AND
MEANS OF DEPARTURE OF SUBJECT OFFICERS IN
COMPLIANCE WITH THESE ORDERS.

BY DIRECTION:

J. J. STEWART, BRIG GEN, USMC

"Jesus!" Galloway said, disgustedly. "How do we get out of this, Skipper? Or at least how do I?"

"I spoke with General McInerny," Dawkins said. "He thinks he may be able to get you out of it. I told him I need you to refit the squadron. These two heroes are stuck."

"Stuck with what?" Pickering asked. Galloway handed him the radio message.

"No! Jesus H. Christ!" Pickering said when he had read the message. He handed it to Dunn.

"You're on the Pan American clipper departing at 0700, Mr. Pickering," Dawkins said.

"Can I take my ten days' leave here?" Dunn asked. Dawkins looked at him. "I'm in love," Dunn explained.

"Will you stop that?" Lieutenant Ursery said.

"Love will have to wait," Dawkins said, smiling. "Duty calls, Mr. Dunn. You will be on that PAA clipper."

"I don't know why he talks like that, Colonel," Lieutenant Ursery said. "He's crazy."

"Yes, I know," Dawkins said. "If the offer is still good, I think I would like a drink."

"Denny," Pickering said. "Would you get the Colonel a nice glass of cyanide, please?"

"We've got just about everything, Colonel, pay no attention to Mr. Pick," Denny said. "What can I fix you?"

"Bourbon?"

"Finest Kentucky sour mash coming up."

"Skipper," Galloway pursued. "There's no way I can get out of this?"

"I told you, Charley, General McInerney thinks he can get you out of the war bond tour, but you're going to have to go to the States tomorrow."

"I know General McInerney," Pick said. "Maybe if I asked him . . ."

"Try saying 'aye, aye, Sir,' just once, Mr. Pickering," Dawkins said.

"If you know him, Pick," Bill Dunn said, "ask him if he can fix it so I can spend my ten days' leave with Whatsername here."

" 'Whatsername'?" Carol Ursery exploded.

"Tell him I'm in love," Dun said, unabashed.

"Can you call the States from here?" Galloway asked.

"There's a hell of a wait for personal calls, Charley," Dawkins replied. "It took me four hours to get through to my wife."

"Who do you want to call, Skipper?" Pickering asked, and then, smugly, "Ah! Ward's aunt!"

"Watch your mouth, Pickering!"

"Do you wish to be nasty to me, Sir, or do you want to talk to the sainted Aunt Carolyn?"

For a moment, Colonel Dawkins was convinced that Galloway was going to really rip into Pickering. But what Galloway said was, "Don't tell me you can get a call through?"

"You got a number, Skipper?" Pickering asked. "I'll just bet that P and FE has a priority. If I can get through to the switchboard in San Francisco, they can put you through to anywhere in the States."

Galloway dug out his wallet.

"Pickering," Colonel Dawkins asked. "What's your connection with Pacific & Far East Shipping?"

Pickering looked at him.

"Sir, my father owns it," he said simply. "But I would appreciate it if that didn't get around."

(THREE)
Jenkintown, Pennsylvania
2345 Hours 20 October 1942

Mrs. Carolyn Ward McNamara was thirty-two, blond, long-haired, long-legged, and at the moment fiercely annoyed. It had taken a long time to get to sleep, and when the telephone at her bedside table rang, she did not welcome the intrusion.

It was probably a wrong number. Or worse, some goddamned man who'd decided it was his duty to comfort the grass widow in her loneliness.

Some goddamned man who'd needed liquid courage to find the nerve and had drunk enough so that he either didn't know what time it was, or didn't care.

She sat up in bed, turned on the bedside lamp, grabbed the telephone, and snarled into it, "Who is this, for God's sake?"

"Mrs. Carolyn W. McNamara, please," a female voice asked. It was an operator.

"Who is this?" Carolyn snapped.

"Are you Mrs. McNamara?" the operator persisted.

"Yes, who the hell is this?"

"Go ahead, Honolulu, we have Mrs. McNamara on the line."

"One moment, San Francisco," another female voice said.

San Francisco? Honolulu? What the hell is this? It has to be about Charley! Oh, God!

"Muku Muku," a male voice said.

What did he say?

"We're ready with Mrs. McNamara on the mainland."

"One moment, please."

"Galloway."

"We're ready with your party, Captain Galloway. Go ahead, please."

"Oh, God, Charley!"

"Carolyn?"

"Yes, yes, yes. Charley, where are you? Are you all right?"

"I'm fine. How are you?"

"Where are you?"

"Hawaii."

"Thank God! I've been so worried. Charley, you're not hurt?"

"No. I'm fine."

"The newspapers have been full . . ."

"I'm fine."

Damn him, he would tell me he's fine if he had just lost both his legs.

"What are you doing in Hawaii?" Carolyn asked suspiciously.

"Chasing bare-breasted girls in grass skirts, what else?"

"Charley, damn you!"

"Look, the reason I called, I'm going to have a couple of days, maybe a couple of weeks, in the States. I wondered if I could come to see you. . . ."

"You *wondered* if you could come to see me?"

"Well, you know. I thought about your family."

"When are you going to be in the States?"

"We're catching a plane to San Francisco in the morning. We ought to be in there tomorrow night sometime."

"What are you going to do in San Francisco?"

"You're not going to believe this, but they're sending me on a war bond tour."

"Why shouldn't I believe it? Jimmy Ward's been on one."

"Yeah, I forgot. Where is he?"

Jimmy Ward was First Lieutenant James G. Ward, USMCR, Carolyn Ward McNamara's nephew. Jimmy Ward had brought then Technical Sergeant Galloway to his parents' home, where Aunt Carolyn had first met Sergeant Galloway. Jimmy Ward was thus responsible for substantially changing her life.

Who the hell cares where Jimmy is? Carolyn thought furiously.

"Right now he's in Washington," she said. "Tell me about the war bond tour. Where are you going to be?"

"I don't know. We're supposed to get a ten-day leave before it starts, and I thought maybe I could come to see you."

There you go again! You thought maybe *you could come to see me? Goddamn you, Charley!*

"Tell me something, Charley," Carolyn said. "Do you love me? Or are you just lining up the standard Marine Corps girl in every port?"

"You don't have to ask that!"

"Yes, I do, damn you, Charley!"

"What are you mad about?"

"Can you say those three words or not?"

"Sure I can say them. But there are people here, Carolyn."

"I don't care who's there!"

"Yeah, sure, Carolyn."

"Wrong three words."

"Jesus Christ! All right." Captain Galloway's voice dropped ten decibels. "I love you."

It was very faint, but it was enough.

"I love you, too, Charley."

"Yeah."

"You're going to San Francisco? And then you'll be on leave?"

"Right."

"Charley, when you get to San Francisco, you go to the hotel."

"What hotel?"

"How many hotels have we been in together in San Francisco?"

"We probably couldn't get a room in there, Carolyn," he said first, and then understood what she was saying. "You want to come all the way out here?"

"Get a room for us, Charley," she said. "I'll meet you there."

"And if I can't?"

"Then sit in the damned lobby and wait for me."

"How long will it take you to get there?"

"I don't know. Two or three days. I'm leaving right now."

"What time is it where you are?"

"Almost midnight."

"It's ten to five in the afternoon here. You mean you'll leave in the morning?"

"No. I mean I'm going to get up and get dressed and leave right now. That's what you do when you love somebody."

"Carolyn, you don't have to do that."

"Just get us a room, my darling," Carolyn said.

"I'll see what I can do."

"Get us a room, Charley. Wait for me," Carolyn said, and hung up.

(FOUR)
Muku Muku
2235 Hours 20 October 1942

Lieutenant Carol Ursery, Nurse Corps, USNR, fresh from a shower, walked over to a full-length mirror and looked at herself. She was wearing a set of men's pajamas and a terry bathrobe with a P & FE insignia embroidered on the breast, and a puffy towel was turbaned about her head. But she didn't pay much attention to any of that . . . because what she saw in that big mirror was one very confused human being. Too much was going on around her this evening. And inside her . . . especially inside her. She was all in a swirl.

There had to be an explanation for all that, and the most logical one was alcohol. She had had more to drink since coming to Muku Muku than she could ever remember having at one time in her life.

Not as much as poor Flo. Flo really got plastered.

Understandable, of course. Flo had learned all at once that her man—her husband—had come through Guadalcanal intact, was on his way to Pearl Harbor, and that he'd been promoted to master gunner. It wasn't just a promotion. With a bar on his collar rather than stripes on his sleeve, Flo and her husband would no longer have to hide from the Navy the very fact of their marriage.

Officer–enlisted marriages were forbidden.

All the same, Carol didn't think it likely that the Navy would court-martial a nurse who'd earned on December 7th both the Purple Heart for wounds and the Silver Star for valor, no matter what she did. But there would still have been serious trouble for both of them if it came out they had defied Navy regulations and gotten married.

I wonder if they'll have to get married again, or whether they can just confess they've been married all along?

Flo would probably have had too much to drink in any event . . . even if that nice old Denny the Steward and his assistants hadn't passed out liquor as if the one who passed out the most would get a prize.

Everybody got drunk, even that nice Colonel Dawkins, and she didn't think he was the type who got drunk very often. And while they were throwing it back, they talked about Guadalcanal, even the Colonel. Carol had never heard anyone who'd been there talk about it. She suspected they didn't like to do that in front of people who hadn't been there . . . in front of people—women, especially—who wouldn't understand. But Flo was different. Flo was a regular Navy nurse; and her husband was a regular Marine who'd been a flying sergeant probably before Pick Pickering and Billy Dunn were born. They could talk in front of her, she was one of them. And after a while, when they all got drunker, they seemed to forget about Carol Ursery . . . or at least that Carol Ursery wasn't one of them.

She heard things about Billy Dunn that she had a hard time believing, to look at him. He was a double ace. He'd shot down ten Japanese airplanes. Nobody would believe that, to look at him. He looked like a boy.

And Pick Pickering, who came across initially as such a wise-ass: He wasn't that way, really. He told Colonel Dawkins he was going to turn in his wings after his buddy was hurt so badly—that poor kid wrapped up like a mummy in Ward 9D. He told him he didn't want to fly anymore; that he was afraid. But Galloway wouldn't let him.

And then Captain Galloway, who was just as drunk as the others, said with great affection: "The truth, Colonel, is this sonofabitch can really fly; I couldn't let him go; The Corps needs him."

And she learned that Galloway had taken Pickering with him when they flew to some Japanese-occupied island and rescued some people who were there reporting on Japanese aircraft movement.

And that Billy Dunn had been the squadron commander while they were gone. He really looked like a college cheerleader, Carol thought. How could this kid be a Marine officer, much less a double ace and an acting squadron commander?

The first time she saw him in the hospital, she actually thought that he looked like a cheerleader wearing his big brother's uniform. A drunken boy.

And then she remembered that Billy didn't seem as drunk as the others, later on . . . that he'd been quiet and thoughtful. They stopped dancing after Colonel Dawkins came. At the time, she was grateful; she thought she was probably going to have to fight him off, the way he was dancing so close to her.

Especially early on, when he had an erection. But he was a perfect gentleman about that, Carol now recalled. He was terribly embarrassed, and swiftly moved his middle away from hers.

But it meant he was interested in her, excited by her. And that alarmed her: While she wasn't a virgin, neither did she sleep around, especially with a kid she'd just met . . . especially with a kid five or six years younger than she was—at least five or six years.

Well, he hadn't even made a pass at her, tried to steal a quick feel or anything like that. He was really a nice kid. . . . A kid? how could she call this *man* a kid? A double ace, who was going to get both the Distinguished Flying Cross and possibly the Navy Cross too, Colonel Dawkins said?

And then he just disappeared, even before Colonel Dawkins left. And this solved Carol's problem of how to handle him when he made a pass at her. She didn't want to hurt his feelings, but she was not about to go to bed with a kid . . . even if he was cute as a button and a genuine hero. And more mature, more of a man, than he looked like.

Well, it really didn't matter. No harm done. No feelings hurt. Thank God. Colonel

Dawkins said there would be a car at Muku Muku at five in the morning that would take them to Honolulu to catch the Pan American commercial flight to San Francisco. She'd probably never see him again. Which was probably a good thing, because the truth seemed to be that she was more attracted to him than was good for her.

She looked at herself in the mirror one more time, lifted the towel off of her head and brushed her hair out, then turned the light off and went out of the bathroom into the bedroom.

She could hear the surf crashing on the beach below. This was the first time this evening she was conscious of it. She went out onto the balcony and looked down. There was just enough light to see the surf. It was a beautiful night.

She stood there, looking out at the stars and the water for several minutes, and then she turned around and started back to her room. She would have to somehow wake up early enough to rouse Flo and get the both of them back to the Nurses' Quarters before the other girls started to get up—and started to make wise-ass remarks about where they'd been all night.

And then, farther down the balcony, she saw the coal of a cigarette glow bright; and in the light, she could make out Billy's face.

I could pretend I didn't see that and just go back in my room. But he has seen me. And he knows that I have seen him.

She walked down the balcony to him. He was wearing a robe like hers; and when he saw her coming, he got up from the chaise lounge where he had been sitting.

"Couldn't sleep?" Carol asked.

"No," he said.

I am making him uncomfortable. It's almost as if he's afraid of me.

"This is really a beautiful place, isn't it?"

"Yes."

"Billy, are you all right?"

"Yes, of course I'm all right. Why shouldn't I be all right?"

"I'm sorry I asked."

"That's all right. Forget it."

"Billy, did I say something wrong? Did I do something?"

"Of course not."

"You had a lot to drink. . . ."

"Yeah."

"Is that why you . . . just disappeared?"

He didn't answer for a moment.

"When I disappeared, I was getting sober," he said finally.

"Then why?"

"Sober enough to realize I'd been making an ass of myself with you."

"Don't be silly. I didn't feel that way at all."

Why did I say that? Not only isn't it true, but it's encouraging him.

"The reason I left was because you had just decided to stay over," he said. "I was afraid."

What the hell is he talking about?

"Afraid? I don't understand."

"I was drunk, and we were fooling around. But that was all right, because you were going to leave, and that would be the end of it."

I will be damned! He thought I was interested in him!

"And you thought I was staying because of you?" she blurted.

"Pretty dumb, huh?"

"Billy, I did nothing that gave you any right to think anything like that."

"I know. Now I know. I'm sorry. The thing is, I don't know much about women. I don't know *anything* about women."

What does that mean? That you've never had a girlfriend? That you're a virgin, for God's sake?

"You've never had a girlfriend? Come on!"

He did not reply.

"I can't believe that, Billy."

"Yeah. Well."

My God, he means it!

"Oh, Billy," she heard herself say; her hand, as if with a mind of its own, reached out and touched his cheek.

"I don't know what to do now," Dunn said.

She pulled her hand away from his face.

"What does that mean?"

"I don't know whether that meant you felt sorry for me, or whether it meant . . . that maybe I should try to kiss you."

"Billy, I feel like your big sister."

Or maybe your mother. What I would like to do is put my arms around you and comfort you, and tell you everything is going to be all right.

Carol, who do you think you're kidding?

"Yeah. Well. I figured that was probably it. Sorry."

"You're very sweet," she said.

She leaned forward and kissed him chastely on the forehead. His arms, awkwardly, went around her. He had his face in her neck.

"God, you're so beautiful!" he said.

What I should do now is push him away. This is getting out of control!

"Billy, now stop," Carol said, and pushed away from him. This caused him to raise his face so that it was level with hers. She felt his breath on her lips.

"Oh, Billy, this is insane," Carol said in the instant before her hand went to the back of his head and pulled it toward her.

(FIVE)
The Commissary
Metro-Magnum Studios
Los Angeles, California
1330 Hours 22 October 1942

Veronica Wood had come to the commissary to eat. She was famished. She'd gotten up at half past four, had one lousy four-minute egg, one piece of dry toast, a glass of skim milk, and not a goddamned thing else since.

Since then, there was the twenty-minute ride in the studio limousine, at least an hour and a goddamn half for makeup, and then twenty-two—count 'em, twenty-two—takes of one lousy scene.

Veronica was convinced that the first take was the one that would finally be used: The others were imposed on her because (a) Stefan Klodny the director wanted to polish his reputation as a perfectionist, or (b) the Hungarian pansy had overheard her saying that the worst kind of queer was a faggot Hungarian with a beard. Or both.

She ordered the Metro-Magnum Burger. This came on a Kaiser roll with sesame seeds, and with onions, lettuce, cheese, and some kind of sauce, and with french fried potatoes. The temptation was to wolf the whole goddamn thing down, and then top it off with cherry pie à la mode.

But she was an artist, and aware that artists are called upon to sacrifice. Her fans wanted Veronica Wood svelte, not chubby. When the Metro-Magnum Burger was served, she carefully salted and delicately let her mouth savor one french fry. She chewed it with relish, then pushed the rest of the french fries to the side of the plate. After that she removed the hamburger from the Kaiser roll and deposited the roll on top of the french fries. So far as she knew, onions and lettuce were not fattening, but that goddamned sauce was probably a hundred calories a taste. Consequently, she carefully scraped off as much of the sauce as she could. Then she ate the hamburger patty and the lettuce and the onions ... slowly, slowly, savoring each bite. And if the onions made her breath bad, fuck it, she wasn't planning on kissing anybody anyway.

When she finished her lunch she was still hungry. She ordered a cup of black coffee. It would probably make her even hungrier, she thought. And, God, it was five hours until supper!

She was in a foul mood. Not in the mood for company, and especially not in the mood for the company of H. Morton Cooperman, of the Metro-Magnum Studios public relations staff.

"May I join you, darling?"

"What if I said no?"

"I was on Stage Eleven, looking for you," Mort said as he slid into a chair and picked up one of her french fries. "Do you mind?"

"I hope you choke on it," Veronica said.

"Stefan told me he'd been hard on you," Mort said. "He said the final result was magnificent."

"How would he know?"

"We all admire your professionalism, darling," Mort said. "Your willingness to strive for perfection."

"What do you want, Mort? I'm really in no mood for your bullshit."

"How do you feel about going on a war bond tour?"

"No way. I'm tired. I get a month off. Read my contract."

"Mr. Roth thought you'd be pleased we've been able to arrange this for you."

"Mr. Roth is as full of shit as you are."

"This is not an ordinary war bond tour, darling. This one is worthy of you. These are Marines, fresh from Guadalcanal. An absolutely magnificent Marine named Machine Gun McCoy, who's going to get the Medal of Honor. And a group of pilots, all of them aces. The publicity will be wonderful."

"Listen carefully, Mort: No!"

"All orchestrated by the master flack of them all, our own beloved Jake Dillon. You'll almost certainly get a *Life* cover."

"Jake is in Australia, or some goddamned place like that."

"Jake is in Los Angeles."

"Since when?"

"I don't know since when, darling, all I know is that he'll be here tomorrow at half past nine to set this thing up. I'd love to be able to tell him that you'll be going with it."

He didn't call me, the sonofabitch!

"Fuck you, Mort, and fuck Jake, too," Miss Wood said, then rose from the table and marched magnificently out of the commissary to a waiting studio Lincoln limousine.

The chauffeur pushed himself off the fender and opened the door for her, after which he ran around the front and slipped behind the wheel.

When he paused at the gatehouse, the chauffeur turned around.

"Would you like me to stop anywhere, Miss Wood?"

"Just take me home, please," Veronica replied. But then asked: "Do you think you could find Mr. Dillon's place in Malibu?"

"Yes, Ma'am. Would you like me to take you there?"

No, you jackass, I'm just asking for the hell of it; I'm writing a goddamn book.

"Would you, please?" she asked sweetly.

The nature of Miss Wood's relationship with Jake Dillon was such that she did not feel it necessary to knock at the front door and seek admission from one of Jake's Mexicans. When the limousine pulled up before the house, she was out of the car before the chauffeur could get out from behind the wheel.

"Wait!" she called over her shoulder, and went around the side of the house, down the path to the beach, and up the circular stairs to the sun deck.

A black-haired woman in shorts (young, good skin, nice legs, boobs a little too big) was sitting in one of Jake's chairs. A skinny kid in swim trunks and a T-shirt was in the other.

If these two didn't just get out of the sack, my name is Ethel Barrymore.

"Who the hell are you?" Miss Wood inquired.

The broad with the too-big boobs stood up.

"My name is Dawn Morris, Miss Wood," she said. "I'm a nurse."

"You're a what?"

"I'm taking care of Corporal Easterbrook, Miss Wood," Dawn said, indicating the Easterbunny.

"I'll bet you are," Miss Wood said. "Where's Jake Dillon?"

"He went into Los Angeles," the kid said. "Are you who I think you are?"

"That would depend, honey, wouldn't it, on who you think I am?" Veronica said, and immediately regretted it. He was just a kid.

But what the hell is going on here with Jake and a hooker and a kid?

"She said she was taking care of you," Veronica said. "You're sick?"

"I had a little malaria," the Easterbunny said.

"Well, look what the cat dragged in," Jake Dillon said from behind her, in the house.

She turned and looked at him.

"You could have called me, you sonofabitch!" Miss Wood said.

"Hi there, Veronica!" Jake Dillon said with a cheerful wave, then smiled and opened his arms.

"Oh, goddamn you, Jake!" Miss Wood said, rushing over to him and wrapping her arms around him. "You bastard! I was so worried about you!"

Over Veronica Wood's shoulder, Major Dillon winked at the Easterbunny.

I don't believe any of this, the Easterbunny thought. *That's really Veronica Wood, the movie star, even if she does swear like a drill instructor. And I just talked to her. And now Major Dillon is hugging her and she's crying and he's patting her on the back.*

And I'm not on the 'Canal anymore, and it doesn't even seem like there is a war, or there ever was a war.

And thirty minutes ago I did it again with Dawn, who is the most beautiful woman I have ever seen, better looking even than Veronica Wood, now that I can see her in real life. And she liked it. She didn't push me away or anything, just asked if she was sure I could, that she didn't want me to exert myself too much, and get sick again.

Veronica Wood let go of Jake Dillon and turned to face Dawn Morris and the Easterbunny, but she kept her arm around his back.

"I was just introducing myself to your friends, Jake."

"That's Bobby Easterbrook, a Marine from Guadalcanal," Jake said. "He's been a little under the weather, and Dawn has been taking care of him."

"He's a Marine?" Veronica asked incredulously.

"He's a Marine," Jake said firmly. "You saw the *Life* cover of the Marine firing the Browning Automatic Rifle?"

"The one who was bleeding? What about it?"

"Easterbrook made that shot," Jake said. "He's a hell of a photographer."

"I'll be damned," Veronica said, and then, sweetly, asked, "Would you two excuse Jake and me for a minute?"

"Certainly, Miss Wood," Dawn said.

"Actually, it'll probably take longer than a minute," Veronica Wood said. "So you two just go on with whatever you were doing before I showed up."

She took her arm from around Dillon's back, caught his hand, and led him into the master bedroom. A moment later, the door slid closed, immediately followed by the drapes.

"I didn't know they were such good friends," Dawn Morris said, as if to herself.

Major Dillon's going to bang Veronica Wood, just as sure as Christ made little apples, the Easterbunny thought. *And she doesn't care if we know it or not. Jesus Christ!*

Dawn Morris was standing next to him. He could see the smooth skin of her legs.

Jesus, I like the way her legs feel. I'd really like to just . . . why the hell not?

Dawn Morris leaned down and caught the Easterbunny's hand as it moved under her shorts.

"Behave," she said.

"Why don't we go take a nap ourselves?"

"We just did that."

"So we'll do it again."

Dawn smiled at him, but she thought: *Goddamn you, you're as horny as a rabbit. Why don't you just leave me alone? Twice last night and twice this morning should be more than enough.*

But on the other hand, it wasn't all that bad, nothing disgusting. You're sort of sweet, and here I am, with Jake Dillon and Veronica Wood, which could be very, very useful in the future. And I could throw that out the window if I don't keep him happy.

"Are you sure you're all right?"

"I'm fine," the Easterbunny said. "What the hell, I'm a Marine."

IX

Second Lieutenant John Marston Moore, USMCR, pulled on the emergency brake of the Studebaker President, opened the door, and then, very carefully, wincing with the pain, lifted up on his left leg and swung it out of the car.

"Sonofabitch!" he said softly. He turned on the seat, put the other leg out, reached over and grasped the handle of the briefcase that was handcuffed to his wrist, and then stood up. He glanced up at the porch and swore again. Brigadier General Fleming Pickering, wearing a pale-blue silk dressing robe, was standing there, drinking a cup of coffee, looking at him.

Moore smiled, then walked as briskly as he could to the house and up the wide steps to the porch.

"Good morning, General."

"When was the last time a doctor looked at your legs?" Pickering asked.

"I go in for a checkup regularly, Sir."

"That's not what I asked, Johnny."

"About a week ago, Sir. Maybe ten days."

"And what did he say?"

"That considering the nature of the wound, a certain amount of discomfort is to be expected."

"That didn't look like discomfort; that looked like pain."

"I'm all right, Sir."

"When you've had your breakfast, we will both go see the doctor."

"That's not necessary, Sir."

"Why couldn't Pluto have gone to the dungeon?" Pickering asked, ignoring his reply.

"I was awake when the phone rang, Sir," Moore said. "And Pluto had just gone to sleep."

"There's a significant difference, Johnny, between stoicism and foolishness, or worse, idiocy."

Moore didn't reply.

"Sit down," Pickering ordered. "Was the trip worthwhile?"

"From my point of view, Sir, very worthwhile. I'm not sure how you will feel about it."

Trying—and not quite succeeding—to make it look painless, Moore sat down on a rattan couch before a rattan coffee table, unlocked the handcuffs attaching the briefcase to his wrist, and then unlocked the briefcase itself. He handed Pickering a large, sealed manila envelope.

"George!" Pickering said, raising his voice. "If there's any coffee left, bring it. And a cup and saucer."

He tore open the envelope and took from it several sheets of paper.

URGENT- VIA SPECIAL CHANNEL
NAVY DEPARTMENT WASH DC 2115 22OCT42
FOR: SUPREME COMMANDER SOUTH WEST PACIFIC AREA
EYES ONLY BRIGADIER GENERAL FLEMING PICKERING, USMCR

1. SECNAV HAS DIRECTED ME TO INFORM YOU OF THE FOLLOWING:
   A. CHIEF OF STAFF, USA, SECWAR CONCURRING, ANNOUNCES THE PROMO-
TION OF 1/LT HONG SON DO, SIGC, USAR TO CAPT, SIGC, USAR, WITH DATE OF
RANK 1AUG42.
   B. CHIEF OF STAFF, USA, SECWAR CONCURRING, ANNOUNCES THE PROMO-
TION OF CAPT HONG SON DO, SIGC, USAR TO MAJ, SIGC, USAR, WITH DATE OF
RANK 21OCT42.
   C. ACTING COMMANDANT, USMC, SECNAV CONCURRING, HAVING WAIVED
TIME IN GRADE REQUIREMENTS IN VIEW OF EXEMPLARY SERVICE, ANNOUNCES
PROMOTION OF 2/LT JOHN MARSTON MOORE, USMCR, TO 1/LT USMCR WITH
DATE OF RANK 21OCT42.
   D. ACTING COMMANDANT, USMC, SECNAV CONCURRING, ORDERS THE IMME-
DIATE SEPARATION FROM ACTIVE SERVICE OF SGT GEORGE F. HART, USMCR,
FOR PURPOSE OF ACCEPTING COMMISSION AS 2/LT USMCR WITH CONCURRENT
CALL TO ACTIVE DUTY IN PRESENT STATION.
   E. SECNAV, CHIEF OF STAFF TO COMMANDER-IN-CHIEF CONCURRING, AU-
THORIZES 2/LT GEORGE F. HART, USMCR, ACCESS TO SUCH CLASSIFIED MATE-
RIAL AS BRIG GEN FLEMING PICKERING, USMCR, AT HIS DISCRETION, MAY DECIDE
THE EXIGENCIES OF THE NAVAL SERVICE REQUIRE.

2. SENIOR NAVAL OFFICER PRESENT, SUPREME HEADQUARTERS, SWPOA,
WILL BE ADVISED THROUGH ROUTINE CHANNELS OF PARAS C. THROUGH
D. HEREOF FOR ADMINISTRATIVE PURPOSES.

3. SECNAV DESIRES TO EXPRESS HIS APPRECIATION TO BRIG GEN PICKERING
FOR HIS REPORT OF 17OCT42, AND TO RESTATE HIS COMPLETE CONFIDENCE
IN GEN PICKERING'S DISCRETION. SECNAV WISHES TO EMPHASIZE INTEREST IN
HIGHEST QUARTERS OF SUCCESSFUL COMPLETION OF GEN PICKERING'S BASIC
MISSION TO SUPREME HEADQUARTERS, SWPOA.

BY DIRECTION:

DAVID HAUGHTON, CAPTAIN, USN
ADMINISTRATIVE ASSISTANT TO THE SECRETARY OF THE NAVY

Sergeant George Hart, in a khaki shirt and green trousers, came onto the porch, carrying a silver coffeepot in one hand and a cup and saucer in the other. There was a snub-nosed .38 caliber revolver in a holster on his belt.

Pickering glanced at him.

"Lieutenant, would you present my compliments to Major Hong Son Do, and ask him to join us, please?"

"Excuse me, Sir?" Hart said, confused.

"Go get Pluto, George," Moore said.

Hart went back into the cottage. Pickering turned his attention to the other documents. By the time he finished reading them, Pluto and Hart had come onto the porch. Pickering waved them into rattan chairs.

"Moore brought the midnight After-Action Reports," Pickering said. "And the latest MAGICs . . ."

Pluto Hon looked at Pickering and then at Hart. The very code word, MAGIC, was not supposed to be used in the presence of anyone not holding that specific security clearance. Curiosity was on Hart's face.

". . . There has been no action to speak of on Guadalcanal," Pickering continued. "Some small patrol actions, another bombing attack, but no major attack. And nothing in the MAGIC intercepts . . ."

Christ, there he goes again! Hon thought.

". . . that suggests there have been any changes in IJGS orders to General Hyakutake changing the plan." (IJGS: The *I*mperial *J*apanese *G*eneral *S*taff.) "Does anybody have any idea what's going on?"

"Sir," Hon began carefully.

"Go on, Major," Pickering said cordially.

Hon now looked really confused, which was Pickering's intention.

"Really, Major," Pickering said, handing him Haughton's radio message, "when the phone rings in the wee hours saying something has come into the dungeon for us, you really should make an effort to get out of bed and go see what it is. All sorts of interesting things *do* come in."

Hon read the radio message.

"I'll be damned," he said. "I thought Hart had a screw loose. . . ."

"Lieutenant Hart, you mean?" Pickering asked.

"Yes, Sir. General, I'm grateful."

"Sir, I don't have any idea what's going on," Hart said.

"That's par for the course, for second lieutenants, isn't it, Moore?"

"Yes, Sir. You ought to think about writing that on the palm of your hand, Hart. So you won't forget it."

"General," Pluto said, looking at Moore. "Sir, if I had heard the phone, I'd have gone down there."

"We were just talking about that, weren't we, Johnny? From now on, until you can get Hart up to speed, Pluto, I want you to make all the middle-of-the-night runs to the dungeon. Understand?"

"Yes, Sir."

"Sir, I'm all right," Moore protested.

"Your second order of business, Major, is to take Lieutenant Gimpy here to the dispensary and get an accurate report on his condition."

"Yes, Sir."

"Your first order of business is to answer my first question: What's going on with the Japanese at Guadalcanal? I want to know what to tell El Supremo when he asks me. And I'm sure he'll ask."

"Just before I quit last night, Sir, I checked with Hawaii to make sure I had all the MAGIC intercepts they had."

"Sir, can I ask what a MAGIC intercept is?" Hart asked.

"OK," Pickering said. "Let's do that right now. Give him Haughton's radio, Pluto."

Pluto handed it over, and Hart read it, and then looked at Pickering for an explanation.

"Paragraph e, I think it was e," Pickering began, "where Mr. Knox authorized me to grant you access to certain classified information, is the important one."

"Yes, Sir?"

"If I don't explain this correctly, Pluto," Pickering went on, "please correct me." Pluto nodded.

"There is no way the Japanese can stop anyone with the right kind of radio from listening to their radio messages," Pickering began. "Just as there's no way we can stop the Japanese from listening to ours. As a consequence, even relatively unimportant messages, on both sides, are coded. The word Pluto and Moore use is 'encrypted.'"

"However, probably the most important secret of this war, George, and I'm not exaggerating in the least, is that Navy cryptographers at Pearl Harbor have broken many—by no means all, but many—of the important Japanese codes."

"Jesus!" Hart said.

"The program is called MAGIC," Pickering went on. "A MAGIC intercept is a Japanese message we have intercepted and decoded. Such messages have the highest possible security classification. If the Japanese even suspect that we have broken their codes, they will of course change them. I really don't understand why they hold to the notion that their encryption is so perfect that it cannot be broken. . . ."

"Face, Sir, I think," Pluto said. "Pride. Ego. It is their code, conceived by Japanese minds, and therefore beyond the capacity of the barbarians to comprehend."

"That's as good a reason as any, I suppose," Pickering said. "Do you agree, Moore?"

"Japanese face is certainly involved," Moore said. "But when I think about it, what makes most sense to me is a variation on that idea: Absent any suspicion that we have cracked their codes (and I would say almost certainly ignoring the advice of our counterparts, Japanese encryption people), there is no Japanese officer of senior enough rank to be listened to, who has the nerve to suggest to the really big brass that their encryption isn't really as secure as some other big brass has touted it to be. Admitting error, the way we do, is absolutely alien to the Japanese. You are either right, or you are in disgrace for having made a bad decision earlier on."

"I don't understand a thing you said," Hart confessed.

"OK," Moore said. "Japanese are not stupid. I'll bet my last dime that somewhere in Japan right now there are a dozen cryptographic lieutenants—maybe even majors, people like us—who know damned well that in time you crack any code. But they can't go to IJGS and say 'we think it's logical that by now the Americans have broken this code.' They don't have enough rank to go to the IJGS and say anything. And they can't go to their own brass, either—their colonels and buck generals— and make their suspicions known. They know that will open them to accusations of harboring a defeatist attitude, having a disrespectful opinion of their seniors, that sort of thing. And even if they went to their colonels and generals, and were believed, the colonels and generals know that if *they* go up the chain of command to somebody who can order new codes, they will be open to the same charges. So everybody keeps their mouths shut, and we get to keep reading their mail."

"Uh," Hart grunted.

"That, what you just heard, George, was analysis," Pickering offered. "Pluto and Moore are more than cryptographers. They—plus the people in Hawaii, of course—read the MAGIC intercepts and try to understand their meaning. Their analyses are made available to three people, three people only, in SWPOA. General MacArthur, his G-2 General Willoughby, and me."

"That's all?" Hart asked, surprised.

"They're the only people authorized access to MAGIC," Pickering explained. "In addition, of course, to Pluto and Moore, and now you."

"And Mrs. Feller, Sir," Moore said.

"I haven't forgotten her, Moore," Pickering said. "Is she back yet?"

"Yes, Sir. She came back from Melbourne on the evening train."

"OK. Then I'll deal with her today. That will leave it the way I said it, Hart. The three of you have access. And MacArthur, Willoughby, and me. If *anyone else* ever mentions MAGIC to you, in any connection whatever, you will instantly report that to either Pluto or Moore or me. You understand?"

"Yes, Sir."

"Let's get back to what's going on at Guadalcanal. I don't think it will be long before there's a call from El Supremo."

"I checked with Hawaii last night before I closed down," Pluto said. "We have all their MAGICs. None were to Generals Hyakutake, Tadashi, or Maruyama. Or from them. We have to presume, therefore, that the original orders—"

"Which called for the attack on 18 October," Pickering interrupted.

"—which called for the attack to be launched 18 October," Pluto affirmed. "We have to presume that they remain in force. *And* that there has been no request by Hyakutake to IJGS for a delay in execution. I think we can further infer that IJGS, having had no word from Hyakutake to the contrary, believes the attack is underway."

"Moore?" Pickering asked.

Moore shrugged, looked thoughtful for a moment, then made a gesture with his fist balled, thumb up.

"Absolute agreement?" Pickering challenged.

"We talked about it last night," Moore said. "It fits in with the most logical scenario on Guadalcanal."

"Which is?" Pickering asked.

Hart noticed that the relationship between the three of them had subtly changed, as if they had changed from uniforms into casual clothes. It was not a couple of junior officers talking to a general—they had even stopped using the terms "Sir" and "General"—but rather three equals dealing with a subject as dispassionately as biologists discussing mysterious lesions on a frog.

"They're obviously having more trouble moving through the mountains than they thought they would," Moore went on, "especially their artillery. If they had moved it as easily as they thought they could—were ordered to—the attack would have started. But to make it official that they hadn't would mean a loss of face all around—for Maruyama for having failed, for Hyakutake for having issued an order that has not been obeyed. Et cetera."

"You're saying there won't be an attack?"

"No. They'll attack," Pluto said. "If it's a six-man squad with one mortar. But the attack is not on schedule. And from that I think we can safely infer that when launched it will not be in the strength they anticipated. And I think it will be very uncoordinated. . . ."

"When?"

"Today," Moore said firmly.

"Tomorrow," Pluto said, equally firmly.

"And that's what I tell El Supremo?" Pickering asked.

"It's our best shot," Pluto said.

"OK," Pickering said. "Now, how long will it take you to get Hart up to speed on the machine?"

"Not long. He can already type. Not as long as it will take to get him into an officer's uniform, and through the paper shuffling at SWPOA."

"Can I help with that?" Pickering asked.

"Yes, Sir. A word in General Sutherland's ear . . . ."

"No," Pickering said, and smiled at him. "You're a major now, Major. You see what you can do. If you have trouble, *then* I'll go to Sutherland."

"I'm not a major yet," Pluto said. "It'll take days for the paperwork to get here from Washington."

It took a long time for Pickering to reply.

"How long will it take to get an officer's uniform for Hart?" he asked finally.

"There's an officer's sales store," Moore replied. "No time at all."

"Come with me, please, Major," Pickering said, and motioned the others to come along.

He went to a telephone and dialed a number.

"Colonel Huff, this is General Pickering," he said when there was an answer. "Would you put me through to the Supreme Commander, please?"

There was a slight pause.

"Good morning, General," Pickering said. "Sir, I would like to ask a personal favor."

There was another slight pause.

"Sir, I have just received word that Pluto Hon's long-overdue promotion has come through. I know he would be honored, and I would regard it as a personal favor, if you would pin his new insignia on."

Another pause, slightly longer.

"Thank you very much, Sir. I very much appreciate your kindness."

He hung up. He turned to Pluto Hon.

"Do you think anyone would dare ask you for the paperwork after El Supremo has pinned the brass on you himself?"

"No, Sir."

"Get the right insignia for you and Moore, get a uniform for George. And when you have all that, come back here and get me."

"We're all going to El Supremo's office?" Moore asked. "But you only asked about Pluto."

"It is an old military tactic, Lieutenant, known as Getting the Camel's Nose Under the Tent," General Pickering said. "General MacArthur knows all about it. He'll understand."

(TWO)
USMC Public Relations Office
U.S. Post Office Building
Los Angeles, California
0845 Hours 24 October 1942

When he saw Major Homer C. Dillon, USMCR, walk into the outer office and speak to one of the sergeants, the mind of First Lieutenant Richard B. Macklin, USMC, took something like an abrupt lurch. Dillon was almost certainly asking for him. And the Major inspired decidedly mixed emotions in him.

Macklin, a tall, not quite handsome officer, whose tunic was adorned with parachutist's wings and two rows of ribbons, the most senior of which was the Purple Heart Medal with one oak leaf cluster, had encountered Dillon twice before. Their initial meeting was at the Parachute School at the old Navy Dirigible Base in Lakewood, N.J., before he was ordered to the Pacific. And they met again six weeks previously, in the U.S. Army 4th General Hospital in Melbourne, Australia. Macklin was then recuperating from the wounds he'd received during the invasion of Gavutu. That very day Dillon sent him to the States to participate in the First War Bond Tour (an inspired act on Dillon's part, Macklin had to admit).

Still, Macklin was of several minds about Dillon himself. For one thing, Lieutenant

Macklin was an Annapolis graduate, a career Marine officer, and Major Dillon was not. Consequently, he wasn't entirely sure of the wisdom of directly commissioning a former China Marine sergeant as a major simply because the sergeant had become a press agent for a Hollywood studio after leaving The Corps. At the same time, it could be argued that The Corps needed the expertise of such a man. Such, anyhow, had been the opinion of the Assistant Commandant, who had arranged for Dillon's commissioning. Brigadier General J. J. Stewart, head of Marine Corps Public Relations, had been good enough to pass this information on to Macklin, and Macklin was grateful to have learned it.

Lieutenant Macklin was also not at all sure how Major Dillon felt about him. Both at Lakewood and at the 4th General Hospital, he sensed that Dillon did not wholly approve of him. It was of course likely that ex–Sergeant Dillon was a little uncomfortable with major's leaves on his shoulders, especially in the presence of a regular officer of a lesser rank.

And then, too, Lieutenant Macklin was more than a little disappointed when General Stewart telephoned to tell him that, in addition to his other duties, Major Dillon would be ''taking responsibility'' for the Second War Bond Tour, and that for the time being at least Dillon would be operating out of Los Angeles. Macklin had thought—indeed, he'd been told—that he would be running the Second War Bond Tour. He wondered if this—it was in effect a kind of demotion—would affect his chances for promotion. God knows, that was overdue.

On the other hand, problems had already arisen in taking what Macklin had come to think of as ''Tour Two'' out of the starting gate. These problems were certainly not his fault; but if they got out of hand, they would almost certainly reflect adversely on him. Dillon's presence would at least take him out of the line of fire. If anything went bad, Dillon, as the senior officer, would obviously be responsible.

Macklin rose from behind his desk and walked somewhat stiffly to the door. His leg was still giving him a little trouble. When he had to be on his feet for any length of time, he supported himself with a cane.

''Good morning, Sir,'' Macklin called. ''It's good to see you, again, Sir.''

Dillon crossed the room to him.

''How are you, Macklin? How's your leg?'' Dillon asked, offering his hand.

''Coming along just fine, Sir. A little stiff. Thank you for asking. Sir, General Stewart has been trying to get in touch with you. He asks that you call him immediately.''

''Did he say what he wanted?''

''He said it was good news, Sir. About Easterbrook.''

Well, that is good news, Dillon thought. *Stewart is telling me he finally got Personnel off their ass and they've come up with a set of records for the Easterbunny. That means I can get him paid and get leave orders cut for him, and let him go home.*

''I'll call him later in the morning. And I've got some good news, too. Veronica Wood has graciously agreed to lend her presence to this war bond tour.''

''That's wonderful!''

''You better get a press release out on it right away . . . check with Mort Cooperman at Metro-Magnum, he's got their still-photo lab running off a hundred eight-by-ten glossies to send out with them. I told him to use the shot of her in the negligee where you can see her nipples.''

''Aye, aye, Sir,'' Lieutenant Macklin said. He was familiar with the photograph Dillon referred to. On the one hand, in his opinion, it bordered upon the lewd and lascivious; but on the other, he felt sure that newspapers across the country would print it.

''So bring me up to speed,'' Dillon said. ''What have you got laid on so far?''

"I have the tentative schedule in my desk, Sir," Macklin said. "There are, I'm afraid, two problems."

"Which are?"

"There are six Guadalcanal aces assigned to the tour, Sir, as you know. Three of them are here. I've put them up in the Hollywood Roosevelt Hotel. They gave us a very attractive rate, Major."

"They like to get their hotel in the newspapers, too, Macklin. They should have comped the whole damned tour."

"Yes, Sir," Macklin said.

I never thought about that, he thought. *This is going to be a learning experience for me.*

"Well, they are putting me up, Sir, free of charge."

"What about the other three pilots?"

Macklin walked stiffly to his desk and came out with a sheet of paper, which he handed to Dillon. It was the radio message from General Stewart ordering Captain Charles M. Galloway and Lieutenants William C. Dunn and Malcolm S. Pickering to participate in the tour.

"These officers are in San Francisco, Sir," Macklin said. "They reported in by telephone. And when I told them what was on the agenda—coming to Los Angeles—and that the question of whether they could have a leave before the tour starts hadn't been resolved, they said—"

"'They'?" Dillon interrupted. "Who did you talk to?"

"The Captain, Sir. Galloway. He said they all had diarrhea and weren't in any condition to come to Los Angeles. Sir, I don't mean to impugn the Captain's word, but I really wonder if all three of them could be so incapacitated simultaneously."

"Have you got a telephone number for them?"

"Yes, Sir. They're staying at the Andrew Foster Hotel."

"Well, maybe the Andrew Foster is comping them, Lieutenant. I'll deal with that. Anything else?"

"Yes, Sir. There is a major problem with Sergeant Machine Gun McCoy."

"What kind of a problem?"

"He's in the Brig at San Diego, Major. He apparently got drunk and tore up a brothel."

"Christ, they're going to give him the Medal of Honor!"

"And assaulted an officer, Sir."

"Do they know about the medal?"

"Yes, Sir. Captain Jellner, the San Diego Public Affairs Officer, has told them about that. It didn't seem to change their intention to bring him before a General Court-Martial."

"OK. That's my first order of business. I'll go down there right now. Call Jellner and tell him I'm on my way."

"Aye, aye, Sir. And, Sir, I requested Captain Galloway to check in with me every morning at zero nine hundred. What should I say to him?"

"Tell him I said I don't want any of them drinking anything but Pepto-Bismol, and that I will be in touch."

"Aye, aye, Sir," Lieutenant Macklin said.

"I'll call you later," Dillon said.

"Sir, would it be appropriate for me to call Miss Wood and express our gratitude to her?"

"I'll take care of that, Lieutenant," Dillon said. "Thanks, anyway."

(THREE)
Office of the Commanding General
USMC Recruit Training Depot
San Diego, California
1215 Hours 24 October 1942

Brigadier General J. L. Underwood, USMC, looked up from his desk when he heard a knock at his open office door.

"You wanted to see me, Sir?" Colonel Daniel M. Frazier, USMC, his deputy, asked.

"Come in, Dan," General Underwood said, "and close the door."

Colonel Frazier did as he was ordered, then looked at General Underwood.

"What's up, Boss?"

"We are about to be honored with the visit of a feather-merchant major from Headquarters Public Affairs. He wants to discuss 'the ramifications of the Sergeant McCoy affair.'"

"Uh-oh."

"I think it would be a good thing if you sat in on this."

"Yes, Sir. He's coming now?"

"He's on his way."

"Has the General had cause to rethink his decision vis-à-vis Sergeant McCoy?"

"The General has decided to give the sonofabitch a fair trial and then hang him," General Underwood said. "I figure he'll get twenty years. I'm going to let him contemplate his next twenty years from his cell at Portsmouth . . . for about six months. And then I'm going to have a change of heart and restore him to duty as a private. I figure what he did at Guadalcanal earned him that much. But The Corps cannot tolerate staff sergeants calling officers what . . . what he called that MP lieutenant. Not to mention all those people he put in the hospital."

"Yes, Sir," Colonel Frazier said.

There was a knock at the door.

"Yes?"

"Major Dillon to see the General, Sir," a voice called.

"Show the Major in, please," General Underwood called, and then added softly, as if to himself, "and I don't need some feather-merchant public affairs puke to tell me about the good of The Corps."

Major Jake Dillon marched into General Underwood's office, stopped exactly eight inches from the desk, came to rigid attention, stared over General Underwood's head, and barked, "Sir, Major Dillon, Homer C."

General Underwood examined Major Dillon carefully, and reluctantly came to the decision that, public relations feather merchant or not, he looked like a Marine. Nevertheless, to set the stage properly, he kept him standing there at attention for sixty seconds—which seemed much longer—before saying, softly, "You may stand at ease, Major."

"Yes, Sir. Thank you, Sir," Dillon said, and assumed the position of parade rest. Instead of standing rigidly with his arms at his side, thumbs on the seam of his trousers, feet together, he was now standing rigidly with his feet precisely twelve inches apart and with his hands crossed precisely over the small of his back. He continued to stare over General Underwood's head.

"I understand you wish to discuss the matter of Staff Sergeant McCoy?" General Underwood said quietly, with ice in his voice.

"The General is correct, Sir. Yes, Sir."

"And I am to presume you are speaking for the Director of Public Affairs? He sent you here?"

"No, Sir. If the Major gave the General that impression, Sir, it was inadvertent, Sir."

"Excuse me, Major," Colonel Frazier said. "Have we met?"

"Yes, Sir. The Major has had the privilege of knowing the Colonel."

"Where would that have been, Major?"

"Sir, in Shanghai, China, Sir. When the Colonel was S-4 of the 4th Marines, Sir."

"Goddamn it, of course! Jake Dillon."

"You know this officer, Colonel Frazier?" General Underwood asked.

"Yes, Sir. In '38 and '39 he had the heavy-weapons section under Master Gunnery Sergeant Jack (NMI) Stecker."

"Jack (NMI) Stecker has the Medal," General Underwood said.

"Now Captain Stecker," Colonel Frazier said.

"He made major," General Underwood corrected him. "I can't imagine Jack (NMI) Stecker even using the term 'motherfucker,' much less screaming it at an officer."

"Begging the General's pardon," Dillon said. "It is now Lieutenant Colonel Stecker."

"Well, I hadn't heard that," Colonel Frazier said. "Are you sure?"

"Sir, yes, Sir. I saw Colonel Stecker a few days ago, Sir."

"On Guadalcanal?" General Underwood said.

"Sir, yes, Sir. Colonel Stecker commands Second of the Fifth, Sir."

"Dillon, I said 'at ease,' not 'parade rest,'" General Underwood said.

"Aye, aye, Sir. Sorry, Sir," Dillon said, and allowed the stiffness to go out of his body.

"Are things as bad over there as we hear, Dillon?" General Underwood said.

"They're pretty goddamn bad, General. The goddamned Navy sailed off with all the heavy artillery and most of the rations still aboard ship. For the first couple of weeks, we were eating Jap rations; we didn't have any of our own."

"You were there, I gather, Dillon?" General Underwood asked.

"Yes, Sir. I went into Tulagi with Jack (NMI) Stecker's battalion."

General Underwood and Major Dillon were now looking at each other.

"This was easier, frankly, when I thought you were a goddamn feather merchant," General Underwood said.

"Jake, are you really here to try to talk us into letting this sonofabitch go?" Colonel Frazier asked. "Do you know what all he did?"

"Yes, Sir, I read the reports. But on the other hand, Sir, I heard what he did on Bloody Ridge. He's one hell of a Marine, Colonel."

"He's a goddamn animal who belongs in Portsmouth!" General Underwood said angrily.

Dillon and Colonel Frazier both looked at him.

"Sir, the word is already out that they're going to give him the Medal of Honor," Dillon said. "If it comes out why he—"

"That's enough, Dillon," General Underwood said sharply.

"Yes, Sir."

General Underwood stood up.

"I can't waste any more time on this individual," General Underwood said. "You deal with it, Frazier. If Dillon has any reasonable proposals to make, that you feel you can go along with, I will support any decision you make. That will be all, gentlemen. Thank you."

Colonel Frazier stood up. Both he and Major Dillon came to attention.

"By your leave, Sir?" Colonel Frazier asked.

General Underwood, his eyes on his desk, made an impatient gesture of dismissal. Colonel Frazier and Major Dillon made precise about-face movements and marched out of his office.

"The General said if you had 'any reasonable proposal,' Jake," Colonel Frazier said. They were now in his office, drinking coffee to which sour-mash bourbon had been added.

"Sir, the first thing we have to keep in mind is that some people, who are a lot more senior than you and me, think this war bond tour business is good for The Corps."

"Do you?"

Dillon met his eyes.

"I really don't know. They told me to do it. I'm saying 'aye, aye, Sir,' and giving it my best shot."

"OK. We'll go with that, for the sake of argument: The war bond tour is good for The Corps."

"If we go with that, Colonel, then we have to go with the idea that putting a major, me, in charge, with a lieutenant and half a dozen sergeants to help, is a justified use of Marines. Plus, of course, the heroes. They could be doing other things, too."

"I'm listening, Jake," Colonel Frazier said.

"If we go with that, and if it means that instead of The Corps looking foolish for giving the Medal to somebody who turns out to be an asshole, The Corps looks good for giving the Medal to a guy who killed thirty, forty Japs all by himself, then it seems to me that The Corps would be justified in assigning two more Marines to the tour . . . that would mean for about a month."

"Two more Marines, Jake? Who are you talking about?"

"I don't have any names, but I'll bet you wouldn't have to look hard around the Recruit Depot to find two gunnery sergeants who are larger and tougher than Staff Sergeant McCoy."

"And what would these two gunnies do, Jake?"

"Well, I think that by now, as long as he's been in the Brig, Sergeant McCoy must be pretty dirty. The two gunnies would probably start off by giving Sergeant McCoy a bath. With a fire hose. That would probably put him in a good frame of mind. Then they could talk to him about how important it is to him and The Corps for him to behave himself. And if he ever felt he needed some exercise, they could give it to him."

Colonel Frazier looked at Major Dillon for a long moment. Then he pushed a lever on his intercom.

"Sergeant Major," he announced. "I'm sending a Major Dillon to see you. He will tell you what he wants. I don't know what that is, and I don't want to know. But you will give him whatever he asks for. Do you understand?"

"Aye, aye, Sir," a metallic voice replied.

"Thank you, Colonel," Jake said.

"I have no idea what you're talking about, Major Dillon," Colonel Frazier said. "But I'm sure you'll be able to work it out with the Sergeant Major. He's in the third office down the hall to the right."

(FOUR)
Water Lily Cottage
Brisbane, Australia
1615 Hours 23 October 1942

When he heard the crunch of tires on the driveway, Brigadier General Fleming Pickering, USMCR, was drinking coffee. Not five minutes earlier, he almost took a stiff drink. But now that Ellen was arriving, he knew he'd made the right decision in not doing that.

He checked himself in the mirror, tugging at the skirt of his blouse, then adjusting his necktie to a precise location he decided would please the Commandant of The Marine Corps himself.

He was wearing his ribbons, too. There was an impressive display of them—the Navy Cross, the Silver Star, the Legion of Merit, the Navy & Marine Corps Medal, the Purple Heart with three oak leaf clusters, the World War I Victory Medal, the Legion d'Honneur in the grade of Chevalier, and the Croix de Geurre. And they were neatly arrayed above what Pickering thought of as the "I-Was-There" ribbons: for service in France in World War I, for service since World War II started, and the Pacific Theatre of Operations ribbon.

He rarely wore all this, and he wasn't sure why he was doing so now. Certainly his visit to General MacArthur required it (he'd correctly suspected that El Supremo would not only have a photographer present for the pinning-on-of-the-insignia, but that he would insist that Pickering get in the picture). But then there was Ellen Feller, who was just now approaching (like a pirate ship on the horizon; up goes the Jolly Roger). Mrs. Feller was impressed with brass. And he was aware that he made a visually impressive brass hat in his general's uniform, with stars on collar points and epaulets, and all his ribbons.

"On deck, George," Pickering said softly. "Here she comes."

He heard footsteps on the stairs, and then on the porch, and then the old-fashioned, manual, twist-it-with-your-fingers doorbell rang.

Wearing not only his hours-old lieutenant's uniform, but a silver cord identifying him as an aide-de-camp to a general officer, George Hart went to the door and opened it.

"May I help you?" George asked.

Pickering looked up and let his gaze rest casually on Ellen. She was a tall woman in her middle thirties, dark haired and smooth skinned; and she was wearing little makeup. She seemed surprised to see Hart. At the same time, Pickering was surprised to see how she was dressed. She was in uniform. An Army officer's uniform, complete to cap with officer's insignia. But on the lapels, where an officer would have the U.S. insignia above the branch of service, there were small blue triangles. The uniform was authorized for wear by civilians attached to the Army.

Now that he thought about it, Pickering was not surprised that Ellen had decided to put herself in uniform. He noticed, too, that the uniform did not conceal her long, shapely calves or the contours of her bosom.

He had a quick mental image of her naked, and as quickly forced it from his mind . . . consciously replacing it with an image of Johnny Moore wincing with pain as he pulled his torn-up leg from the Studebaker.

What happened to Johnny is as much Ellen's fault as it was the fault of the Japanese. This is a world-class bitch.

"Mrs. Feller to see General Pickering," Ellen said.

"Just a moment, please," George said, "I'll see if the General is free."

"He expects me, Lieutenant," Ellen said, not at all pleasantly.

"One moment, please," Hart said, and closed the door in her face.

He turned to look at Pickering, smiling. Pickering nodded, held up his hand for ten seconds or so, and then dropped it. Hart turned back to the door and opened it again.

"Would you come in, please?" Hart said, and turned to Pickering. "General, Mrs. Feller."

"Hello, Ellen, how are you?" Pickering said, and added, "That will be all, Hart, thank you."

"Aye, aye, Sir," Hart said, and marched across the living room to the kitchen, closing the door after him.

"He's new," Ellen said. She crossed the room to him and shook his hand.

That was better than being kissed.

"Yes. Moore has been promoted, and Hart is my new aide."

"I heard only yesterday that you had come back," Ellen said. "I was in Melbourne."

"Yes, I know," Pickering said. "With Colonel Jasper, of Willoughby's staff."

"Oh, you've spoken to him?"

"Not yet," Pickering said.

I'll be damned if there isn't something really erotic about her in the uniform.

"Well, I'm sure you know that the OSS is setting up here. Jasper met with them in Melbourne. I thought I should know what's going on."

"If you're fond of Colonel Jasper, Ellen, you might tell him that General MacArthur is opposed to the OSS setting up here."

"What is that supposed to mean, Fleming?" Ellen asked. "If I'm fond of him?"

"Well, you've been sleeping with him. That generally presumes a certain fondness."

Ellen could not quite conceal her surprise at that.

"Fleming, you weren't here," she said after a moment. "So far as I knew, you were never coming back. Charley Jasper doesn't mean anything to me."

She didn't deny it; I rather thought she would. I wish she had. And she assumes I'm jealous. I suppose maybe I am. That's a perfectly natural male reaction.

"Ellen, your sleeping around is posing problems we have to deal with."

"I'm not going to beg for your forgiveness, Fleming, if that's what you're talking about. If you were here, what happened with Jasper never would have happened."

I wonder what would have happened if I hadn't gone to Guadalcanal? You know damned well what would have happened. The only reason it only happened once was that I did go to Guadalcanal.

"Problems with MAGIC," Pickering said. "As of this moment, the only MAGIC material to which you will have access will be that provided to you by Pluto or Moore for the purpose of briefing General MacArthur."

"You didn't give me my MAGIC clearance, Fleming, and I don't think you have the authority to take it away. I can't believe you're letting your personal feelings cloud your professional judgment."

"I have the authority, Ellen."

"Well," she said, for the first time losing control, "we'll see what General Willoughby has to say about that."

And then control came back. She smiled at him and wet her lips with her tongue.

"Fleming, I'll tell you what I'm going to do. I'm going to go back outside. While I'm gone, you will send your aide someplace; and when I come back, we'll start this all over again. We both have said things we really don't mean."

"Ellen . . ."

"I wept when you left for Guadalcanal," she said. "I had finally found a man I really admired, and we . . . we had only that one time together."

"That shouldn't have happened," he said.

"It did. Fleming, are you afraid I want more from you than you're in a position to give? I'm satisfied with the crumbs. . . . I know you would never leave your wife. . . . She would never find out about us, I swear on my life."

Was there an implied threat in there?

"That's enough, Ellen. Now shut up and listen to me."

She found his eyes. With an effort, he forced himself to meet hers.

"You have two options, Ellen. You will become the briefer for MacArthur and Willoughby. You will not have access to any MAGIC material except that which Pluto gives you; you are no longer authorized access to the dungeon in any way."

"Or?"

"You will be on the next plane to the States, under sedation. On your arrival in the United States, you will be taken to a federal mental hospital, and you will spend the war there."

"You have to be kidding!"

"General Willoughby will be made privy to the rather extensive report the Army's Counterintelligence Corps has compiled on you. He will understand why this was necessary."

"What CIC report?" she snapped.

Pickering went to his briefcase, unlocked it, and took from it a thick stack of paper. This was held together with metal clips and covered by a sheet of folder paper imprinted with diagonal stripes and the words TOP SECRET, top and bottom.

"This one," he said, handing it to her. "They are remarkably thorough, you'll see."

She snatched the report from his hand and glanced through it . . . but long enough to take in what it contained.

"You'd let this garbage out? After what we've meant to each other?"

"The only reason I'm not doing it is that it would ruin the careers of Colonel Jasper and the others. They don't deserve that."

"Your name is in this filthy file! Have you considered that?"

"You still don't understand, do you?" Pickering said. "We're not talking about you, or me, we're talking about the security of MAGIC. You have proved that you can't be trusted with that. . . ."

"Don't be absurd. That's absolutely untrue."

"Oh? By a conscious act, *you* did nothing when they were going to send Moore to Guadalcanal. You knew he wasn't supposed to go. No one with access to MAGIC is supposed to be placed in any threat of capture by the enemy."

"You went to Guadalcanal," she said.

Yeah, I did. And I was wrong.

"You allowed Moore to be sent to Guadalcanal because he posed a potential threat to your reputation, and MAGIC be damned."

"Flem, you were gone. I was lonely. He was persistent. It happened. I was trying to stop it. I knew it was wrong. All I was trying to do—"

"Was save your skin. And MAGIC be damned," Pickering interrupted her.

"Why don't you just have me shot, then?"

"I considered it. Banning would almost certainly see that as the best solution. It is still an option."

She looked at him, and he met her eyes. And after a moment he saw in them that she believed him. But he saw too, in her eyes, that she wasn't going to grant the point.

"We're both saying things we don't mean again, aren't we?"

"I have said nothing I don't mean. I'm getting tired of this, Ellen. You either accept the option of becoming our briefer, and thus saving Pluto's and Moore's time, as well as the careers of the people you've been sleeping with . . ."

"Including yours?"

". . . or you don't."

"This conversation is unbelievable," Ellen said. "I'll tell you what I'm going to do, Fleming. I'm going to do you a favor. I'm going to walk out of here and forget we ever had it."

She glared at him defiantly for a moment, as if waiting for his response. Then she turned and walked to the door.

Just as she reached it, it opened inward and three men in civilian clothing moved inside. One of them spun her around and twisted her arm behind her back. Ellen screamed. The man put his hand over her mouth. The second man pulled her uniform skirt up, high enough to clear her stocking. Then he jabbed a hypodermic needle like a dart into the skin of her upper thigh and carefully depressed the plunger.

He removed the needle, then looked at Ellen Feller's eyes.

The third man moved to Fleming Pickering.

"Are you all right?" he asked.

Pickering glared at him.

"What was that he injected?"

"Not what it should have been," the man said. "It won't kill her."

"Goddamn it!"

The man walked past him and picked up the CIC report.

"What happens to that, now?" Pickering asked.

"I don't think we'll have to use it," the man said.

Pickering looked on while Ellen Feller, as if she were drunk, was half carried, half walked out of the house between the first two men. The man with the report walked after them. He stopped at the door and turned to face Pickering.

"General, for what it's worth, I've been thinking that this is the difference between us and the Japs. If I was in the Kempe Tai, she would be long dead. What we do with people like this is lock them up somewhere until the war is over, and then turn them loose."

Then he was gone.

Pickering moved to the bar and took a bottle of scotch and poured three inches in a water glass. Then he picked up the glass and very carefully poured the whiskey back into the bottle. He felt eyes on him, and looked over his shoulder.

George Hart had come into the room.

"They know what they're doing, don't they?" Hart said. "That was pretty impressive, the way they handled her."

Don't open your mouth, Fleming Pickering. No matter what comes out, it will be the wrong thing to say.

He turned back to the bottle and put his hand on it.

"I was talking with the Colonel before you came back," Hart said. "He used to be a homicide captain in Chicago."

"Is that so?"

"Yeah, cops can spot each other. He was surprised that I hadn't gone in the Army, and the MPs."

"Well, now that you have learned what a sterling fellow and four-star hypocrite I am, Hart, would you like me to see if I can use my influence and have you transferred to the CIC?"

Hart didn't reply. He walked up to the bar, freed the bottle from Pickering's grip, and poured an inch in the glass.

"No, Sir," he said. "I'd like to stick around, if that's all right with you."

He put the glass in Pickering's hand.

"You know what my father told me when I joined the force?" he asked. "He said that I should never forget that women are twice as dangerous as men."

Pickering drained the glass.

"I'll try to remember that, George," Pickering said. "Thank you very much."

"What you should remember, General, is that she was really dangerous. I was hoping that the Colonel could talk you out of sending her home. She didn't give a good goddamn how many people she got killed."

Brigadier General Fleming Pickering, USMCR, looked at Second Lieutenant George Hart, USMCR, for a moment.

I'll be a sonofabitch, he means it! He thinks I should have gone along with that bastard's recommendation that I let them "remove" her.

At least I didn't do that.

So what does that make me, the Good Samaritan?

"Would you like a drink, George? And can we please change the subject?"

"Yes, Sir," Hart said, and reached for the bottle. "Except for one thing."

"Which is?"

"I don't think Lieut—*Major* Pluto or Moore could handle knowing about this. I don't think we should tell them. Let him think she got sick and they flew her home."

"Whatever you think, George. You're probably right."

"Can I ask, Sir, for a favor?"

"What?"

"I'd really like to have a couple copies of those pictures of me with General MacArthur to send to my folks. And my girl. Could I get some, do you think?"

"I'm sure we can," Pickering said. "The next time you're in the Palace, go to the Signal Section and tell them I sent you."

"Yes, Sir."

I wonder what El Supremo would think if he knew what just happened. Will he find out? Or is that something else not worthy of the Supreme Commander's attention, and from which he will be spared by his loyal staff?

If the decision was MacArthur's, would he have done what I did? Or would he have gone along with the Colonel and George and "removed" her?

The telephone rang. Hart picked it up and answered it.

"General Pickering's quarters, Lieutenant Hart speaking."

Pickering looked at him.

"General," Hart reported, covering the microphone with his hand, "this is Colonel Huff. General MacArthur's compliments, and are you and Major Hon free for supper and bridge?"

"Tell Colonel Huff," Pickering said, "that Major Hon and I will be delighted."

Maybe if I let him win, I could bring up the subject of Donovan's people again.

Pickering had a flash in his mind of Ellen Feller with her skirt hiked high, a needle in her thigh. And then he replaced it with an image of Jack Stecker's boy, wrapped up like a mummy in the hospital at Pearl Harbor.

He reached for the scotch bottle and then stopped himself. He would have to be absolutely sober if he expected to find the tiny chink in El Supremo's armor he would need to bring up the subject of Donovan yet again.

(ONE)

FROM: COM GEN 1ST MAR DIV 2355 23OCT42

SUBJECT: AFTER-ACTION REPORT

TO: COMMANDER-IN-CHIEF, PACIFIC, PEARL HARBOR
INFO: SUPREME COMMANDER SWPOA, BRISBANE
                     COMMANDANT, USMC, WASH, DC

1. AT APPROXIMATELY 1800 23OCT42 HEAVY JAPANESE ARTILLERY BARRAGE WITH PRIMARY IMPACT IN VICINITY US LINES ON MATANIKAU RIVER, SECONDARY IMPACT HENDERSON FIELD, AND HARASSING AND INTERMITTED FIRE STRIKING OTHER US EMPLACEMENTS. IT IS BELIEVED THAT WEAPONRY INVOLVED WAS 150-MM REPEAT 150-MM AND SMALLER, AUGMENTED BY MORTAR FIRE.

2. AT APPROXIMATELY 1900 23OCT42, JAPANESE FORCES IN ESTIMATED REIN-FORCED REGIMENTAL STRENGTH ACCOMPANIED BY SEVEN (7) TYPE 97 LIGHT TANKS ATTACKED ACROSS SANDBAR (PRIMARILY) 3RD BN, 7TH MARINES 500 YARDS FROM MOUTH OF MATANIKAU RIVER AND (SECONDARILY) 3RD BN, 5TH MARINES 1000 YARDS FROM MOUTH OF RIVER.

3. FORTY (40) 105-MM HOWITZERS OF 2ND, 3RD AND 5TH BATTALIONS 11TH MARINES PLUS ATTACHED
I BATTERY 10TH MARINES (COL. DELVALLE) WHICH HAD PREVIOUSLY BEEN REG-ISTERED ON ATTACK AREA IMMEDIATELY OPENED FIRE. APPROXIMATELY 6,000 ROUNDS 105-MM AND HEAVY MORTAR EXPENDED DURING PERIOD 1900–2200.

4. WEATHER AND MOONLIGHT CONDITIONS PERMITTED SUPPORT BY NAVY, MARINE AND USAAC AIRCRAFT FROM HENDERSON FIELD. NUMBER OF SORTIES NOT YET AVAILABLE, BUT EFFECT OF WELL AIMED BOMBARDMENT AND STRAF-ING WAS APPARENT TO ALL HANDS.

5. AT APPROXIMATELY 2100 23OCT42 ATTACK HAD BEEN TURNED. INITIAL MA-RINE PATROL ACTIVITY INDICATES JAPANESE LOSS OF AT LEAST THREE (3) TYPE 97 LIGHT TANKS, AND IT IS RELIABLY ESTIMATED THAT JAPANESE INFANTRY LOSSES WILL EXCEED SIX HUNDRED (600) KIA.

6. US LOSSES:
   A. FIELD GRADE OFFICER KIA ZERO (0)
   B. FIELD GRADE OFFICER WIA ZERO (0)
   C. COMPANY GRADE OFFICER KIA ZERO (0)
   D. COMPANY GRADE OFFICER WIA ONE (1)
   E. ENLISTED KIA TWO (2)

F. ENLISTED WIA ELEVEN (11)

G. MISSING IN ACTION: ZERO (0)

H. MINIMAL DAMAGE TO HENDERSON FIELD AND AIRCRAFT. HENDERSON FIELD IS OPERABLE.

VANDEGRIFT MAJ GEN USMC COMMANDING

(TWO)
Radio City Music Hall
New York City, New York
1825 Hours 24 October 1942

"Did you like the show?" Mrs. Carolyn Spencer Howell asked Major Edward F. Banning, USMC, as they left the world's largest theater. Mrs. Howell was tall, willowy, chic, black haired, and exquisitely dressed. Her clothes were seriously expensive, but tastefully understated. "When my husband turned me in for a new model," as she liked to put it, "his new tail cost him his ears and his nose."

Her annual salary—for her labor in the research department of the New York Public Library—would not have paid for the ankle-length silver fox coat she was now wearing.

"Great legs," Ed Banning said.

"We can come back tomorrow," Carolyn said as she put her hand on his arm. "The Christmas Show starts tomorrow. Great legs in Santa Claus costumes. I thought you would like the Rockettes."

"Once is enough, thank you," Banning said.

"What would you like to do now?"

"That's supposed to be my line," Banning said.

"This is my town. I'm trying to do my bit for the boys in service."

"Well, if you really feel that way, three guesses what I would like to do."

She squeezed his arm.

"Aside from that," Carolyn said. "Are you hungry, Ed?"

"You're speaking of food," he said.

"Yes, I'm speaking of food. The word was 'hungry.'"

"Oh," he said. "Could I ply you with spirits?"

"Jack and Charlie's," she said.

"What's that?"

"A saloon," she said. "A real saloon. It was a speakeasy during Prohibition. Not far, we can walk."

"Fine," he said.

"My mother told me that Jack's boy has just joined the Marines."

"Sounds like my kind of place."

"I think you'll like it."

She leaned her head against his shoulder as they waited for the light to change.

"I thought New Yorkers didn't pay attention to red lights," Banning said.

"They do when they're with boys from the country they want to keep from getting run over."

The light changed and they crossed the street. A few minutes later they came to what looked to Banning like a typical New York City brownstone house . . . except for a rank of neatly painted cast-iron jockeys surveying a line of cold-looking people waiting to move down a shallow flight of stairs to a basement entrance.

"Is this it?" Banning asked.

"This is Jack and Charlie's."

"We can't get in here," Banning said. "Look at the line."

"I think we can," she said. "I used to spend a lot of time in here in the olden days."

"With your husband?"

"Yes, with my husband. Does that bother you, Ed?"

"What if he's in there?"

"I don't mind being seen with a handsome Marine," Carolyn said. "As a matter of fact, now that you've brought that up, I'm determined to get in."

She let go of his arm, then elbowed her way past the people on the stairs and disappeared from sight. Banning was left feeling distinctly uncomfortable.

She was gone a long time, long enough for Banning to conclude that her onetime clout at this place had dissolved with her divorce.

Out of the corner of his eye, he became aware that he was being saluted. He returned the salute without taking a good look at the saluter, except to notice idly that he was a Marine.

"Excuse me, Sir," a familiar voice said; there was a touch of amusement in it. "Is this where I catch the streetcar to the Bund?"

The Bund was in Shanghai, and the voice was very familiar. Banning turned and saw First Lieutenant Kenneth R. McCoy, USMCR.

Goddamn it, of all people!

He smiled, and held out his hand.

"Hello, Ken," he said. "What cliché should I use? 'Fancy meeting you here'? Or 'small world, isn't it'?"

"Are you waiting to go in?"

"My . . . lady friend . . . is trying to buck the line."

"Come on," McCoy said, starting to shoulder his way through the people by the stairs. He turned and motioned Banning to follow him.

If I were these people, and somebody tried to move ahead of me, I'd be annoyed.

Halfway down the stairs, he met Carolyn coming up.

"Come on," she said. As she spoke, her eyes fell on McCoy; and then she swung her gaze back to Banning. "I got us a table."

A large man in a dinner jacket was standing next to a headwaiter's table. He stepped aside as Carolyn reached him. Banning moved after her, followed by McCoy.

If he stops McCoy, Banning decided graciously, *I'll tell him he's with us.*

The headwaiter spotted McCoy and gave him a smile of recognition.

"Miss Sage called, Lieutenant. She'll be a few minutes late."

"I'm a few minutes late, myself," McCoy said. "Thank you, Gregory."

Another man in a dinner jacket appeared, this one looking a little confused.

"Are you together?" he asked.

"Why not?" McCoy said, smiling at Banning.

The sonofabitch looks like he swallowed the goddamn cat. He's curious. Why not? I would be, in his shoes.

"This way, please," the man in the dinner jacket said. He led them to a table near the bar, snatched from it a brass RESERVED sign, and moved the table so that Carolyn could slide into the banquette seat against the wall. McCoy waved Banning in beside her, then sat down.

"Where did you come from?" Carolyn asked with a smile.

"The rock turned over," Banning said, "and there he was."

"Ed!" Carolyn said, shocked.

"Would you like a menu right away?" the man in the dinner jacket asked. "Or would you like something from the bar?"

"I'd like a drink," Carolyn said. "Martini, please, olive."

"For me, too, please," Banning said.

The man in the dinner jacket started to move away.

"You didn't ask what this gentleman is having," Carolyn protested.

"I know what the Lieutenant drinks," the man in the dinner jacket said, somewhat smugly.

McCoy smiled at Banning, even more smugly.

You're enjoying this, aren't you, McCoy?

"Ken, may I present Mrs. Carolyn Howell?" Banning said. "Carolyn, this is Lieutenant Ken McCoy."

Carolyn smiled and offered McCoy her hand; then the bell rang in her head.

"You're Killer McCoy?" she asked incredulously.

"Thanks a lot, *Sir,"* McCoy said angrily.

A young woman who wore her jet-black hair in a pageboy suddenly appeared at the table and leaned over to kiss McCoy on the top of his head. "You're not supposed to call him that," she said. "It really pisses him off."

What did she say? Carolyn wondered, shocked. *Did she really say what I think she did?*

"Hi," the young woman said. "I'm Ernie Sage."

Banning rose to his feet.

"How do you do?" he said politely. "I'm Ed Banning. This is Carolyn Howell."

"Oh, I know who you are," Ernie Sage said. "Ken's told me all about you."

All about me? That I'm married? And that my stateless wife is somewhere in China . . . if she's managed to survive at all?

A waiter delivered the drinks. Ernie Sage grabbed McCoy's and took a swallow.

"I need this more than you do," she said. "Today has been a real bitch!"

The waiter smiled. "Shall I bring you one of your own, Miss Sage?"

"Please," Ernie said. She turned to Carolyn. "I guess you know these two go back a long way together. But I never met him before. I admire your taste."

Carolyn was uncomfortable.

"Are you a New Yorker, Miss Sage?"

"Please call me 'Ernie,' " Ernie said. "I was raised in New Jersey. I've got an apartment here. When I'm not being a camp follower, I'm a copywriter for BBD and O."

"Excuse me, what did you say?" Carolyn blurted.

"When Ken has a camp I can follow him to, I'm there," said Ernie Sage. "So far I've failed to persuade him to make an honest woman of me."

"Jesus, Ernie," McCoy said.

"I even have a red T-shirt with MARINES in gold letters across the bosom," Ernie said, demonstrating with her hand across the front of her dress.

After a long moment, Carolyn said, "You don't happen to know where I can find one like it, do you?"

"I'm sure we can get one for you, can't we, honey?" Ernie asked, grabbing McCoy's hand.

The waiter delivered another drink.

"I'd like to wash my hands," Carolyn said. "Ed and I just came out of Radio City Music Hall."

"That made your hands dirty?" Ernie asked. She rose to her feet. "I'll go with you."

The men waited until the women had disappeared around the end of the bar.

"Very pretty, that girl," Banning said.

"Pickering introduced us, when we were in OCS at Quantico," McCoy said. "His mother went to college with her mother. Her family is somewhat less than thrilled about us."

"Carolyn knows about my wife, Ken," Banning said.

"I figured you would probably tell her," McCoy said. "You know that Rickabee has people checking on her in Shanghai?"

"No, I didn't."

"He probably didn't want to raise your hopes," McCoy said. "There's been word that some of the Peking Marines didn't surrender; that they're running loose with the warlords. Maybe she got in contact with them."

"That sounds pretty unlikely," Banning said.

"She's a White Russian. She's been through this sort of thing before. I'll bet she's all right."

What the White Russians did to survive when their money gave out, and they had nothing left to sell, was to sell themselves. Preferably to an American or a European. But when that wasn't possible, to a Chinese. Now that the Japanese are running things in China . . .

Banning had a very sharp, very clear picture of Milla, sweet goddamned Milla, who'd already survived so goddamned much . . . desperately hanging on to his hand as they were married in the Anglican Cathedral in Shanghai . . . seven hours before the goddamned Corps ordered him out of Shanghai for the Philippines, with no goddamned way to get her out.

"Shit," Banning said softly, bitterly.

McCoy looked at him.

"Drink your martini. There's nothing you can do about anything."

"Fuck you, Killer," Banning said.

McCoy let that particular "Killer" pass unnoted. And Banning, meanwhile, picked up his martini and drained it, then held it over his head, signaling he wanted another.

"So what brings you to the Big City, Lieutenant?" he asked, closing the subject of the former Baroness Milla Christiana Lendenkowitz, now Mrs. Edward F. Banning, present address unknown.

"I've been down at the Armed Forces Induction Station," McCoy replied. "What about you?"

"Rickabee ordered me to take a week off," Banning answered. "The week's over tomorrow."

"That figures. I paddle the goddamned rubber boat into the jaws of danger, while the Major sits on his ass in the Port Moresby Aussie O Club bar. And the Major gets a week off."

Does he mean that? Or is he pulling my leg?

"Didn't Rickabee offer you time off?"

McCoy smiled. "Rickabee suspected, correctly, that the goddamn Navy has been grabbing everybody who speaks Japanese and Chinese. He said if I could grab as many as I could for our side in a week or less, he'd call it duty and pay me travel and per diem. He knew my girl lives here."

"I presume, then, Lieutenant, that you're on duty?"

"Yeah," McCoy said, and gestured around the 21 Club. "Tough, huh?"

"And then you go back to Washington?"

"To Parris Island. They've got a dozen boots down there who are supposed to speak Chinese. You know what we need them for."

Banning nodded: As soon as arrangements could be made, McCoy was to be sent to China—to Mongolia, specifically—where he'd set up a weather-reporting radio station. It was of course hoped that he'd find a way to keep the Japanese from finding it and shutting it down.

Considering that no one was sure the Marines could hold on to Guadalcanal, it seemed pretty farfetched that the top-level planners were already considering the problems of long-range bombing of the Japanese home islands. But in one sense it was encouraging; somebody thought the war could be won.

"When does that start?"

"They don't confide in me," McCoy said. "Rickabee probably knows, but he won't tell me." He laughed.

"What's funny?"

"Do you know what an oxymoron is? Sessions just told me."

Banning thought it over a moment. "Yeah, I think I do."

"Rickabee had him in his office while he told me who to look for at Parris Island: boots who would volunteer for this thing. 'The important thing to find there,' he said, 'is intelligence. I don't just want volunteers; I want smart volunteers.' And Sessions said, 'Colonel, that's an oxymoron.' I thought it meant sort of a supermoron or something. I didn't know what the hell he was talking about. But Rickabee was pissed and threw him out of his office. Sessions told me later that an oxymoron is something like 'military intelligence.' Anybody intelligent who volunteered for this thing would prove by volunteering that he was pretty stupid."

Banning laughed.

But you volunteered, didn't you, Killer? And you're not stupid. Or are you? What is the difference between valor and stupidity?

Carolyn Howell met Ernestine Sage's eyes in the ladies'-room mirror.

"I know about Mrs. Banning," she said.

"I thought maybe you did," Ernie said as she repaired her lipstick. "According to my Marine, your Marine is a man of great integrity."

"I met him in the library. He was researching the *Shanghai Post* to find out any scraps he could about what happened after the Japanese occupied the city."

"You're a librarian?" Ernie interrupted.

"Yes. I went back to work after my divorce," Carolyn replied absently. "And it just . . . happened . . . between us. I already knew about his having to leave his wife over there."

"You didn't have to tell me that," Ernie said.

"You didn't have to call yourself a camp follower," Carolyn said. "Why did you?"

"Well, for one thing it's the truth," Ernie said. "He won't marry me. So I take what I can get. Whither he goest, there goeth I, as it says in the Good Book, more or less. Except that he doesn't often go someplace where I can follow him." She gave her head a little regretful shake. "I lived with him outside Camp Pendleton for a while."

"Why won't he marry you?"

"The Killer thinks he's going to get killed . . . or rather, that's his professional opinion. He has integrity, too, goddamn him; he doesn't want to leave a widow."

"Have you two got plans for tonight?" Carolyn asked.

"The office boy has a reputation for coming up with anything you want, for a price. I gave him twenty dollars and told him to find me some steaks. He couldn't get any steaks, but he came up with a rib roast. I am going to pretend I'm a housewife and make it for him."

"I'll give you thirty dollars for it," Carolyn said. "And invite the two of you to join us for dinner in the bargain."

"Deal," Ernie said. "And in the bargain, I will smile enchantingly at Gregory and charm him into letting me raid their wine cellar."

(THREE)
The Andrew Foster Hotel
San Francisco, California
1730 Hours 24 October 1942

Mrs. Carolyn Ward McNamara was by nature a very fastidious woman. Consequently, she was at the moment a very annoyed one. Not only had she not bathed in seventy-two hours, or changed her clothing (except underwear, once) during that time, but her skin felt gritty from the coal ash that blew through the window of the passenger car on the final, St. Louis–San Francisco leg of her journey. The last time she combed her hair—as they were coming into San Francisco—she could literally hear the scraping noise the ash made against her comb.

Before she actually entered Philadelphia's 30th Street Station *(how long ago? it seems like weeks),* she really had no idea how overloaded the railroads were. Even in the middle of the night, 30th Street Station was jammed. Still, she was able to buy a ticket to San Francisco, thank God! ... even if she didn't have a seat for most of the way to Chicago. And the passenger car was *old!*—even older than the one that brought her from Chicago to here; it had probably been retired from service after the Civil War and resurrected for this one. Anyhow, she found a place at the rear of that ancient passenger car, behind the last seat, where she was able to crawl in and rest her back against the wall.

During the trip, she subsisted on cheese and baloney sandwiches, orangeade, and an infrequent piece of fruit. She'd sell her soul right now for five ounces of scalloped veal, some new potatoes, and a green salad.

At the station, she waited thirty minutes for a taxi, then had to share the cab with two people who apparently lived at opposite ends of San Francisco.

And now she was finally arriving at the Andrew Foster, but God only knew what she was going to find there. If she managed to connect with Charley at all, he'd probably be in the same shape that she was: tired, dirty, and with no place to go.

"Here we are, lady," the driver said as the cab pulled up in front of the hotel.

Coming here, she realized at that moment, was not the smartest idea she ever had. But when she heard Charley's voice, and he told her he was on his way to San Francisco, it seemed like an inspiration. They would meet where they had parted, in San Francisco's most elegant hotel.

The doorman opened the door (looking askance, Carolyn was sure, at the filthy lady with the coal ash in her hair). She glanced out. People were standing in line in front of the revolving door.

Not only is there going to be no room at this inn, but what made you think they would obligingly provide a message-forwarding service for you and Charley?

"Good afternoon, Madam," the doorman said. "Will Madam be checking in?"

Not goddamn likely. But if I tell him that, what do I do?

"Yes, thank you."

She saw a Marine captain waiting in line for the revolving door, and her heart jumped. And then she saw he was shorter than Charley, and older, and not an aviator.

A bellman appeared and took her luggage. Mustering all the dignity she could, Carolyn marched after him. He passed through a swinging door next to the revolving door. But when she tried to follow him, another bellman smiled and waved his hand to tell her that was not permitted and pointed at the revolving door.

What the hell is the difference? But you're certainly in no position to make a scene over it.

She took her place in line and eventually made it into the lobby. Which was jammed. Just about all the chairs were occupied, and mountains of luggage were stacked everywhere.

She found the REGISTRATION sign . . . and the line, of course—actually, two of them—of those waiting for the attention of the formally dressed desk clerks. As she worked her way up to the desk, she kept hearing what she expected: "I'm sorry, there's absolutely nothing, and I can't tell you when there will be a vacancy."

Finally, it was her turn.

"May I help you, Madam?"

For half a second she was tempted to try to brazen it out: to announce that she had a reservation, then to act highly indignant when he couldn't find it.

But that won't work. It's not the most original idea in the world anyway. And I certainly wouldn't be the first person in the world to try it.

"Are there any messages for me? My name is Mrs. Carolyn McNamara?"

"If you'll check with our concierge, Madam? He would have messages."

He pointed out the concierge's desk, before which, naturally, there was a line of people.

"Thank you," Carolyn said, and walked over to the end of that line.

"May I help you, Madam?" the concierge asked five minutes later. The man looked and sounded vastly overworked.

"I'm Mrs. Carolyn McNamara. Are there any messages for me? Or for Captain Charles Galloway of the Marine Corps?"

"I will check, Madam," he said.

He consulted a leather-bound folder.

"There seems to be a message, Madam," he said. "But I'm not sure if it's from Captain Galloway, or for the Captain."

Oh, thank God!

"I'll take it, whatever it is."

"Madam, as you can understand, I couldn't give you a message intended for Captain Galloway. But if Madam will have a seat, I'll look into this as quickly as I can."

He gestured rather grandly to a setting of chairs and couches around a coffee table. One of the chairs was not occupied.

She walked to the chair and sat down, then let her eyes quickly sweep the lobby. She saw at least a dozen Marine officers. None of these was Captain Charles M. Galloway.

She glanced back at the concierge. He was simultaneously talking on the telephone and dealing with a highly excited female.

He'll forget me.

Carolyn did not like to smoke in public. She was raised to consider this unladylike.

To hell with it, she decided. *I'll have a cigarette and then I'll go back to the concierge and threaten to throw a scene unless he gives me Charley's message.*

She took a Chesterfield from her purse and lit it.

Two young Marine officers came into her sight. Both of them were aviators (although she wondered about the smaller of the two; if he was nineteen, she was fifty). As she looked at them, they gazed at her, shrugged at each other, and marched toward her.

Oh, God, that's all I need, two Marine Aviators trying to pick me up!

"Mrs. McNamara?" the taller of them said.

How does he know my name?

"Yes."

"I knew it," the one who looked like a high school kid said in a southern accent you could cut with a knife. "The family resemblance is remarkable!"

"I beg your pardon?"

"Ma'am, I am Lieutenant William C. Dunn. I had the privilege of serving with your nephew, Lieutenant Jim Ward."

"What?"

"Ma'am, may I introduce Lieutenant Malcolm S. Pickering?"

"How do you do, Mrs. McNamara?" Lieutenant Pickering asked politely.

Carolyn ignored him.

"You know Jimmy?"

"Yes, Ma'am, I was with him when he had his unfortunate accident."

"That was on Guadalcanal! You were on Guadalcanal?"

A bellman appeared carrying a tray with a glass of champagne on it.

"Mrs. McNamara?" he asked.

"Yes."

"Compliments of the management, Madam," the bellman said. "We hope you enjoy your stay with us."

Without thinking, Carolyn took the champagne.

She looked at the young lieutenant.

"If you were on Guadalcanal . . . did you know Captain Charles Galloway?"

"Ma'am, I had the privilege of serving as Captain Galloway's executive officer," Dunn said.

"Do you know where he is?" Carolyn asked.

"At the moment, no, Ma'am, I do not, I regret to say."

A middle-aged man wearing a gray frock coat and striped pants walked up to them; he was obviously an assistant manager, or some other senior hotel functionary.

"Mrs. McNamara, we're ready for you. Whenever you're finished with your champagne, of course."

"By all means, drink the champagne, Mrs. McNamara," Lieutenant Pickering said. "Never waste champagne, I always say."

She glowered at him.

"You don't know where he is, either, I suppose?"

"No, but I'll bet he does," Pick replied, nodding at the assistant manager.

Carolyn stood up.

"Let's go."

"Finish your champagne," Pick said.

"I don't want any damned champagne, thank you very much!"

"It's been a pleasure, Ma'am," Dunn said. "We hope to have the pleasure of your company soon again."

"Yeah," Carolyn said. "Right."

"This way, Madam," the man in the gray frock coat said.

He led her toward the bank of elevators, but ignored one that was waiting. Instead he put a key in what appeared to be an ordinary door. He opened it and gestured for her to precede him inside. She stepped through the door and realized it was a small elevator.

The man in the frock coat reached into the elevator, pushed a button (the only one Carolyn could see), then closed the door. As he did, an interior door closed automatically, and the elevator began to rise.

When the door opened, Captain Charles M. Galloway was standing in what looked like somebody's living room. He was wearing a perfectly fitting, perfectly pressed uniform; his gold wings were gleaming on his chest.

God, he's so good-looking!

God, and I look like the wrath of God!

And what's going on? What is this place?

"What is this place, Charley?"

"Pickering's mother's apartment. It's ours for as long as we need it."

"Pickering's mother? What are you talking about?"

"You remember the first time we were here? We had dinner with Mr. Foster and his daughter?"

"The one who had a son who was an aviator? Wanted to know about his training?"

"Right. Pickering. You just met him in the lobby, right?"

"What was that all about?"

"They went down to meet you while I came here. We were shooting pool in the Old Man's apartment."

"You were shooting pool in what old man's apartment?"

"Mr. Foster's."

And then Charley slipped his fingers inside his collar, reaching for something. *What the hell is he doing?*

He removed his fingers from his collar, impatiently pulled his necktie down, jerked his collar open, reached inside, and came out with a some kind of chain.

"I've got it," he said.

Oh, my God! My Episcopal Serviceman's Cross. He actually wore it!

"So I see," she said.

Thank you, God, for bringing him back to me!

"Carolyn, I love you."

Nobody's here. You feel safe in saying so, right?

"I know, my darling."

"Aren't we . . . aren't we supposed to kiss each other? Are you sore at me or something?"

"Charley, you don't want be close to me right now, much less kiss me. I haven't been out of these clothes for three days."

"I don't give a damn," he said simply.

"Charley, I desperately need a bath."

"Not for me, you don't."

"For me, I do."

"Jesus!"

"Charley, give me ten minutes, please."

He had somehow managed to move very close to her. She didn't remember him doing it. But all of a sudden, there he was, with his hands on her upper arms.

"I have to kiss you," he said matter-of-factly. "I can't wait ten minutes."

He kissed her, but not the Johnny Weismuller "You-Jane-Me-Tarzan" squeezing-the-breath-out-of-her kiss she expected. He slowly moved his head to hers and, barely touching her, very gently kissed her forehead, and her eyebrows, and her cheeks, and even her nose. And then he found her lips.

By then, her knees seemed to have lost all their strength. She was sort of sagging against him.

"Oh, God, Charley," she said when he took his lips away.

"What I thought about," he said, "was taking your clothes off and then taking a shower with you. Like the last time. Remember?"

"What are you waiting for, Charley?" Carolyn asked.

(FOUR)
The Lobby Bar
The Andrew Foster Hotel
San Francisco, California
1735 Hours 24 October 1942

Lieutenants Pickering and Dunn shouldered their way through the crowd at the bar and finally caught the attention of the bartender.

"Gentlemen?" the bartender asked, then took a good look at Lieutenant Dunn. "Lieutenant, I'm sorry, but I'm going to have to see your ID card."

"He's with me," Pick said.

"And I better have a look at yours, too," the bartender said. "They're really on us about serving minors."

Identity cards were produced.

"I'm sorry about that," the bartender said. "What can I fix you?"

"No problem," Pick said. "Famous Grouse and water. A lot of the former, just a little of the latter. Twice."

"Sir, I'm sorry, we're out of Famous Grouse."

"There's a couple of bottles in the cabinet under the cash register," Pick said.

The bartender stared at him for two or three beats, smiled uneasily, and walked down the bar for a quick word with a second bartender. He was a gray-haired man with a manner that said he'd been standing behind that bar from at least the time when the first was in kindergarten. He glanced up the bar, then quickly walked to Pickering and Dunn, pausing en route to take a quart bottle of Famous Grouse from the cabinet under the cash register.

"He didn't know who you were, Pick," he said, smiling. "And you were asking for the Boss's private stock."

"It looks as if the boss is making a lot of money," Pick said, indicating the crowd at the bar. "I thought he might be in here, checking the house."

"You just missed him," the bartender said. "But I'll tell you who is in here, and was asking about you."

"Female and attractive, I hope?" Bill Dunn asked.

"Paul, this is Bill Dunn," Pickering said. "Bill, Paul taught me everything I know about mixing drinks. And washing glasses. Are you aware that I am one of the world's best glass polishers?"

The two shook hands.

"No, he's not. He's a lousy glass polisher," Paul said. "But I did make him memorize the Bartender's Guide."

"Tell me about the attractive female who's been asking about him," Dunn said.

"Over there," Paul said, chuckling and nodding his head toward a table in the corner of the room. It was occupied by two attractive women and six attentive Naval officers, all of whom wore wings of gold.

The taller of the two women at that moment waved, then stood up. Her hair was dark, and red.

"She is not what she appears to be, Bill," Pick said. "Or, phrased another way, she does not deliver what she appears to be offering."

The bartender chuckled. "Don't tell me you struck out with her, Pick? That's hard to believe."

"She ruined my batting average, if you have to know. And God knows, I gave it the old school try."

"What's her name?" Dunn asked as the redhead made her way to the bar.

"Alexandra, after the Virgin Princess of Constantinople," Pick said.

"Pick," Alexandra said, giving him her cheek to kiss. "I heard you were in town. You could have called me."

"Just passing through," Pick said.

"I'm Bill Dunn."

"Hello," Alexandra said, and looked at him closely.

"Bill, this is Alexandra Spears, as in spears through the heart."

"That's not kind, Pick," Alexandra said.

"Alexandra, do you believe in love at first sight?" Bill Dunn asked.

"Does your mother know you're out, little boy?" Alexandra replied.

"Watch it, Alex," Pick said. "He's a friend of mine."

"Sorry," Alexandra said. "We were talking about why you didn't call me."

"I told you. We're just passing through town. And obviously, you're not hurting for company. If I thought you were sitting at home, all alone, just waiting for the phone to ring, I might have called. Did you pick up those sailors in here, or bring them with you?"

"I'd forgotten what a sonofabitch you can be, Pick," she replied. "But to answer your question, Bitsy and I just stopped in for a drink on our way to Jack and Marjorie's, and they offered to buy us a drink."

"Bitsy is the blonde offering false hope to the swabbie?"

"Bitsy is Bitsy Thomas, Pick. You know her."

He shook his head, no.

"We were about to leave, as a matter of fact. Why don't you come with us? I know Jack and Marjorie would love to see you."

"I'll pass, thank you," Pick said.

"I'd like to go," Bill Dunn said.

"No, you wouldn't," Pick said.

"Yes, I would," Bill Dunn replied. "I think I'm in love."

"You're not old enough to be in love," Alexandra said, looking hard at him again. "Oh, come on, Pick. It'll be fun."

"Please, Sir," Bill Dunn said.

"How are we going to get Whatsername . . ."

"Bitsy," Alexandra furnished.

". . . away from the Navy?"

"I told you, they only bought us a drink," Alexandra said.

"They apparently feel there's more to it than that," Pick said. "The Navy is throwing menacing looks over here. And there are six of them, and only two of us."

"I'll go over and tell them we're in love," Bill Dunn said. "They're supposed to be gentlemen; they'll understand."

"No, you won't!" Alexandra said. "What you're going to do, sonny boy, is go to the garage and wait for us. Then I will leave, and when Bitsy sees that I'm gone, she'll get the message. And when she leaves, then Pick can."

"You're pretty good at this sort of thing, aren't you?" Pick asked.

"I'd really like to, Sir," Bill Dunn said, making it a plaintive request.

"Oh, Christ!"

"I don't know how well you know this guy," Alexandra said to Bill Dunn, "but he really is not a very nice person."

"Run along, Lieutenant," Pick said. "I suppose we must do what we can to keep up the morale of the home front."

"Yes, Sir," Bill Dunn said.

When he was out of earshot, Alexandra looked at Pickering.

"Pick, that's just a boy. You don't mean to tell me that the Marines are really going to send him off to the war?"

"You want a straight answer, Alex? Or are you just idly curious?"

"I want a straight answer."

"He is just a boy. I would be surprised if he's ever . . . had a woman. In the biblical sense. But yes, war is war, and The Corps will inevitably, sooner or later—almost certainly sooner—send him to the war."

"Is he really a pilot? For that matter, are you?"

"Yes, he is. We are. And I'm sure, when the time comes, that Billy Dunn will do his best."

"He's so young," Alexandra said. "He looks so . . . vulnerable."

"Do me a favor, Alex, and don't play around with his emotions."

"What's that supposed to mean?"

"You know damned well what I mean. The way you played around with me."

"Screw you, Pick," Alexandra said. "You got what you deserved. I'll see you in the garage."

She walked out of the bar. Two minutes later Bitsy Thomas left the six Naval Aviators at the table and left the bar. The Naval Aviators stared unpleasantly at Pickering for a minute or two until he finished his drink and left the bar.

(FIVE)
"Edgewater"
Malibu, California
1830 Hours 24 October 1942

Major Homer C. Dillon, USMCR, was not in a very good mood as he turned off the coast highway onto the access road between the highway and the houses that lined the beach. For one thing, the goddamned car was acting up.

You'd think if you paid nearly four thousand dollars for the sonofabitch and it wasn't even a year old, that you could expect to drive the sonofabitch back and forth to San Diego with all eight cylinders firing and the goddamned roof mechanism working.

Dillon drove a yellow 1942 Packard 120 Victoria—the big-engine and long-wheel-base Packard with a special convertible body by Darrin. The Darrin body meant some pretty details: At the window line, for instance, the doors had a little dip in them, so you could rest your elbow there. All this cost a full thousand, maybe twelve hundred, dollars more than the ordinary "big" Packard convertible. And initially he was very pleased with it.

But today, even before he got to San Diego, it started to miss. And when he tried to put the roof up at the Brig at the Recruit Depot—to keep the seats cool when he was inside getting good ol' Machine Gun McCoy, that sonofabitch, turned loose—there was a grinding noise, then a screech, and then smoke. And there was the goddamned roof, stuck half up and half down.

He couldn't drive it that way. So he borrowed tools and dug in the back, behind the backseat, to disconnect the roof from the pump. When he was finishing that, hydraulic fluid squirted all over his shirt and trousers. They were probably ruined.

Though Dillon did not remember Colonel Frazier as being nearly so accommodating when it had been Sergeant Dillon and Major Frazier in the 4th Marines, the Colonel had really come through. There were now, and for the duration of the war bond tour, two gunnery sergeants on temporary duty with the Los Angeles Detachment, Marine Corps Public Affairs Division; they had already done a fine job of providing Staff Sergeant McCoy with a few pointers about the kind of good behavior it was in his own best interests to display. Aside from a few minor scrapes on his face, where the force of the stream from the fire hose had skidded him across the cell floor, there wasn't a mark on him.

Frazier also arranged for a Marine Green 1941 Plymouth station wagon—normally assigned to Recruiting—to transport the two sergeants and the Hero of Bloody Ridge. That immediately proved useful. For McCoy crapped out in the back all the way to Los Angeles. But, as they followed him up the highway—with the goddamned Packard running on not more than five cylinders, backfiring like a water-cooled .50 caliber Browning, trailing a cloud of white smoke—it looked like the closing credits of *Abbott & Costello Join the Marines.*

And then he had to walk through the lobby of the Hollywood Roosevelt Hotel, looking like he'd pissed his pants, to arrange for a small suite (instead of the single already reserved) for McCoy and his new buddies.

When he finally drove into his under-the-house, four-car garage, the only car there was the 1941 Ford Super Deluxe wood-sided station wagon he'd bought for Maria-Theresa and Alejandro to use. So as he went up the stairs, it was in the presumption that there wouldn't be anyone else in the house besides servants.

Except, of course, for the Easterbunny and the Nurse. Whatsername? Dawn.
Oh, Christ! I never called that idiot Stewart!

At the top of the stairs, when he stepped into the kitchen, he bellowed, "Alejandro!" And in a moment Alejandro appeared.

"Señor Jake?"

"If you can start the sonofabitch, start the Packard and have Maria-Theresa follow you in the Ford. Take it to the Packard place and tell them I want it fixed now."

"Señor Jake, is Saturday. Is half past six. They no open."

"Oh, shit. Do it anyway. Park the sonofabitch right in the middle of the lawn in front of the showroom, and leave the hood open."

"Señor Jake joke, yes?"

"Señor Jake joke no. Do it, Alejandro."

"Si, Señor."

Jake went into his bedroom, took his trousers off, sniffed them, saw how the stain had spread, uttered an obscenity, and threw them across the room.

Then he sat down on the bed, dialing the long-distance operator with one hand and unbuttoning his shirt with the other.

"Person to person, Brigadier General Stewart, Public Relations Division, Headquarters, U.S. Marine Corps, Washington, D.C.," he said.

He had all his shirt buttons open before the Eighth and I operator answered. He was working on his tie when he became aware that he was not alone in his bedroom.

Veronica Wood was standing over him. One towel, wrapped around her head, covered all her hair. Another towel, wrapped around her torso, concealed her bosom and the juncture of her legs—or so she apparently believed.

"You could have said 'hello, baby' or something," she said.

"I didn't know you were here. I didn't see a car, and Alejandro didn't say anything."

"General Stewart's office, Sergeant Klauber speaking, Sir."

"Major Dillon, Sergeant, returning the General's call."

"One moment, Sir. I'll see if the General is free."

"It's Saturday. I let him go," Veronica said. "What's that smell?"

"Brake fluid, hydraulic fluid, I don't know what that stuff is. And how was your day?"

"What did you do, roll around in it? Don't ask about my day."

"OK, I won't."

"General Stewart."

"Major Dillon, Sir," Jake said.

"Major Dillon, Sir," Veronica parroted, then giggled, and saluted. This action caused the towel around her body to rise even higher, and then to slip loose. She adjusted the towel, an action that Jake found to be quite pleasurable.

"Dillon, I have been trying to get in touch with you all day."

"Sir, I was in San Diego. There was a problem there that had to be resolved."

"Sir, I was in San Diego," Veronica parroted.

"What sort of a problem?"

Oh, shit, I don't want to get into that.

"It's a solved problem, General. I spoke with General Underwood and Colonel Frazier. They not only gave me a couple of gunnery sergeants, but a station wagon as well, for as long as the tour lasts."

"Well, that was certainly nice of General Underwood," General Stewart said.

"I think the General has a good appreciation of the importance of the war bond tour," Jake said.

"I think the General has a good appreciation of the importance of the war bond tour," Veronica parroted, then sat down on the bed beside Major Dillon and inserted her tongue in his ear.

"The reason I've been trying so hard to get in touch with you, Dillon, is that I have some good news."

I've been called back to work for Pickering, I hope?

"Yes, Sir?"

Miss Veronica Wood groped Major Homer C. Dillon, USMCR. He pushed her hand away.

"I had a very good conversation with the Assistant Commandant about your man Easterbrook," General Stewart said.

"Sir, did you manage to get his records straightened out?"

"Yes, of course," General Stewart said, a hint of pique in his voice. "I told you I'd handle that."

"Yes, Sir," Major Dillon said.

"Yes, Sir," Miss Veronica Wood said. She stood up and walked in front of Jake Dillon, removing the towel from her hair as she did. She swung her head back and forth, and her long blond hair swept this way and that. Sweetly.

"The Assistant Commandant was aware, of course, that Easterbrook's splendid work has come to the attention of the Secretary of the Navy," General Stewart said.

What the hell is he talking about? Oh, yeah! The Easterbunny's 16mm film and still pictures Ed Banning took to Washington with him. Knox probably said, "nice pictures, Banning." And Banning probably said, "they were taken by a young corporal, Sir," passing the credit where it was due.

"Yes, Sir?"

"That letter reflected well on the shop, Dillon. It made us all look good."

What the fuck is this idiot talking about?

"Yes, Sir," Major Dillon said.

"And I told him that I had just arranged to have his lost-in-combat records reconstructed, which would reflect his promotion to staff sergeant early on in the Guadalcanal campaign."

"Thank you, Sir."

Miss Wood untucked the towel that more or less covered her body and held it by its corners. She lowered a corner, briefly, enough to expose her left breast. And then she quickly gathered it back over her and winked at Major Dillon.

"Get off the phone, Jake," Miss Wood said.

"And the Assistant Commandant then asked me, Jake, if I had considered the question of decorating Easterbrook and commissioning him . . ."

Jesus Christ, he's nineteen years old!

". . . and I said the thought had occurred to me, but that I hadn't really thought it through."

Miss Wood raised the towel over her head and let it fall across her face. And then, her hands locked behind her neck, she demonstrated the dance technique known as "bump and grind."

"Get off the phone Jake!" she called plaintively from beneath the towel.

"He's a little young, General," Dillon said.

"I made that point myself, Dillon," General Stewart said.

"Who's a little young? Are you talking about Bobby?" Miss Wood inquired, pulling the towel off her head so she could see.

"The Assistant Commandant said he could think of no greater recommendation for commissioning a second lieutenant than his earning staff sergeant's stripes on the battlefield, and taking over from officers who had fallen in battle."

"And you're thinking of recommending Sergeant Easterbrook for a commission, General?"

"What about Bobby?" Miss Wood asked, letting the towel fall to the floor, then moving to sit, stark naked, beside Dillon on the bed.

"It's a *fait accompli,* Dillon! You just get that young man to San Diego as soon as you can. By the time you reach there, everything will be laid on. He'll be walked through the commissioning process."

"Yes, Sir."

"And then we'll assign him to train the combat correspondents. The elusive round peg in the round hole, right, Dillon? Who better to train them than someone like Easterbrook?"

"Yes, Sir," Dillon said.

"And it should make a fine public affairs press release, wouldn't you say?"

"Yes, Sir. I'll write it myself."

Marine Corps eats loco weed; goes bananas in spades.

"My other phone has been ringing, Dillon. I'll be in touch."

"Yes, Sir. Thank you, Sir. Good-bye, Sir."

He hung up.

"That was about Bobby, wasn't it?" Veronica asked.

"'Bobby'? I didn't know you knew his name."

"I wanted to talk to you about him," she said. "Or, specifically, about Florence Nightingale."

"Dawn Morris, you mean?"

"What has Bobby got that that bitch wants?"

"A friend who promised her a screen test," Dillon said.

"You're kidding!"

"Not at all. Easterbrook was pretty sick . . . sick and shaken up . . . when I got him here. I asked Harry to send a nurse . . ."

"Harry who?"

"Harald Barthelmy, M.D. . . . over here to take care of him. The bastard dressed up his receptionist in a nurse suit and tried to palm her off on me. I was going to throw her out and then kick Harry's ass; but I saw the way the kid looked at her. And I thought, what the hell, why not? It was in a good cause."

"You sicked that slut on that nice kid? Jesus Christ, Jake! He's nice. He's sweet!"

"She's not so bad. And she's been good for Easterbrook."

"He told me about Guadalcanal," Veronica said.

"Did he?"

That's surprising.

"Yeah. Whatsername went into town—in *my* studio car, by the way—and we were alone and started to talk. Florence Nightingale has him drinking gin and orange juice. And he got a little tight, more than a little tight, and told me about it. Including the part about his not knowing he was coming home until you pulled him on the airplane."

"He was pretty close to the edge," Jake said. "I didn't see it, a friend of mine did. Where is he now?"

"Sound asleep on the balcony," Veronica said, gesturing toward the drapes over the sliding door. "I lowered the awning and put a blanket on him."

"They're going to make an officer out of him."

"An officer? Jesus, he's just a kid!"

"Right."

"Was that your idea?"

"No, but there's nothing I can do about it."

"Why not?"

"Because we're both in The Marine Corps. All you get to do in The Marine Corps is say 'aye, aye, Sir.'"

"They really say that, Jake, 'aye, aye'? It sounds like bad dialogue from a DeMille sailboat epic."

Dillon laughed. "They really say it. I really say it."

"You were really kissing the ass of whoever you were talking to on the phone. Who was that?"

"One of the idiots who wants to put a bar on the kid's shoulders."

"So what happens to Florence Nightingale? How long is that going to go on? I think he thinks he's in love with her."

"Tony Weil called me. They're getting stage nineteen set up for some Technicolor tests. He said he needs some bodies for that, and if I send her over on Monday, he'll give her dialogue and put her in costume, get her somebody decent to play against, and direct it himself. After that, I can send her back to Dr. Harry. I'll think of some story to tell the kid, to let him down easy. I've got to send him to San Diego Monday anyway. She just won't be here when he gets back. She had to see her sick grandmother in Dubuque, or something."

"Tony's actually going to direct her a test?" Veronica asked.

Dillon nodded. "He'll also cut it for me. Do it right."

"Tony's all right. Not like some unnamed overrated hysterical Hungarian fags we have on the lot. That was nice of him."

"He owes me a couple of favors. But he is a nice guy."

"So are you," Veronica Wood said, reaching out to touch his face. "A nice guy." He looked into her eyes for a moment. "Speaking of costumes: Does the one I'm wearing give you any ideas?"

He looked thoughtful a moment. "Beats me."

"You bastard!" she said.

"If you vant to geddin in my pants, sveetheart," Dillon said, in a thick and very credible mimicry of the director with whom Miss Wood was currently experiencing artistic differences, "you shouldn't ought to talk to me like dat."

"You *three-star* bastard!" Veronica said delightedly, and pushed him back on the bed. Then she shrieked and looked at her fingers. "What the *hell* is that sticky crap?"

"It comes out of the plumbing that makes the roof of the car go up and down."

"Well, I don't want it on me," Veronica said. "Go take a bath."

He went into the bathroom, into the stall shower, and turned the water on. Veronica stepped in beside him.

"What the hell," she said. "I was already in costume."

(SIX)
Apartment 7B
The Bay View Apartments
Russian Hill, San Francisco, California
1145 Hours 24 October 1942

"I'm a little embarrassed," Miss Bitsy Thomas said to First Lieutenant Malcolm S. Pickering, USMCR. "I've never known Alex to behave like that before."

She was referring to Miss Alexandra Spears. Two minutes before, Miss Spears announced that Miss Thomas and Lieutenant Pickering would have to amuse themselves, then led First Lieutenant William C. Dunn into her bedroom.

"Neither have I," Pick said. "Perhaps it is love at first sight."

"She had a lot to drink," Bitsy said loyally.

"I've noticed that women who want to do something they think is a little out of the ordinary tend to take a belt or two," Pick said. "It gives them an excuse."

"That's a dirty shot," Bitsy said.

"In vino veritas," Pick said. "Speaking of which, can I fix you another?"

"I think I've had enough, thank you."

"There is no such thing as 'enough,'" he said. "It goes directly from 'not enough' to 'too much.'"

"Have it your way. Too much."

Pick started to make himself a drink at Alexandra's bar.

"Can I ask you a question?" Bitsy asked.

"You can ask," he said.

"Do you always drink this much? You've really been socking it away."

"Only when I can get it."

"I've got another question, but I'm afraid to ask it."

"Ask it. I didn't promise to answer your questions."

"Is it because you're going overseas?" Bitsy asked. "Oh, God, that came out wrong. I didn't mean to suggest you're afraid."

"If I was going overseas, I would be afraid."

"You're not going overseas?"

Pick took a sip of his drink, then met her eyes before replying. "I just got back."

"You did? Where were you?"

"VMF-229, on the 'Canal."

"I don't know what that means."

"I flew fighters, Wildcats, F4Fs, on Guadalcanal."

There was doubt in her eyes.

"That's kind of hard to believe, Pick."

"It's even harder to believe when you're there," he said.

After a pause, she said, shocked, "My God, I believe you!"

"All's well that ends well, to coin a phrase."

"What are you going to do now?"

"I don't know. First they're putting us on display. And after that, who knows?"

"What do you mean, 'on display'?"

"There's a war bond tour," Pick said, a bitter tone in his voice. "We are going to build up civilian morale and encourage people to buy war bonds."

Bitsy considered this a moment, then walked over to him.

"I have the prerogative of changing my mind," she said. "I'm a female." She took his glass from his hand and took a sip. "That's good. Would you make me one?"

He was pouring the drink when, thoughtfully, Bitsy asked, "You said 'we.' You don't mean that . . ."

She pointed toward the bedroom. Faintly but unmistakably, the sounds of carnal delight were issuing from it. She became aware of them and blushed.

"Put another record on," Pick said.

She did so.

"He was over there, too?" she pursued when she walked back to him.

"They're going to pin the Navy Cross on him in a couple of days," he said. "Little Billy in there is a double ace. Three kills at Midway, seven on the 'Canal. He was my squadron executive officer."

"But Alex asked him what I asked you, if he was . . . concerned . . . about going to the war."

"And he said he was. People who have been there are more 'concerned' than those who haven't."

"You know what I mean; that was dishonest of him. Of the both of you."

"First of all, I haven't made a pass at you, by way of trying to turn on your maternal instincts. So that is a moot point. Secondly, haven't you ever heard what the Jesuits say, the end justifies the means?"

"That's dirty!"

"They are both doing what they want to do. What's wrong with that?"

She exhaled audibly, shaking her head, then sipped at her drink.

"You're not what I expected, either," she said.

"What did you expect?"

"I was surprised I didn't have to defend my virtue," she said.

"Sorry to have disappointed you."

She laughed. "That I expected. The arrogance. I didn't say 'disappointed.' I said 'surprised.' "

"People think I'm arrogant?" he asked, as if this surprised him.

"The only reason Alex walked across that bar to you was because she knew you were the only man in there who would not walk across the bar to her. Or am I missing something here? Are you actually arrogant enough to think you can wait for me to make a pass at you?"

"Truth time?"

"Why not?"

"I really wish you had turned out to be a bitch like Alex instead of a nice girl. I don't make passes at nice girls."

"Baloney!"

"Boy Scout's Honor," he said, holding up three fingers like a Boy Scout. "I have learned that I have this great talent for hurting nice girls. There's enough of the other kind around so that I don't have to do that."

She found his eyes and looked into them.

"How do you hurt nice girls?"

"They seem to expect more of me than I can offer," he said.

"You've never had a nice girl?"

"I was, maybe still am, in love with a nice girl."

"And?"

"She was married to a guy in my line of work," Pick said. "He got killed on Wake Island. Once was enough for her. Oddly enough, now I understand."

He drained his drink.

"Are you staying here with Alex?" he asked. "Or can I take you home? The trumpeting of the mating elephants in there is getting me down."

She smiled.

"Where are you staying?" she asked. "With your mother?"

"No. In the hotel."

"Is anybody staying with you?"

"The king of the herd," Pick said, nodding toward the bedroom.

"You can take me home, if you'd like," Bitsy said. "But if you offered to show me your etchings, I just might accept."

Pick's surprise registered on his face.

"You have the saddest eyes I have ever seen," Bitsy went on. "I'm not what you think I am, Pick. Neither a virgin nor a quasi-virgin. As a matter of fact, I understand how your girlfriend feels."

"I don't understand."

"What happened to my husband wasn't heroic, like Wake Island. What happened to Dick was that a World War One cannon he was training on—or with, whatever— blew up at Fort Sill, Oklahoma."

"I'm sorry," he said.

"I think maybe tonight, we need each other," she said. She patted his cheek, smiled, and walked to the door, picking up her jacket on the way.

"Shall we go?" she asked.

Pick put his drink down and walked toward the door.

XI

"Good morning, General," MacArthur's secretary, a technical sergeant, said in a voice loud enough to alert everyone in the office to the presence of a general officer—meaning that everybody was supposed to stop what he was doing and come to attention.

"As you were," Brigadier General Fleming Pickering said quickly. The sergeant dropped back into his seat, and a couple of other enlisted men and a captain resumed what they were doing. But Lieutenant Colonel Sidney Huff, MacArthur's senior aide-de-camp, remained on his feet behind his desk.

"You too, Sid," Pickering said with a smile. "Sit down."

He's looking at my ribbons. Have a good look, Sid.

I should have started wearing the damned things long before this; people are impressed. It's not so much, look at me, the hero, but rather don't try to pull that "I'm a regular, you're nothing but a civilian in uniform" business on me. As these colorful little pieces of cloth attest, I have been there when people were trying to kill me, and failed. And this makes me a warrior, too, if only part time.

"The Supreme Commander is in conference with General Willoughby, General. I'll see if he can be disturbed."

"Thank you."

Huff depressed a lever on what must have been the world's oldest intercom device and announced Pickering's presence.

"Show the General in," MacArthur's voice replied metallically.

Huff started for MacArthur's door.

"Sid, I know where it is," Pickering said.

Huff ignored him. He tapped twice on MacArthur's door, immediately opened it, stepped halfway inside, and announced, "General Pickering, Sir."

"Come in, Fleming," MacArthur said. "I am delighted to receive a Marine this morning. You are entitled to bask in reflected glory."

"Good morning, General," Pickering replied with a polite nod in MacArthur's direction, and then added, "General," to Brigadier General Charles A. Willoughby, who was standing at a large map of the Solomon Islands mounted on a sheet of plywood, which itself rested on what seemed to be an oversize artist's tripod.

Willoughby nodded and said, "Pickering."

Was that to remind me that generals get to call each other by their last names? Or is he emulating El Supremo, who calls everybody but a favored few by their last names?

"That will be all, Huff, thank you," General MacArthur said. Colonel Huff stepped back into the outer office and closed the door.

"I presume you have a MAGIC intercept," MacArthur said. "When I had Huff try to find you earlier, he reported you were in the building but not available."

"Yes, Sir. You sent for me, Sir?"

"Have you seen Vandergrift's latest After-Action Report?"

"I glanced at it, Sir. You're referring to the twenty-three hundred twenty-five October AA?"

"Yes. I've got it here somewhere."

He walked to his desk and started to rummage through manila folders.

"There were a number of intercepts, General. Pluto and I were trying to find something interesting."

"And presumably you did?" MacArthur said. There was a hint of annoyance in his voice. This surprised Pickering until he realized that El Supremo was not annoyed at him; he was annoyed because he couldn't instantly find what he was looking for.

"One, Sir, I thought would be of particular interest to you," Pickering said.

MacArthur finally found what he was looking for.

"Ah-ha!" he said triumphantly, and handed a manila folder to Pickering. It was stamped SECRET. "Here you go. Take the time to read it."

He either didn't hear anything I said, or chose not to.

"Aye, aye, Sir."

It was the After-Action that had come in just after one in the morning. He had scanned it, and then gone back to trying to find something of special interest in the MAGIC intercepts.

I better read this carefully. I suspect there'll be an oral exam. El Supremo is in one of his good moods. And that usually triggers a lecture.

FROM: COM GEN 1ST MAR DIV 2325 25OCT42

SUBJECT: AFTER-ACTION REPORT

TO: COMMANDER-IN-CHIEF, PACIFIC, PEARL HARBOR
INFO: SUPREME COMMANDER SWPOA, BRISBANE
                    COMMANDANT, USMC, WASH, DC

1. AT APPROXIMATELY 0030 25OCT42, WITHOUT ARTILLERY OR MORTAR PREP-
ARATION, JAPANESE FORCES, BELIEVED TO BE THE 29TH INFANTRY REGIMENT,
ATTACKED POSITIONS TO THE LEFT CENTER OF 1ST BN, 7TH MARINES (LT COL
LEWIS B. PULLER) EAST OF BLOODY RIDGE. THE ATTACK WAS CONTAINED BY
1/7, WITH SMALL ARMS AND MORTAR FIRE ASSISTANCE FROM 2ND BN, 164TH
INFANTRY, US ARMY.

A regiment attacking a battalion. Three-to-one odds, right by the book. . . . And they were "contained" by Puller's battalion. Chesty Puller is one hell of a Marine.

2. 3RD BN, 164TH INF, USA, THEN IN REGIMENTAL RESERVE ONE (1) MILE
EAST OF HENDERSON FIELD (LT COL ROBERT K. HALL, USA) WAS ORDERED TO
REINFORCE 1/7, IN ANTICIPATION OF CONTINUED, OR AUGMENTED JAPANESE
ATTACK.

National Guardsmen. Their enlisted men are older than the Marines—by at least five years. Which means they've probably had more training. But this is the first time they've been in combat.

3. BY AGREEMENT BETWEEN LT COL PULLER AND LT COL HALL, TROOPS OF 3/164 USA WERE DISTRIBUTED IN SMALL DETACHMENTS TO UNITS OF 1/7 RATHER THAN TAKING THEIR OWN POSITION ON LINE. RAIN WAS FALLING HEAVILY AND VISIBILITY WAS POOR. IT WAS IN MANY CASES NECESSARY FOR MARINES TO LEAD USA INFANTRY INTO DEFENSE POSITIONS BY HOLDING THEIR HANDS. THE EMPLACEMENT OF USA TROOPS WAS ACCOMPLISHED BY 0330 25OCT42.

I wonder how that happened. Was it the force of Chesty Puller's personality that made this Army battalion commander in effect give up his command? Or was he actually wise enough to know that was the thing to do under the circumstances, and to hell with personal dignity and the honor of the Army? I wonder if Chesty would do the same thing if the boot were on the other foot?

4. ALL AVAILABLE 105-MM HOWITZERS OF 11TH MARINES MAINTAINED FIRE UPON ATTACK AREA THROUGHOUT THIS PERIOD, AUGMENTED BY 37-MM CANNON OF HEAVY WEAPONS COMPANY, 164TH INF USA, FIRING PRIMARILY CANISTER. M COMPANY 7TH MARINES EXPENDED APPROXIMATELY 1,200 ROUNDS 81-MM MORTAR AMMUNITION DURING THE NIGHT.

God, that's a lot of 81mm mortar ammo! Even more when you think that somebody had to carry it from the dump after the on-site supply was exhausted.

5. USA 37-MM CANISTER FIRE ESPECIALLY EFFECTIVE IN CONTAINING SERIES OF JAPANESE ATTACKS DURING PERIOD 0100-0700 25OCT42.

Well, that's Vandergrift giving credit where it's due. That's six hours of 37mm cannon fire. I wonder how many rounds?

6. AT APPROXIMATELY 0700 25OCT42, JAPANESE ATTACKS DIMINISHED IN INTENSITY. GREATEST PENETRATION OF US LINES WAS APPROXIMATELY 150 YARD SALIENT IN LINES OF COMBINED 1/7 AND 3/164 USA, AND SALIENT WAS REDUCED BY APPROXIMATELY 0830.

The best the Japs could do with a regiment in six hours was make a 150-yard dent in our lines; and then they couldn't hold it! But what did that cost us?

7. AT APPROXIMATELY 0830 25OCT42, 3/164 USA BEGAN TO ESTABLISH ITS OWN LINES TO LEFT OF 1/7, ESTABLISHMENT CONTINUING THROUGHOUT MORNING.

Well, the Army battalion commander got command of his battalion back. Did he demand it? Or did Vandergrift decide that it was the best thing to do, tactically? If that's the case, Vandergrift must think the Army commander knows what he's doing. Otherwise, he would have kept the soldiers under Puller's command.

8. HEAVY JAPANESE ARTILLERY FIRE, PROBABLY 150-MM COMMENCED AT 0800 25OCT42 ON BOTH US LINES AND HENDERSON FIELD. FIRE WAS AT TEN-MINUTE INTERVALS AND CONTINUED UNTIL 1100 25OCT42.

Their big guns. We have nothing to counter them. Our 155mm's sailed off with the Navy the day we landed. Goddamn the Navy!

9. HEAVY RAIN RENDERED FIGHTER STRIP NUMBER ONE INOPERABLE, AND RAIN PLUS DAMAGE FROM JAPANESE HEAVY ARTILLERY RENDERED HENDERSON FIELD RUNWAYS INOPERABLE DURING MORNING. LIMITED US AIR ACTIVITY AFTER 1345.

Well, at least Pick wasn't there!

10. INTENSITY OF JAPANESE AIR ACTIVITY DURING AFTERNOON 25OCT42 SUGGESTED BY ROUGH NOTES OF LT COL L.C. MERILLAT, FOLLOWING:
1423—CONDITION RED. 16 JAP BOMBERS AT 20000 FT, FIVE MILES
1430—INTENSE BOMBING OF KUKUM BEACH
1434—1 BOMBER SHOT DOWN, REMAINDER LEAVING
1435—1 BOMBER HAS PORT MOTOR SHOT OUT
1436—2 ZERO SHOT DOWN OVER HENDERSON
1442—ANOTHER JAP FORMATION APPROACHING
1451—1 ZERO SHOT DOWN
1456—HENDERSON STRAFED BY THREE ZEROS
1502—NINE ZEKES BOMB HENDERSON AIRCRAFT GRAVEYARD
1507—HENDERSON STRAFED BY SIX ZEROS
1516—CONDITION GREEN

Thank God, Pick wasn't there. I wonder where he is.

11. AT APPROXIMATELY 2000 25OCT42, LIGHT (105-MM AND SMALLER) JAPANESE ARTILLERY BARRAGE COMMENCED ON NOW SEPARATE POSITIONS OF 1/7 AND 3/164 USA AND CONTINUED INTERMITTENTLY UNTIL 2100.

The standard artillery "softening up" barrage. How the hell did the Japanese move that much ammunition over that terrain? The most one man can carry is one 105mm shell at a time. For that matter, how did they get their cannon in position?

12. AT 2100 25OCT42 SMALL JAPANESE ATTACKS, IN STRENGTH OF 30 TO 200, UNDER MACHINEGUN COVER COMMENCED PRIMARILY AGAINST 3/164 USA AND CONTINUED UNTIL APPROXIMATELY 2400. 37-MM CANNON OF WEAPONS COMPANY, 7TH MARINES KILLED AT LEAST 250 OF THE ENEMY WITH CANISTER AT CLOSE RANGE. NO SIGNIFICANT PENETRATION OF US LINES OCCURRED.

Jesus, you have to give the Japs credit for tenacity! They kept attacking for three hours! Did they know they were attacking soldiers and not Marines? Sure, they did. They have good scouts, too. They knew what they were doing. And the Army fooled them. It cost the Japs 250 men to learn that this wasn't the Philippines; that if they haven't been starved and they have ammunition to fight with, American soldiers, American National Guardsmen, are not a pushover.

13. AT APPROXIMATELY 0300 26OCT42, JAPANESE STRUCK IN FORCE AT LINES OF 2ND BN 7TH MARINES (LT COL HANNEKAN) WITH MAJOR EFFORT AT F COMPANY 2/7TH, WHICH WAS FORCED TO TEMPORARILY WITHDRAW AT 0500.

"Temporarily withdraw" is a euphemism. Maybe it wasn't a retreat, but Fox company certainly got pushed out of their positions.

14. A COUNTERATTACK WAS LAUNCHED UNDER EXEC OFF 2/7TH (MAJ O.M. CONELY). TROOPS CONSISTED OF RADIOMEN, MESSMEN, BANDSMEN, WHO

WERE JOINED BY ELEMENTS OF COMPANY G AND 2 PLATOONS OF COMPANY C, 1/5TH MARINES. AMONG PARTICIPANTS WAS PLATOON SERGEANT MITCHELL PAIGE, USMC, WHO IS BEING RECOMMENDED FOR MEDAL OF HONOR FOR VALOR IN ACTION DESCRIBED IN 13 ABOVE.

Conely apparently rounded up everybody who could hold a rifle—cooks and hornplayers and stragglers and the lost—and sounded charge.

I wonder what the sergeant actually did to get his name in this? The British call that sort of thing "mentioned in despatches." We don't normally do it. Sergeant Paige must be one incredible Marine!

15. BY APPROXIMATELY 0600 THE SITUATION WAS WELL IN HAND, WITH ALL POSITIONS LOST IN US HANDS. APPROXIMATELY 300 JAPANESE BODIES WERE FOUND IN AREA OF F COMPANY 2/7TH.

Jesus, what amounted to less than a company of Marines—dragged up on the battlefield and just told to go out and fight—killed 300 Japs!

16. BY APPROXIMATELY 0800, SIGNIFICANT JAPANESE ACTIVITY HAD CEASED.
17. JAPANESE LOSSES ARE ESTIMATED AT APPROXIMATELY TWO THOUSAND TWO HUNDRED (2200) KIA.

Sonofabitch! Twenty-two hundred dead. Six companies . . . a battalion and a half . . . dead! But what did it cost us? Here it is:

18. US LOSSES: USMC AND USA ESTIMATED TOTAL 105 KIA, 242 WIA, 7 MIA AS FOLLOWS:
   A. FIELD GRADE OFFICER KIA FOUR (4)
   B. FIELD GRADE OFFICER WIA THREE (3)
   C. COMPANY GRADE OFFICER KIA TWELVE (12)
   D. COMPANY GRADE OFFICER WIA SIXTEEN (16)
   E. ENLISTED KIA EIGHTY-NINE (89)
   F. ENLISTED WIA TWO HUNDRED FIFTEEN (215)
   G. MISSING IN ACTION: SEVEN (7)
   H. HENDERSON FIELD IS OPERABLE; FIGHTER STRIP MINIMALLY SO.

VANDEGRIFT MAJ GEN USMC COMMANDING

SECRET

Jesus Christ, the Japanese took a whipping! Almost ten to one! How do they get their men to keep fighting when they're taking losses like that?

Pickering looked up from the After-Action Report to find MacArthur's eyes on him.

"You said something about an interesting MAGIC intercept, Fleming?"

"I have it here," Pickering said, then took several folded-together sheets of paper from the right bellows pocket of his blouse.

MacArthur chuckled, and Pickering looked at him.

"Pluto and Lieutenant Whatsisname, the one who was wounded . . ."

"Moore, Sir," Pickering furnished.

"... the one who limps. When they arrive with a MAGIC, they normally come not only armed to the teeth but with the MAGICs in a briefcase chained to their wrists. You are a delightfully informal fellow, Fleming."

"My aide, Sir, is in your outer office—armed to the teeth and with the briefcase chained to his wrist. That is known, I believe, as delegation of responsibility."

MacArthur's face froze.

Watch your mouth, Pickering. You may think El Supremo is more than a little pompous, but El Supremo thinks of himself as The Supreme Commander. One does not say anything to The Supreme Commander that he might possibly interpret as insolent.

After almost visibly making up his mind, MacArthur apparently decided the humor was neither out of place nor disrespectful. He laughed.

"Pay attention, Willoughby," he said. "I think we can all learn something from the Marines."

"General," Willoughby replied, "I'm fully aware that General Pickering can be quite ruthless as far as security is concerned."

Christ! That can't be anything but a reference to Ellen Feller. God, let's not open that bag of worms!

MacArthur looked at Willoughby, curiosity on his face.

"I think that is expected of someone with his responsibilities," MacArthur said finally. "He is also very tenacious, bringing up again and again a subject he knows I would rather he didn't. I find both characteristics admirable, in their way." He met Pickering's eyes. "You were about to tell me about the intercept."

I have just had my wrist slapped. I've been told he doesn't want to hear me try to sell Donovan's people to him again. But he didn't ask Willoughby what he meant. Or does he already know about Ellen Feller?

"Sir, there's a Japanese Naval officer that the people at CINCPAC and Pluto have been keeping track of—Commander Tadakae Ohmae, an intelligence officer."

"What about him?" MacArthur asked impatiently.

"He's apparently on Guadalcanal. Just after midnight last night, he sent a radio to Tokyo, using Japanese 17th Army facilities. It was addressed to the Intelligence Officer of their Navy. Pluto and I think it's significant; CINCPAC doesn't."

"What colors CINCPAC's thinking?"

"Pluto believes that Commander Ohmae is more important than his rank suggests: that he is in effect the Japanese Navy's man on Guadalcanal, sent there to find out what's really going on. . . ."

"Someone like you, in other words, Fleming?" MacArthur asked.

"Yes, Sir. Although I don't consider myself possessed of Ohmae's expertise or influence."

MacArthur grunted. "Go on."

"The tone of Ohmae's radio suggests that he reports things as he sees them . . ."

"Another similarity, wouldn't you say?"

I'm going to ignore that. I think he's trying to throw me off balance. Why?

"... which, in Pluto's judgment, tends to support the idea that he is a man of some influence."

"And CINCPAC disagrees?"

"CINCPAC feels that if this fellow were as important as Pluto believes he is, he wouldn't have used a fairly standard code. He'd have used something more complex—and less likely to be broken now or in the future."

"Like your own personal code, you're saying, the one that is denied even to my cryptographers?"

I wondered how long it would take before you brought that up. You can't really be the Emperor, can you, if one of the mice around the throne can send off letters you can't read?

"Access to that code is controlled by Secretary Knox, Sir."

"I'm just trying to understand what you're driving at, Fleming," MacArthur said disarmingly.

"Yes, Sir. Pluto feels, and I agree, that he didn't use a better code, because a better code is not available to the Japanese on Guadalcanal; Ohmae used what was available."

MacArthur grunted again. "What did Commander Ohmae say in his radio to Tokyo?"

"It was a rather blanket indictment of the 17th Army, Sir. He cited a number of reasons why he believed the attack failed."

"Such as?"

Pickering dropped his eyes to the MAGIC intercept.

"He feels that General Nasu and his regimental commanders were, quote, grossly incompetent, unquote."

"That accusation is always made when a battle is lost," MacArthur said, "almost invariably by those who have not shouldered the weight of command themselves. Unless a commander has access to the matériel of war, his professional competence and the valor of his men is for nothing."

He's talking about himself, about his losing the Philippines.

"Commander Ohmae touches on those areas, Sir," Pickering said, and dropped his eyes to the intercept again. "He says, quote, the severe fatigue of the troops immediately before the attack is directly attributable to the gross underestimation by 17th Army of terrain difficulties, unquote."

"Willoughby and I were saying, just before you came in, that it was amazing the enemy could move as much ammunition as they did to the battle line."

El Supremo's beginning to approve of Commander Ohmae; the true test of somebody else's intelligence is how closely he agrees with you.

"He also faults 17th Army for their, quote, faulty assessment, unquote, of our lines despite, quote, aerial photography showing the enemy had completed a complex, in-depth, perimeter defense of their positions, unquote."

"Willoughby and I were just talking about that, too. When they struck the lines, they attacked in inadequate force at the wrong place. Isn't that so, Willoughby?"

"Yes, Sir."

"We had decided that it was due to lack of adequate intelligence. But if they had adequate aerial photos and ignored them, then that is incompetence."

"Ohmae also stated, bluntly," Pickering said, "quote, General Oka was chronically indifferent to his orders, and General Kawaguchi was chronically insubordinate, unquote."

"'Chronically insubordinate'?"

"Yes, Sir."

"A serious allegation," MacArthur said thoughtfully. "But it happens, even among general officers. We know that, don't we, Willoughby. We've had our experience with that, haven't we?"

"Yes, Sir. Unfortunately, we have."

"General Wainwright," MacArthur went on, "disobeyed my order to fight on. He apparently decided he had to. But then, with every expectation his own order would be obeyed, he ordered General Sharpe on Mindanao to surrender. General Sharpe had thirty thousand effectives, rations, ammunition, and had no reason to surrender. Yet he remembered his oath—the words 'to obey the orders of the officers appointed over me'—and hoisted the white flag."

"It's a tough call," Pickering said without thinking.

MacArthur looked at him.

"I was ordered to leave the Philippines, Fleming. Did you know that?"

"Yes, Sir."

"What I wanted to do was resign my commission and enlist as a private and meet my fate on Bataan. . . ."

By God, he means that!

"It was, as you put it, 'a tough call.' But in the end, I had no choice. I had my orders. I obeyed them."

"Thank God you did," Willoughby said. "The Army, the nation, needs you."

He believes that. He is not kissing El Supremo's ass. He believes it. And he's right.

MacArthur looked at Willoughby for a long moment. Finally, he spoke.

"Willoughby, I think I would like a doughnut and some fresh coffee," he said. "Would you see if Sergeant Gomez can accommodate us? Will you have some coffee and a doughnut with us, Fleming?"

"Yes, Sir. Thank you," General Pickering replied.

(TWO)
Los Angeles Airport
Los Angeles, California
0910 Hours 27 October 1942

Major Jake Dillon, USMCR, waited impatiently behind the waist-high chain-link fence as Transcontinental & Western Airline's *City of Portland* taxied up the ramp and stopped. This was Flight 217, nonstop DC-3 service from San Francisco.

The door opened, and a stewardess appeared in the doorway. *(Nice-looking,* Jake noticed almost automatically, *good facial features, nice boobs, and long, shapely calves.)*

The steps were nowhere in sight. Jake looked around impatiently and saw they were being rolled up by hand from a hundred yards away.

They were finally brought up to the door, and passengers began to debark. These were almost entirely men in uniform; but a few self-important-looking civilians with briefcases were mixed in.

A familiar face appeared. It belonged to First Lieutenant Malcolm S. Pickering, USMCR. Lieutenant Pickering was in the process of buttoning his unbuttoned blouse and pulling his field scarf up to the proper position. After that he correctly adjusted his fore-and-aft cap, then glanced around until he spotted Dillon, whereupon he waved cheerfully.

He walked over to Dillon. At the last moment, as if just remembering what was expected of him as a Marine officer, he saluted.

"And good morning to you, Sir. And how is the Major this fine, sunny morning?"

Dillon returned the salute.

"Have you been drinking, Pick?" he asked.

"Not 'drinking,' Sir, which would suggest that I have been hanging around in saloons. I did, however, dilute that awful canned orange juice they served on the airplane with a little gin."

"Where's the others?"

Pickering pointed back toward the airplane, where First Lieutenant William C. Dunn was in intimate conversation with the stewardess. As they watched, she surreptitiously slipped him a matchbook containing her name and telephone number.

"He's wasting his time," Dillon said. "You're on another airplane in thirty-five minutes."

"Really? That's a shame. The stewardess has her heart set on mothering Little Billy before The Marine Corps sends him off to the war."

"Where's Charley?"

"The Major is referring to Captain Charles M. Galloway?"

"Where is he, Pick?"

"The Captain came down with a severe case of diarrhea, Major. He—"

"You can hand that diarrhea crap to Macklin, Pick. Don't try to pull it on me. Where's Galloway?"

"He's not coming," Pick said.

"What do you mean, he's not coming?"

"I didn't tell him you called."

Dillon looked at him to make sure he wasn't having his chain pulled.

"You want to explain that?"

"He's with his girlfriend. I decided that whatever this public relations bullshit you've set up is, it's not as important as that. So I didn't tell him you called. I left him a note, to be delivered with his room-service breakfast, saying that Little Billy and I would be out of town for a couple days, and to have fun."

"Goddamn you!" Dillon exploded.

"So court-martial me, Major," Pick said, not entirely pleasantly.

"You're liable to regret playing Fairy Godfather," Dillon said, after the moment he gave himself to control his temper.

"How so?"

"You are now, officially, the escort officer assigned to take Staff Sergeant McCoy and Lieutenant Dunn to Washington for their decoration ceremonies, Vice Captain Galloway."

"Is that what this is all about?"

"You will escort Lieutenant Dunn and Sergeant McCoy to Washington. You will see that they appear—sober, in the appointed uniform, at the appointed place, at the appointed time—or so help me Christ, I will call in every favor I have owed me, and you will spend the rest of this war ferrying Stearmans from the factory to Pensacola."

"Do you think I could have that in writing?"

Dillon glowered at him. After a moment, Pick shrugged.

"OK, Jake. I'll take care of them."

"The proper response, Mr. Pickering, is 'aye, aye, Sir.'"

"Aye, aye, Sir," Pick said. "I said I'd take care of them. I will."

"Sergeant McCoy and his escorts will be billeted at Eighth and I. I have no objection to you and Dunn staying in your dad's apartment, but I am holding you responsible for McCoy."

"Then I had better stay at Eighth and I, too, hadn't I? What escorts?"

"I've got two gunnies, large ones, sitting on McCoy. You work out the details with them. Somebody from Public Relations will meet your plane. You call me on arrival, and at least once a day. And whenever anything happens you think I should know about. I'll give you the numbers of the Public Relations office here, and my house in Malibu. The officer-in-charge is a lieutenant named Macklin."

"OK, Jake," Pick said.

"When we're around Macklin, it's 'Major' and 'Yes, Sir.' Get the picture?"

"Aye, aye, Sir."

Dunn walked up.

"Can I meet you guys later someplace? The lady wants to show me around Hollywood."

"In half an hour, you'll be on another airplane," Dillon said. "Follow me, please, gentlemen."

"Major, this is a sure thing!" Dunn protested.

"The only sure things are death and taxes," Dillon said. "I broke my ass to get seats on the airplane. You'll be on it."

"What if I, for example, had diarrhea and missed it?"

"Then you would spend the next four days having diarrhea crossing the country by train," Dillon said. "Follow me, please."

There were four Marines inside the terminal: three noncommissioned officers standing by a not-in-use-at-the-moment ticket counter, and one second lieutenant sitting in a chrome and plastic chair in a waiting area on the other side of the terminal space.

As Major Dillon and Lieutenants Dunn and Pickering approached the enlisted men, the largest of these, a barrel-chested, 220-pound, six-foot-two-inch master gunnery sergeant, softly said, "Ten-hut!" and came to attention. The next-largest Marine, a six-foot-one, 205-pound, barrel-chested gunnery sergeant, decided that the smallest Marine, a six-foot, 195-pound staff sergeant, was not complying with the order with sufficient dispatch. He corrected this perceived breach of the code of military courtesy by punching the staff sergeant just above the kidneys with his thumb, which caused the staff sergeant not only to grunt painfully but rapidly assume the position of attention.

"As you were," Major Dillon said. "Gunny, there's been a slight change in plans. This is Lieutenant Pickering, who will be in charge."

"Aye, aye, Sir," the master gunnery sergeant said.

"Lieutenant Pickering, this is Master Gunnery Sergeant Louveau, who is Sergeant McCoy's escort, and this is Gunnery Sergeant Devlin."

Pickering shook hands with both Louveau and Devlin, then offered a hand to McCoy.

"I have the advantage on you, Sergeant," he said. "Not only do I know who you are, but I'm a friend of your brother's. This is Lieutenant Dunn."

"I know who you are, too, Sergeant," Dunn said.

Staff Sergeant McCoy said not a word, for which breach of courtesy he received another thumb over the kidney.

"The officers spoke to you, McCoy," the gunnery sergeant said.

"Aye, aye, Sir," Staff Sergeant McCoy said.

"Gunny, I'm sure they're ready to board the aircraft," Dillon said. "Would you see that Sergeant McCoy finds his seat?"

"Aye, aye, Sir," the master gunnery sergeant said. He took Staff Sergeant McCoy's elbow and, followed by the gunnery sergeant, propelled him down the terminal toward an area occupied by United Airlines.

"You want to tell me what that's all about?" Pick asked.

"He's a mean sonofabitch when he's sober," Dillon said. "Drunk, he's worse. The gunnies are going to keep him sober while the President or the Secretary of the Navy—just who is still up in the air—hangs The Medal around his neck. And while you all are out selling war bonds."

"Major, did you hear what he did on Bloody Ridge?" Dunn asked. "He's one hell of a Marine."

"I also heard what he did in a whorehouse in San Diego," Dillon replied. "The only reason he's not on his way to Portsmouth Naval Prison is because of what he did on Bloody Ridge." He paused for a moment, catching each of their eyes in turn, as he said: "Let me tell both of you something: A smart Marine officer knows when to look the other way when good Marine sergeants, like those two, deal with a problem. You understand what I'm saying?"

"I get the picture," Pickering said.

"Good," Dillon said. "I really hope you do. I know Charley would have. Whether you like it or not, Pick; you're going to have to start behaving like a Marine officer; flying airplanes isn't all The Corps expects you to do."

He raised his hand over his shoulder and made a *come on over* gesture to the second lieutenant sitting in the chrome and plastic chair across the terminal.

"Surprise two," Dillon said.

Pick and Dunn turned to see Second Lieutenant Robert F. Easterbrook, USMCR, standing up and then walking over to them.

"I'll be damned," Bill Dunn said. "What do you call that, a three-day wonder?"

"Good morning, Sirs," the Easterbunny said.

My God, Pick thought, *he's actually blushing.*

"Where's your camera, Easterbunny?" Dunn asked. "You have to have a camera around somewhere."

"Shit," the Easterbunny said, blushing even redder as he ran back to where he'd been sitting and retrieved a 35mm Leica from under the seat. He returned looking sheepish.

"Lieutenant Easterbrook is one more responsibility of yours, Lieutenant Pickering," Jake said. "Since you so graciously excused Captain Galloway from this detail."

"What do I do with him?"

"The Director of Public Affairs, a brigadier general named J. J. Stewart whom you will find at Eighth and I, is not only determined to have a look at this most recent addition to the officer corps, but he's going to pin a medal on him. You will work that into your busy schedule, too. After that, Easterbrook, you have until Thursday, 5 November, to make your way back out here."

"Aye, aye, Sir," the Easterbunny said.

"The same applies to you two," Jake said. "Today is Tuesday the twenty-seventh. I want you in Los Angeles a week from Thursday. The tour starts Friday. And you will be on it."

"This officer, too, Sir?" Dunn asked.

"For a day or two. Then he's going to start training combat correspondents."

"Hey, good for you, Easterbunny," Pick said.

"In the meantime, I don't want him to pick up any bad habits," Dillon said.

"We won't let him out of our sight until we send him home to his mommy, will we, Lieutenant Dunn?" Pick replied.

"That's what I'm afraid of."

Miss Dorothy Northcutt, a stewardess for two of her twenty-eight years, thought the two young Marine officers in 9B and 9C were just adorable. Neither of them looked old enough to be out of school, much less Marine officers.

She did the approved stewardess squat in the aisle.

"Well, the Marines seem to have just about taken over this flight, haven't they?" she asked.

"I think they have just come back from the war," the blond one said, indicating the three sergeants in 8A, -B, and -C. "There's something about their eyes . . ."

Meaning, of course, Miss Northcutt concluded, *that you are on your way to the war. And you're so young!*

"Can I get you anything before we serve breakfast?"

"Do you think I could have a little gin in a glass of orange juice?" the blond one asked. When he saw the look on Miss Northcutt's face, he added, "My mother always gave me that when my tummy felt a little funny."

"You don't feel well?"

"I'll be all right," he said bravely. "It's a little bumpy up here."

"But you're wearing wings. Aren't you a pilot?"

"In training," Dunn said. "I've never flown on one of these before."

"I'll get you one," she said, and looked at Second Lieutenant Easterbrook.

"Could I have the same thing, please?"

Ignoring the Marine officer in 9A (who was obviously older—and even more obviously trying to look down her blouse while she was squatting in the aisle), Miss Northcutt stood up and walked forward to fetch orange juice and gin.

"This isn't your day, Bill," Pickering said, leaning across the aisle. "We're making a fuel stop at Kansas City; I'll bet they change crews there."

"With a little bit of luck, we'll hit some bad weather, or blow a jug or something, and get stranded overnight," Dunn replied. "Think positive, Pickering! Butt out!"

(THREE)
The Foster Lafayette Hotel
Washington, D.C.
1300 Hours 28 October 1942

Senator Richardson S. Fowler (R., Cal.) knocked on the door of the suite adjacent to his.

"Come!" a familiar voice called, and he pushed the door open.

Three young men, in their underwear, were seated around a room-service table eating steak and eggs and french fried potatoes. When one of them stood up and smiled, Senator Fowler had trouble finding his voice.

"Well, Pick," he said finally, trying and not quite succeeding to attain the jocular tone he wanted, "home, I see, is the sailor. . . ."

"Uncle Dick . . ." Pick said, and approached him with his hand extended. But that gesture turned into an embrace.

"Uncle Dick, sailors are those guys in the round white hats and the pants with all the buttons on the fly. We are Marines."

The other two young men looked at them in curiosity.

"Senator Fowler, may I present Lieutenants Dunn and Easterbrook?" Pick said. "They, too, are Marines."

Both of them stood up and he shook their hands.

My God, they're even younger-looking than Pick! Are these kids the men we're asking to fight our wars?

"You could have called me, Pick," Fowler said.

"We just came in this morning," Pick said. "The airplane broke . . . unfortunately, at the wrong airport. And then duty calls. I have to take these two heroes to have medals pinned on them."

"So I understand," Fowler said. "Frank Knox called me."

And what Frank Knox said was, "I'm going to decorate two heroes at three-thirty. One of them is Fleming Pickering's son. I thought you might want to be there."

There was another knock at the door.

"Come!" Pick called.

It was a bellman carrying freshly pressed uniforms, thus explaining the underwear.

"Easterbrook?" Fowler asked, remembering. "You're the Marine combat correspondent who shot the film Fleming Pickering sent back?"

"Blush for the Senator, Easterbunny," Pick said.

"That was you?"

"Yes, Sir," Easterbrook said, furious with himself when he felt his cheeks warm.

"Marvelous work, Son. You should be proud of yourself."

"Can we offer you something, Uncle Dick?" Pick said.

"Not if it's an excuse for you to have something. If you're going to see Frank Knox, I want you sober."

"I am on my very good behavior," Pick said.

"That will be a change," Fowler said, and immediately regretted it. But he moved hastily on: "So the two of you are to be decorated?"

"Not me," Pick said. "Johnny Reb here—"

"Screw you, Pick," Dunn interrupted.

"—gets the Navy Cross at half past three from Frank Knox. And at half past five, Easterbrook gets the Bronze Star from a general named Stewart at Eighth and I."

"Oh," Fowler said.

He doesn't know he's being decorated. Was that intentional, or a foul-up? Should I tell him?

"Can I see you a minute, Uncle Dick?" Pick asked.

"Certainly. You want to come next door?"

Pickering followed through the door connecting the two apartments, then closed it after him.

"What's that fellow . . . Dunn, you said?"

"Dunn," Pick confirmed.

". . . done to earn the Navy Cross?"

"He shot down ten Japanese aircraft. Three at Midway, seven on the 'Canal."

"And how many have you shot down?" Fowler asked softly.

"Six."

"Doesn't that make you an ace?"

"I have always been an ace," Pick said.

"There are those who are saying that air power saved Guadalcanal," Fowler said.

"Has it been saved?"

"It's not over. But the Japanese apparently took their best shot, and it wasn't good enough."

"I hadn't heard," Pick said.

"I should have thought you'd be fascinated to hear the news from there."

Pick ignored the question. "If anybody saved the 'Canal—if, in fact, it has been saved—it was the Marine with a rifle in his hand who saved it."

"That's pretty modest of you, isn't it?"

"No. That's the way it is. I have a hard time looking a rifle platoon leader in the eye; it makes me feel like a feather merchant."

"I'm sure he feels the same way about you," Fowler said, then changed the subject. "What did you want to ask me, Pick?"

"I need some influence. I need an air priority for Dunn—he lives near Mobile, Alabama—to get him from there to Los Angeles on November 5. And the same thing for the Easterbunny. He lives near Jefferson City, Missouri, wherever the hell that is."

"'The Easterbunny'? Why do you call him that?"

"What else would you call a nineteen-year-old who blushes and whose name is Easterbrook?"

"But those were officer's uniforms the bellman carried in there. He's only nineteen and he's an officer?"

"He's been an officer for maybe three days. I need an air priority for him from here to Jefferson City, leaving as soon as possible after five-thirty today, and then from there to Los Angeles."

"Call my office, they'll arrange it. I'll tell them to expect the call."

"Thank you."

"Where are you going?"

"I'll probably stay here. Mother's in Honolulu. God only knows where The General is, and I'm sure I'm beginning to get on Grandpa's nerves living in his apartment."

"You better not let him hear you say that," Fowler said, chuckling. "Your father-the-general is in Brisbane. The President sent him there."

"To do what?"

"I'm sorry, Pick, I can't tell you; that's privileged."

Pick shrugged.

"Well, if you stick around here, we'll have dinner," Fowler said.

"Love to. Thanks for the help."

"I'm invited to that awards ceremony in Knox's office, Pick. You want to ride over with me?"

"Fine, thank you."

"I'll pick you up at quarter to three," Fowler said. "Now let me make some telephone calls."

The first call the Senator made was to his office, to tell his administrative assistant that Young Pickering would be calling. The second was to the Hon. Frank Knox, Secretary of the Navy.

The Director of Marine Corps Public Relations was also on the phone to Secretary Knox's office that afternoon. It was quite easy for Captain David Haughton, USN, Secretary Knox's administrative assistant, to clarify for him the confusion about which Marine officers were to be decorated and by whom. The Secretary desired to make the presentations to all three officers personally.

And it turned out to be just as easy for the Director of Public Affairs, USMC, to carry out the Secretary's desires in regard to this ceremony. The President's presentation of the Medal of Honor to Staff Sergeant Thomas M. "Machine Gun" McCoy was scheduled for 1100 the next day. General Stewart had already laid on a dry run for the still and motion picture photographers and the sound team who'd be recording that event. And now, instead of practicing with Marines playing the roles of the people involved, those technicians would simply go to the Secretary of the Navy's office today. Two birds with one stone. General Stewart was pleased with himself.

(FOUR)
Office of the Secretary of the Navy
Navy Department
Washington, D.C.
1515 Hours 28 October 1942

Having decided the presentation ceremony was of sufficient importance to justify his personal attention, Brigadier General J. J. Stewart had arrived at Secretary Knox's office thirty minutes earlier, on the heels of the still and motion picture photography crew.

Those to be decorated, however, had not yet shown up. And so General Stewart's temper flared once again at Captain O. L. Greene. The first time Captain Greene provoked his anger (at least in regard to the present circumstances) was after he'd returned from meeting the plane from California at the airport. When he came back from the airport, Greene reported that the three young officers did not, as they were supposed to, accompany him to the VIP Transient Quarters at Eighth and I, where they were to be installed.

"I told them about the quarters, General," Greene explained, "but Pickering, the officers' escort, told me he'd already made arrangements for the officers. Sergeant McCoy and the two gunnies are in the transient staff NCO Quarters. I gave the officers' escort the schedule."

By then, of course, it had been too late to do anything about the escort officer running around loose with Dunn and Easterbrook. So he'd limited his expression of displeasure to suggesting to Captain Greene that the next time he was given specific instructions, it would well behoove him not to let a lieutenant talk him out of following them.

Now he wished he'd given in to the impulse to ream Captain Greene a new anal orifice back when it might have done some good. In fifteen minutes, the Secretary of the Navy was going to invest Lieutenant Dunn with the Navy Cross, the nation's second-highest award for valor, and no one had the faintest goddamn idea where Dunn was.

The Secretary's conference room had been turned into something like a motion picture set for the presentation. The conference table itself was now pushed to one side of the room; a dark-blue drape suspended from iron pipe was put up as a backdrop; lights were set up and tested; and two motion picture cameras—an industry-standard 35mm Mitchell and a 16mm EyeMo as a backup—were in place. It then took the master sergeant in charge of it all an extraordinary amount of time to arrange the flags against the backdrop—the National Colors, and the flags of the Navy Department, The Marine Corps, and the Secretary of the Navy.

But that delay was as nothing in comparison with the one that really mattered.

And then, as General Stewart glared impatiently—for the umpteenth time—at his wristwatch, the door to the Secretary's conference room opened and three Marine officers walked in.

"General," the tallest of the three barked crisply, "Lieutenant Pickering reporting with a detail of two, Sir."

The other first lieutenant, who was also wearing the wings of a Naval Aviator (and thus he had to be the Navy Cross decoratee), seemed for some reason to find this very amusing.

But General Stewart did not dwell on that. He was pleased with what he saw. The three of them were not only shipshape, with fresh shaves and haircuts, but fine-looking, clean-cut young officers in well-fitting uniforms. It could very easily not have been so. When these pictures appeared in movie newsreels and in newspapers across the country, The Corps would look good.

There was only one minor item that had to be corrected. But even as this thought occurred to General Stewart, the master sergeant took care of it:

"Lieutenant," he said, "this time you're on the other side of the lens. Why don't you let me hold that Leica for you?"

Lieutenant Easterbrook pulled the strap of his Leica camera case over his head and turned it over to the master sergeant.

It was at that point that General Stewart realized that a civilian had entered the room. And then, a moment later, he realized just who that civilian was.

"Good afternoon, Senator," he said.

"Good afternoon."

"I'm General Stewart . . ." General Stewart began, but got no further.

Captain David Haughton put his head in the door and interrupted him: "Senator, if you don't mind, the Secretary . . ."

"Certainly," the Senator said, and left the room.

A moment later a Marine first lieutenant wearing the silver cord of an aide-de-camp came in carrying a red flag with two stars on it. He was followed by a Marine captain carrying an identical flag. General Stewart recognized the captain as the aide-de-camp of the Assistant Commandant. But he had no idea who the other two-star was.

He was pleased that he had chosen to appear personally; if he hadn't, the Assistant Commandant might have wondered where he was.

Captain Haughton reappeared, leading the Assistant Commandant, the Director of Marine Corps Aviation, and the senior senator from California. He arranged them before the flags, and then gestured to the young Marine officers.

"Over here, please, gentlemen," he said. "Lieutenant Dunn on the left, Lieutenant Pickering, and then Lieutenant Easterbrook."

"Sir, I'm not involved in this," Lieutenant Pickering said.

"Mr. Pickering," Captain Haughton said sternly. "Your father can argue with me. You can't. Get in ranks."

The Assistant Commandant and the Director of Marine Corps Aviation both laughed.

My God, General Stewart realized somewhat belatedly, *that must be General Pickering's son!*

"You ready for us, Sergeant?" Captain Haughton asked.

"Yes, Sir," the master sergeant said. "Let's have the lights, please."

The backdrop was instantly flooded with brilliant light. The master sergeant gave those bathed in it a moment to recover.

"Roll film," the master sergeant ordered.

Captain Haughton opened the door again.

"Gentlemen," he announced, "the Honorable Frank Knox, Secretary of the Navy."

(FIVE)

URGENT- VIA SPECIAL CHANNEL
NAVY DEPARTMENT WASH DC 2115 22OCT42
FOR: SUPREME COMMANDER SOUTH WEST PACIFIC AREA
EYES ONLY BRIGADIER GENERAL FLEMING PICKERING, USMCR

FOLLOWING PERSONAL FROM SECNAV TO BRIG GEN PICKERING:

DEAR FLEMING:
    THIRTY MINUTES AGO I HAD THE GREAT PERSONAL PLEASURE AND PRIVILEGE OF INVESTING FIRST LIEUTENANT MALCOLM S. PICKERING, USMCR, WITH THE DISTINGUISHED FLYING CROSS FOR HIS EXTRAORDINARY VALOR AND PROFESSIONAL SKILL AT GUADALCANAL. SENATOR FOWLER WAS PRESENT. YOUR SON IS A FINE YOUNG MAN, AND YOU CAN TAKE GREAT PRIDE IN HIM.

    I HAVE BEEN INFORMED THAT FOLLOWING HIS PARTICIPATION IN THE WAR BOND TOUR HE IS TO BE ASSIGNED TO DUTIES INVOLVING THE DEVELOPMENT OF TACTICS FOR THE NEW CORSAIR FIGHTER. VIS A VIS THE WAR BOND TOUR,

WHEN I ASKED, PRO FORMA, IF THERE WAS ANYTHING I COULD DO FOR HIM, HE INSTANTLY ASKED TO BE RELIEVED FROM WAR BOND TOUR DUTIES. I TOLD HIM IT WAS OUT OF MY REALM OF AUTHORITY. VIS A VIS THE CORSAIR ASSIGNMENT, I HAD NOTHING TO DO WITH THAT EITHER. THE DIRECTOR OF MARINE CORPS AVIATION TOLD ME THAT PILOTS LIKE YOUR BOY (AND LIKE THAT OF HIS GUADAL-CANAL COMRADE IN ARMS, LIEUTENANT WILLIAM DUNN, WHO WAS DECORATED TODAY WITH THE NAVY CROSS FOR HIS TEN VICTORIES AND WHO IS BEING SIMILARLY ASSIGNED) ARE WORTH THEIR WEIGHT IN GOLD TO TRAIN OTHER PILOTS AND THAT THE MARINE CORPS HAS NO INTENTION OF SENDING THEM BACK INTO COMBAT UNTIL THEY HAVE TRAINED AN ADEQUATE SUPPLY OF NAVAL AVIATORS.

KEEP BUTTING YOUR HEAD AGAINST THE PALACE WALL FOR YOUR FRIEND DONOVAN'S FRIENDS. YOU CAN IMAGINE WHERE THAT ORDER CAME FROM, AS RECENTLY AS YESTERDAY.

GUERRILLAS IN PHILIPPINES HAVE ATTRACTED ATTENTION IN SAME QUAR-TERS. LEAHY QUOTE SUGGESTED UNQUOTE THAT RICKABEE'S PEOPLE ARE PROBABLY THE BEST TO GET TO BOTTOM OF QUESTION OF THEIR POTENTIAL EFFECTIVENESS, IF ANY. YOUR RECOMMENDATIONS, IF ANY, AND OPINION, IN PARTICULAR, OF MACARTHUR'S RELUCTANCE TO GET INVOLVED EARNESTLY SOLICITED.

BEST PERSONAL REGARDS, FRANK

END PERSONAL FROM SECNAV TO BRIGGEN PICKERING

BY DIRECTION:

DAVID HAUGHTON, CAPTAIN, USN
ADMINISTRATIVE ASSISTANT TO THE SECRETARY OF THE NAVY

(SIX)
The Foster Lafayette Hotel
Washington, D.C.
2015 Hours 28 October 1942

"I'm a little disappointed with this thing," First Lieutenant Malcolm S. Pickering, USMCR, said. As he spoke, he removed the accompanying ribbon from the oblong blue box that contained his Distinguished Flying Cross and held it in his fingers.

"What do you mean, 'disappointed'?" First Lieutenant Kenneth R. McCoy, USMCR, asked.

"The British do it right," Pick said. "Don't you watch English movies? When Tyrone Power gets the British DFC for sweeping the skies of the dirty Hun, you can see the sonofabitch for miles; it's striped; it looks like a 'Danger High Voltage' sign. This thing looks like something you get for not catching the clap for three consecutive months."

"Pick," Miss Ernestine Sage groaned, "you're disgusting!"

McCoy laughed. "He's a little drunk is all."

" 'A little drunk' is the understatement of the week," Ernie said.

"How are the girls going to know I'm a hero with this No Clap ribbon? How will I get laid?"

"Jesus, watch your mouth, Pick!" McCoy snapped.

"That's never been a problem with you before," Ernie said. "Why should it be now?"

He fastened his eyes on her. "You may have a point, Madam," he said solemnly. He turned his eyes to McCoy. "How come you didn't get a medal?"

"For what?"

"For paddling your little rubber boat ashore from the submarine. Now that took balls!"

"Shut up, Pick," McCoy snapped.

"What are you talking about, Pick?" Ernie said seriously. "And you shut up, Ken!"

"That's classified, damn it!" McCoy said.

"Why is it classified? It's history. And, anyway, Ernie doesn't look very Japanese to me."

"What little rubber boat, Pick?" Ernie demanded.

"I'll never forget it. There he was on a sunny South Pacific beach, surrounded by cannibals. He'd paddled there in his little rubber boat from a submarine."

"Oh, damn it!" McCoy said, and walked across the room to the bar, passing en route Lieutenants Dunn and Easterbrook, who were sitting side by side on a couch, sound asleep.

"If he wasn't so mad," Ernie said, "I'd think you were trying to be funny."

"As God is my witness, there he was, teaching the cannibals close-order drill."

"What were you doing there, Pick?" Ernie asked suspiciously.

"He was the copilot of the plane that picked us up," McCoy said from the bar. "Now can we change the subject?"

"Why didn't you get a medal?" Ernie asked McCoy. "And why did I have to hear this from him?"

"You don't get medals for doing what you're supposed to do, all right?" McCoy said. "And everything he told you is supposed to be classified."

"That's what I thought when they gave me this thing," Pick said. "I didn't do a goddamn thing a lot of other people didn't also do, and they didn't get medals. Dick Stecker, for example."

"Stecker will probably get one," McCoy said. "He's an ace too, isn't he?"

"A mummy ace," Pick said.

McCoy glared at him.

"Don't give me the evil eye, Mister McCoy. You saw him. Wrapped up like Tutankhamen."

There was a knock at the door. It was one of the assistant managers.

"I thought you would like to see this, Mr. Pickering," he said, and handed him a thin stack of newspapers. "There's several copies."

"Thank you," Pick said.

He accepted the stack of newspapers and handed one to McCoy and Ernie. It was *The Washington Star,* and there was a four-column picture of Bill Dunn as Secretary Knox was pinning his Navy Cross on him. A headline accompanied the picture: "GUADALCANAL DOUBLE ACE AWARDED NAVY CROSS."

Pick took his copy and walked to the couch and draped it over Lieutenant Dunn's head. By the time he reached the bar, Dunn was in the process of sweeping the newspaper away. Once he finished that, he rose to his feet wide awake and started toward Pickering.

"I have a great idea!" he said.

"Look what woke up! Read the newspaper."

"You come home with me," Dunn said.

"Read the goddamned newspaper."

"What are you going to do, just stay here?"

"I thought that I'd hang around with the Killer," Pick said. "Maybe pick up some girls or something."

"Goddamn you!" McCoy said.

"What you've heard about Alabama isn't true. We wear shoes and have indoor plumbing and everything," Dunn said.

"I'm not going to be here," McCoy said. "I'm on my way to Parris Island in the morning."

"You don't want to stay here alone, Pick," Ernie said. "Come with me. Mother and Daddy would love to see you."

"With all respect, I'll pass on that," Pick said. "Wouldn't I be in the way, Bill?"

"Hell, no. Come on, Pick. I want you to."

Pick shrugged. "OK. Thank you. Now go read the newspaper," Pick said.

"Why?" Dunn asked. But he took the newspaper McCoy offered him.

Dunn looked at his photograph.

"Goddamn!"

"That will be printed all over the country," Ernie said. "You're famous, Bill."

"Goddamn it, this is going to ruin my . . . social . . . life! I knew if I stayed in the goddamned Marine Corps long enough, they'd get around to screwing that up, too!"

"What in the world are you talking about?" Ernie asked.

"Tell her, Lieutenant," Pick said. "She's one of us. She'll understand."

"I think what I need is a drink," Bill Dunn said.

XII

(ONE)
The Officers' Club
Main Side
U.S. Naval Air Station
Pensacola, Florida
1545 Hours 30 October 1942

With a feeling that he'd accomplished, in spades, what he'd set out to do, Lieutenant Colonel J. Danner Porter, USMC (elevated to that rank three weeks previously), marched out of the club. He was accompanied by Captain James Carstairs, USMC, who followed Colonel Porter, a few steps to his rear.

It had come to Colonel Porter's attention that certain of his instructor pilots, in direct violation of written orders to the contrary, had taken up the habit of visiting the club during the afternoon hours.

Colonel Porter devoutly believed that when the duty hours were clearly specified—in this case from 0700 to 1630—*his* officers would perform military duties, not sit around the O Club in their flight suits swilling beer and killing time until 1625, when they could sign out for the day at Flight Training Operations.

In Colonel Porter's opinion, it didn't matter at all whether or not they had completed their scheduled training flights. There were other things they could do: prepare for the next day's operations, for example, or counsel their students, or spend a little time studying the training syllabus to evaluate their performance and that of their students against the specified criteria.

When he looked in on the Club a few minutes earlier, he found nine of his Marine flight instructors in the small bar, where officers were permitted to drink when they weren't in the prescribed uniform of the day. (He saw at least as many Navy flight instructors in there as well, but that was besides the point. The Navy was the Navy and The Marine Corps was The Marine Corps. If the Navy was willing to tolerate such behavior, it was the Navy's business, not his.) Colonel Porter knew all nine by sight. While he stood at the door and called off their names, Captain Carstairs wrote them down.

As soon as the clerks could type them up, each of the nine officers would receive a reply-by-endorsement letter. This would state that it had come to the undersigned's (Colonel Porter's) attention that, in disobedience to Letter Order so and so, of such and such a date, the individual had been observed in the Officers' Club during duty hours consuming intoxicating beverages. The officer would "reply by endorsement hereto" exactly why he had chosen to disregard orders.

Those letters would become part of the officer's official records and would be considered by promotion boards. Colonel Porter regretted the necessity of having to place a black mark against an officer's record; but this was The Marine Corps, and Marine officers were expected to obey their orders.

It was at this moment—when he was at the peak of the savoring of his own effectiveness—that Colonel Porter's pleasure came suddenly crashing down: Walking up to the Officers' Club under the canvas marquee were a pair of Marine officers. They were not, technically speaking, his Marine officers (as the nine in the bar were his); but they *were* Marine officers, or at least they were wearing Marine officers' uniforms, with Naval Aviators' wings of gold. And so, in that sense, he was responsible for them.

Why me, dear Lord? he thought to himself. *Why me?*

The pair were a disgrace to the Corps.

Their violations of the prescribed uniform code were many and flagrant: Their covers, for instance, were at best disreputable . . . at worst insulting to good order. Though the prescribed cover was the cap, brimmed, these two were wearing fore-and-aft caps. The taller of the two officers wore his on the back of his head, while the smaller actually had his on sidewards (to look at him, he was so young he was probably fresh from Basic Flight Training—maybe at Memphis?).

The knot of the tall officer's field scarf was dangling at least an inch away from his collar, the top two buttons of his blouse were unbuttoned, and he was eating a hot dog. This last meant there was no way he could render the hand salute (unless he dropped the hot dog). For he was holding the hot dog in his right hand, while in his left he was carrying a disreputable-looking equipment bag.

The small officer, meanwhile, looked like a goddamned wandering gypsy. In one hand he was carrying a cigarette; in the other, an even more disreputable-looking issue equipment bag. Both lower bellows pockets of his blouse were bulging. The left held a newspaper, and the right almost certainly contained a whiskey bottle in a brown paper bag. *And God alone knows what else; the pocket's seams are straining.*

"Afternoon, Colonel," the little one greeted him, smiling. He had a Rebel twang that was almost a parody of a southern accent. It came out, 'Aft'noon, Cunnel."

"A word, gentlemen, if you please," Colonel Porter said. The two stopped. Colonel Porter stepped close enough to confirm some of his suspicions: Neither had been close to a razor for at least twenty-four hours. And they both reeked of gin.

"What can we do for you, Colonel?" the small one continued. It came out, "Whut kin we do foah you, Cunnel?"

"You can follow me inside, if you will, please, gentlemen."

"I'll be damned, it's Captain Mustache," the tall one said, more than a little thickly.

"What did you say, Lieutenant?" Colonel Porter snapped.

"This officer is known to me, Sir," Captain Carstairs said; he wore a perfectly trimmed pencil-line mustache. "The last name is Carstairs, Lieutenant . . . as you might have recalled under more favorable circumstances. You are apparently confusing me with Captain Mistacher."

"Whatever you say. How have you been?"

Captain Carstairs gave the tall Lieutenant a tight, sharp-edged smile. And Colonel Porter took that as a sign of disapproval.

They were now inside the lobby of the Officers' Club. A large, oblong table was in the center of the room.

"Step up to the table, please, Lieutenant," Colonel Porter said. "As you unload the contents of your pockets, Captain Carstairs will record exactly what you have jammed in there."

"Little Billy," the tall one said. "I think we are on the Colonel's shit list."

"You are an officer, presumably—" Colonel Porter said icily, only to be interrupted by the smaller, younger one.

"I was getting that feeling myself, Pick," he agreed solemnly, in his slurred Southern drawl.

"—and I don't like your language."

"Aye, aye, Sir," Lieutenant Malcolm S. Pickering said, and saluted. Officers of the Naval Service do not salute indoors.

"You are drunk, Lieutenant!"

"I would judge that an accurate assessment of my condition," Pick said, carefully and slowly pronouncing each syllable.

"Close your mouth! You will speak only when spoken to!"

"Excuse me. I thought you were talking to me."

"You unload your pockets," Colonel Porter said to Lieutenant Dunn.

The brown bag turned out to contain gin, not whiskey.

"What is your unit, Lieutenant?" Colonel Porter asked as Dunn put his hand back in his pocket.

"Suh, ah have the distinct honah and priv'lidge of serving with VMF-229, Suh," Dunn said, trying his best to stand to attention.

Dunn laid an oblong, four-by-six-inch blue box on the table; then two more identical boxes. And then he reached for other items.

No wonder he was about to burst the seams on that pocket. Holy God, they look like medal boxes!

Colonel Porter picked one of them up and opened it. It was the Distinguished Flying Cross.

"Is this yours, Lieutenant?"

"No, Suh. That one belongs to Lieutenant Pickering. He left it on the airplane, and I picked it up for him."

Porter opened another of the boxes. It held another DFC. He opened the third box, which contained the Navy Cross.

"Is this yours or his?" Colonel Porter asked softly.

"Those two are mine, Suh," Dunn said. "Mr. Frank Knox, hisself, gave them to me yesterday."

"What are you two doing here?" Porter asked.

"Just passin' through, Cunnel," Dunn said. "We came in on the courier flight. And just as soon as I kin find a telephone, Ah'm going to call mah daddy and have him come fetch us. Ah live over on Mobile Bay."

"Captain Carstairs," Colonel Porter said, "you will assist these gentlemen in any way you can. I suggest that you offer them coffee and something to eat. You will stay with them until they have transportation. If that turns into a problem, you will arrange transportation and accompany them to their destination."

"Aye, aye, Sir," Captain Carstairs said.

"That's right nice of you, Cunnel," Bill Dunn said. "Could I offah you a small libation?"

"Thank you, no. Good afternoon, gentlemen," Colonel Porter said, and marched out of the Officers' Club.

"Nice fella, for a cunnel," Bill Dunn said.

"I know who you are," Captain Carstairs said, with a sympathetic shake of his head and the tight, small smile that Colonel Porter noticed earlier; but there was a warm glint in his eye. "You're Dunn. I saw your picture in the newspaper this morning."

"God-damn!" Dunn said. "Pick, didn't I tell you that was going to happen?"

"Well, you're going to have to change your attack. Try pinning the goddamn medals on. Maybe that will work."

"You think so?" Dunn asked hopefully.

Captain Carstairs grabbed each officer by the arm and propelled them away from the bar and toward the dining room.

(TWO)
Live Oaks Plantation
Baldwin County, Alabama
1205 Hours 31 October 1942

Mrs. Alma Dunn walked into the large kitchen and sat down at the table, then picked up a biscuit and took a bite. She pointed to glasses sitting in front of her son; they were half full of a thick red liquid.

Lieutenant William C. Dunn, wearing a khaki shirt and green trousers, was sitting across the table from Lieutenant Malcolm S. Pickering, who was similarly attired. The table was loaded with food, none of which seemed particularly appetizing to either of them.

"Is that tomato juice or a Bloody Mary?" Mrs. Dunn asked.

"Bloody Mary," her son answered.

"Kate, would you fix me one, please?"

"Yes, Ma'am," Kate said. Kate was a tiny black woman; she looked to Pick Pickering to be at least seventy, and to weigh about that many pounds.

"I hope you both feel awful," Mrs. Dunn said. "You were pretty disgusting when you rolled in here last night."

"I'm sorry, Mrs. Dunn," Pick said.

"You should be," she said matter-of-factly.

Bill Dunn's mother did not look at all like Pick's mother, Mrs. Patricia Pickering. Mrs. Dunn was a large, young-looking woman, whose sandy blond hair was parted in the middle and arranged in a kind of pigtail at the back. She was wearing a tweed skirt and a sweater, with just a hint of lipstick. And her only jewelry was a small metal pin, which showed three blue stars on a white background. Mrs. Patricia Pickering, in contrast, was svelte and elegant; Pick could never remember seeing her, for instance, without her four-carat emerald-cut diamond engagement ring. Yet she, too, wore a similar pin, with two blue stars. The number of stars on the pins signified how many members of the wearer's immediate family were in the military or naval service of the United States.

But they're the same kind of women, Pick thought. *They'd like each other.*

"God is punishing us, Mother. You don't have to trouble."

"What was the occasion?"

"It isn't every day you get to meet the President of the United States," Bill Dunn said.

"The President? When you came in here, you said you got your medal from Mr. Knox. And you're in hot water about that, too, by the way. The Senator called your daddy."

"Senator Foghorn's mad they gave me a medal?"

"Don't be a wise-ass, Billy. He saw your picture in the Washington papers. Senator Whatsisname from California . . ."

"Fowler, Mrs. Dunn," Pick furnished.

". . . Senator Fowler was in the picture. Senator Chadwick called your daddy to tell him he'd have been there himself if he'd known about it. And your daddy is mad that you didn't call the Senator and tell him what was going on."

"Mother, come on! What was I supposed to do, call him up and say, 'Senator, they're giving me a medal, why don't you come watch?' "

"That's what I told your daddy, but it didn't seem to help much."

Kate delivered a Bloody Mary, and Alma Dunn took a sip, nodded her approval, and then saw Pick's eyes on her.

"Does your mother drink, Mr. Pickering?"

"Only when she's thirsty," Pick's mouth ran away from him.

Alma Dunn laughed. "Now I know why you're friends. Two wise apples."

"Where is Daddy?"

"He had to go to the bank in Mobile. I think he's taking your medal to show your uncle Jack. You were telling me about the President?"

"He gave the Medal of Honor to a sergeant. Sergeant 'Machine Gun' McCoy. Pick had to take him. I tagged along."

"I don't understand."

"The Sergeant, Mother, is not *fully readjusted* to life in the States."

"Neither are you, apparently. But I still don't know what you're talking about."

"The only reason I'm telling you this, Mrs. Dunn," Pick said, "is because I want you to believe that we are not the only sinners in The Marine Corps. Ol' Machine Gun is even worse. The Corps assigned two very large gunnery sergeants to make sure he showed up at the White House sober. I was in charge of the sergeants."

"What's that, the blind leading the blind?"

"Yes, Ma'am," Pick said.

"Eat your ham, Billy," Kate ordered. "It'll settle your stomach. And you, too," she added to Pick.

"I don't suppose either of you heard it, but the phone's been ringing off the hook all morning."

"Those of us with clear consciences sleep soundly," Billy said.

"Huh!" Kate snorted. "You ought to be ashamed of yourself, Billy. You came in here, kissed your mama, and fell asleep on the couch. Clear conscience, my foot!"

"Fred called. He's coming down this afternoon from Fort Benning," Mrs. Dunn said.

"Fred is my brother," Bill explained. "He's a major in the National Guard. The Army's teaching him to jump out of airplanes."

"He said, 'Don't tell him I said so, but I'm so proud of Billy I can't spit.'"

"Did he say 'Billy' or 'the runt'?" Dunn asked.

His mother ignored him, and went on: "And both the newspapers called, Mobile and Pensacola. They want to send reporters to talk to you."

"No," Bill Dunn said flatly.

"I told them you were asleep, and to call later. And the Rector called—"

"The Reverend Jasper Willis Thorne," Bill Dunn interrupted. "You ever notice, Pick, that Episcopal priests always have three names?"

"Mine is James Woolworth Stanton," Pick said.

"I told him you would call him back," Mrs. Dunn said, then looked at Pick. "You're Episcopal?"

"Fallen, Ma'am, at the moment."

"A little churching would do the both of you some good, after the way you was yesterday," Kate said.

"And, of course, Sue-Ann," Mrs. Dunn said.

"Oh, God!" Dunn said.

"Tell me about Sue-Ann," Pick said.

"Nothing to tell," Dunn said.

"That's why you had her picture next to your cot, right?"

"We're friends, that's all."

"They grew up together," Mrs. Dunn said. "She's a very sweet girl."

"I can't wait to meet her," Pick said.

"She said she saw your picture in the newspaper and was just thrilled. I told her to come for supper," Mrs. Dunn said.

"If your father brings your medal back, you're going to have to wear it," Pick said. "For Sue-Ann."

Dunn gave him a dirty look.

"I hear a car coming. Maybe it's your daddy," Kate announced, and left the kitchen to investigate. In a moment, she came back. "It's not your daddy. It's an Army car."

"Then it must be my brother the major," Billy said, and stood up.

Pick followed him out of the kitchen and through the living room and then onto the porch. The house was large, rambling, and one story; and he remembered from the night before that it was all on high brick pillars. He also remembered that the wide steps leading up to the porch seemed a lot steeper last night than they appeared now.

The driveway ran between a long row of ancient, enormous, live oak trees. He looked down it and saw that Kate hadn't got it quite right. It was a military car, a 1941 Plymouth sedan. But it was Marine green, not Army olive drab.

"Why does that fella in the back look familiar?" Bill Dunn asked.

"It's Captain Mustache," Pick said. "He drove us here last night."

"And now, I suspect, he's come to extract his pound of flesh," Dunn said. "You didn't say anything to him Sergeant McCoy–like last night, did you, Mr. Pickering?"

"Not that I recall," Pick said.

The Plymouth came out of the tunnel of live oak and stopped parallel to the wide stairs. Pick noticed for the first time that the driveway was paved with clam shells, bleached white by the sun.

A Marine corporal stepped out from behind the wheel, ran around the front, and opened the rear door. Captain Carstairs emerged, tugged at the hem of his blouse, and started toward the house.

"Natty sonofabitch, isn't he?" Bill Dunn said softly, but not softly enough to escape his mother's ears.

"You watch your language, Billy!"

"Yes, Ma'am," he said, sounding genuinely contrite.

Carstairs reached the top of the stairs, came onto the porch, and removed his uniform cap.

"Good morning, Ma'am," he said. "Gentlemen."

"Good morning, Sir," Dunn and Pickering said, almost in unison.

"Lovely day, isn't it?"

"I don't think either of them noticed, Captain," Mrs. Dunn said. "But yes, it is. Can I have Kate bring you something?"

"That's very kind, Ma'am," Captain Carstairs said, and nodded at the Bloody Mary Pickering was holding. "That looks interesting."

"It's not tomato juice, Captain," Bill Dunn said.

"I hoped it wouldn't be," Carstairs said, smiling.

"I'll have Kate bring you one," Mrs. Dunn said. And then, "Captain, if you'll excuse me?"

"You're very kind, Ma'am," Captain Carstairs said.

Kate appeared almost immediately with a tray holding three glasses and a glass pitcher full of a red liquid.

"Kate," Dunn said. "Would you see that the corporal gets something to drink? Why don't you ask him in the kitchen and see if he's hungry?"

"Can I fix you something, Captain?" Kate asked.

"I wouldn't want to impose."

"How about a nice ham sandwich?"

"You ought to try it, Captain," Dunn said. "We cure our own."

"Thank you very much," Carstairs said.

"Why don't we sit over there?" Dunn said, indicating a set of white wicker chairs, couches, and a table, to the right of the wide porch.

"This is a very nice place, Mr. Dunn," Carstairs said. "I guess I've flown over it a thousand times, but this is the first time I've been on the ground."

"It's nice," Dunn agreed. "One of my ancestors stole it from the Indians, and then another ancestor kept the Yankee carpetbaggers from stealing it from us."

"How did he do that?" Carstairs asked.

"There's a story going around that every time the Yankees started out for here from Mobile, their boats seemed to blow up," Dunn said.

"How big is it?" Pick asked.

"Right at a hundred thousand acres," Dunn said. "Most of it in timber now. You ever hear of the boll weevil?"

"No," Pick admitted.

"Up in Dale County, they built a monument to the boll weevil," Dunn said. "Right in the center of town. Everything down here used to be cotton. The boll weevil came along and ate all the cotton, and we had to find something else to do with the land. We put ours in timber. And pecans. We have twelve hundred acres in pecans. And we're running some livestock. Swine, sheep, and cattle. You can graze cattle in pecan groves, get double use of the land."

"I would never have pegged you for a farmer," Pick said.

"My brothers are farmers," Dunn said. "Before I went in the Corps, they hadn't made up their minds what I was going to be. The only thing they knew was that I wasn't cut out to be a farmer. Now I'm not so sure. This all looks pretty good to me, now that I'm home."

"Yours was a pretty spectacular homecoming, Mr. Dunn," Carstairs said.

"He said, preparatory to dropping the other shoe," Pick said. Carstairs gave him a dirty look. "I would like to apologize for calling you Captain Mustache, and thank you for driving us over here," Pick went on.

"Count me in on that," Dunn said. "I have the feeling that light colonel can be a real nasty sonofabitch."

"It doesn't behoove lieutenants, Mr. Dunn," Carstairs said, "to refer to a lieutenant colonel as a 'real nasty sonofabitch' in the hearing of a captain who works for the nasty sonofabitch."

"Yes, Sir," Dunn said. "Can I infer from your presence that all has not been forgiven?"

"Forgiven, no. But there is an opportunity offered for you to make amends."

"And what if we're unrepentant?" Pick asked.

"Let me put it this way, Mr. Pickering," Carstairs said. "I spent the morning delivering 'reply by endorsement' letters to the officers Colonel Porter found drinking beer in the Club yesterday afternoon; these letters asked them to explain why they weren't whitewashing rocks, or doing something else useful, when they were through with their last student of the day."

"Fuck him," Pick said. "If you're suggesting he'll write our CO, even our MAG commander, telling him we were a little tight, let him."

"The letter would go to your new MAG commander, Mr. Pickering, not your old one."

"I don't know what you're talking about."

"You don't know, do you?" Carstairs said. "You two are not going back to your squadrons. None of the Guadalcanal aces are. You're going to train new fighter pilots. Here. I mean in the States. Probably at Memphis, I would guess."

"How do you know that?"

"Take my word for it. My orders to Memphis were canceled. I'm going to the Pacific. The Corps seems to feel the new generation of fighter pilots should be trained by people with combat experience, and not by those of us they've kept around the States until now."

"Oh, shit," Dunn said.

"It could be worse than teaching fighter pilots in Memphis or Florida, Mr. Dunn. It could mean teaching basic flight here—sitting in the backseat of Yellow Perils, and whitewashing rocks when you're through with the day's flying."

"He'd do that to us?" Pick asked.

"In a word, Mr. Pickering, you can bet your ass he would."

"How do we make amends? Kiss his ass at high noon in front of the O Club?"

"Colonel Porter feels that it would be educational—perhaps even inspirational—if you were to speak to the Marine Aviators and the Marine students here. And he sent me to ask if you would, for the good of The Corps, be willing to give up one day of your well-earned leave for that noble purpose."

"Or else he writes the reply-by-endorsement letters, right?" Pick asked.

"That sums it up neatly, Mr. Pickering."

"Or has us assigned here flying students in goddamn Yellow Perils," Dunn said.

"Precisely, Mr. Dunn. Or both. I don't suppose you really give a damn, but one of those letters would probably derail the promotion I'm sure The Corps has in mind for someone who's been a squadron exec and has the Navy Cross."

"Fuck a promotion!"

"You don't mean that, Billy," Pick said, and looked at Carstairs. "When?"

"Colonel Porter suggests the day after tomorrow, if that would be convenient. It will take me that long to set it up."

"What are we supposed to talk about?" Pick said.

"What you would have liked to hear when you were about to get your wings. About the Zero, for example. How do you fight the Zero?"

"If it's one Wildcat and one Zero," Dunn said, "you run. You're outnumbered."

Pick laughed. "Very well said, Mr. Dunn."

"Unfortunately, I didn't say it first," Dunn said. "Joe Foss . . . you remember Foss, Captain Foss? From out west someplace . . . ?" Pick nodded. "That's his line."

"Is it that bad?" Carstairs asked.

"It's that bad," Dunn said. "The Zero is one hell of an airplane."

"Then that's what you talk about," Carstairs said. "This inspirational speech of yours will take place at Corey Field commencing at 0800 the day after tomorrow. I'll send a car for you—"

"There's wheels here," Dunn interrupted. "I know where Corey Field is."

"I think the Colonel expects that you will appear in the prescribed uniform, which means with brimmed cover, and wearing your decorations."

"I don't have one of those hats," Pick said.

"Me either," Dunn said.

"Then if you will each give me your head size, and . . . I think they're $21.95 . . . I will buy them for you at the sales store and have the corporal bring them to you."

"Yes, Sir," Dunn said. "Thank you."

"What I will do," Carstairs said, "is pick you up here at 0700. If you want to follow me over to Corey in your car, fine. That would spare me another trip here to bring you back."

"I know where Corey Field is," Dunn said. "You don't have to come over here."

"That wasn't a suggestion, Mr. Dunn," Carstairs said. "This is The Marine Corps. I am a captain, and you are a lieutenant, and I say what we are going to do, and you say, 'Aye, aye, Sir.'"

"Aye, aye, Sir."

"Now that we have our business out of the way, do you suppose I could have another Bloody Mary?" Carstairs asked.

"Won't Colonel Whatsisname be looking for you?" Pick asked.

"If the nasty sonofabitch thinks it took me all afternoon to find you two, why should I correct him?"

They were on their third Bloody Mary when, almost together, two automobiles appeared in the long driveway under the arch of the enormous live oaks. One was an Oldsmobile sedan, the second a Plymouth convertible.

"Unless I'm mistaken," Dunn said, "here comes the paratroops."

"In two cars?" Pick asked.

"You ever go to see the Andy Hardy movies?" Dunn asked, and then went on without waiting for a reply. "You remember when Andy Hardy got a Plymouth like that when he graduated from high school? Sue-Ann thought it was darling, so Mr. Pendergrast bought her one."

The cars came closer.

"No, it's not the paratroops. It's the Reverend Three Names."

He put his Bloody Mary down and walked down the wide steps to wait for the cars to drive up.

A tall, slim, gray-haired man in a gray suit stepped out of the Oldsmobile and grasped Dunn's hand with both of his own, shaking it with great enthusiasm.

"Here comes another car," Captain Carstairs announced. "Maybe that's the paratroops. What's he talking about?"

"His brother's in the Army at Fort Benning," Pick explained. "He's coming down here."

The Plymouth pulled up. A long-legged blonde in a sweater and skirt got out, squealed "Billy!", and then kissed both the Marine officer and the cleric. She kissed the Marine officer with somewhat more enthusiasm.

Then, hanging on to his arm, she marched him up the stairs.

"Hi, y'all," she called cheerfully to Pickering and Carstairs. "Let me say hello a minute to Miss Alma, and then I'll be with you."

She and the Reverend Mr. Jasper Willis Thorne went into the house.

"Nice," Pick said, vis-à-vis Miss Sue-Ann Pendergrast.

"Very nice," Captain Carstairs agreed.

"I'll be a sonofabitch," Lieutenant Dunn said, visibly shocked. "She gave me tongue, with the rector standing right there."

The second Oldsmobile slid, rather than braked, to a stop. The door opened, and a very large man wearing major's leaves and paratroop boots jumped out and ran up the stairs, taking them three at a time.

Captain Carstairs stood up, decided the porch was outside, and saluted.

"Good afternoon, Sir," he said.

Major Frederick C. Dunn, Infantry, Army of the United States, returned the salute crisply, if idly.

"If you're waiting for me to salute you, Fred, don't hold your breath," Bill Dunn said.

"Goddamn, Runt!" Major Dunn said emotionally. "You're a sight for goddamn sore eyes!"

He went to his brother, wrapped him in a bear hug, and lifted him off the ground.

After a moment, he set him down.

"Gentlemen," he said in an accent that was even thicker than Bill Dunn's, "if you'll excuse me, I'll go say hello to my momma and see if I can't find something decent for us to drink."

He wrapped his arm around his brother's shoulders, giving him no choice but to accompany him into the house.

Carstairs looked at Pickering.

"Nice people, aren't they?" he said.

Pick started to agree, but what came out was, "Do you ever see Martha?"

"I thought you might get around to asking that question. Yes. As a matter of fact, I saw her just before I came over here. And I'm going to have dinner with her tonight."

Pick grunted.

"No, I didn't tell her I'd seen you," Carstairs said. "I wasn't sure if you wanted me to; if it would, so to speak, be the thing to do."

"Tell her, if you like," Pick said. "It doesn't make any difference."

"You don't plan to call her?"

"When a woman tells you she doesn't want to marry you, and means it . . ."

"I didn't know it had gone that far."

"How far is far? There doesn't seem much point in calling her, does there?"

"Is that why you never wrote?"

"You know about that?"

"She told me. She was always asking what I'd heard, where you were . . ."

"There didn't seem to be much point in writing, either."

"She won't marry me either, for whatever that's worth," Carstairs said. "But I haven't given up on asking."

Pick looked at him, and his mouth opened. But he shut it again when Major Frederick Dunn reappeared on the porch, carrying a quart bottle of sour-mash bourbon and three glasses.

"Let the rector have the fruit juice," Major Dunn announced. "I got us some of Daddy's best sipping whiskey."

(THREE)
Jefferson City, Missouri
1710 Hours 1 November 1942

Second Lieutenant Robert F. Easterbrook, USMCR, sat at the wheel of a 1936 Chevrolet Two-Door Deluxe, his father's car, and stared out at the Mississippi River. He was parked with the nose of the car against a cable-and-pole barrier; he'd been parked there for three quarters of an hour. In his hand was a bottle of Budweiser beer, now warm and tasting like horse piss. Two empty Bud bottles lay on the floor on the passenger side, and three full bottles, now for sure warm, were in a bag beside it.

He'd bought a six-pack. Except they didn't come in a box anymore—to conserve paper for the war effort. And to conserve metal, they came in bottles. And to conserve glass, they were deposit-returnable bottles, not the kind you could throw away. And he hadn't been able to purchase the beer on the first try, either. Or the second. There was some kind of a keep-Missouri-clean-and-sober campaign going on. They checked your identity card to see if you were old enough to drink. In the first two places, they seemed overjoyed to learn that he wasn't.

It's pretty fucking unfair. You're old enough to get shot at, and you can't buy six lousy bottles of fucking beer. You're a goddamned commissioned officer, for Christ's sake. People have to salute you, and you still can't buy a beer.

At the third place he tried, a saloon, the bartender said he was supposed to check IDs, *"but what the hell, you're a soldier boy, and what the cops don't see can't hurt me; but don't make a habit of it, huh?"* and gave it to him.

I'm not a "soldier boy"; I'm a Marine. I'm a goddamned officer in The Marine

Corps. Not that anybody around here seems to know what that is, or give a good goddamn.

On the Mississippi, an old-fashioned tug with a paddle wheel was pushing a barge train upriver. Although the paddle wheel on the tug was churning up the water furiously, it was barely making progress against the current.

Back when he was in high school (something like nine thousand years ago), he waited impatiently for his sixteenth birthday so he could get a job working the boats on the river. You could make a lot of money doing that. And he knew he'd need money after he graduated from high school if he was going to study photojournalism at U of M. But it turned out he didn't get a boat job. They told him he should come back when he got his growth.

Later, when he was working for the *Conner Courier* as a flunky with photojournalist dreams, he would have shot pictures of the tired old paddle-wheel tug pushing the barges up the river. In fact, he would have broken his ass then to get pictures of it. And he would have been thrilled to fucking death if Mr. Greene, to be nice to him, found space for one of them on page 11 of the *Courier*. Now, even though he had Sergeant Lomax's 35mm Leica on the seat beside him, he couldn't imagine taking pictures of the paddle-wheel tug and its barge train if the tug and all the barges were gloriously in flame and about to blow up.

He'd wondered earlier why he sort of had to keep carrying Lomax's Leica around with him. Christ knew, no one was going to use anything he shot with it, not that there was anything worth shooting.

But he did get a chance to see the print of the shot he took of Lieutenant Dunn shaking Secretary Knox's hand when Knox gave him the Navy Cross. They'd run that on the front page of *The Kansas City Star*. He didn't get a credit line for it, though. All it said was OFFICIAL USMC PHOTO. But he knew he took it.

Even though he told Mr. Greene that, it was pretty clear that Mr. Greene thought he was bullshitting him.

Still, there was no reason now to be carrying Lomax's Leica around; he wasn't going to use it. So why wasn't he able to just put the fucking thing in his bag? Or maybe see if he could find out where Lomax's wife was, so he could send it to her?

It's funny, he thought to himself now and again, *if Lomax didn't get himself blown away, he wouldn't be able to call me "Easterbunny" anymore; he'd have to call me "Sir."*

You weren't supposed to talk ill of the dead, but the truth was that on occasion, Lomax could be a sadistic prick.

When he pointed out the picture of Dunn to his mother and told her he took it, she smiled vaguely and said, "That's nice." Meaning: "You always wanted to be a photographer; photographers take pictures. What's the big deal?"

For that matter, he wasn't entirely sure that his mother really believed he was an officer, and that she didn't privately suspect he just bought the goddamned gold bars and pinned them on to impress people. At breakfast this morning, she'd made a point of making a big deal about his cousin Harry, who was four, five years older than he was and a graduate of Northwestern University. Harry had been drafted and was going to Officer Candidate School in some Army post someplace; he'd written home that it was nearly killing him, but he was going to try to stick it out, because if he could, he was going to be an officer in the Ordnance Corps.

In other words, here was an older guy than you are, with a goddamned college degree, who had to go through OCS, which was nearly killing him. . . . So how come you're an officer?

As for his father, he wouldn't even let him use the goddamn car. He claimed it was because of the gas rationing and the tire shortage, and because he didn't know what he'd do without it. But the Easterbunny just happened to notice in *The Kansas*

City Star that ran his picture on page one that servicemen on leave could go to the ration board and get gas coupons. So he'd gone down to City Hall, and it turned out that the guy on the ration board was in the Corps in World War I. And one thing ran into another: The guy asked where he'd been; and when he told him, he asked about the 'Canal. And so the Easterbunny walked out of the ration board with coupons for sixty gallons of gas (you were supposed to get only twenty), and coupons for four new tires (you weren't supposed to get tires at all).

And even then, before he'd let him borrow the goddamn car, the old man gave him a "don't speed, don't drink, be careful" speech as if he was seventeen and got his license the day before yesterday.

Once he had the car, he looked up the kids he'd gone around with in high school, of course. But that was a fucking disaster, too.

It was partly his own fault, he was willing to admit. He should have kept his fucking mouth shut. There was no way they were going to believe he'd just been in Hollywood, staying in a place on the ocean in Malibu . . . much less that he not only met Veronica Wood there, but that he and she were now friends . . . and that she took him to Metro-Magnum Studios one morning in a limousine and let him watch them make the movie she was in.

It was partly, too, that they all seemed to be very young and very stupid. They didn't want to know about the 'Canal. That was so far away that it was nowhere, as far as they knew. They wanted to know shit like Eddie Williams asked him: "Since you're in the Marines," he said, "did they ever let you shoot a tommy gun like Robert Montgomery did in *Bataan?*" The Easterbunny hadn't seen that movie, but that didn't matter.

"Yeah," he told him, "they let me shoot a tommy gun; it was great." He didn't tell him about the one he took from Lieutenant Minter when the knee mortar round landed right next to him and blew his legs off. Or that he still had the heavy sonofabitch; it was in the closet of his bedroom at Major Dillon's house on the beach in Malibu. Eddie and the others wouldn't have believed that, either.

He ran into Katherine Cohan, too, on the street; and she sort of rubbed against him then. . . . She wasn't nearly as pretty as he remembered her. He knew that if he called her up and asked her to go to the movies, she'd probably go. She'd probably also let him a cop a little feel, maybe even a little bare teat; but that would be all she'd let him do. So he didn't call her up.

And he certainly couldn't tell anybody about Dawn Morris. Nobody would believe *any* of that, either how good-looking she was . . . or that she'd done it with him at least dozen times . . . or *what* she'd done to him.

Though it made him feel guilty as shit, the thing he really wanted to do was get the hell away from here and go back to Los Angeles and be alone with Dawn Morris in his bedroom at Major Dillon's house. He'd even been prepared to lie to his mother and father, to tell them he'd been called back early. That was a really shitty thing to do to your parents, lie to them, when they were so glad to see you. Still, he'd called the airline and asked if he could move his reservation up. But they told him no; the priority he had was for a specific seat on a specific flight; he'd have to get another priority if he wanted to change that.

Even if he wasn't able to do it, it made him feel shitty that he tried.

Lieutenant Easterbrook looked at his wristwatch. It was time to go home. His father expected to eat ten minutes after he walked in the door, and he'd expect his son to be there, too. If he wasn't, he'd think he was in jail for drunken driving . . . after driving the car a hundred miles an hour the wrong way down a one-way street and hitting an ambulance with it.

Easterbrook drained his warm beer.

He picked up the other two empties, left the car, and threw all three as far as he could out in the river. Then he got back in the car, lit a cigarette, and started the engine. He was backing away from the railing when he braked to a stop; he had to fish through his pockets for the package of Sen-Sen. He spilled maybe a third of it into his mouth.

The old man had a nose like a bird dog. If he smelled beer on his breath, there was sure to be a scene about drunken driving when he got home.

(FOUR)
"Edgewater"
Malibu, California
1815 Hours 1 November 1942

With surprising grace, Veronica Wood ran through the sand from the water to the stairs, making Jake wonder again how women did that. Whenever he ran on sand, it was all he could do to keep from falling on his ass.

She came to him and bent over and kissed him. Then she pointed at his scotch. "Get me one of those, will you?" she said.

While he took care of that, she went to the shower on the porch, closed the curtain, and turned the water on. He pushed the button for Alejandro; and when he came, he told him to bring the bottle and some glasses and ice and the siphon bottle.

"No siphon," Alejandro said.

"You broke it?"

"The things, they are no more," Alejandro said, holding his thumb and index fingers three inches apart, to mime a CO_2 cartridge. "What you call them, 'cartridges'?"

Do you? Cartridges? Cartridges are something you load in a weapon. I guess you do.

"Don't we have any bottles of soda?"

"Is same thing?"

"Just about," Jake said.

"I get," Alejandro said.

Veronica Wood's bathing suit came flying over the top of the shower curtain. Jake imagined an entirely pleasant picture of what was behind the curtain.

Jake found a cigar in his blouse and lit it.

Veronica pushed the shower curtain aside, wrapped herself in her towel, and walked over and sat on his lap. Once she'd made herself comfortable, she kissed him wetly on the mouth.

"Goddamn, now I'll have to have my pants pressed. You're soaking!"

"I'm not worth it to you to have your goddamned pants pressed? Go to hell!"

"I don't know if you know this or not, but when you sit down wearing a towel, people can see everything you've got—Alejandro, for example."

"Why do I think Poppa has had a bad day?" Veronica asked.

"Because it was a bitch," he said. "I now know what the Marine Corps does when they get stuck with idiot officers; they put them in public relations."

"You're in public relations, Poppa. What does that make you?"

"An idiot," he said, and laughed. "How was your day?"

"We looped, all goddamn day," she said. "Jean Jansen can't remember her lines when she's reading them from a script. And Janos, of course, had to be there. . . . It was the first time I ever looped anything, of course, and he had to tell me how to do it."

"You're almost finished, aren't you?"

"We were supposed to be finished today. I told that pansy sonofabitch to get one of his boyfriends to dub it for me, if he can't finish it by noon tomorrow."

"You didn't really?"

"No. I wanted to. But I knew that if I did, he'd throw a hysterical fit, and we'd be in there for the rest of the week. I did tell him I don't give a good goddamn how inconvenient it is, or who else he has to reschedule, if he can't finish my part by tomorrow, I'm going to get sick."

Alejandro opened the balcony door, and Veronica quickly slid out of Jake's lap.

"I wish you hadn't said what you did about the towel," she said. "Not that he hasn't seen something like that before."

"Something similar, maybe," Jake said, "but not something like *that.*"

"Aren't you sweet!"

"Alejandro, I don't care if the Pope calls, I'm not here," Jake said.

"*Sí,* Señor Jake. You eat here?"

"What have we got to eat?"

"We got fish for broil, and a piece pork. Can either roast or make chops?"

"Honey?" Jake asked.

"What did you call me?"

"Slip of the tongue," Jake said.

"Your tongue never slips, Jake, my darling," she said, and turned to Alejandro. "Whichever is easiest, Alejandro."

"*Sí,* señora."

He left.

"What did he call me? 'Señora'?"

"*Sí,* Señora."

"What does that mean in Spanish?"

"Lady Who Goes Around In Towel Showing Everything."

"It means 'Missus,' not 'Miss,' you bastard."

"Slip of the tongue."

"I like that: '*Señora* Dillon.' How does that sound to you?"

"Don't start that kind of thing now," Dillon said.

"Why not? You've got a wife or something I don't know about?"

"Just to keep the record clear. No wife. Ex or otherwise."

"Then why not?"

"Come on, Veronica."

"If it's supposed to be so goddamned self-evident, how come I don't understand?"

The telephone rang.

Now I'm sorry I told him to say I'm not here. What I need right now is an interruption.

"Jake?"

Alejandro appeared, carrying a telephone with a very long cord.

"Is four eleven, Señor Jake," he said, handing him the handset and setting the base down on the table beside him.

"I thought you told him no calls."

"This is my private line," he said, and then, "Hello?"

"Jake, I hope I'm not interrupting anything," said James Allwood Maxwell, Chairman of the Board of Metro-Magnum Studios, Inc.

"How are you, Jim? Of course not."

"Who is that?" Veronica asked, and tried to put her ear to the handset.

"Jake, there were those on the board who thought I was carrying corporate loyalty a step too far when I announced we would continue you on full salary when you went in uniform. . . ."

What the hell is this? What comes next? "We've had a bad year, and there's nothing I can do about it. I tried. But New York, those bastards say there is no way we can justify that nonproducing expense any longer"? Shit, that's all I need. What The Corps is paying me won't pay the taxes on this place. I'll have to let Alejandro and Maria go. What the hell will they do? Shit!

". . . but my position then, my position now, and what I told them, was that I never—Metro-Magnum never—paid Jake Dillon a dime that didn't come back like the bread Christ threw on the water."

But? Is this where we talk about those cold-blooded bastards in New York who don't understand because they are incapable of understanding? All they know is the bottom line?

"I don't mind telling you, Jake, that when you smoothed things over between Veronica and Janos Kazar, I felt my decision to keep you on as a member of the Metro-Magnum family was absolutely justified. . . . The way those two were at each other's throats, it was costing us more money than I like to think about. . . ."

"Veronica is a sensitive artist, Jim. I really don't think Janos fully appreciates that."

Hearing her name, Veronica made another attempt to place her ear against the headset. Jake stood and walked away from her.

"Jake, I certainly don't want to argue the point, but calling him a Hungarian cocksucker at the top of her lungs in the commissary didn't make him look fondly at her. He's sensitive, too."

"Who is that? Are you talking about me?" Veronica asked.

She caught up with Jake, and he gave in. He held the receiver an inch from his ear so she could hear.

"Well, Jim, I think that's all water under the dam. I talked to Veronica today, and she tells me that they're going to wind up the looping tomorrow."

"So I understand," he said. "But let me continue. My point is that my judgment in keeping you on salary was justified by what you did for Metro-Magnum when you made peace between Veronica and Janos. And now this!"

Now this what? What the fuck is he talking about?

"She photographs like Bergman," Mr. Maxwell went on. "And her speaking voice. I wouldn't want that you should repeat this, but I ran the test again for Shirley, for her opinion . . ."

Shirley was Mrs. James Allwood Maxwell, a long-legged blonde who was almost a foot taller than her husband.

". . . and Shirley said, about her voice, I mean, that it would even make Janos horny."

This can't be what I think he's talking about.

"Well, we all respect Shirley's judgment, Jim."

"So I thank you, my friend, on behalf of the entire Metro-Magnum family, for Dawn Morris."

"I thought that you would appreciate the same things I saw in her, Jim."

"We have major plans for her, Jake. Major plans. She's our answer to Lauren Bacall."

"I'm pleased it turned out well, Jim."

" 'Well' is a gross understatement," Mr. Maxwell said. "And Mort Cooperman had a splendid idea, Jake. And I'm sure it will please you. We can get some instant publicity out of it, and so can you. By you I mean the Marines. Mort wants to send her on the war bond tour with you. I told him I thought you would be pleased."

"Delighted."

"Good. Mort will be in touch. Such a pleasure hearing your voice, Jake."

"Good to talk to you, Jim."

The line went dead.

"I'll be a sonofabitch," Jake said.

"Why not, Jake?"

"It happens. Some people change when they're on film."

"That's not what I meant, Jake, and, goddamn it, you know it!"

"Oh," Jake Dillon said. "That."

"Yeah, that. Why not?"

"In addition to two thousand other reasons, I'm in the Marine Corps; I won't be around."

"Fuck the two thousand reasons. I know what you're thinking, and they're bullshit. And you won't be in the Marine Corps forever."

"Once a Marine, always a Marine. Haven't you ever heard that?"

"Goddamn you, Jake," Veronica said, her voice breaking.

"You think you could wait until the goddamn war is over?"

She met his eyes.

"What is that, a proposal? Can I consider myself proposed to?"

"If it makes you feel better."

"Is it, or isn't it?"

"Yeah, I guess it is."

"You're not just saying that?"

"No."

"You're supposed to drop on your knees when you propose."

"You've been watching too many movies. People don't do that."

"You will, or I'll know you're just bullshitting me."

Major Jake Dillon looked at her for a moment, then shrugged and dropped to one knee.

"This OK?" he asked.

"Honey, that's fine," Veronica Wood said.

XIII

When Lieutenant Colonel Jack (NMI) Stecker, USMCR, walked into Division Headquarters, he was wearing frayed, sweat- and oil-stained utilities and a pair of boondockers covered with mud and mildew.

He was armed with a U.S. Rifle, Caliber .30-06, M1, commonly known as the Garand. He carried it slung over his shoulder, with two eight-round, *en bloc* clips attached to its leather strap.

Early on in the battle for Guadalcanal, when then Major Stecker put a pair of bullets from his Garand into the heads of two Japanese soldiers (and did it firing offhand, with only two shots, at a distance that was later measured as 190 yards), he cast considerable doubt upon the widely held, near-sacred belief among Marines that the U.S. Rifle, Caliber .30-06, M1903 Springfield was the finest rifle in the world.

He also wore a shoulder holster, which held a Colt M1911A1 pistol. These were originally issued to Second Lieutenant Richard J. Stecker, USMCR. When Colonel Stecker went to visit his son a few minutes before he was evacuated by air, he found them lying under Lieutenant Stecker's cot in the hospital.

Certain minor disciplinary and logistical problems within the First Marine Division resulted from Colonel Stecker's carrying of the Garand and his wearing of the shoulder holster. These problems were in no way due to any action or behavior of the Colonel. They just kind of grew like topsy:

As it happened, Marine regulations proscribed shoulder holsters, except for those engaged in special operations, such as tank crewmen and aviators. Naturally, no superior officer was about to challenge Colonel Stecker's right to wear one. Most senior officers, including his regimental commander, had a pretty good idea how he came by it and why he was wearing it. And this wasn't Quantico, anyway, this was Guadalcanal, and what difference did it make?

As for the Garand, no one, of course, was going to question the right of a battalion commander to arm himself with any weapon that struck his fancy. And this would have been true even for those battalion commanders who did not win the Medal of Honor in France in World War I.

But there is a tendency in the military, just as in civilian life, to emulate those we hold in high regard. Imitation is indeed the most sincere form of flattery. Colonel Stecker not only enjoyed a reputation as one hell of a Marine, but he very much looked the part: He was personally imposing—tall, erect, and muscular.

If Colonel Stecker felt that the way to go about armed was with a Garand and a .45 in a shoulder holster, then a large number of majors, captains, lieutenants, sergeants major, and gunnery sergeants (those, in other words, who believed with some reason they could get away with it) clearly felt that this was a practice to be emulated.

Though extra shoulder holsters were not available to the Division's tankers (much to their regret), the Cactus Air Force did in fact have access to a goodly supply of them. And for the proper price, they were in a position to meet the perceived demand. A barter commerce was already well established between Henderson Field and Espíritu Santo (and other rear-area bases). Japanese flags (many, to be honest, of local manufacture) and other artifacts were sent to the rear via R4D or other supply aircraft, while various items (many of which had a tendency to gurgle) were sent forward in payment thereof. It was not at all difficult to add shoulder holsters to the list of rear-area goods that could be exchanged for souvenirs of the battlefield.

In exchange for a bona fide (as opposed to locally manufactured) Japanese flag or other genuine artifact of war, the Marines of the Air Group would provide shoulder holsters to their comrades-in-arms of the First Marine Division.

Until the Army came to Guadalcanal, laying one's hands on a Garand posed a much greater problem. But the Army came equipped with Garands.

Mysteriously, almost immediately upon the Army's arrival, these weapons seemed to vanish from the possession of the men they'd been issued to. And after the Army became engaged in military actions, virtually no Garands were recovered from the various scenes of battle and returned to Army control.

By then, of course, the value of the Garand was apparent to all hands: Among other demonstrable advantages, for instance, it fired eight shots as fast as you could pull the trigger. On the other hand, a Springfield held only five rounds, and you had to work the bolt mechanism to fire one. Thus, when he happened to notice a Garand in the hands of one of his riflemen, it is perhaps not surprising that even the saltiest second lieutenant (the kind of officer who devoutly believed in the sacredness of regulations) did not point an accusing finger, shout "that weapon is stolen!", and take steps to return it to its proper owner.

The more senior officers, meanwhile, seemed to be so overwhelmed by the press of their duties that they were unable to devote time to investigating reports of theft of small arms from the U.S. Army. This understandable negligence did, however, lead to occasional differences of opinion between the Army and the Marines. Indeed, when one Marine colonel informed an Army captain that Marines never lost their rifles and that the Marine Corps could not be held responsible for the Army's lax training in that area, the Army captain was seen to leave the regimental headquarters in a highly aroused state of indignation.

"The General will see you now, Colonel," Major General Archer A. Vandergrift's sergeant major said to Colonel Stecker.

Lieutenant Colonel Stecker nodded his thanks to the sergeant major for holding open for him the piece of canvas that was General Vandergrift's office door and stepped inside.

"Good morning, Sir."

"Good morning," Vandergrift said.

Vandergrift was not alone in his office. There was another colonel there; he stood up when he saw Stecker and smiled.

His was a familiar face to Stecker, but he was a newcomer to Guadalcanal. That was evident by his brand-new utilities and boondockers, and by the unmarred paint on his steel helmet. And because he was wearing a spotless set of web gear, complete to suspenders.

"You two know each other, don't you?" Vandergrift asked, but it was more of a statement than a question.

"Yes, Sir," they said, almost in unison.

"I worked for the Colonel at Quantico," Jack Stecker said. "When he was in Marine Corps Schools."

"That seems like a long time ago, doesn't it, Jack?" Lieutenant Colonel G. H. Newberry said.

"Yes, Sir," Stecker said.

"Newberry will be taking over your battalion, Colonel," General Vandergrift said.

There was a just-perceptible hesitation before Stecker replied, "Aye, aye, Sir."

Well, what the hell did I expect? I never expected to command a battalion in the first place. Battalions go to career officers, not people who have an "R" for reserve after USMC in their signature block.

"From what I've been hearing, Jack," Colonel Newberry said, "you've done a hell of a job with it."

You didn't have to say that. Why am I surprised that you're a gentleman, trying to make this easier for me? I always thought you were a pretty good officer. As a matter of fact, the only thing I don't like about you is that you're taking my battalion away from me.

"I've had some pretty fine Marines to work with, Colonel."

"My experience is that Marines reflect their officers," General Vandergrift said. "Good or bad."

That was nice of him, too.

"I want you to turn it over to Newberry as soon as possible, Colonel," Vandergrift said.

"Aye, aye, Sir. I'd like a day or two, Sir, if that's possible."

Vandergrift looked at his wristwatch. "Would you settle for thirty hours? There's a PBY scheduled to leave Henderson at seventeen hundred tomorrow. I want you on it."

"Aye, aye, Sir," Stecker said. "We ought to be able to do it in that time."

"Newberry," Vandergrift said, "I'd like a word with Colonel Stecker, if you don't mind."

"Aye, aye, Sir. By your leave, Sir," Newberry said, and then added, "I'll wait for you outside, Jack."

"All right," Stecker said.

Newberry left. Vandergrift waved Stecker into a folding chair.

"OK, Jack," he said. "What is it that you know about Newberry that I don't? He came highly recommended."

"Sir, to the best of my knowledge, Colonel Newberry is a fine officer. I'd be very surprised if he didn't do a fine job with Second of the Fifth."

"You looked pretty damned unhappy a minute ago," Vandergrift said. "All that was was having to give up your battalion?"

"Yes, Sir."

"The Corps doesn't give people battalions until they die or retire, Jack. At least, not anymore. You ought to know that."

"Yes, Sir."

"Or had you hoped to turn it over to your exec? What's his name?"

"Young, Sir," Stecker replied automatically, and then went on without thinking. "No, Sir, Young's not ready for a battalion yet. He just made major."

"Good company commanders do not necessarily make good battalion commanders, is that what you're saying?"

"You need experience, Sir, seeing how a battalion is run. Give Young a couple more months . . ." He stopped. "General, I don't know what made me start crying in my soup. I apologize, Sir."

"You looked just like that, Jack, like you were going to cry in your soup."

"I'm sorry, Sir. By your leave?"

"I'll tell you when, Colonel. Please keep your seat."

"Aye, aye, Sir."

"I'll tell you why you're crying in your soup, Jack. You're worn out, that's why."

"I'm fine, Sir. Is that why I was relieved?"

"There's two kinds of relief, Colonel. You are not being relieved because you weren't doing the job, or even because you're tired . . . but, frankly, being tired entered into it. You have been relieved because Newberry—through no fault of his own—has never heard a shot fired in anger, and it's time he was given the opportunity. And because The Corps has other places where you can be useful. By taking you out of there now, The Corps is going to wind up with two qualified battalion commanders, Newberry and Young. They will teach each other; Young will show Newberry how to function under fire, and Newberry will show Young how to run a battalion . . . what is expected of him as a field-grade officer."

"Yes, Sir."

"We're going to need a lot of battalion commanders. The last thing I heard, there may be as many as six Marine divisions."

"Six, Sir?" Stecker was surprised. Even in World War I, there had only been one Marine division.

"I wouldn't be surprised if it went higher than six. We're going to have to have that many battalion commanders. That means we're going to have to train them."

"Yes, Sir. Is that what I'll be doing?"

"I'd bet on it, before we're through. But that's not what's on the agenda for you right now. You probably won't like this, but you're the best man I can think of for the job."

"As the captain said to the second lieutenant when he appointed him VD control officer."

Vandergrift looked at Stecker in surprise and with a hint of annoyance. But then he chuckled.

"At least you don't look as if you're going to weep all over the place anymore," he said, "and now that I think about it, this will almost certainly involve protecting our people from social diseases."

"Sir?"

"We're winding down here, Jack, and probably just in time. The Division is exhausted. Malaria is just about out of control. We haven't been able to feed them properly, and we have demanded physical exertion from them unlike anything I've ever seen before."

"Yes, Sir," Stecker agreed.

"The Army's sending more troops here. I think we can probably call the island secure before they take over, but maybe not. In any event, the Division is going to have to be refitted and brought back to something resembling health. That means Australia and New Zealand. I'm sending you there as the advance party . . . we're not calling it that, yet, but that's what it is."

"Aye, aye, Sir."

"I don't have to tell you what's needed. Just get it ready."

"Aye, aye, Sir."

"Fleming Pickering is there," Vandergrift said. "I never asked you how you felt about him being a general officer. You were his sergeant in France, weren't you?"

"No, Sir. We were there at the same time, but he was never one of my corporals."

"And you worked for him here, when he was filling in for Colonel Goetke, didn't you?"

"General, I happen to feel that General Pickering is a fine general officer. But I couldn't say a word against him if I didn't. He really took care of Elly when our boy was injured. He got her to Hawaii, and then found an apartment for her."

"Then I guess that makes it you and me against the rest of The Corps, doesn't it, Jack?"

"I wondered about that, Sir. How the . . . how senior officers feel about him."

"I've heard the word 'brass' before, Jack. And the answer is that most of the brass who haven't worked with him think he's the worst thing to hit The Marine Corps since . . ." Vandergrift stopped, and then, smiling, finished, ". . . since the Garand rifle."

Stecker chuckled. "Well, I guess they're going to be proved wrong on both counts, then, aren't they, Sir?"

"There is one occasion when I am not very opposed to influence, Jack, and that is when it's for the good of The Corps, or, more specifically, for the good of the First Division. Pickering has a lot of influence. I want you to keep that in mind when somebody in Australia tells you you can't have something the First Marine Division should have on hand when it gets there. It doesn't seem to be much of a secret that he has MacArthur's ear."

"Is that why I'm being sent there, Sir, because of my relationship with General Pickering?"

"You're being sent there, as I said a moment ago, because you're the best man for the job. Pickering is . . . the olive in the martini."

"Yes, Sir."

"You will proceed via Espíritu Santo to Pearl Harbor, thence to Brisbane. I don't see any reason why you can't have a week, or longer, on leave in Hawaii when you're there."

"Thank you, Sir."

"Give my regards to Elly, please, Jack, and offer my congratulations to your son."

"Sir?"

"By now they've given him the DFC. It now comes just about automatically with being an ace."

"Thank you, Sir."

"Now go turn over to Newberry, Colonel, and pack your gear. You are dismissed."

"Aye, aye, Sir."

(TWO)
Office of the Assistant Chief of Staff, Intelligence
Supreme Headquarters
South West Pacific Ocean Area
Brisbane, Australia
1615 Hours 2 November 1942

"Pull up a chair, Pickering, I'll be with you in a minute," Brigadier General Charles A. Willoughby, MacArthur's intelligence officer, said to Brigadier General Fleming Pickering, USMCR.

Why am I offended when this sonofabitch calls me by my last name?

Pickering walked over to General Willoughby's office window and looked out, although this meant searching for and operating the cords that controlled the drapes.

A minute or so later, General Willoughby raised his eyes from his desk and found Pickering at the window.

"So, Pickering, what's on your mind?"

"General, thank you for seeing me."

Willoughby made a deprecating gesture.

"I want to talk about guerrillas in the Philippines," Pickering said.

Willoughby shrugged.

"Sure," he said, "but there's not much to talk about."

Willoughby always spoke with a faintly German accent, but now, for some reason, his accent was more than usually apparent. Pickering's mind went off at a tangent: *Willoughby sounds like an English name, not a German one. Where did he get that accent?*

"Let's talk about this General Fertig," Pickering said.

"He's not a general. He's a captain. A reserve captain. Technically, I suppose, he's guilty of impersonating an officer."

Well, I know how that feels. Every time I check my uniform in the mirror and see the stars, I feel like I'm impersonating an officer.

"What did he do before the war?"

"He was a mining engineer, I think. Or a civil engineer. Some kind of an engineer."

Pickering had a sudden suspicion, and jumped on it.

"You knew him, didn't you, General?"

"Yes. I met him at parties, that sort of thing."

Now, that's interesting. The question now becomes what kind of parties. Patricia and I met El Supremo half a dozen times at parties in Manila. But they were business parties Pacific & Far East Shipping gave. El Supremo and his wife were invited there under the general category, Military/Diplomatic. I don't recall that you were ever invited to one of those, Willoughby. Colonels didn't make that list.

Come to think of it, did I ever meet this guy? I don't think so. I would have remembered that name. Wendell Fertig isn't John Jones. And "Fertig" in German means "finished." I would have remembered that, I think.

"What kind of parties?"

"At the Polo Club, for one."

I belonged to the Polo Club. But only for business reasons—and for Patricia. She liked to have lunch out there. I arranged guest cards for our masters and chief engineers when they were in port. The only time I can remember going out there myself was when Pick was in boarding school—he couldn't have been older than fourteen. During summer vacation he came out on the Pacific Venturer—*worked his way out as a messboy. While she was in port, I took him out there so he could play.*

He had a sudden clear memory of Pick at fourteen—a skinny, ungainly kid wearing borrowed boots and breeches that were much too large for him, sweat-soaked, galloping down that long grass field. He was unseated when his pony shied; he skidded twenty yards on his back, while Patricia moaned, so slowly, "Ohhhhh myyyyy Lordddddd!!!!"

"This man Fertig belonged the Polo Club?"

"I suppose he did. I saw him out there a good deal. And he played, of course."

OK. We have now established that General/Captain Fertig was a member of Manila social hierarchy. Polo Club membership wasn't cheap, and there was a certain snobbish ambience to it. You didn't just apply for membership; you had to be invited to apply. And then the membership committee had to approve you. They were notorious for keeping the riffraff out.

"How did he come by his commission?" Pickering asked.

"He was directly commissioned just before the war, in October or November 1941. The General saw the war coming . . ."

Why am I tempted to interrupt and ask, "Which general would that be, General?"

". . . and we set up a program to directly commission civilians with useful skills. Fertig came in as a first lieutenant, Corps of Engineers, Reserve, as I recall."

Yeah, you knew him, all right. And now he wasn't one of the overpaid civilians at the Polo Club, he was a lieutenant who had to call you "Sir."

"What was his skill, engineering?"

"Yes. Demolitions, as I recall. There was another one, a chap named Ralph Fralick. They were both commissioned into the Corps of Engineers as first lieutenants."

"And what did they do when the war started?"

"That category of reserve officers came on active duty 1 December 1941. Their call to active duty was originally scheduled for 1 January 1942. But with the situation so obviously deteriorating, the General moved it up a month."

"What did Fertig and this other fellow . . . Fralick?"

"Fralick," Willoughby confirmed.

". . . do when the Japanese invaded?"

"I don't know specifically, of course . . ."

Someone as important as you was obviously too busy to keep track of a lowly reserve lieutenant, right?

". . . but I presume demolitions. That's what they were recruited for. The best people to blow a bridge up, of course, are the engineers who built it."

"He apparently did it well enough to get himself promoted," Pickering thought aloud.

"No one is casting aspersions against his competence, Pickering. As an Engineer officer. Without men like Fertig and Fralick blowing bridges and roads—literally in the teeth of the Japanese—Bataan would have fallen sooner than it did, and at a considerably cheaper cost to the enemy."

"And then, presumably, rather than accept capture by the Japanese when Bataan was lost, Fertig somehow got to Mindanao."

"A less generous interpretation would be that Captain Fertig chose to ignore his orders to proceed to the fortress of Corregidor, and elected to go to the island of Mindanao."

"He was ordered to Corregidor?"

"All the specialist officers were ordered to Corregidor. There was work for them there."

"What about the other one? Fralick?"

"He never showed up on Corregidor. I don't know what happened to him. Presumably he's either dead or a POW."

"He's not on Mindanao with Fertig?"

"That's possible, of course, but so far his name has not come up."

"I'm very curious why Fertig is now calling himself 'General Fertig.'"

"God only knows," Willoughby said, audibly exhaling. "If you accept the premise that he knows better, then I just don't know."

"You're suggesting he might not know any better?"

"I'm saying, Pickering, that despite the valor he displayed on Bataan, he may well have been at the end of his string. He was under enormous psychological pressure. He was not a professional military man. He was a civilian in an officer's uniform, upon whose shoulders was suddenly thrust enormous burdens . . ."

I know where you got that, Charley. That's El Supremo talking. That's what I'm hearing right now, El Supremo's evaluation of Fertig. And El Supremo's like the Pope, isn't he? Infallible, when speaking on matters of military faith and Army morality?

". . . that he could not realistically be expected to handle."

"You're suggesting, General, that he's a little off base, mentally speaking?"

"He did not obey his orders to move to Corregidor. The only way he could have gotten from Bataan to Mindanao, as you well know, is by boat. A thirty-, forty-footer. That means he . . . the word is 'stole' . . . that means he stole one—one that he knew was certainly required for our military. Given the fact that he performed his duties well—even admirably—prior to this, one is drawn to the conclusion that he was not then, and is not now, thinking clearly."

"And the proof would be that he is now under the delusion that he is a general?"

"I shouldn't have to tell you, General . . ."

"General"? *Charley, did you really call me* "General"?

". . . that when men, brave men, finally crack under the strains of combat, they often display manifestations of delusion. They think they're home, or still in battle . . . or that they're Napoleon."

"Then the bottom line would seem to be that you don't think Fertig's guerrilla operation is worth much?"

"Think about it," Willoughby said. "There are a number of field-grade officers, professional soldiers, on Bataan, Mindanao, and other islands . . . professional Naval officers, too, and I daresay some professional Marine officers, as well . . . who have so far escaped capture by the Japanese. Don't you think it's odd we haven't heard from any of them? From any one of them?"

"Yes," Pickering said. "It is odd."

"They would have the military training and experience to set up guerrilla operations, not to mention the contacts among the Filipino Scouts, et cetera, et cetera. Don't you think they would have acted along those lines if there was any possibility, any possibility at all, to do so?"

"I can see your point," Pickering said.

"God knows I admire this man Fertig," Willoughby said. "But right now, I just feel sorry for him. I hope he manages to stay out of Japanese hands."

"General, I won't take any more of your time."

"Nonsense, Pickering. My door is always open to you, you know that."

(THREE)
Cryptographic Center
Supreme Headquarters
South West Pacific Ocean Area
Brisbane, Australia
1725 Hours 2 November 1942

As he turned to bolt the steel door behind him, Brigadier General Fleming Pickering offered a greeting to Major Hong Son Do, Signal Corps, Army of the United States. "Still here, Pluto?" he asked.

"Sir?" Pluto asked, surprised at the question.

"It's almost five-thirty. I thought you'd almost certainly be over at the Field Grade Officer's Mess with the other brass hats, sucking on a martini and figuring out clever ways to annoy the lieutenants."

"I feel like a whore in church in there," Pluto said. "I've been doing my eating and drinking with Moore and Hart in the Navy's Junior Officer's Mess."

Pickering laughed. "Anything interesting come in?"

"Koffler doesn't have the clap, or tuberculosis, or syphilis."

"Well, I'm glad to hear that. Is there some reason you felt that you had to tell me?"

"You can't have any of the three and get married here. Everything is fixed. They're getting married next week."

"You didn't mention our other two lovesick warriors."

"They're not getting married. Barbara Cotter was smart enough to ask some discreet questions. The minute they get married, the nurses would get shipped home.''

''You're kidding! This doesn't affect Koffler and the Farnsworth girl?''

''Daphne Farnsworth is what SWPOA insists on calling 'an indigenous female.' Indigenous females don't count. And anyway, she's an Australian, she's already home.''

''Anything I can do?''

''I don't think so, Boss. And when I asked Howard if I should come to you, he said he didn't want special treatment.''

''Maybe there's a reason for it.''

''Well, anyway, when you see two nurses weeping loudly at Koffler's wedding, you'll know why. Aside from that, nothing special. I think the Japanese are licking their wounds. Is there something I can do for you, General?''

''Let me at the typewriter,'' Pickering said. ''It's time for me to tell Washington how to run the war . . . yet again.''

Pluto stood up.

''And afterward, you and I will go have a drink, or three, at the Navy Mess. I need one.''

EYES ONLY - THE SECRETARY OF THE NAVY
DUPLICATION FORBIDDEN
ORIGINAL TO BE DESTROYED AFTER ENCRYPTION AND TRANSMITTAL
TO SECNAV

Brisbane, Australia
Monday 2 November 1942

Dear Frank:

I think I have gotten to the bottom of why El Supremo shows no interest at all in this fellow Fertig in the Philippines. I'm not going to waste your time telling you about it, but it's nonsense. Admiral Leahy is right, there is potential there, and I think Rickabee's people should be involved from the start.

If he encounters trouble doing what I think he has to do, I'm going to tell Rickabee to come to you. I suspect he will encounter the same kind of parochial nonsense among the professional warriors in Washington that I have encountered here.

I have been butting my head—vis-à-vis Donovan's people—against the Palace wall so often and so long that it's bloody; and I'm getting nowhere. Is there any chance I can stop? It would take a direct order from Roosevelt to make him change his mind. And then he and his people will drag their feet, at which, you may have noticed, they're very good.

More soon.

Best regards,

Fleming Pickering, Brigadier General, USMCR

TOP SECRET

EYES ONLY - CAPTAIN DAVID HAUGHTON, USN
OFFICE OF THE SECRETARY OF THE NAVY
DUPLICATION FORBIDDEN
ORIGINAL TO BE DESTROYED AFTER ENCRYPTION AND TRANSMITTAL
TO SECNAV
FOR COLONEL F. L. RICKABEE
OFFICE OF MANAGEMENT ANALYSIS

Brisbane, Australia
Monday 2 November 1942

Dear Fritz:

Don't tell him yet, or even Banning, but I want you to try to find a suitable replacement for McCoy for the Mongolian Operation.

And put him and Banning to work finding out about Guerrilla operations. I believe that this Wendell Fertig in the Philippines is probably going to turn out to be more useful than anybody in the Palace here is willing to even consider. I suspect that the same attitude vis-à-vis unconventional warriors and the competence of reserve officers is prevalent in Washington.

This idea has Leahy's backing, so if you encounter any trouble, feel free to go to Frank Knox.

If you can do it without making any waves, please (a) see if you can find out where my son is being assigned after the war bond tour and (b) tell me if telling his mother would really endanger the entire war effort. She went to see Jack NMI Stecker's boy at the hospital in Pearl and is in pretty bad shape.

Koffler is getting married next week, for a little good news. I decided I had the authority to make him a staff sergeant and have done so.

Regards,

Fleming Pickering, Brigadier General, USMCR

TOP SECRET

(FOUR)
Live Oaks Plantation
Baldwin County, Alabama
0700 Hours 2 November 1942

First Lieutenants William C. Dunn and Malcolm S. Pickering were waiting on the porch when the Marine-green Plymouth drove up. They were freshly showered and shaved, their uniforms bore a perfect press, and their shoes were brilliantly shined. The glasses of orange juice in their hands contained no intoxicants.

A 1940 Buick Limited sedan, newly polished, sat in the driveway, with its twin spare tires installed in their own gleaming shrouds in the front fenders.

"He's got somebody with him," Lieutenant Pickering observed.

"I hope he forgets the fucking hats," Lieutenant Dunn replied.

He was to be disappointed. The individual in the passenger seat leapt out the moment the Plymouth stopped moving and opened the rear door for Captain Carstairs. He emerged holding a Cap, Brimmed, Officers, in each hand.

"I would rather face a thousand deaths," Bill Dunn said, getting to his feet and placing his glass on the wide top of the railing.

"You'd rather what?"

"That is what General Lee said when he went to meet Grant at Appomattox Court House. 'I would rather face a thousand deaths, but now I must go . . .'"

"The way I heard it, what he said was, 'Win a few, lose a few, it all evens up in the end.'"

"Blasphemy, Pickering, blasphemy!" Dunn said, and then called, "Captain Carstairs. Good morning, Sir."

"Good morning, gentlemen," Carstairs said. "How nice to see you looking so bright-eyed and bushy-tailed. I have your covers." He looked inside the cap in his right hand. "Who is the five and seven-eighths?"

"That would be the pinhead here, Sir," Pick said, and then smiled at the driver. "Hey, Corporal. How are you?"

"Gentlemen," Carstairs said, "this is Mr. Larsen. Mr. Larsen is about to be graduated as a Naval Aviator and commissioned in The Corps."

Pickering looked at him closely for the first time. He was wearing impeccably pressed enlisted men's greens. You could literally see a reflection in his shoes. And though there was no evidence whatever that Mr. Larsen had a beard, Pick knew this was because Mr. Larsen had shaved with great care earlier this morning— maybe two or three times. And he was built like a tank . . . reminding Pick of Technical Sergeant—now Master Gunner, he remembered—Big Steve Oblensky.

"How do you do, Mr. Larsen?" Lieutenant Dunn said, and offered his hand.

I forgot about that polish and shaving crap. Billy went through P'Cola as a cadet; he knows about that chickenshit bullshit because he had to put up with it himself. Dick Stecker and I had our commissions when we showed up. And that, I recall, really pissed off Captain Mustache.

And now that I think about it, was that because Dick and I were living in the San Carlos Hotel and didn't have to put up with his chickenshit? Or maybe because we were living in the San Carlos and so I got to meet Martha? And because I didn't have to spend my evenings shining my shoes and the toilet seats in the barracks, I could chase after her?

"Sir, I am fine, Sir," Mr. Larsen said. "Sir, I consider this a great honor to meet you, Sir."

"Marine officers," Pick heard himself saying, "do not gush like women. Try to control yourself, Mr. Larsen."

"Sir, yes, Sir. Sir, no excuse, Sir," Mr. Larsen said.

Captain Carstairs and Lieutenant Dunn gave Lieutenant Pickering dirty looks.

Well, fuck you both! I went through my fair share of the pop-to-attention, shine-the-heels-of-your-shoes chickenshit bullshit at Quantico myself, and nothing that's happened to me since has made me change my mind. It was unnecessary bullshit then, and it is now.

"Here is your cover, Mr. Pickering," Carstairs said.

"Thank you, Sir," Pick said, and took the cover and put it on.

"Mr. Larsen, are you aware of the history of the corded ropes on the upper portion of covers such as these?" Pick asked.

"Sir, they identify commissioned officers of The Corps, Sir."

"I heard a most interesting variation of that, Mr. Larsen . . ."

Carstairs is glowering at me. Fuck him!

". . . from a Marine officer . . . a career Marine officer . . . who already wears two Purple Hearts for wounds suffered in this war; he was an officer in the Marine Raiders during the raid on Makin Island; and most recently he was involved in a Top Secret operation rescuing two Marines who were trapped on an enemy-held island. Would you be interested in hearing what this distinguished officer of the Regular Marine Corps told me about the knotted ropes on commissioned officers' caps, Mr. Larsen?"

"Sir, yes, Sir, I would, Sir."

"May I proceed, Sir? Is Mr. Larsen close enough to joining our officer corps that he may be entrusted with this hoary lore?"

"Go ahead, Mr. Pickering," Carstairs said.

"Killer McCoy told me, Mr. Larsen, that the ropes date back to the days when Marines served aboard sailing ships. The first ropes, according to McCoy, were sewn onto officers' covers so that Marine marksmen aloft in the rigging could safely shoot chickenshit officers in the head, and not some good Marine by mistake."

Lieutenant Dunn laughed. Mr. Larsen looked very uncomfortable. After a valiant effort not to, Captain Carstairs smiled.

"Oh, God, Pickering!" he said. "I should have expected something like that from you."

"Did Captain Carstairs tell you that I taught him to fly, Mr. Larsen?"

"Sir, no, Sir. He did not, Sir."

"Just to keep the record straight, Mr. Larsen, I taught him how to fly," Carstairs said, not quite succeeding in keeping himself from laughing.

"Whatever you say, Sir," Pickering said.

"Mr. Dunn," Carstairs said, "Mr. Larsen has informed me that he would consider it a privilege if you were to permit him to drive your personal automobile to Corey Field. I told him I felt sure you would grant him that privilege."

Well, that explains what the kid is doing here; Carstairs wants us in the staff car with him.

"Sure," Dunn said, and then had a second thought. "Can you drive an automatic shift? That's my mother's car, all the new gadgets."

Larsen's face fell.

"Sir, no, Sir, I never drove a car with an automatic shift, Sir."

"Show him how, Dunn," Carstairs ordered.

"You just put it in 'R' for 'Race' and step on the gas," Pick offered helpfully.

"God, you must really want to be a basic flight instructor, Mr. Pickering," Carstairs said.

"I'd forgotten about that," Pick said. "I am now on my very best behavior."

"You'd better be, when we get over there," Carstairs said.

"OK," Pick said.

"I had dinner with Martha last night. She was disgustingly pleased to hear that you were safely home. I think she expects you to call her. Have you?"

"No. I told you. She's made herself pretty clear about how she feels about me. I don't see any point in calling her."

"Suit yourself, Pick," Carstairs said.

Dunn came back.

"He can handle the car all right," he said. "When it works, any idiot can do it."

"When it works?"

"It broke when my mother was driving over the causeway to Mobile; just refused to move another inch. It's supposed to have been fixed."

"Well, he'll be following us," Carstairs said. "It shouldn't be a problem. You ride in the front, Pickering. Dunn and I will ride in the back."

"Aye, aye, Sir."

(FIVE)
Corey Field
Escambia County, Florida
0820 Hours 2 November 1942

Because he had a good view from the front seat of the car, Pickering saw the four Grumman F4F4 Wildcats almost from the moment the Plymouth passed inside the gate.

And he instantly understood what they were doing there. They were props in a bullshit session. He had gone through much the same thing himself, once upon a time. Aviation cadets (or in his and Dick Stecker's case, student officers) were gathered someplace shortly after reporting aboard, and a couple of fighters or dive-bombers were flown in from someplace and put on display: *This is what you will be privileged to fly if you work ever so hard and shine your shoes properly and don't kill yourself in a Yellow Peril learning how.*

He was surprised that the Plymouth headed in the direction of the Wildcats. Two of them were parked nose to nose, in front of bleachers . . . as though they were on a stage, or were part of a classroom display. The other two were parked to one side, on the grass between the ramp and a runway. As they drove closer, he saw that the bleachers were full of Naval Aviation cadets. Some of these were in flight suits, and some were in their sailor suits. There were only a few Marines.

Of course there's only a few Marines, stupid! We're always outnumbered at least ten to one by the goddamned Navy. I wonder what the hell is going on here. There's an admiral's flag, and a staff car to go with it, and I'll be damned, a little tent. I'll bet they put up the tent so the Admiral can take a piss without having to walk a hundred yards. It must be a graduation ceremony or something.

The Plymouth headed right for the other staff car and pulled up beside it.

What the hell is this?

"Out, gentlemen," Carstairs ordered from the rear seat.

The door of the Plymouth beside them was opened by a white hat. An admiral stepped out, and then Colonel Porter got out the other side.

Captain Carstairs saluted.

"Good morning, Admiral," he said. "May I present, Sir, Lieutenant William C. Dunn and Lieutenant Malcolm S. Pickering?"

"Lieutenant Dunn, I consider it an honor to make your acquaintance," Rear Admiral Richard B. Sayre, USN, said, offering his hand. Then he turned to Lieutenant Pickering and put his arm around his shoulder as he shook his hand.

"Welcome home, Pick," Martha Sayre Culhane's father said, "I can't tell you how glad I am to see you."

"Thank you, Sir," Pick said.

Dunn and Colonel Porter looked at them with wide eyes.

"How have you set this up, Porter?" Admiral Sayre asked.

"Captain Carstairs will go out there whenever you're ready, Admiral. Attention on deck will be called. Captain Carstairs will then introduce you. We will then proceed to the microphone, with Dunn following you, and Pickering following Dunn. The three of us will take our seats."

"Where's the band? Why isn't the band here?"

"They had a commitment elsewhere, Sir, I'm afraid," Colonel Porter replied.

"Well, it's too late to do anything about it now," Admiral Sayre said somewhat petulantly. "But the band should have been here."

"Sorry, Sir," Colonel Porter said.

"OK. Let's get rolling," Admiral Sayre ordered.

As Captain Carstairs marched out to a lectern set up on a small stage, the others formed in line behind Admiral Sayre. Colonel Porter was next, and he was followed by Dunn, Pickering, and Admiral Sayre's aide-de-camp, a Lieutenant J. G., who was carrying a manila envelope.

Carstairs reached the microphone.

"Attention on deck!" he ordered, his voice amplified over a loudspeaker system. Everybody in the bleachers came to attention . . . including, Pick noticed, four guys in flight suits sitting at the end of the bleachers in the front row.

The guys who flew the Wildcats in, he decided. *They are almost certainly as deeply impressed with this bullshit as I am.*

"Gentlemen," Carstairs' amplified voice announced, "Rear Admiral Richard B. Sayre, U.S. Navy."

Admiral Sayre immediately started to march to the platform. The others followed. Pick became aware that Dunn, ahead of him, was going through the little shuffle known as "getting in step." He realized that he was doing the same thing.

A Pavlovian reflex, he thought. *It's like riding a bicycle. Once you learn how, it is indelibly engraved on your brain. When the occasion arises you do it, just like one of Pavlov's goddamned dogs.*

Admiral Sayre marched toward the lectern. Colonel Porter then led the others toward a row of folding chairs while Sayre's aide marched up and stood behind Admiral Sayre. A moment later, Sayre glanced over his shoulder to see that everyone was where they were supposed to be.

"Good morning, gentlemen," Admiral Sayre said to the microphone.

Three hundred male voices responded, "Good morning, Sir!"

"Take your seats, please," Admiral Sayre ordered.

Cooling metal in the engine of the Wildcat behind Pick creaked. Without thinking about it, he looked over his shoulder. The first thing he thought was, *Jesus, it's brand new. Or at least it's been superbly maintained. They even polished the sonofabitch.*

Then he noticed that someone had painted miniature Japanese flags—a red circle on a white background—below the canopy. There were six of them: a row of five, and then a sixth meatball under the first meatball in the top row.

Now, what's that bullshit supposed to mean? We didn't paint meatballs on our airplanes. Nobody had his own airplane. We flew anything Big Steve could fix up well enough to get it in the air. Who is this asshole, flying a polished airplane around the States with meatballs painted on it?

Then he saw the neat lettering above the meatballs: 1/LT M. S. PICKERING, USMCR.

He switched his eyes to the other Wildcat, which was parked with its nose next to this one. There were two rows of meatballs painted on the fuselage below the canopy, ten in all, and 1/LT W. C. DUNN, USMCR was neatly lettered above them.

Jesus H. Christ!

"Gentlemen," Admiral Sayre began his little talk, "I'm going to tell you something about our brothers in The Marine Corps. If you have not yet learned this, you should keep it in mind during your Naval service. When they get their hands on something valuable, they very rarely offer to share it with their brothers in the Navy.''

There was the expected laughter.

''In this case, when I learned that Colonel Porter had his hands on something valuable, I decided to invite the Navy to his party, in case doing so himself might slip his mind.''

There was more expected laughter.

Pick glanced at the bleachers and noticed a Navy cadet staring at him as if he gave milk. He quickly turned his gaze at another Navy cadet. He, too, was staring at him. He then dropped his eyes to the stage.

''Another hint, if you will permit me, that will certainly prove valuable to you in your later careers: If you have to teach somebody something, and you want it to stick in the minds of your students, you go seek out the most qualified expert you can find and have him teach what he knows. Colonel Porter is familiar with this principle of instruction and has brought two such experts with him here today.''

He held his hand out to his aide, who put two sheets of paper in it. Admiral Sayre held them down on the lectern and began to read:

''Navy Department, Washington, D. C. 24 October 1942. Award of the Distinguished Flying Cross. By Direction of the President of the United States, the Distinguished Flying Cross is awarded to First Lieutenant Malcolm S. Pickering, USMCR. Citation: During the period 14 August–16 October 1942, while assigned to VMF-229, then engaged in combat against the enemy in the vicinity of Guadalcanal, Solomon Islands, Lieutenant Pickering demonstrated both extraordinary professional skill and great personal valor. Almost daily engaging in aerial combat against the enemy, who almost invariably outnumbered Lieutenant Pickering and his fellow pilots by a factor of at least five to one, flying aircraft so ravaged by battle that only the exigencies of the situation permitted their use, Lieutenant Pickering's professional skill and complete disregard of his personal safety contributed materially to the successful defense of the Guadalcanal perimeter. During this period he downed four Japanese Zero aircraft, one Japanese Kate aircraft, and one Japanese Betty aircraft. Entered the Naval Service from California.''

Before the Admiral began reading, there was rustling and whispered conversation in the bleachers. Now there was absolute silence.

Admiral Sayre then began to read from the second sheet of paper:

''Navy Department, Washington, D. C. 24 October 1942. Award of the Navy Cross. By Direction of the President of the United States, the Navy Cross is awarded to First Lieutenant William Charles Dunn, USMCR. Citation: On 4 June 1942, while serving with VMF-221 during the Battle of Midway, Lieutenant Dunn, facing an enemy force which outnumbered his and his comrades' by a factor of at least ten to one, with complete disregard for his personal safety, during a battle which saw the loss of ninety percent of his squadron, downed two Japanese Zero and one Japanese Kate aircraft. Lieutenant Dunn relentlessly attacked and downed the second Japanese Zero aircraft despite serious and painful wounds from Japanese 20mm cannon fire, which destroyed his aircraft canopy and many of his aircraft instruments and left him partially blinded and in great pain. He then successfully flew his severely damaged aircraft to Midway Island and effected a wheels-up landing.

''During the period 14 August–16 October 1942, while serving as Executive Officer, VMF-229, then engaged in combat against the enemy in the vicinity of Guadalcanal, Solomon Islands, Lieutenant Dunn demonstrated both extraordinary professional skill and great personal valor, which combined with his leadership skills to inspire his subordinates. Almost daily leading his men into aerial combat against the enemy, who almost invariably outnumbered the pilots of VMF-229 by a factor of at least five to one, Lieutenant Dunn's professional skill, complete disregard of his own personal safety, and magnificent leadership skills were an inspiration to his men and contributed materially to the successful defense of the Guadalcanal perimeter. During this period he frequently assumed command of his squadron in the absence of the squadron commander, and downed three Japanese Zero aircraft, two Japanese Kate aircraft, and two Japanese Betty aircraft. Lieutenant Dunn's valor in action, above and beyond the call of duty, his superb leadership, and his superior professional skills reflect great credit upon himself, the United States Marine Corps, and the Naval Service. Entered the Naval Service from Alabama.''

At the word ''Alabama'' there came sort of an Indian war cry from the bleachers.

''Gentlemen,'' Admiral Sayre went on, electing to ignore the Indian war cry, ''I think you will agree with me when I say that Colonel Porter has brought here today two masters of the two crafts you are attempting to learn, piloting airplanes and serving as officers of the Naval Service. Lieutenant Dunn has a few words he would like to say, and then we are going to see a demonstration of their flying skills. Lieutenant Dunn, would you please come up here?''

Bill Dunn, who was visibly uncomfortable and clearly would have preferred to be anywhere but where he found himself, walked to the lectern.

Well, I'm sorry about that, Billy Boy. But better thee than me. And they don't want to hear from me. All I have is the lousy DFC. This'll teach you to be a fucking Navy Cross hero!

As Dunn stepped before the microphone, he was racked by a coughing fit. This lasted a good thirty seconds. When he finally spoke, his voice was faint, harsh, and strained.

''Gentlemen,'' he said. ''It's good to be back at P'Cola. And I want to say that I know the only reason I am back is because of my instructor pilots when I went through here. As you can hear, I'm in no shape to talk much. But Lieutenant Pickering would, I am sure, be happy to say a few words and answer whatever questions you might have. I don't mind saying that he is the finest pilot I have seen, except for Captain Charles M. Galloway, our squadron commander. Would you come up here, please, Mr. Pickering?''

XIV

It turned out that First Lieutenant Malcolm S. Pickering, USMCR, was wrong about the tent to the side of the bleachers: It wasn't there to provide the Admiral with a convenient place to void his bladder. Instead, in keeping with the general theatricality of the whole affair, it was a dressing room for the actors involved in the melodrama being presented for the fledgling birdmen. When he went inside, he saw that it contained three chairs, a pipe-iron rack from which hung three flight suits, and a full-length mirror.

Two of the Suits, Flying, Winter, were brand new; each of these had a leather patch over the breast, on which was stamped in gold representations of Naval Aviator's wings. Above one of the wings, Pickering's name was sewn, while Dunn's name was sewn above the other. The other suit belonged to Lieutenant Colonel J. Danner Porter, USMC. It was not quite new, but it was spotless and holeless and shipshape.

They were accompanied into the tent by Captain J. J. O'Fallon, USMC. Captain O'Fallon, a heavyset redhead, was the squadron commander of VMF-289, which was based at the Memphis Naval Air Station, Millington, Tennessee. In exchange for flying four of his Wildcats (two of them suitably painted up for the occasion with meatballs and Pickering's and Dunn's names) from Memphis in the early-morning hours, Captain O'Fallon was going to be granted the great privilege of joining Colonel Porter in engaging the two aces in mock aerial combat.

Pick's first thought when he saw the brand-new flight suits was to wonder if there were any more around here, and if so, how he could steal them. His fellow pilots of VMF-229 had been almost pathetically grateful when he returned with the boxes of RAAF flight suits he stole at Port Moresby, New Guinea; theirs were literally in tatters.

But then he realized that VMF-229 was no longer operating out of Henderson Field, and that he was at NAS Pensacola, where there were more than adequate supplies of flight suits and everything else. And after that, he recalled that VMF-229 was no longer his squadron . . . and that for all practical purposes it no longer existed.

Colonel Porter already had the script for the aerial melodrama firmly set in his mind: First he and O'Fallon would fly off somewhere out of sight. And then they'd attack Corey Field (representing Henderson Field) in a strafing maneuver. Dunn and Pickering, on patrol, would defend Corey/Henderson.

Since it would be impossible to actually shoot down Colonel Porter and Captain O'Fallon, they would next climb to 5,000 feet and get in a dogfight. (Pickering realized that he and Dunn would be allowed to win. How would it look to the student pilots if two heroic aces lost?)

In order to make this bit of theater possible, the Wildcats had been equipped with "gun cameras." These were 16mm motion picture cameras mounted in the wings.

When the gun trigger was pulled, the camera operated. Colonel Porter's intention was to have the gun camera film developed immediately so that it could be shown to everybody after lunch.

Between the time they finished playing war and started lunch, Lieutenants Pickering and Dunn would be debriefed on the platform by an intelligence officer. Captain Mustache Carstairs would play that role.

While they changed into the flight suits, the students were permitted to leave the bleachers and examine the Wildcats.

But when it came time for him to examine it up close, Pickering was nearly as impressed with his Wildcat as any of them. As he went through the preflight and then climbed into the cockpit, he could find nothing at all wrong with it. The aircraft was perfect in every respect: There wasn't a trace of dirt anywhere. The Plexiglas of the canopy and windscreen was clear and without cracks. Even the leather on the seat and headrest looked new. And, of course, everything worked the way it was designed to work; and there were no patched bullet holes on the skin of the wings or fuselage.

After a time, the student pilots were ordered away from the aircraft. Then sailors in pressed and starched blue work uniforms appeared with fire extinguishers. Porter and Captain O'Fallon started their engines, warmed them up, and moved to the threshold of the active runway. One after the other they took off and disappeared from sight in the direction of Alabama.

Ten minutes later, Bill Dunn looked over at Pickering and gave the wind-'em-up signal. Pickering followed him to the threshold of the active runway and stopped, to permit Dunn to take off first.

"Do you ever remember taking off one at a time?" Dunn's voice came metallically over the radio. "Come on."

Pick released the brakes and moved onto the runway beside him. Dunn looked over at him, smiled, and gave him a thumbs-up.

"Corey, Cactus rolling," Dunn told the tower, and shoved the throttle to TAKEOFF POWER. Pickering followed suit. They started down the runway together.

Something is wrong! Something's missing! Pick thought, and for a moment he felt fear.

Shit, goddamn it, you goddamn fool! This is a paved *runway. Paved runways don't cause the goddamned gear to complain the way pierced steel planking and large rocks do.*

Life came into the controls. Twenty feet apart, the two Wildcats lifted off the ground.

"Colonel," Dunn's voice came over the radio ten minutes later. "Sir, I'm sorry, I forgot your call sign."

"Cactus Leader," Colonel Porter replied, "this is Red Leader. Over."

"Red Leader," Dunn replied, "this is Cactus Leader. Colonel, I'm out of bullets. Or at least a red light comes on when I pull the trigger."

Pickering laughed and touched his mike button.

"Cactus Leader, this is Cactus Two. I'm out of bullets, too."

"Cactus Leader, Red Leader," Colonel Porter replied. "Break this off, and return to field."

"Roger, Red Leader."

"Cactus Leader, we will go first. Cactus Leader, there will be no, repeat no, unauthorized aerobatic maneuvers at any altitude in the vicinity of Corey Field. Acknowledge."

What the hell does that mean? Oh, Christ, he thinks we were planning on doing a victory barrel roll over the field. Why not? We really whipped their ass. I expected to win, but not that easily.

"Red Leader, say again?"

"Cactus Leader, you will land at Corey and you will not, repeat not, perform any aerobatic maneuvers of any kind. Acknowledge."

"Aye, aye, Sir," Dunn said. "Cactus Leader, out."

Dunn suddenly made a sharp, steep, diving turn to his right. This confused Pickering for a moment. He'd been flying on Dunn's wing since they formed up again after what must have been the third or fourth time they shot Porter and O'Fallon down; and, confused or not, he followed him instinctively. Dunn straightened out heading west. Pickering could see Mobile Bay near the horizon.

Now what, Billy Boy? Are you going to do a barrel roll over Ye Olde Family Manse?

Lieutenant Dunn did precisely that, with Lieutenant Pickering repeating the maneuver on his tail.

Then Dunn did more than confuse Pickering; he astonished him. After putting his Wildcat into a steep turn (permitting him to lower his gear utilizing centrifugal force, rather than having to crank it down), he lined himself up with an auxiliary field and landed.

What the hell is that all about? Did he get a warning light?

"Billy?"

There was no reply.

Pickering overflew the auxiliary field.

It's not in use. Otherwise, there'd be an ambulance and some other ground crew, in case a student pranged his Yellow Peril.

Billy, you just about managed to run out of runway! What the hell is going on?

Pickering picked up a little altitude and flew around the field. Then he put his Wildcat in a steep turn in order to release his gear in the usual (but specifically proscribed) manner. And then he made an approach and landing that he considered to be much safer than the one executed by Lieutenant Dunn.

Christ, you're not supposed to put a Wildcat down on one of these auxiliary fields at all!

He stood on the brakes and pulled up beside Dunn's Wildcat. The engine was still running. Dunn was a hundred yards away, walking toward an enormous live oak tree.

Pickering unstrapped himself, climbed out of the cockpit, and trotted after Dunn. He had to wait to speak to him, however; for as he caught up with him, Dunn was having a hell of a time trying to close the zipper of his new flight suit after having urinated on the live oak.

"You want to tell me what you're doing?"

"Officially, I had a hydraulic system failure warning light and made a precautionary landing. When you were unable to contact me by radio, you very courageously landed your aircraft to see what assistance you might be able to render. All in keeping with the honorable traditions of The Marine Corps. *Semper Fi.*"

"What the hell is this?"

"Actually, I am planning for the future," Bill Dunn said, very seriously. "Fifty years from now . . . what'll that be, 1992? . . . Colonel William C. Dunn—anybody who has ever worn a uniform in the Deep South gets to call himself 'Colonel,' you know . . ."

"Billy . . ."

"Colonel Dunn, a fine old silver-haired gentleman, is going to stand where you and I are standing. He will have a grandfatherly hand on the shoulder of his grandson, William C. Dunn . . . let me see, that'll be William C. Dunn the *Sixth* . . . and he will say, 'Grandson, during the Great War, your granddaddy was a fighter pilot, and he was over at Pensacola and out flying a Grumman Wildcat, which at the time was one hell of a fighter, and nature called. So he landed his airplane right here where this pecan orchard is now. That used to be a landing strip, boy. And he took out his talleywacker and pissed right up against this fine old live oak tree.' "

"Jesus Christ, Billy!"

" 'And the moral of that story, Grandson, is that when you are up to your ears in bullshit, the only thing you can do is piss on it.' "

"You're insane." Pick laughed.

"You landed here when you knew goddamned well the strip wasn't long enough for a Wildcat. You're insane, too."

A sudden image came to Pick of Bill Dunn as a silver-haired seventy-odd-year-old with his hand on the shoulder of a blond-haired boy.

And his mouth ran away with him.

"You're presuming you're going to live through this war," he said.

Dunn met his eyes.

"I considered that possibility, Pick," he said. "Or improbability. But then I decided, if I do somehow manage to come through alive, and I didn't land here and piss on the oak, I'd regret it for the rest of my life. So I put the wheels down. I certainly didn't think you'd be dumb enough to follow me. This was supposed to be a private moment."

"Sorry to intrude."

"And then I realized, when I heard you coming, that I should have known better. If you are so inclined, Pick, you may piss on my live oak."

"I consider that a great honor, Billy."

As Pick was standing by the tree, Dunn said, "Under the circumstances, I don't think we should even make a low-level pass over Corey Field, much less a barrel roll. Colonel Whatsisname would shit a brick, and I really don't want to wind up in the backseat of a Yellow Peril."

"Yeah," Pick said. "I guess he would."

"And the sonofabitch is probably right. It would set a bad example for those kids."

(TWO)
Main Dining Room
The Officers' Club
Main Side, U.S. Naval Air Station
Pensacola, Florida
1625 Hours 2 November 1942

The gun camera footage proved interesting; but Pick had private doubts about how accurately it represented the flow of bullets.

The cameras were apparently bore-sighted: They showed the view as you'd see it if you were looking down the machine gun's barrel. But that made shooting and killing instantaneous. And .50 caliber bullets didn't really fly that way. In combat, you didn't aim where the enemy aircraft was, you aimed where it was going to be. Like shooting skeet, you lead the target.

Somewhat immodestly, he wondered if the reason he never had any trouble with aerial gunnery, in training or in combat, was that he'd shot a hell of a lot of skeet. That was probably true, he concluded. And true of Billy, too. There was a wall full of shotguns in his house.

Knocking little clay disks out of the air with a shotgun probably had a lot to do with me being here and in one piece, instead of dead. Or wrapped in two miles of white gauze, tied up like a goddamned mummy, like Dick.

The lights came on.

Colonel Porter stepped to the lectern and tapped the microphone with his fingernail.

"Gentlemen," he said, "I have to confess—and I am sure that Captain O'Fallon shares my feeling—that it is somewhat embarrassing to have to stand here after everybody has seen proof of how Lieutenants Dunn and Pickering cleaned our clocks."

There came the expected laughter.

"One final observation, gentlemen, and then we can begin our cocktail hour. I'm sure you all noticed how brief those film segments were. None of them lasted more than a couple of seconds. I hope you understand how that works. The cameras were activated only when the gun trigger was depressed. And Lieutenants Dunn and Pickering only fired when they were sure of their target, when they knew they were within range and were going to hit what they aimed at."

The students and some of the IPs looked at Dunn and Pickering. One of them started to applaud, and others joined in.

I wonder if I look as uncomfortable as Grandpa Bill.

"To the victor goes the spoils," Colonel Porter said. "Tradition requires that the senior officer present is served first. But I think we can waive that tonight. Waiter, would you please serve Lieutenant Dunn and Lieutenant Pickering?"

A white-jacketed waiter appeared. He was carrying a silver tray on which were two glasses filled with a dark liquid and ice cubes.

Thank God! I can really use a drink!

"A toast, Mr. Dunn, if you please," Colonel Porter said.

Bill Dunn raised his glass.

"To The Corps," he said.

Pick took a sip.

Jesus, what the hell is this?

It's tea, that's what it is! I'll be a sonofabitch!

He looked at the lectern. Lieutenant Colonel J. Danner Porter, USMC, was smiling benignly at him.

"I think," Lieutenant Dunn said softly, "that that's what is known as 'inspired chickenshit.'"

"I just hope it means we are forgiven," Pick said.

"You mean for getting drunk?"

"We paid for that by being here. What I mean is for cleaning his clock."

Dunn laughed, and then his face changed.

"I have just fallen in love again," he said. "Will you look at that in the doorway?"

Pick turned.

"That one's off-limits, Billy," Pick said as Mrs. Martha Sayre Culhane started walking across the floor to him. She looked every bit as incredibly beautiful as he remembered her.

"Lieutenant Pickering, how nice to see you," she said. "It's been some time, hasn't it?"

"Hello, Martha."

"I'm Bill Dunn, Ma'am."

"I know," she said.

"Bill, Martha," Pick said.

"Do you suppose you could get me one of those?" Martha said, nodding at Pick's tea with ice cubes.

"It's tea," Pick said.

Colonel Porter walked up.

"Good afternoon, Miss Sayre," he said.

"It's Mrs. Culhane," Martha said.

"Oh, God! Excuse me!"

"My father sent me to ask when you're going to be through with Lieutenant Pickering, Colonel. Anytime soon?"

"Why, I think the Admiral could have him right now, Mrs. Culhane."

"Thank you," Martha said. She turned to Bill Dunn. "You don't have to worry about his getting home, Mr. Dunn. I'll see that he gets there, either tonight or perhaps in the morning."

Pick looked at Colonel Porter.

"By your leave, Sir?"

"Certainly," Porter said, and put out his hand. "Thank you very much, Pickering," he said. "I hope you understand why what happened here today was worth all the effort, and your time?"

"Yes, Sir."

"Good luck, Mr. Pickering," Colonel Porter said, and then added, "Good evening, Mrs. Culhane. My compliments to your father."

"Thank you," Martha said. She put her hand on Pick's arm. "Ready, Mr. Pickering?"

A dark-maroon 1940 Mercury convertible was parked just outside the front door of the Club. It was in a spot marked RESERVED FOR FLAG AND GENERAL OFFICERS.

Martha had the driver's door open before Pick could open it for her. He went around the rear of the car and got in the front. Martha ground the starter, but then put both of her hands on the top of the steering wheel and looked over at him.

"I had to come see you," she said. "But you don't have to come with me."

"I'm here because I want to be," he said. "And besides, I thought your father, your father and your mother, wanted to see me."

"I lied about that," she said. "I lied to Colonel Porter. I told my father I was going to see . . . a friend of mine, and that I might stay over. I don't think Colonel Porter knew I was lying; I'm sure my father did."

"What do you want to do, Martha?"

"I want to get it settled between us, once and for all."

"I thought we'd . . . I was pretty sure you had . . . already done that."

"So did I, but here I am."

"I don't think this is the place to have a conversation like this," he said.

"Neither do I," Martha said, and put the Mercury in reverse with a clash of gears.

When they passed out of the gate onto Pensacola's Navy Boulevard, Pick asked, "Where are we going?"

"The San Carlos," she said, without looking at him.

"Well, at least I can get a drink. That was really tea Colonel Porter gave me."

"I'm going to drop you off in front," Martha said. "You're going to go in and get a room, and then meet me in the bar."

"Why doesn't that sound like the schedule for an illicit assignation?"

She laughed. "Because it isn't. We're going there to talk. You know, I'd forgotten that about you, that you're really funny sometimes."

"We're going to talk, right?"

"I can't think of anyplace else to go, and I want to look at you while we're talking."

"Well, you could pull to the curb and turn the headlights on, and I could stand in front of the car."

She laughed again.

"I've really missed you."

"I could tell by all the letters you didn't answer."

"Four is not very many letters."

"It is, if none of them get a reply."

Martha dropped Pick off at the front of the white, rambling, Spanish-architecture San Carlos Hotel.* He walked into the lobby and looked up at the stained-glass arching overhead. All its pieces were intact. This was not always the case.

Sometimes, exuberant Naval Aviators and/or their lady friends caused pieces of glass to be broken by bombing the lobby with beer bottles. The Navy bombed the Marines, or vice versa. And sometimes the Marines and the Navy bombed instructor pilots.

He walked to the desk, and smiled when he recognized the man behind it, Chester Gayfer, the resident manager.

"Well, look what the tide washed up," Gayfer said. "When did you get back, Pick? It's good to see you."

"How are you, Chet? Good to see you, too."

"Back for good? Or just passing through?"

"Just passing through. I need a room."

"Your old 'room' just happens to free, primarily because we don't have much call for the Penthouse."

Jesus, I don't want to go up there. Dick and I lived there. It would be haunted.

"I think an ordinary room, Chet, thank you," Pick said.

Gayfer turned to the key rack, took one, and then handed it to him.

"The Penthouse," he said. "Take it." When Pick reached for his wallet, he held his hands up, fingers spread. "My pleasure. I want you to comp me at the Andrew Foster."

What the hell. The Penthouse at least doesn't look like a hotel room—as in taking a girl to a hotel room.

"It's done," Pick said. "Thank you."

"Where's your luggage?"

"It will be coming."

"Have a good time, Pick," Gayfer said with a knowing smile. But then he asked, "How's Dick Stecker? You ever see him?"

"Yeah, he's in Hawaii."

"Give him my regards if you see him," Gayfer said.

"I will," Pick said, and walked across the lobby to the bar.

Martha was sitting at the bar. She already had a drink, as well as the fascinated attention of a number of young men in Navy and Marine uniforms who were sitting to either side of her.

He walked up to her.

"I ordered you a scotch," she said.

The bright smiles faded from the faces of quite a few young officers.

"Did you get a room?" she asked. "Let me have the key."

The faces now registered gross surprise.

A good many Naval Aviators (and some Army and Air Force pilots, too) have fond memories of the San Carlos Hotel. . . . And so as I was actually writing this chapter (September, 1992), I was saddened to hear over a Pensacola radio station the news that the San Carlos is to be demolished and turned into a parking lot, all efforts to preserve it having failed. Since I thought that at least some of my readers would be interested to learn of this tragedy, I've added this footnote, which has nothing whatever to do with this story.

He handed Martha the key. She looked at it.

"There's no number on it."

"It's the Penthouse," he said.

"Maybe it would be a good idea if you bring something to drink with you when you come up," she said.

Does she not know these clowns can hear her? Or doesn't she give a damn?

She walked out of the bar and through the door to the lobby, carrying her drink with her.

"Give me a bottle of this," Pick said to the bartender, "and let me pay for the drinks the lady ordered."

"I can't do that, Sir," the bartender said. "Sorry."

"Call Mr. Gayfer," Pick said. "And tell him the bottle's going to the Penthouse." When he saw hesitation on the bartender's face, he said, more sharply than he intended, "Do it!"

The bartender went to the telephone and returned a moment later, his hands refusing the money Pick held out to him.

"Mr. Gayfer said he'd put it on your bill, Sir," he said. Then he took a fresh bottle of Johnnie Walker from under the bar and handed it to Pick.

"Thank you," Pick said, then smiled at the officers at the bar. "Good hunting, gentlemen," he said, and walked out to the lobby.

The door to the Penthouse was open. Martha was by the windows overlooking the street, half sitting on the sill.

"I think you find my etchings interesting, as the bishop said to the nun."

She smiled.

He glanced around the sitting room and into the kitchenette. Both bedroom doors were closed. It was a hotel suite now, nothing more. There was no hint that a pair of Marine second lieutenants had once lived here while learning to fly.

"Brings back memories?" Martha asked.

"Yeah. Some. We had a lot of fun here."

"I was only here once. You're talking about you and Dick?"

He nodded.

"How is he?"

He met her eyes. "He got his gear shot out; made it back to Henderson, dumped it, rolled his airplane into a ball, and is now in the Navy Hospital at Pearl, wrapped up like a mummy."

"I'm sorry," Martha said. "I liked Dick."

"Everybody likes Dick."

"You didn't get hurt?"

He shook his head no.

"Jim told me you were a natural pilot," she said.

Jim? Oh. Carstairs. Captain James Carstairs.

"And you're an ace," she went on. "I saw the way they looked at you."

"You saw how who looked at me?" he asked. And then, before she could reply, he held up the bottle and asked, "You want some of this?"

"In a minute; I still have some," she said, raising her glass; it was a quarter full. Then she went on: "The kids, the students at Corey Field this morning."

He walked into the kitchenette and started making himself a drink.

"You were at the Field this morning? I didn't see you," he said from there.

"I didn't want you to see me."

"I hope you were suitably impressed."

"I was," Martha said. "You had those kids hanging on your every word."

"I was talking about the flying."

"I was talking about Lieutenant Pickering, the Marine officer. You weren't that way when you left. You've changed. You reminded me of my husband today."

"He's dead."

"Why did you have to say that?"

"Because sometimes I think you think he's coming back."

"I guess I did for a while. No more."

He finished making his drink and went back into the sitting room. Martha hadn't moved from the window.

"So now you get on with your life, right?" Pick asked.

"Right."

"And does that include me?"

She turned, carefully put her glass on the windowsill, and then pushed herself erect and looked at him.

"I'm sorry I brought you here, Pick," she said. "Sorry I put you through this."

She touched his cheek with her hand, then stepped around him and walked across the room and out into the corridor. She stopped and turned.

"Take care of yourself," she said, and then she was gone.

Pick exhaled audibly. Then he put his untouched drink on the windowsill beside hers, waited for the sound of the elevator to tell him that she was gone, and walked out of the apartment.

At the door he turned, went into the kitchenette and picked up the bottle of scotch, took a last look around the Penthouse, and left.

(THREE)
Belle-Vue Garden Apartments
Los Angeles, California
1325 Hours 4 November 1942

When the door buzzer sounded, Dawn Morris was at her card table, autographing a stack of eight-by-ten-inch photographs.

Actually, they weren't real photographs, run through an enlarger; they were printed, like the cover of a magazine, but on heavy paper with white borders, so they looked like photographs. And this disappointed her just a little when she first saw them.

Dawn managed to talk herself out of that little disappointment, however, after it sank in that there were two thousand of them, and that not just any old photographer took them, but Metro-Magnum Studios' Chief Still Photographer himself, and that Mr. Cooperman, who was Jake Dillon's stand-in as publicity chief, told her they would order more as necessary.

They'd printed up all those photographs so she could pass them out on the war bond tour. The picture showed her in something like a military uniform, except that she wasn't wearing a shirt under the jacket, and you could see really quite a lot of her cleavage.

Mr. Cooperman said they were going to start calling her "The GI's Sweetheart." And just as soon as she came off the tour, they were going to start shooting her first feature film. She would play a Red Cross girl who breaks the rules and dates a GI. She falls in love with him and gets caught, and gets in trouble. They hadn't resolved that yet—how she was going to get out of trouble—but they would by the time she came off the war bond tour.

Anyway, she was under contract to Metro-Magnum Studios. And they were paying her five hundred dollars a week. While that certainly wasn't nearly as much money as they were paying some star like Veronica Wood, for example, it was a lot more than she ever made in a month, much less a week.

Mr. Cooperman said they wanted to take advantage of the war bond tour publicity, so they were going to make the movie just as fast as they could. They would get it out right away, not let it gather dust in the vault. Dawn wasn't sure how she felt about that. You obviously couldn't make a high-quality movie if you did it in a hurry. But on the other hand, it was better to be the star of a movie made in a hurry than not to be in any movie at all.

When the doorbell rang, Dawn had no idea who it could be. Somebody she didn't want to see anyway, probably; so she didn't answer the door at first.

Then whoever it was just sat on the damned button and banged on the door with keys or something . . . which was probably going to chip the paint and make the superintendent give her trouble. Not that she really had to give a shit anymore; she'd be out of this dump by the time she came off the war bond tour. Get a place maybe closer to Beverly Hills. Or maybe even she'd get lucky and find some place on the beach.

Mr. Cooperman said not to worry about gas rationing. Motion pictures had been declared a war industry, just like the airplane companies. Since she was driving to work in a war industry, she would get a "C" Ration Sticker for her car.

Dawn stood up and went to the picture window; she'd made a hole in the curtain over it that let her peek out at whoever was at her door.

At least most of the time: It was possible to stand in a place that was out of range of her peephole. And the person who was there today was doing that. But she did recognize Mr. Jake Dillon's yellow Packard 120 convertible in the parking lot. It stood out like a rose in a garbage dump from all the junks there . . . including Dawn's 1935 Chevrolet coupe.

She wondered what he wanted. But then, that wasn't all that hard to figure out. So the question was really how to give it to him. How coy should she appear? Probably not very coy at all, she decided. They'd understood each other right from the start. She scratched his back by being nice to the kid he brought home from the war, and he scratched hers by getting her a film test. A really good film test. Which meant she owed him. And now he was coming to collect.

So what was wrong with that? She'd been around Hollywood long enough to know all about the casting couch. And having Jake Dillon as a friend certainly wouldn't hurt her career any. And she certainly wouldn't be the only actress who was being nice to Dillon. Veronica Wood was screwing him.

I wonder if she'd be pissed if she found out I was doing it with him, too.

She called, "Just a moment, please!" And then she went to the door and unfastened the chain and all the dead-bolt locks you needed in a dump like this to keep people from stealing you blind. As she was finishing with that, she had a final pleasant thought: *Three weeks ago, I couldn't even get in an agent's office. And here I am about to do it with Mr. Jake Dillon and worrying if Veronica Wood will be pissed if she finds out!*

"Hello, Dawn, darling," Miss Veronica Wood greeted her. "I hope I didn't rip you out of bed or anything?"

"Oh, no," Dawn said. "I'm really surprised to see you here, Miss Wood."

"I had a hell of a time finding it, I'll tell you that," Veronica said. "Can I come in?"

What the hell does she want?

"Oh, of course. Excuse me," Dawn said. "Please come in. You'll have to excuse the appearance of the place. . . ."

"I've lived in worse," Veronica said, and walked to the card table and picked up one of the photographs.

"Isn't that Mr. Dillon's car?"

"Yeah. They finally got it fixed," Veronica said. Then, tossing the photograph back on the table, she said, "Not bad. Who did that, Roger Marshutz?"

"Yes. Yes, he did."

"He's a horny little bastard; keep your knees crossed when you're around him. But he's one hell of a photographer. He did a nice job with your boobs on this one."

"I liked it," Dawn said.

"You'll pass them out on the war bond tour, I suppose?"

"Yes."

"I thought so. I was over at Publicity just before I came here, and they were signing mine."

What the hell does that mean?

"Excuse me? I don't quite understand."

Veronica looked at Dawn as if her suspicions that she was retarded were just confirmed.

"The girls, the girls in Publicity, were signing my handouts."

"Oh."

Of course, Veronica Wood is a star. Stars don't autograph their own pictures. How the hell would the fans know if the real star had signed them or not? I am not a star—at least not yet. And that's why I'm signing my own photographs. What the hell, I sort of like signing them. But this will be the last time. Next time the girls in Publicity can sign "Warm regards, Dawn Morris" two thousand times. They probably have nicer handwriting than I do, anyway.

"Can I offer you something to drink?"

"Have you got any scotch?"

"No, I'm sorry, I don't think I do."

"Then I'll pass, thanks anyway."

"I know I have gin."

"Gin makes me horny, and then it gives me a headache," Veronica Wood said. "I don't like to get horny unless I can do something about it. Thanks anyway."

"Is there something you wanted, Miss Wood?"

"No, I was just in the neighborhood and thought I'd pop in and say 'howdy,' " Veronica said, meeting her eyes. "I wanted to talk to you about Bobby."

Bobby? Who the hell is Bobby? Oh.

"Corporal Easterbrook, you mean? What about him?"

"Actually, Lieutenant Easterbrook," Veronica said. "They gave him a commission. You didn't know?"

Dawn shrugged helplessly. "What about him?"

"Now you and I know why you were screwing him at Jake's place," Veronica said. "But I don't think he does."

"I don't . . ." Dawn began.

"Let me put it this way, Dawn darling," Veronica interrupted her. And then she changed the entire pitch and timbre of her voice, sounding as well bred and cultured as she did in her last film, where she played the Sarah Lawrence–educated daughter of a Detroit industrialist who fell in love with her father's chauffeur. It earned her an Academy Award nomination. "As you take your first steps toward what we all hope will be a distinguished motion picture career, the one thing you don't need is to have me pissed at you."

"I don't know what you're talking about."

"I like that kid," Veronica said, her diction and timbre returning to normal. "He's a good kid. He's been through stuff in the war you and I can't even imagine, and he's just dumb and sweet enough to think that you were screwing him because you liked him."

"I don't know what you're driving at," Dawn said.

"Yeah, you do. It's time for Bobby to get thrown out of your bed. And don't tell me you haven't thought about it. You couldn't keep it up if you wanted to. Even in his lieutenant's costume, he looks like a little boy. You can't afford a reputation for robbing the cradle, either."

"He is young, isn't he," Dawn said. "And he's so sweet!"

"So," Veronica said. "The question is how to let Bobby down gently. You want to be an actress, act. You figure out how to do it. Just keep in mind that if you don't do a really nice job of letting him down, you will not only break his heart, but you will really piss me off. You really don't want to do that."

Dawn had her first rebellious thought, and it was not entirely unpleasant: *Jesus, is it possible that she's looking at me as a threat to her? Of course it's possible. But I'm not as vulnerable as she thinks I am. The studio has plans for me—based on my screen test, and on the fact that Shirley Maxwell liked it. She may have an Academy Award nomination, and she may be screwing the ears off Jake Dillon, but she doesn't come close to having the influence Shirley Maxwell has on her husband. And he runs the studio!*

"I have no intention of hurting Bob Easterbrook, Miss Wood," Dawn said. "I really like him. You didn't have to come here and threaten me."

"It wasn't a threat, it was statement of fact."

"Not that I think you could do a thing to harm me . . ."

"Oh! I'll be goddamned! Darling, let me let you in on a little secret. The real power at Metro-Magnum is Shirley Maxwell. Don't ever forget that. And just for the record, Shirley and I go way back. She was under contract, too, you know. We were in the chorus of a swimming-pool epic with Esther Williams . . . and we were sharing a dump like this. Anyhow, she once confided in me back then that she really loved that porcine dwarf she finally married. And I confided in her that I really loved Jake Dillon, and I was going to catch him in a weak mood and get him to marry me. The consequence of that is that Shirley knows that I'm the only female on the lot who's not trying to get her husband's undersized dork out of his pants and into her mouth. And Shirley likes Jake, too . . . and not only because of me. When I heard that Shirley said nice things to the dwarf about your test, I knew it was because of Jake. You're not bad-looking, and you have a fine set of boobs, but so do five thousand other girls out here. How long do you think you'd last if I went to Shirley and told her to keep an eye on the dwarf, he's got the hots for Whatsername, Dawn something, the one with the sexy voice and the big teats?"

They locked eyes for a moment.

"I think we understand each other, Miss Wood," Dawn finally said.

"Yeah, I think maybe we do," Veronica said, and then shifted back into the role of Pamela Hornsbury of Sarah Lawrence and Detroit. "And please call me Veronica. Now that you're going to be part of the Metro-Magnum family, it seems only appropriate, don't you think, darling?"

Then she smiled and walked out of Dawn's apartment.

(FOUR)
Cottage B
The Foster Beverly Hills
Beverly Hills, California
1325 Hours 5 November 1942

"May I come in?" the general manager of the Foster Beverly Hills said, inserting his head through the open door.

First Lieutenant Malcolm S. Pickering, USMCR, waved him in, then held up his index finger, asking him to wait. Pick was sitting on a couch whose wildly floral upholstery and faux-bamboo wood manifested, he supposed, a South Pacific ambience. There was a telephone at his ear.

"I know they're in the Federal Building," he said to the telephone. "Or maybe it's the Post Office Building. Would you keep trying? It's the West Coast, or Los Angeles, or something like that, Detachment of the Public Affairs Division of the Marine Corps. Thank you."

He put the handset in its cradle.

"Lieutenant Pickering, I'm Gerald Samson, the general manager. I'm so sorry about the mix-up. We just had no record of your reservation."

"No problem," Pick said. "All fixed." He gestured around the room. "This is very nice. Lieutenant Dunn and I feel right at home in here. There's only one thing missing."

"What's that?"

"Bare-breasted maidens in grass skirts," Pick said.

"And poisonous insects," Lieutenant Bill Dunn said, coming into the room. There was the sound of a toilet flushing. "Lots and lots of large poisonous insects."

Mr. Samson smiled uneasily. Thirty-five minutes previously, Paul Dester, the day manager, had telephoned him at home. Dester explained then that two Marine officers were in the lobby, insisting they had a reservation made by the Andrew Foster in San Francisco. Though Dester found no record of such a reservation (it would have been in the name of a Lieutenant Pickering), he called the Andrew Foster to check. And the day manager there said he was quite positive that no reservation had been made for Lieutenant Pickering. He would have remembered; Lieutenant Pickering was Andrew Foster's grandson.

At that point Dester actually had to call to ask what he was supposed to do:

"Is there a cottage open?"

"Only B, and we're holding that for Spencer Tracy. For Mr. Tracy's friends. They'll be in tomorrow."

"Put Mr. Pickering in B, and send fruit and cheese and champagne. We'll worry about Mr. Tracy's friends later. I'll be right there."

When Mr. Samson came into the room, the fruit-and-cheese basket and champagne were untouched. The reason for that became almost immediately apparent when a bellman appeared with bottles of scotch and bourbon, glasses, and ice.

"How many bedrooms are there here?" Pick asked.

"There are three, Mr. Pickering."

"A guest of mine, and a guest of his, will be arriving sometime this afternoon. Captain Charles Galloway. They'll need the bigger bedroom."

"That would be the Palm Room," Samson said, indicating one of the doors with a nod of his head. "We'll be on the lookout for Captain Galloway, Sir."

"Thank you," Pick said, and then the telephone rang and he grabbed it.

"I've found a Marine Public Affairs Detachment, Sir. It's in the Post Office Building. Should I ring it?" the operator asked.

"Please," Pick said, and covered the mouthpiece with his hand. "We're about to have a little nip to cut the dust of the trail, Mr. Samson. Can we ask you to join us?"

"Los Angeles Detachment, Marine Corps Public Relations, Lieutenant Macklin speaking."

"I'm trying to find Major Dillon," his caller said.

"May I ask who is calling?"

"My name is Pickering."

"*Lieutenant* Pickering?"

"Right."

"Where are you, Lieutenant?"

"I asked first. Where's Dillon?"

"One moment, please," Macklin said, and covered the microphone with his hand. He'd recently read an extract of the service record of First Lieutenant Pickering, Malcolm S., USMCR; and Pickering hadn't been a first lieutenant long enough to wear the lacquer off his bars.

I outrank him, and I don't have to tolerate his being a wise-ass. But on the other hand, we're going to be together for the next two weeks, and it would be better if an amicable relationship existed.

"Major, it's Lieutenant Pickering," Macklin said.

"Let me have it," Jake Dillon said, and took the telephone from Macklin. "Hey, Pick, where are you?"

"In the Beverly Hills."

"Dunn with you?"

"Bright-eyed and bushy-tailed."

"You're supposed to be in the Roosevelt."

"I don't like the Roosevelt," Pick said.

"Have you been at the sauce?"

"Not yet. They just brought it."

"Where in the Hills?"

"Cottage B. It has a charming South Pacific ambience. You ought to see it."

"I will. I'll be right there. And you will be there when I arrive. Both of you."

"Aye, aye, Sir. Whatever the Major desires, Sir."

"Let me add 'sober,'" Dillon said, and hung up. He looked at Macklin. "Well, that's two out of three. Or five out of six, counting the three we already have in the Roosevelt. I don't think we'll have a problem with Captain Galloway."

"They're not in the Hollywood Roosevelt, Sir?"

"No, they're in the Foster Beverly Hills."

"I don't understand, Sir."

The telephone rang, and again Lieutenant Macklin answered it in the prescribed military manner.

"Sir," his caller said, "may I speak with Major Dillon, please. My name is Corp—*Lieutenant* Easterbrook."

Macklin covered the microphone with his hand.

"It's Lieutenant Easterbrook, Sir," he said.

In Lieutenant Macklin's professional judgment, the commissioning of Corporal Easterbrook was an affront to every commissioned officer who'd earned his commission the hard way. The right way (and the hardest way) to earn a commission, of course, was to go through Annapolis, as he himself had. But failing that, you could take a course of instruction at an Officer Candidate School that would at least impart the absolute basic knowledge a commissioned officer needed and weed out those who were not qualified to be officers. Simply doing your duty as an enlisted man on Guadalcanal should not be enough to merit promotion to commissioned status.

These thoughts made Macklin wonder again about his own promotion. If he had been able to answer the telephone *"Captain Macklin speaking, Sir,"* perhaps Pickering's tone would have been a little more respectful.

Dillon took the phone from him again.

"Hey, Easterbunny, where are you? How was the leave?"

"Just fine, Sir. I'm at the airport, Sir. You said to call when I got in."

"Great. Look, hop in a cab and tell him to take you . . . Wait a minute. In ten minutes, be out in front. Lieutenant Macklin will pick you up. You came on TWA, right?"

"Yes, Sir."

"Be out in front in ten minutes," Dillon said, and broke the connection with his finger. He dialed a number from memory.

"Jake Dillon," he said to whoever answered, as Macklin watched with curiosity. "Is Veronica Wood on the lot? Get her for me, will you?"

He turned to Macklin.

"The station wagon is here, right?"

"Yes, Sir."

"Go pick up the Easterbunny, and take him to the Foster Beverly Hills, Cottage B. I'll meet you there. It's about time you met Pickering and Dunn. And they probably know where Galloway is, too."

"Aye, aye, Sir," Macklin said.

"Hey, baby," Jake said to the telephone. "I'm glad I caught you. You want to meet me, as soon as you can, at the Hills?"

There was a pause.

"I don't want to sit around the goddamn Polo Lounge either. I want you to meet a couple of friends of mine, Marines. They're in B."

"Boy," Second Lieutenant Robert F. Easterbrook, USMCR, said to First Lieutenant R. B. Macklin, USMC, as they drove up the palm-tree-lined drive to the entrance of the Foster Beverly Hills Hotel, "this is *classy!*"

Lieutenant Macklin ignored him and looked for a place to park the station wagon. Another of Major Dillon's odd notions was to decree that enlisted men could almost always be put to doing something more useful than chauffeuring officers around, and that henceforth the officers (meaning Macklin, of course; Dillon habitually drove his own car) would drive themselves.

He saw a spot and started to drive into it. A bellman held up his hand and stopped him.

"We'll take care of the car, Sir," the bellman said. "Are you checking in?"

"We're here to see Major Dillon," Macklin said. "I don't think it's permissible for a civilian to drive a military vehicle. I will park it myself, thank you, just the same."

The bellman considered that a moment, then shrugged his shoulders and stepped out of the way.

Macklin parked the station wagon and carefully locked it. And then, with Lieutenant Easterbrook at his side, he walked into the lobby.

"How would I find Cottage B?" he inquired of the doorman.

"May I ask whom you wish to see, Sir?"

"Major Homer Dillon, USMC."

"There must be some mistake, Sir. There is no Major Dillon in Cottage B."

"How about a Lieutenant Pickering?" Macklin snapped.

"One moment, Sir," the doorman said. "I'll see if Lieutenant Pickering is in. May I have your name, please?"

"Macklin," Macklin said. "Lieutenant R. B. Macklin."

The doorman picked up a telephone and dialed a number.

"Excuse me," he said to whoever answered. "There is a Lieutenant Mackeral at the door who wishes to see Lieutenant Pickering. May I pass him through?"

"He called you 'Mackeral,'" Lieutenant Easterbrook observed, chuckling . . . quite unnecessarily.

"Turn right at the reception desk, Lieutenant," the doorman said, pointing. "And then your first left. Cottage B is the second cottage."

"Thank you very much," Lieutenant Macklin said, somewhat icily. "Follow me, Easterbrook."

There was just time for Lieutenant Macklin to be introduced to Lieutenants Dunn and Pickering when Captain Charles M. Galloway and Mrs. Carolyn Ward Spencer walked into the cottage. They were trailed by a bellman carrying luggage.

"The temporary arrangements," Pick said, pointing to the door to the Palm Room, "are that you and Charley are in there. If you'd rather, we could find you some other . . ."

"This is marvelous," Carolyn said. "Thank you, Pick. I keep saying that, but you keep doing things . . ."

"Enjoy it while you can," Pick said. "I no longer have to polish the Skipper's apple; me or Dunn. We are all now Instructor Pilots."

"I heard about that," Charley said. "I think it makes sense."

"I can't believe you're saying that. You like the idea of being an IP?"

"He's not going to be an IP is why," Carolyn said. "Somebody blew a trumpet, and he's going back over there."

"How did you work that, Skipper?" Dunn asked.

"Clean living, Mr. Dunn," Galloway said. "You ought to try it sometime. Works miracles."

Clean living indeed, Lieutenant Macklin thought. *What the Captain is up to with this woman is defined as illicit cohabitation. It's conduct unbecoming an officer and a gentlemen,* de facto *and* de jure.

"Any chance we can go with you, Skipper?" Pick asked.

"No," Galloway said. "I asked, and the answer is no. Somebody decided clowns like you two are worth their weight in gold. But thanks, Pick. I wish it was otherwise."

"This must be the place," a female voice announced from the doorway. "I can smell Marines in rut."

That's Veronica Wood! Lieutenant Macklin realized in surprise. *Did she actually say what I think I heard?*

Veronica crossed the room and kissed Lieutenant Easterbrook wetly, then moved to Jake Dillon and kissed him with a little more enthusiasm.

"Bobby gets kissed first," Veronica said, "because he's prettier than you are, even if you are my fiancé."

"Jesus," Jake said.

What did she say? "Fiancé"? Macklin thought.

Veronica glanced around the room and noticed Carolyn for the first time. She walked to her and kissed her. "The East Coast President of the Marine Corps Camp Followers. When was the last time?"

"The Hotel Willard, in Washington," Carolyn said.

"Right!" Veronica said, and then accused: "You promised to write, and you never did."

"I thought you were just being polite," Carolyn said.

"Don't be silly. We have to stick together. You going on the tour?"

"No, she is not," Jake Dillon said. "Which brings us to that. Enjoy tonight, children, because tomorrow it's all over. Tomorrow at 0900, we will all gather at the Hollywood Roosevelt, luggage all packed and ready to be loaded aboard the bus. . . ."

"Bus?" Pick asked. "What bus?"

"The Greyhound Bus we have chartered to carry everybody on the tour," Dillon said, "on which, regrettably, there is no room for anyone else."

"You better find one more seat, Jake," Veronica said. "Or there will be two empty seats on your bus."

"Oh, Jesus," Jake said, but it was a surrender.

I can't believe this! Macklin thought. *He's actually going to permit this woman to come on the tour—this, to use her own words, camp follower. There will be questions about her, questions that cannot avoid bringing embarrassment to The Corps.*

"Jake, if it would pose prob—" Carolyn said, and was interrupted by Veronica.

"No problems, right, Jake?"

"No problems, Carolyn," Jake said. "But I don't know what the hell we're going to do about hotel rooms. . . ."

"No problem," Veronica said. "I will stay in your room, and Charley and Carolyn will stay in mine."

"Yeah," Jake said. "That'd work."

She is absolutely shameless! Macklin thought. *The both of them are absolutely shameless! If any of this comes out, how am I going to look? If there is a scandal, and that seems entirely possible, my promotion will go down the toilet.*

"Major, Sir," Pick said. "Are there any more logistical problems to be solved? Or can we start thinking about how to enjoy our last night of freedom?"

"Just as long as you understand, Pick, that this is your last night of freedom, and that from now on you behave, that's all I have."

"In that case, I think the condemned man will start drinking his last meal," Pick said.

"Lieutenant," Lieutenant Easterbrook asked, "would it be all right if I used the phone? I'd sort of like to call somebody."

"Somebody named Dawn, no doubt," Veronica said. "Well, we now know how Bobby plans to spend the night, don't we?"

Lieutenant Easterbrook blushed, but no one seemed to notice.

XV

Brigadier General Fleming Pickering, USMCR, was in a particularly sour mood. He was just about finished decrypting a MAGIC intercept from Pearl Harbor. The bitch of it was that he was not very good at operating the cryptographic machine, and this meant that it took him a long, painstaking hour and a half to decode an intercept in which a verbose Japanese admiral was exhorting his underlings to do good—at great length . . . and this obviously had about as much bearing on the conduct of the war as the price of shoe polish in Peoria, Illinois.

General Pickering was aware that he had no one to blame for his present unhappiness but himself: To begin with, General Pickering of the Horse Marines had grandly ordered the people in Pearl Harbor to send him "anything and everything." General Pickering of the Horse Marines would decide what was and what was not important. Next, even though such training had been regularly offered by Major Hong Song Do, General Pickering the prevaricator had successfully escaped on-the-job practice training in the efficient use of the cryptographic machine. If General Pickering the prevaricator had accepted such training, he would an hour ago have been been finished with decrypting the current MAGIC, analyzing the current MAGIC, and shredding the ten pages of verbose Japanese bullshit and putting it in the burn bag. And finally, General Pickering the idiot had learned as a corporal that the one thing you don't do in The Marine Corps is volunteer for anything. Even so, he had volunteered to come to the dungeon. The fact that it still seemed the decent thing to do did not alter the fact that he was in fact spending this lovely Sunday morning in a goddamned steel cell, three floors underground, with water running down the goddamned walls.

The telephone rang.

"Yes?" he snarled into the receiver.

"General Pickering?"

"Speaking," he snapped.

"Sir, this is Sergeant Widakovich."

Who the hell is Sergeant Widakovich? Oh, yeah, that enormous Polish Military Policeman. He looks like he could pull a plow. His hands are so big they make that tommy gun I've never seen him without look like something you'd buy for a kid in Woolworth's.

"What can I do for you, Sergeant?"

"General, I'm sorry to bother you . . ."

Perfectly all right, Sergeant. The sound of the human voice has a certain appeal. I was beginning to think I'd be here alone for the rest of my life.

He looked at his watch.

Oh Christ, it's quarter to twelve. Hart's going to relieve me at noon. Please don't tell me, Sergeant, that Hart called and will be late.

"What's up, Sergeant?"

"Sir, there's an officer out here. A Marine lieutenant colonel . . ."

That must be that idiot who relieved the other idiot CINCPAC sent here as liaison officer. Obviously. When The Corps has a supply of idiot lieutenant colonels on hand they don't know what to do with, they make them liaison officers. What the hell does he want? I told him I was not to be disturbed when I was down here.

". . . He's been waiting over an hour, Sir."

Good, let the sonofabitch wait.

". . . and I thought I should tell you, Sir."

"Thank you, Sergeant."

"His name is Stecker, Sir."

"Say again, Sergeant?"

"It's a Lieutenant Colonel Stecker, Sir."

"I'll be right there, Sergeant. Thank you."

Pickering waited impatiently while the steel door leading to the anteroom of the Cryptographic Section was opened. That required unlocking two locks, then removing the bars these held in place. Finally the door creaked open.

"General," Lieutenant Colonel Jack (NMI) Stecker, USMCR, said, "I didn't want to disturb—"

"Jesus Christ, Jack, am I glad to see you!"

He stepped around the guard's counter and shook Stecker's hand, then wrapped an arm around his shoulder.

"When did you get in? What are you doing here?"

"Last night—" Stecker began.

"Come on back with me," Pickering broke in. "If CINCPAC comes on line, and there's no instant reply, they start pissing their pants."

"Sir," Sergeant Widakovich asked, "are you taking the Colonel in there with you? Sir, he's not on the list."

"If anybody says anything, Sergeant, you tell them you did everything short of turning that Thompson on me, and I still took him back."

"Yes, Sir, General," Sergeant Widakovich said, smiling.

"General. I can wait," Stecker said uneasily. "I have nothing but time."

"Come on in the dungeon, Jack," Pickering said, then took his arm and led him down the interior corridor to the MAGIC room. He unlocked the door and gestured for Stecker to go in. He followed him in, then closed and locked the door.

"What is this place?"

"Don't ask, Jack," Pickering said. "How about some coffee? I just made a fresh pot."

"Thank you," Stecker said. When he saw the crypto machine, which Pickering, in violation of his own rules, had not covered up, curiosity overwhelmed him. "What the hell is that thing?"

"Don't ask, Jack," Pickering said. He took the heavy canvas cover from its hook on the wall and spread it over the machine.

"Sorry," Stecker said.

"We can talk about anything else," Pickering said. "Tell me about Dick, for instance."

"They've got him up, out of bed. In sort of a man-sized baby walker," Stecker said. "Some new theory that the sooner they start moving around, the better." He met Pickering's eyes. "I think he's in a good deal of pain, but he won't take anything but aspirin."

"He wrote you?"

"I saw him. I came here the long way around, via Pearl Harbor."

"So you saw Elly, too?"

"Yes, indeed. That's what I'm doing here. I wanted to thank you for all you've done—"

"Don't be an ass," Pickering said, cutting him off. "Elly's comfortable? I haven't had a chance to check myself."

"Yes, of course, she's comfortable. That apartment you got for her!"

"And she's met Patricia?"

"Yes, indeed. That's another reason I came down here looking for you." He reached in the bellows pocket of his jacket and handed Pickering an envelope. "From Patricia."

"Thank you," Pickering said. He glanced at the envelope and put it in his pocket. "So what are you doing here? When did you get in?"

"I got in last night. I'm sort of stationed here. I'm the first member of the advance party, but they're not calling it that yet."

"What are you going to do?"

"Arrange things, here and in New Zealand, to take care of the Division when it's relieved and comes here for rest and refitting. They took my battalion away from me."

That sounds, Pickering thought, *as if he was relieved for cause. I don't believe that, but I'm damned sure not going to ask.*

"So why didn't you call me when you got in?"

"I had to get a BOQ, look up the Marine liaison officer."

"You wasted your effort getting a BOQ," Pickering said. "You just moved in with me. I have a little house. Four bedrooms, and only two of us—"

He was interrupted by a deep, ugly, bell-like sound. Someone was beating on the steel door, which caused it to vibrate like a drum.

"What the hell?" Stecker exclaimed.

"My replacement has arrived," Pickering said. He walked over to the door, then unlocked and opened it.

Second Lieutenant George F. Hart, USMCR, came in. His uniform was adorned with the insignia of an aide-de-camp.

Why does this surprise me? Stecker wondered. *Pickering is a General. Generals have aides-de-camp.*

"I can't tell you how glad I am to see you, George," Pickering said. "Did you meet Colonel Stecker when you were on Guadalcanal?"

"No, Sir."

"Jack, this is George Hart."

"How are you, Hart?" Stecker asked.

"How do you do, Sir?" Hart replied. A moment later, he surprised Stecker by starting to take off his blouse. A moment after that, he surprised Stecker again, for he could now see that Hart was wearing a snub-nosed revolver in a shoulder holster. And a moment later, he surprised Stecker a third time when he slipped out of the holster and offered it to Pickering.

"I always feel like Edward G. Robinson in a grade-B movie when I wear that," Pickering said.

"But on the other hand, people can't tell you are wearing it. A .45 is pretty obvious," Hart said. "It's up to you."

"I think I'll stick with the .45, George. That makes me feel like Alan Ladd. Or John Wayne."

"Suit yourself," Hart said.

Pickering went to the table on which sat the mysterious machine now covered with canvas, opened a drawer, and took out a Colt Model 1911A1 .45 pistol. He removed the clip, checked to see that there was no cartridge in the action, and replaced the clip. He then put the pistol under the waistband of his trousers, in the small of his back. He sensed Stecker's eyes on him, and looked at him.

"George and I have a deal," he said. "I am allowed to go out and play by myself, but only if I am armed to the teeth. If you think it's a little odd for a general to be ordered around by a second lieutenant, you have to remember Colonel Fritz Rickabee. . . . You know Fritz don't you, Jack?" He didn't wait for an answer. "The truth is that we really work for him, and this gun nonsense is his idea. And both of us are afraid of him, right, George?"

"The Colonel is a formidable man, Sir."

"I know Rickabee," Stecker said. "I agree, he's formidable."

"OK, George. I'll save you a piece of the wedding cake," Pickering said. "Or maybe the party will still be going when Moore relieves you."

"I forgot to tell you. Commander Feldt is at the Cottage, he and some other RAN types. I told him you insisted that he stay there."

"Good man," Pickering said, and again sensed Stecker's curiosity. "Staff Sergeant Koffler is getting married at two. He's the radio operator Killer McCoy and company took off Buka. I am giving the bride away. Afterward, I may very well have more to drink than is good for me."

"That seems like a splendid idea," Stecker said.

(TWO)
Saint Bartholomew's Church
Brisbane, Australia
1345 Hours 8 November 1942

When Pickering and Stecker drove up in Pickering's 1938 Jaguar Drop Head Coupe, Lieutenant Commander Eric Feldt, Royal Australian Navy Reserve, a RAN lieutenant, a RAN chief petty officer, and ten RAN sailors were standing outside the church. They were all in dress uniforms (in the case of the officers and the chief, this included swords).

The chief shouted something unintelligible in the Australian version of the English language, whereupon he, the Lieutenant, and the enlisted men snapped to a frozen position of attention.

Commander Feldt, however, did not feel constricted by the minutiae of military courtesy as it was usually practiced among and between officers of an allied power. He waited until Pickering emerged from the Jaguar. Then, hands on hips, he declared, "I was wondering where the bloody hell you were, Pickering. The bloody bride has been here for an hour."

Lieutenant Colonel Stecker's eyes widened noticeably. He was more than a little shocked.

The RAN lieutenant, looking mortified, raised his hand in the British-style, palm-out salute, and held that position.

Pickering returned the lieutenant's salute. "Good afternoon, Mr. Dodds." He then turned to Feldt. "And good afternoon to you, Commander Feldt. I'm so glad to see that you have found time in your busy schedule for this joyous occasion."

"Well, I couldn't have you going around saying that all Australians are a lot of sodding arseholes, now could I?" He turned his attention to Colonel Stecker. "You're new."

"Colonel Stecker, may I present Commander Feldt?" Pickering said formally, but smiling. "Commander Feldt commands the Coastwatcher Establishment."

"Thank you," Colonel Stecker said when Feldt offered his hand—so idly it was close to insulting.

"For what?" Feldt asked suspiciously. "It was the sodding least we could do for Koffler; he's one of us."

"I commanded Second Battalion, Fifth Marines, on Guadalcanal," Stecker said. "We know what the Coastwatchers did for us. So thank you."

Commander Feldt looked very embarrassed.

"What exactly is it that you're doing for Sergeant Koffler, Eric?" Pickering asked. "Aside from gracing the wedding with your presence?"

"What the sodding hell does it look like? When the lad and his bride come out of the church, they will pass under an arch of swords. Ours and yours. Not actually swords: They're going to use the machetes we got from the ordnance people. They're damned near as big as swords. I sent the one who limps—"

"Lieutenant Moore?"

"Right. The one who limps. I sent him out behind the church to rehearse with your lads."

"To rehearse what?"

"I don't know how the sodding Marine Corps does it, Pickering," Feldt said, "but in the Australian Navy, everyone raises his bloody sword at the same time, on command, not when they sodding well feel like it. When I asked the one who limps if he knew how to do it, and he said no, I sent him around in back to rehearse."

"With the General's permission," Lieutenant Colonel Jack (NMI) Stecker said formally, but not quite succeeding in concealing a smile, "I will go see how the rehearsal is proceeding."

"Go ahead," Pickering said. "We have five or ten minutes yet."

Feldt waited until Stecker was out of earshot.

"He works for you?"

"No. He's here to set up things for the First Marines when they come here to refit."

"I thought he said he was a battalion commander?"

"Until a week or so ago, he was."

"But he got himself relieved, huh? He looked pretty bloody competent to me. What did he do wrong?"

"He is pretty bloody competent," Pickering said coldly. "Jack Stecker has our Medal of Honor, Eric. The equivalent of your Victoria Cross."

"Then he really must have fucked up by the numbers—the way you bloody Yanks say it—to get himself relieved."

"Eric," Pickering flared furiously, "once again you're letting your goddamned mouth run away with you, offering ignorant and unsolicited opinions about matters you don't know a goddamned thing about."

Feldt met his eyes and didn't give an inch. "Good friend of yours, huh?"

"That has absolutely nothing to do with it."

"To change the subject, I spoke with the bride's father this morning."

"I'm afraid to ask what you said."

"I told him Daphne was in service, she worked for me, and I never knew a finer lass. And I told him that the lad she's marrying is as good as they come, even if he's an American, and that I thought he should be here."

"And?"

"And he said that what they've done has shamed him and his wife before all of their friends, and as far as he's concerned he no longer has a daughter."

"God!"

"So I told him that now that I have proof of what a sodding arsehole he is, if he comes anywhere near Brisbane today—much less near the church—I will break his right leg and stick it up his arse."

"Well said, Eric, well said," Pickering answered.

A somewhat delicate-appearing young man in clerical vestments came out of the church and walked quickly to them.

"General Pickering," he said, "the rector is ready for you now."

"Tell the bloody rector to keep his pants on," Commander Feldt said. "The sodding Americans are still practicing with their bloody machetes."

(THREE)
Water Lily Cottage
Brisbane, Australia
1845 Hours 8 November 1942

The six stiff drinks of Famous Grouse scotch after he, Colonel Stecker, Commander Feldt, and Major Hong Song Do arrived at the cottage, added to considerable champagne at the reception for Staff Sergeant and Mrs. Stephen M. Koffler, USMCR, had left Brigadier General Fleming Pickering much mellower than he'd been earlier, in the dungeon.

"Did I ever tell you, Jack, that Patricia and I really hoped that Pick would one day marry Ernie Sage?"

"I don't know who you're talking about," Jack Stecker replied, confused.

"It sounds like he wanted his son to marry a poufter, is what it sounds like," Commander Feldt said. "Pickering, old sod, you're as tight as a tick."

"Ernie Sage is one of the most beautiful, charming young *women* I have ever known," Pickering declared indignantly, if somewhat thickly. "For a local reference, Eric, she is now . . . how shall I put this? . . . *romantically involved* with Killer McCoy."

"Romantically involved?" Feldt inquired. "What the bleeding fuck is that? Why isn't the Killer fucking her, if she's so sodding beautiful?"

"Because he is a Marine officer and a gentleman, Eric," Pickering said solemnly. "Marine officers do not fuck. They spread pollen, in a gentlemanly fashion."

"You ever hear the story, Flem?" Colonel Stecker asked; he was about as mellow as General Pickering. "The one about the Marine second lieutenant in Paris in 1917?"

"Which story about which second lieutenant would that be?" General Pickering inquired, carefully pronouncing each syllable.

"He was down on the Pigalle," Stecker said, "and the Mam'selle, who already noticed that he had a month's pay in his pocket, did not mention money until the act was done."

"The spreading of the pollen, you mean, Colonel?" Major Hong asked.

"Exactly," Colonel Stecker replied. "But finally, she said, *'Mon Lieutenant.* The act is over and soon you shall leave. With great regret I have to bring up the subject of money.' To which he replied, 'Mam'selle, I am an officer of the United States Marine Corps. Marine officers do not take money for rendering a public service.'"

"I like the Killer," Feldt said.

"That was a terrible joke, Colonel, with due respect," Pluto said.

"I'm still trying to figure out Daphne's father," Pickering said.

"He's a sodding arsehole," Feldt said. "Leave it at that."

"I thought it was pretty funny," Stecker said.

"Where is the Killer now, Pickering?" Feldt asked. "I liked that lad."

"Why do they call him 'Killer'?" Pluto inquired.

"He is apparently very good at killing people, which is why Eric likes him," Pickering replied.

"Pickering, I keep asking where the Killer is, and you keep going deaf on me," Feldt said, almost plaintively.

"I suppose he's in Washington," Pickering said. "I'm thinking very seriously of sending him to the Philippines."

"What for?" Stecker asked.

"I am constrained to remind you," Pluto announced solemnly, "that that subject is classified."

"Our own personal Japanese spy having been heard from," Feldt said, "and I hope ignored, please answer the sodding question."

"I am not a fucking Jap spy," Pluto said righteously. "I am a *Korean* spy."

"There's an Army officer there, on Mindanao, who's set up some sort of guerrilla operation," Pickering said. "I think it's worth looking into. So does Leahy."

"Admiral Leahy?" Stecker asked, and when Pickering grunted, he continued, "To what end?"

"To see if they're capable of doing any damage, that sort of thing."

"Seven to one, sometimes ten to one," Stecker said.

"I'll cover that," Feldt said. "What are you betting on?"

"What do you mean, Jack?" Pickering asked. "Seven to one?"

"A reasonably well led guerrilla force can tie down forces at least seven times its own strength," Stecker said. "Often more. We had a hell of a time in Nicaragua, and we outnumbered them more than ten to one. Good fighters, the little brown bastards."

"That's right, you were in Nicaragua, weren't you?"

"Where is Nicaragua?" Feldt asked.

"It is one of the seven moons of Jupiter," Pluto answered.

"Everybody was in Nicaragua," Stecker said. "Chesty Puller, Lou Diamond, just about everybody who was in The Corps between the wars found himself chasing banditos, or guerrillas, at one time or another."

"Pluto," Feldt asked, almost lovingly, "are you well versed in that jiujitsu business, or can I tell you to go sod yourself?"

Pluto leapt to his feet and waved his arms around, mimicking as best he could an Oriental character he had once seen in a Charley Chan movie. "At your peril, Commander Feldt! My hands are lethal weapons!"

"Pluto, sit down before you fall down," Pickering ordered. Then he turned to Stecker again. "And we had trouble with guerrillas in the Philippines, didn't we, Jack?"

"The Corps and the Army did," Stecker said. "That's where the .45 caliber round came from, you know."

"No, I didn't," Feldt said. "Forty-five caliber round what?"

"The pistol cartridge," Stecker said. "The standard sidearm was the .38. The Filipinos—mainly the Moros—used to come out of the bush swinging machetes. The .38 round just wouldn't put them down. The .38 bullet just wasn't heavy enough. So they came up with the .45. There's not much a 230-grain .45 bullet won't put down with one shot."

"Pickering, this old mate of yours is a sodding encyclopedia of military lore, isn't he?" Feldt asked.

"Yes, I suppose he is," Pickering said.

"Commander," Stecker said, "are you familiar with arm wrestling? I think I'd like to break your wrist."

"Oh, you would, would you?"

"We are not going to start breaking up the furniture," Pickering announced.

It was too late. Commander Feldt and Colonel Stecker were already removing the candelabra from a small table suitable for arm wrestling.

(FOUR)

TOP SECRET

EYES ONLY - CAPTAIN DAVID HAUGHTON, USN
OFFICE OF THE SECRETARY OF THE NAVY
DUPLICATION FORBIDDEN
ORIGINAL TO BE DESTROYED AFTER ENCRYPTION AND TRANSMITTAL
TO SECNAV
FOR COLONEL F. L. RICKABEE
OFFICE OF MANAGEMENT ANALYSIS

Brisbane, Australia
Monday 9 November 1942

Dear Fritz:

I don't know if you've heard or not, but Lt Colonel Jack NMI Stecker is here in Brisbane. He went to Staff Sergeant Koffler's wedding with me, as a matter of fact, and is at this moment moving his stuff from the Army BOQ into my house.

He's here to set up facilities for the First Mardiv when they are relieved from Guadalcanal and brought here for rehabilitation and refitting. According to Stecker, they are in really bad physical shape; almost everybody has malaria.

Stecker was relieved of his command of Second Battalion, Fifth Marines, and is now officially assigned to SWPOA in some sort of vaguely defined billet. I am unable to believe he was relieved for cause, and strongly suspect that it is the professional officer corps' pushing a reservist/up-from-the-ranks Mustang to give the command to one of their own. I can't imagine why General Vandergrift permitted this to happen. But it has happened, and it may be a blessing in disguise for us.

I had a talk with Stecker after the wedding, and it came out that he had extensive experience with guerrilla operations in the Banana Republics, especially Nicaragua, between the wars. It seems to me that if you know how to fight against guerrillas, it would follow that you know how to fight as a guerrilla. . . . and certainly to knowledgeably evaluate how someone else is set up, and equipped, to fight as guerrillas.

I haven't said anything to him yet, but I know him well enough to know that he would rather be doing something either with or for this fellow Fertig on Mindanao than arranging tours of picturesque Australia or USO shows, which is what The Corps wants him to do now. So I want him transferred to us, with a caveat: He has already suffered enough humiliation as it is (goddamn it; he has the Medal of Honor; how could they do this to him?), so I want you to take every precaution to make sure there is no scuttlebutt circulating that he has been further demoted by his assignment to us.

Do it as quickly as you can, and I think you had better send McCoy over here too, as quickly as that can be arranged. I think the sooner we get somebody with Captain/General Fertig, the better.

Regards,

Fleming Pickering, Brigadier General, USMCR

TOP SECRET

(FIVE)
The Main Ballroom
The Hotel Portland
Portland, Oregon
1930 Hours 10 November 1942

Veronica Wood excused herself politely from the knot of local dignitaries gathered around her and walked across the crowded floor to First Lieutenant Malcolm S. Pickering, USMCR. She was wearing a silver lamé cocktail dress and, he was convinced, absolutely nothing else.

"Hi, Marine!" she said. "Looking for a good time?"

"Some other time, perhaps, Madam. I am just returned from learning more about the manufacture of truck windows than I really care to know. I have booze, and not lust, on my mind."

He offered his glass to her. She shook her head "no," so he took a healthy swallow.

"I was at the local theater group," Veronica said. "You get no sympathy at all from me."

"Not even if I tell you I have just examined the banquet program, and right after where it says 'baked chicken breast Portland,' it says, 'remarks by yours truly.'"

She chuckled and then kissed him on the cheek.

"You're good at it, Pick," Veronica said. "You really are. You have them in the palm of your hand."

"Did Jake send you over to stroke my feathers? He promised to get me out of making after-dinner speeches."

"No," she said. "But if he thought of it, he probably would have. I came over to tell you Bobby said he was sorry he missed you, and good-bye."

"'Good-bye?' What happened to him?"

"The first group of . . . what do you call them, 'Marine war correspondents'?"

"*Combat* correspondents," Pick furnished.

"*Combat* correspondents . . . are in Los Angeles. Jake put him on the train at half past four. Bobby's supposed to teach them how to do it. At Metro-Magnum."

"I must be getting old," Pick said. "I think making him an officer was idiotic. He's a nice kid, but the word is *kid.*"

"You and Jake," Veronica said. "But Jake said he'll probably do OK."

"Jake's whistling in the dark. Would you, if you were a man, take orders from Bobby?"

"I think you underestimate him, Pick."

"I hope so. Still, for the sake of the combat correspondents, better Bobby than Macklin."

"Ooooh, that's an interesting observation! What have you got against him?"

"Forget it," Pick said. "I was thinking out loud. I shouldn't have."

"Speaking of the devil . . ."

First Lieutenant R. B. Macklin, USMC, walked up to them.

"I wondered where you were, Pickering," he said.

"I was out inspiring the workers to make more and better truck windows," Pick said. "Was that idle curiosity that sent you in my direction? Or did you have something on your mind?"

"Washington has asked for a transcript of your remarks . . ."

"Washington?"

"General Stewart's office. Since this tour is going so well, I think they intend to use it as sort of a model for the East Coast and Midwest war bond tours. They're next, you know."

"I just stand up and open my mouth," Pick said. "I never wrote anything down."

"Well, that's what I'm asking, Pickering, that you write it down, so I can send it to General Stewart."

Pickering motioned with his index finger for Macklin to put his head close to his. When he did, he whispered a few words into his ear.

Macklin colored, glared at him, and then said, "Well, we'll see what Major Dillon has to say about that! Excuse me, Miss Wood."

Veronica watched him go. "What was that all about, Pick? Did you whisper sweet obscenities in his ear?"

"And now he's going to tell Daddy that I have been a bad boy," Pick said.

"Tell me something, Pick," Veronica said. "Did Bobby ever say anything to you about Dawn Morris?"

"About Dawn Morris?" Pick answered, thought a moment, and then replied, "No, what do you mean?"

"Well, he was hanging around with you and Dunn. I thought maybe he said something."

"No. He hung around with us because we protected him from Macklin. Macklin likes to prove he's a Marine officer by ordering Bobby around and making him call him 'Sir.' . . . And I think maybe Bobby was hoping he could latch on to one of Little Billy's rejects."

"And did he?"

"You act like his mother. No, Mother, Bobby has been a good boy. I think—I know—that a couple of Billy's rejects would have been perfectly happy to play house with him . . . with anyone wearing a Marine uniform. But I don't think he could work up the courage to make a pass."

"Maybe you should have found the courage for him," Veronica said. "Where is Billy Dunn, by the way?"

"The last time I saw him was at the . . . what the hell were they making at that factory? Before lunch?"

"Before lunch was the place that used to make thermostats and is now making artillery fuzes."

"Lieutenant Dunn was last seen entering a Buick owned by the wife of a well-known thermostat manufacturer," Pick said, in a credible mimicry of Walter Winchell. Winchell was a radio news broadcaster who specialized in celebrity gossip. His trademarks were the sound of a telegraph key and an intense, staccato speaking voice. "The word going around is that they were going to test each other's temperatures."

"You sound jealous," Veronica said, laughing.

"I am," Pick said.

"Maybe you ought to smile back at Dawn Morris."

"Lips that have touched Macklin's shall never touch mine."

Veronica was truly surprised. "You really think she's . . . uh . . ."

"They could, I suppose, be holding Midnight Vespers in her room."

"Do you think Bobby knew that?"

"Yeah, sure he did. We saw Macklin going into her room at one in the morning—in Sacramento, I think, on the second or third day of this odyssey—in his dressing gown, no less. Why did you ask that?"

"No reason, Pick. Just feminine curiosity. Oh, there's Billy."

"I hate that sexually satiated look on his face," Pick said.

Dunn crossed the room to them, snatching a drink from a waiter's tray on the way.

He took a sip from it, grimaced, and handed it to Pick.

"Scotch," he said.

"God is punishing you," Pick said.

"I'll take it," Veronica said, taking the drink from Pickering.

"God has been very kind to me lately, actually," Dunn said. "And how was your afternoon, Mr. Pickering?"

"What would you like to know about truck windows?"

Dunn looked at his watch.

"Isn't it about time for the triumphal entry?" he asked.

"Any minute now," Pick said. "If you want a drink before the baked chicken breast Portland, you'd better get it now."

"Not chicken again!"

"I told you, God is punishing you. When he said, 'Thou Shalt Not Commit Adultery,' He meant it. He knows how you spent the afternoon."

"Oh, Pick, shut up." Veronica giggled.

Another waiter passed with a tray full of drinks. Dunn took another chance. To judge by the pleased look on his face after he tasted it, this time he was successful.

"See, He does love me after all. This is pretty good sour mash."

There was a small ripple of applause. It gradually swelled as everyone in the Main Ballroom turned to the door.

Staff Sergeant Thomas Michael "Machine Gun" McCoy, USMCR, stood in the doorway. He was wearing a dress blue uniform, and the Medal of Honor on its white-starred ribbon was hanging around his neck. Behind him, in greens, were a pair of gunnery sergeants.

The Mayor of Portland walked to the door and shook Sergeant McCoy's hand. The applause died down. The strains of the Marine Hymn, from an electric organ, filled the room.

With the exception of Lieutenants Dunn and Pickering, everyone there seemed to come to attention. A few people actually put their hands over their hearts.

When the music was over, Sergeant McCoy waved shyly and modestly at the crowd. And then, with the mayor at his side and the two gunnies one step behind him, he crossed the room to the bar. Once he was there, a bartender handed him a Pilsner glass of beer.

"I would really like to know what Jake Dillon said to him, to get him to behave," Dunn said.

"It is probably what the gunnies have done to him," Pickering said.

"You mean you don't know?" Veronica asked.

"Know what?" Pick asked.

"If he behaves all day, and all the way to dinner, Jake sees that he gets two drinks after dinner. And that isn't the only carrot Jake dangles in front of his nose, either."

"The lady speaketh, I believeth, the truth," Pick said.

"Major Dillon *is* a man with an *uncommon* problem-solving ability, isn't he?" Dunn asked admiringly.

"Every night?" Pick asked.

"Every night, if he has behaved all day," Veronica said.

"How come nobody ever dangles a carrot in front of my nose?" Pick asked.

"God doesn't love you," Dunn said. "And look who's coming!"

Lieutenant R. B. Macklin was walking across the room to them.

"Would you mind posing with Sergeant McCoy and the mayor, Miss Wood, for some photographs?" he asked when he reached them.

"Certainly."

"Maybe it would be better if you left your drink here," Macklin suggested. Veronica handed it to Pickering. Dunn drained his bourbon.

"We would like you in the photos too, Dunn," Macklin said.

"I've been through this before, Macklin," Dunn said.

"You two could have expressed a certain respect for The Corps by coming to attention when the Marine Hymn was played," Macklin said.

"Unless you want to be photographed on your rear end, Lieutenant," Dunn said softly and icily, "you had better not say one more word to either me or Mr. Pickering for the entire balance of the evening."

He turned to Veronica Wood. "Would you take my arm, Ma'am, and we'll sashay across the ballroom and have our picture taken."

"I would be honored, Lieutenant Dunn," Veronica said. She took his arm, and they marched across the room, with Lieutenant Macklin trailing along behind.

"Is that what they mean when they say a 'two-fisted drinker'?" a female voice behind Pick asked. He turned to see who it was. She was in a cocktail dress, an older woman, thirty-five anyway; her hair seemed to be prematurely gray.

"I guess it is," Pick said. He finished his drink and set it down.

"You're Lieutenant Pickering, right?" the woman asked, offering her hand.

"Yes, Ma'am," he said.

"I've been wanting to introduce myself," she said. "We're going to dinner together. I'm Alice Feaster. Mrs. Alice Feaster. For what it's worth, I'm the President of the City Council's sister. That's how I got a ticket."

"How do you do?" Pick said. "I didn't know we were going into dinner in pairs."

"I arranged it," Mrs. Feaster said.

What the hell does that mean?

"And the Major . . . what's his name?"

"Major Dillon."

". . . pointed you out to me, but I didn't want to interrupt. You were having a private conversation with Miss Wood."

"You should have come up. If I had known, I would have gone looking for you."

"May I ask you a personal question?"

"Certainly."

"Is there . . . uh . . . anything between you and Miss Wood?"

"Miss Wood is going to marry Major Dillon. We're just friends."

"You seem to be very good friends," she said.

"We are. Can I get you a drink, Mrs. Feaster?"

"I'd love one. A martini. Gin. Onions."

On the way back from the bar, Pickering observed that Mrs. Feaster was very well preserved, for an older woman.

"Thank you very much," she said, looking at him over the rim of the martini glass.

"Did your brother the City Council President manage a ticket for Mr. Feaster, too?"

"Mr. Feaster is in Spokane tonight."

"I'm sorry."

"You wouldn't really like him; he's rather dull." She reacted to the surprised look in his face by asking: "Don't you think people should say what they want to?"

"Absolutely."

"And where is your wife, while you're off on the war bond tour?"

"No wife."

"I'm surprised. You're a very good-looking young man. I'm surprised that some sweet young thing hasn't led you to the altar."

"So is my mother."

Chimes sounded.

"I think that's for us," Mrs. Feaster said.

"It sounded like an elevator," Pick replied. "You know, 'third floor, ladies' lingerie'?"

Why did I say "ladies' lingerie"?

She laughed as she took his arm.

"May I?"

She walked very close to him as they crossed the room to the place where the guests at the head table were gathering. The President of the City Council was a tall, balding man with a skinny wife.

"We're really honored to have you in Portland, Lieutenant," he said.

"Thank you, Sir."

"And grateful for the excitement, right, Frank?" Mrs. Feaster said. "We don't have much excitement in Portland, do we?"

"Oh, I wouldn't say that, Alice."

"I would," Alice said with a sharp laugh; then she gave Pick's arm a little squeeze. When he looked down at her, he (almost entirely innocently, he told himself) got a look down the opening of her dress.

Black lace and white flesh are inarguably erotic.

Lieutenant Pickering made his way back to his seat at the head table, next to Mrs. Alice Feaster. He held a plaque on which was mounted a gold key to the City of Portland. The audience was giving him a nice hand.

"I would like to thank Lieutenant Pickering for these inspiring remarks," the mayor said after the applause died down.

"Give me that," Mrs. Feaster said. "I'll put it on the floor."

As she did so, he caught another glimpse of black lace and white flesh.

Watch yourself, Pickering. You've had three drinks and probably two bottles of wine. You weren't nearly as brilliant a speaker up there as you think you were. They thought you were funny as hell when you told them it was a pleasure to be in Spokane. But the truth is that you forgot where you are. And you said Spokane because that's where she told you her husband is tonight.

"I would now like to recognize the other Guadalcanal aces," the mayor went on. "I will ask them to stand as I call their names and come here for their keys to our city. I'll ask you to hold your applause until everyone has received his key."

Mrs. Feaster turned in her seat so she could watch the other aces. In doing so, her knee touched Pick's leg.

"I loved your speech," she said.

"Thank you."

"Are they taking good care of you? I mean in the hotel?"

"Very nice."

"Nice rooms?"

"Very nice."

Mrs. Feaster's knee had not broken contact with his leg, Pick realized.

"Anyone sharing it with you?"

"No."

You don't want to do this, Pickering. You will regret it in the morning. As a matter of fact, even despite that last remark of hers, you don't know whether the knee is accidental or not. So get thee behind me, Satan.

Pickering turned in his seat to watch the others have their hands shaken and take their keys. Doing so removed his leg from Mrs. Feaster's knee. Mrs. Feaster's knee did not pursue Lieutenant Pickering's leg.

"And now, the Reverend Stanley O. White," the mayor announced, "of the Sage Avenue Baptist Church, will lead us in our closing prayer."

The Reverend White stepped to the lectern.

"May we please bow our heads in prayer," he began.

The Reverend, Pick adjudged after the opening phrases, *is not afflicted with brevity.*

Mrs. Feaster's hand suddenly appeared on Pick's leg, just above the knee, and then slid slowly upward. By the time her fingers found what she was looking for, his male appendage had reacted to the stimuli.

"Thank God," Mrs. Feaster whispered. "I was beginning to wonder if you were queer."

Oh, fuck it! Why not?

(SIX)
The John Charles Fremont Suite
The Foster Washingtonian Hotel
Seattle, Washington
1715 Hours 13 November 1942

"I didn't think you were going to show up," First Lieutenant Malcolm S. Pickering, USMCR, said to First Lieutenant William C. Dunn, when Dunn came into the suite, "so I had supper without you."

Pickering was sitting on a couch, wearing a shirt and trousers. On the coffee table in front of him were the remnants of a T-bone steak and a baked potato.

"I am a Marine officer. I am at the proper place, at the proper time, although I must change into the properly appointed uniform. Why should that surprise you?" Dunn replied.

"The lady did not express her appreciation in the physical sense, in other words?"

After somehow recalling a previously long-forgotten lecture that the only civilians permitted to fly aboard Navy or Marine aircraft without specific permission were members of the press, Lieutenant Dunn had taken Miss Roberta Daiman to the Boeing Plant for an orientation ride in a Yellow Peril. Miss Daiman was a reporter for *The Seattle Times.*

"Let us say I was given a preview of the coming attraction," Dunn said. "What's on the menu for tonight? Or is that why you're eating a steak?"

"Chicken," Pick replied. "What else?"

"Do I have time to order a steak?"

"I think so," Pick said, and reached for the telephone.

"On the way over here," Dunn said. "It came over the radio that we lost the cruiser *Atlanta.*"

Pick dropped the handset back into the cradle. "No shit?"

"There wasn't much. Just a bulletin, 'The Navy Department has just announced the loss of the USS *Atlanta* . . .'"

"They say where?"

"Off Savo Island."

"Shit," Pickering said, then shrugged and picked up the telephone and asked for room service.

"I better change," Dunn said. "Which bedroom is mine?"

"The larger one. I thought from the look on the lady's face that you might be expecting an overnight guest."

"Shall I ask if she has a friend?"

"It is a sacred rule of the gentle gender that when two or more of them gather together, none of them would dream of doing that sort of thing outside of holy matrimony. And besides, I'm tired."

"Suit yourself," Dunn said, and repeated, "I better change."

About five minutes later, while Pickering was making himself a drink, there was a knock at the door. He went to open it, a little surprised at the quick service.

But it was not room service. It was Second Lieutenant Robert F. Easterbrook, USMCR . . . as surprised to see Pickering as Pickering was to see him.

"Easterbunny! I thought you were in Hollywood."

"I thought this was Major Dillon's room."

"Actually, it was Veronica Wood's, but when she and Dillon went to Los Angeles on business, Dunn and I moved in."

"He's in Hollywood?"

"That's the story for public consumption. If you really have to talk to him, he left a telephone number. A friend of his—maybe of hers—has a place on the water outside of town."

"I hate to bother him," Easterbrook said.

"Then, if it's not important, don't."

"Maybe later. Can I have a drink?"

Pick waved at the row of whiskey bottles on the bar. Easterbrook walked over to it and poured scotch in a glass.

"I found out that Sergeant Lomax's widow lives here," he said. "I want to give her the Leica."

"What Leica?"

"Lomax had a Leica. When he got killed, I took it. Or Lieutenant Hale took it. And when he got killed, I took it from him. Now I want to give it back."

"I wondered where that camera came from; I didn't think it was issued."

Dunn walked into the sitting room, tucking his shirt into his trousers.

Pickering spoke for Easterbrook, which was fortunate. For at that moment Lieutenant Easterbrook was incapable of speech—having swallowed all at once at least two ounces of scotch: "He found out that the widow of the sergeant who got killed lives here. He's going to return the sergeant's camera to her."

"I don't envy that job," Dunn said.

Easterbrook smiled weakly at him.

The story he'd just related was not the truth, the whole truth, and nothing but the truth. About the only true part of it was that he had found out that Sergeant Lomax's widow did live in Seattle.

But the real reason he was in Seattle was to tell Major Dillon that he wanted to resign his commission. He shouldn't have been made an officer in the first place.

For Christ's sake. I'm only nineteen years old! And they didn't send me to OCS. . . .

If they did, I probably would have flunked out. . . . *They just pinned a gold bar on me and told me I was an officer.*

He had suspected all along that the commission was a big mistake. But the first time he met the combat correspondents at Metro-Magnum Studios, he was goddamn certain it was.

They looked at me and smirked. "Who the fuck is this kid? He's going to be our detachment commander? You've got to be kidding!" I could see it in their faces and the way they talked to me, like I was a goddamned joke. And I am, as an officer.

Pick and Dunn are officers. Maybe it's because they're older than I am and went to college, or maybe they were just born that way. But they can give people orders: there is something about them that says "officer," and people do what they say. And I bet that when I'm not around, between themselves, they laugh at Second Lieutenant Easterbunny, too. Why not? I'm a fucking joke.

Those combat correspondents The Corps recruited are real journalists: they worked on real newspapers. The New York Times *and the* Louisville Courier-Journal, *papers like those. There's even one from* The Kansas City Star. *He knows about the* Conner Courier, *that it's a shitty little weekly.* . . . *And what if he writes home and asks about me and finds out that I was nothing more than an after-school kid who helped out for sixty-five cents an hour?*

And I don't give a fuck about what The Corps says . . . that shit about you not having to respect the man, only the bar on his collar. That's bullshit. I've been around enough good officers—not just Dunn and Pickering, but on the 'Canal, where it counted—to know the first thing enlisted men look for in their officers is competence. If they don't think he knows what he's doing, it doesn't matter if he has fucking colonel's eagles on his collar, they won't pay a fucking bit of attention to what he's got to say.

And not one of those combat correspondents at Metro-Magnum is dumb enough to see anything in me but what I am. . . . *They're real reporters, for Christ's sake, trained to separate the bullshit from the real thing . . . which is a kid with a bar on his shoulder because some asshole like Macklin who doesn't know the first thing about what The Corps is really all about got a wild hair up his ass and pinned a gold bar on him.*

And unless I resign my commission, The Corps will send those poor innocent bastards off to combat under me. And they're going to get killed because they don't teach at Parris Island or San Diego what a combat correspondent has to know to stay alive when you're in deep shit. And they certainly won't pay one fucking bit of attention to me if I try to tell them. I wouldn't pay attention to me either, if I was one of them.

What they need is somebody like Lomax. If that nasty sonofabitch hadn't got himself killed, they could have pinned a bar on him, and he could have done this. They would have listened to him, not only because he would have kicked the shit out of them, the way he did to me, but because he was a real newspaperman. Right here. On The Seattle Times.

What the hell is his wife going to say to me when I give her his camera? "How come you're still alive and passing yourself off as an officer, you little shit; and my husband—a grown man, but only a sergeant—is dead?"

What I should do is just keep the fucking Leica. She didn't expect to get it back, anyway. She told me that on the phone. But I don't have the balls to do something like that. I still think like a fucking Boy Scout. And Boy Scouts don't keep things that don't belong to them. And Boy Scouts should not lead men into combat. Me, an officer? Shit. I don't even know how to resign my commission! What do I do? Write somebody? . . . *Who?* . . . *A letter, or what?*

''Easterbunny,'' Pickering said. ''Go easy on the sauce. That's your third. I don't want you falling on your ass.''

''Sorry.''

''You don't have to be sorry, Easterbunny,'' Dunn said. ''Just take it easy.''

They're tolerating me. Treating me like a kid. They know fucking well I have no right to be an officer.

''Something bothering you, my boy?'' Pickering asked. ''In the absence of our beloved leader, would you like to pour your heart out to Lieutenant Dunn or myself?''

''Have you perhaps been painfully pricked by Cupid's arrow, Easterbunny?'' Dunn asked.

''Go fuck yourself,'' Easterbrook said. ''Both of you.''

''That does it,'' Pickering said, laughing. ''Easterbunny, you have just been shut off. You never tell people who are larger than you to go fuck themselves.''

''What's the matter, Easterbunny?'' Dunn asked. ''Maybe we can fix it.''

''If Major Dillon's gone, Captain Galloway's in charge, right?''

''Perhaps, technically, Lieutenant,'' Pickering said. ''But in the real world, knowing that Captain Galloway is floating around on the wings of love, and that Macklin is . . .''

''A feather merchant,'' Dunn supplied.

''Well said. And that I am smarter than Little Billy here, I am running things. So if you have something on your mind, tell me.''

''I don't like that 'smarter than' crap,'' Dunn said. ''If you're so smart, how come you got stuck with running this circus?''

''I'm going to see Captain Galloway,'' Easterbrook announced, then walked somewhat unsteadily toward the door.

''Easterbunny, Galloway will burn you a new asshole if you show up at his door shit-faced,'' Pickering said.

Easterbrook looked at him. And then he opened the door and walked out into the corridor.

He was almost at the elevator when it occurred to him that he would never see Captain Galloway unless he found out Captain Galloway's room number.

There was a house telephone on a narrow table against the mirrored wall across from the bank of elevators. He picked it up and asked the operator for Captain Galloway's room number.

''I will connect you, Sir.''

''I don't want to be connected. I want to know what room he's in.''

''I will connect you, Sir,'' the operator persisted.

In the mirror, Easterbrook saw the elevator door behind him open. Staff Sergeant Thomas M. ''Machine Gun'' McCoy stepped off. He was wearing his dress blues, and the Medal of Honor was hanging down his chest.

He was closely followed by his gunnery sergeant escorts.

''Well, I'll be goddamned,'' Sergeant McCoy said. ''The ninety-day wonder is back. I thought we'd seen the last of you.''

Easterbrook tried to replace the handset in its cradle; he missed by two inches. He turned around.

''Fuck you, McCoy,'' the Easterbunny said. ''You're really an asshole, you know that?''

Two strong hands grasped each of McCoy's arms.

''Lieutenant, why don't you get on the elevator,'' one of the gunnery sergeants said.

''Because I have just decided to tell this asshole what I really think of him. You're a fucking disgrace to The Marine Corps, McCoy.''

"You fucking little feather merchant!"

"I was there, McCoy, when you got that fucking medal. Don't you call me a feather merchant!"

"What do you mean, you were there?"

"I mean I was on Bloody Ridge with the Raiders is what I mean, shit-for-brains. I know what happened. I saw what happened."

"Shit, I didn't know you was there."

"I was there with Lieutenant Donaldson. You remember Lieutenant Donaldson, McCoy? Now, there was one hell of a Marine officer. And you know what he said to me the first time you ignored your orders and stood up with your fucking machine gun?"

"Lieutenant Donaldson got killed," McCoy said.

"He said, 'If the Japs don't kill that sonofabitch, I will,' is what he said."

"Donaldson was wounded," McCoy said, as if to himself.

"Yeah, he was bad wounded. But he saw you get up when you were supposed to stay where the fuck he told you to stay."

"And then some sonofabitch with more balls than brains started to carry him down the hill, and the Japs killed him, too. I seen them go down. That's when I stood up again."

"I wasn't hit, you asshole. The Lieutenant was too heavy for me to carry. I fell down with him on top of me and couldn't get up. But I saw you, you sonofabitch, leave your hole and charge off like it was your own fucking war! Good Marines would have died if you hadn't been so fucking lucky. If I had a weapon then, I'd have killed you myself."

Lieutenant Easterbrook suddenly felt a little woozy. He turned around and supported himself on the telephone table. When he looked at the mirror, he saw McCoy being hustled away by the gunnies. And when he looked at his own reflection he saw that tears were running down his cheeks.

And then he knew he was going to be sick. He ran down the corridor to Dunn's and Pickering's room and hammered on the door until Pickering opened it. And then he ran into one of the bedrooms, and just made it to the toilet in time.

"I hope that the wages of sin caught up with him before Captain Galloway saw him shit-faced," he heard Lieutenant Pickering say.

And then his stomach erupted again.

XVI

(ONE)
The John Charles Fremont Suite
The Foster Washingtonian Hotel
Seattle Washington
2145 Hours 13 November 1942

Lieutenant Malcolm S. Pickering, USMCR, sat at the writing desk in the sitting room. A bottle of scotch was beside him. Several sheets of ornately engraved stationery were before him.

He had started to write a long-overdue letter. When the knock at the door interrupted him, he'd gotten as far as:

> Dear Dad,
>   I feel I have been shamelessly remiss in writing my favorite boy in the overseas service. I hope that you can understand that those of us on the home front are also making our sacrifices for the war effort, too. Would you believe that I've eaten chicken—in one form or another—for the pièce de résistance eleven days in a row? And the shortages! . . .

He uttered a vulgarism and stood up and went and opened the door. One of "The Gorillas's Gunnies," as he thought of them, was standing there.

Now what? What has that sonofabitch done now?

"What's up, Gunny?"

"Mr. Pickering, is Mr. Easterbrook in here by any chance?"

Thank God. I was afraid for a moment that I was about to be informed that Gargantua has pulled the arms off his plaything of the evening.

"He is, Gunny. But to put it delicately, he is indisposed at the moment. To put a point on it, he got shit-faced, and he's sleeping it off."

That's an understatement. After throwing up all over himself, and all over the bathroom, he went on a crying jag and announced that he intends to resign his commission and go back to the 'Canal as a corporal.

"Could I come in, Mr. Pickering?"

"Sure. Come on in. I presume our gorilla has had his evening's rations, she has been sent safely back to the village, and our gorilla is safely in his cage."

The gunny laughed.

"Would you like a drink, Gunny?"

"No, Sir. Thank you, Sir."

"This must be serious. This is only the second time in my Marine Corps experience that a gunny has turned down good booze."

"Well, maybe a little one, Mr. Pickering. I always hate to see good hootch go to waste."

Pickering fixed him a drink and handed it to him.

The gunny raised the glass and said, "The Corps."

Pick was surprised at the toast, and strangely moved by it. He repeated the toast,

''The Corps.'' And then he asked, ''What do you want with Mr. Easterbrook, Gunny? Can I help?''

''This is good booze,'' the gunny said. Then he met Pickering's eyes. ''McCoy wants to apologize to Mr. Easterbrook, Sir. I think maybe it would be a good idea.''

Lieutenant Pickering quite naturally assumed that Staff Sergeant McCoy had spoken disrespectfully to Lieutenant Easterbrook; that he'd said it in the hearing of one or both of the gunnies; that they had been offended; and that they had subsequently ''counseled'' Staff Sergeant McCoy by bouncing him off the walls and the floor until he became truly repentant and wished to make any amends that were called for—including an apology.

''What did the gorilla say to him, Gunny?''

''Mr. Easterbrook ate McCoy a new asshole, Mr. Pickering.''

''What did you say?''

''Would you believe McCoy crying, Mr. Pickering?''

''No,'' Pick said. ''I would indeed find that very hard to believe.'' A thought occurred to him, which he turned into a kind of accusation: ''Was he drunk? He's supposed to have two beers and two drinks a day, and not a goddamned drop more.''

''Stone sober. But he bawled like a baby. He said that he thought Mr. Easterbrook was dead, and that Mr. Easterbrook was the bravest man he's ever seen.''

''Easterbrook?'' Pick asked incredulously.

''Did you know that Mr. Easterbrook was with the Raiders on Bloody Ridge?''

''I knew he spent a lot of time with the Raiders,'' Pick replied, remembering the Easterbunny eating in VMF-229's mess—tired, dirty, and scared shitless. And remembering how he'd felt sorry for him and asked where he'd been.

''Well, it looks like he was on Bloody Ridge when McCoy did whatever he did to get the Medal, and McCoy seen him try to carry some wounded officer down the hill. Saw him fall; thought he was killed. McCoy said that when Mr. Easterbrook stood up to carry this officer, he had to know he was going to get his ass killed, the way the Japs were laying in fire. But he did it anyway, trying to get this officer to a Corpsman.''

''Jesus H. Christ!''

''And Mr. Easterbrook told McCoy that he seen what McCoy done. . . . I guess he left his position when he wasn't supposed to when he killed all them Japanese. . . . And Mr. Easterbrook told him if he'd had a weapon, he would have killed him himself.''

''How did this all come out?'' Pick asked, sensing that what he was hearing was the truth.

''We was bringing McCoy up in the elevator from the press conference. And when the door opened, there was Mr. Easterbrook. And McCoy called him a feather merchant, and . . . I guess Mr. Easterbrook had a couple of drinks and decided he'd had enough of McCoy's shit. And he really went after him.'' The gunny paused, and then added, with admiration in his voice, ''He really ate him a new asshole. Called him everything in the book . . . starting with asshole.''

''And this reduced McCoy to tears?''

''Yes, Sir. Not by the elevator. When we got him back to the room. He really wants to apologize, Mr. Pickering. I think maybe it would be a good idea.''

''Where is our weeping hero?''

''In the room, Sir.''

''Give me fifteen minutes, Gunny, and then bring him down.''

''Aye, aye, Sir. Thank you, Mr. Pickering.''

(TWO)

When First Lieutenant William C. Dunn, USMCR, unlocked the door to the John Charles Fremont Suite of the Foster Washingtonian Hotel and waved Miss Roberta Daiman inside, it was with the reasonable expectation that First Lieutenant Malcolm S. Pickering, being an officer and a gentleman, would have retired for the evening, leaving the sitting room free for whatever purposes Lieutenant Dunn might have vis-à-vis Miss Daiman.

Instead, he found—for all practical purposes—a crowd. Lieutenants Pickering and Easterbrook, the gorilla, and the gorilla's keepers were all there. The Easterbunny, who looked wan and pale, was being fed a Prairie Oyster—at least to judge by the horrible grimace on his face, and by the materials on the table: the eggshells, the tomato juice, and the Tabasco and Worcestershire sauce bottles.*

"Easterbunny, damn you!" Lieutenant Dunn said. "What the hell have you been up to?"

"Speak kindly to our boy," Pickering said. "Or you will offend Sergeant McCoy, and he will pull your arms off . . . with my blessing."

"Just what the hell is going on around here?" Dunn asked.

"We have been trying to think of some way to impress upon Mr. Easterbrook's detachment of would-be combat correspondents that they are singularly fortunate in having an officer of his proven valor to lead them."

"You bet your fucking ass," Staff Sergeant McCoy said.

"I didn't think anyone would be here," Lieutenant Dunn said to Miss Daiman.

Pickering went on. "We have also concluded that there would be no cries of outrage from the Raiders if Lieutenant Easterbrook were to sew a Raider Patch on his uniform. After all, he was on Bloody Ridge with them."

"He's as much entitled to that fucking patch as any fucking Raider," Staff Sergeant McCoy agreed.

"What, exactly, is the problem with the combat correspondents?" Dunn asked.

"They seem to have formed the notion—or at least Mr. Easterbrook feels they have formed the notion—that he is a feather merchant."

"Feather merchant, my ass," Sergeant McCoy interjected. "This little fucker is the bravest man I ever seen. I thought he was dead!"

"What did you say, Sergeant?" Miss Daiman asked.

"Excuse him, Miss, please," the Master Gunnery Sergeant said. "Watch your goddamn language, McCoy!"

"What did you say, Sergeant?" Miss Daiman asked again.

Sergeant McCoy pointed his finger at Lieutenant Easterbrook. "That's the bravest man I ever seen," he said. He made a sound that could have been a sob. And then, finding his voice, he passionately announced, "He deserves this goddamn medal, not me."

"Do you really mean that, Sergeant McCoy?" Miss Daiman asked innocently.

"You bet your sweet ass I mean it."

"Excuse me," Lieutenant Easterbrook said, pushing himself off the couch, "I'm going to be sick again."

---

*Another note having no proper connection with this story: As I was writing this book, word came that Brigadier Walter S. McIlhenny, USMCR, Retired, of Avery Island, New Iberia, Louisiana, where his family owns the Tabasco Company, had died. General McIlhenny served with distinction on Guadalcanal and elsewhere, and left a substantial portion of his fortune to the scholarship fund of the Marine Military Academy, a Marine Corps–affiliated boarding school for boys.

(THREE)

ASSOCIATED PRESS SEATTLE 34224
PRIORITY FOR NATIONAL WIRE

SLUG MEDAL OF HONOR WINNER "MACHINE GUN" MCCOY IDENTI-
FIES "REAL HERO OF BLOODY RIDGE"

BY ROBERTA DAIMAN, STAFF REPORTER, THE SEATTLE TIMES

SEATTLE, WASH NOV. 13—STAFF SERGEANT THOMAS J. MCCOY
USMCR WHOSE VALOR FIGHTING AS A MARINE RAIDER ON GUA-
DALCANAL'S BLOODY RIDGE EARNED HIM BOTH THE SOBRIQUET
"MACHINE GUN MCCOY" AND THE MEDAL OF HONOR FROM THE
HANDS OF PRESIDENT FRANKLIN D. ROOSEVELT POINTED A FIN-
GER AT A BOYISH MARINE SECOND LIEUTENANT AND PRO-
CLAIMED HIM TO BE THE BRAVEST MAN ON BLOODY RIDGE.

"HE DESERVES THIS (THE MEDAL OF HONOR) MORE THAN I DO"
SERGEANT MCCOY SAID OF NINETEEN YEAR OLD 2ND LT ROBERT
F. EASTERBROOK, OF CONNER, MO. EASTERBROOK, THEN AN EN-
LISTED MARINE COMBAT CORRESPONDENT, WAS WITH MCCOY ON
"BLOODY RIDGE" DURING THE ENGAGEMENT WHICH SAW MCCOY
EARN THE NATION'S HIGHEST AWARD FOR VALOR.

TEARS FILLING HIS EYES, MCCOY WENT ON TO DESCRIBE HOW
EASTERBROOK, WITH COMPLETE DISREGARD OF HIS OWN SAFETY,
ATTEMPTED TO CARRY A BADLY WOUNDED MARINE OFFICER TO
SAFETY THROUGH A HAIL OF JAPANESE SMALL ARMS AND MORTAR
FIRE.

"I THOUGHT HE WAS DEAD," MCCOY SAID. "I DON'T KNOW HOW
ANYONE COULD HAVE LIVED THROUGH THAT. WHEN HE STOOD
UP, WITH LIEUTENANT DONALDSON SLUNG OVER HIS SHOULDER,
I KNEW THEY WERE BOTH AS GOOD AS DEAD."

MARINE FIRST LIEUTENANT ARTHUR M. DONALDSON DIED OF
WOUNDS RECEIVED DURING THE BATTLE, STRUCK A THIRD TIME
BY ENEMY FIRE AS EASTERBROOK TRIED TO CARRY HIM TO
SAFETY.

THE STORY CAME OUT IN SEATTLE AS THE TWO MARINE VETERANS
OF GUADALCANAL WERE PREPARING TO BRING TO A CLOSE THE
SECOND WAR BOND TOUR. UNTIL TODAY, MCCOY HAD BELIEVED
EASTERBROOK TO BE DEAD, AND HAD NOT RECOGNIZED THE
SLIGHT MARINE OFFICER ACCOMPANYING THE TOUR IN A PUBLIC
RELATIONS CAPACITY AS THE COMBAT CORRESPONDENT WHO
HAD BEEN WILLING TO LAY DOWN HIS LIFE FOR A FELLOW MARINE
ON GUADALCANAL.

THIS REPORTER ASKED MARINE LIEUTENANT WILLIAM C. DUNN,
A GUADALCANAL DOUBLE ACE AND HOLDER OF THE NAVY CROSS,
THE NATION'S SECOND HIGHEST DECORATION FOR VALOR, WHO
IS ALSO ON THE WAR BOND TOUR, HOW EASTERBROOK'S EXPLOITS
COULD HAVE GONE UNNOTICED.

"MOST HEROISM GOES UNNOTICED," DUNN REPLIED. "FOR EVERY MARINE YOU SEE WITH A MEDAL, THERE ARE A DOZEN MARINES WHO DID AT LEAST AS MUCH WHEN NO ONE WAS AROUND TO SEE THEM DO IT. EVERYONE WHO WAS ON BLOODY RIDGE DESERVED A MEDAL."

ALL THE GUADALCANAL HEROES CONFESSED THEY WERE HAPPY THE WAR BOND TOUR IS ABOUT OVER. MCCOY WILL REJOIN HIS MARINE RAIDER BATTALION IN THE PACIFIC. EASTERBROOK, "THE BRAVEST MAN ON BLOODY RIDGE" IS IN THE PROCESS OF TRAIN-ING A DETACHMENT OF COMBAT CORRESPONDENTS IN LOS ANGELES. HE WILL LEAD THEM OVERSEAS WHEN THEIR TRAINING IS COMPLETED. WITH THE EXCEPTION OF CAPTAIN CHARLES M. GALLOWAY, WHO IS RETURNING TO THE FIGHTER SQUADRON HE COMMANDED ON GUADALCANAL, THE MARINE ACES ARE BEING ASSIGNED TO VARIOUS TRAINING BASES IN THE UNITED STATES TO TRAIN THE NEXT GENERATION OF FIGHTER PILOTS.
END END END

CAPTION, PIC ONE ACCOMPANYING: (L-R) MEDAL OF HONOR WIN-NER STAFF SERGEANT THOMAS J. MCCOY USMCR AND THE MAN HE DECLARES WAS THE "BRAVEST MAN ON BLOODY RIDGE," 2ND LT ROBERT F. EASTERBROOK, USMC, (PHOTO BY ROBERTA DAIMAN, SEATTLE TIMES)

CAPTION, PIC TWO ACCOMPANYING: MEDAL OF HONOR WINNER STAFF SERGEANT THOMAS J "MACHINE GUN" MCCOY USMC (LEFT) AND NAVY CROSS WINNER 1ST LT WILLIAM C. DUNN, USMCR, FLANK 2ND LT ROBERT F. EASTERBROOK, USMCR, THE MARINE COMBAT CORRESPONDENT MCCOY SAYS WAS "THE BRAV-EST MAN ON BLOODY RIDGE." (PHOTO BY ROBERTA DAIMAN, SEAT-TLE TIMES)

(FOUR)

TOP SECRET

EYES ONLY - THE SECRETARY OF THE NAVY
DUPLICATION FORBIDDEN
ORIGINAL TO BE DESTROYED AFTER ENCRYPTION AND
TRANSMITTAL TO SECNAV

Brisbane, Australia
Saturday 14 November 1942

Dear Frank:

Word just reached here that the battleships Washington and South Dakota have sunk the Japanese battleship Kirishima, even though the South Dakota apparently was pretty badly hit in the process. I'd like to think that Admiral Dan Callahan somehow knows about this. I was pretty upset when I heard he was killed the day before. Revenge is sweet.

The more I get into this Fertig in the Philippines business—specifically, the more I have learned from Lt Col Jack NMI Stecker about the efficacy of a well run guerrilla operation—the more I become convinced that it's worth a good deal of effort and expense.

Where it stands right now is that a young Marine officer, Lieutenant Kenneth McCoy, whom they call 'Killer,' by the way, just arrived here. He has already made the Makin Island Marine Raider operation, and went ashore on Buka from another submarine when we replaced the Marines there. He is as expert in rubber boat operations as they come, in other words. He sees no problem in getting ashore from a submarine off Mindanao.

He and Stecker have come up with a list of matériel they feel should go to Fertig, essentially, and in this order, gold, radios, medicine and small arms and ammunition. Because of the small stature of the average Filipino, both feel that the US Carbine is the proper weapon. I have the radios and the carbines and ammunition for them, and have been promised an array of medicines whenever I want them. I have also been promised a submarine, probably the USS Narwahl, which is a cargo submarine. The promise came from CINCPAC himself, who shares my belief that any guerrilla operation in the Philippines should be supported on strategic, tactical and moral grounds.

I only need two things more: I need $250,000 in gold. Actually, what I need is a cable transfer of that much money to the Bank of Australia, who will give me the gold. The sooner the better.

The second thing I need is for you to goose the Marine Corps personnel people. They still haven't transferred Lt Col Stecker to me. Colonel Rickabee reports that he's been getting a very cold shoulder about this, although no explanation has been given, and your normally incredibly able Captain Haughton hasn't been able to get them off their upholstered chairs, either. I need Stecker for this. He's an expert in guerrilla operations, and this is certainly more important than what the Corps wants him to do vis a vis setting up prophylactic facilities and amateur theatricals. McCoy going ashore alone would not be nearly as effective as the two of them going together.

I earnestly solicit your immediate action in this regard.

Best regards,

Fleming Pickering, Brigadier General, USMCR

TOP SECRET

(FIVE)
The Peabody Hotel
Memphis, Tennessee
1725 Hours 17 November 1942

''This is a first for me,'' First Lieutenant Malcolm S. Pickering said to First Lieutenant William C. Dunn, after the bellman who had led them to the small suite had left. ''I have been in many, many hotels, and I have seen some strange things in their lobbies; but I have never before seen ducks.''
   ''It is an old southern custom. We call it 'ducks in the lobby.' ''
   ''With a 'd,' right?''

"Don't be obscene, Mr. Pickering. And if you are reaching for the phone to order booze, forget it."

"Why?"

"Because this is the South, Mr. Pickering. We do not corrupt our youth—such as yourself—by giving them whiskey."

"You're kidding."

"I am not kidding."

"Well, as soon as I find out if my car has arrived, I will ask for a bellman. I'll bet the bellman has an idea how we can circumvent that perverted Southern custom."

"Why don't we wait until we report in? We can buy booze on the base, I'm sure," Dunn said.

"Why don't we just go out there in the morning?"

"Because if we report in today, anytime before midnight, it is a day of duty, and we don't lose a day of leave."

"Why don't we go out there in the morning and say we reported in last night and there was nobody there to properly receive us?" Pick asked.

"That would be a case of an officer knowingly uttering a statement he knows to be false."

"So what?"

"Pick, you better understand, you've never been in a squadron under anybody but Charley Galloway. There are a number of squadron commanders who are real pricks. . . ."

"And it will be our luck to get one, right?"

"Right. And I won't be the exec, either. Just one more airplane jockey. So, until we find out how much of a prick our new squadron commander is going to be, be smart, keep your mouth shut, and your eyes and ears open."

"OK. Now can I ask if my car is here?"

"Yes, you may," Dunn said grandly.

The car had been delivered; it would be at the front door in five minutes.

"I have just had another unpleasant, if realistic, thought," Dunn said. "Our new skipper maybe won't permit us to live here."

"Fuck him," Pick said. "Wave your Navy Cross in his face."

"Pick, you weren't listening. You're going to have to change your whole attitude, or you're going to get us both in trouble. Maybe you don't give a damn, but I don't want to get sent back to P'Cola to fly Yellow Perils."

"I surrender. I am now on my good behavior. Note the glow of my halo."

"Just make sure it keeps glowing," Dunn said. "Let's go."

There was a staff sergeant on duty at the headquarters of Marine Air Group 59. He told them that the Major was out inspecting the flight line.

"What for?" Pick asked.

"Sir," the sergeant replied, looking askance at the question from the young, new pilot, obviously fresh from P'Cola, "the SOP says the Officer of the Day will inspect the flight line every two hours during off-duty hours, Sir."

"Right," Pickering said.

"Your name is Dunn, you said, Lieutenant?" the sergeant asked. And then, before Dunn could reply, he asked another question. "Sir, isn't that the Navy Cross? Are you that Mr. Dunn, Sir?"

"That's him, Sergeant. We call him 'Modest Bill.' He always wears his medals—"

"Shut up, Pick," Dunn said, and it was in the voice of command.

"—when trying to make a favorable first impression on his new squadron commander," Pick finished.

"I told you to shut up, Mr. Pickering."

Pick shrugged, but said nothing else.

"This is for you, Mr. Dunn," the sergeant said, and handed him a large manila envelope.

Dunn tore it open and read the single sheet of Teletype paper it contained.

"Well," he said, "I'm all right with the new skipper, but your ass, Mr. Pickering, is in a crack."

"What are you talking about?"

"What are you talking about, *Sir?*, if you please, Mr. Pickering."

"What do you mean, Sir?"

"Stick this in your ear, Mr. Pickering," Dunn said, handing him the Teletype. "And then call me 'Sir.' Get in the habit of calling me Sir, as a matter of fact."

ROUTINE CONFIDENTIAL
HEADQUARTERS USMC WASH DC 1535 13 NOV 42
COMMANDING OFFICER MAG-59
MEMPHIS NAVAL AIR STATION TENN

    1. FOLLOWING EXTRACTS GENERAL ORDER 205 HQ USMC DATED 10 NOV 42 QUOTED FOR INFORMATION AND APPROPRIATE ACTION.
    ****
    17. 1/LT WILLIAM C. DUNN, USMCR, HQ MAG-59 IS PROMOTED CAPTAIN, USMCR, WITH DATE OF RANK 1 NOV 42.
    18. CAPT WILLIAM C. DUNN, USMCR, DETACHED HQ MAG-59 ATTACHED VMF-262, MAG-59, MEMPHIS NAVAL AIR STATION, TENN, FOR DUTY AS COMMANDING OFFICER.
    ****
    171. 1/LT MALCOM S. PICKERING, USMCR, DETACHED HQ MAG-59 ATTACHED VMF-262, MAG-59, MEMPHIS AIR STATION, TENN, FOR DUTY.
    ****
BY DIRECTION OF THE COMMANDANT

VORHEES, LT COL. USMC

"I'll be goddamned, *Sir,*" Lieutenant Pickering said.

"Better, Mr. Pickering, better," Captain Dunn said.

(SIX)
Water Lily Cottage
Brisbane, Australia
1015 Hours 19 November 1942

When Brigadier General Fleming Pickering, USMCR, entered the house, he had to look for Lieutenant Colonel Jack (NMI) Stecker, USMCR; Lieutenant Kenneth R. McCoy, USMCR; and Staff Sergeant Stephen M. Koffler, USMCR. He found them in the bathroom.

The bathtub was full. In it was floating a black object, about a foot square.

"Hold it under again, Koffler," Colonel Stecker ordered.

Sergeant Koffler knelt by the tub and with some effort submerged the black object. From the evidence on the floor, as well as Koffler's rolled-up sleeves and water-soaked shirt, it was clear to General Pickering that this was not the first time they had done whatever they were doing.

Lieutenant McCoy looked at his wristwatch.

"Two minutes this time," McCoy ordered, and Koffler nodded.

"What is that?" Pickering asked.

Stecker and McCoy, in a reflex action, came almost to attention.

"Actually, this is aspirin," McCoy said. "The other stuff is in short supply. We have a buoyancy problem. So we filled the pack with aspirin. If this stuff leaks, all we lose is aspirin."

"What is that stuff?"

"Something new; they're packing radios in it. Plastic is what they call it. Koffler found out you can reseal it—sort of remelt it together. So far it's working like a Swiss watch."

"I've had a number of Swiss watches that leaked," Pickering said, and then smiled at Koffler. "Good work, Koffler."

"Thank you, Sir," Koffler said, and then blurted, "General, can I ask you something?"

"Ask away."

"Can I go with the Colonel and Mr. McCoy?"

"What makes you think the Colonel and Mr. McCoy are going anywhere?" Pickering replied.

Staff Sergeant Koffler didn't even acknowledge General Pickering's evasive reply.

"General, they're going to need a radio operator," Koffler said. "And I'm pretty good in a rubber boat."

My God, you haven't fully recovered from Buka, and you just got married, and you're volunteering to do something like that again?

"You just got married, Steve."

"If they can't get ashore in the rubber boat . . ." Koffler went on.

"McCoy, have you been running off at the mouth to Sergeant Koffler?"

"I think the sergeant has been getting information the way I've been getting mine," Colonel Stecker said. "Putting two and two together. The only difference between him and me is that I'm pretty sure I know where we're going—although no one has come out and said so—and that all he knows is that it's a beach somewhere."

"Jack, I've been pulling every string I know how to pull, and I can't get you released from this SWPOA assignment. Until I can, I can't just order you to go with McCoy."

"Sir, you can order me to go with McCoy . . ." Koffler said.

"I'm aware of that, Sergeant Koffler, thank you very much," Pickering said.

". . . and Mr. McCoy can't paddle the boat by himself."

Stecker smiled at Koffler, then the smile faded as he turned to Pickering.

"I can't imagine why they won't release me," he said. "God knows, there's fifty officers I can think of who could set up for the Division coming here. And since I'm already on somebody's shit list . . ."

"What makes you think you're on somebody's shit list?" Pickering asked.

"I'm in limbo. I am neither fish nor fowl nor good red meat. What does that look like to you?"

I don't have an answer, Jack, goddamn it!

"Two minutes," McCoy announced. "Any bubbles?"

"Not a goddamn bubble," Koffler announced triumphantly. "I knew it would work."

"Hold it down for another three minutes," McCoy ordered. "That'll prove it, one way or another."

"I have something to tell you," Stecker said.

"Which is?"

"I sent a personal to General Vandergrift," Stecker said. "I asked him, if he wouldn't release me to you, would he let me resign my commission."

"There's no way they'll let you do that," Pickering said. "Christ, Jack, you commanded a battalion—and goddamned well. When did you send the message to Vandergrift?"

"Yesterday."

"Did you mention this operation?" Pickering asked.

"I said I knew of a billet where I could make a contribution as a master gunnery sergeant. Nothing specific."

"Well, resigning your commission is out of the question," Pickering said. "I'm working on this, Jack. All I can tell you is trust me."

"This is important," Stecker said, pointing at the bathtub. "What I'm supposed to be doing isn't."

I completely agree, but I can't tell you that.

"In other words, you don't care if half the First Marine contracts the clap?" Pickering asked. "Because you failed to provide adequate prophylactic stations for them?"

"Now that you ask . . ." Stecker said.

"General?" Hart's voice called from the living room.

"In here, Hart," Pickering called back. "We're all playing with McCoy's rubber duck."

Hart came in and handed Pickering a large manila envelope.

"I thought you'd want to see this right away, Sir. It just came in."

Pickering ripped the envelope open and started to read it.

"Koffler, what the hell are you doing?" Hart asked.

URGENT- VIA SPECIAL CHANNEL
NAVY DEPARTMENT WASH DC 2115 18NOV42
FOR: SUPREME COMMANDER SOUTH WEST PACIFIC AREA
EYES ONLY BRIGADIER GENERAL FLEMING PICKERING, USMCR

1. FOLLOWING PERSONAL FROM SECNAV TO BRIG GEN FLEMING PICKERING USMCR:

DEAR FLEMING:

THE FOLLOWING IS ABSOLUTELY CONFIDENTIAL. THE PRESIDENT IS SENDING THE NAME OF MAJOR GENERAL ARCHER VANDEGRIFT TO THE SENATE FOR THEIR ADVICE AND CONSENT TO HIS PROMOTION TO LIEUTENANT GENERAL AND COMMANDANT OF THE MARINE CORPS, TO TAKE EFFECT AT SUCH TIME AS MAY BE AGREED UPON BY GENERAL VANDEGRIFT AND GENERAL HOLCOMB.

IN PREPARATION FOR THE ASSUMPTION OF HIS NEW DUTIES GENERAL VANDE-GRIFT HAS ASKED FOR THE EXTRAORDINARY PROMOTION OF AN OFFICER HE FEELS HE MUST HAVE ON HIS PERSONAL STAFF. IN THE BELIEF THAT THIS OFFICER WAS ON THE BRINK OF EXHAUSTION, GENERAL VANDEGRIFT HAD AR-RANGED FOR HIM TO PURSUE PHYSICALLY UNTIRING DUTIES IN AUSTRALIA.

I WILL TODAY ANNOUNCE THE PROMOTION OF LT COL JACK NMI STECKER, PRESENTLY ASSIGNED SUPREME HEADQUARTERS SWPOA, TO COLONEL. IT IS ANTICIPATED THAT, UPON GENERAL VANDEGRIFT'S ACCESSION TO COMMAN-DANT USMC, HE WILL SUBMIT COLONEL STECKER'S NAME FOR PROMOTION TO BRIGADIER GENERAL. I WILL ENTHUSIASTICALLY ENDORSE SUCH A RECOMMEN-DATION.

THE SECRETARY OF THE TREASURY INFORMED ME THIS AFTERNOON THAT TWO HUNDRED FIFTY THOUSAND DOLLARS FROM THE PRESIDENT'S CONFIDEN-TIAL FUND HAS BEEN CABLE TRANSFERRED TO YOUR ACCOUNT AT THE BANK OF AUSTRALIA MELBOURNE.

THE PRESIDENT HAS DIRECTED ME TO INQUIRE THE STATUS OF YOUR CAM-PAIGN TO HAVE THE OSS RECOGNIZED BY THE SWPOA AS A MEMBER OF THE TEAM.

PLEASE PASS TO LIEUTENANT MCCOY, 'GODSPEED AND GOOD LUCK!'

REGARDS

FRANK

END PERSONAL FROM SECNAV

BY DIRECTION:

DAVID HAUGHTON, CAPTAIN, USN
ADMINISTRATIVE ASSISTANT TO THE SECRETARY OF THE NAVY

"Well, I'll be a son of a bitch," Pickering said.

Koffler turned. "General?"

"I think you had better read this, *Sergeant Major* Stecker," Pickering said. "General Vandergrift has been heard from."

Stecker scanned the sheets, his eyebrows rising. "I don't think you were supposed to show me this," he said. "It says—"

"I know what it says. Show it to McCoy and Koffler, Colonel. Consider that an order."

Koffler had to read it last. As the other men stood dumbfounded, he looked at Pickering.

"Sir, if the Colonel's not going, then—"

"Sergeants are supposed to speak only when spoken to, Koffler."

"—then you're *really* going to need somebody who knows how to paddle a rubber boat."

Pickering stared at him for what seemed the longest moment of Koffler's life. Then a deep laugh rumbled out of his throat, and rolled on and on.

Behind him, the black plastic pack bobbed in the bathtub.